W. SOMERSET MAUGHAM W. SOMERSET MAUGHAM

love
Alix

February 2007

Mary Dingwall

W. Somerset Maugham

Cakes and Ale
The Painted Veil
Liza of Lambeth
The Razor's Edge
Theatre
The Moon and Sixpence

W. Somerset Maugham

BOOK CLUB ASSOCIATES
LONDON

Cakes and Ale first published in 1930
by William Heinemann Limited
The Painted Veil first published in 1925
by William Heinemann Limited
Liza of Lambeth first published in 1897
by William Heinemann Limited
The Razor's Edge first published in 1944
by William Heinemann Limited
Theatre first published in 1937
by William Heinemann Limited
The Moon and Sixpence first published in 1919
by William Heinemann Limited

This edition published 1980 by
Book Club Associates
By arrangement with

William Heinemann Limited
10 Upper Grosvenor Street
London W1

Martin Secker & Warburg Limited
54 Poland Street
London W1

and

Octopus Books Limited
59 Grosvenor Street
London W1

Printed in the United States of America

Contents

W. Somerset Maugham

Cakes and Ale

or

The Skeleton in the Cupboard

W. Somerset Maugham

Preface

It was as a short story, and not a very long one either, that I first thought of this novel. Here is the note I made when it occurred to me: 'I am asked to write my reminiscences of a famous novelist, a friend of my boyhood, living at W. with a common wife, very unfaithful to him. There he writes his great books. Later he marries his secretary, who guards him and makes him into a figure. My wonder whether even in old age he is not slightly restive at being made into a monument.' I was writing at the time a series of short stories for 'The Cosmopolitan'. My contract stipulated that they were to be between twelve hundred and fifteen hundred words, so that with the illustration they should not occupy more than a page of the magazine, but I allowed myself some latitude and then the illustration spread across the opposite page and gave me a little more space. I thought this story would do for this purpose, and put it aside for future use. But I had long had in mind the character of Rosie. I had wanted for years to write about her, but the opportunity never presented itself; I could contrive no setting in which she found a place to suit her, and I began to think I never should. I did not very much care. A character in a writer's head, unwritten, remains a possession; his thoughts recur to it constantly, and while his imagination gradually enriches it he enjoys the singular pleasure of feeling that there, in his mind, someone is living a varied and tremulous life, obedient to his fancy and yet in a queer wilful way independent of him. But when once that character is set down on paper it belongs to the writer no more. He forgets it. It is curious how completely a person who may have occupied your reveries for many years can thus cease to be. It suddenly struck me that the little story I had jotted down offered me just the framework for this character that I had been looking for. I would make her the wife of my distinguished novelist. I saw that my story could never be got into a couple of thousand words, so I made up my mind to wait a little and use my material for one of the much longer tales, fourteen or fifteen thousand words, with which, following upon *Rain*, I had been not unsuccessful. But the more I thought of it the less inclined I was to waste Rosie on a story even of this length. Old recollections returned to me. I found I had not said all I wanted to say about the W. of the note, which in *Of Human Bondage* I had called Blackstable. After so many years I did not see why I should not get closer to the facts. The Uncle William, Rector of Blackstable, and his wife Isabella, became Uncle Henry, Vicar, and his wife, Sophie. The Philip Carey of the earlier book became the I of *Cakes and Ale*.

When the book appeared I was attacked in various quarters because I was supposed in the character of Edward Driffield to have drawn a portrait of Thomas Hardy. This was not my intention. He was no more in my mind than George Meredith or Anatole France. As my note suggests, I had been stuck by the notion that the veneration to which an author full of years and

honour is exposed must be irksome to the little alert soul within him that is
alive still to the adventures of his fancy. Many odd and disconcerting ideas
must cross his mind, I thought, while he maintains the dignified exterior
that his admirers demand of him. I read *Tess of the D'Urbevilles* when I was
eighteen with such enthusiasm that I determined to marry a milkmaid, but I
had never been so much taken with Hardy's other books as were most of my
contemporaries, and I did not think his English very good. I was never so
much interested in him as I was at one time in George Meredith, and later in
Anatole France. I knew little of Hardy's life. I know now only enough to be
certain that the points in common between his and that of Edward Driffield
are negligible. They consist only in both having been born in humble
circumstances and both having had two wives. I met Thomas Hardy but
once. This was at a dinner-party at Lady St Helier's, better known in the
social history of the day as Lady Jeune, who liked to ask to her house (in a
much more exclusive world than the world of today) everyone that in some
way or another had caught the public eye. I was then a popular and
fashionable playwright. It was one of those great dinner-parties that people
gave before the war, with a vast number of courses, thick and clear soup, fish,
a couple of entrées, sorbet (to give you a chance to get your second wind),
joint, game, sweet, ice and savoury; and there were twenty-four people all of
whom by rank, political eminence or artistic achievement, were
distinguished. When the ladies retired to the drawing-room I found myself
sitting next to Thomas Hardy. I remember a little man with an earthy face.
In his evening clothes, with his boiled shirt and high collar, he had still a
strange look of the soil. He was amiable and mild. It struck me at the time
that there was in him a curious mixture of shyness and self-assurance. I do
not remember what we talked about, but I know that we talked for three-
quarters of an hour. At the end of it he paid me a great compliment: he asked
me (not having heard my name) what was my profession.

I am told that two or three writers thought themselves aimed at in the
character of Alroy Kear. They were under a misapprehension. This
character was a composite portrait: I took the appearance from one writer,
the obsession with good society from another, the heartiness from a third,
the pride in athletic prowess from a fourth, and a great deal from myself. For
I have a grim capacity for seeing my own absurdity and I find in myself much
to excite my ridicule. I am inclined to think that this is why I see people (if I
am to believe what I am frequently told and frequently read of myself) in a
less flattering light than many authors who have not this unfortunate
idiosyncrasy. For all the characters that we create are but copies of
ourselves. It may be of course also that they really are nobler, more
disinterested, virtuous and spiritual than I. It is very natural that being
godlike they should create men in their own image. When I wanted to draw
the portrait of a writer who used every means of advertisement possible to
assist the diffusion of his works I have no need to fix my attention on any
particular person. The practice is too common for that. Nor can one help
feeling sympathy for it. Every year hundreds of books, many of considerable
merit, pass unnoticed. Each one has taken the author months to write, he
may have had it in his mind for years; he has put into it something of himself
which is lost for ever, it is heart-rending to think how great are the chances
that it will be disregarded in the press of matter that weighs down the critics'
tables and burdens the booksellers' shelves. It is not unnatural that he
should use what means he can to attract the attention of the public.

Experience has taught him what to do. He must make himself a public figure. He must keep in the public eye. He must give interviews and get his photograph in the papers. He must write letters to 'The Times', address meetings and occupy himself with social questions; he must make after-dinner speeches; he must recommend books in the publishers' advertisements; and he must be seen without fail at the proper places at the proper times. He must never allow himself to be forgotten. It is hard and anxious work, for a mistake may cost him dear; it would be brutal to look with anything but kindliness at an author who takes so much trouble to persuade the world at large to read books that he honestly considers so well worth reading.

But there is one form of advertisement that I deplore. This is the cocktail party that is given to launch a book. You secure the presence of a photographer. You invite the gossip writers and as many eminent people as you know. The gossip writers give you a paragraph in their columns and the illustrated papers publish the photographs, but the eminent people expect to get a signed copy of the book for nothing. This ignoble practice is not rendered less objectionable when it is presumed (sometimes no doubt with justice) to be given at the expense of the publisher. It did not flourish at the time I wrote *Cakes and Ale*. It would have given me the material for a lively chapter.

Chapter One

I have noticed that when someone asks for you on the telephone and, finding you out, leaves a message begging you to call him up the moment you come in, and it's important, the matter is more often important to him than to you. When it comes to making you a present or doing you a favour most people are able to hold their impatience within reasonable bounds. So when I got back to my lodgings with just enough time to have a drink, a cigarette, and to read my paper before dressing for dinner, and was told by Miss Fellows, my landlady, that Mr Alroy Kear wished me to ring him up at once, I felt that I could safely ignore his request.

'Is that the writer?' she asked me.

'It is.'

She gave the telephone a friendly glance.

'Shall I get him?'

'No, thank you.'

'What shall I say if he rings again?'

'Ask him to leave a message.'

'Very good, sir.'

She pursed her lips. She took the empty siphon, swept the room with a look to see that it was tidy, and went out. Miss Fellows was a great novel reader. I was sure that she had read all Roy's books. Her disapproval of my casualness suggested that she had read them with admiration. When I got home again, I found a note in her bold, legible writing on the sideboard.

Mr Kear rang up twice. Can you lunch with him tomorrow? If not what day will suit you?

I raised my eyebrows. I had not seen Roy for three months and then only for a few minutes at a party; he had been very friendly, he always was, and when we separated he had expressed his hearty regret that we met so seldom.

'London's awful,' he said. 'One never has time to see any of the people one wants to. Let's lunch together one day next week, shall we?'

'I'd like to,' I replied.

'I'll look at my book when I get home and ring you up.'

'All right.'

I had not known Roy for twenty years without learning that he always kept in the upper left-hand pocket of his waistcoat the little book in which he put down his engagements; I was therefore not surprised when I heard from him no further. It was impossible for me now to persuade myself that this urgent desire of his to dispense hospitality was disinterested. As I smoked a pipe before going to bed I turned over in my mind the possible reasons for which Roy might want me to lunch with him. It might be that an admirer of his had pestered him to introduce me to her or that an American editor, in

London for a few days, had desired Roy to put me in touch with him; but I could not do my old friend the injustice of supposing him so barren of devices as not to be able to cope with such a situation. Besides, he told me to choose my own day, so it could hardly be that he wished me to meet anyone else.

Than Roy no one could show a more genuine cordiality to a fellow novelist whose name was on everybody's lips, but no one could more genially turn a cold shoulder on him when idleness, failure, or someone else's success had cast a shade on his notoriety. The writer has his ups and downs, and I was but too conscious that at the moment I was not in the public eye. It was obvious that I might have found excuses without affront to refuse Roy's invitation, though he was a determined fellow and if he was resolved for purposes of his own to see me, I well knew that nothing short of a downright 'go to hell' would check his persistence; but I was beset by curiosity. I had also a considerable affection for Roy.

I had watched with admiration his rise in the world of letters. His career might well have served as a model for any young man entering upon the pursuit of literature. I could think of no one among my contemporaries who had achieved so considerable a position on so little talent. This, like the wise man's daily dose of Bemax, might have gone into a heaped-up tablespoon. He was perfectly aware of it, and it must have seemed to him sometimes little short of a miracle that he had been able with it to compose already some thirty books. I cannot but think that he saw the white light of revelation when first he read that Thomas Carlyle in an after-dinner speech had stated that genius was an infinite capacity for taking pains. He pondered the saying. If that was all, he must have told himself, he could be a genius like the rest, and when the excited reviewer of a lady's paper, writing a notice of one of his works, used the word (and of late the critics have been doing it with agreeable frequency) he must have sighed with the satisfaction of one who after long hours of toil has completed a cross-word puzzle. No one who for years had observed his indefatigable industry could deny that at all events he deserved to be a genius.

Roy started with certain advantages. He was the only son of a civil servant who after being Colonial Secretary for many years in Hong-Kong ended his career as Governor of Jamaica. When you looked up Alroy Kear in the serried pages of *Who's Who* you saw *o.s.* of Sir Raymond Kear, K.C.M.G., K.C.V.O. *q.v.* and of Emily, *y.d.* of the late Major-General Percy Camperdown, Indian Army. He was educated at Winchester and at New College, Oxford. He was president of the Union and but for an unfortunate attack of measles might very well have got his rowing blue. His academic career was respectable rather than showy, and he left the university without a debt in the world. Roy was even then of a thrifty habit, without any inclination to unprofitable expense, and he was a good son. He knew that it had been a sacrifice to his parents to give him so costly an education. His father, having retired, lived in an unpretentious, but not mean, house near Stroud in Gloucestershire, but at intervals went to London to attend official dinners connected with the colonies he had administered, and on these occasions was in the habit of visiting the Athenaeum, of which he was a member. It was through an old crony at this club that he was able to get his boy, when he came down from Oxford, appointed tutor to the delicate and only son of a very noble lord. This gave Roy a chance to become acquainted at an early age with the great world. He made good use of his opportunities.

You will never find in his works any of the solecisms that disfigure the productions of those who have studied the upper circles of society only in the pages of the illustrated papers. He knew exactly how dukes spoke to one another, and the proper way they should be addressed respectively by a member of Parliament, an attorney, a bookmaker and a valet. There is something captivating in the jauntiness with which in his early novels he handles viceroys, ambassadors, prime ministers, royalties and great ladies. He is friendly without being patronising and familiar without being impertinent. He does not let you forget their rank, but shares with you his comfortable feeling that they are of the same flesh as you and I. I always think it a pity that, fashion having decided that the doings of the aristocracy are no longer a proper subject for serious fiction, Roy, always keenly sensitive to the tendency of the age, should in his later novels have confined himself to the spiritual conflicts of solicitors, chartered accountants and produce brokers. He does not move in these circles with his old assurance.

I knew him first soon after he resigned his tutorship to devote himself exclusively to literature, and he was then a fine, upstanding young man, six feet high in his stockinged feet and of an athletic build, with broad shoulders and a confident carriage. He was not handsome, but in a manly way agreeable to look at, with wide blue frank eyes and curly hair of a lightish brown; his nose was rather short and broad, his chin square. He looked honest, clean, and healthy. He was something of an athlete. No one who has read in his early books the descriptions of a run with the hounds, so vivid and so accurate, can doubt that he wrote from personal experience; and until quite lately he was willing now and then to desert his desk for a day's hunting. He published his first novel at the period when men of letters, to show their virility, drank beer and played cricket, and for some years there was seldom a literary eleven in which his name did not figure. This particular school, I hardly know why, has lost its bravery, their books are neglected, and cricketers though they have remained, they find difficulty in placing their articles. Roy ceased playing cricket a good many years ago and he has developed a fine taste for claret.

Roy was very modest about his first novel. It was short, neatly written, and, as is everything he has produced since, in perfect taste. He sent it with a pleasant letter to all the leading writers of the day, and in this he told each one how greatly he admired his works, how much he had learned from his study of them, and how ardently he aspired to follow, albeit at a humble distance, the trail his correspondent had blazed. He laid his book at the feet of a great artist as the tribute of a young man entering upon the profession of letters to one whom he would always look up to as his master. Deprecatingly fully conscious of his audacity in asking so busy a man to waste his time on a neophyte's puny effort, he begged for criticism and guidance. Few of the replies were perfunctory. The authors he wrote to, flattered by his praise, answered at length. They commended his book; many of them asked him to luncheon. They could not fail to be charmed by his frankness and warmed by his enthusiasm. He asked for their advice with a humility that was touching and promised to act upon it with a sincerity that was impressive. Here, they felt, was someone worth taking a little trouble over.

His novel had a considerable success. It made him many friends in literary circles and in a very short while you could not go to a tea party in Bloomsbury, Campden Hill, or Westminster without finding him handing round bread and butter or disembarrassing an elderly lady of an empty cup.

He was so young, so bluff, so gay, he laughed so merrily at other people's jokes that no one could help liking him. He joined dining clubs where in the basement of a hotel in Victoria Street or Holborn men of letters, young barristers and ladies in Liberty silks and strings of beads, ate a three-and-sixpenny dinner and discussed art and literature. It was soon discovered that he had a pretty gift for after-dinner speaking. He was so pleasant that his fellow writers, his rivals and contemporaries, forgave him even the fact that he was a gentleman. He was generous in his praise of their fledgeling works, and when they sent him manuscripts to criticise could never find a thing amiss. They thought him not only a good sort, but a sound judge.

He wrote a second novel. He took great pains with it and he profited by the advice his elders in the craft had given him. It was only just that more than one should at his request write a review for a paper with whose editor Roy had got into touch and only natural that the review should be flattering. His second novel was successful, but not so successful as to arouse the umbrageous susceptibilities of his competitors. In fact it confirmed them in their suspicions that he would never set the Thames on fire. He was a jolly good fellow; no side, or anything like that: they were quite content to give a leg up to a man who would never climb so high as to be an obstacle to themselves. I know some who smile bitterly now when they reflect on the mistake they made.

But when they say that he is swollen-headed they err. Roy has never lost the modesty which in his youth was his most engaging trait.

'I know I'm not a great novelist,' he will tell you. 'When I compare myself with the giants I simply don't exist. I used to think that one day I should write a really great novel, but I've long ceased even to hope for that. All I want people to say is that I do my best. I do work. I never let anything slipshod get past me. I think I can tell a good story and I can create characters that ring true. And after all the proof of the pudding is in the eating: *The Eye of the Needle* sold thirty-five thousand in England and eighty thousand in America, and for the serial rights of my next book I've got the biggest terms I've ever had yet.'

And what, after all, can it be other than modesty that makes him even now write to the reviewers of his books, thanking them for their praise, and ask them to luncheon? Nay, more: when someone has written a stinging criticism and Roy, especially since his reputation became so great, has had to put up with some very virulent abuse, he does not, like most of us, shrug his shoulders, fling a mental insult at the ruffian who does not like our work, and then forget about it; he writes a long letter to his critic, telling him that he is very sorry he thought his book bad, but his review was so interesting in itself, and if he might venture to say so, showed so much critical sense and so much feeling for words, that he felt bound to write to him. No one is more anxious to improve himself than he, and he hopes he is still capable of learning. He does not want to be a bore, but if the critic has nothing to do on Wednesday or Friday will he come and lunch at the Savoy and tell him why exactly he thought his book so bad? No one can order a lunch better than Roy, and generally by the time the critic has eaten half a dozen oysters and a cut from a saddle of baby lamb, he has eaten his words too. It is only poetic justice that when Roy's next novel comes out the critic should see in the new work a very great advance.

One of the difficulties that a man has to cope with as he goes through life is what to do about the persons with whom he has once been intimate and whose interest for him has in due course subsided. If both parties remain in a modest station the break comes about naturally, and no ill feeling subsists, but if one of them achieves eminence the position is awkward. He makes a multitude of new friends, but the old ones are inexorable; he has a thousand claims on his time, but they feel that they have the first right to it. Unless he is at their beck and call they sigh and with a shrug of the shoulders say:

'Ah, well, I suppose you're like everyone else. I must expect to be dropped now that you're a success.'

That of course is what he would like to do if he had the courage. For the most part he hasn't. He weakly accepts an invitation to supper on Sunday evening. The cold roast beef is frozen and comes from Australia and was over-cooked at middle day; and the burgundy–ah, why will they call it burgundy? Have they never been to Beaune and stayed at the Hôtel de la Poste? Of course it is grand to talk of the good old days when you shared a crust of bread in a garret together, but it is a little disconcerting when you reflect how near to a garret is the room you are sitting in. You feel ill at ease when your friend tells you that his books don't sell and that he can't place his short stories; the managers won't even read his plays, and when he compares them with some of the stuff that's put on (here he fixes you with an accusing eye) it really does seem a bit hard. You are embarrassed and you look away. You exaggerate the failures you have had in order that he may realise that life has its hardships for you too. You refer to your work in the most disparaging way you can and are a trifle taken aback to find that your host's opinion of it is the same as yours. You speak of the fickleness of the public so that he may comfort himself by thinking that your popularity cannot last. He is a friendly but severe critic.

'I haven't read your last book,' he says, 'but I read the one before. I've forgotten its name.'

You tell him.

'I was rather disappointed in it. I didn't think it was quite so good as some of the things you've done. Of course you know which my favourite is.'

And you, having suffered from other hands than his, answer at once with the name of the first book you ever wrote: you were twenty then, and it was crude and ingenuous, and on every page was written your inexperience.

'You'll never do anything so good as that,' he says heartily, and you feel that your whole career has been a long decadence from that one happy hit. 'I always think you've never *quite* fulfilled the promise you showed then.'

The gas fire roasts your feet, but your hands are icy. You look at your wrist-watch surreptitiously and wonder whether your old friend would think it offensive if you took your leave as early as ten. You have told your car to wait round the corner so that it should not stand outside the door and by its magnificence affront his poverty, but at the door he says:

'You'll find a 'bus at the bottom of the street. I'll just walk down with you.'

Panic seizes you and you confess that you have a car. He finds it very odd that the chauffeur should wait round the corner. You answer that this is one of his idiosyncrasies. When you reach it your friend looks at it with tolerant superiority. You nervously ask him to dinner with you one day. You promise to write to him and you drive away wondering whether when he comes he will think you are swanking if you ask him to Claridge's or mean if you suggest Soho.

Roy Kear suffered from none of these tribulations. It sounds a little brutal to say that when he had got all he could get of people he dropped them; but it would take so long to put the matter more delicately, and would need so subtle an adjustment of hints, half-tones and allusions, playful or tender, that such being at bottom the fact, I think it as well to leave it at that. Most of us when we do a caddish thing harbour resentment against the person we have done it to, but Roy's heart, always in the right place, never permitted him much pettiness. He could use a man very shabbily without afterward bearing him the slightest ill-will.

'Poor old Smith,' he would say. 'He is a dear; I'm so fond of him. Pity he's growing so bitter. I wish one could do something for him. No, I haven't seen him for years. It's no good trying to keep up old friendships. It's painful for both sides. The fact is, one grows out of people, and the only thing is to face it.'

But if he ran across Smith at some gathering like the private view of the Royal Academy no one could be more cordial. He wrung his hand and told him how delighted he was to see him. His face beamed. He shed good fellowship as the kindly sun its rays. Smith rejoiced in the glow of this wonderful vitality and it was damned decent of Roy to say he'd give his eye-teeth to have written a book half as good as Smith's last. On the other hand, if Roy thought Smith had not seen him, he looked the other way; but Smith *had* seen him, and Smith resented being cut. Smith was very acid. He said that in the old days Roy had been glad enough to share a steak with him in a shabby restaurant and spend a month's holiday in a fisherman's cottage at St Ives. Smith said that Roy was a time server. He said he was a snob. He said he was a humbug.

Smith was wrong here. The most shining characteristic of Alroy Kear was his sincerity. No one can be a humbug for five and twenty years. Hypocrisy is the most difficult and nerve-racking vice that any man can pursue; it needs an unceasing vigilance and a rare detachment of spirit. It cannot, like adultery or gluttony, be practised at spare moments; it is a whole-time job. It needs also a cynical humour; although Roy laughed so much I never thought he had a very quick sense of humour, and I am quite sure that he was incapable of cynicism. Though I have finished few of his novels, I have begun a good many, and to my mind his sincerity is stamped on every one of their multitudinous pages. This is clearly the chief ground of his stable popularity. Roy has always sincerely believed what everyone else believed at the moment. When he wrote novels about the aristocracy he sincerely believed that its members were dissipated and immoral, and yet had a certain nobility and an innate aptitude for governing the British Empire; when later he wrote of the middle classes he sincerely believed that they were the backbone of the country. His villains have always been villainous, his heroes heroic, and his maidens chaste.

When Roy asked the author of a flattering review to lunch it was because he was sincerely grateful to him for his good opinion, and when he asked the author of an unflattering one it was because he was sincerely concerned to improve himself. When unknown admirers from Texas or Western Australia came to London it was not only to cultivate his public that he took them to the National Gallery, it was because he was sincerely anxious to observe their reactions to art. You had only to hear him lecture to be convinced of his sincerity.

When he stood on the platform, in evening dress admirably worn, or in a loose, much used but perfectly cut lounge suit if it better fitted the occasion, and faced his audience seriously, frankly, but with an engaging diffidence you could not but realise that he was giving himself up to his task with complete earnestness. Though now and then he pretended to be at a loss for a word, it was only to make it more effective when he uttered it. His voice was full and manly. He told a story well. He was never dull. He was fond of lecturing upon the younger writers of England and America, and he explained their merits to his audience with an enthusiasm that attested his generosity. Perhaps he told almost too much, for when you had heard his lecture you felt that you really knew all you wanted to about them and it was quite unnecessary to read their books. I suppose that is why when Roy had lectured in some provincial town not a single copy of the books of the authors he had spoken of was ever asked for, but there was always a run on his own. His energy was prodigious. Not only did he make successful tours of the United States, but he lectured up and down Great Britain. No club was so small, no society for the self-improvement of its members so insignificant, that Roy disdained to give it an hour of his time. Now and then he revised his lectures and issued them in neat little books. Most people who are interested in these things have at least looked through the works entitled *Modern Novelists*, *Russian Fiction*, and *Some Writers*; and few can deny that they exhibit a real feeling for literature and a charming personality.

But this by no means exhausted his activities. He was an active member of the organisations that have been founded to further the interests of authors or to alleviate their hard lot when sickness or old age has brought them to penury. He was always willing to give his help when matters of copyright were the subject of legislation and he was never unprepared to take his place in those missions to a foreign country which are devised to establish amicable relations between writers of different nationalities. He could be counted on to reply for literature at a public dinner and he was invariably on the reception committee formed to give a proper welcome to a literary celebrity from overseas. No bazaar lacked an autographed copy of at least one of his books. He never refused to grant an interview. He justly said that no one knew better than he the hardships of the author's trade and if he could help a struggling journalist to earn a few guineas by having a pleasant chat with him he had not the inhumanity to refuse. He generally asked his interviewer to luncheon and seldom failed to make a good impression on him. The only stipulation he made was that he should see the article before it was published. He was never impatient with the persons who call up the celebrated on the telephone at inconvenient moments to ask them for the information of newspaper readers whether they believe in God or what they eat for breakfast. He figured in every symposium and the public knew what he thought of prohibition, vegetarianism, jazz, garlic, exercise, marriage, politics and the place of women in the home.

His views on marriage were abstract, for he had successfully evaded the state which so many artists have found difficult to reconcile with the arduous pursuit of their calling. It was generally known that he had for some years cherished a hopeless passion for a married woman of rank, and though he never spoke of her but with chivalrous admiration, it was understood that she had treated him with harshness. The novels of his middle period reflected in their unwonted bitterness the strain to which he had been put. The anguish of spirit he had passed through then enabled him without offence to elude the advances of ladies of little reputation, frayed ornaments of a hectic circle, who were willing to exchange an uncertain present for the

security of marriage with a successful novelist. When he saw in their bright
eyes the shadow of the registry office he told them that the memory of his one
great love would always prevent him from forming any permanent tie. His
quixotry might exasperate, but could not affront, them. He sighed a little
when he reflected that he must be for ever denied the joys of domesticity and
the satisfaction of parenthood, but it was a sacrifice that he was prepared to
make not only to his ideal, but also to the possible partner of his joys. He had
noticed that people really do not want to be bothered with the wives of
authors and painters. The artist who insisted on taking his wife wherever he
went only made himself a nuisance and indeed was in consequence often not
asked to places he would have liked to go; and if he left his wife at home, he
was on his return exposed to recriminations that shattered the repose so
essential for him to do the best that was in him. Alroy Kear was a bachelor
and now at fifty was likely to remain one.

He was an example of what an author can do, and to what heights he can
rise, by industry, commonsense, honesty and the efficient combination of
means and ends. He was a good fellow and none but a cross-grained carper
could grudge him his success. I felt that to fall asleep with his image in my
mind would insure me a good night. I scribbled a note to Miss Fellows,
knocked the ashes out of my pipe, put out the light in my sitting-room and
went to bed.

Chapter Two

When I rang for my letters and the papers next morning a message was
delivered to me, in answer to my note to Miss Fellows, that Mr Alroy Kear
expected me at one-fifteen at his club in St James's Street; so a little before
one I strolled round to my own and had the cocktail, which I was pretty sure
Roy would not offer me. Then I walked down St James's Street, looking idly
at the shop windows, and since I had still a few minutes to spare (I did not
want to keep my appointment too punctually) I went into Christie's to see if
there was anything I liked the look of. The auction had already begun and a
group of dark, small men were passing round to one another pieces of
Victorian silver, while the auctioneer, following their gestures with bored
eyes, muttered in a drone: 'Ten shillings offered, eleven, eleven and six' . . .
It was a fine day, early in June, and the air in King Street was bright. It made
the pictures on the walls of Christie's look very dingy. I went out. The
people in the street walked with a kind of nonchalance, as though the ease of
the day had entered into their souls and in the midst of their affairs they had a
sudden and surprised inclination to stop and look at the picture of life.

Roy's club was sedate. In the ante-chamber were only an ancient porter
and a page; and I had a sudden and melancholy feeling that the members
were all attending the funeral of the head-waiter. The page, when I had
uttered Roy's name, led me into an empty passage to leave my hat and stick
and then into an empty hall hung with life-sized portraits of Victorian
statesmen. Roy got up from a leather sofa and warmly greeted me.

'Shall we go straight up?' he said.

I was right in thinking that he would not offer me a cocktail and I commended my prudence. He led me up a noble flight of heavily carpeted stairs, and we passed nobody on the way; we entered the strangers' dining-room, and we were its only occupants. It was a room of some size, very clean and white, with an Adam window. We sat down by it and a demure waiter handed us the bill of fare. Beef, mutton and lamb, cold salmon, apple tart, rhubarb tart, gooseberry tart. As my eye travelled down the inevitable list I sighed as I thought of the restaurants round the corner where there were French cooking, the clatter of life and pretty painted women in summer frocks.

'I can recommend the veal-and-ham pie,' said Roy.

'All right.'

'I'll mix the salad myself,' he told the waiter in an off-hand and yet commanding way, and then, casting his eye once more on the bill of fare, generously: 'And what about some asparagus to follow?'

'That would be very nice.'

His manner grew a trifle grander.

'Asparagus for two and tell the chef to choose them himself. Now what would you like to drink? What do you say to a bottle of hock? We rather fancy our hock here.'

When I had agreed to this he told the waiter to call the wine-steward. I could not but admire the authoritative and yet perfectly polite manner in which he gave his orders. You felt that thus would a well-bred king send for one of his field-marshals. The wine-steward, portly in black, with the silver chain of his office round his neck, bustled in with the wine-list in his hand. Roy nodded to him with a curt familiarity.

'Hulloa, Armstrong, we want some of the Liebfraumilch, the '21.'

'Very good, sir.'

'How's it holding up? Pretty well? We shan't be able to get any more of it, you know.'

'I'm afraid not, sir.'

'Well, it's no good meeting trouble halfway, is it, Armstrong?'

Roy smiled at the steward with breezy cordiality. The steward saw from his long experience of members that the remark needed an answer.

'No, sir.'

Roy laughed and his eye sought mine. Quite a character, Armstrong.

'Well, chill it, Armstrong; not too much, you know, but just right. I want my guest to see that we know what's what here.' He turned to me. 'Armstrong's been with us for eight and forty years.' And when the wine-steward had left us: 'I hope you don't mind coming here. It's quiet and we can have a good talk. It's ages since we did. You're looking very fit.'

This drew my attention to Roy's appearance.

'Not half so fit as you,' I answered.

'The result of an upright, sober and godly life,' he laughed. 'Plenty of work. Plenty of exercise. How's the golf? We must have a game one of these days.'

I knew that Roy was scratch and that nothing would please him less than to waste a day with so indifferent a player as myself. But I felt I was quite safe in accepting so vague an invitation. He looked the picture of health. His curly hair was getting very grey, but it suited him and made his frank, sun-burned face look younger. His eyes, which looked upon the world with such a hearty candour, were bright and clear. He was not so slim as in his youth and I was not surprised that when the waiter offered us rolls he asked for

Rye-Vita. His slight corpulence only added to his dignity. It gave weight to his observations. Because his movements were a little more deliberate than they had been you had a comfortable feeling of confidence in him; he filled his chair with so much solidity that you had almost the impression that he sat upon a monument.

I do not know whether, as I wished, I have indicated by my report of his dialogue with the waiter that his conversation was not as a rule brilliant or witty, but it was fluent and he laughed so much that you sometimes had the illusion that what he said was funny. He was never at a loss for a remark and he could discourse on the topics of the day with an ease that prevented his hearers from experiencing any sense of strain.

Many authors from their preoccupation with words have the bad habit of choosing those they use in conversation too carefully. They form their sentences with unconscious care and say neither more nor less than they mean. It makes intercourse with them somewhat formidable to persons in the upper ranks of society whose vocabulary is limited by their simple spiritual needs, and their company consequently is sought only with hesitation. No constraint of this sort was ever felt with Roy. He could talk with a dancing guardee in terms that were perfectly comprehensible to him and with a racing countess in the language of her stable boys. They said of him with enthusiasm and relief that he was not a bit like an author. No compliment pleased him better. The wise always use a number of ready-made phrases (at the moment I write 'nobody's business' is the most common), popular adjectives (like 'divine' or 'shy-making'), verbs that you only know the meaning of if you live in the right set (like 'dunch'), which give a homely sparkle to small talk and avoid the necessity of thought. The Americans, who are the most efficient people on the earth, have carried this device to such a height of perfection and have invented so wide a range of pithy and hackneyed phrases that they can carry on an amusing and animated conversation without giving a moment's reflection to what they are saying and so leave their minds free to consider the more important matters of big business and fornication. Roy's repertory was extensive and his scent for the word of the minute unerring; it peppered his speech, but aptly, and he used it each time with a sort of bright eagerness, as though his fertile brain had just minted it.

Now he talked of this and that, of our common friends and the latest books, of the opera. He was very breezy. He was always cordial, but today his cordiality took my breath away. He lamented that we saw one another so seldom and told me with the frankness that was one of his pleasant characteristics how much he liked me and what a high opinion he had of me. I felt I must not fail to meet this friendliness halfway. He asked me about the book I was writing, I asked him about the book he was writing. We told one another that neither of us had had the success he deserved. We ate the veal-and-ham pie and Roy told me how he mixed a salad. We drank the hock and smacked appreciative lips.

And I wondered when he was coming to the point.

I could not bring myself to believe that at the height of the London season Alroy Kear would waste an hour on a fellow writer who was not a reviewer and had no influence in any quarter whatever in order to talk of Matisse, the Russian Ballet and Marcel Proust. Besides, at the back of his gaiety I vaguely felt a slight apprehension. Had I not known that he was in a prosperous state I should have suspected that he was going to borrow a hundred pounds from me. It began to look as though luncheon would end without his finding the opportunity to say what he had in mind. I knew he was cautious. Perhaps he thought that this meeting, the first after so long a separation, had better be employed in establishing friendly relations, and was prepared to look upon the pleasant, substantial meal merely as ground bait.

'Shall we go and have our coffee in the next room?' he said.

'If you like.'

'I think it's more comfortable.'

I followed him into another room, much more spacious, with great leather armchairs and huge sofas; there were papers and magazines on the tables. Two old gentlemen in a corner were talking in undertones. They gave us a hostile glance, but this did not deter Roy from offering them a cordial greeting.

'Hullo, General,' he cried, nodding breezily.

I stood for a moment at the window, looking at the gaiety of the day, and wished I knew more of the historical associations of St James's Street. I was ashamed that I did not even know the name of the club across the way and was afraid to ask Roy lest he should despise me for not knowing what every decent person knew. He called me back by asking me whether I would have a brandy with my coffee, and when I refused, insisted. The club's brandy was famous. We sat side by side on a sofa by the elegant fireplace and lit cigars.

'The last time Edward Driffield ever came to London he lunched with me here,' said Roy casually. 'I made the old man try our brandy and he was delighted with it. I was staying with his widow over last week-end.'

'Were you?'

'She sent you all sorts of messages.'

'That's very kind of her. I shouldn't have thought she remembered me.'

'Oh, yes, she does. You lunched there about six years ago, didn't you? She says the old man was so glad to see you.'

'I didn't think *she* was.'

'Oh, you're quite wrong. Of course she had to be very careful. The old man was pestered with people who wanted to see him and she had to husband his strength. She was always afraid he'd do too much. It's a wonderful thing if you come to think of it that she should have kept him alive and in possession of all his faculties to the age of eighty-four. I've been seeing a good deal of her since he died. She's awfully lonely. After all, she devoted herself to looking after him for twenty-five years. Othello's occupation, you know. I really feel sorry for her.'

'She's still comparatively young. I dare say she'll marry again.'

'Oh, no, she couldn't do that. That would be dreadful.'

There was a slight pause while we sipped our brandy.

'You must be one of the few persons still alive who knew Driffield when he was unknown. You saw quite a lot of him at one time, didn't you?'

'A certain amount. I was almost a small boy and he was a middle-aged man. We weren't boon companions, you know.'

'Perhaps not, but you must know a great deal about him that other people don't.'

'I suppose I do.'

'Have you ever thought of writing your recollections of him?'

'Good heavens, no!'

'Don't you think you ought to? He was one of the greatest novelists of our day. The last of the Victorians. He was an enormous figure. His novels have as good a chance of surviving as any that have been written in the last hundred years.'

'I wonder. I've always thought them rather boring.'

Roy looked at me with eyes twinkling with laughter.

'How like you that is! Anyhow you must admit that you're in the minority. I don't mind telling you that I've read his novels not once or twice, but half a dozen times, and every time I read them I think they're finer. Did you read the articles that were written about him at his death?'

'Some of them.'

'The consensus of opinion was absolutely amazing. I read every one.'

'If they all said the same thing, wasn't that rather unnecessary?'

Roy shrugged his massive shoulders good-humouredly, but did not answer my question.

'I thought the *Times Lit. Sup.* was splendid. It would have done the old man good to read it. I hear that the *Quarterly* is going to have an article in its next number.'

'I still think his novels rather boring.'

Roy smiled indulgently.

'Doesn't it make you slightly uneasy to think that you disagree with everyone whose opinion matters?'

'Not particularly. I've been writing for thirty-five years now, and you can't think how many geniuses I've seen acclaimed, enjoy their hour or two of glory and vanish into obscurity. I wonder what's happened to them. Are they dead, are they shut up in mad-houses, are they hidden away in offices? I wonder if they furtively lend their books to the doctor and the maiden lady in some obscure village. I wonder if they are still great men in some Italian pension.'

'Oh, yes, they're the flash in the pans. I've known them.'

'You've even lectured about them.'

'One has to. One wants to give them a leg up if one can and one knows they won't amount to anything. Hang it all, one can afford to be generous. But after all, Driffield wasn't anything like that. The collected edition of his works is in thirty-seven volumes and the last set that came up at Sotheby's sold for seventy-eight pounds. That speaks for itself. His sales have increased steadily every year and last year was the best he ever had. You can take my word for that. Mrs Driffield showed me his accounts last time I was down there. Driffield has come to stay all right.'

'Who can tell?'

'Well, you think you can,' replied Roy acidly.

I was not put out. I knew I was irritating him and it gave me a pleasant sensation.

'I think the instinctive judgments I formed when I was a boy were right. They told me Carlyle was a great writer and I was ashamed that I found the *French Revolution* and *Sartor Resartus* unreadable. Can anyone read them now? I thought the opinions of others must be better than mine and I persuaded myself that I thought George Meredith magnificent. In my heart I found him affected, verbose and insincere. A good many people think so too now. Because they told me that to admire Walter Pater was to prove myself a cultured young man, I admired Walter Pater, but heavens, how *Marius* bored me!'

'Oh, well, I don't suppose anyone reads Pater now, and of course Meredith has gone all to pot and Carlyle was a pretentious windbag.'

'You don't know how secure of immortality they all looked thirty years ago.'

'And have you never made mistakes?'

'One or two. I didn't think half as much of Newman as I do now, and I thought a great deal more of the tinkling quatrains of Fitzgerald. I could not read Goethe's *Wilhelm Meister*; now I think it his masterpiece.'

'And what did you think much of then that you think much of still?'

'Well, *Tristram Shandy* and *Amelia* and *Vanity Fair*. *Madame Bovary*, *La Chartreuse de Parme*, and *Anna Karenina*. And Wordsworth and Keats and Verlaine.'

'If you don't mind my saying so, I don't think that's particularly original.'

'I don't mind your saying so at all. I don't think it is. But you asked me why I believed in my own judgment, and I was trying to explain to you that, whatever I said out of timidity and in deference to the cultured opinion of the day, I didn't really admire certain authors who were then thought admirable and the event seems to show that I was right. And what I honestly and instinctivelty liked then has stood the test of time with me and with critical opinion in general.'

Roy was silent for a moment. He looked in the bottom of his cup, but whether to see if there were any more coffee in it or to find something to say, I did not know. I gave the clock on the chimney-piece a glance. In a minute it would be fitting for me to take my leave. Perhaps I had been wrong and Roy had invited me only that we might idly chat of Shakespeare and the musical glasses. I chid myself for the uncharitable thoughts I had had of him. I looked at him with concern. If that was his only object it must be that he was feeling tired or discouraged. If he was disinterested it could only be that for the moment at least the world was too much for him. But he caught my look at the clock and spoke.

'I don't see how you can deny that there must be something in a man who's able to carry on for sixty years, writing book after book, and who's able to hold an ever-increasing public. After all, at Ferne Court there are shelves filled with the translations of Driffield's books into every language of civilised people. Of course I'm willing to admit that a lot he wrote seems a bit old-fashioned nowadays. He flourished in a bad period and he was inclined to be long-winded. Most of his plots are melodramatic; but there's one quality you must allow him: beauty.'

'Yes?' I said.

'When all's said and done, that's the only thing that counts and Driffield never wrote a page that wasn't instinct with beauty.'

'Yes?' I said.

'I wish you'd been there when we went down to present him with his portrait on his eightieth birthday. It really was a memorable occasion.'

'I read about it in the papers.'

'It wasn't only writers, you know, it was a thoroughly representative gathering—science, politics, business, art, the world; I think you'd have to go a long way to find gathered together such a collection of distinguished people as got out from that train at Blackstable. It was awfully moving when the P.M. presented the old man with the Order of Merit. He made a charming speech. I don't mind telling you there were tears in a good many eyes that day.'

'Did Driffield cry?'

'No, he was singularly calm. He was like he always was, rather shy, you know, and quiet, very well-mannered, grateful, of course, but a little dry. Mrs Driffield didn't want him to get overtired and when we went into lunch he stayed in his study, and she sent him something in on a tray. I slipped away while the others were having their coffee. He was smoking his pipe and looking at the portrait. I asked him what he thought of it. He wouldn't tell me, he just smiled a little. He asked me if I thought he could take his teeth out and I said, No, the deputation would be coming in presently to say good-bye to him. Then I asked him if he didn't think it was a wonderful moment. "Rum," he said, "very rum." The fact is, I suppose, he was shattered. He was a messy eater in his later days and a messy smoker—he scattered the tobacco all over himself when he filled his pipe; Mrs Driffield didn't like people to see him when he was like that, but of course she didn't mind me; I tidied him up a bit and then they all came in and shook hands with him, and we went back to town.'

I got up.

'Well, I really must be going. It's been awfully nice seeing you.'

'I'm just going to the private view at the Leicester Galleries. I know the people there. I'll take you in if you like.'

'It's very kind of you, but they sent me a card. No, I don't think I'll come.'

We walked down the stairs and I got my hat. When we came out into the street and I turned toward Piccadilly, Roy said:

'I'll just walk up to the top with you.' He got into step with me. 'You knew his first wife, didn't you?'

'Whose?'

'Driffield's.'

'Oh!' I had forgotten him. 'Yes.'

'Well?'

'Fairly.'

'I suppose she was awful.'

'I don't recollect that.'

'She must have been dreadfully common. She was a barmaid, wasn't she?'

'Yes.'

'I wonder why the devil he married her. I've always been given to understand that she was extremely unfaithful to him.'

'Extremely.'

'Do you remember at all what she was like?'

'Yes, very distinctly,' I smiled. 'She was sweet.'

Roy gave a short laugh.

'That's not the general impression.'

I did not answer. We had reached Piccadilly, and stopping I held out my hand to Roy. He shook it, but I fancied without his usual heartiness. I had the impression that he was disappointed with our meeting. I could not imagine why. Whatever he had wanted of me I had not been able to do, for the reason that he had given me no inkling of what it was, and as I strolled under the arcade of the Ritz Hotel and along the park railings till I came opposite Half Moon Street I wondered if my manner had been more than ordinarily forbidding. It was quite evident that Roy had felt the moment inopportune to ask me to grant him a favour.

I walked up Half Moon Street. After the gay tumult of Piccadilly it had a pleasant silence. It was sedate and respectable. Most of the houses let apartments, but this was not advertised by the vulgarity of a card; some had a brightly polished brass plate, like a doctor's, to announce the fact and others the word *Apartments* neatly painted on the fanlight. One or two with an added discretion merely gave the name of the proprietor, so that if you were ignorant you might have thought it a tailor's or a money lender's. There was none of the congested traffic of Jermyn Street, where also they let rooms, but here and there a smart car, unattended, stood outside a door and occasionally at another a taxi deposited a middle-aged lady. You had the feeling that the people who lodged here were not gay and a trifle disreputable as in Jermyn Street, racing men who rose in the morning with headaches and asked for a hair of the dog that bit them, but respectable women from the country who came up for six weeks for the London season and elderly gentlemen who belonged to exclusive clubs. You felt that they came year after year to the same house and perhaps had known the proprietor when he was still in private service. My own Miss Fellows had been cook in some very good places, but you would never have guessed it had you seen her walking along to do her shopping in Shepherd's Market. She was not stout, red-faced and blousy as one expects a cook to be; she was spare and very upright, neatly but fashionably dressed, a woman of middle age with determined features; her lips were rouged and she wore an eyeglass. She was businesslike, quiet, coolly cynical and very expensive.

The rooms I occupied were on the ground floor. The parlour was papered with an old marbled paper and on the walls were water colours of romantic scenes, cavaliers bidding good-bye to their ladies and knights of old banqueting in stately halls; there were large ferns in pots, and the armchairs were covered with faded leather. There was about the room an amusing air of the eighteen eighties, and when I looked out of the window I expected to see a private hansom rather than a Chrysler. The curtains were of a heavy red rep.

Chapter Three

I had a good deal to do that afternoon, but my conversation with Roy and the impression of the day before yesterday, the sense of a past that still dwelt in the minds of men not yet old, that my room, I could not tell why, had given me even more strongly than usual as I entered it, inveigled my thoughts to saunter down the road of memory. It was as though all the people who had at one time and another inhabited my lodging pressed upon me with their old-fashioned ways and odd clothes, men with mutton-chop whiskers in frock coats and women in bustles and flounced skirts. The rumble of London, which I did not know if I imagined or heard (my house was at the top of Half Moon Street), and the beauty of the sunny June day (*le vierge, le vivace et le bel aujourd'hui*), gave my reverie a poignancy which was not quite painful. The past I looked at seemed to have lost its reality and I saw it as though it were a scene in a play and I a spectator in the back row of a dark gallery. But it was all very clear as far as it went. It was not misty like life as one leads it when the ceaseless throng of impressions seems to rob them of outline, but sharp and definite like a landscape painted in oils by a painstaking artist of the middle-Victorian era.

I fancy that life is more amusing now than it was forty years ago and I have a notion that people are more amiable. They may have been worthier then, possessed of more solid virtue as, I am told, they were possessed of more substantial knowledge; I do not know. I know they were more cantankerous; they ate too much, many of them drank too much, and they took too little exercise. Their livers were out of order and their digestions often impaired. They were irritable. I do not speak of London, of which I knew nothing till I was grown up, nor of grand people who hunted and shot, but of the countryside and of the modest persons, gentlemen of small means, clergymen, retired officers and such like who made up the local society. The dullness of their lives was almost incredible. There were no golf links; at a few houses was an ill-kept tennis court, but it was only the very young who played; there was a dance once a year in the Assembly Rooms; carriage folk went for a drive in the afternoon; the others went for a 'constitutional!' You may say that they did not miss amusements they had never thought of, and that they created excitement for themselves from the small entertainment (tea when you were asked to bring your music and you sang the songs of Maude Valérie White and Tosti) which at infrequent intervals they offered one another; the days were very long; they were bored. People who were condemned to spend their lives within a mile of one another quarrelled bitterly, and seeing each other every day in the town, cut one another for twenty years. They were vain, pig-headed and odd. It was a life that perhaps formed queer characters; people were not so like one another as now and they acquired a small celebrity by their idiosyncrasies, but they were not easy to get on with. It may be that we are flippant and careless, but we accept one another without the old suspicion; our manners, rough and ready, are kindly; we are more prepared to give and take and we are not so crabbed.

I lived with an uncle and aunt on the outskirts of a little Kentish town by the sea. It was called Blackstable and my uncle was the vicar. My aunt was a German. She came of a very noble but impoverished family, and the only portion she brought her husband was a marquetry writing-desk, made for an ancestor in the Seventeenth Century, and a set of tumblers. Of these only a few remained when I entered upon the scene and they were used as ornaments in the drawing-room. I liked the grand coat-of-arms with which they were heavily engraved. There were I don't know how many quarterings, which my aunt used demurely to explain to me, and the supporters were fine and the crest emerging from a crown incredibly romantic. She was a simple old lady, of a meek and Christian disposition, but she had not, though married for more than thirty years to a modest parson with very little income beyond his stipend, forgotten that she was *hochwohlgeboren*. When a rich banker from London, with a name that in these days is famous in financial circles, took a neighbouring house for the summer holidays, though my uncle called on him (chiefly, I surmise, to get a subscription to the Additional Curates Society), she refused to do so because he was in trade. No one thought her a snob. It was accepted as perfectly reasonable. The banker had a little boy of my own age, and, I forget how, I became acquainted with him. I still remember the discussion that ensued when I asked if I might bring him to the vicarage; permission was reluctantly given me, but I was not allowed to go in return to his house. My aunt said I'd be wanting to go to the coal merchant's next, and my uncle said:

'Evil communications corrupt good manners.'

The banker used to come to church every Sunday morning, and he always put half a sovereign in the plate, but if he thought his generosity made a good impression he was much mistaken. All Blackstable knew, but only thought him purse-proud.

Blackstable consisted of a long winding street that led to the sea, with little two-storey houses, many of them residential but with a good many shops; and from this ran a certain number of short streets, recently built, that ended on one side in the country and on the other in the marshes. Round about the harbour was a congeries of narrow winding alleys. Colliers brought coal from Newcastle to Blackstable and the harbour was animated. When I was old enough to be allowed out by myself I used to spend hours wandering about there looking at the rough grimy men in their jerseys and watching the coal being unloaded.

It was at Blackstable that I first met Edward Driffield. I was fifteen and had just come back from school for the summer holidays. The morning after I got home I took a towel and bathing drawers and went down to the beach. The sky was unclouded and the air hot and bright, but the North Sea gave it a pleasant tang so that it was a delight just to live and breathe. In winter the natives of Blackstable walked down the empty street with a hurried gait, screwing themselves up in order to expose as little surface as possible to the bitterness of the east wind, but now they dawdled; they stood about in groups in the space between the 'Duke of Kent' and the 'Bear and Key.' You heard a hum of their East-Anglian speech, drawling a little with an accent that may be ugly, but in which from old association I still find a leisurely charm. They were fresh-complexioned, with blue eyes and high cheek bones, and their hair was light. They had a clean, honest and ingenuous look. I do not think they were very intelligent, but they were guileless. They looked healthy, and though not tall for the most part were strong and active. There was little wheeled traffic in Blackstable in those days and the groups that stood about the road chatting seldom had to move for anything but the doctor's dogcart or the baker's trap.

Passing the bank, I called in to say how-do-you-do to the manager, who was my uncle's churchwarden, and when I came out met my uncle's curate. He stopped and shook hands with me. He was walking with a stranger. He did not introduce me to him. He was a smallish man with a beard and he was dressed rather loudly in a bright brown knickerbocker suit, the breeches very tight, with navy-blue stockings, black boots and a billycock hat. Knickerbockers were uncommon then, at least in Blackstable, and being young and fresh from school I immediately set the fellow down as a cad. But while I chatted with the curate he looked at me in a friendly way, with a smile in his pale blue eyes. I felt that for two pins he would have joined in the conversation and I assumed a haughty demeanour. I was not going to run the risk of being spoken to by a chap who wore knickerbockers like a gamekeeper and I resented the familiarity of his good-humoured expression. I was myself faultlessly dressed in white flannel trousers, a blue blazer with the arms of my school on the breast pocket, and a black-and-white straw hat with a very wide brim. The curate said that he must be getting on (fortunately, for I never knew how to break away from a meeting in the street and would endure agonies of shyness while I looked in vain for an opportunity), but said that he would be coming up to the vicarage that afternoon and would I tell my uncle. The stranger nodded and smiled as we parted, but I gave him a stony stare. I supposed he was a summer visitor and in Blackstable we did not mix with the summer visitors. We thought London people vulgar. We said it was horrid to have all that rag-tag and bobtail down from town every year, but of course it was all right for the tradespeople. Even they, however, gave a faint sigh of relief when September came to an end and Blackstable sank back into its usual peace.

When I went home to dinner, my hair insufficiently dried and clinging dankly to my head, I remarked that I had met the curate and he was coming up that afternoon.

'Old Mrs Shepherd died last night,' said my uncle in explanation.

The curate's name was Galloway; he was a tall, thin, ungainly man with untidy black hair and a small sallow dark face. I suppose he was quite young, but to me he seemed middle-aged. He talked very quickly and gesticulated a great deal. This made people think him rather queer and my uncle would not have kept him but that he was very energetic, and my uncle, being extremely lazy, was glad to have someone to take so much work off his shoulders. After he had finished the business that had brought him to the vicarage Mr Galloway came in to say how-do-you-do to my aunt and she asked him to stay to tea.

'Who was that you were with this morning?' I asked him as he sat down.

'Oh, that was Edward Driffield. I didn't introduce him. I wasn't sure if your uncle would wish you to know him.'

'I think it would be most undesirable,' said my uncle.

'Why, who is he? He's not a Blackstable man, is he?'

'He was born in the parish,' said my uncle. 'His father was old Miss Wolfe's bailiff at Ferne Court. But they were chapel people.'

'He married a Blackstable girl,' said Mr Galloway.

'In church, I believe,' said my aunt. 'Is it true that she was a barmaid at the Railway Arms?'

'She looks as if she might have been something like that,' said Mr Galloway with a smile.

'Are they going to stay long?'

'Yes, I think so. They've taken one of those houses in that street where the Congregational chapel is,' said the curate.

At that time in Blackstable, though the new streets doubtless had names, nobody knew or used them.

'Is he coming to church?' asked my uncle.

'I haven't actually talked to him about it yet,' answered Mr Galloway. 'He's quite an educated man, you know.'

'I can hardly believe that,' said my uncle.

'He was at Haversham School, I understand, and he got any number of scholarships and prizes. He got a scholarship at Wadham, but he ran away to sea instead.'

'I'd heard he was rather a harum-scarum,' said my uncle.

'He doesn't look much like a sailor,' I remarked.

'Oh, he gave up the sea many years ago. He's been all sorts of things since then.'

'Jack of all trades and master of none,' said my uncle.

'Now, I understand, he's a writer.'

'That won't last long,' said my uncle.

I had never known a writer before; I was interested.

'What does he write?' I asked. 'Books?'

'I believe so,' said the curate, 'and articles. He had a novel published last spring. He's promised to lend it to me.'

'I wouldn't waste my time on rubbish in your place,' said my uncle, who never read anything but the *Times* and the *Guardian*.

'What's it called?' I asked.

'He told me the title, but I forget it.'

'Anyhow, it's quite unnecessary that you should know,' said my uncle. 'I should very much object to your reading trashy novels. During your holidays the best thing you can do is to keep out in the open air. And you have a holiday task, I presume?'

I had. It was *Ivanhoe*. I had read it when I was ten, and the notion of reading it again and writing an essay on it bored me to distraction.

When I consider the greatness that Edward Driffield afterwards achieved I cannot but smile as I remember the fashion in which he was discussed at my uncle's table. When he died a little while ago and an agitation arose among his admirers to have him buried in Westminster Abbey the present incumbent at Blackstable, my uncle's successor twice removed, wrote to the *Daily Mail* pointing out that Driffield was born in the parish and not only had passed long years, especially the last twenty-five of his life, in the neighbourhood, but had laid there the scene of some of his most famous books; it was only becoming then that his bones should rest in the churchyard where under the Kentish elms his father and mother dwelt in peace. There was relief in Blackstable when, the Dean of Westminster having somewhat curtly refused the Abbey, Mrs Driffield sent a dignified letter to the press in which she expressed her confidence that she was carrying out the dearest wishes of her dead husband in having him buried among the simple people he knew and loved so well. Unless the notabilities of Blackstable have very much changed since my day I do not believe they vastly liked that phrase about 'simple people,' but, as I afterward learnt, they had never been able to 'abide' the second Mrs Driffield.

Chapter Four

To my surprise, two or three days after I lunched with Alroy Kear I received a letter from Edward Driffield's widow. It ran as follows:

> Dear Friend,
> I hear that you had a long talk with Roy last week about Edward Driffield and I am so glad to know that you spoke of him so nicely. He often talked to me of you. He had the greatest admiration for your talent and he was so very pleased to see you when you came to lunch with us. I wonder if you have in your possession any letters that he wrote to you and if so whether you would let me have copies of them. I should be very pleased if I could persuade you to come down for two or three days and stay with me. I live very quietly now and have no one here, so please choose your own time. I shall be delighted to see you again and have a talk of old times. I have a particular service I want you to do me and I am sure that for the sake of my dear dead husband you will not refuse.
> Yours ever sincerely,
> Amy Driffield

I had seen Mrs Driffield only once and she but mildly interested me; I do not like being addressed as 'dear friend'; that alone would have been enough to make me decline her invitation; and I was exasperated by its general character which, however ingenious an excuse I invented, made the reason I did not go quite obvious, namely, that I did not want to. I had no letters of Driffield's. I suppose years ago he had written to me several times, brief notes, but he was then an obscure scribbler and even if I ever kept letters it would never have occurred to me to keep his. How was I to know that he was going to be acclaimed as the greatest novelist of our day? I hesitated only because Mrs Driffield said she wanted me to do something for her. It would certainly be a nuisance, but it would be churlish not to do it if I could, and after all her husband was a very distinguished man.

The letter came by the first post and after breakfast I rang up Roy. As soon as I mentioned my name I was put through to him by his secretary. If I were writing a detective story I should immediately have suspected that my call was awaited, and Roy's virile voice calling hullo would have confirmed my suspicion. No one could naturally be quite so cheery so early in the morning.

'I hope I didn't wake you,' I said.

'Good God, no.' His healthy laugh rippled along the wires. 'I've been up since seven. I've been riding in the park. I'm just going to have breakfast. Come along and have it with me.'

'I have a great affection for you, Roy,' I answered, 'but I don't think you're the sort of person I'd care to have breakfast with. Besides, I've already had mine. Look here, I've just had a letter from Mrs Driffield asking me to go down and stay.'

'Yes, she told me she was going to ask you. We might go down together. She's got quite a good grass court and she does one very well. I think you'd like it.'

'What is it that she wants me to do?'

'Ah, I think she'd like to tell you that herself.'

There was a softness in Roy's voice such as I imagined he would use if he were telling a prospective father that his wife was about to gratify his wishes. It cut no ice with me.

'Come off it, Roy,' I said. 'I'm too old a bird to be caught with chaff. Spit it out.'

There was a moment's pause at the other end of the telephone. I felt that Roy did not like my expression.

'Are you busy this morning?' he asked suddenly. 'I'd like to come and see you.'

'All right, come on. I shall be in till one.'

'I'll be round in about an hour.'

I replaced the receiver and relit my pipe. I gave Mrs Driffield's letter a second glance.

I remembered vividly the luncheon to which she referred. I happened to be staying for a long week-end not far from Tercanbury with a certain Lady Hodmarsh, the clever and handsome American wife of a sporting baronet with no intelligence and charming manners. Perhaps to relieve the tedium of domestic life she was in the habit of entertaining persons connected with the arts. Her parties were mixed and gay. Members of the nobility and gentry mingled with astonishment and an uneasy awe with painters, writers and actors. Lady Hodmarsh neither read the books nor looked at the pictures of the people to whom she offered hospitality, but she liked their company and enjoyed the feeling it gave her of being in the artistic know. When on this occasion the conversation happened to dwell for a moment on Edward Driffield, her most celebrated neighbour, and I mentioned that I had at one time known him very well she proposed that we should go over and lunch with him on Monday when a number of her guests were going back to London. I demurred, for I had not seen Driffield for five and thirty years and I could not believe that he would remember me; and if he did (though this I kept to myself) I could not believe that it would be with pleasure. But there was a young peer there, a certain Lord Scallion, with literary inclinations so violent that, instead of ruling this country as the laws of man and nature have decreed, he devoted his energy to the composition of detective novels. His curiosity to see Driffield was boundless and the moment Lady Hodmarsh made her suggestion he said it would be too divine. The star guest of the party was a big young fat duchess and it appeared that her admiration for the famous writer was so intense that she was prepared to cut an engagement in London and not go up till the afternoon.

'That would make four of us,' said Lady Hodmarsh. 'I don't think they could manage more than that. I'll wire to Mrs Driffield at once.'

I could not see myself going to see Driffield in that company and tried to throw cold water on the scheme.

'It'll only bore him to death,' I said. 'He'll hate having a lot of strangers barging in on him like this. He's a very old man.'

'That's why if they want to see him they'd better see him now. He can't last much longer. Mrs Driffield says he likes to meet people. They never see anybody but the doctor and the parson and it's a change for them. Mrs Driffield said I could always bring anyone interesting. Of course she has to be very careful. He's pestered by all sorts of people who want to see him just out of idle curiosity, and interviewers and authors who want him to read their books, and silly hysterical women. But Mrs Driffield is wonderful. She keeps everyone away from him but those she thinks he ought to see. I mean, he'd be dead in a week if he saw everyone who wants to see him. She has to think of his strength. Naturally we're different.'

Of course I thought I was; but as I looked at them I perceived that the duchess and Lord Scallion thought they were too; so it seemed best to say no more.

We drove over in a bright yellow Rolls. Ferne Court was three miles from Blackstable. It was a stucco house built, I suppose, about 1840, plain and unpretentious, but substantial; it was the same back and front, with two large bows on each side of a flat piece in which was the front door, and there were two large bows on the first floor. A plain parapet hid the low roof. It stood in about an acre of garden, somewhat overgrown with trees, but neatly tended, and from the drawing-room window you had a pleasant view of woods and green downland. The drawing-room was furnished so exactly as you felt a drawing-room in a country house of modest size should be furnished, that it was slightly disconcerting. Clean bright chintzes covered the comfortable chairs and the large sofa, and the curtains were of the same bright clean chintz. On little Chippendale tables stood large Oriental bowls filled with pot-pourri. On the cream-coloured walls were pleasant water-colours by painters well known at the beginning of this century. There were great masses of flowers charmingly arranged, and on the grand piano in silver frames photographs of celebrated actresses, deceased authors and minor royalties.

It was no wonder that the duchess cried out that it was a lovely room. It was just the kind of room in which a distinguished writer should spend the evening of his days. Mrs Driffield received us with modest assurance. She was a woman of about five and forty, I judged, with a small sallow face and neat sharp features. She had a black cloche hat pressed tight down on her head and wore a grey coat and skirt. Her figure was slight and she was neither tall nor short, and she looked trim, competent and alert. She might have been the squire's widowed daughter, who ran the parish and had a peculiar gift for organisation. She introduced us to a clergyman and a lady, who got up as we were shown in. They were the Vicar of Blackstable and his wife. Lady Hodmarsh and the duchess immediately assumed the cringing affability that persons of rank assume with their inferiors in order to show them that they are not in the least conscious of any difference in station between them.

Then Edward Driffield came in. I had seen portraits of him from time to time in the illustrated papers but it was with dismay that I saw him in the flesh. He was smaller than I remembered and very thin, his head was barely covered with fine silvery hair, he was cleanshaven and his skin was almost transparent. His blue eyes were very pale and the rims of his eyelids red. He looked an old, old man, hanging on to mortality by a thread; he wore very white false teeth and they made his smile seem forced and stiff. I had never seen him but bearded, and his lips were thin and pallid. He was dressed in a new, well-cut suit of blue serge and his low collar, two or three sizes too large for him, showed a wrinkled, scraggy neck. He wore a neat black tie with a pearl in it. He looked a little like a dean in mufti on his summer holiday in Switzerland.

Mrs Driffield gave him a quick glance as he came in and smiled encouragingly; she must have been satisfied with the neatness of his appearance. He shook hands with his guests and to each said something civil. When he came to me he said:

'It's very good of a busy and successful man like you to come all this way to see an old fogey.'

I was a trifle taken aback, for he spoke as though he had never seen me before, and I was afraid my friends would think I had been boasting when I claimed at one time to have known him intimately. I wondered if he had completely forgotten me.

'I don't know how many years it is since we last met,' I said, trying to be hearty.

He looked at me for what I suppose was no more than a few seconds, but for what seemed to me quite a long time, and then I had a sudden shock; he gave me a little wink. It was so quick that nobody but I could have caught it, and so unexpected in that distinguished old face that I could hardly believe my eyes. In a moment his face was once more composed, intelligently benign and quietly observant. Luncheon was announced and we trooped into the dining-room.

This also was in what can only be described as the acme of good taste. On the Chippendale sideboard were silver candlesticks. We sat on Chippendale chairs and ate off a Chippendale table. In a silver bowl in the middle were roses and round this were silver dishes with chocolates in them and peppermint creams; the silver salt cellars were brightly polished and evidently Georgian. On the cream-coloured walls were mezzo-tints of ladies painted by Sir Peter Lely and on the chimney-piece a garniture of blue delf. The service was conducted by two maids in brown uniform and Mrs Driffield in the midst of her fluent conversation kept a wary eye on them. I wondered how she had managed to train the buxom Kentish girls (their healthy colour and high cheek bones betrayed the fact that they were 'local') to such a pitch of efficiency. The lunch was just right for the occasion, smart but not showy, fillets of sole rolled up and covered with a white sauce, roast chicken, with new potatoes and green peas, asparagus and gooseberry fool. It was the dining-room and the lunch and the manner which you felt exactly fitted a literary gent of great celebrity but moderate wealth.

Mrs Driffield, like the wives of most men of letters, was a great talker and she did not let the conversation at her end of the table flag; so that, however much we might have wanted to hear what her husband was saying at the other, we had no opportunity. She was gay and sprightly. Though Edward Driffield's indifferent health and great age obliged her to live most of the year in the country, she managed notwithstanding to run up to town often enough to keep abreast of what was going on and she was soon engaged with Lord Scallion in an animated discussion of the plays in the London theatres and the terrible crowd at the Royal Academy. It had taken her two visits to look at all the pictures and even then she had not had time to see the water-colours. She liked water-colours so much; they were unpretentious; she hated things to be pretentious.

So that host and hostess should sit at the head and foot of the table, the vicar sat next to Lord Scallion and his wife next to the duchess. The duchess engaged her in conversation on the subject of working-class dwellings, a subject on which she seemed to be much more at home than the parson's lady, and my attention being thus set free I watched Edward Driffield. He was talking to Lady Hodmarsh. She was apparently telling him how to write a novel and giving him a list of a few that he really ought to read. He listened to her with what looked like polite interest, putting in now and then a remark in a voice too low for me to catch, and when she made a jest (she made them frequently and often good ones) he gave a little chuckle and shot her a quick look that seemed to say: this woman isn't such a damned fool after all. Remembering the past, I asked myself curiously what he thought of this grand company, his neatly turned-out wife, so competent and discreetly managing, and the elegant surroundings in which he lived. I wondered if he regretted his early days of adventure. I wondered if all this amused him or if the amiable civility of his manner masked a hideous boredom. Perhaps he felt my eyes upon him, for he raised his. They rested on me for a while with a thoughtful look, mild and yet oddly scrutinising, and then suddenly, unmistakably this time, he gave me another wink. The frivolous gesture in that old, withered face was more than startling, it was embarrassing; I did not know what to do. My lips outlined a dubious smile.

But the duchess joining in the conversation at the head of the table, the vicar's wife turned to me.

'You knew him many years ago, didn't you?' she asked me in a low tone. 'Yes.'

She gave the company a glance to see that no one was attending to us.

'His wife is anxious that you shouldn't call up old memories that might be painful to him. He's very frail, you know, and the least thing upsets him.'

'I'll be very careful.'

'The way she looks after him is simply wonderful. Her devotion is a lesson to all of us. She realises what a precious charge it is. Her unselfishness is beyond words.' She lowered her voice a little more. 'Of course he's a very old man and old men sometimes are a little trying; I've never seen her out of patience. In her way she's just as wonderful as he is.'

These were the sort of remarks to which it was difficult to find a reply, but I felt that one was expected of me.

'Considering everything I think he looks very well,' I murmured.

'He owes it all to her.'

At the end of the luncheon we went back into the drawing-room and after we had been standing about for two or three minutes Edward Driffield joined me. I was talking with the vicar and for want of anything better to say was admiring the charming view. I turned to my host.

'I was just saying how picturesque that little row of cottages is down there.'

'From here.' Driffield looked at their broken outline and an ironic smile curled his thin lips. 'I was born in one of them. Rum isn't it?'

But Mrs Driffield came up to us with bustling geniality. Her voice was brisk and melodious.

'Oh Edward, I'm sure the duchess would like to see your writing-room. She has to go almost immediately.'

'I'm so sorry, but I must catch the three-eighteen from Tercanbury,' said the duchess.

We filed into Driffield's study. It was a large room on the other side of the house, looking out on the same view as the dining-room, with a bow window. It was the sort of room that a devoted wife would evidently arrange for her literary husband. It was scrupulously tidy and large bowls of flowers gave it a feminine touch.

'This is the desk at which he's written all his later works,' said Mrs Driffield, closing a book that was open face downward on it. 'It's the frontispiece in the third volume of the *édition de luxe*. It's a period piece.'

We all admired the writing-table and Lady Hodmarsh, when she thought no one was looking, ran her fingers along its under edge to see if it was genuine. Mrs Driffield gave us a quick, bright smile.

'Would you like to see one of his manuscripts?'

'I'd love to,' said the duchess, 'and then I simply must bolt.'

Mrs Driffield took from a shelf a manuscript bound in blue morocco, and while the rest of the party reverently examined it I had a look at the books with which the room was lined. As authors will, I ran my eye round quickly to see if there were any of mine, but could not find one; I saw, however, a complete set of Alroy Kear's and a great many novels in bright bindings, which looked suspiciously unread; I guessed that they were the works of authors who had sent them to the master in homage to his talent and perhaps the hope of a few words of eulogy that could be used in the publisher's advertisements. But all the books were so neatly arranged, they were so clean, that I had the impression they were very seldom read. There was the Oxford Dictionary and there were standard editions in grand bindings of most of the English classics, Fielding, Boswell, Hazlitt and so on, and there were a great many books on the sea; I recognised the variously coloured, untidy volumes of the sailing directions issued by the Admiralty, and there were a number of works on gardening. The room had the look not of a writer's workshop, but of a memorial to a great name, and you could almost see already the desultory tripper wandering in for want of something better to do and smell the rather musty, close smell of a museum that few visited. I had a suspicion that nowadays if Driffield read anything at all it was the *Gardener's Chronicle* or the *Shipping Gazette*, of which I saw a bundle on a table in the corner.

When the ladies had seen all they wanted we bade our hosts farewell. But Lady Hodmarsh was a woman of tact and it must have occurred to her that I, the excuse for the party, had scarcely had a word with Edward Driffield, for at the door, enveloping me with a friendly smile, she said to him:

'I was so interested to hear that you and Mr Ashenden had known one another years and years ago. Was he a nice little boy?'

Driffield looked at me for a moment with that level, ironic gaze of his. I had the impression that if there had been nobody there he would have put his tongue out at me.

'Shy,' he replied. 'I taught him to ride a bicycle.'

We got once more into the huge yellow Rolls and drove off.

'He's too sweet,' said the duchess. 'I'm so glad we went.'

'He has such nice manners, hasn't he?' said Lady Hodmarsh.

'You didn't really expect him to eat his peas with a knife, did you?' I asked.

'I wish he had,' said Scallion. 'It would have been so picturesque.'

'I believe it's very difficult,' said the duchess. 'I've tried over and over again and I can never get them to stay on.'

'You have to spear them,' said Scallion.

'Not at all,' retorted the duchess. 'You have to balance them on the flat, and they roll like the devil.'

'What did you think of Mrs Driffield?' asked Lady Hodmarsh.

'I suppose she serves her purpose,' said the duchess.

'He's so old, poor darling, he must have someone to look after him. You know she was a hospital nurse?'

'Oh, was she?' said the duchess. 'I thought perhaps she'd been his secretary or typist or something.'

'She's quite nice,' said Lady Hodmarsh, warmly defending a friend.

'Oh, quite.'

'He had a long illness about twenty years ago, and she was his nurse then, and after he got well he married her.'

'Funny how men will do that. She must have been years younger than him. She can't be more than—what?—forty or forty-five.'

'No, I shouldn't think so. Forty-seven, say. I'm told she's done a great deal for him. I mean, she's made him quite presentable. Alroy Kear told me that before that he was almost too bohemian.'

'As a rule authors' wives are odious.'

'It's such a bore having to have them, isn't it?'

'Crashing. I wonder they don't see that themselves.'

'Poor wretches, they often suffer from the delusion that people find them interesting,' I murmured.

We reached Tercanbury, dropped the duchess at the station and drove on.

Chapter Five

It was true that Edward Driffield had taught me to bicycle. That was indeed how I first made his acquaintance. I do not know how long the safety bicycle had been invented, but I know that it was not common in the remote part of

Kent in which I lived and when you saw someone speeding along on solid tyres you turned round and looked till he was out of sight. It was still a matter for jocularity on the part of middle-aged gentlemen who said Shank's pony was good enough for them, and for trepidation on the part of elderly ladies who made a dash for the side of the road when they saw one coming. I had been for some time filled with envy of the boys whom I saw riding into the school grounds on their bicycles. It gave a pretty opportunity for showing off when you entered the gateway without holding on to the handles. I had persuaded my uncle to let me have one at the beginning of the summer holidays, and though my aunt was against it, since she said I should only break my neck, he had yielded to my pertinacity more willingly because I was of course paying for it out of my own money. I ordered it before school broke up and a few days later the carrier brought it over from Tercanbury.

I was determined to learn to ride it by myself and chaps at school had told me that they had learned in half an hour. I tried and tried and at last came to the conclusion that I was abnormally stupid but even after my pride was sufficiently humbled for me to allow the gardener to hold me up I seemed at the end of the first morning no nearer to being able to get on by myself than at the beginning. Next day, however, thinking that the carriage drive at the vicarage was too winding to give a fellow a proper chance, I wheeled the bicycle to a road not far away which I knew was perfectly flat and straight and so solitary that no one would see me making a fool of myself. I tried several times to mount, but fell off each time. I barked my shins against the pedals and got very hot and bothered. After I had been doing this for about an hour, though I began to think that God did not intend me to ride a bicycle, but was determined (unable to bear the thought of the sarcasms of my uncle, his representative at Blackstable) to do so all the same, to my disgust I saw two people on bicycles coming along the deserted road. I immediately wheeled my machine to the side and sat down on a stile, looking out to sea in a nonchalant way as though I had been for a ride and were just sitting there wrapped in contemplation of the vasty ocean. I kept my eyes dreamily averted from the two persons who were advancing toward me, but I felt that they were coming nearer, and through the corner of my eye I saw that they were a man and a woman. As they passed me the woman swerved violently to my side of the road and, crashing against me, fell to the ground.

'Oh, I'm sorry,' she said. 'I knew I should fall off the moment I saw you.'

It was impossible under the circumstances to preserve my appearance of abstraction and, blushing furiously, I said that it didn't matter at all.

The man had got off as she fell.

'You haven't hurt yourself?' he asked.

'Oh, no.'

I recognised him then as Edward Driffield, the author I had seen walking with the curate a few days before.

'I'm just learning to ride,' said his companion. 'And I fall off whenever I see anything in the road.'

'Aren't you the vicar's nephew?' said Driffield. 'I saw you the other day. Galloway told me you were. This is my wife.'

She held out her hand with an oddly frank gesture and when I took it it gave mine a warm and hearty pressure. She smiled with her lips and with her eyes and there was in her smile something that even then I recognised as singularly pleasant. I was confused. People I did not know made me dreadfully self-conscious, and I could not take in any of the details of her appearance. I just had an impression of a rather large blonde woman. I do not know if I noticed then or only remembered afterward that she wore a full skirt of blue serge, a pink shirt with a starched front and a starched collar, and a straw hat, called in those days, I think, a boater, perched on the top of a lot of golden hair.

'I think bicycling's lovely don't you?' she said, looking at my beautiful new machine which leaned against the stile. 'It must be wonderful to be able to ride well.'

I felt that this inferred an admiration for my proficiency.

'It's only a matter of practice,' I said.

'This is only my third lesson. Mr Driffield says I'm coming on wonderful, but I feel so stupid I could kick myself. How long did it take you before you could ride?'

I blushed to the roots of my hair. I could hardly utter the shameful words.

'I can't ride,' I said. 'I've only just got this bike and this is the first time I've tried.'

I equivocated a trifle there, but I made it all right with my conscience by adding the mental reservation: except yesterday at home in the garden.

'I'll give you a lesson if you like,' said Driffield in his good-humoured way. 'Come on.'

'Oh, no,' I said. 'I wouldn't dream of it.'

'Why not?' asked his wife, her blue eyes still pleasantly smiling. 'Mr Driffield would like to and it'll give me a chance to rest.'

Driffield took my bicycle, and I, reluctant but unable to withstand his friendly violence, clumsily mounted. I swayed from side to side, but he held me with a firm hand.

'Faster,' he said.

I pedalled and he ran by me as I wobbled from side to side. We were both very hot when, notwithstanding his efforts, I at last fell off. It was very hard under such circumstances to preserve the standoffishness befitting the vicar's nephew with the son of Miss Wolfe's bailiff, and when I started back again and for thirty or forty thrilling yards actually rode by myself and Mrs Driffield ran into the middle of the road with her arms akimbo shouting, 'Go it, got it, two to one on the favourite,' I was laughing so much that I positively forgot all about my social status. I got off of my own accord, my face no doubt wearing an air of immodest triumph, and received without embarrassment the Driffields' congratulation on my cleverness in riding a bicycle the very first day I tried.

'I want to see if I can get on by myself,' said Mrs Driffield, and I sat down again on the stile while her husband and I watched her unavailing struggles.

Then, wanting to rest again, disappointed but cheerful, she sat down beside me. Driffield lit his pipe. We chatted. I did not of course realise it then, but I know now that there was a disarming frankness in her manner that put one at one's ease. She talked with a kind of eagerness, like a child bubbling over with the zest of life, and her eyes were lit all the time by her engaging smile. I did not know why I liked it. I should say it was a little sly, if slyness were not a displeasing quality; it was too innocent to be sly. It was mischievous rather, like that of a child who has done something that he thinks funny, but is quite well aware that you will think rather naughty; he knows all the same that you won't be really cross and if you don't find out about it quickly he'll come and tell you himself. But of course then I only knew that her smile made me feel at home.

Presently Driffield, looking at his watch, said that they must be going and suggested that we should all ride back together in style. It was just the time that my aunt and uncle would be coming home from their daily walk down the town and I did not like to run the risk of being seen with people whom they would not at all approve of; so I asked them to go on first, as they would go more quickly than I. Mrs Driffield would not hear of it, but Driffield gave me a funny, amused little look, which made me think that he saw through my excuse so that I blushed scarlet, and he said:

'Let him go by himself, Rosie. He can manage better alone.'

'All right. Shall you be here tomorrow? We're coming.'

'I'll try to,' I answered.

They rode off, and in a few minutes I followed. Feeling very much pleased with myself, I rode all the way to the vicarage gates without falling. I think I boasted a good deal at dinner, but I did not say that I had met the Driffields.

Next day at about eleven I got my bicycle out of the coachhouse. It was so called though it held not even a pony trap and was used by the gardener to keep the mower and the roller, and by Mary-Ann for her sack of meal for the chickens. I wheeled it down to the gate and, mounting none too easily, rode along the Tercanbury Road till I came to the old turnpike and turned into Joy Lane.

The sky was blue and the air, warm and yet fresh, crackled, as it were, with the heat. The light was brilliant without harshness. The sun's beams seemed to hit the white road with a directed energy and bounce back like a rubber ball.

I rode backward and forward, waiting for the Driffields, and presently saw them come. I waved to them and turned round (getting off to do so) and we pedalled along together. Mrs Driffield and I complimented one another on our progress. We rode anxiously, clinging like grim death to the handle-bars, but exultant, and Driffield said that as soon as we felt sure of ourselves we must go for rides all over the country.

'I want to get rubbings of one or two brasses in the neighbourhood,' he said.

I did not know what he meant, but he would not explain.

'Wait and I'll show you,' he said. 'Do you think you could ride fourteen miles tomorrow, seven there and seven back?'

'Rather,' I said.

'I'll bring a sheet of paper for you and some wax and you can make a rubbing. But you'd better ask your uncle if you can come.'

'I needn't do that.'

'I think you'd better all the same.'

Mrs Driffield gave me that peculiar look of hers, mischievous and yet friendly, and I blushed scarlet. I knew that if I asked my uncle he would say no. It would be much better to say nothing about it. But as we rode along I saw coming toward us the doctor in his dogcart. I looked straight in front of me as he passed in the vain hope that if I did not look at him he would not look at me. I was uneasy. If he had seen me the fact would quickly reach the ears of my uncle or my aunt and I considered whether it would not be safer to disclose myself a secret that could no longer be concealed. When we parted at the vicarage gates (I had not been able to avoid riding as far as this in their company) Driffield said that if I found I could come with them next day I had better call for them as early as I could.

'You know where we live, don't you? Next door to the Congregational church. It's called Lime Cottage.'

When I sat down to dinner I looked for an opportunity to slip in casually the information that I had by accident run across the Driffields; but news travelled fast in Blackstable.

'Who were those people you were bicycling with this morning?' asked my aunt. 'We met Dr Anstey in the town and he said he'd seen you.'

My uncle, chewing his roast beef with an air of disapproval, looked sullenly at his plate.

'The Driffields,' I said with nonchalance. 'You know, the author. Mr Galloway knows them.'

'They're most disreputable people,' said my uncle. 'I don't wish you to associate with them.'

'Why not?' I asked.

'I'm not going to give you my reasons. It's enough that I don't wish it.'

'How did you ever get to know them?' asked my aunt.

'I was just riding along and they were riding along, and they asked me if I'd like to ride with them,' I said, distorting the truth a little.

'I call it very pushing,' said my uncle.

I began to sulk. And to show my indignation when the sweet was put on the table, though it was raspberry tart which I was extremely fond of, I refused to have any. My aunt asked me if I was not feeling very well.

'Yes,' I said, as haughtily as I could, 'I'm feeling all right.'

'Have a little bit,' said my aunt.

'I'm not hungry,' I answered.

'Just to please me.'

'He must know when he's had enough,' said my uncle.

I gave him a bitter look.

'I don't mind having a small piece,' I said.

My aunt gave me a generous helping, which I ate with the air of one who, impelled by a stern sense of duty, performs an act that is deeply distasteful to him. It was a beautiful raspberry tart. Mary-Ann made short pastry that melted in the mouth. But when my aunt asked me whether I could not manage a little more I refused with cold dignity. She did not insist. My uncle said grace and I carried my outraged feelings into the drawing-room.

But when I reckoned that the servants had finished their dinner I went into the kitchen. Emily was cleaning the silver in the pantry. Mary-Ann was washing up.

'I say, what's wrong with the Driffields?' I asked her.

Mary-Ann had come to the vicarage when she was eighteen. She had bathed me when I was a small boy, given me powders in plum jam when I needed them, packed my box when I went to school, nursed me when I was ill, read to me when I was bored and scolded me when I was naughty. Emily, the housemaid, was a flighty young thing, and Mary-Ann didn't know whatever would become of me if *she* had the looking after of me. Mary-Ann was a Blackstable girl. She had never been to London in her life and I do not think she had been to Tercanbury more than three or four times. She was never ill. She never had a holiday. She was paid twelve pounds a year. One evening a week she went down the town to see her mother, who did the vicarage washing; and on Sunday evenings she went to church. But Mary-Ann knew everything that went on in Blackstable. She knew who everybody was, who had married whom, what anyone's father had died of, and how many children, and what they were called, any woman had had.

I asked Mary-Ann my question and she slopped a wet clout noisily into the sink.

'I don't blame your uncle,' she said. 'I wouldn't let you go about with them, not if you was my nephew. Fancy their askin' you to ride your bicycle with them! Some people will do anything.'

I saw that the conversation in the dining-room had been repeated to Mary-Ann.

'I'm not a child,' I said.

'That makes it all the worse. The impudence of their comin' 'ere at all!' Mary-Ann dropped her aitches freely. 'Takin' a house and pretendin' to be ladies and gentlemen. Now leave that pie alone.'

The raspberry tart was standing on the kitchen table and I broke off a piece of crust with my fingers and put it in my mouth.

'We're goin' to eat that for our supper. If you'd wanted a second 'elpin' why didn't you 'ave one when you was 'avin' your dinner? Ted Driffield never could stick to anything. He 'ad a good education, too. The one I'm sorry for is his mother. He's been a trouble to 'er from the day he was born. And then to go an' marry Rosie Gann. They tell me that when he told his mother what he was goin' to do she took to 'er bed and stayed there for three weeks and wouldn't talk to anybody.'

'Was Mrs Driffield Rosie Gann before she married? Which Ganns were those?'

Gann was one of the commonest names at Blackstable. The churchyard was thick with their graves.

'Oh, you wouldn't 'ave known them. Old Josiah Gann was her father. He was a wild one, too. He went for a soldier and when he come back he 'ad a wooden leg. He used to go out doing painting, but he was out of work more often than not. They lived in the next 'ouse to us in Rye Lane. Me an' Rosie used to go to Sunday school together.'

'But she's not as old as you are,' I said with the bluntness of my age.

'She'll never see thirty again.'

Mary-Ann was a little woman with a snub nose and decayed teeth, but fresh-coloured, and I do not suppose she could have been more than thirty-five.

'Rosie ain't more than four or five years younger than me, whatever she may pretend she is. They tell me you wouldn't know her now all dressed up and everything.'

'Is it true that she was a barmaid?' I asked.

'Yes, at the Railway Arms and then at the Prince of Wales's Feathers at Haversham. Mrs Reeves 'ad her to 'elp in the bar at the Railway Arms, but it got so bad she had to get rid of her.'

The Railway Arms was a very modest little public-house just opposite the station of the London, Chatham & Dover Railway. It had a sort of sinister gaiety. On a winter's night as you passed by you saw through the glass doors men lounging about the bar. My uncle very much disapproved of it, and had for years been trying to get its licence taken away. It was frequented by the railway porters, colliers and farm labourers. The respectable residents of Blackstable would have disdained to enter it and, when they wanted a glass of bitter, went to the Bear and Key or the Duke of Kent.

'Why, what did she do?' I asked, my eyes popping out of my head.

'What didn't she do?' said Mary-Ann. 'What d'you think your uncle would say if he caught me tellin' you things like that? There wasn't a man who come in to 'ave a drink what she didn't carry on with. No matter who they was. She couldn't stick to anybody, it was just one man after another. They tell me it was simply 'orrible. That was when it begun with Lord George. It wasn't the sort of place he was likely to go to, he was too grand for that, but they say he went in accidental like one day when his train was late, and he saw her. And after that he was never out of the place, mixin' with all them common rough people, and of course they all knew what he was there for, and him with a wife and three children. Oh, I was sorry for her! And the talk it made. Well, it got so Mrs Reeves said she wasn't going to put up with it another day and she give her her wages and told her to pack her box and go. Good riddance to bad rubbish, that's what I said.'

I knew Lord George very well. His name was George Kemp and the title by which he was always known had been given him ironically owing to his grand manner. He was our coal merchant, but he also dabbled in house property, and he owned a share in one or two colliers. He lived in a new brick house that stood in its own grounds and he drove his own trap. He was a stoutish man with a pointed beard, florid, with a high colour and bold blue eyes. Remembering him, I think he must have looked like some jolly rubicund merchant in an old Dutch picture. He was always very flashily dressed and when you saw him driving at a smart pace down the middle of the High Street in a fawn-coloured covert-coat with large buttons, his brown bowler on the side of his head and a red rose in his button hole, you could not but look at him. On Sunday he used to come to church in a lustrous topper and a frock coat. Everyone knew that he wanted to be made churchwarden, and it was evident that his energy would have made him useful, but my uncle said not in his time, and though Lord George as a protest went to chapel for a year my uncle remained obdurate. He cut him dead when he met him in the town. A reconciliation was effected and Lord George came to church again, but my uncle only yielded so far as to appoint him sidesman. The gentry thought him vulgar and I have no doubt that he was vain and boastful. They complained of his loud voice and his strident laugh—when he was talking to somebody on one side of the street you heard every word he said from the other—and they thought his manners dreadful. He was much too friendly; when he talked to them it was as though he were not in trade at all; they said he was very pushing. But if he thought his hail-fellow-well-met air, his activity in public works, his open purse when subscriptions were needed for the annual regatta or for the harvest festival, his willingness to do anyone a good turn were going to break the barriers at Blackstable he was mistaken. His efforts at sociability were met with blank hostility.

I remember once that the doctor's wife was calling on my aunt and Emily came in to tell my uncle that Mr George Kemp would like to see him.

'But I heard the front door ring, Emily,' said my aunt.

'Yes'm, he came to the front door.'

There was a moment's awkwardness. Everyone was at a loss to know how to deal with such an unusual occurrence, and even Emily, who knew who should come to the front door, who should go to the side door, and who to the back, looked a trifle flustered. My aunt, who was a gentle soul, I think felt honestly embarrassed that anyone should put himself in such a false position; but the doctor's wife gave a little sniff of contempt. At last my uncle collected himself.

'Show him into the study, Emily,' he said. 'I'll come as soon as I've finished my tea.'

But Lord George remained exuberant, flashy, loud and boisterous. He said the town was dead and he was going to wake it up. He was going to get the company to run excursion trains. He didn't see why it shouldn't become another Margate. And why shouldn't they have a mayor? Ferne Bay had one.

'I suppose he thinks he'd be mayor himself,' said the people of Blackstable. They pursed their lips. 'Pride goeth before a fall,' they said.

And my uncle remarked that you could take a horse to the water but you couldn't make him drink.

I should add that I looked upon Lord George with the same scornful derision as everyone else. It outraged me that he should stop me in the street and call me by my Christian name and talk to me as though there were no social difference between us. He even suggested that I should play cricket with his sons, who were of about the same age as myself. But they went to the grammar school at Haversham and of course I couldn't possibly have anything to do with them.

I was shocked and thrilled by what Mary-Ann told me, but I had difficulty in believing it. I had read too many novels and had learnt too much at school not to know a good deal about love, but I thought it was a matter that only concerned young people. I could not conceive that a man with a beard, who had sons as old as I, could have any feelings of that sort. I thought when you married all that was finished. That people over thirty should make love seemed to me rather disgusting.

'You don't mean to say they did anything?' I asked Mary-Ann.

'From what I hear there's very little that Rosie Gann didn't do. And Lord George wasn't the only one.'

'But, look here, why didn't she have a baby?'

In the novels I had read whenever a lovely woman stooped to folly she had a baby. The cause was put with infinite precaution, sometimes indeed suggested only by a row of asterisks, but the result was inevitable.

'More by good luck than by good management, I lay,' said Mary-Ann. Then she recollected herself and stopped drying the plates she was busy with. 'It seems to me you know a lot more than you ought to,' she said.

'Of course I know,' I said importantly. 'Hang it all, I'm practically grown up, aren't I?'

'All I can tell you,' said Mary-Ann, 'is that when Mrs Reeves give her the sack Lord George got her a job at the Prince of Wales's Feathers at Haversham and he was always poppin' over there in his trap. You can't tell me the ale's any different over there from what it is here.'

'Then why did Ted Driffield marry her?' I asked.

'Ask me another,' said Mary-Ann. 'It was at the Feathers he saw her. I suppose he couldn't get no one else to marry him. No respectable girl would 'ave 'ad 'im.'

'Did he know about her?'

'You'd better ask him.'

I was silent. It was all very puzzling.

'What does she look like now?' asked Mary-Ann. 'I never seen her since she married. I never even speak to 'er after I 'eard what was goin' on at the Railway Arms.'

'She looks all right,' I said.

'Well, you ask her if she remembers me and see what she says.'

Chapter Six

I had quite made up my mind that I was going out with the Driffields next morning, but knew that it was no good asking my uncle if I might. If he found out that I had been and made a row it couldn't be helped, and if Ted Driffield asked me whether I had got my uncle's permission I was quite prepared to say I had. But I had after all no need to lie. In the afternoon, the tide being high, I walked down to the beach to bathe and my uncle, having something to do in the town, walked part of the way with me. Just as we were passing the Bear and Key, Ted Driffield stepped out of it. He saw us and came straight up to my uncle. I was startled at his coolness.

'Good afternoon, Vicar,' he said. 'I wonder if you remember me. I used to sing in the choir when I was a boy. Ted Driffield. My old governor was Miss Wolfe's bailiff.'

My uncle was a very timid man, and he was taken aback.

'Oh, yes, how do you do? I was sorry to hear your father died.'

'I've made the acquaintance of your young nephew. I was wondering if you'd let him come for a ride with me tomorrow. It's rather dull for him riding alone, and I'm going to do a rubbing of one of the brasses at Ferne Church.'

'It's very kind of you, but—'

My uncle was going to refuse, but Driffield interrupted him.

'I'll see he doesn't get up to any mischief. I thought he might like to make a rubbing himself. It would be an interest for him. I'll give him some paper and wax so that it won't cost him anything.'

My uncle had not a consecutive mind and the suggestion that Ted Driffield should pay for my paper and wax offended him so much that he quite forgot his intention to forbid me to go at all.

'He can quite well get his own paper and wax,' he said. 'He has plenty of pocket money, and he'd much better spend it on something like that than on sweets and make himself sick.'

'Well, if he goes to Hayward, the stationer's, and says he wants the same paper as I got and the wax they'll let him have it.'

'I'll go now,' I said, and to prevent any change of mind on my uncle's part dashed across the road.

Chapter Seven

I do not know why the Driffields bothered about me unless it was from pure kindness of heart. I was a dull little boy, not very talkative, and if I amused Ted Driffield at all it must have been unconsciously. Perhaps he was tickled by my attitude of superiority. I was under the impression that it was condescension on my part to consort with the son of Miss Wolfe's bailiff, and he what my uncle called a penny-a-liner; and when, perhaps with a trace of superciliousness, I asked him to lend me one of his books and he said it wouldn't interest me I took him at his word and did not insist. After my uncle had once consented to my going out with the Driffields he made no further objection to my association with them. Sometimes we went for sails together, sometimes we went to some picturesque spot and Driffield painted a little water-colour. I do not know if the English climate was better in those days or if it is only an illusion of youth, but I seem to remember that all through that summer the sunny days followed one another in an unbroken line. I began to feel a curious affection for the undulating, opulent and gracious country. We went far afield, to one church after another, taking rubbings of brasses, knights in armour and ladies in stiff farthingales. Ted Driffield fired me with his own enthusiasm for this simple pursuit and I rubbed with passion. I showed my uncle proudly the results of my industry, and I suppose he thought that whatever my company, I could not come to much harm when I was occupied in church. Mrs Driffield used to remain in the churchyard while we were at work, not reading or sewing, but just mooning about; she seemed able to do nothing for an indefinite time without feeling bored. Sometimes I would go out and sit with her for a little on the grass. We chattered about my school, my friends there and my masters, about the people at Blackstable and about nothing at all. She gratified me by calling me Mr Ashenden. I think she was the first person who had ever done so and it made me feel grown up. I resented it vastly when people called me Master Willie. I thought it a ridiculous name for anyone to have. In fact I did not like either of my names and spent much time inventing others that would have suited me better. The ones I preferred were Roderic Ravensworth and I covered sheets of paper with this signature in a suitably dashing hand. I did not mind Ludovic Montgomery either.

I could not get over what Mary-Ann had told me about Mrs Driffield. Though I knew theoretically what people did when they were married, and was capable of putting the facts in the bluntest language, I did not really understand it. I thought it indeed rather disgusting and I did not quite, quite believe it. After all, I was aware that the earth was round, but I *knew* it was flat. Mrs Driffield seemed so frank, her laugh so open, there was in her demeanour something so young and childlike, that I could not see her 'going with' sailors and above all anyone so gross and horrible as Lord George. She was not at all the type of wicked woman I had read of in novels. Of course I knew she wasn't 'good form' and she spoke with the Blackstable accent, she dropped an aitch now and then, and sometimes her grammar gave me a shock, but I couldn't help liking her. I came to the conclusion that what Mary-Ann had told me was a pack of lies.

One day I happened to tell her that Mary-Ann was our cook.

'She says she lived next door to you in Rye Lane,' I added, quite prepared to hear Mrs Driffield say that she had never even heard of her.

But she smiled and her blue eyes gleamed.

'That's right. She used to take me to Sunday school. She used to have a rare job keeping me quiet. I heard she'd gone to service at the vicarage. Fancy her being there still! I haven't seen her for donkey's years. I'd like to see her again and have a chat about old days. Remember me to her, will you, and ask her to look in on her evening out. I'll give her a cup of tea.'

I was taken aback at this. After all, the Driffields lived in a house that they were talking of buying and they had a 'general.' It wouldn't be at all the thing for them to have Mary-Ann to tea, and it would make it very awkward for me. They seemed to have no sense of the things one could do and the things one simply couldn't. It never ceased to embarrass me, the way in which they talked of incidents in their past that I should have thought they would not dream of mentioning. I do not know that the people I lived among were pretentious in the sense of making themselves out to be richer or grander than they really were, but looking back it does seem to me that they lived a life full of pretences. They dwelt behind a mask of respectability. You never caught them in their shirt sleeves with their feet on the table. The ladies put on afternoon dresses and were not visible till then; they lived privately with rigid economy so that you could not drop in for a casual meal, but when they entertained their tables groaned with food. Though catastrophe over-whelmed the family, they held their heads high and ignored it. One of the sons might have married an actress, but they never referred to the calamity, and though the neighbours said it was dreadful, they took ostentatious care not to mention the theatre in the presence of the afflicted. We all knew that the wife of Major Greencourt who had taken the Three Gables was connected with trade, but neither she nor the major ever so much as hinted at the discreditable secret; and though we sniffed at them behind their backs, we were too polite even to mention crockery (the source of Mrs Greencourt's adequate income) in their presence. It was still not unheard of for an angry parent to cut off his son with a shilling or to tell his daughter (who like my own mother had married a solicitor) never to darken his doors again. I was used to all this and it seemed to me natural. What did shock me was to hear Ted Driffield speak of being a waiter in a restaurant in Holborn as though it were the most ordinary thing in the world. I knew he had run away to sea: that was romantic; I knew that boys, in books at all events, often did this and had thrilling adventures before they married a fortune and an earl's daughter; but Ted Driffield had driven a cab at Maidstone and had been clerk in a booking-office at Birmingham. Once when we bicycled past the Railway Arms, Mrs Driffield mentioned quite casually, as though it were something that anyone might have done, that she had worked there for three years.

'It was my first place,' she said. 'After that I went to the Feathers at Haversham. I only left there to get married.'

She laughed as though she enjoyed the recollection. I did not know what to say; I did not know which way to look; I blushed scarlet. Another time when we were going through Ferne Bay on our way back from a long excursion, it being a hot day and all of us thirsty, she suggested that we should go into the Dolphin and have a glass of beer. She began talking to the girl behind the bar and I was horrified to hear her remark that she had been in the business herself for five years. The landlord joined us and Ted Driffield offered him a drink, and Mrs Driffield said that the barmaid must have a glass of port, and for some time they all chatted amiably about trade and tied houses and how the price of everything was going up. Meanwhile, I stood, hot and cold all over and not knowing what to do with myself. As we went out Mrs Driffield remarked:

'I took quite a fancy to that girl, Ted. She ought to do well for herself. As I said to her, it's a hard life but a merry one. You do see a bit of what's going on and if you play your cards right you ought to marry well. I noticed she had an engagement ring on, but she told me she just wore that because it gave the fellows a chance to tease her.'

Driffield laughed. She turned to me.

'I had a rare old time when I was a barmaid, but of course you can't go on for ever. You have to think of your future.'

But a greater jolt awaited me. It was halfway through September and my holidays were drawing to an end. I was very full of the Driffields, but my desire to talk about them at home was snubbed by my uncle.

'We don't want your friends pushed down our throats all day long,' said he. 'There are other topics of conversation that are more suitable. But I do think that, as Ted Driffield was born in the parish and is seeing you almost every day, he might come to church occasionally.'

One day I told Driffield: 'My uncle wants you to come to church.'

'All right. Let's go to church next Sunday night, Rosie.'

'I don't mind,' she said.

I told Mary-Ann they were going. I sat in the vicarage pew just behind the squire's and I could not look round, but I was conscious by the behaviour of my neighbours on the other side of the aisle that they were there, and as soon as I had a chance next day I asked Mary-Ann if she had seen them.

'I see 'er all right,' said Mary-Ann grimly.

'Did you speak to her afterwards?'

'Me?' She suddenly burst into anger. 'You get out of my kitchen. What d'you want to come bothering me all day long? How d'you expect me to do my work with you getting in my way all the time?'

'All right,' I said. 'Don't get in a wax.'

'I don't know what your uncle's about lettin' you go all over the place with the likes of them. All them flowers in her 'at. I wonder she ain't ashamed to show her face. Now run along, I'm busy.'

I did not know why Mary-Ann was so cross. I did not mention Mrs Driffield again. But two or three days later I happened to go into the kitchen to get something I wanted. There were two kitchens at the vicarage, a small one in which the cooking was done and a large one, built I suppose for a time when country clergymen had large families and gave grand dinners to the surrounding gentry, where Mary-Ann sat and sewed when her day's work was over. We had cold supper at eight so that after tea she had little to do. It was getting on for seven and the day was drawing in. It was Emily's evening out and I expected to find Mary-Ann alone, but as I went along the passage I heard voices and the sound of laughter. I supposed Mary-Ann had someone in to see her. The lamp was lit, but it had a thick green shade and the kitchen was almost in darkness. I saw a teapot and cups on the table. Mary-Ann was having a late cup of tea with her friend. The conversation stopped as I opened the door, then I heard a voice.

'Good-evening.'

With a start I saw that Mary-Ann's friend was Mrs Driffield. Mary-Ann laughed a little at my surprise.

'Rosie Gann dropped in to have a cup of tea with me,' she said.

'We've been having a talk about old times.'

Mary-Ann was a little shy at my finding her thus, but not half so shy as I. Mrs Driffield gave me that childlike, mischievous smile of hers; she was perfectly at her ease. For some reason I noticed her dress. I suppose because I had never seen her so grand before. It was of pale blue cloth, very tight at the waist, with high sleeves and a long skirt with a flounce at the bottom. She wore a large black straw hat with a great quantity of roses and leaves and bows on it. It was evidently the hat she had worn in church on Sunday.

'I thought if I went on waiting till Mary-Ann came to see me I'd have to wait till doomsday, so I thought the best thing I could do was to come and see her myself.'

Mary-Ann grinned self-consciously, but did not look displeased. I asked for whatever it was I wanted and as quickly as I could left them. I went out into the garden and wandered about aimlessly. I walked down to the road and looked over the gate. The night had fallen. Presently I saw a man strolling along. I paid no attention to him, but he passed backward and forward and it looked as though he were waiting for someone. At first I thought it might be Ted Driffield and I was on the point of going out when he stopped and lit a pipe; I saw it was Lord George. I wondered what he was doing there and at the same moment it struck me that he was waiting for Mrs Driffield. My heart began to beat fast, and though I was hidden by the darkness I withdrew into the shade of the bushes. I waited a few minutes longer, then I saw the side door open and Mrs Driffield let out by Mary-Ann. I heard her footsteps on the gravel. She came to the gate and opened it. It opened with a little click. At the sound Lord George stepped across the road and before she could come out slipped in. He took her in his arms and gave her a great hug. She gave a little laugh.

'Take care of my hat,' she whispered.

I was not more than three feet away from them and I was terrified lest they should notice me. I was so ashamed for them. I was trembling with agitation. For a minute he held her in his arms.

'What about the garden?' he said, still in a whisper.

'No, there's that boy. Let's go in the fields.'

They went out by the gate, he with his arm round her waist, and were lost in the night. Now I felt my heart pounding against my chest so that I could hardly breathe. I was so astonished at what I had seen that I could not think sensibly. I would have given anything to be able to tell someone, but it was a secret and I must keep it. I was thrilled with the importance it gave me. I walked slowly up to the house and let myself in by the side door. Mary-Ann, hearing it open, called me.

'Is that you, Master Willie?'

'Yes.'

I looked in the kitchen. Mary-Ann was putting the supper on a tray to take it into the dining-room.

'I wouldn't say anything to your uncle about Rosie Gann 'avin' been here,' she said.

'Oh, no.'

'It was a surprisement to me. When I 'eared a knock at the side door and opened it and saw Rosie standing there, you could 'ave knocked me down with a feather. "Mary-Ann," she says, an' before I knew what she was up to she was kissing me all over me face. I couldn't but ask 'er in and when she was in I couldn't but ask her to 'ave a nice cup of tea.'

Mary-Ann was anxious to excuse herself. After all she had said of Mrs Driffield it must seem strange to me that I should find them sitting there together chatting away and laughing. I did not want to crow.

'She's not so bad, is she?' I said.

Mary-Ann smiled. Notwithstanding her black, decayed teeth her smile was sweet and touching.

'I don't 'ardly know what it is, but there's somethin' you can't 'elp likin' about her. She was 'ere the best part of an hour and I will say that for 'er, she never once give 'erself airs. And she told me with 'er own lips the material of that dress she 'ad on cost thirteen and eleven a yard and I believe it. She remembers everything, how I used to brush her 'air for her when she was a tiny tot and how I used to make her wash her little 'ands before tea. You see, sometimes her mother used to send 'er in to 'ave her tea with us. She was as pretty as a picture in them days.'

Mary-Ann looked back into the past and her funny crumpled face grew wistful.

'Oh, well,' she said after a pause, 'I dare say she's been no worse than plenty others if the truth was only known. She 'ad more temptation than most, and I dare say a lot of them as blame her would 'ave been no better than what she was if they'd 'ad the opportunity.'

Chapter Eight

The weather broke suddenly; it grew chilly and heavy rain fell. It put an end to our excursions. I was not sorry, for I did not know how I could look Mrs Driffield in the face now that I had seen her meeting with George Kemp. I was not so much shocked as astonished. I could not understand how it was possible for her to like being kissed by an old man, and the fantastic notion passed through my mind, filled with the novels I had read, that somehow Lord George held her in his power and forced her by his knowledge of some fearful secret to submit to his loathsome embraces. My imagination played with terrible possibilities. Bigamy, murder and forgery. Very few villains in books failed to hold the threat of exposure of one of these crimes over some hapless female. Perhaps Mrs Driffield had backed a bill; I never could quite understand what this meant, but I knew that the consequences were disastrous. I toyed with the fancy of her anguish (the long sleepless nights when she sat at her window in her nightdress, her fair hair hanging to her knees, and watched hopelessly for the dawn) and saw myself (not a boy of fifteen with sixpence a week pocket money, but a tall man with a waxed moustache and muscles of steel in faultless evening dress) with a happy blend of heroism and dexterity rescuing her from the toils of the rascally blackmailer. On the other hand, it had not looked as though she had yielded quite unwillingly to Lord George's fondling and I could not get out of my ears the sound of her laugh. It had a note that I had never heard before. It gave me a queer feeling of breathlessness.

During the rest of my holidays I only saw the Driffields once more. I met them by chance in the town and they stopped and spoke to me. I suddenly felt very shy again, but when I looked at Mrs Driffield I could not help blushing with embarrassment, for there was nothing in her countenance that indicated a guilty secret. She looked at me with those soft blue eyes of hers in which there was a child's playful naughtiness. She often held her mouth a little open, as though it were just going to break into a smile, and her lips were full and red. There was honesty and innocence in her face and an ingenuous frankness and though then I could not have expressed this, I felt it quite strongly. If I had put it into words at all I think I should have said: She looks as straight as a die. It was impossible that she could be 'carrying on' with Lord George. There must be an explanation; I did not believe what my eyes had seen.

Then the day came when I had to go back to school. The carter had taken my trunk and I walked to the station by myself. I had refused to let my aunt see me off, thinking it more manly to go alone, but I felt rather low as I walked down the street. It was a small branch line to Tercanbury and the station was at the other end of the town near the beach. I took my ticket and settled myself in the corner of a third-class carriage. Suddenly I heard a voice: There he is; and Mr and Mrs Driffield bustled gaily up.

'We thought we must come and see you off,' she said. 'Are you feeling miserable?'

'No, of course not.'

'Oh, well, it won't last long. We'll have no end of a time when you come back for Christmas. Can you skate?'

'No.'

'I can. I'll teach you.'

Her high spirits cheered me, and at the same time the thought that they had come to the station to say good-bye to me gave me a lump in my throat. I tried hard not to let the emotion I felt appear on my face.

'I expect I shall be playing a lot of rugger this term,' I said. 'I ought to get into the second fifteen.'

She looked at me with kindly shining eyes, smiling with her full red lips. There was something in her smile I had always rather liked, and her voice seemed almost to tremble with a laugh or a tear. For one horrible moment I was afraid that she was going to kiss me. I was scared out of my wits. She talked on, she was mildly facetious as grown-up people are with schoolboys, and Driffield stood there without saying anything. He looked at me with a smile in his eyes and pulled his beard. Then the guard blew a cracked whistle and waved a red flag. Mrs Driffield took my hand and shook it. Driffield came forward.

'Good-bye,' he said. 'Here's something for you.'

He pressed a tiny packet into my hand and the train steamed off. When I opened it I found two half-crowns wrapped in a piece of toilet-paper. I blushed to the roots of my hair. I was glad enough to have an extra five shillings, but the thought that Ted Driffield had dared to give me a tip filled me with rage and humiliation. I could not possibly accept anything from him. It was true that I had bicycled with him and sailed with him, but he wasn't a sahib (I had got that from Major Greencourt) and it was an insult to give me five shillings. At first I thought of returning the money without a word, showing by my silence how outraged I was at the solecism he had committed, then I composed in my head a dignified and frigid letter in which I thanked him for his generosity, but said that he must see how impossible it was for a gentleman to accept a tip from someone who was practically a stranger. I thought it over for two or three days and every day it seemed more difficult to part with the two half-crowns. I felt sure that Driffield had meant it kindly, and of course he was very bad form and didn't know about things; it would be rather hard to hurt his feelings by sending the money back, and finally I spent it. But I assuaged my wounded pride by not writing to thank Driffield for his gift.

When Christmas came, however, and I went back to Blackstable for the holidays, it was the Driffields I was most eager to see. In that stagnant little place they alone seemed to have a connection with the outside world which already was beginning to touch my day-dreams with anxious curiosity. But I could not overcome my shyness enough to go to their house and call, and I hoped that I should meet them in the town. But the weather was dreadful, a boisterous wind whistled down the street, piercing you to the bone, and the few women who had an errand were swept along by their full skirts like fishing boats in half a gale. The cold rain scudded in sudden squalls and the sky, which in summer had enclosed the friendly country so snugly, now was a great pall that pressed upon the earth with awful menace. There was small hope of meeting the Driffields by chance and at last I took my courage in both hands and one day after tea slipped out. As far as the station the road was pitch dark, but there the street lamps, few and dim, made it easier to keep to the pavement. The Driffields lived in a little two-storey house in a side street; it was of dingy yellow brick and had a bow window. I knocked and presently a little maid opened the door; I asked if Mrs Driffield was in. She gave me an uncertain look and, saying she would go and see, left me standing in the passage. I had already heard voices in the next room, but they were stilled as she opened the door and, entering, shut it behind her. I had a faint impression of mystery; in the houses of my uncle's friends, even if there was no fire and the gas had to be lit as you went in, you were shown into the drawing-room when you called. But the door was opened and Driffield came out. There was only a speck of light in the passage and at first he could not see who it was; but in an instant he recognised me.

'Oh, it's you. We wondered when we were going to see you.' Then he called out: 'Rosie, it's young Ashenden.'

There was a cry and before you could say knife Mrs Driffield had come into the passage and was shaking my hands.

'Come in, come in. Take off your coat. Isn't it awful, the weather? You must be perishing.'

She helped me with my coat and took off my muffler and snatched my cap out of my hand and drew me into the room. It was hot and stuffy, a tiny room full of furniture, with a fire burning in the grate; they had gas there, which we hadn't at the vicarage, and the three burners in round globes of frosted glass filled the room with harsh light. The air was grey with tobacco smoke. At first, dazzled and then taken aback by my effusive welcome, I did not see who the two men were who got up as I came in. Then I saw they were the curate, Mr Galloway, and Lord George Kemp. I fancied that the curate shook my hand with constraint.

'How are you? I just came in to return some books that Mr Driffield had lent me and Mrs Driffield very kindly asked me to stay to tea.'

I felt rather than saw the quizzical look that Driffield gave him. He said something about the mammon of unrighteousness, which I recognised as a quotation, but did not gather the sense of. Mr Galloway laughed.

'I don't know about that,' he said. 'What about the publicans and sinners?'

I thought the remark in very bad taste, but I was immediately seized upon by Lord George. There was no constraint about him.

'Well, young fellow, home for the holidays? My word, what a big chap you're growing.'

I shook hands with him rather coldly. I wished I had not come.

'Let me give you a nice strong cup of tea,' said Mrs Driffield.

'I've already had tea.'

'Have some more,' said Lord George, speaking as though he owned the place (that was just like him). 'A big fellow like you can always tuck away another piece of bread and butter and jam and Mrs D. will cut you a slice with her own fair hands.'

The tea things were still on the table and they were sitting round it. A chair was brought up for me and Mrs Driffield gave me a piece of cake.

'We were just trying to persuade Ted to sing us a song,' said Lord George. 'Come on, Ted.'

'Sing, "All Through Stickin' to a Soljer," Ted,' said Mrs Driffield. 'I love that.'

'No, sing "First We Mopped the Floor with Him."'

'I'll sing 'em both if you're not careful,' said Driffield.

He took his banjo, which was lying on the top of the cottage piano, tuned it and began to sing. He had a rich baritone voice. I was quite used to people singing songs. When there was a tea party at the vicarage, or I went to one at the major's or the doctor's, people always brought their music with them. They left it in the hall, so that it should not seem that they wanted to be asked to play or sing; but after tea the hostess asked them if they had brought it. They shyly admitted that they had, and if it was at the vicarage I was sent to fetch it. Sometimes a young lady would say that she had quite given up playing and hadn't brought anything with her, and then her mother would break in and say that *she* had brought it. But when they sang it was not comic songs; it was 'I'll Sing Thee Songs of Araby,' or 'Good-Night, Beloved,' or 'Queen of My Heart.' Once at the annual concert at the Assembly Rooms, Smithson, the draper, had sung a comic song, and though the people at the back of the hall had applauded a great deal, the gentry had seen nothing funny in it. Perhaps there wasn't. Anyhow, before the next concert he was asked to be a little more careful about what he sang ('Remember there are ladies present, Mr Smithson') and so gave 'The Death of Nelson.' The next ditty that Driffield sang had a chorus and the curate and Lord George joined in lustily. I heard it a good many times afterward, but I can only remember four lines:

> *First we mopped the floor with him;*
> *Dragged him up and down the stairs;*
> *Then we lugged him round the room,*
> *Under tables, over chairs.*

When it was finished, assuming my best company manners, I turned to Mrs Driffield.

'Don't you sing?' I asked.

'I do, but it always turns the milk, so Ted doesn't encourage me.'

Driffield put down his banjo and lit a pipe.

'Well, how's the old book getting along, Ted?' said Lord George heartily.

'Oh, all right. I'm working away, you know.'

'Good old Ted and his books,' Lord George laughed. 'Why don't you settle down and do something respectable for a change? I'll give you a job in my office.'

'Oh, I'm all right.'

'You let him be, George,' said Mrs Driffield. 'He likes writing, and what I say is, as long as it keeps him happy, why shouldn't he.'

'Well, I don't pretend to know anything about books,' began George Kemp.

'Then don't talk about them,' interrupted Driffield with a smile.

'I don't think anyone need be ashamed to have written *Fairhaven,*' said Mr Galloway, 'and I don't care what the critics said.'

'Well, Ted, I've known you since I was a boy and *I* couldn't read it, try as I would.'

'Oh, come on, we don't want to start talking about books,' said Mrs Driffield. 'Sing us another song, Ted.'

'I must be going,' said the curate. He turned to me. 'We might walk along together. Have you got anything for me to read, Driffield?'

Driffield pointed to a pile of new books that were heaped up on a table in the corner.

'Take your pick.'

'By Jove, what a lot!' I said, looking at them greedily.

'Oh, it's all rubbish. They're sent down for review.'

'What d'you do with them?'

'Take 'em into Tercanbury and sell 'em for what they'll fetch. It all helps to pay the butcher.'

When we left, the curate and I, he with several books under his arm, he asked me:

'Did you tell your uncle you were coming to see the Driffields?'

'No, I just went out for a walk and it suddenly occurred to me that I might look in.'

This of course was some way from the truth, but I did not care to tell Mr Galloway that, though I was practically grown up, my uncle realised the fact so little that he was quite capable of trying to prevent me from seeing people he objected to.

'Unless you have to I wouldn't say anything about it in your place. The Driffields are perfectly all right, but your uncle doesn't quite approve of them.'

'I know,' I said. 'It's such rot.'

'Of course they're rather common, but he doesn't write half badly, and when you think what he came from it's wonderful that he writes at all.'

I was glad to know how the land lay. Mr Galloway did not wish my uncle to know that he was on friendly terms with the Driffields. I could feel sure at all events that he would not give me away.

The patronising manner in which my uncle's curate spoke of one who has been now so long recognised as one of the greatest of the later Victorian novelists must arouse a smile; but it was the manner in which he was generally spoken of at Blackstable. One day we went to tea at Mrs Greencourt's, who had staying with her a cousin, the wife of an Oxford don, and we had been told that she was very cultivated. She was a Mrs Encombe, a little woman with an eager wrinkled face; she surprised us very much because she wore her grey hair short and a black serge skirt that only just came down below the tops of her square-toed boots. She was the first example of the New Woman that had ever been seen in Blackstable. We were staggered and immediately on the defensive, for she looked intellectual, and it made us feel shy. (Afterward we all scoffed at her, and my uncle said to my aunt: 'Well, my dear, I'm thankful you're not clever, at least I've been spared that'; and my aunt in a playful mood put my uncle's slippers which were warming for him by the fire over her boots and said: 'Look, I'm the new woman.' And then we all said: 'Mrs Greencourt is very funny; you never know what she'll do next. But of course she isn't quite quite.' We could hardly forget that her father made china and that her grandfather had been a factory hand.)

But we all found it very interesting to hear Mrs Encombe talk of the people she knew. My uncle had been at Oxford, but everyone he asked about seemed to be dead. Mrs Encombe knew Mrs Humphry Ward and admired *Robert Elsmere*. My uncle considered it a scandalous work, and he was surprised that Mr Gladstone, who at least called himself a Christian, had found a good word to say for it. They had quite an argument about it. My uncle said he thought it would unsettle people's opinions and give them all sorts of ideas that they were much better without. Mrs Encombe answered that he wouldn't think that if he knew Mrs Humphry Ward. She was a woman of the very highest character, a niece of Mr Matthew Arnold, and whatever you might think of the book itself (and she, Mrs Encombe, was quite willing to admit that there were parts which had better have been omitted) it was quite certain that she had written it from the very highest motives. Mrs Encombe knew Miss Broughton too. She was of very good family and it was strange that she wrote the books she did.

'I don't see any harm in them,' said Mrs Hayforth, the doctor's wife. 'I enjoy them, especially *Red as a Rose is She*.'

'Would you like your girls to read them?' asked Mrs Encombe.

'Not just yet perhaps,' said Mrs Hayforth. 'But when they're married I should have no objection.'

'Then it might interest you to know,' said Mrs Encombe, 'that when I was in Florence last Easter I was introduced to Ouida.'

'That's quite another matter,' returned Mrs Hayforth. 'I can't believe that any lady would read a book by Ouida.'

'I read one out of curiosity,' said Mrs Encombe. 'I must say, it's more what you'd expect from a Frenchman than from an English gentlewoman.'

'Oh, but I understand she isn't really English. I've always heard her real name is Mademoiselle de la Ramée.'

It was then that Mr Galloway mentioned Edward Driffield.

'You know we have an author living here,' he said.

'We're not very proud of him,' said the major. 'He's the son of old Miss Wolfe's bailiff and he married a barmaid.'

'Can he write?' asked Mrs Encombe.

'You can tell at once that he's not a gentleman,' said the curate, 'but when you consider the disadvantages he's had to struggle against it's rather remarkable that he should write as well as does.'

'He's a friend of Willie's,' said my uncle.

Everyone looked at me, and I felt very uncomfortable.

'They bicycled together last summer, and after Willie had gone back to school I got one of his books from the library to see what it was like. I read the first volume and then I sent it back. I wrote a pretty stiff letter to the librarian and I was glad to hear that he'd withdrawn it from circulation. If it had been my own property I should have put it promptly in the kitchen stove.'

'I looked through one of his books myself,' said the doctor. 'It interested me because it was set in this neighbourhood and I recognised some of the people. But I can't say I liked it; I thought it unnecessarily coarse.'

'I mentioned that to him,' said Mr Galloway, 'and he said the men in the colliers that run up to Newcastle and the fishermen and farm hands don't behave like ladies and gentlemen and don't talk like them.'

'But why write about people of that character?' said my uncle.

'That's what I say,' said Mrs Hayforth. 'We all know that there are coarse and wicked and vicious people in the world, but I don't see what good it does to write about them.'

'I'm not defending him,' said Mr Galloway. 'I'm only telling you what explanation he gives himself. And then of course he brought up Dickens.'

'Dickens is quite different,' said my uncle. 'I don't see how anyone can object to the *Pickwick Papers*.'

'I suppose it's a matter of taste,' said my aunt. 'I always found Dickens very coarse. I don't want to read about people who drop their aitches. I must say I'm very glad the weather's so bad now and Willie can't take any more rides with Mr Driffield. I don't think he's quite the sort of person he ought to associate with.'

Both Mr Galloway and I looked down our noses.

Chapter Nine

As often as the mild Christmas gaieties of Blackstable allowed me I went to the Driffields' little house next door to the Congregational chapel. I always found Lord George and often Mr Galloway. Our conspiracy of silence had made us friends and when we met at the vicarage or in the vestry after church we looked at one another archly. We did not talk about our secret, but we enjoyed it; I think it gave us both a good deal of satisfaction to know that we were making a fool of my uncle. But once it occurred to me that George Kemp, meeting my uncle in the street, might remark casually that he had been seeing a lot of me at the Driffields'.

'What about Lord George?' I said to Mr Galloway.

'Oh, I made that all right.'

We chuckled. I began to like Lord George. At first I was very cold with him and scrupulously polite, but he seemed so unconscious of the social difference between us that I was forced to conclude that my haughty courtesy failed to put him in his place. He was always cordial, breezy, even boisterous; he chaffed me in his common way and I answered him back with schoolboy wit; we made the others laugh and this disposed me kindly toward him. He was for ever bragging about the great schemes he had in mind, but he took in good part my jokes at the expense of his grandiose imaginations. It amused me to hear him tell stories about the swells of Blackstable that made them look foolish and when he mimicked their oddities I roared with laughter. He was blatant and vulgar and the way he dressed was always a shock to me (I had never been to Newmarket nor seen a trainer, but that was my idea of how a Newmarket trainer dressed), and his table manners were offensive, but I found myself less and less affronted by him. He gave me the *Pink 'Un* every week and I took it home, carefully tucked away in my great-coat pocket, and read it in my bedroom.

I never went to the Driffields till after tea at the vicarage, but I always managed to make a second tea when I got there. Afterward Ted Driffield sang comic songs, accompanying himself sometimes on the banjo and sometimes on the piano. He would sing, peering at the music with his rather short-sighted eyes, for an hour at a time; there was a smile on his lips and he liked us all to join in the chorus. We played whist. I had learned the game when I was a child and my uncle and aunt and I used to play at the vicarage during the long winter evenings. My uncle always took dummy, and though of course we played for love, when my aunt and I lost I used to retire under the dining-room table and cry. Ted Driffield did not play cards, he said he had no head for them, and when we started a game he would sit down by the fire and, pencil in hand, read one of the books that had been sent down to him from London to review. I had never played with three people before and of course I did not play well, but Mrs Driffield had a natural card sense. Her movements as a rule were rather deliberate, but when it came to playing cards she was quick and alert. She played the rest of us right off our heads. Ordinarily she did not speak very much and then slowly, but when, after a hand was played, she took the trouble good humouredly to point out to me my mistakes, she was not only lucid but voluble. Lord George chaffed her as he chaffed everybody; she would smile at his banter, for she very seldom laughed, and sometimes make a neat retort. They did not behave like lovers, but like familiar friends, and I should have quite forgotten what I had heard about them and what I had seen but that now and then she gave him a look that embarrassed me. Her eyes rested on him quietly, as though he were not a man but a chair or a table, and in them was a mischievous, childlike smile. Then I would notice that his face seemed suddenly to swell and he moved uneasily in his chair. I looked quickly at the curate, afraid that he would notice something, but he was intent on the cards or else was lighting his pipe.

The hour or two I spent nearly every day in that hot, poky, smoke-laden room passed like lightning, and as the holidays drew nearer to their end I was seized with dismay at the thought that I must spend the next three months dully at school.

'I don't know what we shall do without you,' said Mrs Driffield. 'We shall have to play dummy.'

I was glad that my going would break up the game. While I was doing prep I did not want to think that they were sitting in that little room and enjoying themselves just as if I did not exist.

'How long do you get at Easter?' asked Mr Galloway.

'About three weeks.'

'We'll have a lovely time then,' said Mrs Driffield. 'The weather ought to be all right. We can ride in the mornings and then after tea we'll play whist. You've improved a lot. If we play three or four times a week during your Easter holidays you won't need to be afraid to play with anybody.'

Chapter Ten

But the term came to an end at last. I was in high spirits when once more I got out of the train at Blackstable. I had grown a little and I had had a new suit made at Tercanbury, blue serge and very smart, and I had bought a new tie. I meant to go and see the Driffields immediately I had swallowed my tea and I was full of hope that the carrier would have brought my box in time for me to put the new suit on. It made me look quite grown up. I had already begun putting vaseline on my upper lip every night to make my moustache grow. On my way through the town I looked down the street in which the Driffields lived in the hope of seeing them. I should have liked to go in and say how-do-you-do, but I knew that Driffield wrote in the morning and Mrs Driffield was not 'presentable.' I had all sorts of exciting things to tell them. I had won a heat in the hundred-yard race in the sports and I had been second in the hurdles. I meant to have a shot for the history prize in the summer and I was going to swot up my English history during the holidays. Though there was an east wind blowing, the sky was blue and there was a feeling of spring in the air. The High Street, with its colours washed clean by the wind and its lines sharp as though drawn with a new pen, looked like a picture by Samuel Scott, quiet and naïve and cosy: now, looking back; then it looked like nothing but High Street, Blackstable. When I came to the railway bridge I noticed that two or three houses were being built.

'By Jove,' I said, 'Lord George *is* going it.'

In the fields beyond little white lambs were frisking. The elm trees were just beginning to turn green. I let myself in by the side door. My uncle was sitting in his armchair by the fire reading the *Times*. I shouted to my aunt and she came downstairs, a pink spot from the excitement of seeing me on each of her withered cheeks, and threw her thin old arms round my neck. She said all the right things.

'How you've grown!' and 'Good gracious me, you'll be getting a moustache soon!'

I kissed my uncle on his bald forehead and I stood in front of the fire with my legs well apart and my back to it, and was extremely grown up and rather condescending. Then I went upstairs to say how-do-you-do to Emily, and into the kitchen to shake hands with Mary-Ann, and out into the garden to see the gardener.

When I sat down hungrily to dinner and my uncle carved the leg of mutton I asked my aunt:

'Well, what's happened at Blackstable since I was here?'

'Nothing very much. Mrs Greencourt went down to Mentone for six weeks, but she came back a few days ago. The major had an attack of gout.'

'And your friends the Driffields have bolted,' added my uncle.

'They've done what?' I cried.

'Bolted. They took their luggage away one night and just went up to

London. They've left bills all over the place. They hadn't paid their rent and they hadn't paid for their furniture. They owed Harris the butcher the best part of thirty pounds.'

'How awful,' I said.

'That's bad enough,' said my aunt, 'but it appears they hadn't even paid the wages of the maid they had for three months.'

I was flabbergasted. I thought I felt a little sick.

'I think in future,' said my uncle, 'you would be wiser not to consort with people whom your aunt and I don't think proper associates for you.'

'One can't help feeling sorry for all those tradesmen they cheated,' said my aunt.

'It serves them right,' said my uncle. 'Fancy giving credit to people like that! I should have thought anyone could see they were nothing but adventurers.'

'I always wonder why they came down here at all.'

'They just wanted to show off, and I suppose they thought as people knew who they were here it would be easier to get things on credit.'

I did not think this quite logical, but was too much crushed to argue.

As soon as I had the chance I asked Mary-Ann what she knew of the incident. To my surprise she did not take it at all in the same way as my uncle and aunt. She giggled.

'They let everyone in proper,' she said. 'They was as free as you like with their money and everyone thought they 'ad plenty. It was always the best end of the neck for them at the butcher's and when they wanted a steak nothing would do but the undercut. Asparagus and grapes and I don't know what all. They ran up bills in every shop in the town. I don't know 'ow people can be such fools.'

But it was evidently of the tradesmen she was speaking and not of the Driffields.

'But how did they manage to bunk without anyone knowing?' I asked.

'Well, that's what everybody's askin'. They do say it was Lord George 'elped them. How did they get their boxes to the station, I ask you, if 'e didn't take them in that there trap of 'is?'

'What does he say about it?'

'He says 'e knows no more about it than the man in the moon. There was a rare to-do all over the town when they found out the Driffields had shot the moon. It made me laugh. Lord George says 'e never knew they was broke, and 'e makes out 'e was as surprised as anybody. But I for one don't believe a word of it. We all know about 'im and Rosie before she was married, and between you and me and the gatepost I don't know that it ended there. They do say they was seen walkin' about the fields together last summer and 'e was in and out of the 'ouse pretty near every day.'

'How did people find out?'

'Well, it's like this. They 'ad a girl there and they told 'er she could go 'ome and spend the night with her mother, but she wasn't to be back later than eight o'clock in the morning. Well, when she come back she couldn't get in. She knocked and she rung but nobody answered, and so she went in next door and asked the lady there what she'd better do, and the lady said she'd better go to the police station. The sergeant come back with 'er and 'e knocked and 'e rung, but 'e couldn't get no answer. Then he asked the girl 'ad they paid 'er 'er wages, and she said no, not for three months, and then 'e said, you take my word for it, they've shot the moon, that's what they've done. An' when they come to get inside they found they'd took all their clothes, an' their books—they say as Ted Driffield 'ad a rare lot of books—an' every blessed thing that belonged to them.'

'And has nothing been heard of them since?'

'Well, not exactly, but when they'd been gone about a week the girl got a letter from London, and when she opened it there was no letter or anything, but just a postal order for 'er wages. An' if you ask me, I call that very 'andsome not to do a poor girl out of her wages.'

I was much more shocked than Mary-Ann. I was a very respectable youth. The reader cannot have failed to observe that I accepted the conventions of my class as if they were the laws of Nature, and though debts on the grand scale in books had seemed to me romantic, and duns and moneylenders were familiar to my fancy, I could not but think it mean and paltry not to pay the tradesmen's books. I listened with confusion when people talked in my presence of the Driffields, and when they spoke of them as my friends I said: 'Hang it all, I just knew them'; and when they asked: 'Weren't they fearfully common?' I said: 'Well, they didn't exactly suggest the Vere de Veres, you know.' Poor Mr Galloway was dreadfully upset.

'Of course I didn't think they were wealthy,' he told me, 'but I thought they had enough to get along. The house was very nicely furnished and the piano was new. It never struck me that they hadn't paid for a single thing. They never stinted themselves. What hurts me is the deceit. I used to see quite a lot of them and I thought they liked me. They always made one welcome. You'd hardly believe it, but the last time I saw them when they shook hands with me Mrs Driffield asked me to come next day and Driffield said: "Muffins for tea tomorrow." And all the time they had everything packed upstairs and that very night they took the last train to London.'

'What does Lord George say about it?'

'To tell you the truth I haven't gone out of my way to see him lately. It's been a lesson to me. There's a little proverb about evil communications that I've thought well to bear in mind.'

I felt very much the same about Lord George, and I was a little nervous too. If he took it into his head to tell people that at Christmas I had been going to see the Driffields almost every day, and it came to my uncle's ears, I foresaw an unpleasant fuss. My uncle would accuse me of deceit and prevarication and disobedience and of not behaving like a gentleman, and I did not at the moment see what answer I could make. I knew him well enough to be aware that he would not let the matter drop, and that I should be reminded of my transgression for years. I was just as glad not to see Lord George. But one day I ran into him face to face in the High Street.

'Hulloa, youngster,' he cried, addressing me in a way I particularly resented. 'Back for the holidays, I suppose.'

'You suppose quite correctly,' I answered with what I thought withering sarcasm.

Unfortunately he only bellowed with laughter.

'You're so sharp you'll cut yourself if you don't look out,' he answered heartily. 'Well, it looks as if there was no more whist for you and me just yet. Now you see what comes of living beyond your means. What I always say to my boys is, if you've got a pound and you spend nineteen and six you're a rich man, but if you spend twenty shillings and sixpence you're a pauper. Look after the pence, young fellow, and the pounds'll look after themselves.'

But though he spoke after this fashion there was in his voice no note of disapproval, but a bubble of laughter as though in his heart he were tittering at these admirable maxims.

'They say you helped them to bunk,' I remarked.

'Me?' His face assumed a look of extreme surprise, but his eyes glittered with sly mirth. 'Why, when they came and told me the Driffields had shot the moon you could have knocked me down with a feather. They owed me four pounds seventeen and six for coal. We've all been let in, even poor old Galloway who never got his muffins for tea.'

I had never thought Lord George more blatant. I should have liked to say something final and crushing, but as I could not think of anything I just said that I must be getting along and with a curt nod left him.

Chapter Eleven

Musing thus over the past, while I waited for Alroy Kear, I chuckled when I considered this shabby incident of Edward Driffield's obscurity in the light of the immense respectability of his later years. I wondered whether it was because in my boyhood he was as a writer held in such small esteem by the people about me that I had never been able to see in him the astonishing merit that the best critical opinion eventually ascribed to him. He was for long thought to write very bad English, and indeed he gave you the impression of writing with the stub of a blunt pencil; his style was laboured, an uneasy mixture of the classical and the slangy, and his dialogue was such as could never have issued from the mouth of a human being. Toward the end of his career, when he dictated his books, his style, acquiring a conversational ease, became flowing and limpid; and then the critics, going back to the novels of his maturity, found that their English had a nervous, racy vigour that eminently suited the matter. His prime belonged to a period when the purple patch was in vogue and there are descriptive passages in his works that have found their way into all the anthologies of English prose. His pieces on the sea, and spring in the Kentish woods, and sunset on the lower reaches of the Thames are famous. It should be a mortification to me that I cannot read them without discomfort.

When I was a young man, though his books sold but little and one or two were banned by the libraries, it was very much a mark of culture to admire him. He was thought boldly realistic. He was a very good stick to beat the Philistines with. Somebody's lucky inspiration discovered that his sailors and peasants were Shakespearean, and when the advanced got together they uttered shrill cries of ecstasy over the dry and spicy humour of his yokels. This was a commodity that Edward Driffield had no difficulty in supplying. My own heart sank when he led me into the forecastle of a sailing ship or the taproom of a public-house and I knew I was in for half a dozen pages in dialect of facetious comment on life, ethics and immortality. But, I admit, I have always thought the Shakespearean clowns tedious and their innumerable progeny insupportable.

Driffield's strength lay evidently in his depiction of the class he knew best, farmers and farm labourers, shopkeepers and bartenders, skippers of sailing ships, mates, cooks and able seamen. When he introduces characters belonging to a higher station in life even his warmest admirers, one would have thought, must experience a certain malaise; his fine gentlemen are so incredibly fine, his high-born ladies are so good, so pure, so noble that you are not surprised that they can only express themselves with polysyllabic dignity. His women hardly come to life. But here again I must add that this is only my opinion; the world at large and the most eminent critics have agreed that they are very winsome types of English womanhood, spirited, gallant, high-souled, and they have been often compared with the heroines of Shakespeare. We know of course that women are habitually constipated, but to represent them in fiction as being altogether devoid of a back passage seems to me really an excess of chivalry. I am surprised that they care to see themselves thus limned.

The critics can force the world to pay attention to a very indifferent writer, and the world may lose its head over one who has no merit at all, but the result in neither case is lasting; and I cannot help thinking that no writer can hold the public for as long as Edward Driffield without considerable gifts. The elect sneer at popularity; they are inclined even to assert that it is a proof of mediocrity; but they forget that posterity makes its choice not from among the unknown writers of a period, but from among the known. It may be that some great masterpiece which deserves immortality has fallen still-born from the press, but posterity will never hear of it; it may be that posterity will scrap all the best sellers of our day, but it is among them that it must choose. At all events Edward Driffield is in the running. His novels happen to bore me; I find them long; the melodramatic incidents with which he sought to stir the sluggish reader's interest leave me cold; but he certainly had sincerity. There is in his best books the stir of life, and in none of them can you fail to be aware of the author's enigmatic personality. In his earlier days he was praised or blamed for his realism; according to the idiosyncrasy of his critics he was extolled for his truth or censured for his coarseness. But realism has ceased to excite remark, and the library reader will take in his stride obstacles at which a generation back he would have violently shied. The cultured reader of these pages will remember the leading article in the *Literary Supplement* of *The Times* which appeared at the moment of Driffield's death. Taking the novels of Edward Driffield as his text, the author wrote what was very well described as a hymn to beauty. No one who read it could fail to be impressed by those swelling periods, which reminded one of the noble prose of Jeremy Taylor, by that reverence and piety, by all those high sentiments, in short, expressed in a style that was ornate without excess and dulcet without effeminacy. It was itself a thing of beauty. If some suggested that Edward Driffield was by way of being a humorist and that a jest would here and there have lightened this eulogious article it must be replied that after all it was a funeral oration. And it is well known that Beauty does not look with a good grace on the timid advances of Humour. Roy Kear, when he was talking to me of Driffield, claimed that, whatever his faults, they were redeemed by the beauty that suffused his pages. Now I come to look back on our conversation, I think it was this remark that had most exasperated me.

Thirty years ago in literary circles God was all the fashion. It was good form to believe and journalists used Him to adorn a phrase or balance a sentence; then God went out (oddly enough with cricket and beer) and Pan came in. In a hundred novels his cloven hoof left its imprint on the sward; poets saw him lurking in the twilight on London commons, and literary ladies in Surrey, nymphs of an industrial age, mysteriously surrendered their virginity to his rough embrace. Spiritually they were never the same again. But Pan went out and now beauty has taken his place. People find it in a phrase, or a turbot, a dog, a day, a picture, an action, a dress. Young women in cohorts, each of whom has written so promising and competent a novel, prattle of it in every manner from allusive to arch, from intense to charming; and the young men, more or less recently down from Oxford, but still trailing its clouds of glory, who tell us in the weekly papers that we should think of art, life and the universe, fling the word with a pretty negligence about their close-packed pages. It is sadly frayed. Gosh, they have worked it hard! The ideal has many names and beauty is but one of them. I wonder if this clamour is anything more than the cry of distress of those who cannot make themselves at home in our heroic world of machines, and I wonder if their passion for beauty, the Little Nell of this shamefaced day, is anything more than sentimentality. It may be that another generation, accommodating itself more adequately to the stress of life, will look for inspiration not in a flight from reality, but in an eager acceptance of it.

I do not know if others are like myself, but I am conscious that I cannot contemplate beauty long. For me no poet made a falser statement than Keats when he wrote the first line of *Endymion*. When the thing of beauty has given me the magic of its sensation my mind quickly wanders; I listen with incredulity to the persons who tell me that they can look with rapture for hours at a view of a picture. Beauty is an ecstasy; it is as simple as hunger. There is really nothing to be said about it. It is like the perfume of a rose: you can smell it and that is all: that is why the criticism of art, except in so far as it is unconcerned with beauty and therefore with art, is tiresome. All the critic can tell you with regard to Titian's *Entombment of Christ*, perhaps of all the pictures in the world that which has most pure beauty, is to go and look at it. What else he has to say is history, or biography, or what not. But people add other qualities to beauty–sublimity, human interest, tenderness, love–because beauty does not long content them. Beauty is perfect, and perfection (such is human nature) holds our attention but for a little while. The mathematician who after seeing *Phèdre* asked: *'Qu'est-ce que ça prouve?'* was not such a fool as he has been generally made out. No one has ever been able to explain why the Doric temple of Paestum is more beautiful than a glass of cold beer except by bringing in considerations that have nothing to do with beauty. Beauty is a blind alley. It is a mountain peak which once reached leads nowhere. That is why in the end we find more to entrance us in El Greco than in Titian, in the incomplete achievement of Shakespeare than in the consummate success of Racine. Too much has been written about beauty. That is why I have written a little more. Beauty is that which satisfies the aesthetic instinct. But who wants to be satisfied? It is only to the dullard that enough is as good as a feast. Let us face it: beauty is a bit of a bore.

But of course what the critics wrote about Edward Driffield was eye-wash. His outstanding merit was not the realism that gave vigour to his work, nor the beauty that informed it, nor his graphic portraits of seafaring men, nor his poetic descriptions of salty marshes, of storm and calm and of nestling hamlets; it was his longevity. Reverence for old age is one of the most admirable traits of the human race and I think it may safely be stated that in no other country than ours is that trait more marked. The awe and love with which other nations regard old age is often platonic; but ours is practical. Who but the English would fill Covent Garden to listen to an aged prima

donna without a voice? Who but the English would pay to see dancers so
decrepit that they can hardly put one foot before the other and say to one
another admiringly in the intervals: 'By George, sir, d'you know he's a long
way past sixty?' But compared with politicians and writers these are but
striplings, and I often think that a *jeune premier* must be of a singularly
amiable disposition if it does not make him bitter to consider that when at
the age of seventy he must end his career the public man and the author are
only at their prime. A man who is a politician at forty is a statesman at three
score and ten. It is at this age, when he would be too old to be a clerk or a
gardener or a police-court magistrate, that he is ripe to govern a country.
This is not so strange when you reflect that from the earliest times the old
have rubbed it into the young that they are wiser than they, and before the
young had discovered what nonsense this was they were old too, and it
profited them to carry on the imposture; and besides, no one can have moved
in the society of politicians without discovering that (if one may judge by
results) it requires little mental ability to rule a nation. But why writers
should be more esteemed the older they grow, has long perplexed me. At one
time I thought that the praise accorded to them when they had ceased for
twenty years to write anything of interest was largely due to the fact that the
younger men, having no longer to fear their competition, felt it safe to extol
their merit; and it is well known that to praise someone whose rivalry you do
not dread is often a very good way of putting a spoke in the wheel of someone
whose rivalry you do. But this is to take a low view of human nature and I
would not for the world lay myself open to a charge of cheap cynicism. After
mature consideration I have come to the conclusion that the real reason for
the universal applause that comforts the declining years of the author who
exceeds the common span of man is that intelligent people after the age of
thirty read nothing at all. As they grow older the books they read in their
youth are lit with its glamour and with every year that passes they ascribe
greater merit to the author that wrote them. Of course he must go on; he
must keep in the public eye. It is no good his thinking that it is enough to
write one or two masterpieces; he must provide a pedestal for them of forty
or fifty works of no particular consequence. This needs time. His production
must be such that it he cannot captivate a reader by his charm he can stun
him by his weight.

If, as I think, longevity is genius, few in our time have enjoyed it in a more
conspicuous degree than Edward Driffield. When he was a young fellow in
the sixties (the cultured having had their way with him and passed him by)
his position in the world of letters was only respectable; the best judges
praised him, but with moderation; the younger men were inclined to be
frivolous at his expense. It was agreed that he had talent, but it never
occurred to anyone that he was one of the glories of English literature. He
celebrated his seventieth birthday; an uneasiness passed over the world of
letters, like a ruffling of the waters when on an Eastern sea a typhoon lurks in
the distance, and it grew evident that there had lived among us all these years
a great novelist and none of us had suspected it. There was a rush for
Driffield's books in the various libraries and a hundred busy pens, in
Bloomsbury, in Chelsea and in other places where men of letters congregate,
wrote appreciations, studies, essays and works, short and chatty or long and
intense, on his novels. These were reprinted, in complete editions, in select
editions, at a shilling and three and six and five shillings and a guinea. His
style was analysed, his philosophy was examined, his technique was

dissected. At seventy-five everyone agreed that Edward Driffield had genius. At eighty he was the Grand Old Man of English Letters. This position he held till his death.

Now we look about and think sadly that there is no one to take his place. A few septuagenarians are sitting up and taking notice, and they evidently feel that they could comfortably fill the vacant niche. But it is obvious that they lack something.

Though these recollections have taken so long to narrate they took but a little while to pass through my head. They came to me higgledy-piggledy, an incident and then a scrap of conversation that belonged to a previous time, and I have set them down in order for the convenience of the reader and because I have a neat mind. One thing that surprised me was that even at that far distance I could remember distinctly what people looked like and even the gist of what they said, but only with vagueness what they wore. I knew of course that the dress, especially of women, was quite different forty years ago from what it was now, but if I recalled it at all it was not from life but from pictures and photographs that I had seen much later.

I was still occupied with my idle fancies when I heard a taxi stop at the door, the bell ring, and in a moment Alroy Kear's booming voice telling the butler that he had an appointment with me. He came in, big, bluff and hearty; his vitality shattered with a single gesture the frail construction I had been building out of the vanished past. He brought in with him, like a blustering wind in March, the aggressive and inescapable present.

'I was just asking myself,' I said, 'who could possibly succeed Edward Driffield as the Grand Old Man of English Letters and you arrive to answer my question.'

He broke into a jovial laugh, but into his eyes came a quick look of suspicion.

'I don't think there's anybody,' he said.

'How about yourself?'

'Oh, my dear boy, I'm not fifty yet. Give me another twenty-five years.' He laughed, but his eyes held mine keenly. 'I never know when you're pulling my leg.' He looked down suddenly. 'Of course one can't help thinking about the future sometimes. All the people who are at the top of the tree now are anything from fifteen to twenty years older than me. They can't last for ever, and when they're gone who is there? Of course there's Aldous; he's a good deal younger than me, but he's not very strong and I don't believe he takes great care of himself. Barring accidents, by which I mean barring some genius who suddenly springs up and sweeps the board, I don't quite see how in another twenty or twenty-five years I can help having the field pretty well to myself. It's just a question of pegging away and living on longer than the others.'

Roy sank his virile bulk into one of my landlady's armchairs and I offered him a whisky and soda.

'No, I never drink spirits before six o'clock,' he said. He looked about him. 'Jolly, these digs are.'

'I know. What have you come to see me about?'

'I thought I'd better have a little chat with you about Mrs Driffield's invitation. It was rather difficult to explain over the telephone. The truth of the matter is that I've arranged to write Driffield's life.'

'Oh! Why didn't you tell me the other day?'

I felt friendly disposed toward Roy. I was happy to think that I had not misjudged him when I suspected that it was not merely for the pleasure of my company that he had asked me to luncheon.

'I hadn't entirely made up my mind. Mrs Driffield is very keen on my doing it. She's going to help me in every way she can. She's giving me all the material she has. She's been collecting it for a good many years. It's not an easy thing to do and of course I can't afford not to do it well. But if I can make a pretty good job of it, it can't fail to do me a lot of good. People have so much more respect for a novelist if he writes something serious now and then. Those critical works of mine were an awful sweat, and they sold nothing, but I don't regret them for a moment. They've given me a position I could never have got without them.'

'I think it's a very good plan. You've known Driffield more intimately than most people for the last twenty years.'

'I think I have. But of course he was over sixty when I first made his acquaintance. I wrote and told him how much I admired his books and he asked me to go and see him. But I know nothing about the early part of his life. Mrs Driffield used to try to get him to talk about those days and she made very copious notes of all he said, and then there are diaries that he kept now and then, and of course a lot of the stuff in the novels is obviously autobiographical. But there are immense lacunae. I'll tell you the sort of book I want to write, a sort of intimate life, with a lot of those little details that make people feel warm inside, you know, and then woven in with this a really exhaustive criticism of his literary work, not ponderous, of course, but although sympathetic, searching and . . . subtle. Naturally it wants doing, but Mrs Driffield seems to think I can do it.'

'I'm sure you can,' I put in.

'I don't see why not,' said Roy. 'I am a critic, and I'm a novelist. It's obvious that I have certain literary qualifications. But I can't do anything unless everyone who can is willing to help me.'

I began to see where I came in. I tried to make my face look quite blank. Roy leaned forward.

'I asked you the other day if you were going to write anything about Driffield yourself and you said you weren't. Can I take that as definite?'

'Certainly.'

'Then have you got any objection to giving me your material?'

'My dear boy, I haven't got any.'

'Oh, that's nonsense,' said Roy good-humouredly, with the tone of a doctor who is trying to persuade a child to have its throat examined. 'When he was living at Blackstable you must have seen a lot of him.'

'I was only a boy then.'

'But you must have been conscious of the unusual experience. After all, no one could be for half an hour in Edward Driffield's society without being impressed by his extraordinary personality. It must have been obvious even to a boy of sixteen, and you were probably more observant and sensitive than the average boy of that age.'

'I wonder if his personality would have seemed extraordinary without the reputation to back it up. Do you imagine that if you went down to a spa in the west of England as Mr Atkins, a chartered accountant taking the waters for his liver, you would impress the people you met there as a man of character?'

'I imagine they'd soon realise that I was not quite the common or garden chartered accountant,' said Roy, with a smile that took from his remark any appearance of self-esteem.

'Well, all I can tell you is that what chiefly bothered me about Driffield in those days was that the knickerbocker suit he wore was dreadfully loud. We used to bicycle a lot together and it always made me feel a trifle uncomfortable to be seen with him.'

'It sounds comic now. What did he talk about?'

'I don't know; nothing very much. He was rather keen on architecture, and he talked about farming, and if a pub looked nice he generally suggested stopping for five minutes and having a glass of bitter, and then he would talk to the landlord about the crops and the price of coal and things like that.'

I rambled on, though I could see by the look of Roy's face that he was disappointed with me; he listened, but he was a trifle bored, and it struck me that when he was bored he looked peevish. But though I couldn't remember that Driffield had ever said anything significant during those long rides of ours, I had a very acute recollection of the *feel* of them. Blackstable was peculiar in this, that though it was on the sea, with a long shingly beach and marshland at the back, you had only to go about half a mile inland to come into the most rural country in Kent. Winding roads that ran between the great fat green fields and clumps of huge elms, substantial and with a homely stateliness like good old Kentish farmers' wives, high-coloured and robust, who had grown portly on good butter and home-made bread and cream and fresh eggs. And sometimes the road was only a lane, with thick hawthorn hedges, and the green elms overhung it on either side so that when you looked up there was only a strip of blue sky between. And as you rode along in the warm, keen air you had a sensation that the world was standing still and life would last for ever. Although you were pedalling with such energy you had a delicious feeling of laziness. You were quite happy when no one spoke, and if one of the party from sheer high spirits suddenly put on speed and shot ahead it was a joke that everyone laughed at and for a few minutes you pedalled as hard as you could. And we chaffed one another innocently and giggled at our own humour. Now and then one would pass cottages with little gardens in front of them and in the gardens were hollyhocks and tiger lilies; and a little way from the road were farmhouses, with their spacious barns and oasthouses; and one would pass through hop-fields with the ripening hops hanging in garlands. The public-houses were friendly and informal, hardly more important than cottages, and on the porches often honeysuckle would be growing. The names they bore were usual and familiar: The Jolly Sailor, The Merry Ploughman, The Crown and Anchor, The Red Lion.

But of course all that could matter nothing to Roy, and he interrupted me.

'Did he ever talk of literature?' he asked.

'I don't think so. He wasn't that sort of writer. I suppose he thought about his writing, but he never mentioned it. He used to lend the curate books. In the winter, one Christmas holidays, I used to have tea at his house nearly every day and sometimes the curate and he would talk about books, but we used to shut them up.'

'Don't you remember anything he said?'

'Only one thing. I remember it because I hadn't ever read the things he was talking about and what he said made me do so. He said that when Shakespeare retired to Stratford-on-Avon and became respectable, if he ever thought of his plays at all, probably the two that he remembered with most interest were *Measure for Measure* and *Troilus and Cressida*.'

'I don't think that's very illuminating. Didn't he say anything about anyone more modern than Shakespeare?'

'Well, not then, that I can remember; but when I was lunching with the
Driffields a few years ago I overheard him saying that Henry James had
turned his back on one of the great events of the world's history, the rise of
the United States, in order to report tittle-tattle at tea parties in English
country houses. Driffield called it *il gran rifiuto*. I was surprised at hearing
the old man use an Italian phrase and amused because a great big bouncing
duchess who was there was the only person who knew what the devil he was
talking about. He said: "Poor Henry, he's spending eternity wandering
round and round a stately park and the fence is just too high for him to peep
over and they're having tea just too far away for him to hear what the
countess is saying."'

Roy listened to my little anecdote with attention. He shook his head
reflectively.

'I don't think I could use that. I'd have the Henry James gang down on me
like a thousand of bricks. . . . But what used you to do during those
evenings?'

'Well, we played whist while Driffield read books for review and he used
to sing.'

'That's interesting,' said Roy, leaning forward eagerly. 'Do you
remember what he sang?'

'Perfectly. "All Through Stickin' to a Soljer" and "Come Where the
Booze Is Cheaper" were his favourites.'

'Oh!'

I could see that Roy was disappointed.

'Did you expect him to sing Schumann?' I asked.

'I don't know why not. It would have been rather a good point. But I think
I should have expected him to sing sea chanties or old English country airs,
you know, the sort of thing they used to sing at fairings—blind fiddlers and
the village swains dancing with the girls on the threshing floor and all that
sort of thing. I might have made something rather beautiful out of that, but I
can't *see* Edward Driffield singing music-hall songs. After all, when you're
drawing a man's portrait you must get the values right; you only confuse the
impression if you put in stuff that's all out of tone.'

'You know that shortly after this he shot the moon. He let everybody in.'

Roy was silent for fully a minute and he looked down at the carpet
reflectively.

'Yes, I knew there'd been some unpleasantness. Mrs Driffield mentioned
it. I understand everything was paid up later before he finally bought Ferne
Court and settled down in the district. I don't think it's necessary to dwell on
an incident that is not really of any importance in the history of his
development. After all, it happened nearly forty years ago. You know, there
were some very curious sides to the old man. One would have thought that
after a rather sordid little scandal like that the neighbourhood of Blackstable
would be the last place he'd choose to spend the rest of his life in when he'd
become celebrated, especially when it was the scene of his rather humble
origins; but he didn't seem to mind a bit. He seemed to think the whole thing
rather a good joke. He was quite capable of telling people who came to lunch
about it and it was very embarrassing for Mrs Driffield. I should like you to
know Amy better. She's a very remarkable woman. Of course the old man
had written all his great books before he ever set eyes on her, but I don't
think anyone can deny that it was she who created the rather imposing and

dignified figure that the world saw for the last twenty-five years of his life. She's been very frank with me. She didn't have such an easy job of it. Old Driffield had some queer ways and she had to use a good deal of tact to get him to behave decently. He was very obstinate in some things and I think a woman of less character would have been discouraged. For instance, he had a habit that poor Amy had a lot of trouble to break him of: after he'd finished his meat and vegetables he'd take a piece of bread and wipe the plate clean with it and eat it.'

'Do you know what that means?' I said. 'It means that for long he had so little to eat that he couldn't afford to waste any food he could get.'

'Well, that may be, but it's not a very pretty habit for a distinguished man of letters. And then, he didn't exactly tipple, but he was rather fond of going down to the Bear and Key at Blackstable and having a few beers in the public bar. Of course there was no harm in it, but it did make him rather conspicuous, especially in summer when the place was full of trippers. He didn't mind who he talked to. He didn't seem able to realise that he had a position to keep up. You can't deny it was rather awkward after they'd been having a lot of interesting people to lunch—people like Edmund Gosse, for instance, and Lord Curzon—that he should go down to a public-house and tell the plumber and the baker and the sanitary inspector what he thought about them. But of course that could be explained away. One could say that he was after local colour and was interested in types. But he had some habits that really were rather difficult to cope with. Do you know that it was with the greatest difficulty that Amy Driffield could ever get him to take a bath?'

'He was born at a time when people thought it unhealthy to take too many baths. I don't suppose he ever lived in a house that had a bathroom till he was fifty.'

'Well, he said he never had had a bath more than once a week and he didn't see why he should change his habits at his time of life. Then Amy said that he must change his under linen every day, but he objected to that too. He said he'd always been used to wearing his vest and drawers for a week and it was nonsense, it only wore them out to have them washed so often. Mrs Driffield did everything she could to tempt him to have a bath every day, with bath salts and perfumes, you know, but nothing would induce him to, and as he grew older he wouldn't even have one once a week. She tells me that for the last three years of his life he never had a bath at all. Of course, all this is between ourselves; I'm merely telling it to show you that in writing his life I shall have to use a good deal of tact. I don't see how one can deny that he was just a wee bit unscrupulous in money matters and he had a kink in him that made him take a strange pleasure in the society of his inferiors and some of his personal habits were rather disagreeable, but I don't think that side of him was the most significant. I don't want to say anything that's untrue, but I do think there's a certain amount that's better left unsaid.'

'Don't you think it would be more interesting if you went the whole hog and drew him warts and all?'

'Oh, I couldn't. Amy Driffield would never speak to me again. She only asked me to do the life because she felt she could trust my discretion. I must behave like a gentleman.'

'It's very hard to be a gentleman and a writer.'

'I don't see why. And besides, you know what the critics are. If you tell the truth they only say you're cynical and it does an author no good to get a reputation for cynicism. Of course I don't deny that if I were thoroughly unscrupulous I could make a sensation. It would be rather amusing to show the man with his passion for beauty and his careless treatment of his obligations, his fine style and his personal hatred for soap and water, his idealism and his tippling in disreputable pubs; but honestly, would it pay? They'd only say I was imitating Lytton Strachey. No, I think I shall do much better to be allusive and charming and rather subtle, you know the sort of thing, and tender. I think one ought always to *see* a book before one starts it. Well, I see this rather like a portrait by Van Dyck, with a good deal of atmosphere, you know, and a certain gravity, and with a sort of aristocratic distinction. Do you know what I mean? About eighty thousand words.'

He was absorbed for a moment in the ecstasy of aesthetic contemplation. In his mind's eye he saw a book, in royal octavo, slim and light in the hand printed with large margins on handsome paper in a type that was both clear and comely, and I think he saw a binding in smooth black cloth with a decoration in gold and gilt lettering. But being human, Alroy Kear could not, as I suggested a few pages back, hold the ecstasy that beauty yields for more than a little while. He gave me a candid smile.

'But how the devil am I to get over the first Mrs Driffield?'

'The skeleton in the cupboard,' I murmured.

'She is damned awkward to deal with. She was married to Driffield for a good many years. Amy has very decided views on the subject, but I don't see how I can possibly meet them. You see, her attitude is that Rose Driffield exerted a most pernicious influence on her husband, and that she did everything possible to ruin him morally, physically and financially; she was beneath him in every way, at least intellectually and spiritually, and it was only because he was a man of immense force and vitality that he survived. It was of course a very unfortunate marriage. It's true that she's been dead for ages and it seems a pity to rake up old scandals and wash a lot of dirty linen in public; but the fact remains that all Driffield's greatest books were written when he was living with her. Much as I admire the later books, and no one is more conscious of their genuine beauty than I am, and they have a restraint and a sort of classical sobriety which are admirable, I must admit that they haven't the tang and the vigour and the smell and bustle of life of the early ones. It does seem to me that you can't altogether ignore the influence his first wife had on his work.'

'What are you going to do about it?' I asked.

'Well, I can't see why all that part of his life shouldn't be treated with the greatest possible reserve and delicacy, so as not to offend the most exacting susceptibility, and yet with a sort of manly frankness, if you understand what I mean, that would be rather moving.'

'It sounds a very tall order.'

'As I see it, there's no need to dot the i's or to cross the t's. It can only be a question of getting just the right touch. I wouldn't state more than I could help, but I would suggest what was essential for the reader to realise. You know, however gross a subject is you can soften its unpleasantness if you treat it with dignity. But I can do nothing unless I am in complete possession of the facts.'

'Obviously you can't cook them unless you have them.'

Roy had been speaking with a fluent ease that revealed the successful lecturer. I wished (a) that I could express myself with so much force and aptness, never at a loss for a word, rolling off the sentences without a moment's hesitation; and (b) that I did not feel so miserably incompetent with my one small insignificant person to represent the large and appreciative audience that Roy was instinctively addressing. But now he paused. A genial look came over his face, which his enthusiasm had reddened and the heat of the day caused to perspire, and the eyes that had held me with a dominating brilliance softened and smiled.

'This is where you come in, old boy,' he said pleasantly.

I have always found it a very good plan in life to say nothing when I had nothing to say and when I do not know how to answer a remark to hold my tongue. I remained silent and looked back at Roy amiably.

'You know more about his life at Blackstable than anybody else.'

'I don't know about that. There must be a number of people at Blackstable who saw as much of him in the old days as I did.'

'That may be, but after all they're presumably not people of any importance, and I don't think they matter very much.'

'Oh, I see. You mean that I'm the only person who might blow the gaff.'

'Roughly, that is what I do mean, if you feel that you must put it in a facetious way.'

I saw that Roy was not inclined to be amused. I did not mind, for I am quite used to people not being amused at my jokes. I often think that the purest type of the artist is the humorist who laughs at his own jests.

'And you saw a good deal of him later on in London, I believe.'

'Yes.'

'That is when he had an apartment somewhere in Lower Belgravia.'

'Well, lodgings in Pimlico.'

Roy smiled dryly.

'We won't quarrel about the exact designation of the quarter of London in which he lived. You were very intimate with him then.'

'Fairly.'

'How long did that last?'

'About a couple of years.'

'How old were you then?'

'Twenty.'

'Now look here, I want you to do me a great favour. It won't take you very long and it will be of quite inestimable value to me. I want you to jot down as fully as you can all your recollections of Driffield, and all you remember about his wife and his relations with her and so on, both at Blackstable and in London.'

'It needn't take you very long. You can write it quite roughly, I mean. You needn't bother about style, you know, or anything like that. I'll put the style in. All I want are the facts. After all, you know them and nobody else does. I don't want to be pompous or anything like that, but Driffield was a great man and you owe it to his memory and to English literature to tell everything you know. I shouldn't have asked you, but you told me the other day that you weren't going to write anything about him yourself. It would be rather like a dog in a manger to keep to yourself a whole lot of material that you have no intention of using.

Thus Roy appealed at once to my sense of duty, my indolence, my generosity and my rectitude.

'But why does Mrs Driffield want me to go down and stay at Ferne Court?' I asked.

'Well, we talked it over. It's a very jolly house to stay in. She does one very well, and it ought to be divine in the country just now. She thought it would be very nice and quiet for you if you felt inclined to write your recollections there; of course, I said I couldn't promise that, but naturally being so near Blackstable would remind you of all sorts of things that you might otherwise forget. And then, living in his house, among his books and things, it would make the past seem much more real. We could all talk about him, and you know how in the heat of conversation things come back. Amy's very quick and clever. She's been in the habit of making notes of Driffield's talk for years, and after all it's quite likely that you'll say things on the spur of the moment that you wouldn't think of writing and she can just jot them down afterward. And we can play tennis and bathe.'

'I'm not very fond of staying with people,' I said. 'I hate getting up for a nine-o'clock breakfast to eat things I have no mind to. I don't like going for walks, and I'm not interested in other people's chickens.'

'She's a lonely woman now. It would be a kindness to her and it would be a kindness to me too.'

I reflected.

'I'll tell you what I'll do: I'll go down to Blackstable, but I'll go down on my own. I'll put up at the Bear and Key and I'll come over and see Mrs Driffield while you're there. You can both talk your heads off about Edward Driffield, but I shall be able to get away when I'm fed up with you.'

Roy laughed good-naturedly.

'All right. That'll do. And will you jot down anything you can remember that you think will be useful to me?'

'I'll try.'

'When will you come? I'm going down on Friday.'

'I'll come with you if you'll promise not to talk to me in the train.'

'All right. The five-ten's the best one. Shall I come and fetch you?'

'I'm capable of getting to Victoria by myself. I'll meet you on the platform.'

I don't know if Roy was afraid of my changing my mind, but he got up at once, shook my hand heartily and left. He begged me on no account to forget my tennis racket and bathing suit.

Chapter Twelve

My promise to Roy sent my thoughts back to my first years in London. Having nothing much to do that afternoon, it occurred to me to stroll along and have a cup of tea with my old landlady. Mrs Hudson's name had been given to me by the secretary of the medical school at St Luke's when, a callow youth just arrived in town, I was looking for lodgings. She had a house in Vincent Square. I lived there for five years, in two rooms on the ground floor, and over me on the drawing-room floor lived a master at Westminster School. I paid a pound a week for my rooms and he paid twenty-five shillings. Mrs Hudson was a little, active, bustling woman, with a sallow face, a large aquiline nose and the brightest, the most vivacious black eyes that I ever saw. She had a great deal of very dark hair, in the afternoons and all day on Sunday arranged in a fringe on the forehead with a bun at the nape of the neck as you may see in old photographs of the Jersey

Lily. She had a heart of gold (though I did not know it then, for when you are young you take the kindness people show you as your right) and she was an excellent cook. No one could make a better *omelette soufflée* than she. Every morning she was up betimes to get the fire lit in her gentlemen's sitting-rooms so that 'they needn't eat their breakfasts simply perishin' with the cold, my word it's bitter this morning'; and if she didn't hear you having your bath, a flat tin bath that slipped under the bed, the water put in the night before to take the chill off, she'd say: 'There now, there's my dining-room floor not up yet, 'e'll be late for his lecture again,' and she would come tripping upstairs and thump on the door and you would hear her shrill voice: 'If you don't get up at once you won't 'ave time to 'ave breakfast, an' I've got a lovely 'addick for you.' She worked all day long and she sang at her work and she was gay and happy and smiling. Her husband was much older than she. He had been a butler in very good families, and wore side-whiskers and a perfect manner; he was verger at a neighbouring church, highly respected, and he waited at table and cleaned the boots and helped with the washing-up. Mrs Hudson's only relaxation was to come up after she had served the dinners (I had mine at half-past six and the schoolmaster at seven) and have a little chat with her gentlemen. I wish to goodness I had had the sense (like Amy Driffield with her celebrated husband) to take notes of her conversation, for Mrs Hudson was a mistress of Cockney humour. She had a gift of repartee that never failed her, she had a racy style and an apt and varied vocabulary, she was never at a loss for the comic metaphor or the vivid phrase. She was a pattern of propriety and she would never have women in her house, you never knew what they were up to ('It's men, men, men all the time with them, and afternoon tea and thin bread and butter, and openin' the door and ringin' for 'ot water and I don't know what all'); but in conversation she did not hesitate to use what was called in those days the blue bag. One could have said of her what she said of Marie Lloyd: 'What I like about 'er is that she gives you a good laugh. She goes pretty near the knuckle sometimes, but she never jumps over the fence.' Mrs Hudson enjoyed her own humour and I think she talked more willingly to her lodgers because her husband was a serious man ('It's as it should be,' she said, ''im bein' a verger and attendin' weddings and funerals and what all') and wasn't much of a one for a joke. 'Wot I says to 'Udson is, laugh while you've got the chance, you won't laugh much when you're dead and buried.'

Mrs Hudson's humour was cumulative and the story of her feud with Miss Butcher who let lodgings at number fourteen was a great comic saga that went on year in and year out.

'She's a disagreeable old cat, but I give you my word I'd miss 'er if the Lord took 'er one fine day. Though what 'e'd do with 'er when 'e got 'er I can't think. Many's the good laugh she's give me in 'er time.'

Mrs Hudson had very bad teeth and the question whether she should have them taken out and have false ones was discussed by her for two or three years with an unimaginable variety of comic invention.

'But as I said to 'Udson on'y last night, when he said, "Oh, come on, 'ave 'em out and 'ave done with it," I shouldn't 'ave anythin' to talk about.'

I had not seen Mrs Hudson for two or three years. My last visit had been in answer to a little letter in which she asked me to come and drink a nice strong cup of tea with her and announced: 'Hudson died three months ago next Saturday, aged seventy-nine, and George and Hester send their respectful compliments.' George was the issue of her marriage with

Hudson. He was now a man approaching middle age who worked at Woolwich Arsenal, and his mother had been repeating for twenty years that George would be bringing a wife home one of these days. Hester was the maid-of-all-work she had engaged toward the end of my stay with her, and Mrs Hudson still spoke of her as 'that dratted girl of mine.' Though Mrs Hudson must have been well over thirty when I first took her rooms, and that was five and thirty years ago, I had no feeling as I walked leisurely through the Green Park that I should not find her alive. She was as definitely part of the recollections of my youth as the pelicans that stood at the edge of the ornamental water.

I walked down the area steps and the door was opened to me by Hester, a woman getting on for fifty now and stoutish, but still bearing on her shyly grinning face the irresponsibility of the dratted girl. Mrs Hudson was darning George's socks when I was shown into the front room of the basement and she took off her spectacles to look at me.

'Well, if that isn't Mr Ashenden! Who ever thought of seeing you? Is the water boiling, 'Ester? You will 'ave a nice cup of tea, won't you?'

Mrs Hudson was a little heavier than when I first knew her and her movements were more deliberate, but there was scarcely a white hair on her head, and her eyes, as black and shining as buttons, sparkled with fun. I sat down in a shabby little armchair covered with maroon leather.

'How are you getting on, Mrs Hudson?' I asked.

'Oh, I've got nothin' much to complain of except that I'm not so young as I used to was,' she answered. 'I can't do so much as I could when you was 'ere. I don't give my gentlemen dinner now, only breakfast.'

'Are all your rooms let?'

'Yes, I'm thankful to say.'

Owing to the rise of prices Mrs Hudson was able to get more for her rooms than in my day, and I think in her modest way she was quite well off. But of course people wanted a lot nowadays.

'You wouldn't believe it, first I 'ad to put in a bathroom, and then I 'ad to put in the electric light, and then nothin' would satisfy them but I must 'ave a telephone. What they'll want next I can't think.'

'Mr George says it's pretty near time Mrs 'Udson thought of retiring,' said Hester, who was laying the tea.

'You mind your own business, my girl,' said Mrs Hudson tartly. 'When I retire it'll be to the cemetery. Fancy me livin' all alone with George and 'Ester without nobody to talk to.'

'Mr George says she ought to take a little 'ouse in the country an' take care of 'erself,' said Hester, unperturbed by the reproof.

'Don't talk to me about the country. The doctor said I was to go there for six weeks last summer. It nearly killed me, I give you my word. The noise of it. All them birds singin' all the time, and the cocks crowin' and the cows mooin'. I couldn't stick it. When you've lived all the years I 'ave in peace and quietness you can't get used to all that racket goin' on all the time.'

A few doors away was the Vauxhall Bridge Road and down it trams were clanging, ringing their bells as they went, motor buses were lumbering along, taxis were tooting their horns. If Mrs Hudson heard it, it was London she heard, and it soothed her as a mother's crooning soothes a restless child.

I looked around the cosy, shabby, homely little parlour in which Mrs Hudson had lived so long. I wondered if there was anything I could do for her. I noticed that she had a gramophone. It was the only thing I could think of.

'Is there anything you want, Mrs Hudson?' I asked.

She fixed her beady eyes on me reflectively.

'I don't know as there is, now you come to speak of it, except me 'ealth and strength for another twenty years so as I can go on workin'.'

I do not think I am a sentimentalist, but her reply, unexpected but so characteristic, made a sudden lump come to my throat.

When it was time for me to go I asked if I could see the rooms I had lived in for five years.

'Run upstairs, 'Ester, and see if Mr Graham's in. If he ain't, I'm sure 'e wouldn't mind you 'avin' a look at them.'

Hester scurried up, and in a moment, slightly breathless, came down again to say that Mr Graham was out. Mrs Hudson came with me. The bed was the same narrow iron bed that I had slept in and dreamed in and there was the same chest of drawers and the same washing stand. But the sitting-room had the grim heartiness of the athlete; on the walls were photographs of cricket elevens and rowing men in shorts; golf clubs stood in the corner and pipes and tobacco jars, ornamented with the arms of a college, were littered on the chimney-piece. In my day we believed in art for art's sake and this I exemplified by draping the chimney-piece with a Moorish rug, putting up curtains of art serge and a bilious green, and hanging on the walls autotypes of pictures by Perugino, Van Dyck and Hobbema.

'Very artistic you was, wasn't you?' Mrs Hudson remarked, not without irony.

'Very,' I murmured.

I could not help feeling a pang as I thought of all the years that had passed since I inhabited that room, and of all that had happened to me. It was at that same table that I had eaten my hearty breakfast and my frugal dinner, read my medical books and written my first novel. It was in that same armchair that I had read for the first time Wordsworth and Stendhal, the Elizabethan dramatists and the Russian novelists, Gibbon, Boswell, Voltaire and Rousseau. I wondered who had used them since. Medical students, articled clerks, young fellows making their way in the city and elderly men retired from the colonies or thrown unexpectedly upon the world by the break up of an old home. The room made me, as Mrs Hudson would have put it, go queer all over. All the hopes that had been cherished there, the bright visions of the future, the flaming passion of youth; the regrets, the disillusion, the weariness, the resignation; so much had been felt in that room, by so many, the whole gamut of human emotion, that it seemed strangely to have acquired a troubling and enigmatic personality of its own. I have no notion why, but it made me think of a woman at a cross-road with a finger on her lips, looking back and with her other hand beckoning. What I obscurely (and rather shamefacedly) felt, communicated itself to Mrs Hudson, for she gave a laugh and with a characteristic gesture rubbed her prominent nose.

'My word, people are funny,' she said. 'When I think of all the gentlemen I've 'ad here, I give you my word you wouldn't believe it if I told you some of the things I know about them. One of them's funnier than the other. Sometimes I lie abed thinkin' of them, and *laugh*. Well, it would be a bad world if you didn't get a good laugh now and then, but, lor', lodgers really are the limit.'

Chapter Thirteen

I lived with Mrs Hudson for nearly two years before I met the Driffields again. My life was very regular. I spent all day at the hospital and about six walked back to Vincent Square. I bought the *Star* at Lambeth Bridge and read it till my dinner was served. Then I read seriously for an hour or two, works to improve my mind, for I was a strenuous, earnest and industrious youth, and after that wrote novels and plays till bedtime. I do not know for what reason it was that one day toward the end of June, happening to leave the hospital early, I thought I would walk down the Vauxhall Bridge Road. I liked it for its noisy bustle. It had a sordid vivacity that was pleasantly exciting and you felt that at any moment an adventure might there befall you. I strolled along in a daydream and was surprised suddenly to hear my name. I stopped and looked, and there to my astonishment stood Mrs Driffield. She was smiling at me.

'Don't you know me?' she cried.

'Yes. Mrs Driffield.'

And though I was grown up I was conscious that I was blushing as furiously as when I was sixteen. I was embarrassed. With my lamentably Victorian notions of honesty I had been much shocked by the Driffields' behaviour in running away from Blackstable without paying their bills. It seemed to me very shabby. I felt deeply the shame I thought they must feel and I was astounded that Mrs Driffield should speak to someone who knew of the discreditable incident. If I had seen her coming I should have looked away, my delicacy presuming that she would wish to avoid the mortification of being seen by me; but she held out her hand and shook mine with obvious pleasure.

'I am glad to see a Blackstable face,' she said. 'You know we left there in a hurry.'

She laughed and I laughed too; but her laugh was mirthful and childlike, while mine, I felt, was strained.

'I hear there *was* a to-do when they found out we'd skipped. I thought Ted would never stop laughing when he heard about it. What did your uncle say?'

I was quick to get the right tone. I wasn't going to let her think that I couldn't see a joke as well as anyone.

'Oh, you know what he is. He's very old-fashioned.'

'Yes, that's what's wrong with Blackstable. They want waking up.' She gave me a friendly look. 'You've grown a lot since I saw you last. Why, you're growing a moustache.'

'Yes,' I said, giving it as much of a twirl as its size allowed me. 'I've had that for ages.'

'How time does fly, doesn't it? You were just a boy four years ago and now you're a man.'

'I ought to be,' I replied somewhat haughtily. 'I'm nearly twenty-one.'

I was looking at Mrs Driffield. She wore a very small hat with feathers in it, and a pale grey dress with large leg-of-mutton sleeves and a long train. I thought she looked very smart. I had always thought that she had a nice face, but I noticed now, for the first time, that she was pretty. Her eyes were bluer than I remembered and her skin was like ivory.

'You know we live just round the corner,' she said.

'So do I.'

'We live in Limpus Road. We've been there almost ever since we left Blackstable.'

'Well, I've been in Vincent Square for nearly two years.'

'I knew you were in London. George Kemp told me so, and I often wondered where you were. Why don't you walk back with me now? Ted will be so pleased to see you.'

'I don't mind,' I said.

As we walked along she told me that Driffield was now literary editor of a weekly paper; his last book had done much better than any of his others and he was expecting to get quite a bit as an advance on royalties for the next one. She seemed to know most of the Blackstable news, and I remembered how it had been suspected that Lord George had helped the Driffields in their flight. I guessed that he wrote to them now and then. I noticed as we walked along that sometimes the men who passed us stared at Mrs Driffield. It occurred to me presently that they must think her pretty too. I began to walk with a certain swagger.

Limpus Road was a long, wide, straight street that ran parallel with the Vauxhall Bridge Road. The houses were all alike, of stucco, dingily painted, solid and with substantial porticos. I suppose they had been built to be inhabited by men of standing in the city of London, but the street had gone down in the world or had never attracted the right sort of tenant; and its decayed respectability had an air at once furtive and shabbily dissipated, that made you think of persons who had seen better days and now, genteelly fuddled, talked of the social distinction of their youth. The Driffields lived in a house painted a dull red, and Mrs Driffield letting me into a narrow dark hall, opened a door and said:

'Go in. I'll tell Ted you're here.'

She walked down the hall and I entered the sitting-room. The Driffields had the basement and the ground floor of the house, which they rented from the lady who lived in the upper part.. The room into which I went looked as if it had been furnished with the scourings of auction sales. There were heavy velvet curtains with great fringes, all loops and festoons, and a gilt suite, upholstered in yellow damask, heavily buttoned; and there was a great pouffe in the middle of the room. There were gilt cabinets in which were masses of little articles, pieces of china, ivory figures, wood carvings, bits of Indian brass; and on the walls hung large oil paintings of highland glens and stags and gillies. In a moment Mrs Driffield brought her husband and he greeted me warmly. He wore a shabby alpaca coat and grey trousers; he had shaved his beard and wore now a moustache and a small imperial. I noticed for the first time how short he was; but he looked more distinguished than he used to. There was something a trifle foreign in his appearance and I thought this was much more what I should expect an author to look like.

'Well, what do you think of our new abode?' he asked. 'It looks rich, doesn't it? I think it inspires confidence.'

He looked round him with satisfaction.

'And Ted's got his den at the back where he can write, and we've got a dining-room in the basement,' said Mrs Driffield. 'Miss Cowley was companion for many years to a lady of title and when she died she left her all her furniture. You can see everything's good, can't you? You can see it came out of a gentleman's house.'

'Rosie fell in love with the place the moment we saw it,' said Driffield.

'You did too, Ted.'

'We've lived in sordid circumstances so long; it's a change to be surrounded by luxury. Madame de Pompadour and all that sort of thing.'

When I left them it was with a very cordial invitation to come again. It appeared that they were at home every Saturday afternoon and all sorts of people whom I would like to meet were in the habit of dropping in.

Chapter Fourteen

I went. I enjoyed myself. I went again. When the autumn came and I returned to London for the winter session at St Luke's I got into the habit of going every Saturday. It was my introduction into the world of art and letters; I kept it a profound secret that in the privacy of my lodgings I was busily writing; I was excited to meet people who were writing also and I listened entranced to their conversation. All sorts of persons came to these parties: at that time week-ends were rare, golf was still a subject for ridicule and few had much to do on Saturday afternoons. I do not think anyone came who was of any great importance; at all events, of all the painters, writers and musicians I met at the Driffields' I cannot remember one whose reputation has endured; but the effect was cultured and animated. You found young actors who were looking for parts and middle-aged singers who deplored the fact that the English were not a musical race, composers who played their compositions on the Driffields' cottage piano and complained in a whispered aside that they sounded nothing except on a concert grand, poets who on pressure consented to read a little thing that they had just written and painters who were looking for commissions. Now and then a person of title added a certain glamour; seldom, however, for in those days the aristocracy had not yet become bohemian and if a person of quality cultivated the society of artists it was generally because a notorious divorce or a little difficulty over cards had made life in his own station (or hers) a bit awkward. We have changed all that. One of the greatest benefits that compulsory education has conferred upon the world is the wide diffusion among the nobility and gentry of the practice of writing. Horace Walpole once wrote a *Catalogue of Royal and Noble Authors*; such a work now would have the dimensions of an encyclopaedia. A title, even a courtesy one, can make a well-known author of almost anyone and it may be safely asserted that there is no better passport to the world of letters than rank.

I have indeed sometimes thought that now that the House of Lords must inevitably in a short while be abolished, it would be a good plan if the profession of literature were by law confined to its members and their wives and children. It would be a graceful compensation that the British people might offer the peers in return for the surrender of their hereditary privileges. It would be a means of support for those (too many) whom devotion to the public cause in keeping chorus girls and race horses and playing *chemin de fer* has impoverished, and a pleasant occupation for the rest who by the process of natural selection have in the course of time become unfit to do anything but govern the British Empire. But this is an age of specialisation and if my plan is adopted it is obvious that it cannot but be to the greater glory of English literature that its various provinces should be apportioned among the various ranks of the nobility. I would suggest, therefore, that the humbler branches of literature should be practised by the lower orders of the peerage and that the barons and viscounts should devote themselves exclusively to journalism and the drama. Fiction might be the privileged demesne of the earls. They have already shown their aptitude for this difficult art and their numbers are so great that they would very competently supply the demand. To the marquises might safely be left the production of that part of literature which is known (I have never quite seen why) as *belles lettres*. It is perhaps not very profitable from a pecuniary standpoint, but it has a distinction that very well suits the holders of this romantic title.

The crown of literature is poetry. It is its end and aim. It is the sublimest activity of the human mind. It is the achievement of beauty. The writer of prose can only step aside when the poet passes; he makes the best of us look like a piece of cheese. It is evident then that the writing of poetry should be left to the dukes, and I should like to see their rights protected by the most severe pains and penalties, it is intolerable that the noblest of arts should be practised by any but the noblest of men. And since here, too, specialisation must prevail, I foresee that the dukes (like the successors of Alexander) will divide the realm of poetry between them, each confining himself to that aspect with which hereditary influence and natural bent have rendered him competent to deal: thus I see the dukes of Manchester writing poems of a didactic and moral character, the dukes of Westminster composing stirring odes on Duty and the Responsibilities of Empire; whereas I imagine that the dukes of Devonshire would be more likely to write love lyrics and elegies in the Propertian manner while it is almost inevitable that the dukes of Marlborough should pipe in an idyllic strain on such subjects as domestic bliss, conscription and content with modest station.

But if you say that this is somewhat formidable and remind me that the muse does not only stalk with majestic tread, but on occasion trips on a light fantastic toe; if, recalling the wise person who said that he did not care who made a nation's laws so long as he wrote its songs, you ask me (thinking rightly that it would ill become the dukes to do so) who shall twang those measures on the lyre that the diverse and inconstant soul of man occasionally hankers after—I answer (obviously enough, I should have thought) the duchesses. I recognise that the day is past when the amorous peasants of the Romagna sang to their sweethearts the verses of Torquato Tasso and Mrs Humphry Ward crooned over young Arnold's cradle the choruses of Œdipus in Colonus. The age demands something more up-to-date. I suggest, therefore, that the more domestic duchesses should write our hymns and our nursery rhymes; while the skittish ones, those who incline to mingle vine leaves with the strawberry, should write the lyrics for musical comedies, humorous verse for the comic papers and mottoes for Christmas cards and crackers. Thus would they retain in the hearts of the British public that place which they have held hitherto only on account of their exalted station.

It was at these parties on Saturday afternoon that I discovered very much to my surprise that Edward Driffield was a distinguished person. He had written something like twenty books, and though he had never made more than a pittance out of them his reputation was considerable. The best judges admired them and the friends who came to his house were agreed that one of these days he would be recognised. They upbraided the public because it would not see that here was a great writer, and since the easiest way to exalt one man is to kick another in the pants, they reviled freely all the novelists whose contemporary fame obscured his. If, indeed, I had known as much of literary circles as I learned later I should have guessed by the not infrequent visits of Mrs Barton Trafford that the time was approaching when Edward Driffield, like a runner in a long-distance race breaking away suddenly from the little knot of plodding athletes, must forge ahead. I admit that when first I was introduced to this lady her name meant nothing to me. Driffield presented me as a young neighbour of his in the country and told her that I was a medical student. She gave me a mellifluous smile, murmured in a soft voice something about Tom Sawyer, and, accepting the bread and butter I offered her, went on talking with her host. But I noticed that her arrival had made an impression and the conversation, which had been noisy and hilarious, was hushed. When in an undertone I asked who she was, I found that my ignorance was amazing; I was told that she had 'made' So-and-So and So-and-So. After half an hour she rose, shook hands very graciously with such of the people as she was acquainted with, and with a sort of lithe sweetness sidled out of the room. Driffield accompanied her to the door and put her in a hansom.

Mrs Barton Trafford was then a woman of about fifty; she was small and slight, but with rather large features, which made her head look a little too big for her body; she had crisp white hair which she wore like the Venus of Milo, and she was supposed in her youth to have been very comely. She dressed discreetly in black silk, and wore round her neck jangling chains of beads and shells. She was said to have been unhappily married in early life, but now for many years had been congenially united to Barton Trafford, a clerk in the Home Office and a well-known authority on prehistoric man. She gave you the curious impression of having no bones in her body and you felt that if you pinched her shin (which of course my respect for her sex as well as something of quiet dignity in her appearance would have never allowed me to do) your fingers would meet. When you took her hand it was like taking a fillet of sole. Her face, notwithstanding its large features, had something fluid about it. When she sat it was as though she had no backbone and were stuffed, like an expensive cushion, with swansdown.

Everything was soft about her, her voice, her smile, her laugh; her eyes, which were small and pale, had the softness of flowers; her manner was as soft as the summer rain. It was this extraordinary, and charming, characteristic that made her the wonderful friend she was. It was this that had gained her the celebrity that she now enjoyed. The whole world was aware of her friendship with the great novelist whose death a few years back had come as such a shock to the English-speaking peoples. Everyone had read the innumerable letters which he had written to her and which she was induced to publish shortly after his demise. Every page revealed his admiration for her beauty and his respect for her judgment; he could never say often enough how much he owed to her encouragement, her ready sympathy, her tact, her taste; and if certain of his expressions of passion were such as some persons might think would not be read by Mr Barton Trafford with unmixed feelings, that only added to the human interest of the work. But Mr Barton Trafford was above the prejudices of vulgar men (his misfortune, if such it was, was one that the greatest personages in history have endured with philosophy) and, abandoning his studies of aurignacian flints and neolithic axe heads, he consented to write a Life of the deceased novelist in which he showed quite definitely how great a part of the writer's genius was due to his wife's influence.

But Mrs Barton Trafford's interest in literature, her passion for art, were not dead because the friend for whom she had done so much had become part, with her far from negligible assistance, of posterity. She was a great reader. Little that was noteworthy escaped her attention and she was quick to establish personal relations with any young writer who showed promise. Her fame, especially since the Life, was now such that she was sure that no one would hesitate to accept the sympathy she was prepared to offer. It was inevitable that Mrs Barton Trafford's genius for friendship should in due course find an outlet. When she read something that struck her, Mr Barton Trafford, himself no mean critic, wrote a warm letter of appreciation to the author and asked him to luncheon. After luncheon, having to get back to the Home Office, he left him to have a chat with Mrs Barton Trafford. Many were called. They all had *something*, but that was not enough. Mrs Barton Trafford had a *flair*, and she trusted her *flair*; her *flair* bade her wait.

She was so cautious indeed that with Jasper Gibbons she almost missed the bus. The records of the past tell us of writers who grew famous in a night, but in our more prudent day this is unheard of. The critics want to see which way the cat will jump, and the public has been sold a pup too often to take unnecessary chances. But in the case of Jasper Gibbons it is almost the exact truth that he did thus jump into celebrity. Now that he is so completely forgotten and the critics who praised him would willingly eat their words if they were not carefully guarded in the files of innumerable newspaper offices, the sensation he made with his first volume of poems is almost unbelievable. The most important papers gave to reviews of it as much space as they would have to the report of a prize fight, the most influential critics fell over one another in their eagerness to welcome him. They likened him to Milton (for the sonority of his blank verse), to Keats (for the opulence of his sensuous imagery), and to Shelley (for his airy fantasy); and, using him as a stick to beat idols of whom they were weary, they gave in his name many a resounding whack on the emaciated buttocks of Lord Tennyson and a few good husky smacks on the bald pate of Robert Browning. The public fell like the walls of Jericho. Edition after edition was sold, and you saw Jasper Gibbons's handsome volume in the boudoirs of countesses in Mayfair, in vicarage drawing-rooms from Land's End to John o' Groats and in the parlours of many an honest but cultured merchant in Glasgow, Aberdeen and Belfast. When it became known that Queen Victoria had accepted a specially bound copy of the book from the hands of the loyal publisher, and had given him (not the poet, the publisher) a copy of *Leaves from a Journal in the Highlands* in exchange, the national enthusiasm knew no bounds.

And all this happened as it were in the twinkling of an eye. Seven cities in Greece disputed the honour of having given birth to Homer, and though Jasper Gibbons's birthplace (Walsall) was well known, twice seven critics claimed the honour of having discovered him; eminent judges of literature who for twenty years had written eulogies of one another's works in the weekly papers quarrelled so bitterly over this matter that one cut the other dead in the Athenaeum. Nor was the great world remiss in giving him its recognition. Jasper Gibbons was asked to luncheon and invited to tea by dowager duchesses, the wives of cabinet ministers and the widows of bishops. It is said that Harrison Ainsworth was the first English man of letters to move in English society on terms of equality (and I have sometimes wondered that an enterprising publisher on this account has not thought of bringing out a complete edition of his works); but I believe that Jasper Gibbons was the first poet to have his name engraved at the bottom of an At Home card as a draw as enticing as an opera singer or a ventriloquist.

It was out of the question then for Mrs Barton Trafford to get in on the ground floor. She could only buy in the open market. I do not know what prodigious strategy she employed, what miracles of tact, what tenderness, what exquisite sympathy, what demure blandishments; I can only surmise and admire; she nobbled Jasper Gibbons. In a little while he was eating out of her soft hand. She was admirable. She had him to lunch to meet the right people; she gave At Homes where he recited his poems before the most distinguished persons in England; she introduced him to eminent actors who gave him commissions to write plays; she saw that his poems should only appear in the proper places; she dealt with the publishers and made contracts for him that would have staggered even a cabinet minister; she took care that he should accept only the invitations of which she approved; she even went so far as to separate him from his wife with whom he had lived happily for ten years, since she felt that a poet to be true to himself and his art must not be encumbered with domestic ties. When the crash came Mrs Barton Trafford, had she chosen, might have said that she had done everything for him that it was humanly possible to do.

For there was a crash. Jasper Gibbons brought out another volume of poetry; it was neither better nor worse than the first; it was very much like the first; it was treated with respect, but the critics made reservations; some of them even carped. The book was a disappointment. Its sale also. And unfortunately Jasper Gibbons was inclined to tipple. He had never been accustomed to having money to spend, he was quite unused to the lavish entertainments that were offered him, perhaps he missed his homely common little wife; once or twice he came to dinner at Mrs Barton Trafford's in a condition that anyone less worldly, less simple-minded than she, would have described as blind to the world. She told her guests gently that the bard was not quite himself that evening. His third book was a failure. The critics tore him limb from limb, they knocked him down and stamped on him, and, to quote one of Edward Driffield's favourite songs, then they lugged him round the room and then they jumped upon his face: they were quite naturally annoyed that they had mistaken a fluent versifier for a deathless poet and were determined that he should suffer for their error. Then Jasper Gibbons was arrested for being drunk and disorderly in Piccadilly and Mr Barton Trafford had to go to Vine Street at midnight to bail him out.

Mrs Barton Trafford at this juncture was perfect. She did not repine. No harsh word escaped her lips. She might have been excused if she had felt a certain bitterness because this man for whom she had done so much had let her down. She remained tender, gentle and sympathetic. She was the woman who understood. She dropped him, but not like a hot brick, or a hot potato. She dropped him with infinite gentleness, as softly as the tear that she doubtless shed when she made up her mind to do something so repugnant to her nature; she dropped him with so much tact, with such sensibility, that Jasper Gibbons perhaps hardly knew he was dropped. But there was no doubt about it. She would say nothing against him, indeed she would not discuss him at all, and when mention was made of him she merely smiled, a little sadly, and sighed. But her smile was the *coup de grâce*, and her sigh buried him deep.

Mrs Barton Trafford had a passion for literature too sincere to allow a setback of this character long to discourage her; and however great her disappointment she was a woman of too disinterested a nature to let the gifts of tact, sympathy and understanding with which she was blessed by nature lie fallow. She continued to move in literary circles, going to tea parties here and there, to soirées and to At Homes, charming always and gentle, listening intelligently, but watchful, critical and determined (if I may put it crudely) next time to back a winner. It was then that she met Edward Driffield and formed a favourable opinion of his gifts. It is true that he was not young, but then he was unlikely like Jasper Gibbons to go to pieces. She offered him her friendship. He could not fail to be moved when, in that gentle way of hers, she told him that it was a scandal that his exquisite work remained known only in the narrow circle. He was pleased and flattered. It is always pleasant to be assured that you are a genius. She told him that Barton Trafford was reflecting on the possibility of writing an important article on him for the *Quarterly Review*. She asked him to luncheon to meet people who might be useful to him. She wanted him to know his intellectual equals. Sometimes she took him for a walk on the Chelsea Embankment and they talked of poets dead and gone and love and friendship, and had tea in an A.B.C. shop. When Mrs Barton Trafford came to Limpus Street on Saturday afternoon she had the air of the queen bee preparing herself for the nuptial flight.

Her manner with Mrs Driffield was perfect. It was affable, but not condescending. She always thanked her very prettily for having allowed her to come and see her and complimented her on her appearance. If she praised Edward Driffield to her, telling her with a little envy in her tone what a privilege it was to enjoy the companionship of such a great man, it was certainly from pure kindness, and not because she knew that there is nothing that exasperates the wife of a literary man more than to have another woman tell her flattering things about him. She talked to Mrs Driffield of the simple things her simple nature might be supposed to be interested in, of cooking and servants and Edward's health and how careful she must be with him. Mrs Barton Trafford treated her exactly as you would expect a woman of very good Scotch family, which she was, to treat an ex-barmaid with whom a distinguished man of letters had made an unfortunate marriage. She was cordial, playful and gently determined to put her at her ease.

It was strange that Rosie could not bear her; indeed, Mrs Barton Trafford was the only person that I ever knew her dislike. In those days even barmaids did not habitually use the 'bitches' and 'bloodys' that are part and parcel of the current vocabulary of the best-brought-up young ladies, and I never heard Rosie use a word that would have shocked my Aunt Sophie. When anyone told a story that was a little near the knuckle she would blush to the roots of her hair. But she referred to Mrs Barton Trafford as 'that damned old cat.' It needed the most urgent persuasion of her more intimate friends to induce her to be civil to her.

'Don't be a fool, Rosie,' they said. They all called her Rosie and presently I, though very shyly, got in the habit of doing so too. 'If she wants to she can make him. He must play up to her. She can work the trick if anyone can.'

Though most of the Driffields' visitors were occasional, appearing every other Saturday, say, or every third, there was a little band that, like myself, came almost every week. We were the stand-bys; we arrived early and stayed late. Of these the most faithful were Quentin Forde, Harry Retford and Lionel Hillier.

Quentin Forde was a stocky little man with a fine head of the type that was afterward for a time much admired in the moving pictures, a straight nose and handsome eyes, neatly cropped grey hair and a black moustache; if he had been four or five inches taller he would have been the perfect type of the villain of melodrama. He was known to be very 'well connected,' and he was affluent; his only occupation was to cultivate the arts. He went to all the first nights and all the private views. He had the amateur's severity, and cherished for the productions of his contemporaries a polite but sweeping contempt. I discovered that he did not come to the Driffields' because Edward was a genius, but because Rosie was beautiful.

Now that I look back I cannot get over my surprise that I should have had to be told what was surely so obvious. When I first knew her it never occurred to me to ask myself whether she was pretty or plain, and when, seeing her again after five years, I noticed for the first time that she was very pretty, I was interested but did not trouble to think much about it. I took it as part of the natural order of things, just as I took the sun setting over the North Sea or the towers of Tercanbury Cathedral. I was quite startled when I heard people speak of Rosie's beauty, and when they complimented Edward on her looks and his eyes rested on her for a moment, mine followed his. Lionel Hillier was a painter and he asked her to sit for him. When he talked of the picture he wanted to paint and told me what he saw in her, I listened to him stupidly. I was puzzled and confused. Harry Retford knew one of the fashionable photographers of the period and, arranging special terms, he took Rosie to be photographed. A Saturday or two later the proofs were there and we all looked at them. I had never seen Rosie in evening dress. She was wearing a dress in white satin, with a long train and puffy sleeves, and it was cut low; her hair was more elaborately done than usual. She looked very different from the strapping young woman I had first met in Joy Lane in a boater and a starched skirt. But Lionel Hillier tossed the photographs aside impatiently.

'Rotten,' he said. 'What can a photograph give of Rosie? The thing about her is her colour.' He turned to her. 'Rosie, don't you know that your colour is *the* great miracle of the age?'

She looked at him without answering, but her full red lips broke into their childlike, mischievous smile.

'If I can only get a suggestion of it I'm made for life,' he said. 'All the rich stockbrokers' wives will come on their bended knees and beg me to paint them like you.'

Presently I learned that Rosie was sitting to him, but when, never having been in a painter's studio and looking upon it as the gateway of romance, I asked if I might not come one day and see how the picture was getting on, Hillier said that he did not want anyone to see it yet. He was a man of five and thirty and of a flamboyant appearance. He looked like a portrait of Van Dyck in which the distinction had been replaced by good humour. He was slightly above the middle height, slim; and he had a fine mane of black hair and flowing moustaches and a pointed beard. He favoured broad-brimmed sombreros and Spanish capes. He had lived a long time in Paris and talked admiringly of painters, Monet, Sisley, Renoir, of whom we had never heard, and with contempt of Sir Frederick Leighton and Mr Alma-Tadema and Mr G. F. Watts, whom in our heart of hearts we very much admired. I have often wondered what became of him. He spent a few years in London trying to make his way, failed, I suppose, and then drifted to Florence. I was told that he had a drawing school there, but when, years later, chancing to be in that city, I asked about him, I could find no one who had ever heard of him. I think he must have had some talent, for I have even now a very vivid recollection of the portrait he painted of Rosie Driffield. I wonder what has happened to it. Has it been destroyed or is it hidden away, its face to the wall, in the attic of a junk shop in Chelsea? I should like to think that it has at least found a place on the walls of some provincial gallery.

When I was at last allowed to come and see it, I put my foot in it fine and proper. Hillier's studio was in the Fulham Road, one of a group at the back of a row of shops, and you went in through a dark and smelly passage. It was a Sunday afternoon in March, a fine blue day, and I walked from Vincent Square through deserted streets. Hillier lived in his studio; there was a large divan on which he slept, and a tiny little room at the back where he cooked his breakfast, washed his brushes and, I suppose, himself.

When I arrived Rosie still wore the dress in which she had been sitting and they were having a cup of tea. Hillier opened the door for me, and still holding my hand led me up to the large canvas.

'There she is,' he said.

He had painted Rosie full length, just a little less than life-size, in an evening dress of white silk. It was not at all like the academy portraits I was accustomed to. I did not know what to say, so I said the first thing that came into my head.

'When will it be finished?'

'It is finished,' he answered.

I blushed furiously. I felt a perfect fool. I had not then acquired the technique that I flatter myself now enables me to deal competently with the works of modern artists. If this were the place I could write a very neat little guide to enable the amateur of pictures to deal to the satisfaction of their painters with the most diverse manifestations of the creative instinct. There is the intense 'By God' that acknowledges the power of the ruthless realist, the 'It's so awfully sincere' that covers your embarrassment when you are shown the coloured photograph of an alderman's widow, the low whistle that exhibits your admiration of the post-impressionist, the 'Terribly amusing' that expresses what you feel about the cubist, the 'Oh!' of one who is overcome, the 'Ah!' of him whose breath is taken away.

'It's awfully like,' was all that then I could lamely say.

'It's not chocolate-boxy enough for you,' said Hillier.

'I think it's awfully good,' I answered quickly, defending myself. 'Are you going to send it to the Academy?'

'Good God, no! I might send it to the Grosvenor.'

I looked from the painting to Rosie and from Rosie to the painting.

'Get into the pose, Rosie,' said Hillier, 'and let him see you.'

She got up on to the model stand. I stared at her and I stared at the picture.

I had such a funny little feeling in my heart. It was as though someone softly plunged a sharp knife into it, but it was not an unpleasant sensation at all, painful but strangely agreeable; and then suddenly I felt quite weak at the knees. But now I do not know if I remember Rosie in the flesh or in the picture. For when I think of her it is not in the shirt and boater that I first saw her in, nor in any of the other dresses I saw her in then or later, but in the white silk that Hillier painted, with a black velvet bow in her hair, and in the pose he had made her take.

I never exactly knew Rosie's age, but reckoning the years out as well as I can, I think she must have been then thirty-five. She did not look anything like it. Her face was quite unlined and her skin as smooth as a child's. I do not think she had very good features. They certainly had none of the aristocratic distinction of the great ladies whose photographs were at that time sold in all the shops; they were rather blunt. Her short nose was a little thick, her eyes were smallish, her mouth was large; but her eyes had the blue of cornflowers, and they smiled with her lips, very red and sensual, and her smile was the gayest, the most friendly, the sweetest thing I ever saw. She had by nature a heavy, sullen look, but when she smiled this sullenness became on a sudden infinitely attractive. She had no colour in her face; it was of a very pale brown except under the eyes where it was faintly blue. Her hair was pale gold and it was done in the fashion of the day high on the head with an elaborate fringe.

'She's the very devil to paint,' said Hillier, looking at her and at his picture. 'You see, she's all gold, her face and her hair, and yet she doesn't give you a golden effect, she gives you a silvery effect.'

I knew what he meant. She glowed, but palely, like the moon rather than the sun, or if it was like the sun it was like the sun in the white mist of dawn. Hillier had placed her in the middle of his canvas and she stood, with her arms by her sides, the palms of her hands toward you and her head a little thrown back, in an attitude that gave value to the pearly beauty of her neck and bosom. She stood like an actress taking a call, confused by unexpected applause, but there was something so virginal about her, so exquisitely springlike, that the comparison was absurd. This artless creature had never known grease paint or footlights. She stood like a maiden apt for love offering herself guilelessly, because she was fulfilling the purposes of Nature, to the embraces of a lover. She belonged to a generation that did not fear a certain opulence of line, she was slender, but her breasts were ample and her hips well marked. When, later, Mrs Barton Trafford saw the picture she said it reminded her of a sacrificial heifer.

Chapter Fifteen

Edward Driffield worked at night, and Rosie, having nothing to do, was glad to go out with one or other of her friends. She liked luxury and Quentin Forde was well-to-do. He would fetch her in a cab and take her to dine at Kettner's or the Savoy, and she would put on her grandest clothes for him; and Harry Retford, though he never had a bob, behaved as if he had, and took her about in hansoms too and gave her dinner at Romano's or in one or other of the little restaurants that were becoming modish in Soho. He was an actor and a clever one, but he was difficult to suit and so was often out of work. He was about thirty, a man with a pleasantly ugly face and a clipped way of speaking that made what he said sound funny. Rosie liked his devil-may-care attitude toward life, the swagger with which he wore clothes made by the best tailor in London and unpaid for, the recklessness with which he would put a fiver he hadn't got on a horse, and the generosity with which he flung his money about when a lucky win put him in funds. He was gay, charming, vain, boastful and unscrupulous. Rosie told me that once he had pawned his watch to take her out to dinner and then borrowed a couple of pounds from the actor manager who had given them seats for the play in order to take him out to supper with them afterward.

But she was just as well pleased to go with Lionel Hillier to his studio and eat a chop that he and she cooked between them and spend the evening talking, and it was only very rarely that she would dine with me at all. I used to fetch her after I had had my dinner in Vincent Square and she hers with Driffield, and we would get on a bus and go to a music-hall. We went here and there, to the Pavilion or the Tivoli, sometimes to the Metropolitan if there was a particular turn we wanted to see; but our favourite was the Canterbury. It was cheap and the show was good. We ordered a couple of beers and I smoked my pipe. Rosie looked round with delight at the great dark smoky house, crowded to the ceiling with the inhabitants of South London.

'I like the Canterbury,' she said. 'It's so homey.'

I discovered that she was a great reader. She liked history, but only history of a certain kind, the lives of queens and of mistresses of royal personages; and she would tell me with a childlike wonder of the strange things she read. She had a wide acquaintance with the six consorts of King Henry VIII and there was little she did not know about Mrs Fitzherbert and Lady Hamilton. Her appetite was prodigious and she ranged from Lucrezia Borgia to the wives of Philip of Spain; then there was the long list of the royal mistresses of France. She knew them all, and all about them, from Agnes Sorel down to Madame du Barry.

'I like to read about real things,' she said. 'I don't much care for novels.'

She liked to gossip about Blackstable and I thought it was on account of my connection with it that she liked to come out with me. She seemed to know all that was going on there.

'I go down every other week or so to see my mother,' she said. 'Just for the night, you know.'

'To Blackstable?'

I was surprised.

'No, not to Blackstable,' Rosie smiled. 'I don't know that I'd care to go there just yet. To Haversham. Mother comes over to meet me. I stay at the hotel where I used to work.'

She was never a great talker. Often when, the night being fine, we decided to walk back from the music-hall at which we had been spending the evening, she never opened her mouth. But her silence was intimate and comfortable. It did not exclude you from thoughts that engaged her apart from you; it included you in a pervasive well-being.

I was talking about her once to Lionel Hillier and I said to him that I could not understand how she had turned from the fresh pleasant-looking young woman I had first known at Blackstable into the lovely creature whose beauty now practically everyone acknowledged. (There were people who made reservations. 'Of course she has a very good figure,' they said, 'but it's not the sort of face I very much admire personally.' And others said: 'Oh, yes, a very pretty woman; but it's a pity she hasn't a little more distinction.')

'I can explain that to you in half a jiffy,' said Lionel Hillier. 'She was only a fresh, buxom wench when you first met her. *I* made her beauty.'

I forget what my answer was, but I know it was ribald.

'All right. That just shows you don't know anything about beauty. No one ever thought very much of Rosie till I saw her like the sun shining silver. It wasn't till I painted it that anyone knew that her hair was the most lovely thing in the world.'

'Did you make her neck and her breasts and her carriage and her bones?' I asked.

'Yes, damn you, that's just what I did do.'

When Hillier talked of Rosie in front of her she listened to him with a smiling gravity. A little flush came into her pale cheeks. I think that at first when he spoke to her of her beauty she believed he was just making game of her; but when she found out that he wasn't, when he painted her silvery gold, it had no particular effect on her. She was a trifle amused, pleased of course, and a little surprised, but it did not turn her head. She thought him a little mad. I often wondered whether there was anything between them. I could not forget all I had heard of Rosie at Blackstable and what I had seen in the vicarage garden; I wondered about Quentin Forde, too, and Harry Retford. I used to watch them with her. She was not exactly familiar with them, comradely rather; she used to make her appointments with them quite openly in anybody's hearing; and when she looked at them it was with that mischievous, childlike smile which I had now discovered held such a mysterious beauty. Sometimes when we were sitting side by side in a music-hall I looked at her face; I do not think I was in love with her, I merely enjoyed the sensation of sitting quietly beside her and looking at the pale gold of her hair and the pale gold of her skin. Of course Lionel Hillier was right; the strange thing was that this gold did give one a strange moonlight feeling. She had the serenity of a summer evening when the light fades slowly from the unclouded sky. There was nothing dull in her immense placidity; it was as living as the sea when under the August sun it lay calm and shining along the Kentish coast. She reminded me of a sonatina by an old Italian composer with its wistfulness in which there is yet an urbane flippancy and its light rippling gaiety in which echoes still the trembling of a sigh. Sometimes, feeling my eyes on her, she would turn round and for a moment or two look me full in the face. She did not speak. I did not know of what she was thinking.

Once, I remember, I fetched her at Limpus Road, and the maid, telling me she was not ready, asked me to wait in the parlour. She came in. She was in black velvet, with a picture hat covered with ostrich feathers (we were going to the Pavilion and she had dressed up for it) and she looked so lovely that it took my breath away. I was staggered. The clothes of that day gave a woman dignity and there was something amazingly attractive in the way her virginal beauty (sometimes she looked like the exquisite statue of Psyche in the museum at Naples) contrasted with the stateliness of her gown. She had a trait that I think must be very rare: the skin under her eyes, faintly blue, was all dewy. Sometimes I could not persuade myself that it was natural, and once I asked her if she had rubbed vaseline under her eyes. That was just the effect it gave. She smiled, took a handkerchief and handed it to me.

'Rub them and see,' she said.

Then one night when we had walked home from the Canterbury, and I was leaving her at her door, when I held out my hand she laughed a little, a low chuckle it was, and leaned forward.

'You old silly,' she said.

She kissed me on the mouth. It was not a hurried peck, nor was it a kiss of passion. Her lips, those very full red lips of hers, rested on mine long enough for me to be conscious of their shape and their warmth and their softness. Then she withdrew them, but without hurry, in silence pushed open the door, slipped inside and left me. I was so startled that I had not been able to say anything. I accepted her kiss stupidly. I remained inert. I turned away and walked back to my lodgings. I seemed to hear still in my ears Rosie's laughter. It was not contemptuous or wounding, but frank and affectionate; it was as though she laughed because she was fond of me.

Chapter Sixteen

I did not go out with Rosie again for more than a week. She was going down to Haversham to spend a night with her mother. She had various engagements in London. Then she asked me if I would go to the Haymarket Theatre with her. The play was a success and free seats were not to be had so we made up our minds to go in the pit. We had a steak and a glass of beer at the Café Monico and then stood with the crowd. In those days there was no orderly queue and when the doors were opened there was a mad rush and scramble to get in. We were hot and breathless and somewhat battered when at last we pushed our way into our seats.

We walked back through St James's Park. The night was so lovely that we sat down on a bench. In the starlight Rosie's face and her fair hair glowed softly. She was suffused, as it were (I express it awkwardly, but I do not know how to describe the emotion she gave me) with a friendliness at once candid and tender. She was like a silvery flower of the night that only gave its perfume to the moonbeams. I slipped my arm round her waist and she turned her face to mine. This time it was I who kissed. She did not move; her soft red lips submitted to the pressure of mine with a calm, intense passivity as the water of a lake accepts the light of the moon. I don't know how long we stayed there.

'I'm awfully hungry,' she said suddenly.

'So am I,' I laughed.

'Couldn't we go and have some fish and chips somewhere?'

'Rather.'

In those days I knew my way very well about Westminster, not yet a fashionable quarter for parliamentary and otherwise cultured persons, but slummy and down-at-heel; and after we had come out of the park, crossing Victoria Street, I led Rosie to a fried fish shop in Horseferry Row. It was late and the only other person there was the driver of a four-wheeler waiting outside. We ordered our fish and chips and a bottle of beer. A poor woman came in and bought two penn'orth of mixed and took it away with her in a piece of paper. We ate with appetite.

Our way back to Rosie's led through Vincent Square and as we passed my house I asked her:

'Won't you come in for a minute? You've never seen my rooms.'

'What about your landlady? I don't want to get you into trouble.'

'Oh, she sleeps like a rock.'

'I'll come in for a little.'

I slipped my key into the lock and because the passage was dark took Rosie's hand to lead her in. I lit the gas in my sitting-room. She took off her hat and vigorously scratched her head. Then she looked for a glass, but I was very artistic and had taken down the mirror that was over the chimney-piece and there was no means in the room for anyone to see what he looked like.

'Come into my bedroom,' I said. 'There's a glass there.'

I opened the door and lit the candle. Rosie followed me in and I held it up so that she should be able to see herself. I looked at her in the glass as she arranged her hair. She took two or three pins out, which she put in her mouth, and taking one of my brushes, brushed her hair up from the nape of her neck. She twisted it, patted it, and put back the pins, and as she was intent on this her eyes caught mine in the glass and she smiled at me. When she had replaced the last pin she turned and faced me; she did not say anything; she looked at me tranquilly, still with that little friendly smile in her blue eyes. I put down the candle. The room was very small and the dressing-table was by the bed. She raised her hand and softly stroked my cheek.

I wish now that I had not started to write this book in the first person singular. It is all very well when you can show yourself in an amiable or touching light and nothing can be more effective than the modest heroic or pathetic humorous which in this mode is much cultivated; it is charming to write about yourself when you see on the reader's eyelash the glittering tear and on his lips the tender smile; but it is not so nice when you have to exhibit yourself as a plain damned fool.

A little while ago I read in the *Evening Standard* an article by Mr Evelyn Waugh in the course of which he remarked that to write novels in the first person was a contemptible practice. I wish he had explained why, but he merely threw out the statement with just the same take-it-or-leave-it casualness as Euclid used when he made his celebrated observation about parallel straight lines. I was much concerned and forthwith asked Alroy Kear (who read everything, even the books he writes prefaces for) to recommend to me some works on the art of fiction. On his advice I read *The Craft of Fiction* by Mr Percy Lubbock, from which I learned that the only way to write novels was like Henry James; after that I read *Aspects of the Novel* by Mr E. M. Forster, from which I learned that the only way to write novels was like Mr E. M. Forster; then I read *The Structure of the Novel* by Mr Edwin Muir, from which I learned nothing at all. In none of them could I discover anything to the point at issue. All the same I can find one reason why certain novelists, such as Defoe, Sterne, Thackeray, Dickens, Emily Brontë and Proust, well known in their day but now doubtless forgotten, have used the method that Mr Evelyn Waugh reprehends. As we grow older we become more conscious of the complexity, incoherence and unreasonableness of human beings; this indeed is the only excuse that offers for the middle-aged or elderly writer, whose thoughts should more properly be turned to graver matters, occupying himself with the trivial concerns of imaginary people. For if the proper study of mankind is man it is evidently more sensible to occupy yourself with the coherent, substantial and significant creatures of fiction than with the irrational and shadowy figures of real life. Sometimes the novelist feels himself like God and is prepared to tell you everything about his characters; sometimes, however, he does not; and then he tells you not everything that is to be known about them but the little he knows himself; and since as we grow older we feel ourselves less and less like God I should not be surprised to learn that with advancing years the novelist grows less and less inclined to describe more than his own experience has given him. The first person singular is a very useful device for this limited purpose.

Rosie raised her hand and softly stroked my face. I do not know why I should have behaved as I then did; it was not at all how I had seen myself behaving on such an occasion. A sob broke from my tight throat. I do not know whether it was because I was shy and lonely (not lonely in the body, for I spent all day at the hospital with all kinds of people, but lonely in the spirit) or because my desire was so great, but I began to cry. I felt terribly ashamed of myself; I tried to control myself, I couldn't; the tears welled up in my eyes and poured down my cheeks. Rosie saw them and gave a little gasp.

'Oh, honey, what is it? What's the matter? Don't. Don't!'

She put her arms round my neck and began to cry too, and she kissed my lips and my eyes and my wet cheeks. She undid her bodice and lowered my head till it rested on her bosom. She stroked my smooth face. She rocked me back and forth as though I were a child in her arms. I kissed her breasts and I kissed the white column of her neck; and she slipped out of her bodice and out of her skirt and her petticoats and I held her for a moment by her corseted waist; then she undid it, holding her breath for an instant to enable her to do so, and stood before me in her shift. When I put my hands on her sides I could feel the ribbing of the skin from the pressure of the corsets.

'Blow out the candle,' she whispered.

It was she who awoke me when the dawn peering through the curtains revealed the shape of the bed and of the wardrobe against the darkness of the lingering night. She woke me by kissing me on the mouth and her hair falling over my face tickled me.

'I must get up,' she said. 'I don't want your landlady to see me.'

'There's plenty of time.'

Her breasts when she leaned over me were heavy on my chest. In a little while she got out of bed. I lit the candle. She turned to the glass and tied up her hair and then she looked for a moment at her naked body. Her waist was naturally small; though so well developed she was very slender; her breasts were straight and firm and they stood out from the chest as though carved in marble. It was a body made for the act of love. In the light of the candle, struggling now with the increasing day, it was all silvery gold; and the only colour was the rosy pink of the hard nipples.

We dressed in silence. She did not put on her corsets again, but rolled them up and I wrapped them in a piece of newspaper. We tiptoed along the passage and when I opened the door and we stepped out into the street the dawn ran to meet us like a cat leaping up the steps. The square was empty; already the sun was shining on the eastern windows. I felt as young as the day. We walked arm in arm till we came to the corner of Limpus Road.

'Leave me here,' said Rosie. 'One never knows.'

I kissed her and I watched her walk away. She walked rather slowly, with the firm tread of the country woman who likes to feel the good earth under her feet, and held herself erect. I could not go back to bed. I strolled on till I came to the Embankment. The river had the bright hues of the early morning. A brown barge came down stream and passed under Vauxhall Bridge. In a dinghy two men were rowing close to the side. I was hungry.

Chapter Seventeen

After that for more than a year whenever Rosie came out with me she used on the way home to drop into my rooms, sometimes for an hour, sometimes till the breaking day warned us that the slaveys would soon be scrubbing the doorsteps. I have a recollection of warm sunny mornings when the tired air of London had a welcome freshness, and of our footfalls that seemed so noisy in the empty streets, and then of scurrying along huddled under an umbrella, silent but gay, when the winter brought cold and rain. The policeman on point duty gave us a stare as we passed, sometimes of suspicion; but sometimes also there was a twinkle of comprehension in his eyes. Now and then we would see a homeless creature huddled up asleep in a portico and Rosie gave my arm a friendly little pressure when (chiefly for show and because I wanted to make a good impression on her, for my shillings were scarce) I placed a piece of silver on a shapeless lap or in a skinny fist. Rosie made me very happy. I had a great affection for her. She was easy and comfortable. She had a placidity of temper that communicated itself to the people she was with; you shared her pleasure in the passing moment.

Before I became her lover I had often asked myself if she was the mistress of the others, Forde, Harry Retford and Hillier, and afterwards I questioned her. She kissed me.

'Don't be so silly. I like them, you know that. I like to go out with them, but that's all.'

I wanted to ask her if she had been the mistress of George Kemp, but I did not like to. Though I had never seen her in a temper, I had a notion that she had one and I vaguely felt that this was a question that might anger her. I did not want to give her the opportunity of saying things so wounding that I could not forgive her. I was young, only just over one and twenty, Quentin Forde and the others seemed old to me; it did not seem unnatural to me that to Rosie they were only friends. It gave me a thrill of pride to think that I was her lover. When I used to look at her chatting and laughing with all and sundry at tea on Saturday afternoons, I glowed with self-satisfaction. I thought of the nights we passed together and I was inclined to laugh at the people who were so ignorant of my great secret. But sometimes I thought that Lionel Hillier looked at me in a quizzical way, as if he were enjoying a good joke at my expense, and I asked myself uneasily if Rosie had told him that she was having an affair with me. I wondered if there was anything in my manner that betrayed me. I told Rosie that I was afraid Hillier suspected something; she looked at me with those blue eyes of hers that always seemed ready to smile.

'Don't bother about it,' she said. 'He's got a nasty mind.'

I had never been intimate with Quentin Forde. He looked upon me as a dull and insignificant young man (which of course I was) and though he had always been civil he had never taken any notice of me. I thought it could only be my fancy that now he began to be a little more frigid with me than before. But one day Harry Retford to my surprise asked me to dine with him and go to the play. I told Rosie.

'Oh, of course you must go. He'll give you an awfully good time. Good old Harry, he always makes me laugh.'

So I dined with him. He made himself very pleasant and I was impressed to hear him talk of actors and actresses. He had a sarcastic humour and was very funny at the expense of Quentin Forde, whom he did not like; I tried to get him to talk of Rosie, but he had nothing to say of her. He seemed to be a gay dog. With leers and laughing innuendoes he gave me to understand that he was a devil with the girls. I could not but ask myself if he was standing me this dinner because he knew I was Rosie's lover and so felt friendly disposed toward me. But if he knew, of course the others knew too. I hope I did not show it, but in my heart I certainly felt somewhat patronising toward them.

Then in winter, toward the end of January, someone new appeared at Limpus Road. This was a Dutch Jew named Jack Kuyper, a diamond merchant from Amsterdam, who was spending a few weeks in London on business. I do not know how he had come to know the Driffields and whether it was esteem for the author that brought him to the house, but it was certainly not that which caused him to come again. He was a tall, stout, dark man with a bald head and a big hooked nose, a man of fifty, but of a powerful appearance, sensual, determined and jovial. He made no secret of his admiration for Rosie. He was rich apparently, for he sent her roses every day; she chid him for his extravagance, but was flattered. I could not bear him. He was blatant and loud. I hated his fluent conversation in perfect but foreign English; I hated the extravagant compliments he paid Rosie; I hated the heartiness with which he treated her friends. I found that Quentin Forde liked him as little as I; we almost became cordial with one another.

'Mercifully he's not staying long,' Quentin Forde pursed his lips and raised his black eyebrows; with his white hair and long sallow face he looked incredibly gentlemanly. 'Women are always the same; they adore a bounder.'

'He's so frightfully vulgar,' I complained.

'That is his charm,' said Quentin Forde.

For the next two or three weeks I saw next to nothing of Rosie. Jack Kuyper took her out night after night, to this smart restaurant and that, to one play after another. I was vexed and hurt.

'He doesn't know anyone in London,' said Rosie, trying to soothe my ruffled feelings. 'He wants to see everything he can while he's here. It wouldn't be very nice for him to go alone all the time. He's only here for a fortnight more.'

I did not see the object of this self-sacrifice on her part.

'But don't you think he's awful?' I said.

'No. I think he's fun. He makes me laugh.'

'Don't you know that he's absolutely gone on you?'

'Well, it pleases him and it doesn't do me any harm.'

'He's old and fat and horrible. It gives me the creeps to look at him.'

'I don't think he's so bad,' said Rosie.

'You couldn't have anything to do with him,' I protested. 'I mean, he's such an awful cad.'

Rosie scratched her head. It was an unpleasant habit of hers.

'It's funny how different foreigners are from English people,' she said.

I was thankful when Jack Kuyper went back to Amsterdam. Rosie had promised to dine with me the day after and as a treat we arranged to dine in Soho. She fetched me in a hansom and we drove on.

'Has your horrible old man gone?' I asked.

'Yes,' she laughed.

I put my arm round her waist. (I have elsewhere remarked how much more convenient the hansom was for this pleasant and indeed almost essential act in human intercourse than the taxi of the present day, so unwillingly refrain from labouring the point.) I put my arm round her waist and kissed her. Her lips were like spring flowers. We arrived. I hung my hat and my coat (it was very long and tight at the waist, with a velvet collar and velvet cuffs; very smart) on a peg and asked Rosie to give me her cape.

'I'm going to keep it on,' she said.

'You'll be awfully hot. You'll only catch cold when we go out.'

'I don't care. It's the first time I've worn it. Don't you think it's lovely. And look: the muff matches.'

I gave the cape a glance. It was of fur. I did not know it was sable.

'It looks awfully rich. How did you get that?'

'Jack Kuyper gave it to me. We went and bought it yesterday just before he went away.' She stroked the smooth fur; she was as happy with it as a child with a toy. 'How much d'you think it cost?'

'I haven't an idea.'

'Two hundred and sixty pounds. Do you know I've never had anything that cost so much in my life? I told him it was far too much, but he wouldn't listen. He made me have it.'

Rosie chuckled with glee and her eyes shone. But I felt my face go stiff and a shiver run down my spine.

'Won't Driffield think it's rather funny, Kuyper giving you a fur cape that costs all that?' said I, trying to make my voice sound natural.

Rosie's eyes danced mischievously.

'You know what Ted is, he never notices anything; if he says anything about it I shall tell him I gave twenty pounds for it in a pawnshop. He won't know any better.' She rubbed her face against the collar. 'It's so soft. And everyone can see it cost money.'

I tried to eat in order not to show the bitterness in my heart. I did my best to keep the conversation going on one topic or another. Rosie did not much mind what I said. She could only think of her new cape and every other minute her eyes returned to the muff that she insisted on holding on her lap. She looked at it with an affection in which there was something lazy, sensual and self-complacent. I was angry with her. I thought her stupid and common.

'You look like a cat that's swallowed a canary,' I could not help snapping.

She only giggled.

'That's what I feel like.'

Two hundred and sixty pounds was an enormous sum to me. I did not know one *could* pay so much for a cape. I lived on fourteen pounds a month and not at all badly either; and in case any reader is not a ready reckoner I will add that this is one hundred and sixty-eight pounds a year. I could not believe that anyone would make as expensive a present as that from pure friendship; what did it mean but that Jack Kuyper had been sleeping with Rosie, night after night, all the time he was in London, and now when he went away was paying her? How could she accept it? Didn't she see how it degraded her? Didn't she see how frightfully vulgar it was of him to give her a thing that cost so much? Apparently not, for she said to me:

'It was nice of him, wasn't it? But then Jews are always generous.'

'I suppose he could afford it,' I said.

'Oh yes, he's got lots of money. He said he wanted to give me something before he went away and asked me what I wanted. Well, I said, I could do with a cape and a muff to match, but I never thought he'd buy me anything like this. When we went into the shop I asked them to show me something in astrakhan, but he said: No, sable, and the best money can buy. And when we saw this he absolutely insisted on my having it.'

I thought of her with her white body, her skin so milky, in the arms of that old fat gross man and his thick loose lips kissing hers. And then I knew that the suspicion that I had refused to believe was true; I knew that when she went out to dinner with Quentin Forde and Harry Retford and Lionel Hillier she went to bed with them just as she came to bed with me. I could not speak; I knew that if I did I should insult her. I do not think I was jealous so much as mortified. I felt that she had been making a damned fool of me. I used all my determination to prevent the bitter jibes from passing my lips.

We went on to the theatre. I could not listen to the play. I could only feel against my arm the smoothness of the sable cape; I could only see her fingers for ever stroking the muff. I could have borne the thought of the others; it was Jack Kuyper who horrified me. How could she? It was abominable to be poor. I longed to have enough money to tell her that if she would send the fellow back his beastly furs I would give her better ones instead. At last she noticed that I did not speak.

'You're very silent tonight.'

'Am I?'

'Aren't you well?'

'Perfectly.'

She gave me a sidelong look. I did not meet her eyes, but I knew they were smiling with that smile at once mischievous and childlike that I knew so well. She said nothing more. At the end of the play, since it was raining, we took a hansom and I gave the driver her address in Limpus Road. She did not speak till we got to Victoria Street, then she said:

'Don't you want me to come home with you?'

'Just as you like.'

She lifted up the trap and gave the driver my address. She took my hand and held it, but I remained inert. I looked straight out of the window with angry dignity. When we reached Vincent Square I handed her out of the cab and let her into the house without a word. I took off my hat and coat. She threw her cape and her muff on the sofa.

'Why are you so sulky?' she asked, coming up to me.

'I'm not sulky,' I answered, looking away.

She took my face in her two hands.

'How can you be so silly? Why should you be angry because Jack Kuyper gives me a fur cape? You can't afford to give me one, can you?'

'Of course I can't.'

'And Ted can't either. You can't expect me to refuse a fur cape that cost two hundred and sixty pounds. I've wanted a fur cape all my life. It means nothing to Jack.'

'You don't expect me to believe that he gave it you just out of friendship.'

'He might have. Anyhow, he's gone back to Amsterdam, and who knows when he'll come back?'

'He isn't the only one, either.'

I looked at Rosie now, with angry, hurt, resentful eyes; she smiled at me, and I wish I knew how to describe the sweet kindliness of her beautiful smile; her voice was exquisitely gentle.

'Oh, my dear, why d'you bother your head about any others? What harm does it do you? Don't I give you a good time! Aren't you happy when you're with me?'

'Awfully.'

'Well, then. It's so silly to be fussy and jealous. Why not be happy with what you can get? Enjoy yourself while you have the chance, I say; we shall all be dead in a hundred years and what will anything matter then? Let's have a good time while we can.'

She put her arms round my neck and pressed her lips against mine. I forgot my wrath. I only thought of her beauty and her enveloping kindness.

'You must take me as I am, you know,' she whispered.

'All right,' I said.

Chapter Eighteen

During all this time I saw really very little of Driffield. His editorship occupied much of his day and in the evening he wrote. He was, of course, there every Saturday afternoon, amiable and ironically amusing; he appeared glad to see me and chatted with me for a little while pleasantly of indifferent things; but naturally most of his attention was given to guests older and more imporant than I. But I had a feeling that he was growing more aloof; he was no longer the jolly, rather vulgar companion that I had known at Blackstable. Perhaps it was only my increasing sensibility that discerned as it were an invisible barrier that existed between him and the people he chaffed and joked with. It was as though he lived a life of the imagination that made the life of every day a little shadowy. He was asked to speak now and then at public dinners. He joined a literary club. He began to know a good many people outside the narrow circle into which his writing had drawn him, and he was increasingly asked to luncheon and tea by the ladies who like to gather about them distinguished authors. Rosie was asked too, but seldom went; she said she didn't care for parties, and after all they didn't want her, they only wanted Ted. I think she was shy and felt out of it. It may be that hostesses had more than once let her see how tiresome they thought it that she must be included; and after inviting her because it was polite, ignored her because to be polite irked them.

It was just then that Edward Driffield published *The Cup of Life*. It is not my business to criticise his works, and of late as much has been written about them as must satisfy the appetite of any ordinary reader; but I will permit myself to say that *The Cup of Life*, though certainly not the most celebrated of his books, nor the most popular, is to my mind the most interesting. It has a cold ruthlessness that in all the sentimentality of English fiction strikes an original note. It is refreshing and astringent. It tastes of tart apples. It sets your teeth on edge, but it has a subtle, bitter-sweet savour that is very agreeable to the palate. Of all Driffield's books it is the only one I should like to have written. The scene of the child's death, terrible and heart-rending, but written without slop or sickliness, and the curious incident that follows it, cannot easily be forgotten by anyone who has read them.

It was this part of the book that caused the sudden storm that burst on the wretched Driffield's head. For a few days after publication it looked as though it would run its course like the rest of his novels, namely that it would have substantial reviews, laudatory on the whole but with reservations, and that the sales would be respectable, but modest. Rosie told me that he expected to make three hundred pounds out of it and was talking of renting a house on the river for the summer. The first two or three notices were non-committal; then in one of the morning papers appeared a violent attack. There was a column of it. The book was described as gratuitously offensive, obscene, and the publishers were rated for putting it before the public. Harrowing pictures were drawn of the devastating effect it must have on the youth of England. It was described as an insult to womanhood. The reviewer protested against the possibility of such a work falling into the hands of young boys and innocent maidens. Other papers followed suit. The more foolish demanded that the book should be suppressed and some asked themselves gravely if this was not a case where the public prosecutor might with fitness intervene. Condemnation was universal; if here and there a courageous writer, accustomed to the more realistic tone of continental fiction, asserted that Edward Driffield had never written anything better, he was ignored. His honest opinion was ascribed to a base desire to play to the gallery. The libraries barred the book and the lessors of the railway bookstalls refused to stock it.

All this was naturally very unpleasant for Edward Driffield, but he bore it with philosophic calm. He shrugged his shoulders.

'They say it isn't true,' he smiled. 'They can go to hell. It is true.'

He was supported in this trial by the fidelity of his friends. To admire *The Cup of Life* became a mark of aesthetic acumen: to be shocked by it was to confess yourself a philistine. Mrs Barton Trafford had no hesitation in saying that it was a masterpiece, and though this wasn't quite the moment for Barton's article in the *Quarterly*, her faith in Edward Driffield's future remained unshaken. It is strange (and instructive) to read now, the book that created such a sensation; there is not a word that could bring a blush to the cheek of the most guileless, not an episode that could cause the novel reader of the present day to turn a hair.

Chapter Nineteen

About six months later, when the excitement over *The Cup of Life* had subsided and Driffield had already begun the novel which he published under the name of *By Their Fruits*, I, being then an in-patient dresser and in my fourth year, in the course of my duties went one day into the main hall of the hospital to await the surgeon whom I was accompanying on his round of the wards. I glanced at the rack in which letters were placed, for sometimes people, not knowing my address in Vincent Square, wrote to me at the hospital. I was surprised to find a telegram for me. It ran as follows:

PLEASE COME AND SEE ME AT FIVE O'CLOCK THIS AFTERNOON WITHOUT FAIL. IMPORTANT.   ISABEL TRAFFORD.

I wondered what she wanted me for. I had met her perhaps a dozen times during the last two years, but she had never taken any notice of me, and I had never been to her house. I knew that men were scarce at teatime and a hostess, short of them at the last moment, might think that a young medical student was better than nothing; but the wording of the telegram hardly suggested a party.

The surgeon for whom I dressed was prosy and verbose. It was not till past five that I was free and then it took me a good twenty minutes to get down to Chelsea. Mrs Barton Trafford lived in a block of flats on the Embankment. It was nearly six when I rang at her door and asked if she was at home. But when I was ushered into her drawing-room and began to explain why I was late she cut me short.

'We supposed you couldn't get away. It doesn't matter.'

Her husband was there.

'I expect he'd like a cup of tea,' he said.

'Oh, I think it's rather late for tea, isn't it?' She looked at me gently, her mild, rather fine eyes full of kindness. 'You don't want any tea, do you?'

I was thirsty and hungry, for my lunch had consisted of a scone and butter and a cup of coffee, but I did not like to say so. I refused tea.

'Do you know Allgood Newton?' asked Mrs Barton Trafford, with a gesture toward a man who had been sitting in a big armchair when I was shown in, and now got up. 'I expect you've met him at Edward's.'

I had. He did not come often, but his name was familiar to me and I remembered him. He made me very nervous and I do not think I had ever spoken to him. Though now completely forgotten, in those days he was the best-known critic in England. He was a large, fat, blond man, with a fleshy white face, pale blue eyes and greying fair hair. He generally wore a pale blue tie to bring out the colour of his eyes. He was very amiable to the authors he met at Driffield's and said charming and flattering things to them, but when they were gone he was very amusing at their expense. He spoke in a low, even voice, with an apt choice of words: no one could with more point tell a malicious story about a friend.

Allgood Newton shook hands with me and Mrs Barton Trafford, with her ready sympathy, anxious to put me at my ease, took me by the hand and made me sit on the sofa beside her. The tea was still on the table and she took a jam sandwich and delicately nibbled it.

'Have you seen the Driffields lately?' she asked me as though making conversation.

'I was there last Saturday.'

'You haven't seen either of them since?'

'No.'

Mrs Barton Trafford looked from Allgood Newton to her husband and back as though mutely demanding their help.

'Nothing will be gained by circumlocution, Isabel,' said Newton, a faintly malicious twinkle in his eye, in his fat precise way.

Mrs Barton Trafford turned to me.

'Then you don't know that Mrs Driffield has run away from her husband.'
'What!'

I was flabbergasted. I could not believe my ears.

'Perhaps it would be better if you told him the facts, Allgood,' said Mrs Trafford.

The critic leaned back in his chair and placed the tips of the fingers of one hand against the tips of the fingers of the other. He spoke with unction.

'I had to see Edward Driffield last night about a literary article that I am doing for him and after dinner, since the night was fine, I thought I would walk round to his house. He was expecting me; and I knew besides that he never went out at night except for some function as important as the Lord Mayor's banquet or the Academy dinner. Imagine my surprise then, nay, my utter and complete bewilderment, when as I approached I saw the door of his house open and Edward in person emerge. You know of course that Immanuel Kant was in the habit of taking his daily walk at a certain hour with such punctuality that the inhabitants of Königsberg were accustomed to set their watches by the event and when once he came out of his house an hour earlier than usual they turned pale, for they knew that this could only mean that some terrible thing had happened. They were right; Immanuel Kant had just received intelligence of the fall of the Bastille.'

Allgood Newton paused for a moment to mark the effect of his anecdote. Mrs Barton Trafford gave him her understanding smile.

'I did not envisage so world-shaking a catastrophe as this when I saw Edward hurrying toward me, but it immediately occurred to me that something untoward was afoot. He carried neither cane nor gloves. He wore his working coat, a venerable garment in black alpaca, and a wide-awake hat. There was something wild in his mien and distraught in his bearing. I asked myself, knowing the vicissitudes of the conjugal state, whether a matrimonial difference had driven him headlong from the house or whether he was hastening to a letter-box in order to post a letter. He sped like Hector flying the noblest of the Greeks. He did not seem to see me and the suspicion flashed across my mind that he did not want to. I stopped him. "Edward," I said. He looked startled. For a moment I could have sworn he did not know who I was. "What avenging furies urge you with such hot haste through the rakish purlieus of Pimlico?" I asked. "Oh, it's you," he said. "Where are you going?" I asked. "Nowhere," he replied.'

At this rate I thought Allgood Newton would never finish his story and Mrs Hudson would be vexed with me for turning up to dinner half an hour late.

'I told him on what errand I had come, and proposed that we should return to his house where we could more conveniently discuss the question that perturbed me. "I'm too restless to go home," he said; "let's walk. You can talk to me as we go along." Assenting, I turned round and we began to walk; but his pace was so rapid that I had to beg him to moderate it. Even Dr Johnson could not have carried on a conversation when he was walking down Fleet Street at the speed of an express train: Edward's appearance was so peculiar and his manner so agitated that I thought it wise to lead him through the less frequented streets. I talked to him of my article. The subject that occupied me was more copious than had at first sight appeared, and I was doubtful whether after all I could do justice to it in the columns of a weekly journal. I put the matter before him fully and fairly and asked him his opinion. "Rosie has left me," he answered. For a moment I did not know what he was talking about, but in a trice it occurred to me that he was speaking of the buxom and not unprepossessing female from whose hands I had on occasion accepted a cup of tea. From his tone I divined that he expected condolence from me rather than felicitation.'

Allgood Newton paused again and his blue eyes twinkled.

'You're wonderful, Allgood,' said Mrs Barton Trafford.

'Priceless,' said her husband.

'Realising that the occasion demanded sympathy, I said: "My dear fellow." He interrupted me. "I had a letter by the last post," he said. "She's run away with Lord George Kemp."'

I gasped, but said nothing. Mrs Trafford gave me a quick look.

'"Who is Lord George Kemp?" "He's a Blackstable man," he replied. I had little time to think. I determined to be frank. "You're well rid of her," I said. "Allgood!" he cried. I stopped and put my hand on his arm. "You must know that she was deceiving you with all your friends. Her behaviour was a public scandal. My dear Edward, let us face the fact: your wife was nothing but a common strumpet." He snatched his arm away from me and gave a sort of low roar, like an orang-utan in the forests of Borneo forcibly deprived of a coconut, and before I could stop him he broke away and fled. I was so startled that I could do nothing but listen to his cries and his hurrying footsteps.'

'You shouldn't have let him go,' said Mrs Barton Trafford. 'In the state he was he might have thrown himself in the Thames.'

'The thought occurred to me, but I noticed that he did not run in the direction of the river, but plunged into the meaner streets of the neighbourhood in which we had been walking. And I reflected also that there is no example in literary history of an author committing suicide while engaged on the composition of a literary work. Whatever his tribulations, he is unwilling to leave to posterity an uncompleted opus.'

I was astounded at what I heard and shocked and dismayed; but I was worried too because I could not make out why Mrs Trafford had sent for me. She knew me much too little to think that the story could be of any particular interest to me; nor would she have troubled to let me hear it as a piece of news.

'Poor Edward,' she said. 'Of course no one can deny that it is a blessing in disguise, but I'm afraid he'll take it very much to heart. Fortunately he's done nothing rash.' She turned to me. 'As soon as Mr Newton told us about it I went round to Limpus Road. Edward was out, but the maid said he'd only just left; that means that he must have gone home between the time he ran away from Allgood and this morning. You'll wonder why I asked you to come and see me.'

I did not answer. I waited for her to go on.

'It was at Blackstable you first knew the Driffields, wasn't it? You can tell us who is this Lord George Kemp. Edward said he was a Blackstable man.'

'He's middle-aged. He's got a wife and two sons. They're as old as I am.'

'But I don't understand who he can be. I can't find him in Debrett.'

I almost laughed.

'Oh, he's not really a lord. He's the local coal merchant. They call him Lord George at Blackstable because he's so grand. It's just a joke.'

'The quiddity of bucolic humour is often a trifle obscure to the uninitiated,' said Allgood Newton.

'We must all help dear Edward in every way we can,' said Mrs Barton

Trafford. Her eyes rested on me thoughtfully. 'If Kemp has run away with Rosie Driffield he must have left his wife.'

'I suppose so,' I replied.

'Will you do something very kind?'

'If I can.'

'Will you go down to Blackstable and find out exactly what has happened? I think we ought to get in touch with the wife.'

I have never been very fond of interfering in other people's affairs.

'I don't know how I could do that,' I answered.

'Couldn't you see her?'

'No, I couldn't.'

If Mrs Barton Trafford thought my reply blunt she did not show it. She smiled a little.

'At all events that can be left over. The urgent thing is to go down and find out about Kemp. I shall try to see Edward this evening. I can't bear the thought of his staying on in that odious house by himself. Barton and I have made up our minds to bring him here. We have a spare room and I'll arrange it so that he can work there. Don't you agree that that would be the best thing for him, Allgood?'

'Absolutely.'

'There's no reason why he shouldn't stay here indefinitely, at all events for a few weeks, and then he can come away with us in the summer. We're going to Brittany. I'm sure he'd like that. It would be a thorough change for him.'

'The immediate question,' said Barton Trafford, fixing on me an eye nearly as kindly as his wife's, 'is whether this young sawbones will go to Blackstable and find out what he can. We must know where we are. That is essential.'

Barton Trafford excused his interest in archaeology by a hearty manner and a jocose, even slangy way of speech.

'He couldn't refuse,' said his wife, giving me a soft, appealing glance. 'You won't refuse, will you? It's so important and you're the only person who can help us.'

Of course she did not know that I was as anxious to find out what had happened as she; she could not tell what a bitter jealous pain stabbed my heart.

'I couldn't possibly get away from the hospital before Saturday,' I said.

'That'll do. It's very good of you. All Edward's friends will be grateful to you. When shall you return?'

'I have to be back in London early on Monday morning.'

'Then come and have tea with me in the afternoon. I shall await you with impatience. Thank God, that's settled. Now I must try and get hold of Edward.'

I understood that I was dismissed. Allgood Newton took his leave and came downstairs with me.

'Our Isabel has *un petit air* of Catherine of Aragon today that I find vastly becoming,' he murmured when the door was closed behind us. 'This is a golden opportunity and I think we may safely trust our friend not to miss it. A charming woman with a heart of gold. *Vénus toute entière à sa proie attachée.*'

I did not understand what he meant, for what I have already told the reader about Mrs Barton Trafford I only learned much later, but I realised that he was saying something vaguely malicious about her, and probably amusing, so I sniggered.

'I suppose your youth inclines you to what my good Dizzy named in an unlucky moment the gondola of London.'

'I'm going to take a bus,' I answered.

'Oh? Had you proposed to go by hansom I was going to ask you to be good enough to drop me on your way, but if you are going to use the homely conveyance which I in my old-fashioned manner still prefer to call an omnibus, I shall hoist my unwieldy carcase into a four-wheeler.'

He signalled to one and gave me two flabby fingers to shake.

'I shall come on Monday to hear the result of what dear Henry would call your exquisitely delicate mission.'

Chapter Twenty

But it was years before I saw Allgood Newton again, for when I got to Blackstable I found a letter from Mrs Barton Trafford (who had taken the precaution to note my address) asking me, for reasons that she would explain when she saw me, not to come to her flat but to meet her at six o'clock in the first-class waiting-room at Victoria Station. As soon then as I could get away from the hospital on Monday I made my way there, and after waiting for a while saw her come in. She came toward me with little tripping steps.

'Well, have you anything to tell me? Let us find a quiet corner and sit down.'

We sought a place and found it.

'I must explain why I asked you to come here,' she said. 'Edward is staying with me. At first he did not want to come, but I persuaded him. But he's nervous and ill and irritable. I did not want to run the risk of his seeing you.'

I told Mrs Trafford the bare facts of my story and she listened attentively. Now and then she nodded her head. But I could not hope to make her understand the commotion I had found at Blackstable. The town was beside itself with excitement. Nothing so thrilling had happened there for years and no one could talk of anything else. Humpty-dumpty had had a great fall. Lord George Kemp had absconded. About a week before he had announced that he had to go up to London on business, and two days later a petition in bankruptcy was filed against him. It appeared that his building operations had not been successful, his attempt to make Blackstable into a frequented seaside resort meeting with no response, and he had been forced to raise money in every way he could. All kinds of rumours ran through the little town. Quite a number of small people who had entrusted their savings to him were faced with the loss of all they had. The details were vague, for neither my uncle nor my aunt knew anything of business matters, nor had I the knowledge to make what they told me comprehensible. But there was a mortgage on George Kemp's house and a bill of sale on his furniture. His wife was left without a penny. His two sons, lads of twenty and twenty-one, were in the coal business, but that too was involved in the general ruin. George Kemp had gone off with all the cash he could lay hands on, something like fifteen hundred pounds, they said, though how they knew I cannot imagine; and it was reported that a warrant had been issued for his arrest. It was supposed that he had left the country; some said he had gone to Australia and some to Canada.

'I hope they catch him,' said my uncle. 'He ought to get penal servitude for life.'

The indignation was universal. They could not forgive him because he had always been so noisy and boisterous, because he had chaffed them and stood them drinks and given them garden parties, because he had driven such a smart trap and worn his brown billycock hat at such a rakish angle. But it was on Sunday night after church in the vestry that the churchwarden told my uncle the worst. For the last two years he had been meeting Rosie Driffield at Haversham almost every week and they had been spending the night together at a public-house. The licensee of this had put money into one of Lord George's wildcat schemes, and on discovering that he had lost it blurted out the whole story. He could have borne it if Lord George had defrauded others, but that he should defraud him who had done him a good turn and whom he looked upon as a chum, that was the limit.

'I expect they've run away together,' said my uncle.

'I shouldn't be surprised,' said the churchwarden.

After supper, while the housemaid was clearing away, I went into the kitchen to talk to Mary-Ann. She had been at church and had heard the story too. I cannot believe that the congregation had listened very attentively to my uncle's sermon.

'The vicar says they've run away together,' I said. I had not breathed a word of what I knew.

'Why, of course they 'ave,' said Mary-Ann. 'He was the only man she ever really fancied. He only 'ad to lift 'is little finger and she'd leave anyone no matter who it was.'

I lowered my eyes. I was suffering from bitter mortification; and I was angry with Rosie: I thought she had behaved very badly to me.

'I suppose we shall never see her again,' I said.

It gave me a pang to utter the words.

'I don't suppose we shall,' said Mary-Ann cheerfully.

When I had told Mrs Barton Trafford as much of this story as I thought she need know, she sighed, but whether from satisfaction or distress I had no notion.

'Well, that's the end of Rosie at all events,' she said. She got up and held out her hand. 'Why will these literary men make these unfortunate marriages? It's all very sad, very sad. Thank you so much for what you've done. We know where we are now. The great thing is that it shouldn't interfere with Edward's work.'

Her remarks seemed a trifle disconnected to me. The fact was, I have no doubt, that she was giving me not the smallest thought. I led her out of Victoria Station and put her into a bus that went down the King's Road, Chelsea; then I walked back to my lodgings.

Chapter Twenty-one

I lost touch with Driffield. I was too shy to seek him out; I was busy with my examinations, and when I had passed them I went abroad. I remember vaguely to have seen in the paper that he had divorced Rosie. Nothing more was heard of her. Small sums reached her mother occasionally, ten or twenty pounds, and they came in a registered letter with a New York postmark; but no address was given, no message enclosed, and they were presumed to come from Rosie only because no one else could possibly send Mrs Gann money. Then in the fullness of years Rosie's mother died, and it may be supposed that in some way the news reached her, for the letters ceased to come.

Chapter Twenty-two

Alroy Kear and I, as arranged, met on Friday at Victoria Station to catch the five ten to Blackstable. We made ourselves comfortable in opposite corners of a smoking compartment. From him I now learned roughly what had happened to Driffield after his wife ran away from him. Roy had in due course become very intimate with Mrs Barton Trafford. Knowing him and remembering her, I realised that this was inevitable. I was not surprised to hear that he had travelled with her and Barton on the continent, sharing with them to the full their passion for Wagner, post-impressionist painting and baroque architecture. He had lunched assiduously at the flat in Chelsea and when advancing years and failing health had imprisoned Mrs Trafford to her drawing-room, notwithstanding the many claims on his time he had gone regularly once a week to sit with her. He had a good heart. After her death he wrote an article about her in which with admirable emotion he did justice to her great gifts of sympathy and discrimination.

It pleased me to think that his kindliness should receive its due and unexpected reward, for Mrs Barton Trafford had told him much about Edward Driffield that could not fail to be of service to him in the work of love on which he was now engaged. Mrs Barton Trafford, exercising a gentle violence, not only took Edward Driffield into her house when the flight of his faithless wife left him what Roy could only describe by the French word *désemparé*, but persuaded him to stay for nearly a year. She gave him the loving care, the unfailing kindness and the intelligent understanding of a woman who combined feminine tact with masculine vigour, a heart of gold with an unerring eye for the main chance. It was in her flat that he finished *By Their Fruits*. She was justified in looking upon it as her book and the dedication to her is a proof that Driffield was not unmindful of his debt. She took him to Italy (with Barton of course, for Mrs Trafford knew too well how malicious people were, to give occasion for scandal) and with a volume of Ruskin in her hand revealed to Edward Driffield the immortal beauties of that country. Then she found him rooms in the Temple and arranged little luncheons there, she acting very prettily the part of hostess, where he could receive the persons whom his increasing reputation attracted.

It must be admitted that this increasing reputation was very largely due to her. His great celebrity came only during his last years when he had long ceased to write, but the foundations of it were undoubtedly laid by Mrs Trafford's untiring efforts. Not only did she inspire (and perhaps write not a little, for she had a dexterous pen) the article that Barton at last contributed to the *Quarterly* in which the claim was first made that Driffield must be ranked with the masters of British fiction, but as each book came out she organised its reception. She went here and there, seeing editors and, more important still, proprietors of influential organs; she gave soirées to which everyone was invited who could be of use. She persuaded Edward Driffield to give readings at the houses of the very great for charitable purposes; she saw to it that his photographs should appear in the illustrated weeklies; she revised personally any interview he gave. For ten years she was an indefatigable press agent. She kept him steadily before the public.

Mrs Barton Trafford had a grand time, but she did not get above herself. It was useless indeed to ask him to a party without her; he refused. And when she and Barton and Driffield were invited anywhere to dinner they came together and went together. She never let him out of her sight. Hostesses might rave; they could take it or leave it. As a rule they took it. If Mrs Barton Trafford happened to be a little out of temper it was through him she showed it, for while she remained charming, Edward Driffield would be uncommonly gruff. But she knew exactly how to draw him out and when the company was distinguished could make him brilliant. She was perfect with him. She never concealed from him her conviction that he was the greatest writer of his day; she not only referred to him invariably as the master, but, perhaps a little playfully and yet how flatteringly, addressed him always as such. To the end she retained something kittenish.

Then a terrible thing happened. Driffield caught pneumonia and was extremely ill; for some time his life was despaired of. Mrs Barton Trafford did everything that such a woman could do, and would willingly have nursed him herself, but she was frail, she was indeed over sixty, and he had to have professional nurses. When at last he pulled through, the doctors said that he must go into the country, and since he was still extremely weak insisted that a nurse should go with him. Mrs Trafford wanted him to go to Bournemouth so that she could run down for week-ends and see that everything was well with him, but Driffield had a fancy for Cornwall, and the doctors agreed that the mild airs of Penzance would suit him. One would have thought that a woman of Isabel Trafford's delicate intuition would have had some foreboding of ill. No. She let him go. She impressed on the nurse that she entrusted her with a grave responsibility; she placed in her hands, if not the future of English literature, at least the life and welfare of its most distinguished living representative. It was a priceless charge.

Three weeks later Edward Driffield wrote and told her that he had married his nurse by special licence.

I imagine that never did Mrs Barton Trafford exhibit more pre-eminently her greatness of soul than in the manner in which she met this situation. Did she cry, Judas, Judas? Did she tear her hair and fall on the floor and kick her heels in an attack of hysterics? Did she turn on the mild and learned Barton and call him a blithering old fool? Did she inveigh against the faithlessness of men and the wantonness of women or did she relieve her wounded feelings by shouting at the top of her voice a string of those obscenities with which the alienists tell us the chastest females are surprisingly acquainted? Not at all. She wrote a charming letter of congratulation to Driffield and she wrote to his bride telling her that she was glad to think that now she would have two loving friends instead of one. She begged them both to come and stay with her on their return to London. She told everyone she met that the marriage had made her very, very happy, for Edward Driffield would soon be an old man and must have someone to take care of him; who could do this better than a hospital nurse? She never had anything but praise for the new Mrs Driffield; she was not exactly pretty, she said, but she had a very nice face; of course she wasn't quite, quite a lady, but Edward would only have been uncomfortable with anyone too grand. She was just the sort of wife for him. I think it may be not unjustly said that Mrs Barton Trafford fairly ran over with the milk of human kindness, but all the same I have an inkling that if ever the milk of human kindness was charged with vitriol, here was a case in point.

Chapter Twenty-three

When we arrived at Blackstable, Roy and I, a car, neither ostentatiously grand nor obviously cheap, was waiting for him and the chauffeur had a note for me asking me to lunch with Mrs Driffield next day. I got into a taxi and went to the 'Bear and Key.' I had learned from Roy that there was a new Marine Hotel on the front, but I did not propose for the luxuries of civilisation to abandon a resort of my youth. Change met me at the railway station, which was not in its old place, but up a new road, and of course it was strange to be driven down the High Street in a car. But the 'Bear and Key' was unaltered. It received me with its old churlish indifference: there was no one at the entrance, the driver put my bag down and drove away; I called, no one answered; I went into the bar and found a young lady with shingled hair reading a book by Mr Compton Mackenzie. I asked her if I could have a room. She gave me a slightly offended look and said she thought so, but as that seemed to exhaust her interest in the matter I asked politely whether there was anyone who could show it to me. She got up and, opening a door, in a shrill voice called: 'Katie.'

'What is it?' I heard.

'There's a gent wants a room.'

In a little while appeared an ancient and haggard female in a very dirty print dress, with an untidy mop of grey hair, and showed me, two flights up, a very small grubby room.

'Can't you do something better than that for me?' I asked.

'It's the room commercials generally 'ave,' she answered with a sniff.

'Haven't you got any others?'

'Not a single.'

'Then give me a double room.'

'I'll go and ask Mrs Brentford.'

I accompanied her down to the first floor and she knocked at a door. She was told to come in, and when she opened it I caught sight of a stout woman with grey hair elaborately marcelled. She was reading a book. Apparently everyone at the 'Bear and Key' was interested in literature. She gave me an indifferent look when Katie said I wasn't satisfied with number seven.

'Show him number five,' she said.

I began to feel that I had been a trifle rash in declining so haughtily Mrs Driffield's invitation to stay with her and then putting aside in my sentimental way Roy's wise suggestion that I should stay at the Marine Hotel. Katie took me upstairs again and ushered me into a largish room looking on the High Street. Most of its space was occupied by a double bed. The windows had certainly not been opened for a month.

I said that would do and asked about dinner.

'You can 'ave what you like,' said Katie. 'We 'aven't got nothing in, but I'll run round and get it.'

Knowing English inns, I ordered a fried sole and a grilled chop. Then I went for a stroll. I walked down to the beach and found that they had built an esplanade and there was a row of bungalows and villas where I remembered only windswept fields. But they were seedy and bedraggled and I guessed that even after all these years Lord George's dream of turning Blackstable into a popular seaside resort had not come true. A retired military man, a pair of elderly ladies walked along the crumbling asphalt. It was incredibly dreary. A chill wind was blowing and a light drizzle swept over from the sea.

I went back into the town and here, in the space between the 'Bear and Key' and the 'Duke of Kent,' were little knots of men standing about notwithstanding the inclement weather; and their eyes had the same pale blue, their high cheek bones the same ruddy colour as that of their fathers before them. It was strange to see that some of the sailors in blue jerseys still wore little gold rings in their ears; and not only old ones but boys scarcely out of their teens. I sauntered down the street and there was the bank refronted, but the stationery shop where I had bought paper and wax to make rubbings with an obscure writer whom I had met by chance was unchanged; there were two or three cinemas and their garish posters suddenly gave the prim street a dissipated air so that it looked like a respectable elderly woman who had taken a drop too much.

It was cold and cheerless in the commercial room where I ate my dinner alone at a large table laid for six. I was served by the slatternly Katie. I asked if I could have a fire.

'Not in June,' she said. 'We don't 'ave fires after April.'

'I'll pay for it,' I protested.

'Not in June. In October, yes, but not in June.'

When I had finished I went into the bar to have a glass of port.

'Very quiet,' I said to the shingled barmaid.

'Yes, it is quiet,' she answered.

'I should have thought on a Friday night you'd have quite a lot of people in here.'

'Well, one would think that, wouldn't one?'

Then a stout red-faced man with a close-cropped head of grey hair came in from the back and I guessed that this was my host.

'Are you Mr Brentford?' I asked him.

'Yes, that's me.'

'I knew your father. Will you have a glass of port?'

I told him my name, in the days of his boyhood better known than any other at Blackstable, but somewhat to my mortification I saw that it aroused no echo in his memory. He consented, however, to let me stand him a glass of port.

'Down here on business?' he asked me. 'We get quite a few commercial gents at one time and another. We always like to do what we can for them.'

I told him that I had come down to see Mrs Driffield and left him to guess on what errand.

'I used to see a lot of the old man,' said Mr Brentford. 'He used to be very partial to dropping in here and having his glass of bitter. Mind you, I don't say he ever got tiddly, but he used to like to sit in the bar and talk. My word, he'd talk by the hour and he never cared who he talked to. Mrs Driffield didn't half like his coming here. He'd slip away, out of the house, without saying a word to anybody, and come toddling down. You know it's a bit of a walk for a man of that age. Of course when they missed him Mrs Driffield knew where he was, and she used to telephone and ask if he was here. Then she'd drive over in the car and go in and see my wife. "You go in and fetch him, Mrs Brentford," she'd say; "I don't like to go in the bar meself, not with all those men hanging about"; so Mrs Brentford would come in and she'd say, "Now Mr Driffield, Mrs Driffield's come for you in the car, so you'd better finish your beer and let her take you home." He used to ask Mrs Brentford not to say he was here when Mrs Driffield rang up, but of course we couldn't do that. He was an old man and all that and we didn't want to take the responsibility. He was born in this parish, you know, and his first wife, she was a Blackstable girl. She's been dead these many years. I never knew her. He was a funny old fellow. No side, you know; they tell me they thought a rare lot of him in London and when he died the papers were full of him; but you'd never have known it to talk to him. He might have been just nobody like you and me. Of course we always tried to make him comfortable; we tried to get him to sit in one of them easy chairs, but no, he must sit up at the bar; he said he liked to feel his feet on a rail. My belief is he was happier here than anywhere. He always said he liked a bar. He said you saw life there and he said he'd always loved life. Quite a character he was. Reminded me of my father, except that my old governor never read a book in his life and he drank a bottle of French brandy a day and he was seventy-eight when he died and his last illness was his first. I quite missed old Driffield when he popped off. I was only saying to Mrs Brentford the other day, I'd like to read one of his books some time. They tell me he wrote several about these parts.'

Chapter Twenty-four

Next morning it was cold and raw, but it was not raining, and I walked down the High Street toward the vicarage. I recognised the names over the shops, the Kentish names that have been borne for centuries–the Ganns, the Kemps, the Cobbs, the Igguldens–but I saw no one that I knew. I felt like a ghost walking down that street where I had once known nearly everyone, if not to speak to, at least by sight. Suddenly a very shabby little car passed me, stopped and backed, and I saw someone looking at me curiously. A tall, heavy elderly man got out and came toward me.

'Aren't you Willie Ashenden?' he asked.

Then I recognised him. He was the doctor's son, and I had been at school with him; we had passed from form to form together, and I knew that he had succeeded his father in his practice.

'Hullo, how are you?' he asked. 'I've just been along to the vicarage to see my grandson. It's a preparatory school now, you know, and I put him there at the beginning of this term.'

He was shabbily dressed and unkempt, but he had a fine head and I saw that in youth he must have had unusual beauty. It was funny that I had never noticed it.

'Are you a grandfather?' I asked.

'Three times over,' he laughed.

It gave me a shock. He had drawn breath, walked the earth and presently grown to man's estate, married, had children and they in turn had had children; I judged from the look of him that he had lived, with incessant toil, in penury. He had the peculiar manner of the country doctor, bluff, hearty and unctuous. His life was over. I had plans in my head for books and plays, I was full of schemes for the future; I felt that a long stretch of activity and fun still lay before me; and yet, I supposed, to others I must seem the elderly man that he seemed to me. I was so shaken that I had not the presence of mind to ask about his brothers whom as a child I had played with, or about the old friends who had been my companions; after a few foolish remarks I left him. I walked on to the vicarage, a roomy, rambling house too far out of the way for the modern incumbent who took his duties more seriously than did my uncle and too large for the present cost of living. It stood in a big garden and was surrounded by green fields. There was a great square notice board that announced that it was a preparatory school for the sons of gentlemen and gave the name and the degrees of the head master. I looked over the paling; the garden was squalid and untidy and the pond in which I used to fish for roach was choked up. The glebe fields had been cut up into building lots. There were rows of little brick houses with bumpy ill-made roads, I walked along Joy Lane and there were houses here too, bungalows facing the sea; and the old turnpike house was a trim tea shop.

I wandered about here and there. There seemed innumerable streets of little houses of yellow brick, but I do not know who lived in them for I saw no one about. I went down to the harbour. It was deserted. There was but one tramp lying a little way out from the pier. Two or three sailormen were sitting outside a warehouse and they stared at me as I passed. The bottom had fallen out of the coal trade and colliers came to Blackstable no longer.

Then it was time for me to go to Ferne Court and I went back to the 'Bear and Key.' The landlord had told me that he had a Daimler for hire and I had arranged that it should take me to my luncheon. It stood at the door when I came up, a brougham, but the oldest, most dilapidated car of its make that I had ever seen; it panted along with squeaks and thumps and rattlings, with sudden angry jerks, so that I wondered if I should ever reach my destination. But the extraordinary, the amazing thing about it was that it smelled exactly like the old landau which my uncle used to hire every Sunday morning to go to church in. This was a rank odour of stables and of stale straw that lay at the bottom of the carriage; and I wondered in vain why, after all these years, the motor car should have it too. But nothing can bring back the past like a perfume or a stench, and, oblivious to the country I was trundling through, I saw myself once more a little boy on the front seat with the communion plate beside me and, facing me, my aunt, smelling slightly of clean linen and eau-de-Cologne, in her black silk cloak and her little bonnet with a feather, and my uncle in his cassock, a broad band of ribbed silk round his ample waist and a gold cross hanging over his stomach from the gold chain round his neck.

'Now, Willie, mind you behave nicely today. You're not to turn round, and sit up properly in your seat. The Lord's House isn't the place to loll in and you must remember that you should set an example to other little boys who haven't had your advantages.'

When I arrived at Ferne Court, Mrs Driffield and Roy were walking round the garden and they came up to me as I got out of the car.

'I was showing Roy my flowers,' said Mrs Driffield, as she shook hands with me. And then with a sigh: 'They're all I have now.'

She looked no older than when last I saw her six years before. She wore her tweeds with quiet distinction. At her neck was a collar of white crêpe and at her wrists cuffs of the same. Roy, I noticed, wore with his neat blue suit a black tie; I supposed it was a sign of respect for the illustrious dead.

'I'll just show you my herbaceous borders,' said Mrs Driffield, 'and then we'll go in to lunch.'

We walked round and Roy was very knowledgeable. He knew what all the flowers were called, and the Latin names tripped off his tongue like cigarettes out of a cigarette-making machine. He told Mrs Driffield where she ought to get certain varieties that she absolutely must have and how perfectly lovely were certain others.

'Shall we go in through Edward's study?' suggested Mrs Driffield. 'I keep it exactly as it was when he was here. I haven't changed a thing. You'd be surprised how many people come over to see the house, and of course above all they want to see the room he worked in.'

We went in through an open window. There was a bowl of roses on the desk and on a little round table by the side of the armchair a copy of the *Spectator*. In the ash trays were the master's pipes and there was ink in the inkstand. The scene was perfectly set. I do not know why the room seemed so strangely dead; it had already the mustiness of a museum. Mrs Driffield went to the bookshelves and with a little smile, half playful, half sad, passed a rapid hand across the back of half a dozen volumes bound in blue.

'You know that Edward admired your work so much,' said Mrs Driffield. 'He re-read your books quite often.'

'I'm very glad to think that,' I said politely.

I knew very well that they had not been there on my last visit and in a casual way I took one of them out and ran my fingers along the top to see whether there was dust on it. There was not. Then I took another book down, one of Charlotte Brontë's, and making a little plausible conversation tried the same experiment. No, there was no dust there either. All I learned was that Mrs Driffield was an excellent housekeeper and had a conscientious maid.

We went in to luncheon, a hearty British meal of roast beef and Yorkshire pudding, and we talked of the work on which Roy was engaged.

'I want to spare dear Roy all the labour I can,' said Mrs Driffield, 'and I've been gathering together as much of the material as I could myself. Of course it's been rather painful, but it's been very interesting, too. I came across a lot of old photographs that I must show you.'

After luncheon we went into the drawing-room and I noticed again with what perfect tact Mrs Driffield had arranged it. It suited the widow of a distinguished man of letters almost more than it had suited the wife. Those chintzes, those bowls of pot-pourri, those Dresden China figures—there was about them a faint air of regret; they seemed to reflect pensively upon a past of distinction. I could have wished on this chilly day that there were a fire in the grate, but the English are a hardy as well as a conservative race; and it is not difficult for them to maintain their principles at the cost of the discomfort of others. I doubted whether Mrs Driffield would have conceived the possibility of lighting a fire before the first of October. She asked me whether I had lately seen the lady who had brought me to lunch with the Driffields, and I surmised from her faint acerbity that since the death of her eminent husband the great and fashionable had shown a distinct tendency to take no further notice of her. We were just settling down to talk about the defunct; Roy and Mrs Driffield were putting artful questions to incite me to disclose my recollections and I was gathering my wits about me so that I should not in an unguarded moment let slip anything that I had made up my mind to keep to myself; when suddenly the trim parlour-maid brought in two cards on a small salver.

'Two gentlemen in a car, mum, and they say, could they look at the house and garden?'

'What a bore!' cried Mrs Driffield, but with astonishing alacrity. 'Isn't it funny I should have been speaking just now about the people who want to see the house? I never have a moment's peace.'

'Well, why don't you say you're sorry you can't see them?' said Roy, with what I thought a certain cattiness.

'Oh. I couldn't do that. Edward wouldn't have like me to.' She looked at the cards. 'I haven't got my glasses on me.'

She handed them to me, and on one I read 'Henry Beard MacDougal, University of Virginia'; and in pencil was written: 'Assistant professor in English Literature.' The other was 'Jean-Paul Underhill,' and there was at the bottom an address in New York.

'Americans,' said Mrs Driffield. 'Say I shall be very pleased if they'll come in.'

Presently the maid ushered the strangers in. They were both tall young men and broad-shouldered, with heavy, clean-shaven, swarthy faces and handsome eyes; they both wore horn-rimmed spectacles and they both had thick black hair combed straight back from their foreheads. They both wore English suits that were evidently brand-new; they were both slightly embarrassed, but verbose and extremely civil. They explained that they were making a literary tour of England and, being admirers of Edward Driffield, had taken the liberty of stopping off on their way to Rye to visit Henry James's house in the hope that they would be permitted to see a spot sanctified by so many associations. The reference to Rye did not go down very well with Mrs Driffield.

'I believe they have some very good links there,' she said.

She introduced the Americans to Roy and me. I was filled with admiration for the way in which Roy rose to the occasion. It appeared that he had lectured before the University of Virginia and had stayed with a distinguished member of the faculty. It had been an unforgettable experience. He did not know whether he had been more impressed by the lavish hospitality with which those charming Virginians had entertained him or by their intelligent interest in art and literature. He asked how So-and-So was, and So-and-So; he had made lifelong friends there, and it looked as though everyone he had met was good and kind and clever. Soon the young professor was telling Roy how much he liked his books, and Roy was modestly telling him what in this one and the other his aim had been and how conscious he was that he had come far short of achieving it. Mrs Driffield listened with smiling sympathy, but I had a feeling that her smile was growing a trifle strained. It may be that Roy had too, for he suddenly broke off.

'But you don't want me to bore you with my stuff,' he said in his loud hearty way. 'I'm only here because Mrs Driffield has entrusted to me the great honour of writing Edward Driffield's Life.'

This of course interested the visitors very much.

'It's some job, believe me,' said Roy, playfully American. 'Fortunately I have the assistance of Mrs Driffield, who was not only a perfect wife, but an admirable amanuensis and secretary; the materials she has placed at my disposal are so amazingly full that really little remains for me to do but take advantage of her industry and her—her affectionate zeal.'

Mrs Driffield looked down demurely at the carpet and the two young Americans turned on her their large dark eyes in which you could read their sympathy, their interest and their respect. After a little more conversation—partly literary but also about golf, for the visitors admitted that they hoped to get a round or two at Rye, and here again Roy was on the spot, for he told them to look out for such and such a bunker and when they came to London hoped they would play with him at Sunningdale; after this, I say, Mrs Driffield got up and offered to show them Edward's study and bedroom, and of course the garden. Roy rose to his feet, evidently bent on accompanying them, but Mrs Driffield gave him a little smile; it was pleasant but firm.

'Don't you bother to come, Roy,' she said. 'I'll take them round. You stay here and talk to Mr Ashenden.'

'Oh, all right. Of course.'

The strangers bade us farewell and Roy and I settled down again in the chintz armchairs.

'Jolly room this is,' said Roy.

'Very.'

'Amy had to work hard to get it. You know the old man bought this house two or three years before they were married. She tried to make him sell it, but he wouldn't. He was very obstinate in some ways. You see, it belonged to a certain Miss Wolfe, whose bailiff his father was, and he said that when he was a little boy his one idea was to own it himself and now he'd got it he was going to keep it. One would have thought the last thing he'd want to do was to live in a place where everyone knew all about his origins and everything. Once poor Amy very nearly engaged a housemaid before she discovered she was Edward's great-niece. When Amy came here the house was furnished from attic to cellar in the best Tottenham Court Road manner; you know the sort of thing, Turkey carpets and mahogany sideboards, and a plush-covered suite in the drawing-room, and modern marquetry. It was his idea of how a gentleman's house should be furnished. Amy says it was simply awful. He wouldn't let her change a thing and she had to go to work with the greatest care; she says she simply couldn't have lived in it and she was determined to have things right, so she had to change things one by one so that he didn't pay any attention. She told me the hardest job she had was with his writing-desk. I don't know whether you've noticed the one there is in his study now. It's a very good period piece; I wouldn't mind having it myself. Well, he had a horrible American roll-top desk. He'd had it for years and he'd written a dozen books on it and he simply wouldn't part with it, he had no feeling for things like that; he just happened to be attached to it because he'd had it so long. You must get Amy to tell you the story how she managed to get rid of it in the end. It's really priceless. She's a remarkable woman, you know; she generally gets her own way.'

'I've noticed it,' I said.

It had not taken her long to dispose of Roy when he showed signs of wishing to go over the house with the visitors. He gave me a quick look and laughed. Roy was not stupid.

'You don't know America as well as I do,' he said. 'They always prefer a live mouse to a dead lion. That's one of the reasons why I like America.'

Chapter Twenty-five

When Mrs Driffield, having sent the pilgrims on their way, came back she bore under her arm a portfolio.

'What very nice young men!' she said. 'I wish young men in England took such a keen interest in literature. I gave them that photo of Edward when he was dead and they asked me for one of mine, and I signed it for them.' Then very graciously: 'You made a great impression on them, Roy. They said it was a real privilege to meet you.'

'I've lectured in America so much,' said Roy, with modesty.

'Oh, but they've read your books. They say that what they like about them is that they're so virile.'

The portfolio contained a number of old photographs, groups of schoolboys among whom I recognised an urchin with untidy hair as Driffield only because his widow pointed him out, Rugby fifteens with Driffield a little older, and then one of a young sailor in a jersey and a reefer jacket, Driffield when he ran away to sea.

'Here's one taken when he was first married,' said Mrs Driffield.

He wore a beard and black-and-white check trousers; in his buttonhole was a large white rose backed my maidenhair and on the table beside him a chimney-pot hat.

'And here is the bride,' said Mrs Driffield, trying not to smile.

Poor Rosie, seen by a country photographer over forty years ago, was grotesque. She was standing very stiffly against a background of baronial hall, holding a large bouquet; her dress was elaborately draped, pinched at the waist, and she wore a bustle. Her fringe came down to her eyes. On her head was a wreath of orange blossoms, perched high on a mass of hair, and from it was thrown back a long veil. Only I knew how lovely she must have looked.

'She looks fearfully common,' said Roy.

'She was,' murmured Mrs Driffield.

We looked at more photographs of Edward, photographs that had been taken of him when he began to be known, photographs when he wore only a moustache and others, all the later ones, when he was clean-shaven. You saw his face grown thinner and more lined. The stubborn commonplace of the early portraits melted gradually into a weary refinement. You saw the change in him wrought by experience, thought and achieved ambition. I looked again at the photograph of the young sailorman and fancied that I saw in it already a trace of that aloofness that seemed to me so marked in the older ones and that I had had years before the vague sensation of in the man himself. The face you saw was a mask and the actions he performed were without significance. I had an impression that the real man, to his death unknown and lonely, was a wraith that went a silent way unseen between the writer of his books and the man who led his life, and smiled with ironical detachment at the two puppets that the world took for Edward Driffield. I am conscious that in what I have written of him I have not presented a living man, standing on his feet, rounded, with comprehensible motives and logical activities; I have not tried to: I am glad to leave that to the abler pen of Alroy Kear.

I came across the photographs that Harry Retford, the actor, had had taken of Rosie, and then a photograph of the picture that Lionel Hillier had painted of her. It gave me a pang. That was how I best remembered her. Notwithstanding the old-fashioned gown, she was alive there and tremulous with the passion that filled her. She seemed to offer herself to the assault of love.

'She gives you the impression of a hefty wench,' said Roy.

'If you like the milkmaid type,' answered Mrs Driffield. 'I've always thought she looked rather like a white nigger.'

That was what Mrs Barton Trafford had been fond of calling her, and with Rosie's thick lips and broad nose there was indeed a hateful truth in the description. But they did not know how silvery golden her hair was, nor how golden silver her skin; they did not know her enchanting smile.

'She wasn't a bit like a white nigger,' I said. 'She was virginal like the dawn. She was like Hebe. She was like a tea rose.'

Mrs Driffield smiled and exchanged a meaning glance with Roy.

'Mrs Barton Trafford told me a great deal about her. I don't wish to seem spiteful, but I'm afraid I don't think that she can have been a very nice woman.'

'That's where you make a mistake,' I replied. 'She was a very nice woman. I never saw her in a bad temper. You only had to say you wanted something for her to give it to you. I never heard her say a disagreeable thing about anyone. She had a heart of gold.'

'She was a terrible slattern. Her house was always in a mess; you didn't like to sit down in a chair because it was so dusty and you dared not look in the corners. And it was the same with her person. She could never put a skirt on straight and you'd see about two inches of petticoat hanging down on one side.'

'She didn't bother about things like that. They didn't make her any the less beautiful. And she was as good as she was beautiful.'

Roy burst out laughing and Mrs Driffield put her hand up to her mouth to hide her smile.

'Oh, come, Mr Ashenden, that's really going too far. After all, let's face it, she was a nymphomaniac.'

'I think that's a very silly word,' I said.

'Well, then, let me say that she can hardly have been a very good woman to treat poor Edward as she did. Of course it was a blessing in disguise. If she hadn't run away from him he might have had to bear that burden for the rest of his life, and with such a handicap he could never have reached the position he did. But the fact remains that she was notoriously unfaithful to him. From what I hear she was absolutely promiscuous.'

'You don't understand,' I said. 'She was a very simple woman. Her instincts were healthy and ingenuous. She loved to make people happy. She loved love.'

'Do you call that love?'

'Well, then, the act of love. She was naturally affectionate. When she liked anyone it was quite natural for her to go to bed with him. She never thought twice about it. It was not vice; it wasn't lasciviousness; it was her nature. She gave herself as naturally as the sun gives heat or the flowers their perfume. It was a pleasure to her and she liked to give pleasure to others. It had no effect on her character; she remained sincere, unspoiled and artless.'

Mrs Driffield looked as though she had taken a dose of castor oil and had just been trying to get the taste of it out of her mouth by sucking a lemon.

'I don't understand,' she said. 'But then I'm bound to admit that I never understood what Edward saw in her.'

'Did he know that she was carrying on with all sorts of people?' asked Roy.

'I'm sure he didn't,' she replied quickly.

'You think him a bigger fool than I do, Mrs Driffield,' I said.

'Then why did he put up with it?'

'I think I can tell you. You see, she wasn't a woman who ever inspired love. Only affection. It was absurd to be jealous over her. She was like a clear deep pool in a forest glade into which it's heavenly to plunge, but it is neither less cool nor less crystalline because a tramp and a gipsy and a gamekeeper have plunged into it before you.'

Roy laughed again and this time Mrs Driffield without concealment smiled thinly.

'It's comic to hear you so lyrical,' said Roy.

I stifled a sigh. I have noticed that when I am most serious people are apt to laugh at me, and indeed when after a lapse of time I have read passages that I wrote from the fullness of my heart I have been tempted to laugh at myself. It must be that there is something naturally absurd in a sincere emotion, though why there should be I cannot imagine, unless it is that man, the ephemeral inhabitant of an insignificant planet, with all his pain and all his striving is but a jest in an eternal mind.

I saw that Mrs Driffield wished to ask me something. It caused her a certain embarrassment.

'Do you think he'd have taken her back if she'd been willing to come?'

'You knew him better than I. I should say no. I think that when he had exhausted an emotion he took no further interest in the person who had aroused it. I should say that he had a peculiar combination of strong feeling and extreme callousness.'

'I don't know how you can say that,' cried Roy. 'He was the kindest man I ever met.'

Mrs Driffield looked at me steadily and then dropped her eyes.

'I wonder what happened to her when she went to America,' he asked.

'I believe she married Kemp,' said Mrs Driffield. 'I heard they had taken another name. Of course they couldn't show their faces over here again.'

'When did she die?'

'Oh, about ten years ago.'

'How did you hear?' I asked.

'From Harold Kemp, the son; he's in some sort of business at Maidstone. I never told Edward. She's been dead to him for many years and I saw no reason to remind him of the past. It always helps you if you put yourself in other people's shoes and I said to myself that if I were he I shouldn't want to be reminded of an unfortunate episode of my youth. Don't you think I was right?'

Chapter Twenty-six

Mrs Driffield very kindly offered to send me back to Blackstable in her car, but I preferred to walk. I promised to dine at Ferne Court next day and meanwhile to write down what I could remember of the two periods during which I had been in the habit of seeing Edward Driffield. As I walked along the winding road, meeting no one by the way, I mused upon what I should say. Do they not tell us that style is the art of omission? If that is so I should certainly write a very pretty piece, and it seemed almost a pity that Roy should use it only as material. I chuckled when I reflected what a bombshell I could throw if I chose. There was one person who could tell them all they wanted to know about Edward Driffield and his first marriage; but this fact I proposed to keep to myself. They thought Rosie was dead; they erred; Rosie was very much alive.

Being in New York for the production of a play and my arrival having been advertised to all and sundry by my manager's energetic press representative, I received one day a letter addressed in a handwriting I knew but could not place. It was large and round, firm but uneducated. It was so familiar to me that I was exasperated not to remember whose it was. It would have been more sensible to open the letter at once, but instead I looked at the envelope and racked my brain. There are handwritings I cannot see without a little shiver of dismay and some letters that look so tiresome that I cannot bring myself to open them for a week. When at last I tore open the envelope what I read gave me a strange feeling. It began abruptly:

> I have just seen that you are in New York and would like to see you again. I am not living in New York any more, but Yonkers is quite close and if you have a car you can easily do it in half an hour. I expect you are very busy so leave it to you to make a date. Although it is many years since we last met I hope you have not forgotten your old friend.
>
> Rose Iggulden (formerly Driffield)

I looked at the address; it was Albermarle, evidently a hotel or an apartment house, then there was the name of a street, and Yonkers. A shiver passed through me as though someone had walked over my grave. During the years that had passed I had sometimes thought of Rosie, but of late I had said to myself that she must surely be dead. I was puzzled for a moment by the name. Why Iggulden and not Kemp? Then it occurred to me that they had taken this name, a Kentish one too, when they fled from England. My first impulse was to make an excuse not to see her; I am always shy of seeing again people I have not seen for a long time; but then I was seized with curiosity. I wanted to see what she was like and to hear what had happened to her. I was going down to Dobb's Ferry for the week-end, to reach which I had to pass through Yonkers, and so answered that I would come at about four on the following Saturday.

The Albermarle was a huge block of apartments, comparatively new, and it looked as though it were inhabited by persons in easy circumstances. My name was telephoned up by a negro porter in uniform and I was taken up in the elevator by another. I felt uncommonly nervous. The door was opened for me by a coloured maid.

'Come right in,' she said. 'Mrs Iggulden's expecting you.'

'I was ushered into a living-room that served also as dining-room, for at one end of it was a square table of heavily carved oak, a dresser and four chairs of the kind that the manufacturers in Grand Rapids would certainly describe as Jacobean. But the other end was furnished with a Louis XV suite, gilt and upholstered in pale blue damask; there were a great many small tables, richly carved and gilt, on which stood Sèvres vases with ormolu decorations and nude bronze ladies with draperies flowing as though in a howling gale that artfully concealed those parts of their bodies that decency required; and each one held at the end of a playfully outstretched arm an electric lamp. The gramophone was the grandest thing I had ever seen out of a shop window, all gilt and shaped like a sedan chair and painted with Watteau courtiers and their ladies.

After I had waited for about five minutes a door was opened and Rosie came briskly in. She gave me both her hands.

'Well, this is a surprise,' she said. 'I hate to think how many years it is since we met. Excuse me one moment.' She went to the door and called: 'Jessie, you can bring the tea in. Mind the water's boiling properly.' Then, coming back: 'The trouble I've had to teach that girl to make tea properly, you'd never believe.'

Rosie was at least seventy. She was wearing a very smart sleeveless frock of green chiffon, heavily *diamanté*, cut square at the neck and very short; it fitted like a bursting glove. By her shape I gathered that she wore rubber corsets. Her nails were blood-coloured and her eyebrows plucked. She was stout, and she had a double chin; the skin of her bosom, although she had powdered it freely, was red, and her face was red too. But she looked well and healthy and full of beans. Her hair was still abundant, but it was quite white, shingled and permanently waved. As a young woman she had had soft, naturally waving hair and these stiff undulations, as though she had just come out of a hairdresser's, seemed more than anything else to change her. The only thing that remained was her smile, which had still its old childlike and mischievous sweetness. Her teeth had never been very good, irregular and of bad shape; but these now were replaced by a set of perfect evenness and snowy brilliance; they were obviously the best money could buy.

The coloured maid brought in an elaborate tea with *pâté* sandwiches and cookies and candy and little knives and forks and tiny napkins. It was all neat and smart.

'That's one thing I've never been able to do without—my tea,' said Rosie, helping herself to a hot buttered scone. 'It's my best meal, really, though I know I shouldn't eat it. My doctor keeps on saying to me: "Mrs Iggulden, you can't expect to get your weight down if you will eat half a dozen cookies at tea."' She gave me a smile, and I had a sudden inkling that, notwithstanding the marcelled hair and the powder and the fat, Rosie was the same as ever. 'But what I say is: A little of what you fancy does you good.'

I had always found her easy to talk to. Soon we were chatting away as though it were only a few weeks since we had last seen one another.

'Were you surprised to get my letter? I put Driffield so as you should know who it was from. We took the name of Iggulden when we came to America. George had a little unpleasantness when he left Blackstable, perhaps you heard about it, and he thought in a new country he'd better start with a new name, if you understand what I mean.'

I nodded vaguely.

'Poor George, he died ten years ago, you know.'

'I'm sorry to hear that.'

'Oh, well, he was getting on in years. He was past seventy, though you'd never have guessed it to look at him. It was a great blow to me. No woman could want a better husband than what he made me. Never a cross word from the day we married till the day he died. And I'm pleased to say he left me very well provided for.'

'I'm glad to know that.'

'Yes, he did very well over here. He went into the building trade, he always had a fancy for it, and he got in with Tammany. He always said the greatest mistake he ever made was not coming here over twenty years before. He liked the country from the first day he set foot in it. He had plenty of go and that's what you want here. He was just the sort to get on.'

'Have you never been back to England?'

'No, I've never wanted to. George used to talk about it sometimes, just for a trip, you know, but we never got down to it, and now he's gone I haven't got the inclination. I expect London would seem very dead and alive to me after New York. We used to live in New York, you know. I only came here after his death.'

'What made you choose Yonkers?'

'Well, I always fancied it. I used to say to George, when we retire we'll go and live at Yonkers. It's like a little bit of England to me, you know. Maidstone or Guildford or some place like that.'

I smiled, but I understood what she meant. Notwithstanding its trams and its tootling cars, its cinemas and electric signs, Yonkers, with its winding main street, has a faint air of an English market town gone jazz.

'Of course I sometimes wonder what's happened to all the folks at Blackstable. I suppose they're most of them dead by now and I expect they think I am too.'

'I haven't been there for thirty years.'

I did not know then that the rumour of Rosie's death had reached Blackstable. I dare say that someone had brought back the news that George Kemp was dead and thus a mistake had arisen.

'I suppose nobody knows here that you were Edward Driffield's first wife?'

'Oh, no; why, if they had I should have had the reporters buzzing around my apartment like a swarm of bees. You know sometimes I've hardly been able to help laughing when I've been out somewhere playing bridge and they're started talking about Ted's books. They like them no end in America. I never thought so much of them myself.'

'You never were a great novel reader, were you?'

I used to like history better, but I don't seem to have much time for reading now. Sunday's my great day. I think the Sunday papers over here are lovely. You don't have anything like them in England. Then of course I play a lot of bridge; I'm crazy about contract.'

I remember that when as a young boy I had first met Rosie her uncanny skill at whist had impressed me. I felt that I knew the sort of bridge player she was, quick, bold and accurate: a good partner and a dangerous opponent.

'You'd have been surprised at the fuss they made over here when Ted died. I knew they thought a lot of him, but I never knew he was such a big bug as all that. The papers were full of him, and they had pictures of him and Ferne Court; he always said he meant to live in that house some day. Whatever made him marry that hospital nurse? I always thought he'd marry Mrs Barton Trafford. They never had any children, did they?'

'No.'

'Ted would have liked to have some. It was a great blow to him that I couldn't have any more after the first.'

'I didn't know you'd ever had a child,' I said with surprise.

'Oh, yes. That's why Ted married me. But I had a very bad time when it came and the doctors said I couldn't have another. If she'd lived, poor little thing, I don't suppose I'd ever have run away with George. She was six when she died. A dear little thing she was and as pretty as a picture.'

'You never mentioned her.'

'No, I couldn't bear to speak about her. She got meningitis and we took her to the hospital. They put her in a private room and they let us stay with her. I shall never forget what she went through, screaming, screaming all the time, and nobody able to do anything.'

Rosie's voice broke.

'Was it that death Driffield described in *The Cup of Life*?'

'Yes, that's it. I always thought it so funny of Ted. He couldn't bear to speak of it, any more than I could, but he wrote it all down; he didn't leave out a thing; even little things I hadn't noticed at the time he put in and then I remembered them. You'd think he was just heartless, but he wasn't, he was upset just as much as I was. When we used to go home at night he'd cry like a child. Funny chap, wasn't he?'

It was *The Cup of Life* that had raised such a storm of protest; and it was the child's death and the episode that followed it that had especially brought down on Driffield's head such virulent abuse. I remembered the description very well. It was harrowing. There was nothing sentimental in it; it did not excite the reader's tears, but his anger rather that such cruel suffering should be inflicted on a little child. You felt that God at the Judgment Day would have to account for such things as this. It was a very powerful piece of writing. But if this incident was taken from life, was the one that followed it also? It was this that had shocked the public of the 'nineties and this that the critics had condemned as not only indecent but incredible. In *The Cup of Life* the husband and wife (I forget their names now) had come back from the hospital after the child's death—they were poor people and they lived from hand to mouth in lodgings—and had their tea. It was latish: about seven o'clock. They were exhausted by the strain of a week's ceaseless anxiety and shattered by their grief. They had nothing to say to one another. They sat in a miserable silence. The hours passed. Then on a sudden the wife got up and going into their bedroom put on her hat.

'I'm going out,' she said.

'All right.'

They lived near Victoria Station. She walked along the Buckingham Palace Road and through the park. She came into Piccadilly and went slowly toward the Circus. A man caught her eye, paused and turned round.

'Good-evening,' he said.

'Good-evening.'

She stopped and smiled.

'Will you come and have a drink?' he asked.

'I don't mind if I do.'

They went into a tavern in one of the side streets of Piccadilly, where harlots congregated and men came to pick them up, and they drank a glass of beer. She chatted with the stranger and laughed with him. She told him a cock-and-bull story about herself. Presently he asked if he could go home with her; no, she said, he couldn't do that, but they could go to a hotel. They got into a cab and drove to Bloomsbury and there they took a room for the night. And next morning she took a bus to Trafalgar Square and walked through the park; when she got home her husband was just sitting down to breakfast. After breakfast they went back to the hospital to see about the child's funeral.

'Will you tell me something, Rosie?' I asked. 'What happened in the book after the child's death—did that happen too?'

She looked at me for a moment doubtfully; then her lips broke into her still beautiful smile.

'Well, it's all so many years ago, what odds does it make? I don't mind telling you. He didn't get it quite right. You see, it was only guesswork on his part. I was surprised that he knew as much as he did; I never told him anything.'

Rosie took a cigarette and pensively tapped its end on the table, but she did not light it.

'We came back from the hospital just like he said. We walked back; I felt I couldn't sit still in a cab, and I felt all dead inside me. I'd cried so much I couldn't cry any more, and I was tired. Ted tried to comfort me, but I said: "For God's sake shut up." After that he didn't say any more. We had rooms in the Vauxhall Bridge Road then, on the second floor, just a sitting-room and a bedroom, that's why we'd had to take the poor little thing to the hospital; we couldn't nurse her in lodgings; besides, the landlady said she wouldn't have it, and Ted said she'd be looked after better at the hospital. She wasn't a bad sort, the landlady; she'd been a tart and Ted used to talk to her by the hour together. She came up when she heard us come in.

'"How's the little girl tonight?" she said.

'"She's dead," said Ted.

'I couldn't say anything. Then she brought up the tea. I didn't want anything, but Ted made me eat some ham. Then I sat at the window. I didn't look round when the landlady came up to clear away, I didn't want anyone to speak to me. Ted was reading a book; at least he was pretending to, but he didn't turn the pages, and I saw the tears dropping on it. I kept on looking out of the window. It was the end of June, the twenty-eighth, and the days were long. It was just near the corner where we lived and I looked at the people going in and out of the public-house and the trams going up and down. I thought the day would never come to an end; then all of a sudden I noticed that it was night. All the lamps were lit. There was an awful lot of people in the street. I felt so tired. My legs were like lead.

'"Why don't you light the gas?" I said to Ted.

'"Do you want it?" he said.

'"It's no good sitting in the dark," I said.

'He lit the gas. He began smoking his pipe. I knew that would do him good. But I just sat and looked at the street. I don't know what came over me. I felt that if I went on sitting in that room I'd go mad. I wanted to go somewhere where there were lights and people. I wanted to get away from Ted; no, not so much that, I wanted to get away from all that Ted was thinking and feeling. We only had two rooms. I went into the bedroom; the child's cot was still there, but I wouldn't look at it. I put on my hat and a veil and I changed my dress and then I went back to Ted.

'"I'm going out," I said.

'Ted looked at me. I dare say he noticed I'd got my new dress on and perhaps something in the way I spoke made him see I didn't want him.

'"All right," he said.

'In the book he made me walk through the park, but I didn't do that really. I went down to Victoria and I took a hansom to Charing Cross. It was only a shilling fare. Then I walked up the Strand. I'd made up my mind what I wanted to do before I came out. Do you remember Harry Retford? Well, he was acting at the Adelphi then, he had the second comedy part. Well, I went to the stage door, and sent up my name. I always liked Harry Retford. I expect he was a bit unscrupulous and he was rather funny over money matters, but he could make you laugh and with all his faults he was a rare good sort. You know he was killed in the Boer War, don't you?'

'I didn't. I only knew he'd disappeared and one never saw his name on playbills; I thought perhaps he'd gone into business or something.'

'No, he went out at once. He was killed at Ladysmith. After I'd been waiting a bit he came down and I said: "Harry, let's go on the razzle tonight. What about a bit of supper at Romano's?" "Not 'alf," he said. "You wait here and the minute the show's over and I've got my make-up off I'll come down." It made me feel better just to see him; he was playing a racing tout and it made me laugh just to look at him in his check suit and his billycock hat and his red nose. Well, I waited till the end of the show and then he came down and we walked along to Romano's.

'"Are you hungry?" he said to me.

'"Starving," I said; and I was.

'"Let's have the best," he said, "and blow the expense. I told Bill Terris I was taking my best girl out to supper and I touched him for a couple of quid."

'"Let's have champagne," I said.

'"Three cheers for the widow!" he said.

'I don't know if you ever went to Romano's in the old days. It was fine. You used to see all the theatrical people and the racing men, and the girls from the Gaiety used to go there. It was *the* place. And the Roman. Harry knew him and he came up to our table; he used to talk in funny broken English; I believe he put it on because he knew it made people laugh. And if someone he knew was down and out he'd always lend him a fiver.

'"How's the kid?" said Harry.

'"Better," I said.

'I didn't want to tell him the truth. You know how funny men are; they don't understand some things. I knew Harry would think it dreadful of me to come out to supper when the poor child was lying dead in hospital. He'd be awfully sorry and all that, but that's not what I wanted; I wanted to laugh.'

Rosie lit the cigarette that she had been playing with.

'You know how when a woman is having a baby, sometimes the husband can't stand it any more and he goes out and has another woman. And then when she finds out, and it's funny how often she does, she kicks up no end of a fuss; she says, that the man should go and do it just then, when she's going through hell, well, it's the limit. I always tell her not to be silly. It doesn't mean he doesn't love her, and isn't terribly upset, it doesn't mean anything, it's just nerves; if he wasn't so upset he wouldn't think of it. I know because that's how I felt then.

'When we'd finished our supper Harry said: "Well, what about it?"'

'"What about what?" I said.

'There wasn't any dancing in those days and there was nowhere to go.

'"What about coming round to my flat and having a look at my photograph album?" said Harry.

'"I don't mind if I do," I said.

'He had a bit of a flat in the Charing Cross Road, just two rooms and a bath and a kitchenette, and we drove round there, and I stayed the night.

'When I got back the next morning the breakfast was already on the table and Ted had just started. I'd made up my mind that if he said anything I was going to fly out at him. I didn't care what happened. I'd earned my living before, and I was ready to earn it again. For two pins I'd have packed my box and left him there and then. But he just looked up as I came in.

'"You've just come in time," he said. "I was going to eat your sausage."

'I sat down and poured him out his tea. And he went on reading the paper. After we'd finished breakfast we went to the hospital. He never asked me where I'd been. I didn't know what he thought. He was terribly kind to me all that time. I was miserable, you know. Somehow I felt that I just couldn't get over it, and there was nothing he didn't do to make it easier for me.'

'What did you think when you read the book?' I asked.

'Well, it did give me a turn to see that he did know pretty well what happened that night. What beat me was his writing it at all. You'd have thought it was the last thing he'd put in a book. You're queer fish, you writers.'

At that moment the telephone bell rang. Rosie took up the receiver and listened.

'Why, Mr Vanuzzi, how very nice of you to call me up! Oh, I'm pretty well, thank you. Well, pretty and well, if you like. When you're my age you take all the compliments you can get.'

She embarked upon a conversation which, I gathered from her tone, was of a facetious and even flirtatious character. I did not pay much attention, and since it seemed to prolong itself I began to meditate upon the writer's life. It is full of tribulation. First he must endure poverty and the world's indifference; then, having achieved a measure of success, he must submit with a good grace to its hazards. He depends upon a fickle public. He is at the mercy of journalists who want to interview him and photographers who want to take his picture, of editors who harry him for copy and tax gatherers who harry him for income tax, of persons of quality who ask him to lunch and secretaries of institutes who ask him to lecture, of women who want to marry him and women who want to divorce him, of youths who want his autograph, actors who want parts and strangers who want a loan, of gushing ladies who want advice on their matrimonial affairs and earnest young men who want advice on their compositions, of agents, publishers, managers, bores, admirers, critics, and his own conscience. But he has one compensation. Whenever he has anything on his mind, whether it be a harassing reflection, grief at the death of a friend, unrequited love, wounded pride, anger at the treachery of someone to whom he has shown kindness, in short any emotion or any perplexing thought, he has only to put it down in black and white, using it as a theme of a story or the decoration of an essay, to forget all about it. He is the only free man.

Rosie put back the receiver and turned to me.

'That was one of my beaux. I'm going to play bridge tonight and he rang up to say he'd call round for me in his car. Of course he's a Wop, but he's real nice. He used to run a big grocery store down town, in New York, but he's retired now.'

'Have you never thought of marrying again, Rosie?'

'No.' She smiled. 'Not that I haven't had offers. I'm quite happy as I am. The way I look on it is this, I don't want to marry an old man, and it would be silly at my age to marry a young one. I've had my time and I'm ready to call it a day.'

'What made you run away with George Kemp?'

'Well, I'd always liked him. I knew him long before I knew Ted, you know. Of course, I never thought there was any chance of marrying him. For one thing he was married already and then he had his position to think of. And then when he came to me one day and said that everything had gone wrong and he was bust and there'd be a warrant out for his arrest in a few days and he was going to America and would I go with him, well, what could I do? I couldn't let him go all that way by himself, with no money perhaps, and him having been always so grand and living in his own house and driving his own trap. It wasn't as if I was afraid of work.'

'I sometimes think he was the only man you ever cared for,' I suggested.

'I dare say there's some truth in that.'

'I wonder what it was you saw in him.'

Rosie's eyes travelled to a picture on the wall that for some reason had escaped my notice. It was an enlarged photograph of Lord George in a carved gilt frame. It looked as if it might have been taken soon after his arrival in America; perhaps at the time of their marriage. It was a three-quarter length. It showed him in a long frock coat, tightly buttoned, and a tall silk hat cocked rakishly on one side of his head; there was a large rose in his buttonhole; under one arm he carried a silver-headed cane and smoke curled from a big cigar that he held in his right hand. He had a heavy moustache, waxed at the ends, a saucy look in his eye, and in his bearing an arrogant swagger. In his tie was a horseshoe in diamonds. He looked like a publican dressed up in his best to go to the Derby.

'I'll tell you,' said Rosie. 'He was always such a perfect gentleman.'

The
Painted
Veil

W.
Somerset
Maugham

The Painted Veil

'. . . the painted veil which those who live call Life.'

Preface

This story was suggested by the lines of Dante that run as follows:

Deh, quando tu sarai tornato al mondo,
E riposato della lunga via,
Seguito il terzo spirito al secondo,
Ricorditi di me, che son la Pia:
Siena mi fè; disfecemi Maremma:
Salsi colui, che, innanellata pria
Disposando m'avea con la sua gemma.

'Pray, when you are returned to the world, and rested from the long journey,' followed the third spirit on the second, 'remember me, who am Pia. Siena made me, Maremma unmade me: this he knows who after betrothal espoused me with his ring.'

I was a student at St Thomas's Hospital and the Easter vacation gave me six weeks to myself. With my clothes in a gladstone bag and twenty pounds in my pocket I set out. I was twenty. I went to Genoa and Pisa and then to Florence. Here I took a room in the via Laura, from the window of which I could see the lovely dome of the Cathedral, in the apartment of a widow lady, with a daughter, who offered me board and lodging (after a good deal of haggling) for four lire a day. I am afraid that she did not make a very good thing out of it, since my appetite was enormous, and I could devour a mountain of macaroni without inconvenience. She had a vineyard on the Tuscan hills, and my recollection is that the Chianti she got from it was the best I have ever drunk in Italy. Her daughter gave me an Italian lesson every day. She seemed to me then of mature age, but I do not suppose that she was more than twenty-six. She had had trouble. Her betrothed, an officer, had been killed in Abyssinia and she was consecrated to virginity. It was an understood thing that on her mother's death (a buxom, grey-haired, jovial lady who did not mean to die a day before the dear Lord saw fit) Ersilia would enter religion. But she looked forward to this with cheerfulness. She loved a good laugh. We were very gay at luncheon and dinner, but she took her lessons seriously, and when I was stupid or inattentive rapped me over the knuckles with a black ruler. I should have been indignant at being treated like a child if it had not reminded me of the old-fashioned pedagogues I had read of in books and so made me laugh.

I lived laborious days. I started each one by translating a few pages of one of Ibsen's plays so that I might acquire mastery of technique and ease in writing dialogue; then, with Ruskin in my hand, I examined the sights of Florence. I admired according to instructions the tower of Giotto and the bronze doors of Ghiberti. I was properly enthusiastic over the Botticellis in the Uffizi and I turned the scornful shoulder of extreme youth on what the master disapproved of. After luncheon I had my Italian lesson and then going out once more I visited the churches and wandered day-dreaming along the Arno. When dinner was done I went out to look for adventure, but such was my innocence, or at least my shyness, I always came home as virtuous as I had gone out. The Signora, though she had given me a key, sighed with relief when she heard me come in and bolt the door, for she was always afraid I should forget to do this, and I returned to my perusal of the history of the Guelphs and Ghibellines. I was bitterly conscious that not thus behaved the writers of the romantic era, though I doubt whether any of them managed to spend six weeks in Italy on twenty pounds, and I much enjoyed my sober and industrious life.

I had already read the Inferno (with the help of a translation, but conscientiously looking out in a dictionary the words I did not know), so with Ersilia started on the Purgatorio. When we came to the passage I have quoted above she told me that Pia was a gentlewoman of Siena whose husband, suspecting her of adultery and afraid on account of her family to put her to death, took her down to his castle in the Maremma the noxious vapours of which he was confident would do the trick; but she took so long to die that he grew impatient and had her thrown out of the window. I do not know where Ersilia learnt all this, the note in my own Dante was less circumstantial, but the story for some reason caught my imagination. I turned it over in my mind and for many years from time to time would brood over it for two or three days. I used to repeat to myself the line: *Siena mi fè; disfecemi Maremma.* But it was one among many subjects that occupied my fancy and for long periods I forgot it. Of course I saw it as a modern story, and I could not think of a setting in the world of today in which such events might plausibly happen. It was not till I made a long journey in China that I found this.

I think this is the only novel I have written in which I started from a story rather than from a character. It is difficult to explain the relation between character and plot. You cannot very well think of a character in the void; the moment you think of him, you think of him in some situation, doing something; so that the character and at least his principle action seem to be the result of a simultaneous act of the imagination. But in this case the characters were chosen to fit the story I gradually evolved; they were constructed from persons I had long known in different circumstances.

I had with this book some of the difficulties that are apt to befall an author. I had originally called my hero and heroine Lane, a common enough name, but it appeared that there were people of that name in Hong-Kong. They brought an action, which the proprietors of the magazine in which my novel was serialised, settled for two hundred and fifty pounds, and I changed the name to Fane. Then the Assistant Colonial Secretary, thinking himself libelled, threatened to institute proceedings. I was surprised, since in England we can put a Prime Minister on the stage or use him as the character of a novel, an Archbishop of Canterbury or a Lord Chancellor, and the tenants of these exalted offices do not turn a hair. It seemed to me strange that the temporary occupant of so insignificant a post should think himself aimed at, but in order to save trouble I changed Hong-Kong to an imaginary colony of Tching-Yen.* The book had already been published when the

---

*Tching-Yen has now been replaced by Hong-Kong.

incident arose and was recalled. A certain number of astute reviewers who had received it did not on one pretext and another return their copies. These have now acquired a bibliographical value, I think there are about sixty of them in existence, and are bought by collectors at a high price.

Chapter One

She gave a startled cry.

'What's the matter?' he asked.

Notwithstanding the darkness of the shuttered room he saw her face on a sudden distraught with terror.

'Some one just tried the door.'

'Well, perhaps it was the amah, or one of the boys.'

'They never come at this time. They know I always sleep after tiffin.'

'Who else could it be?'

'Walter,' she whispered, her lips trembling.

She pointed to his shoes. He tried to put them on, but his nervousness, for her alarm was affecting him, made him clumsy, and besides, they were on the tight side. With a faint gasp of impatience she gave him a shoe-horn. She slipped into a kimono and in her bare feet went over to her dressing-table. Her hair was shingled and with a comb she had repaired its disorder before he had laced his second shoe. She handed him his coat.

'How shall I get out?'

'You'd better wait a bit. I'll look out and see that it's all right.'

'It can't possibly be Walter. He doesn't leave the laboratory till five.'

'Who is it then?'

They spoke in whispers now. She was quaking. It occurred to him that in an emergency she would lose her head and on a sudden he felt angry with her. If it wasn't safe why the devil had she said it was? She caught her breath and put her hand on his arm. He followed the direction of her glance. They stood facing the windows that led out on the verandah. They were shuttered and the shutters were bolted. They saw the white china knob of the handle slowly turn. They had heard no one walk along the verandah. It was terrifying to see that silent motion. A minute passed and there was no sound. Then, with the ghastliness of the supernatural, in the same stealthy, noiseless and horrifying manner, they saw the white china knob of the handle at the other window turn also. It was so frightening that Kitty, her nerves failing her, opened her mouth to scream; but, seeing what she was going to do, he swiftly put his hand over it and her cry was smothered in his fingers.

Silence. She leaned against him, her knees shaking, and he was afraid she would faint. Frowning, his jaw set, he carried her to the bed and sat her down upon it. She was as white as the sheet and notwithstanding his tan his cheeks were pale too. He stood by her side looking with fascinated gaze at the china knob. They did not speak. Then he saw that she was crying.

'For God's sake don't do that,' he whispered irritably. 'If we're in for it we're in for it. We shall just have to brazen it out.'

She looked for her handkerchief and knowing what she wanted he gave her her bag.

'Where's your topee?'

'I left it downstairs.'

'Oh, my God!'

'I say, you must pull yourself together. It's a hundred to one it wasn't Walter. Why on earth should he come back at this hour? He never does come home in the middle of the day, does he?'

'Never.'

'I'll bet you anything you like it was the amah.'

She gave him the shadow of a smile. His rich, caressing voice reassured her and she took his hand and affectionately pressed it. He gave her a moment to collect herself.

'Look here, we can't stay here for ever,' he said then. 'Do you feel up to going out on the verandah and having a look?'

'I don't think I can stand.'

'Have you got any brandy in here?'

She shook her head. A frown for an instant darkened his brow, he was growing impatient, he did not quite know what to do. Suddenly she clutched his hand more tightly.

'Suppose he's waiting there?'

He forced his lips to smile and his voice retained the gentle, persuasive tone the effect of which he was so fully conscious of.

'That's not very likely. Have a little pluck, Kitty. How can it possibly be your husband? If he'd come in and seen a strange topee in the hall and come upstairs and found your room locked, surely he would have made some sort of row. It must have been one of the servants. Only a Chinese would turn a handle in that way.'

She did feel more herself now.

'It's not very pleasant even if it was only the amah.'

'She can be squared and if necessary I'll put the fear of God into her. There are not many advantages in being a government official, but you may as well get what you can out of it.'

He must be right. She stood up and turning to him stretched out her arms: he took her in his and kissed her on the lips. It was such rapture that it was pain. She adored him. He released her and she went to the window. She slid back the bolt and opening the shutter a little looked out. There was not a soul. She slipped on to the verandah, looked into her husband's dressing-room and then into her own sitting-room. Both were empty. She went back to the bedroom and beckoned to him.

'Nobody.'

'I believe the whole thing was an optical delusion.'

'Don't laugh. I was terrified. Go into my sitting-room and sit down. I'll put on my stockings and some shoes.'

Chapter Two

He did as she bade and in five minutes she joined him. He was smoking a cigarette.

'I say, could I have a brandy and soda?'

'Yes, I'll ring.'

'I don't think it would hurt *you* by the look of things.'

They waited in silence for the boy to answer. She gave the order.

'Ring up the laboratory and ask if Walter is there,' she said then. 'They won't know your voice.'

He took up the receiver and asked for the number. He inquired whether Dr Fane was in. He put down the receiver.

'He hasn't been in since tiffin,' he told her. 'Ask the boy whether he has been here.'

'I daren't. It'll look so funny if he has and I didn't see him.'

The boy brought the drinks and Townsend helped himself. When he offered her some she shook her head.

'What's to be done if it was Walter?' she asked.

'Perhaps he wouldn't care.'

'Walter?'

Her tone was incredulous.

'It's always struck me he was rather shy. Some men can't bear scenes, you know. He's got sense enough to know that there's nothing to be gained by making a scandal. I don't believe for a minute it was Walter, but even if it was, my impression is that he'll do nothing. I think he'll ignore it.'

She reflected for a moment.

'He's awfully in love with me.'

'Well, that's all to the good. You'll get round him.'

He gave her that charming smile of his which she had always found so irresistible. It was a slow smile which started in his clear blue eyes and travelled by perceptible degrees to his shapely mouth. He had small white even teeth. It was a very sensual smile and it made her heart melt in her body.

'I don't very much care,' she said, with a flash of gaiety. 'It was worth it.'

'It was my fault.'

'Why did you come? I was amazed to see you.'

'I couldn't resist it.'

'You dear.'

She leaned a little towards him, her dark and shining eyes gazing passionately into his, her mouth a little open with desire, and he put his arms round her. She abandoned herself with a sigh of ecstasy to their shelter.

'You know you can always count on me.' he said.

'I'm so happy with you. I wish I could make you as happy as you make me.'

'You're not frightened any more?'

'I hate Walter,' she answered.

He did not quite know what to say to this, so he kissed her. Her face was very soft against his.

But he took her wrist on which was a little gold watch and looked at the time.

'Do you know what I must do now?'

'Bolt?' she smiled.

He nodded. For one instant she clung to him more closely, but she felt his desire to go, and she released him.

'It's shameful the way you neglect your work. Be off with you.'

He could never resist the temptation to flirt.

'You seem in a devil of a hurry to get rid of me,' he said lightly.

'You know that I hate to let you go.'

Her answer was low and deep and serious. He gave a flattered laugh.

'Don't worry your pretty little head about our mysterious visitor. I'm quite sure it was the amah. And if there's any trouble I guarantee to get you out of it.'

'Have you had a lot of experience?'

His smile was amused and complacent.

'No, but I flatter myself that I've got a head screwed on my shoulders.'

Chapter Three

She went out on to the verandah and watched him leave the house. He waved his hand to her. It gave her a little thrill as she looked at him; he was forty-one, but he had the lithe figure and the springing step of a boy.

The verandah was in shadow; and lazily, her heart at ease with satisfied love, she lingered. Their house stood in the Happey Valley, on the side of the hill, for they could not afford to live on the more eligible but expensive Peak. But her abstracted gaze scarcely noticed the blue sea and the crowded shipping in the harbour. She could think only of her lover.

Of course it was stupid to behave as they had done that afternoon, but if he wanted her how could she be prudent? He had come two or three times after tiffin, when in the heat of the day no one thought of stirring out, and not even the boys had seen him come and go. It was very difficult at Hong-Kong. She hated the Chinese city and it made her nervous to go into the filthy little house off the Victoria Road in which they were in the habit of meeting. It was a curio dealer's; and the Chinese who were sitting about stared at her unpleasantly; she hated the ingratiating smile of the old man who took her to the back of the shop and then up a dark flight of stairs. The room into which he led her was frowsy and the large wooden bed against the wall made her shudder.

'This is dreadfully sordid, isn't it?' she said to Charlie the first time she met him there.

'It was till you came in,' he answered.

Of course the moment he took her in his arms she forgot everything.

Oh, how hateful it was that she wasn't free, that they both weren't free! She didn't like his wife. Kitty's wandering thoughts dwelt now for a moment on Dorothy Townsend. How unfortunate to be called Dorothy! It dated you. She was thirty-eight at least. But Charlie never spoke of her. Of course he didn't care for her; she bored him to death. But he was a gentleman. Kitty smiled with affectionate irony: it was just like him, silly old thing; he might be unfaithful to her, but he would never allow a word in disparagement of her to cross his lips. She was a tallish woman, taller than Kitty, neither stout nor thin, with a good deal of pale brown hair; she could never have been pretty with anything but the prettiness of youth; her features were good enough without being remarkable and her blue eyes were cold. She had a skin that you would never look at twice and no colour in her cheeks. And she dressed like—well, like what she was, the wife of the Assistant Colonial Secretary at Hong-Kong. Kitty smiled and gave her shoulders a faint shrug.

Of course no one could deny that Dorothy Townsend had a pleasant voice. She was a wonderful mother, Charlie always said that of her, and she was what Kitty's mother called a gentlewoman. But Kitty did not like her. She did not like her casual manner; and the politeness with which she treated you when you went there, to tea or dinner, was exasperating because you could not but feel how little interest she took in you. The fact was, Kitty supposed, that she cared for nothing but her children: there were two boys at school in England, and another boy of six whom she was going to take home next year. Her face was a mask. She smiled and in her pleasant, well-mannered way said the things that were expected of her; but for all her cordiality held you at a distance. She had a few intimate friends in the Colony and they greatly admired her. Kitty wondered whether Mrs Townsend thought her a little common. She flushed. After all there was no reason for her to put on airs. It was true that her father had been a Colonial Governor and of course it was very grand while it lasted—every one stood up when you entered a room and men took off their hats to you as you passed in your car—but what could be more insignificant than a Colonial Governor when he had retired? Dorothy Townsend's father lived on a pension in a small house at Earl's Court. Kitty's mother would think it a dreadful bore if she asked her to call. Kitty's father, Bernard Garstin, was a K.C. and there was no reason why he should not be made a judge one of these days. Anyhow they lived in South Kensington.

Chapter Four

Kitty, coming to Hong-Kong on her marriage, had found it hard to reconcile herself to the fact that her social position was determined by her husband's occupation. Of course every one had been very kind and for two or three months they had gone out to parties almost every night; when they dined at Government House the Governor took her in as a bride; but she had understood quickly that as the wife of the government bacteriologist she was of no particular consequence. It made her angry.

'It's too absurd,' she told her husband. 'Why, there's hardly any one here that one would bother about for five minutes at home. Mother wouldn't dream of asking any of them to dine at our house.'

'You mustn't let it worry you,' he answered. 'It doesn't really matter, you know.'

'Of course it doesn't matter, it only shows how stupid they are, but it is rather funny when you think of all the people who used to come to our house at home that here we should be treated like dirt.'

'From a social standpoint the man of science does not exist,' he smiled.

She knew that now, but she had not known it when she married him.

'I don't know that it exactly amuses me to be taken in to dinner by the agent of the P. and O.,' she said, laughing in order that what she said might not seem snobbish.

Perhaps he saw the reproach behind her lightness of manner, for he took her hand and shyly pressed it.

'I'm awfully sorry, Kitty dear, but don't let it vex you.'

'Oh. I'm not going to let it do that.'

Chapter Five

It couldn't have been Walter that afternoon. It must have been one of the servants and after all they didn't matter. Chinese servants knew everything anyway. But they held their tongues.

Her heart beat a little faster as she remembered the way in which that white china knob slowly turned. They mustn't take risks like that again. It was better to go to the curio shop. No one who saw her go in would think anything of it, and they were absolutely safe there. The owner of the shop knew who Charlie was and he was not such a fool as to put up the back of the Assistant Colonial Secretary. What did anything matter really but that Charlie loved her?

She turned away from the verandah and went back into her sitting-room. She threw herself down on the sofa and stretched out her hand to get a cigarette. Her eye caught sight of a note lying on the top of a book. She opened it. It was written in pencil.

> Dear Kitty,
> Here is the book you wanted. I was just going to send it when I met Dr Fane and he said he'd bring it round himself as he was passing the house.
>
> V.H.

She rang the bell and when the boy came asked him who had brought the book and when.

'Master bring it, missy, after tiffin,' he answered.

Then it had been Walter. She rang up the Colonial Secretary's Office at once and asked for Charlie. She told him what she had just learned. There was a pause before he answered.

'What shall I do?' she asked.

'I'm in the middle of an important consultation. I'm afraid I can't talk to you now. My advice to you is to sit tight.'

She put down the receiver. She understood that he was not alone and she was impatient with his business.

She sat down again, at a desk, and resting her face in her hands sought to think out the situation. Of course Walter might merely have thought she was sleeping: there was no reason why she should not lock herself in. She tried to remember if they had been talking. Certainly they had not been talking loud. And there was the hat. It was maddening of Charlie to have left it downstairs. But it was no use blaming him for that, it was natural enough, and there was nothing to tell that Walter had noticed it. He was probably in a hurry and had just left the book and note on his way to some appointment connected with his work. The strange thing was that he should have tried the door and then the two windows. If he thought she was asleep it was unlike him to disturb her. What a fool she had been!

She shook herself a little and again she felt that sweet pain in her heart which she always felt when she thought of Charlie. It had been worth it. He had said that he would stand by her, and if the worse came to the worse, well... Let Walter kick up a row if he chose. She had Charlie; what did she care? Perhaps it would be the best thing for him to know. She had never cared for Walter and since she had loved Charlie Townsend it had irked and bored her to submit to her husband's caresses. She wanted to have nothing more to do with him. She didn't see how he could prove anything. If he accused her she would deny, and if it came to a pass that she could deny no longer, well, she would fling the truth in his teeth, and he could do what he chose.

Chapter Six

Within three months of her marriage she knew that she had made a mistake; but it had been her mother's fault even more than hers.

There was a photograph of her mother in the room and Kitty's harassed eyes fell on it. She did not know why she kept it there, for she was not very fond of her mother; there was one of her father too, but that was downstairs on the grand piano. It has been done when he took silk and it represented him in a wig and gown. Even they could not make him imposing; he was a little, wizened man, with tired eyes, a long upper lip, and a thin mouth; a facetious photographer had told him to look pleasant, but he had succeeded only in looking severe. It was on this account, for as a rule the down-turned corners of his mouth and the dejection of his eyes gave him an air of mild depression, that Mrs Garstin, thinking it made him look judicial, had chosen it from among the proofs. But her own photograph showed her in the dress in which she had gone to Court when her husband was made a King's Counsel. She was very grand in the velvet gown, the long train so disposed as to show to advantage, with feathers in her hair and flowers in her hand. She held herself erect. She was a woman of fifty, thin and flat-chested, with prominent cheek-bones and a large, well-shaped nose. She had a great quantity of very smooth black hair and Kitty had always suspected that, if not dyed, it was at least touched up. Her fine black eyes were never still and this was the most noticeable thing about her; for when she was talking to you it was disconcerting to see those restless eyes in that impassive, unlined and yellow face. They moved from one part of you to another, to other persons in the room, and then back to you; you felt that she was criticising you, summing you up, watchful meanwhile of all that went on around her, and that the words she spoke had no connection with her thoughts.

Chapter Seven

Mrs Garstin was a hard, cruel, managing, ambitious, parsimonious and stupid woman. She was the daughter, one of five, of a solicitor in Liverpool and Bernard Garstin had met her when he was on the Northern Circuit. He had seemed then a young man of promise and her father said he would go far. He hadn't. He was painstaking, industrious and capable, but he had not the will to advance himself. Mrs Garstin despised him. But she recognised, though with bitterness, that she could only achieve success through him, and she set herself to drive him on the way she desired to go. She nagged him without mercy. She discovered that if she wanted him to do something which his sensitiveness revolted against she had only to give him no peace and eventually, exhausted, he would yield. On her side she set herself to cultivate the people who might be useful. She flattered the solicitors who would send her husband briefs and was familiar with their wives. She was obsequious to the judges and their ladies. She made much of promising politicians.

In twenty-five years Mrs Garstin never invited any one to dine at her house because she liked him. She gave large dinner parties at regular intervals. But parsimony was as strong in her as ambition. She hated to spend money. She flattered herself that she could make as much show as any one else at half the price. Her dinners were long and elaborate, but thrifty, and she could never persuade herself that people when they were eating and talking knew what they drank. She wrapped sparkling Moselle in a napkin and thought her guests took it for champagne.

Bernard Garstin had a fair, though not a large practice. Men who had been called after him had long outstripped him. Mrs Garstin made him stand for parliament. The expense of the election was borne by the party, but here again her parsimony balked her ambition, and she could not bring herself to spend enough money to nurse the constituency. The subscriptions Bernard Garstin made to the innumerable funds a candidate is expected to contribute to, were always just a little less than adequate. He was beaten. Though it would have pleased Mrs Garstin to be a member's wife she bore her disappointment with fortitude. The fact of her husband's standing had brought her in contact with a number of prominent persons and she appreciated the addition to her social consequence. She knew that Bernard would never make his mark in the House. She wanted him to be a member only that he might have a claim on the gratitude of his party and surely to fight two or three losing seats would give him that.

But he was still a junior and many younger men than he had already taken silk. It was necessary that he should too, not only because otherwise he could scarcely hope to be made a judge, but on her account also; it mortified her to go in to dinner after women ten years younger than herself. But here she encountered in her husband an obstinacy which she had not for years been accustomed to. He was afraid that as a K.C. he would get no work. A bird in the hand was worth two in the bush, he told her, to which she retorted that a proverb was the last refuge of the mentally destitute. He suggested to her the possibility that his income would be halved and he knew that there was no argument which could have greater weight with her. She would not listen. She called him pusillanimous. She gave him no peace and at last, as always, he yielded. He applied for silk and it was promptly awarded him.

His misgivings were justified. He made no headway as a leader and his briefs were few. But he concealed any disappointment he may have felt, and if he reproached his wife it was in his heart. He grew perhaps a little more silent, but he had always been silent at home, and no one in his family noticed a change in him. His daughters had never looked upon him as anything but a source of income; it had always seemed perfectly natural that he should lead a dog's life in order to provide them with board and lodging, clothes, holidays and money for odds and ends; and now, understanding that through his fault money was less plentiful, the indifference they had felt for him was tinged with an exasperated contempt. It never occurred to them to ask themselves what were the feelings of the subdued little man who went out early in the morning and came home at night only in time to dress for dinner. He was a stranger to them, but because he was their father they took it for granted that he should love and cherish them.

Chapter Eight

But there was a quality of courage in Mrs Garstin which in itself was admirable. She let no one in her immediate circle, which to her was the world, see how mortified she was by the frustration of her hopes. She made no change in her style of living. By careful management she was able to give as showy dinners as she had done before, and she met her friends with the same bright gaiety which she had so long cultivated. She had a hard and facile fund of chit-chat which in the society she moved in passed for conversation. She was a useful guest among persons to whom small talk did not come easily, for she was never at a loss with a new topic and could be trusted immediately to break an awkward silence with a suitable observation.

It was unlikely now that Bernard Garstin would ever be made a judge of the High Court, but he might still hope for a County Court judgeship or at the worst an appointment in the Colonies. Meanwhile she had the satisfaction of seeing him appointed Recorder of a Welsh town. But it was on her daughters that she set her hopes. By arranging good marriages for them she expected to make up for all the disappointments of her career. There were two, Kitty and Doris. Doris gave no sign of good looks, her nose was too long and her figure was lumpy; so that Mrs Garstin could hope no more for her than that she should marry a young man who was well off in a suitable profession.

But Kitty was a beauty. She gave promise of being so when she was still a child, for she had large, dark eyes, liquid and vivacious, brown, curling hair in which there was a reddish tint, exquisite teeth and a lovely skin. Her features would never be very good, for her chin was too square and her nose, though not so long as Doris's, too big. Her beauty depended a good deal on her youth, and Mrs Garstin realised that she must marry in the first flush of her maidenhood. When she came out she was dazzling: her skin was still her greatest beauty, but her eyes with their long lashes were so starry and yet so melting that it gave you a catch at the heart to look into them. She had a charming gaiety and the desire to please. Mrs Garstin bestowed upon her all the affection, a harsh, competent, calculating affection, of which she was capable; she dreamed ambitious dreams; it was not a good marriage she aimed at for her daughter, but a brilliant one.

Kitty had been brought up with the knowledge that she was going to be a beautiful woman and she more than suspected her mother's ambition. It accorded with her own desires. She was launched upon the world and Mrs

Garstin performed prodigies in getting herself invited to dances where her
daughter might meet eligible men. Kitty was a success. She was amusing as
well as beautiful, and very soon she had a dozen men in love with her. But
none was suitable, and Kitty, charming and friendly with all, took care to
commit herself with none. The drawing-room in South Kensington was
filled on Sunday afternoons with amorous youth, but Mrs Garstin observed,
with a grim smile of approval, that it needed no effort on her part to keep
them at a distance from Kitty. Kitty was prepared to flirt with them, and it
diverted her to play one off against the other, but when they proposed to her,
as none failed to do, she refused them with tact but decision.

Her first season passed without the perfect suitor presenting himself, and
the second also; but she was young and could afford to wait. Mrs Garstin
told her friends that she thought it a pity for a girl to marry till she was
twenty-one. But a third year passed and then a fourth. Two or three of her
old admirers proposed again, but they were still penniless, one or two boys
younger than herself proposed; a retired Indian Civilian, a K.C.I.E., did the
same: he was fifty-three. Kitty still danced a great deal, she went to
Wimbledon and Lord's, to Ascot and Henley; she was thoroughly enjoying
herself; but still no one whose position and income were satisfactory asked
her to marry him. Mrs Garstin began to grow uneasy. She noticed that Kitty
was beginning to attract men of forty and over. She reminded her that she
would not be any longer so pretty in a year or two and that young girls were
coming out all the time. Mrs Garstin did not mince her words in the
domestic circle and she warned her daughter tartly that she would miss her
market.

Kitty shrugged her shoulders. She thought herself as pretty as ever,
prettier perhaps, for she had learnt how to dress in the last four years, and
she had plenty of time. If she wanted to marry just to be married there were a
dozen boys who would jump at the chance. Surely the right man would come
along sooner or later. But Mrs Garstin judged the situation more shrewdly:
with anger in her heart for the beautiful daughter who had missed her
chances she set her standard a little lower. She turned back to the
professional class at which she had sneered in her pride and looked about for
a young lawyer or a business man whose future inspired her with confidence.

Kitty reached the age of twenty-five and was still unmarried. Mrs Garstin
was exasperated and she did not hesitate often to give Kitty a piece of her
very unpleasant mind. She asked her how much longer she expected her
father to support her. He had spent sums he could ill afford in order to give
her a chance and she had not taken it. It never struck Mrs Garstin that
perhaps her own hard affability had frightened the men, sons of wealthy
fathers or heirs to a title, whose visits she had too cordially encouraged. She
put down Kitty's failure to stupidity. Then Doris came out. She had a long
nose still, and a poor figure, and she danced badly. In her first season she
became engaged to Geoffrey Dennison. He was the only son of a prosperous
surgeon who had been given a baronetcy during the war. Geoffrey would
inherit a title–it is not very grand to be a medical baronet, but a title, thank
God, is still a title–and a very comfortable fortune.

Kitty in a panic married Walter Fane.

Chapter Nine

She had known him but a little while and had never taken much notice of him. She had no idea when or where they had first met till after their engagement he told her that it was at a dance to which some friends had brought him. She certainly paid no attention to him then and if she danced with him it was because she was good-natured and was glad to dance with any one who asked her. She didn't know him from Adam when a day or two later at another dance he came up and spoke to her. Then she remarked that he was at every dance she went to.

'You know, I've danced with you at least a dozen times now and you must tell me your name,' she said to him at last in her laughing way.

He was obviously taken aback.

'Do you mean to say you don't know it? I was introduced to you.'

'Oh, but people always mumble. I shouldn't be at all surprised if you hadn't the ghost of an idea what mine was.'

He smiled at her. His face was grave and a trifle stern, but his smile was very sweet.

'Of course I know it.' He was silent for a moment or two. 'Have you no curiosity?' he asked then.

'As much as most women.'

'It didn't occur to you to ask somebody or other what my name was?'

She was faintly amused; she wondered why he thought it could in the least interest her; but she liked to please, so she looked at him with that dazzling smile of hers and her beautiful eyes, dewy ponds under forest trees, held an enchanting kindness.

'Well, what is it?'

'Walter Fane.'

She did not know why he came to dances, he did not dance very well, and he seemed to know few people. She had a passing thought that he was in love with her; but she dismissed it with a shrug of the shoulders: she had known girls who thought every man they met was in love with them and had always found them absurd. But she gave Walter Fane just a little more of her attention. He certainly did not behave like any of the other youths who had been in love with her. Most of them told her so frankly and wanted to kiss her: a good many did. But Walter Fane never talked of her and very little of himself. He was rather silent; she did not mind that because she had plenty to say and it pleased her to see him laugh when she made a facetious remark; but when he talked it was not stupidly. He was evidently shy. It appeared that he lived in the East and was home on leave.

One Sunday afternoon he appeared at their house in South Kensington. There were a dozen people there, and he sat for some time, somewhat ill at ease, and then went away. Her mother asked her later who he was.

'I haven't a notion. Did you ask him to come here?'

'Yes, I met him at the Baddeleys. He said he'd seen you at various dances. I said I was always at home on Sundays.'

'His name is Fane and he's got some sort of job in the East.'

'Yes, he's a doctor. Is he in love with you?'

'Upon my word, I don't know.'

'I should have thought you knew by now when a young man was in love with you.'

'I wouldn't marry him if he were,' said Kitty lightly.

Mrs Garstin did not answer. Her silence was heavy with displeasure. Kitty flushed: she knew that her mother did not care now whom she married so long as somehow she got her off her hands.

Chapter Ten

During the next week she met him at three dances and now, his shyness perhaps wearing off a little, he was somewhat more communicative. He was a doctor, certainly, but he did not practise; he was a bacteriologist (Kitty had only a very vague idea what that meant) and he had a job at Hong-Kong. He was going back in the autumn. He talked a good deal about China. She made it a practice to appear interested in whatever people talked to her of, but indeed the life in Hong-Kong sounded quite jolly; there were clubs and tennis and racing and polo and golf.

'Do people dance much there?'

'Oh, yes, I think so.'

She wondered whether he told her these things with a motive. He seemed to like her society, but never by a pressure of the hand, by a glance or by a word, did he give the smallest indication that he looked upon her as anything but a girl whom you met and danced with. On the following Sunday he came again to their house. Her father happened to come in, it was raining and he had not been able to play golf, and he and Walter Fane had a long chat. She asked her father afterwards what they had talked of.

'It appears he's stationed at Hong-Kong. The Chief Justice is an old friend of mine at the Bar. He seems an unusually intelligent young man.'

She knew that her father was as a rule bored to death by the young people whom for her sake and now her sister's he had been forced for years to entertain.

'It's not often you like any of my young men, father,' she said.

His kind, tired eyes rested upon her.

'Are you going to marry him by any chance?'

'Certainly not.'

'Is he in love with you?'

'He shows no sign of it.'

'Do you like him?'

'I don't think I do very much. He irritates me a little.'

He was not her type at all. He was short, but not thick-set, slight rather and thin; dark and clean-shaven, with very regular, clean-cut features. His eyes were almost black, but not large, they were not very mobile and they rested on objects with a singular persistence; they were curious, but not very pleasant eyes. With his straight, delicate nose, his fine brow and well-shaped mouth he ought to have been good-looking. But surprisingly enough he was not. When Kitty began to think of him at all she was surprised that he should have such good features when you took them one by one. His expression was slightly sarcastic and now that Kitty knew him better she realised that she was not quite at ease with him. He had no gaiety.

By the time the season drew to its end they had seen a good deal of one another, but he had remained as aloof and impenetrable as ever. He was not exactly shy with her, but embarrassed; his conversation remained strangely impersonal. Kitty came to the conclusion that he was not in the least in love with her. He liked her and found her easy to talk to, but when he returned to China in November he would not think of her again. She thought it not impossible that he was engaged all the time to some nurse in a hospital at Hong-Kong, the daughter of a clergyman, dull, plain, flat-footed and strenuous; that was the wife that would exactly suit him.

Then came the announcement of Doris's engagement to Geoffrey Dennison. Doris, at eighteen, was making quite a suitable marriage, and she was twenty-five and single. Supposing she did not marry at all? That season the only person who had proposed to her was a boy of twenty who was still at Oxford: she couldn't marry a boy five years younger than herself. She had made a hash of things. Last year she had refused a widowed Knight of the Bath with three children. She almost wished she hadn't. Mother would be horrible now, and Doris, Doris who had always been sacrificed because she, Kitty, was expected to make the brilliant match, would not fail to crow over her. Kitty's heart sank.

Chapter Eleven

But one afternoon when she was walking home from Harrod's she chanced to meet Walter Fane in the Brompton Road. He stopped and talked to her. Then, casually, he asked her if she would take a turn with him in the Park. She had no particular wish to go home; it was not just then a very agreeable place. They strolled along, talking as they always talked, of casual things, and he asked her where she was going for the summer.

'Oh, we always bury ourselves in the country. You see, father is exhausted after the term's work and we just go to the quietest place we can find.'

Kitty spoke with her tongue in her cheek, for she knew quite well that her father had not nearly enough work to tire him and even if he had his convenience would never have been consulted in the choice of a holiday. But a quiet place was a cheap place.

'Don't you think those chairs look rather inviting?' said Walter suddenly.

She followed his eyes and saw two green chairs by themselves under a tree on the grass.

'Let us sit in them,' she said.

But when they were seated he seemed to grow strangely abstracted. He was an odd creature. She chattered on, however, gaily enough and wondered why he had asked her to walk with him in the Park. Perhaps he was going to confide in her his passion for the flat-footed nurse in Hong-Kong. Suddenly her turned to her, interrupting her in the middle of a sentence, so that she could not but see that he had not been listening, and his face was chalk white.

'I want to say something to you.'

She looked at him quickly and she saw that his eyes were filled with a painful anxiety. His voice was strained, low and not quite steady. But before she could ask herself what this agitation meant he spoke again.

'I want to ask you if you'll marry me.'

'You could knock me down with a feather,' she answered so surprised that she looked at him blankly.

'Didn't you know I was awfully in love with you?'

'You never showed it.'

'I'm very awkward and clumsy. I always find it more difficult to say the things I mean than the things I don't.'

Her heart began to beat a little more quickly. She had been proposed to often before, but gaily or sentimentally, and she had answered in the same fashion. No one had ever asked her to marry him in a manner which was so abrupt and yet strangely tragic.

'It's very kind of you,' she said, doubtfully.

'I fell in love with you the first time I saw you. I wanted to ask you before, but I could never bring myself to it.'

'I'm not sure if that's very well put,' she chuckled.

She was glad to have an opportunity to laugh a little, for on that fine, sunny day the air about them seemed on a sudden heavy with foreboding. He frowned darkly.

'Oh, you know what I mean. I didn't want to lose hope. But now you're going away and in the autumn I have to go back to China.'

'I've never thought of you in that way,' she said helplessly.

He said nothing more. He looked down on the grass sullenly. He was a very odd creature. But now that he had told her she felt in some mysterious way that his love was something she had never met before. She was a little frightened, but she was elated also. His impassivity was vaguely impressive.

'You must give me time to think.'

Still he did not say anything. He did not stir. Did he mean to keep her there till she had decided? That was absurd. She must talk it over with her mother. She ought to have got up when she spoke, she had waited thinking he would answer, and now, she did not know why, she found it difficult to make a movement. She did not look at him, but she was conscious of his appearance; she had never seen herself marrying a man so little taller than herself. When you sat close to him you saw how good his features were, and how cold his face. It was strange when you couldn't help being conscious of the devastating passion which was in his heart.

'I don't know you, I don't know you at all,' she said tremulously.

He gave her a look and she felt her eyes drawn to his. They had a tenderness which she had never seen in them before, but there was something beseeching in them, like a dog's that has been whipped, which slightly exasperated her.

'I think I improve on acquaintance,' he said.

'Of course you're shy, aren't you?'

It was certainly the oddest proposal she had ever had. And even now it seemed to her that they were saying to one another the last things you would have expected on such an occasion. She was not in the least in love with him. She did not know why she hesitated to refuse him at once.

'I'm awfully stupid,' he said, 'I want to tell you that I love you more than anything in the world, but I find it so awfully difficult to say.'

Now that was odd too, for inexplicably enough it touched her; he wasn't really cold, of course, it was his manner that was unfortunate: she liked him at that moment better than she had ever liked him before. Doris was to be married in November. He would be on his way to China then and if she married him she would be with him. It wouldn't be very nice to be a bridesmaid at Doris's wedding. She would be glad to escape that. And then Doris as a married woman and herself single! Every one knew how young Doris was and it would make her seem older. It would put her on the shelf. It wouldn't be a very good marriage for her, but it was a marriage, and the fact that she would live in China made it easier. She was afraid of her mother's bitter tongue. Why, all the girls who had come out with her were married long ago and most of them had children; she was tired of going to see them and gushing over their babies. Walter Fane offered her a new life. She turned to him with a smile which she well knew the effect of.

'If I were so rash as to say I'd marry you, when would you want to marry me?'

He gave a sudden gasp of delight, and his white cheeks flushed.

'Now. At once. As soon as possible. We'd go to Italy for our honeymoon. August and September.'

That would save her from spending the summer in a country vicarage, hired at five guineas a week, with her father and mother. In a flash she saw in her mind's eye the announcement in the *Morning Post* that, the bridegroom having to return to the East, the wedding would take place at once. She knew her mother well enough, she could be counted on to make a splash; for the moment at least Doris would be in the background and when Doris's much grander wedding took place she would be far away.

She stretched out her hand.

'I think I like you very much. You must give me time to get used to you.'

'Then it's yes?' he interrupted.

'I suppose so.'

Chapter Twelve

She knew him very little then, and now, though they had been married for nearly two years, she knew him but little more. At first she had been touched by his kindness and flattered, though surprised, by his passion. He was extremely considerate; he was very attentive to her comfort; she never expressed the slightest wish without his hastening to gratify it. He was constantly giving her little presents. When she happened to feel ill no one could have been kinder or more thoughtful. She seemed to do him a favour when she gave him the opportunity of doing something tiresome for her. And he was always exceedingly polite. He rose to his feet when she entered a room, he gave her his hand to help her out of a car, if he chanced to meet her in the street he took off his hat, he was solicitous to open the door for her when she left a room, he never came into her bedroom or her boudoir without a knock. He treated her not as Kitty had seen most men treat their wives, but as though she were a fellow-guest in a country house. It was pleasing and yet a trifle comic. She would have felt more at home with him if he had been more casual. Nor did their conjugal relations draw her closer to him. He was passionate then, fierce, oddly hysterical too, and sentimental.

It disconcerted her to realise how emotional he really was. His self-control was due to shyness or to long training, she did not know which; it seemed to her faintly contemptible that when she lay in his arms, his desire appeased, he who was so timid of saying absurd things, who so feared to be ridiculous, should use baby talk. She had offended him bitterly once by laughing and telling him that he was talking the most fearful slush. She had felt his arms grow limp about her, he remained quite silent for a little while, and then without a word released her and went into his own room. She didn't want to hurt his feelings and a day or two later she said to him:

'You silly old thing, I don't mind what nonsense you talk to me.'

He had laughed in a shamefaced way. She had discovered very soon that he had an unhappy disability to lose himself. He was self-conscious. When there was a party and every one started singing Walter could never bring himself to join in. He sat there smiling to show that he was pleased and amused, but his smile was forced; it was more like a sarcastic smirk, and you could not help feeling that he thought all those people enjoying themselves a pack of fools. He could not bring himself to play the round games which Kitty with her high spirits found such a lark. On their journey out to China he had absolutely refused to put on fancy dress when every one else was wearing it. It disturbed her pleasure that he should so obviously think the whole thing a bore.

Kitty was lively; she was willing to chatter all day long and she laughed easily. His silence disconcerted her. He had a way which exasperated her of returning no answer to some casual remark of hers. It was true that it needed no answer, but an answer all the same would have been pleasant. If it was raining and she said: 'It's raining cats and dogs,' she would have liked him to say: 'Yes, isn't it?' He remained silent. Sometimes she would have liked to shake him.

'I said it was raining cats and dogs,' she repeated.

'I heard you,' he answered, with his affectionate smile.

It showed that he had not meant to be offensive. He did not speak because he had nothing to say. But if nobody spoke unless he had something to say, Kitty reflected, with a smile, the human race would very soon lose the use of speech.

Chapter Thirteen

The fact was, of course, that he had no charm. That was why he was not popular, and she had not been long in Hong-Kong before she discovered that he was not. She remained very vague about his work. It was enough for her to realise, and she did this quite distinctly, that to be the government bacteriologist was no great fry. He seemed to have no desire to discuss that part of his life with her. Because she was willing to be interested in anything at first she had asked him about it. He put her off with a jest.

'It's very dull and technical,' he said on another occasion. 'And it's grossly underpaid.'

He was very reserved. All she knew about his antecedents, his birth, his education, and his life before he met her, she had elicited by direct questioning. It was odd, the only thing that seemed to annoy him was a question; and when, in her natural curiosity, she fired a string of them at him, his answers became at every one more abrupt. She had the wit to see that he did not care to reply because he had anything to hide from her, but merely from a natural secretiveness. It bored him to talk about himself. It made him shy and uncomfortable. He did not know how to be open. He was fond of reading, but he read books which seemed to Kitty very dull. If he was not busy with some scientific treatise he would read books about China or historical works. He never relaxed. She did not think he could. He was fond of games: he played tennis and bridge.

She wondered why he had ever fallen in love with her. She could not imagine any one less suited than herself to this restrained, cold and self-possessed man. And yet it was quite certain that he loved her madly. He would do anything in the world to please her. He was like wax in her hands. When she thought of one side he showed her, a side which only she had seen, she a little despised him. She wondered whether his sarcastic manner, with its contemptuous tolerance for so many persons and things she admired, was merely a façade to conceal a profound weakness. She supposed he was clever, every one seemed to think he was, but except very occasionally when he was with two or three people he liked and was in the mood, she had never found him entertaining. He did not precisely bore her, he left her indifferent.

Chapter Fourteen

Though Kitty had met his wife at various tea-parties she had been some weeks in Hong-Kong before she saw Charles Townsend. She was introduced to him only when with her husband she went to dine at his house. Kitty was on the defensive. Charles Townsend was Assistant Colonial Secretary and she had no mind to allow him to use her with the condescension which, notwithstanding her good manners she discerned in Mrs Townsend. The room in which they were received was spacious. It was furnished as was every other drawing-room she had been in at Hong-Kong in a comfortable and homely style. It was a large party. They were the last to come and as they entered Chinese servants in uniform were handing round cocktails and olives. Mrs Townsend greeted them in her casual fashion and looking at a list told Walter whom he was to take in to dinner.

Kitty saw a tall and very handsome man bear down on them.

'This is my husband.'

'I am to have the privilege of sitting next to you,' he said.

She immediately felt at ease and the sense of hostility vanished from her bosom. Though his eyes were smiling she had seen in them a quick look of surprise. She understood it perfectly and it made her inclined to laugh.

'I shan't be able to eat any dinner,' he said, 'and if I know Dorothy the dinner's damned good.'

'Why not?'

'I ought to have been told. Some one really ought to have warned me.'

'What about?'

'No one said a word. How was I to know that I was going to meet a raging beauty?'

'Now what am I to say to that?'

'Nothing. Leave me to do the talking. And I'll say it over and over again.'

Kitty, unmoved, wondered what exactly his wife had told him about her. He must have asked. And Townsend looking down on her with his laughing eyes, suddenly remembered.

'What is she like?' he had inquired when his wife told him she had met Dr Fane's bride.

'Oh, quite a nice little thing. Actressy.'

'Was she on the stage?'

'Oh, no, I don't think so. Her father's a doctor or a lawyer or something. I suppose we shall have to ask them to dinner.'

'There's no hurry, is there?'

When they were sitting side by side at table he told her that he had known Walter Fane ever since he came to the Colony.

'We play bridge together. He's far and away the best bridge player at the Club.'

She told Walter on the way home.

'That's not saying very much, you know.'

'How does he play?'

'Not badly. He plays a winning hand very well, but when he has bad cards he goes all to pieces.'

'Does he play as well as you?'

'I have no illusions about my play. I should describe myself as a very good player in the second class. Townsend thinks he's in the first. He isn't.'

'Don't you like him?'

'I neither like him nor dislike him. I believe he's not bad at his job and every one says he's a good sportsman. He doesn't very much interest me.'

It was not the first time that Walter's moderation had exasperated her. She asked herself why it was necessary to be so prudent: you either liked people or you didn't. She had liked Charles Townsend very much. And she had not expected to. He was probably the most popular man in the Colony. It was supposed that the Colonial Secretary would retire soon and every one hoped that Townsend would succeed him. He played tennis and polo and golf. He kept racing ponies. He was always ready to do any one a good turn. He never let red tape interfere with him. He put on no airs. Kitty did not know why she had resented hearing him so well spoken of, she could not help thinking he must be very conceited: she had been extremely silly; that was the last thing you could accuse him of.

She had enjoyed her evening. They had talked of the theatres in London, and of Ascot and Cowes, all the things she knew about, so that really she might have met him at some nice house in Lennox Gardens; and later, when the men came into the drawing-room after dinner, he had strolled over and sat beside her again. Though he had not said anything very amusing, he had made her laugh; it must have been the way he said it: there was a caressing sound in his deep, rich voice, a delightful expression in his kind, shining blue eyes, which made you feel very much at home with him. Of course he had charm. That was what made him so pleasant.

He was tall, six foot two at least, she thought, and he had a beautiful figure; he was evidently in very good condition and he had not a spare ounce of fat on him. He was well-dressed, the best-dressed man in the room, and he wore his clothes well. She liked a man to be smart. Her eyes wandered to Walter: he really should try to be a little better turned out. She noticed Townsend's cuff-links and waistcoat buttons; she had seen similar ones at Cartier's. Of course the Townsends had private means. His face was deeply sunburned, but the sun had not taken the healthy colour from his cheeks. She liked the little trim curly moustache which did not conceal his full red lips. He had black hair, short and brushed very sleek. But of course his eyes, under thick bushy eyebrows, were his best feature: they were so very blue, and they had a laughing tenderness which persuaded you of the sweetness of his disposition. No man who had those blue eyes could bear to hurt any one.

She could not but know that she had made an impression on him. If he had not said charming things to her his eyes, warm with admiration, would have betrayed him. His ease was delightful. He had no self-consciousness. Kitty was at home in these circumstances and she admired the way in which amid the banter which was the staple of their conversation he insinuated every now and then a pretty, flattering speech. When she shook hands with him on leaving he gave her hand a pressure that she could not mistake.

'I hope we shall see you again soon,' he said casually, but his eyes gave his words a meaning which she could not fail to see.

'Hong-Kong is very small, isn't it?' she said.

Chapter Fifteen

Who would have thought then that within three months they would be on such terms? He had told her since that he was crazy about her on that first evening. She was the most beautiful thing he had ever seen. He remembered the dress she wore; it was her wedding dress, and he said she looked like a lily of the valley. She knew that he was in love with her before he told her, and a little frightened she kept him at a distance. He was impetuous and it was difficult. She was afraid to let him kiss her, for the thought of his arms about her made her heart beat so fast. She had never been in love before. It was wonderful. And now that she knew what love was she felt a sudden sympathy for the love that Walter bore her. She teased him, playfully, and saw that he enjoyed it. She had been perhaps a little afraid of him, but now she had more confidence. She chaffed him and it amused her to see the slow smile with which at first he received her banter. He was surprised and pleased. One of these days, she thought, he would become quite human. Now that she had learnt something of passion it diverted her to play lightly, like a harpist running his fingers across the strings of his harp, on his affections. She laughed when she saw how she bewildered and confused him.

And when Charlie became her lover the situation between herself and Walter seemed exquisitely absurd. She could hardly look at him, so grave and self-controlled, without laughing. She was too happy to feel unkindly towards him. Except for him, after all, she would never have known Charlie. She had hesitated some time before the final step, not because she did not want to yield to Charlie's passion, her own was equal to his, but because her upbringing and all the conventions of her life intimidated her. She was amazed afterwards (and the final act was due to accident; neither of them had seen the opportunity till it was face to face with them) to discover that she felt in no way different from what she had before. She had expected that it would cause some, she hardly knew what, fantastic change in her so that she would feel like somebody else; and when she had a chance to look at herself in the glass she was bewildered to see the same woman she had seen the day before.

'Are you angry with me?' he asked her.

'I adore you,' she whispered.

'Don't you think you were very silly to waste so much time?'

'A perfect fool.'

Chapter Sixteen

Her happiness, sometimes almost more than she could bear, renewed her beauty. Just before she married, beginning to lose her first freshness, she had looked tired and drawn. The uncharitable said that she was going off. But there is all the difference between a girl of twenty-five and a married woman of that age. She was like a rosebud that is beginning to turn yellow at the edges of the petals, and then suddenly she was a rose in full bloom. Her starry eyes gained a more significant expression; her skin (that feature which had always been her greatest pride and most anxious care) was dazzling: it could not be compared to the peach or to the flower; it was they that demanded comparison with it. She looked eighteen once more. She was at the height of her glowing loveliness. It was impossible not to remark it and her women friends asked her in little friendly asides if she was going to have a baby. The indifferent who had said she was just a very pretty woman with a long nose admitted that they had misjudged her. She was what Charlie had called her the first time he saw her, a raging beauty.

They managed their intrigue with skill. He had a broad back, he told her ('I will not have you swank about your figure,' she interrupted lightly), and it did not matter about him; but for her sake they mustn't take the smallest risk. They could not meet often alone, not half often enough for him, but he had to think of her first, sometimes in the curio shop, now and then after luncheon in her house when no one was about; but she saw him a good deal here and there. It amused her then to see the formal way he spoke to her, jovial, for he was always that, with the same manner he used with every one. Who could imagine when they heard him chaff her with that charming humour of his that so lately he had held her in his passionate arms?

She worshipped him. He was splendid, in his smart top boots and his white breeches, when he played polo. In tennis clothes he looked a mere boy. Of course he was proud of his figure: it was the best figure she had ever seen. He took pains to keep it. He never ate bread or potatoes or butter. And he took a great deal of exercise. She liked the care he took of his hands; he was manicured once a week. He was a wonderful athlete and the year before he had won the local tennis championship. Certainly he was the best dancer she had ever danced with; it was a dream to dance with him. No one would think he was forty. She told him she did not believe it.

'I believe it's all bluff and you're really twenty-five.'

He laughed. He was well pleased.

'Oh, my dear, I have a boy of fifteen. I'm a middle-aged gent. In another two or three years I shall just be a fat old party.'

'You'll be adorable when you're a hundred.'

She liked his black, bushy eyebrows. She wondered whether it was they that gave his blue eyes their disturbing expression.

He was full of accomplishments. He could play the piano quite well, ragtime, of course, and he could sing a comic song with a rich voice and good humour. She did not believe there was anything he could not do: He was very clever at his work too and she shared his pleasure when he told her that the Governor had particularly congratulated him on the way he had done some difficult job.

'Although it's I as says it,' he laughed, his eyes charming with the love he bore her, 'there's not a fellow in the Service who could have done it better.'

Oh, how she wished that she were his wife rather than Walter's!

Chapter Seventeen

Of course it was not certain yet that Walter knew the truth, and if he didn't it was better perhaps to leave well alone; but if he did, well, in the end it would be the best thing for all of them. At first she had been, if not satisfied, at least resigned to seeing Charlie only by stealth; but time had increased her passion and for some while now she had been increasingly impatient of the obstacles which prevented them from being always together. He had told her so often that he cursed his position which forced him to be so discreet, the ties which bound him, and the ties which bound her: how marvellous it would have been, he said, if they were both free! She saw his point of view; no one wanted a scandal, and of course it required a good deal of thinking over before you changed the course of your life; but if freedom were thrust upon them, ah, then, how simple everything would be!

It was not as though any one would suffer very much. She knew exactly what his relations were with his wife. She was a cold woman and there had been no love between them for years. It was habit that held them together, convenience, and of course the children. It was easier for Charlie than for her: Walter loved her; but after all, he was absorbed in his work; and a man always had his club; he might be upset at first, but he would get over it; there was no reason why he should not marry somebody else. Charlie had told her that he could not make out how she came to throw herself away on Walter Fane.

She wondered, half-smiling, why a little while before she had been terrified at the thought that Walter had caught them. Of course it was startling to see the handle of the door slowly turn. But after all they knew the worst that Walter could do, and they were ready for it. Charlie would feel as great a relief as she that what they both desired more than anything in the world should be thus forced upon them.

Walter was a gentleman, she would do him the justice to acknowledge that, and he loved her; he would do the right thing and allow her to divorce him. They had made a mistake and the lucky thing was that they had found it out before it was too late. She made up her mind exactly what she was going to say to him and how she would treat him. She would be kind, smiling, and firm. There was no need for them to quarrel. Later on she would always be glad to see him. She hoped honestly that the two years they had spent together would remain with him as a priceless memory.

'I don't suppose Dorothy Townsend will mind divorcing Charlie a bit,' she thought. 'Now the youngest boy is going back to England it will be much nicer for her to be in England too. There's absolutely nothing for her to do in Hong-Kong. She'll be able to spend all the holidays with her boys. And then she's got her father and mother in England.'

It was all very simple and everything could be managed without scandal or ill-feeling. And then she and Charlie could marry. Kitty drew a long sigh. They would be very happy. It was worth going through a certain amount of bother to achieve that. Confusedly, one picture jostling another, she thought of the life they would lead together, of the fun they would have and the little journeys they would take together, the house they would live in, the positions he would rise to and the help she would be to him. He would be very proud of her and she, she adored him.

But through all these day-dreams ran a current of apprehension. It was funny: it was as though the wood and the strings of the orchestra played Arcadian melodies and in the bass the drums, softly but with foreboding, beat a grim tattoo. Sooner or later Walter must come home and her heart beat fast at the thought of meeting him: It was strange that he had gone away that afternoon without saying a word to her. Of course she was not frightened of him; after all what could he do, she repeated to herself; but she could not quite allay her uneasiness. Once more she repeated what she would say to him. What was the good of making a scene? She was very sorry, Heaven knew she didn't want to cause him pain, but she couldn't help it if she didn't love him. It was no good pretending and it was always better to tell the truth. She hoped he wouldn't be unhappy, but they had made a mistake and the only sensible thing was to acknowledge it. She would always think kindly of him.

But even as she said this to herself a sudden gust of fear made the sweat start out in the palms of her hands. And because she was frightened she grew angry with him. If he wanted to make a scene, that was his lookout; he must not be surprised if he got more than he bargained for. She would tell him that she had never cared two pins for him and that not a day had passed since their marriage without her regretting it. He was dull. Oh, how he'd bored her, bored her, bored her! He thought himself so much better than any one else, it was laughable; he had no sense of humour; she hated his supercilious air, his coldness, and his self-control. It was easy to be self-controlled when you were interested in nothing and nobody but yourself. He was repulsive to her. She hated to let him kiss her. What had he to be so conceited about? He danced rottenly, he was a wet blanket at a party, he couldn't play or sing, he couldn't play polo and his tennis was no better than anybody else's. Bridge? Who cared about bridge?

Kitty worked herself up into a towering passion. Let him dare to reproach her. All that had happened was his own fault. She was thankful that he knew the truth at last. She hated him and wished never to see him again. Yes, she was thankful that it was all over. Why couldn't he leave her alone? He had pestered her into marrying him and now she was fed up.

'Fed up,' she repeated aloud, trembling with anger. 'Fed up! Fed up!'

She heard the car draw up to the gate of their garden. He was coming up the stairs.

Chapter Eighteen

He came into the room: Her heart was beating wildly and her hands were shaking; it was lucky that she lay on the sofa. She was holding an open book as though she had been reading. He stood for an instant on the threshold and their eyes met. Her heart sank; she felt on a sudden a cold chill pass through her limbs and she shivered. She had that feeling which you describe by saying that some one was walking over your grave. His face was deathly pale; she had seen it like that once before, when they sat together in the Park and he asked her to marry him. His dark eyes, immobile and inscrutable, seemed preternaturally large. He knew everything.

'You're back early,' she remarked.

Her lips trembled so that she could hardly frame the words. She was terrified. She was afraid she would faint.

'I think it's about the usual time.'

His voice sounded strange to her. It was raised on the last word in order to give his remark a casual air, but it was forced. She wondered if he saw that she was shaking in every limb. It was only by an effort that she did not scream. He dropped his eyes.

'I'm just going to dress.'

He left the room. She was shattered. For two or three minutes she could not stir, but at last, raising herself from the sofa with difficulty, as though she had had an illness and were still weak, she found her feet. She did not know if her legs would support her. She felt her way by means of chairs and tables to the verandah and then with one hand on the wall went to her room. She put on a tea-gown and when she went back into her boudoir (they only used the drawing-room when there was a party) he was standing at a table looking at the pictures of the *Sketch*. She had to force herself to enter.

'Shall we go down? Dinner is ready.'

'Have I kept you waiting?'

It was dreadful that she could not control the trembling of her lips.

When was he going to speak?

They sat down and for a moment there was silence between them. Then he made a remark and because it was so commonplace it had a sinister air.

'The *Empress* didn't come in today,' he said. 'I wonder if she's been delayed by a storm.'

'Was she due today?'

'Yes.'

She looked at him now and saw that his eyes were fixed on his plate. He made another observation, equally trivial, about a tennis tournament that was about to be played, and he spoke at length. His voice as a rule was agreeable, with a variety of tone, but now he spoke on one note. It was strangely unnatural. It gave Kitty the impression that he was speaking from a long way off. And all the time his eyes were directed to his plate or the table, or to a picture on the wall. He would not meet hers. She realised that he could not bear to look at her.

'Shall we go upstairs?' he said when dinner was finished.

'If you like.'

She rose and he held open the door for her. His eyes were cast down as she passed him. When they reached the sitting-room he took up the illustrated paper once more.

'Is this a new *Sketch*? I don't think I've seen it.'

'I don't know. I haven't noticed.'

It had been lying about for a fortnight and she knew that he had looked it through and through. He took it and sat down. She lay again on the sofa and took her book. As a rule in the evening, when they were alone, they played coon-can or patience. He was leaning back in an arm-chair, in a comfortable attitude, and his attention seemed absorbed by the illustration he was looking at. He did not turn the page. She tried to read, but she could not see the print before her eyes. The words were blurred. Her head began to ache violently.

When would he speak?

They sat in silence for an hour. She gave up the pretence of reading, and letting her novel fall on her lap, gazed into space. She was afraid to make the smallest gesture or the smallest sound. He sat quite still, in that same easy attitude, and stared with those wide, immobile eyes of his at the picture. His stillness was strangely menacing. It gave Kitty the feeling of a wild beast prepared to spring.

When suddenly he stood up she started. She clenched her hands and she felt herself grow pale. Now!

'I have some work to do,' he said in that quiet, toneless voice, his eyes averted. 'If you don't mind I'll go into my study. I daresay you'll have gone to bed by the time I've finished.'

'I *am* rather tired tonight.'

'Well, good-night.'

'Good-night.'

He left the room.

Chapter Nineteen

As soon as she could next morning she rang Townsend up at his office:

'Yes, what is it?'

'I want to see you.'

'My dear, I'm awfully busy. I'm a working man.'

'It's very important. Can I come down to the office?'

'Oh, no, I wouldn't do that if I were you.'

'Well, come here then.'

'I can't possibly get away. What about this afternoon? And don't you think it would be better if I didn't come to your house?'

'I must see you at once.'

There was a pause and she was afraid that she had been cut off.

'Are you there?' she asked anxiously.

'Yes, I was thinking. Has anything happened?'

'I can't tell you over the telephone.'

There was another silence before he spoke again.

'Well, look here, I can manage to see you for ten minutes at one if that'll do. You'd better go to Ku-Chou's and I'll come along as soon as I can.'

'The curio shop?' she asked in dismay.

'Well, we can't meet in the lounge at the Hong-Kong Hotel very well,' he answered.

She noticed a trace of irritation in his voice.

'Very well. I'll go to Ku-Chou's.'

Chapter Twenty

She got out of her rickshaw in the Victoria Road and walked up the steep, narrow lane till she came to the shop. She lingered outside a moment as though her attention were attracted by the bric-à-brac which was displayed. But a boy who was standing there on the watch for customers, recognising her at once, gave her a broad smile of connivance. He said something in Chinese to some one within and the master, a little, fat-faced man in a black gown, came out and greeted her. She walked in quickly.

'Mr Townsend no come yet. You go top-side, yes?'

She went to the back of the shop and walked up the rickety, dark stairs. The Chinese followed her and unlocked the door that led into the bedroom. It was stuffy and there was an acrid smell of opium. She sat down on a sandalwood chest.

In a moment she heard a heavy step on the creaking stairs. Townsend came in and shut the door behind him. His face bore a sullen look, as he saw her it vanished, and he smiled in that charming way of his. He took her quickly in his arms and kissed her lips.

'Now what's the trouble?'

'It makes me feel better just to see you,' she smiled.

He sat down on the bed and lit a cigarette.

'You look rather washed out this morning.'

'I don't wonder,' she answered. 'I don't think I closed my eyes all night.'

He gave her a look. He was smiling still, but his smile was a little set and unnatural. She thought there was a shade of anxiety in his eyes.

'He knows,' she said.

There was an instant's pause before he answered.

'What did he say?'

'He hasn't said anything.'

'What!' He looked at her sharply. 'What makes you think he knows?'

'Everything. His look. The way he talked at dinner.'

'Was he disagreeable?'

'No, on the contrary, he was scrupulously polite. For the first time since we married he didn't kiss me good-night.'

She dropped her eyes. She was not sure if Charles understood. As a rule

Walter took her in his arms and pressed his lips to hers and would not let them go. His whole body grew tender and passionate with his kiss.

'Why do you imagine he didn't say anything?'

'I don't know.'

There was a pause. Kitty sat very still on the sandalwood box and looked with anxious attention at Townsend. His face once more was sullen and there was a frown between his brows. His mouth drooped a little at the corners. But all at once he looked up and a gleam of malicious amusement came into his eyes.

'I wonder if he *is* going to say anything.'

She did not answer. She did not know what he meant.

'After all, he wouldn't be the first man who's shut his eyes in a case of this sort. What has he to gain by making a row? If he'd wanted to make a row he would have insisted on coming into your room.' His eyes twinkled and his lips broke into a broad smile. 'We should have looked a pair of damned fools.'

'I wish you could have seen his face last night.'

'I expect he was upset. It was naturally a shock. It's a damned humiliating position for any man. He always looks a fool. Walter doesn't give me the impression of a fellow who'd care to wash a lot of dirty linen in public.'

'I don't think he would,' she answered reflectively. 'He's very sensitive, I've discovered that.'

'That's all to the good as far as we're concerned. You know, it's a very good plan to put yourself in somebody else's shoes and ask yourself how you would act in his place. There's only one way in which a man can save his face when he's in that sort of position and that is to pretend he knows nothing. I bet you anything you like that that is exactly what he's going to do.'

The more Townsend talked the more buoyant he became. His blue eyes sparkled and he was once more his gay and jovial self. He irradiated an encouraging confidence.

'Heavens knows, I don't want to say anything disagreeable about him, but when you come down to brass tacks a bacteriologist is no great shakes. The chances are that I shall be Colonial Secretary when Simmons goes home, and it's to Walter's interest to keep on the right side of me. He's got his bread and butter to think of, like the rest of us: do you think the Colonial Office are going to do much for a fellow who makes a scandal? Believe me, he's got everything to gain by holding his tongue and everything to lose by kicking up a row.'

Kitty moved uneasily. She knew how shy Walter was and she could believe that the fear of a scene, and the dread of public attention, might have influence upon him; but she could not believe that he would be affected by the thought of a material advantage. Perhaps she didn't know him very well, but Charlie didn't know him at all.

'Has it occurred to you that he's madly in love with me?'

He did not answer, but he smiled at her with roguish eyes. She knew and loved that charming look of his.

'Well, what is it? I know you're going to say something awful.'

'Well, you know, women are often under the impression that men are much more madly in love with them than they really are.'

For the first time she laughed. His confidence was catching.

'What a monstrous thing to say.'

'I put it to you that you haven't been bothering much about your husband lately. Perhaps he isn't quite so much in love with you as he was.'

'At all events I shall never delude myself that *you* are madly in love with me,' she retorted.

'That's where you're wrong.'

Ah, how good it was to hear him say that! She knew it and her belief in his passion warmed her heart. As he spoke he rose from the bed and came and sat down beside her on the sandalwood box. He put his arm round her waist.

'Don't worry your silly little head a moment longer,' he said. 'I promise you there's nothing to fear. I'm as certain as I am of anything that he's going to pretend he knows nothing. You know, this sort of thing is awfully difficult to prove. You say he's in love with you; perhaps he doesn't want to lose you altogether. I swear I'd accept anything rather than that if you were my wife.'

She leaned towards him. Her body became limp and yielding against his arm. The love she felt for him was almost torture. His last words had struck her: perhaps Walter loved her so passionately that he was prepared to accept any humiliation if sometimes she would let him love her. She could understand that; for that was how she felt towards Charlie. A thrill of pride passed through her, and at the same time a faint sensation of contempt for a man who could love so slavishly.

She put her arm lovingly round Charlie's neck.

'You're simply wonderful. I was shaking like a leaf when I came here and you've made everything all right.'

He took her face in his hand and kissed her lips.

'Darling.'

'You're such a comfort to me,' she sighed.

'I'm sure you need not be nervous. And you know I'll stand by you. I won't let you down.'

She put away her fears, but for an instant unreasonably she regretted that her plans for the future were shattered. Now that all danger was past she almost wished that Walter were going to insist on a divorce.

'I knew I could count on you,' she said.

'So I should hope.'

'Oughtn't you to go and have your tiffin?'

'Oh, damn my tiffin.'

He drew her more closely to him and now she was held tight in his arms. His mouth sought hers.

'Oh, Charlie, you must let me go.'

'Never.'

She gave a little laugh, a laugh of happy love and of triumph; his eyes were heavy with desire. He lifted her to her feet and not letting her go but holding her close to his breast he locked the door.

Chapter Twenty-one

All through the afternoon she thought of what Charlie had said about Walter. They were dining out that evening and when he came back from the Club she was dressing. He knocked at her door.

'Come in.'

He did not open.

'I'm going straight along to dress. How long will you be?'

'Ten minutes.'

He said nothing more, but went to his own room. His voice had that constrained note which she had heard in it the night before. She felt fairly sure of herself now. She was ready before he was and when he came downstairs she was already seated in the car.

'I'm afraid I've kept you waiting,' he said.

'I shall survive it,' she replied, and she was able to smile as she spoke.

She made an observation or two as they drove down the hill, but he answered curtly. She shrugged her shoulders; she was growing a trifle impatient: if he wanted to sulk, let him, she didn't care. They drove in silence till they reached their destination. It was a large dinner party. There were too many people and too many courses. While Kitty chatted gaily with her neighbours she watched Walter. He was deathly pale and his face was pinched.

'Your husband is looking rather washed out. I thought he didn't mind the heat. Has he been working very hard?'

'He always works hard.'

'I suppose you're going away soon?'

'Oh, yes, I think I shall go to Japan as I did last year,' she said. 'The doctor says I must get out of the heat if I don't want to go all to pieces.'

Walter did not as usual when they were dining out give her a little smiling glance now and then. He never looked at her. She had noticed that when he came down to the car he kept his eyes averted, and he did the same when, with his usual politeness, he gave her his hand to alight. Now, talking with the women on either side of him, he did not smile, but looked at them with steady and unblinking eyes; and really his eyes looked enormous and in that pale face coal black. His face was set and stern.

'He must be an agreeable companion,' thought Kitty ironically.

The idea of those unfortunate ladies trying to indulge in small talk with that grim mask not a little diverted her.

Of course he knew; there was no doubt about that, and he was furious with her. Why hadn't he said anything? Was it really because, though angry and hurt, he loved her so much that he was afraid she would leave him. The thought made her ever so slightly despise him, but good-naturedly: after all, he was her husband and he provided her with board and lodging; so long as he didn't interfere with her and let her do as she liked she would be quite nice to him. On the other hand perhaps his silence was due merely to a morbid timidity. Charlie was right when he said that no one would hate a scandal more than Walter. He never made a speech if he could help it. He had told her once that when he was subpoenaed as a witness on a case where he was to give expert evidence he had hardly slept for a week before. His shyness was a disease.

And there was another thing: men were very vain, and so long as no one knew what had happened it might be that Walter would be content to ignore it. Then she wondered whether by any possibility Charlie was right when he suggested that Walter knew which side his bread was buttered. Charlie was the most popular man in the Colony and soon would be Colonial Secretary. He could be very useful to Walter: on the other hand he could make himself very unpleasant if Walter put his back up. Her heart exulted as she thought of her lover's strength and determination; she felt so defenceless in his virile arms. Men were strange: it would never have occurred to her that Walter was capable of such baseness, and yet you never knew; perhaps his seriousness was merely a mask for a mean and pettifogging nature. The more she considered it the more likely it seemed that Charlie was right; and she turned her glance once more on her husband. There was no indulgence in it.

It happened that just then the women on either side of him were talking with their neighbours and he was left alone. He was staring straight in front of him, forgetful of the party, and his eyes were filled with a mortal sadness. It gave Kitty a shock.

Chapter Twenty-two

Next day when she was lying down after luncheon, dozing, she was aroused by a knock at her door.

'Who is it?' she cried irritably.

At that hour she was unaccustomed to be disturbed.

'I.'

She recognised her husband's voice and she sat up quickly.

'Come in.'

'Did I wake you?' he asked as he entered.

'In point of fact you did,' she answered in the natural tone she had adopted with him for the last two days.

'Will you come into the next room. I want to have a little talk with you.'

Her heart gave a sudden beat against her ribs.

'I'll put on a dressing-gown.'

He left her. She slipped her bare feet into mules and wrapped herself in a kimono. She looked in the glass; she was very pale and she put on some rouge. She stood at the door for a moment, nerving herself for the interview, and then with a bold face joined him.

'How did you manage to get away from the Laboratory at this hour?' she said. 'I don't often see you at this sort of time.'

'Won't you sit down?'

He did not look at her. He spoke gravely. She was glad to do as he asked: her knees were a little shaky, and unable to continue in that jocular tone she kept silent. He sat also and lit a cigarette. His eyes wandered restlessly about the room. He seemed to have some difficulty in starting.

Suddenly he looked full at her; and because he had held his eyes so long averted, his direct gaze gave her such a fright that she smothered a cry.

'Have you ever heard of Mei-tan-fu?' he asked. 'There's been a good deal about it in the papers lately.'

She stared at him in astonishment. She hesitated.

'Is that the place where there's cholera? Mr Arbuthnot was talking about it last night.'

'There's an epidemic. I believe it's the worst they've had for years. There was a medical missionary there. He died of cholera three days ago. There's a French convent there and of course there's the Customs man. Every one else has got out.'

His eyes were still fixed on her and she could not lower hers. She tried to read his expression, but she was nervous, and she could only discern a strange watchfulness. How could he look so steadily? He did not even blink.

'The French nuns are doing what they can. They've turned the orphanage into a hospital. But the people are dying like flies. I've offered to go and take charge.'

'You?'

She started violently. Her first thought was that if he went she would be free and without let or hindrance could see Charlie. But the thought shocked her. She felt herself go scarlet. Why did he watch her like that? She looked away in embarrassment.

'Is that necessary?' she faltered.

'There's not a foreign doctor in the place.'

'But you're not a doctor, you're a bacteriologist.'

'I am an M.D., you know, and before I specialised I did a good deal of general work in a hospital. The fact that I'm first and foremost a bacteriologist is all to the good. It will be an admirable chance for research work.'

He spoke almost flippantly and when she glanced at him she was surprised to see in his eyes a gleam of mockery. She could not understand.

'But won't it be awfully dangerous?'

'Awfully.'

He smiled. It was a derisive grimace. She leaned her forehead on her hand. Suicide. It was nothing short of that. Dreadful! She had not thought he would take it like that. She couldn't let him do that. It was cruel. It was not her fault if she did not love him. She couldn't bear the thought that he should kill himself for her sake. Tears flowed softly down her cheeks.

'What are you crying for?'

His voice was cold.

'You're not obliged to go, are you?'

'No, I go of my own free will.'

'Please don't, Walter. It would be too awful if something happened. Supposing you died?'

Though his face remained impassive the shadow of a smile once more crossed his eyes. He did not answer.

'Where is this place?' she asked after a pause.

'Mei-tan-fu? It's on a tributary of the Western River. We should go up the Western River and then by chair.'

'Who is we?'

'You and I.'

She looked at him quickly. She thought she had heard amiss. But now the smile in his eyes had travelled to his lips. His dark eyes were fixed on her.

'Are you expecting me to come too?'

'I thought you'd like to.'

Her breath began to come very fast. A shudder passed through her.

'But surely it's no place for a woman. The missionary sent his wife and children down weeks ago and the A.P.C. man and his wife came down. I met her at a tea-party. I've just remembered that she said they left some place on account of cholera.'

'There are five French nuns there.'

Panic seized her.

'I don't know what you mean. It would be madness for me to go. You know how delicate I am. Dr Hayward said I must get out of Hong-Kong on account of the heat. I could never stand the heat up there. And cholera: I should be frightened out of my wits. It's just asking for trouble. There's no reason for me to go. I should die.'

He did not answer. She looked at him in her desperation and she could hardly restrain a cry. His face had a sort of black pallor which suddenly terrified her. She saw in it a look of hatred. Was it possible that he wanted her to die? She answered her own outrageous thought.

'It's absurd. If you think you ought to go it's your own lookout. But really you can't expect me to. I hate illness. A cholera epidemic. I don't pretend to be very brave and I don't mind telling you that I haven't pluck for that. I shall stay here until it's time for me to go to Japan.'

'I should have thought that you would want to accompany me when I am about to set out on a dangerous expedition.'

He was openly mocking her now. She was confused. She did not quite know whether he meant what he said or was merely trying to frighten her.

'I don't think any one could reasonably blame me for refusing to go to a dangerous place where I had no business or where I could be of no use.'

'You could be of the greatest use; you could cheer and comfort me.'

She grew even a little paler.

'I don't understand what you're talking about.'

'I shouldn't have thought it needed more than average intelligence.'

'I'm not going, Walter. It's monstrous to ask me.'

'Then I shall not go either. I shall immediately file my petition.'

Chapter Twenty-three

She looked at him blankly. What he said was so unexpected that at the first moment she could hardly gather its sense.

'What on earth are you talking about?' she faltered.

Even to herself her reply rang false, and she saw the look of disdain which it called forth on Walter's stern face.

'I'm afraid you've thought me a bigger fool than I am.'

She did not quite know what to say. She was undecided whether indignantly to assert her innocence or to break out into angry reproaches. He seemed to read her thoughts.

'I've got all the proof necessary.'

She began to cry. The tears flowed from her eyes without any particular anguish and she did not dry them: to weep gave her a little time to collect herself. But her mind was blank. He watched her without concern, and his calmness frightened her. He grew impatient.

'You're not going to do much good by crying, you know.'

His voice, so cold and hard, had the effect of exciting in her a certain indignation. She was recovering her nerve.

'I don't care. I suppose you have no objection to my divorcing you. It means nothing to a man.'

'Will you allow me to ask why I should put myself to the smallest inconvenience on your account?'

'It can't make any difference to you. It's not much to ask you to behave like a gentleman.'

'I have much too great a regard for your welfare.'

She sat up now and dried her eyes.

'What *do* you mean?' she asked him.

'Townsend will marry you only if he is co-respondent and the case is so shameless that his wife is forced to divorce him.'

'You don't know what you're talking about,' she cried.

'You stupid fool.'

His tone was so contemptuous that she flushed with anger. And perhaps her anger was greater because she had never before heard him say to her any but sweet, flattering and delightful things. She had been accustomed to find him subservient to all her whims.

'If you want the truth you can have it. He's only too anxious to marry me. Dorothy Townsend is perfectly willing to divorce him and we shall be married the moment we're free.'

'Did he tell you that in so many words or is that the impression you have gained from his manner?'

Walter's eyes shone with bitter mockery. They made Kitty a trifle uneasy. She was not quite sure that Charlie had ever said exactly that in so many words.

'He's said it over and over again.'

'That's a lie and you know it's a lie.'

'He loves me with all his heart and soul. He loves me as passionately as I love him. You've found out. I'm not going to deny anything. Why should I? We've been lovers for a year and I'm proud of it. He means everything in the world to me and I'm glad that you know at last. We're sick to death of secrecy and compromise and all the rest of it. It was a mistake that I ever married you, I never should have done it, I was a fool. I never cared for you. We never had anything in common. I don't like the people you like and I'm bored by the things that interest you. I'm thankful it's finished.'

He watched her without a gesture and without a movement of his face. He listened attentively and no change in his expression showed that what she said affected him.

'Do you know why I married you?'

'Because you wanted to be married before your sister Doris.'

It was true, but it gave her a funny little turn to realise that he knew it. Oddly enough, even in that moment of fear and anger, it excited her compassion. He faintly smiled.

'I had no illusions about you,' he said. 'I knew you were silly and frivolous and empty-headed. But I loved you. I knew that your aims and ideals were vulgar and commonplace. But I loved you. I knew that you were second-rate. But I loved you. It's comic when I think how hard I tried to be amused by the things that amused you and how anxious I was to hide from you that I wasn't ignorant and vulgar and scandal-mongering and stupid. I knew how frightened you were of intelligence and I did everything I could to make you think me as big a fool as the rest of the men you knew. I knew that you'd only married me for convenience. I loved you so much, I didn't care. Most people, as far as I can see, when they're in love with some one and the love isn't returned feel that they have a grievance. They grow angry and bitter. I wasn't like that. I never expected you to love me, I didn't see any reason that you should, I never thought myself very lovable. I was thankful to be allowed to love you and I was enraptured when now and then I thought you were pleased with me or when I noticed in your eyes a gleam of good-humoured affection. I tried not to bore you with my love; I knew I couldn't afford to do that and I was always on the lookout for the first sign that you were impatient with my affection. What most husbands expect as a right I was prepared to receive as a favour.'

Kitty, accustomed to flattery all her life, had never heard such things said to her before. Blind wrath, driving out fear, arose in her heart: it seemed to choke her, and she felt the blood-vessels in her temples swell and throb. Wounded vanity can make a woman more vindictive than a lioness robbed of her cubs. Kitty's jaw, always a little too square, protruded with an apish hideousness and her beautiful eyes were black with malice. But she kept her temper in check.

'If a man hasn't what's necessary to make a woman love him, it's his fault, not hers.'

'Evidently.'

His derisive tone increased her irritation. She felt that she could wound him more by maintaining her calm.

'I'm not very well-educated and I'm not very clever. I'm just a perfectly ordinary young woman. I like the things that the people like among whom I've lived all my life. I like dancing and tennis and theatres and I like the men who play games. It's quite true that I've always been bored by you and by the things you like. They mean nothing to me and I don't want them to. You dragged me round those interminable galleries in Venice: I should have enjoyed myself much more playing golf at Sandwich.

'I know.'

'I'm sorry if I haven't been all that you expected me to be. Unfortunately I always found you physically repulsive. You can hardly blame me for that.'

'I don't.'

Kitty could more easily have coped with the situation if he had raved and stormed. She could have met violence with violence. His self-control was inhuman and she hated him now as she had never hated him before.

'I don't think you're a man at all. Why didn't you break into the room when you knew I was there with Charlie? You might at least have tried to thrash him. Were you afraid?'

But the moment she had said this she flushed, for she was ashamed. He did not answer, but in his eyes she read an icy disdain. The shadow of a smile flickered on his lips.

'It may be that, like a historical character, I am too proud to fight.'

Kitty, unable to think of anything to answer, shrugged her shoulders. For a moment longer he held her in his immobile gaze.

'I think I've said all I had to say: if you refuse to come to Mei-tan-fu I shall file my petition.'

'Why won't you consent to let me divorce you?'

He took his eyes off her at last. He leaned back in his chair and lit a cigarette. He smoked it to the end without saying a word. Then, throwing away the butt, he gave a little smile. He looked at her once more.

'If Mrs Townsend will give me her assurance that she will divorce her husband and if he will give me his written promise to marry you within a week of the two decrees being made absolute, I will do that.'

There was something in the way he spoke which disconcerted her. But her self-respect obliged her to accept his offer in the grand manner.

'That is very generous of you, Walter.'

To her astonishment he burst suddenly into a shout of laughter. She flushed angrily.

'What are you laughing at? I see nothing to laugh at.'

'I beg your pardon. I daresay my sense of humour is peculiar.'

She looked at him frowning. She would have liked to say something bitter and wounding, but no rejoinder occurred to her. He looked at his watch.

'You had better look sharp if you want to catch Townsend at his office. If you decide to come with me to Mei-tan-fu it would be necessary to start the day after tomorrow.'

'Do you want me to tell him today?'

'They say there is no time like the present.'

Her heart began to beat a little faster. It was not uneasiness that she felt, it was, she didn't quite know what it was. She wished she could have had a little longer; she would have liked to prepare Charlie. But she had the fullest confidence in him, he loved her as much as she loved him, and it was treacherous even to let the thought cross her mind that he would not welcome the necessity that was forced upon them. She turned to Walter gravely.

'I don't think you know what love is. You have no conception how desperately in love Charlie and I are with one another. It really is the only thing that matters and every sacrifice that our love calls for will be as easy as falling off a log.'

He gave a little bow, but said nothing, and his eyes followed her as she walked with measured step from the room.

Chapter Twenty-four

She sent in a little note to Charlie on which she had written: '*Please see me. It is urgent.*' A Chinese boy asked her to wait and brought the answer that Mr Townsend would see her in five minutes. She was unaccountably nervous. When at last she was ushered into his room Charlie came forward to shake hands with her, but the moment the boy, having closed the door, left them alone he dropped the affable formality of his manner.

'I say, my dear, you really mustn't come here in working hours. I've got an awful lot to do and we don't want to give people a chance to gossip.'

She gave him a long look with those beautiful eyes of hers and tried to smile, but her lips were stiff and she could not.

'I wouldn't have come unless it was necessary.'

He smiled and took her arm.

'Well, since you're here come and sit down.'

It was a bare room, narrow, with a high ceiling; its walls were painted in two shades of terra cotta. The only furniture consisted of a large desk, a revolving chair for Townsend to sit in and a leather arm-chair for visitors. It intimidated Kitty to sit in this. He sat at the desk. She had never seen him in spectacles before; she did not know that he used them. When he noticed that her eyes were on them he took them off.

'I only use them for reading,' he said.

Her tears came easily and now, she hardly knew why, she began to cry. She had no deliberate intention of deceiving, but rather an instinctive desire to excite his sympathy. He looked at her blankly.

'Is anything the matter? Oh, my dear, don't cry.'

She took out her handkerchief and tried to check her sobs. He rang the bell and when the boy came to the door went to it.

'If any one asks for me say I'm out.'

'Very good, sir.'

The boy closed the door. Charlie sat on the arm of the chair and put his arm round Kitty's shoulders.

'Now, Kitty dear, tell me all about it.'

'Walter wants a divorce,' she said.

She felt the pressure of his arm on her shoulder cease. His body stiffened. There was a moment's silence, then Townsend rose from her chair and sat down once more in his.

'What exactly do you mean?' he said.

She looked at him quickly, for his voice was hoarse, and she saw that his face was dully red.

'I've had a talk with him. I've come straight from the house now. He says he has all the proof he wants.'

'You didn't commit yourself, did you? You didn't acknowledge anything?'

Her heart sank.

'No,' she answered.

'Are you quite sure?' he asked, looking at her sharply.

'Quite sure,' she lied again.

He leaned back in his chair and stared vacantly at the map of China which was hanging on the wall in front of him. She watched him anxiously. She was somewhat disconcerted at the manner in which he had received the news. She had expected him to take her in his arms and tell her he was thankful, for now they could be together always; but of course men were funny. She was crying softly, not now to arouse sympathy, but because it seemed the natural thing to do.

'This is a bloody mess we've got into,' he said at length. 'But it's no good losing our heads. Crying isn't going to do us any good, you know.'

She noticed the irritation in his voice and dried her eyes.

'It's not my fault, Charlie. I couldn't help it.'

'Of course you couldn't. It was just damned bad luck. I was just as much to blame as you were. The thing to do now is to see how we're going to get out of it. I don't suppose you want to be divorced any more than I do.'

She smothered a gasp. She gave him a searching look. He was not thinking of her at all.

'I wonder what his proofs really are. I don't know how he can actually prove that we were together in that room. On the whole we've been about as careful as any one could be. I'm sure that old fellow at the curio shop wouldn't have given us away. Even if he'd seen us go in there's no reason why we shouldn't hunt curios together.'

He was talking to himself rather than to her.

'It's easy enough to bring charges, but it's damned difficult to prove them; any lawyer will tell you that. Our line is to deny everything, and if he threatens to bring an action we'll tell him to go to hell and we'll fight it.'

'I couldn't go into court, Charlie.'

'Why on earth not? I'm afraid you'll have to. God knows, I don't want a row, but we can't take it lying down.'

'Why need we defend it?'

'What a question to ask. After all, it's not only you that are concerned, I'm concerned too. But as a matter of fact I don't think you need be afraid of that. We shall be able to square your husband somehow. The only thing that worries me is the best way to set about it.'

It looked as though an idea occurred to him, for he turned towards her with his charming smile and his tone, a moment before abrupt and business-like, became ingratiating.

'I'm afraid you've been awfully upset, poor little woman. It's too bad.' He stretched out his hand and took hers. 'It's a scrape we've got into, but we shall get out of it. It's not . . .' He stopped and Kitty had a suspicion that he had been about to say that it was not the first he had got out of. 'The greatest thing is to keep our heads. You know I shall never let you down.'

'I'm not frightened. I don't care what he does.'

He smiled still, but perhaps his smile was a trifle forced.

'If the worst comes to the worst I shall have to tell the Governor. He'll curse me like hell, but he's a good fellow and a man of the world. He'll fix it up somehow. It wouldn't do him any good if there was a scandal.'

'What can he do?' asked Kitty.

'He can bring pressure to bear on Walter. If he can't get at him through his ambition he'll get at him through his sense of duty.'

Kitty was a little chilled. She did not seem able to make Charlie see how desperately grave the situation was. His airiness made her impatient. She was sorry that she had come to see him in his office. The surroundings intimidated her. It would have been much easier to say what she wanted if she could have been in his arms with hers round his neck.

'You don't know Walter,' she said.

'I know that every man has his price.'

She loved Charlie with all her heart, but his reply disconcerted her; for such a clever man it was a stupid thing to say.

'I don't think you realise how angry Walter is. You haven't seen his face and the look of his eyes.'

He did not reply for the moment, but looked at her with a slight smile. She knew what he was thinking. Walter was the bacteriologist and occupied a subordinate position; he would hardly have the impudence to make himself a nuisance to the upper officials of the Colony.

'It's no good deceiving yourself, Charlie,' she said earnestly. 'If Walter has made up his mind to bring an action nothing that you or anybody else can say will have the slightest influence.'

His face once more grew heavy and sulky.

'Is it his idea to make me co-respondent?'

'At first it was. At last I managed to get him to consent to let me divorce him.'

'Oh, well, that's not so terrible.' His manner relaxed again and she saw the relief in his eyes. 'That seems to me a very good way out. After all, it's the least a man can do, it's the only decent thing.'

'But he makes a condition.'

He gave her an inquiring glance and he seemed to reflect.

'Of course I'm not a very rich man, but I'll do anything in my power.'

Kitty was silent. Charlie was saying things which she would never have expected him to say. And they made it difficult for her to speak. She had expected to blurt it out in one breath, held in his loving arms, with her burning face hid on his breast.

'He agrees to my divorcing him if your wife will give him the assurance that she will divorce you.'

'Anything else?'

Kitty could hardly find her voice.

'And—it's awfully hard to say, Charlie, it sounds dreadful—if you'll promise to marry me within a week of the decrees being made absolute.'

Chapter Twenty-five

For a moment he was silent. Then he took her hand again and pressed it gently.

'You know, darling,' he said, 'whatever happens we must keep Dorothy out of this.'

She looked at him blankly.

'But I don't understand. How can we?'

'Well, we can't only think of ourselves in this world. You know, other things being equal, there's nothing in this world I'd love more than to marry you. But it's quite out of the question. I know Dorothy: nothing would induce her to divorce me.'

Kitty was becoming horribly frightened. She began to cry again. He got up and sat down beside her with his arm round her waist.

'Try not to upset yourself, darling. We *must* keep our heads.'

'I thought you loved me . . .'

'Of course I love you,' he said tenderly. 'You surely can't have any doubt of that now.'

'If she won't divorce you Walter will make you co-respondent.'

He took an appreciable time to answer. His tone was dry.

'Of course that would ruin my career, but I'm afraid it wouldn't do you much good. If the worst came to the worst I should make a clean breast of it to Dorothy; she'd be dreadfully hurt and wretched, but she'd forgive me.' He had an idea. 'I'm not sure if the best plan wouldn't be to make a clean breast of it anyhow. If she went to your husband I daresay she could persuade him to hold his tongue.'

'Does that mean you don't want her to divorce you?'

'Well, I have got my boys to think of, haven't I? And naturally I don't want to make her unhappy. We've always got on very well together. She's been an awfully good wife to me, you know.'

'Why did you tell me that she meant nothing to you?'

'I never did. I said I wasn't in love with her. We haven't slept together for years except now and then, on Christmas Day for instance, or the day before she was going home or the day she came back. She isn't a woman who cares for that sort of thing. But we've always been excellent friends. I don't mind telling you that I depend on her more than any one has any idea of.'

'Don't you think it would have been better to leave me alone then?'

She found it strange that with terror catching her breath she could speak so calmly.

'You were the loveliest little thing I'd seen for years. I just fell madly in love with you. You can't blame me for that.'

'After all, you said you'd never let me down.'

'But, good God, I'm not going to let you down. We've got in an awful scrape and I'm going to do everything that's humanly possible to get you out of it.'

'Except the one obvious and natural thing.'

He stood up and returned to his own chair.

'My dear, you must be reasonable. We'd much better face the situation frankly. I don't want to hurt your feelings, but really I must tell you the truth. I'm very keen on my career. There's no reason why I shouldn't be a Governor one of these days, and it's a damned soft job to be a Colonial Governor. Unless we can hush this up I don't stand a dog's chance. I may not have to leave the service, but there'll always be a black mark against me. If I do have to leave the service then I must go into business in China where I know people. In either case my only chance is for Dorothy to stick to me.'

'Was it necessary to tell me that you wanted nothing in the world but me?'

The corners of his mouth drooped peevishly.

'Oh, my dear, it's rather hard to take quite literally the things a man says when he's in love with you.'

'Didn't you mean them?'

'At the moment.'

'And what's to happen to me if Walter divorces me?'

'If we really haven't a leg to stand on of course we won't defend. There shouldn't be any publicity and people are pretty broad-minded nowadays.'

For the first time Kitty thought of her mother. She shivered. She looked again at Townsend. Her pain now was tinged with resentment.

'I'm sure you'd have no difficulty in bearing any inconvenience that I had to suffer,' she said.

'We're not going to get much further by saying disagreeable things to one another,' he answered.

She gave a cry of despair. It was dreadful that she should love him so devotedly and yet feel such bitterness towards him. It was not possible that he understood how much he meant to her.

'Oh, Charlie, don't you know how I love you?'

'But, my dear, I love you. Only we're not living in a desert island and we've got to make the best we can out of the circumstances that are forced upon us. You really must be reasonable.'

'How can I be reasonable? To me our love was everything and you were my whole life. It is not very pleasant to realise that to you it was only an episode.'

'Of course it wasn't an episode. But you know, when you ask me to get my wife, to whom I'm very much attached, to divorce me, and ruin my career by marrying you, you're asking a good deal.'

'No more than I'm willing to do for you.'

'The circumstances are rather different.'

'The only difference is that you don't love me.'

'One can be very much in love with a woman without wishing to spend the rest of one's life with her.'

She gave him a quick look and despair seized her. Heavy tears rolled down her cheeks.

'Oh, how cruel! How can you be so heartless?'

She began to sob hysterically. He gave an anxious glance at the door.

'My dear, do try and control yourself.'

'You don't know how I love you,' she gasped. 'I can't live without you. Have you no pity for me?'

She could not speak any more. She wept without restraint.

'I don't want to be unkind and, Heaven knows I don't want to hurt your feelings, but I must tell you the truth.'

'It's the ruin of my whole life. Why couldn't you leave me alone? What harm had I ever done you?'

'Of course if it does you any good to put all the blame on me you may.'

Kitty blazed with sudden anger.

'I suppose I threw myself at your head. I suppose I gave you no peace till you yielded to my entreaties.'

'I don't say that. But I certainly should never have thought of making love to you if you hadn't made it perfectly clear that you were ready to be made love to.'

Oh, the shame of it! She knew that what he said was true. His face now was sullen and worried and his hands moved uneasily. Every now and then he gave her a little glance of exasperation.

'Won't your husband forgive you?' he said after a while.

'I never asked him.'

Instinctively he clenched his hands. She saw him suppress the exclamation of annoyance which came to his lips.

'Why don't you go to him and throw yourself on his mercy? If he's as much in love with you as you say he's bound to forgive you.'

'How little you know him!'

Chapter Twenty-six

She wiped her eyes. She tried to pull herself together.

'Charlie, if you desert me I shall die.'

She was driven now to appeal to his compassion. She ought to have told him at once. When he knew the horrible alternative that was placed before her his generosity, his sense of justice, his manliness, would be so vehemently aroused that he would think of nothing but her danger. Oh, how passionately she desired to feel his dear, protecting arms around her!

'Walter wants me to go to Mei-tan-fu.'

'Oh, but that's the place where the cholera is. They've got the worst epidemic that they've had for fifty years. It's no place for a woman. You can't possibly go there.'

'If you let me down I shall have to.'

'What do you mean? I don't understand.'

'Walter is taking the place of the missionary doctor who died. He wants me to go with him.'

'When?'

'Now. At once.'

Townsend pushed back his chair and looked at her with puzzled eyes.

'I may be very stupid, but I can't make head or tail out of what you're saying. If he wants you to go to this place with him what about a divorce?'

'He's given me my choice. I must either go to Mei-tan-fu or else he'll bring an action.'

'Oh, I see.' Townsend's tone changed ever so slightly. 'I think that's rather decent of him, don't you?'

'Decent?'

'Well, it's a damned sporting thing of him to go there. It's not a thing I'd fancy. Of course he'll get a C.M.G. for it when he comes back.'

'But me, Charlie?' she cried, with anguish in her voice.

'Well, I think if he wants you to go, under the circumstances I don't see how you can very well refuse.'

'It means death. Absolutely certain death.'

'Oh, damn it all, that's rather an exaggeration. He would hardly take you if he thought that. It's no more risk for you than for him. In point of fact there's no great risk if you're careful. I've been here when there's been cholera and I haven't turned a hair. The great thing is not to eat anything uncooked, no raw fruit or salads, or anything like that, and see that your drinking water is boiled.' He was gaining confidence as he proceeded, and his speech was fluent; he was even becoming less sullen and more alert; he was almost breezy. 'After all, it's his job, isn't it? He's interested in bugs. It's rather a chance for him if you come to think of it.'

'But me, Charlie?' she repeated, not with anguish now, but with consternation.

'Well, the best way to understand a man is to put yourself in his shoes. From his point of view you've been rather a naughty little thing and he wants to get you out of harm's way. I always thought he never wanted to divorce you, he doesn't strike me as that sort of chap; but he made what he thought was a very generous offer and you put his back up by turning it down. I don't want to blame you, but really for all our sakes I think you ought to have given it a little consideration.'

'But don't you see it'll kill me? Don't you know that he's taking me there because he *knows* it'll kill me.'

'Oh, my dear, don't talk like that. We're in a damned awkward position and really it's no time to be melodramatic.'

'You've made up your mind not to understand.' Oh, the pain in her heart, and the fear! She could have screamed. 'You can't send me to certain death. If you have no love or pity for me you must have just ordinary human feeling.'

'I think it's rather hard on me to put it like that. As far as I can make out your husband is behaving very generously. He's willing to forgive you if you'll let him. He wants to get you away and this opportunity has presented itself to take you to some place where for a few months you'll be out of harm's way. I don't pretend that Mei-tan-fu is a health resort, I never knew a Chinese city that was, but there's no reason to get the wind up about it. In fact that's the worst thing you can do. I believe as many people die from sheer fright in an epidemic as because they get infected.'

'But I'm frightened now. When Walter spoke of it I almost fainted.'

'At the first moment I can quite believe it was a shock, but when you come to look at it calmly you'll be all right. It'll be the sort of experience that not every one has had.'

'I thought, I thought . . .'

She rocked to and fro in an agony. He did not speak, and once more his face wore that sullen look which till lately she had never known. Kitty was not crying now. She was dry-eyed, calm, and though her voice was low it was steady.

'Do you want me to go?'

'It's Hobson's choice, isn't it?'

'Is it?'

'It's only fair to you to tell you that if your husband brought an action for divorce and won it I should not be in a position to marry you.'

It must have seemed an age to him before she answered. She rose slowly to her feet.

'I don't think that my husband ever thought of bringing an action.'

'Then why in God's name have you been frightening me out of my wits?' he asked.

She looked at him coolly.

'He knew that you'd let me down.'

She was silent. Vaguely, as when you are studying a foreign language and read a page which at first you can make nothing of, till a word or a sentence gives you a clue; and on a sudden a suspicion, as it were, of the sense flashes across your troubled wits, vaguely she gained an inkling into the workings of Walter's mind. It was like a dark and ominous landscape seen by a flash of lightning and in a moment hidden again by the night. She shuddered at what she saw.

'He made that threat only because he knew that you'd crumple up at it, Charlie. It's strange that he should have judged you so accurately. It was just like him to expose me to such a cruel disillusion.'

Charlie looked down at the sheet of blotting paper in front of him. He was frowning a little and his mouth was sulky. But he did not reply.

'He knew that you were vain, cowardly and self-seeking. He wanted me to see it with my own eyes. He knew that you'd run like a hare at the approach of danger. He knew how grossly deceived I was in thinking that you were in love with me, because he knew that you were incapable of loving any one but yourself. He knew you'd sacrifice me without a pang to save your own skin.'

'If it really gives you any satisfaction to say beastly things to me I suppose I've got no right to complain. Women always are unfair and they generally manage to put a man in the wrong. But there is something to be said on the other side.'

She took no notice of his interruption.

'And now I know all that he knew. I know that you're callous and heartless, I know that you're selfish, selfish beyond words, and I know that you haven't the nerve of a rabbit, I know you're a liar and a humbug, I know that you're utterly contemptible. And the tragic part is'—her face was on a sudden distraught with pain—'the tragic part is that notwithstanding I love you with all my heart.'

'Kitty.'

She gave a bitter laugh. He had spoken her name in that melting, rich tone of his which came to him so naturally and meant so little.

'You fool,' she said.

He drew back quickly, flushing and offended; he could not make her out.

She gave him a look in which there was a glint of amusement.

'You're beginning to dislike me, aren't you? Well, dislike me. It doesn't make any difference to me now.'

She began to put on her gloves.

'What are you going to do?' he asked.

'Oh, don't be afraid, you'll come to no harm. You'll be quite safe.'

'For God's sake, don't talk like that, Kitty,' he answered and his deep voice rang with anxiety. 'You must know that everything that concerns you concerns me. I shall be frightfully anxious to know what happens. What are you going to say to your husband?'

'I'm going to tell him that I'm prepared to go to Mei-tan-fu with him.'

'Perhaps when you consent he won't insist.'

He could not have known why, when he said this, she looked at him so strangely.

'You're not really frightened?' he asked her.

'No,' she said. 'You've inspired me with courage. To go into the midst of a cholera epidemic will be a unique experience and if I die it—well, I die.'

'I was trying to be as kind to you as I could.'

She looked at him again. Tears sprang into her eyes once more and her heart was very full. The impulse was almost irresistible to fling herself on his breast and crush her lips against his. It was no use.

'If you want to know,' she said, trying to keep her voice steady, 'I go with death in my heart and fear. I do not know what Walter has in that dark, twisted mind of his, but I'm shaking with terror. I think it may be that death will be really a release.'

She felt that she could not hold on to her self-control for another moment. She walked swiftly to the door and let herself out before he had time to move from his chair. Townsend gave a long sigh of relief. He badly wanted a brandy and soda.

Chapter Twenty-seven

Walter was in when she got home. She would have liked to go straight to her room, but he was downstairs, in the hall, giving instructions to one of the boys. She was so wretched that she welcomed the humiliation to which she must expose herself. She stopped and faced him.

'I'm coming with you to that place,' she said.

'Oh, good.'

'When do you want me to be ready?'

'Tomorrow night.'

She did not know what spirit of bravado entered into her. His indifference was like a prick of a spear. She said a thing that surprised herself.

'I suppose I needn't take more than a few summer things and a shroud, need I?'

She was watching his face and knew that her flippancy angered him.

'I've already told your amah what you'll want.'

She nodded and went up to her room. She was very pale.

Chapter Twenty-eight

They were reaching their destination at last. They were borne in chairs, day after day, along a narrow causeway between interminable rice-fields. They set out at dawn and travelled till the heat of the day forced them to take shelter in a wayside inn and then went on again till they reached the town where they had arranged to spend the night. Kitty's chair headed the procession and Walter followed her; then in a struggling line came the coolies that bore their bedding, stores and equipment. Kitty passed through the country with unseeing eyes. All through the long hours, the silence broken only by an occasional remark from one of the bearers or a snatch of uncouth song, she turned over in her tortured mind the details of that heart-rending scene in Charlie's office. Recalling what he had said to her and what she had said to him, she was dismayed to see what an arid and business-like turn their conversation had taken. She had not said what she wanted to say and she had not spoken in the tone she intended. Had she been able to make him see her boundless love, the passion in her heart, and her helplessness, he could never have been so inhuman as to leave her to her fate. She had been taken unawares. She could hardly believe her ears when he told her, more clearly than with words, that he cared nothing for her. That was why she had not even cried very much, she had been so dazed. She had wept since, wept miserably.

At night in the inns, sharing the principal guest chamber with her husband and conscious that Walter, lying on his camp bed, a few feet away from her, lay awake, she dug her teeth in the pillow so that no sound might escape her. But in the day-time, protected by the curtains of her chair, she allowed herself to give way. Her pain was so great that she could have screamed at the top of her voice; she had never known that one could suffer so much; and she asked herself desperately what she had done to deserve it. She could not make out why Charlie did not love her: it was her fault, she supposed, but she had done everything she knew to make him fond of her. They had always got on so well, they laughed all the time they were together, they were not only lovers but good friends. She could not understand; she was broken. She told herself that she hated and despised him; but she had no idea how she was going to live if she was never to see him again. If Walter was taking her to Mei-tan-fu as a punishment he was making a fool of himself, for what did she care now what became of her? She had nothing to live for any more. It was rather hard to be finished with life at twenty-seven.

Chapter Twenty-nine

On the steamer that took them up the Western River Walter read incessantly, but at meal-times he endeavoured to make some kind of conversation. He talked to her as though she were a stranger with whom he happened to be making the journey, of indifferent things, from politeness, Kitty imagined, or because so he could render more marked the gulf that separated them.

In a flash of insight she had told Charlie that Walter had sent her to him with the threat of divorce as the alternative to her accompanying him to the stricken city in order that she might see for herself how indifferent, cowardly and selfish he was. It was true. It was a trick which accorded very well with his sardonic humour. He knew exactly what would happen and he had given her amah necessary instructions before her return. She had caught in his eyes a disdain which seemed to include her lover as well as herself. He said to himself, perhaps, that if he had been in Townsend's place nothing in the world would have hindered him from making any sacrifice to gratify her smallest whim. She knew that was true also. But then, when her eyes were opened, how could he make her do something which was so dangerous, and which he must know frightened her so terribly? At first she thought he was only playing with her and till they actually started, no, later, till they left the river and took to the chairs for the journey across country, she thought he would give that little laugh of his and tell her that she need not come. She had no inkling what was in his mind. He could not really desire her death. He had loved her so desperately. She knew what love was now and she remembered a thousand signs of his adoration. For him really, in the French phrase, she did make fine weather and foul. It was impossible that he did not love her still. Did you cease to love a person because you had been treated cruelly? She had not made him suffer as Charlie had made her suffer and yet, if Charlie made a sign, notwithstanding everything, even though she knew him now, she would abandon all the world had to offer and fly to his arms. Even though he had sacrificed her and cared nothing for her, even though he was callous and unkind, she loved him.

At first she thought that she had only to bide her time, and sooner or later Walter would forgive her. She had been too confident of her power over him to believe that it was gone for ever. Many waters could not quench love. He was weak if he loved her, and felt that love her he must. But now she was not quite sure. When in the evening he sat reading in the straight-backed blackwood chair of the inn with the light of a hurricane lamp on his face she was able to watch him at her ease. She lay on the pallet on which her bed presently would be set and she was in shadow. Those straight, regular features of his made his face look very severe. You could hardly believe that it was possible for them on occasion to be changed by so sweet a smile. He was able to read as calmly as though she were a thousand miles away; she saw him turn the pages and she saw the eyes move regularly as they travelled from line to line. He was not thinking of her. And when, the table being set and dinner brought in, he put aside his book and gave her a glance (not knowing how the light on his face threw into distinctness his expression), she was startled to see in his eyes a look of physical distaste. Yes, it startled her. Was it possible that his love had left him entirely? Was it possible that he really designed her death? It was absurd. That would be the act of a madman. It was odd, the little shiver that ran through her as the thought occurred to her that perhaps Walter was not quite sane.

Chapter Thirty

Suddenly her bearers, long silent, began to speak and one of them, turning round, with words she could not understand and with a gesture, sought to attract her attention. She looked in the direction he pointed and there, on the top of a hill, saw an archway; she knew by now that it was a memorial in compliment of a fortunate scholar or a virtuous widow, she had passed many of them since they left the river; but this one, silhouetted against the westering sun, was more fantastic and beautiful than any she had seen. Yet, she knew not why, it made her uneasy; it had a significance which she felt but could not put into words: Was it a menace that she vaguely discerned or was it derision? She was passing a grove of bamboos and they leaned over the causeway strangely as if they would detain her; though the summer evening was windless their narrow green leaves shivered a little. It gave her the sensation that some one hidden among them was watching her as she passed. Now they came to the foot of the hill and the rice-fields ceased. The bearers took it with a swinging stride. The hill was covered close with little green mounds, close, close to one another, so that the ground was ribbed like the sea-sand when the tide has gone out; and this she knew too for she had passed just such a spot as they approached each populous city and left it. It was the graveyard. Now she knew why the bearers had called her attention to the archway that stood on the crest of the hill: they had reached the end of their journey.

They passed through the archway and the chair-bearers paused to change the pole from shoulder to shoulder. One of them wiped his sweating face with a dirty rag. The causeway wound down. There were bedraggled houses on each side. Now the night was falling. But the bearers on a sudden broke into excited talk and with a jump that shook her ranged themselves as near as they could to the wall. In a moment she knew what had startled them, for as they stood there, chattering to one another, four peasants passed, quick and silent, bearing a new coffin, unpainted, and its fresh wood gleamed white in the approaching darkness. Kitty felt her heart beat in terror against her ribs. The coffin passed, but the bearers stood still; it seemed as though they could not summon up the will to go on. But there was a shout from behind and they started. They did not speak now.

They walked for a few minutes longer and then turned sharply into an open gateway. The chair was set down. She had arrived.

Chapter Thirty-one

It was a bungalow and she entered the sitting-room. She sat down while the coolies, straggling in one by one, brought in their loads. Walter in the courtyard gave directions where this or that was to be placed. She was very tired. She was startled to hear an unknown voice.

'May I come in?'

She flushed and grew pale. She was overwrought and it made her nervous to meet a stranger. A man came out of the darkness, for the long low room was lit only by a shaded lamp, and held out his hand.

'My name is Waddington. I am the Deputy Commissioner.'

'Oh, the Customs. I know. I heard that you were here.'

In that dim light she could see only that he was a little thin man, no taller than she, with a bald head and a small, bare face.

'I live just at the bottom of the hill, but coming in this way you wouldn't have seen my house. I thought you'd be too fagged to come and dine with me, so I've ordered your dinner here and I've invited myself.'

'I'm delighted to hear it.'

'You'll find the cook's not bad. I kept on Watson's boys for you.'

'Watson was the missionary who was here?'

'Yes. Very nice fellow. I'll show you his grave tomorrow if you like.'

'How kind you are,' said Kitty, with a smile.

At that moment Walter came in. Waddington had introduced himself to him before coming in to see Kitty and now he said:

'I've just been breaking it to your missus that I'm dining with you. Since Watson died I haven't had anybody much to talk to but the nuns, and I can never do myself justice in French. Besides, there is only a limited number of subjects you can talk to them about.'

'I've just told the boy to bring in some drinks,' said Walter.

The servant brought whisky and soda and Kitty noticed that Waddington helped himself generously. His manner of speaking and his easy chuckle had suggested to her when he came in that he was not quite sober.

'Here's luck,' he said. Then, turning to Walter: 'You've got your work cut out for you here. They're dying like flies. The magistrate's lost his head and Colonel Yü, the officer commanding the troops, is having a devil of a job to prevent them from looting. If something doesn't happen soon we shall all be murdered in our beds. I tried to get the nuns to go, but of course they wouldn't. They all want to be martyrs, damn them.'

He spoke lightly and there was in his voice a sort of ghostly laughter so that you could not listen to him without smiling.

'Why haven't you gone?' asked Walter.

'Well, I've lost half my staff and the others are ready to lie down and die at any minute. Somebody's got to stay and keep things together.'

'Have you been inoculated?'

'Yes. Watson did me. But he did himself too, and it didn't do him much good, poor blighter.' He turned to Kitty and his funny little face was gaily puckered. 'I don't think there's any great risk if you take proper precautions. Have your milk and water boiled and don't eat fresh fruit or uncooked vegetables. Have you brought any gramophone records with you?'

'No, I don't think so,' said Kitty.

'I'm sorry for that. I was hoping you would. I haven't had any for a long time and I'm sick of my old ones.'

The boy came in to ask if they would have dinner.

'You won't dress tonight, will you?' asked Waddington. 'My boy died last week and the boy I have now is a fool, so I haven't been dressing in the evening.'

'I'll go and take off my hat,' said Kitty.

Her room was next door to that in which they sat. It was barely furnished. An amah was kneeling on the floor, the lamp beside her, unpacking Kitty's things.

Chapter Thirty-two

The dining-room was small and the greater part of it was filled by an immense table. On the walls were engravings of scenes from the Bible and illuminated texts.

'Missionaries always have large dining-tables,' Waddington explained. 'They get so much a year more for every child they have and they buy their tables when they marry so that there shall be plenty of room for little strangers.'

From the ceiling hung a large paraffin lamp, so that Kitty was able to see better what sort of a man Waddington was. His baldness had deceived her into thinking him no longer young, but she saw now that he must be well under forty. His face, small under a high, rounded forehead, was unlined and fresh-coloured; it was ugly like a monkey's, but with an ugliness that was not without charm; it was an amusing face. His features, his nose and his mouth, were hardly larger than a child's, and he had small, very bright blue eyes. His eyebrows were fair and scanty. He looked like a funny little old boy. He helped himself constantly to liquor and as dinner proceeded it became evident that he was far from sober. But if he was drunk it was without offensiveness, gaily, as a satyr might be who had stolen a wine-skin from a sleeping shepherd.

He talked of Hong-Kong; he had many friends there and he wanted to know about them. He had been down for the races a year before and he talked of ponies and their owners.

'By the way, what about Townsend?' he asked suddenly. 'Is he going to become Colonial Secretary?'

Kitty felt herself flush, but her husband did not look at her.

'I shouldn't wonder,' he answered.

'He's the sort that gets on.'

'Do you know him?' asked Walter.

'Yes, I know him pretty well. We travelled out from home together once.'

From the other side of the river they heard the beating of gongs and the clatter of fire-crackers. There, so short a way from them, the great city lay in terror; and death, sudden and ruthless, hurried through its tortuous streets. But Waddington began to speak of London. He talked of the theatres. He knew everything that was being played at the moment and he told them what pieces he had seen when he was last home on leave. He laughed as he recollected the humour of this low comedian and sighed as he reflected on the beauty of that star of musical comedy. He was pleased to be able to boast that a cousin of his had married one of the most celebrated. He had lunched with her and she had given him her photograph. He would show it to them when they came and dined with him at the Customs.

Walter looked at his guest with a cold and ironic gaze, but he was evidently not a little amused by him, and he made an effort to show a civil interest in topics of which Kitty was well aware he knew nothing. A faint smile lingered on his lips. But Kitty, she knew not why, was filled with awe. In the house of that dead missionary, over against the stricken city, they seemed immeasurably apart from all the world. Three solitary creatures and strangers to each other.

Dinner was finished and she rose from the table.

'Do you mind if I say goodnight to you? I'm going to bed.'

'I'll take myself off, I expect the doctor wants to go to bed too,' answered Waddington. 'We must be out early tomorrow.'

He shook hands with Kitty. He was quite steady on his feet, but his eyes were shining more than ever.

'I'll come and fetch you,' he told Walter, 'and take you to see the Magistrate and Colonel Yü, and then we'll go along to the Convent. You've got your work cut out, I can tell you.'

Chapter Thirty-three

Her night was tortured with strange dreams. She seemed to be carried in her chair and she felt the swaying motion as the bearers marched with their long, uneven stride. She entered cities, vast and dim, where the multitude thronged about her with curious eyes. The streets were narrow and tortuous and in the open shops, with their strange wares, all traffic stopped as she went by and those who bought and those who sold, paused. Then she came to the memorial arch and its fantastic outline seemed on a sudden to gain a monstrous life; its capricious contours were like the waving arms of a Hindu god, and, as she passed under it, she heard the echo of mocking laughter. But then Charlie Townsend came towards her and took her in his arms, lifting her out of the chair, and said it was all a mistake, he had never meant to treat her as he had, for he loved her and he couldn't live without her. She felt his kisses on her mouth and she wept with joy, asking him why he had been so cruel, but though she asked she knew it did not matter. And then there was a hoarse, abrupt cry and they were separated, and between, hurrying silently, coolies passed in their ragged blue and they bore a coffin.

She awoke with a start.

The bungalow stood half way down a steep hill and from her window she saw the narrow river below her and opposite, the city. The dawn had just broken and from the river rose a white mist shrouding the junks that lay moored close to one another like peas in a pod. There were hundreds of them, and they were silent, mysterious in that ghostly light, and you had a feeling that their crews lay under an enchantment, for it seemed that it was not sleep, but something strange and terrible, that held them so still and mute.

The morning drew on and the sun touched the mist so that it shone whitely like the ghost of snow on a dying star. Though on the river it was light so that you could discern palely the lines of the crowded junks and the thick forest of their masts, in front it was a shining wall the eye could not pierce. But suddenly from that white cloud a tall, grim and massive bastion emerged. It seemed not merely to be made visible by the all-discovering sun but rather to rise out of nothing at the touch of a magic wand. It towered, the stronghold of a cruel and barbaric race, over the river. But the magician who built worked swiftly and now a fragment of coloured wall crowned the bastion; in a moment, out of the mist, looming vastly and touched here and there by a yellow ray of sun, there was seen a cluster of green and yellow roofs. Huge they seemed and you could make out no pattern; the order, if order there was, escaped you; wayward and extravagant, but of an unimaginable richness. This was no fortress, nor a temple, but the magic palace of some emperor of the gods where no man might enter. It was too airy, fantastic and unsubstantial to be the work of human hands; it was the fabric of a dream.

The tears ran down Kitty's face and she gazed, her hands clasped to her breast and her mouth, for she was breathless, open a little. She had never felt so light of heart and it seemed to her as though her body were a shell that lay at her feet and she pure spirit. Here was Beauty. She took it as the believer takes in his mouth the wafer which is God.

Chapter Thirty-four

Since Walter went out early in the morning, came back at tiffin only for half an hour, and did not then return till dinner was just ready, Kitty found herself much alone. For some days she did not stir from the bungalow. It was very hot and for the most part she lay in a long chair by the open window, trying to read. The hard light of mid-day had robbed the magic palace of its mystery and now it was no more than a temple on the city wall, garish and shabby, but because she had seen it once in such an ecstasy it was never again quite common-place; and often at dawn or at dusk, and again at night, she found herself able to recapture something of that beauty. What had seemed to her a mighty bastion was but the city wall and on this, massive and dark, her eyes rested continually. Behind its crenellations lay the city in the dread grip of the pestilence.

Vaguely she knew that terrible things were happening there, not from Walter who when she questioned him (for otherwise he rarely spoke to her) answered with a humorous nonchalance which sent a shiver down her spine; but from Waddington and from the amah. The people were dying at the rate of a hundred a day, and hardly any of those who were attacked by the disease recovered from it; the gods had been brought out from the abandoned temples and placed in the streets; offerings were laid before them and sacrifices made, but they did not stay the plague. The people died so fast that it was hardly possible to bury them. In some houses the whole family had been swept away and there was none to perform the funeral rights. The officer commanding the troops was a masterful man and if the city was not given over to riot and arson it was due to his determination. He forced his soldiers to bury such as there was no one else to bury and he had shot with his own hand an officer who demurred at entering a stricken house.

Kitty sometimes was so frightened that her heart sank within her and she would tremble in every limb. It was all very well to say that the risk was small if you took reasonable precautions: she was panic-stricken. She turned over in her mind crazy plans of escape. To get away, just to get away, she was prepared to set out as she was and make her way alone, without anything but what she stood up in, to some place of safety. She thought of throwing herself on the mercy of Waddington, telling him everything and beseeching him to help her to get back to Hong-Kong. If she flung herself on her knees before her husband, and admitted that she was frightened, frightened, even though he hated her now he must have enough human feeling in him to pity her.

It was out of the question. If she went, where could she go? Not to her mother; her mother would make her see very plainly that, having married her off, she counted on being rid of her; and besides she did not want to go to her mother. She wanted to go to Charlie, and he did not want her. She knew what he would say if she suddenly appeared before him. She saw the sullen look of his face and the shrewd hardness behind his charming eyes. It would be difficult for him to find words that sounded well. She clenched her hands. She would have given anything to humiliate him as he had humiliated her. Sometimes she was seized with such a frenzy that she wished she had let Walter divorce her, ruining herself if only she could have ruined him too. Certain things he had said to her made her blush with shame when she recalled them.

Chapter Thirty-five

The first time she was alone with Waddington she brought the conversation round to Charlie. Waddington had spoken of him on the evening of their arrival. She pretended that he was no more than an acquaintance of her husband.

'I never much cared for him,' said Waddington. 'I've always thought him a bore.'

'You must be very hard to please,' returned Kitty, in the bright, chaffing way she could assume so easily. 'I suppose he's far and away the most popular man in Hong-Kong.'

'I know. That is his stock in trade. He's made a science of popularity. He has the gift of making every one he meets feel that he is the one person in the world he wants to see. He's always ready to do a service that isn't any trouble to himself, and even if he doesn't do what you want he manages to give you the impression that it's only because it's not humanly possible.'

'That is surely an attractive trait.'

'Charm and nothing but charm at last grows a little tiresome, I think. It's a relief then to deal with a man who isn't quite so delightful but a little more sincere. I've known Charlie Townsend for a good many years and once or twice I've caught him with the mask off–you see, I never mattered, just a subordinate official in the Customs–and I know that he doesn't in his heart give a damn for any one in the world but himself.'

Kitty, lounging easily in her chair, looked at him with smiling eyes. She turned her wedding-ring round and round her finger.

'Of course he'll get on. He knows all the official ropes. Before I die I have every belief that I shall address him as Your Excellency and stand up when he enters the room.'

'Most people think he deserves to get on. He's generally supposed to have a great deal of ability.'

'Ability? What nonsense! He's a very stupid man. He gives you the impression that he dashes off his work and gets it through from sheer brilliancy. Nothing of the kind. He's as industrious as a Eurasian clerk.'

'How has he got the reputation of being so clever?'

'There are many foolish people in the world and when a man in a rather high position puts on no frills, slaps them on the back, and tells them he'll do anything in the world for them, they are very likely to think him clever. And then of course, there's his wife. There's an able woman if you like. She has a good sound head and her advice is always worth taking. As long as Charlie Townsend's got her to depend on he's pretty safe never to do a foolish thing, and that's the first thing necessary for a man to get on in Government service. They don't want clever men; clever men have ideas, and ideas cause trouble; they want men who have charm and tact and who can be counted on never to make a blunder. Oh, yes, Charlie Townsend will get to the top of the tree all right.'

'I wonder why you dislike him?'

'I don't dislike him.'

'But you like his wife better?' smiled Kitty.

'I'm an old-fashioned little man and I like a well-bred woman.'

'I wish she were well-dressed as well as well-bred.'

'Doesn't she dress well? I never noticed.'

'I've always heard that they were a devoted couple,' said Kitty, watching him through her eye-lashes.

'He's very fond of her: I will give him that credit. I think that is the most decent thing about him.'

'Cold praise.'

'He has his little flirtations, but they're not serious. He's much too cunning to let them go to such lengths as might cause him inconvenience. And of course he isn't a passionate man; he's only a vain one. He likes admiration. He's fat and forty now, he does himself too well, but he was very good-looking when he first came to the Colony. I've often heard his wife chaff him about his conquests.'

'She doesn't take his flirtations very seriously?'

'Oh, no, she knows they don't go very far. She says she'd like to be able to make friends of the poor little things who fall to Charlie; but they're always so common. She says it's really not very flattering to her that the women who fall in love with her husband are so uncommonly second-rate.'

Chapter Thirty-six

When Waddington left her Kitty thought over what he had so carelessly said. It hadn't been very pleasant to hear and she had had to make something of an effort not to show how much it touched her. It was bitter to think that all he said was true. She knew that Charlie was stupid and vain, hungry for flattery, and she remembered the complacency with which he had told her little stories to prove his cleverness. He was proud of a low cunning. How worthless must she be if she had given her heart so passionately to such a man because–because he had nice eyes and a good figure! She wished to despise him, because so long as she only hated him she knew that she was very near loving him. The way he had treated her should have opened her eyes. Walter had always held him in contempt. Oh, if she could only get him out of her mind altogether! And had his wife chaffed him about her obvious infatuation for him? Dorothy would have liked to make a friend of her, but that she found her second-rate. Kitty smiled a little: how indignant her mother would be to know that her daughter was considered that!

But at night she dreamt of him again. She felt his arms pressing her close and the hot passion of his kisses on her lips. What did it matter if he was fat and forty? She laughed with soft affection because he minded so much; she loved him all the more for his childlike vanity and she could be sorry for him and comfort him. When she awoke tears were streaming from her eyes.

She did not know why it seemed to her so tragic to cry in her sleep.

Chapter Thirty-seven

She saw Waddington every day, for he strolled up the hill to the Fanes' bungalow when his day's work was done; and so after a week they had arrived at an intimacy which under other circumstances they could scarcely have achieved in a year. Once when Kitty told him she didn't know what she would do there without him he answered, laughing:

'You see, you and I are the only people here who walk quite quietly and peaceably on solid ground. The nuns walk in heaven and your husband–in darkness.'

Though she gave a careless laugh she wondered what he meant. She felt that his merry little blue eyes were scanning her face with an amiable, but disconcerting attention. She had discovered already that he was shrewd and she had a feeling that the relations between herself and Walter excited his cynical curiosity. She found a certain amusement in baffling him. She liked him and she knew that he was kindly disposed towards her. He was not witty nor brilliant, but he had a dry and incisive way of putting things which was diverting, and his funny, boyish face under that bald skull, all screwed up with laughter, made his remarks sometimes extremely droll. He had lived for many years in outports, often with no man of his own colour to talk to, and his personality had developed in eccentric freedom. He was full of fads and oddities. His frankness was refreshing. He seemed to look upon life in a spirit of banter, and his ridicule of the Colony at Hong-Kong was acid; but he laughed also at the Chinese officials in Mei-tan-fu and at the cholera which decimated the city. He could not tell a tragic story or one of heroism without making it faintly absurd. He had many anecdotes of his adventures during twenty years in China, and you concluded from them that the earth was a very grotesque, bizarre and ludicrous place.

Though he denied that he was a Chinese scholar (he swore that the Sinologues were as mad as march hares) he spoke the language with ease. He read little and what he knew he had learned from conversation. But he often told Kitty stories from the Chinese novels and from Chinese history and though he told them with that airy badinage which was natural to him it was good-humoured and even tender. It seemed to her that, perhaps unconsciously, he had adopted the Chinese view that the Europeans were barbarians and their life a folly: in China alone was it so led that a sensible man might discern in it a sort of reality. Here was food for reflection: Kitty had never heard the Chinese spoken of as anything but decadent, dirty and unspeakable. It was as though the corner of a curtain were lifted for a moment, and she caught a glimpse of a world rich with a colour and significance she had not dreamt of.

He sat there, talking, laughing and drinking.

'Don't you think you drink too much?' said Kitty to him boldly.

'It's my great pleasure in life,' he answered. 'Besides, it keeps the cholera out.'

When he left her he was generally drunk, but he carried his liquor well. It made him hilarious, but not disagreeable.

One evening Walter, coming back earlier than usual, asked him to stay to dinner. A curious incident happened. They had their soup and their fish and then with the chicken a fresh green salad was handed to Kitty by the boy.

'Good God, you're not going to eat that,' cried Waddington, as he saw Kitty take some.

'Yes, we have it every night.'

'My wife likes it,' said Walter.

The dish was handed to Waddington, but he shook his head.

'Thank you very much, but I'm not thinking of committing suicide just yet.'

Walter smiled grimly and helped himself. Waddington said nothing more, in fact he became strangely taciturn, and soon after dinner he left them.

It was true that they ate salad every night. Two days after their arrival the cook, with the unconcern of the Chinese, had sent it in and Kitty, without thinking, took some. Walter leaned forward quickly.

'You oughtn't to eat that. The boy's crazy to serve it.'

'Why not?' asked Kitty, looking at him full in the face.

'It's always dangerous, it's madness now. You'll kill yourself.'

'I thought that was the idea,' said Kitty.

She began to eat it coolly. She was seized with she knew not what spirit of bravado. She watched Walter with mocking eyes. She thought that he grew a trifle pale, but when the salad was handed to him he helped himself. The cook, finding they did not refuse it, sent them some in every day and every day, courting death, they ate it. It was grotesque to take such a risk. Kitty, in terror of the disease, took it with the feeling not only that she was thus maliciously avenging herself on Walter, but that she was flouting her own desperate fears.

Chapter Thirty-eight

It was the day after this that Waddington, coming to the bungalow in the afternoon, when he had sat a little asked Kitty if she would not go for a stroll with him. She had not been out of the compound since their arrival. She was glad enough.

'There are not many walks, I'm afraid,' he said. 'But we'll go to the top of the hill.'

'Oh, yes, where the archway is. I've seen it often from the terrace.'

One of the boys opened the heavy doorway for them and they stepped out into the dusty lane. They walked a few yards and then Kitty, seizing Waddington's arm in fright, gave a startled cry.

'Look!'

'What's the matter?'

At the foot of the wall that surrounded the compound a man lay on his back with his legs stretched out and his arms thrown over his head. He wore the patched blue rags and the wild mop of hair of the Chinese beggar.

'He looks as if he were dead,' Kitty gasped.

'He is dead. Come along; you'd better look the other way. I'll have him moved when we come back.'

But Kitty was trembling so violently that she could not stir.

'I've never seen any one dead before.'

'You'd better hurry up and get used to it then, because you'll see a good many before you've done with this cheerful spot.'

He took her hand and drew it in his arm. They walked for a little in silence.

'Did he die of cholera?' she said at last.

'I suppose so.'

They walked up the hill till they came to the archway. It was richly carved. Fantastic and ironical it stood like a landmark in the surrounding country. They sat down on the pedestal and faced the wide plain. The hill was sown close with the little green mounds of the dead, not in lines but disorderly, so that you felt that beneath the surface they must strangely jostle one another. The narrow causeway meandered sinuously among the green rice-fields. A small boy seated on the neck of a water-buffalo drove it slowly home, and three peasants in wide straw hats lolloped with sidelong gait under their heavy loads. After the heat of the day it was pleasant in that spot to catch the faint breeze of the evening and the wide expanse of country brought a sense of restful melancholy to the tortured heart. But Kitty could not rid her mind of the dead beggar.

'How can you talk and laugh and drink whisky when people are dying all around you?' she asked suddenly.

Waddington did not answer. He turned round and looked at her, then he put his hand on her arm.

'You know, this is no place for a woman,' he said gravely. 'Why don't you go?'

She gave him a sidelong glance from beneath her long lashes and there was the shadow of a smile on her lips.

'I should have thought under the circumstances a wife's place was by her husband's side.'

'When they telegraphed to me that you were coming with Fane I was astonished. But then it occurred to me that perhaps you'd been a nurse and all this sort of thing was in the day's work. I expected you to be one of those grim-visaged females who lead you a dog's life when you're ill in hospital. You could have knocked me down with a feather when I came into the bungalow and saw you sitting down and resting. You looked very frail and white and tired.'

'You couldn't expect me to look my best after nine days on the road.'

'You look frail and white and tired now, and if you'll allow me to say so, desperately unhappy.'

Kitty flushed because she could not help it, but she was able to give a laugh that sounded merry enough.

'I'm sorry you don't like my expression. The only reason I have for looking unhappy is that since I was twelve I've known that my nose was a little too long. But to cherish a secret sorrow is a most effective pose: you can't think how many sweet young men have wanted to console me.'

Waddington's blue and shining eyes rested on her and she knew that he did not believe a word she said. She did not care so long as he pretended to.

'I knew that you hadn't been married very long and I came to the conclusion that you and your husband were madly in love with each other. I couldn't believe that he had wished you to come, but perhaps you had absolutely refused to stay behind.'

'That's a very reasonable explanation,' she said lightly.

'Yes, but it isn't the right one.'

She waited for him to go on, fearful of what he was about to say, for she had a pretty good idea of his shrewdness and was aware that he never hesitated to speak his mind, but unable to resist the desire to hear him talk about herself.

'I don't think for a moment that you're in love with your husband. I think you dislike him, I shouldn't be surprised if you hated him. But I'm quite sure you're afraid of him.'

For a moment she looked away. She did not mean to let Waddington see that anything he said affected her.

'I have a suspicion that you don't very much like my husband,' she said with cool irony.

'I respect him. He has brains and character; and that, I may tell you, is a very unusual combination. I don't suppose you know what he is doing here, because I don't think he's very expansive with you. If any man single-handed can put a stop to this frightful epidemic he's going to do it. He's doctoring the sick, cleaning the city up, trying to get the drinking water pure. He doesn't mind where he goes nor what he does. He's risking his life twenty times a day. He's got Colonel Yü in his pocket and he's induced him to put the troops at his disposal. He's even put a little pluck into the magistrate and the old man is really trying to do something. And the nuns at the convent swear by him. They think he's a hero.'

'Don't you?'

'After all this isn't his job, is it? He's a bacteriologist. There was no call for him to come here. He doesn't give me the impression that he's moved by compassion for all these dying Chinamen. Watson was different. He loved the human race. Though he was a missionary it didn't make any difference to him if they were Christian, Buddhist or Confucian; they were just human beings. Your husband isn't here because he cares a damn if a hundred thousand Chinese die of cholera; he isn't here either in the interests of science. Why is he here?'

'You'd better ask him.'

'It interests me to see you together. I sometimes wonder how you behave when you're alone. When I'm there you're acting, both of you, and acting damned badly, by George. You'd neither of you get thirty bob a week in a touring company if that's the best you can do.'

'I don't know what you mean,' smiled Kitty, keeping up a pretence of frivolity which she knew did not deceive.

'You're a very pretty woman. It's funny that your husband should never look at you. When he speaks to you it sounds as though it were not his voice but somebody else's.'

'Do you think he doesn't love me?' asked Kitty in a low voice, hoarsely, putting aside suddenly her lightness.

'I don't know. I don't know if you fill him with such a repulsion that it gives him goose-flesh to be near you or if he's burning with a love that for some reason he will not allow himself to show. I've asked myself if you're both here to commit suicide.'

Kitty had seen the startled glance and then the scrutinising look Waddington gave them when the incident of the salad took place.

'I think you're attaching too much importance to a few lettuce leaves,' she said flippantly. She rose. 'Shall we go home? I'm sure you want a whisky and soda.'

'You're not a heroine at all events. You're frightened to death. Are you sure you don't want to go away?'

'What has it got to do with you?'

'I'll help you.'

'Are *you* going to fall to my look of secret sorrow? Look at my profile and tell me if my nose isn't a trifle too long.'

He gazed at her reflectively, that malicious, ironical look in his bright eyes, but mingled with it, a shadow, like a tree standing at a river's edge and its reflection in the water, was an expression of singular kindliness. It brought sudden tears to Kitty's eyes.

'Must you stay?'

'Yes.'

They passed under the flamboyant archway and walked down the hill. When they came to the compound they saw the body of the dead beggar. He took her arm, but she released herself. She stood still.

'It's dreadful, isn't it?'

'What? Death.'

'Yes. It makes everything else seem so horribly trivial. He doesn't look human. When you look at him you can hardly persuade yourself that he's ever been alive. It's hard to think that not so very many years ago he was just a little boy tearing down the hill and flying a kite.'

She could not hold back the sob that choked her.

Chapter Thirty-nine

A few days later Waddington, sitting with Kitty, a long glass of whisky and soda in his hand, began to speak to her of the convent.

'The Mother Superior is a very remarkable woman,' he said. 'The Sisters tell me that she belongs to one of the greatest families in France, but they won't tell me which; the Mother Superior, they say, doesn't wish it to be talked of.'

'Why don't you ask her if it interests you?' smiled Kitty.

'If you knew her you'd know it was impossible to ask her an indiscreet question.'

'She must certainly be very remarkable if she can impress you with awe.'

'I am the bearer of a message from her to you. She has asked me to say that, though of course you may not wish to adventure into the very centre of the epidemic, if you do not mind that it will give her great pleasure to show you the convent.'

'It's very kind of her. I shouldn't have thought she was aware of my existence.'

'I've spoken about you; I go there two or three times a week just now to see if there's anything I can do; and I daresay your husband has told them about you. You must be prepared to find that they have an unbounded admiration for him.'

'Are you a Catholic?'

His malicious eyes twinkled and his funny little face was puckered with laughter.

'Why are you grinning at me?' asked Kitty.

'Can any good come out of Galilee? No, I'm not a CAtholic. I describe myself as a member of the Church of England, which I suppose is an inoffensive way of saying that you don't believe in anything very much. . . . When the Mother Superior came here ten years ago she brought seven nuns with her and of those all but three are dead. You see, at the best of times, Mei-tan-fu is not a health resort. They live in the very middle of the city, in the poorest district, they work very hard and they never have a holiday.'

'But are there only three and the Mother Superior now?'

'Oh, no, more have taken their places. There are six of them now. When one of them died of cholera at the beginning of the epidemic two others came up from Canton.'

Kitty shivered a little.

'Are you cold?'

'No, it was only some one walking over my grave.'

'When they leave France they leave it for ever. They're not like the Protestant missionaries who have a year's leave every now and then. I always think that must be the hardest thing of all. We English have no very strong attachment to the soil, we can make ourselves at home in any part of the world, but the French, I think, have an attachment to their country which is almost a physical bond. They're never really at ease when they're out of it. It always seems to me very moving that these women should make just that sacrifice. I suppose if I *were* a Catholic it would seem very natural to me.'

Kitty looked at him coolly. She could not quite understand the emotion with which the little man spoke and she asked herself whether it was a pose. He had drunk a good deal of whisky and perhaps he was not quite sober.

'Come and see for yourself,' he said, with his bantering smile, quickly reading her thought. 'It's not nearly so risky as eating a tomato.'

'If you're not frightened there's no reason why I should be.'

'I think it'll amuse you. It's like a little bit of France.'

Chapter Forty

They crossed the river in a sampan. A chair was waiting for Kitty at the landing-stage and she was carried up the hill to the water-gate. It was through this that the coolies came to fetch water from the river and they hurried to and fro with huge buckets hanging from the yoke on their shoulder, splashing the causeway so that it was as wet as though it had heavily rained. Kitty's bearers gave short, sharp cries to urge them to make way.

'Of course all business is at a standstill,' said Waddington, walking by her side. 'Under normal circumstances you have to fight your way through the coolies carrying loads up and down to the junks.'

The street was narrow and winding so that Kitty lost all sense of the direction in which she was going. Many of the shops were closed. She had grown used on the journey up to the untidiness of a Chinese street, but here was the litter of weeks, garbage and refuse; and the stench was so horrible that she had to put her handkerchief to her face. Passing through Chinese cities she had been incommoded by the staring of the crowd, but now she noticed that no more than an indifferent glance was thrown at her. The passers-by, scattered rather than as usual thronging, seemed intent on their own affairs. They were cowed and listless. Now and then as they went by a house they heard the beating of gongs and the shrill, sustained lament of unknown instruments. Behind those closed doors one was lying dead.

'Here we are,' said Waddington at last.

The chair was set down at a small doorway, surmounted by a cross, in a long white wall, and Kitty stepped out. He rang the bell.

'You mustn't expect anything very grand, you know. They're miserably poor.'

The door was opened by a Chinese girl, and after a word or two from Waddington she led them into a little room on the side of the corridor. It contained a large table covered with a chequered oilcloth and round the walls was a set of stiff chairs. At one end of the room was a statue, in plaster, of the Blessed Virgin. In a moment a nun came in, short and plump, with a homely face, red cheeks and merry eyes. Waddington, introducing Kitty to her, called her Sœur St Joseph.

'*C'est la dame du docteur?*' she asked, beaming, and then added that the Mother Superior would join them directly.

Sister St Joseph could speak no English and Kitty's French was halting; but Waddington, fluent, voluble and inaccurate, maintained a stream of facetious comment which convulsed the good-humoured nun. Her cheerful, easy laughter not a little astonished Kitty. She had an idea that the religious were always grave and this sweet and childlike merriment touched her.

Chapter Forty-one

The door opened, to Kitty's fancy not quite naturally but as though it swung back of itself on its hinges, and the Mother Superior entered the little room. She stood for an instant on the threshold and a grave smile hovered upon her lips as she looked at the laughing Sister and Waddington's puckered, clownish face. Then she came forward and held out her hand to Kitty.

'Mrs Fane?' She spoke in English with a good deal of accent, but with a correct pronunciation, and she gave the shadow of a bow. 'It is a great pleasure to me to make the acquaintance of the wife of our good and brave doctor.'

Kitty felt that the Superior's eyes held her in a long and unembarrassed look of appraisal. It was so frank that it was not uncivil; you felt that here was a woman whose business it was to form an opinion of others and to whom it never occurred that subterfuge was necessary. With a dignified affability she motioned to her visitors to take chairs and herself sat down. Sister St Joseph, smiling still but silent, stood at the side but a little behind the Superior.

'I know you English like tea,' said the Mother Superior, 'and I have ordered some. But I must make my excuses if it is served in the Chinese fashion. I know that Mr Waddington prefers whisky, but that I am afraid I cannot offer him.'

She smiled and there was a hint of malice in her grave eyes.

'Oh, come, *ma mère*, you speak as if I were a confirmed drunkard.'

'I wish you could say that you never drink, Mr Waddington.'

'I can at all events say that I never drink except to excess.'

The Mother Superior laughed and translated into French for Sister St Joseph the flippant remark. She looked at him with lingering, friendly eyes.

'We must make allowances for Mr Waddington because two or three times when we had no money at all and did not know how we were to feed our orphans Mr Waddington came to our rescue.'

The convert who had opened the door for them now came in with a tray on which were Chinese cups, a tea-pot, and a little plate of the French cakes called *Madeleines*.

'You must eat the *Madeleines*,' said the Mother Superior, 'because Sister St Joseph made them for you herself this morning.'

They talked of commonplace things. The Mother Superior asked Kitty how long she had been in China and if the journey from Hong-Kong had greatly tired her. She asked her if she had been in France and if she did not find the climate of Hong-Kong trying. It was a conversation, trivial but friendly, which gained a peculiar savour from the circumstances. The parlour was very quiet, so that you could hardly believe that you were in the midst of a populous city. Peace dwelt there. And yet all round about the epidemic was raging and the people, terrified and restless, were kept in check but by the strong will of a soldier who was more than half a brigand. Within the convent walls the infirmary was crowded with sick and dying soldiers, and of the orphans in the nuns' charge a quarter were dead.

Kitty, impressed she hardly knew why, observed the grave lady who asked her these amiable questions. She was dressed in white and the only colour on her habit was the red heart that burned on her breast. She was a woman of middle age, she might have been forty or fifty, it was impossible to say, for there were few wrinkles on her smooth, pale face, and you received the impression that she was far from young chiefly from the dignity of her bearing, her assurance, and the emaciation of her strong and beautiful hands. The face was long, with a large mouth and large, even teeth; the nose, though not small, was delicate and sensitive; but it was the eyes, under their thin black brows, which gave her face its intense and tragic character. They were very large, black, and though not exactly cold, by their calm steadiness strangely compelling. Your first thought when you looked at the Mother Superior was that as a girl she must have been beautiful, but in a moment you realised that this was a woman whose beauty, depending on character, had grown with advancing years. Her voice was deep, low and controlled, and whether she spoke in English or in French she spoke slowly. But the most striking thing about her was the air she had of authority tempered by Christian charity; you felt in her the habit of command. To be obeyed was natural to her, but she accepted obedience with humility. You could not fail to see that she was deeply conscious of the authority of the church which upheld her. But Kitty had a surmise that notwithstanding her austere demeanour she had for human frailty a human tolerance; and it was impossible to look at her grave smile when she listened to Waddington, unabashed, talking nonsense, without being sure that she had a lively sense of the ridiculous.

But there was some other quality in her which Kitty vaguely felt, but could not put a name to. It was something that notwithstanding the Mother Superior's cordiality and the exquisite manners which made Kitty feel like an awkward school-girl, held her at a distance.

Chapter Forty-two

'*Monsieur ne mange rien,*' said Sister St Joseph.

'Monsieur's palate is ruined by Manchu cooking,' replied the Mother Superior.

The smile left Sister St Joseph's face and she assumed an expression of some primness. Waddington, a roguish glance in his eyes, took another cake. Kitty did not understand the incident.

'To prove to you how unjust you are, *ma mère,* I will ruin the excellent dinner that awaits me.'

'If Mrs Fane would like to see over the convent I shall be glad to show her.' The Mother Superior turned to Kitty with a deprecating smile. 'I am sorry you should see it just now when everything is in disorder. We have so much work and not enough Sisters to do it. Colonel Yü has insisted on our putting our infirmary at the disposal of sick soldiers and we have had to make the *réfectoire* into an infirmary for our orphans.'

She stood at the door to allow Kitty to pass and together, followed by Sister St Joseph and Waddington, they walked along cool white corridors. They went first into a large, bare room where a number of Chinese girls were working at elaborate embroideries. They stood up when the visitors entered and the Mother Superior showed Kitty specimens of the work.

'We go on with it notwithstanding the epidemic because it takes their minds off the danger.'

They went to a second room in which younger girls were doing plain sewing, hemming and stitching, and then into a third where there were only tiny children under the charge of a Chinese convert. They were playing noisily and when the Mother Superior came in they crowded round her, mites of two and three, with their black Chinese eyes and their black hair; and they seized her hands and hid themselves in her great skirts. An enchanting smile lit up her grave face, and she fondled them; she spoke little chaffing words which Kitty, ignorant though she was of Chinese, could tell were like caresses. She shuddered a little, for in their uniform dress, sallow-skinned, stunted, with their flat noses, they looked to her hardly human. They were repulsive. But the Mother Superior stood among them like Charity itself. When she wished to leave the room they would not let her go, but clung to her, so that, with smiling expostulations, she had to use a gentle force to free herself. They at all events found nothing terrifying in this great lady.

'You know of course,' she said, as they walked along another corridor, 'that they are only orphans in the sense that their parents have wished to be rid of them. We give them a few cash for every child that is brought in, otherwise they will not take the trouble, but do away with them.' She turned to the Sister. 'Have any come today?' she asked.

'Four.'

'Now, with the cholera, they are more than ever anxious not to be burdened with useless girls.'

She showed Kitty the dormitories and then they passed a door on which was painted the word *infirmerie*. Kitty heard groans and loud cries and sounds as though beings not human were in pain.

'I will not show you the infirmary,' said the Mother Superior in her placid tones. 'It is not a sight that one would wish to see.' A thought struck her. 'I wonder if Dr Fane is there?'

She looked interrogatively at the Sister and she, with her merry smile, opened the door and slipped in. Kitty shrank back as the open door allowed her to hear more horribly the tumult within. Sister St Joseph came back.

'No, he has been and will not be back again till later.'

'What about number six?'

'*Pauvre garçon*, he's dead.'

The Mother Superior crossed herself and her lips moved in a short and silent prayer.

They passed by a courtyard and Kitty's eyes fell upon two long shapes that lay side by side on the ground covered with a piece of blue cotton. The Superior turned to Waddington.

'We are so short of beds that we have to put two patients in one and the moment a sick man dies he must be bundled out in order to make room for another.' But she gave Kitty a smile. 'Now we will show you our chapel. We are very proud of it. One of our friends in France sent us a little while ago a life-size statue of the Blessed Virgin.'

Chapter Forty-three

The chapel was no more than a long low room with whitewashed walls and rows of deal benches; at the end was the altar on which stood the image; it was in plaster of Paris painted in crude colours; it was very bright and new and garish. Behind it was a picture in oils of the Crucifixion with the two Marys at the foot of the Cross in extravagant attitudes of grief. The drawing was bad and the dark pigments were put on with an eye that knew nothing of the beauty of colour. Around the walls were the Stations of the Cross painted by the same unfortunate hand. The chapel was hideous and vulgar.

The nuns on entering knelt down to say a prayer and then, rising, the Mother Superior began once more to chat with Kitty.

'Everything that can be broken is broken when it comes here, but the statue presented to us by our benefactor came from Paris without so much as the smallest chip. There is no doubt that it was a miracle.'

Waddington's malicious eyes gleamed, but he held his tongue.

'The altarpiece and the Stations of the Cross were painted by one of our Sisters, Sœur St Anselme.' The Mother Superior crossed herself. 'She was a real artist. Unfortunately, she fell a victim to the epidemic. Do you not think that they are very beautiful?'

Kitty faltered an affirmative. On the altar were bunches of paper flowers and the candlesticks were distractingly ornate.

'We have the privilege of keeping here the Blessed Sacrament.'

'Yes?' said Kitty, not understanding.

'It has been a great comfort to us during this time of so terrible trouble.'

They left the chapel and retraced their step to the parlour in which they had first sat.

'Would you like to see the babies that came in this morning before you go?'

'Very much,' said Kitty.

The Mother Superior led them into a tiny room on the other side of the passage. On a table, under a cloth, there was a singular wriggling. The Sister drew back the cloth and displayed four tiny, naked infants. They were very red and they made funny restless movements with their arms and legs; their quaint little Chinese faces were screwed up into strange grimaces. They looked hardly human; queer animals of an unknown species, and yet there was something singularly moving in the sight. The Mother Superior looked at them with an amused smile.

'They seem very lively. Sometimes they are brought in only to die. Of course we baptise them the moment they come.'

'The lady's husband will be pleased with them,' said Sister St Joseph. 'I think he could play by the hour with the babies. When they cry he has only to take them up, and he makes them comfortable in the crook of his arm, so that they laugh with delight.'

Then Kitty and Waddington found themselves at the door. Kitty gravely thanked the Mother Superior for the trouble she had taken. The nun bowed with a condescension that was at once dignified and affable.

'It has been a great pleasure. You do not know how kind and helpful your husband has been to us. He has been sent to us by Heaven. I am glad that you came with him. When he goes home it must be a great comfort to him to have you there with your love and your—your sweet face. You must take care of him and not let him work too hard. You must look after him for all our sakes.'

Kitty flushed. She did not know what to say. The Mother Superior held out her hand and while she held it Kitty was conscious of those cool, thoughtful eyes which rested on her with detachment and yet with something that looked like a profound understanding.

Sister St Joseph closed the door behind them and Kitty got into her chair. They went back through the narrow, winding streets. Waddington made a casual remark: Kitty did not answer. He looked round, but the side curtains of the chair were drawn and he could not see her. He walked on in silence. But when they reached the river and she stepped out to his surprise he saw that her eyes were streaming with tears.

'What is the matter?' he asked, his face puckered into an expression of dismay.

'Nothing.' She tried to smile. 'Only foolishness.'

Chapter Forty-four

Alone once more in the sordid parlour of the dead missionary, lying on the long chair that faced the window, her abstracted eyes on the temple across the river (now again at the approach of evening aerial and lovely), Kitty tried to set in order the feelings in her heart. She would never have believed that this visit to the convent could so have moved her. She had gone from curiosity. She had nothing else to do and after looking for so many days at the walled city across the water she was not unwilling to have at least a glimpse of its mysterious streets.

But once within the convent it had seemed to her that she was transported into another world situated strangely neither in space nor time. Those bare rooms and the white corridors, austere and simple, seemed to possess the spirit of something remote and mystical. The little chapel, so ugly and vulgar, in its very crudeness was pathetic; it had something which was wanting in the greatness of a cathedral, with its stained glass and its pictures: it was very humble; and the faith which had adorned it, the affection which cherished it, had endued it with a delicate beauty of the soul. The methodical way in which the convent's work was carried on in the midst of the pestilence showed a coolness in the face of danger and a practical sense, almost ironical it was so matter of fact, which were deeply impressive. In Kitty's ears rang still the ghastly sounds she heard when for a moment Sister St Joseph opened the infirmary door.

It was unexpected the way they had spoken of Walter. First the Sister and then the Mother Superior herself, and the tone of her voice had been very gentle when she praised him. Oddly enough it gave her a little thrill of pride to know that they thought so well of him. Waddington also had told something of what Walter was doing; but it was not only his competence that the nuns praised (in Hong-Kong she had known that he was thought clever), they spoke of his thoughtfulness and his tenderness. Of course he could be very tender. He was at his best when you were ill; he was too intelligent to exasperate, and his touch was pleasant, cool and soothing. By some magic he seemed able by his mere presence to relieve your suffering. She knew that she would never see again in his eyes the look of affection which she had once been so used to that she found it merely exasperating. She knew now how immense was his capacity for loving; in some odd way he was pouring it out on these wretched sick who had only him to look to. She did not feel jealousy, but a sense of emptiness; it was as though a support that she had grown so accustomed to as not to realise its presence were suddenly withdrawn from her so that she swayed this way and that like a thing that was top-heavy.

She had only contempt for herself because once she had felt contempt for Walter. He must have known how she regarded him and he had accepted her estimate without bitterness. She was a fool and he knew it and because he loved her it had made no difference to him. She did not hate him now, nor feel resentment of him, but fear rather and perplexity. She could not admit but that he had remarkable qualities, sometimes she thought that there was even in him a strange and unattractive greatness; it was curious then that she could not love him, but loved still a man whose worthlessness was now so clear to her. After thinking, thinking, all through those long days she rated accurately Charles Townsend's value; he was a common fellow and his qualities were second-rate. If she could only tear from her heart the love that still lingered there! She tried not to think of him.

Waddington too thought highly of Walter. She alone had been blind to his merit. Why? Because he loved her and she did not love him. What was it in the human heart that made you despise a man because he loved you? But Waddington had confessed that he did not like Walter. Men didn't. It was easy to see that those two nuns had for him a feeling which was very like affection. He was different with women; notwithstanding his shyness you felt in him an exquisite kindliness.

Chapter Forty-five

But after all it was the nuns that had most deeply touched her. Sister St Joseph, with her merry face and apple red cheeks; she had been one of the little band that came out to China with the Mother Superior ten years before and she had seen one after another of her companions die of disease, privation and homesickness; and yet she remained cheerful and happy. What was it that gave her that naïve and charming humour? And the Mother Superior. Kitty in fancy stood again in her presence and once more she felt humble and ashamed. Though she was so simple and unaffected she had a native dignity which inspired awe, and you could not imagine that any one could treat her without respect. Sister St Joseph by the way she stood, by every small gesture and the intonation of her answers, had shown the deep submission in which she held herself; and Waddington, frivolous and impertinent, had shown by his tone that he was not quite at his ease. Kitty thought it unnecessary to have told her that the Mother Superior belonged to one of the great families of France; there was that in her bearing which suggested ancient race, and she had the authority of one who has never known that it is possible to be disobeyed. She had the condescension of a great lady and the humility of a saint. There was in her strong, handsome and ravaged face an austerity that was passionate; and at the same time she had a solicitude and a gentleness which permitted those little children to cluster, noisy and unafraid, in the assurance of her deep affection. When she had looked at the four new-born babies she had worn a smile that was sweet and yet profound: it was like a ray of sunshine on a wild and desolate heath. What Sister St Joseph had said so carelessly of Walter moved Kitty strangely; she knew that he had desperately wanted her to bear a child, but she had never suspected from his reticence that he was capable with a baby of showing without embarrassment a charming and playful tenderness. Most men were silly and awkward with babies. How strange he was!

But to all that moving experience there had been a shadow (a dark lining to the silver cloud), insistent and plain, which disconcerted her. In the sober gaiety of Sister St Joseph, and much more in the beautiful courtesy of the Mother Superior, she had felt an aloofness which oppressed her. They were friendly and even cordial, but at the same time they held something back, she knew not what, so that she was conscious that she was nothing but a casual stranger. There was a barrier between her and them. They spoke a different language not only of the tongue but of the heart. And when the door was closed upon her she felt that they had put her out of their minds so completely, going about their neglected work again without delay, that for them she might never have existed. She felt shut out not only from that poor little convent, but from some mysterious garden of the spirit after which with all her soul she hankered. She felt on a sudden alone as she had never felt alone before. That was why she had wept.

And now, throwing back her head wearily, she sighed: 'Oh, I'm so worthless.'

Chapter Forty-six

That evening Walter came back to the bungalow a little earlier than usual. Kitty was lying on the long chair by the open window. It was nearly dark.

'Don't you want a lamp?' he asked.

'They'll bring it when dinner is ready.'

He talked to her always quite casually, of trifling things, as though they were friendly acquaintances, and there was never anything in his manner to suggest that he harboured malice in his heart. He never met her eyes and he never smiled. He was scrupulously polite.

'Walter, what do you propose we should do if we get through the epidemic?' she asked.

He waited for a moment before answering. She could not see his face.

'I haven't thought.'

In the old days she said carelessly whatever came into her head; it never occurred to her to think before she spoke; but now she was afraid of him; she felt her lips tremble and her heart beat painfully.

'I went to the convent this afternoon.'

'So I heard.'

She forced herself to speak though she could hardly frame the words.

'Did you really want me to die when you brought me here?'

'If I were you I'd leave well alone, Kitty. I don't think any good will come of talking about what we should do much better to forget.'

'But you don't forget; neither do I. I've been thinking a great deal since I came here. Won't you listen to what I have to say?'

'Certainly.'

'I treated you very badly. I was unfaithful to you.'

He stood stock still. His immobility was strangely terrifying.

'I don't know whether you'll understand what I mean. That sort of thing doesn't mean very much to a woman when it's over. I think women have never quite understood the attitude that men take up.' She spoke abruptly, in a voice she would hardly have recognised as her own. 'You know what Charlie was and you knew what he'd do. Well, you were quite right. He's a worthless creature. I suppose I shouldn't have been taken in by him if I hadn't been as worthless as he. I don't ask you to forgive me. I don't ask you to love me as you used to love me. But couldn't we be friends? With all these people dying in thousands round us, and with those nuns in their convent . . .'

'What have they got to do with it?' he interrupted.

'I can't quite explain. I had such a singular feeling when I went there to-day. It all seems to mean so much. It's all so terrible and their self-sacrifice is so wonderful; I can't help feeling it's absurd and disproportionate, if you understand what I mean, to distress yourself because a foolish woman has been unfaithful to you. I'm much too worthless and insignificant for you to give me a thought.'

He did not answer, but he did not move away; he seemed to be waiting for her to continue.

'Mr Waddington and the nuns have told me such wonderful things about you. I'm very proud of you, Walter.'

'You used not to be; you used to feel contempt for me. Don't you still?'

'Don't you know that I'm afraid of you?'

Again he was silent.

'I don't understand you,' he said at last. 'I don't know what it is you want.'

'Nothing for myself. I only want you to be a little less unhappy.'

She felt him stiffen and his voice was very cold when he answered.

'You're mistaken in thinking I'm unhappy. I have a great deal too much to do to think of you very often.'

'I have wondered if the nuns would allow me to go and work at the convent. They are very shorthanded and if I could be of any help I should be grateful to them.'

'It is not easy work or pleasant work. I doubt if it would amuse you long.'

'Do you absolutely despise me, Walter?'

'No.' He hesitated and his voice was strange. 'I despise myself.'

Chapter Forty-seven

It was after dinner. As usual Walter sat by the lamp and read. He read every evening till Kitty went to bed and then went into a laboratory which he had fitted up in one of the bungalow's empty rooms. Here he worked late into the night. He slept little. He was occupied with she knew not what experiments. He told her nothing of his work; but even in the old days he had been reticent on this: he was not by nature expansive. She thought deeply of what he had just said to her: the conversation had led to nothing. She knew him so little that she could not be sure if he was speaking the truth or not. Was it possible that, whereas he now existed so ominously for her, she had entirely ceased to exist for him? Her conversation which had entertained him once because he loved her, now that he loved her no longer might be merely tedious to him. It mortified her.

She looked at him. The light of the lamp displayed his profile as though it were a cameo. With his regular and finely-cut features it was very distinguished, but it was more than severe, it was grim: that immobility of his, only his eyes moving as he perused each page, was vaguely terrifying. Who would have thought that this hard face could be melted by passion to such tenderness of expression? She knew and it excited in her a little shiver of distaste. It was strange that though he was good-looking as well as honest, reliable and talented, it had been so impossible for her to love him. It was a relief that she need never again submit to his caresses.

He would not answer when she had asked him whether in forcing her to come here he had really wished to kill her. The mystery of this fascinated and horrified her. He was so extraordinarily kind; it was incredible that he could have had such a devilish intention. He must have suggested it only to frighten her and to get back on Charlie (that would be like his sardonic humour) and then from obstinacy or from fear of looking foolish insisted on her going through with it.

Yes, he said he despised himself. What did he mean by that? Once again Kitty looked at his calm cool face. She might not even be in the room, he was so unconscious of her.

'Why do you despise yourself?' she asked, hardly knowing that she spoke, as though she were continuing without a break the earlier conversation.

He put down his book and observed her reflectively. He seemed to gather his thoughts from a remote distance.

'Because I loved you.'

She flushed and looked away. She could not bear his cold, steady and appraising gaze. She understood what he meant. It was a little while before she answered.

'I think you do me an injustice,' she said. 'It's not fair to blame me because I was silly and frivolous and vulgar. I was brought up like that. All the girls I know are like that. . . . It's like reproaching some one who has no ear for music because he's bored at a symphony concert. Is it fair to blame me because you ascribed to me qualities I hadn't got? I never tried to deceive you by pretending I was anything I wasn't. I was just pretty and gay. You don't ask for a pearl necklace or a sable coat at a booth in a fair; you ask for a tin trumpet and a toy balloon.'

'I don't blame you.'

His voice was weary. She was beginning to feel a trifle impatient with him. Why could he not realise, what suddenly had become so clear to her, that beside all the terror of death under whose shadow they lay and beside the awe of the beauty which she had caught a glimpse of that day, their own affairs were trivial? What did it really matter if a silly woman had committed adultery and why should her husband, face to face with the sublime, give it a thought? It was strange that Walter with all his cleverness should have so little sense of proportion. Because he had dressed a doll in gorgeous robes and set her in a sanctuary to worship her, and then discovered that the doll was filled with sawdust he could neither forgive himself nor her. His soul was lacerated. It was all make-believe that he had lived on, and when the truth shattered it he thought reality itself was shattered. It was true enough, he would not forgive her because he could not forgive himself.

She thought that she heard him give a faint sigh and she shot a rapid glance at him. A sudden thought struck her and it took her breath away. She only just refrained from giving a cry.

Was it what they called–a broken heart–that he suffered from?

Chapter Forty-eight

All the next day Kitty thought of the convent; and the morning after, early, soon after Walter had gone, taking the amah with her to get chairs, she crossed the river. It was barely day and the Chinese crowding the ferry boat, some in the blue cotton of the peasant, others in the black robes of respectability, had a strange look of the dead being borne over the water to the land of shadow. And when they stepped ashore they stood for a little at the landing-place uncertainly as though they did not quite know where to go, before desultorily, in twos and threes, they wandered up the hill.

At that hour the streets of the city were very empty so that more than ever it seemed a city of the dead. The passers-by had an abstracted air so that you might almost have thought them ghosts. The sky was unclouded and the early sun shed a heavenly mildness on the scene; it was difficult to imagine, on that blithe, fresh and smiling morn, that the city lay gasping, like a man whose life is being throttled out of him by a maniac's hands, in the dark clutch of the pestilence. It was incredible that nature (the blue of the sky was clear like a child's heart) should be so indifferent when men were writhing in agony and going to their death in fear. When the chairs were set down at the convent door a beggar arose from the ground and asked Kitty for alms. He was clad in faded and shapeless rags that looked as though he had raked them out of a muck-heap, and through their rents you saw his skin hard and rough and tanned like the hide of a goat; his bare legs were emaciated, and his head, with its shock of coarse grey hair (the cheeks hollow, the eyes wild), was the head of a madman. Kitty turned from him in frightened horror, and the chair-bearers in gruff tones bade him begone, but he was importunate, and to be rid of him, shuddering, Kitty gave him a few cash.

The door was opened and the amah explained that Kitty wished to see the Mother Superior. She was taken once more into the stiff parlour in which it seemed a window had never been opened, and here she sat so long that she began to think her message had not been delivered. At last the Mother Superior came in.

'I must ask you to excuse me for keeping you waiting,' she said. 'I did not expect you and I was occupied.'

'Forgive me for troubling you. I am afraid I have come at an inconvenient moment.'

The Mother Superior gave her a smile, austere but sweet, and begged her to sit down. But Kitty saw that her eyes were swollen. She had been weeping. Kitty was startled, for she had received from the Mother Superior the impression that she was a woman whom earthly troubles could not greatly move.

'I am afraid something has happened,' she faltered. 'Would you like me to go away? I can come another time.'

'No, no. Tell me what I can do for you. It is only–only that one of our Sisters died last night.' Her voice lost its even tone and her eyes filled with tears. 'It is wicked of me to grieve, for I know that her good and simple soul has flown straight to heaven; she was a saint; but it is difficult always to control one's weakness. I am afraid I am not always very reasonable.'

'I'm so sorry, I'm so dreadfully sorry,' said Kitty.

Her ready sympathy brought a sob into her voice.

'She was one of the Sisters who came out from France with me ten years ago. There are only three of us left now. I remember, we stood in a little group at the end of the boat (what do you call it, the bow?) and as we steamed out of the harbour at Marseilles and we saw the golden figure of Saint-Marie la Grace, we said a prayer together. It had been my greatest wish since I entered religion to be allowed to come to China, but when I saw the land grow distant I could not prevent myself from weeping. I was their Superior; it was not a very good example I was giving my daughters. And then Sister St Francis Xavier–that is the name of the Sister who died last night–took my hand and told me not to grieve; for wherever we were, she said, there was France and there was God.'

That severe and handsome face was distorted by the grief which human nature wrung from her and by the effort to restrain the tears which her reason and her faith refused. Kitty looked away. She felt that it was indecent to peer into that struggle.

'I have been writing to her father. She, like me, was her mother's only daughter. They were fisher folk in Brittany, and it will be hard for them. Oh, when will this terrible epidemic cease? Two of our girls have been attacked this morning and nothing but a miracle can save them. These Chinese have no resistance. The loss of Sister St Francis is very severe. There is so much to do and now fewer than ever to do it. We have Sisters at our other houses in China who are eager to come, all our Order, I think, would give anything in the world (only they have nothing) to come here; but it is almost certain death; and so long as we can manage with the Sisters we have I am unwilling that others should be sacrificed.'

'That encourages me, *ma mère*,' said Kitty. 'I have been feeling that I had come at a very unfortunate moment. You said the other day that there was more work than the Sisters could do, and I was wondering if you would allow me to come and help them. I do not mind what I do if I can only be useful. I should be thankful if you just set me to scrub the floors.'

The Mother Superior gave an amused smile and Kitty was astonished at the mobile temperament which could so easily pass from mood to mood.

'There is no need to scrub the floors. That is done after a fashion by the orphans.' She paused and looked kindly at Kitty. 'My dear child, do you not think that you have done enough in coming with your husband here? That is more than many wives would have had the courage to do, and for the rest how can you be better occupied than in giving him peace and comfort when he comes home to you after the day's work? Believe me, he needs then all your love and all your consideration.'

Kitty could not easily meet the eyes which rested on her with a detached scrutiny and with an ironical kindliness.

'I have nothing whatever to do from morning till night,' said Kitty. 'I feel that there is so much to be done that I cannot bear to think that I am idle. I don't want to make a nuisance of myself, and I know that I have no claim either on your kindness or on your time, but I mean what I say and it would be a charity that you were doing me if you would let me be of some help to you.'

'You do not look very strong. When you did us the pleasure of coming to see us the day before yesterday it seemed to me that you were very pale. Sister St Joseph thought that perhaps you were going to have a baby.'

'No, no,' cried Kitty, flushing to the roots of her hair.

The Mother Superior gave a little, silvery laugh.

'It is nothing to be ashamed of, my dear child, nor is there anything improbable in the supposition. How long have you been married?'

'I am very pale because I am naturally pale, but I am very strong, and I promise you I am not afraid of work.'

Now the Superior was complete mistress of herself. She assumed unconsciously the air of authority which was habitual to her and she held Kitty in an appraising scrutiny. Kitty felt unaccountably nervous.

'Can you speak Chinese?'

'I'm afraid not,' answered Kitty.

'Ah, that is a pity. I could have put you in charge of the elder girls. It is very difficult just now, and I am afraid they will get—what do you call? Out of hand?' she concluded with a tentative sound.

'Could I not be of help to the Sisters in nursing? I am not at all afraid of the cholera. I could nurse the girls or the soldiers.'

The Mother Superior, unsmiling now, a reflective look on her face, shook her head.

'You do not know what the cholera is. It is a dreadful thing to see. The work in the infirmary is done by soldiers and we need a Sister only to supervise. And so far as the girls are concerned . . . no, no, I am sure your husband would not wish it; it is a terrible and frightening sight.'

'I should grow used to it.'

'No, it is out of the question. It is our business and our privilege to do such things, but there is no call for you to do so.'

'You make me feel very useless and very helpless. It seems incredible that there should be nothing that I can do.'

'Have you spoken to your husband of your wish?'

'Yes.'

The Mother Superior looked at her as though she were delving into the secrets of her heart, but when she saw Kitty's anxious and appealing look she gave a smile.

'Of course you are a Protestant?' she asked.

'Yes.'

'It doesn't matter. Dr Watson, the missionary who died, was a Protestant, and it made no difference. He was all that was most charming to us. We owe him a deep debt of gratitude.'

Now the flicker of a smile passed over Kitty's face, but she did not say anything. The Mother Superior seemed to reflect. She rose to her feet.

'It is very good of you. I think I can find something for you to do. It is true that now Sister St Francis has been taken from us, it is impossible for us to cope with the work. When will you be ready to start?'

'Now.'

'*A la bonne heure.* I am content to hear you say that.'

'I promise you I will do my best. I am very grateful to you for the opportunity that you are giving me.'

The Mother Superior opened the parlour door, but as she was going out she hesitated. Once more she gave Kitty a long, searching and sagacious look. Then she laid her hand gently on her arm.

'You know, my dear child, that one cannot find peace in work or in pleasure, in the world or in a convent, but only in one's soul.'

Kitty gave a little start, but the Mother Superior passed swiftly out.

Chapter Forty-nine

Kitty found the work a refreshment to her spirit. She went to the convent every morning soon after sunrise and did not return to the bungalow till the westering sun flooded the narrow river and its crowded junks with gold. The Mother Superior gave into her care the smaller children. Kitty's mother had brought to London from her native Liverpool a practical sense of housewifery and Kitty, notwithstanding her air of frivolity, had always had certain gifts to which she referred only in bantering tones. Thus she could cook quite well and she sewed beautifully. When she disclosed this talent she was set to supervise the stitching and hemming of the younger girls. They knew a little French and every day she picked up a few words of Chinese so that it was not difficult for her to manage. At other times she had to see that the smaller children did not get into mischief; she had to dress and undress them and take care that they rested when rest was needed. There were a good many babies and these were in charge of amahs, but she was bidden to keep an eye on them. None of the work was very important and she would have liked to do something which was more arduous; but the Mother Superior paid no attention to her entreaties and Kitty stood sufficiently in awe of her not to be importunate.

For the first few days she had to make something of an effort to overcome the faint distaste she felt for these little girls, in their ugly uniforms, with their stiff black hair, their round yellow faces, and their staring, sloe-black eyes. But she remembered the soft look which had transfigured so beautifully the countenance of the Mother Superior when on Kitty's first visit to the convent she had stood surrounded by those ugly little things, and she would not allow herself to surrender to her instinct. And presently, taking in her arms one or other of the tiny creatures, crying because of a fall or a cutting tooth, when Kitty found that a few soft words, though in a language the child could not understand, the pressure of her arms and the softness of her cheek against the weeping yellow face, could comfort and console, she began to lose all her feeling of strangeness. The small children, without any fear of her, came to her in their childish troubles and it gave her a peculiar happiness to discern their confidence. It was the same with the older girls, those to whom she taught sewing; their bright, clever smiles and the pleasure she could give them by a word of praise, touched her. She felt that they liked her and, flattered and proud, she liked them in return.

But there was one child that she could not grow used to. It was a little girl of six, an idiot with a huge hydrocephalic head that swayed top-heavily on a small, squat body, large vacant eyes and a drooling mouth; the creature spoke hoarsely a few mumbled words; it was revolting and horrible; and for some reason it conceived an idiot attachment for Kitty so that it followed her about as she changed her place from one part of the large room to another. It clung to her skirt and rubbed its face against her knees. It sought to fondle her hands. She shivered with disgust. She knew it yearned for caresses and she could not bring herself to touch it.

Once, speaking of it to Sister St Joseph, she said that it was a pity it lived. Sister St Joseph smiled and stretched out her hand to the misformed thing. It came and rubbed its bulging forehead against it.

'Poor little mite,' said the nun. 'She was brought here positively dying. By the mercy of Providence I was at the door just as she came. I thought there was not a moment to lose so I baptised her at once. You would not believe what trouble we have had to keep her with us. Three or four times we thought that her little soul would escape to heaven.'

Kitty was silent. Sister St Joseph in her loquacious way began to gossip of other things. And next day when the idiot child came to her and touched her hand Kitty nerved herself to place it in a caress on the great bare skull. She forced her lips into a smile. But suddenly the child, with an idiot perversity, left her; it seemed to lose interest in her, and that day and the following days paid her no attention. Kitty did not know what she had done and tried to lure it to her with smiles and gestures, but it turned away and pretended not to see her.

Chapter Fifty

Since the nuns were busy from morning till night with a hundred duties Kitty saw little of them, but at the services in the bare, humble chapel. On her first day the Mother Superior, catching sight of her seated at the back behind the girls on the benches according to their ages, stopped and spoke to her.

'You must not think it necessary for you to come to the chapel when we do,' she said. 'You are a Protestant and you have your own convictions.'

'But I like to come, Mother. I find that it rests me.'

The Mother Superior gave her a moment's glance and slightly inclined her grave head.

'Of course you will do exactly as you choose. I merely wanted you to understand that you are under no obligation.'

But with Sister St Joseph Kitty soon became on terms not of intimacy perhaps but of familiarity. The economy of the convent was in her charge and to look after the material well-being of that big family kept the Sister on her feet all day. She said that the only time she had to rest was that which she devoted to prayer. But it pleased her towards evening when Kitty was with the girls at their work to come in and, vowing that she was tired out and had not a moment to spare, sit down for a few minutes and gossip. When she was not in the presence of the Mother Superior she was a talkative, merry creature, fond of a joke, and she did not dislike a bit of scandal. Kitty stood in no fear of her, her habit did not prevent Sister St Joseph from being a good-natured, homely woman, and she chattered with her gaily. She did not mind with her showing how badly she talked French and they laughed with one another over Kitty's mistakes. The Sister taught her every day a few useful words of Chinese. She was a farmer's daughter and at heart she was still a peasant.

'I used to keep the cows when I was little,' she said, 'like St Joan of Arc. But I was too wicked to have visions. It was fortunate, I think, for my father would certainly have whipped me if I had. He used often to whip me, the good old man, for I was a very naughty little girl. I am ashamed sometimes when I think now of the pranks I used to play.'

Kitty laughed at the thought that this corpulent, middle-aged nun could ever have been a wayward child. And yet there was something childlike in her still so that your heart went out to her: she seemed to have about her an aroma of the countryside in autumn when the apple trees are laden with fruit and the crops are in and safely housed. She had not the tragic and austere saintliness of the Mother Superior, but a gaiety that was simple and happy.

'Do you never wish to go home again, *ma sœur?*' asked Kitty.

'Oh, no. It would be too hard to come back. I love to be here and I am never so happy as when I am among the orphans. They're so good, they're so grateful. But it is all very well to be a nun (*on a beau être religieuse*) still one has a mother and one cannot forget that one drank the milk of her breasts. She is old, my mother, and it is hard never to see her again; but then she is fond of her daughter-in-law, and my brother is good to her. His son is growing up now, I should think they will be glad of an extra pair of strong arms on the farm; he was only a child when I left France, but he promised to have a fist that you could fell an ox with.'

It was almost impossible in that quiet room, listening to the nun, to realise that on the other side of these four walls cholera was raging. Sister St Joseph had an unconcern which conveyed itself to Kitty.

She had a naïve curiosity about the world and its inhabitants. She asked Kitty all kinds of questions about London and England, a country, she thought, where so thick was the fog that you could not see your hand at mid-day, and she wanted to know if Kitty went to balls and whether she lived in a grand house and how many brothers and sisters she had. She spoke often of Walter. The Mother Superior said he was wonderful and every day they prayed for him. How lucky Kitty was to have a husband who was so good and so brave and so clever.

Chapter Fifty-one

But sooner or later Sister St Joseph returned to the subject of the Mother Superior. Kitty had been conscious from the beginning that the personality of this woman dominated the convent. She was regarded by all that dwelt there with love certainly and with admiration, but also with awe and not a little dread. Notwithstanding her kindliness Kitty herself felt like a schoolgirl in her presence. She was never quite at her ease with her, for she was filled with a sentiment which was so strange that it embarrassed her: reverence. Sister St Joseph with an ingenuous desire to impress, told Kitty how great the family was to which the Mother Superior belonged; she had among her ancestors persons of historic importance and she was *un peu cousine* with half the kings in Europe: Alphonso of Spain had hunted at her father's, and they had *châteaux* all over France. It must have been hard to leave so much grandeur. Kitty listened smilingly, but not a little impressed.

'*Du reste*, you have only to look at her,' said the Sister, 'to see that, *comme famille, c'est le dessus du panier*'.

'She has the most beautiful hands that I have ever seen,' said Kitty.

'Ah, but if you only knew how she had used them. She is not afraid of work, *notre bonne mère.*'

When they had come to this city there had been nothing. They had built the convent. The Mother Superior had made the plans and supervised the work. The moment they arrived they began to save the poor little unwanted girls from the baby-tower and the cruel hands of the midwife. At first they had had no beds to sleep in and no glass to keep out the night air ('and there is nothing,' said Sister St Joseph, 'which is more unwholesome'); and often they had no money left, not only to pay the builders, but even to buy their simple fare; they lived like peasants, what was she saying? the peasants in France, *tenez*, the men who worked for her father, would have thrown to the pigs the food they ate. And then the Mother Superior would collect her daughters round her and they would kneel and pray; and the Blessed Virgin would send money. A thousand francs would arrive by post next day, or a stranger, an Englishman (a Protestant, if you please) or even a Chinaman would knock at the door while they were actually on their knees and bring them a present. Once they were in such straits that they all made a vow to the Blessed Virgin that they would recite a *neuvaine* in her honour if she succoured them, and, would you believe it? that funny Mr Waddington came to see us next day and saying that we looked as though we all wanted a good plate of roast beef gave us a hundred dollars.

What a comic little man he was, with his bald head and his little shrewd eyes (*ses petits yeux malins*) and his jokes. *Mon Dieu*, how he murdered the French language, and yet you could not help laughing at him. He was always in a good humour. All through this terrible epidemic he carried himself as if he were enjoying a holiday. He had a heart quite French and a wit so that you would hardly believe he was English. Except for his accent. But sometimes Sister St Joseph thought he spoke badly on purpose to make you laugh. Of course his morals were not all one could wish; but still that was his business (with a sigh, a shrug and a shake of the head) and he was a bachelor and a young man.

'What is wrong with his morals, *ma sœur?*' asked Kitty smiling.

'Is it possible that you do not know? It is a sin for me to tell you. I have no business to say such things. He lives with a Chinese woman, that is to say, not a Chinese woman, but a Manchu. A princess, it appears, and she loves him to distraction.'

'That sounds quite impossible,' cried Kitty.

'No, no, I promise you, it is everything that is most true. It is very wicked of him. Those things are not done. Did you not hear, when you first came to the convent and he would not eat the *madeleines* that I had made expressly, that *notre bonne mère* said his stomach was deranged by Manchu cooking? That was what she meant and you should have seen the head that he made. It is a story altogether curious. It appears that he was stationed at Hankow during the revolution when they were massacring the Manchus and this good little Waddington saved the lives of one of their great families. They are related to the Imperial Family. The girl fell violently in love with him and—well, the rest you can imagine. And then when he left Hankow she ran away and followed him and now she follows him everywhere, and he has had to resign himself to keep her, poor fellow, and I daresay he is very fond of her; they are quite charming sometimes, these Manchu women. But what am I thinking of? I have a thousand things to do and I sit here. I am a bad religious. I am ashamed of myself.'

Chapter Fifty-two

Kitty had a queer feeling that she was growing. The constant occupation distracted her mind and the glimpses she had of other lives and other outlooks awakened her imagination. She began to regain her spirits; she felt better and stronger. It had seemed to her that she could do nothing now but weep; but to her surprise, and not a little to her confusion, she caught herself laughing at this and that. It began to seem quite natural to live in the midst of a terrible epidemic. She knew that people were dying to the right and left of her, but she ceased very much to think of it. The Mother Superior had forbidden her to go into the infirmaries and the closed doors excited her curiosity. She would have liked to peep in, but could not do so without being seen, and she did not know what punishment the Mother Superior would inflict upon her. It would be dreadful to be sent away. She was devoted to the children now and they would miss her if she went; in fact she did not know what they would do without her.

And one day it occurred to her that she had neither thought of Charles Townsend nor dreamt of him for a week. Her heart gave a sudden thud against her ribs: she was cured. She could think of him now with indifference. She loved him no longer. Oh, the relief and the sense of liberation! It was strange to look back and remember how passionately she had yearned for him; she thought she would die when he failed her; she thought life thenceforward had nothing to offer but misery. And now already she was laughing. A worthless creature. What a fool she had made of herself! And now, considering him calmly, she wondered what on earth she had seen in him. It was lucky that Waddington knew nothing, she could never have endured his malicious eyeing and his ironical innuendoes. She was free, free at last, free! She could hardly prevent herself from laughing aloud.

The children were playing some romping game and it was her habit to look on with an indulgent smile, restraining them when they made too much noise and taking care that in their boisterousness none was hurt; but now in her high spirits, feeling as young as any of them, she joined in the game. The little girls received her with delight. They chased up and down the room, shouting at the top of their shrill voices, with fantastic and almost barbarous glee. They grew so excited that they leaped into the air with joy. The noise was terrific.

Suddenly the door opened and the Mother Superior stood on the threshold. Kitty, abashed, extricated herself from the clutches of a dozen little girls who with wild shrieks had seized her.

'Is this how you keep these children good and quiet?' asked the Mother Superior, a smile on her lips.

'We were having a game, Mother. They got excited. It is my fault, I led them on.'

The Mother Superior came forward and as usual the children clustered about her. She put her hands round their narrow shoulders and playfully pulled their little yellow ears. She looked at Kitty with a long, soft look. Kitty was flushed and she was breathing quickly. Her liquid eyes were shining and her lovely hair, disarranged in all the struggling and the laughter, was in adorable confusion.

'*Que vous êtes belle, ma chère enfant,*' said the Mother Superior. 'It does the heart good to look at you. No wonder these children adore you.'

Kitty blushed deeply and, she knew not why, tears suddenly filled her eyes. She covered her face with her hands.

'Oh, Mother, you make me ashamed.'

'Come, do not be silly. Beauty is also a gift of God, one of the most rare and precious, and we should be thankful if we are happy enough to possess it and thankful, if we are not, that others possess it for our pleasure.'

She smiled again and as though Kitty were a child too gently patted her soft cheek.

Chapter Fifty-three

Since she had been working at the convent Kitty had seen less of Waddington. Two or three times he had come down to the river bank to meet her and they had walked up the hill together. He came in to drink a whisky and soda, but he would seldom stay to dinner. One Sunday, however, he suggested that they should take their luncheon with them and go in chairs to a Buddhist monastery. It was situated ten miles from the city and had some reputation as a place of pilgrimage. The Mother Superior, insisting that Kitty must have a day's rest, would not let her work on Sundays and Walter of course was as busy then as usual.

They started early in order to arrive before the heat of the day and were carried along a narrow causeway between the rice-fields. Now and then they passed comfortable farm-houses nestling with friendly intimacy in a groove of bamboos. Kitty enjoyed the idleness; it was pleasant after being cooped up in the city to see about her the wide country. They came to the monastery, straggling low buildings by the side of the river, agreeably shaded by trees, and were led by smiling monks through courtyards, empty with a solemn emptiness, and shown temples with grimacing gods. In the sanctuary sat the Buddha, remote and sad, wistful, abstracted and faintly smiling. There was about everything a sense of dejection; the magnificence was shoddy and ruined; the gods were dusty and the faith that had made them was dying. The monks seemed to stay on sufferance, as though they awaited a notice to quit; and in the smile of the abbot, with his beautiful politeness, was the irony of resignation. One of these days the monks would wander away from the shady, pleasant wood, and the buildings, crumbling and neglected, would be battered by fierce storms and beseiged by the surrounding nature. Wild creepers would twine themselves about the dead images and the trees would grow in the courtyards. Then the gods would dwell there no longer, but evil spirits of darkness.

Chapter Fifty-four

They sat on the steps of a little building (four lacquered columns and a high, tiled roof under which stood a great bronze bell) and watched the river flow sluggish and with many a bend towards the stricken city. They could see its crenellated walls. The heat hung over it like a pall. But the river, though it flowed so slowly, had still a sense of movement and it gave one a melancholy feeling of the transitoriness of things. Everything passed, and what trace of its passage remained? It seemed to Kitty that they were all, the human race, like the drops of water in that river and they flowed on, each so close to the other and yet so far apart, a nameless flood, to the sea. When all things lasted so short a time and nothing mattered very much, it seemed pitiful that men, attaching an absurd importance to trivial objects, should make themselves and one another so unhappy.

'Do you know Harrington Gardens?' she asked Waddington, with a smile in her beautiful eyes.

'No. Why?'

'Nothing; only it's a long way from here. It's where my people live.'

'Are you thinking of going home?'

'No.'

'I suppose you'll be leaving here in a couple of months. The epidemic seems to be abating and the cool weather should see the end of it.'

'I almost think I shall be sorry to go.'

For a moment she thought of the future. She did not know what plans

Walter had in mind. He told her nothing. He was cool, polite, silent and inscrutable. Two little drops in that river that flowed silently towards the unknown; two little drops that to themselves had so much individuality and to the onlooker were but an undistinguishable part of the water.

'Take care the nuns don't start converting you,' said Waddington, with his malicious little smile.

'They're much too busy. Nor do they care. They're wonderful and so kind; and yet – I hardly know how to explain it – there is a wall between them and me. I don't know what it is. It is as though they possessed a secret which made all the difference in their lives and which I was unworthy to share. It is not faith; it is something deeper and more – more significant: they walk in a different world from ours and we shall always be strangers to them. Each day when the convent door closes behind me I feel that for them I have ceased to exist.'

'I can understand that it is something of a blow to your vanity,' he returned mockingly.

'My vanity.'

Kitty shrugged her shoulders. Then, smiling once more, she turned to him lazily.

'Why did you never tell me that you lived with a Manchu Princess?'

'What have those gossiping old women been telling you? I am sure that it is a sin for nuns to discuss the private affairs of the Customs officials.'

'Why should you be so sensitive?'

Waddington glanced down, sideways, so that it gave him an air of slyness. He faintly shrugged his shoulders.

'It's not a thing to advertise. I do not know that it would greatly add to my chances of promotion in the service.'

'Are you very fond of her?'

He looked up now and his ugly little face had the look of a naughty schoolboy's.

'She's abandoned everything for my sake, home, family, security and self-respect. It's a good many years now since she threw everything to the winds to be with me. I've sent her away two or three times, but she's always come back; I've run away from her myself, but she's always followed me. And now I've given it up as a bad job; I think I've got to put up with her for the rest of my life.'

'She must really love you to distraction.'

'It's a rather funny sensation, you know,' he answered, wrinkling a perplexed forehead. 'I haven't the smallest doubt that if I really left her, definitely, she would commit suicide. Not with any ill-feeling towards me, but quite naturally, because she was unwilling to live without me. It is a curious feeling it gives one to know that. It can't help meaning something to you.'

'But it's loving that's the important thing, not being loved. One's not even grateful to the people who love one; if one doesn't love them, they only bore one.'

'I have no experience of the plural,' he replied. 'Mine is only in the singular.'

'Is she really an Imperial Princess?'

'No, that is a romantic exaggeration of the nuns. She belongs to one of the great families of the Manchus, but they have, of course, been ruined by the revolution. She is all the same a very great lady.'

He said it in a tone of pride, so that a smile flickered in Kitty's eyes.

'Are you going to stay here for the rest of your life then?'

'In China? Yes. What would she do elsewhere? When I retire I shall take a little Chinese house in Peking and spend the rest of my days there.'

'Have you any children?'

'No.'

She looked at him curiously. It was strange that this little bald-headed man with his monkey face should have aroused in the alien woman so devastating a passion. She could not tell why the way he spoke of her, notwithstanding his casual manner and his flippant phrases, gave her the impression so strongly of the woman's intense and unique devotion. It troubled her a little.

'It does seem a long way to Harrington Gardens,' she smiled.

'Why do you say that?'

'I don't understand anything. Life is so strange. I feel like some one who's lived all his life by a duck-pond and suddenly is shown the sea. It makes me a little breathless, and yet it fills me with elation. I don't want to die, I want to live. I'm beginning to feel a new courage. I feel like one of those old sailors who set sail for undiscovered seas and I think my soul hankers for the unknown.'

Waddington looked at her reflectively. Her abstracted gaze rested on the smoothness of the river. Two little drops that flowed silently towards the dark, eternal sea.

'May I come and see the Manchu lady?' asked Kitty, suddenly raising her head.

'She can't speak a word of English.'

'You've been very kind to me, you've done a great deal for me, perhaps I could show her by my manner that I had a friendly feeling towards her.'

Waddington gave a thin, mocking little smile, but he answered with good-humour.

'I will come and fetch you one day and she shall give you a cup of jasmine tea.'

She would not tell him that this story of an alien love had from the first moment strangely intrigued her fancy, and the Manchu Princess stood now as the symbol of something that vaguely, but insistently, beckoned to her. She pointed enigmatically to a mystic land of the spirit.

Chapter Fifty-five

But a day or two later Kitty made an unforseen discovery.

She went to the convent as usual and set about her first work of seeing that the children were washed and dressed. Since the nuns held firmly that the night air was harmful, the atmosphere in the dormitory was close and fetid. After the freshness of the morning it always made Kitty a little uncomfortable and she hastened to open such windows as would. But to-day she felt on a sudden desperately sick and with her head swimming she stood at the window trying to compose herself. It had never been as bad as this before. Then nausea overwhelmed her and she vomited. She gave a cry so that the children were frightened, and the older girl who was helping her ran up and, seeing Kitty white and trembling, stopped short with an exclamation. Cholera! The thought flashed through Kitty's mind and then a deathlike feeling came over her; she was seized with terror, she struggled for a moment against the night that seemed agonisingly to run through her veins; she felt horribly ill; and then darkness.

When she opened her eyes she did not at first know where she was. She seemed to be lying on the floor and, moving her head slightly, she thought that there was a pillow under it. She could not remember. The Mother Superior was kneeling by her side, holding smelling salts to her nose, and Sister St Joseph stood looking at her. Then it came back. Cholera! She saw the consternation on the nuns' faces. Sister St Joseph looked huge and her outline was blurred. Once more terror overwhelmed her.

'Oh, Mother, Mother,' she sobbed. 'Am I going to die? I don't want to die.'

'Of course you're not going to die,' said the Mother Superior.

She was quite composed and there was even amusement in her eyes.

'But it's cholera. Where's Walter? Has he been sent for? Oh, Mother, Mother.'

She burst into a flood of tears. The Mother Superior gave her hand and Kitty seized it as though it were a hold upon the life she feared to lose.

'Come, come, my dear child, you mustn't be so silly. It's not cholera or anything of the kind.'

'Where's Walter?'

'Your husband is much too busy to be troubled. In five minutes you'll be perfectly well.'

Kitty looked at her with staring, harassed eyes. Why did she take it so calmly? It was cruel.

'Keep perfectly quiet for a minute,' said the Mother Superior. 'There is nothing to alarm yourself about.'

Kitty felt her heart beat madly. She had grown so used to the thought of cholera that it had ceased to seem possible that she could catch it. Oh, the fool she had been! She knew she was going to die. She was frightened. The girls brought in a long rattan chair and placed it by the window.

'Come, let us lift you,' said the Mother Superior. 'You will be more comfortable on the *chaise longue*. Do you think you can stand?'

She put her hands under Kitty's arms and Sister St Joseph helped her to her feet. She sank exhausted into the chair.

'I had better shut the window,' said Sister St Joseph. 'The early morning air cannot be good for her.'

'No, no,' said Kitty. 'Please leave it open.'

It gave her confidence to see the blue sky. She was shaken, but certainly she began to feel better. The two nuns looked at her for a moment in silence, and Sister St Joseph said something to the Mother Superior which she could not understand. Then the Mother Superior sat on the side of the chair and took her hand.

'Listen, *ma chère enfant*. . .'

She asked her one or two questions. Kitty answered them without knowing what they meant. Her lips were trembling so that she could hardly frame the words.

'There is no doubt about it,' said Sister St Joseph. 'I am not one to be deceived in such a matter.'

She gave a little laugh in which Kitty seemed to discern a certain excitement and not a little affection. The Mother Superior, still holding Kitty's hand, smiled with soft tenderness.

'Sister St Joseph has more experience of these things than I have, dear child, and she said at once what was the matter with you. She was evidently quite right.'

'What do you mean?' asked Kitty anxiously.

'It is quite evident. Did the possibility of such a thing never occur to you? You are with child, my dear.'

The start that Kitty gave shook her from head to foot, and she put her feet to the ground as though to spring up.

'Lie still, lie still,' said the Mother Superior.

Kitty felt herself blush furiously and she put her hands to her breasts.

'It's impossible. It isn't true.'

Qu'est ce qu'elle dit? asked Sister St Joseph.

The Mother Superior translated. Sister St Joseph's broad simple face, with its red cheeks, was beaming.

'No mistakes is possible. I give you my word of honour.'

'How long have you been married, my child?' asked the Mother Superior. 'Why, when my sister-in-law had been married as long as you she had already two babies.'

Kitty sank back into the chair. There was death in her heart.

'I'm so ashamed,' she whispered.

'Because you are going to have a baby? Why, what can be more natural?'

'Quelle joie pour le docteur,' said Sister St Joseph.

'Yes, think what a happiness for your husband. He will be overwhelmed with joy. You have only to see him with babies, and the look on his face when he plays with them, to see how enchanted he will be to have one of his own.'

For a little while Kitty was silent. The two nuns looked at her with tender interest and the Mother Superior stroked her hand.

'It was silly of me not to have suspected it before,' said Kitty. 'At all events I'm glad it's not cholera. I feel very much better. I will get back to my work.'

'Not today, my dear child. You have had a shock, you had much better go home and rest yourself.'

'No, no, I would much rather stay and work.'

'I insist. What would our good doctor say if I let you be imprudent? Come tomorrow, if you like, or the day after, but today you must be quiet. I will send for a chair. Would you like me to let one of our young girls go with you?'

'Oh, no, I shall be all right alone.'

Chapter Fifty-six

Kitty was lying on her bed and the shutters were closed. It was after luncheon and the servants slept. What she had learnt that morning (and now she was certain that it was true) filled her with consternation. Ever since she came home she had been trying to think; but her mind was a blank, and she could not collect her thoughts. Suddenly she heard a step, the feet were booted so that it could not be one of the boys; with a gasp of apprehension she realised that it could only be her husband. He was in the sitting-room and she heard herself called. She did not reply. There was a moment's silence and then a knock on her door.

'Yes?'

'May I come in?'

Kitty rose from her bed and slipped into a dressing-gown.

'Yes.'

He entered. She was glad that the closed shutters shadowed her face.

'I hope I didn't wake you. I knocked very, very gently.'

'I haven't been asleep.'

He went to one of the windows and threw open the shutter. A flood of warm light streamed into the room.

'What is it?' she asked. 'Why are you back so early?'

'The Sisters said that you weren't very well. I thought I had better come and see what was the matter.'

A flash of anger passed through her.

'What would you have said if it had been cholera?'

'If it had been you certainly couldn't have made your way home this morning.'

She went to the dressing-table and passed the comb through her shingled hair. She wanted to gain time. Then, sitting down, she lit a cigarette.

'I wasn't very well this morning and the Mother Superior thought I'd better come back here. But I'm perfectly all right again. I shall go to the convent as usual tomorrow.'

'What was the matter with you?'

'Didn't they tell you?'

'No. The Mother Superior said that you must tell me yourself.'

He did now what he did seldom; he looked her full in the face; his professional instincts were stronger than his personal. She hesitated. Then she forced herself to meet his eyes.

'I'm going to have a baby,' she said.

She was accustomed to his habit of meeting with silence a statement which you would naturally expect to evoke an exclamation, but never had it seemed to her more devastating. He said nothing; he made no gesture; no movement on his face nor change of expression in his dark eyes indicated that he had heard. She felt suddenly inclined to cry. If a man loved his wife and his wife loved him, at such a moment they were drawn together by a poignant emotion. The silence was intolerable and she broke it.

'I don't know why it never occurred to me before. It was stupid of me, but . . . what with one thing and another . . .'

'How long have you . . . when do you expect to be confined?'

The words seemed to issue from his lips with difficulty. She felt that his throat was as dry as hers. It was a nuisance that her lips trembled so when she spoke; if he was not of stone it must excite his pity.

'I suppose I've been like this between two and three months.'

'Am I the father.'

She gave a little gasp. There was just a shadow of a tremor in his voice; it was dreadful that cold self-control of his which made the smallest token of emotion so shattering. She did not know why she thought suddenly of an instrument she had been shown in Hong-Kong upon which a needle oscillated a little and she had been told that this represented an earthquake a thousand miles away in which perhaps a thousand persons had lost their lives. She looked at him. He was ghastly pale. She had seen that pallor on him once, twice before. He was looking down, a little sideways.

'Well.'

She clasped her hands. She knew that if she could say yes it would mean everything in the world to him. He would believe her, of course he would believe her, because he wanted to; and then he would forgive. She knew how deep was his tenderness and how ready he was, for all his shyness, to expend it. She knew that he was not vindictive; he would forgive her if she could but give him an excuse to, an excuse that touched his heart, and he would forgive completely. She could count on him never to throw the past in her teeth. Cruel he might be, cold and morbid, but he was neither mean nor petty. It would alter everything if she said yes.

And she had an urgent need for sympathy. The unexpected knowledge that she was with child had overwhelmed her with strange hopes and unforeseen desires. She felt weak, frightened a little, alone and very far from any friends. That morning, though she cared little for her mother, she had had a sudden craving to be with her. She needed help and consolation. She did not love Walter, she knew that she never could, but at this moment she longed with all her heart for him to take her in his arms so that she could lay her head on his breast; clinging to him she could have cried happily; she wanted him to kiss her and she wanted to twine her arms around his neck.

She began to weep. She had lied so much and she could lie easily. What could a lie matter when it could only do good? A lie, a lie, what was a lie? It was so easy to say yes. She saw Walter's eyes melt and his arms outstretched towards her. She couldn't say it; she didn't know why, she just couldn't. All she had gone through during these bitter weeks, Charlie and his unkindness, the cholera and all these people dying, the nuns, oddly enough even that funny, drunken little Waddington, it all seemed to have changed her so that she did not know herself; though she was so deeply moved, some bystander in her soul seemed to watch her with terror and surprise. She *had* to tell the truth. It did not seem worth while to lie. Her thoughts wandered strangely: on a sudden she saw that dead beggar at the foot of the compound wall. Why should she think of him? She did not sob; the tears streamed down her face, quite easily, from wide eyes. At last she answered the question. He had asked her if he was the child's father.

'I don't know,' she said.

He gave the ghost of a chuckle. It made Kitty shudder.

'It's a bit awkward, isn't it?'

His answer was characteristic, it was exactly what she would have expected him to say, but it made her heart sink. She wondered if he realised how hard it had been for her to tell the truth (at the same moment she recognised that it had not been in the least hard, but inevitable) and if he gave her credit for it. Her answer, *I don't know, I don't know*, hammered away in her head. It was impossible now to take it back. She got her handkerchief from her bag and dried her eyes. They did not speak. There was a syphon on the table by her bed and he got her a glass of water. He brought it to her and held the glass while she drank. She noticed how thin his hand was, it was a fine hand, slender, with long fingers, but now it was nothing but skin and bone; it trembled a little: he could control his face, but his hand betrayed him.

'Don't mind my crying,' she said. 'It's nothing really; it's only that I can't help the water running out of my eyes.'

She drank the water and he put the glass back. He sat down on a chair and lit a cigarette. He gave a little sigh. Once or twice before she had heard him sigh like that and it always gave her a catch at the heart. Looking at him now, for he was staring with abstracted gaze out of the window, she was surprised that she had not noticed before how terribly thin he had grown during the last weeks. His temples were sunken and the bones of his face showed through the skin. His clothes hung on him loosely as though they had been made for a larger man. Through his sunburn his face had a greenish pallor. He looked exhausted. He was working too hard, sleeping little and eating nothing. In her own grief and perturbation she found room to pity him. It was cruel to think that she could do nothing for him.

He put his hand over his forehead, as though his head were aching, and she had a feeling that in his brain too those words hammered madly: *I don't know, I don't know.* It was strange that this moody, cold and shy man should have such a natural affection for very little babies; most men didn't care much even for their own, but the nuns, touched and a little amused, had more than once spoken of it. If he felt like that about those funny little Chinese babies what would he have felt about his own? Kitty bit her lips in order to prevent herself from crying again.

He looked at his watch.

'I'm afraid I must go back to the city. I have a great deal to do today . . . Shall you be all right?'

'Oh, yes. Don't bother about me.'

'I think you'd better not wait for me this evening. I may be very late and I'll get something to eat from Colonel Yü.'

'Very well.'

He rose.

'If I were you, I wouldn't try to do anything today. You'd better take it easy. Is there anything you want before I go?'

'No, thanks. I shall be quite all right.'

He paused for an instant, as though he were undecided, and then, abruptly and without looking at her, took his hat and walked out of the room. She heard him go through the compound. She felt terribly alone. There was no need for self-restraint now and gave herself up to a passion of tears.

Chapter Fifty-seven

The night was sultry and Kitty sat at the window looking at the fantastic roofs, dark against the starlight, of the Chinese temple, when at last Walter came in. Her eyes were heavy with weeping, but she was composed. Notwithstanding all there was to harass her she felt, perhaps only from exhaustion, strangely at peace.

'I thought you'd be already in bed,' said Walter as he came in.

'I wasn't sleepy. I thought it cooler to sit up. Have you had any dinner?'

'All I want.'

He walked up and down the long room and she saw that he had something to say to her. She knew that he was embarrassed. Without concern she waited for him to summon up his resolution. He began abruptly.

'I've been thinking about what you told me this afternoon. It seems to me that it would be better if you went away. I have spoken to Colonel Yü and he will give you an escort. You could take the amah with you. You will be quite safe.'

'Where is there for me to go?'

'You can go to your mother's.'

'Do you think she would be pleased to see me?'

He paused for a moment, hesitating, as though for reflection.

'Then you can go to Hong-Kong.'

'What should I do there?'

'You will need a good deal of care and attention. I don't think it's fair to ask you to stay here.'

She could not prevent the smile, not only of bitterness but of frank amusement, that crossed her face. She gave him a glance and very nearly laughed.

'I don't know why you should be so anxious about my health.'

He came over to the window and stood looking out at the night. There had never been so many stars in the unclouded sky.

'This isn't the place for a woman in your condition.'

She looked at him, white in his thin clothes against the darkness; there was something sinister in his fine profile, and yet oddly enough at this moment it excited in her no fear.

'When you insisted on my coming here did you want it to kill me?' she asked suddenly.

He was so long answering that she thought he had refused to hear.

'At first.'

She gave a little shudder, for it was the first time he had admitted his intention. But she bore him no ill will for it. Her feeling surprised herself; there was a certain admiration in it and a faint amusement. She did not quite know why, but suddenly thinking of Charlie Townsend he seemed to her an abject fool.

'It was a terrible risk you were taking,' she answered. 'With your sensitive conscience I wonder if you could ever have forgiven yourself if I had died.'

'Well, you haven't. You've thrived on it.'

'I've never felt better in my life.'

She had an instinct to throw herself on the mercy of his humour. After all they had gone through, when they were living amid these scenes of horror and desolation, it seemed inept to attach importance to the ridiculous act of fornication. When death stood round the corner, taking lives like a gardener digging up potatoes, it was foolishness to care what dirty things this person or that did with his body. If she could only make him realise how little Charlie meant to her, so that now already she had difficulty in calling up his features to her imagination, and how entirely the love of him had passed out of her heart! Because she had no feeling for Townsend the various acts she had committed with him had lost their significance. She had regained her heart and what she had given of her body seemed not to matter a rap. She was inclined to say to Walter: 'Look here, don't you think we've been silly long enough? We've sulked with one another like children. Why can't we kiss and be friends. There's no reason why we shouldn't be friends just because we're not lovers.'

He stood very still and the lamplight made the pallor of his impassive face startling. She did not trust him; if she said the wrong thing he would turn upon her with such an icy sternness. She knew by now his extreme sensitiveness, for which his acid irony was a protection, and how quickly he could close his heart if his feelings were hurt. She had a moment's irritation at his stupidity. Surely what troubled him most was the wound to his vanity: she vaguely realised that this is the hardest of all wounds to heal. It was singular that men attached so much importance to their wives' faithfulness; when first she had gone with Charlie she had expected to feel quite different, a changed woman; but she had seemed to herself exactly the same, she had experienced only well-being and a greater vitality. She wished now that she had been able to tell Walter that the child was his; the lie would have meant so little to her, and the assurance would have been so great a comfort to him. And after all it might not be a lie: it was funny, that something in her heart which had prevented her from giving herself the benefit of the doubt. How silly men were! Their part in procreation was so unimportant; it was the woman who carried the child through long months of uneasiness and bore it with pain, and yet a man because of his momentary connection made such preposterous claims. Why should that make any difference to him in his feeling towards the child? Then Kitty's thoughts wandered to the child which she herself would bear; she thought of it not with emotion nor with a passion of maternity, but with an idle curiosity.

'I daresay you'd like to think it over a little,' said Walter, breaking the long silence.

'Think what?'

He turned a little as if he were surprised.

'About when you want to go?'

'But I don't want to go.'

'Why not?'

'I like my work at the convent. I think I'm making myself useful. I should prefer to stay as long as you do.'

'I think I should tell you that in your present condition you are probably more liable to catch any infection that happen to be about.'

'I like the discreet way you put it,' she smiled ironically.

'You're not staying for my sake?'

She hesitated. He little knew that now the strongest emotion he excited in her, and the most unexpected, was pity.

'No. You don't love me. I often think I rather bore you.'

'I shouldn't have thought you were the sort of person to put yourself out for a few stuffy nuns and a parcel of Chinese brats.'

Her lips outlined a smile.

'I think it's rather unfair to despise me so much because you made such a mistake in your judgment of me. It's not my fault that you were such an ass.'

'If you're determined to stay you are of course at liberty to do so.'

'I'm sorry I can't give you the opportunity of being magnanimous.' She found it strangely hard to be quite serious with him. 'As a matter of fact you're quite right, it's not only for the orphans that I'm staying: you see, I'm in the peculiar position that I haven't got a soul in the world that I can go to. I know no one who wouldn't think me a nuisance. I know no one who cares a row of pins if I'm alive or dead.'

He frowned. But he did not frown in anger.

'We have made a dreadful hash of things, haven't we?' he said.

'Do you still want to divorce me? I don't think I care any more.'

'You must know that by bringing you here I've condoned the offence.'

'I didn't know. You see, I haven't made a study of infidelity. What are we going to do then when we leave here? Are we going on living together?'

'Oh, don't you think we can let the future take care of itself?'

There was the weariness of death in his voice.

Chapter Fifty-eight

Two or three days later Waddington fetched Kitty from the convent (for her restlessness had induced her immediately to resume her work) and took her to drink the promised cup of tea with his mistress. Kitty had on more than one occasion dined at Waddington's house. It was a square, white and pretentious building, such as the Customs build for their officials all over China; and the dining-room in which they ate, the drawing-room in which they sat, were furnished with prim and solid furniture. They had the appearance of being partly offices and partly hotel; there was nothing homelike in them and you understood that these houses were merely places of haphazard sojourn to their successive occupants. It would never have occurred to you that on an upper floor mystery and perhaps romance dwelt shrouded. They ascended a flight of stairs and Waddington opened a door. Kitty went into a large, bare room with whitewashed walls on which hung scrolls in various calligraphies. At a square table, on a stiff arm-chair, both of blackwood and heavily carved, sat the Manchu. She rose as Kitty and Waddington entered, but made no step forward.

'Here she is,' said Waddington, and added something in Chinese.

Kitty shook hands with her. She was slim in her long embroidered gown and somewhat taller than Kitty, used to the Southern people, had expected. She wore a jacket of pale green silk with tight sleeves that came over her wrists and on her black hair, elaborately dressed, was the head-dress of the Manchu women. Her face was coated with powder and her cheeks from the eyes to the mouth heavily rouged; her plucked eyebrows were a thin dark line and her mouth was scarlet. From this mask her black, slightly slanting, large eyes burned like lakes of liquid jet. She seemed more like an idol than a woman. Her movements were slow and assured. Kitty had the impression that she was slightly shy but very curious. She nodded her head two or three times, looking at Kitty, while Waddington spoke of her. Kitty noticed her hands; they were preternaturally long, very slender, of the colour of ivory; and the exquisite nails were painted. Kitty thought she had never seen anything so lovely as those languid and elegant hands. They suggested the breeding of uncounted centuries.

She spoke a little, in a high voice, like the twittering of birds in an orchard, and Waddington, translating, told Kitty that she was glad to see her; how old was she and how many children had she got? They sat down on three straight chairs at the square table and a boy brought in bowls of tea, pale and scented with jasmine. The Manchu lady handed Kitty a green tin of Three Castles cigarettes. Besides the table and the chairs the room contained little furniture; there was a wide pallet bed on which was an embroidered head rest and two sandalwood chests.

'What does she do with herself all day long?' asked Kitty.

'She paints a little and sometimes she writes a poem. But she mostly sits. She smokes, but only in moderation, which is fortunate, since one of my duties is to prevent the traffic in opium.'

'Do you smoke?' asked Kitty.

'Seldom. To tell you the truth I much prefer whisky.'

There was in the room a faintly acrid smell; it was not unpleasant, but peculiar and exotic.

'Tell her that I am sorry I cannot talk to her. I am sure we have many things to say to one another.'

When this was translated to the Manchu she gave Kitty a quick glance in which there was the hint of a smile. She was impressive as she sat, without embarrassment, in her beautiful clothes; and from the painted face the eyes looked out wary, self-possessed and unfathomable. She was unreal, like a picture, and yet had an elegance which made Kitty feel all thumbs. Kitty had never paid anything but passing and somewhat contemptuous attention to the China in which fate had thrown her. It was not done in her set. Now she seemed on a sudden to have an inkling of something remote and mysterious. Here was the East, immemorial, dark and inscrutable. The beliefs and the ideals of the West seemed crude beside ideals and beliefs of which in this exquisite creature she seemed to catch a fugitive glimpse. Here was a different life, lived on a different plane. Kitty felt strangely that the sight of this idol, with her painted face and slanting, wary eyes, made the efforts and the pains of the everyday world she knew slightly absurd. That coloured mask seemed to hide the secret of an abundant profound and significant experience: those long, delicate hands with their tapering fingers held the key of riddles undivined.

'What does she think about all day long?' asked Kitty.

'Nothing,' smiled Waddington.

'She's wonderful. Tell her I've never seen such beautiful hands. I wonder what she sees in *you*.'

Waddington, smiling, translated the question.

'She says I'm good.'

'As if a woman ever loved a man for his virtue,' Kitty mocked.

The Manchu laughed but once. This was when Kitty, for something to say, expressed admiration of a jade bracelet she wore. She took it off and Kitty, trying to put it on, found, though her hands were small enough, that it would not pass over her knuckles. Then the Manchu burst into childlike laughter. She said something to Waddington and called for an amah. She gave her an instruction and the amah in a moment brought in a pair of very beautiful Manchu shoes.

'She wants to give you these if you can wear them,' said Waddington. 'You'll find they make quite good bedroom slippers.'

'They fit me perfectly,' said Kitty, not without satisfaction.

But she noticed a roguish smile on Waddington's face.

'Are they too big for her?' she asked quickly.

'Miles.'

Kitty laughed and when Waddington translated, the Manchu and the amah laughed also.

When Kitty and Waddington, a little later, were walking up the hill together, she turned to him with a friendly smile.

'You did not tell me that you had a great affection for her.'

'What makes you think I have?'

'I saw it in your eyes. It's strange, it must be like loving a phantom or a dream. Men are incalculable; I thought you were like everybody else and now I feel that I don't know the first thing about you.'

As they reached the bungalow he asked her abruptly:

'Why did you want to see her?'

Kitty hesitated for a moment before answering.

'I'm looking for something and I don't quite know what it is. But I know that it's very important for me to know it, and if I did it would make all the difference. Perhaps the nuns know it; when I'm with them I feel that they hold a secret which they will not share with me. I don't know why it came into my head that if I saw this Manchu woman I should have an inkling of what I am looking for. Perhaps she would tell me if she could.'

'What makes you think she knows it?'

Kitty gave him a sidelong glance, but did not answer. Instead she asked him a question.

'Do you know it?'

He smiled and shrugged his shoulders.

'Tao. Some of us look for the Way in opium and some in God, some of us in whisky and some in love. It is all the same Way and it leads nowhither.'

Chapter Fifty-nine

Kitty fell again into the comfortable routine of her work and though in the early morning feeling far from well she had spirit enough not to let it discompose her. She was astonished at the interest the nuns took in her: sisters who, when she saw them in a corridor, had done no more than bid her good morning now on a flimsy pretext came into the room in which she was occupied and looked at her, chatting a little, with a sweet and childlike excitement. Sister St Joseph told her with a repetition which was sometimes tedious how she had been saying to herself for days past: 'Now, I wonder,' or: 'I shouldn't be surprised'; and then, when Kitty fainted: 'There can be no doubt, it jumps to the eyes.' She told Kitty long stories of her sister-in-law's confinements, which but for Kitty's quick sense of humour would have been not a little alarming. Sister St Joseph combined in a pleasant fashion the realistic outlook of her upbringing (a river wound through the meadows of her father's farm and the poplars that stood on its bank trembled in the faintest breeze) with a charming intimacy with religious things. One day, firmly convinced that a heretic could know nothing of such matters, she told Kitty of the Annunciation.

'I can never read those lines in the Holy Writ without weeping,' she said. 'I do not know why, but it gives me such a funny feeling.'

And then in French, in words that to Kitty sounded unfamiliar and in their precision a trifle cold, she quoted:

'*And the angel came in unto her, and said, Hail full of grace, the Lord is with thee: blessed art thou among women.*'

The mystery of birth blew through the convent like a little fitful wind playing among the white blossoms of an orchard. The thought that Kitty was with child disturbed and excited those sterile women. She frightened them a little now and fascinated them. They looked upon the physical side of her condition with robust common sense, for they were the daughters of peasants and fishermen; but in their childlike hearts was awe. They were troubled by the thought of her burden and yet happy and strangely exalted. Sister St Joseph told her that they all prayed for her, and Sister St Martin had said what a pity it was she was not a Catholic; but the Mother Superior had reproved her; she said that it was possible to be a good woman—*une brave femme*, she put it—even though one was Protestant and *le Bon Dieu* would in some way or other arrange all that.

Kitty was both touched and diverted by the interest she aroused, but surprised beyond measure when she found that even the Mother Superior, so austere in her saintliness, treated her with a new complaisance. She had always been kind to Kitty, but in a remote fashion; now she used her with a tenderness in which there was something maternal. Her voice had in it a new and gentle note and in her eyes was a sudden playfulness as though Kitty were a child who had done a clever and amusing thing. It was oddly moving. Her soul was like a calm, grey sea rolling majestically, awe-inspiring in its sombre greatness, and then suddenly a ray of sunshine made it alert, friendly and gay. Often now in the evening she would come and sit with Kitty.

'I must take care that you do not tire yourself, *mon enfant*,' she said, making a transparent excuse to herself, 'or Dr Fane will never forgive me. Oh, this British self-control! There he is delighted beyond measure and when you speak to him of it he becomes quite pale.'

She took Kitty's hand and patted it affectionately.

'Dr Fane told me that he wished you to go away, but you would not because you could not bear to leave us. That was kind of you, my dear child, and I want you to know that we appreciate the help you have been to us. But I think that you did not want to leave him either, and that is better, for your place is by his side, and he needs you. Ah, I do not know what we should have done without that admirable man.'

'I am glad to think that he has been able to do something for you,' said Kitty.

'You must love him with all your heart, my dear. He is a saint.'

Kitty smiled and in her heart sighed. There was only one thing she could do for Walter now and that she could not think how to. She wanted him to forgive her, not for her sake any more, but for his own; for she felt that this alone could give him peace of mind. It was useless to ask him for his forgiveness, and if he had a suspicion that she desired it for his good rather than hers his stubborn vanity would make him refuse at all costs (it was curious that his vanity now did not irritate her, it seemed natural and only made her sorrier for him); and the only chance was that some unexpected occurrence might throw him off his guard. She had an idea that he would welcome an uprush of emotion which would liberate him from his nightmare of resentment, but that, in his pathetic folly, he would fight when it came with all his might against it.

Was it not pitiful that men, tarrying so short a space in a world where there was so much pain, should thus torture themselves?

Chapter Sixty

Though the Mother Superior talked with Kitty not more than three or four times and once or twice for but ten minutes the impression she made upon Kitty was profound. Her character was like a country which on first acquaintance seems grand, but inhospitable; but in which presently you discover smiling little villages among fruit trees in the folds of the majestic mountains, and pleasant ambling rivers that flow kindly through lush meadows. But these comfortable scenes, though they surprise and even reassure you, are not enough to make you feel at home in the land of tawny heights and windswept spaces. It would have been impossible to become intimate with the Mother Superior; she had that something impersonal about her which Kitty had felt with the other nuns, even with the good-humoured, chatty Sister St Joseph, but with her it was a barrier which was almost palpable. It gave you quite a curious sensation, chilling but awe-inspiring, that she could walk on the same earth as you, attend to mundane affairs, and yet live so obviously upon a plane you could not reach. She once said to Kitty:

'It is not enough that a religious should be continually in prayer with Jesus; she should be herself a prayer.'

Though her conversation was interwoven with her religion, Kitty felt that this was natural to her and that no effort was made to influence the heretic. It seemed strange to her that the Mother Superior, with her deep sense of charity, should be content to leave Kitty in a condition of what must seem to her sinful ignorance.

One evening the two of them were sitting together. The days were shortening now and the mellow light of the evening was agreeable and a little melancholy. The Mother Superior looked very tired. Her tragic face was drawn and white; her fine dark eyes had lost their fire. Her fatigue perhaps urged her to a rare mood of confidence.

'This is a memorable day for me, my child,' she said, breaking from a long reverie, 'for this is the anniversary of the day on which I finally determined to enter religion. For two years I had been thinking of it, but I had suffered as it were a fear of this calling, for I dreaded that I might be recaptured by the spirit of the world. But that morning when I communicated I made the vow that I would before nightfall announce my wish to my dear mother. After I had received the Holy Communion I asked Our Lord to give me peace of mind: Thou shalt have it only, the answer seemed to come to me, when thou hast ceased to desire it.'

The Mother Superior seemed to lose herself in thoughts of the past.

'That day, one of our friends, Madame de Viernot, had left for the Carmel without telling any of her relatives. She knew that they were opposed to her step, but she was a widow and thought that as such she had the right to do as she chose. One of my cousins had gone to bid farewell to the dear fugitive and did not come back till the evening. She was much moved. I had not spoken to my mother, I trembled at the thought of telling her what I had in mind, and yet I wished to keep the resolution I had made at Holy Communion. I asked my cousin all manner of questions. My mother, who appeared to be absorbed in her tapestry, lost no word. While I talked I said to myself: If I want to speak today I have not a minute to lose.

'It is strange how vividly I remember the scene. We were sitting round the table, a round table covered with a red cloth, and we worked by the light of a lamp with a green shade. My two cousins were staying with us and we were all working at tapestries to re-cover the chairs in the drawing-room. Imagine, they had not been re-covered since the days of Louis XIV, when they were bought, and they were so shabby and faded, my mother said it was a disgrace.

'I tried to form the words, but my lips would not move; and then, suddenly, after a few minutes of silence my mother said to me: "I really cannot understand the conduct of your friend. I do not like this leaving without a word all those to whom she is so dear. The gesture is theatrical and offends my taste. A well-bred woman does nothing which shall make people talk of her. I hope that if ever you caused us the great sorrow of leaving us you would not take flight as though you were committing a crime."

'It was the moment to speak, but such was my weakness that I could only say: "Ah, set your mind at rest, *maman*, I should not have the strength."

'My mother made no answer and I repented because I had not dared to explain myself. I seemed to hear the word of Our Lord to St Peter: "Peter, lovest thou me?" Oh, what weakness, what ingratitude was mine! I loved my comfort, the manner of my life, my family and my diversions. I was lost in these bitter thoughts when a little later, as though the conversation had not been interrupted, my mother said to me: "Still, my Odette, I do not think that you will die without having done something that will endure."

'I was still lost in my anxiety and my reflections, while my cousins, never knowing the beating of my heart, worked quietly, when suddenly my mother, letting her tapestry fall and looking at me attentively, said: "Ah, my dear child, I am very sure that you will end by becoming a religious."

'"Are you speaking seriously, my good mother," I answered. "You are laying bare the innermost thought and desire of my heart."

'"*Mais oui*," cried my cousins without giving me time to finish, "For two years Odette has thought of nothing else. But you will not give your permission, *ma tante*, you must not give your permission."

'"By what right, my dear children, should we refuse it," said my mother, "if it is the Will of God?"

'My cousins then, wishing to make a jest of the conversation, asked me what I intended to do with the trifles that belonged to me and quarrelled gaily about which should take possession of this and which of that. But these first moments of gaiety lasted a very little while and we began to weep. Then we heard my father come up the stairs.'

The Mother Superior paused for a moment and sighed.

'It was very hard for my father. I was his only daughter and men often have a deeper feeling for their daughters than they ever have for their sons.'

'It is a great misfortune to have a heart,' said Kitty, with a smile.

'It is a great good fortune to consecrate that heart to the love of Jesus Christ.'

At that moment a little girl came up to the Mother Superior and confident in her interest showed her a fantastic toy that she had somehow got hold of. The Mother Superior put her beautiful, delicate hand round the child's shoulder and the child nestled up to her. It moved Kitty to observe how sweet her smile was and yet how impersonal.

'It is wonderful to see the adoration that all your orphans have for you, Mother,' she said. 'I think I should be very proud if I could excite so great a devotion.'

The Mother Superior gave once more her aloof and yet beautiful smile.

'There is only one way to win hearts and that is to make oneself like unto those of whom one would be loved.'

Chapter Sixty-one

Walter did not come back to dinner that evening. Kitty waited for him a little, for when he was detained in the city he always managed to send her word, but at last she sat down. She made no more than a pretence of eating the many courses which the Chinese cook, with his regard for propriety notwithstanding pestilence and the difficulty of provisioning, invariably set before her; and then, sinking into the long rattan chair by the open window, surrendered herself to the beauty of the starry night. The silence rested her.

She did not try to read. Her thoughts floated upon the surface of her mind like little white clouds reflected on a still lake. She was too tired to seize upon one, follow it up and absorb herself in its attendant train. She wondered vaguely what there was for her in the various impressions which her conversations with the nuns had left upon her. It was singular that, though their way of life so profoundly moved her, the faith which occasioned it left her untouched. She could not envisage the possibility that she might at any time be captured by the ardour of belief. She gave a little sigh: perhaps it would make everything easier if that great white light should illuminate her soul. Once or twice she had had the desire to tell the Mother Superior of her unhappiness and its cause; but she dared not: she could not bear that this austere woman should think ill of her. To her what she had done would naturally seem a grievous sin. The odd thing was that she herself could not regard it as wicked so much as stupid and ugly.

Perhaps it was due to an obtuseness in herself that she looked upon her connection with Townsend as regrettable and shocking even, but to be forgotten rather than to be repented of. It was like making a blunder at a party; there was nothing to do about it, it was dreadfully mortifying, but it showed a lack of sense to ascribe too much importance to it. She shuddered as she thought of Charlie with his large frame too well covered, the vagueness of his jaw and the way he had of standing with his chest thrown out so that he might not seem to have a paunch. His sanguine temperament showed itself in the little red veins which soon would form a network on his ruddy cheeks. She had liked his bushy eyebrows: there was to her in them now something animal and repulsive.

And the future? It was curious how indifferent it left her; she could not see into it at all. Perhaps she would die when her baby was born. Her sister Doris had always been much stronger than she, and Doris had nearly died. (She had done her duty and produced an heir to the new baronetcy; Kitty smiled as she thought of her mother's satisfaction.) If the future was so vague it meant perhaps that she was destined never to see it. Walter would probably ask her mother to take care of the child—if the child survived; and she knew him well enough to be sure that, however uncertain of his paternity, he would treat it with kindness. Walter could be trusted under any circumstances to behave admirably. It was a pity that with his great qualities, his unselfishness and honour, his intelligence and sensibility, he should be so unlovable. She was not in the least frightened of him now, but sorry for him, and at the same time she could not help thinking him slightly absurd. The depth of his emotion made him vulnerable and she had a feeling that somehow and at some time she so could work upon it as to induce him to forgive her. The thought haunted her now that in thus giving him peace of mind she would make the only possible amends for the anguish she had caused him. It was a pity he had so little sense of humour: she could see them both, some day, laughing together at the way they had tormented themselves.

She was tired. She took the lamp into her room and undressed. She went to bed and presently fell asleep.

Chapter Sixty-two

But she was awakened by a loud knocking. At first, since it was interwoven with the dream from which she was aroused, she could not attach the sound to reality. The knocking went on and she was conscious that it must be at the gateway of the compound. It was quite dark. She had a watch with phosphorised hands and saw that it was half past two. It must be Walter coming back—how late he was—and he could not awake the boy. The knocking went on, louder and louder, and in the silence of the night it was really not a little alarming. The knocking stopped and she heard the withdrawing of the heavy bolt. Walter had never come back so late. Poor thing, he must be tired! She hoped he would have the sense to go straight to bed instead of working as usual in that laboratory of his.

There was a sound of voices, and people came into the compound. That was strange, for Walter coming home late, in order not to disturb her, took pains to be quiet. Two or three persons ran swiftly up the wooden steps and came into the room next door. Kitty was a little frightened. At the back of her mind was always the fear of an anti-foreign riot. Had something happened? Her heart began to beat quickly. But before she had time to put her vague apprehension into shape some one walked across the room and knocked at her door.

'Mrs Fane.'

She recognised Waddington's voice.

'Yes. What is it?'

'Will you get up at once. I have something to say to you.'

She rose and put on a dressing-gown. She unlocked the door and opened it. Her glance took in Waddington in a pair of Chinese trousers and a pongee coat, the houseboy holding a hurricane lamp, and a little further back three

Chinese soldiers in khaki. She started as she saw the consternation on Waddington's face; his head was tousled as though he had jumped out of bed.

'What is the matter?' she gasped.

'You must keep calm. There's not a moment to lose. Put on your clothes at once and come with me.'

'But what is it? Has something happened in the city?'

The sight of the soldiers suggested to her at once that there had been an outbreak and they were come to protect her.

'Your husband's been taken ill. We want you to come at once.'

'Walter?' she cried.

'You mustn't be upset. I don't exactly know what's the matter. Colonel Yü sent this officer to me and asked me to bring you to the Yamen at once.'

Kitty stared at him for a moment, she felt a sudden cold in her heart, and then she turned.

'I shall be ready in two minutes.'

'I came just as I was,' he answered. 'I was asleep, I just put on a coat and some shoes.'

She did not hear what he said. She dressed by the light of the stars, taking the first things that came to hand; her fingers on a sudden were so clumsy that it seemed to take her an age to find the little clasps that closed her dress. She put round her shoulders the Cantonese shawl she had worn in the evening.

'I haven't put a hat on. There's no need, is there?'

'No.'

The boy held the lantern in front of them and they hurried down the steps and out of the compound gate.

'Take care you don't fall,' said Waddington. 'You'd better hang on to my arm.'

The soldiers followed immediately behind them.

'Colonel Yü has sent chairs. They're waiting on the other side of the river.'

They walked quickly down the hill. Kitty could not bring herself to utter the question that trembled so horribly on her lips. She was mortally afraid of the answer. They came to the bank and there, with a thread of light at the bow, a sampan was waiting for them.

'Is it cholera?' she said then.

'I'm afraid so.'

She gave a little cry and stopped short.

'I think you ought to come as quickly as you can.' He gave her his hand to help her into the boat. The passage was short and the river almost stagnant; they stood in a bunch at the bow, while a woman with a child tied on her hip with one oar impelled the sampan across.

'He was taken ill this afternoon, the afternoon of yesterday that is,' said Waddington.

'Why wasn't I sent for at once?'

Although there was no reason for it they spoke in whispers. In the darkness Kitty could only feel how intense was her companion's anxiety.

'Colonel Yü wanted to, but he wouldn't let him. Colonel Yü has been with him all the time.'

'He ought to have sent for me all the same. It's heartless.'

'Your husband knew that you had never seen any one with cholera. It's a terrible and revolting sight. He didn't want you to see it.'

'After all he is my husband,' she said in a choking voice.

Waddington made no reply.

'Why am I allowed to come now?'

Waddington put his hand on her arm.

'My dear, you must be very brave. You must be prepared for the worst.'

She gave a wail of anguish and turned away a little, for she saw that the three Chinese soldiers were looking at her. She had a sudden strange glimpse of the whites of their eyes.

'Is he dying?'

'I only know the message Colonel Yü gave to this officer who came and fetched me. As far as I can judge collapse has set in.'

'Is there no hope at all?'

'I'm dreadfully sorry, I'm afraid that if we don't get there quickly we shan't find him alive.'

She shuddered. The tears began to stream down her cheeks.

'You see, he's been overworking, he has no powers of resistance.'

She withdrew from the pressure of his arm with a gesture of irritation. It exasperated her that he should talk in that low, anguished voice.

They reached the side and two men, Chinese coolies, standing on the bank helped her to step on shore. The chairs were waiting. As she got into hers Waddington said to her:

'Try and keep a tight hold on your nerves. You'll want all your self-control.'

'Tell the bearers to make haste.'

'They have orders to go as fast as they can.'

The officer, already in his chair, passed by and as he passed called out to Kitty's bearers. They raised the chair smartly, arranged the poles on their shoulders, and at a swift pace set off. Waddington followed close behind. They took the hill at a run, a man with a lantern going before each chair, and at the water-gate the gatekeeper was standing with a torch. The officer shouted to him as they approached and he flung open one side of the gate to let them through. He uttered some sort of interjection as they passed and the bearers called back. In the dead of the night those gutteral sounds in a strange language were mysterious and alarming. They slithered up the wet and slippery cobbles of the alley and one of the officer's bearers stumbled. Kitty heard the officer's voice raised in anger, the shrill retort of the bearer, and then the chair in front hurried on again. The streets were narrow and tortuous. Here in the city was deep night. It was a city of the dead. They hastened along a narrow lane, turned a corner, and then at a run took a flight of steps; the bearers were beginning to blow hard; they walked with long, rapid strides, in silence; one took out a ragged handkerchief and as he walked wiped from his forehead the sweat that ran down into his eyes; they wound this way and that so that it might have been a maze through which they sped; in the shadow of the shuttered shops sometimes a form seemed to be lying, but you did not know whether it was a man who slept to awake at dawn or a man who slept to awake never; the narrow streets were ghostly in their silent emptiness and when on a sudden a dog barked loudly it sent a shock of terror through Kitty's tortured nerves. She did not know where they went. The way seemed endless. Could they not go faster? Faster. Faster. The time was going and any moment it might be too late.

Chapter Sixty-three

Suddenly, walking along a blank long wall they came to a gateway flanked by sentry boxes, and the bearers set down the chairs. Waddington hurried up to Kitty. She had already jumped out. The officer knocked loudly on the door and shouted. A postern was opened and they passed into a courtyard. It was large and square. Huddled against the walls, under the eaves of the overhanging roofs, soldiers wrapped in their blankets were lying in huddled groups. They stopped for a moment while the officer spoke to a man who might have been a sergeant on guard. He turned and said something to Waddington.

'He's still alive,' said Waddington in a low voice. 'Take care how you walk.'

Still preceded by the men with lanterns they made their way across the yard, up some steps, through a great doorway and then down into another wide court. On one side of this was a long chamber with lights in it; the lights within shining through the rice paper silhouetted the elaborate pattern of the lattice. The lantern-bearers led them across the yard towards this room and at the door the officer knocked. It was opened immediately and the officer with a glance at Kitty stepped back.

'Will you walk in,' said Waddington.

It was a long, low room and the smoky lamps that lit it made the gloom ominous. Three or four orderlies stood about. On a pallet against the wall opposite the door a man was lying huddled under a blanket. An officer was standing motionless at the foot.

Kitty hurried up and leaned over the pallet. Walter lay with his eyes closed and in that sombre light his face had the greyness of death. He was horribly still.

'Walter, Walter,' she gasped, in a low, terrified tone.

There was a slight movement in the body, or the shadow of a movement; it was so slight it was like a breath of air which you cannot feel and yet for an instant ruffles the surface of still water.

'Walter, Walter, speak to me.'

The eyes were opened slowly, as though it were an infinite effort to raise those heavy lids, but he did not look, he stared at the wall a few inches from his face. He spoke; his voice, low and weak, had the hint of a smile in it.

'This is a pretty kettle of fish,' he said.

Kitty dared not breathe. He made no further sound, no beginning of a gesture, but his eyes, those dark, cold eyes of his (seeing now what mysteries?) stared at the whitewashed wall. Kitty raised herself to her feet. With haggard gaze she faced the man who stood there.

'Surely something can be done. You're not going to stand there and do nothing?'

She clasped her hands. Waddington spoke to the officer who stood at the end of the bed.

'I'm afraid they've done everything that was possible. The regimental surgeon has been treating him. Your husband has trained him and he's done all that your husband could do himself.'

'Is that the surgeon?'

'No, that is Colonel Yü. He's never left your husband's side.'

Distracted, Kitty gave him a glance. He was a tallish man, but stockily built, and he seemed ill at ease in his khaki uniform. He was looking at Walter and she saw that his eyes were wet with tears. It gave her a pang. Why should that man with his yellow, flat face have tears in his eyes? It exasperated her.

'It's awful to be able to do nothing.'

'At least he's not in pain any more,' said Waddington.

She leaned once more over her husband. Those ghastly eyes of his still stared vacantly in front of him. She could not tell if he saw with them. She did not know whether he had heard what was said. She put her lips close to his ears.

'Walter, isn't there something we can do?'

She thought that there must be some drug they could give him which would stay the dreadful ebbing of his life. Now that her eyes were more accustomed to the dimness she saw with horror that his face had fallen. She would hardly have recognised him. It was unthinkable that in a few short hours he should look like another man; he hardly looked like a man at all; he looked like death.

She thought that he was making an effort to speak. She put her ear close.

'Don't fuss. I've had a rough passage, but I'm all right now.'

Kitty waited for a moment, but he was silent. His immobility rent her heart with anguish; it was terrifying that he should lie so still. He seemed prepared already for the stillness of the grave. Some one, the surgeon or a dresser, came forward and with a gesture motioned her aside; he leaned over the dying man and with a dirty rag wet his lips. Kitty stood up once more and turned to Waddington despairingly.

'Is there no hope at all?' she whispered.

He shook his head.

'How much longer can he live?'

'No one can tell. An hour perhaps.'

Kitty looked round the bare chamber and her eyes rested for an instant on the substantial form of Colonel Yü.

'Can I be left alone with him for a little while?' she asked. 'Only for a minute.'

'Certainly, if you wish it.'

Waddington stepped over to the Colonel and spoke to him. The Colonel gave a little bow and then in a low tone an order.

'We shall wait on the steps,' said Waddington as they trooped out. 'You have only to call.'

Now that the incredible had overwhelmed her consciousness, like a drug coursing through her veins, and she realised that Walter was going to die she had but one thought, and that was to make his end easier for him by dragging from his soul the rancour which poisoned it. If he could die at peace with her it seemed to her that he would die at peace with himself. She thought now not of herself at all but only of him.

'Walter, I beseech you to forgive me,' she said, leaning over him. For fear that he could not bear the pressure she took care not to touch him. 'I'm so desperately sorry for the wrong I did you. I so bitterly regret it.'

He said nothing. He did not seem to hear. She was obliged to insist. It seemed to her strangely that his soul was a fluttering moth and its wings were heavy with hatred.

'Darling.'

A shadow passed over his wan and sunken face. It was less than a movement, and yet it gave all the effect of a terrifying convulsion. She had never used that word to him before. Perhaps in his dying brain there passed the thought, confused and difficultly grasped, that he had only heard her use it, a commonplace of her vocabulary, to dogs and babies and motor-cars. Then something horrible occurred. She clenched her hands, trying with all her might to control herself, for she saw two tears run slowly down his wasted cheeks.

'Oh, my precious, my dear, if you ever loved me – I know you loved me and I was hateful – I beg you to forgive me. I've no chance now to show my repentance. Have mercy on me. I beseech you to forgive.'

She stopped. She looked at him, all breathless, waiting passionately for a reply. She saw that he tried to speak. Her heart gave a great bound. It seemed to her that it would be in a manner a reparation for the suffering she had caused him if at this last moment she could effect his deliverance from that load of bitterness. His lips moved. He did not look at her. His eyes stared unseeing at the white-washed wall. She leaned over him so that she might hear. But he spoke quite clearly.

'The dog it was that died.'

She stayed as still as though she were turned to stone. She could not understand and gazed at him in terrified perplexity. It was meaningless. Delirium. He had not understood a word she said.

It was impossible to be so still and yet to live. She stared and stared. His eyes were open. She could not tell if he breathed. She began to grow frightened.

'Walter,' she whispered. 'Walter.'

At last, suddenly, she raised herself. A sudden fear seized her. She turned and went to the door.

'Will you come, please. He doesn't seem to . . .'

They stepped in. The Chinese surgeon went up to the bed. He had an electric torch in his hand and he lit it and looked at Walter's eyes. Then he closed them. He said something in Chinese. Waddington put his arm round Kitty.

'I'm afraid he's dead.'

Kitty gave a deep sigh. A few tears fell from her eyes. She felt dazed rather than overcome. The Chinese stood about, round the bed, helplessly, as though they did not quite know what to do next. Waddington was silent. In a minute the Chinese began to speak in a low tone among themselves.

'You'd better let me take you back to the bungalow,' said Waddington. 'He'll be brought there.'

Kitty passed her hand wearily across her forehead. She went up to the pallet bed and leaned over it. She kissed Walter gently on the lips. She was not crying now.

'I'm sorry to give you so much trouble.'

The officers saluted as she passed and she gravely bowed. They walked back across the courtyard and got into their chairs. She saw Waddington light a cigarette. A little smoke lost in the air, that was the life of man.

Chapter Sixty-four

Dawn was breaking now, and here and there a Chinese was taking down the shutters of his shop. In its dark recesses, by the light of a taper, a woman was washing her hands and face. In a tea-house at a corner a group of men were eating an early meal. The grey, cold light of the rising day sidled along the narrow lanes like a thief. There was a pale mist on the river and the masts of the crowded junks loomed through it like the lances of a phantom army. It was chilly as they crossed and Kitty huddled herself up in her gay and coloured shawl. They walked up the hill and they were above the mist. The sun shone from an unclouded sky. It shone as though this were a day like another and nothing had happened to distinguish it from its fellows.

'Wouldn't you like to lie down?' said Waddington when they entered the bungalow.

'No. I'll sit at the window.'

She had sat at the window so often and so long during the weeks that had passed and her eyes now were so familiar with the fantastic, garish, beautiful and mysterious temple on its great bastion that it rested her spirit. It was so unreal, even in the crude light of midday, that it withdrew her from the reality of life.

'I'll get the boy to make you some tea. I'm afraid it will be necessary to bury him this morning. I'll make all arrangements.'

'Thank you.'

Chapter Sixty-five

They buried him three hours later. It seemed horrible to Kitty that he must be put into a Chinese coffin, as though in so strange a bed he must rest uneasily, but there was no help for it. The nuns, learning of Walter's death as they learned everything that happened in the city, sent by a messenger a cross of dahlias, stiff and formal, but made as though by the accustomed hands of a florist; and the cross, alone on the Chinese coffin, looked grotesque and out of place. When all was ready they had to wait for Colonel Yü who had sent to Waddington to say that he desired to attend the funeral. He came accompanied by an A.D.C. They walked up the hill, the coffin borne by half a dozen coolies, to a little plot of land where lay buried the missionary whose place Walter had taken. Waddington had found among the missionary's effects an English prayer-book and in a low voice, with an embarrassment that was unusual to him, read the burial service. Perhaps, reciting those solemn but terrible words, the thought hovered in his mind that if he in his turn fell a victim to the pestilence there would be no one now to say them over him. The coffin was lowered into the grave and the grave-diggers began to throw in the earth.

Colonel Yü, who had stood with bared head by the grave-side, put on his hat, saluted Kitty gravely, said a word or two to Waddington and followed by his A.D.C. walked away. The coolies, curious to watch a Christian burial, had lingered and now in a straggling group, their yokes trailing in their hands, sauntered off. Kitty and Waddington waited till the grave was filled and then placed on the mound, smelling of fresh earth, the nuns' prim dahlias. She had not wept, but when the first shovelful of earth rattled on the coffin she felt a dreadful pang at her heart.

She saw that Waddington was waiting for her to come away.

'Are you in a hurry?' she asked. 'I don't want to go back to the bungalow just yet.'

'I have nothing to do. I am entirely in your hands.'

Chapter Sixty-six

They sauntered along the causeway till they came to the top of the hill on which stood that archway, the memorial to a virtuous widow, which had occupied so large a part of Kitty's impression of the place. It was a symbol, but of what she scarcely knew; she could not tell why it bore a note of so sardonic irony.

'Shall we sit down a little? We haven't sat here for ages.' The plain was spread before her widely; it was tranquil and serene in the morning light. 'It's only a few weeks that I've been here and it seems a lifetime.'

He did not answer and for a while she allowed her thoughts to wander. She gave a sigh.

'Do you think that the soul is immortal?' she asked.

He did not seem surprised at the question.

'How should I know?'

'Just now, when they'd washed Walter, before they put him into the coffin I looked at him. He looked very young. Too young to die. Do you remember that beggar that we saw the first time you took me for a walk? I was frightened not because he was dead, but because he looked as though he'd never been a human being. He was just a dead animal. And now again, with Walter, it looked so like a machine that has run down. That's what is so frightening. And if it is only a machine how futile is all this suffering and the heart pains and the misery.'

He did not answer, but his eyes travelled over the landscape at their feet. The wide expanse on that gay and sunny morning filled the heart with exultation. The trim little rice-fields stretched as far as the eye could see and in many of them the blue-clad peasants with their buffaloes were working industriously. It was a peaceful and a happy scene. Kitty broke the silence.

'I can't tell you how deeply moved I've been by all I've seen at the convent. They're wonderful, those nuns, they make me feel utterly worthless. They give up everything, their home, their country, love, children, freedom; and all the little things which I sometimes think must be harder still to give up, flowers and green fields, going for a walk on an autumn day, books and music, comfort, everything they give up, everything. And they do it so that they may devote themselves to a life of sacrifice and poverty, obedience, killing work and prayer. To all of them this world is really and truly a place of exile. Life is a cross which they willingly bear, but in their hearts all the time is the desire–oh, it's so much stronger than desire, it's a longing, an eager, passionate longing for the death which shall lead them to life everlasting.'

Kitty clasped her hands and looked at him with anguish.

'Well?'

'Supposing there is no life everlasting? Think what it means if death is really the end of all things. They've given up all for nothing. They've been cheated. They're dupes.'

Waddington reflected for a little while.

'I wonder. I wonder if it matters that what they have aimed at is illusion. Their lives are in themselves beautiful. I have an idea that the only thing which makes it possible to regard this world we live in without disgust is the beauty which now and then men create out of the chaos. The pictures they paint, the music they compose, the books they write, and the lives they lead. Of all these the richest in beauty is the beautiful life. That is the perfect work of art.'

Kitty sighed. What he said seemed hard. She wanted more.

'Have you ever been to a symphony concert?' he continued.

'Yes,' she smiled. 'I know nothing of music, but I'm rather fond of it.'

'Each member of the orchestra plays his own little instrument, and what do you think he knows of the complicated harmonies which unroll themselves on the indifferent air? He is concerned only with his own small share. But he knows that the symphony is lovely, and though there's none to hear it, it is lovely still, and he is content to play his part.'

'You spoke of Tao the other day,' said Kitty, after a pause. 'Tell me what it is.'

Waddington gave her a little look, hesitated an instant, and then with a faint smile on his comic face answered:

'It is the Way and the Waygoer. It is the eternal road along which walk all beings, but no being made it, for itself is being. It is everything and nothing. From it all things spring, all things conform to it, and to it at last all things return. It is a square without angles, a sound which ears cannot hear, and an image without form. It is a vast net and though its meshes are as wide as the sea it lets nothing through. It is the sanctuary where all things find refuge. It is nowhere, but without looking out of the window you may see it. Desire not to desire, it teaches, and leave all things to take their course. He that humbles himself shall be preserved entire. He that bends shall be made straight. Failure is the foundation of success and success is the lurking-place of failure; but who can tell when the turning point will come? He who strives after tenderness can become even as a little child. Gentleness brings victory to him who attacks and safety to him who defends. Mighty is he who conquers himself.'

'Does it mean anything?'

'Sometimes, when I've had half a dozen whiskies and look at the stars, I think perhaps it does.'

Silence fell upon them and when it was broken it was again by Kitty.

'Tell me, is: the dog it was that died, a quotation?'

Waddington's lips outlined a smile and he was ready with his answer. But perhaps at that moment his sensibilities were abnormally acute. Kitty was not looking at him, but there was something about her expression which made him change his mind.

'If it is I don't know it,' he answered warily. 'Why?'

'Nothing. It crossed my mind. It had a familiar ring.'

There was another silence.

'When you were alone with your husband,' said Waddington presently, 'I had a talk with the regimental surgeon. I thought we ought to have some details.'

'Well?'

'He was in a very hysterical state. I couldn't really quite understand what he meant. So far as I can make out your husband got infected during the course of experiments he was making.'

'He was always experimenting. He wasn't really a doctor, he was a bacteriologist; that is why he was so anxious to come here.'

'But I can't quite make out from the surgeon's statements whether he was infected accidentally or whether he was actually experimenting on himself.'

Kitty grew very pale. The suggestion made her shudder. Waddington took her hand.

'Forgive me for talking about this again,' he said gently, 'but I thought it might comfort you—I know how frightfully difficult it is on these occasions to say anything that is of the least use—I thought it might mean something to you that Walter died a martyr to science and to his duty.'

Kitty shrugged her shoulders with a suspicion of impatience.

'Walter died of a broken heart,' she said.

Waddington did not answer. She turned and looked at him slowly. Her face was white and set.

'What did he mean by saying: the dog it was that died? What is it?'

'It's the last line of Goldsmith's *Elegy*.'

Chapter Sixty-seven

Next morning Kitty went to the convent. The girl who opened the door seemed surprised to see her and when Kitty had been for a few minutes about her work the Mother Superior came in. She went up to Kitty and took her hand.

'I am glad to see you, my dear child. You show a fine courage in coming back here so soon after your great sorrow; and wisdom, for I am sure that a little work will keep you from brooding.'

Kitty cast down her eyes, reddening a little; she did not want the Mother Superior to see into her heart.

'I need not tell you how sincerely all of us here sympathise with you.'

'You are very kind,' whispered Kitty.

'We all pray for you constantly and for the soul of him you have lost.'

Kitty made no reply. The Mother Superior released her hand and in her cool, authoritative tone imposed various tasks upon her. She patted two or three children on the head, gave them her aloof, but winning smile, and went about her more pressing affairs.

Chapter Sixty-eight

A week went by. Kitty was sewing. The Mother Superior entered the room and sat down beside her. She gave Kitty's work a shrewd glance.

'You sew very well, my dear. It is a rare accomplishment for young women of your world nowadays.'

'I owe it to my mother.'

'I am sure that your mother will be very glad to see you again.'

Kitty looked up. There was that in the Mother Superior's manner which prevented the remark from being taken as a casual politeness. She went on.

'I allowed you to come here after the death of your dear husband because I thought occupation would distract your mind. I did not think you were fit at that moment to take the long journey to Hong-Kong by yourself, nor did I wish you to sit alone in your house with nothing to do but to remember your loss. But now eight days have passed. It is time for you to go.'

'I don't want to go, Mother. I want to stay here.'

'There is nothing for you to stay for. You came to be with your husband. Your husband is dead. You are in a condition in which you will shortly need a care and attention which it is impossible for you to get here. It is your duty, my dear child, to do everything in your power for the welfare of the being that God has entrusted to your care.'

Kitty was silent for a moment. She looked down.

'I was under the impression that I was of some use here. It has been a great pleasure to me to think that I was. I hoped that you would allow me to go on with my work till the epidemic had come to an end.'

'We are all very grateful for what you have done for us,' answered the Superior, with a slight smile, 'but now that the epidemic is waning the risk of coming here is not so great and I am expecting two sisters from Canton. They should be here very shortly and when they arrive I do not think that I shall be able to make any use of your services.'

Kitty's heart sank. The Mother Superior's tone admitted of no reply; she knew her well enough to know that she would be insensible to entreaty. That she found it necessary to reason with Kitty had brought into her voice a note, if hardly of irritation, at least of the peremptoriness which might lead to it.

'Mr Waddington was good enough to ask my advice.'

'I wish he could have minded his own business,' interrupted Kitty.

'If he hadn't I should all the same have felt obliged to give it him,' said the Mother Superior gently. 'At the present moment your place is not here, but with your mother. Mr Waddington has arranged with Colonel Yü to give you a strong escort so that you will be perfectly safe on the journey, and he has arranged for bearers and coolies. The amah will go with you and arrangements will be made at the cities you pass through. In fact, everything possible for your comfort has been done.'

Kitty's lips tightened. She thought that they might at least have consulted her in a matter which only concerned herself. She had to exercise some self-control in order not to answer sharply.

'And when am I to start?'

The Mother Superior remained quite placid.

'The sooner you can get back to Hong-Kong and then sail to England the better, my dear child. We thought you would like to start at dawn the day after tomorrow.'

'So soon.'

Kitty felt a little inclined to cry. But it was true enough; she had no place there.

'You all seem in a great hurry to be rid of me,' she said ruefully.

Kitty was conscious of a relaxation in the Superior's demeanour. She saw that Kitty was prepared to yield and unconsciously she assumed a more gracious tone. Kitty's sense of humour was acute and her eyes twinkled as she reflected that even the saints liked to have their own way.

'Don't think that I fail to appreciate the goodness of your heart, my dear child, and the admirable charity which makes you unwilling to abandon your self-imposed duties.'

Kitty stared straight in front of her. She faintly shrugged her shoulders. She knew that she could ascribe to herself no such exalted virtues. She wanted to stay because she had nowhere else to go. It was a curious sensation this, that nobody in the world cared two straws whether she was alive or dead.

'I cannot understand that you should be reluctant to go home,' pursued the Superior amiably. 'There are many foreigners in this country who would give a great deal to have your chance!'

'But not you, Mother?'

'Oh, with us it is different, my dear child. When we come here we know that we have left our homes for ever.'

Out of her own wounded feelings emerged the desire in Kitty's mind, malicious perhaps, to seek the joint in the armour of faith which rendered the nuns so aloofly immune to all the natural feelings. She wanted to see whether there was left in the Superior any of the weakness of humanity.

'I should have thought that sometimes it was hard never to see again those that are dear to you and the scenes amid which you were brought up.'

The Mother Superior hesitated for a moment, but Kitty watching her could see no change in the serenity of her beautiful and austere face.

'It is hard for my mother who is old now, for I am her only daughter and she would dearly like to see me once more before she dies. I wish I could give her that joy. But it cannot be and we shall wait till we can meet in paradise.'

'All the same, when one thinks of those to whom one is so dear, it must be difficult not to ask oneself if one was right in cutting oneself off from them.'

'Are you asking me if I have ever regretted the step I took?' On a sudden the Mother Superior's face grew radiant. 'Never, never. I have exchanged a life that was trivial and worthless for one of sacrifice and prayer.'

There was a brief silence and then the Mother Superior, assuming a lighter manner, smiled.

'I am going to ask you to take a little parcel and post it for me when you get to Marseilles. I do not wish to entrust it to the Chinese post-office. I will fetch it at once.'

'You can give it to me tomorrow,' said Kitty.

'You will be too busy to come here tomorrow, my dear. It will be more convenient for you to bid us farewell tonight.'

She rose and with the easy dignity which her voluminous habit could not conceal left the room. In a moment Sister St Joseph came in. She was come to say good-bye. She hoped that Kitty would have a pleasant journey; she would be quite safe, for Colonel Yü was sending a strong escort with her; and the sisters constantly did the journey alone and no harm came to them. And did she like the sea? *Mon Dieu*, how ill she was when there was a storm in the Indian Ocean, *Madame* her mother would be pleased to see her daughter, and she must take care of herself; after all she had another little soul in her care now, and they would all pray for her; she would pray constantly for her and the dear little baby and for the soul of the poor, brave doctor. She was voluble, kindly, and affectionate; and yet Kitty was deeply conscious that for Sister St Joseph (her gaze intent on eternity) she was but a wraith without body or substance. She had a wild impulse to seize the stout, good-natured nun by the shoulders and shake her, crying: 'Don't you know that I'm a human being, unhappy and alone, and I want comfort and sympathy and encouragement; oh, can't you turn a minute away from God and give me a little compassion; not the Christian compassion that you have for all suffering things, but just human compassion for me?' The thought brought a smile to Kitty's lips: how very surprised Sister St Joseph would be! She would certainly be convinced of what now she only suspected, that all English people were mad.

'Fortunately I am a very good sailor,' Kitty answered. 'I've never been sea-sick yet.'

The Mother Superior returned with a small, neat parcel.

'They're handkerchiefs that I've had made for the name-day of my mother,' she said. 'The initials have been embroidered by our young girls.'

Sister St Joseph suggested that Kitty would like to see how beautifully the work was done and the Mother Superior with an indulgent, deprecating smile untied the parcel. The handkerchiefs were of very fine lawn and the initials embroidered in a complicated cypher were surmounted by a crown of strawberry leaves. When Kitty had properly admired the workmanship the handkerchiefs were wrapped up again and the parcel handed to her. Sister St Joseph, with an '*eh bien, Madame, je vous quitte*' and a repetition of her polite and impersonal salutations, went away. Kitty realised that this was the moment to take her leave of the Superior. She thanked her for her kindness to her. They walked together along the bare, white-washed corridors.

'Would it be asking too much of you to register the parcel when you arrive at Marseilles?' said the Superior.

'Of course I'll do that,' said Kitty.

She glanced at the address. The name seemed very grand, but the place mentioned attracted her attention.

'But that is one of the *châteaux* I've seen. I was motoring with friends in France.'

'It is very possible,' said the Mother Superior. 'Strangers are permitted to view it on two days a week.'

'I think if I had ever lived in such a beautiful place I should never have had the courage to leave it.'

'It is of course a historical monument. It is scarcely intimate. If I regretted anything it would not be that, but the little *château* that we lived in when I was a child. It was in the Pyrenees. I was born within sound of the sea. I do not deny that sometimes I should like to hear the waves beating against the rocks.'

Kitty had an idea that the Mother Superior, divining her thought and the reason for her remarks, was slyly making fun of her. But they reached the little, unpretentious door of the convent. To Kitty's surprise the Mother Superior took her in her arms and kissed her. The pressure of her pale lips on Kitty's cheeks, she kissed her first on one side and then on the other, was so unexpected that it made her flush and inclined to cry.

'Good-bye, God bless you, my dear child.' She held her for a moment in her arms. 'Remember that it is nothing to do your duty, that is demanded of you and is no more meritorious than to wash your hands when they are dirty; the only thing that counts is the love of duty; when love and duty are one, then grace is in you and you will enjoy a happiness which passes all understanding.'

The convent door closed for the last time behind her.

Chapter Sixty-nine

Waddington walked with Kitty up the hill and they turned aside for a moment to look at Walter's grave; at the memorial arch he said good-bye to her, and looking at it for the last time she felt that she could reply to the enigmatic irony of its appearance with an equal irony of her own. She stepped into her chair.

One day passed after the other. The sights of the wayside served as a background to her thoughts. She saw them as it were in duplicate, rounded as though in a stereoscope, with an added significance because to everything she saw was added the recollection of what she had seen when but a few short weeks before she had taken the same journey in the contrary direction. The coolies with their loads straggled disorderly, two or three together, and then a hundred yards behind one by himself, and then two or three more; the soldiers of the escort shuffled along with a clumsy walk that covered five and twenty miles a day; the amah was carried by two bearers and Kitty, not because she was heavier, but for face' sake, by four. Now and then they met a string of coolies lolloping by in line with their heavy burdens, now and then a Chinese official in a sedan who looked at the white woman with inquisitive eyes; now they came across peasants in faded blue and huge hats on their way to market and now a woman, old or young, tottering along on her bound feet. They passed up and down little hills laid out with trim rice-fields and farmhouses nestling cosily in a grove of bamboos; they passed through ragged villages and populous cities walled like the cities in a missal. The sun of the early autumn was pleasant, and if at daybreak, when the shimmering dawn lent the neat fields the enchantment of a fairy tale, it was cold, the warmth later was very grateful. Kitty was filled by it with a sense of beatitude which she made no effort to resist.

The vivid scenes with their elegant colour, their unexpected distinction, and their strangeness, were like an arras before which, like mysterious, shadowy shapes, played the phantoms of Kitty's fancy. They seemed wholly unreal. Mei-tan-fu with its crenellated walls was like the painted canvas placed on the stage in an old play to represent a city. The nuns, Waddington, and the Manchu woman who loved him, were fantastic characters in a masque; and the rest, the people sidling along the tortuous streets and those who died, were nameless supers. Of course it had, they all had, a significance of some sort, but what was it? It was as though they performed a ritual dance, elaborate and ancient, and you knew that those complicated measures had a meaning which it was important for you to know; and yet you could see no clue, no clue.

It seemed incredible to Kitty (an old woman was passing along the causeway, in blue, and the blue in the sunshine was like lapis lazuli; her face with its thousand little wrinkles was like a mask of old ivory; and she leaned, as she walked on her tiny feet, on a long black staff) it seemed incredible to Kitty that she and Walter had taken part in that strange and unreal dance. They had played important parts too. She might easily have lost her life: he had. Was it a joke? Perhaps it was nothing but a dream from which she would suddenly awake with a sigh of relief. It seemed to have taken place a long time ago and in a far-off place. It was singular how shadowy the persons of that play seemed against the sunny background of real life. And now it seemed to Kitty like a story that she was reading; it was a little startling that it seemed to concern her so little. She found already that she could not recall with distinctness Waddington's face which had been so familiar to her.

This evening they should reach the city on the Western River from which she was to take the steamer. Thence it was but a night's run to Hong-Kong.

Chapter Seventy

At first because she had not wept when Walter died she was ashamed. It seemed dreadfully callous. Why, the eyes of the Chinese officer, Colonel Yü, had been wet with tears. She was dazed by her husband's death. It was difficult to understand that he would not come into the bungalow again and that when he got up in the morning she would not hear him take his bath in the Suchow tub. He was alive and now he was dead. The sisters wondered at her Christian resignation and admired the courage with which she bore her loss. But Waddington was shrewd; for all his grave sympathy she had a feeling that—how should she put it?—that he had his tongue in his cheek. Of course, Walter's death had been a shock to her. She didn't want him to die. But after all she didn't love him, she had never loved him; it was decent to bear herself with becoming sorrow; it would be ugly and vulgar even to let any one see in her heart; but she had gone through too much to make pretences to herself. It seemed to her that this at least the last few weeks had taught her, that if it is necessary sometimes to lie to others it is always despicable to lie to oneself. She was sorry that Walter had died in that tragic manner, but she was sorry with a purely human sorrow such as she might have felt if it had been an acquaintance. She would acknowledge that Walter had admirable qualities; it just happened that she did not like him; he had always bored her. She would not admit that his death was a relief to her, she could say honestly that if by a word of hers she could bring him back to life she would say it, but she could not resist the feeling that his death made her way to some extent a trifle easier. They would never have been happy together and yet to part would have been terribly difficult. She was startled at herself for feeling as she did; she supposed that people would think her heartless and cruel if they knew. Well, they shouldn't know. She wondered if all her fellows had in their hearts shameful secrets which they spent their time guarding from curious glances.

She looked very little into the future and she made no plans. The only thing she knew was that she wanted to stay in Hong-Kong as short a while as might be. She looked forward to arriving there with horror. It seemed to her that she would like to wander for ever through that smiling and friendly country in her rattan chair, and, an indifferent spectator for ever of the phantasmagoria of life, pass each night under a different roof. But of course the immediate future must be faced: she would go to the hotel when she reached Hong-Kong, she would arrange about getting rid of the house and selling the furniture; there would be no need to see Townsend. He would have the grace to keep out of her way. She would like, all the same, to see him once more in order to tell him what a despicable creature she thought him.

But what did Charles Townsend matter?

Like a rich melody on a harp that rang in exultant arpeggios through the complicated harmonies of a symphony, one thought beat in her heart insistently. It was this thought which gave their exotic beauty to the rice-fields, which made a little smile break on her pale lips as a smooth-faced lad swung past her on his way to the market town with exultation in his carriage and audacity in his eyes, and which gave the magic of a tumultuous life to the cities she passed through. The city of the pestilence was a prison from which she was escaped, and she had never known before how exquisite was the blueness of the sky and what a joy there was in the bamboo copses that leaned with such an adorable grace across the causeway. Freedom! That was the thought that sung in her heart so that even though the future was so dim, it was iridescent like the mist over the river where the morning sun fell upon it. Freedom! Not only freedom from a bond that irked, and a companionship which depressed her; freedom, not only from the death which had threatened, but freedom from the love that had degraded her; freedom from all spiritual ties, the freedom of a disembodied spirit; and with freedom, courage and a valiant unconcern for whatever was to come.

Chapter Seventy-one

When the boat docked at Hong-Kong, Kitty, who had been standing on deck to look at the coloured, gay and vivacious traffic of the river, went into her cabin to see that the amah had left nothing behind. She gave herself a look in the glass. She wore black, the nuns had dyed a dress for her, but not mourning; and the thought crossed her mind that the first thing she must do was to see to this. The habiliments of woe could not but serve as an effective disguise to her unexpected feelings. There was a knock on her cabin door. The amah opened it.

'Mrs Fane.'

Kitty turned round and saw a face which at the first moment she did not recognise. Then her heart gave a sudden quick beat and she flushed. It was Dorothy Townsend. Kitty so little expected to see her that she knew neither what to do nor what to say. But Mrs Townsend came into the cabin and with an impulsive gesture took Kitty in her arms.

'Oh, my dear, my dear, I'm so dreadfully sorry for you.'

Kitty allowed herself to be kissed. She was a little surprised at this effusiveness in a woman who she had always thought cold and distant.

'It's very kind of you,' murmured Kitty.

'Come on deck. The amah will look after your things and my boys are here.'

She took Kitty's hand and Kitty, allowing herself to be led, noticed that her good-natured, weather-beaten face bore an expression of real concern.

'Your boat's early, I very nearly didn't get down in time,' said Mrs Townsend. 'I couldn't have borne it if I'd missed you.'

'But you didn't come to meet me?' exclaimed Kitty.

'Of course I did.'

'But how did you know I was coming?'

'Mr Waddington sent me a telegram.'

Kitty turned away. She had a lump in her throat. It was funny that a little unexpected kindness should so affect her. She did not want to cry; she wished Dorothy Townsend would go away. But Dorothy took the hand that was hanging by Kitty's side and pressed it. It embarrassed Kitty that this shy woman should be so demonstrative.

'I want you to do me a great favour. Charlie and I want you to come and stay with us while you're in Hong-Kong.'

Kitty snatched her hand away.

'It's awfully kind of you. I couldn't possibly.'

'But you must. You can't go and live all by yourself in your own house. It would be dreadful for you. I've prepared everything. You shall have your own sitting-room. You can have your meals there if you don't care to have them with us. We both want you to come.'

'I wasn't thinking of going to the house. I was going to get myself a room at the Hong-Kong Hotel. I couldn't possibly put you to so much trouble.'

The suggestion had taken her by surprise. She was confused and vexed. If Charlie had had any sense of decency he would never have allowed his wife to make the invitation. She did not wish to be under an obligation to either of them.

'Oh, but I couldn't bear the idea of your living at a hotel. And you'd hate the Hong-Kong Hotel just now. With all those people about and the band playing jazz all the time. Please say you'll come to us. I promise you that Charlie and I won't bother you.'

'I don't know why you should be so kind to me.' Kitty was getting a little short of excuses; she could not bring herself to utter a blunt and definite no. 'I'm afraid I'm not very good company among strangers just now.'

'But need we be strangers to you? Oh, I do so want not to be, I so want you to allow me to be your friend.' Dorothy clasped her hands and her voice, her cool, deliberate and distinguished voice, was tremulous with tears. 'I so awfully want you to come. You see, I want to make amends to you.'

Kitty did not understand. She did not know what amends Charlie's wife owed her.

'I'm afraid I didn't very much like you at first. I thought you rather fast. You see, I'm old-fashioned and I suppose I'm intolerant.'

Kitty gave her a passing glance. What she meant was that at first she had thought Kitty vulgar. Though Kitty allowed no shadow of it to show on her face in her heart she laughed. Much she cared for what any one thought of her now!

'And when I heard that you'd gone with your husband into the jaws of death, without a moment's hesitation, I felt such a frightful cad. I felt so humiliated. You've been so wonderful, you've been so brave, you make all the rest of us look so dreadfully cheap and second-rate.' Now the tears were pouring down her kind, homely face. 'I can't tell you how much I admire you and what a respect I have for you. I know I can do nothing to make up for your terrible loss, but I want you to know how deeply, how sincerely I feel for you. And if you'll only allow me to do a little something for you it will be a privilege. Don't bear me a grudge because I misjudged you. You're heroic and I'm just a silly fool of a woman.'

Kitty looked down at the deck. She was very pale. She wished that Dorothy would not show such uncontrollable emotion. She was touched, it was true, but she could not help a slight feeling of impatience that this simple creature should believe such lies.

'If you really mean that you'd like to have me, of course I shall be glad to come,' she sighed.

Chapter Seventy-two

The Townsends lived on the Peak in a house with a wide view over the sea, and Charlie did not as a rule come up to luncheon, but on the day of Kitty's arrival Dorothy (they were Kitty and Dorothy to one another by now) told her that if she felt up to seeing him he would like to come and bid her welcome. Kitty reflected that since she must see him she might just as well see him at once and she looked forward with grim amusement to the embarrassment she must cause him. She saw very well that the invitation to stay had arisen in his wife's fancy and notwithstanding his own feelings he had immediately approved. Kitty knew how great his desire was always to do the right thing and to offer her a gracious hospitality was obviously very much the right thing. But he could hardly remember that last interview of theirs without mortification: to a man so vain as Townsend it must be galling like an ulcer that would not heal. She hoped that she had hurt him as much as he had hurt her. He must hate her now. She was glad to think that she did not hate, but only despised him. It gave her a sardonic satisfaction to reflect that whatever his feelings he would be obliged to make much of her. When she left his office that afternoon he must have hoped with all his heart that he would never set eyes on her again.

And now, sitting with Dorothy, she waited for him to come in. She was conscious of her delight in the sober luxury of the drawing-room. She sat in an armchair, there were lovely flowers here and there, on the walls were pleasing pictures; the room was shaded and cool, it was friendly and homelike. She remembered with a faint shudder the bare and empty parlour of the missionary's bungalow; the rattan chairs and the kitchen table with its cotton cloth, the stained shelves with all those cheap editions of novels, and the little skimpy red curtains that had such a dusty look. Oh, it had been so uncomfortable! She supposed that Dorothy had never thought of that.

They heard a motor drive up, and Charlie strode into the room.

'Am I late? I hope I haven't kept you waiting. I had to see the Governor and I simply couldn't get away.'

He went up to Kitty, and took both her hands.

'I'm so very, very glad you've come here. I know Dorothy has told you that we want you to stay as long as ever you like and that we want you to look upon our house as your home. But I want to tell you so myself as well. If there's anything in the world I can do for you I shall only be too happy.' His eyes wore a charming expression of sincerity; she wondered if he saw the irony in hers. 'I'm awfully stupid at saying some things and I don't want to seem a clumsy fool, but I do want you to know how deeply I sympathise with you in your husband's death. He was a thundering good chap, and he'll be missed here more than I can say.'

'Don't, Charlie,' said his wife. 'I'm sure Kitty understands. . . . Here are the cocktails.'

Following the luxurious custom of the foreigners in China two boys in uniform came into the room with savouries and cocktails. Kitty refused.

'Oh, you must have one,' insisted Townsend in his breezy, cordial way. 'It'll do you good and I'm sure you haven't had such a thing as a cocktail since you left Hong-Kong. Unless I'm very much mistaken you couldn't get ice at Mei-tan-fu.'

'You're not mistaken,' said Kitty.

For a moment she had a picture before her mind's eye of that beggar with the tousled head in the blue rags through which you saw the emaciated limbs, who had lain dead against the compound wall.

Chapter Seventy-three

They went in to luncheon. Charlie, sitting at the head of his table, easily took charge of the conversation. After those first few words of sympathy he treated Kitty, not as though she had just suffered a devastating experience, but rather as though she had come in from Shanghai for a change after an operation for appendicitis. She needed cheering and he was prepared to cheer her. The best way of making her feel at home was to treat her as one of the family. He was a tactful man. He began talking of the autumn race meeting, and the polo—by Jove, he would have to give up playing polo if he couldn't get his weight down—and a chat he had had that morning with the Governor. He spoke of a party they had been to on the Admiral's flag-ship, the state of affairs in Canton, and of the links at Lushan. In a few minutes Kitty felt that she might have been away for no longer than a weekend. It was incredible that over there, up country, six hundred miles away only (the distance from London to Edinburgh, wasn't it?) men, women and children had been dying like flies. Soon she found herself asking about so and so who had broken a collar bone at polo and if Mrs This had gone home or Mrs That was playing in the tennis tournament. Charlie made his little jokes and she smiled at them. Dorothy with her faint air of superiority (which now included Kitty and so was no longer slightly offensive, but a bond of union rather) was gently ironic about various persons in the colony. Kitty began to feel more alert.

'Why, she's looking better already,' said Charlie to his wife. 'She was so pale before tiffin that I was quite startled; she's really got some colour in her cheeks now.'

But while she took her part in the conversation, if not with gaiety (for she felt that neither Dorothy nor Charlie with his admirable sense of decorum would approve of that) at least with cheerfulness, Kitty observed her host. In all those weeks during which her fancy had been revengefully occupied with him she had built up in her mind a very vivid impression of him. His thick curling hair was a little too long and too carefully brushed, in order to hide the fact that it was greying there was too much oil on it; his face was too red, with its network of mauve veins on the cheeks, and his jowl was too massive: when he did not hold his head up to hide it you saw that he had a double chin; and there was something apelike in those bushy, grizzled eyebrows of his that vaguely disgusted her. He was heavy in his movements, and all the care he took in his diet and all his exercise did not prevent him from being fat; his bones were much too well covered and his joints had a middle-aged stiffness. His smart clothes were a little tight for him and a little too young.

But when he came into the drawing-room before luncheon Kitty received quite a shock (this perhaps was why her pallor had been so marked), for she discovered that her imagination had played an odd trick on her: he did not in the least look as she had pictured him. She could hardly help laughing at herself. His hair was not grey at all, oh, there were a few white hairs on the temple, but they were becoming; and his face was not red, but sunburned; his head was very well placed on his neck; and he wasn't stout and he wasn't old: in fact he was almost slim and his figure was admirable–could you blame him if he was a trifle vain of it?–he might have been a young man. And of course he did know how to wear his clothes; it was absurd to deny that: he looked neat and clean and trim. Whatever could have possessed her to think him this and that? He was a very handsome man. It was lucky that she knew how worthless he was. Of course she had always admitted that his voice had a winning quality, and his voice was exactly as she remembered it: it made the falseness of every word he said more exasperating; its richness of tone and its warmth rang now in her ears with insincerity and she wondered how she could ever have been taken in by it. His eyes were beautiful: that was where his charm lay, they had such a soft, blue brilliance and even when he was talking balderdash an expression which was so delightful; it was almost impossible not to be moved by them.

At last the coffee was brought in and Charlie lit his cheroot. He looked at his watch and rose from the table.

'Well, I must leave you two young women to your own devices. It's time for me to get back to the office.' He paused and then with his friendly, charming eyes on Kitty said to her: 'I'm not going to bother you for a day or two till you're rested, but then I want to have a little business talk with you.'

'With me?'

'We must make arrangements about your house, you know, and then there's the furniture.'

'Oh, but I can go to a lawyer. There's no reason why I should bother you about that.'

'Don't think for a moment I'm going to let you waste your money on legal

expenses. I'm going to see to everything. You know you're entitled to a
pension: I'm going to talk to H.E. about it and see if by making
representations in the proper quarter we can't get something extra for you.
You put yourself in my hands. But don't bother about anything just yet. All
we want you to do now is to get fit and well: isn't that right, Dorothy?'

'Of course.'

He gave Kitty a little nod and then passing by his wife's chair took her
hand and kissed it. Most Englishmen look a little foolish when they kiss a
woman's hand; he did it with a graceful ease.

Chapter Seventy-four

It was not till Kitty was fairly settled at the Townsends that she discovered
that she was weary. The comfort and the unaccustomed amenity of this life
broke up the strain under which she had been living. She had forgotten how
pleasant it was to take one's ease, how lulling to be surrounded by pretty
things, and how agreeable it was to receive attention. She sank back with a
sigh of relief into the facile existence of the luxurious East. It was not
displeasing to feel that in a discreet and well-bred fashion she was an object
of sympathetic interest. Her bereavement was so recent that it was
impossible for entertainments to be given for her, but ladies of consequence
in the Colony (His Excellency's wife, the wives of the Admiral and of the
Chief Justice) came to drink a quiet cup of tea with her. His Excellency's
wife said that His Excellency was most anxious to see her and if she would
come very quietly to luncheon at Government House ('not a party, of
course, only ourselves and the A.D.C.'s!'), it would be very nice. These
ladies used Kitty as though she were a piece of porcelain which was as fragile
as it was precious. She could not fail to see that they looked upon her as a
little heroine, and she had sufficient humour to play the part with modesty
and discretion. She wished sometimes that Waddington were there; with his
malicious shrewdness he would have seen the fun of the situation; and when
alone they might have had a good laugh over it together. Dorothy had had a
letter from him, and he had said all manner of things about her devoted work
at the convent, about her courage and her self-control. Of course he was
skilfully pulling their legs: the dirty dog.

Chapter Seventy-five

Kitty did not know whether it was by chance or by design that she never
found herself for a moment alone with Charlie. His tact was exquisite. He
remained kindly, sympathetic, pleasant and amiable. No one could have
guessed that they had ever been more than acquaintances. But one afternoon
when she was lying on a sofa outside her room reading he passed along the
verandah and stopped.

'What is that you're reading?' he asked.

'A book.'

She looked at him with irony. He smiled.

'Dorothy's gone to a garden-party at Government House.'

'I know. Why haven't you gone too?'

'I didn't feel I could face it and I thought I'd come back and keep you company. The car's outside, would you like to come for a drive round the island?'

'No, thank you.'

He sat down on the foot of the sofa on which she lay.

'We haven't had the chance of a talk by ourselves since you got here.'

She looked straight into his eyes with cool insolence.

'Do you think we have anything to say to one another?'

'Volumes.'

She shifted her feet a little so that she should not touch him.

'Are you still angry with me?' he asked, the shadow of a smile on his lips and his eyes melting.

'Not a bit,' she laughed.

'I don't think you'd laugh if you weren't.'

'You're mistaken; I despise you much too much to be angry with you.'

He was unruffled.

'I think you're rather hard on me. Looking back calmly, don't you honestly think I was right?'

'From your standpoint.'

'Now that you know Dorothy, you must admit she's rather nice?'

'Of course. I shall always be grateful for her great kindness to me.'

'She's one in a thousand. I should never have had a moment's peace if we'd bolted. It would have been a rotten trick to play on her. And after all I had to think of my children; it would have been an awful handicap for them.'

For a minute she held him in her reflective gaze. She felt completely mistress of the situation.

'I've watched you very carefully during the week I've been here. I've come to the conclusion that you really are fond of Dorothy. I should never have thought you capable of it.'

'I told you I was fond of her. I wouldn't do anything to cause her a moment's uneasiness. She's the best wife a man ever had.'

'Have you never thought that you owed her any loyalty?'

'What the eye doesn't see the heart doesn't grieve for,' he smiled.

She shrugged her shoulders.

'You're despicable.'

'I'm human. I don't know why you should think me such a cad because I fell head over ears in love with you. I didn't particularly want to, you know.'

It gave her a little twist of the heart-strings to hear him say that.

'I was fair game,' she answered bitterly.

'Naturally I couldn't foresee that we were going to get into such a devil of a scrape.'

'And in any case you had a pretty shrewd idea that if any one suffered it wouldn't be you.'

'I think that's a bit thick. After all, now it's all over, you must see I acted for the best for both of us. You lost your head and you ought to be jolly glad that I kept mine. Do you think it would have been a success if I'd done what you wanted me to? We were dashed uncomfortable in the frying-pan, but we should have been a damned sight worse off in the fire. And you haven't come to any harm. Why can't we kiss and make friends?'

She almost laughed.

'You can hardly expect me to forget that you sent me to almost certain death without a shadow of compunction?'

'Oh, what nonsense! I told you there was no risk if you took reasonable precautions. Do you think I'd have let you go for a moment if I hadn't been perfectly convinced of that?'

'You were convinced because you wanted to be. You're one of those cowards who only think what it's profitable for them to think.'

'Well, the proof of the pudding is in the eating. You have come back, and if you don't mind my saying anything so objectionable you've come back prettier than ever.'

'And Walter?'

He could not resist the facetious answer which came to his mind. Charlie smiled.

'Nothing suits you so well as black.'

She stared at him for a moment. Tears filled her eyes and she began to cry. Her beautiful face was distorted with grief. She did not seek to hide it, but lay on her back with her hands along her sides.

'For God's sake don't cry like that. I didn't mean to say anything unkind. It was only a joke. You know how sincerely I feel for you in your bereavement.'

'Oh, hold your stupid tongue.'

'I'd give anything to have Walter back again.'

'He died because of you and me.'

He took her hand, but she snatched it away from him.

'Please go away,' she sobbed. 'That's the only thing you can do for me now. I hate and despise you. Walter was worth ten of you and I was too big a fool to see it. Go away. Go away.'

She saw he was going to speak again and she sprang to her feet and went into her room. He followed her, and as he entered, with instinctive prudence, drew the shutter so that they were almost in darkness.

'I can't leave you like this,' he said, putting his arms round her. 'You know I didn't mean to hurt you.'

'Don't touch me. For God's sake go. Go away.'

She tried to tear herself from him, but he would not let her. She was crying hysterically now.

'Darling, don't you know that I've always loved you,' he said in his deep, charming voice. 'I love you more than ever.'

'How can you tell such lies! Let me go. Damn you, let me go.'

'Don't be unkind to me, Kitty. I know I've been a brute to you, but forgive me.'

She was shaking and sobbing, struggling to get away from him, but the pressure of his arms was strangely comforting. She had so longed to feel them round her once more, just once, and all her body trembled. She felt dreadfully weak. It seemed as though her bones were melting, and the sorrow she felt for Walter shifted into pity for herself.

'Oh, how could you be so unkind to me?' she sobbed. 'Don't you know that I loved you with all my heart. No one has ever loved you as I loved you.'

'Darling.'

He began to kiss her.

'No, no,' she cried.

He sought her face, but she turned away; he sought her lips; she did not know what he was saying, broken, passionate words of love; and his arms held her so firmly that she felt like a child that has been lost and now at last is safe at home. She moaned faintly. Her eyes were closed and her face was wet with tears. And then he found her lips and the pressure of his upon them shot through her body like the flame of God. It was an ecstasy and she was burnt to a cinder and she glowed as though she were transfigured. In her dreams, in her dreams she had known this rapture. What was he doing with her now? She did not know. She was not a woman, her personality was dissolved, she was nothing but desire. He lifted her off her feet, she was very light in his arms, he carried her and she clung to him, desperate and adoring; her head sank on the pillow and his lips clung to hers.

Chapter Seventy-six

She sat on the edge of the bed hiding her face with her hands.

'Would you like a drop of water?'

She shook her head. He went over to the washing-stand, filled the tooth-glass and brought it to her.

'Come along, have a little drink and you'll feel better.'

He put the glass to her lips and she sipped the water. Then, with horrified eyes, she stared at him. He was standing over her, looking down, and in his eyes was a twinkle of self-satisfaction.

'Well, do you think I'm such a dirty dog as you did?' he asked.

She looked down.

'Yes. But I know that I'm not a bit better than you. Oh, I'm so ashamed.'

'Well, I think you're very ungrateful.'

'Will you go now?'

'To tell you the truth I think it's about time. I'll just go and tidy up before Dorothy comes in.'

He went out of the room with a jaunty step.

Kitty sat for a while, still on the edge of the bed, hunched up like an imbecile. Her mind was vacant. A shudder passed through her. She staggered to her feet and, going to the dressing-table, sank into a chair. She stared at herself in the glass. Her eyes were swollen with tears; her face was stained and there was a red mark on one cheek where his had rested. She looked at herself with horror. It was the same face. She had expected in it she knew not what change of degradation.

'Swine,' she flung at her reflection. 'Swine.'

Then, letting her face fall on her arms, she wept bitterly. Shame, shame! She did not know what had come over her. It was horrible. She hated him and she hated herself. It had been ecstasy. Oh, hateful! She could never look him in the face again. He was so justified. He had been right not to marry her, for she was worthless; she was no better than a harlot. Oh, worse, for those poor women gave themselves for bread. And in this house too into which Dorothy had taken her in her sorrow and cruel desolation! Her shoulders shook with her sobs. Everything was gone now. She had thought herself changed, she had thought herself strong, she thought she had returned to Hong-Kong a woman who possessed herself; new ideas flitted about her heart like little yellow butterflies in the sunshine and she had hoped to be so much better in the future; freedom like a spirit of light had beckoned her on, and the world was like a spacious plain through which she could walk light of foot and with head erect. She had thought herself free from lust and vile passions, free to live the clean and healthy life of the spirit; she had likened herself to the white egrets that fly with leisurely flight across the rice-fields at dusk and they are like the soaring thoughts of a mind at rest with itself; and she was a slave. Weak, weak! It was hopeless, it was no good to try, she was a slut.

She would not go in to dinner. She sent the boy to tell Dorothy that she had a headache and preferred to remain in her room. Dorothy came in and, seeing her red, swollen eyes, talked for a little in her gentle, commiserating way of trivial things. Kitty knew that Dorothy thought she had been crying on account of Walter and, sympathising like the good and loving wife she was, respected the natural sorrow.

'I know it's very hard, dear,' she said as she left Kitty. 'But you must try to have courage. I'm sure your dear husband wouldn't wish you to grieve for him.'

Chapter Seventy-seven

But next morning Kitty rose early and leaving a note for Dorothy to say that she was gone out on business took a tram down the hill. She made her way through the crowded streets with their motor cars, rickshaws and chairs, and the motley throng of Europeans and Chinese, to the offices of the P. & O. Company. A ship was sailing in two days, the first ship out of the port, and she had made up her mind that at all costs she must go on it. When the clerk told her that every berth was booked she asked to see the chief agent. She sent in her name and the agent, whom she had met before, came out to fetch her into his office. He knew her circumstances and when she told him what she wished he sent for the passenger list. He looked at it with perplexity.

'I beseech you to do what you can for me,' she urged him.

'I don't think there's any one in the Colony who wouldn't do anything in the world for you, Mrs Fane,' he answered.

He sent for a clerk and made enquiries. Then he nodded.

'I'm going to shift one or two people. I know you want to get home and I think we ought to do our best for you. I can give you a little cabin to yourself. I expect you'd prefer that.'

She thanked him. She left him with an elated heart. Flight: that was her only thought. Flight! She sent a cable to her father to announce her immediate return; she had already cabled to him to say that Walter was dead; and then went back again to the Townsends to tell Dorothy what she had done.

'We shall be dreadfully sorry to lose you,' the kind creature said, 'but of course I understand that you want to be with your mother and father.'

Since her return to Hong-Kong Kitty had hesitated from day to day to go to her house. She dreaded entering it again and meeting face to face the recollections with which it was peopled. But now she had no alternative. Townsend had arranged for the sale of the furniture and he had found some one eager to take on the lease, but there were all her clothes and Walter's, for they had taken next to nothing to Mei-tan-fu, and there were books, photographs, and various odds and ends. Kitty, indifferent to everything and anxious to cut herself off completely from the past, realised that it would outrage the susceptibilities of the Colony if she allowed these things to go with the rest to an auction-room. They must be packed and sent to her. So after tiffin she prepared to go to the house. Dorothy, eager to give her help, offered to accompany her, but Kitty begged to be allowed to go alone. She agreed that two of Dorothy's boys should come and assist in the packing.

The house had been left in charge of the head boy and he opened the door for Kitty. It was curious to go into her own house as though she were a stranger. It was neat and clean. Everything was in its place, ready for her use, but although the day was warm and sunny there was about the silent rooms a chill and desolate air. The furniture was stiffly arranged, exactly where it should be, and the vases which should have held flowers were in their places; the book which Kitty had laid face downwards she did not remember when still lay face downwards. It was as though the house had been left empty but a minute before and yet that minute was fraught with eternity so that you could not imagine that ever again that house would echo with talk and resound with laughter. On the piano the open music of a foxtrot seemed to wait to be played, but you had a feeling that if you struck the keys no sound would come. Walter's room was as tidy as when he was there. On the chest of drawers were two large photographs of Kitty, one in her presentation dress and one in her wedding-gown.

But the boys fetched up the trunks from the box-room and she stood over them watching them pack. They packed neatly and quickly. Kitty reflected that in the two days she had it would be easy to get everything done. She must not let herself think; she had no time for that. Suddenly she heard a step behind her and turning round saw Charles Townsend. She felt a sudden chill at her heart.

'What do you want?' she said.

'Will you come into your sitting-room? I have something to say to you.'

'I'm very busy.'

'I shall only keep you five minutes.'

She said no more, but with a word to the boys to go on with what they were doing, preceded Charles into the next room. She did not sit down, in order to show him that she expected him not to detain her. She knew that she was very pale and her heart was beating fast, but she faced him coolly, with hostile eyes.

'What is it you want?'

'I've just heard from Dorothy that you're going the day after tomorrow. She told me that you'd come here to do your packing and she asked me to ring up and find out if there was anything I could do for you.'

'I'm grateful to you, but I can manage quite well by myself.'

'So I imagined. I didn't come here to ask you that.

'I came to ask if your sudden departure is due to what happened yesterday.'

'You and Dorothy have been very good to me. I didn't wish you to think I was taking advantage of your good nature.'

'That's not a very straight answer.'

'What does it matter to you?'

'It matters a great deal. I shouldn't like to think that anything I'd done had driven you away.'

She was standing at the table. She looked down. Her eyes fell on the *Sketch*. It was months old now. It was that paper which Walter had stared at all through the terrible evening when – and Walter now was . . . She raised her eyes.

'I feel absolutely degraded. You can't possibly despise me as much as I despise myself.'

'But I don't despise you. I meant every word that I said yesterday. What's the good of running away like this? I don't know why we can't be good friends. I hate the idea of your thinking I've treated you badly.'

'Why couldn't you leave me alone?'

'Hang it all, I'm not a stick or a stone. It's so unreasonable, the way you look at it; it's so morbid. I thought after yesterday you'd feel a little more kindly to me. After all, we're only human.'

'I don't feel human. I feel like an animal. A pig or a rabbit or a dog. Oh, I don't blame you, I was just as bad. I yielded to you because I wanted you. But it wasn't the real me. I'm not that hateful, beastly, lustful woman. I disown her. It wasn't me that lay on that bed panting for you when my husband was hardly cold in his grave and your wife had been so kind to me, so indescribably kind. It was only the animal in me, dark and fearful like an evil spirit, and I disown, and hate, and despise it. And ever since, when I've thought of it, my gorge rises and I feel that I must vomit.'

He frowned a little and gave a short, uneasy snigger.

'Well, I'm fairly broadminded, but sometimes you say things that positively shock me.'

'I should be sorry to do that. You'd better go now. You're a very unimportant little man and I'm silly to talk to you seriously.'

He did not answer for a while and she saw by the shadow in his blue eyes that he was angry with her. He would heave a sigh of relief when, tactful and courteous as ever, he had finally seen her off. It amused her to think of the politeness with which, while they shook hands and he wished her a pleasant journey, she would thank him for his hospitality. But she saw his expression change.

'Dorothy tells me you're going to have a baby,' he said.

She felt herself colour, but she allowed no gesture to escape her.

'I am.'

'Am I by any chance the father?'

'No, no. It's Walter's child.'

She spoke with an emphasis which she could not prevent, but even as she spoke she knew that it was not the tone with which to carry conviction.

'Are you sure?' He was now roguishly smiling. 'After all, you were married to Walter a couple of years and nothing happened. The dates seem to fit all right. I think it's much more likely to be mine than Walter's.'

'I would rather kill myself than have a child of yours.'

'Oh, come now, that's nonsense. I should be awfully pleased and proud. I'd like it to be a girl, you know. I've only had boys with Dorothy. You won't be able to be in doubt very long, you know: my three kiddies are absolutely the living image of me.'

He had regained his good humour and she knew why. If the child was his, though she might never see him again, she could never entirely escape him. His power over her would reach out and he would still, obscurely but definitely, influence every day of her life.

'You really are the most vain and fatuous ass that it's ever been my bad luck to run across,' she said.

Chapter Seventy-eight

As the ship steamed into Marseilles, Kitty, looking at the rugged and beautiful outline of the coast glowing in the sunlight, on a sudden caught sight of the golden statue of the Blessed Virgin which stands upon the church of Sainte Marie de la Grace as a symbol of safety to the mariner at sea. She remembered how the Sisters of the convent at Mei-tan-fu, leaving their own land for ever, had knelt as the figure faded in the distance so that it was no more than a little golden flame in the blue sky and sought in prayer to allay the pang of separation. She clasped her hands in supplication to what power she knew not.

During the long, quiet journey she had thought incessantly of the horrible thing that had happened to her. She could not understand herself. It was so unexpected. What was it that had seized her, so that, despising him, despising him with all her heart, she had yielded passionately to Charlie's foul embrace? Rage filled her and disgust of herself obsessed her. She felt that she could never forget her humiliation. She wept. But as the distance from Hong-Kong increased she found that she was insensibly losing the vividness of her resentment. What had happened seemed to have happened in another world. She was like a person who has been stricken with sudden madness and recovering is distressed and ashamed at the grotesque things he vaguely remembers to have done when he was not himself. But because he knows he was not himself he feels that in his own eyes at least he can claim indulgence. Kitty thought that perhaps a generous heart might pity rather than condemn her. But she sighed as she thought how woefully her self-confidence had been shattered. The way had seemed to stretch before her straight and easy and now she saw that it was a tortuous way and that pitfalls awaited her. The vast spaces and the tragic and beautiful sunsets of the Indian Ocean rested her. She seemed borne then to some country where she might in freedom possess her soul. If she could only regain her self-respect at the cost of a bitter conflict, well, she must find the courage to affront it.

The future was lonely and difficult. At Port Said she had received a letter from her mother in answer to her cable. It was a long letter written in the large and fanciful writing which was taught to young ladies in her mother's youth. Its ornateness was so neat that it gave you an impression of insincerity. Mrs Garstin expressed her regret at Walter's death and sympathised properly with her daughter's grief. She feared that Kitty was left inadequately provided for, but naturally the Colonial Office would give her a pension. She was glad to know that Kitty was coming back to England and of course she must come and stay with her father and mother till her child was born. Then followed certain instructions that Kitty must be sure to follow and various details of her sister Doris's confinement. The little boy weighed so and so much and his paternal grandfather said he had never seen a finer child. Doris was expecting again and they hoped for another boy in order to make the succession to the baronetcy quite sure.

Kitty saw that the point of the letter lay in the definite date set for the invitation. Mrs Garstin had no intention of being saddled with a widowed daughter in modest circumstances. It was singular, when she reflected how her mother had idolised her, that now, disappointed in her, she found her merely a nuisance. How strange was the relation between parents and children! When they were small the parents doted on them, passed through agonies of apprehension at each childish ailment, and the children clung to their parents with love and adoration; a few years passed, the children grew up, and persons not of their kin were more important to their happiness than father or mother. Indifference displaced the blind and instinctive love of the past. Their meetings were a source of boredom and irritation. Distracted once at the thought of a month's separation they were able now to look forward with equanimity to being parted for years. Her mother need not worry: as soon as she could she would make herself a home of her own. But she must have a little time; at present everything was vague and she could not form any picture of the future: perhaps she would die in childbirth; that would be a solution of many difficulties.

But when they docked two letters were handed to her. She was surprised to recognise her father's writing: she did not remember that he had ever written to her. He was not effusive, and began: dear Kitty. He told her that he was writing instead of her mother who had not been well and was obliged to go into a nursing home to have an operation. Kitty was not to be frightened and was to keep to her intention of going round by sea; it was much more expensive to come across by land and with her mother away it would be inconvenient for Kitty to stay at the house in Harrington Gardens. The other was from Doris and it started: Kitty darling, not because Doris had any particular affection for her, but because it was her way thus to address every one she knew.

> Kitty darling,
> I expect Father has written to you. Mother has got to have an operation. It appears that she has been rotten for the last year, but you know she hates doctors and she's been taking all sorts of patent medicines. I don't know what's the matter with her as she insists on making a secret of the whole thing and flies into a passion if you ask her questions. She has been looking simply awful and if I were you I think I'd get off at Marseilles and come back as quick as you can. But don't let on that I told you to come as she pretends there's nothing much the matter with her and she doesn't want you to get here till she's back at home. She's made the doctors promise that she shall be moved in a week. Best love.
> Doris

> I'm awfully sorry about Walter. You must have had a hell of a time, poor darling. I'm simply dying to see you. It's rather funny our both having babies together. We shall be able to hold one another's hands.

Kitty, lost in reflection, stood for a little while on the deck. She could not imagine her mother ill. She never remembered to have seen her other than active and resolute; she had always been impatient of other people's ailments. Then a steward came up to her with a telegram.

DEEPLY REGRET TO INFORM YOU THAT YOUR MOTHER DIED THIS MORNING. FATHER.

Chapter Seventy-nine

Kitty rang the bell at the house in Harrington Gardens. She was told that her father was in his study and going to the door she opened it softly: he was sitting by the fire reading the last edition of the evening paper. He looked up as she entered, put down the paper, and sprang nervously to his feet.

'Oh, Kitty, I didn't expect you till the later train.'

'I thought you wouldn't want the bother of coming to meet me so I didn't wire the time I expected to arrive.'

He gave her his cheek to kiss in the manner she so well remembered.

'I was just having a look at the paper,' he said. 'I haven't read the paper for the last two days.'

She saw that he thought it needed some explanation if he occupied himself with the ordinary affairs of life.

'Of course,' she said. 'You must be tired out. I'm afraid mother's death has been a great shock to you.'

He was older and thinner than when she had last seen him. A little, lined, dried-up man, with a precise manner.

'The surgeon said there had never been any hope. She hadn't been herself for more than a year, but she refused to see a doctor. The surgeon told me that she must have been in constant pain, he said it was a miracle that she had been able to endure it.'

'Did she never complain?'

'She said she wasn't very well. But she never complained of pain.' He paused and looked at Kitty. 'Are you very tired after your journey?'

'Not very.'

'Would you like to go up and see her?'

'Is she here?'

'Yes, she was brought here from the nursing home.'

'Yes, I'll go now.'

'Would you like me to come with you?'

There was something in her father's tone that made her look at him quickly. His face was slightly turned from her; he did not want her to catch his eye. Kitty had acquired of late a singular proficiency at reading the thoughts of others. After all, day after day she had applied all her sensibilities to divine from a casual word or an unguarded gesture the hidden thoughts of her husband. She guessed at once what her father was trying to hide from her. It was relief he felt, an infinite relief, and he was frightened of himself. For hard on thirty years he had been a good and faithful husband, he had never uttered a single word in dispraise of his wife, and now he should grieve for her. He had always done the things that were expected of him. It would have been shocking to him by the flicker of an eyelid or by the smallest hint to betray that he did not feel what under the circumstances a bereaved husband should feel.

'No, I would rather go by myself,' said Kitty.

She went upstairs and into the large, cold and pretentious bedroom in which her mother for so many years had slept. She remembered so well those massive pieces of mahogany and the engravings after Marcus Stone which adorned the walls. The things on the dressing-table were arranged with the stiff precision which Mrs Garstin had all her life insisted upon. The flowers looked out of place; Mrs Garstin would have thought it silly, affected and unhealthy to have flowers in her bedroom. Their perfume did not cover that acrid, musty smell, as of freshly washed linen, which Kitty remembered as characteristic of her mother's room.

Mrs Garstin lay on the bed, her hands folded across her breasts with a meekness which in life she would have had no patience with. With her strong sharp features, the cheeks hollow with suffering and the temples sunken, she looked handsome and even imposing. Death had robbed her face of its meanness and left only an impression of character. She might have been a Roman empress. It was strange to Kitty that of the dead persons she had seen this was the only one who in death seemed to preserve a look as though that clay had been once a habitation of the spirit. Grief she could not feel, for there had been too much bitterness between her mother and herself to leave in her heart any deep feeling of affection; and looking back on the girl she had been she knew that it was her mother who had made her what she was. But when she looked at that hard, domineering and ambitious woman who lay there so still and silent with all her petty aims frustrated by death, she was aware of a vague pathos. She had schemed and intrigued all her life and never had she desired anything but what was base and unworthy. Kitty wondered whether perhaps in some other sphere she looked upon her earthly course with consternation.

Doris came in.

'I thought you'd come by this train. I felt I must look in for a moment. Isn't it dreadful? Poor darling mother.'

Bursting into tears, she flung herself into Kitty's arms. Kitty kissed her. She knew how her mother had neglected Doris in favour of her and how harsh she had been with her because she was plain and dull. She wondered whether Doris really felt the extravagant grief she showed. But Doris had always been emotional. She wished she could cry: Doris would think her dreadfully hard. Kitty felt that she had been through too much to feign a distress she did not feel.

'Would you like to come and see father?' she asked her when the strength of the outburst had somewhat subsided.

Doris wiped her eyes. Kitty noticed that her sister's pregnancy had blunted her features and in her black dress she looked gross and blousy.

'No, I don't think I will. I shall only cry again. Poor old thing, he's bearing it wonderfully.'

Kitty showed her sister out of the house and then went back to her father. He was standing in front of the fire and the newspaper was neatly folded. He wanted her to see that he had not been reading it again.

'I haven't dressed for dinner,' he said. 'I didn't think it was necessary.'

Chapter Eighty

They dined. Mr Garstin gave Kitty the details of his wife's illness and death, and he told her of the kindness of the friends who had written (there were piles of sympathetic letters on his table and he sighed when he considered the burden of answering them) and of the arrangements he had made for the funeral. Then they went back into his study. This was the only room in the house which had a fire. He mechanically took from the chimney-piece his pipe and began to fill it, but he gave his daughter a doubtful look and put it down.

'Aren't you going to smoke?' she asked.

'Your mother didn't very much like the smell of a pipe after dinner and since the war I've given up cigars.'

His answer gave Kitty a little pang. It seemed dreadful that a man of sixty should hesitate to smoke what he wanted in his own study.

'I like the smell of a pipe.' she smiled.

A faint look of relief crossed his face and taking his pipe once more he lit it. They sat opposite one another on each side of the fire. He felt that he must talk to Kitty of her own troubles.

'You received the letter your mother wrote to you to Port Said, I suppose. The news of poor Walter's death was a great shock to both of us. I thought him a very nice fellow.'

Kitty did not know what to say.

'Your mother told me that you were going to have a baby.'

'Yes.'

'When do you expect it?'

'In about four months.'

'It will be a great consolation to you. You must go and see Doris's boy. He's a fine little fellow.'

They were talking more distantly than if they were strangers who had just met, for if they had been he would have been interested in her just because of that, and curious, but their common past was a wall of indifference between them. Kitty knew too well that she had done nothing to beget her father's affection, he had never counted in the house and had been taken for granted, the bread-winner who was a little despised because he could provide no more luxuriously for his family; but she had taken for granted that he loved her just because he was her father, and it was a shock to discover that his heart was empty of feeling for her. She had known that they were all bored by him, but it had never occurred to her that he was equally bored by them. He was as ever kind and subdued, but the sad perspicacity which she had learnt in suffering suggested to her that, though he had probably never acknowledged it to himself and never would, in his heart he disliked her.

His pipe was not drawing and he rose to find something to poke it with. Perhaps it was an excuse to hide his nervousness.

'Your mother wished you to stay here till your baby was born and she was going to have your old room got ready for you.'

'I know. I promise you I won't be a bother.'

'Oh, it's not that. Under the circumstances it was evident that the only place for you to come to was your father's house. But the fact is that I've just been offered the post of Chief Justice of the Bahamas and I have accepted it.'

'Oh, father, I'm so glad. I congratulate you with all my heart.'

'The offer arrived too late for me to tell your poor mother. It would have given her a great satisfaction.'

The bitter irony of fate! After all her efforts, intrigues and humiliations, Mrs Garstin had died without knowing that her ambition, however modified by past disappointments, was at last achieved.

'I am sailing early next month. Of course this house will be put in the agent's hands and my intention was to sell the furniture. I'm sorry that I shan't be able to have you to stay here, but if you'd like any of the furniture to furnish a flat I shall be extremely pleased to give it you.'

Kitty looked into the fire. Her heart beat quickly; it was curious that on a sudden she should be so nervous. But at last she forced herself to speak. In her voice was a little tremor.

'Couldn't I come with you, father?'

'You? Oh, my dear Kitty.' His face fell. She had often heard the expression, but thought it only a phrase, and now for the first time in her life she saw the movement that it described. It was so marked that it startled her. 'But all your friends are here and Doris is here. I should have thought you'd be much happier if you took a flat in London. I don't exactly know what your circumstances are, but I shall be very glad to pay the rent of it.'

'I have enough money to live on.'

'I'm going to a strange place. I know nothing of the conditions.'

'I'm used to strange places. London means nothing to me any more. I couldn't breathe here.'

He closed his eyes for a moment and she thought he was going to cry. His face bore an expression of utter misery. It wrung her heart. She had been right; the death of his wife had filled him with relief and now this chance to break entirely with the past had offered him freedom. He had seen a new life spread before him and at last after all these years rest and the mirage of happiness. She saw dimly all the suffering that had preyed on his heart for thirty years. At last he opened his eyes. He could not prevent the sigh that escaped him.

'Of course if you wish to come I shall be very pleased.'

It was pitiful. The struggle had been short and he had surrendered to his sense of duty. With those few words he abandoned all his hopes. She rose from her chair and going over to him knelt down and seized his hands.

'No, father, I won't come unless you want me. You've sacrificed yourself enough. If you want to go alone, go. Don't think of me for a minute.'

He released one of her hands and stroked her pretty hair.

'Of course I want you, my dear. After all I'm your father and you're a widow and alone. If you want to be with me it would be very unkind of me not to want you.'

'But that's just it, I make no claims on you because I'm your daughter, you owe me nothing.'

'Oh, my dear child.'

'Nothing,' she repeated vehemently. 'My heart sinks when I think how we've battened on you all our lives and have given you nothing in return. Not even a little affection. I'm afraid you've not had a very happy life. Won't you let me try to make up a little for all I've failed to do in the past?'

He frowned a little. Her emotion embarrassed him.

'I don't know what you mean. I've never had any complaint to make of you.'

'Oh, father, I've been through so much, I've been so unhappy. I'm not the Kitty I was when I went away. I'm terribly weak, but I don't think I'm the filthy cad I was then. Won't you give me a chance? I have nobody but you in the world now. Won't you let me try to make you love me? Oh, father, I'm so lonely and so miserable; I want your love so badly.'

She buried her face in his lap and cried as though her heart were breaking.

'Oh, my Kitty, my little Kitty,' he murmured.

She looked up and put her arms round his neck.

'Oh, father, be kind to me. Let us be kind to one another.'

He kissed her, on the lips as a lover might, and his cheeks were wet with her tears.

'Of course you shall come with me.'

'Do you want me to? Do you really want me to?'

'Yes.'

'I'm so grateful to you.'

'Oh, my dear, don't say things like that to me. It makes me feel quite awkward.'

He took out his handkerchief and dried her eyes. He smiled in a way that she had never seen him smile before. Once more she threw her arms round his neck.

'We'll have such a lark, father dear. You don't know what fun we're going to have together.'

'You haven't forgotten that you're going to have a baby.'

'I'm glad she'll be born out there within sound of the sea and under a wide blue sky.'

'Have you already made up your mind about the sex?' he murmured, with his thin, dry smile.

'I want a girl because I want to bring her up so that she shan't make the mistakes I've made. When I look back upon the girl I was I hate myself. But I never had a chance. I'm going to bring up my daughter so that she's free and can stand on her own feet. I'm not going to bring a child into the world, and love her, and bring her up, just so that some man may want to sleep with her so much that he's willing to provide her with board and lodging for the rest of her life.'

She felt her father stiffen. He had never spoken of such things and it shocked him to hear these words in his daughter's mouth.

'Let me be frank just this once, father. I've been foolish and wicked and hateful. I've been terribly punished. I'm determined to save my daughter from all that. I want her to be fearless and frank. I want her to be a person, independent of others because she is possessed of herself, and I want her to take life like a free man and make a better job of it than I have.'

'Why, my love, you talk as though you were fifty. You've got all your life before you. You mustn't be down-hearted.'

Kitty shook her head and slowly smiled.

'I'm not. I have hope and courage.'

The past was finished; let the dead bury their dead. Was that dreadfully callous? She hoped with all her heart that she had learnt compassion and charity. She could not know what the future had in store for her, but she felt in herself the strength to accept whatever was to come with a light and buoyant spirit. Then, on a sudden, for no reason that she knew of, from the depths of her unconscious arose a reminiscence of the journey they had taken, she and poor Walter, to the plague-ridden city where he had met his death: one morning they set out in their chairs while it was still dark, and as the day broke she divined rather than saw a scene of such breath-taking loveliness that for a brief period the anguish of her heart was assuaged. It reduced to insignificance all human tribulation. The sun rose, dispelling the mist, and she saw winding onwards as far as the eye could reach, among the rice-fields, across a little river and through undulating country the path they were to follow: perhaps her faults and follies, the unhappiness she had suffered, were not entirely vain if she could follow the path that now she dimly discerned before her, not the path that kind funny old Waddington had spoken of that led nowhither, but the path those dear nuns at the convent followed so humbly, the path that led to peace.

Liza of
Lambeth

W.
Somerset
Maugham

Chapter One

It was the first Saturday afternoon in August; it had been broiling hot all day, with a cloudless sky, and the sun had been beating down on the houses, so that the top rooms were like ovens; but now with the approach of evening it was cooler, and everyone in Vere Street was out of doors.

Vere Street, Lambeth, is a short, straight street leading out of the Westminster Bridge Road; it has forty houses on one side and forty houses on the other, and these eighty houses are very much more like one another than ever peas are like peas, or young ladies like young ladies. They are newish, three-storied buildings of dingy grey brick with slate roofs, and they are perfectly flat, without a bow-window or even a projecting cornice or window-sill to break the straightness of the line from one end of the street to the other.

This Saturday afternoon the street was full of life; no traffic came down Vere Street, and the cemented space between the pavements was given up to children. Several games of cricket were being played by wildly excited boys, using coats for wickets, an old tennis-ball or a bundle of rags tied together for a ball, and, generally, an old broomstick for bat. The wicket was so large and the bat so small that the man in was always getting bowled, when heated quarrels would arise, the batter absolutely refusing to go out and the bowler absolutely insisting on going in. The girls were more peaceable; they were chiefly employed in skipping, and only abused one another mildly when the rope was not properly turned or the skipper did not jump sufficiently high. Worst off of all were the very young children, for there had been no rain for weeks, and the street was as dry and clean as a covered court, and, in the lack of mud to wallow in, they sat about the road, disconsolate as poets. The number of babies was prodigious; they sprawled about everywhere, on the pavement, round the doors, and about their mothers' skirts. The grown-ups were gathered round the open doors; there were usually two women squatting on the doorstep, and two or three more seated on either side on chairs; they were invariably nursing babies, and most of them showed clear signs that the present object of the maternal care would be soon ousted by a new arrival. Men were less numerous but such as there were leant against the walls, smoking, or sat on the sills of the ground-floor windows. It was the dead season in Vere Street as much as in Belgravia, and really if it had not been for babies just come or just about to come, and an opportune murder in a neighbouring doss-house, there would have been nothing whatever to talk about. As it was, the little groups talked quietly, discussing the atrocity or the merits of the local midwives, comparing the circumstances of their various confinements.

'You'll be 'avin' your little trouble soon, eh, Polly?' asked one good lady of another.

'Oh, I reckon I've got another two months ter go yet,' answered Polly.

'Well,' said a third, 'I wouldn't 'ave thought you'd go so long by the look of yer!'

'I 'ope you'll have it easier this time, my dear,' said a very stout old person, a woman of great importance.

'She said she wasn't goin' to 'ave no more, when the last one come.' This remark came from Polly's husband.

'Ah,' said the stout old lady, who was in the business, and boasted vast experience. 'That's wot they all says; but, Lor' bless yer, they don't mean it.'

'Well, I've got three, and I'm not goin' to 'ave no more bli'me if I will; 'tain't good enough–that's wot I says.'

'You're abaht right there, ole gal,' said Polly. 'My word, 'Arry, if you 'ave any more I'll git a divorce, that I will.'

At that moment an organ-grinder turned the corner and came down the street.

'Good biz; 'ere's an organ!' cried half a dozen people at once.

The organ-man was an Italian, with a shock of black hair and a ferocious moustache. Drawing his organ to a favourable spot, he stopped, released his shoulder from the leather straps by which he dragged it, and cocking his large soft hat on the side of his head, began turning the handle. It was a lively tune, and in less than no time a little crowd had gathered round to listen, chiefly the young men and the maidens, for the married ladies were never in a fit state to dance, and therefore disinclined to trouble themselves to stand round the organ. There was a moment's hesitation at opening the ball; then one girl said to another:

'Come on, Florrie, you and me ain't shy; we'll begin, and bust it!'

The two girls took hold of one another, one acting gentleman, the other lady; three or four more pairs of girls immediately joined them, and they began a waltz. They held themselves very upright; and with an air of grave dignity which was quite impressive, glided slowly about, making their steps with the utmost precision, bearing themselves with sufficient decorum for a court ball. After a while the men began to itch for a turn, and two of them, taking hold of one another in the most approved fashion, waltzed round the circle with the gravity of judges.

All at once there was a cry: 'There's Liza!' And several members of the group turned and called out: 'Oo, look at Liza!'

The dancers stopped to see the sight, and the organ-grinder, having come to the end of his tune, ceased turning the handle and looked to see what was the excitement.

'Oo, Liza!' they called out. 'Look at Liza; oo, I sy!'

It was a young girl of about eighteen, with dark eyes, and an enormous fringe, puffed-out and curled and frizzed, covering her whole forehead from side to side, and coming down to meet her eyebrows. She was dressed in brilliant violet, with great lappets of velvet, and she had on her head an enormous black hat covered with feathers.

'I sy, ain't she got up dossy?' called out the groups at the doors, as she passed.

'Dressed ter death, and kill the fashion; that's wot I calls it.'

Liza saw what a sensation she was creating; she arched her back and lifted her head, and walked down the street, swaying her body from side to side, and swaggering along as though the whole place belonged to her.

''Ave yer bought the street, Bill?' shouted one youth; and then half a dozen burst forth at once, as if by inspiration:

'Knocked 'em in the Old Kent Road!'

It was immediately taken up by a dozen more, and they all yelled it out:
'Knocked 'em in the Old Kent Road. Yah, ah, knocked 'em in the Old Kent Road!'

'Oo, Liza!' they shouted; the whole street joined in, and they gave long, shrill, ear-piercing shrieks and strange calls, that rung down the street and echoed back again.

'Hextra special!' called out a wag.

'Oh, Liza! Oo! Ooo!' yells and whistles, and then it thundered forth again:
'Knocked 'em in the Old Kent Road!'

Liza put on the air of a conquering hero, and sauntered on, enchanted at the uproar. She stuck out her elbows and jerked her head on one side, and said to herself as she passed through the bellowing crowd:

'This is jam!'

'Knocked 'em in the Old Kent Road!'

When she came to the group round the barrel-organ, one of the girls cried out to her:

'Is that yer new dress, Liza?'

'Well, it don't look like my old one, do it?' said Liza.

'Where did yer git it?' asked another friend, rather enviously.

'Picked it up in the street, of course,' scornfully answered Liza.

'I believe it's the same one as I saw in the pawnbroker's dahn the road,' said on of the men, to tease her.

'Thet's it; but wot was you doin' in there? Pledgin' yer shirt, or was it yer trousers?'

'Yah, I wouldn't git a second-'and dress at a pawnbroker's!'

'Garn!' said Liza indignantly. 'I'll swipe yer over the snitch if yer talk ter me. I got the mayterials in the West Hend, didn't I? And I 'ad it mide up by my Court Dressmiker, so you jolly well dry up, old jelly-belly.'

'Garn!' was the reply.

Liza had been so intent on her new dress and the comment it was exciting that she had not noticed the organ.

'Oo, I say, let's 'ave some dancin',' she said as soon as she saw it 'Come on, Sally,' she added, to one of the girls, 'you an' me'll dance together. Grind away, old cock!'

The man turned on a new tune, and the organ began to play the Intermezzo from the 'Cavalleria'; other couples quickly followed Liza's example, and they began to waltz round with the same solemnity as before; but Liza outdid them all; if the others were as stately as queens, she was as stately as an empress; the gravity and dignity with which she waltzed were something appalling, you felt that the minuet was a frolic in comparison; it would have been a fitting measure to tread round the grave of a *première danseuse*, or at the funeral of a professional humorist. And the graces she put on, the languor of the eyes, the contemptuous curl of the lips, the exquisite turn of the hand, the dainty arching of the foot! you felt there could be no questioning her right to the tyranny of Vere Street.

Suddenly she stopped short, and disengaged herself from her companion.

'Oh, I sy,' she said, 'this is too bloomin' slow; it gives me the sick.'

That is not precisely what she said, but it is impossible always to give the exact unexpurgated words of Liza and the other personages of the story; the reader is therefore entreated with his thoughts to piece out the necessary imperfections of the dialogue.

'It's too bloomin' slow,' she said again; 'it gives me the sick. Let's 'ave somethin' a bit more lively than this 'ere waltz. You stand over there, Sally, an' we'll show 'em 'ow ter skirt dance.'

They all stopped waltzing.

'Talk of the ballet at the Canterbury and the South London. You just wite till you see the ballet at Vere Street, Lambeth—we'll knock 'em!'

She went up to the organ-grinder.

'Na then, Italiano,' she said to him, 'you buck up; give us a tune that's got some guts in it! See?'

She caught hold of his big hat and squashed it down over his eyes. The man grinned from ear to ear, and, touching the little catch at the side began to play a lively tune such as Liza had asked for.

The men had fallen out, but several girls had put themselves in position, in couples, standing face to face; and immediately the music struck up, they began. They held up their skirts on each side, so as to show their feet, and proceeded to go through the difficult steps and motions of the dance. Liza was right; they could not have done it better in a trained ballet. But the best dancer of them all was Liza; she threw her whole soul into it; forgetting the stiff bearing which she had thought proper to the waltz, and casting of its elaborate graces, she gave herself up entirely to the present pleasure. Gradually the other couples stood aside, so that Liza and Sally were left alone. They paced it carefully, watching each other's steps, and as if by instinct performing corresponding movements, so as to make the whole a thing of symmetry.

'I'm abaht done,' said Sally, blowing and puffing. 'I've 'ad enough of it.'

'Go on, Liza!' cried out a dozen voices when Sally stopped.

She gave no sign of having heard them other than calmly to continue her dance. She glided through the steps, and swayed about, and manipulated her skirt, all with the most charming grace imaginable, then, the music altering, she changed the style of her dancing, her feet moved more quickly, and did not keep so strictly to the ground. She was getting excited at the admiration of the onlookers, and her dance grew wilder and more daring. She lifted her skirts higher, brought in new and more difficult movements into her improvisation, kicking up her legs she did the wonderful twist, backwards and forwards, of which the dancer is proud.

'Look at 'er legs!' cried one of the men.

'Look at 'er stockin's!' shouted another; and indeed they were remarkable, for Liza had chosen them of the same brilliant hue as her dress, and was herself most proud of the harmony.

Her dance became gayer: her feet scarcely touched the ground, she whirled round madly.

'Tike care yer don't split!' cried out one of the wags, at a very audacious kick.

The words were hardly out of his mouth when Liza, with a gigantic effort, raised her foot and kicked off his hat. The feat was greeted with applause, and she went on, making turns and twists, flourishing her skirts, kicking higher and higher, and finally, among a volley of shouts, fell on her hands and turned head over heels in a magnificent catherine-wheel; then scrambling to her feet again, she tumbled into the arms of a young man standing in the front of the ring.

'That's right, Liza,' he said. 'Give us a kiss, now,' and promptly tried to take one.

'Git aht!' said Liza, pushing him away, not too gently.

'Yus, give us a kiss,' cried another, running up to her.

'I'll smack yer in the fice!' said Liza, elegantly, as she dodged him.

'Ketch 'old on 'er, Bill,' cried out a third, 'an' we'll all kiss her.'

'Na, you won't!' shrieked Liza, beginning to run.

'Come on,' they cried, 'we'll ketch 'er.'

She dodged in and out, between their legs, under their arms, and then, getting clear of the little crowd, caught up her skirts so that they might not hinder her, and took to her heels along the street. A score of men set in chase, whistling, shouting, yelling; the people at the doors looked up to see the fun, and cried out to her as she dashed past; she ran like the wind. Suddenly a man from the side darted into the middle of the road, stood straight in her way, and before she knew where she was, she had jumped shrieking into his arms, and he, lifting her up to him, had imprinted two sounding kisses on her cheeks.

'Oh, you—!' she said. Her expression was quite unprintable; nor can it be euphemised.

There was a shout of laughter from the bystanders, and the young men in chase of her, and Liza, looking up, saw a big, bearded man whom she had never seen before. She blushed to the very roots of her hair, quickly extricated herself from his arms, and, amid the jeers and laughter of everyone, slid into the door of the nearest house and was lost to view.

Chapter Two

Liza and her mother were having supper. Mrs Kemp was an elderly woman, short, and rather stout, with a red face, and grey hair brushed tight back over her forehead. She had been a widow for many years, and since her husband's death had lived with Liza in the ground-floor front room in which they were now sitting. Her husband had been a soldier, and from a grateful country she received a pension large enough to keep her from starvation, and by charring and doing such odd jobs as she could get she earned a little extra to supply herself with liquor. Liza was able to make her own living by working at a factory.

Mrs Kemp was rather sulky this evening.

'Wot was yer doin' this afternoon, Liza?' she asked.

'I was in the street.'

'You're always in the street when I want yer.'

'I didn't know as 'ow yer wanted me, mother,' answered Liza.

'Well, yer might 'ave come ter see! I might 'ave been dead, for all you knew.'

Liza said nothing.

'My rheumatics was thet bad to-dy, thet I didn't know wot ter do with myself. The doctor said I was to be rubbed with that stuff 'e give me, but yer won't never do nothin' for me.'

'Well, mother,' said Liza, 'your rheumatics was all right yesterday.'

'I know wot you was doin'; you was showin' of thet new dress of yours. Pretty waste of money thet is, instead of givin' it me ter sive up. An' for the matter of thet, I wanted a new dress far worse than you did. But, of course, I don't matter.'

Liza did not answer, and Mrs Kemp, having nothing more to say, continued her supper in silence.

It was Liza who spoke next.

'There's some new people moved in the street. 'Ave you seen 'em?' she asked.

'No, wot are they?'

'I dunno; I've seen a chap, a big chap with a beard. I think 'e lives up at the other end.'

She felt herself blushing a little.

'No one any good you be sure,' said Mrs Kemp. 'I can't swaller these new people as are comin' in; the street ain't wot it was when I fust come.'

When they had done, Mrs Kemp got up, and having finished her half-pint of beer, said to her daughter:

'Put the things away, Liza. I'm just goin' round to see Mrs Clayton; she's just 'ad twins, and she 'ad nine before these come. It's a pity the Lord don't see fit ter tike some on 'em—thet's wot I say.'

After which pious remark Mrs Kemp went out of the house and turned into another a few doors up.

Liza did not clear the supper things away as she was told, but opened the window and drew her chair to it. She leant on the sill, looking out into the street. The sun had set, and it was twilight, the sky was growing dark, bringing to view the twinkling stars; there was no breeze, but it was pleasantly and restfully cool. The good folk still sat at their doorsteps, talking as before on the same inexhaustible subjects, but a little subdued with the approach of night. The boys were still playing cricket, but they were mostly at the other end of the street, and their shouts were muffled before they reached Liza's ears.

She sat, leaning her head on her hands, breathing in the fresh air and feeling a certain exquisite sense of peacefulness which she was not used to. It was Saturday evening, and she thankfully remembered that there would be no factory on the morrow; she was glad to rest. Somehow she felt a little tired, perhaps it was through the excitement of the afternoon, and she enjoyed the quietness of the evening. It seemed so tranquil and still; the silence filled her with a strange delight, she felt as if she could sit there all through the night looking out into the cool, dark street, and up heavenwards at the stars. She was very happy, but yet at the same time experienced a strange new sensation of melancholy, and she almost wished to cry.

Suddenly a dark form stepped in front of the open window. She gave a little shriek.

''Oo's thet?' she asked, for it was quite dark, and she did not recognise the man standing in front of her.

'Me, Liza,' was the answer.

'Tom?'

'Yus!'

It was a young man with light yellow hair and a little fair moustache, which made him appear almost boyish; he was light-complexioned and blue-eyed, and had a frank and pleasant look mingled with a curious bashfulness that made him blush when people spoke to him.

'Wot's up?' asked Liza.

'Come aht for a walk, Liza, will yer?'

'No!' she answered decisively.

'You promised ter yesterday, Liza.'

'Yesterday an' ter-day's two different things,' was her wise reply.

'Yus, come on, Liza.'

'Na, I tell yer, I won't.'

'I want ter talk ter yer, Liza.' Her hand was resting on the window-sill, and he put his upon it. She quickly drew it back.

'Well, I don't want yer ter talk ter me.'

But she did, for it was she who broke the silence.

'Say, Tom, 'oo are them new folk as 'as come into the street? It's a big chap with a brown beard.'

'D'you mean the bloke as kissed yer this afternoon?'

Liza blushed again.

'Well, why shouldn't 'e kiss me?' she said, with some inconsequence.

'I never said as 'ow 'e shouldn't; I only arst yer if it was the sime.'

'Yes, thet's 'oo I mean.'

''Is nime is Blakeston—Jim Blakeston. I've only spoke to 'im once; he's took the two top rooms at No. 19 'ouse.'

'Wot's 'e want two top rooms for?'

''Im? Oh, 'e's got a big family—five kids. Ain't yer seen 'is wife abaht the street? She's a big, fat woman, as does 'er 'air funny.'

'I didn't know 'e 'ad a wife.'

There was another silence; Liza sat thinking, and Tom stood at the window, looking at her.

'Won't yer come aht with me, Liza?' he asked, at last.

'Na, Tom,' she said, a little more gently, 'it's too lite.'

'Liza,' he said, blushing to the roots of his hair.

'Well?'

'Liza'—he couldn't go on, and stuttered in his shyness—'Liza, I—I—I loves yer, Liza.'

'Garn awy!'

He was quite brave now, and took hold of her hand.

'Yer know, Liza, I'm earnin' twenty-three shillin's at the works now, an' I've got some furniture as mother left me when she was took.'

The girl said nothing.

'Liza, will you 'ave me? I'll make yer a good 'usband, Liza, swop me bob, I will; an' yer know I'm not a drinkin' sort. Liza, will yer marry me?'

'Na, Tom,' she answered quietly.

'Oh, Liza, won't you 'ave me?'

'Na, Tom, I can't.'

'Why not? You've come aht walkin' with me ever since Whitsun.'

'Ah, things is different now.'

'You're not walkin' aht with anybody else, are you, Liza?' he asked quickly.

'Na, not that.'

'Well, why won't yer, Liza, I do love yer, I've never loved anybody as I love you!'

'Oh, I can't, Tom!'

'There ain't no one else?'

'Na.'

'Then why not?'

'I'm very sorry, Tom, but I don't love yer so as ter marry yer.'

'Oh, Liza!'

She could not see the look upon his face, but she heard the agony in his voice; and, moved with sudden pity, she bent out, threw her arms round his neck, and kissed him on both cheeks.

'Never mind old chap!' she said. 'I'm not worth troublin' abaht.'

And quickly drawing back, she slammed the window to, and moved into the further part of the room.

Chapter Three

The following day was Sunday. Liza when she was dressing herself in the morning, felt the hardness of fate in the impossibility of eating one's cake and having it; she wished she had reserved her new dress, and had still before her the sensation of a first appearance in it. With a sigh she put on her ordinary everyday working dress, and proceeded to get the breakfast ready, for her mother had been out late the previous night, celebrating the new arrivals in the street, and had the 'rheumatics' this morning.

'Oo, my 'ead!' she was saying, as she pressed her hands on each side of her forehead. 'I've got the neuralgy again, wot shall I do? I dunno 'ow it is, but it always comes on Sunday mornings. Oo, an' my rheumatics, they give me sich a doin' in the night!'

'You'd better go to the 'orspital, mother.'

'Not I!' answered the worthy lady, with great decision. 'You 'as a dozen young chaps messin' you abaht, and lookin' at yer; and then they tells yer ter leave off beer and spirrits. Well, wot I says, I says I can't do withaht my glass of beer.' She thumped her pillow to emphasise the statement.

'Wot with the work I 'ave ter do, lookin' after you and the cookin' an' gettin' everythin' ready and doin' all the 'ousework, and goin' aht charring besides—well, I says, if I don't 'ave a drop of beer, I says, ter pull me together, I should be under the turf in no time.'

She munched her bread-and-butter and drank her tea.

'When you've done breakfast, Liza,' she said, 'you can give the grate a cleanin', an' my boots'd do with a bit of polishin'. Mrs Tike, in the next 'ouse, 'll give yer some blackin'.'

She remained silent for a bit, then said:

'I don't think I shall get up ter-day, Liza. My rheumatics is bad. You can put the room straight and cook the dinner.'

'Arright, mother; you stay where you are, an' I'll do everythin' for yer.'

'Well, it's only wot yer ought to do, considerin' all the trouble you've been ter me when you was young, and considerin' thet when you was born the doctor thought I never should get through it. Wot 'ave you done with your week's money, Liza?'

'Oh, I've put it awy,' answered Liza quietly.

'Where?' asked her mother.

'Where it'll be safe.'

'Where's that?'

Liza was driven into a corner.

'Why d'you want ter know?' she asked.

'Why shouldn't I know; d'you think I want ter steal it from yer?'

'Na, not thet.'

'Well, why won't you tell me?'

'Oh, a thing's sifer when only one person knows where it is.'

This was a very discreet remark, but it set Mrs Kemp in a whirlwind of passion. She raised herself and sat up in the bed, flourishing her clenched fist at her daughter.

'I know wot yer mean, you–you!' Her language was emphatic, her epithets picturesque, but too forcible for reproduction. 'You think I'd steal it,' she went on. 'I know yer! D'yer think I'd go an' tike yer dirty money?'

'Well, mother,' said Liza, 'when I've told yer before, the money's perspired like.'

'Wot d'yer mean?'

'It got less.'

'Well, I can't 'elp thet, can I? Anyone can come in 'ere and tike the money.'

'If it's 'idden awy, they can't, can they, mother?' said Liza.

Mrs Kemp shook her fist.

'You dirty slut, you,' she said, 'yer think I tike yer money! Why, you ought ter give it me every week instead of savin' it up and spendin' it on all sorts of muck, while I 'ave ter grind my very bones down to keep yer.'

'Yer know, mother, if I didn't 'ave a little bit saved up, we should be rather short when you're dahn in yer luck.'

Mrs Kemp's money always ran out on Tuesday, and Liza had to keep things going till the following Saturday.

'Oh, don't talk ter me!' proceeded Mrs Kemp. 'When I was a girl I give all my money ter my mother. She never 'ad ter ask me for nothin'. On Saturday when I come 'ome with my wiges, I give it 'er every farthin'. That's wot a daughter ought ter do. I can say this for myself, I be'aved by my mother like a gal should. None of your prodigal sons for me! She didn't 'ave ter ask me for three 'apence ter get a drop of beer.'

Liza was wise in her generation; she held her tongue, and put on her hat.

'Now, you're goin' aht, and leavin' me; I dunno wot you get up to in the street with all those men. No good, I'll be bound. An' 'ere I am left alone, an' I might die for all you care.'

In her sorrow at herself the old lady began to cry, and Liza slipped out of the room and into the street.

Leaning against the wall of the opposite house was Tom; he came towards her.

'Ulloa!' she said, as she saw him. 'Wot are you doin' 'ere?'

'I was waitin' for you ter come aht, Liza,' he answered.

She looked at him quickly.

'I ain't comin' aht with yer ter-day, if thet's wot yer mean,' she said.

'I never thought of arskin' yer, Liza–after wot you said ter me last night.'

His voice was a little sad, and she felt so sorry for him.

'But yer did want ter speak ter me, didn't yer Tom?' she said, more gently.

'You've got a day off ter-morrow, ain't yer?'

'Bank 'Oliday. Yus! Why?'

'Why, 'cause they've got a drag startin' from the "Red Lion" that's goin' down ter Chingford for the day–an' I'm goin'.'

'Yus!' she said.

He looked at her doubtfully.

'Will yer come too, Liza? It'll be a regular beeno; there's only goin' ter be people in the street. Eh, Liza?'

'Na, I can't.'

'Why not?'

'I ain't got—I ain't got the ooftish.'

'I mean, won't yer come with me?'

'Na, Tom, thank yer; I can't do thet neither.'

'Yer might as well, Liza; it wouldn't 'urt yer.'

'Na, it wouldn't be right like; I can't come aht with yer, and then mean nothin'! It would be doin' yer aht of an outing.'

'I don't see why,' he said, very crestfallen.

'I can't go on keepin' company with you—after what I said last night.'

'I shan't enjoy it a bit without you, Liza.'

'You git somebody else, Tom. You'll do withaht me all right.'

She nodded to him, and walked up the street to the house of her friend Sally. Having arrived in front of it, she put her hands to her mouth in trumpet form, and shouted:

''I! 'I! 'I! Sally!'

A couple of fellows standing by copied her.

''I! 'I! 'I! Sally!'

'Garn!' said Liza, looking round at them.

Sally did not appear and she repeated her call. The men imitated her, and half a dozen took it up, so that there was enough noise to wake the seven sleepers.

''I! 'I! 'I! Sally!'

A head was put out of a top window, and Liza, taking off her hat, waved it, crying:

'Come on dahn, Sally!'

'Arright, old gal!' shouted the other. 'I'm comin'!'

'So's Christmas!' was Liza's repartee.

There was a clatter down the stairs, and Sally, rushing through the passage, threw herself on to her friend. They began fooling, in reminiscence of a melodrama they had lately seen together.

'Oh, my darlin' duck!' said Liza, kissing her and pressing her, with affected rapture, to her bosom.

'My sweetest sweet!' replied Sally, copying her.

'An' 'ow does your lidyship ter-day?'

'Oh!'—with immense languor—'fust class; and is your royal 'ighness quite well?'

'I deeply regret,' answered Liza, 'but my royal 'ighness 'as got the collywobbles.'

Sally was a small, thin girl, with sandy hair and blue eyes, and a very freckled complexion. She had an enormous mouth, with terrible, square teeth set wide apart, which looked as if they could masticate an iron bar. She was dressed like Liza, in a shortish black skirt and an old-fashioned bodice, green and grey and yellow with age; her sleeves were tucked up to the elbow, and she wore a singularly dirty apron, that had once been white.

'Wot 'ave you got yer 'air in them things for?' asked Liza, pointing to the curl-papers. 'Goin' aht with yer young man ter-day?'

'No, I'm going ter stay 'ere all day.'

'Wot for, then?'

'Why, 'Arry's going ter tike me ter Chingford ter-morrer.'

'Oh? In the "Red Lion" brake?'

'Yus. Are you goin'?'

'Na!'

'Not! Well, why don't you get round Tom? 'E'll tike yer, and jolly glad 'e'll be, too.'

''E arst me ter go with 'im, but I wouldn't.'

'Swop me bob—why not?'

'I ain't keepin' company with 'im.'

'Yer might 'ave gone with 'im all the sime.'

'Na. You're goin' with 'Arry, ain't yer?'

'Yus!'

'An' you're goin' to 'ave 'im?'

'Right again!'

'Well, I couldn't go with Tom, an' then throw 'im over.'

'Well, you are a mug!'

The two girls had strolled down towards the Westminster Bridge Road, and Sally, meeting her young man, had gone to him. Liza walked back, wishing to get home in time to cook the dinner. But she went slowly, for she knew every dweller in the street, and as she passed the groups sitting at their doors, as on the previous evening, but this time mostly engaged in peeling potatoes or shelling peas, she stopped and had a little chat. Everyone liked her, and was glad to have her company. 'Good old Liza,' they would say, as she left them, 'she's a rare good sort, ain't she?'

She asked after the aches and pains of all the old people, and delicately inquired after the babies, past and future; the children hung on to her skirts and asked her to play with them, and she would hold one end of the rope while tiny little ragged girls skipped, invariably entangling themselves after two jumps.

She had nearly reached home, when she heard a voice cry:

'Mornin'!'

She looked round and recognised the man whom Tom had told her was called Jim Blakeston. He was sitting on a stool at the door of one of the houses, playing with two young children, to whom he was giving rides on his knee. She remembered his heavy brown beard from the day before, and she had also an impression of great size; she noticed this morning that he was, in fact, a big man, tall and broad, and she saw besides that he had large, masculine features and pleasant brown eyes. She supposed him to be about forty.

'Mornin'!' he said again, as she stopped and looked at him.

Liza blushed scarlet, and was too confused to answer.

'Well, yer needn't look as if I was goin' ter eat yer up, 'cause I ain't,' he said.

''Oo are you? I'm not afeard of yer.'

'Wot are yer so bloomin' red abaht?' he asked pointedly.

'Well, I'm 'ot.'

'You ain't shirty 'cause I kissed yer last night?'

'I'm not shirty; but it was pretty cool, considerin' like as I didn't know yer.'

'Well, you run into my arms.'

'Thet I didn't; you run aht and caught me.'

'An' kissed yer before you could say "Jack Robinson".' He laughed at the thought. 'Well, Liza,' he went on, 'seein' as 'ow I kissed yer against yer will, the best thing you can do ter make it up is to kiss me not against yer will.'

'Me?' said Liza, looking at him, open-mouthed. 'Well you are a pill.'

The children began to clamour for the riding, which had been discontinued on Liza's approach.

'Are them your kids?' she asked.

'Yus; them's two on 'em.'

''Ow many 'ave yer got?'

'Five; the eldest gal's fifteen, and the next one 'oo's a boy's twelve, and then there are these two and baby.'

'Well, you've got enough for your money.'

'Too many for me—and more comin'.'

'Ah, well,' said Liza, laughing, 'thet's your fault, ain't it?'

Then she bade him good morning, and strolled off.

He watched her as she went, and saw half a dozen little boys surround her and beg her to join them in their game of cricket. They caught hold of her arms and skirts, and pulled her to their pitch.

'Na, I can't,' she said, trying to disengage herself. 'I've got the dinner ter cook.'

'Dinner ter cook?' shouted one small boy. 'Why, they always cooks the cats' meat at the shop.'

'You little so-and-so!' said Liza, somewhat inelegantly, making a dash at him.

He dodged her and gave a whoop; then turning he caught her round the legs, and another boy catching hold of her round the neck they dragged her down, and all three struggled on the ground, rolling over and over; the other boys threw themselves on the top, so that there was a great heap of legs and arms and heads waving and bobbing up and down.

Liza extricated herself with some difficulty, and taking off her hat she began cuffing the boys with it, using all the time the most lively expressions. Then, having cleared the field, she retired victorious into her own house and began cooking the dinner.

Chapter Four

Bank Holiday was a beautiful day: the cloudless sky threatened a stifling heat for noontide, but early in the morning, when Liza got out of bed and threw open the window, it was fresh and cool. She dressed herself, wondering how she should spend her day; she thought of Sally going off to Chingford with her lover, and of herself remaining alone in the dull street with half the people away. She almost wished it were an ordinary work-day, and that there were no such things as bank holidays. And it seemed to be a little like two Sundays running, but with the second rather worse than the first. Her mother was still sleeping, and she was in no great hurry about getting the breakfast, but stood quietly looking out of the window at the house opposite.

In a little while she saw Sally coming along. She was arrayed in purple and fine linen—a very smart red dress, trimmed with velveteen, and a tremendous hat covered with feathers. She had reaped the benefit of keeping

her hair in curl-papers since Saturday, and her sandy fringe stretched from
ear to ear. She was in enormous spirits.

''Ulloa, Liza!' she called as soon as she saw her at the window.

Liza looked at her a little enviously.

''Ulloa!' she answered quietly.

'I'm just goin' to the "Red Lion" to meet 'Arry.'

'At what time d'yer start?'

'The brake leaves at 'alf-past eight sharp.'

'Why, it's only eight; it's only just struck at the church.
'Arry won't be there yet, will he?'

'Oh, 'e's sure ter be early. I couldn't wite. I've been witing abaht since
'alf-past six. I've been up since five this morning.'

'Since five! What 'ave you been doin'?'

'Dressin' myself and doin' my 'air. I woke up so early. I've been dreamin'
all the night abaht it. I simply couldn't sleep.'

'Well, you are a caution!' said Liza.

'Bust it, I don't go on the spree every day! Oh, I do 'ope I shall enjoy
myself.'

'Why, you simply dunno where you are!' said Liza, a little crossly.

'Don't you wish you was comin', Liza?' asked Sally.

'Na! I could if I liked, but I don't want ter.'

'You are a coughdrop–that's all I can say. Ketch me refusin' when I 'ave
the chanst.'

'Well, it's done now. I ain't got the chanst any more.' Liza said this with
just a little regret in her voice.

'Come on dahn to the "Red Lion", Liza, and see us off,' said Sally.

'No, I'm damned if I do!' answered Liza, with some warmth.

'You might as well. P'raps 'Arry won't be there, an' you can keep me
company till 'e comes. An' you can see the 'orses.'

Liza was really very anxious to see the brake and the horses and the people
going; but she hesitated a little longer. Sally asked her once again. Then she
said:

'Arright, I'll come with yer, and wite till the bloomin' old thing starts.'

She did not trouble to put on a hat, but just walked out as she was,
and accompanied Sally to the public-house which was getting up the
expedition.

Although there was still nearly half and hour to wait, the brake was drawn
up before the main entrance; it was large and long, with seats arranged
crosswise, so that four people could sit on each; and it was drawn by two
powerful horses, whose harness the coachman was now examining. Sally
was not the first on the scene, for already half a dozen people had taken their
places, but Harry had not yet arrived. The two girls stood by the public-
door, looking at the preparations. Huge baskets full of food were brought
out and stowed away; cases of beer were hoisted up and put in every possible
place–under the seats, under the driver's legs, and even beneath the brake.
As more people came up, Sally began to get excited about Harry's non-
appearance.

'I say, I wish 'e'd come!' she said. ''E is lite.'

Then she looked up and down the Westminster Bridge Road to see if he
was in view.

'Suppose 'e don't turn up! I will give it 'im when 'e comes for keepin' me
witin' like this.'

'Why, there's a quarter of an hour yet,' said Liza, who saw nothing at all to get excited about.

At last Sally saw her lover, and rushed off to meet him. Liza was left alone, rather disconsolate at all this bustle and preparation. She was not sorry that she had refused Tom's invitation, but she did wish that she had conscientiously been able to accept it. Sally and her friend came up; attired in his Sunday best, he was a fit match for his lady-love—he wore a shirt and collar, unusual luxuries—and he carried under his arm a concertina to make things merry on the way.

'Ain't you goin', Liza?' he asked in surprise at seeing her without a hat and with her apron on.

'Na,' said Sally, 'ain't she a soft? Tom said 'e'd tike 'er, an' she wouldn't.'

'Well, I'm dashed!'

Then they climbed the ladder and took their seats, so that Liza was left alone again. More people had come along, and the brake was nearly full. Liza knew them all, but they were too busy taking their places to talk to her. At last Tom came. He saw her standing there and went up to her.

'Won't yer change yer mind, Liza, an' come along with us?'

'Na, Tom, I told yer I wouldn't—it's not right like.' She felt she must repeat that to herself often.

'I shan't enjoy it a bit without you,' he said.

'Well, I can't 'elp it!' she answered, somewhat sullenly.

At that moment a man came out of the public-house with a horn in his hand; her heart gave a great jump, for if there was anything she adored it was to drive along to the tootling of a horn. She really felt it was very hard lines that she must stay at home when all these people were going to have such a fine time; and they were all so merry, and she could picture to herself so well the delights of the drive and the picnic. She felt very much inclined to cry. But she mustn't go, and she wouldn't go: she repeated that to herself twice as the trumpeter gave a preliminary tootle.

Two more people hurried along, and when they came near Liza saw that they were Jim Blakeston and a woman whom she supposed to be his wife.

'Are you comin' Liza?' Jim said to her.

'No,' she answered. 'I didn't know you was goin'.'

'I wish you was comin',' he replied, 'we shall 'ave a game.'

She could only just keep back the sobs; she so wished she were going. It did seem hard that she must remain behind; and all because she wasn't going to marry Tom. After all, she didn't see why that should prevent her; there really was no need to refuse for that. She began to think she had acted foolishly: it didn't do anyone any good that she refused to go out with Tom, and no one thought it anything specially fine that she should renounce her pleasure. Sally merely thought her a fool.

Tom was standing by her side, silent, and looking disappointed and rather unhappy. Jim said to her, in a low voice:

'I am sorry you're not comin'!'

It was too much. She did want to go so badly, and she really couldn't resist any longer. If Tom would only ask her once more, and if she could only change her mind reasonably and decently, she would accept; but he stood silent, and she had to speak herself. It was very undignified.

'Yer know, Tom,' she said, 'I don't want ter spoil your day.'

'Well, I don't think I shall go alone; it 'ud be so precious slow.'

Supposing he didn't ask her again! What should she do? She looked up at the clock on the front of the pub, and noticed that it only wanted five minutes to the half-hour. How terrible it would be if the brake started and he didn't ask her! Her heart beat violently against her chest, and in her agitation she fumbled with the corner of her apron.

'Well, what can I do, Tom dear?'

'Why, come with me, of course. Oh, Liza, do say yes.'

She had got the offer again, and it only wanted a little seemly hesitation, and the thing was done.

'I shouldn't like ter, Tom,' she said. 'But d'you think it 'ud be arright?'

'Yus, of course it would. Come on. Liza!' In his eagerness he clasped her hand.

'Well,' she remarked, looking down, 'if it'd spoil your 'oliday—'

'I won't go if you don't—swop me bob, I won't!' he answered.

'Well, if I come, it won't mean that I'm keepin' company with you.'

'Na, it won't mean anythin' you don't like.'

'Arright!' she said.

'You'll come?' he could hardly believe her.

'Yus!' she answered, smiling all over her face.

'You're a good sort, Liza! I say, 'Arry, Liza's comin'!' he shouted.

'Liza? 'Oorray!' shouted Harry.

''S'at right, Liza?' called Sally.

And Liza feeling quite joyful and light of heart called back:

'Yus!'

''Oorray!' shouted Sally in answer.

'Thet's right, Liza,' called Jim; and he smiled pleasantly as she looked at him.

'There's just room for you two 'ere,' said Harry, pointing to the vacant places by his side.

'Arright!' said Tom.

'I must jest go an' get a 'at an' tell mother,' said Liza.

'There's just three minutes. Be quick!' answered Tom, and as she scampered off as hard as she could go, he shouted to the coachman: ''Old 'ard; there's another passenger comin' in a minute.'

'Arright, old cock,' answered the coachman; 'no 'urry!'

Liza rushed into the room, and called to her mother, who was still asleep: 'Mother! mother! I'm going to Chingford!'

Then tearing off her old dress she slipped into her gorgeous violet one; she kicked off her old ragged shoes and put on her new boots. She brushed her hair down and rapidly gave her fringe a twirl and a twist—it was luckily still moderately in curl from the previous Saturday—and putting on her black hat with all the feathers, she rushed along the street, and scrambling up the brake steps fell panting on Tom's lap.

The coachman cracked his whip, the trumpeter tootled his horn, and with a cry and a cheer from the occupants, the brake clattered down the road.

Chapter Five

As soon as Liza had recovered herself she started examining the people on the brake; and first of all she took stock of the woman whom Jim Blakeston had with him.

'This is my missus!' said Jim, pointing to her with his thumb.

'You ain't been dahn in the street much, 'ave yer?' said Liza, by way of making the acquaintance.

'Na,' answered Mrs Blakeston, 'My youngster's been dahn with the measles, an' I've 'ad my work cut out lookin' after 'im.'

'Oh, an' is 'e all right now?'

'Yus, 'e's getting on fine, an' Jim wanted ter go ter Chingford ter-day, an' 'e says ter me, well, 'e says, "You come along ter Chingford, too; it'll do you good," An' 'e says, "You can leave Polly"–she's my eldest, yer know–"you can leave Polly," says 'e. "ter look after the kids." So I says, "Well, I don't mind if I do," says I.'

Meanwhile Liza was looking at her. First she noticed her dress: she wore a black cloak and a funny, old-fashioned black bonnet; then examining the woman herself, she saw a middle-sized, stout person anywhere between thirty and forty years old. She had a large, fat face with a big mouth, and her hair was curiously done, parted in the middle and plastered down on each side of the head in little plaits. One could see that she was a woman of great strength, notwithstanding evident traces of hard work and much child-bearing.

Liza knew all the other passengers, and now that everyone was settled down and had got over the excitement of departure, they had time to greet one another. They were delighted to have Liza among them, for where she was there was no dullness. Her attention was first off all taken up by a young coster who had arrayed himself in the traditional costume–grey suit, tight trousers, and shiny buttons in profusion.

'Wot cheer, Bill!' she cried to him.

'Wot cheer, Liza!' he answered.

'You are got up dossy; you'll knock 'em.'

'Na then, Liza Kemp,' said his companion, turning round with mock indignation, 'you let my Johnny alone. If you come gettin' round 'im I'll give you wot for.'

'Arright, Clary Sharp, I don't want 'im,' answered Liza. 'I've got one of my own, an' thet's a good 'andful–ain't it, Tom?'

Tom was delighted, and, unable to find a repartee, in his pleasure gave Liza a great nudge with his elbow.

''Oo, I say,' said Liza, putting her hand to her side. 'Tike care of my ribs; you'll brike 'em.'

'Them's not yer ribs,' shouted a candid friend–'them's yer whale-bones yer afraid of breakin'.'

'Garn!'

''Ave yer got whale-bones?' said Tom, with affected simplicity, putting his arm round her waist to feel.

'Na then,' she said, 'keep off the grass!'

'Well, I only wanted ter know if you'd got any.'

'Garn; yer don't git round me like thet.'

He still kept as he was.

'Na then,' she repeated, 'tike yer 'and away. If yer touch me there you'll 'ave to marry me.'

'Thet's just wot I wants ter do, Liza!'

'Shut it!' she answered cruelly, and drew his arm away from her waist.

The horses scampered on, and the man behind blew his horn with vigour. 'Don't bust yerself, guv'nor!' said one of the passengers to him when he made a particularly discordant sound. They drove along eastwards, and as the hour grew later the streets became more filled and the traffic greater. At last they got on the road to Chingford, and caught up numbers of other vehicles going in the same direction—donkey-shays, pony-carts, tradesmen's carts, dog-carts, drags, brakes, every conceivable kind of wheel thing, all filled with people, the wretched donkey dragging along four solid rate-payers to the pair of stout horses easily managing a couple of score. They exchanged cheers and greetings as they passed, the 'Red Lion' brake being noticeable above all for its uproariousness. As the day wore on the sun became hotter, and the road seemed more dusty and threw up a greater heat. 'I am gettin 'ot!' was the common cry, and everyone began to puff and sweat.

The ladies removed their cloaks and capes, and the men, following their example, took off their coats and sat in their shirt-sleeves. Whereupon ensued much banter of a not particularly edifying kind respecting the garments which each person would like to remove—which showed that the innuendo of Frech farce is not so unknown to the upright, honest Englishman as might be supposed.

At last came in sight the half-way house, where the horses were to have a rest and a sponge down. They had been talking of it for the last quarter of a mile, and when at length it was observed on the top of a hill a cheer broke out, and some thirsty wag began to sing 'Rule Britannia', whilst others burst forth with a different national ditty, 'Beer, Glorious Beer!' They drew up before the pub entrance, and all climbed down as quickly as they could. The bar was besieged, and potmen and barmaids were quickly busy drawing beer and handing it over to the eager folk outside.

THE IDYLL OF CORYDON AND PHYLLIS

Gallantry ordered that the faithful swain and the amorous shepherdess should drink out of one and the same pot.

''Urry up an' 'ave your whack,' said Corydon, politely handing the foaming bowl for his fair one to drink from.

Phyllis, without replying, raised it to her lips and drank deep. The swain watched anxiously.

''Ere, give us a chanst!' he said, as the pot was raised higher and higher and its contents appeared to be getting less and less.

At this the amorous shepherdess stopped and handed the pot to her lover.

'Well, I'm dashed!' said Corydon, looking into it; and added: 'I guess you know a thing or two.' Then with courtly grace putting his own lips to the place where had been those of his beloved, finished the pint.

'Go' lumme!' remarked the shepherdess, smacking her lips, 'that was somethin' like!' And she put out her tongue and licked her lips, and then breathed deeply.

The faithful swain having finished, gave a long sigh, and said:

'Well, I could do with some more!'

'For the matter of thet, I could do with a gargle!'

Thus encouraged, the gallant returned to the bar, and soon brought out a second pint.

'You 'ave a fust pop,' amorously remarked Phyllis, and he took a long drink and handed the pot to her.

She, with maiden modesty, turned it so as to have a different part to drink from; but he remarked as he saw her:

'You are bloomin' particular.'

Then, unwilling to grieve him, she turned it back again and applied her ruby lips to the place where his had been.

'Now we shan't be long!' she remarked, as she handed him back the pot.

The faithful swain took out of his pocket a short clay pipe, blew through it, filled it, and began to smoke, while Phyllis sighed at the thought of the cool liquid gliding down her throat, and with the pleasing recollection gently stroked her stomach. Then Corydon spat, and immediately his love said:

'I can spit farther than thet.'

'I bet yer yer can't.'

She tried, and did. He collected himself and spat again, further than before, she followed him, and in this idyllic contest they remained till the tootling horn warned them to take their places.

At last they reached Chingford, and here the horses were taken out and the drag, on which they were to lunch, drawn up in a sheltered spot. They were all rather hungry, but as it was not yet feeding-time, they scattered to have drinks meanwhile. Liza and Tom, with Sally and her young man, went off together to the nearest public-house, and as they drank beer, Harry, who was a great sportsman, gave them a graphic account of a prize-fight he had seen on the previous Saturday evening, which had been rendered specially memorable by one man being so hurt that he had died from the effects. It had evidently been a very fine affair, and Harry said that several swells from the West End had been present, and he related their ludicrous efforts to get in without being seen by anyone, and their terror when someone to frighten them called out 'Copper!' Then Tom and he entered into a discussion on the subject of boxing, in which Tom, being a shy and undogmatic sort of person, was entirely worsted. After this they strolled back to the brake, and found things being prepared for luncheon; the hampers were brought out and emptied, and the bottles of beer in great profusion made many a thirsty mouth thirstier.

'Come along, lidies an' gentlemen—if you are gentlemen,' shouted the coachman; 'the animals is now goin' ter be fed!'

'Garn awy,' answered somebody, 'we're not hanimals; we don't drink water.'

'You're too clever,' remarked the coachman; 'I can see you've just come from the board school.'

As the former speaker was a lady of quite mature appearance, the remark was not without its little irony. The other man blew his horn by way of grace, at which Liza called out to him:

'Don't do thet, you'll bust, I know you will, an' if you bust you'll quite spoil my dinner!'

Then they all set to. Pork-pies, saveloys, sausages, cold potatoes, hard-boiled eggs, cold-bacon, veal, ham, crabs and shrimps, cheese, butter, cold suet-puddings and treacle, gooseberry-tarts, cherry-tarts, butter, bread, more sausages, and yet again pork-pies! They devoured the provisions like ravening beasts, stolidly, silently, earnestly, in large mouthfuls which they shoved down their throats unmasticated. The intelligent foreigner seeing them thus dispose of their food would have understood why England is a great nation. He would have understood why Britons never, never will be slaves. They never stopped except to drink, and then at each gulp they emptied their glass; no heel-taps! And still they ate, and still they drank— but as all things must cease, they stopped at last, and a long sigh of content broke from their two-and-thirty throats.

Then the gathering broke up, and the good folk paired themselves and separated. Harry and his lady strolled off to secluded byways in the forest, so that they might discourse of their loves and digest their dinner. Tom had all the morning been waiting for this happy moment; he had counted on the expansive effect of a full stomach to thaw his Liza's coldness, and he had pictured himself sitting on the grass with his back against the trunk of a spreading chestnut-tree, with his arm round his Liza's waist, and her head resting affectionately on his manly bosom. Liza, too, had foreseen the separation into couples after dinner, and had been racking her brains to find a means of getting out of it.

'I don't want 'im slobberin' abaht me.' she said; 'it gives me the sick, all this kissin' an' cuddlin'!'

She scarcely knew why she objected to his caresses; but they bored her and made her cross. But luckily the blessed institution of marriage came to her rescue, for Jim and his wife naturally had no particular desire to spend the afternoon together, and Liza, seeing a little embarrassment on their part, proposed that they should go for a walk together in the forest.

Jim agreed at once, and with pleasure, but Tom was dreadfully disappointed. He hadn't the courage to say anything, but he glared at Blakeston. Jim smiled benignly at him, and Tom began to sulk. Then they began a funny walk through the woods. Jim tried to go on with Liza, and Liza was not at all disinclined to this, for she had come to the conclusion that Jim, notwithstanding his 'cheek', was not ''alf a bad sort'. But Tom kept walking alongside of them, and as Jim slightly quickened his pace so as to get Liza on in front, Tom quickened his, and Mrs Blakeston, who didn't want to be left behind, had to break into a little trot to keep up with them. Jim tried also to get Liza all to himself in the conversation, and let Tom see that he was out in the cold, but Tom would break in with cross, sulky remarks, just to make the others uncomfortable. Liza at last got rather vexed with him.

'Strikes me you got aht of bed the wrong way this mornin',' she said to him.

'Yer didn't think thet when yer said you'd come aht with me.' He emphasised the 'me'.

Liza shrugged her shoulders.

'You give me the 'ump,' she said. 'If yer wants ter mike a fool of yerself, you can go elsewhere an' do it.'

'I suppose yer want me ter go away now,' he said angrily.

'I didn't say I did.'

'Arright, Liza, I won't stay where I'm not wanted.' And turning on his heel he marched off, striking through the underwood into the midst of the forest.

He felt extremely unhappy as he wandered on, and there was a choky feeling in his throat as he thought of Liza: she was very unkind and ungrateful, and he wished he had never come to Chingford. She might so easily have come for a walk with him instead of going with that beast of a Blakeston; she wouldn't ever do anything for him, and he hated her—but all the same, he was a poor foolish thing in love, and he began to feel that perhaps he had been a little exacting and little forward to take offence. And then he wished he had never said anything, and he wanted so much to see her and make it up. He made his way back to Chingford, hoping she would not make him wait too long.

Liza was a little surprised when Tom turned and left them.

'Wot 'as 'e got the needle abaht?' she said.

'Why, 'e's jealous,' answered Jim, with a laugh.

'Tom jealous?'

'Yus; 'e's jealous of me.'

'Well, 'e ain't got no cause ter be jealous of anyone—that 'e ain't!' said Liza, and continued by telling him all about Tom: how he had wanted to marry her and she wouldn't have him, and how she had only agreed to come to Chingford with him on the understanding that she should preserve her entire freedom. Jim listened sympathetically, but his wife paid no attention; she was doubtless engaged in thought respecting her household or her family.

When they got back to Chingford they saw Tom standing in solitude looking at them. Liza was struck by the woebegone expression on his face; she felt she had been cruel to him, and leaving the Blakestons went up to him.

'I say, Tom,' she said, 'don't tike on so; I didn't mean it.'

He was bursting to apologise for his behaviour.

'Yer know, Tom,' she went on, 'I'm rather 'asty, an' I'm sorry I said wot I did.'

'Oh, Liza, you are good! You ain't cross with me?'

'Me? Na; it's you thet oughter be cross.'

'You are a good sort, Liza!'

'You ain't vexed with me?'

'Give me Liza every time; that's wot I say,' he answered, as his face lit up.

'Come along an' 'ave tea, an' then we'll go for a donkey-ride.'

The donkey-ride was a great success. Liza was a little afraid at first, so Tom walked by her side to take care of her, she screamed the moment the beast began to trot, and clutched hold of Tom to save herself from falling, and as he felt her hand on his shoulder, and heard her appealing cry: 'Oh, do 'old me! I'm fallin'!' he felt that he had never in his life been so deliciously happy. The whole party joined in, and it was proposed that they should have races; but in the first heat, when the donkeys broke into a canter, Liza fell off into Tom's arms and the donkey scampered on without her.

'I know wot I'll do,' she said, when the runaway had been recovered, 'I'll ride 'im straddlewyse.'

'Garn!' said Sally, 'yer can't with petticoats.'

'Yus, I can, an' I will too!'

So another donkey was procured, this time with a man's saddle, and putting her foot in the stirrup, she cocked her leg over and took her seat triumphantly. Neither modesty nor bashfulness was to be reckoned among Liza's faults, and in this position she felt quite at ease.

'I'll git along arright now, Tom,' she said; 'you garn and git yerself a moke, and come an' jine in.'

The next race was perfectly uproarious. Liza kicked and beat her donkey with all her might, shrieking and laughing the while, and finally came in winner by a length. After that they felt rather warm and dry, and repaired to the public-house to restore themselves and talk over the excitements of the racecourse.

When they had drunk several pints of beer Liza and Sally, with their respective adorers and the Blakestons, walked round to find other means of amusing themselves; they were arrested by a coconut-shy.

'Oh, let's 'ave a shy!' said Liza, excitedly, at which the unlucky men had to pull out their coppers, while Sally and Liza made ludicrously bad shots at the coconuts.

'It looks so bloomin' easy,' said Liza, brushing up her hair, 'but I can't 'it the blasted thing. You 'ave a shot, Tom.'

He and Harry were equally unskilful, but Jim got three coconuts running, and the proprietors of the show began to look on him with some concern.

'You are a dab at it,' said Liza, in admiration.

They tried to induce Mrs Blakeston to try her luck, but she stoutly refused.

'I don't 'old with such foolishness. It's wiste of money ter me,' she said.

'Na then, don't crack on, old tart,' remarked her husband, 'let's go an' eat the coconuts.'

There was one for each couple, and after the ladies had sucked the juice they divided them and added their respective shares to their dinners and teas. Supper came next. Again they fell to sausage-rolls, boiled eggs, and saveloys, and countless bottles of beer were added to those already drunk.

'I dunno 'ow many bottles of beer I've drunk—I've lost count,' said Liza; whereat there was a general laugh.

They still had an hour before the brake was to start back, and it was then the concertinas came in useful. They sat down on the grass, and the concert was begun by Harry, who played a solo; then there was a call for a song, and Jim stood up and sang that ancient ditty, 'O dem Golden Kippers, O'. There was no shyness in the company, and Liza, almost without being asked, gave another popular comic song. Then there was more concertina playing, and another demand for a song, Liza turned to Tom, who was sitting quietly by her side.

'Give us a song, old cock,' she said.

'I can't,' he answered. 'I'm not a singin' sort.' At which Blakeston got up and offered to sing again.

'Tom is rather a soft,' said Liza to herself, 'not like that cove Blakeston.'

They repaired to the public-house to have a few last drinks before the brake started, and when the horn blew to warn them, rather unsteadily, they proceeded to take their places.

Liza, as she scrambled up the steps, said: 'Well, I believe I'm boozed.'

The coachman had arrived at the melancholy stage of intoxication, and was sitting on his box holding his reins, with his head bent on his chest. He was thinking sadly of the long-lost days of his youth, and wishing he had been a better man.

Liza had no respect for such holy emotions, and she brought down her fist on the crown of his hat, and bashed it over his eyes.

'Na then, old jellybelly,' she said, 'wot's the good of 'avin' a fice as long as a kite?'

He turned round and smote her.

'Jellybelly yerself!' said he.

'Puddin' fice!' she cried.

'Kite fice!'

'Boss eye!'

She was tremendously excited, laughing and singing, keeping the whole company in an uproar. In her jollity she had changed hats with Tom, and he in her big feathers made her shriek with laughter. When they started they began to sing 'For 'e's a jolly good feller', making the night resound with their noisy voices.

Liza and Tom and the Blakestons had got a seat together, Liza being between the two men. Tom was perfectly happy, and only wished that they might go on so for ever. Gradually as they drove along they became quieter, their singing ceased, and they talked in undertones. Some of them slept; Sally and her young man were leaning up against one another, slumbering quite peacefully. The night was beautiful, the sky still blue, very dark, scattered over with countless brilliant stars, and Liza, as she looked up at the heavens, felt a certain emotion, as if she wished to be taken in someone's arms, or feel some strong man's caress; and there was in her heart a strange sensation as though it were growing big. She stopped speaking, and all four were silent. Then slowly she felt Tom's arm steal round her waist, cautiously, as though it were afraid of being there; this time both she and Tom were happy. But suddenly there was a movement on the other side of her, a hand was advanced along her leg, and her hand was grasped and gently pressed. It was Jim Blakeston. She started a little and began trembling so that Tom noticed it, and whispered:

'You're cold, Liza.'

'Na, I'm not, Tom; it's only a sort of shiver thet went through me.'

His arm gave her waist a squeeze, and at the same time the big rough hand pressed her little one. And so she sat between them till they reached the 'Red Lion' in the Westminster Bridge Road, and Tom said to himself: 'I believe she does care for me after all.'

When they got down they all said good night, and Sally and Liza, with their respective slaves and the Blakestons, marched off homewards. At the corner of Vere Street Harry said to Tom and Blakeston:

'I say, you blokes, let's go an' 'ave another drink before closin' time.'

'I don't mind,' said Tom, 'after we've took the gals 'ome.'

'Then we shan't 'ave time, it's just on closin' time now,' answered Harry.

'Well, we can't leave 'em 'ere.'

'Yus, you can,' said Sally. 'No one'll run away with us.'

Tom did not want to part from Liza, but she broke in with:

'Yus, go on, Tom. Sally an' me'll git along arright, an' you ain't got too much time.'

'Yus, good night, 'Arry,' said Sally to settle the matter.

'Good night, old gal,' he answered, 'give us another slobber.'

And she, not at all unwilling, surrendered herself to him, while he imprinted two sounding kisses on her cheeks.

'Good night, Tom,' said Liza, holding out her hand.

'Good night, Liza,' he answered, taking it, but looking very wistfully at her.

She understood, and with a kindly smile lifted up her face to him. He bent down and, taking her in his arms, kissed her passionately.

'You do kiss nice, Liza,' he said, making the others laugh.

'Thanks for tikin' me aht, old man,' she said as they parted.

'Arright, Liza,' he answered, and added, almost to himself: 'God bless yer!'

"Ulloa, Blakeston, ain't you comin'?' said Harry, seeing that Jim was walking off with his wife instead of joining him and Tom.

'Na,' he answered, 'I'm goin' 'ome. I've got ter be up at five ter-morrer.'

'You are a chap!' said Harry, disgustedly, strolling off with Tom to the pub, while the others made their way down the sleeping street.

The house where Sally lived came first, and she left them; then, walking a few yards more, they came to the Blakeston's, and after a little talk at the door Liza bade the couple good night, and was left to walk the rest of the way home. The street was perfectly silent, and the lamp-posts, far apart, threw a dim light which only served to make Liza realise her solitude. There was such a difference between the street at midday, with its swarms of people, and now, when there was neither sound nor soul besides herself, that even she was struck by it. The regular line of houses on either side, with the even pavements and straight, cemented road, seemed to her like some desert place, as if everyone were dead, or a fire had raged and left it all desolate. Suddenly she heard a footstep, she started and looked back. It was a man hurrying behind her, and in a moment she had recognised Jim. He beckoned to her, and in a low voice called:

'Liza!'

She stopped till he had come up to her.

'Wot 'ave yer come aht again for?' she said.

'I've come aht ter say good night to you, Liza,' he answered.

'But yer said good night a moment ago.'

'I wanted to say it again—properly.'

'Where's yer missus?'

'Oh, she's gone in. I said I was dry and was goin' ter 'ave a drink after all.'

'But she'll know yer didn't go ter the pub.'

'Na, she won't, she's gone straight upstairs to see after the kid. I wanted ter see yer alone, Liza.'

'Why?'

He didn't answer, but tried to take hold of her hand. She drew it away quickly. They walked in silence till they came to Liza's house.

'Good night,' said Liza.

'Won't you come for a little walk, Liza?'

'Tike care no one 'ears you,' she added, in a whisper, though why she whispered she did not know.

'Will yer?' he asked again.

'Na—you've got to get up at five.'

'Oh, I only said thet not ter go inter the pub with them.'

'So as yer might come 'ere with me?' asked Liza.

'Yus!'

'No, I'm not comin'. Good night.'

'Well, say good night nicely.'

'Wot d'yer mean?'

'Tom said you did kiss nice.'

She looked at him without speaking, and in a moment he had clasped his arms round her, almost lifting her off her feet, and kissed her. She turned her face away.

'Give us yer lips, Liza,' he whispered–'give us yer lips.'

He turned her face without resistance and kissed her on the mouth.

At last she tore herself from him, and opening the door slid away into the house.

Chapter Six

Next morning on her way to the factory Liza came up with Sally. They were both of them rather stale and bedraggled after the day's outing; their fringes were ragged and untidily straying over their foreheads, their back hair, carelessly tied in a loose knot, fell over their necks and threatened completely to come down. Liza had not had time to put her hat on, and was holding it in her hand. Sally's was pinned on sideways, and she had to bash it down on her head every now and then to prevent its coming off. Cinderella herself was not more transformed than they were; but Cinderella even in her rags was virtuously tidy and patched up, while Sally had a great tear in her shabby dress, and Liza's stockings were falling over her boots.

'Wot cheer, Sal!' said Liza, when she caught her up.

'Oh, I 'ave got such a 'ead on me this mornin'!' she remarked, turning round a pale face: heavily lined under the eyes.

'I don't feel too chirpy neither,' said Liza, sympathetically.

'I wish I 'adn't drunk so much beer,' added Sally, as a pang shot through her head.

'Oh, you'll be arright in a bit,' said Liza. Just then they heard the clock strike eight, and they began to run so that they might not miss getting their tokens and thereby their day's pay; they turned into the street at the end of which was the factory, and saw half a hundred women running like themselves to get in before it was too late.

All the morning Liza worked in a dead-and-alive sort of fashion, her head like a piece of lead with electric shocks going through it when she moved, and her tongue and mouth hot and dry. At last lunch-time came.

'Come on, Sal,' said Liza, 'I'm goin' to 'ave a glass o' bitter. I can't stand this no longer.'

So they entered the public-house opposite, and in one draught finished their pots. Liza gave a long sigh of relief.

'That bucks you up, don't it?'

'I was dry! I ain't told yer yet, Liza, 'ave I? 'E got it aht last night.'

'Who d'yer mean?'

'Why, 'Arry. 'E spit it aht at last.'

'Arst yer ter nime the day?' said Liza, smiling.

'Thet's it.'

'And did yer?'

'Didn't I jest!' answered Sally, with some emphasis. 'I always told yer I'd git off before you.'

'Yus!' said Liza, thinking.

'Yer know, Liza, you'd better tike Tom; 'e ain't a bad sort.' She was quite patronising.

'I'm goin' ter tike 'oo I like; an' it ain't nobody's business but mine.'

'Arright, Liza, don't get shirty over it; I don't mean no offence.'

'What d'yer say it for then?'

'Well, I thought as seeing as yer'd gone aht with 'im yesterday thet yer meant ter after all.'

''E wanted ter tike me; I didn't arsk 'im.'

'Well, I didn't arsk my 'Arry, either.'

'I never said yer did,' replied Liza.

'Oh, you've got the 'ump, you 'ave!' finished Sally, rather angrily.

The beer had restored Liza; she went back to work without a headache, and, except for a slight languor, feeling no worse for the previous day's debauch. As she worked on she began going over in her mind the events of the preceding day, and she found entwined in all her thoughts the burly person of Jim Blakeston. She saw him walking by her side in the Forest, presiding over the meals, playing the concertina, singing, joking, and finally, on the drive back, she felt the heavy form by her side, and the big, rough hand holding hers, while Tom's arm was round her waist. Tom! That was the first time he had entered her mind, and he sank into a shadow beside the other. Last of all she remembered the walk home from the pub, the good nights, and the rapid footstep as Jim caught her up, and the kiss. She blushed and looked up quickly to see whether any of the girls were looking at her; she could not help thinking of that moment when he took her in his arms; she still felt the roughness of his beard pressing on her mouth. Her heart seemed to grow larger in her breast, and she caught for breath as she threw back her head as if to receive his lips again. A shudder ran through her from the vividness of the thought.

'Wot are you shiverin' for, Liza?' asked one of the girls. 'You ain't cold.'

'Not much,' answered Liza, blushing awkwardly on her meditations being broken into. 'Why, I'm sweatin' so—I'm drippin' wet.'

'I expect yer caught cold in the Faurest yesterday.'

'I see your mash as I was comin' along this mornin'.'

Liza stared a little.

'I ain't got one, 'oo d'yer mean, ay?'

'Yer only Tom, of course. 'E did look washed aht. Wot was yer doin' with 'im yesterday?'

''E ain't got nothin' ter do with me, 'e ain't.'

'Garn, don't you tell me!'

The bell rang, and, throwing over their work, the girls trooped off, and after chattering in groups outside the factory gates for a while, made their way in different directions to their respective homes. Liza and Sally went along together.

'I sy, we are comin' aht!' cried Sally, seeing the advertisement of a play being acted at the neighbouring theatre.

'I should like ter see thet!' said Liza, as they stood arm-in-arm in front of the flaring poster. It represented two rooms and a passage in between; in one room a dead man was lying on the floor, while two others were standing horror-stricken, listening to a youth who was in the passage, knocking at the door.

'You see, they've killed 'im,' said Sally, excitedly.

'Yus, any fool can see thet! an' the one ahtside, wot's 'e doin' of?'

'Ain't 'e beautiful? I'll git my 'Arry ter tike me, I will. I should like ter see it. 'E said 'e'd tike me to the ply.'

They strolled on again, and Liza, leaving Sally, made her way to her mother's. She knew she must pass Jim's house, and wondered whether she would see him. But as she walked along the street she saw Tom coming the opposite way, with a sudden impulse she turned back so as not to meet him, and began walking the way she had come. Then thinking herself a fool for what she had done, she turned again and walked towards him. She wondered if he had seen her or noticed her movement, but when she looked down the street he was nowhere to be seen; he had not caught sight of her, and had evidently gone in to see a mate in one or other of the houses. She quickened her step, and passing the house where lived Jim, could not help looking up; he was standing at the door watching her, with a smile on his lips.

'I didn't see yer, Mr Blakeston,' she said, as he came up to her.

'Didn't yer? Well, I knew yer would; an' I was witin' for yer ter look up. I see yer before ter-day.'

'Na, when?'

'I passed be'ind yer as you an' thet other girl was lookin' at the advertisement of thet ply.'

'I never see yer.'

'Na, I know yer didn't. I 'ear yer say, you says: "I should like to see thet."'

'Yus, an' I should too.'

'Well, I'll tike yer.'

'You?'

'Yus; why not?'

'I like thet; wot would yer missus sy?'

'She wouldn't know.'

'But the neighbours would!'

'No, they wouldn't, no one'd see us.'

He was speaking in a low voice so that people could not hear.

'You could meet me ahtside the theatre,' he went on.

'Na, I couldn't go with you; you're a married man.'

'Garn! wot's thet matter—jest ter go ter the ply? An' besides, my missus can't come if she wanted, she's got the kids ter look after.'

'I should like ter see it,' said Liza meditatively.

They had reached her house, and Jim said:

'Well, come aht this evenin' and tell me if yer will—eh, Liza?'

'Na, I'm not comin' aht this evening.'

'Thet won't 'urt yer. I shall wite for yer.'

''Tain't a bit of good your witin', 'cause I shan't come.'

'Well, then, look 'ere, Liza; next Saturday night's the last night, an' I shall go to the theatre, any'ow. An' if you'll come, you just come to the door at 'alf-past six, an' you'll find me there. See?'

'Na, I don't,' said Liza, firmly.

'Well, I shall expect yer.'

'I shan't come, so you needn't expect.' And with that she walked into the house and slammed the door behind her.

Her mother had not come in from her day's charring, and Liza set about getting her tea. She thought it would be rather lonely eating it alone, so pouring out a cup of tea and putting a little condensed milk into it, she cut a huge piece of bread-and-butter, and sat herself down outside on the doorstep. Another woman came downstairs, and seeing Liza, sat down by her side and began to talk.

'Why, Mrs Stanley, wot 'ave yer done to your 'ead?' asked Liza, noticing a bandage round her forehead.

'I 'ad an accident last night,' answered the woman, blushing uneasily.

'Oh, I am sorry! Wot did yer do to yerself?'

'I fell against the coal-scuttle and cut my 'ead open.'

'Well, I never!'

'To tell yer the truth, I 'ad a few words with my old man. But one doesn't like them things to get abaht; yer won't tell anyone, will yer?'

'Not me!' answered Liza. 'I didn't know yer husband was like thet.'

'Oh, 'e's as gentle as a lamb when 'e's sober,' said Mrs Stanley, apologetically. 'But, Lor' bless yer, when 'e's 'ad a drop too much 'e's a demond, an' there's no two ways abaht it.'

'An' you ain't been married long, neither?' said Liza.

'Na, not above eighteen months; ain't it disgriceful? Thet's wot the doctor at the 'orspital says ter me. I 'ad ter go ter the 'orspital. You should have seen 'ow it bled—it bled all dahn' my fice, and went streamin' like a bust water-pipe. Well, it fair frightened my old man, an' I says ter 'im, "I'll charge yer," an' although I was bleedin' like a bloomin' pig I shook my fist at 'im, an' I says, "I'll charge ye—see if I don't!" An' 'e says, "Na," says 'e, "don't do thet, for God's sike, Kitie, I'll git three months." "An' serve yer damn well right!" says I, an' I went aht an' left 'im. But, Lor' bless yer, I wouldn't charge 'im! I know 'e don't mean it: 'e's as gentle as a lamb when 'e's sober.' She smiled quite affectionately as she said this.

'Wot did yer do, then?' asked Liza.

'Well, as I wos tellin' yer, I went to the 'orspital, an' the doctor 'e says to me, "My good woman," says 'e, "you might have been very seriously injured." An' me not been married eighteen months! An' as I was tellin' the doctor all about it, "Missus," 'e says ter me, lookin' at me straight in the eyeball, "Missus," says 'e, "'ave you been drinkin'?" "Drinkin'?" says I; "no! I've 'ad a little drop, but as for drinkin'"! "Mind," says I, "I don't say I'm a teetotaller—I'm not, I 'ave my glass of beer, and I like it. I couldn't do withaht it, wot with the work I 'ave, I must 'ave somethin' ter keep me tergether. But as for drinkin' 'eavily! Well, I can say this, there ain't a soberer woman than myself in all London. Why, my first 'usband never touched a drop. Ah, my fust 'usband, 'e was a beauty, 'e was."'

She stopped the repetition of her conversation and addressed herself to Liza.

''E was thet different ter this one. 'E was a man as 'ad seen better days. 'E was a gentleman!' She mouthed the word and emphasised it with an expressive nod.

''E was a gentleman and a Christian. 'E'd been in good circumstances in 'is time; an' 'e was a man of education and a teetotaller, for twenty-two years.'

At that moment Liza's mother appeared on the scene.

'Good evenin', Mrs Stanley,' she said, politely.

'The sime ter you, Mrs Kemp,' replied that lady, with equal courtesy.

'An' 'ow is your poor 'ead?' asked Liza's mother, with sympathy.

'Oh, it's been achin' cruel. I've hardly known wot ter do with myself.'

'I'm sure 'e ought ter be ashimed of 'imself for treatin' yer like thet.'

'Oh, it wasn't 'is blows I minded so much, Mrs Kemp,' replied Mrs Stanley, 'an' don't you think it. It was wot 'e said ter me. I can stand a blow as well as any woman. I don't mind thet, an' when 'e don't tike a mean advantage of me I can stand up for myself an' give as good as I tike; an' many's the time I give my fust husband a black eye. But the language 'e used, an' the things 'e called me! It made me blush to the roots of my 'air; I'm not used ter bein' spoken ter like thet. I was in good circumstances when my fust 'usband was alive, 'e earned between two an' three pound a week, 'e did. As I said to 'im this mornin', "'Ow a gentleman can use sich language, I dunno."'

''Usbands is cautions, 'owever good they are,' said Mrs Kemp, aphoristically. 'But I mustn't stay aht 'ere in the night air.'

''As yer rheumatism been troublin' yer litely?' asked Mrs Stanley.

'Oh, cruel. Liza rubs me with embrocation every night, but it torments me cruel.'

Mrs Kemp then went into the house, and Liza remained talking to Mrs Stanley, she, too, had to go in, and Liza was left alone. Some while she spent thinking of nothing, staring vacantly in front of her, enjoying the cool and quiet of the evening. But Liza could not be left alone long, several boys came along with a bat and a ball, and fixed upon the road just in front of her for their pitch. Taking off their coats they piled them up at the two ends, and were ready to begin.

'I say, old gal,' said one of them to Liza, 'come an' have a gime of cricket, will yer?'

'Na, Bob, I'm tired.'

'Come on!'

'Na, I tell you I won't.'

'She was on the booze yesterday, an' she ain't got over it,' cried another boy.

'I'll swipe yer over the snitch!' replied Liza to him, and then on being asked again, said:

'Leave me alone, won't yer?'

'Liza's got the needle ter-night, thet's flat,' commented a third member of the team.

'I wouldn't drink if I was you, Liza,' added another, with mock gravity. 'It's a bad 'abit ter git into,' and he began rolling and swaying about like a drunken man.

If Liza had been 'in form' she would have gone straight away and given the whole lot of them a sample of her strength; but she was only rather bored and vexed that they should disturb her quietness, so she let them talk. They saw she was not to be drawn, and leaving her, set to their game. She watched them for some time, but her thoughts gradually lost themselves, and insensibly her mind was filled with a burly form, and she was again thinking of Jim.

''E is a good sort ter want ter tike me ter the ply,' she said to herself. 'Tom never arst me!'

Jim had said he would come out in the evening; he ought to be here soon, she thought. Of course she wasn't going to the theatre with him, but she didn't mind talking to him; she rather enjoyed being asked to do a thing and refusing, and she would have liked another opportunity of doing so. But he didn't come, and he had said he would!

'I say, Bill,' she said at last to one of the boys who was fielding close beside her, 'that there Blakeston—d'you know 'im?'

'Yes, rather; why, he works at the sime plice as me.'

'Wot's 'e do with 'isself in the evening; I never see 'im abaht?'

'I dunno. I see 'im this evenin' go into the "Red Lion". I suppose 'e's there, but I dunno.'

Then he wasn't coming. Of course she had told him she was going to stay indoors, but he might have come all the same—just to see.

'I know Tom 'ud 'ave come,' she said to herself, rather sulkily.

'Liza! Liza!' she heard her mother's voice calling her.

'Arright, I'm comin',' said Liza.

'I've been witin' for you this last 'alf-hour ter rub me.'

'Why didn't yer call?' asked Liza.

'I did call. I've been callin' this last I dunno 'ow long; it's give me quite a sore throat.'

'I never 'eard yer.'

'Na, yer didn't want ter 'ear me, did yer? Yer don't mind if I dies with rheumatics, do yer? I know.'

Liza did not answer, but took the bottle, and, pouring some of the liniment on her hand, began to rub it into Mrs Kemp's rheumatic joints, while the invalid kept complaining and grumbling at everything Liza did.

'Don't rub so 'ard, Liza, you'll rub all the skin off.'

Then when Liza did it as gently as she could, she grumbled again.

'If you do it like thet, it won't do no good at all. You want ter sive yerself trouble—I know yer. When I was young girls didn't mind a little bit of 'ard work—but, law bless yer, you don't care abaht my rheumatics, do yer?'

At last she finished, and Liza went to bed by her mother's side.

Chapter Seven

Two days passed, and it was Friday morning. Liza had got up early and strolled off to her work in good time, but she did not meet her faithful Sally on the way, nor find her at the factory when she herself arrived. The bell rang and all the girls trooped in, but still Sally did not come. Liza could not make it out, and was thinking she would be shut out, when just as the man who gave out the tokens for the day's work was pulling down the shutter in front of his window, Sally arrived, breathless and perspiring.

'Whew! Go' lumme, I am 'ot!' she said, wiping her face with her apron.

'I thought you wasn't comin',' said Liza.

'Well, I only just did it; I overslep' myself. I was aht lite last night.'

'Were yer?'

'Me an' 'Arry went ter see the ply. Oh, Liza, it's simply spiffin'! I've never see sich a good ply in my life. Lor'! Why, it mikes yer blood run cold: they 'ang a man on the stige; oh, it mide me creep all over!'

And then she began telling Liza all about it—the blood and thunder, the shooting, the railway train, the murder, the bomb, the hero, the funny man–jumbling everything up in her excitement, repeating little scraps of dialogue–all wrong–gesticulating, getting excited and red in the face at the recollection. Liza listened rather crossly, feeling bored at the detail into which Sally was going; the piece really didn't much interest her.

'One 'ud think yer'd never been to a theatre in your life before,' she said.

'I never seen anything so good, I can tell yer. You tike my tip, and git Tom ter tike yer.'

'I don't want ter go; an' if I did I'd py for myself an' go alone.'

'Cheese it! That ain't 'alf so good. Me an' 'Arry, we set together, 'im with 'is arm round my wiste and me 'oldin' 'is 'and. It was jam, I can tell yer!'

'Well, I don't want anyone sprawlin' me abaht, thet ain't my mark!'

'But I do like 'Arry; you dunno the little ways 'e 'as; an' we're goin' ter be married in three weeks now. 'Arry said, well, 'e says, "I'll git a licence." "Na," says I, "'ave the banns read aht in church; it seems more reg'lar like to 'ave banns"; so they're goin' ter to be read aht next Sunday. You'll come with me an' 'ear them, won't yer, Liza?'

'Yus, I don't mind.'

On the way home Sally insisted on stopping in front of the poster and explaining to Liza all about the scene represented.

'Oh, you give me the sick with your "Fital Card", you do! I'm goin' 'ome.' And she left Sally in the midst of her explanation.

'I dunno wot's up with Liza,' remarked Sally to a mutual friend. 'She's always got the needle, some-'ow.'

'Oh, she's barmy,' answered the friend.

'Well, I do think she's a bit dotty sometimes–I do really,' rejoined Sally.

Liza walked homewards, thinking of the play; at length she tossed her head impatiently.

'I don't want ter see the blasted thing; an' if I see that there Jim I'll tell 'im so; swop me bob, I will.'

She did see him; he was leaning with his back against the wall of his house, smoking. Liza knew he had seen her, and as she walked by pretended not to have noticed him. To her disgust, he let her pass, and she was thinking he hadn't seen her after all, when she heard him call her name.

'Liza!'

She turned round and started with surprise very well imitated. 'I didn't see you was there!' she said.

'Why did yer pretend not ter notice me, as yer went past–eh, Liza?'

'Why, I didn't see yer.'

'Garn! But you ain't shirty with me?'

'Wot 'ave I got to be shirty abaht?'

He tried to take her hand, but she drew it away quickly. She was getting used to the movement. They went on talking, but Jim did not mention the theatre; Liza was surprised, and wondered whether he had forgotten.

'Er–Sally went to the ply last night,' she said, at last.

'Oh!' he said, and that was all.

She got impatient.

'Well, I'm off!' she said.

'Na, don't go yet; I want ter talk ter yer,' he replied.

'Wot abaht? anythin' in partickler?' She would drag it out of him if she possibly could.

'Not thet I knows on,' he said, smiling.

'Good night!' she said, abruptly, turning away from him.

'Well, I'm damned if 'e ain't forgotten!' she said to herself, sulkily, as she marched home.

The following evening about six o'clock, it suddenly struck her that it was the last night of the 'New and Sensational Drama'.

'I do like thet Jim Blakeston,' she said to herself; 'fancy tretin' me like thet! You wouldn't catch Tom doin' sich a thing. Bli'me if I speak to 'im again, the— Now I shan't see it at all. I've a good mind ter go on my own 'ook. Fancy 'is forgettin' all abaht it, like thet!'

She was really quite indignant; though, as she had distinctly refused Jim's offer, it was rather hard to see why.

''E said 'e'd wite for me ahtside the doors; I wonder if 'e's there. I'll go an' see if 'e is, see if I don't–an' then if 'e's there, I'll go in on my own 'ook, jist ter spite 'im!'

She dressed herself in her best, and, so that the neighbours shouldn't see her, went up a passage between some model lodging-house buildings, and in this roundabout way got into the Westminster Bridge Road, and soon found herself in front of the theatre.

'I've been witin' for yer this 'alf-hour.'

She turned round and saw Jim standing just behind her.

''Oo are you talkin' to? I'm not goin' to the ply with you. Wot d'yer tike me for, eh?'

''Oo are yer goin' with, then?'

'I'm goin' alone.'

'Garn! don't be a bloomin' jackass!'

Liza was feeling very injured.

'Thet's 'ow you treat me! I shall go 'ome. Why didn't you come aht the other night?'

'Yer told me not ter.'

She snorted at the ridiculous ineptitude of the reply.

'Why didn't you say nothin' abaht it yesterday?'

'Why, I thought you'd come if I didn't talk on it.'

'Well, I think you're a —— brute!' She felt very much inclined to cry.

'Come on, Liza, don't tike on; I didn't mean no offence.' And he put his arm round her waist and led her to take their places at the gallery door. Two tears escaped from the corners of her eyes and ran down her nose, but she felt very relieved and happy, and let him lead her where he would.

There was a long string of people waiting at the door, and Liza was delighted to see a couple of niggers who were helping them to while away the time of waiting. The niggers sang and danced, and made faces, while the people looked on with appreciative gravity, like royalty listening to de Reszké, and they were very generous of applause and halfpence at the end of the performance. Then, when the niggers moved to the pit doors, paper boys came along offering *Tit-Bits* and 'extra specials'; after that three little girls came round and sang sentimental songs and collected more halfpence. At last a movement ran through the serpent-like string of people, sounds were heard behind the door, everyone closed up, the men told the women to keep close and hold tight; there was a great unbarring and unbolting, the doors were thrown open, and, like a bursting river, the people surged in.

Half an hour more and the curtain went up. The play was indeed thrilling. Liza quite forgot her companion, and was intent on the scene; she watched the incidents breathlessly, trembling with excitement, almost beside herself at the celebrated hanging incident. When the curtain fell on the first act she sighed and mopped her face.

'See 'ow 'ot I am,' she said to Jim, giving him her hand.

'Yus, you are!' he remarked, taking it.

'Leave go!' she said, trying to withdraw it from him.

'Not much,' he answered, quite boldly.

'Garn! Leave go!' But he didn't, and she really did not struggle very violently.

The second act came, and she shrieked over the comic man; and her laughter rang higher than anyone else's, so that people turned to look at her, and said:

'She is enjoyin' 'erself.'

Then when the murder came she bit her nails and the sweat stood on her forehead in great drops; in her excitement she even called out as loud as she could to the victim, 'Look aht!' it caused a laugh and slackened the tension, for the whole house was holding its breath as it looked at the villians listening at the door, creeping silently forward, crawling like tigers to their prey.

Liza trembled all over, and in her terror threw herself against Jim, who put both arms round her, and said:

'Don't be afride, Liza; it's all right.'

At last the men sprang, there was a scuffle, and the wretch was killed, then came the scene depicted on the posters–the victim's son knocking at the door, on the inside of which were the murderers and the murdered man. At last the curtain came down, and the house in relief burst forth into cheers and cheers; the handsome hero in his top hat was greeted thunderously; the murdered man, with his clothes still all disarranged, was hailed with sympathy; and the villains–the house yelled and hissed and booed, while the poor brutes bowed and tried to look as if they liked it.

'I am enjoyin' myself,' said Liza, pressing herself quite close to Jim; 'you are a good sort ter tike me–Jim.'

He gave her a little hug, and it struck her that she was sitting just as Sally had done, and, like Sally, she found it 'jam'.

The *entre'actes* were short and the curtain was soon up again, and the comic man raised customary laughter by undressing and exposing his nether garments to the public view; then more tragedy, and the final act with its darkened room, its casting lots, and its explosion.

When it was all over and they had got outside Jim smacked his lips and said:

'I could do with a gargle; let's go into thet pub there.'

'I'm as dry as bone,' said Liza; and so they went.

When they got in they discovered they were hungry, and seeing some appetising sausage-rolls, ate of them, and washed them down with a couple of pots of beer; then Jim lit his pipe and they strolled off. They had got quite near the Westminster Bridge Road when Jim suggested that they should go and have one more drink before closing time.

'I shall be tight,' said Liza.

'Thet don't matter,' answered Jim, laughing. 'You ain't got ter go ter work in ter mornin' an' you can sleep it aht.'

'Arright, I don't mind if I do then, in for a penny, in for a pound.'

At the pub door she drew back.

'I say, guv'ner,' she said, 'there'll be some of the coves from dahn our street, and they'll see us.'

'Na, there won't be nobody there, don't yer 'ave no fear.'

'I don't like ter go in for fear of it.'

'Well, we ain't doin' no 'arm if they does see us, an' we can go into the private bar, an' you bet your boots there won't be no one there.'

She yielded, and they went in.

'Two pints of bitter, please, miss,' ordered Jim.

'I say, 'old 'ard. I can't drink more than 'alf a pint,' said Liza.

'Cheese it,' answered Jim. 'You can do with all you can get, I know.'

At closing time they left and walked down the broad road which led homewards.

'Let's 'ave a little sit dahn,' said Jim, pointing to an empty bench between two trees.

'Na, it's gettin' lite; I want ter be 'ome.'

'It's such a fine night, it's a pity ter go in already;' and he drew her unresisting towards the seat. He put his arm round her waist.

'Un'and me, villin!' she said, in apt misquotation of the melodrama, but Jim only laughed, and she made no effort to disengage herself.

They sat there for a long while in silence; the beer had got to Liza's head, and the warm night air filled her with a double intoxication. She felt the arm round her waist, and the big, heavy form pressing against her side; she experienced again the curious sensation as if her heart were about to burst, and it choked her—a feeling so oppressive and painful that it almost made her feel sick. Her hands began to tremble, and her breathing grew rapid, as though she were suffocating. Almost fainting, she swayed over towards the man, and a cold shiver ran through her from top to toe. Jim bent over her, and, taking her in both arms, he pressed his lips to hers in a long, passionate kiss. At last, panting for breath, she turned her head away and groaned.

Then they again sat for a long while in silence, Liza full of a strange happiness, feeling as if she could laugh aloud hysterically, but restrained by the calm and silence of the night. Close behind struck a church clock—one.

'Bless my soul!' said Liza, starting, 'there's one o'clock I must get 'ome.'

'It's so nice out 'ere; do sty, Liza.' he pressed her closer to him. 'Yer know, Liza, I love yer—fit ter kill.'

'Na, I can't stay; come on.' She got up from the seat, and pulled him up too. 'Come on,' she said.

Without speaking they went along, and there was no one to be seen either in front or behind them. He had not got his arm round her now, and they were walking side by side, slightly separated. It was Liza who spoke first.

'You'd better go dahn the Road and by the church an' git into Vere Street the other end, an' I'll go through the passage, so thet no one shouldn't see us comin' together,' she spoke almost in a whisper.

'Arright, Liza,' he answered, 'I'll do just as you tell me.'

They came to the passage of which Liza spoke; it was a narrow way between blank walls, the backs of factories, and it led into the upper end of Vere Street. The entrance to it was guarded by two iron posts in the middle, so that horses or barrows should not be taken through.

They had just got to it when a man came out into the open road. Liza quickly turned her head away.

'I wonder if 'e see us,' she said, when he had passed out of earshot. ''E's lookin' back,' she added.

'Why, 'oo is it?' asked Jim.

'It's a man aht of our street,' she answered. 'I dunno 'im, but I know where 'e lodges. D'yer think 'e see us?'

'Na, 'e wouldn't know 'oo it was in the dark.'

'But he looked round; all the street'll know it if he see us.'

'Well, we ain't doin' no 'arm.'

She stretched out her hand to say good night.

'I'll come a little wy with yer along the passage,' said Jim.

'Na, you mustn't; you go straight round.'

'But it's so dark; p'raps summat'll 'appen to yer.'

'Not it! You go on 'ome an' leave me,' she replied, and entering the passage, stood facing him with one of the iron pillars between them.

'Good night, old cock,' she said, stretching out her hand. He took it, and said:

'I wish yer wasn't goin' ter leave me, Liza.'

'Garn! I must!' She tried to get her hand away from his, but he held it firm, resting it on the top of the pillar.

'Leave go my 'and,' she said. He made no movement, but looked into her eyes steadily, so that it made her uneasy. She repented having come out with him. 'Leave go my 'and.' And she beat down on his hand with her closed fist.

'Liza!' he said, at last.

'Well, wot is it?' she answered, still thumping down on his hand with her fist.

'Liza,' he said in a whisper, 'will yer?'

'Will I wot?' she said, looking down.

'You know, Liza. Sy, will yer?'

'Na,' she said.

He bent over her and repeated—

'Will yer?'

She did not speak, but kept beating down on his hand.

'Liza,' he said again, his voice growing hoarse and thick—'Liza, will yer?'

She still kept silence, looking away and continually bringing down her fist. He looked at her a moment, and she, ceasing to thump his hand, looked up at him with half-opened mouth. Suddenly he shook himself, and closing his fist gave her a violent, swinging blow in the belly.

'Come on,' he said.

And together they slid down into the darkness of the passage.

Chapter Eight

Mrs Kemp was in the habit of slumbering somewhat heavily on Sunday mornings, or Liza would not have been allowed to go on sleeping as she did. When she woke, she rubbed her eyes to gather her senses together and gradually she remembered having gone to the theatre on the previous evening; then suddenly everything came back to her. She stretched out her legs and gave a long sigh of delight. Her heart was full; she thought of Jim, and the delicious sensation of love came over her. Closing her eyes, she imagined his warm kisses, and she lifted up her arms as if to put them round his neck and draw him down to her; she almost felt the rough beard on her face, and the strong heavy arms round her body. She smiled to herself and took a long breath; then, slipping back the sleeves of her nightdress, she looked at her own thin arms, just two pieces of bone with not a muscle on them, but very white and showing distinctly the interlacement of blue veins; she did not notice that her hands were rough, and red and dirty with the nails broken, and bitten to the quick. She got out of bed and looked at herself in the glass over the mantelpiece; with one hand she brushed back her hair and smiled at herself; her face was very small and thin, but the complexion was nice, clear and white, with a delicate tint of red on the cheeks, and her eyes were big and dark like her hair. She felt very happy.

She did not want to dress yet, but rather to sit down and think, so she twisted up her hair into a little knot, slipped a skirt over her nightdress, and sat on a chair near the window and began looking around. The decorations of the room had been centred on the mantelpiece; the chief ornament consisted of a pear and an apple, a pineapple, a bunch of grapes, and several fat plums, all very beautifully done in wax, as was the fashion about the middle of this most glorious reign. They were appropriately coloured—the apple blushing red, the grapes an inky black, emerald green leaves were scattered here and there to lend finish, and the whole was mounted on an ebonised stand covered with black velvet, and protected from dust and dirt by a beautiful glass cover bordered with red plush. Liza's eyes rested on this with approbation, and the pineapple quite made her mouth water. At either end of the mantelpiece were pink jars with blue flowers on the front; round the top in Gothic letters of gold were inscribed: 'A Present from a Friend'—these were products of a later, but not less artistic age. The intervening spaces were taken up with little jars and cups and saucers—gold inside, with a view of the town outside, and surrounding them, 'A Present from Clacton-on-Sea,' or, alliteratively, 'A Memento of Margate.' Of these many were broken, but they had been mended with glue, and it is well known that pottery in the eyes of the connoisseur loses none of its value by a crack or two. Then there were portraits innumerable—little yellow cartes-de-visite in velvet frames, some of which were decorated with shells; they showed strange people with old-fashioned clothes, the women with bodices and sleeves fitting close to the figure, stern-featured females with hair carefully parted in the middle and plastered down on each side, firm chins and mouths, with small, pig-like eyes and wrinkled faces, and the men were uncomfortably clad in Sunday garments, very stiff and uneasy in their awkward postures, with large whiskers and shaved chins and upper lips and a general air of horny-handed toil. Then there were one or two daguerreotypes, little full-length figures framed in gold paper. There was one of Mrs Kemp's father and one of her mother, and there were several photographs of betrothed or newly-married couples, the lady sitting down and the man standing behind her with his hand on the chair, or the man sitting and the woman with her hand on his shoulder. And from all sides of the room, standing on the mantelpiece, hanging above it, on the wall and over the bed, they stared full-face into the room, self-consciously fixed for ever in their stiff discomfort.

The walls were covered with dingy, antiquated paper, and ornamented with coloured supplements from Christmas Numbers—there was a very patriotic picture of a soldier shaking the hand of a fallen comrade and waving his arm in defiance of a band of advancing Arabs; there was a 'Cherry Ripe', almost black with age and dirt; there were two almanacks several years old, one with a coloured portrait of the Marquess of Lorne, very handsome and elegantly dressed, the object of Mrs Kemp's adoration since her husband's demise; the other a Jubilee portrait of the Queen, somewhat losing in dignity by a moustache which Liza in an irreverent moment had smeared on with charcoal.

The furniture consisted of a wash-hand stand and a little deal chest of drawers, which acted as sideboard to such pots and pans and crockery as could not find room in the grate; and besides the bed there was nothing but two kitchen chairs and a lamp. Liza looked at it all and felt perfectly satisfied; she put a pin into one corner of the noble Marquess to prevent him from falling, fiddled about with the ornaments a little, and then started washing herself. After putting on her clothes she ate some bread-and-butter, swallowed a dishful of cold tea, and went out into the street.

She saw some boys playing cricket and went up to them.

'Let me ply,' she said.

'Arright, Liza,' cried half a dozen of them in delight; and the captain added: 'You go an' scout over by the lamp-post.'

'Go an' scout my eye!' said Liza, indignantly. 'When I ply cricket I does the battin'.'

'Na, you're not goin' ter bat all the time. 'Oo are you gettin' at?' replied the captain, who had taken advantage of his position to put himself in first, and was still at the wicket.

'Well, then I shan't ply,' answered Liza.

'Garn, Ernie, let 'er go in!' shouted two or three members of the team.

'Well, I'm busted!' remarked the captain, as she took his bat. 'You won't sty in long, I lay,' he said, as he sent the old bowler fielding and took the ball himself. He was a young gentleman who did not suffer from excessive backwardness.

'Aht!' shouted a dozen voices as the ball went past Liza's bat and landed in the pile of coats which formed the wicket. The captain came forward to resume his innings, but Liza held the bat away from him.

'Garn!' she said; 'thet was only a trial.'

'You never said trial,' answered the captain indignantly.

'Yus, I did,' said Liza; 'I said it just as the ball was comin'—under my breath.'

'Well, I am busted!' repeated the captain.

Just then Liza saw Tom among the lookers-on, and as she felt very kindly disposed to the world in general that morning, she called out to him:

''Ulloa, Tom!' she said. 'Come an' give us a ball; this chap can't bowl.'

'Well, I got yer aht, any'ow,' said that person.

'Ah, yer wouldn't 'ave got me aht plying square. But a trial ball—well, one don't ever know wot a trial ball's goin' ter do.'

Tom began bowling very slowly and easily, so that Liza could swing her bat round and hit mightily; she ran well, too, and pantingly brought up her score to twenty. Then the fielders interposed.

'I sy, look 'ere, 'e's only givin' 'er lobs; 'e's not tryin' ter git 'er aht.'

'You're spoilin' our gime.'

'I don't care; I've got twenty runs—thet's more than you could do. I'll go aht now of my own accord, so there! Come on, Tom.'

Tom joined her, and as the captain at last resumed his bat and the game went on, they commenced talking, Liza leaning against the wall of a house, while Tom stood in front of her, smiling with pleasure.

'Where 'ave you been 'idin' yerself, Tom? I ain't seen yer for I dunno 'ow long.'

'I've been abaht as usual; an' I've seen you when you didn't see me.'

'Well, yer might 'ave come up and said good mornin' when you see me.'

'I didn't want ter force myself on yer, Liza.'

'Garn! you are a bloomin' cuckoo, I'm blowed!'

'I thought yer didn't like me 'angin' round yer; so I kep' away.'

'Why, yer talks as if I didn't like yer. Yer don't think I'd 'ave come aht beanfeastin' with yer if I 'adn't liked yer?'

Liza was really very dishonest, but she felt so happy this morning that she loved the whole world, and of course Tom came in with the others. She looked very kindly at him, and he was so affected that a great lump came in his throat and he could not speak.

Liza's eyes turned to Jim's house, and she saw coming out of the door a girl of about her own age; she fancied she saw in her some likeness to Jim.

'Say, Tom,' she asked, 'thet ain't Blakeston's daughter, is it?'

'Yus, thet's it.'

'I'll go an' speak to 'er.' said Liza, leaving Tom and going over the road. 'You're Polly Blakeston, ain't yer?' she said.

'Thet's me!' said the girl.

'I thought you was. Your dad, 'e says ter me, "You dunno my daughter, Polly, do yer?" says 'e. "Na," says I, "I don't." "Well," says 'e, "You can't miss 'er when you see 'er." An' right enough I didn't.'

'Mother says I'm all father, an' there ain't nothin' of 'er in me. Dad says it's lucky it ain't the other wy abaht, or 'e'd 'ave got a divorce.'

They both laughed.

'Where are you goin' now?' asked Liza, looking at the slop-basin she was carrying.

'I was just goin' dahn into the road ter get some ice-cream for dinner. Father 'ad a bit of luck last night, 'e says, and 'e'd stand the lot of us ice-cream for dinner ter-day.'

'I'll come with yer if yer like.'

'Come on!' And, already friends, they walked arm-in-arm to the Westminster Bridge Road. Then they went along till they came to a stall where an Italian was selling the required commodity, and having had a taste apiece to see if they liked it, Polly planked down sixpence and had her basin filled with a poisonous-looking mixture of red and white ice-cream.

On the way back, looking up the street, Polly cried:

'There's father!'

Liza's heart beat rapidly and she turned red; but suddenly a sense of shame came over her, and casting down her head so that she might not see him, she said:

'I think I'll be off 'ome an' see 'ow mother's gettin' on.' And before Polly could say anything she had slipped away and entered her own house.

Mother was not getting on at all well.

'You've come in at last, you ——, you!' snarled Mrs Kemp, as Liza entered the room.

'Wot's the matter, mother?'

'Matter! I like thet—matter indeed! Go an' matter yerself an' be mattered! Nice way ter treat an old woman like me—an' yer own mother, too!'

'Wot's up now?'

'Don't talk ter me; I don't want ter listen ter you. Leavin' me all alone, me with my rheumatics, an' the neuralgy! I've 'ad the neuralgy all the mornin', and my 'ead's been simply splittin', so thet I thought the bones 'ud come apart and all my brains go streamin' on the floor. An' when I wake up there's no one ter git my tea for me, an' I lay there witin' an' witin', an' at last I 'ad ter git up and mike it myself. And, my 'ead simply cruel! Why, I might 'ave been burnt ter death with the fire alight an' me asleep.'

'Well, I am sorry, mother; but I went aht just for a bit, an' didn't think you'd wike. An' besides, the fire wasn't alight.'

'Garn with yer! I didn't treat my mother like thet. Oh, you've been a bad daughter ter me—an' I 'ad more illness carryin' you than with all the other children put togither. You was a cross at yer birth, an' you've been a cross ever since. An' now in my old age, when I've worked myself ter the bone, yer leaves me to starve and burn to death.' Here she began to cry, and the rest of her utterances was lost in sobs.

The dusk had darkened into night, and Mrs Kemp had retired to rest with the dicky-birds. Liza was thinking of many things; she wondered why she had been unwilling to meet Jim in the morning.

'I was a bally fool,' she said to herself.

It really seemed an age since the previous night, and all that had happened seemed very long ago. She had not spoken to Jim all day, and she had so much to say to him. Then, wondering whether he was about, she went to the window and looked out; but there was nobody there. She closed the window again and sat just beside it; the time went on, and she wondered whether he would come, asking herself whether he had been thinking of her as she of him; gradually her thoughts grew vague, and a kind of mist came over them. She nodded. Suddenly she roused herself with a start, fancying she had heard something; she listened again, and in a moment the sound was repeated, three or four gentle taps on the window. She opened it quickly and whispered:

'Jim.'

'Thet's me,' he answered, 'come aht.'

Closing the window, she went into the passage and opened the street door; it was hardly unlocked before Jim had pushed his way in; partly shutting it behind him, he took her in his arms and hugged her to his breast. She kissed him passionately.

'I thought yer'd come ter-night, Jim; summat in my 'eart told me so. But you 'ave been long.'

'I wouldn't come before, 'cause I thought there'd be people abaht. Kiss us!' And again he pressed his lips to hers, and Liza nearly fainted with the delight of it.

'Let's go for a walk, shall we?' he said.

'Arright!' They were speaking in whispers. 'You go into the road through the passage, an' I'll go by the street.'

'Yus, thet's right,' and kissing her once more, he slid out, and she closed the door behind him.

Then going back to get her hat, she came again into the passage, waiting behind the door till it might be safe for her to venture. She had not made up her mind to risk it, when she heard a key put in the lock, and she hardly had time to spring back to prevent herself from being hit by the opening door. It was a man, one of the upstairs lodgers.

''Uloa!' he said, ''oo's there?'

'Mr 'Odges! Strike me, you did give me a turn; I was just goin' aht.' She blushed to her hair, but in the darkness he could see nothing.

'Good night,' she said, and went out.

She walked close along the sides of the houses like a thief, and the policeman as she passed him turned and looked at her, wondering whether she was meditating some illegal deed. She breathed freely on coming into the open road, and seeing Jim skulking behind a tree, ran up to him, and in the shadows they kissed again.

Chapter Nine

Thus began a time of love and joy. As soon as her work was over and she had finished tea, Liza would slip out and at some appointed spot meet Jim. Usually it would be at the church, where the Westminster Bridge Road bends down to get to the river, and they would go off, arm-in-arm, till they came to some place where they could sit down and rest. Sometimes they would walk along the Albert Embankment to Battersea Park, and here sit on the benches, watching the children play. The female cyclist had almost abandoned Battersea for the parks on the other side of the river, but often enough one went by, and Liza, with the old-fashioned prejudice of her class, would look after the rider and make some remark about her, not seldom more forcible than ladylike. Both Jim and she liked children, and tiny, ragged urchins would gather round to have rides on the man's knees or mock fights with Liza.

They thought themselves far away from anyone in Vere Street, but twice, as they were walking along, they were met by people they knew. Once it was two workmen coming home from a job at Vauxhall; Liza did not see them till they were quite near; she immediately dropped Jim's arm, and they both cast their eyes to the ground as the men passed, like ostriches, expecting that if they did not look they would not be seen.

'D'you see 'em, Jim?' asked Liza, in a whisper, when they had gone by. 'I wonder if they see us.' Almost instinctively she turned round, and at the same moment one of the men turned too; then there was no doubt about it.

'Thet did give me a turn,' she said.

'So it did me,' answered Jim; 'I simply went 'ot all over.'

'We was bally fools,' said Liza; 'we oughter 'ave spoken to 'em! D'you think they'll let aht?'

They heard nothing of it, when Jim afterwards met one of the men in a public-house he did not mention a meeting, and they thought that perhaps they had not been recognised. But the second time was worse.

It was on the Albert Embankment again. They were met by a party of four, all of whom lived in the street. Liza's heart sank within her, for there was no chance of escape; she thought of turning quickly and walking in the opposite direction, but there was not time, for the men had already seen them. She whispered to Jim:

'Back us up,' as and they met she said to one of the men: ''Ulloa there! Where are you off to?'

The men stopped, and one of them asked the question back.

'Where are you off to?'

'Me? Oh, I've just been to the 'orspital. One of the gals at our place is queer, an' so I says ter myself, "I'll go an' see 'er." ' She faltered a little as she began, but quickly gathered herself together, lying fluently and without hesitation.

'An' when I come aht,' she went on, ' 'o should I see just passin' the 'orspital but this 'ere cove, an' 'e says to me, "Wot cheer," says 'e, "I'm goin' ter Vaux'all, come an' walk a bit of the wy with us." "Arright," says I, "I don't mind if I do." '

One man winked, and another said: 'Go it, Liza!'

She fired up with the dignity of outraged innocence.

'Wot d'yer mean by thet?' she said; 'd'yer think I'm kiddin'?'

'Kiddin'? No! You've only just come up from the country, ain't yer?'

'Think I'm kidding? What d'yer think I want ter kid for? Liars never believe anyone, thet's fact.'

'Na then, Liza, don't be saucy.'

'Saucy! I'll smack yer in the eye if yer sy much ter me. Come on,' she said to Jim, who had been standing sheepishly by; and they walked away.

The men shouted: 'Now we shan't be long!' and went off laughing.

After that they decided to go where there was no chance at all of their being seen. They did not meet till they got over Westminster Bridge, and thence they made their way into the park; they would lie down on the grass in one another's arms, and thus spend the long summer evenings. After the heat of the day there would be a gentle breeze in the park, and they would take in long breaths of the air; it seemed far away from London, it was so quiet and cool; and Liza, as she lay by Jim's side, felt her love for him overflowing to the rest of the world and enveloping mankind itself in a kind of grateful happiness. If it could only have lasted! They would stay and see the stars shine out dimly, one by one, from the blue sky, till it grew late and the blue darkened into black, and the stars glittered in thousands all above them. But as the nights grew cooler, they found it cold on the grass, and the time they had there seemed too short for the long journey they had to make; so, crossing the bridge as before, they strolled along the Embankment till they came to a vacant bench, and there they would sit, with Liza nestling close up to her lover and his great arms around her. The rain of September made no difference to them; they went as usual to their seat beneath the trees, and Jim would take Liza on his knee, and, opening his coat, shelter her with it, while she, with her arms round his neck, pressed very close to him, and occasionally gave a little laugh of pleasure and delight. They hardly spoke at all through these evenings, for what had they to say to one another? Often without exchanging a word they would sit for an hour with their faces touching, the one feeling on his cheek the hot breath from the other's mouth; while at the end of the time the only motion was an upraising of Liza's lips, a bending down of Jim's, so that they might meet and kiss. Sometimes Liza fell into a light doze, and Jim would sit very still for fear of waking her, and when she roused herself she would smile, while he bent down again and kissed her. They were very happy. But the hours passed by so quickly, that Big Ben striking twelve came upon them as a surprise, and unwillingly they got up and made their way homewards; their partings were never ending—each evening Jim refused to let her go from his arms, and tears stood in his eyes at the thought of the separation.

'I'd give somethin',' he would say, 'if we could be togither always.'

'Never mind, old chap!' Liza would answer, herself half crying, 'it can't be 'elped, so we must jolly well lump it.'

But notwithstanding all their precautions people in Vere Street appeared to know. First of all Liza noticed that the women did not seem quite so cordial as before, and she often fancied they were talking of her; when she passed by they appeared to look at her, then say something or other, and perhaps burst out laughing; but when she approached they would immediately stop speaking, and keep silence in a rather awkward, constrained manner. For a long time she was unwilling to believe that there was any change in them, and Jim who had observed nothing, persuaded her that it was all fancy. But gradually it became clearer, and Jim had to agree with her that somehow or other people had found out. Once when Liza had been talking to Polly, Jim's daughter, Mrs Blakeston had called her, and when the girl had come to her mother Liza saw that she spoke angrily, and they both looked across at her. When Liza caught Mrs Blakeston's eye she saw in her face a surly scowl, which almost frightened her; she wanted to brave it out, and stepped forward a little to go and speak with the woman, but Mrs Blakeston, standing still, looked so angrily at her that she was afraid to. When she told Jim his face grew dark, and he said: 'Blast the woman! I'll give 'er wot for if she says anythin' ter you.'

'Don't strike 'er, wotever 'appens, will yer, Jim?' said Liza

'She'd better tike care then!' he answered, and he told her that lately his wife had been sulking, and not speaking to him. The previous night, on coming home after the day's work and bidding her 'Good evenin',' she had turned her back on him without answering.

'Can't you answer when you're spoke to?' he had said.

'Good evenin',' she had replied sulkily, with her back still turned.

After that Liza noticed that Polly avoided her.

'Wot's up, Polly?' she said to her one day. 'You never speaks now; 'ave you 'ad yer tongue cut aht?'

'Me? I ain't got nothin' ter speak abaht, thet I knows of,' answered Polly, abruptly walking off. Liza grew very red and quickly looked to see if anyone had noticed the incident. A couple of youths, sitting on the pavement, had seen it, and she saw then nudge one another and wink.

Then the fellows about the street began to chaff her.

'You look pale,' said one of a group to her one day.

'You're overworkin' yerself, you are,' said another.

'Married life don't agree with Liza, that's wot it is,' added a third.

''Oo d'yer think yer gettin' at? I ain't married, an' never like ter be,' she answered.

'Liza 'as all the pleasures of a 'usband an' none of the trouble.'

'Bli'me if I know wot yer mean!' said Liza.

'Na, of course not; you don't know nothin', do yer?'

'Innocent as a bibe. Our Father which art in 'eaven!'

''Aven't been in London long, 'ave yer?'

They spoke in chorus, and Liza stood in front of them, bewildered, not knowing what to answer.

'Don't you mike no mistake abaht it, Liza knows a thing or two.'

'O me darlin', I love yer fit to kill, but tike care your missus ain't round the corner.' This was particularly bold, and they all laughed.

Liza felt very uncomfortable, and fiddled about with her apron, wondering how she should get away.

'Tike care yer don't git into trouble, thet's all,' said one of the men, with burlesque gravity.

'Yer might give us a chanst, Liza, you come aht with me one evenin'.' You oughter give us all a turn, jist ter show there's no ill-feelin'.'

'Bli'me if I know wot yer all talkin' abaht. You're all barmy on the crumpet,' said Liza indignantly, and, turning her back on them, made for home.

Among other things that had happened was Sally's marriage. One Saturday a little procession had started from Vere Street, consisting of Sally, in a state of giggling excitement, her fringe magnificent after a whole week of curling-papers, clad in a perfectly new velveteen dress of the colour known as electric blue; and Harry, rather nervous and ill at ease in the unaccustomed restraint of a collar; these two walked arm-in-arm, and were followed by Sally's mother and uncle, also arm-in-arm, and the procession was brought up by Harry's brother and a friend. They started with a flourish of trumpets and an old boot, and walked down the middle of Vere Street, accompanied by the neighbours' good wishes; but as they got into the Westminster Bridge Road and nearer to the church, the happy couple grew silent, and Harry began to perspire freely, so that his collar gave him perfect torture. There was a public-house just opposite the church, and it was suggested that they should have a drink before going in. As it was a solemn occasion they went into the private bar, and there Sally's uncle, who was a man of means, ordered six pots of beer.

'Feel a bit nervous, 'Arry?' asked his friend.

'Na,' said Harry, as if he had been used to getting married every day of his life; 'bit warm, thet's all.'

'Your very good 'ealth, Sally,' said her mother, lifting her mug; 'this is the last time as I shall ever address you as miss.'

'An' may she be as good a wife as you was,' added Sally's uncle.

'Well, I don't think my old man ever 'ad no complaint ter mike abaht me. I did my duty by 'im, although it's me as says it,' answered the good lady.

'Well, mates,' said Harry's brother, 'I reckon it's abaht time to go in. So 'ere's to the 'ealth of Mr 'Enry Atkins an' 'is future missus.'

'An' God bless 'em!' said Sally's mother.

Then they went into the church, and as they solemnly walked up the aisle a pale-faced young curate came out of the vestry and down to the bottom of the chancel. The beer had had a calming effect on their troubled minds, and both Harry and Sally began to think it rather a good joke. They smiled on each other, and at those parts of the service which they thought suggestive violently nudged one another in the ribs. When the ring had to be produced, Harry fumbled about in different pockets, and his brother whispered:

'Swop me bob, 'e's gone and lorst it!'

However, all went right, and Sally having carefully pocketed the certificate, they went out and had another drink to celebrate the happy event.

In the evening Liza and several friends came into the couple's room, which they had taken in the same house as Sally had lived in before, and drank the health of the bride and bridegroom till they thought fit to retire.

Chapter Ten

It was November. The fine weather had quite gone now, and with it much of the sweet pleasure of Jim and Liza's love. When they came out at night on the Embankment they found it cold and dreary; sometimes a light fog covered the river-banks, and made the lamps glow out dim and large; a light rain would be falling, which sent a chill into their very souls; foot passengers came along at rare intervals, holding up umbrellas, and staring straight in front of them as they hurried along in the damp and cold; a cab would pass rapidly by, splashing up the mud on each side. The benches were deserted, except, perhaps, for some poor homeless wretch who could afford no shelter, and, huddled up in a corner, with his head buried in his breast, was sleeping heavily, like a dead man. The wet mud made Liza's skirts cling about her feet, and the damp would come in and chill her legs and creep up her body, till she shivered, and for warmth pressed herself close against Jim. Sometimes they would go into the third-class waiting-rooms at Waterloo or Charing Cross and sit there, but it was not like the park or the Embankment on summer nights; they had warmth, but the heat made their wet clothes steam and smell, and the gas flared in their eyes, and they hated the people perpetually coming in and out, opening the doors and letting in a blast of cold air; they hated the noise of the guards and porters shouting out the departure of the trains, the shrill whistling of the steam-engine, the hurry and bustle and confusion. About eleven o'clock, when the trains grew less frequent, they got some quietness; but then their minds were troubled, and they felt heavy, sad and miserable.

One evening they had been sitting at Waterloo Station; it was foggy outside—a thick, yellow November fog, which filled the waiting-room, entering the lungs, and making the mouth taste nasty and the eyes smart. It was about half-past eleven, and the station was unusually quiet; a few passengers, in wraps and overcoats, were walking to and fro, waiting for the last train, and one or two porters were standing about yawning. Liza and Jim had remained for an hour in perfect silence, filled with a gloomy unhappiness, as of a great weight on their brains. Liza was sitting forward, with her elbows on her knees, resting her face on her hands.

'I wish I was straight,' she said at last, not looking up.

'Well, why won't yer come along of me altogether, an' you'll be arright then?' he answered.

'Na, that's no go; I can't do thet.' He had often asked her to live with him entirely, but she had always refused.

'You can come along of me, an' I'll tike a room in a lodgin' 'ouse in 'Olloway, an' we can live there as if we was married.'

'Wot abaht yer work?'

'I can get work over the other side as well as I can 'ere. I'm abaht sick of the wy things is goin' on.'

312	Liza of Lambeth

'So am I; but I can't leave mother.'

'She can come, too.'

'Not when I'm not married. I shouldn't like 'er ter know as I'd—as I'd gone wrong.'

'Well, I'll marry yer. Swop me bob, I wants ter badly enough.'

'Yer can't; yer married already.'

'Thet don't matter! If I give the missus so much a week aht of my screw, she'll sign a piper ter give up all clime ter me, an' then we can get spliced. One of the men as I works with done thet, an' it was arright.'

Liza shook her head.

'Na, yer can't do thet now; it's bigamy, an' the cop tikes yer, an' yer gits twelve months' 'ard for it.'

'But swop me bob, Liza, I can't go on like this. Yer knows the missus—well, there ain't no bloomin' doubt abaht it, she knows as you an' me are carryin' on, an' she mikes no bones abaht lettin' me see it.'

'She don't do thet?'

'Well, she don't exactly sy it, but she sulks an' won't speak, an' then when I says anythin' she rounds on me an' calls me all the nimes she can think of. I'd give 'er a good 'idin', but some'ow I don't like ter! She mikes the plice a 'ell ter me, an' I'm not goin' ter stand it no longer!'

'You'll 'ave ter sit it, then; yer can't chuck it.'

'Yus I can, an' I would if you'd come along of me. I don't believe you like me at all, Liza, or you'd come.'

She turned towards him and put her arms round his neck.

'Yer know I do, old cock,' she said. 'I like yer better than anyone else in the world; but I can't go awy an' leave mother.'

'Bli'me me if I see why; she's never been much ter you. She mikes yer slave awy ter pay the rent, an' all the money she earns she boozes.'

'Thet's true, she ain't been wot yer might call a good mother ter me—but some'ow she's my mother, an' I don't like ter leave 'er on 'er own, now she's so old—an' she can't do much with the rheumatics. An' besides, Jim dear, it ain't only mother, but there's yer own kids, yer can't leave them.'

He thought for a while, and then said:

'You're abaht right there, Liza; I dunno if I could get on without the kids. If I could only tike them an' you too, swop me bob, I should be 'appy.'

Liza smiled sadly.

'So yer see, Jim, we're in a bloomin' 'ole, an' there ain't no way aht of it thet I can see.'

He took her on his knees, and pressing her to him, kissed her very long and very lovingly.

'Well, we must trust ter luck,' she said again, 'p'raps somethin' 'll 'appen soon, an' everythin' 'll come right in the end—when we gets four balls of worsted for a penny.'

It was past twelve, and separating, they went by different ways along the dreary, wet, deserted roads till they came to Vere Street.

The street seemed quite different to Liza from what it had been three months before. Tom, the humble adorer, had quite disappeared from her life. One day, three or four weeks after the August Bank Holiday, she saw him dawdling along the pavement, and it suddenly struck her that she had not seen him for a long time; but she had been so full of her happiness that she had been unable to think of anyone but Jim. She wondered at his absence, since before wherever she had been there was he certain to be also.

She passed him, but to her astonishment he did not speak to her. She thought by some wonder he had not seen her, but she felt his gaze resting upon her. She turned back, and suddenly he dropped his eyes and looked down, walking on as if he had not seen her, but blushing furiously.

'Tom,' she said, 'why don't yer speak ter me.'

He started and blushed more than ever.

'I didn't know yer was there,' he stuttered.

'Don't tell me,' she said, 'wot's up?'

'Nothin' as I knows of,' he answered uneasily.

'I ain't offended yer, 'ave I, Tom?'

'Na, not as I knows of,' he replied, looking very unhappy.

'You don't ever come my way now,' she said.

'I didn't know as yer wanted ter see me.'

'Garn! Yer knows I likes you as well as anybody.'

'Yer likes so many people, Liza,' he said, flushing.

'What d'yer mean?' said Liza indignantly, but very red; she was afraid he knew now, and it was from him especially she would have been so glad to hide it.

'Nothin',' he answered.

'One doesn't say things like thet without any meanin', unless one's a blimed fool.'

'You're right there, Liza,' he answered. 'I am a blimed, fool.' He looked at her a little reproachfully, she thought, and then he said 'Good-bye,' and turned away.

At first she was horrified that he should know of her love for Jim, but then she did not care. After all, it was nobody's business, and what did anything matter as long as she loved Jim and Jim loved her? Then she grew angry that Tom should suspect her; he could know nothing but that some of the men had seen her with Jim near Vauxhall, and it seemed mean that he should condemn her for that. Thenceforward, when she ran against Tom, she cut him; he never tried to speak to her, but as she passed him, pretending to look in front of her, she could see that he always blushed, and she fancied his eyes were very sorrowful. Then several weeks went by, and as she began to feel more and more lonely in the street, she regretted the quarrel; she cried a little as she thought that she had lost his faithful, gentle love, and she would have much liked to be friends with him again. If he had only made some advance she would have welcomed him so cordially, but she was too proud to go to him herself and beg him to forgive her—and then, how could he forgive her?

She had lost Sally too, for on her marriage Harry had made her give up the factory; he was a young man with principles worthy of a Member of Parliament, and he had said:

'A woman's plice is 'er 'ome, an' if 'er old man can't afford ter keep 'er without 'er workin' in a factory—well, all I can say is thet 'e'd better go an' git single.'

'Quite right, too,' agreed his mother-in-law; 'an' wot's more, she'll 'ave a baby ter look after soon, an' thet'll tike 'er all 'er time, an' there's no one as knows thet better than me, for I've 'ad twelve, ter sy nothin' of two stills an' one miss.'

Liza quite envied Sally her happiness, for the bride was brimming over with song and laughter; her happiness overwhelmed her.

'I am 'appy,' she said to Liza one day a few weeks after her marriage. 'You dunno wot a good sort 'Arry is. 'E's just a darlin', an' there's no mistikin' it. I

don't care wot other people sy, but wot I says is, there's nothin' like
marriage. Never a cross word passes his lips, an' mother 'as all 'er meals with
us, an' 'e says all the better. Well, I'm thet 'appy I simply dunno if I'm
standin' on my 'ead or on my 'eels.'

But alas! it did not last too long. Sally was not so full of joy when next Liza
met her, and one day her eyes looked very much as if she had been crying.

'Wot's the matter?' asked Liza, looking at her. 'Wot 'ave yer been
blubberin' abaht?'

'Me?' said Sally, getting very red. 'Oh, I've got a bit of a toothache,
an'—well, I'm rather a fool like, an' it 'urt so much that I couldn't 'elp cryin'.'

Liza was not satisfied, but could get nothing further out of her. Then one
day it came out. It was a Saturday night, the time when women in Vere
Street weep. Liza went up into Sally's room for a few minutes on her way to
the Westminster Bridge Road, where she was to meet Jim. Harry had taken
the top back room, and Liza, climbing up the second flight of stairs, called
out as usual,

'Wot ho, Sally!'

The door remained shut, although Liza could see that there was a light in
the room; but on getting to the door she stood still, for she heard the sound of
sobbing. She listened for a minute and then knocked: there was a little flurry
inside, and someone called out:

''Oo's there?'

'Only me,' said Liza, opening the door. As she did so she saw Sally rapidly
wipe her eyes and put her handkerchief away. Her mother was sitting by her
side, evidently comforting her.

'Wot's up, Sal?' asked Liza.

'Nothin',' answered Sally, with a brave little gasp to stop the crying,
turning her face downwards so that Liza should not see the tears in her eyes;
but they were too strong for her, and, quickly taking out her handkerchief,
she hid her face in it and began to sob broken-heartedly. Liza looked at the
mother in interrogation.

'Oh, it's thet man again!' said the lady, snorting and tossing her head.

'Not 'Arry?' asked Liza, in surprise.

'Not 'Arry—'oo is it if it ain't 'Arry? The villin!'

'Wot's 'e been doin', then?' asked Liza again.

'Beatin' 'er, that's wot 'e's been doin'! Oh, the villin, 'e oughter be
ashimed of 'isself, 'e ought!'

'I didn't know 'e was like that!' said Liza.

'Didn't yer? I thought the 'ole street knew it by now,' said Mrs Cooper
indignantly. 'Oh, 'e's a wrong 'un, 'e is.'

'It wasn't 'is fault,' put in Sally, amidst her sobs; 'it's only because 'e's 'ad
a little drop too much. 'E's arright when 'e's sober.'

'A little drop too much! I should just think 'e'd 'ad, the beast! I'd give it
'im if I was a man. They're all like thet—'usbinds is all alike; they're arright
when they're sober—sometimes—but when they've got the liquor in 'em,
they're beasts, an' no mistike. I 'ad a 'usband myself for five-an'-twenty
years, an' I know 'em.'

'Well, mother,' sobbed Sally, 'it was all my fault. I should 'ave come 'ome
earlier.'

'Na, it wasn't your fault at all. Just you look 'ere, Liza: this is wot 'e done
an' call 'isself a man. Just because Sally'd gone aht to 'ave a chat with Mrs
McLeod in the next 'ouse, when she come in 'e start bangin' 'er abaht. An'

me, too, wot d'yer think of that!' Mrs Cooper was quite purple with indignation.

'Yus,' she went on, 'thet's a man for yer. Of course, I wasn't goin' ter stand there an' see my daughter bein' knocked abaht; it wasn't likely–was it? An' 'e rounds on me, an' 'e 'its me with 'is fist. Look 'ere.' She pulled up her sleeves and showed two red and brawny arms. ''E's bruised my arms; I thought 'e'd broken it at fust. If I 'adn't put my arm up, 'e'd 'ave got me on the 'ead, an' 'e might 'ave killed me. An' I says to 'im, "If you touch me again, I'll go ter the police-station, thet I will!" Well, that frightened 'im a bit, an' then didn't I let 'im 'ave it! "You call yerself a man," says I, "an' you ain't fit ter clean the drains aht." You should 'ave 'eard the language 'e used. "You dirty old woman," says 'e, "you go away; you're always interferin' with me." Well, I don't like ter repeat wot 'e said, and thet's the truth. An' I says ter 'im, "I wish yer'd never married my daughter, an' if I'd known you was like this I'd 'ave died sooner than let yer."'

'Well, I didn't know 'e was like thet!' said Liza.

''E was arright at fust,' said Sally.

'Yus, they're always arright at fust! But ter think it should 'ave come to this now, when they ain't been married three months, an' the first child not born yet! I think it's disgraceful.'

Liza stayed a little while longer, helping to comfort Sally, who kept pathetically taking to herself all the blame of the dispute; and then, bidding her good night and better luck, she slid off to meet Jim.

When she reached the appointed spot he was not to be found. She waited for some time, and at last saw him come out of the neighbouring pub.

'Good night, Jim,' she said as she came up to him.

'So you've turned up, 'ave yer?' he answered roughly, turning round.

'Wot's the matter, Jim?' she asked in a frightened way, for he had never before spoken to her in that manner.

'Nice thing ter keep me witin' all night for yer to come aht.'

She saw that he had been drinking, and answered humbly:

'I'm very sorry, Jim, but I went in to Sally, an' 'er bloke 'ad been knockin' 'er abaht, an' so I sat with 'er a bit.'

'Knockin' 'er abaht, 'ad 'e? and serve 'er damn well right too; an' there's many more as could do with a good 'idin'!'

Liza did not answer. He looked at her, and then suddenly said:

'Come in an' 'ave a drink.'

'Na, I'm not thirsty; I don't want a drink,' she answered.

'Come on,' he said angrily.

'Na, Jim, you've had quite enough already.'

''Oo are you talkin' ter?' he said. 'Don't come if yer don't want ter; I'll go an' 'ave one by myself.'

'Na, Jim, don't.' She caught hold of his arm.

'Yus, I shall,' he said, going towards the pub, while she held him back. 'Let me go, can't yer! Let me go!' He roughly pulled his arm away from her. As she tried to catch hold of it again, he pushed her back, and in the little scuffle caught her a blow over the face.

'Oh!' she cried, 'you did 'urt!'

He was sobered at once.

'Liza,' he said. 'I ain't 'urt yer?' She didn't answer, and he took her in his arms. 'Liza, I ain't 'urt you, 'ave I? Say I ain't 'urt yer. I'm so sorry, I beg your pardon, Liza.'

'Arright, old chap,' she said, smiling charmingly on him. 'It wasn't the blow that 'urt me much; it was the wy you was talkin'.'

'I didn't mean it, Liza.' He was so contrite, he could not humble himself enough. 'I 'ad another bloomin' row with the missus ter-night, an' then when I didn't find you 'ere, an' I kept witin' an' witin' – well, I fair downright lost my 'air. An' I 'ad two or three pints of four 'alf, an' – well, I dunno—'

'Never mind, old cock, I can stand more than thet as long as yer loves me.'

He kissed her and they were quite friends again. But the little quarrel had another effect which was worse for Liza. When she woke up next morning she noticed a slight soreness over the ridge of bone under the left eye, and on looking in the glass saw that it was black and blue and green. She bathed it, but it remained, and seemed to get more marked. She was terrified lest people should see it, and kept indoors all day; but next morning it was blacker than ever. She went to the factory with her hat over eyes and her head bent down; she escaped observation, but on the way home she was not so lucky. The sharp eyes of some girls noticed it first.

'Wot's the matter with yer eye?' asked one of them.

'Me?' answered Liza, putting her hand up as if in ignorance. 'Nothin' thet I knows of.'

Two or three young men were standing by, and hearing the girl, looked up.

'Why, yer've got a black eye, Liza!'

'Me? I ain't got no black eye!'

'Yus, you 'ave; 'ow d'yer get it?'

'I dunno,' said Liza. 'I didn't know I 'ad one.'

'Garn! tell us another!' was the answer. 'One doesn't git a black eye without knowin' 'ow they got it.'

'Well, I did fall against the chest of drawers yesterday; I suppose I must 'ave got it then.'

'Oh yes, we believe thet, don't we?'

'I didn't know 'e was so 'andy with 'is dukes, did you, Ted?' asked one man of another.

Liza felt herself grow red to the tips of her toes.

'Who?' she asked.

'Never you mind; nobody you know.'

At that moment Jim's wife passed and looked at her with a scowl. Liza wished herself a hundred miles away, and blushed more violently than ever.

'Wot are yer blushin' abaht?' ingenuously asked one of the girls.

And they all looked from her to Mrs Blakeston and back again. Someone said: ''Ow abaht our Sunday boots on now?' And a titter went through them. Liza's nerve deserted her; she could think of nothing to say, and a sob burst from her. To hide the tears which were coming from her eyes she turned away and walked homewards. Immediately a great shout of laughter broke from the group, and she heard them positively screaming till she got into her own house.

Chapter Eleven

A few days afterwards Liza was talking with Sally, who did not seem very much happier than when Liza had last seen her.

''E ain't wot I thought 'e wos,' she said. 'I don't mind sayin' thet; but 'e 'as a lot ter put up with; I expect I'm rather tryin' sometimes, an' 'e means well. P'raps 'e'll be kinder like when the biby's born.'

'Cheer up, old gal,' answered Liza, who had seen something of the lives of many married couples; 'it won't seem so bad after yer gets used to it; it's a bit disappointin' at fust, but yer gits not ter mind it.'

After a little Sally said she must go and see about her husband's tea. She said good-bye, and then rather awkwardly:

'Say, Liza, tike care of yerself!'

'Tike care of meself—why?' asked Liza, in surprise.

'Yer know wot I mean.'

'Na, I'm darned if I do.'

'Thet there Mrs Blakeston, she's lookin' aht for you.'

'Mrs Blakeston!' Liza was startled.

'Yus; she says she's goin' ter give you somethin' if she can git 'old on yer. I should advise yer ter tike care.'

'Me?' said Liza.

Sally looked away, so as not to see the other's face.

'She says as 'ow yer've been messin' abaht with 'er old man.'

Liza didn't say anything, and Sally, repeating her good-bye, slid off.

Liza felt a chill run through her. She had several times noticed a scowl and a look of anger on Mrs Blakeston's face, and she had avoided her as much as possible; but she had no idea that the woman meant to do anything to her. She was very frightened, a cold sweat broke out over her face. If Mrs Blakeston got hold of her she would be helpless, she was so small and weak, while the other was strong and muscular. Liza wondered what she would do if she did catch her.

That night she told Jim, and tried to make a joke of it.

'I say, Jim, your missus—she says she's goin' ter give me socks if she catches me.'

'My missus! 'Ow d'yer know?'

'She's been tellin' people in the street.'

'Go' lumme,' said Jim, furious, 'if she dares ter touch a 'air of your 'ead, swop me dicky I'll give 'er sich a 'idin' as she never 'ad before! By God, give me the chanst, an' I would let 'er 'ave it; I'm bloomin' well sick of 'er sulks!' He clenched his fist as he spoke.

Liza was a coward. She could not help thinking of her enemy's threat; it got on her nerves, and she hardly dared go out for fear of meeting her; she would look nervously in front of her, quickly turning round is she saw in the distance anyone resembling Mrs Blakeston. She dreamed of her at night; she saw the big, powerful form, the heavy, frowning face, and the curiously braided brown hair; and she would wake up with a cry and find herself bathed in sweat.

It was the Saturday afternoon following this, a chill November day, with the roads sloshy, and a grey, comfortless sky that made one's spirits sink. It was about three o'clock, and Liza was coming home from work; she got into Vere Street, and was walking quickly towards her house when she saw Mrs Blakeston coming towards her. Her heart gave a great jump. Turning, she walked rapidly in the direction she had come; with a screw round of her eyes she saw that she was being followed, and therefore went straight out of Vere Street. She went right round, meaning to get into the street from the other end, and, unobserved, slip into her house, which was then quite close; but she dared not risk it immediately for fear Mrs Blakeston should still be there; so she waited about for half an hour. It seemed an age. Finally, taking her courage in both hands, she turned the corner and entered Vere Street. She nearly ran into the arms of Mrs Blakeston, who was standing close to the public-house door.

Liza gave a little cry, and the woman said, with a sneer:

'Yer didn't expect ter see me, did yer?'

Liza did not answer, but tried to walk past her. Mrs Blakeston stepped forward and blocked her way.

'Yer seem ter be in a mighty fine 'urry,' she said.

'Yus, I've got ter git 'ome,' said Liza, again trying to pass.

'But supposin' I don't let yer?' remarked Mrs Blakeston, preventing her from moving.

'Why don't yer leave me alone?' Liza said. 'I ain't interferin' with you!'

'Not interferin' with me, aren't yer? I like thet!'

'Let me go by,' said Liza. 'I don't want ter talk ter you.'

'Na, I know thet,' said the other; 'but I want ter talk ter you, an' I shan't let yer go until I've said wot I wants ter sy.'

Liza looked round for help. At the beginning of the altercation the loafers about the public-house had looked up with interest, and gradually gathered round in a little circle. Passers-by had joined in, and a number of other people in the street, seeing the crowd, added themselves to it to see what was going on. Liza saw that all eyes were fixed on her, the men amused and excited, the women unsympathetic, rather virtuously indignant. Liza wanted to ask for help, but there were so many people, and they all seemed so much against her, that she had not the courage to. So, having surveyed the crowd, she turned her eyes to Mrs Blakeston, and stood in front of her, trembling a little, and very white.

'Na, 'e ain't there,' said Mrs Blakeston, sneeringly, 'so yer needn't look for 'im.'

'I dunno wot yer mean,' answered Liza, 'an' I want ter go awy. I ain't done nothin' ter you.'

'Not done nothin' ter me?' furiously repeated the woman. 'I'll tell yer wot yer've done ter me—you've robbed me of my 'usbind, you 'ave. I never 'ad a word with my 'usbind until you took 'im from me. An' now it's all you with 'im. 'E's got no time for 'is wife an' family—it's all you. An' 'is money too. I never git a penny of it; if it weren't for the little bit I 'ad saved up in the siving-bank, me an' my children 'ud be starvin' now! An' all through you!'

She shook her fist at her.

'I never 'ad any money from anyone.'

'Don't talk ter me; I know yer did. Yer dirty bitch! you oughter be ashimed of yourself tikin' a married man from 'is family, an' 'im old enough ter be yer father.'

'She's right there!' said one or two of the onlooking women. 'There can't be no good in 'er if she tikes somebody else's 'usbind.'

'I'll give it yer!' proceeded Mrs Blakeston, getting more hot and excited, brandishing her fist, and speaking in a loud voice, hoarse with rage. 'Oh, I've been tryin' ter git 'old on yer this four weeks. Why, you're a prostitute–thet's wot you are!'

'I'm not!' answered Liza indignantly.

'Yus, you are,' repeated Mrs Blakeston, advancing menacingly, so that Liza shrank back. 'An' wot's more, 'e treats yer like one. I know 'oo give yer thet black eye; thet shows what 'e thinks of yer! An' serve yer bloomin' well right if 'e'd give yer one in both eyes!'

Mrs Blakeston stood close in front of her, her heavy jaw protruded and the frown of her eyebrows dark and stern. For a moment she stood silent, contemplating Liza, while the surrounders looked on in breathless interest.

'Yer dirty little bitch, you!' she said at last. 'Tike that!' and with her open hand she gave her a sharp smack on the cheek.

Liza started back with a cry and put her hand up to her face.

'An' tike thet!' added Mrs Blakeston, repeating the blow. Then, gathering up the spittle in her mouth, she spat in Liza's face.

Liza sprang on her, and with her hands spread out like claws buried her nails in the woman's face and drew them down her cheeks. Mrs Blakeston caught hold of her hair with both hands and tugged it as hard as she could. But they were immediately separated.

''Ere, 'old 'ard!' said some of the men. 'Fight it aht fair and square. Don't go scratchin' and maulin' like thet.'

'I'll fight 'er, I don't mind!' shouted Mrs Blakeston, tucking up her sleeves and savagely glaring at her opponent.

Liza stood in front of her, pale and trembling; as she looked at her enemy, and saw the long red marks of her nails, with blood coming from one or two of them, she shrank back.

'I don't want ter fight,' she said hoarsely.

'Na, I don't suppose yer do,' hissed the other, 'but yer'll damn well 'ave ter!'

'She's ever so much bigger than me; I've got no chanst,' added Liza tearfully.

'You should 'ave thought of thet before. Come on!' and with these words Mrs Blakeston rushed upon her. She hit her with both fists one after the other. Liza did not try to guard herself, but imitating the woman's motion, hit out with her own fists; and for a minute or two they continued thus, raining blows on one another with the same windmill motion of the arms. But Liza could not stand against the other woman's weight; the blows came down heavy and rapid all over the face and head. She put up her hands to cover her face and turned her head away, while Mrs Blakeston kept on hitting mercilessly.

'Time!' shouted some of the men–'Time!' and Mrs Blakeston stopped to rest herself.

'It don't seem 'ardly fair to set them two on tergether. Liza's got no chanst against a big woman like thet,' said a man among the crowd.

'Well, it's 'er own fault,' answered a woman; 'she didn't oughter mess about with 'er 'usbind.'

'Well, I don't think it's right,' added another man. 'She's gettin' it too much.'

'An' serve 'er right too!' said one of the women. 'She deserves all she gets, an' a damn sight more inter the bargain.'

'Quite right,' put in a third; 'a woman's got no right ter tike someone's 'usbind from 'er. An' if she does she's bloomin' lucky if she gits off with a 'idin'–thet's wot I think.'

'So do I. But I wouldn't 'ave thought it of Liza. I never thought she was a wrong 'un.'

'Pretty specimen she is!' said a little dark woman, who looked like a Jewess. 'If she messed abaht with my old man, I'd stick 'er–I swear I would!'

'Now she's been carryin' on with one, she'll try an' git others–you see if she don't.'

'She'd better not come round my 'ouse; I'll soon give 'er wot for.'

Meanwhile Liza was standing at one corner of the ring, trembling all over and crying bitterly. One of her eyes was bunged up, and her hair, all dishevelled, was hanging down over her face. Two young fellows, who had constituted themselves her seconds, were standing in front of her, offering rather ironical comfort. One of them had taken the bottom corners of her apron and was fanning her with it, while the other was showing her how to stand and hold her arms.

'You stand up to 'er, Liza,' he was saying; 'there ain't no good funkin' it, you'll simply get it all the worse. You 'it 'er back. Give 'er one on the boko, like this–see; yer must show a bit of pluck, yer know.'

Liza tried to check her sobs.

'Yus, 'it 'er 'ard, that's wot yer've got ter do,' said the other. 'An' if yer find she's gettin' the better on yer, you close on 'er and catch 'old of 'er 'air and scratch 'er.'

'You've marked 'er with yer nails, Liza. By gosh, you did fly on her when she spat at yer! thet's the way ter do the job!'

Then turning to his fellow, he said:

'D'yer remember thet fight as old Mother Gregg 'ad with another woman in the street last year?'

'Na,' he answered, 'I never saw thet.'

'It was a cawker; an' the cops come in and took 'em both off ter quod.'

Liza wished the policemen would come and take her off; she would willingly have gone to prison to escape the fiend in front of her; but no help came.

'Time's up!' shouted the referee. 'Fire away!'

'Tike care of the cops!' shouted a man.

'There's no fear abaht them,' answered somebody else. 'They always keeps out of the way when there's anythin' goin' on.'

'Fire away!'

Mrs Blakeston attacked Liza madly; but the girl stood up bravely, and as well as she could gave back the blows she received. The spectators grew tremendously excited.

'Got 'im again!' they shouted. 'Give it 'er, Liza, thet's a good 'un!–'it 'er 'ard!'

'Two ter one on the old 'un!' shouted a sporting gentleman; but Liza found no backers.

'Ain't she standin' up well now she's roused?' cried someone.

'Oh, she's got some pluck in 'er, she 'as!'

'Thet's a knock-aht!' they shouted as Mrs Blakeston brought her fist down on to Liza's nose; the girl staggered back, and blood began to flow. Then, losing all fear, mad with rage, she made a rush on her enemy, and rained down blows all over her nose and mouth. The woman recoiled at the sudden violence of the onslaught, and the men cried:

'By God, the little 'un's gettin' the best of it!'

But quickly recovering herself the woman closed with Liza, and dug her nails into her flesh. Liza caught hold of her hair and pulled with all her might, and turning her teeth on Mrs Blakeston tried to bite her. And thus for a minute they swayed about, scratching, tearing, biting, sweat and blood pouring down their faces, and their eyes fixed on one another, bloodshot and full of rage. The audience shouted and cheered and clapped their hands.

'Wot the 'ell's up 'ere?'

'I sy, look there,' said some of the women in a whisper. 'It's the 'usbind!'

He stood on tiptoe and looked over the crowd.

'My Gawd,' he said, 'it's Liza!'

Then roughly pushing the people aside, he made his way through the crowd into the centre, and thrusting himself between the two women, tore them apart. He turned furiously on his wife.

'By Gawd, I'll give yer somethin' for this!'

And for a moment they all three stood silently looking at one another.

Another man had been attracted by the crowd, and he, too, pushed his way through.

'Come 'ome, Liza,' he said.

'Tom!'

He took hold of her arm, and led her through the people, who gave way to let her pass. They walked silently through the street, Tom very grave. Liza weeping bitterly.

'Oh, Tom,' she sobbed after a while, 'I couldn't 'elp it!' Then, when her tears permitted, 'I did love 'im so!'

When they got to the door she plaintively said: 'Come in,' and he followed her to her room. Here she sank on to a chair, and gave herself up to her tears.

Tom wetted the end of a towel and began wiping her face, grimy with blood and tears. She let him do it, just moaning amid her sobs:

'You are good ter me, Tom.'

'Cheer up, old gal,' he said kindly, 'it's all over now.'

After a while the excess of crying brought its cessation. She drank some water, and then taking up a broken hand-glass she looked at herself, saying:

'I am a sight!' and proceeded to wind up her hair. 'You 'ave been good ter me, Tom,' she repeated, her voice still broken with sobs; and as he sat down beside her she took his hand.

'Na, I ain't,' he answered; 'it's only wot anybody 'ud 'ave done.'

'Yer know, Tom,' she said, after a little silence, 'I'm so sorry I spoke cross like when I met yer in the street; you ain't spoke ter me since.'

'Oh, thet's all over now, old lidy, we needn't think of thet.'

'Oh, but I 'ave treated yer bad. I'm a regular wrong 'un, I am.'

He pressed her hand without speaking.

'I say, Tom,' she began, after another pause. 'Did yer know thet—well, you know—before ter-day?'

He blushed as he answered:

'Yus.'

She spoke very sadly and slowly.

'I thought yer did; yer seemed so cut up like when I used to meet yer. Yer did love me then, Tom, didn't yer?'

'I do now, dearie,' he answered.

'Ah, it's too lite now,' she sighed.

'D'yer know, Liza,' he said, 'I just abaht kicked the life aht of a feller 'cause 'e said you was messin' abaht with—with 'im.'

'An' yer knew I was?'

'Yus—but I wasn't goin' ter 'ave anyone say it before me.'

'They've all rounded on me except you, Tom. I'd 'ave done better if I'd tiken you when you arst me; I shouldn't be where I am now, if I 'ad.'

'Well, won't yer now? Won't yer 'ave me now?'

'Me? After wot's 'appened?'

'Oh, I don't mind abaht thet. Thet don't matter ter me if you'll marry me. I fair can't live without yer, Liza—won't yer?'

She groaned.

'Na, I can't, Tom, it wouldn't be right.'

'Why, not, if I don't mind?'

'Tom,' she said, looking down, almost whispering, I'm like that—you know!'

'Wot d'yer mean?'

She could scarcely utter the words—

'I think I'm in the family wy.'

He paused a moment; then spoke again.

'Well—I don't mind, if yer'll only marry me.'

'Na, I can't, Tom,' she said, bursting into tears; 'I can't, but you are so good ter me; I'd do anythin' ter mike it up ter you.'

She put her arms round his neck and slid on to his knees.

'Yer know, Tom, I couldn't marry yer now; but anythin' else—if yer wants me ter do anythin' else, I'll do it if it'll mike you 'appy.'

He did not understand, but only said:

'You're a good gal, Liza,' and bending down he kissed her gravely on the forehead.

Then with a sigh he lifted her down, and getting up left her alone. For a while she sat where he left her, but as she thought of all she had gone through her loneliness and misery overcame her, the tears welled forth, and throwing herself on the bed she buried her face in the pillows.

Jim stood looking at Liza as she went off with Tom, and his wife watched him jealously.

'It's 'er you're thinkin' abaht. Of course you'd 'ave liked ter tike 'er 'ome yourself, I know, an' leave me to shift for myself.'

'Shut up!' said Jim, angrily turning upon her.

'I shan't shut up,' she answered, raising her voice. 'Nice 'usbind you are. Go' lumme, as good as they mike 'em! Nice thing ter go an' leave yer wife and children for a thing like thet! At your age, too! You oughter be ashimed of yerself. Why, it's like messin' abaht with yer own daughter!'

'By God!'—he ground his teeth with rage—'if yer don't leave me alone, I'll kick the life aht of yer!'

'There!' she said, turning to the crowd–'there, see 'ow 'e treats me! Listen ter that! I've been 'is wife for twenty years, an' yer couldn't 'ave 'ad a better wife, an' I've bore 'im nine children, yet say nothin' of a miscarriage, an' I've got another one comin', an' thet's 'ow 'e treats me! Nice 'usbind, ain't it?' She looked at him scornfully, then again at the surrounders as if for their opinion.

'Well, I ain't goin' ter stay 'ere all night; get aht of the light!' He pushed aside the people who barred his way, and the one or two who growled a little at his roughness, looking at his angry face, were afraid to complain.

'Look at 'im!' said his wife. ''E's afraid, 'e is. See 'im slinkin' awy like a bloomin' mongrel with 'is tail between 'is legs. Ugh!' She walked just behind him, shouting and brandishing her arms.

'Yer dirty beast, you,' she yelled, 'ter go foolin' abaht with a little girl! Ugh! I wish yer wasn't my 'usbind; I wouldn't be seen drowned with yer, if I could 'elp it. Yer mike me sick ter look at yer.'

The crowd followed them on both sides of the road, keeping at a discreet distance, but still eagerly listening.

Jim turned on her once or twice and said:

'Shut up!'

But it only made her more angry. 'I tell yer I shan't shut up. I don't care 'oo knows it, you're a ——, you are! I'm ashimed the children should 'ave such a father as you. D'yer think I didn't know wot you was up ter them nights you was awy–courtin', yus, courtin'? You're a nice man, you are!'

Jim did not answer her, but walked on. At last he turned round to the people who were following and said:

'Na then, wot d'you want 'ere? You jolly well clear off, or I'll give some of you somethin'!'

They were mostly boys and women, and at his words they shrank back.

''E's afraid ter sy anythin' ter me,' jeered Mrs Blakeston. ''E's a beauty!'

Jim entered his house, and she followed him till they came up into their room. Polly was giving the children their tea. They all started up as they saw their mother with her hair and clothes in disorder, blotches of dried blood on her face, and the long scratch-marks.

'Oh, mother,' said Polly, 'wot is the matter?'

''E's the matter,' she answered, pointing to her husband. 'It's through 'im I've got all this. Look at yer father, children; e's a father to be proud of, leavin' yer ter starve an' spendin' 'is week's money on a dirty little strumper.'

Jim felt easier now he had not got so many strange eyes on him.

'Now, look 'ere,' he said, 'I'm not goin' ter stand this much longer, so just you tike care.'

'I ain't frightened of yer. I know yer'd like ter kill me, but yer'll get strung up if you do.'

'Na, I won't kill yer, but if I 'ave any more of your sauce I'll do the next best thing to it.'

'Touch me if you dare,' she said, 'I'll 'ave the law on you. An' I shouldn't mind 'ow many month's 'ard you got.'

'Be quiet!' he said, and, closing his hand, gave her a heavy blow in the chest that made her stagger.

'Oh, you —— !' she screamed.

She seized the poker, and in a fury of rage rushed at him.

'Would yer?' he said, catching hold of it and wrenching it from her grasp. He threw it to the end of the room and grappled with her. For a moment they

swayed about from side to side, then with an effort he lifted her off her feet
and threw her to the ground; but she caught hold of him and he came down
on the top of her. She screamed as her head thumped down on the floor, and
the children, who were standing huddled up in a corner, terrified, screamed
too.

Jim caught hold of his wife's head and began beating it against the floor.
She cried out: 'You're killing me! Help! Help!'

Polly in terror ran up to her father and tried to pull him off.

'Father, don't 'it 'er! Anythin' but thet—for God's sike!'

'Leave me alone,' he said, 'or I'll give you somethin' too.'

She caught hold of his arm, but Jim, still kneeling on his wife, gave Polly a
backhanded blow which sent her staggering back.

'Tike that!'

Polly ran out of the room, downstairs to the first-floor front, where two
men and two women were sitting at tea.

'Oh, come an' stop father!' she cried. ''E's killin' mother!'

'Why, wot's 'e doin'?'

'Oh, 'e's got 'er on the floor, an' 'e's bangin' 'er 'ead. 'E's payin' 'er aht for
givin' Liza Kemp a 'idin'.

One of the women started up and said to her husband: 'Come on, John,
you go an' stop it.'

'Don't you, John,' said the other man. 'When a man's givin' 'is wife socks
it's best not ter interfere.'

'But 'e's killin' 'er,' repeated Polly, trembling with fright.

'Garn!' rejoined the man, 'she'll git over it; an' p'raps she deserves it, for
all you know.'

John sat undecided, looking now at Polly, now at his wife, and now at the
other man.

'Oh, do be quick—for God's sike!' said Polly.

At that moment a sound as of something smashing was heard upstairs, and
a woman's shriek. Mrs Blakeston, in an effort to tear herself away from her
husband, had knocked up against the wash-hand stand, and the whole thing
had crashed down.

'Go on, John,' said the wife.

'No, I ain't goin'; I shan't do no good, an' 'e'll only round on me.'

'Well, you are a bloomin' lot of cowards, thet's all I can say,' indignantly
answered the wife. 'But I ain't goin' ter see a woman murdered; I'll go an'
stop 'im.'

With that she ran upstairs and threw open the door. Jim was still kneeling
on his wife, hitting her furiously, while she was trying to protect her head
and face with her hands.

'Leave off!' shouted the woman.

Jim looked up. ''Oo the devil are you?' he said.

'Leave off, I tell yer. Aren't yer ashimed of yerself, knockin' a woman
abaht like that?' And she sprang at him, seizing his fist.

'Let go,' he said, 'or I'll give you a bit.'

'Yer'd better not touch me,' she said. 'Yer dirty coward! Why, look at 'er,
she's almost senseless.'

Jim stopped and gazed at his wife. He got up and gave her a kick.

'Git up!' he said; but she remained huddled up on the floor, moaning
feebly. The woman from downstairs went on her knees and took her head in
her arms.

'Never mind, Mrs Blakeston. 'E's not goin' ter touch yer. 'Ere, drink this little drop of water.' Then turning to Jim, with infinite disdain: 'Yer dirty blackguard, you! If I was a man I'd give you something for this.'

Jim put on his hat and went out, slamming the door, while the woman shouted after him: 'Good riddance!'

'Lord love yer,' said Mrs Kemp, 'wot is the matter?'

She had just come in, and opening the door had started back in surprise at seeing Liza on the bed, all tears. Liza made no answer, but cried as if her heart were breaking. Mrs Kemp went up to her and tried to look at her face.

'Don't cry, dearie; tell us wot it is.'

Liza sat up and dried her eyes.

'I am so un'appy!'

'Wot 'ave yer been doin' ter yer fice? My!'

'Nothin'.'

'Garn! yer can't 'ave got a fice like thet all by itself.'

'I 'ad a bit of a scrimmage with a woman dahn the street,' sobbed out Liza.

'She 'as give yer a doin'; an' yer all upset – an' look at yer eye! I brought in a little bit of stike for ter-morrer's dinner; you can just cut a bit off an' put it over yer optic, that'll soon put it right. I always used ter do thet myself when me an' your poor father 'ad words.'

'Oh, I'm all over in a tremble, an' my 'ead, oo, my 'ead does feel bad!'

'I know what yer want,' remarked Mrs Kemp, nodding her head, 'an' it so 'appens as I've got the very thing with me.' She pulled a medicine bottle out of her pocket, and taking out the cork smelt it. 'Thet's good stuff, none of your fire-water or your methylated spirit. I don't often indulge in sich things, but when I do I likes to 'ave the best.'

She handed the bottle to Liza, who took a mouthful and gave it her back; she had a drink herself, and smacked her lips.

'Thet's good stuff. 'Ave a drop more.'

'Na,' said Liza, 'I ain't used ter drinkin' spirits.'

She felt dull and miserable, and a heavy pain throbbed through her head. If she could only forget!

'Na, I know you're not, but, bless your soul, thet won' 'urt yer. It'll do you no end of good. Why, often when I've been feelin' thet done up thet I didn't know wot ter do with myself, I've just 'ad a little drop of whisky or gin – I'm not partic'ler wot spirit it is – an' it's pulled me up wonderful.'

Liza took another sip, a slightly longer one; it burnt as it went down her throat, and sent through her a feeling of comfortable warmth.

'I really do think it's doin' me good,' she said, wiping her eyes and giving a sigh of relief as the crying ceased.

'I knew it would. Tike my word for it, if people took a little drop of spirits in time, there'd be much less sickness abaht.'

They sat for a while in silence, then Mrs Kemp remarked:

'Yer know, Liza, it strikes me as 'ow we could do with a drop more. You not bein' in the 'abit of tikin' anythin' I only brought just this little drop for me; an' it ain't took us long ter finish thet up. But as you're an invalid like we'll git a little more this time; it's sure ter turn aht useful.'

'But you ain't got nothin' ter put it in.'

'Yus, I 'ave,' answered Mrs Kemp; 'there's thet bottle as they gives me at the 'orspital. Just empty the medicine aht into the pile, an' wash it aht, an' I'll tike it round to the pub myself.'

Liza, when she was left alone, began to turn things over in her mind. She did not feel so utterly unhappy as before, for the things she had gone through seemed further away.

'After all,' she said, 'it don't so much matter.'

Mrs Kemp came in.

''Ave a little drop more, Liza,' she said.

'Well, I don't mind if I do. I'll get some tumblers, shall I? There's no mistike abaht it,' she added, when she had taken a little, 'it do buck yer up.'

'You're right, Liza—you're right. An' you wanted it badly. Fancy you 'avin' a fight with a woman! Oh, I've 'ad some in my day, but then I wasn't a little bit of a thing like you is. I wish I'd been there, I wouldn't 'ave stood by an' looked on while my daughter was gettin' the worst of it; although I'm turned sixty-five, an' gettin' on for sixty-six, I'd 'ave said to 'er: "If you touch my daughter you'll 'ave me ter deal with, so just look aht!"'

She brandished her glass, and that reminding her, she refilled it and Liza's.

'Ah, Liza,' she remarked, 'you're a chip off the old block. Ter see you settin' there an' 'avin' your little drop, it mikes me feel as if I was livin' a better life. Yer used ter be rather 'ard on me, Liza, 'cause I took a little drop on Saturday nights. An, mind, I don't sy I didn't tike a little drop too much sometimes—accidents will occur even in the best regulated of families, but wot I say is this—it's good stuff, I say, an' it don't 'urt yer.'

'Buck up, old gal!' said Liza, filling the glasses, 'no 'eel-taps. I feel like a new woman now. I was thet dahn in the dumps—well, I shouldn't 'ave cared if I'd been at the bottom of the river, an' thet's the truth.'

'You don't sy so,' replied her affectionate mother.

'Yus, I do, an' I mean it too, but I don't feel like thet now. You're right, mother, when you're in trouble there's nothin' like a bit of spirits.'

'Well, if I don't know, I dunno 'oo does, for the trouble I've 'ad, it 'ud be enough to kill many women. Well, I've 'ad thirteen children, an' you can think wot thet was; every one I 'ad I used ter sy I wouldn't 'ave no more—but one does, yer know. You'll 'ave a family some day, Liza, an' I shouldn't wonder if you didn't 'ave as many as me. We come from a very prodigal family, we do, we've all gone in ter double figures, except your Aunt Mary, who only 'ad three—but then she wasn't married, so it didn't count, like.'

They drank each other's health. Everything was getting blurred to Liza, she was losing her head.

'Yus,' went on Mrs Kemp, 'I've 'ad thirteen children an' I'm proud of it. As your poor dear father used ter sy, it shows as 'ow one's got the blood of a Briton in one. Your poor dear father, 'e was a great 'and at speakin' 'e was: 'e used ter speak at parliamentary meetin's—I really believe 'e'd 'ave been a Member of Parliament if 'e'd been alive now. Well, as I was sayin', your father 'e used ter sy, "None of your small families for me, I don't approve of them," says 'e. 'E was a man of very 'igh principles, an' by politics 'e was a Radical. "No," says 'e, when 'e got talkin', "when a man can 'ave a family risin' into double figures, it shows 'e's got the backbone of a Briton in 'im. That's the stuff as 'as built up England's nime and glory! When one thinks of the mighty British Hempire, " says 'e, "on which the sun never sets from mornin' till night, one 'as ter be proud of 'isself, an' one 'as ter do one's duty in thet walk of life in which it 'as pleased Providence ter set one—an' every man's fust duty is ter get as many children as 'e bloomin' well can." Lord lover yer—'e could talk, I can tell yer.'

'Drink up, mother,' said Liza. 'You're not 'alf drinkin'.' She flourished the bottle. 'I don't care a twopenny 'ang for all them blokes; I'm quite 'appy, an' I don't want anythin' else.'

'I can see you're my daughter now,' said Mrs Kemp. 'When yer used ter round on me I used ter think as 'ow if I 'adn't carried yer for nine months, it must 'ave been some mistike, an' yer wasn't my daughter at all. When you come ter think of it, a man 'e don't know if it's 'is child or somebody else's, but yer can't deceive a woman like thet. Yer couldn't palm off somebody else's kid on 'er.'

'I am beginnin' ter feel quite lively,' said Liza. 'I dunno wot it is, but I feel as if I wanted to laugh till I fairly split my sides.'

And she began to sing: 'For 'e's a jolly good feller—for 'e's a jolly good feller!'

Her dress was all disarranged; her face was covered with the scars of scratches, and clots of blood had fixed under her nose; her eye had swollen up so that it was nearly closed, and red; her hair was hanging over her face and shoulders, and she laughed stupidly and leered with heavy, sodden ugliness.

> 'Disy, Disy! I can't afford a kerridge,
> But you'll look neat, on the seat
> Of a bicycle mide for two.'

She shouted out the tunes, beating time on the table, and her mother, grinning, with her thin, grey hair hanging dishevelled over her head, joined in with her weak, cracked voice—

> 'Oh, dem golden kippers, oh!'

Then Liza grew more melancholy and broke into 'Auld Lang Syne'.

> 'Should old acquaintance be forgot
> And never brought to mind?
>
> For old lang syne'.

Finally they both grew silent, and in a little while there came a snore from Mrs Kemp; her head fell forward to her chest; Liza tumbled from her chair on to the bed, and sprawling across it fell asleep.

> *'Although I am drunk and bad, be you kind,*
> *Cast a glance at this heart which is bewildered and distressed.*
> *O God, take away from my mind my cry and my complaint.*
> *Offer wine, and take sorrow from my remembrance.*
> *Offer wine.*

Chapter Twelve

About the middle of the night Liza woke; her mouth was hot and dry, and a sharp, cutting pain passed through her head as she moved. Her mother had evidently roused herself, for she was lying in bed by her side, partially undressed, with all the bedclothes rolled round her. Liza shivered in the cold night, and taking off some of her things—her boots, her skirt, and jacket—got right into bed; she tried to get some of the blanket from her mother, but as she pulled Mrs Kemp gave a growl in her sleep and drew the clothes more tightly round her. So Liza put over herself her skirt and a shawl, which was lying over the end of the bed, and tried to go to sleep.

But she could not; her head and hands were broiling hot, and she was terribly thirsty; when she lifted herself up to get a drink of water such a pang went through her head that she fell back on the bed groaning, and lay there with beating heart. And strange pains that she did not know went through her. Then a cold shiver seemed to rise in the very marrow of her bones and run down every artery and vein, freezing the blood; her skin puckered up, and drawing up her legs she lay huddled together in a heap, the shawl wrapped tightly round her, and her teeth chattering. Shivering, she whispered:

'Oh, I'm so cold, so cold. Mother, give me some clothes; I shall die of the cold. Oh, I'm freezing!'

But after a while the cold seemed to give way, and a sudden heat seized her, flushing her face, making her break out into perspiration, so that she threw everything off and loosened the things about her neck.

'Give us a drink,' she said. 'Oh, I'd give anythin' for a little drop of water!'

There was no one to hear; Mrs Kemp continued to sleep heavily, occasionally breaking out into a little snore.

Liza remained there, now shivering with cold, now panting for breath, listening to the regular, heavy breathing by her side, and in her pain she sobbed. She pulled at her pillow and said:

'Why can't I go to sleep? Why can't I sleep like 'er?'

And the darkness was awful; it was a heavy, ghastly blackness, that seemed palpable, so that it frightened her, and she looked for relief at the faint light glimmering through the window from a distant street-lamp. She thought the night would never end—the minutes seemed like hours, and she wondered how she should live through till morning. And strange pains that she did not know went through her.

Still the night went on, the darkness continued, cold and horrible, and her mother breathed loudly and steadily by her side.

At last with the morning sleep came; but the sleep was almost worse than the wakefulness, for it was accompanied by ugly, disturbing dreams. Liza thought she was going through the fight with her enemy, and Mrs Blakeston grew enormous in size, and multiplied, so that every way she turned the figure confronted her. And she began running away, and she ran and ran till she found herself reckoning up an account she had puzzled over in the morning, and she did it backwards and forwards, upwards and downwards, starting here, starting there, and the figures got mixed up with other things, and she had to begin over again, and everything jumbled up, and her head whirled, till finally, with a start, she woke.

The darkness had given way to a cold, grey dawn, her uncovered legs were chilled to the bone, and by her side she heard again the regular, nasal breathing of the drunkard.

For a long while she lay where she was, feeling very sick and ill, but better than in the night. At last her mother woke.

'Liza!' she called.

'Yus, mother,' she answered feebly.

'Git us a cup of tea, will yer?'

'I can't, mother, I'm ill.'

'Garn!' said Mrs Kemp, in surprise. Then looking at her: 'Swop me bob, wot's up with yer? Why, yer cheeks is flushed, an' yer forehead–it is 'ot! Wot's the matter with yer, gal?'

'I dunno,' said Liza. 'I've been thet bad all night, I thought I was goin' ter die.'

'I know wot it is,' said Mrs Kemp, shaking her head; 'the fact is, you ain't used ter drinkin', an' of course it's upset yer. Now me, why I'm as fresh as a disy. Tike my word, there ain't no good in teetotalism; it finds yer aht in the end, an' it's found you aht.'

Mrs Kemp considered it a judgement of Providence. She got up and mixed some whisky and water.

''Ere, drink this,' she said. 'When one's 'ad a drop too much at night, there's nothin' like havin' a drop more in the mornin' ter put one right. It just acts like magic.'

'Tike it awy,' said Liza, turning from it in disgust; 'the smell of it gives me the sick. I'll never touch spirits again.'

'Ah, thet's wot we all says sometime in our lives, but we does, an' wot's more we can't do withaht it. Why, me, the 'ard life I've 'ad—' It is unnecessary to repeat Mrs Kemp's repetitions.

Liza did not get up all day. Tom came to inquire after her, and was told she was very ill. Liza plaintively asked whether anyone else had been, and sighed a little when her mother answered no. But she felt too ill to think much or trouble much about anything. The fever came again as the day wore on, and the pains in her head grew worse. Her mother came to bed, and quickly went off to sleep, leaving Liza to bear her agony alone. She began to have frightful pains all over her, and she held her breath to prevent herself from crying out and waking her mother. She clutched the sheets in her agony, and at last, about six o'clock in the morning, she could bear it no longer, and in the anguish of labour screamed out, and woke her mother.

Mrs Kemp was frightened out of her wits. Going upstairs she woke the woman who lived on the floor above her. Without hesitating, the good lady put on a skirt and came down.

'She's 'ad a miss,' she said, after looking at Liza. 'Is there anyone you could send to the 'orspital?'

'Na, I dunno 'oo I could get at this hour?'

'Well, I'll git my old man ter go.'

She called her husband, and sent him off. She was a stout, middle-aged

Liza of Lambeth

woman, rough-visaged and strong-armed. Her name was Mrs Hodges.

'It's lucky you came ter me,' she said, when she had settled down. 'I go aht nursin', yer know, so I know all abaht it.'

'Well, you surprise me,' said Mrs Kemp. 'I didn't know as Liza was thet way. She never told me nothin' abaht it.'

'D'yer know 'oo it is 'as done it?'

'Now you ask me somethin' I don't know,' replied Mrs Kemp. 'But now I come ter think of it, it must be thet there Tom. 'E's been keepin' company with Liza. 'E's a single man, so they'll be able ter get married—thet's somethin'.'

'It ain't Tom,' feebly said Liza.

'Not 'im; 'oo is it, then?'

Liza did not answer.

'Eh?' repeated the mother, ''oo is it?'

Liza lay still without speaking.

'Never mind, Mrs Kemp,' said Mrs Hodges, 'don't worry 'er now; you'll be able ter find aht all abaht it when she gits better.'

For a while the two women sat still, waiting the doctor's coming, and Liza lay gazing vacantly at the wall, panting for breath. Sometimes Jim crossed her mind, and she opened her mouth to call for him, but in her despair she restrained herself.

The doctor came.

'D'you think she's bad, doctor?' asked Mrs Hodges.

'I'm afraid she is rather,' he answered. 'I'll come in again this evening.'

'Oh, doctor,' said Mrs Kemp, as he was going, 'could yer give me somethin' for my rheumatics? I'm a martyr to rheumatism, an' these cold days I 'ardly knows wot ter do with myself. An', doctor, could you let me 'ave some beef-tea? My 'usbind's dead, an' of course I can't do no work with my daughter ill like this, an' we're very short—'

The day passed, and in the evening Mrs Hodges, who had been attending to her own domestic duties, came downstairs again. Mrs Kemp was on the bed sleeping.

'I was just 'avin' a little nap,' she said to Mrs Hodges, on waking.

''Ow is the girl?' asked that lady.

'Oh,' answered Mrs Kemp, 'my rheumatics 'as been thet bad I really 'aven't known wot ter do with myself, an' now Liza can't rub me I'm worse than ever. It is unfortunate thet she should get ill just now when I want so much attendin' ter myself, but there, it's just my luck!'

Mrs Hodges went over and looked at Liza; she was lying just as when she left in the morning, her cheeks flushed, her mouth open for breath, and tiny beads of sweat stood on her forehead.

''Ow are yer, ducky?' asked Mrs Hodges; but Liza did not answer.

'It's my belief she's unconscious,' said Mrs Kemp. 'I've been askin' 'er 'oo it was as done it, but she don't seem to 'ear wot I say. It's been a great shock ter me, Mrs 'Odges.'

'I believe you,' replied that lady, sympathetically.

'Well, when you come in and said wot it was, yer might 'ave knocked me dahn with a feather. I knew no more than the dead wot 'ad 'appened.'

'I saw at once wot it was,' said Mrs Hodges, nodding her head.

'Yus, of course, you knew. I expect you've 'ad a great deal of practice one way an' another.'

'You're right, Mrs Kemp, you're right. I've been on the job now for nearly twenty years, an' if I don't know somethin' abaht it I ought.'

'D'yer finds it pays well?'

'Well, Mrs Kemp, tike it all in all, I ain't got no grounds for complaint. I'm in the 'abit of askin' five shillings, an' I will say this, I don't think it's too much for wot I do.'

The news of Liza's illness had quickly spread, and more than once in the course of the day a neighbour had come to ask after her. There was a knock at the door now, and Mrs Hodges opened it. Tom stood on the threshold asking to come in.

'Yus, you can come,' said Mrs Kemp.

He advanced on tiptoe, so as to make no noise, and for a while stood silently looking at Liza. Mrs Hodges was by his side.

'Can I speak to 'er?' he whispered.

'She can't 'ear you.'

He groaned.

'D'yer think she'll get arright?' he asked.

Mrs Hodges shrugged her shoulders.

'I shouldn't like ter give an opinion,' she said, cautiously.

Tom bent over Liza, and, blushing, kissed her; then, without speaking further, went out of the room.

'Thet's the young man as was courtin' 'er,' said Mrs Kemp, pointing over her shoulder with her thumb.

Soon after the doctor came.

'Wot do yer think of 'er, doctor?' said Mrs Hodges, bustling forwards authoritatively in her position of midwife and sick-nurse.

'I'm afraid she's very bad.'

'D'yer think she's goin' ter die?' she asked, dropping her voice to a whisper.

'I'm afraid so!'

As the doctor sat down by Liza's side Mrs Hodges turned round and significantly nodded to Mrs Kemp, who put her handkerchief to her eyes. Then she went outside to the little group waiting at the door.

'Wot does the doctor sy?' they asked, among them Tom.

''E says just wot I've been sayin' all along; I knew she wouldn't live.'

And Tom burst out: 'Oh, Liza!'

As she retired a woman remarked:

'Mrs 'Odges is very clever, I think.'

'Yus,' remarked another, 'she got me through my last confinement simply wonderful. If it come to choosin' between 'em I'd back Mrs 'Odges against forty doctors.'

'Ter tell yer the truth, so would I. I've never known 'er wrong yet.'

Mrs Hodges sat down beside Mrs Kemp and proceeded to comfort her.

'Why don't yer tike a little drop of brandy ter calm yer nerves, Mrs Kemp?' she said, 'you want it.'

'I was just feelin' rather faint, an' I couldn't 'elp thinkin' as 'ow two-penneth of whisky 'ud do me good.'

'Na, Mrs Kemp,' said Mrs Hodges, earnestly, putting her hand on the other's arm. 'You take my tip—when you're queer there's nothin' like brandy for pullin' yer togither. I don't object to whisky myself, but as a medicine yer can't beat brandy.'

'Well, I won't set up myself as knowin' better than you Mrs 'Odges; I'll do wot you think right.'

Quite accidentally there was some in the room, and Mrs Kemp poured it out for herself and her friend.

'I'm not in the 'abit of tikin' anythin' when I'm aht on business,' she apologised, 'but just ter keep you company I don't mind if I do.'

'Your 'ealth, Mrs 'Odges.'

'Sime ter you, an' thank yer, Mrs Kemp.'

Liza lay still, breathing very quietly, her eyes closed. The doctor kept his fingers on her pulse.

'I've been very fortunate of lite,' remarked Mrs Hodges, as she licked her lips, 'this mikes the second death I've 'ad in the last ten days—women, I mean, of course I don't count bibies.'

'Yer don't sy so.'

'Of course the other one—well, she was only a prostitute, so it didn't so much matter. It ain't like another woman, is it?'

'Na, you're right.'

'Still, one don't like 'em ter die, even if they are thet. One mustn't be too 'ard on 'em.'

'Strikes me you've got a very kind 'eart, Mrs 'Odges,' said Mrs Kemp.

'I 'ave thet; an' I often says it 'ud be better for my peace of mind an' my business if I 'adn't. I 'ave ter go through a lot, I do; but I can say this for myself, I always gives satisfaction, an' thet's somethin' as all lidies in my line can't say.'

They sipped their brandy for a while.

'It's a great trial ter me that this should 'ave 'appened,' said Mrs Kemp, coming to the subject that had been disturbing her for some time. 'Mine's always been a very respectable family, an' such a thing as this 'as never 'appened before. No, Mrs 'Odges, I was lawfully married in church, an' I've got my marriage lines now ter show I was, an' thet one of my daughters should 'ave gone wrong in this way—well, I can't understand it. I give 'er a good education, an' she 'ad all the comforts of a 'ome. She never wanted for nothin'; I worked myself to the bone ter keep 'er in luxury, an' then thet she should go an' disgrace me like this!'

'I understand wot yer mean, Mrs Kemp.'

'I can tell you my family was very respectable; an' my 'usbind, 'e earned twenty-five shillings a week, an' was in the sime plice seventeen years; an' 'is employers sent a beautiful wreath ter put on 'is coffin; an' they tell me they never 'ad such a good workman an' sich an 'onest man before. An' me! Well, I can sy this—I've done my duty by the girl, an' she's never learnt anythin' but good from me. Of course I ain't always been in wot yer might call flourishing circumstances, but I've always set her a good example, as she could tell yer so 'erself if she wasn't speechless.'

Mrs Kemp paused for a moment's reflection.

'As they sy in the Bible,' she finished, 'it's enough ter mike one's grey 'airs go dahn into the ground in sorrer. I can show yer my marriage certificate. Of course one doesn't like ter say much, because of course she's very bad; but if she got well I should 'ave given 'er a talkin' ter.'

There was another knock.

'Do go an' see 'oo thet is; I can't, on account of my rheumatics.'

Mrs Hodges opened the door. It was Jim.

He was very white, and the blackness of his hair and beard, contrasting with the deathly pallor of his face, made him look ghastly. Mrs Hodges stepped back.

''Oo's 'e?' she said, turning to Mrs Kemp.

Jim pushed her aside and went up to the bed.

'Doctor, is she very bad?' he asked.

The doctor looked at him questioningly.

Jim whispered: 'It was me as done it. She ain't goin' ter die, is she?'

The doctor nodded.

'O God! wot shall I do? It was my fault! I wish I was dead!'

Jim took the girl's head in his hands, and the tears burst from his eyes.

'She ain't dead yet, is she?'

'She's just living,' said the doctor.

Jim bent down.

'Liza, Liza, speak ter me! Liza, say you forgive me! Oh, speak ter me!'

His voice was full of agony. The doctor spoke.

'She can't hear you.'

'Oh, she must hear me! Liza! Liza!'

He sank on his knees by the bedside.

They all remained silent: Liza lying stiller than ever, her breast unmoved by the feeble respiration, Jim looking at her very mournfully; the doctor grave, with his fingers on the pulse. The two women looked at Jim.

'Fancy it bein' 'im!' said Mrs Kemp. 'Strike me lucky, ain't 'e a sight!'

'You 'ave got 'er insured, Mrs Kemp?' asked the midwife. She could bear the silence no longer.

'Trust me fur thet!' replied the good lady. 'I've 'ad 'er insured ever since she was born. Why, only the other dy I was sayin' ter myself thet all thet money 'ad been wisted, but you see it wasn't; yer never know yer luck, you see!'

'Quite right, Mrs Kemp; I'm a rare one for insurin'. It's a great thing. I've always insured all my children.'

'The way I look on it is this,' said Mrs Kemp—'wotever yer do when they're alive, an' we all know as children is very tryin' sometimes, you should give them a good funeral when they dies. Thet's my motto, an' I've always acted up to it.'

'Do you deal with Mr Stearman?' asked Mrs Hodges.

'No, Mrs 'Odges, for undertikin' give me Mr Footley every time. In the black line 'e's fust an' the rest nowhere!'

'Well, thet's very strange now—thet's just wot I think. Mr Footley does 'is work well, an' 'e's very reasonable. I'm a very old customer of 'is, an' 'e lets me 'ave things as cheap as anybody.'

'Does 'e indeed! Well, Mrs 'Odges, if it ain't askin' too much of yer, I should look upon it as very kind if you'd go an' mike the arrangements for Liza.'

'Why, certainly, Mrs Kemp. I'm always willin' ter do a good turn to anybody, if I can.'

'I want it done very respectable,' said Mrs Kemp; 'I'm not goin' ter stint for nothin' for my daughter's funeral. I like plumes, you know, although they is a bit extra.'

'Never you fear, Mrs Kemp, it shall be done as well as if it was for my own 'usbind, an' I can't say more than thet. Mr Footley thinks a deal of me, 'e does! Why, only the other dy as I was goin' inter 'is shop, 'e says, "Good mornin', Mrs 'Odges." "Good mornin', Mr Footley," says I. "You've jest come in the nick of time," says 'e. "This gentleman an' myself," pointin' to another gentleman as was standin' there, "we was 'avin' a bit of an argument. Now you're a very intelligent woman, Mrs 'Odges, and a good customer too." "I can say thet for myself," says I, "I gives yer all the work I can." "I believe you," says 'e. "Well," 'e says, "now which do you think? Does hoak look better than helm, or does helm look better than hoak? Hoak *versus* helm, thet's the question." "Well, Mr Footley," says I, "for my own private opinion, when you've got a nice brass plite in the middle, an' nice brass 'andles each end, there's nothin' like hoak." "Quite right," says 'e. "Thet's wot I think; for coffins give me hoak any day, an' I 'ope," says 'e, "when the Lord sees fit ter call me to 'Imself, I shall be put in a hoak coffin myself." "Amen," says I.'

'I like hoak,' said Mrs Kemp. 'My poor 'usbind 'e 'ad a hoak coffin. We did 'ave a job with 'im, I can tell yer. You know 'e 'ad dropsy, an' 'e swell up—oh, 'e did swell; 'is own mother wouldn't 'ave known 'im. Why, 'is leg swell up till it was as big round as 'is body, swop me bob, it did.'

'Did it indeed!' ejaculated Mrs Hodges.

'Yus, an' when 'e died they sent the coffin up. I didn't 'ave Mr Footley at thet time; we didn't live 'ere then, we lived in Battersea, an' all our undertikin' was done by Mr Brownin'; well, 'e sent the coffin up, an' we got my old man in, but we couldn't get the lid down, he was so swell up. Well, Mr Brownin', 'e was a great big man, thirteen stone if 'e was a ounce. Well, 'e stood on the coffin, an' a young man 'e 'ad with 'im stood on it too, an' the lid simply wouldn't go dahn; so Mr Brownin', 'e said, "Jump on, missus," so I was in my widow's weeds, yer know, but we 'ad ter get it dahn, so I stood on it, an' we all jumped, an' at last we got it to, an' screwed it; but, lor', we did 'ave a job; I shall never forget it.'

Then all was silence. And a heaviness seemed to fill the air like a grey blight, cold and suffocating; and the heaviness was Death. They felt the presence in the room, and they dared not move, they dared not draw their breath. The silence was terrifying.

Suddenly a sound was heard—a loud rattle. It was from the bed and rang through the room, piercing the stillness.

The doctor opened one of Liza's eyes and touched it, then he laid on her breast the hand he had been holding, and drew the sheet over her head.

Jim turned away with a look of intense weariness on his face, and the two women began weeping silently. The darkness was sinking before the day, and a dim, grey light came through the window. The lamp spluttered out.

The
Razor's
Edge

W.
Somerset
Maugham

The Razor's Edge

The sharp edge of a razor is difficult to pass over;
thus the wise say the path to Salvation is hard.

KATHA-UPANISHAD

Chapter One

One

I have never begun a novel with more misgiving. If I call it a novel it is only because I don't know what else to call it. I have little story to tell and I end neither with a death nor a marriage. Death ends all things and so is the comprehensive conclusion of a story, but marriage finishes it very properly too and the sophisticated are ill-advised to sneer at what is by convention termed a happy ending. It is a sound instinct of the common people which persuades them that with this all that needs to be said is said. When male and female, after whatever vicissitudes you like, are at last brought together they have fulfilled their biological function and interest passes to the generation that is to come. But I leave my reader in the air. This book consists of my recollections of a man with whom I was thrown into close contact only at long intervals, and I have little knowledge of what happened to him in between. I suppose that by the exercise of invention I could fill the gaps plausibly enough and so make my narrative more coherent; but I have no wish to do that. I only want to set down what I know of my own knowledge.

Many years ago I wrote a novel called *The Moon and Sixpence*. In that I took a famous painter, Paul Gauguin, and, using the novelist's privilege, devised a number of incidents to illustrate the character I had created on the suggestions afforded me by the scanty facts I knew about the French artist. In the present book I have attempted to do nothing of the kind. I have invented nothing. To save embarrassment to people still living I have given to the persons who play a part in this story names of my own contriving, and I have in other ways taken pains to make sure that no one should recognize them. The man I am writing about is not famous. It may be that he never will be. It may be that when his life at last comes to an end he will leave no more trace of his sojourn on earth than a stone thrown into a river leaves on the surface of the water. Then my book, if it is read at all, will be read only for what intrinsic interest it may possess. But it may be that the way of life that he has chosen for himself and the peculiar strength and sweetness of his character may have an ever-growing influence over his fellow men so that, long after his death perhaps, it may be realized that there lived in this age a very remarkable creature. Then it will be quite clear of whom I write in this book and those who want to know at least a little about his early life may find in it something to their purpose. I think my book, within its acknowledged limitations, will be a useful source of information to my friend's biographers.

I do not pretend that the conversations I have recorded can be regarded as verbatim reports. I never kept notes of what was said on this or the other occasion, but I have a good memory for what concerns me, and though I have put these conversations in my own words they faithfully represent, I believe, what was said. I remarked a little while back that I have invented nothing; I want now to modify that statement. I have taken the liberty that historians have taken from the time of Herodotus to put into the mouths of the persons of my narrative speeches that I did not myself hear and could not possibly have heard. I have done this for the same reasons as the historians have, to give liveliness and verisimilitude to scenes that would have been ineffective if they had been merely recounted. I want to be read and I think I am justified in doing what I can to make my book readable. The intelligent reader will easily see for himself where I have used this artifice, and he is at perfect liberty to reject it.

Another reason that has caused me to embark upon this work with apprehension is that the persons I have chiefly to deal with are American. It is very difficult to know people and I don't think one can ever really know any but one's own countrymen. For men and women are not only themselves; they are also the region in which they were born, the city apartment or the farm in which they learnt to walk, the games they played as children, the old wives' tales they overheard, the food they ate, the schools they attended, the sports they followed, the poets they read, and the God they believed in. It is all these things that have made them what they are, and these are the things that you can't come to know by hearsay, you can only know them if you have lived them. You can only know them if you are them. And because you cannot know persons of a nation foreign to you except from observation, it is difficult to give them credibility in the pages of a book. Even so subtle and careful an observer as Henry James, though he lived in England for forty years, never managed to create an Englishman who was through and through English. For my part, except in a few short stories I have never attempted to deal with any but my own countrymen, and if I have ventured to do otherwise in short stories it is because in them you can treat your characters more summarily. You give the reader broad indications and leave him to fill in the details. It may be asked why, if I turned Paul Gauguin into an Englishman, I could not do the same with the persons of this book. The answer is simple: I couldn't. They would not then have been the people they are. I do not pretend that they are American as Americans see themselves; they are American seen through an English eye. I have not attempted to reproduce the peculiarities of their speech. The mess English writers make when they try to do this is only equalled by the mess American writers make when they try to reproduce English as spoken in England. Slang is the great pitfall. Henry James in his English stories made constant use of it, but never quite as the English do, so that instead of getting the colloquial effect he was after, it too often gives the English reader an uncomfortable jolt.

Two

In 1919 I happened to be in Chicago on my way to the Far East, and for reasons that have nothing to do with this narrative I was staying there for two or three weeks. I had recently brought out a successful novel and being for the moment news I had no sooner arrived than I was interviewed. Next morning my telephone rang. I answered.

'Elliott Templeton speaking.'

'Elliott? I thought you were in Paris.'

'No, I'm visiting with my sister. We want you to come along and lunch with us today.'

'I should love to.'

He named the hour and gave me the address.

I had known Elliott Templeton for fifteen years. He was at this time in his late fifties, a tall, elegant man with good features and thick waving dark hair only sufficiently greying to add to the distinction of his appearance. He was always beautifully dressed. He got his haberdashery at Charvet's, but his suits, his shoes and his hats in London. He had an apartment in Paris on the Rive Gauche in the fashionable Rue St Guillaume. People who did not like him said he was a dealer, but this was a charge that he resented with indignation. He had taste and knowledge, and he did not mind admitting that in bygone years, when he first settled in Paris, he had given rich collectors who wanted to buy pictures the benefit of his advice; and when through his social connections he heard that some impoverished nobleman, English or French, was disposed to sell a picture of first-rate quality he was glad to put him in touch with the directors of American museums who, he happened to know, were on the lookout for a fine example of such and such a master. There were many old families in France and some in England whose circumstances compelled them to part with a signed piece of Buhl or a writing-table made by Chippendale himself if it could be done quietly, and they were glad to know a man of great culture and perfect manners who could arrange the matter with discretion. One would naturally suppose that Elliott profited by the transactions, but one was too well bred to mention it. Unkind people asserted that everything in his apartment was for sale and that after he had invited wealthy Americans to an excellent lunch, with vintage wines, one or two of his valuable drawings would disappear or a marquetry commode would be replaced by one in lacquer. When he was asked why a particular piece had vanished he very plausibly explained that he hadn't thought it quite up to his mark and had exchanged it for one of much finer quality. He added that it was tiresome always to look at the same things.

'*Nous autres américains,* we Americans,' he said, 'like change. It is at once our weakness and our strength.'

Some of the American ladies in Paris, who claimed to know all about him, said that his family was quite poor and if he was able to live in the way he did it was only because he had been very clever. I do not know how much money he had, but his ducal landlord certainly made him pay a lot for his apartment and it was furnished with objects of value. On the walls were drawings by the great French masters, Watteau, Fragonard, Claude Lorraine and so on; Savonnerie and Aubusson rugs displayed their beauty on the parquet floors; and in the drawing-room there was a Louis Quinze suite in *petit point* of such elegance that it might well have belonged, as he claimed, to Madame de Pompadour. Anyhow he had enough to live in what he considered was the proper style for a gentleman without trying to earn money, and the method by which he had done so in the past was a matter which, unless you wished to lose his acquaintance, you were wise not to refer to. Thus relieved of material cares he gave himself over to the ruling passion of his life, which was social relationships. His business connections with the impecunious great both in France and in England had secured the foothold he had obtained on his arrival in Europe as a young man with letters of introduction to persons of consequence. His origins recommended him to the American ladies of title to whom he brought letters, for he was of an old Virginian family and through his mother traced his descent from one of the signatories of the Declaration of Independence. He was well favoured, bright, a good dancer, a fair shot and a fine tennis player. He was an asset at any party. He was lavish with flowers and expensive boxes of chocolates, and though he entertained little, when he did it was with an originality that pleased. It amused these rich ladies to be taken to bohemian restaurants in Soho or *bistros* in the Latin Quarter. He was always prepared to make himself useful and there was nothing, however tiresome, that you asked him to do for you that he would not do with pleasure. He took an immense amount of trouble to make himself agreeable to ageing women, and it was not long before he was the *ami de la maison*, the household pet, in many an imposing mansion. His amiability was extreme; he never minded being asked at the last moment because someone had thrown you over and you could put him next to a very boring old lady and count on him to be as charming and amusing with her as he knew how.

In two or more years, both in London to which he went for the last part of the season and to pay a round of country house visits in the early autumn, and in Paris, where he had settled down, he knew everyone whom a young American could know. The ladies who had first introduced him into society were surprised to discover how wide the circle of his acquaintance had grown. Their feelings were mixed. On the one hand they were pleased that their young protégé had made so great a success, and on the other a trifle nettled that he should be on intimate terms with persons with whom their own relations had remained strictly formal. Though he continued to be obliging and useful to them, they were uneasily conscious that he had used them as stepping-stones to his social advancement. They were afraid he was a snob. And of course he was. He was a colossal snob. He was a snob without shame. He would put up with any affront, he would ignore any rebuff, he would swallow any rudeness to get asked to a party he wanted to go to or to make a connection with some crusty old dowager of great name. He was indefatigable. When he had fixed his eye on his prey he hunted it with the persistence of a botanist who will expose himself to dangers of flood, earthquake, fever and hostile natives to find an orchid of peculiar rarity. The war of 1914 gave him his final chance. When it broke out he joined an ambulance corps and served first in Flanders and then in the Argonne; he came back after a year with a red ribbon in his buttonhole and secured a position in the Red Cross in Paris. By then he was in affluent circumstances and he contributed generously to the good works patronized by persons of consequence. He was always ready with his exquisite taste and his gift for organization to help in any charitable function that was widely publicized. He became a member of the two most exclusive clubs in Paris. He was *ce cher Elliott* to the greatest ladies in France. He had finally arrived.

Three

When I first met Elliott I was just a young author like another and he took no notice of me. He never forgot a face and when I ran across him here or there he shook hands with me cordially, but showed no desire to further our acquaintance; and if I saw him at the opera, say, he being with a person of high rank, he was apt not to catch sight of me. But then I happened to make a somewhat startling success as a playwright, and presently I became aware that Elliott regarded me with a warmer feeling. One day I received a note from him asking me to lunch at Claridge's, where he lived when in London. It was a small party and not a very smart one, and I conceived the notion that he was trying me out. But from then on, since my success had brought me many new friends, I began to see him more frequently. Shortly after this I spent some weeks of the autumn in Paris and met him at the house of a common acquaintance. He asked me where I was staying and in a day or two I received another invitation to lunch, this time at his apartment; when I arrived I was surprised to see that it was a party of considerable distinction. I giggled to myself. I knew that with his perfect sense of social relations he had realized that in English society as an author I was not of much account, but that in France, where an author just because he is an author has prestige, I was. During the years that followed our acquaintance became fairly intimate without ever developing into friendship. I doubt whether it was possible for Elliott Templeton to be a friend. He took no interest in people apart from their social position. When I chanced to be in Paris or he in London, he continued to ask me to parties when he wanted an extra man or was obliged to entertain travelling Americans. Some of these were, I suspected, old clients and some were strangers sent to him with letters of introduction. They were the cross of his life. He felt he had to do something for them and yet was unwilling to have them meet his grand friends. The best way of disposing of them of course was to give them dinner and take them to a play, but that was often difficult when he was engaged every evening for three weeks ahead, and also he had an inkling that they would scarcely be satisfied with that. Since I was an author and so of little consequence he didn't mind telling me his troubles on this matter.

'People in America are so inconsiderate in the way they give letters. It's not that I'm not delighted to see the people who are sent to me, but I really don't see why I should inflict them on my friends.'

He sought to make amends by sending them great baskets of roses and huge boxes of chocolates, but sometimes he had to do more. It was then, somewhat naïvely after what he had told me, that he asked me to come to the party he was organizing.

'They want to meet you so much,' he wrote to flatter me. 'Mrs So and So is a very cultivated woman and she's read every word you've written.'

Mrs So and So would then tell me she'd so much enjoyed my book *Mr*

Perrin and Mr Traill and congratulate me on my play *The Mollusc*. The first
of these was written by Hugh Walpole and the second by Hubert Henry
Davies.

Four

If I have given the reader an impression that Elliott Templeton was a
despicable character I have done him an injustice.

He was for one thing what the French call *serviable*, a word for which, so
far as I know, there is no exact equivalent in English. The dictionary tells me
that *serviceable* in the sense of helpful, obliging and kind is archaic. That is
just what Elliott was. He was generous, and though early in his career he had
doubtless showered flowers, candy and presents on his acquaintance from an
ulterior motive, he continued to do so when it was no longer necessary. It
caused him pleasure to give. He was hospitable. His chef was as good as any
in Paris and you could be sure at his table of having set before you the earliest
delicacies of the season. His wine proved the excellence of his judgment. It is
true that his guests were chosen for their social importance rather than
because they were good company, but he took care to invite at least one or
two for their powers of entertainment, so that his parties were almost always
amusing. People laughed at him behind his back and called him a filthy snob,
but nevertheless accepted his invitations with alacrity. His French was
fluent and correct and his accent perfect. He had taken great pains to adopt
the manner of speech as it is spoken in England and you had to have a very
sensitive ear to catch now and then an American intonation. He was a good
talker if only you could keep him off the subject of dukes and duchesses, but
even about them, now that his position was unassailable, he allowed himself,
especially when you were alone with him, to be amusing. He had a pleasantly
malicious tongue and there was no scandal about these exalted personages
that did not reach his ears. From him I learnt who was the father of the
Princess X's last child and who was the mistress of the Marquis de Y. I don't
believe even Marcel Proust knew more of the inner life of the aristocracy
than Elliott Templeton.

When I was in Paris we used often to lunch together, sometimes at his
apartment and sometimes at a restaurant. I like to wander about the
antiquity shops, occasionally to buy but more often to look, and Elliott was
always enchanted to go with me. He had knowledge and a real love of
beautiful objects. I think he knew every shop of the kind in Paris and was on
familiar terms with the proprietor. He adored haggling and when we started
out would say to me:

'If there's anything you want don't try to buy it yourself. Just give me a
hint and let me do the rest.'

He would be delighted when he had got for me something I fancied for
half the asking price. It was a treat to watch him bargain. He would argue,
cajole, lose his temper, appeal to the seller's better nature, ridicule him,
point out the defects of the object in question, threaten never to cross his
threshold again, sigh, shrug his shoulders, admonish, start for the door in
frowning anger and when finally he had won his point shake his head sadly as

though he accepted defeat with resignation. Then he would whisper to me in English.

'Take it with you. It would be cheap at double the money.'

Elliott was a zealous Catholic. He had not lived long in Paris before he met an abbé who was celebrated for his success in bringing infidels and heretics back to the fold. He was a great diner-out and a noted wit. He confined his ministrations to the rich and the aristocratic. It was inevitable that Elliott should be attracted by a man who, though of humble origins, was a welcome guest in the most exclusive houses, and he confided to a wealthy American lady who was one of the abbé's recent converts that, though his family had always been Episcopalian, he had for long been interested in the Catholic Church. She asked Elliott to meet the abbé at dinner one evening, just three of them, and the abbé was scintillating. Elliott's hostess brought the conversation around to Catholicism and the abbé spoke of it with unction, but without pedantry, as a man of the world, though a priest, speaking to another man of the world. Elliott was flattered to discover that the abbé knew all about him.

'The Duchesse de Vendôme was speaking of you the other day. She told me that she thought you highly intelligent.'

Elliott flushed with pleasure. He had been presented to Her Royal Highness, but it had never occurred to him that she would give him a second thought. The abbé spoke of the faith with wisdom and benignity; he was broad-minded, modern in his outlook and tolerant. He made the Church seem to Elliott very like a select club that a well-bred man owed it to himself to belong to. Six months later he was received into it. His conversion, combined with the generosity he showed in his contributions to Catholic charities, opened several doors that had been closed to him before.

It may be that his motives in abandoning the faith of his fathers were mixed, but there could be no doubt of his devoutness when he had done so. He attended Mass every Sunday at the church frequented by the best people, went to confession regularly and made periodical visits to Rome. In course of time he was rewarded for his piety by being made a papal chamberlain, and the assiduity with which he performed the duties of his office was rewarded by the order of, I think, the Holy Sepulchre. His career as a Catholic was in fact no less successful than his career as an *homme du monde*.

I often asked myself what was the cause of the snobbishness that obsessed this man who was so intelligent, so kindly and so cultivated. He was no upstart. His father had been president of one of the southern universities and his grandfather a divine of some eminence. Elliott was too clever not to see that many of the persons who accepted his invitations did so only to get a free meal and that of these some were stupid and some worthless. The glamour of their resounding titles blinded him to their faults. I can only guess that to be on terms of intimate familiarity with these gentlemen of ancient lineage, to be the faithful retainer of their ladies, gave him a sensation of triumph that never palled; and I think that at the back of it all was a passionate romanticism that led him to see in the weedy little French duke the crusader who had gone to the Holy Land with Saint Louis and in the blustering, fox-hunting English earl the ancestor who had attended Henry the Eighth to the Field of the Cloth of Gold. In the company of such as these he felt that he lived in a spacious and gallant past. I think when he turned the pages of the Almanach de Gotha his heart beat warmly as one name after another brought back to him recollections of old wars, historic sieges and celebrated duels, diplomatic intrigues and the love affairs of kings. Such anyhow was Elliott Templeton.

Five

I was having a wash and a brush-up before starting out to go to the luncheon Elliott had invited me to, when they rang up from the desk to say that he was below. I was a little surprised, but as soon as I was ready went down.

'I thought it would be safer if I came and fetched you,' he said as we shook hands. 'I don't know how well you know Chicago.'

He had the feeling I have noticed in some Americans who have lived many years abroad that America is a difficult and even dangerous place in which the European cannot safely be left to find his way about by himself.

'It's early yet. We might walk part of the way,' he suggested.

There was a slight nip in the air, but not a cloud in the sky, and it was pleasant to stretch one's legs.

'I thought I'd better tell you about my sister before you meet her,' said Elliott as we walked along. 'She's stayed with me once or twice in Paris, but I don't think you were there at the time. It's not a big party, you know. Only my sister and her daughter Isabel and Gregory Brabazon.'

'The decorator?' I asked.

'Yes. My sister's house is awful, and Isabel and I want her to have it done over. I happened to hear that Gregory was in Chicago and so I got her to ask him to lunch today. He's not quite a gentleman, of course, but he has taste. He did Raney Castle for Mary Olifant and St Clement Talbot for the St Erths. The duchess was delighted with him. You'll see Louisa's house for yourself. How she can have lived in it all these years I shall never understand. For the matter of that how she can live in Chicago I shall never understand either.'

It appeared that Mrs Bradley was a widow with three children, two sons and a daughter; but the sons were much older and married. One was in a government post in the Philippines and the other, in the diplomatic service as his father had been, was at Buenos Aires. Mrs Bradley's husband had occupied posts in various parts of the world, and after being first secretary in Rome for some years was made minister to one of the republics on the west coast of South America and had there died.

'I wanted Louisa to sell the house in Chicago when he passed over,' Elliott went on, 'but she had a sentiment about it. It had been in the Bradley family for quite a long while. The Bradleys are one of the oldest families in Illinois. They came from Virginia in 1839 and took up land about sixty miles from what is now Chicago. They still own it.' Elliott hesitated a little and looked at me to see how I would take it. 'The Bradley who settled here was what I suppose you might call a farmer. I'm not sure whether you know, but about the middle of last century, when the Middle West began to be opened up, quite a number of Virginians, younger sons of good family, you know, were tempted by the lure of the unknown to leave the fleshpots of their native state. My brother-in-law's father, Chester Bradley, saw that Chicago had a future and entered a law office here. At all events he made enough money to leave his son very adequately provided for.'

Elliott's manner, rather than his words, suggested that perhaps it was not quite the thing for the late Chester Bradley to have left the stately mansion and the broad acres he had inherited to enter an office, but the fact that he had amassed a fortune at least partly compensated for it. Elliott was none too pleased when on a later occasion Mrs Bradley showed me some snapshots of what he called their 'place' in the country, and I saw a modest frame house with a pretty little garden, but with a barn and a cowhouse and hog pens within a stone's throw, surrounded by a desolate waste of flat fields. I couldn't help thinking that Mr Chester Bradley knew what he was about when he abandoned this to make his way in the city.

Presently we hailed a taxi. It put us down before a brown-stone house. Narrow and rather high, and you ascended to the front door by a flight of steep steps. It was in a row of houses, in a street that led off Lake Shore Drive, and its appearance, even on that bright autumn day, was so drab that you wondered how anyone could feel any sentiment about it. The door was opened by a tall and stout Negro butler with white hair, and we were ushered into the drawing-room. Mrs Bradley got up from her chair as we came in and Elliott presented me to her. She must have been a handsome woman when young, for her features, though on the large side, were good and she had fine eyes. But her sallowish face, almost aggressively destitute of make-up, had sagged and it was plain that she had lost the battle with the corpulence of middle age. I surmised that she was unwilling to accept defeat, for when she sat down she sat very erect in a straight-backed chair which the cruel armour of her corsets doubtless made more comfortable than an upholstered one. She wore a blue gown, heavily braided, and her high collar was stiff with whalebone. She had a fine head of white hair tightly marcelled and intricately dressed. Her other guest had not arrived and while waiting for him we talked of one thing and another.

'Elliott tells me that you came over by the southern route,' said Mrs Bradley. 'Did you stop in Rome?'

'Yes, I spent a week there,'

'And how is dear Queen Margherita?'

Somewhat surprised by her question, I said I didn't know.

'Oh, didn't you go and see her? Such a very nice woman. She was so kind to us when we were in Rome. Mr Bradley was first secretary. Why didn't you go and see her? You're not like Elliott, so black that you can't go to the Quirinal?'

'Not at all,' I smiled. 'The fact is I don't know her.'

'Don't you?' said Mrs Bradley as though she could hardly believe her ears. 'Why not?'

'To tell you the truth authors don't hobnob with kings and queens as a general rule.'

'But she's such a sweet woman,' Mrs Bradley expostulated, as though it were very hoity-toity of me not to know that royal personage. 'I'm sure you'd like her.'

At this moment the door was opened and the butler ushered in Gregory Brabazon.

Gregory Brabazon, notwithstanding his name, was not a romantic creature. He was a short, very fat man, as bald as an egg except for a ring of black curly hair round his ears and at the back of his neck, with a red, naked face that looked as though it were on the point of breaking out into a violent sweat, quick grey eyes, sensual lips and a heavy jowl. He was an Englishman and I had sometimes met him at bohemian parties in London. He was very jovial, very hearty and laughed a great deal, but you didn't have to be a great judge of character to know that his noisy friendliness was merely cover for a very astute man of business. He had been for some years the most successful decorator in London. He had a great booming voice and little fat hands that were wonderfully expressive. With telling gestures, with a spate of excited words he could thrill the imagination of a doubting client so that it was almost impossible to withhold the order he seemed to make it a favour to accept.

The butler came in again with a tray of cocktails.

'We won't wait for Isabel,' said Mrs Bradley as she took one.

'Where is she?' asked Elliott.

'She went to play golf with Larry. She said she might be late.'

Elliott turned to me.

'Larry is Laurence Darrell. Isabel is supposed to be engaged to him.'

'I didn't know you drank cocktails, Elliott,' I said.

'I don't,' he answered grimly, as he sipped the one he had taken, 'but in this barbarous land of prohibition what can one do?' He sighed. 'They're beginning to serve them in some houses in Paris. Evil communications corrupt good manners.'

'Stuff and nonsense, Elliott,' said Mrs Bradley.

She said it good-naturedly enough, but with a decision that suggested to me that she was a woman of character and I suspected from the look she gave him, amused but shrewd, that she had no illusions about him. I wondered what she would make of Gregory Brabazon. I had caught the professional look he gave the room as he came in and the involuntary lifting of his bushy eyebrows. It was indeed an amazing room. The paper on the walls, the cretonne of the curtains and on the upholstered furniture were of the same pattern; on the walls were oil paintings in massive gold frames that the Bradleys had evidently bought when they were in Rome. Virgins of the school of Raphael, Virgins of the school of Guido Reni, landscapes of the school of Zuccarelli, ruins of the school of Pannini. There were the trophies of their sojourn in Peking, blackwood tables too profusely carved, huge cloisonné vases, and there were the purchases they had made in Chili or Peru, obese figures in hard stone and earthenware vases. There was a Chippendale writing-table and a marquetry vitrine. The lamp-shades were of white silk on which some ill-advised artist had painted shepherds and shepherdesses in Watteau costumes. It was hideous and yet, I don't know why, agreeable. It had a homely, lived-in air and you felt that that incredible jumble had a significance. All those incongruous objects belonged together because they were part of Mrs Bradley's life.

We had finished our cocktails when the door was flung open and a girl came in, followed by a boy.

'Are we late?' she asked. 'I've brought Larry back. Is there anything for him to eat?'

'I expect so,' smiled Mrs Bradley. 'Ring the bell and tell Eugene to put another place.'

'He opened the door for us. I've already told him.'

'This is my daughter Isabel,' said Mrs Bradley, turning to me. 'And this is Laurence Darrell.'

Isabel gave me a rapid handshake and turned impetuously to Gregory Brabazon.

'Are you Mr Brabazon? I've been crazy to meet you. I love what you've done for Clementine Dormer. Isn't this room terrible? I've been trying to get Mamma to do something about it for years and now you're in Chicago it's our chance. Tell me honestly what you think of it.'

I knew that was the last thing Brabazon would do. He gave Mrs Bradley a quick glance, but her impassive face told him nothing. He decided that Isabel was the person who counted and broke into a boisterous laugh.

'I'm sure it's very comfortable and all that,' he said, 'but if you ask me point-blank, well, I do think it's pretty awful.'

Isabel was a tall girl with the oval face, straight nose, fine eyes and full mouth that appeared to be characteristic of the family. She was comely though on the fat side, which I ascribed to her age, and I guessed that she would fine down as she grew older. She had strong, good hands, though they also were a trifle fat, and her legs, displayed by her short skirt, were fat too. She had a good skin and a high colour, which exercise and the drive back in an open car had doubtless heightened. She was sparkling and vivacious. Her radiant health, her playful gaiety, her enjoyment of life, the happiness you felt in her were exhilarating. She was so natural that she made Elliott, for all his elegance, look rather tawdry. Her freshness made Mrs Bradley, with her pasty, lined face, look tired and old.

We went down to lunch. Gregory Brabazon blinked when he saw the dining-room. The walls were papered with a dark red paper that imitated stuff and hung with portraits of grim, sour-faced men and women, very badly painted, who were the immediate forebears of the late Mr Bradley. He was there, too, with a heavy moustache, very stiff in a frock coat and a white starched collar. Mrs Bradley, painted by a French artist of the nineties, hung over the chimney piece in full evening dress of pale blue satin with pearls around her neck and a diamond star in her hair. With one bejewelled hand she fingered a lace scarf so carefully painted that you could count every stitch and with the other negligently held an ostrich-feather fan. The furniture, of black oak, was overwhelming.

'What do you think of it?' asked Isabel of Gregory Brabazon as we sat down.

'I'm sure it cost a great deal of money,' he answered.

'It did,' said Mrs Bradley. 'It was given to us as a wedding present by Mr Bradley's father. It's been all over the world with us. Lisbon, Peking, Quito, Rome. Dear Queen Margherita admired it very much.'

'What would you do if it was yours?' Isabel asked Brabazon, but before he could answer, Elliott answered for him.

'Burn it,' he said.

The three of them began to discuss how they would treat the room. Elliott was all for Louis Quinze, while Isabel wanted a refectory table and Italian chairs. Brabazon thought Chippendale would be more in keeping with Mrs Bradley's personality.

'I always think that's so important,' he said, 'a person's personality.' He turned to Elliott. 'Of course you know the Duchess of Olifant?'

'Mary? She's one of my most intimate friends.'

'She wanted me to do her dining-room and the moment I saw her I said George the Second.'

'How right you were. I noticed the room the last time I dined there. It's in perfect taste.'

So the conversation went on. Mrs Bradley listened, but you could not tell what she was thinking. I said little and Isabel's young man, Larry, I'd forgotten his surname, said nothing at all. He was sitting on the other side of the table between Brabazon and Elliott and every now and then I glanced at him. He looked very young. He was about the same height as Elliott, just under six feet, thin and loose-limbed. He was a pleasant-looking boy, neither handsome nor plain, rather shy and in no way remarkable. I was interested in the fact that though, so far as I could remember, he hadn't said half a dozen words since entering the house, he seemed perfectly at ease and in a curious way appeared to take part in the conversation without opening his mouth. I noticed his hands. They were long, but not large for his size, beautifully shaped and at the same time strong. I thought that a painter would be pleased to paint them. He was slightly built but not delicate in appearance; on the contrary I should have said he was wiry and resistant. His face, grave in repose, was tanned, but otherwise there was little colour in it, and his features, though regular enough, were undistinguished. He had rather high cheekbones and his temples were hollow. He had dark brown hair with a slight wave in it. His eyes looked larger than they really were because they were deep set in the orbits and his lashes were thick and long. His eyes were peculiar, not of the rich hazel that Isabel shared with her mother and her uncle, but so dark that the iris made one colour with the pupil, and this gave them a peculiar intensity. He had a natural grace that was attractive and I could see why Isabel had been taken by him. Now and again her glance rested on him for a moment and I seemed to see in her expression not only love but fondness. Their eyes met and there was in his a tenderness that was beautiful to see. There is nothing more touching than the sight of young love, and I, a middle-aged man then, envied them, but at the same time, I couldn't imagine why, I felt sorry for them. It was silly because, so far as I knew, there was no impediment to their happiness; their circumstances seemed easy and there was no reason why they should not marry and live happily ever afterwards.

Isabel, Elliott and Gregory Brabazon went on talking of the redecoration of the house, trying to get out of Mrs Bradley at least an admission that something should be done, but she only smiled amiably.

'You mustn't try to rush me. I want to have time to think it over.' She turned to the boy. 'What do you think of it all, Larry?'

He looked round the table, a smile in his eyes.

'I don't think it matters one way or the other,' he said.

'You beast, Larry,' cried Isabel. 'I particularly told you to back us up.'

'If Aunt Louisa is happy with what she's got, what is the object of changing?'

His question was so much to the point and so sensible that it made me laugh. He looked at me then and smiled.

'And don't grin like that just because you've made a very stupid remark,' said Isabel.

But he only grinned the more, and I noticed then that he had small and white and regular teeth. There was something in the look he gave Isabel that made her flush and catch her breath. Unless I was mistaken she was madly in love with him, but I don't know what it was that gave me the feeling that in her love for him there was also something maternal. It was a little unexpected in so young a girl. With a soft smile on her lips she directed her attention once more to Gregory Brabazon.

'Don't pay any attention to him. He's very stupid and entirely uneducated. He doesn't know anything about anything except flying.'

'Flying?' I said.

'He was an aviator in the war.'

'I should have thought he was too young to have been in the war.'

'He was. Much too young. He behaved very badly. He ran away from school and went to Canada. By lying his head off he got them to believe he was eighteen and got into the air corps. He was fighting in France at the time of the armistice.'

'You're boring your mother's guests, Isabel,' said Larry.

'I've known him all my life, and when he came back he looked lovely in his uniform, with all those pretty ribbons on his tunic, so I just sat on his doorstep, so to speak, till he consented to marry me just to have a little peace and quiet. The competition was awful.'

'Really, Isabel,' said her mother.

Larry leant over towards me.

'I hope you don't believe a word she says. Isabel isn't a bad girl really, but she's a liar.'

Luncheon was finished and soon after Elliott and I left. I had told him before that I was going to the museum to look at the pictures and he said he would take me. I don't particularly like going to a gallery with anyone else, but I could not say I would sooner go alone, so I accepted his company. On our way we spoke of Isabel and Larry.

'It's rather charming to see two young things so much in love with one another,' I said.

'They're much too young to marry.'

'Why? It's such fun to be young and in love and to marry.'

'Don't be ridiculous. She's nineteen and he's only just twenty. He hasn't got a job. He has a tiny income, three thousand a year Louisa tells me, and Louisa's not a rich woman by any manner of means. She needs all she has.'

'Well, he can get a job.'

'That's just it. He's not trying to. He seems to be quite satisfied to do nothing.'

'I dare say he had a pretty rough time in the war. He may want a rest.'

'He's been resting for a year. That's surely long enough.'

'I thought he seemed a nice sort of boy.'

'Oh, I have nothing against him. He's quite well born and all that sort of thing. His father came from Baltimore. He was assistant professor of Romance languages at Yale or something like that. His mother was a Philadelphian of old Quaker stock.'

'You speak of them in the past. Are they dead?'

'Yes, his mother died in childbirth and his father about twelve years ago. He was brought up by an old college friend of his father's who's a doctor at Marvin. That's how Louisa and Isabel knew him.'

'Where's Marvin?'

'That's where the Bradley place is. Louisa spends the summer there. She was sorry for the child. Dr Nelson's a bachelor and didn't know the first thing about bringing up a boy. It was Louisa who insisted that he should be sent to St Paul's and she always had him out here for his Christmas vacation.' Elliott shrugged a Gallic shoulder. 'I should have thought she would foresee the inevitable result.'

We had now arrived at the museum and our attention was directed to the pictures. Once more I was impressed by Elliott's knowledge and taste. He shepherded me around the rooms as though I were a group of tourists, and no professor of art could have discoursed more instructively then he did. Making up my mind to come again by myself when I could wander at will and have a good time, I submitted; after a while he looked at his watch.

'Let us go,' he said. 'I never spend more than one hour in a gallery. That is as long as one's power of appreciation persists. We will finish another day.'

I thanked him warmly when we separated. I went my way perhaps a wiser but certainly a peevish man.

When I was saying good-bye to Mrs Bradley she told me that next day Isabel was having a few of her young friends in to dinner and they were going on to dance afterwards, and if I would come Elliott and I could have a talk when they had gone.

'You'll be doing him a kindness,' she added. 'He's been abroad so long, he feels rather out of it here. He doesn't seem able to find anyone he has anything in common with.'

I accepted and before we parted on the museum steps Elliott told me he was glad I had.

'I'm like a lost soul in this great city,' he said. 'I promised Louisa to spend six weeks with her, we hadn't seen one another since 1912, but I'm counting the days till I can get back to Paris. It's the only place in the world for a civilized man to live. My dear fellow, d'you know how they look upon me here? They look upon me as a freak. Savages.'

I laughed and left.

Six

The following evening, having refused Elliott's telephoned offer to fetch me, I arrived quite safely at Mrs Bradley's house. I had been delayed by someone who had come to see me and was a trifle late. So much noise came from the sitting-room as I walked upstairs that I thought it must be a large party and I was surprised to find that there were, including myself, only twelve people. Mrs Bradley was very grand in green satin with a dog-collar of seed pearls round her neck, and Elliott in his well-cut dinner jacket looked elegant as he alone could look. When he shook hands with me my nostrils were assailed by all the perfumes of Arabia. I was introduced to a stoutish, tall man with a red face who looked somewhat ill at ease in evening clothes. He was a Dr Nelson, but at the moment that meant nothing to me. The rest of the party consisted of Isabel's friends, but their names escaped me as soon as I heard them. The girls were young and pretty and the men young and upstanding. None of them made any impression on me except one boy and that only because he was so tall and so massive. He must have been six foot three or four and he had great broad shoulders. Isabel was looking very pretty; she was dressed in white silk, with a long, hobbled skirt that concealed her fat legs; the cut of her frock showed that she had well-developed breasts; her bare arms were a trifle fat, but her neck was lovely. She was excited and her fine eyes sparkled. There was no doubt about it, she was a very pretty and desirable young woman, but it was obvious that unless she took care she would develop an unbecoming corpulence.

At dinner I found myself placed between Mrs Bradley and a shy drab girl who seemed even younger than the others. As we sat down, to make the way easier Mrs Bradley explained that her grandparents lived at Marvin and that she and Isabel had been at school together. Her name, the only one I heard mentioned, was Sophie. A lot of chaff was bandied across the table, everyone talked at the top of his voice and there was a great deal of laughter. They seemed to know one another very well. When I was not occupied with my hostess I attempted to make conversation with my neighbour, but I had no great success. She was quieter than the rest. She was not pretty, but she had an amusing face, with a little tilted nose, a wide mouth and greenish blue eyes; her hair, simply done, was of a sandy brown. She was very thin and her chest was almost as flat as a boy's. She laughed at the badinage that went on, but in a manner that was a little forced so that you felt she wasn't as much amused as she pretended to be. I guessed that she was making an effort to be a good sport. I could not make out if she was a trifle stupid or only painfully timid and, having tried various topics of conversation only to have them dropped, for want of anything better to say I asked her to tell me who all the people at table were.

'Well, you know Dr Nelson,' she said, indicating the middle-aged man who was opposite me on Mrs Bradley's other side. 'He's Larry's guardian. He's our doctor at Marvin. He's very clever, he invents gadgets for planes that no one will have anything to do with and when he isn't doing that he drinks.'

There was a gleam in her pale eyes as she said this that made me suspect that there was more in her than I had at first supposed. She went on to give me the names of one young thing after another, telling me who their parents were, and in the case of the men what college they had been to and what work they did. It wasn't very illuminating.

'She's very sweet,' or: 'He's a very good golfer.'

'And who is that big fellow with the eyebrows?'

'That? Oh, that's Gray Maturin. His father's got an enormous house on the river at Marvin. He's our millionaire. We're very proud of him. He gives us class. Maturin, Hobbes, Rayner and Smith. He's one of the richest men in Chicago and Gray's his only son.'

She put such a pleasant irony into that list of names that I gave her an inquisitive glance. She caught it and flushed.

'Tell me more about Mr Maturin.'

'There's nothing to tell. He's rich. He's highly respected. He built us a new church at Marvin and he's given a million dollars to the University of Chicago.'

'His son's a fine-looking fellow.'

'He's nice. You'd never think his grandfather was shanty Irish and his grandmother a Swedish waitress in an eating house.'

Gray Maturin was striking rather than handsome. He had a rugged, unfinished look; a short blunt nose, a sensual mouth and the florid Irish complexion; a great quantity of raven black hair, very sleek, and under heavy eyebrows clear, very blue eyes. Though built on so large a scale he was finely proportioned, and stripped he must have been a fine figure of a man. He was obviously very powerful. His virility was impressive. He made Larry who was sitting next to him, though only three of four inches shorter, look puny.

'He's very much admired,' said my shy neighbour. 'I know several girls who would stop at nothing short of murder to get him. But they haven't a chance.'

'Why not?'

'You don't know anything, do you?'

'How should I?'

'He's so much in love with Isabel, he can't see straight, and Isabel's in love with Larry.'

'What's to prevent him from setting to and cutting Larry out?'

'Larry's his best friend.'

'I suppose that complicates matters.'

'If you're as high-principled as Gray is.'

I was not sure whether she said this in all seriousness or whether there was in her tone a hint of mockery. There was nothing saucy in her manner, forward or pert, and yet I got the impression that she was lacking neither in humour nor in shrewdness. I wondered what she was really thinking while she made conversation with me, but that I knew I should never find out. She was obviously unsure of herself and I conceived the notion that she was an only child who had lived a secluded life with people a great deal older than herself. There was a modesty, an unobtrusiveness about her that I found engaging, but if I was right in thinking that she had lived much alone I guessed that she had quietly observed the older persons she lived with and had formed decided opinions upon them. We who are of mature age seldom suspect how unmercifully and yet with what insight the very young judge us. I looked again into her greenish blue eyes.

'How old are you?' I asked.

'Seventeen.'

'Do you read much?' I asked at a venture.

But before she could answer, Mrs Bradley, attentive to her duties as a hostess, drew me to her with some remark and before I could disengage myself dinner was at an end. The young people went off at once to wherever they were going and the four of us who were left went up to the sitting-room.

I was surprised that I had been asked to this party, for after a little desultory conversation they began to talk of a matter that I should have thought they would have preferred to discuss in private. I could not make up my mind whether it would be more discreet in me to get up and go or whether, as a disinterested audience of one, I was useful to them. The question at issue was Larry's odd disinclination to go to work, and it had been brought to a point by an offer from Mr Maturin, the father of the boy who had been at dinner, to take him into his office. It was a fine opportunity. With ability and industry Larry could go forward to making in due course a great deal of money. Young Gray Maturin was eager for him to take it.

I cannot remember all that was said, but the gist of it is clear in my memory. On Larry's return from France Dr Nelson, his guardian, had suggested that he should go to college, but he had refused. It was natural that he should want to do nothing for a while; he had had a hard time and had been twice, though not severely, wounded. Dr Nelson thought that he was still suffering from shock and it seemed a good idea that he should rest till he had completely recovered. But the weeks passed into months and now it was over a year since he'd been out of uniform. It appeared that he had done well in the air corps and on his return he cut something of a figure in Chicago, the result of which was that several businessmen offered him positions. He thanked them, but refused. He gave no reason except that he hadn't made up his mind what he wanted to do. He became engaged to Isabel. This was no surprise to Mrs Bradley since they had been inseparable for years and she knew that Isabel was in love with him. She was fond of him and thought he would make Isabel happy.

'Her character's stronger than his. She can give him just what he lacks.'

Though they were both so young Mrs Bradley was quite willing that they should marry at once, but she wasn't prepared for them to do so until Larry had gone to work. He had a little money of his own, but even if he had had ten times more than he had she would have insisted on this. So far as I could gather, what she and Elliott wished to find out from Dr Nelson was what Larry intended to do. They wanted him to use his influence to get him to accept the job that Mr Maturin offered him.

'You know I never had much authority over Larry,' he said. 'Even as a boy he went his own way.'

'I know. You let him run wild. It's a miracle he's turned out as well as he has.'

Dr Nelson, who had been drinking quite heavily, gave her a sour look. His red face grew a trifle redder.

'I was very busy. I had my own affairs to attend to. I took him because there was nowhere else for him to go and his father was a friend of mine. He wasn't easy to do anything with.'

'I don't know how you can say that,' Mrs Bradley answered tartly. 'He has a very sweet disposition.'

'What are you to do with a boy who never argues with you, but does exactly what he likes and when you get mad at him just says he's sorry and lets you storm? If he'd been my own son I could have beaten him. I couldn't beat a boy who hadn't got a relation in the world and whose father had left him to me because he thought I'd be kind to him.'

'That's neither here nor there,' said Elliott, somewhat irritably. 'The position is this: he's dawdled around long enough; he's got a fine chance of a position in which he stands to make a lot of money and if he wants to marry Isabel he must take it.'

'He must see that in the present state of the world,' Mrs Bradley put in, 'a man has to work. He's perfectly strong and well now. We all know how after the war between the States there were men who never did a stroke after they came back from it. They were a burden to their families and useless to the community.'

Then I added my word.

'But what reason does he give for refusing the various offers that are made him?'

'None. Except that they don't appeal to him.'

'But doesn't he want to do anything?'

'Apparently not.'

Dr Nelson helped himself to another highball. He took a long drink and then looked at his two friends.

'Shall I tell you what my impression is? I dare say I'm not a great judge of human nature, but at any rate after thirty-odd years of practice I think I know something about it. The war did something to Larry. He didn't come back the same person that he went. It's not only that he's older. Something happened that changed his personality.'

'What sort of thing?' I asked.

'I wouldn't know. He's very reticent about his war experiences.' Dr Nelson turned to Mrs Bradley. 'Has he ever talked to you about them, Louisa?'

She shook her head.

'No. When he first came back we tried to get him to tell us some of his adventures, but he only laughed in that way of his and said there was nothing to tell. He hasn't even told Isabel. She's tried and tried, but she hasn't got a thing out of him.

The conversation went on in this unsatisfactory way and presently Dr Nelson, looking at his watch, said he must go. I prepared to leave with him, but Elliott pressed me to stay. When he had gone, Mrs Bradley apologized for troubling me with their private affairs and expressed her fear that I had been bored.

'But you see it's all very much on my mind,' she finished.

'Mr Maugham is very discreet, Louisa; you needn't be afraid of telling him anything. I haven't the feeling that Bob Nelson and Larry are very close, but there are some things that Louisa and I thought we'd better not mention to him.'

'Elliott.'

'You've told him so much, you may as well tell him the rest. I don't know whether you noticed Gray Maturin at dinner?'

'He's so big, one could hardly fail to.'

'He's a beau of Isabel's. All the time Larry was away he was very attentive. She likes him and if the war had lasted much longer she might very well have married him. He proposed to her. She didn't accept and she didn't refuse. Louisa guessed she didn't want to make up her mind till Larry came home.'

'How is it that he wasn't in the war?' I asked.

'He strained his heart playing football. It's nothing serious, but the Army wouldn't take him. Anyhow when Larry came home he had no chance. Isabel turned him down flat.'

I didn't know what I was expected to say to that, so I said nothing. Elliott went on. With his distinguished appearance and his Oxford accent he couldn't have been more like an official of high standing at the Foreign Office.

'Of course Larry's a very nice boy and it was damned sporting of him to run away and join the air corps, but I'm a pretty good judge of character. . . .' He gave a knowing little smile and made the only reference I ever heard him make to the fact that he had made a fortune by dealing in works of art. 'Otherwise I shouldn't have at this moment a tidy sum in gilt-edged securities. And my opinion is that Larry will never amount to very much. He has no money to speak of and no standing. Gray Maturin is a very different proposition. He has a good old Irish name. They've had a bishop in the family, and a dramatist and several distinguished soldiers and scholars.'

'How do you know all that?' I asked.

'It's the sort of thing one knows,' he answered casually. 'As a matter of fact I happened to be glancing through the Dictionary of National Biography the other day at the club and I came across the name.'

I didn't think it was my business to repeat what my neighbour at dinner had told me of the shanty Irishman and the Swedish waitress who were Gray's grandfather and grandmother. Elliott proceeded.

'We've all known Henry Maturin for many years. He's a very fine man and a very rich one. Gray's stepping into the best brokerage house in Chicago. He's got the world at his feet. He wants to marry Isabel and one can't deny that from her point of view it would be a very good match. I'm all in favour of it myself and I know Louisa is too.'

'You've been away from America so long, Elliott,' said Mrs Bradley, with a dry smile, 'you've forgotten that in this country girls don't marry because their mothers and their uncles are in favour of it.'

'That is nothing to be proud of, Louisa,' said Elliott sharply. 'As the result of thirty years' experience I may tell you that a marriage arranged with proper regard to position, fortune and community of circumstances has every advantage over a love match. In France, which after all is the only civilized country in the world, Isabel would marry Gray without thinking twice about it; then, after a year or two, if she wanted it, she'd take Larry as her lover, Gray would install a prominent actress in a luxurious apartment, and everyone would be perfectly happy.'

Mrs Bradley was no fool. She looked at her brother with sly amusement.

'The objection to that, Elliott, is that as the New York plays only come here for limited periods, Gray could only hope to keep the tenants of his luxurious apartment for a very uncertain length of time. That would surely be very unsettling for all parties.'

Elliott smiled.

'Gray could buy a seat on the New York stock exchange. After all, if you must live in America I can't see any object in living anywhere but in New York.

I left soon after this, but before I did Elliott, I hardly know why, asked me if I would lunch with him to meet the Maturins, father and son.

'Henry is the best type of the American businessman,' he said, 'and I think you ought to know him. He's looked after our investments for many years.'

I hadn't any particular wish to do this, but no reason to refuse, so I said I would be glad to.

Seven

I had been put up for the length of my stay at a club which possessed a good library and next morning I went there to look at one or two of the university magazines that for the person who does not subscribe to them have always been rather hard to come by. It was early and there was only one other person there. He was seated in a big leather chair absorbed in a book. I was surprised to see it was Larry. He was the last person I should have expected to find in such a place. He looked up as I passed, recognized me and made as if to get up.

'Don't move,' I said, and then almost automatically: 'What are you reading?'

'A book,' he said, with a smile, but a smile so engaging that the rebuff of his answer was in no way offensive.

He closed it and looking at me with his peculiarly opaque eyes held it so that I couldn't see the title.

'Did you have a good time last night?' I asked.

'Wonderful. Didn't get home till five.'

'It's very strenuous of you to be here so bright and early.'

'I come here a good deal. Generally I have the place to myself at this time.'

'I won't disturb you.'

'You're not disturbing me,' he said, smiling again, and now it occurred to me that he had a smile of great sweetness. It was not a brilliant, flashing smile, it was a smile that lit his face as with an inner light. He was sitting in an alcove made by jutting out shelves and there was a chair next to him. He put his hand on the arm. 'Won't you sit down for a minute?'

'All right.'

He handed me the book he was holding.

'That's what I was reading.'

I looked at it and saw it was William James's *Principles of Psychology*. It is, of course, a standard work and important in the history of the science with which it deals; it is moreover exceedingly readable; but it is not the sort of book I should have expected to see in the hands of a very young man, an aviator, who had been dancing till five in the morning.

'Why are you reading this?' I asked.

'I'm very ignorant.'

'You're also very young,' I smiled.

He did not speak for so long a time that I began to find the silence awkward and I was on the point of getting up and looking for the magazines I had come to find. But I had a feeling that he wanted to say something. He looked into vacancy, his face grave and intent, and seemed to meditate. I waited. I was curious to know what it was all about. When he began to speak it was as though he were continuing the conversation without awareness of that long silence.

'When I came back from France they all wanted me to go to college. I couldn't. After what I'd been through I felt I couldn't go back to school. I learnt nothing at my prep school anyway. I felt I couldn't enter into a freshman's life. They wouldn't have liked me. I didn't want to act a part I didn't feel. And I didn't think the instructors would teach me the sort of things I wanted to know.'

'Of course I know this is no business of mine,' I answered, 'but I'm not convinced you were right. I think I understand what you mean and I can see that, after being in the war for two years, it would have been rather a nuisance to become the sort of glorified schoolboy an undergraduate is during his first and second years. I can't believe they wouldn't have liked you. I don't know much about American universities, but I don't believe American undergraduates are very different from English ones, perhaps a little more boisterous and a little more inclined to horse-play, but on the whole very decent, sensible boys, and I take it that if you don't want to lead their lives they're quite willing, if you exercise a little tact, to let you lead yours. I never went to Cambridge as my brothers did. I had the chance, but I refused it. I wanted to get out into the world. I've always regretted it. I think it would have saved me a lot of mistakes. You learn more quickly under the guidance of experienced teachers. You waste a lot of time going down blind alleys if you have no one to lead you.'

'You may be right. I don't mind if I make mistakes. It may be that in one of the blind alleys I may find something to my purpose.'

'What is your purpose?'

He hesitated a moment.

'That's just it. I don't quite know it yet.'

I was silent, for there didn't seem to be anything to say in answer to that. I, who from a very early age have always had before me a clear and definite purpose, was inclined to feel impatient; but I chid myself; I had what I can only call an intuition that there was in the soul of that boy some confused striving, whether of half-thought-out ideas or of dimly felt emotions I could not tell, which filled him with a restlessness that urged him he did not know whither. He strangely excited my sympathy. I had never before heard him speak much and it was only now that I became conscious of the melodiousness of his voice. It was very persuasive. It was like balm. When I considered that, his engaging smile and the expressiveness of his very black eyes I could well understand that Isabel was in love with him. There was indeed something very lovable about him. He turned his head and looked at me without embarrassment, but with an expression in his eyes that was at once scrutinizing and amused.

'Am I right in thinking that after we all went off to dance last night you talked about me?'

'Part of the time.'

'I thought that was why Uncle Bob had been pressed to come to dinner. He hates going out.'

'It appears that you've got the offer of a very good job.'

'A wonderful job.'

'Are you going to take it?'

'I don't think so.'

'Why not?'

'I don't want to.'

I was butting into an affair that was no concern of mine, but I had a notion that just because I was a stranger from a foreign country Larry was not disinclined to talk to me about it.

'Well, you know when people are no good at anything else they become writers,' I said, with a chuckle.

'I have no talent.'

'Then what do you want to do?'

He gave me his radiant, fascinating smile.

'Loaf,' he said.

I had to laugh.

'I shouldn't have thought Chicago the best place in the world to do that in,' I said. 'Anyhow, I'll leave you to your reading. I want to have a look at the *Yale Quarterly*.'

I got up. When I left the library Larry was still absorbed in William James's book. I lunched by myself at the club and since it was quiet in the library went back there to smoke my cigar and idle an hour or two away, reading and writing letters. I was surprised to see Larry still immersed in his book. He looked as if he hadn't moved since I left him. He was still there when about four I went away. I was struck by his evident power of concentration. He had neither noticed me go nor come. I had various things to do during the afternoon and did not go back to the Blackstone till it was time to change for the dinner party I was going to. On my way I was seized with an impulse of curiosity. I dropped into the club once more and went into the library. There were quite a number of people there then, reading the papers and what not. Larry was still sitting in the same chair, intent on the same book. Odd!

Nine

Next day Elliott asked me to lunch at the Palmer House to meet the elder Maturin and his son. We were only four. Henry Maturin was a big man, nearly as big as his son, with a red fleshy face and a great jowl, and he had the same blunt aggressive nose, but his eyes were smaller than his son's, not so blue and very, very shrewd. Though he could not have been much more than fifty he looked ten years older and his hair rapidly thinning, was snow-white. At first sight he was not prepossessing. He looked as though for many years he had done himself too well, and I received the impression of a brutal, clever, competent man who, in business matters at all events, would be pitiless. At first he said little and I had a notion that he was taking my measure. I could not but perceive that he looked upon Elliott as something of a joke. Gray, amiable and polite, was almost completely silent and the party would have been sticky if Elliott, with his perfect social tact, hadn't kept up a flow of easy conversation. I guessed that in the past he had acquired a good deal of experience in dealing with Middle Western businessmen who had to be cajoled into paying a fancy price for an old master. Presently Mr Maturin began to feel more at his ease and he made one or two remarks that showed he was brighter than he looked and indeed had a dry sense of humour. For a while the conversation turned on stocks and shares. I should have been surprised to discover that Elliott was very knowledgeable on the subject if I had not long been aware that for all his nonsense he was nobody's fool. It was then that Mr Maturin remarked:

'I had a letter from Gray's friend Larry Darrell this morning.'

'You didn't tell me, Dad,' said Gray.

Mr Maturin turned to me.

'You know Larry, don't you?' I nodded. 'Gray persuaded me to take him into my business. They're great friends. Gray thinks the world of him.'

'What did he say, Dad?'

'He thanked me. He said he realized it was a great chance for a young fellow and he'd thought it over very carefully and come to the conclusion he'd have been a disappointment to me and thought it better to refuse.'

'That's very foolish of him,' said Elliott.

'It is,' said Mr Maturin.

'I'm awfully sorry, Dad,' said Gray. 'It would have been grand if we could have worked together.'

'You can lead a horse to the water, but you can't make him drink.'

Mr Maturin looked at his son while he said this and his shrewd eyes softened. I realized that there was another side to the hard businessman; he doted on this great hulking son of his. He turned to me once more.

'D'you know, that boy did our course in two under par on Sunday. He beat me seven and six. I could have brained him with my niblick. And to think that I taught him to play golf myself.'

He was brimming over with pride. I began to like him.

'I had a lot of luck, Dad.'

'Not a bit of it. Is it luck when you get out of a bunker and lay your ball six inches from the hole? Thirty-five yards if it was an inch, the shot was. I want him to go into the amateur championship next year.'

'I shouldn't be able to spare the time.'

'I'm your boss, ain't I?'

'Don't I know it! The hell you raise if I'm a minute late at the office.'

Mr Maturin chuckled.

'He's trying to make me out a tyrant,' he said to me. 'Don't you believe him. I'm my business, my partners are no good, and I'm very proud of my business. I've started this boy of mine at the bottom and I expect him to work his way up just like any young fellow I've hired, so that when the time comes for him to take my place he'll be ready for it. It's a great responsibility, a business like mine. I've looked after the investments of some of my clients for thirty years and they trust me. To tell you the truth, I'd rather lose my own money than see them lose theirs.'

Gray laughed.

'The other day when an old girl came in and wanted to invest a thousand dollars in a wildcat scheme that her minister had recommended he refused to take the order, and when she insisted he gave her such hell that she went out sobbing. And then he called up the minister and gave him hell too.'

'People say a lot of hard things about us brokers, but there are brokers and brokers. I don't want people to lose money, I want them to make it, and the way they act, most of them, you'd think their one object in life was to get rid of every cent they have.'

'Well, what did you think of him?' Elliott asked me as we walked away after the Maturins had left us to go back to the office.

'I'm always glad to meet new types. I thought the mutual affection of father and son was rather touching. I don't know that that's so common in England.'

'He adores that boy. He's a queer mixture. What he said about his clients was quite true. He's got hundreds of old women, retired service men and ministers whose savings he looks after. I'd have thought they were more trouble than they're worth, but he takes pride in the confidence they have in him. But when he's got some big deal on and he's up against powerful interests there isn't a man who can be harder and more ruthless. There's no mercy in him then. He wants his pound of flesh and there's nothing much he'll stop at to get it. Get on the wrong side of him and he'll not only ruin you, but get a big laugh out of doing it.'

On getting home Elliott told Mrs Bradley that Larry had refused Henry Maturin's offer. Isabel had been lunching with girl friends and came in while they were still talking about it. They told her. I gathered from Elliott's account of the conversation that ensued that he had expressed himself with considerable eloquence. Though he had certainly not done a stroke of work for ten years, and the work by which he had amassed an ample competence had been far from arduous, he was firmly of opinion that for the run of mankind industry was essential. Larry was a perfectly ordinary young fellow, of no social consequence, and there was no possible reason why he shouldn't conform to the commendable customs of his country. It was evident to a man as clear-sighted as Elliott that America was entering upon a period of prosperity such as it had never known. Larry had a chance of getting in on the ground floor, and if he kept his nose to the grindstone he might well be many times a millionaire by the time he was forty. If he wanted to retire then and live like a gentleman, in Paris, say, with an apartment in the Avenue du Bois and a château in Touraine, he (Elliott) would have nothing to say against it. But Louisa Bradley was more succinct and more unanswerable.

'If he loves you, he ought to be prepared to work for you.'

I don't know what Isabel answered to all this, but she was sensible enough to see that her elders had reason on their side. All the young men of her acquaintance were studying to enter some profession or already busy in an office. Larry could hardly expect to live the rest of his life on his distinguished record in the air corps. The war was over, everyone was sick of it and anxious only to forget about it as quickly as possible. The result of the discussion was that Isabel agreed to have the matter out with Larry once and for all. Mrs Bradley suggested that Isabel should ask him to drive her down to Marvin. She was ordering new curtains for the living-room and had mislaid the measurements, so she wanted Isabel to take them again.

'Bob Nelson will give you luncheon,' she said.

'I have a better plan than that,' said Elliott. 'Put up a luncheon basket for them and let them lunch on the stoop and after lunch they can talk.'

'That would be fun,' said Isabel.

'There are few things so pleasant as a picnic lunch eaten in perfect comfort,' Elliott added sententiously. 'The old Duchesse d'Uzès used to tell me that the most recalcitrant male becomes amenable to suggestion in these conditions. What will you give them for luncheon?'

'Stuffed eggs and a chicken sandwich.'

'Nonsense. You can't have a picnic without *pâté de foie gras*. You must give them curried shrimps to start with, breast of chicken in aspic, with a heart-of-lettuce salad for which I'll make the dressing myself, and after the *pâté* if you like, as a concession to your American habits, an apple pie.'

'I shall give them stuffed eggs and a chicken sandwich, Elliott,' said Mrs Bradley with decision.

'Well, mark my words, it'll be a failure and you'll only have yourself to blame.'

'Larry eats very little, Uncle Elliott,' said Isabel, 'and I don't believe he notices what he eats.'

'I hope you don't think that is to his credit, my poor child,' her uncle returned.

But what Mrs Bradley said they should have was what they got. When Elliott later told me the outcome of the excursion he shrugged his shoulders in a very French way.

'I told them it would be a failure. I begged Louisa to put in a bottle of the Montrachet I sent her just before the war, but she wouldn't listen to me. They took a thermos of hot coffee and nothing else. What would you expect?'

It appeared that Louisa Bradley and Elliott were sitting by themselves in the living-room when they heard the car stop at the door and Isabel came into the house. It was just after dark and the curtains were drawn. Elliott was lounging in an armchair by the fireside reading a novel and Mrs Bradley was at work on a piece of tapestry that was to be made into a fire-screen. Isabel did not come in, but went on up to her room. Elliott looked over his spectacles at his sister.

'I expect she's gone to take off her hat. She'll be down in a minute,' she said.

But Isabel did not come. Several minutes passed.

'Perhaps she's tired. She may be lying down.'

'Wouldn't you have expected Larry to have come in?'

'Don't be exasperating, Elliott.'

'Well, it's your business, not mine.'

He returned to his book. Mrs Bradley went on working. But when half an hour had gone by she got up suddenly.

'I think perhaps I'd better go up and see that she's all right. If she's resting I won't disturb her.'

She left the room, but in a very short while came down again.

'She's been crying. Larry's going to Paris. He's going to be away for two years. She's promised to wait for him.'

'Why does he want to go to Paris?'

'It's no good asking me questions, Elliott. I don't know. She won't tell me anything. She says she understands and she isn't going to stand in his way. I said to her, "If he's prepared to leave you for two years he can't love you very much." "I can't help that," she said, "the thing that matters is that I love *him* very much." "Even after what's happened today?" I said. "Today's made me love him more than ever I did," she said, "and he does love me, Mamma. I'm sure of that."'

Elliott reflected for a while.

'And what's to happen at the end of two years?'

'I tell you I don't know, Elliott.'

'Don't you think it's very unsatisfactory?'

'Very.'

'There's only one thing to be said and that is that they're both very young. It won't hurt them to wait two years and in that time a lot may happen.'

They agreed that it would be better to leave Isabel in peace. They were going out to dinner that night.

'I don't want to upset her,' said Mrs Bradley. 'People would only wonder if her eyes were all swollen.'

But next day after luncheon, which they had by themselves, Mrs Bradley brought the subject up again. But she got little out of Isabel.

'There's really nothing more to tell you than I've told you already, Mamma,' she said.

'But what does he want to do in Paris?'

Isabel smiled, for she knew how preposterous her answer would seem to her mother.

'Loaf.'

'Loaf? What on earth do you mean?'

'That's really what he told me.'

'Really I have no patience with you. If you had any spirit you'd have broken off your engagement there and then. He's just playing with you.'

Isabel looked at the ring she wore on her left hand.

'What can I do? I love him.'

Then Elliott entered the conversation. He approached the matter with his famous tact, 'Not as if I was her uncle, my dear fellow, but as a man of the world speaking to an inexperienced girl,' but he did no better than her mother had done. I received the impression that she had told him, no doubt politely but quite unmistakably, to mind his own business. Elliott told me all this later on in the day in the little sitting-room I had at the Blackstone.

'Of course Louisa is quite right,' he added. 'It's all very unsatisfactory, but that's the sort of thing you run up against when young people are left to arrange their marriages on no better basis than mutual inclination. I've told Louisa not to worry; I think it'll turn out better than she expects. With Larry out of the way and young Gray Maturin on the spot—well, if I know anything about my fellow creatures the outcome is fairly obvious. When you're eighteen your emotions are violent, but they're not durable.'

'You're full of worldly wisdom, Elliott,' I smiled.

'I haven't read my La Rochefoucauld for nothing. You know what Chicago is; they'll be meeting all the time. It flatters a girl to have a man so devoted to her, and when she knows there isn't one of her girl friends who wouldn't be only too glad to marry him—well, I ask you, is it in human nature to resist the temptation of cutting out everyone else? I mean it's like going to a party where you know you'll be bored to distraction and the only refreshments will be lemonade and biscuits; but you go because you know your best friends would give their eyeteeth to and haven't been asked.'

'When does Larry go?'

'I don't know. I don't think that's been decided yet.' Elliott took a long, thin cigarette case in platinum and gold out of his pocket and extracted an Egyptian cigarette. Not for him were Fatimas, Chesterfields, Camels or Lucky Strikes. He looked at me with a smile full of insinuation. 'Of course I wouldn't care to say so to Louisa, but I don't mind telling you that I have a sneaking sympathy for the young fellow. I understand that he got a glimpse of Paris during the war, and I can't blame him if he was captivated by the only city in the world fit for a civilized man to live in. He's young and I have no doubt he wants to sow his wild oats before he settles down to married life. Very natural and very proper. I'll keep an eye on him. I'll introduce him to the right people; he has nice manners and with a hint or two from me he'll be quite presentable; I can guarantee to show him a side of French life that very few Americans have a chance of seeing. Believe me, my dear fellow, the average American can get into the kingdom of heaven much more easily than he can get into the Boulevard St Germain. He's twenty and he has charm. I think I could probably arrange a liaison for him with an older woman. It would form him. I always think there's no better education for a young man than to become the lover of a woman of a certain age and of course if she is the sort of person I have in view, a *femme du monde*, you know, it would immediately give him a situation in Paris.'

'Did you tell that to Mrs Bradley?' I asked, smiling.

Elliott chuckled.

'My dear fellow, if there's one thing I pride myself on it's my tact. I did not tell her. She wouldn't understand, poor dear. It's one of the things I've never understood about Louisa; though she's lived half her life in diplomatic society, in half the capitals of the world, she's remained hopelessly American.'

Nine

That evening I went to dine at a great stone house on Lake Shore Drive which looked as though the architect had started to build a medieval castle and then, changing his mind in the middle, had decided to turn it into a Swiss chalet. It was a huge party and I was glad when I got into the vast and sumptuous drawing-room, all statues, palms, chandeliers, old masters, and overstuffed furniture, to see that there were at least a few people I knew. I was introduced by Henry Maturin to his thin, raddled, frail wife. I said how d'you do to Mrs Bradley and Isabel. Isabel was looking very pretty in a red silk dress that suited her dark hair and rich hazel eyes. She appeared to be in high spirits and no one could have guessed that she had so recently gone through a harassing experience. She was talking gaily to the two or three young men, Gray among them, who surrounded her. She sat at dinner at another table and I could not see her, but afterwards, when we men, after lingering interminably over our coffee, liqueurs and cigars, returned to the drawing-room, I had a chance to speak to her. I knew her too little to say anything directly about what Elliott had told me, but I had something to say that I thought she might be glad to hear.

'I saw your young man the other day in the club,' I remarked casually.

'Oh, did you?'

She spoke as casually as I had, but I perceived that she was instantly alert. Her eyes grew watchful and I thought I read in them something like apprehension.

'He was reading in the library. I was very much impressed by his power of concentration. He was reading when I went in soon after ten, he was still reading when I went back after lunch, and he was reading when I went in again on my way out to dinner. I don't believe he'd moved from his chair for the best part of ten hours.'

'What was he reading?'

'William James's *Principles of Psychology*.'

She looked down so that I had no means of knowing how what I said affected her, but I had a notion that she was at once puzzled and relieved. I was at that moment fetched by my host who wanted me to play bridge and by the time the game broke up Isabel and her mother had gone.

Ten

A couple of days later I went to say good-bye to Mrs Bradley and Elliott. I found them sitting over a cup of tea. Isabel came in shortly after me. We talked about my approaching journey, I thanked them for their kindness to me during my stay in Chicago and after a decent interval got up to go.

'I'll walk with you as far as the drugstore,' said Isabel. 'I've just remembered there's something I want to get.'

The last words Mrs Bradley said to me were: 'You will give my love to dear Queen Margherita the next time you see her, won't you?'

I had given up disclaiming any acquaintance with that august lady and answered glibly that I would be sure to.

When we got into the street Isabel gave me a sidelong smiling glance.

'D'you think you could drink an ice-cream soda?' she asked me.

'I could try,' I answered prudently.

Isabel did not speak till we reached the drugstore, and I, having nothing to say, said nothing. We went in and sat at a table on chairs with twisted wire backs and twisted wire legs. They were very uncomfortable. I ordered two ice-cream sodas. There were a few people at the counters buying; two or three couples were seated at other tables, but they were busy with their own concerns; and to all intents and purposes we were alone. I lit a cigarette and waited while Isabel with every appearance of satisfaction sucked at a long straw. I had a notion that she was nervous.

'I wanted to talk to you,' she said abruptly.

'I gathered that,' I smiled.

For a moment or two she looked at me reflectively.

'Why did you say that about Larry at the Satterthwaites' the night before last?'

'I thought it would interest you. It occurred to me that perhaps you didn't quite know what his idea of loafing was.'

'Uncle Elliott's a terrible gossip. When he said he was going to the Blackstone to have a chat with you I knew he was going to tell you all about everything.'

'I've known him a good many years, you know. He gets a lot of fun out of talking about other people's business.'

'He does,' she smiled. But it was only a gleam. She looked at me steadily and her eyes were serious. 'What do you think of Larry?'

'I've only seen him three times. He seems a very nice boy.'

'Is that all?'

There was a note of distress in her voice.

'No, not quite. It's hard for me to say; you see, I know him so little. Of course, he's attractive. There's something modest and friendly and gentle in him that is very appealing. He's got a lot of self-possession for so young a man. He isn't quite like any of the other boys I've met here.'

While I was thus fumblingly trying to put into words an impression that was not distinct in my own mind, Isabel looked at me intently. When I had finished she gave a little sigh, as if of relief, and then flashed a charming, almost roguish smile at me.

'Uncle Elliott says he's often been surprised at your power of observation. He says nothing much escapes you, but that your great asset as a writer is your common sense.'

'I can think of a quality that would be more valuable,' I answered dryly. 'Talent, for instance.'

'You know, I have no one to talk this over with. Mamma can only see things from her own point of view. She wants my future to be assured.'

'That's natural, isn't it?'

'And Uncle Elliott only looks at it from the social side. My own friends, those of my generation, I mean, think Larry's a washout. It hurts terribly.'

'Of course.'

'It's not that they're not nice to him. One can't help being nice to Larry. But they look upon him as a joke. They josh him a lot and it exasperates them that he doesn't seem to care. He only laughs. You know how things are at present?'

'I only know what Elliott has told me.'

'May I tell you exactly what happened when we went down to Marvin?'

'Of course.'

I have reconstructed Isabel's account partly from my recollection of what she said to me and partly with the help of my imagination. But it was a long talk that she and Larry had, and I have no doubt that they said a great deal more than I now propose to relate. I suspect that as people do on these occasions they not only said much that was irrelevant, but said the same things over and over again.

When Isabel awoke and saw that it was a fine day she gave Larry a ring and, telling him that her mother wanted her to go to Marvin to do something for her, asked him to drive down. She took the precaution to add a thermos of martinis to the thermos of coffee her mother had told Eugene to put in the basket. Larry's roadster was a recent acquisition and he was proud of it. He was a fast driver and the speed at which he went exhilarated them both. When they arrived, Isabel, with Larry to write down the figures, measured the curtains that were to be replaced. Then they set out the luncheon on the stoop. It was sheltered from any wind there was and the sun of the Indian summer was good to bask in. The house, on a dirt road, had none of the elegance of the old frame houses of New England and the best you could say of it was that it was roomy and comfortable, but from the stoop you had a pleasing view of a great red barn with a black roof, a clump of old trees and beyond them, as far as the eye could reach, brown fields. It was a dull landscape, but the sunshine and the glowing tints of the waning year gave it that day an intimate loveliness. There was an exhilaration in the great space that was spread before you. Cold, bleak and dreary as it must have been in winter, dry, sunbaked and oppressive as it may have been in the dog days, just then it was strangely exciting, for the vastness of the view invited the soul to adventure.

They enjoyed their lunch like the healthy young things they were and they were happy to be together. Isabel poured out the coffee and Larry lit his pipe.

'Now go right ahead, darling,' he said, with an amused smile in his eyes.

Isabel was taken aback.

'Go right ahead about what?' she asked with as innocent a look as she could assume.

He chuckled.

'Do you take me for a perfect fool, honey? If your mother didn't know perfectly well the measurements of the living-room windows I'll eat my hat. That isn't why you asked me to drive you down here.'

Recovering her self-assurance, she gave him a brilliant smile.

'It might be that I thought it would be nice if we spent a day together by ourselves.'

'It might be, but I don't think it is. My guess is that Uncle Elliott has told you that I've turned down Henry Maturin's offer.'

He spoke gaily and lightly and she found it convenient to continue in the same tone.

'Gray must be terribly disappointed. He thought it would be grand to have you in the office. You must get down to work some time, and the longer you leave it the harder it'll be.'

He puffed at his pipe and looked at her, tenderly smiling, so that she could not tell if he was serious or not.

'Do you know, I've got an idea that I want to do more with my life than sell bonds.'

'All right then. Go into a law office or study medicine.'

'No, I don't want to do that either.'

'What do you want to do then?'

'Loaf,' he replied calmly.

'Oh, Larry, don't be funny. This is desperately serious.'

Her voice quivered and her eyes filled with tears.

'Don't cry, darling. I don't want to make you miserable.'

He went and sat down beside her and put his arm round her. There was a tenderness in his voice that broke her and she could no longer hold back her tears. But she dried her eyes and forced a smile to her lips.

'It's all very fine to say you don't want to make me miserable. You are making me miserable. You see, I love you.'

'I love you too, Isabel.'

She sighed deeply. Then she disengaged herself from his arm and drew away from him.

'Let's be sensible. A man must work, Larry. It's a matter of self-respect. This is a young country, and it's a man's duty to take part in its activities. Henry Maturin was saying only the other day that we were beginning an era that would make the achievements of the past look like two bits. He said he could see no limit to our progress and he's convinced that by 1930 we shall be the richest and greatest country in the world. Don't you think that's terribly exciting?'

'Terribly.'

'There's never been such a chance for a young man. I should have thought you'd be proud to take part in the work that lies before us. It's such a wonderful adventure.'

He laughed lightly.

'I dare say you're right. The Armours and the Swifts will pack more and better meat, the McCormicks will make more and better harvesters, and Henry Ford will turn out more and better cars. And everyone'll get richer and richer.'

'And why not?'

'As you say, and why not? Money just doesn't happen to interest me.'

Isabel giggled.

'Darling, don't talk like a fool. One can't live without money.'

'I have a little. That's what gives me the chance to do what I want.'

'Loaf?'

'Yes,' he answered, smiling.

'You're making it so difficult for me, Larry,' she sighed.

'I'm sorry. I wouldn't if I could help it.'

'You can help it.'

He shook his head. He was silent for a while, lost in thought. When at last he spoke it was to say something that startled her.

'The dead look so terribly dead when they're dead.'

'What do you mean exactly?' she asked, troubled.

'Just that.' He gave her a rueful smile. 'You have a lot of time to think when you're up in the air by yourself. You get odd ideas.'

'What sort of ideas?'

'Vague,' he said, smiling. 'Incoherent. Confused.'

Isabel thought this over for a while.

'Don't you think if you took a job they might sort themselves out and you'd know where you were?'

'I've thought of that. I had a notion that I might go to work with a carpenter or in a garage.'

'Oh, Larry, people would think you were crazy.'

'Would that matter?'

'To me, yes.'

Once more silence fell upon them. It was she who broke it. She sighed.

'You're so different from what you were before you went out to France.'

'That's not strange. A lot happened to me then, you know.'

'Such as?'

'Oh, just the ordinary casual run of events. My greatest friend in the air corps was killed saving my life. I didn't find that easy to get over.'

'Tell me, Larry.'

He looked at her with deep distress in his eyes.

'I'd rather not talk about it. After all, it was only a trivial incident.'

Emotional by nature, Isabel's eyes again filled with tears.

'Are you unhappy, darling?'

'No,' he answered, smiling. 'The only thing that makes me unhappy is that I'm making you unhappy.' He took her hand and there was something so friendly in the feel of his strong firm hand against hers, something so intimately affectionate, that she had to bite her lips to prevent herself from crying. 'I don't think I shall ever find peace till I make up my mind about things,' he said gravely. He hesitated. 'It's very difficult to put into words. The moment you try you feel embarrassed. You say to yourself: "Who am I that I should bother my head about this, that and the other? Perhaps it's only because I'm a conceited prig. Wouldn't it be better to follow the beaten track and let what's coming to you come?" And then you think of a fellow who an hour before was full of life and fun, and he's lying dead; it's all so cruel and so meaningless. It's hard not to ask yourself what life is all about and whether there's any sense to it or whether it's all a tragic blunder of blind fate.'

It was impossible not to be moved when Larry, with that wonderfully melodious voice of his, spoke, haltingly as though he forced himself to say what he would sooner have left unsaid and yet with such an anguished sincerity; and for a while Isabel did not trust herself to speak.

'Would it help you if you went away for a bit?'

She put the question with a sinking heart. He took a long time to answer.

'I think so. You try to be indifferent to public opinion, but it's not easy. When it's antagonistic it arouses antagonism in you and that disturbs you.'

'Why don't you go then?'

'Well, on account of you.'

'Let's be frank with one another, darling. There's no place for me in your life just now.'

'Does that mean you don't want to be engaged to me any more?'

She forced a smile to her trembling lips.

'No, foolish, it means I'm prepared to wait.'

'It may be a year. It may be two.'

'That's all right. It may be less. Where'd you want to go?'

He looked at her intently as though he were trying to see into her inmost heart. She smiled lightly to hide her deep distress.

'Well, I thought I'd start by going to Paris. I know no one there. There'd be no one to interfere with me. I went to Paris several times on leave. I don't know why, but I've got it into my head that there everything that's muddled in my mind would grow clear. It's a funny place, it gives you the feeling that there you can think out your thoughts to the end without let or hindrance. I think there I may be able to see my way before me.'

'And what's to happen if you don't?'

He chuckled.

'Then I shall fall back on my good American horse sense, give it up as a bad job and come back to Chicago and take any work I can get.'

The scene had affected Isabel too much for her to be able to tell it to me without getting somewhat emotional, and when she finished she looked at me pitifully.

'Do you think I did right?'

'I think you did the only thing you could do, but what's more I think you've been wonderfully kind, generous and understanding.'

'I love him and I want him to be happy. And you know, in a way I'm not sorry he should go. I want him to be out of this hostile atmosphere, and that not only for his sake, but for mine too. I can't blame people when they say he'll never amount to anything; I hate them for it, and yet all the time deep down in me I have an awful fear that they're right. But don't say I'm understanding. I don't begin to understand what he's after.'

'Perhaps you understand with your heart rather than with your reason,' I smiled. 'Why don't you marry him right away and go off to Paris with him?'

The shadow of a smile came into her eyes.

'There's nothing I'd like to do more. But I couldn't. And you know, though I hate to acknowledge it, I do really think he's better off without me. If Dr Nelson is right and he's suffering from delayed shock surely new surroundings and new interests will cure him, and when he's got his balance again he'll come back to Chicago and go into business like everybody else. I wouldn't want to marry an idler.'

Isabel had been brought up in a certain way and she accepted the principles that had been instilled into her. She did not think of money, because she had never known what it was not to have all she needed, but she was instinctively aware of its importance. It meant power, influence and social consequence. It was the natural and obvious thing that a man should earn it. That was his plain life's work.

'It doesn't surprise me that you don't understand Larry,' I said, 'because I'm pretty sure he doesn't understand himself. If he's reticent about his aims it may be that it's because they're obscure to him. Mind you, I hardly know him and this is only guesswork: isn't it possible that he's looking for something, but what it is he doesn't know, and perhaps he isn't even sure it's there? Perhaps whatever it is that happened to him during the war has left him with a restlessness that won't let him be. Don't you think he may be pursuing an ideal that is hidden in a cloud of unknowing—like an astronomer looking for a star that only a mathematical calculation tells him exists?'

'I feel that something's troubling him.'

'His soul? It may be that he's a little frightened of himself. It may be that he has no confidence in the authenticity of the vision that he dimly perceives in his mind's eye.'

'He gives me such an odd impression sometimes; he gives me the impression of a sleep-walker who's suddenly wakened in a strange place and can't think where he is. He was so normal before the war. One of the nice things about him was his enormous zest for life. He was so scatter-brained and gay, it was wonderful to be with him; he was so sweet and ridiculous. What can have happened to change him so much?'

'I wouldn't know. Sometimes a very small thing will have an effect on you out of all proportion to the event. It depends on the circumstances and your mood at the time. I remember going to mass on All Saints' Day, which the French called the Day of the Dead, in a village church that the Germans had knocked about a bit on their first advance into France. It was filled with soldiers and with women in black. In the graveyard were rows of little wooden crosses and as the sad, solemn service went on, and women wept and men too, I had a feeling that perhaps those men who lay under the little crosses were better off than we who lived. I told a friend what I felt and he asked me what I meant. I couldn't explain and I saw that he thought me a perfect damned fool. And I remember after a battle seeing a pile of dead French soldiers heaped upon one another. They looked like the marionettes in a bankrupt puppet show that had been cast pell-mell into a dusty corner because they were of no use any more. I thought then just what Larry said to you: the dead look so awfully dead.'

I do not want the reader to think I am making a mystery of whatever it was that happened to Larry during the war that so profoundly affected him, a mystery that I shall disclose at a convenient moment. I don't think he ever told anybody. He did, however, many years later tell a woman, Suzanne Rouvier, whom Larry and I both knew, about the young airman who had met his death saving his life. She repeated it to me and so I can only relate it at second hand. I have translated it from her French. Larry had apparently struck up a great friendship with another boy in his squadron. Suzanne knew him only by the ironical nickname by which Larry spoke of him.

'He was a little chap with red hair, an Irishman. We used to call him Patsy,' Larry said, 'and he had more vitality than anyone I've ever known. Gosh, he was a live wire. He had a funny face and a funny grin, so that it made you laugh just to look at him. He was a harum-scarum devil and he'd do the craziest things; he was always getting hell from the higher-ups. He was absolutely without fear and when he'd escaped death by a hair's breadth he'd grin all over his face as if it was the best joke in the world. But he was a natural-born flyer and up in the air he was cool and wary. He taught me a lot. He was a bit older than me and he took me under his wing; it was rather comic really, because I was a good six inches taller than he was and if it had come to a scrap I could have knocked him out cold. Once in Paris when he was drunk and I was afraid he was going to get into trouble I did.

'I felt a bit out of it when I joined the squadron and I was afraid I wouldn't make good, but he just joshed me into having confidence in myself. He was funny about the war, he had no feeling of hatred for the Jerries; he loved a scrap and to fight them tickled him to death. He simply couldn't look upon bringing down one of their planes as anything but a practical joke. He was impudent and wild and irresponsible, but there was something so genuine about him that you couldn't help liking him. He'd give you his last penny as freely as he'd take yours. And if you were lonely or homesick or scared, and I was sometimes, he'd see it and with his ugly little face puckered up with laughter he'd say just the right thing to make you feel all right again.'

Larry puffed at his pipe and Suzanne waited for him to go on.

'We used to wangle it so that we could get our leave together, and when we were in Paris he went wild. We had a grand time. We were due for a spot of leave early in March, in 'eighteen that was, and we made our plans beforehand. There wasn't a thing we weren't going to do. The day before we were to go we were sent up to fly over the enemy lines and bring back reports of what we saw. Suddenly we came bang up against some German planes, and before we knew where we were we were in the middle of a dogfight. One of them came after me, but I got in first. I took a look to see if he was going to crash and then out of the corner of my eye I saw another plane on my tail. I dived to get away from him, but he was on to me like a flash and I thought I was done for; then I saw Patsy come down on him like a streak of lightning and give him all he'd got. They'd had enough and sheered off and we made for home. My machine had got pretty well knocked about and I only just made it. Patsy got in before me. When I got out of my plane they'd just got him out of his. He was lying on the ground and they were waiting for the ambulance to come up. When he saw me he grinned.

'"I got that blighter who was on your tail," he said.

'"What's the matter, Patsy?" I asked.

'"Oh, it's nothing. He winged me."

'He was looking deathly white. Suddenly a strange look came over his face. It had just come to him that he was dying, and the possibility of death had never so much as crossed his mind. Before they could stop him he sat up and gave a laugh.

'"Well, I'm jiggered," he said.

'He fell back dead. He was twenty-two. He was going to marry a girl in Ireland after the war.'

The day after my talk with Isabel I left Chicago for San Francisco, where I was to take ship for the Far East.

Chapter Two

One

I did not see Elliott till he came to London towards the end of June in the following year. I asked him whether Larry had after all gone to Paris. He had. I was faintly amused at Elliott's exasperation with him.

'I had a kind of sneaking sympathy for the boy. I couldn't blame him for wanting to spend a couple of years in Paris and I was prepared to launch him. I told him to let me know the moment he arrived, but it was only when Louisa wrote and told me he was there that I knew he'd come. I wrote to him care of the American Express, which was the address she gave me, and asked him to come and dine to meet some of the people I thought he ought to know; I thought I'd try him out first with the Franco-American set, Emily de Montadour and Gracie de Château-Gaillard and so on, and d'you know what he answered? He said he was sorry he couldn't come, but he hadn't brought any evening clothes with him.'

Elliott looked me full in the face to see the stupefaction with which he expected this communication to fill me. He raised a supercilious eyebrow when he observed that I took it with calm.

'He replied to my letter on a sheet of nasty paper with the heading of a café in the Latin Quarter and when I wrote back I asked him to let me know where he was staying. I felt I must do something about him for Isabel's sake, and I thought perhaps he was shy–I mean I couldn't believe that any young fellow in his senses could come to Paris without evening clothes, and in any case there are tolerable tailors there, so I asked him to lunch and said it would be quite a small party, and would you believe it, not only did he ignore my request to give me some other address than the American Express, but he said he never ate luncheon. That finished him as far as I was concerned.'

'I wonder what he's been doing with himself.'

'I don't know, and to tell you the truth I don't care. I'm afraid he's a thoroughly undesirable young man and I think it would be a great mistake for Isabel to marry him. After all, if he led a normal sort of life I'd have run across him at the Ritz bar or at Fouquet's or somewhere.'

I go sometimes to these fashionable places myself, but I go to others also, and it happened that I spent several days in Paris early in the autumn of that year on my way to Marseilles, where I was proposing to take one of the Messagerie ships for Singapore. I dined one evening with friends in Montparnasse and after dinner we went to the Dôme to drink a glass of beer. Presently my wandering eye caught sight of Larry sitting by himself at a little marble-topped table on the crowded terrace. He was looking idly at the people who strolled up and down enjoying the coolness of the night after a sultry day. I left my party and went up to him. His face lit up when he saw me and he gave me an engaging smile. He asked me to sit down, but I said I couldn't as I was with a party.

'I just wanted to say how d'you do to you,' I said.

'Are you staying here?' he asked.

'Only for a very few days.'

'Will you lunch with me tomorrow?'

'I thought you never lunched.'

He chuckled.

'You've seen Elliott. I don't generally, I can't afford the time, I just have a glass of milk and a brioche, but I'd like you to lunch with me.'

'All right.'

We arranged to meet at the Dôme next day to have an apéritif and eat at some place on the boulevard. I rejoined my friends. We sat on talking. When next I looked for Larry he had gone.

Two

I spent the next morning very pleasantly. I went to the Luxembourg and passed an hour looking at some pictures I liked. Then I strolled in the gardens, recapturing the memories of my youth. Nothing had changed. They might have been the same students who walked along the gravel paths in pairs, eagerly discussing the writers who excited them. They might have been the same children who trundled the same hoops under the watchful eyes of the same nurses. They might have been the same old men who basked in the sunshine, reading the morning paper. They might have been the same middle-aged women in mourning who sat on the free benches and gossiped with one another about the price of food and the misdeeds of servants. Then I went to the Odéon and looked at the new books in the galleries and I saw the lads who like myself thirty years before were trying under the petulant eyes of the smock-frocked attendants to read as much as they could of books they could not afford to buy. Then I strolled leisurely along those dear, dingy streets till I came to the Boulevard du Montparnasse and so to the Dôme. Larry was waiting. We had a drink and walked along to a restaurant where we could lunch in the open air.

He was perhaps a little paler than I remembered him and this made his very dark eyes, in their deep orbits, more striking; but he had the same self-possession, curious in one so young, and the same ingenuous smile. When he ordered his lunch I noticed that he spoke French fluently and with a good accent. I congratulated him on it.

'I knew a certain amount of French before, you know,' he explained. 'Aunt Louisa had a French governess for Isabel, and when they were at Marvin she used to make us talk French with her all the time.'

I asked him how he liked Paris.

'Very much.'

'D'you live in Montparnasse?'

'Yes,' he said, after a moment's hesitation which I interpreted into a disinclination to tell exactly where he lived.

'Elliott was rather put out that the only address you gave was the American Express.'

Larry smiled but did not answer.

'What do you do with yourself all the time?'

'I loaf.'

'And you read?'

'Yes, I read.'

'Do you ever hear from Isabel?'

'Sometimes. We're neither of us great letter-writers. She's having a grand time in Chicago. They're coming over next year to stay with Elliott.'

'That'll be nice for you.'

'I don't believe Isabel's ever been to Paris. It'll be fun taking her around.'

He was curious to know about my journey in China and listened attentively to what I told him; but when I tried to get him to talk about himself, I failed. He was so uncommunicative that I was forced to the conclusion that he had asked me to lunch with him merely to enjoy my company. I was pleased, but baffled. We had no sooner finished our coffee than he called for the bill, paid it and got up.

'Well, I must be off,' he said.

We parted. I knew no more of what he was up to than before. I did not see him again.

Three

I was not in Paris in the spring when, sooner than they had planned, Mrs Bradley and Isabel arrived to stay with Elliott; and again I have to eke out my knowledge of what passed during the few weeks they spent there by the exercise of my imagination. They landed at Cherbourg and Elliott, always considerate, went to meet them. They passed through the customs. The train started. Elliott with some complacency told them that he had engaged a very good lady's maid to look after them and when Mrs Bradley said that was quite unnecessary, since they didn't need one, he was very sharp with her.

'Don't be tiresome the moment you arrive, Louisa. No one can be well turned out without a maid, and I've engaged Antoinette not only for your sake and Isabel's but for mine. It would mortify me that you shouldn't be perfectly dressed.'

He gave the clothes they were wearing a disparaging glance.

'Of course you'll want to buy some new frocks. On mature consideration I've come to the conclusion that you can't do better than Chanel.'

'I always used to go to Worth,' said Mrs Bradley.

She might as well not have spoken, for he took no notice.

'I've talked to Chanel myself and I've made an appointment for you tomorrow at three. Then there are hats. Obviously Reboux.'

'I don't want to spend a lot of money, Elliott.'

'I know. I am proposing to pay for everything myself. I'm determined that you shall be a credit to me. Oh, and Louisa, I've arranged several parties for you and I've told my French friends that Myron was an ambassador, which, of course, he would have been if he'd lived a little longer, and it makes a better effect. I don't suppose it'll come up, but I thought I'd better warn you.'

'You're ridiculous, Elliott.'

'No, I'm not. I know the world. I know that the widow of an ambassador has more prestige than the widow of a minister.'

As the train steamed into the Gare du Nord, Isabel, who was standing at the window, called out:

'There's Larry.'

It had hardly stopped when she sprang out and ran to meet him. He threw his arms around her.

'How did he know you were coming?' Elliott asked his sister acidly.

'Isabel wirelessed him from the ship.'

Mrs Bradley kissed him affectionately, and Elliott gave him a limp hand to shake. It was ten o'clock at night.

'Uncle Elliott, can Larry come to lunch tomorrow?' cried Isabel, her arm in the young man's, her face eager and her eyes shining.

'I should be charmed, but Larry has given me to understand that he doesn't eat lunch.'

'He will tomorrow, won't you, Larry?'

'I will,' he smiled.

'I shall look forward to seeing you at one o'clock then.'

He stretched out his hand once more, intending to dismiss him, but Larry grinned at him impudently.

'I'll help with the luggage and get a cab for you.'

'My car is waiting and my man will see to the luggage,' said Elliott with dignity.

'That's fine. Then all we've got to do is to go. If there's room for me I'll come as far as your door with you.'

'Yes, do, Larry,' said Isabel.

They walked down the platform together, followed by Mrs Bradley and Elliott. Elliott's face bore a look of frigid disapproval.

'*Quelles manières*,' he said to himself, for in certain circumstances he felt he could express his sentiments more forcibly in French.

Next morning at eleven, having finished dressing, for he was not an early riser, he sent a note to his sister, via his man Joseph and her maid Antoinette, to ask her to come to the library so that they could have a talk. When she appeared he closed the door carefully and, putting a cigarette into an immensely long agate holder, lit it and sat down.

'Am I to understand that Isabel and Larry are still engaged?' he asked.

'So far as I know.'

'I'm afraid I haven't a very good account to give you of the young man.' He told her then how he had been prepared to launch him in society and the plans he had made to establish him in a fit and proper manner. 'I even had my eye on a *rez-de-chaussée* that would have been the very thing for him. It belongs to the young Marquis de Rethel and he wanted to sublet it because he'd been appointed to the embassy at Madrid.'

But Larry had refused his invitations in a manner that made it quite clear that he did not want his help.

'What the object of coming to Paris is if you're not going to take advantage of what Paris has to give you is beyond my comprehension. I don't know what he does with himself. He doesn't seem to know anybody. Do you know where he lives?'

'The only address we've ever had is the American Express.'

'Like a travelling salesman or a school-teacher on vacation. I shouldn't be surprised if he was living with some little trollop in a studio in Montmarte.'

'Oh, Elliott.'

'What other explanation can there be for the mystery he's making of his dwelling place and for his refusal to consort with people of his own class?'

'It doesn't sound like Larry. And last night, didn't you get the impression that he was just as much in love with Isabel as ever? He couldn't be so false.'

Elliott by a shrug of the shoulders gave her to understand that there was no limit to the duplicity of men.

'What about Gray Maturin? Is he still in the picture?'

'He'd marry Isabel tomorrow if she'd have him.'

Mrs Bradley told him then why they had to come to Europe sooner than they had at first intended. She had found herself in ill-health, and the doctors had informed her that she was suffering from diabetes. It was not serious, and by attention to her diet and taking moderate doses of insulin there was no reason why she should not live for a good many years, but the knowledge that she had an incurable disease made her anxious to see Isabel settled. They had talked the matter over. Isabel was sensible. She had agreed that if Larry refused to come back to Chicago at the end of the two years in Paris they had agreed upon and get a job, there was only one thing to do and that was to break with him. But it offended Mrs Bradley's sense of personal dignity that they should wait till the appointed time and then come to fetch him, like a fugitive from justice, back to his own country. She felt that Isabel would put herself in a humiliating position. But it was very natural that they should spend the summer in Europe, where Isabel had not been since she was a child. After their visit in Paris they could go to some watering-place suitable to Mrs Bradley's complaint, then on to the Austrian Tyrol for a while and from there travel slowly through Italy. Mrs Bradley's intention was to ask Larry to accompany them, so that he and Isabel could see whether the long separation had left their feelings unchanged. It would be manifest in due course whether Larry, having had his fling, was prepared to accept the responsibilities of life.

'Henry Maturin was sore with him for turning down the position he offered him, but Gray has talked him round, and he can go into the business the moment he comes back to Chicago.'

'Gray's a very nice fellow.'

'He certainly is.' Mrs Bradley sighed. 'I know he'd make Isabel happy.'

Elliott then told her what parties he had arranged for them. He was giving a big luncheon on the following day and at the end of the week a grand dinner party. He was taking them to a reception at the Château-Gaillards and he had got cards for them to a ball that the Rothschilds were giving.

'You'll ask Larry, won't you?'

'He tells me he hasn't any evening clothes,' Elliott sniffed.

'Well, ask him all the same. After all, he is a nice boy, and it wouldn't help to give him the cold shoulder. It would only make Isabel obstinate.'

'Of course I'll ask him if you wish it.'

Larry came to lunch at the appointed time, and Elliott, whose manners were admirable, was pointedly cordial to him. It was not difficult, since Larry was so gay, in such high spirits that it would have needed a much more ill-natured man than Elliott not to be charmed by him. The conversation dealt with Chicago and their common friends there, so that there was not much for Elliott to do other than to look amiable and pretend to be interested in the concerns of persons whom he thought of no social consequence. He did not mind listening; indeed, he thought it rather touching to hear them tell of this young couple's engagement, that young couple's marriage, and another young couple's divorce. Who had ever heard of them? *He* knew that that pretty little Marquise de Clinchant had tried to poison herself because her lover, the Prince de Colombey, had left her to marry the daughter of a South American millionaire. That was something to talk about. Looking at Larry, he was obliged to admit that there was something peculiarly attractive in him; with his deep-set strangely black eyes, his high cheekbones, pale skin and mobile mouth he reminded Elliott of a portrait by Botticelli, and it occurred to him that if he were dressed in the costume of the period he would look extravagantly romantic. He remembered his notion of getting him off with a distinguished Frenchwoman and he smiled slyly on reflecting that he was expecting at dinner on Saturday Marie Louise de Florimond, who combined irreproachable connections with notorious immorality. She was forty, but looked ten years younger; she had the delicate beauty of her ancestress painted by Nattier which, owing to Elliott himself, now hung in one of the great American collections; and her sexual voracity was insatiable. Elliott decided to put Larry next to her. He knew she would waste no time in making her desires clear to him. He had already invited a young attaché at the British Embassy whom he thought Isabel might like. Isabel was very pretty, and as he was an Englishman, and well off, it wouldn't matter that she had no fortune. Mellowed by the excellent Montrachet with which they had started lunch and by the fine Bordeaux that followed, Elliott thought with tranquil pleasure of the possibilities that presented themselves to his mind. If things turned out as he thought they very well might, dear Louisa would have no more cause for anxiety. She had always slightly disapproved of him; poor dear, she was very provincial; but he was fond of her. It would be a satisfaction to him to arrange everything for her by help of his knowledge of the world.

To waste no time, Elliott had arranged to take his ladies to look at clothes immediately after lunch, so as they got up from the table he intimated to Larry with the tact of which he was a master that he must make himself scarce, but at the same time he asked him with pressing affability to come to the two grand parties he had arranged. He need hardly have taken so much trouble, since Larry accepted both invitations with alacrity.

But Elliott's plan failed. He was relieved when Larry appeared at the dinner party in a very presentable dinner-jacket, for he had been a little nervous that he would wear the same blue suit that he had worn at lunch; and after dinner, getting Marie Louise de Florimond into a corner, he asked her how she had liked his young American friend.

'He has nice eyes and good teeth.'

'Is that all? I put him beside you because I thought he was just your cup of tea.'

She looked at him suspiciously.

'He told me he was engaged to your pretty niece.'

'*Voyons, ma chère*, the fact that a man belongs to another woman has never prevented you from taking him away from her if you could.'

'Is that what you want me to do? Well, I'm not going to do your dirty work for you, my poor Elliott.'

Elliott chuckled.

'The meaning of that, I presume, is that you tried your stuff and found there was nothing doing.'

'Why I like you, Elliott, is that you have the morals of a bawdy-house keeper. You don't want him to marry your niece. Why not? He is well bred and quite charming. But he's really too innocent. I don't think he had the least suspicion of what I meant.'

'You should have been more explicit, dear friend.'

'I have enough experience to know when I'm wasting my time. The fact is that he has eyes only for your little Isabel, and between you and me, she has twenty years advantage over me. And she's sweet.'

'Do you like her dress? I chose it for her myself.'

'It's pretty and it's suitable. But of course she has no chic.'

Elliott took this as a reflection on himself, and he was not prepared to let Madame de Florimond get away without a dig. He smiled genially.

'One has to have reached your ripe maturity to have your chic, dear friend,' he said.

Madame de Florimond wielded a bludgeon rather than a rapier. Her retort made Elliott's Virginian blood boil.

'But I'm sure that in your fair land of gangsters [*vôtre beau pays d'apaches*] they will hardly miss something that is so subtle and so inimitable.'

But if Madame de Florimond carped, the rest of Elliott's friends were delighted both with Isabel and with Larry. They liked her fresh prettiness, her abounding health and her vitality; they liked his picturesque appearance, his good manners and his quiet, ironic humour. Both had the advantage of speaking good and fluent French. Mrs Bradley, after living so many years in diplomatic circles, spoke it correctly enough but with an unabashed American accent. Elliott entertained them lavishly. Isabel, pleased with her new clothes and her new hats, amused by all the gaiety Elliott provided and happy to be with Larry, thought she had never enjoyed herself so much.

Four

Elliott was of opinion that breakfast was a meal that you should share only with total strangers, and then only if there was no help for it, so Mrs Bradley, somewhat against her will, and Isabel, far from displeased, were obliged to have theirs in their bedrooms. But Isabel, when she awoke, sometimes told Antoinette the grand maid Elliott had engaged for them, to take her *café au lait* into her mother's room so that she could talk to her while she had it. In the busy life she led it was the only moment of the day in which she could be alone with her. One such morning, when they had been in Paris nearly a month, after Isabel had done narrating the events of the previous night, most of which she and Larry had spent going the round of the night clubs with a party of friends, Mrs Bradley let fall the question she had had in mind to ask ever since their arrival.

'When is he coming back to Chicago?'

'I don't know. He hasn't spoken of it.'

'Haven't you asked him?'

'No.'

'Are you scared to?'

'No, of course not.'

Mrs Bradley, lying on a chaise longue, in a modish dressing-gown that Elliott had insisted on giving her, was polishing her nails.

'What do you talk about all the time when you're alone?'

'We don't talk all the time. It's nice to be together. You know, Larry was always rather silent. When we talk I think I do most of the talking.'

'What had he been doing with himself?'

'I don't really know. I don't think anything very much. I suppose he's been having a good time.'

'And where is he living?'

'I don't know that either.'

'He seems very reticent, doesn't he?'

Isabel lit a cigarette and, as she blew a cloud of smoke from her nostrils, looked coolly at her mother.

'What exactly do you mean by that, Mamma?'

'Your uncle Elliott thinks he has an apartment and is living there with a woman.'

Isabel burst out laughing.

'You don't believe that, do you?'

'No. I honestly don't.' Mrs Bradley looked reflectively at her nails. 'Don't you ever talk to him about Chicago?'

'Yes, a lot.'

'Hasn't he given any sort of indication that he intends to come back?'

'I can't say he has.'

'He will have been gone two years next October.'

'I know.'

'Well, it's your business, dear, and you must do what you think right. But things don't get any easier by putting them off.' She glanced at her daughter, but Isabel would not meet her eyes. Mrs Bradley gave her an affectionate smile. 'If you don't want to be late for lunch you'd better go and have your bath.'

'I'm lunching with Larry. We're going to some place in the Latin Quarter.'

'Enjoy yourself.'

An hour later Larry came to fetch her. They took a cab to the Pont St Michel and sauntered up the crowded boulevard till they came to a café they liked the look of. They sat down on the terrace and ordered a couple of Dubonnets. Then they took another cab and went to a restaurant. Isabel had a healthy appetite and she enjoyed the good things Larry ordered for her. She enjoyed looking at the people sitting cheek by jowl with them, for the place was packed, and it made her laugh to see the intense pleasure they so obviously took in their food; but she enjoyed above all sitting at a tiny table alone with Larry. She loved the amusement in his eyes while she chattered away gaily. It was enchanting to feel so much at home with him. But at the back of her mind was a vague disquiet, for though he seemed very much at home too, she felt it was not so much with her as with the surroundings. She had been faintly disturbed by what her mother had said, and though seeming to prattle so guilelessly she observed his every expression. He was not quite the same as when he had left Chicago, but she couldn't tell in what the difference lay. He looked exactly as she remembered him, as young, as frank, but his expression was changed. It was not that he was more serious, his face in repose had always been serious, it had a calmness that was new to her; it was as though he had settled something with himself and were at ease in a way he had never been before.

When they had finished lunch he suggested that they should take a stroll through the Luxembourg.

'No, I don't want to go and look at pictures.'

'All right then, let's go and sit in the gardens.'

'No, I don't want to do that either. I want to go and see where you live.'

'There's nothing to see. I live in a scrubby little room in a hotel.'

'Uncle Elliott says you've got an apartment and are living in sin with an artist's model.'

'Come on then and see for yourself,' he laughed. 'It's only a step from here. We can walk.'

He took her through narrow, tortuous streets, dingy notwithstanding the streak of blue sky that showed between the high houses, and after a while stopped at a small hotel with a pretentious façade.

'Here we are.'

Isabel followed him into a narrow hall, on one side of which was a desk and behind it a man in shirt-sleeves, with a waistcoat in thin black and yellow stripes and a dirty apron, reading a paper. Larry asked for his key, and the man handed it to him from the rack immediately behind him. He gave Isabel an inquisitive glance that turned into a knowing smirk. It was clear that he thought she was going to Larry's room for no honest purpose.

They climbed up two flights of stairs, on which was a threadbare red carpet, and Larry unlocked his door. Isabel entered a smallish room with two windows. They looked out on the grey apartment house opposite, on the ground floor of which was a stationer's shop. There was a single bed in the room, with a night table beside it, a heavy wardrobe with a large mirror, an upholstered but straight-backed armchair and a table between the windows on which were a typewriter, papers and a number of books. The chimney-piece was piled with paper-bound volumes.

'You sit in the armchair. It's not very comfortable, but it's the best I can offer.'

He drew up another chair and sat down.

'Is this where you live?' asked Isabel.

He chuckled at the look on her face.

'It is. I've been here ever since I came to Paris.'

'But why?'

'It's convenient. It's near the Bibliothèque Nationale and the Sorbonne.' He pointed to a door she had not noticed. 'It's got a bathroom. I can get breakfast here and I generally dine at that restaurant where we had lunch.'

'It's awfully sordid.'

'Oh no, it's all right. It's all I want.'

'But what sort of people live here?'

'Oh, I don't know. Up in the attics a few students. Two or three old bachelors in government offices and a retired actress at the Odéon; the only other room with a bath is occupied by a kept woman whose gentleman friend comes to see her every other Thursday; I suppose a few transients. It's a very quiet and respectable place.'

Isabel was a trifle disconcerted and because she knew Larry noticed it and was amused she was half inclined to take offence.

'What's that great big book on the table?' she asked.

'That? Oh, that's my Greek dictionary.'

'Your what?' she cried.

'It's all right. It won't bite you.'

'Are you learning Greek?'

'Yes.'

'Why?'

'I thought I'd like to.'

He was looking at her with a smile in his eyes and she smiled back at him.

'Don't you think you might tell me what you've been up to all the time you've been in Paris?'

'I've been reading a good deal. Eight or ten hours a day. I've attended lectures at the Sorbonne. I think I've read everything that's important in French literature and I can read Latin, at least Latin prose, almost as easily as I can read French. Of course Greek's more difficult. But I have a very good teacher. Until you came here I used to go to him three evenings a week.'

'And what is that going to lead to?'

'The acquisition of knowledge,' he smiled.

'It doesn't sound very practical.'

'Perhaps it isn't and on the other hand perhaps it is. But it's enormous fun. You can't imagine what a thrill it is to read the *Odyssey* in the original. It makes you feel as if you only had to get on tiptoe and stretch out your hands to touch the stars.'

He got up from his chair, as though impelled by an excitement that seized him, and walked up and down the small room.

'I've been reading Spinoza the last month or two. I don't suppose I understand very much of it yet, but it fills me with exultation. It's like landing from your plane on a great plateau in the mountains. Solitude, and an air so pure that it goes to your head like wine and you feel like a million dollars.'

'When are you coming back to Chicago?'

'Chicago? I don't know. I haven't thought of it.'

'You said that if you hadn't got what you wanted after two years you'd give it up as a bad job.'

'I couldn't go back now. I'm on the threshold. I see vast lands of the spirit stretching out before me, beckoning, and I'm eager to travel them.'

'What do you expect to find in them?'

'The answers to my questions.' He gave her a glance that was almost playful, so that except that she knew him so well, she might have thought he was speaking in jest. 'I want to make up my mind whether God is or God is not. I want to find out why evil exists. I want to know whether I have an immortal soul or whether when I die it's the end.'

Isabel gave a little gasp. It made her uncomfortable to hear Larry say such things, and she was thankful that he spoke so lightly, in the tone of ordinary conversation, that it was possible for her to overcome her embarrassment.

'But Larry,' she smiled. 'People have been asking those questions for thousands of years. If they could be answered, surely they'd have been answered by now.'

Larry chuckled.

'Don't laugh as if I'd said something idiotic,' she said sharply.

'On the contrary I think you've said something shrewd. But on the other hand you might say that if men have been asking them for thousands of years it proves that they can't help asking them and have to go on asking them. Besides, it's not true that no one has found the answers. There are more answers than questions, and lots of people have found answers that were perfectly satisfactory for them. Old Ruysbroek for instance.'

'Who was he?'

'Oh, just a guy I didn't know at college,' Larry answered flippantly.

Isabel didn't know what he meant, but passed on.

'It all sounds so adolescent to me. Those are the sort of things sophomores get excited about and then when they leave college they forget about them. They have to earn a living.'

'I don't blame them. You see, I'm in the happy position that I have enough to live on. If I hadn't I'd have had to do like everybody else and make money.'

'But doesn't money mean anything to you?'

'Not a thing,' he grinned.

'How long d'you think all this is going to take you?'

'I wouldn't know. Five years. Ten years.'

'And after that? What are you going to do with all this wisdom?'

'If I ever acquire wisdom I suppose I shall be wise enough to know what to do with it.'

Isabel clasped her hands passionately and leant forwards in her chair.

'You're so wrong, Larry. You're an American. Your place isn't here. Your place is in America.'

'I shall come back when I'm ready.'

'But you're missing so much. How can you bear to sit here in a backwater just when we're living through the most wonderful adventure the world has ever known? Europe's finished. We're the greatest, the most powerful people in the world. We're going forward by leaps and bounds. We've got everything. It's your duty to take part in the development of your country. You've forgotten, you don't know how thrilling life is in America today. Are you sure you're not doing this because you haven't the courage to stand up to the work that's before every American now? Oh, I know you're working in a way, but isn't it just an escape from your responsibilities? Is it more than just a sort of laborious idleness? What would happen to America if everyone shirked as you're shirking?'

'You're very severe, honey,' he smiled. 'The answer to that is that everyone doesn't feel like me. Fortunately for themselves, perhaps, most people are prepared to follow the normal course; what you forget is that I want to learn as passionately as—Gray, for instance, wants to make pots of money. Am I really a traitor to my country because I want to spend a few years educating myself? It may be that when I'm through I shall have something to give that people will be glad to take. It's only a chance, of course, but if I fail I shall be no worse off than a man who's gone into business and hasn't made a go of it.'

'And what about me? Am I of no importance to you at all?'

'You're of very great importance. I want you to marry me.'

'When? In ten years?'

'No. Now. As soon as possible.'

'On what? Mamma can't afford to give me anything. Besides, she wouldn't if she could. She'd think it wrong to help you to live without doing anything.'

'I wouldn't want to take anything from your mother,' said Larry. 'I've got three thousand a year. That's plenty in Paris. We could have a little apartment and a *bonne à tout faire*. We'd have such a lark, darling.'

'But, Larry, one can't live on three thousand a year.'

'Of course one can. Lots of people live on much less.'

'But I don't want to live on three thousand a year. There's no reason why I should.'

'I've been living on half that.'

'But how!'

She looked at the dingy little room with a shudder of distaste.

'It means I've got a bit saved up. We could go down to Capri for our honeymoon and then in the fall we'd go to Greece. I'm crazy to go there. Don't you remember how we used to talk about travelling all over the world together?'

'Of course I want to travel. But not like that. I don't want to travel second-class on steamships and put up at third-rate hotels, without a bathroom, and eat at cheap restaurants.'

'I went all through Italy last October like that. I had a wonderful time. We could travel all over the world on three thousand a year.'

'But I want to have babies, Larry.'

'That's all right. We'd take them along with us.'

'You're so silly,' she laughed. 'D'you know what it costs to have a baby? Violet Tomlinson had one last year and she did it as cheaply as she could and it cost her twelve hundred and fifty. And what d'you think a nurse costs?' She grew more vehement as one idea after another occurred to her. 'You're so impractical. You don't know what you're asking me to do. I'm young, I want to have fun. I want to do all the things that people do. I want to go to parties, I want to go to dances, I want to play golf and ride horseback. I want to wear nice clothes. Can't you imagine what it means to a girl not to be as well dressed as the rest of her crowd? D'you know what it means, Larry, to buy your friends' old dresses when they're sick of them and be thankful when someone out of pity makes you a present of a new one? I couldn't even afford to go to a decent hairdresser to have my hair properly done. I don't want to go about in street-cars and omnibuses; I want to have my own car. And what d'you supqose I'd find to do with myself all day long while you were reading at the Library? Walk about the streets window-shopping or sit in the Luxembourg Garden seeing that my children didn't get into mischief? We wouldn't have any friends.'

'Oh, Isabel,' he interrupted.

'Not the sort of friends I'm used to. Oh yes, Uncle Elliott's friends would ask us now and then for his sake, but we couldn't go because we couldn't afford to return their hospitality. I don't want to know a lot of scrubby, unwashed people; I've got nothing to say to them and they've got nothing to say to me. I want to live, Larry.' She grew suddenly conscious of the look in his eyes, tender as it always was when fixed on her, but gently amused. You think I'm silly, don't you? You think I'm being trivial and horrid.'

'No, I don't. I think what you say is very natural.'

He was standing with his back to the fireplace, and she got up and went up to him so that they were face to face.

'Larry, if you hadn't a cent to your name and got a job that brought you in three thousand a year I'd marry you without a minute's hesitation. I'd cook for you, I'd make the beds, I wouldn't care what I wore, I'd go without anything, I'd look upon it as wonderful fun, because I'd know that it was only a question of time and you'd make good. But this means living in a sordid beastly way all our lives with nothing to look forward to. It means that I should be a drudge to the day of my death. And for what? So that you can spend years trying to find answers to questions that you say yourself are insoluble. It's so wrong. A man ought to work. That's what he's here for. That's how he contributes to the welfare of the community.'

'In short it's his duty to settle down in Chicago and enter Henry Maturin's business. Do you think that by getting my friends to buy the securities that Henry Maturin is interested in I should add greatly to the welfare of the community?'

'There must be brokers and it's a perfectly decent and honourable way of earning a living.'

'You've drawn a very black picture of life in Paris on a moderate income. You know, it isn't really like that. One can dress very nicely without going to Chanel. And all the interesting people don't live in the neighbourhood of the Arc de Triomphe and the Avenue Foch. In fact few interesting people do, because interesting people generally don't have a lot of money. I know quite a number of people here, painters and writers and students, French, English, American, and what not whom I think you'd find much more amusing than Elliott's seedy marquises and long-nosed duchesses. You've got a quick mind and a lively sense of humour. You'd enjoy hearing them swap ideas across the dinner table even though the wine was only *vin ordinaire* and you didn't have a butler and a couple of footmen to wait on you.'

'Don't be stupid, Larry. Of course I would. You know I'm not a snob. I'd love to meet interesting people.'

'Yes, in a Chanel dress. D'you think they wouldn't catch on to it that you looked upon it as a sort of cultured slumming? They wouldn't be at their ease, any more than you would, and you wouldn't get anything out of it except to tell Emily de Montadour and Gracie de Château-Gaillard afterwards what fun you'd had meeting a lot of weird bohemians in the Latin Quarter.'

Isabel slightly shrugged her shoulders.

'I dare say you're right. They're not the sort of people I've been brought up with. They're not the sort of people I have anything in common with.'

'Where does that leave us?'

'Just where we started. I've lived in Chicago ever since I can remember. All my friends are there. All my interests are there. I'm at home there. It's where I belong and it's where you belong. Mamma's ill and she's never going to get any better. I couldn't leave her even if I wanted to.'

'Does that mean that unless I'm prepared to come back to Chicago you don't want to marry me?'

Isabel hesitated. She loved Larry. She wanted to marry him. She wanted him with all the power of her senses. She knew that he desired her. She couldn't believe that when it came down to a showdown he wouldn't weaken. She was afraid, but she had to risk it.

'Yes, Larry, that's just what it does mean.'

He struck a match on the chimney-piece, one of those old-fashioned French sulphur matches that fill your nostrils with an acrid odour, and lit his pipe. Then, passing her, he went over and stood by one of the windows. He looked out. He was silent for what seemed an endless time. She stood as she had stood before, when she was facing him, and looked in the mirror over the chimney-piece, but she did not see herself. Her heart was beating madly and she was sick with apprehension. He turned at last.

'I wish I could make you see how much fuller the life I offer you is than anything you have a conception of. I wish I could make you see how exciting the life of the spirit is and how rich in experience. It's illimitable. It's such a happy life. There's only one thing like it, when you're up in a plane by yourself, high, high, and only infinity surrounds you. You're intoxicated by the boundless space. You feel such a sense of exhilaration that you wouldn't exchange it for all the power and glory in the world. I was reading Descartes the other day. The ease, the grace, the lucidity. Gosh!'

'But Larry,' she interrupted him desperately, 'don't you see you're asking something of me that I'm not fitted for, that I'm not interested in and don't want to be interested in? How often have I got to repeat to you that I'm just an ordinary, normal girl, I'm twenty, in ten years I shall be old, I want to have a good time while I have the chance. Oh, Larry, I do love you so terribly. All this is just trifling. It's not going to lead you anywhere. For your own sake I beseech you to give it up. Be a man, Larry, and do a man's work. You're just wasting the precious years that others are doing so much with. Larry, if you love me you won't give me up for a dream. You've had your fling. Come back with us to America.'

'I can't, darling. It would be death to me. It would be the betrayal of my soul.'

'Oh, Larry, why d'you talk in that way? That's the way hysterical, highbrow women talk. What does it mean? Nothing. Nothing. Nothing.'

'It happens to mean exactly what I feel,' he answered, his eyes twinkling.

'How can you laugh? Don't you realize this is desperately serious? We've come to the cross-roads and what we do now is going to affect our whole lives.'

'I know that. Believe me, I'm perfectly serious.'

She sighed.

'If you won't listen to reason there's nothing more to be said.'

'But I don't think it's reason. I think you've been talking the most terrible nonsense all the time.'

'I?' If she hadn't been so miserable she would have laughed. 'My poor Larry, you're as crazy as a coot.'

She slowly slipped her engagement ring off her finger. She placed it on the palm of her hand and looked at it. It was a square-cut ruby set in a thin platinum band and she had always liked it.

'If you loved me you wouldn't make me so unhappy.'

'I do love you. Unfortunately sometimes one can't do what one thinks is right without making someone else unhappy.'

She stretched out her hand on which the ruby was resting and forced a smile to her trembling lips.

'Here you are, Larry.'

'It's no good to me. Won't you keep it as a memento of our friendship? You can wear it on your little finger. Our friendship needn't stop, need it?'

'I shall always care for you, Larry.'

'Then keep it. I should like you to.'

She hesitated for an instant, then put it on the finger of her right hand.

'It's too large.'

'You can have it altered. Let's go to the Ritz bar and have a drink.'

'All right.'

She was a trifle taken aback that it had all gone so easily. She had not cried. Nothing seemed to be changed except that now she wasn't going to marry Larry. She could hardly believe that everything was over and done with. She resented a little the fact that they hadn't had a terrific scene. They had talked it all over almost as coolly as though they had been discussing the taking of a house. She felt let down, but at the same time was conscious of a slight sense of satisfaction because they had behaved in such a civilized way. She would have given a lot to know exactly what Larry was feeling. But it was always difficult to know that; his smooth face, his dark eyes were a mask that she was aware even she, who had known him for so many years, could not penetrate. She had taken off her hat and laid it on the bed. Now, standing before the mirror, she put it on again.

'Just as a matter of interest,' she said, arranging her hair, 'did you want to break our engagement?'

'No.'

'I thought it might be a relief to you.' He made no reply. She turned round with a gay smile on her lips. 'Now I'm ready.'

Larry locked the door behind him. When he handed the key to the man at the desk he enveloped them both in a look of conniving archness. It was impossible for Isabel not to guess what he thought they had been up to.

'I don't believe that old fellow would bet much on my virginity,' she said.

They took a taxi to the Ritz and had a drink. They spoke of indifferent things, without apparent constraint, like two old friends who saw one another every day. Though Larry was naturally silent, Isabel was a talkative girl, with an ample fund of chit-chat, and she was determined that no silence should fall between them that might be hard to break. She wasn't going to let Larry think she felt any resentment towards him and her pride constrained her to act so that he should not suspect that she was hurt and unhappy. Presently she suggested that he should drive her home. When he dropped her at the door she said to him gaily:

'Don't forget that you're lunching with us tomorrow.'

'You bet your life I won't.'

She gave him her cheek to kiss and passed through the *porte cochère*.

Five

When Isabel entered the drawing-room she found that some people had dropped in to tea. There were two American women who lived in Paris, exquisitely gowned, with strings of pearls round their necks, diamond bracelets on their wrists and costly rings on their fingers. Though the hair of one was darkly hennaed and that of the other unnaturally golden they were strangely alike. They had the same heavily mascaraed eyelashes, the same slim figures, maintained at the cost of extreme mortification, the same clear, sharp features, the same hungry restless eyes; and you could not but be conscious that their lives were a desperate struggle to maintain their fading charms. They talked with inanity in a loud, metallic voice without a moment's pause, as though afraid that if they were silent for an instant the machine would run down and the artificial construction which was all they were would fall to pieces. There was also a secretary from the American Embassy, suave, silent, for he could not get a word in, and very much the man of the world, and a small dark Rumanian prince, all bows and servility, with little darting black eyes and clean-shaven swarthy face, who was for ever jumping up to hand a teacup, pass a plate of cakes, or light a cigarette, and who shamelessly dished out to those present the most flattering, the most gross compliments. He was paying for all the dinners he had received from the objects of his adulation and for all the dinners he hoped to receive.

Mrs Bradley, seated at the tea table and dressed to please Elliott somewhat more grandly than she thought suitable to the occasion, performed her duties as hostess with her usual civil but rather indifferent composure. What she thought of her brother's guests I can only imagine. I never knew her more than slightly and she was a woman who kept herself to herself. She was not a stupid woman; in all the years she had lived in foreign capitals she had met innumerable people of all kinds and I think she summed them up shrewdly enough according to the standards of the small Virginian town where she was born and bred. I think she got a certain amount of amusement from observing their antics and I don't believe she took their airs and graces any more seriously than she took the aches and pains of the characters in a novel which she knew from the beginning (otherwise she wouldn't have read it) would end happily. Paris, Rome, Peking had had no more effect on her Americanism than Elliott's devout Catholicism on her robust, but not inconvenient, Presbyterian faith.

Isabel, with her youth, her strapping good looks and her vitality brought a breath of fresh air into that meretricious atmosphere. She swept in like a young earth goddess. The Rumanian prince leapt to his feet to draw forward a chair for her and with ample gesticulation did his shift. The two American ladies, with shrill amiabilities on their lips, looked her up and down, took in the details of her dress and perhaps in their hearts felt a pang of dismay at being confronted with her exuberant youth. The American diplomat smiled to himself as he saw how false and haggard she made them look. But Isabel thought they were grand; she liked their rich clothes and expensive pearls and felt a twinge of envy for their sophisticated poise. She wondered if she would ever achieve that supreme elegance. Of course the little Rumanian was quite ridiculous, but he was rather sweet and even if he didn't mean the charming things he said it was nice to listen to them. The conversation which her entrance had interrupted was resumed and they talked so brightly, with so much conviction that what they were saying was worth saying, that you almost thought they were talking sense. They talked of the parties they had been to and the parties they were going to. They gossiped about the latest scandal. They tore their friends to pieces. They bandied great names from one to the other. They seemed to know everybody. They were in on all the secrets. Almost in a breath they touched upon the latest play, the latest dressmaker, the latest portrait painter, and the latest mistress of the latest premier. One would have thought there was nothing they didn't know. Isabel listened with ravishment. It all seemed to her wonderfully civilized. This really was life. It gave her a thrilling sense of being in the midst of things. This was real. The setting was perfect. That spacious room with the Savonnerie carpet on the floor, the lovely drawings on the richly-panelled walls, the *petit-point* chairs on which they sat, the priceless pieces of marquetry, commodes and occasional tables, every piece worthy to go into a museum; it must have cost a fortune, that room, but it was worth it. Its beauty, its discretion struck her as never before because she had still so vividly in her mind the shabby little hotel room, with its iron bed and that hard, comfortless chair in which he had sat, that room that Larry saw nothing wrong in. It was bare, cheerless and horrid. It made her shudder to remember it.

The party broke up and Isabel was left with her mother and Elliott.

'Charming women,' said Elliott when he came back from seeing the two poor painted drabs to the door. 'I knew them when they first settled in Paris. I never dreamt they'd turn out as well as they have. It's amazing, the adaptability of our women. You'd hardly know now they were Americans and Middle West into the bargain.'

Mrs Bradley, raising her eyebrows, without speaking gave him a look which he was too quick-witted not to understand.

'No one could ever say that of you, my poor Louisa,' he continued half acidly and half affectionately. 'Though heaven knows, you've had every chance.'

Mrs Bradley pursed her lips.

'I'm afraid I've been a sad disappointment to you, Elliott, but to tell you the truth I'm very satisfied with myself as I am.'

'*Tous les goûts sont dans la nature,*' Elliott murmured.

'I think I ought to tell you that I'm no longer engaged to Larry,' said Isabel.

'Tut,' cried Elliott. 'That'll put my luncheon table out for tomorrow. How on earth am I going to get another man at this short notice?'

'Oh, he's coming to lunch all right.'

'After you've broken off your engagement? That sounds very unconventional.'

Isabel giggled. She kept her gaze on Elliott, for she knew her mother's eyes were fixed upon her and she didn't want to meet them.

'We haven't quarrelled. We talked it over this afternoon and came to the conclusion we'd made a mistake. He doesn't want to come back to America; he wants to stop on in Paris. He's talking of going to Greece.'

'What on earth for? There's no society in Athens. As a matter of fact I never thought so much of Greek art myself. Some of that Hellenistic stuff has a certain decadent charm that's rather attractive. But Phidas: no, no.'

'Look at me, Isabel,' said Mrs Bradley.

Isabel turned and with a faint smile on her lips faced her mother. Mrs Bradley gave her a scrutinizing stare, but all she said was, 'H'm.' The girl hadn't been crying, that she saw; she looked calm and composed.

'I think you're well out of it, Isabel,' said Elliott. 'I was prepared to make the best of it, but I never thought it a good match. He wasn't really up to your mark, and the way he's been behaving in Paris is a pretty clear indication that he'll never amount to anything. With your looks and your connections you can aspire to something better than that. I think you've behaved in a very sensible manner.'

Mrs Bradley gave her daughter a glance that was not devoid of anxiety.

'You haven't done this on my account, Isabel?'

Isabel shook her head decidedly.

'No, darling, I've done it entirely on my own.'

Six

I had come back from the East and was spending some time in London just then. It was perhaps a fortnight after the events I have just related that Elliott called me up one morning. I was not surprised to hear his voice, for I knew that he was in the habit of coming to England to enjoy the fag end of the season. He told me that Mrs Bradley and Isabel were with him and if I would drop in that evening at six for a drink they would be glad to see me. They were, of course, staying at Claridge's. I was at that time living not far from there, so I strolled down Park Lane and through the quiet, dignified streets of Mayfair till I came to the hotel. Elliott had his usual suite. It was panelled in brown wood like the wood of a cigar box and furnished with quiet sumptuousness. He was alone when I was ushered in. Mrs Bradley and Isabel had gone shopping and he was expecting them at any minute. He told me that Isabel had broken her engagement to Larry.

Elliott with his romantic and highly conventional sense of how people should comport themselves under given circumstances had been disconcerted by the young people's behaviour. Not only had Larry come to lunch the very day after the break, but he had acted as though his position were unchanged. He was as pleasant, attentive and soberly gay as usual. He treated Isabel with the same comradely affectionateness with which he had always treated her. He seemed neither harassed, upset nor woebegone. Nor did Isabel appear dispirited. She looked as happy, she laughed as lightly, she jested as merrily as though she had not just taken a decisive and surely searing step in her life. Elliott could not make head or tail of it. From such scraps of their conversation as he caught he gathered that they had no intention of breaking any of the dates they had made. On the first opportunity he talked it over with his sister.

'It's not decent,' he said. 'They can't run around together as if they were still engaged. Larry really should have more sense of propriety. Besides, it damages Isabel's chances. Young Fotheringham, that boy at the British Embassy, is obviously taken with her; he's got money and he's very well connected; if he knew the coast was clear I wouldn't be at all surprised if he made her an offer. I think you ought to talk to her about it.'

'My dear, Isabel's twenty and she has a technique for telling you to mind your own business without offensiveness which I've always found very difficult to cope with.'

'Then you've brought her up extremely badly, Louisa. And besides, it *is* your business.'

'That is a point on which you and she would certainly differ.'

'You're trying my patience, Louisa.'

'My poor Elliott, if you'd ever had a grown-up daughter you'd know that by comparison a bucking steer is easy to manage. And as to knowing what goes on inside her—well, it's much better to pretend you're the simple, innocent old fool she almost certainly takes you for.'

'But you have talked the matter over with her?'

'I tried to. She laughed at me and told me there was really nothing to tell.'

'Is she cut up?'

'I wouldn't know. All I do know is that she eats well and sleeps like a child.'

'Well, take my word for it, if you let them go on like this they'll go off one of these days and get married without saying a word to anybody.'

Mrs Bradley permitted herself to smile.

'It must be a relief to you to think that at present we're living in a country where every facility is afforded to sexual irregularity and every obstacle put in the way of marriage.'

'And quite rightly. Marriage is a serious matter on which rest the security of the family and the stability of the state. But marriage can only maintain its authority if extraconjugal relations are not only tolerated but sanctioned. Prostitution, my poor Louisa—'

'That'll do, Elliott,' interrupted Mrs Bradley. 'I'm not interested in your views on the social and moral values of promiscuous fornication.'

It was then he put forward a scheme that would interrupt Isabel's continued intercourse with Larry, which was so repugnant to his sense of what was fitting. The Paris season was drawing to a close and all the best people were arranging to go to watering-places or to Deauville before repairing for the rest of the summer to their ancestral châteaus in Touraine, Anjou or Brittany. Ordinarily Elliott went to London at the end of June, but his family feeling was strong and his affection for his sister and Isabel sincere; he had been quite ready to sacrifice himself and remain in Paris, if they wished it, when no one who was anyone was there; but he found himself now in the agreeable situation of being able to do what was best for others and at the same time what was convenient to himself. He proposed to Mrs Bradley that the three of them should go to London immediately, where the season was still in full swing and where new interests and new friends would distract Isabel's mind from her unfortunate entanglement. According to the papers the great specialist on Mrs Bradley's disease was then in the British capital and the desirability of consulting him would reasonably account for their precipitate departure and override any disinclination to leave Paris that Isabel might have. Mrs Bradley fell in with the plan. She was puzzled by Isabel. She could not make up her mind whether she was as carefree as she seemed or whether, hurt, angry or heartsick, she was putting on a bold front to conceal her wounded feelings. Mrs Bradley could only agree with Elliott that it would do Isabel good to see new people and new places.

Elliott got busy on the telephone and when Isabel, who had been spending the day at Versailles with Larry, came home, he was able to tell her that he had made an appointment for her mother to see the celebrated doctor three days from then, that he had engaged a suite at Claridge's and that they were starting on the next day but one. Mrs Bradley watched her daughter while this intelligence was being somewhat smugly imparted to her by Elliott, but she did not turn a hair.

'Oh, darling, I'm so glad you're going to see that doctor,' she cried with her usual rather breathless impetuosity. 'Of course, you mustn't miss the chance. And it'll be grand going to London. How long are we going to stay?'

'It would be useless to come back to Paris,' said Elliott. 'There won't be a soul here in a week. I want you to stay with me at Claridge's for the rest of the season. There are always some good balls in July and of course there's Wimbledon. And then Goodwood and Cowes. I'm sure the Ellinghams will be glad to have us on their yacht for Cowes and the Bantocks always have a large party for Goodwood.'

Isabel appeared to be delighted and Mrs Bradley was reassured. It looked as though she were not giving Larry a thought.

Elliott had just finished telling me all this when mother and daughter came in. I had not seen them for more than eighteen months. Mrs Bradley was a little thinner than before and more pasty-faced; she looked tired and none too well. But Isabel was blooming. With her high colour, the rich brown of her hair, her shining hazel eyes, her clear skin, she gave an impression of such youth, of so much enjoyment of the mere fact of being alive, that you felt half inclined to laugh with delight. She gave me the rather absurd notion of a pear, golden and luscious, perfectly ripe and simply asking to be eaten. She radiated warmth so that you thought that if you held out your hands you could feel its comfort. She looked taller than when I had last seen her, whether because she wore higher heels or because the clever dressmaker had cut her frock to conceal her youthful plumpness I don't know, and she held herself with the graceful ease of a girl who has played outdoor games since childhood. She was in short sexually a very attractive young woman. Had I been her mother I should have thought it high time she was married.

Glad of the opportunity to repay some of the kindness I had received from Mrs Bradley in Chicago, I asked them all three to come to a play with me one evening. I arranged to give a luncheon for them.

'You'll be wise to get in at once, my dear fellow,' said Elliott. 'I've already let my friends know we're here and I presume that in a day or two we shall be fixed up for the rest of the season.'

I understood by this that Elliott meant that then they would have no time for the likes of me and I laughed. Elliott gave me a glance in which I discerned a certain hauteur.

'But of course you'll generally find us here about six o'clock and we shall always be glad to see you,' he said graciously, but with the evident intention of putting me, as an author, in my humble place.

But the worm sometimes turns.

'You must try to get in touch with the St Olpherds,' I said. 'I hear they want to dispose of their Constable of Salisbury Cathedral.'

'I'm not buying any pictures just now.'

'I know, but I thought you might dispose of it for them.'

A steely glitter came into Elliott's eyes.

'My dear fellow, the English are a great people, but they have never been able to paint and never will be able to paint. I am not interested in the English school.'

Seven

During the next four weeks I saw little of Elliott and his relations. He did them proud. He took them for a week-end to a grand house in Sussex and for another week-end to an even grander one in Wiltshire. He took them to the royal box at the opera as guests of a minor princess of the House of Windsor. He took them to lunch and dine with the great. Isabel went to several balls. He entertained at Claridge's a series of guests whose names made a fine show in the paper next day. He gave supper parties at Ciro's and the Embassy. In fact he did all the right things and Isabel would have had to be much more sophisticated than she was not to have been a trifle dazzled by the splendour and elegance he provided for her delectation. Elliott could flatter himself that he was taking all this trouble from the purely unselfish motive of distracting Isabel's mind from an unfortunate love affair; but I had a notion he got besides a good deal of satisfaction out of letting his sister see with her own eyes how familiar he was with the illustrious and fashionable. He was an admirable host and he took a delight in displaying his virtuosity.

I went to one or two of his parties myself and now and again I dropped in at Claridge's at six o'clock. I found Isabel surrounded by strapping young men in beautiful clothes who were in the Household Brigade or by elegant young men in less beautiful clothes from the Foreign Office. It was on one of these occasions that she drew me aside.

'I want to ask you something,' she said. 'Do you remember that evening we went to a drugstore and had an ice-cream soda?'

'Perfectly.'

'You were very nice and helpful then. Will you be nice and helpful again?'

'I'll do my best.'

'I want to talk to you about something. Couldn't we lunch one day?'

'Almost any day you like.'

'Somewhere quiet.'

'What d'you say to driving down to Hampton Court and lunching there? The gardens should be at their best just now and you could see Queen Elizabeth's bed.'

The notion suited her and we fixed a day. But when the day came the weather, which had been fine and warm, broke; the sky was grey and a drizzling rain was falling. I called up and asked her if she wouldn't prefer to lunch in town.

'We shouldn't be able to sit in the gardens and the pictures will be so dark, we shan't see a thing.'

'I've sat in lots of gardens and I'm fed to the teeth with old masters. Let's go anyway.'

'All right.'

I fetched her and we drove down. I knew a small hotel where one ate tolerably and we went straight there. On the way Isabel talked with her usual vivacity of the parties she had been to and the people she had met. She had been enjoying herself, but her comments on the various acquaintances she had made suggested to me that she had shrewdness and a quick eye for the absurd. The bad weather kept visitors away and we were the only occupants of the dining-room. The hotel specialized in homely English fare and we had a cut off a leg of excellent lamb with green peas and new potatoes and a deep-dish apple pie with Devonshire cream to follow. With a tankard of pale ale it made an excellent lunch. When we had finished I suggested that we should go into the empty coffee-room where there were armchairs in which we could sit in comfort. It was chilly in there, but the fire was laid, so I put a match to it. The flames made the dingy room more companionable.

'That's that,' I said. 'Now tell me what you want to talk to me about.'

'It's the same as last time,' she chuckled. 'Larry.'

'So I guessed.'

'You know that we've broken off our engagement.'

'Elliott told me.'

'Mamma's relieved and he's delighted.'

She hesitated for a moment and then embarked upon the account of her talk with Larry of which I have done my best faithfully to inform the reader. It may surprise the reader that she knew so little. I don't suppose I had seen her a dozen times and, except for that one occasion at the drugstore, never alone. It did not surprise me. For one thing, as any writer will tell you, people do tell a writer things that they don't tell others. I don't know why, unless it is that having read one or two of his books they feel on peculiarly intimate terms with him; or it may be that they dramatize themselves and, seeing themselves as it were as characters in a novel, are ready to be as open with him as they imagine the characters of his invention are. And I think that Isabel felt that I liked Larry and her, and that their youth touched me, and that I was sympathetic to their distresses. She could not expect to find a friendly listener in Elliott who was disinclined to trouble himself with a young man who had spurned the best chance a young man ever had of getting into society. Nor could her mother help her. Mrs Bradley had high principles and common sense. Her common sense assured her that if you wanted to get on in this world you must accept its conventions, and not to do what everybody else did clearly pointed to instability. Her high principles led her to believe that a man's duty was to go to work in a business where by energy and initiative he had a chance of earning enough money to keep his wife and family in accordance with the standards of his station, give his sons such an education as would enable them on reaching man's estate to make an honest living, and on his death leave his widow adequately provided for.

Isabel had a good memory and the various turns of the long discussion had engraved themselves upon it. I listened in silence till she had finished. She only interrupted herself once to ask me a question.

'Who was Ruysdael?'

'Ruysdael? He was a Dutch landscape painter. Why?'

She told me that Larry had mentioned him. He had said that Ruysdael at least had found an answer to the questions he was asking, and she repeated to me his flippant reply when she had enquired who he was.

'What d'you suppose he meant?'

I had an inspiration.

'Are you sure he didn't say Ruysbroek?'

'He might have. Who was he?'

'He was a Flemish mystic who lived in the fourteenth century.'

'Oh,' she said with disappointment.

It meant nothing to her. But it meant something to me. That was the first indication I had of the turn Larry's reflection was taking, and while she went on with her story, though still listening attentively, part of my mind busied itself with the possibilities that reference of his had suggested. I did not want to make too much of it, for it might be that he had only mentioned the name of the Ecstatic Teacher to make an argumentative point; it might also have a significance that had escaped Isabel. When he answered her question by saying Ruysbroek was just a guy he hadn't known in college he evidently meant to throw her off the scent.

'What do you make of it all?' she asked when she had come to an end.

I paused before replying.

'D'you remember his saying he was just going to loaf? If what he tells you is true his loafing seems to involve some very strenuous work.'

'I'm sure it's true. But don't you see that if he'd worked as hard at any productive form of work he'd be earning a decent income?'

'There are people who are strangely constituted. There are criminals who'll work like beavers to contrive schemes that land them in prison and they no sooner get out than they start all over again and again land in prison. If they put as much industry, as much cleverness, resource and patience into honest practices they could make a handsome living and occupy important positions. But they're just made that way. They like crime.'

'Poor Larry,' she giggled. 'You're not going to suggest that he's learning Greek to cook up a bank robbery.'

I laughed too.

'No, I'm not. What I'm trying to tell you is that there are men who are possessed by an urge so strong to do some particular thing that they can't help themselves, they've got to do it. They're prepared to sacrifice everything to satisfy their yearning.'

'Even the people who love them?'

'Oh, yes.'

'Is that anything more than plain selfishness?'

'I wouldn't know,' I smiled.

'What can be the possible use of Larry's learning dead languages?'

'Some people have a disinterested desire for knowledge. It's not an ignoble desire.'

'What's the good of knowledge if you're not going to do anything with it?'

'Perhaps he is. Perhaps it will be sufficient satisfaction merely to know, as it's a sufficient satisfaction to an artist to produce a work of art. And perhaps it's only a step towards something further.'

'If he wanted knowledge why couldn't he go to college when he came back from the war? It's what Dr Nelson and Mamma wanted him to do.'

'I talked to him about that in Chicago. A degree would be of no use to him. I have an inkling that he had a definite idea of what he wanted and felt he couldn't get it at a university. You know, in learning there's the lone wolf as well as the wolf who runs in the pack. I think Larry is one of those persons who can go no other way than their own.'

'I remember once asking him if he wanted to write. He laughed and said he had nothing to write about.'

'That's the most inconclusive reason for not writing that I've ever heard,' I smiled.

Isabel made a gesture of impatience. She was in no mood even for the mildest jest.

'What I can't make out is why he should have turned out like this. Before the war he was just like everybody else. You wouldn't think it, but he plays a very good game of tennis and he's quite a decent golfer. He used to do all the things the rest of us did. He was a perfectly normal boy and there was no reason to suppose he wouldn't become a perfectly normal man. After all you're a novelist, you ought to be able to explain it.'

'Who am I to explain the infinite complexities of human nature?'

'That's why I wanted to talk to you today,' she added, taking no notice of what I said.

'Are you unhappy?'

'No, not exactly unhappy. When Larry isn't there I'm all right; it's when I'm with him that I feel so weak. Now it's just a sort of ache, like the stiffness you get after a long ride when you haven't been on a horse for months; it's not pain, it's not at all unbearable, but you're conscious of it. I shall get over it all right. I hate the idea of Larry making such a mess of his life.'

'Perhaps he won't. It's a long, arduous road he's starting to travel, but it may be that at the end of it he'll find what he's seeking.'

'What's that?'

'Hasn't it occurred to you? It seems to me that in what he said to you he indicated it pretty plainly. God.'

'God!' she cried. But it was an exclamation of incredulous surprise. Our use of the same word, but in such a different sense, had a comic effect, so that we were obliged to laugh. But Isabel immediately grew serious again and I felt in her whole attitude something like fear. 'What on earth makes you think that?'

'I'm only guessing. But you asked me to tell you what I thought as a novelist. Unfortunately you don't know what experience he had in the war that so profoundly moved him. I think it was some sudden shock for which he was unprepared. I suggest to you that whatever it was that happened to Larry filled him with a sense of the transiency of life, and an anguish to be sure that there was a compensation for the sin and sorrow of the world.'

I could see that Isabel didn't like the turn I had given the conversation. It made her feel shy and awkward.

'Isn't all that awfully morbid? One has to take the world as it comes. If we're here, it's surely to make the most of life.'

'You're probably right.'

'I don't pretend to be anything but a perfectly normal, ordinary girl. I want to have fun.'

'It looks as though there were complete incompatibility of temper between you. It's much better that you should have found it out before marriage.'

'I want to marry and have children and live—'

'In that state of life in which a merciful Providence has been pleased to place you,' I interrupted, smiling.

'Well, there's no harm in that, is there? It's a very pleasant state and I'm quite satisfied with it.'

'You're like two friends who want to take their holiday together, but one of them wants to climb Greenland's icy mountains while the other wants to fish off India's coral strand. Obviously it's not going to work.'

'Anyway, I might get a sealskin coat off Greenland's icy mountains, and I think it's very doubtful if there are any fish off India's coral strand.'

'That remains to be seen.'

'Why d'you say that?' she asked, frowning a little. 'All the time you seem to be making some sort of mental reservation. Of course I know that I'm not playing the star part in this. Larry's got that. He's the idealist, he's the dreamer of a beautiful dream, and even if the dream doesn't come true, it's rather thrilling to have dreamt it. I'm cast for the hard, mercenary, practical part. Common sense is never very sympathetic, is it? But what you forget is that it's I who'd have to pay. Larry would sweep along, trailing clouds of glory, and all there'd be left for me would be to tag along and make both ends meet. I want to live.'

'I don't forget that at all. Years ago, when I was young, I knew a man who was a doctor, and not a bad one either, but he didn't practise. He spent years burrowing away in the library of the British Museum and at long intervals produced a huge pseudo-scientific, pseudo-philosophical book that nobody read and that he had to publish at his own expense. He wrote four or five of them before he died and they were absolutely worthless. He had a son who wanted to go into the army, but there was no money to send him to Sandhurst, so he had to enlist. He was killed in the war. He had a daughter too. She was very pretty and I was rather taken with her. She went on the stage, but she had no talent and she traipsed around the provinces playing small parts in second-rate companies at a miserable salary. His wife, after years of dreary, sordid drudgery broke down in health and the girl had to come home and nurse her and take on the drudgery her mother no longer had the strength for. Wasted, thwarted lives and all to no purpose. It's a toss-up when you decide to leave the beaten track. Many are called but few are chosen.'

'Mother and Uncle Elliott approve of what I've done. Do you approve too?'

'My dear, what can that matter to you? I'm almost a stranger to you.'

'I look upon you as a disinterested observer,' she said, with a pleasant smile. 'I should like to have your approval. You do think I've done right, don't you?'

'I think you've done right for you,' I said, fairly confident that she would not catch the slight distinction I made in my reply.

'Then why have I a bad conscience?'

'Have you?'

With a smile still on her lips, but a slightly rueful smile now, she nodded.

'I know it's only horse sense. I know that every reasonable person would agree that I've done the only possible thing. I know that from every practical standpoint, from the standpoint of worldly wisdom, from the standpoint of common decency, from the standpoint of what's right and wrong, I've done what I ought to do. And yet at the bottom of my heart I've got an uneasy feeling that if I were better, if I were more disinterested, more unselfish, nobler, I'd marry Larry and lead his life. If I only loved him enough I'd think the world well lost.'

'You might put it the other way about. If he loved you enough he wouldn't have hesitated to do what you want.'

'I've said that to myself too. But it doesn't help. I suppose it's more in woman's nature to sacrifice herself than in a man's.' She chuckled. 'Ruth and the alien corn and all that sort of thing.'

'Why don't you risk it?'

We had been talking quite lightly, almost as if we were having a casual conversation about people we both knew but in whose affairs we were not intimately concerned, and even when she narrated to me her talk with Larry Isabel had spoken with a sort of breezy gaiety, enlivening it with humour, as if she did not want me to take what she said too seriously. But now she went pale.

'I'm afraid.'

For a while we were silent. A chill went down my spine as it strangely does when I am confronted with deep and genuine human emotion. I find it terrible and rather awe-inspiring.

'Do you love him very much?' I asked at last.

'I don't know. I'm impatient with him. I'm exasperated with him. I keep longing for him.'

Silence again fell upon us. I didn't know what to say. The coffee-room in which we sat was small, and heavy lace curtains over the window shut out the light. On the walls, covered with yellow marbled paper, were old sporting prints. With its mahogany furniture, its shabby leather chairs and its musty smell it was strangely reminiscent of a coffee-room in a Dickens novel. I poked the fire and put more coal on it. Isabel suddenly began to speak.

'You see, I thought when it came to a showdown he'd knuckle under. I knew he was weak.'

'Weak?' I cried. 'What made you think that? A man who for a year withstood the disapproval of all his friends and associates because he was determined to go his own way.'

'I could always do anything I wanted with him. I could turn him round my little finger. He was never a leader in the things we did. He just tagged along with the crowd.'

I had lit a cigarette and watched the smoke ring I had made. It grew larger and larger and then faded away into the air.

'Mamma and Elliott thought it very wrong of me to go about with him afterwards as though nothing had happened, but I didn't take it very seriously. I kept on thinking up to the end that he'd yield. I couldn't believe that when he'd got it into his thick head that I meant what I said he wouldn't give in.' She hesitated and gave me a smile of roguish, playful malice. 'Will you be awfully shocked if I tell you something?'

'I think it very unlikely.'

'When we decided to come to London I called Larry and asked him if we couldn't spend my last evening in Paris together. When I told them, Uncle Elliott said it was most improper and Mamma said she thought it unnecessary. When Mamma says something is unnecessary it means she thoroughly disapproves. Uncle Elliott asked me what the idea was and I said we were going to dine somewhere and then make a tour of the night clubs. He told Mamma she ought to forbid me to go. Mamma said, "Will you pay any attention if I forbid you to go?" "No, darling," I said, "none." Then she said, "That is what I imagined. In that case there doesn't seem to be much point in my forbidding it."'

'Your mother appears to be a woman of enormous sense.'

'I don't believe she misses much. When Larry called for me I went into her room to say good night to her. I'd made up a bit; you know, you have to in Paris or else you look so naked, and when she saw the dress I had on, I had an uneasy suspicion from the way she took me in from top to toe that she had a pretty shrewd idea what I was after. But she didn't say anything. She just kissed me and said she hoped I'd have a good time.'

'What were you after?'

Isabel looked at me doubtfully, as though she couldn't quite decide how frank she was prepared to be.

'I didn't think I was looking too bad and it was my last chance. Larry had reserved a table at Maxim's. We had lovely things to eat, all the things I particularly liked, and we had champagne. We talked our heads off, at least I did, and I made Larry laugh. One of the things I've liked about him is that I can always amuse him. We danced. When we'd had enough of that we went on to the Château de Madrid. We found some people we knew and joined them and we had more champagne. Then we all went to the Acacia. Larry dances quite well, and we fit. The heat and the music and the wine—I was getting a bit light-headed. I felt absolutely reckless. I danced with my face against Larry's and I knew he wanted me. God knows I wanted him. I had an idea. I suppose it had been at the back of my mind all the time. I thought I'd get him to come home with me and once I'd got him there, well, it was almost inevitable that the inevitable should happen.'

'Upon my word you couldn't put it more delicately.'

'My room was quite a way from Uncle Elliott's and Mamma's, so I knew there was no risk. When we were back in America I thought I'd write and say I was going to have a baby. He'd be obliged to come back and marry me, and when I'd got him home I didn't believe it would be hard to keep him there, especially with Mamma ill. "What a fool I am not to have thought of that before," I said to myself. "Of course that'll settle everything." When the music stopped I just stayed there in his arms. Then I said it was getting late and we had to take the train at noon, so we'd better go. We got into a taxi. I nestled close to him and he put his arms around me and kissed me. He kissed me, he kissed me—oh, it was heaven. It hardly seemed a moment before the taxi stopped at the door. Larry paid it.

'"I shall walk home," he said.

'The taxi rattled off and I put my arms around his neck.

'"Won't you come up and have one last drink?" I said.

'"Yes, if you like," he said.

'He'd rung the bell and the door swung open. He switched on the light as we stepped in. I looked into his eyes. They were so trusting, so honest, so—so guileless; he so obviously hadn't the smallest idea that I was laying a trap for him; I felt I couldn't play him such a dirty trick. It was like taking candy off a child. D'you know what I did? I said, "Oh well, perhaps you'd better not. Mamma's not very well tonight and if she's fallen asleep I don't want to wake her up. Good night." I put my face up for him to kiss and pushed him out of the door. That was the end of that.'

'Are you sorry?' I asked.

'I'm neither pleased nor sorry. I just couldn't help myself. It wasn't me that did what I did. It was just an impulse that took possession of me and acted for me.' She grinned. 'I suppose you'd call it my better nature.'

'I suppose you would.'

'Then my better nature must take the consequences. I trust in the future it'll be more careful.'

That was in effect the end of our talk. It may be that it was some consolation to Isabel to have been able to speak to someone with entire freedom, but that was all the good I had been able to do her. Feeling I had been inadequate, I tried to say at least some small thing that would give her comfort.

'You know, when one's in love,' I said, 'and things go all wrong, one's terribly unhappy and one thinks one won't ever get over it. But you'll be astounded to learn what the sea will do.'

'What do you mean?' she smiled.

'Well love isn't a good sailor and it languishes on a sea voyage. You'll be surprised when you have the Atlantic between you and Larry to find how slight the pang is that before you sailed seemed intolerable.'

'Do you speak from experience?'

'From the experience of a stormy past. When I suffered from the pangs of unrequited love I immediately got on an ocean liner.'

The rain showed no sign of letting up, so we decided that Isabel could survive without seeing the noble pile of Hampton Court or even Queen Elizabeth's bed, and drove back to London. I saw her two or three times after that, but only when other people were present, and then, having had enough of London for a while, I set off for the Tyrol.

Chapter Three

One

For ten years after this I saw neither Isabel nor Larry. I continued to see Elliott, and indeed, for a reason that I shall tell later, more frequently than before, and from time to time I learnt from him what was happening to Isabel. But of Larry he could tell me nothing.

'For all I know he's still living in Paris, but I'm not likely to run across him. We don't move in the same circles,' he added, not without complacency. 'It's very sad that he should have gone so completely to seed. He comes of a very good family. I'm sure I could have made something of him if he'd put himself in my hands. Anyhow it was a lucky escape for Isabel.'

My circle of acquaintance was not so restricted as Elliott's and I know a number of persons in Paris whom he would have thought eminently undesirable. On my brief but not infrequent sojourns I asked one or other of them whether he had run across Larry or had news of him; a few knew him casually, but none could claim any intimacy with him and I could find nobody to give me news of him. I went to the restaurant at which he habitually dined, but found he had not been there for a long time, and they thought he must have gone away. I never saw him at any of the cafés on the Boulevard du Montparnasse which people who live in the neighbourhood are apt to go to.

His intention, after Isabel left Paris, was to go to Greece, but this he abandoned. What he actually did he told me himself many years later, but I will relate it now because it is more convenient to place events as far as I can in chronological order. He stayed on in Paris during the summer and worked without a break till autumn was well advanced.

'I thought I needed a rest from books then,' he said, 'I'd been working from eight to ten hours a day for two years. So I went to work in a coal mine.'

'You did what?' I cried.

He laughed at my astonishment.

'I thought it would do me good to spend a few months in manual labour. I had a notion it would give me an opportunity to sort my thoughts and come to terms with myself.'

I was silent. I wondered whether that was the only reason for this unexpected step or whether it was connected with Isabel's refusal to marry him. The fact was, I didn't know at all how deeply he loved her. Most people when they're in love invent every kind of reason to persuade themselves that it's only sensible to do what they want. I suppose that's why there are so many disastrous marriages. They are like those who put their affairs in the hands of someone they know to be a crook, but who happens to be an intimate friend because, unwilling to believe that a crook is a crook first and a friend afterwards, they are convinced that, however dishonest he may be with others, he won't be so with them. Larry was strong enough to refuse to sacrifice for Isabel's sake the life that he thought was the life for him, but it may be that to lose her was bitterer to endure than he had expected. It may be that like most of us he wanted to eat his cake and have it.

'Well, go on,' I said.

'I packed my books and my clothes in a couple of trunks and got the American Express to store them. Then I put an extra suit and some linen in a grip and started off. My Greek teacher had a sister who was married to the manager of a mine near Lens and he gave me a letter to him. D'you know Lens?'

'No.'

'It's in the North of France, not far from the Belgian border. I only spent a night there, at the station hotel, and next day I took a local to the place where the mine was. Ever been to a mining village?'

'In England.'

'Well, I suppose it's much the same. There's the mine and the manager's house, rows and rows of trim little two-storey houses, all alike, exactly alike, and it's so monotonous it makes your heart sink. There's a newish, ugly church and several bars. It was bleak and cold when I got there and a thin rain was falling. I went to the manager's office and sent in my letter. He was a little, fat man with red cheeks and the look of a guy who enjoys his food. They were short of labour, a lot of miners had been killed in the war, and there were a good many Poles working there, two or three hundred, I should think. He asked me one or two questions, he didn't much like my being an American, he seemed to think it rather fishy, but his brother-in-law's letter spoke well of me and anyhow he was glad to have me. He wanted to give me a job on the surface, but I told him I wanted to work down below. He said I'd find it hard if I wasn't used to it, but I told him I was prepared for that, so then he said I could be helper to a miner. That was boy's work really, but there weren't enough boys to go round. He was a nice fellow; he asked me if I'd done anything about finding a lodging, and when I told him I hadn't he wrote an address on a piece of paper and said that if I went there the woman of the house would let me have a bed. She was the widow of a miner who'd been killed and her two sons were working in the mine.

'I took my grip and went on my way. I found the house, and the door was opened for me by a tall, gaunt woman with greying hair and big, dark eyes. She had good features and she must have been nice-looking once. She wouldn't have been bad then in a haggard way except for two missing front teeth. She told me she hadn't a room, but there were two beds in a room she'd let to a Pole and I could have the other one. Her two sons had one of the upstairs rooms and she had the other. The room she showed me was on the ground floor and supposed, I imagined, to be the living-room; I should have liked a room to myself, but I thought I'd better not be fussy; and the drizzle had turned into a steady, light rain and I was wet already. I didn't want to go farther and get soaked to the skin. So I said that would suit me and I settled in. They used the kitchen as a living-room. It had a couple of rickety armchairs in it. There was a coal shed in the yard which was also the bathhouse. The two boys and the Pole had taken their lunch with them, but she said I could eat with her at midday. I sat in the kitchen afterwards smoking and while she went on with her work she told me all about herself and her family. The others came in at the end of their shift. The Pole first and then the two boys. The Pole passed through the kitchen, nodded to me without speaking when our landlady told him I was to share his room, took a great kettle off the hob and went off to wash himself in the shed. The two boys were tall good-looking fellows notwithstanding the grime on their faces, and seemed inclined to be friendly. They looked upon me as a freak because I was American. One of them was nineteen, off to his military service in a few months, and the other eighteen.

'The Pole came back and then they went to clean up. The Pole had one of those difficult Polish names, but they called him Kosti. He was a big fellow, two or three inches taller than me, and heavily built. He had a pale fleshy face with a broad short nose and a big mouth. His eyes were blue and because he hadn't been able to wash the coal dust off his eyebrows and eyelashes he looked as if he was made up. The black lashes made the blue of his eyes almost startling. He was an ugly, uncouth fellow. The two boys after they'd changed their clothes went out. The Pole sat on in the kitchen, smoking a pipe and reading the paper. I had a book in my pocket, so I took it out and began reading too. I noticed that he glanced at me once or twice and presently he put his paper down.

'"What are you reading?" he asked.

'I handed him the book to see for himself. It was a copy of the *Princesse de Clèves* that I'd bought at the station in Paris because it was small enough to put in my pocket. He looked at it, then at me, curiously, and handed it back. I noticed an ironical smile on his lips.

'"Does it amuse you?"

'"I think it's very interesting–even absorbing."

'"I read it at school at Warsaw. It bored me stiff." He spoke very good French, with hardly a trace of Polish accent. "Now I don't read anything but the newspaper and detective stories."

'Madame Leclerc, that was our old girl's name, with an eye on the soup that was cooking for supper, sat at the table darning socks. She told Kosti that I had been sent to her by the manager of the mine and repeated what else I had seen fit to tell her. He listened, puffing away at his pipe, and looked at me with brilliantly blue eyes. They were hard and shrewd. He asked me a few questions about myself. When I told him I had never worked in a mine before his lips broke again into an ironical smile.

'"You don't know what you're in for. No one would go to work in a mine who could do anything else. But that's your affair and doubtless you have your reasons. Where did you live in Paris?"

'I told him.

'"At one time I used to go to Paris every year, but I kept to the Grands Boulevards. Have you ever been to Larue's? It was my favourite restaurant."

'That surprised me a bit because, you know, it's not cheap.'

'Far from it.'

'I fancy he saw my surprise, for he gave me once more his mocking smile, but evidently didn't think it necessary to explain further. We went on talking in a desultory fashion and then the two boys came in. We had supper and when we'd finished Kosti asked me if I'd like to come to the *bistro* with him and have a beer. It was just a rather large room with a bar at one end of it and a number of marble-topped tables with wooden chairs around them. There was a mechanical piano and someone had put a coin in the slot and it was braying out a dance tune. Only three tables were occupied besides ours. Kosti asked me if I played belote. I'd learnt it with some of my student friends, so I said I did and he proposed that we should play for the beer. I agreed and he called for cards. I lost a beer and a second beer. Then he proposed that we should play for money. He had good cards and I had bad luck. We were playing for very small stakes, but I lost several francs. This and the beer put him in a good humour and he talked. It didn't take me long to guess, both by his way of expressing himself and by his manners, that he was a man of education. When he spoke again of Paris it was to ask me if I knew so and so and so and so, American women I had met at Elliott's when Aunt Louisa and Isabel were staying with him. He appeared to know them better than I did and I wondered how it was that he found himself in his present position. It wasn't late, but we had to get up at the crack of dawn.

'"Let's have one more beer before we go," said Kosti.

'He sipped it and peered at me with this shrewd little eyes. I knew what he reminded me of then, an ill-tempered pig.

'"Why have you come here to work in this rotten mine?" he asked me.

'"For the experience."

'"*Tu es fou, mon petit*," he said.

'"And why are you working in it?"

'He shrugged his massive, ungainly shoulders.

'"I entered the nobleman's cadet school when I was a kid, my father was a general under the Czar and I was a cavalry officer in the last war. I couldn't stand Pilsudski. We arranged to kill him, but someone gave us away. He shot those of us he caught. I managed to get across the frontier just in time. There was nothing for me but the Foreign Legion or a coal mine. I chose the lesser of two evils."

'I had already told Kosti what job I was to have in the mine and he had said nothing, but now, putting his elbow on the marble-topped table, he said:

'"Try to push my hand back."

'I knew the old trial of strength and I put my open palm against his. He laughed. "Your hand won't be as soft as that in a few weeks." I pushed with all my might, but I could make no effect against his huge strength and gradually he pressed my hand back and down to the table.

'"You're pretty strong," he was good enough to say. "There aren't many men who keep up as long as that. Listen, my helper's no good, he's a puny little Frenchman, he hasn't got the strength of a louse. You come along with me tomorrow and I'll get the foreman to let me have you instead."

'"I'd like that," I said. "D'you think he'll do it?"

'"For a consideration. Have you got fifty francs to spare?"

'He stretched out his hand and I took a note out of my wallet. We went home and to bed. I'd had a long day and I slept like a log.'

'Didn't you find the work terribly hard?' I asked Larry.

'Back-breaking at first,' he grinned. 'Kosti worked it with the foreman and I was made his helper. At that time Kosti was working in a space about the size of a hotel bathroom and one got to it through a tunnel so low that you had to crawl through it on your hands and knees. It was as hot as hell in there and we worked in nothing but our pants. There was something terribly repulsive in that great white fat torso of Kosti's; he looked like a huge slug. The row of the pneumatic cutter in that narrow space was deafening. My job was to gather the blocks of coal that he hacked away and load a basket with them and drag the basket through the tunnel to its mouth, where it could be loaded into a truck when the train came along at intervals on its way to the elevators. It's the only coal mine I've ever known, so I don't know if that's the normal practice. It seemed amateurish to me and it was damned hard work. At half time we knocked off for a rest and ate our lunch and smoked. I wasn't sorry when we were through for the day, and gosh, it was good to have a bath. I thought I'd never get my feet clean; they were as black as ink. Of course my hands blistered and they got as sore as the devil, but they healed. I got used to the work.'

'How long did you stick it out?'

'I was only kept on that job for a few weeks. The trucks that carried the coal to the elevators were hauled by a tractor and the driver was a poor mechanic and the engine was always breaking down. Once he couldn't get it going and he didn't seem to know what to do. Well, I'm a pretty good mechanic, so I had a look at it and in half an hour I got it working. The foreman told the manager and he sent for me and asked me if I knew about cars. The result was that he gave me the mechanic's job; of course it was monotonous, but it was easy, and because they didn't have any more engine trouble they were pleased with me.

'Kosti was as sore as hell at my leaving him. I suited him and he'd got used to me. I got to know him pretty well, working with him all day, going to the *bistro* with him after supper, and sharing a room with him. He was a funny fellow. He was the sort of man who'd have appealed to you. He didn't mix with the Poles and we didn't go to the cafés they went to. He couldn't forget he was a nobleman and had been a cavalry officer and he treated them like dirt. Naturally they resented it, but they couldn't do anything about it; he was as strong as an ox, and if it had ever come to a scrap, knives or no knives, he'd have been a match for half a dozen of them together. I got to know some of them all the same, and they told me he'd been a cavalry officer all right in one of the smart regiments, but it was a lie about his having left Poland for political reasons. He'd been kicked out of the Officers' Club at Warsaw and cashiered because he'd been caught cheating at cards. They warned me against playing with him. They said that was why he fought shy of them, because they knew too much about him and wouldn't play with him.

'I'd been losing to him consistently, not much, you know, just a few francs a night, but when he won he always insisted on paying for drinks, so it didn't amount to anything really. I thought I was just having a run of bad luck or that I didn't play as well as he did. But after that I kept my eyes skinned and I was dead sure he was cheating, but d'you know, for the life of me I couldn't see how he did it. Gosh, he was clever. I knew he simply couldn't have the best cards all the time. I watched him like a lynx. He was as cunning as a fox and I guess he saw I'd been put wise to him. One night, after we'd been playing for a while, he looked at me with that rather cruel, sarcastic smile of his which was the only way he knew how to smile, and said:

'"Shall I show you a few tricks?"

'He took the pack of cards and asked me to name one. He shuffled them and he told me to choose one; I did, and it was the card I'd named. He did two or three more tricks and then he asked me if I played poker. I said I did and he dealt me a hand. When I looked at it I saw I'd got four aces and a king.

'"You'd be willing to bet a good deal on that hand, wouldn't you?" he asked.

'"My whole stack," I answered.

'"You'd be silly." He put down the hand he'd dealt himself. It was a straight flush. How it was done I don't know. He laughed at my amazement. "If I weren't an honest man I'd have had your shirt by now."

'"You haven't done so badly as it is," I grinned.

'"Chicken feed. Not enough to buy a dinner at Larue's."

'We continued to play pretty well every night. I came to the conclusion that he cheated not so much for the money as for the fun of it. It gave him a queer satisfaction to know that he was making a fool of me, and I think he got a lot of amusement out of knowing that I was on to what he was doing and couldn't see how it was done.

'But that was only one side of him and it was the other side that made him so interesting to me. I couldn't reconcile the two. Though he boasted he never read anything but the paper and detective stories he was a cultivated man. He was a good talker, caustic, harsh, cynical, but it was exhilarating to listen to him. He was a devout Catholic and had a crucifix hanging over his bed, and he went to Mass every Sunday regularly. On Saturday nights he used to get drunk. The *bistro* we went to was crammed jammed full then, and the air was heavy with smoke. There were quiet, middle-aged miners with their families, and there were groups of young fellows kicking up a hell of a row, and there were men with sweaty faces round tables playing belote with loud shouts, while their wives sat by, a little behind them, and watched. The crowd and the noise had a strange effect on Kosti and he'd grow serious and start talking–of all unlikely subjects–of mysticism. I knew nothing of it then but an essay of Maeterlinck's on Ruysbroek that I'd read in Paris. But Kosti talked of Plotinus and Denis the Areopagite and Jacob Boehme the shoemaker and Meister Eckhart. It was fantastic to hear that great hulking bum, who'd been thrown out of his own world, that sardonic, bitter down-and-out, speaking of the ultimate reality of things and the blessedness of union with God. It was all new to me and I was confused and excited. I was like someone who's lain awake in a darkened room and suddenly a chink of light shoots through the curtains and he knows he only has to draw them and there the country will be spread before him in the glory of the dawn. But if I tried to get him on the subject when he was sober he got mad at me. His eyes were spiteful.

'"How should I know what I was talking about when I didn't know what I was saying?" he snapped.

'But I knew he was lying. He knew perfectly well what he was talking about. He knew a lot. Of course he was soused, but the look in his eyes, the rapt expression on his ugly face, weren't due only to drink. There was more to it than that. The first time he talked in that way he said something that I've never forgotten, because it horrified me; he said that the world isn't a creation, for out of nothing nothing comes; but a manifestation of the eternal nature; well, that was all right, but then he added that evil is as direct a manifestation of the divine as good. They were strange words to hear in that sordid, noisy café, to the accompaniment of dance tunes on the mechanical piano.'

Two

To give the reader a moment's rest I am starting here upon a new section, but I am doing it only for his convenience; the conversation was uninterrupted. I may take this opportunity to say that Larry spoke without haste, often choosing his words with care, and though of course I do not pretend to report them exactly, I have tried to reproduce not only the matter, but the manner of his discourse. His voice, rich in tone, had a musical quality that was grateful to the ear; and as he talked, without gesticulation of any kind, puffing away at his pipe and stopping now and again to relight it, he looked you in the face with a pleasant, often whimsical expression in his dark eyes.

'Then the spring came, late in that flat, dismal part of the country, cold and rainy still; but sometimes a fine warm day made it hard to leave the world above ground and go down hundreds of feet in a rickety elevator, crowded with miners in their grimy overalls, into the bowels of the earth. It was spring all right, but it seemed to come shyly in that grim and sordid landscape as though unsure of a welcome. It was like a flower, a daffodil or a lily, growing in a pot on the window-sill of a slum dwelling and you wondered what it did there. One Sunday morning we were lying in bed, we always slept late on Sunday morning, and I was reading, when Kosti said to me out of a blue sky:

'"I'm getting out of here. D'you want to come with me?"

'I knew a lot of the Poles went back to Poland in the summer to get the harvest in, but it was early for that, and besides, Kosti couldn't go back to Poland.

'"Where are you going?" I asked.

'"Tramping. Across Belgium and into Germany and down the Rhine. We could get work on a farm that would see us through the summer."

'It didn't take a minute to make up my mind.

'"It sounds fine," I said.

'Next day we told the foreman we were through. I found a fellow who was willing to take my grip in exchange for a rucksack. I gave the clothes I didn't want or couldn't carry on my back to the younger of Madame Leclerc's sons who was about my size. Kosti left a bag, packed what he wanted in his rucksack and the day after, as soon as the old girl had given us our coffee, we started off.

'We weren't in any hurry as we knew we couldn't get taken on at a farm at least until the hay was ready to cut, and so we dawdled along through France and Belgium by way of Namur and Liége and got into Germany through

Aachen. We didn't do more than ten or twelve miles a day. When we liked the look of a village we stopped there. There was always some kind of an inn where we could get beds and an alehouse where we could get something to eat and beer to drink. On the whole we had fine weather. It was grand to be out in the open air after all those months in the mine. I don't think I'd ever realized before how good a green meadow is to look at and how lovely a tree is when the leaves aren't out yet, but the branches are veiled in a faint green mist. Kosti started to teach me German and I believe he spoke it as well as he spoke French. As we trudged along he would tell me the German for the various objects we passed, a cow, a horse, a man and so on, and then make me repeat simple German sentences. It made the time pass and by the time we got into Germany I could at least ask for the things I wanted.

'Cologne was a bit out of our way, but Kosti insisted on going there, on account of the Eleven Thousand Virgins, he said, and when we got there he went on a bat. I didn't see him for three days and when he turned up at the room we'd taken in a sort of workmen's rooming-house he was very surly. He'd got in a fight and he had a black eye and a cut on his lip. He wasn't a pretty object, I can tell you. He went to bed for twenty-four hours, and then we started to walk down the valley of the Rhine towards Darmstadt, where he said the country was good and we stood the best chance of getting work.

'I never enjoyed anything more. The fine weather held and we wandered through towns and villages. When there were sights to see we stopped off and looked at them. We put up where we could and once or twice we slept in a loft on the hay. We ate at wayside inns and when we got in the wine country we turned from beer to wine. We made friends with the people in the taverns we drank in. Kosti had a sort of rough joviality that inspired them with confidence and he'd play skat with them, that's a German card game, and skin them with such bluff good humour, with the earthy jokes they appreciated, that they hardly minded losing their pfennigs to him. I practised my German on them. I'd bought a little English-German conversation grammar at Cologne and I was getting on pretty well. And then at night, when he'd got a couple of litres of white wine inside him, Kosti would talk in a morbid way of the flight from the Alone to the Alone, of the Dark Night of the Soul and of the final ecstasy in which the creature becomes one with the Beloved. But when in the early morning, as we walked through the smiling country, with the dew still on the grass, I tried to get him to tell me more, he grew so angry that he could have hit me.

'"Shut up, you fool," he said. "What do you want with all that stuff and nonsense? Come, let's get on with our German."

'You can't argue with a man who's got a fist like a steam hammer and wouldn't think twice about using it. I'd seen him in a rage. I knew he was capable of laying me out cold and leaving me in a ditch and I wouldn't have put it past him to empty my pockets while I was out. I couldn't make head or tail of him. When wine had loosened his tongue and he spoke of the Ineffable, he shed the rough obscene language that he ordinarily used, like the grimy overalls he wore in the mine, and he was well spoken and even eloquent. I couldn't believe he wasn't sincere. I don't know how it occurred to me, but I got the idea somehow that he'd taken on that hard, brutal labour of mine to mortify his flesh. I thought he hated that great, uncouth body of his and wanted to torture it and that his cheating and his bitterness and his cruelty were the revolt of his will against—oh, I don't know what you'd call it—against a deep-rooted instinct of holiness, against a desire for God that terrified and yet obsessed him.

'We'd taken our time, the spring was pretty well over and the trees were in full leaf. The grapes in the vineyards were beginning to fill out. We kept to the dirt roads as much as we could and they were getting dusty. We were in the neighbourhood of Darmstadt and Kosti said we'd better start looking for a job. Our money was getting short. I had half a dozen travellers' cheques in my pocket, but I'd made up my mind not to use them if I could possibly help it. When we saw a farmhouse that looked promising we stopped and asked if they wanted a couple of hands. I dare say we didn't look very inviting. We were dusty and sweaty and dirty. Kosti looked a terrible ruffian and I don't suppose I looked much better either. We were turned down time after time. At one place the farmer said he'd take Kosti but couldn't do with me and Kosti said we were buddies and wouldn't separate. I told him to go ahead, but he wouldn't. I was surprised. I knew Kosti had taken a fancy to me, though I couldn't imagine why, as I didn't begin to be the kind of guy he had any use for, but I would never have thought he liked me well enough to refuse a job on my account. I felt rather conscience-stricken as we walked on, because I didn't really like him, in fact I found him rather repulsive, but when I tried to say something to show I was pleased with what he'd done, he bit my head off.

'But at last our luck turned. We'd just gone through a village in a hollow and we came to a rambling farmhouse that didn't look so bad. We knocked at the door and a woman opened it. We offered ourselves as usual. We said we didn't want any wages, but were willing to work for our board and lodging, and to my surprise instead of slamming the door in our face, she told us to wait. She called to someone inside the house and presently a man came out. He had a good stare at us and asked us where we came from. He asked to see our papers. He gave me another stare when he saw I was American. He didn't seem to like it very much, but anyhow he asked us to come in and have a glass of wine. He took us into the kitchen and we sat down. The woman brought a flagon and some glasses. He told us that his hired man had been gored by a bull and was in hospital and wouldn't be fit for anything till after the harvest was in. With so many men killed, and others going into the factories that were springing up along the Rhine, it was the devil's own job to get labour. We knew that and had been counting on it. Well, to make a long story short he said he'd take us. There was plenty of room in the house, but I suppose he didn't fancy having us there; anyway he told us there were two beds in the hayloft and that was where we were to sleep.

'The work wasn't hard. There were the cows to look after and the hogs; the machinery was in a bad way and we had to do something about that; but I had some leisure. I loved the sweet-smelling meadows and in the evenings I used to wander about and dream. It was a good life.

'The household consisted of old Becker, his wife, his widowed daughter-in-law and her children. Becker was a heavy, grey-haired man in his late forties; he'd been through the war and still limped from a wound in the leg. It hurt him a lot and he drank to kill the pain. He was generally high by the time he got to bed. Kosti got on with him fine and they used to go down to the inn together after supper to play skat and swill wine. Frau Becker had been a hired girl. They'd got her out of an orphanage and Becker had married her soon after his wife's death. She was a good many years younger than he was, rather handsome in a way, full-blown, with red cheeks and fair hair and a hungry sensual look. It didn't take Kosti long to come to the conclusion that there was something doing there. I told him not to be a fool. We had a good job and we didn't want to lose it. He only jeered at me; he said Becker wasn't satisfying her and she was asking for it. I knew it was useless to appeal to his sense of decency, but I told him to be careful; it might be that Becker wouldn't see what he was after, but there was his daughter-in-law, and she wasn't missing anything.

'Ellie, that was her name, was a thickset, big young woman, well under thirty, with black eyes and black hair, a sallow square face and a sullen look. She still wore mourning for her husband killed at Verdun. She was very devout and on Sunday mornings trudged down to the village to early Mass and again in the afternoon to vespers. She had three children, one of whom had been born after her husband's death, and she never spoke at meals except to scold them. She did little work on the farm, but spent most of her time looking after the kids, and in the evening sat by herself in the sitting-room, with the door open so that she could hear if one of them was crying, and read novels. The two women hated one another. Ellie despised Frau Becker because she was a foundling and had been a servant, and bitterly resented her being the mistress of the house and in a position to give orders.

'Ellie was the daughter of a prosperous farmer and had brought a good dowry with her. She hadn't gone to the village school, but to Zwingenberg, the nearest town, where there was a girl's *gymnasium*, and she'd got quite a good education. Poor Frau Becker had come to the farm when she was fourteen and if she could read and write that's about all she could do. That was another cause of discord between the two women. Ellie lost no opportunity of showing off her knowledge, and Frau Becker, red in the face with anger, would ask what use it was to a farmer's wife. Then Ellie would look at her husband's identification disc which she wore on a steel chain round her wrist and with a bitter look on her sullen face say:

'"Not a farmer's wife. Only a farmer's widow. Only the widow of a hero who gave his life for his country."

'Poor old Becker had his work cut out to keep the peace between them.'

'But what did they make of you?' I interrupted Larry.

'Oh, they thought I'd deserted from the American Army and couldn't go back to America or I'd be put in jail. That's how they explained that I didn't care to go down to the inn and drink with Becker and Kosti. They thought I didn't want to attract attention to myself and have the village constable asking questions. When Ellie found out I was trying to learn German she brought out her old schoolbooks and said she'd teach me. So after supper she and I would go in the sitting-room, leaving Frau Becker in the kitchen, and I'd read aloud to her while she corrected my accent and tried to make me understand words I couldn't get the sense of. I guessed she was doing it not so much to help me as to put something over on Frau Becker.

'All this time Kosti was trying to make Frau Becker and wasn't getting anywhere. She was a jolly, merry woman and quite prepared to joke and laugh with him, and he had a way with him with women. I guess she knew what he was after and I dare say she was flattered, but when he started pinching her she told him to keep his hands to himself and smacked his face. And I bet it was a good hard smack.'

Larry hesitated a little and smiled rather shyly.

'I've never been the sort who thinks women are after me, but it occurred to me that—well, that Frau Becker had fallen for me. It made me rather uncomfortable. For one thing she was a lot older than me, and then old

Becker had been very decent to us. She dished out the food at the table and I couldn't help noticing that she helped me more liberally than the others, and she seemed to me to look for opportunities of being along with me. She'd smile at me in what I suppose you'd call a provocative manner. She'd ask me if I had a girl, and say that a young fellow like me must suffer for the want of it in a place like that. You know the sort of thing. I only had three shirts and they were pretty well worn. Once she said it was a disgrace that I should wear such rags and if I'd bring them along she'd mend them. Ellie heard her and next time we were alone said that if I had anything to mend she'd do it. I said it didn't matter. But a day or two later I found that my socks had been darned and my shirts patched and put back on the bench in the loft on which we kept our things; but which of them had done it I don't know. Of course I didn't take Frau Becker seriously; she was a good-natured old soul and I thought it might be just motherliness on her part; but then one day Kosti said to me:

'"Listen, it's not me she wants; it's you. I haven't got a chance."

'"Don't talk such nonsense," I said to him. "She's old enough to be my mother."

'"What of it? You go ahead, my boy, I won't stand in your way. She's not so young as she might be, but she's a fine figure of a woman."

'"Oh, shut up."

'"Why d'you hesitate? Not on my account, I hope. I'm a philosopher and I know there are as good fish in the sea as ever came out. I don't blame her. You're young. I've been young too. *Jeunesse ne dure qu'un moment.*"

'I wasn't too pleased that Kosti was so sure of what I didn't want to believe. I didn't quite know how to deal with the situation, and then I recalled various things that hadn't struck me at the time. Things said by Ellie that I hadn't paid much attention to. But now I understood them and I was pretty sure that she too knew what was happening. She'd turn up suddenly in the kitchen when Frau Becker and I happened to be alone. I got the impression that she was watching us. I didn't like it. I thought she was out to catch us, I knew she hated Frau Becker, and if she had half a chance she'd make trouble. Of course I knew she couldn't catch us, but she was a malevolent creature and I didn't know what lies she mightn't invent and pour into old Becker's ears. I didn't know what to do except to pretend I was such a fool I didn't see what the old girl was up to. I was happy at the farm and enjoying the work and I didn't want to go till after we'd got the harvest in.'

I couldn't help smiling. I could imagine what Larry had looked like then, in his patched shirt and shorts, his face and neck burnt brown by the hot sun of the Rhine valley, with his lithe slim body and his black eyes in their deep sockets. I could well believe that the sight of him set the matronly Frau Becker, so blonde, so full-breasted, all of a flutter with desire.

'Well, what happened?' I asked.

'Well, the summer wore on. We worked like demons there. We cut and stacked the hay. When the cherries were ripe, Kosti and I got up on ladders and picked them, and the two women put them in great baskets and old Becker took them into Zwingenberg and sold them. Then we cut the rye. And of course there were always the animals to look after. We were up before dawn and we didn't stop work till nightfall. I supposed Frau Becker had given me up as a bad job; as far as I could without offending her, I kept her at arm's length. I was too sleepy to read much German in the evenings and soon after supper I'd take myself off to our loft and fall into bed. Most

evenings Becker and Kosti went to the inn down in the village, but I was fast
asleep by the time Kosti came back. It was hot in the loft and I slept naked.

'One night I was awakened. At the first moment I couldn't make out what
it was; I was only half awake. I felt a hot hand on my mouth and I realized
somebody was in bed with me. I tore the hand away and then a mouth was
pressed to mine, two arms were thrown round me and I felt Frau Becker's
great breasts against my body.

'"*Sei still*," she whispered. "Be quiet."

'She pressed up against me and kissed my face with hot full lips and her
hands travelled over my body and she twined her legs in mine.'

Larry stopped. I giggled.

'What did you do?'

He gave me a deprecating smile. He even flushed a little.

'What could I do? I could hear Kosti breathing heavily in his sleep in the
bed next to mine. The situation of Joseph has always seemed to me faintly
ridiculous. I was only twenty-three. I couldn't make a scene and kick her
out. I didn't want to hurt her feelings. I did what was expected of me.

'Then she slipped out of bed and tiptoed out of the loft. I can tell you, I
heaved a sigh of relief. You know, I'd been scared. "Gosh," I said, "what a
risk to take!" I thought it likely that Becker had come home drunk and fallen
asleep in a stupor, but they slept in the same bed, and it might be that he'd
woken up and seen his wife wasn't there. And there was Ellie. She always
said she didn't sleep well. If she'd been awake she'd have heard Frau Becker
go downstairs and out of the house. And then, suddenly, something struck
me. When Frau Becker was in bed with me I'd felt a piece of metal against
my skin. I'd paid no attention, you know one doesn't in those circumstances,
and I'd never thought of asking myself what the devil it was. And now it
flashed across me. I was sitting on the side of my bed thinking and worrying
about the consequences of all this and it was such a shock that I jumped up.
The piece of metal was Ellie's husband's identification disc that she wore
round her wrist and it wasn't Frau Becker that had been in bed with me. It
was Ellie.'

I roared with laughter. I couldn't stop.

'It may seem funny to you,' said Larry. 'It didn't seem funny to me.'

'Well, now you look back on it, don't you think there is just a faint element
of the humorous about it?'

An unwilling smile played on his lips.

'Perhaps. But it was an awkward situation. I didn't know what it was
going to lead to. I didn't like Ellie. I thought her a most unpleasant female.'

'But how could you mistake one for the other?'

'It was pitch dark. She never said a word except to tell me to keep my trap
shut. They were both big stout women. I thought Frau Becker had her eye
on me. It never occurred to me for a moment that Ellie gave me a thought.
She was always thinking of her husband. I lit a cigarette and thought the
position over, and the more I thought of it the less I liked it. It seemed to me
that the best thing I could do was to get out.

'I'd often cursed Kosti because he was so hard to wake. When we were at
the mine I used to have to shake the life out him to get him up in time to go to
work. But I was thankful now that he slept so heavily. I lit my lantern and
dressed, bundled my things into my rucksack—I hadn't got much, so it
didn't take a minute—and slipped my arms through the straps. I walked
across the loft in my stocking feet and didn't put my shoes on till I got to the

bottom of the ladder. I blew out the lantern. It was a dark night, with no moon, but I knew my way to the road and I turned in the direction of the village. I walked fast as I wanted to get through it before anyone was up and about. It was only twelve miles to Zwingenberg and I got there just as it was stirring. I shall never forget that walk. There wasn't a sound except my footsteps on the road and now and then the crowing of a cock in a farm. Then the first greyness when it wasn't yet light and not quite dark, and the first hint of dawn, and the sunrise with the birds all starting to sing, and that lush green country, meadows and woods and the wheat in the fields silvery gold in the cool light of the beginning day. I got a cup of coffee at Zwingenberg and a roll, then I went to the post office and sent a wire to the American Express to have my clothes and my books sent to Bonn.'

'Why Bonn?' I interrupted.

'I'd taken a fancy to it when we stopped off there on our tramp down the Rhine. I liked the way the light shone on the roofs and the river, and its old narrow streets, and its villas and gardens and avenues of chestnut trees and the rococo buildings of the university. It struck me then it wouldn't be a bad place to stay in for a bit. But I thought I'd better present a respectable appearance when I got there, I looked like a tramp and I didn't think I'd inspire much confidence if I went to a pension and asked for a room, so I took a train to Frankfurt and bought myself a grip and a few clothes. I stayed in Bonn off and on for a year.'

'And did you get anything out of your experience, at the mine, I mean, and on the farm?'

'Yes,' said Larry, nodding his head and smiling.

But he didn't tell me what it was and I knew him well enough by then to know that when he felt like telling you something he did, but when he didn't he would turn off questions with a cool pleasantry that made it useless to insist. For I must remind the reader that he narrated all this to me ten years after it happened. Till then, when I once more came in contact with him, I had no notion where he was or how he was engaged. For all I knew he might be dead. Except for my friendship with Elliott, who kept me posted with the course of Isabel's life and so reminded me of Larry, I should doubtless have forgotten his existence.

Three

Isabel was married to Gray Maturin early in the June of the year after the termination of her engagement to Larry. Though Elliott hated leaving Paris at a moment when the season was at its height and he must miss a number of grand parties, his family feeling was too strong to allow him to neglect what he thought a social duty. Isabel's brothers were unable to leave their distant posts and so it behoved him to make the irksome journey to Chicago to give his niece away. Remembering that French aristocrats had gone to the guillotine in all their finery, he made a special journey to London to get himself a new morning coat, a dove-grey double-breasted waistcoat and a silk hat. On his return to Paris he invited me to come and see them on. He was in a state of perturbation because the grey pearl he usually wore in his necktie would not make any sort of effect against the pale grey tie he had chosen as suitable to the festive occasion. I suggested his emerald-and-diamond pin.

'If I were a guest—yes,' he said. 'But in the particular position I shall occupy I feel that a pearl is indicated.'

He was much pleased with the marriage, which concorded with all his ideas of propriety, and he spoke of it with the unctuousness of a dowager duchess expressing herself on the suitability of a union between a scion of the La Rochefoucaulds with a daughter of the Montmorencys. As a visible mark of his satisfaction he was taking over as a wedding present, sparing no expense, a fine portrait by Nattier of a princess of the House of France.

It appeared that Henry Maturin had bought for the young couple a house in Astor Street so that they should be close to where Mrs Bradley lived and not too far from his own palatial residence on Lake Shore Drive. By a happy chance, in which I suspected the deft complicity of Elliott, Gregory Brabazon was in Chicago at the time the purchase was made and the decoration was entrusted to him. When Elliott returned to Europe and, throwing in his hand so far as the season in Paris was concerned, came straight to London, he brought photographs of the result. Gregory Brabazon had let himself go. In the drawing-room he had gone all George the Second and it was very grand. In the library, which was to be Gray's den, he had been inspired by a room in the Amalienburg Palace at Munich, and except that there was no place in it for books it was perfect. Save for the twin beds, Louis Quinze visiting Madame de Pompadour would have found himself perfectly at home in the bedroom Gregory had provided for this young American couple, but Isabel's bathroom would have been an eye-opener to him; it was all glass—walls, ceiling and bath—and on the walls silver fish meandered profusely among gilded aquatic plants.

'Of course it's a tiny house,' said Elliott, 'but Henry told me the decoration set him back a hundred thousand dollars. A fortune to some people.'

The ceremony was performed with such pomp as the Episcopalian church could afford.

'Not like a wedding at Nôtre Dame,' he told me complacently, 'but for a Protestant affair it didn't lack style.'

The press had behaved very handsomely and Elliott negligently tossed the cuttings to me. He showed me photographs of Isabel, hefty but handsome in her wedding-dress, and Gray, a massive but fine figure of a man, a trifle self-conscious in his formal clothes. There was a group of the young couple with bridesmaids and another group with Mrs Bradley in a sumptuous garment and Elliott holding his new top-hat with a grace that only he could have achieved. I asked how Mrs Bradley was.

'She's lost a good deal of weight and I don't like her colour, but she's pretty well. Of course the whole thing was a strain on her, but now it's all over she'll be able to rest up.'

A year later Isabel was delivered of a daughter, to whom, following the fashion of the moment, she gave the name of Joan; and after an interval of two years she had another daughter whom, following another fashion, she called Priscilla.

One of Henry Maturin's partners died and the other two under pressure soon afterwards retired, so that he entered into sole possession of the business over which he had always exercised despotic control. He realized the ambition he had long entertained and took Gray into partnership with him. The firm had never been so prosperous.

'They're making money hand over fist, my dear fellow,' Elliott told me. 'Why, Gray at the age of twenty-five is making fifty thousand a year, and that's only a beginning. The resources of America are inexhaustible. It isn't a boom, it's just the natural development of a great country.'

His chest swelled with an unwonted patriotic fervour.

'Henry Maturin can't live for ever, high blood pressure, you know, and by the time Gray's forty he should be worth twenty million dollars. Princely, my dear fellow, princely.'

Elliott kept up a fairly regular correspondence with his sister and from time to time as the years went on passed on to me what she told him. Gray and Isabel were very happy, and the babies were sweet. They lived in a style that Elliott gladly admitted was eminently suitable; they entertained lavishly and were lavishly entertained; he told me with satisfaction that Isabel and Gray hadn't dined by themselves once in three months. Their whirl of gaiety was interrupted by the death of Mrs Maturin, that colourless, highborn lady whom Henry Maturin had married for her connection when he was making a place for himself in the city to which his father had come as a country bumpkin; and out of respect for her memory for a year the young couple never entertained more than six people to dinner.

'I've always said that eight was the perfect number,' said Elliott, determined to look on the bright side of things. 'It's intimate enough to permit of general conversation and yet large enough to give the impression of a party.'

Gray was wonderfully generous to his wife. On the birth of their first child he gave her a square-cut diamond ring and on the birth of her second a sable coat. He was too busy to leave Chicago much, but such holidays as he could take they spent at Henry Maturin's imposing house at Marvin. Henry could deny nothing to the son whom he adored and one Christmas gave him a plantation in South Carolina so that he could get a fortnight's duck-shooting in the season.

'Of course our merchant princes correspond to those great patrons of the arts of the Italian Renaissance who made fortunes by commerce. The Medici, for instance. Two kings of France were not too proud to marry the daughters of that illustrious family and I foresee the day when the crowned heads of Europe will seek the hands of our dollar princesses. What was it Shelley said? "The world's great age begins anew, the golden years return."'

Henry Maturin had for many years looked after Mrs Bradley's and Elliott's investments and they had a well-justified confidence in his acumen. He had never countenanced speculation and had put their money into sound securities, but with the great increase in values they found their comparatively modest fortunes increased in a manner that both surprised and delighted them. Elliott told me that, without stirring a finger, he was nearly twice as rich in 1926 as he had been in 1918. He was sixty-five, his hair was grey, his face lined and there were pouches under his eyes, but he bore his years gallantly; he was as slim and held himself as erectly as ever; he had always been moderate in his habits and taken care of his appearance. He had no intention of submitting to the ravages of time so long as he could have his clothes made by the best tailor in London, his hair dressed and his face shaved by his own particular barber and a masseur to come in every morning to keep his elegant body in perfect condition. He had long forgotten that he had ever so far demeaned himself as to engage in a trade, and without ever saying so outright, for he was not so stupid as to tell a lie that might be found out, he was inclined to suggest that in his youth he had been in the diplomatic service. I must admit that if I had ever had occasion to draw a portrait of an ambassador I should without hesitation have chosen Elliott as my model.

But things were changing. Such of the great ladies who had advanced Elliott's career as were still alive were well along in years. The English peeresses, having lost their lords, had been forced to surrender their mansions to daughters-in-law, and had retired to villas at Cheltenham or to modest houses in Regent's Park. Stafford House turned into a museum, Curzon House became the seat of an organization, Devonshire House was for sale. The yacht on which Elliott had been in the habit of staying at Cowes had passed into other hands. The fashionable persons who occupied the stage had no use for the elderly man that Elliott now was. They found him tiresome and ridiculous. They were still willing to come to his elaborate luncheon parties at Claridge's but he was quick-witted enough to know that they came to meet one another rather than to see him. He could no longer pick and choose among the invitations that once had littered his writing-table, and much more often than he would have liked anyone to know he suffered the humiliation of dining by himself in the privacy of his suite. Women of rank in England, when a scandal has closed the doors of society to them, develop an interest in the arts and surround themselves with painters, writers and musicians. Elliott was too proud thus to humiliate himself.

'The death duties and the war profiteers have ruined English society,' he told me. 'People don't seem to mind who they know. London still has its tailors, its bootmakers and its hatters, and I trust they'll last my time, but except for them it's finished. My dear fellow, do you know that the St Erths have women to wait at table?'

This he said when we were walking away from Carlton House Terrace after a luncheon party at which an unfortunate incident had occurred. Our noble host had a well-known collection of pictures, and a young American who was there, Paul Barton by name, expressed a desire to see them.

'You've got a Titian, haven't you?'

'We had. It's in America now. Some old Jew offered us a packet of money for it and we were damned hard up at the time, so my governor sold it.'

I noticed that Elliott, bristling, threw a venomous glance at the jovial marquess, and guessed that it was he who had bought the picture. He was furious at hearing himself, Virginian born and the descendant of a signatory of the Declaration, thus described. He had never in his life suffered so great an affront. And what made it worse was that Paul Barton was the object of his virulent hatred. He was a young man who had appeared in London soon after the war. He was twenty-three, blond, very good-looking, charming, a beautiful dancer and had an ample fortune. He had brought a letter of introduction to Elliott, who with the kindness of heart natural to him had presented him to several of his friends. Not content with this he had given him some valuable hints on conduct. Delving back into his own experience, he had shown him how it was possible, by paying small attentions to old ladies and by lending a willing ear to distinguished men, however tedious, for a stranger to make his way in society.

But it was a different world that Paul Barton entered from that into which, a generation before, Elliott Templeton had penetrated–by means of dogged perseverance. It was a world bent on amusing itself. Paul Barton's high spirits, pleasing exterior and engaging manner did for him in a few weeks what Elliott had achieved only after years of industry and determination. Soon he no longer needed Elliott's help and took small pains to conceal the fact. He was pleasant to him when they met, but in an offhand way that deeply offended the older man. Elliott did not ask people to a party because he liked them, but because they helped to make it go, and since Paul Barton was popular he continued to invite him on occasion to his weekly luncheons; but the successful young man was generally engaged and twice he threw Elliott over at the last moment. Elliott had done this himself too often not to know it was because he had just had a more tempting invitation.

'I don't ask you to believe it,' Elliott told me, fuming, 'but it's God's truth that when I see him now he patronizes me. ME. Titian. Titian,' he spluttered. 'He wouldn't know a Titian if he saw one.'

I had never seen Elliott so angry and I guessed his wrath was caused by his belief that Paul Barton had asked about the picture maliciously, having somehow learnt that Elliott had bought it, and would make a funny story at his expense out of the noble lord's reply.

'He's nothing but a dirty little snob, and if there's one thing in the world I detest and despise it's snobbishness. He'd have been nowhere except for me. Would you believe it, his father makes office furniture. Office furniture.' He put withering scorn into the two words. 'And when I tell people he simply doesn't exist in America, his origins couldn't be more humble, they don't seem to care. Take my word for it, my dear fellow, English society is as dead as the dodo.'

Nor did Elliott find France much better. There the great ladies of his youth, if still alive, were given over to bridge (a game he loathed), piety and the care of their grandchildren. Manufacturers, Argentines, Chileans, American women separated or divorced from their husbands, inhabited the stately houses of the aristocracy and entertained with splendour, but at their parties Elliott was confounded to meet politicians who spoke French with a vulgar accent, journalists whose table manners were deplorable, and even actors. The scions of princely families thought it no shame to marry the daughters of shopkeepers. It was true Paris was gay, but with what a shoddy gaiety! The young, devoted to the mad pursuit of pleasure, thought nothing more amusing than to go from one stuffy little night club to another, drinking champagne at a hundred francs a bottle and dancing close-packed with the riff-raff of the town till five o'clock in the morning. The smoke, the heat, the noise made Elliott's head ache. This was not the Paris that he had accepted thirty years before as his spiritual home. This was not the Paris that good Americans went to when they died.

Four

But Elliott had a flair. An inner monitor suggested to him that the Riviera was on the point of becoming once more the resort of rank and fashion. He knew the coast well from having often spent a few days in Monte Carlo at the

Hôtel de Paris on his way back from Rome, whither his duties at the papal court had called him, or at Cannes in the villa of one or the other of his friends. But that was in the winter, and of late rumours had reached him that it was beginning to be well spoken of as a summer resort. The big hotels were remaining open; their summer visitors were listed in the social columns of the *Paris Herald* and Elliott read the familiar names with approval.

'The world is too much with me,' he said. 'I have now reached a time of life when I am prepared to enjoy the beauties of nature.'

The remark may seem obscure. It isn't really. Elliott had always felt that nature was an impediment to the social life, and he had no patience with people who could bother to go to see a lake or a mountain when they had before their eyes a Regency commode or a painting by Watteau. He had at the time a considerable sum of money to spend. Henry Maturin, urged by his son and exasperated by the sight of his friends on the stock exchange who were making fortunes overnight, had surrendered at last to the current of events and, abandoning little by little his old conservatism, had seen no reason why he too should not get on the band wagon. He wrote to Elliott that he was as much opposed to gambling as he had ever been, but this was not gambling, it was an affirmation of his belief in the inexhaustible resources of the country. His optimism was based on common sense. He could see nothing to halt the progress of America. He ended by saying that he had bought on margin a number of sound securities for dear Louisa Bradley and was glad to be able to tell Elliott that she now had a profit of twenty thousand dollars. Finally, if Elliott wanted to make a little money and would allow him to act according to his judgment, he was confident that he would not be disappointed. Elliott, apt to use hackneyed quotations, remarked that he could resist anything but temptation; the consequence of which was that from then on, instead of turning to the social intelligence as he had done for many years when the *Herald* was brought him with his breakfast, he gave his first attention to the reports of the stock market. So successful were Henry Maturin's transactions on his behalf that now Elliott found himself with the tidy sum of fifty thousand dollars which he had done nothing to earn.

He decided to take his profit and buy a house on the Riviera. As a refuge from the world he chose Antibes, which held a strategic position between Cannes and Monte Carlo so that it could be conveniently reached from either; but whether it was the hand of Providence or his own sure instinct that led him to choose a spot that was soon to become the centre of fashion, it is impossible to say. To live in a villa with a garden had a suburban vulgarity that revolted his fastidious taste, so he acquired two houses in the old town looking on the sea, knocked them into one, and installed central heating, bathrooms and the sanitary conveniences that American example has forced on a recalcitrant. Pickling was all the rage just then, so he furnished the house with old Provençal furniture duly pickled and, surrendering discreetly to modernity, with modern fabrics. He was still unwilling to accept such painters as Picasso and Braque–'horrors, my dear fellow, horrors'– whom certain misguided enthusiasts were making such a fuss about, but felt himself at long last justified in extending his patronage to the Impressionists and so adorned his walls with some very pretty pictures. I remember a Monet of people rowing on a river, a Pissarro of a quay and a bridge on the Seine, a Tahitian landscape by Gauguin and a charming Renoir of a young girl in profile with long yellow hair hanging down her back. His house when finished was fresh and gay, unusual, and simple with that simplicity that you know could only have been achieved at great expense.

Then began the most splendid period of Elliott's life. He brought his excellent chef down from Paris and it was soon acknowledged that he had the best cuisine on the Riviera. He dressed his butler and his footman in white with gold straps on their shoulders. He entertained with a magnificence that never overstepped the bounds of good taste. The shores of the Mediterranean were littered with royalties from all parts of Europe: some lured there on account of the climate, some in exile, and some because a scandalous past or an unsuitable marriage made it more convenient for them to inhabit a foreign country. There were Romanoffs from Russia, Hapsburgs from Austria, Bourbons from Spain, the two Sicilys and Parma; there were princes of the House of Windsor and princes of the House of Bragança; there were Royal Highnesses from Sweden and Royal Highnesses from Greece: Elliott entertained them. There were princes and princesses not of royal blood, dukes and duchesses, marquesses and marchionesses, from Austria, Italy, Spain, Russia and Belgium: Elliott entertained them. In winter the King of Sweden and the King of Denmark made sojourns on the coast; now and then Alfonso of Spain paid a hurried visit: Elliott entertained them. I never ceased to admire the way in which, while he bowed with courtly grace to these exalted personages, he managed to maintain the independent demeanour of the citizen of a country where all men are said to be born equal.

I had then, after some years of travel, bought a house on Cap Ferrat and thus saw a good deal of Elliott. I had risen so high in his good graces that sometimes he invited me to his very grandest parties.

'Come as a favour to me, my dear fellow,' he would say. 'Of course I know just as well as you do that royalties ruin a party. But other people like to meet them and I think one owes it to oneself to show the poor things some attention. Though heaven knows they don't deserve it. They're the most ungrateful people in the world; they'll use you, and when they have no further use for you they'll cast you aside like a frayed shirt; they'll accept innumerable favours from you, but there's not one of them who'd cross the road to do the smallest thing for you in return.'

Elliott had taken pains to get on good terms with the local authorities, and the prefect of the district and the bishop of the diocese, accompanied by his vicar general, often graced his table. The bishop had been a cavalry officer before entering the Church and in the war had commanded a regiment. He was a rubicund, stoutish man, who affected the rough-and-ready language of the barracks, and his austere, cadaverous vicar general was always on pins and needles lest he should say something scandalous. He listened with a deprecating smile when his superior told his favourite stories. But the bishop conducted his diocese with remarkable competence and his eloquence in the pulpit was no less moving than his sallies at the luncheon table were amusing. He approved of Elliott for his pious generosity to the Church and liked him for his amiability and the good food he provided; and the two became good friends. Elliott could thus flatter himself that he was making the best of both worlds and, if I may venture so to put it, effecting a very satisfactory working arrangement between God and Mammon.

Elliott was house-proud and he was anxious to show his new house to his sister; he had always felt a certain reserve in her approval of him and he wanted her to see the style in which he now lived and the friends he hobnobbed with. It was the definitive answer to her hesitations. She would have to admit that he had made good. He wrote and asked her to come over with Gray and Isabel, not to stay with him, for he had no room, but to stay as his guests at the near-by Hôtel du Cap. Mrs Bradley replied that her travelling days were over, for her health was indifferent and she thought she was better off at home; and in any case it was impossible for Gray to absent himself from Chicago; business was booming and he was making a great deal of money and had to stay put. Elliott was attached to his sister and her letter alarmed him. He wrote to Isabel. She replied by cable that, though her mother was so far from well that she had to stay in bed one day a week, she was in no immediate danger and indeed with care might be expected to a live a long time yet; but that Gray needed a rest and, with his father there to look after things, there was no reason why he should not take a holiday; so, not that summer but the next, she and Gray would come over.

On October the 23rd, 1929, the New York market broke.

Five

I was in London then and at first we in England did not realize how grave the situation was nor how distressing its results would be. For my own part though chagrined at losing a considerable sum, it was for the most part paper profits that I lost, and when the dust had settled I found myself little the poorer in cash. I knew that Elliott had been gambling heavily and feared that he was badly hit, but I did not see him till we both returned to the Riviera for Christmas. He told me then that Henry Maturin was dead and Gray ruined.

I know little of business matters and I dare say that my account of the events, given me by Elliott, will seem confused. So far as I could make out the catastrophe that had befallen the firm was due in part to Henry Maturin's self-will and in part to Gray's rashness. Henry Maturin at first would not believe that the break was serious, but persuaded himself that it was a plot of the New York brokers to put a quick one over their provincial brethren, and setting his teeth poured forth money to support the market. He raged against the Chicago brokers who were letting themselves be stampeded by those scoundrels in New York. He had always prided himself on the fact that none of his smaller clients, widows with settled incomes, retired officers and such like, had ever lost a penny by following his advice, and now, instead of letting them take a loss, he supported their accounts out of his own pocket. He said he was prepared to go broke, he could make another fortune, but he could never hold up his head again if the little people who trusted him lost their all. He thought he was magnanimous; he was only vain. His great fortune melted and one night he had a heart attack. He was in his sixties, he had always worked hard, played hard, eaten too much and drunk heavily; after a few hours of agony he died of coronary thrombosis.

Gray was left to deal with the situation alone. He had been speculating extensively on the side, without the knowledge of his father, and was personally in the greatest difficulty. His efforts to extricate himself failed. The banks would not lend him money; older men on the exchange told him that the only thing was to throw up the sponge. I am not clear about the rest of the story. He was unable to meet his obligations and was, I understand,

declared bankrupt; he had already mortgaged his own house and was glad to
hand it over to the mortgagees; his father's house on Lake Shore Drive and
the house at Marvin were sold for what they would fetch; Isabel sold her
jewels: all that was left them was the plantation in South Carolina, which was
settled on Isabel and for which a purchaser could not be found. Gray was
wiped out.

'And what about you, Elliott?' I asked.

'Oh, I'm not complaining,' he answered airily. 'God tempers the wind to
the shorn lamb.'

I did not question him further, for his financial affairs were no business of
mine, but whatever his losses were I presumed that like the rest of us he had
suffered.

The depression did not at first hit the Riviera badly. I heard of two or
three people who had lost a good deal, many villas remained closed for the
winter and several were put up for sale. The hotels were far from full and the
Casino at Monte Carlo complained that the season was poor. But it was not
for a couple of years that the draught made itself felt. Then an estate agent
told me that on the stretch of coast that reaches from Toulon to the Italian
border there were forty-eight thousand properties, large and small, to be
sold. The shares of the Casino slumped. The great hotels put down their
prices in a vain attempt to attract. The only foreigners to be seen were those
who had always been so poor that they couldn't be poorer, and they spent no
money because they had no money to spend. The shopkeepers were in
despair. But Elliott neither diminished his staff nor lessened their wages as
many did; he continued to provide choice food and choice wines to royal and
titled persons. He bought himself a large new car, which he imported from
America and on which he had to pay a heavy duty. He gave generously to the
charity the bishop had organized to provide free meals for the families of the
workless. In fact he lived as though there had never been a crisis and half the
world were not staggering from its effects.

I discovered the reason by chance: Elliott had by this time ceased to go to
England except for a fortnight once a year to buy clothes, but he still
transferred his establishment to his apartment in Paris for three months in
the autumn and for May and June, these being the periods when the Riviera
was deserted by Elliott's friends; he liked the summer there, partly on
account of the bathing, but chiefly, I think, because the hot weather gave
him the opportunity to indulge in a gaiety of dress that his sense of decorum
had always forced him to eschew. He would appear then in trousers of
startling colour, red, blue, green or yellow, and with them wear singlets of
contrasting hue, mauve, violet, puce or harlequin, and would accept the
compliments his attire clamoured for with the deprecating grace of an
actress who is told that she has played a new rôle divinely.

I happened to be spending a day in Paris in the spring on my way back to
Cap Ferrat and had asked Elliott to lunch with me. We met in the Ritz bar,
no longer thronged with college boys come from America to have a good
time, but as deserted as a playwright after the first night of an unsuccessful
play. We had a cocktail, a transatlantic habit to which Elliott had at last
become reconciled, and ordered our lunch. When we had finished, he
suggested that we should go round the curio shops, and though I told him I
had no money to spend I was glad enough to accompany him. We walked
through the Place Vendôme and he asked if I would mind going in to
Charvet's for a moment; he had ordered some things and wanted to know if

they were ready. It appeared that he was having some vests made, and some drawers, and he was having his initials embroidered on them. The vests had not come in yet, but the drawers were there and the shop assistant asked Elliott if he would like to see them.

'I would,' said he, and when the man had gone to fetch them added to me: 'I have them made to order on a pattern of my own.'

They were brought, and to me, except that they were of silk, looked exactly like the drawers I had frequently bought for myself at Macy's; but what caught my eye was that above the intertwined E. T. of the initials was a count's crown. I did not say a word.

'Very nice, very nice,' said Elliott. 'Well, when the undershirts are ready you'll send them along.'

We left the shop and Elliott, as he walked away, turned to me with a smile.

'Did you notice the crown? To tell you the truth, I'd forgotten about it when I asked you to come in to Charvet's. I don't think I've had occasion to tell you that His Holiness has been graciously pleased to revive in my favour my old family title.'

'Your what?' I said, startled out of my politeness.

'Didn't you know? I am descended in the female line from the Count de Lauria who came over to England in the suite of Philip the Second and married a maid of honour of Queen Mary's.'

'Our old friend Bloody Mary?'

'That, I believe, is what heretics call her,' Elliott answered stiffly. 'I don't think I ever told you that I spent September of '29 in Rome. I thought it a bore having to go because of course Rome is empty then, but it was fortunate for me that my sense of duty prevailed over my desire for worldly pleasures. My friends at the Vatican told me that the crash was coming and strongly advised me to sell all my American securities. The Catholic Church has the wisdom of twenty centuries behind it and I didn't hesitate for a moment. I cabled to Henry Maturin to sell everything and buy gold, and I cabled to Louisa to tell her to do the same. Henry cabled back asking me if I was crazy and said he'd do nothing until I confirmed the instructions. I immediately cabled in the most peremptory manner, telling him to carry them out and to cable me that he had done so. Poor Louisa paid no attention to my advice and suffered for it.'

'So when the crash came you were sitting pretty?'

'An Americanism, my dear fellow, which I see no occasion for you to use, but it expresses my situation with a good deal of accuracy. I lost nothing; in fact I had made what you would probably call a packet. I was able some time later to buy back my securities for a fraction of their original cost, and since I owed it all to what I can only describe as the direct interposition of Providence I felt it only right and proper that I should do something for Providence in return.'

'Oh, and how did you set about that?'

'Well, you know that the Duce has been reclaiming great tracts of land in the Pontine Marshes and it was represented to me that His Holiness was gravely concerned at the lack of places of worship for the settlers. So, to cut a long story short, I built a little Romanesque church, an exact copy of one I knew in Provence, and perfect in every detail, which, though I say it myself, is a gem. It is dedicated to St Martin because I was lucky enough to find an old stained-glass window representing St Martin in the act of cutting his cloak in two to give half of it to a naked beggar, and as the symbolism seemed so apt I bought it and placed it over the high altar.'

I didn't interrupt Elliott to ask him what connection he saw between the Saint's celebrated action and the rake-off on the pretty penny he had made by selling out in the nick of time which, like an agent's commission, he was paying to a higher power. But to a prosaic person like me symbolism is often obscure. He went on.

'When I was privileged to show the photographs to the Holy Father, he was gracious enough to tell me that he could see at a glance that I was a man of impeccable taste, and he added that it was a pleasure to him to find in this degenerate age someone who combined devotion to the Church with such rare artistic gifts. A memorable experience, my dear fellow, a memorable experience. But no one was more surprised than I when shortly afterwards it was intimated to me that he had been pleased to confer a title upon me. As an American citizen I feel it more modest not to use it, except of course at the Vatican, so I have forbidden my Joseph to address me as *Monsieur le Comte*, and I trust you will respect my confidence. I don't wish it bruited abroad. But I would not like His Holiness to think that I do not value the honour that he had done me and it is purely out of respect for him that I have the crown embroidered on my personal linen. I don't mind telling you that I must take a modest pride in concealing my rank under the sober pin-stripe of an American gentleman.'

We parted. Elliott told me he would come down to the Riviera at the end of June. He did not do so. He had just made his arrangements to transfer his staff from Paris, intending to drive down leisurely in his car so that everything should be in perfect order on his arrival, when he received a cable from Isabel to say that her mother had suddenly taken a turn for the worse. Elliott, besides being fond of his sister, had, as I have said, a strong strain of family feeling. He took the first ship out of Cherbourg and from New York went to Chicago. He wrote to tell me that Mrs Bradley was very ill and grown so thin that it was a shock to him. She might last a few weeks longer or even a few months, but in any case he felt it his sad duty to remain with her till the end. He said he found the great heat more supportable than he had expected, but the lack of congenial society only tolerable because at such a moment he had in any case no heart for it. He said he was disappointed with the way his fellow-countrymen had reacted to the depression; he would have expected them to take their misfortune with more equanimity. Knowing that nothing is easier than to bear other people's calamities with fortitude, I thought that Elliott, richer now than he had ever been in his life, was perhaps hardly entitled to be severe. He ended by giving me messages for several of his friends and bade me by no means forget to explain to everyone I met why it was that his house must remain closed for the summer.

Little more than a month later I received another letter from him to tell me that Mrs Bradley had died. He wrote with sincerity and emotion. I should never have thought him capable of expressing himself with such dignity, real feeling and simplicity, had I not long known that notwithstanding his snobbishness and his absurd affectations Elliott was a kindly, affectionate and honest man. In the course of this letter he told me that Mrs Bradley's affairs appeared to be in some disorder. Her elder son, a diplomatist, being *chargé d'affaires* in Tokyo during the absence of the ambassador, had been of course unable to leave his post. Her second son, Templeton, who had been in the Philippines when I first knew the Bradleys, had been in due course recalled to Washington and occupied a responsible position in the State Department. He had come with his wife to Chicago when his mother's condition was recognized as hopeless, but had been obliged to return to the capital immediately after the funeral. In these circumstances Elliott felt that he must remain in America until things were straightened out. Mrs Bradley had divided her fortune equally between her three children, but it appeared that her losses in the crash of '29 had been substantial. Fortunately they had found a purchaser for the farm at Marvin. Elliott in his letter referred to it as dear Louisa's country place.

'It is always sad when a family has to part with its ancestral home,' he wrote, 'but of late years I have seen this forced upon so many of my English friends that I feel that my nephews and Isabel must accept the inevitable with the same courage and resignation that they have. *Noblesse oblige.*'

They had been lucky too in disposing of Mrs Bradley's house in Chicago. There had long been a scheme afoot to tear down the row of houses in one of which Mrs Bradley lived and build in their stead a great block of apartments, but it had been held up by her obstinate determination to die in the house in which she had lived. But no sooner was the breath out of her body than the promoters came forward with an offer and it was promptly accepted. Yet even at that Isabel was left very ill provided for.

After the crash Gray had tried to get a job, even as a clerk in the office of such of the brokers as had weathered the storm, but there was no business. He applied to his old friends to give him something to do, however humble and however badly paid, but he applied in vain. His frenzied efforts to stave off the disaster that finally overwhelmed him, the burden of anxiety, the humiliation, resulted in a nervous breakdown and he began to have headaches so severe that he was incapacitated for twenty-four hours and as limp as a wet rag when they ceased. It had appeared to Isabel that they could not do better than go down with the children to the plantation in South Carolina till Gray regained his health. In its day it had brought in a hundred thousand dollars a year for its rice crop, but for long now had been no more than a wilderness of marsh and gumwood, useful only to sportsmen who wanted to shoot duck, and no purchaser could be found for it. There they had lived off and on since the crash and there they proposed to return till conditions improved and Gray could find employment.

'I couldn't allow that,' Elliott wrote. 'Why, my dear fellow, they live like pigs. Isabel without a maid, no governess for the children, and only a couple of coloured women to look after them. So I've offered them my apartment in Paris and proposed that they should stay there till things change in this fantastic country. I shall provide them with a staff, as a matter of fact my kitchen-maid is a very good cook, so I shall leave her with them and I can easily find someone to take her place. I shall arrange to settle the accounts myself so that Isabel can spend her small income on her clothes and the *menus plaisirs* of the family. This means of course that I shall spend much more of my time on the Riviera and so hope to see a great deal more of you, my dear fellow, than I have in the past. London and Paris being now what they are I'm really more at home on the Riviera. It's the only place remaining where I can meet people who speak my own language. I dare say I shall go to Paris now and then for a few days, but when I do, I don't in the least mind pigging it at the Ritz. I'm glad to say that I've at long last persuaded Gray and Isabel to accede to my wishes and I'm bringing them all over as soon as the necessary arrangements can be made. The furniture and the pictures (very poor in quality, my dear fellow, and of the most doubtful authenticity) are being sold the week after next and meanwhile, as I thought to live in the house till the last moment would be painful to them, I have brought them to stay with me at the Drake. I shall settle them in when we get to Paris and then come down to the Riviera. Don't forget to remember me to your royal neighbour.'

Who could deny that Elliott, that arch-snob, was also the kindest, most considerate and generous of men?

Chapter Four

One

Elliott, having installed the Maturins in his spacious apartment on the Left Bank, returned to the Riviera at the end of the year. He had planned his house to suit his own convenience and there was no room in it for a family of four, so that, even if he had wanted to, he could not have had them to stay with him there. I do not think he regretted it. He was well aware that as a man by himself he was a more desirable asset than if he must be accompanied by a niece and a nephew, and he could hardly expect to arrange his own distinguished little parties (a matter over which he took immense trouble) if he had to count invariably on the presence of two house guests.

'It's much better for them to settle down in Paris and accustom themselves to civilized life. Besides, the two girls are old enough to go to school and I've found one not far from my apartment which I'm assured is very select.'

In consequence of this I did not see Isabel till the spring when, because I had some work to do that made it desirable for me to spend some weeks there, I went to Paris and took a couple of rooms in a hotel just out of the Place Vendôme. It was a hotel I frequented, not only for its convenient situation, but because it had an air. It was a big old house around a courtyard and it had been an inn for close upon two hundred years. The bathrooms were far from luxurious and the plumbing far from satisfactory; the bedrooms with their iron beds, painted white, their old-fashioned white counterpanes and their huge *armoires à glace* had a poverty-stricken look; but the parlours were furnished with fine old furniture. The sofa, the armchairs, dated from the gaudy reign of Napoleon the Third, and, though I could not say they were comfortable, they had a florid charm. In that room I lived in the past of the French novelists. When I looked at the Empire clock under its glass case I thought that a pretty woman in ringlets and a flounced dress might have watched the minute hand move as she waited for a visit from Rastignac, the well-born adventurer whose career in novel after novel Balzac followed from his humble beginnings to his ultimate grandeur. Dr Bianchon, the physician who was so real to Balzac that when he lay dying he said: 'Only Bianchon can save me,' might well have come into that room to feel the pulse and look at the tongue of a noble dowager from the provinces who had come to Paris to see an attorney about a lawsuit and had called in a doctor for a passing ailment. At that bureau a lovesick woman in a crinoline, her hair parted in the middle, may have written a passionate letter to her faithless lover or a peppery old gentleman in a green frock coat and a stock indited an angry epistle to his extravagant son.

The day after my arrival I called up Isabel and asked if she would give me a cup of tea if I came along at five. It was ten years since I'd seen her. She was reading a French novel when I was ushered into the drawing-room by a staid butler and getting up she took both my hands and greeted me with a warm and winning smile. I had never seen her more than a dozen times, and only twice alone, but she made me feel at once that we were not casual acquaintances but old friends. The ten years that had passed had reduced the gulf that separated the young girl from the middle-aged man and I was no longer conscious of the disparity of age between us. With the delicate flattery of a woman of the world she treated me as if I were her contemporary, and in five minutes we were chatting as frankly and as unconstrainedly as though we were playmates who had been in the habit of meeting without interruption. She had acquired ease, self-possession and assurance.

But what chiefly struck me was the change in her appearance. I remember her as a pretty, bouncing girl who threatened to run to fat; I do not know whether, realizing this, she had taken heroic measures to reduce her weight or whether it was an unusual, though happy, accident of childbearing; but now she was as slender as anyone could wish. The mode of the moment accentuated this. She was in black, and at a glance I noticed that her silk dress, neither too plain nor too fancy, had been made by one of the best dressmakers in Paris, and she wore it with the careless confidence of a woman to whom it is second nature to wear expensive clothes. Ten years before, even with Elliott to advise, her frocks had been somewhat on the showy side and she had worn them as though she were not quite at home in them. Marie Louise de Florimond could not have said now that she lacked chic. She had chic to the tips of her rose-painted nails. Her features had fined down and it occurred to me that she had as pretty and as straight a nose as I had ever seen on a woman's face. There was not a line on her forehead or under her hazel eyes, and though her skin had lost the fresh bloom of extreme youth, its texture was as fine as ever; it obviously owed something now to lotions, creams and massage, but they had given it a soft, transparent delicacy that was singularly attractive. Her thin cheeks were very faintly rouged and her mouth was painted with discretion. She wore her bright brown hair bobbed as was the fashion of the moment and marcelled. She had no rings on her fingers, and I remembered that Elliott had told me that she had sold her jewellery; her hands, though not remarkably small, were well made. At that period women wore short frocks in the day-time and I saw that her legs in champagne-coloured stockings were shapely, long and slender. Legs are the undoing of many a comely woman; Isabel's legs, as a girl her most unfortunate trait, were now uncommonly good. In fact from the pretty girl whose glowing health, high spirits and brilliant colour had given her attractiveness she was become a beautiful woman. That she owed her beauty in some degree to art, discipline and mortification of the flesh did not seem to matter. The result was vastly satisfactory. It might be that the grace of her gestures, the felicity of her carriage, had been acquired by taking thought, but they had a look of perfect spontaneity. I conceived the notion that these four months in Paris had put the finishing touches to a work of conscious art that had been years in the making. Elliott, even in his most censorious mood, could not but have approved of her; I, a person less difficult to please, found her ravishing.

Gray had gone to Mortefontaine to play golf, but she told me he would be in presently.

'And you must see my two little girls. They've gone to the Tuileries Gardens, but they ought to be in soon. They're sweet.'

We talked of one thing and another. She liked being in Paris and they were comfortable in Elliott's apartment. Before leaving them he had made them acquainted with such of his friends as he thought they would like and they had already a pleasant circle of acquaintances. He had pressed them to entertain as abundantly as he had been in the habit of doing.

'You know, it tickles me to death to think that we're living like quite rich people when really we're absolutely broke.'

'Is it as bad as that?'

She chuckled, and now I remembered the light, gay laugh that I had found so pleasing in her ten years before.

'Gray hasn't a penny and I have almost exactly the income Larry had when he wanted me to marry him and I wouldn't because I thought we couldn't possibly live on it and now I've got two children besides. It's rather funny, isn't it?'

'I'm glad you can see the joke of it.'

'What news have you of Larry?'

'I? None. I haven't set eyes on him since before you were last in Paris. I knew slightly some of the people he used to know and I did ask them what had become of him, but that was years ago. No one seemed to know anything about him. He just vanished.'

'We know the manager of the bank in Chicago where Larry has his account and he told us that every now and then he got a draft from some queer place. China, Burma, India. He seems to have been getting around.'

I did not hesitate to put the question that came to the tip of my tongue. After all, if you want to know something the best way is to ask.

'D'you wish now that you had married him?'

She smiled engagingly.

'I've been very happy with Gray. He's been a wonderful husband. You know, until the crash came we had a grand time together. We like the same people, and we like doing the same things. He's very sweet. And it's nice being adored; he's just as much in love with me now as when we first married. He thinks I'm the most wonderful girl in the world. You can't imagine how kind and considerate he is. It was quite absurd how generous he was; you see, he thought nothing was too good for me. D'you know, he's never said an unkind or harsh thing to me all these years we've been married. Oh, I've been very lucky.'

I asked myself if she thought she'd answered my question. I changed the conversation.

'Tell me about your little girls.'

As I spoke the doorbell rang.

'Here they are. You shall see for yourself.'

In a moment they came in followed by a nursery governess and I was introduced first to Joan, the elder, and then to Priscilla. Each in turn gave a polite little knick as she took my hand. One was eight and the other six. They were tall for their age; Isabel of course was tall and Gray, I remembered, was immense; but they were pretty only in the way all children are pretty. They looked frail. They had their father's black hair and their mother's hazel eyes. The presence of a stranger did not make them shy, and they talked eagerly to her of their doings in the gardens. They cast eager eyes on the dainties Isabel's cook had provided for tea, but which neither of us had touched, and being given permission to have one thing were thrown into a small agony of doubt as to which to choose. It was pleasant to see the demonstrative affection they had for their mother and the three of them clustered together made a charming picture. When they had eaten the little cake each had selected, Isabel sent them away and they went without a word of expostulation. I received the impression that she was bringing them up to do as they were told.

When they were gone I said the usual things one says to a mother about her children and Isabel accepted my compliments with evident, but somewhat casual, pleasure. I asked her how Gray was liking Paris.

'Well enough. Uncle Elliott left us a car so he can go and play golf almost every day and he's joined the Travellers' Club and he plays bridge there. Of course, Uncle Elliott's offer to support us in this apartment has been a godsend. Gray's nerves went all to pieces and he still has those terrible headaches; even if he could get a job he isn't really fit to take it; and naturally that worries him. He wants to work, he feels he ought to, and it humiliates him not to be wanted. You see, he feels it's a man's business to work and if he can't work he may just as well be dead. He can't bear his feeling of being a drug on the market, and I only got him to come here by persuading him that rest and change would bring him back to normalcy. But I know he won't be happy till he gets back into harness.'

'I'm afraid you've had a very rough time these last two and a half years.'

'Well, you know, when the crash came at first I simply couldn't believe it. It seemed inconceivable to me that we should be ruined. I could understand that other people should be ruined, but that we should be—well, it just seemed impossible. I went on thinking that something would happen to save us at the last moment. And then, when the final blow came, I felt that life wasn't worth living any more, I didn't think I could face the future; it was too black. For a fortnight I was absolutely miserable. God, it was awful, having to part with everything, knowing there wouldn't be any fun any more, having to do without everything I liked—and then at the end of a fortnight I said: "Oh, to hell with it, I'm not going to give it another thought," and I promise you I never have. I don't regret anything. I had a lot of fun while it lasted and now it's gone, it's gone.'

'It's obvious that ruin is easier to bear in a luxurious apartment in a fashionable quarter, with a competent butler and an excellent cook free and for nothing, and when one can cover one's haggard bones with a dress by Chanel, isn't it?'

'Lanvin,' she giggled. 'I see you haven't changed much in ten years. I don't suppose you'll believe me, being a cynical brute, but I'm not sure if I'd have accepted Uncle Elliott's offer except for Gray and the children. On my twenty-eight hundred a year we could have managed perfectly well on the plantation and we'd have grown rice and rye and corn and kept pigs. After all I was born and raised on a farm in Illinois.'

'In a manner of speaking,' I smiled, knowing that in point of fact she had been born in an expensive clinic in New York.

At this point Gray came in. It is true that I had only seen him two or three times twelve years before, but I had seen a photograph of him with his bride

(Elliott kept it in a splendid frame on his piano along with signed photographs of the King of Sweden, the Queen of Spain and the Duc de Guise) and I had a fair recollection of him. I was taken aback. His hair had receded on the temples and there was a small bald patch on the crown, his face was puffy and red, and he had a double chin. He had put on a lot of weight during years of good living and hard drinking and only his great height saved him from being grossly obese. But the thing I most noticed was the expression of his eyes. I remembered quite well the trusting, open frankness of their Irish blue, when the world was before him and he hadn't a care in the world; now I seemed to see in them a sort of puzzled dismay, and even if I hadn't known the facts I think I might have guessed that something had occurred to destroy his confidence in himself and in the ordered course of events. I felt a kind of diffidence in him, as though he had done wrong, though unwittingly, and were ashamed. It was plain that his nerve was shaken. He greeted me with pleasant cordiality and indeed seemed as glad to see me as if I were an old friend, but I had the impression that his rather noisy heartiness was a habit of manner that scarcely corresponded with his inner feeling.

Drinks were brought in and he mixed us a cocktail. He'd played a couple of rounds of golf and was satisfied with his game. He went into somewhat verbose detail over the difficulties he had surmounted over one of the holes and Isabel listened with an appearance of lively interest. After a few minutes, having made a date to take them to dine and see a play, I left.

Two

I fell into the habit of dropping in to see Isabel three or four times a week in the afternoon after my day's work was over. She was generally alone at that hour and glad to have a gossip. The persons to whom Elliott had introduced her were much older than she and I discovered that she had few friends of her own generation. Mine were for the most part busy till dinnertime and I found it more agreeable to talk with Isabel than to go to my club and play bridge with rather grouchy Frenchmen who did not particularly welcome the intrusion of a stranger. Her charming way of treating me as if she and I were of an age made conversation easy and we joked and laughed and chaffed one another, chatting now about ourselves, now about our common acquaintances, now about books and pictures, so that the time passed very agreeably. One of the defects of my character is that I can never grow used to the plainness of people; however sweet a disposition a friend of mine may have, years of intimacy can never reconcile me to his bad teeth or lopsided nose: on the other hand I never cease to delight in his comeliness and after twenty years of familiarity I am still able to take pleasure in a well-shaped brow or the delicate line of a cheekbone. So I never came into Isabel's presence without feeling anew a little thrill of pleasure in the perfection of her oval face, in the creamy delicacy of her skin and in the bright warmth of her hazel eyes.

Then a very unexpected thing happened.

Three

In all big cities there are self-contained groups that exist without intercommunication, small worlds within a greater world that lead their lives, their members dependent upon one another for companionship, as though they inhabited islands separated from each other by an unnavigable strait. Of no city, in my experience, is this more true than of Paris. There high society seldom admits outsiders into its midst, the politicians live in their own corrupt circle, the bourgeoisie, great and small, frequent one another, writers congregate with writers (it is remarkable in André Gide's Journal to see with how few people he seems to have been intimate who did not follow his own calling), painters hobnob with painters and musicians with musicians. The same thing is true of London, but in a less marked degree; there birds of a feather flock much less together, and there are a dozen houses where at the same table you may meet a duchess, an actress, a painter, a member of Parliament, a lawyer, a dressmaker and an author.

The events of my life have led me at one time and another to dwell transitorily in pretty well all the worlds of Paris, even (through Elliott) in the closed world of the Boulevard St Germain; but that which I like best, better than the discreet circle that has its centre in what is now called the Avenue Foch, better than the cosmopolitan crew than patronize Larue's and the Café de Paris, better than the noisy sordid gaiety of Montmartre, is that section of which the artery is the Boulevard du Montparnasse. In my youth I spent a year in a tiny apartment near the Lion de Belfort, on the fifth floor, from which I had a spacious view of the cemetery. Montparnasse has still for me the tranquil air of a provincial town that was characteristic of it then. When I pass through the dingy narrow Rue d'Odessa I remember with a pang the shabby restaurant where we used to foregather to dine, painters and illustrators and sculptors, I but for Arnold Bennett on occasion, the only writer, and sit late discussing excitedly, absurdly, angrily, painting and literature. It is still a pleasure to me to stroll down the boulevard and look at the young people who are as young as I was then and invent stories for myself about them. When I have nothing better to do I take a taxi and go and sit in the old Café du Dôme. It is no longer what it was then, the meeting place exclusively of Bohemia; the small tradesmen of the neighbourhood have taken to visiting it, and strangers from the other side of the Seine come to it in the hope of seeing a world that has ceased to exist. Students come to it still, of course, painters and writers, but most of them are foreigners; and when you sit there you hear around you as much Russian, Spanish, German and English as French. But I have a notion that they are saying very much the same sort of things as we said forty years ago, only they speak of Picasso instead of Manet and of André Breton instead of Guillaume Apollinaire. My heart goes out to them.

When I had been in Paris about a fortnight I was sitting one evening at the

Dôme and since the terrace was crowded I had been forced to take a table in the front row. It was fine and warm. The plane trees were just bursting into leaf and there was in the air that sense of leisure, lightheartedness and alacrity that was peculiar to Paris. I felt at peace with myself, but not lethargically, with exhilaration rather. Suddenly a man walking past me, stopped and with a grin that displayed a set of very white teeth said: 'Hello!' I looked at him blankly. He was tall and thin. He wore no hat and he had a mop of dark brown hair that badly needed cutting. His upper lip and his chin were concealed by a thick brown beard. His forehead and his neck were deeply tanned. He wore a frayed shirt, without a tie, a brown, threadbare coat and a pair of shabby grey slacks. He looked a bum and to the best of my belief I had never seen him before. I put him down for one of those good-for-nothings who have gone to the devil in Paris and I expected him to pull a hardluck story to wheedle a few francs out of me for a dinner and a bed. He stood in front of me, his hands in his pockets, showing white teeth, with a look of amusement in his dark eyes.

'You don't remember me?' he said.

'I've never set eyes on you in my life.'

I was prepared to give him twenty francs, but I wasn't prepared to let him get away with the bluff that we knew one another.

'Larry,' he said.

'Good God! Sit down.' He chuckled, stepped forward and took the empty chair at my table. 'Have a drink.' I beckoned to the waiter. 'How could you expect me to recognize you with all that hair on your face?'

The waiter came and he ordered an orangeade. Now that I looked at him I remembered the peculiarity of his eyes, which came from the black of the iris being as black as that of the pupil and which gave them at once intensity and opaqueness.

'How long have you been in Paris?' I asked.

'A month.'

'Are you going to stay?'

'For a while.'

While I asked these questions my mind was busy. I noticed that the cuffs of his trousers were ragged and that there were holes in the elbows of his coat. He looked as destitute as any beachcomer I had ever met in an Eastern port. It was hard in those days to forget the depression and I wondered whether the crash of '29 had left him penniless. I didn't much like the thought of that and not being a person to beat about the bush I asked him outright:

'Are you down and out?'

'No, I'm all right. What makes you think that?'

'Well, you look as if you could do with a square meal and the things you've got on are only fit for the garbage can.'

'Are they as bad as all that? I never thought about it. As a matter of fact I have been meaning to get myself a few odds and ends, but I never seem able to get down to it.'

I thought he was shy or proud and I didn't see why I should put up with that sort of nonsense.

'Don't be a fool, Larry. I'm not a millionaire, but I'm not poor. If you're short of cash let me lend you a few thousand francs. That won't break me.'

He laughed outright.

'Thanks a lot, but I'm not short of cash. I've got more money that I can spend.'

'Notwithstanding the crash?'

'Oh, that didn't affect me. Everything I had was in government bonds. I don't know whether they went down in value, I never enquired, but I do know that Uncle Sam went on paying up on the coupons like the decent old party he is. In point of fact I've been spending so little during the last few years, I must have quite a bit in hand.'

'Where have you come from now then?'

'India.'

'Oh, I heard you'd been there. Isabel told me. She apparently knows the manager of your bank in Chicago.'

'Isabel? When did you last see her?'

'Yesterday.'

'She's not in Paris?'

'She is indeed. She's living in Elliott Templeton's apartment.'

'That's grand. I'd love to see her.'

Though I was watching his eyes pretty closely while we were exchanging these remarks I could discern only a natural surprise and pleasure, but no feeling more complicated.

'Gray's there too. You know they're married?'

'Yes, Uncle Bob—Dr Nelson, my guardian—wrote and told me, but he died some years ago.'

It occurred to me that with this break in what appeared his only link with Chicago and his friends there he probably knew nothing of what had happened. I told him of the birth of Isabel's two daughters, of the death of Henry Maturin and Louisa Bradley, of Gray's ruin and of Elliott's generosity.

'Is Elliott here too?'

'No.'

For the first time in forty years Elliott was not spending the spring in Paris. Though looking younger he was now seventy and as usual with men of that age there were days when he felt tired and ill. Little by little he had given up taking any but walking exercise. He was nervous about his health and his doctor came to seen him twice a week to thrust into an alternate buttock a hypodermic needle with the fashionable injection of the moment. At every meal, at home or abroad, he took from his pocket a little gold box from which he extracted a tablet which he swallowed with the reserved air of one performing a religious rite. His doctor had recommended him to take the cure at Montecatini, a watering-place in the north of Italy, and after this he proposed to go to Venice to look for a font of a design suitable to his Romanesque church. He was less unwilling to leave Paris unvisited since each year he found it socially more unsatisfactory. He did not like old people, and resented it when he was invited to meet only persons of his own age, and the young he found vapid. The adornment of the church he had built was now a main interest of his life and here he could indulge his ineradicable passion for buying works of art with the comfortable assurance that he was doing it to the glory of God. He had found in Rome an early altar of honey-coloured stone and had been dickering in Florence for six months for a triptych of the Siennese school to put over it.

Then Larry asked me how Gray was liking Paris.

'I'm afraid he's feeling rather lost here.'

I tried to explain to him how Gray had struck me. He listened to me with his eyes fixed on my face in a meditative, unblinking gaze that suggested to me, I don't know why, that he was listening to me not with his ears, but with some inner more sensitive organ of hearing. It was queer and not very comfortable.

'But you'll see for yourself,' I finished.

'Yes, I'd love to see them. I suppose I shall find the address in the phone book.'

'But if you don't want to scare them out of their wits and drive the children into screaming hysterics, I think you'd be wise to have your hair cut and your beard shaved.'

He laughed.

'I've been thinking of it. There's no object in making myself conspicuous.'

'And while you're about it you might get yourself a new outfit.'

'I suppose I am a bit shabby. When I came to leave India I found that I had nothing but the clothes I stand up in.'

He looked at the suit I was wearing and asked me who my tailor was. I told him, but added that he was in London and so couldn't be of much use to him. We dropped the subject and he began to talk again of Gray and Isabel.

'I've been seeing quite a lot of them,' I said. 'They're very happy together. I've never had a chance of talking to Gray alone, and anyway I dare say he wouldn't talk to me about Isabel, but I know he's devoted to her. His face is rather sullen in repose and his eyes are harassed, but when he looks at Isabel such a gentle, kind look comes into them, it's rather moving. I have a notion that all through their trouble she stood by him like a rock and he never forgets how much he owes her. You'll find Isabel changed.' I didn't tell him she was beautiful as she had never been before. I wasn't sure he had the discernment to see how the pretty, strapping girl had made herself into the wonderfully graceful, delicate and exquisite woman. There are men who are affronted by the aids that art can supply to feminine nature. 'She's very good to Gray. She's taking infinite pains to restore his confidence in himself.'

But it was growing late and I asked Larry if he would come along the boulevard and dine with me.

'No, I don't think I will, thanks,' he answered. 'I must be off.'

He got up, nodded in a friendly way, and stepped out on to the pavement.

Four

I saw Gray and Isabel next day and told them that I had seen Larry. They were as much surprised as I had been.

'It'll be wonderful to see him,' said Isabel. 'Let's call him up at once.'

Then I remembered that I hadn't thought of asking him where he was staying. Isabel gave me hell.

'I'm not sure he'd have told me if I had,' I protested, laughing. 'Probably my subconscious had something to do with it. Don't you remember, he never liked telling people where he lived. It was one of his oddities. He may walk in at any moment.'

'That would be like him,' said Gray. 'Even in the old days you could never count on his being where you expected him to be. He was here today and gone tomorrow. You'd see him in a room and think in a moment you'd go and say hello to him and when you turned round he'd disappeared.'

'He always was the most exasperating fellow,' said Isabel. 'It's no good denying that. I suppose we shall just have to wait till it suits him to turn up.'

He didn't come that day, nor the next, nor the day after. Isabel accused me of having invented the story to annoy. I promised her I hadn't and sought to give her reasons why he hadn't shown up. But they were implausible. Within myself I wondered whether on thinking it over he hadn't made up his mind that he just didn't want to see Gray and Isabel and had wandered off somewhere or other away from Paris. I had a feeling already that he never took root anywhere, but was always prepared at a moment's notice, for a reason that seemed good to him or on a whim, to move on.

He came at last. It was a rainy day and Gray hadn't gone to Mortefontaine. The three of us were together, Isabel and I drinking a cup of tea, Gray sipping a whisky and Perrier, when the butler opened the door and Larry strolled in. Isabel with a cry sprang to her feet and throwing herself into his arms kissed him on both cheeks. Gray, his fat red face redder than ever, warmly wrung his hand.

'Gee, I'm glad to see you, Larry,' he said, his voice choked with emotion.

Isabel bit her lip and I saw she was constraining herself not to cry.

'Have a drink, old man,' said Gray unsteadily.

I was touched by their delight at seeing the wanderer. It must have been pleasant for him to perceive how much he meant to them. He smiled happily. It was plain to me that he was, however, completely self-possessed. He noticed the tea things.

'I'll have a cup of tea,' he said.

'Oh, gosh, you don't want tea,' cried Gray. 'Let's have a bottle of champagne.'

'I'd prefer tea,' smiled Larry.

His composure had on the others the effect he may have intended. They calmed down, but looked at him still with fond eyes. I don't mean to suggest that he responded to their natural exuberance with an ungracious coldness; on the contrary, he was as cordial and charming as one could wish; but I was conscious in his manner of something that I could only describe as remoteness and I wondered what it signified.

'Why didn't you come and see us at once, you horror?' cried Isabel, with a pretence of indignation. 'I've been hanging out of the window for the last five days to see you coming and every time the bell rang my heart leapt to my mouth and I had all I could do to swallow it again.'

Larry chuckled.

'Mr M. told me I looked so tough that your man would never let me through the door. I flew over to London to get some clothes.'

'You needn't have done that,' I smiled. 'You could have got a reach-me-down at the Printemps or the Belle Jardinière.'

'I thought if I was going to do it at all, I'd better do the thing in style. I haven't bought any European clothes for ten years. I went to your tailor and said I wanted a suit in three days. He said it would take a fortnight, so we compromised on four. I got back from London an hour ago.'

He wore a blue serge that nicely fitted his slim figure, a white shirt with a soft collar, a blue silk tie and brown shoes. He had had his hair cut short and shaved off the hair on his face. He looked not only neat, but well-groomed. It was a transformation. He was very thin; his cheekbones were more prominent, his temples hollower and his eyes in the deep sockets larger than I remembered them; but notwithstanding he looked very well; he looked, indeed, with his deeply sunburnt, unlined face, amazingly young. He was a year younger than Gray, they were both in their early thirties, but whereas Gray looked ten years more than his age, Larry looked ten years less. Gray's movements, owing to his great bulk, were deliberate and rather heavy; but Larry's were light and easy. His manner was boyish, gay and debonair, but withal it had a serenity that I was peculiarly conscious of and that I did not recollect in the lad I had known before. And as the conversation proceeded, flowing without difficulty as was natural in old friends with so many common memories, with bits of news about Chicago thrown in by Gray and Isabel, trivial gossip, one thing leading to another, with airy laughter, my impression persisted that in Larry, though his laughter was frank and he listened with evident pleasure to Isabel's breezy chatter, there was a very singular detachment. I did feel that he was playing a part, he was too natural for that and his sincerity was obvious; I felt that there was something within him, I don't know whether to call it awareness or a sensibility or a force, that remained strangely aloof.

The children were brought in and made known to Larry, and gave him their polite little knicks. He held out his hand, looking at them with an engaging tenderness in his soft eyes, and they took it, staring at him gravely. Isabel brightly told him they were getting on nicely with their lessons, gave them a cookie each and sent them away.

'I'll come and read to you for ten minutes when you're in bed.'

She did not at that moment want to be interrupted in her pleasure at seeing Larry. The little girls went up to say good night to their father. It was charming to see the love that lit up the red face of that gross man as he took them in his arms and kissed them. No one could help seeing that he proudly adored them and when they were gone he turned to Larry and with a sweet slow smile on his lips said:

'They're not bad kids, are they?'

Isabel gave him an affectionate glance.

'If I let Gray have his way he'd spoil them to death. He'd let me starve, that great brute would, to feed the children on caviare and *pâté de foie gras*.'

He looked at her with a smile and said: 'You're a liar and you know it. I worship the ground you tread on.'

There was a responsive smile in Isabel's eyes. She knew that and was glad of it. A happy couple.

She insisted that we should stay to dinner. I, thinking they would prefer to be by themselves, made excuses, but she would not listen to them.

'I'll tell Marie to put another carrot in the soup and there'll be plenty for four. There's a chicken and you and Gray can eat the legs while Larry and I eat the wings, and she can make the soufflé large enough for all of us.'

Gray too seemed to want me to stay, so I let myself be persuaded to do what I wanted to.

While we waited Isabel told Larry at length what I had already told him in brief. Though she narrated the lamentable story as gaily as possible Gray's face assumed an expression of sullen melancholy. She tried to cheer him up.

'Anyhow it's all over now. We've fallen on our feet and we've got the future before us. As soon as things improve, Gray's going to get a splendid job and make millions.'

Cocktails were brought in and a couple did something to raise the poor fellow's spirits. I saw that Larry, though he took one, scarcely touched it, and when Gray, unobservant, offered him another he refused. We washed our hands and sat down to dinner. Gray had ordered a bottle of champagne, but when the butler began to fill Larry's glass he told him he didn't want any.

'Oh, but you must have some,' cried Isabel. 'It's Uncle Elliott's best and he only gives it to very special guests.'

'To tell you the truth I prefer water. After having been in the East so long it's a treat to drink water that's safe.'

'This is an occasion.'

'All right, I'll drink a glass.'

The dinner was excellent, but Isabel noticed, as I did too, that Larry ate very little. It struck her, I suppose, that she had been doing all the talking and that Larry had had no chance to do more than listen, so now she began to question him on his actions during the ten years since she had seen him. He answered with his cordial frankness, but so vaguely as not to tell us much.

'Oh, I've been loafing around, you know. I spent a year in Germany and some time in Spain and Italy. And I knocked about the East for a bit.'

'Where have you just come from now?'

'India.'

'How long were you there?'

'Five years.'

'Did you have fun?' asked Gray. 'Shoot any tigers?'

'No,' Larry smiled.

'What on earth were you doing with yourself in India for five years?' said Isabel.

'Playing about,' he answered, with a smile of kindly mockery.

'What about the Rope Trick?' asked Gray. 'Did you see that?'

'No, I didn't.'

'What did you see?'

'A lot.'

I put a question to him then.

'Is it true that the Yogis acquire powers that would seem to us supernatural?'

'I wouldn't know. All I can tell you is that it's commonly believed in India. But the wisest don't attach any importance to powers of that sort; they think they're apt to hinder spiritual progress. I remember one of them telling me of a Yogi who came to the bank of a river; he hadn't the money to pay the ferryman to take him across and the ferryman refused to take him for nothing, so he stepped on the water and walked upon its surface to the other side. The Yogi who told me shrugged his shoulders rather scornfully. "A miracle like that," he said "is worth no more than the penny it would have cost to go on the ferryboat."'

'But d'you think the Yogi really walked over the water?' asked Gray.

'The Yogi who told me believed it implicitly.'

It was a pleasure to hear Larry talk, because he had a wonderfully melodious voice; it was light, rich without being deep, and with a singular variety of tone. We finished dinner and went back to the drawing-room to have our coffee. I had never been to India and was eager to hear more of it.

'Did you come in contact with any writers and thinkers?' I asked.

'I notice that you make a distinction between the two,' said Isabel to tease me.

'I made it my business to,' Larry answered.

'How did you communicate with them? In English?'

'The most interesting, if they spoke at all, didn't speak it very well and understood less. I learnt Hindustani. And when I went south I picked up enough Tamil to get along pretty well.'

'How many languages d'you know now, Larry?'

'Oh, I don't know. Half a dozen or so.'

'I want to know more about the Yogis,' said Isabel. 'Did you get to know any of them intimately?'

'As intimately as you can know persons who pass the best part of their time in the Infinite,' he smiled. 'I spent two years in the Ashrama of one.'

'Two years? What's an Ashrama?'

'Well, I suppose you might call it a hermitage. There are holy men who live alone, in a temple, in the forest or on the slopes of the Himalayas. There are others who attract disciples. A charitable person to acquire merit builds a room, large or small, to lodge a Yogi whose piety has impressed him, and the disciples live with him, sleeping on the verandah or in the cookhouse if there is one or under the trees. I had a tiny hut in the compound just big enough for my camp bed, a chair and a table, and a bookshelf.'

'Where was this?' I enquired.

'In Travancore, a beautiful country of green hills and valleys and soft-flowing rivers. Up in the mountains there are tigers, leopards, elephants and bison, but the Ashrama was on a lagoon and all around it grew coconuts and areca palms. It was three or four miles from the nearest town, but people used to come from there, and even from much farther, on foot or by bullock cart, to hear the Yogi talk when he was inclined to, or just to sit at his feet and share with one another the peace and blessedness that were radiated from his presence as fragrance is wafted upon the air by a tuberose.'

Gray moved uneasily in his chair. I guessed that the conversation was taking a turn that he found uncomfortable.

'Have a drink?' he said to me.

'No, thanks.'

'Well, I'm going to have one. What about you, Isabel?'

He raised his great weight from the chair and went over to the table on which stood whisky and Perrier and glasses.

'Were there other white men there?'

'No. I was the only one.'

'How could you stand it for two years?' cried Isabel.

'They passed like a flash. I've spent days that seemed to be unconscionably longer.'

'What did you do with yourself all the time?'

'I read. I took long walks. I went out in a boat on the lagoon. I meditated. Meditation is very hard work; after two or three hours of it you're as exhausted as if you'd driven a car five hundred miles, and all you want to do is to rest.'

Isabel frowned slightly. She was puzzled and I'm not sure that she wasn't a trifle scared. I think she was beginning to have a notion that the Larry who had entered the room a few hours before, though unchanged in appearance and seemingly as open and friendly as he had ever been, was not the same as the Larry, so candid, easy and gay, wilful to her mind but delightful, that she had known in the past. She had lost him before, and on seeing him again, taking him for the old Larry, she had a feeling that, however altered the circumstances, he was still hers; and now, as though she had sought to catch a sunbeam in her hand and it slipped through her fingers as she grasped it, she was a trifle dismayed. I had looked at her a good deal that evening, which was always a pleasant thing to do, and had seen the fondness in her eyes as they rested on his trim head, with small ears close to the skull, and how the expression in them changed when they dwelt on his hollow temples and the thinness of his cheeks. She glanced at his long lean hands, which notwithstanding their emaciation were strong and virile. Then her gaze lingered on his mobile mouth, well shaped, full without being sensual, and on his serene brow and clean-cut nose. He wore his new clothes not with the bandbox elegance of Elliott, but with a sort of loose carelessness as though he had worn them every day for a year. I felt that he aroused in Isabel motherly instincts I had never felt in her relation with her children. She was an experienced woman; he still looked a boy; and I seemed to read in her air the pride of a mother for her grown-up son because he is talking intelligently and others are listening to him as if he made sense. I don't think the import of what he said penetrated her consciousness.

But I was not done with my questioning.

'What was your Yogi like?'

'In person, d'you mean? Well, he wasn't tall, neither thin nor fat, palish brown in colour and clean-shaven, with close-cropped white hair. He never wore anything but a loincloth, and yet he managed to look as trim and neat and well dressed as a young man in one of Brooks Brothers' advertisements.'

'And what had he got that particularly attracted you?'

Larry looked at me for a full minute before answering. His eyes in their deep sockets seemed as though they were trying to pierce to the depths of my soul.

'Saintliness.'

I was slightly disconcerted by his reply. In that room, with its fine furniture, with those lovely drawings on the walls, the word fell like a plop of water that has seeped through the ceiling from an overflowing bath.

'We've all read about saints, St Francis, St John of the Cross, but that was hundreds of years ago. I never thought it possible to meet one who was alive now. From the first time I saw him I never doubted that he was a saint. It was a wonderful experience.'

'And what did you gain from it?'

'Peace,' he said casually, with a light smile. Then, abruptly, he rose to his feet. 'I must go.'

'Oh, not yet, Larry,' cried Isabel. 'It's quite early.'

'Good night,' he said, smiling still, taking no notice of her expostulation. He kissed her on the cheek. 'I'll see you again in a day or two.'

'Where are you staying? I'll call you.'

'Oh, don't bother to do that. You know how difficult it is to get a call through in Paris, and in any case our telephone is generally out of order.'

I laughed inwardly at the neatness with which Larry had got out of giving an address. It was a queer kink of his to make a secret of his abode. I suggested that they should all dine with me next evening but one in the Bois de Boulogne. It was very pleasant in that balmy spring weather to eat out-of-doors, under the trees, and Gray could drive us there in the coupé. I left with

Larry and would willingly have walked some way with him, but as we got
into the street he shook hands with me and walked quickly off. I got into a
taxi.

Five

We had arranged to meet at the apartment and have a cocktail before
starting. I arrived before Larry. I was taking them to a very smart restaurant
and expected to find Isabel arrayed for the occasion; with all the women
dressed up to the nines I was confident she would not wish to be outshone.
But she had on a plain woollen frock.

'Gray's got one of his headaches,' she said. 'He's in agony. I can't possibly
leave him. I told the cook she could go out when she'd given the children
their supper and I must make something for him myself and try to get him to
take it. You and Larry had better go alone.'

'Is Gray in bed?'

'No, he won't ever go to bed when he has his headaches. God knows, it's
the only place for him, but he won't. He's in the library.'

This was a little panelled room, brown and gold, that Elliott had found in
an old château. The books were protected from anyone who wanted to read
them by gilt latticework, and locked up, but this was perhaps as well, as they
consisted for the most part of illustrated pornographic works of the
eighteenth century. In their contemporary morocco, however, they made a
very pretty effect. Isabel led me in. Gray was sitting humped up in a big
leather chair, with picture papers scattered on the floor beside him. His eyes
were closed and his usually red face had a grey pallor. It was evident that he
was in great pain. He tried to get up, but I stopped him.

'Have you given him any aspirin?' I asked Isabel.

'That never does any good. I have an American prescription, but that
doesn't help either.'

'Oh, don't bother, darling,' said Gray. 'I shall be all right tomorrow.' He
tried to smile. 'I'm sorry to make such a nuisance of myself,' he said to me.
'You all go out to the Bois.'

'I wouldn't dream of it,' said Isabel. 'D'you think I should enjoy myself
when I knew you were suffering the tortures of the damned?'

'Poor slut, I think she loves me,' said Gray, his eyes closed.

Then his face was suddenly contorted and you could almost see the
lancinating pain that pierced his head. The door was softly opened and
Larry stepped in. Isabel told him what was the matter.

'Oh, I am sorry,' he said, giving Gray a look of commiseration. 'Isn't there
anything one can do to relieve him?'

'Nothing,' said Gray, his eyes still closed. 'The only thing you can any of
you do for me is to leave me alone; go off and have a good time by yourselves.'

I thought myself that was the only sensible course to take, but I didn't
suppose Isabel could square it with her conscience.

'Will you let me see if I can help you?' asked Larry.

'No one can help me,' said Gray wearily. 'It's just killing me and
sometimes I wish to God it would.'

'I was wrong in saying that perhaps I could help you. What I meant was that perhaps I could help you to help yourself.'

Gray slowly opened his eyes and looked at Larry.

'How can you do that?'

Larry took what looked like a silver coin out of his pocket and put it in Gray's hand.

'Close your fingers on it tightly and hold your hand palm downwards. Don't fight against me. Make no effort, but hold the coin in your clenched fist. Before I count twenty your hand will open and the coin will drop out of it.'

Gray did as he was told. Larry seated himself at the writing-table and began to count. Isabel and I remained standing. One, two, three, four. Till he got up to fifteen there was no movement in Gray's hand, then it seemed to tremble a little and I had the impression, I can hardly say I saw, that the clenched fingers were loosening. The thumb moved away from the fist. I distinctly saw the fingers quiver. When Larry reached nineteen the coin fell out of Gray's hand and rolled to my feet. I picked it up and looked at it. It was heavy and misshapen, and in bold relief on one side of it was a youthful head which I recognized as that of Alexander the Great. Gray stared at his hand with perplexity.

'I didn't let the coin drop,' he said. 'It fell of itself.'

He was sitting with his right arm resting on the arm of the leather chair.

'Are you quite comfortable in that chair?' asked Larry.

'As comfortable as I can be when my head's giving me hell.'

'Well, let yourself go quite slack. Take it easy. Do nothing. Don't resist. Before I count twenty your right arm will rise from the arm of the chair until your hand is above your head. One, two, three, four.'

He spoke the numbers slowly in that silver-toned, melodious voice of his, and when he had reached nine we saw Gray's hand rise, only just perceptibly, from the leather surface on which it rested until it was perhaps an inch above it. It stopped for a second.

'Ten, eleven, twelve.'

There was a little jerk and then slowly the whole arm began to move upwards. It wasn't resting on the chair any more. Isabel, a little scared, took hold of my hand. It was a curious effect. It had no likeness to a voluntary movement. I've never seen a man walking in his sleep, but I can imagine that he would move in just the same strange way that Gray's arm moved. It didn't look as though the will were the motive power. I should have thought it would be hard to raise the arm so slowly and so evenly by a conscious effort. It gave the impression that a subconscious force, independent of the mind, was raising it. It was the same sort of movement as that of a piston moving very slowly back and forth in a cylinder.

'Fifteen, sixteen, seventeen.'

The words fell, slow, slow, slow, like drops of water in a basin from a defective tap. Gray's arm rose, rose, till his hand was above his head, and as Larry reached the number he had said it fell of its own weight on to the arm of the chair.

'I didn't lift my arm,' said Gray. 'I couldn't help its rising like that. It did it of its own accord.'

Larry faintly smiled.

'It's of no consequence. I thought it might give you confidence in me. Where's that Greek coin?'

I gave it to him.

'Hold it in your hand.' Gray took it. Larry glanced at his watch. 'It's thirteen minutes past eight. In sixty seconds your eyelids will grow so heavy that you'll be obliged to close them and then you'll sleep. You'll sleep for six minutes. At eight twenty you'll wake and you'll have no more pain.'

Neither Isabel nor I spoke. Our eyes were on Larry. He said nothing more. He fixed his gaze on Gray, but did not seem to look at him; he seemed rather to look through and beyond him. There was something eerie in the silence that fell upon us; it was like the silence of flowers in a garden at nightfall. Suddenly I felt Isabel's hand tighten. I glanced at Gray. His eyes were closed. He was breathing easily and regularly; he was asleep. We stood there for a time that seemed interminable. I badly wanted a cigarette, but did not like to light one. Larry was motionless. His eyes looked into I knew not what distance. Except that they were open he might have been in a trance. Suddenly he appeared to relax; his eyes took on their normal expression and he looked at his watch. As he did so, Gray opened his eyes.

'Gosh,' he said, 'I believe I dropped off to sleep.' Then he started. I noticed that his face had lost its ghastly pallor. 'My headache's gone.'

'That's fine,' said Larry. 'Have a cigarette and then we'll all go out to dinner.'

'It's a miracle. I feel perfectly swell. How did you do it?'

'I didn't do it. You did it yourself.'

Isabel went to change and meanwhile Gray and I drank a cocktail. Though it was plain that Larry did not wish it, Gray insisted on talking of what had just happened. He couldn't make it out at all.

'I didn't believe you could do a thing, you know,' he said. 'I just gave in because I felt too lousy to argue.'

He went on to describe the onset of his headaches, the anguish he endured and the wreck he was when the attack subsided. He could not understand how it was that just then he felt his usual robust self. Isabel came back. She was wearing a dress I had not seen before; it reached to the ground, a white sheath of what I think is called marocain, with a flare of black tulle, and I could not but think she would be a credit to us.

It was very gay at the Château de Madrid and we were in high spirits. Larry talked amusing nonsense in a way I had not heard him do before and he made us laugh. I had a notion he was doing this with the idea of diverting our minds from the exhibition of his unexpected power. But Isabel was a determined woman. She was prepared to play ball with him as long as it suited her convenience, but she did not lose sight of her desire to satisfy her curiosity. When we had finished dinner and were drinking coffee and liqueurs and she might well have supposed that the good food, the one glass of wine he drank and the friendly talk had weakened his defences she fixed her bright eyes on Larry.

'Now tell us how you cured Gray's headache.'

'You saw for yourself,' he answered, smiling.

'Did you learn to do that sort of thing in India?'

'Yes.'

'He suffers agonies. D'you think you could cure him permanently?'

'I don't know. I might be able to.'

'It would make a difference to his whole life. He couldn't expect to hold a decent job when he may be incapacitated for forty-eight hours. He'll never be happy till he's at work again.'

'I can't work miracles, you know.'

'But it was a miracle. I saw it with my own eyes.'

'No, it wasn't. I merely put an idea in old Gray's head and he did the rest himself.' He turned to Gray. 'What are you doing tomorrow?'

'Playing golf.'

'I'll look in at six and we'll have a talk.' Then, giving Isabel his winning smile: 'I haven't danced with you for ten years, Isabel. Would you care to see if I still know how to?'

Six

After that we saw a good deal of Larry. For the next week he came to the apartment every day and for half an hour shut himself up with Gray in the library. It appeared that he wanted to persuade him—that was how he smilingly put it—out of having those shattering megrims, and Gray conceived a childlike trust in him. From the little Gray said I got the idea that he was trying besides to restore his broken confidence in himself. About ten days later Gray had another headache, and it so happened that Larry was not to come till the evening. It was not a very bad one, but Gray was so confident now in Larry's odd power that he thought if Larry could be got hold of he could take it away in a few minutes. But neither I, whom Isabel called on the phone, nor they knew where he lived. When Larry at last came and relieved Gray of his pain, Gray asked him for his address so that in case he need he could summon him at once. Larry smiled.

'Call the American Express and leave a message. I'll call them every morning.'

Isabel asked me later why Larry made a secret of his address. He had done that before and then it had turned out that he lived without any mystery in a third-rate hotel in the Latin Quarter.

'I haven't a notion,' I said in answer. 'I can only suggest something very fanciful and there's probably nothing in it. It may be that some queer instinct urges him to carry over to his dwelling-place some privacy of his spirit.'

'What in God's name d'you mean by that?' she cried irritably.

'Hasn't it struck you that when he's with us, easy as he is to get on with, friendly and sociable, one's conscious of a sort of detachment in him, as though he weren't giving all of himself, but withheld in some hidden part of his soul something, I don't know what it is—a tension, a secret, an aspiration, a knowledge—that sets him apart?'

'I've known Larry all my life,' she said impatiently.

'Sometimes he reminds me of a great actor playing perfectly a part in a trumpery play. Like Eleanora Duse in *La Locandiera*.'

Isabel pondered over this for a moment.

'I suppose I know what you mean. One's having fun, and one thinks he's just like one of us, just like everybody else, and then suddenly you have the feeling that he's escaped you like a smoke ring that you try to catch in your hands. What do you think it can be that makes him so queer?'

'Perhaps something so commonplace that one simply doesn't notice it.'

'Such as?'

'Well, goodness, for instance.'

Isabel frowned.

'I wish you wouldn't say things like that. It gives me a nasty feeling in the pit of my stomach.'

'Or is it a little pain in the depth of your heart?'

Isabel gave me a long look as though she were trying to read my thoughts. She took a cigarette from the table beside her and, lighting it, leant back in her chair. She watched the smoke curl up into the air.

'Do you want me to go?' I asked.

'No.'

I was silent for a moment, watching her, and I took my pleasure in the contemplation of her shapely nose and the exquisite line of her jaw.

'Are you very much in love with Larry?'

'God damn you, I've never loved anyone else in all my life.'

'Why did you marry Gray?'

'I had to marry somebody. He was mad about me and Mamma wanted me to marry him. Everybody told me I was well rid of Larry. I was very fond of Gray; I'm very fond of him still. You don't know how sweet he is. No one in the world could be so kind and so considerate. He looks as though he had an awful temper, doesn't he? With me he's always been angelic. When we had money, he wanted me to want things so that he could have the pleasure of giving them to me. Once I said it would be fun if we could have a yacht and go round the world, and if the crash hadn't come he'd have bought one.'

'He sounds almost too good to be true,' I murmured.

'We had a grand time. I shall always be grateful to him for that. He made me very happy.'

I looked at her but did not speak.

'I suppose I didn't really love him, but one can get on all right without love. At the bottom of my heart I hankered for Larry, but as long as I didn't see him it didn't really bother me. D'you remember saying to me that with three thousand miles of ocean between, the pangs of love become quite tolerable? I thought it a cynical remark then, but of course it's true.'

'If it's a pain to see Larry, don't you think it would be wiser not to see him?'

'But it's a pain that's heaven. Besides, you know what he is. Any day he may vanish like a shadow when the sun goes in and we may not see him again for years.'

'Have you never thought of divorcing Gray?'

'I've got no reason for divorcing him.'

'That doesn't prevent your countrywomen from divorcing their husbands when they have a mind to.'

She laughed.

'Why d'you suppose they do it?'

'Don't you know? Because American women expect to find in their husbands a perfection that English women only hope to find in their butlers.'

Isabel gave her head such a haughty toss that I wondered she didn't get a crick in the neck.

'Because Gray isn't articulate you think there's nothing to him.'

'You're wrong there,' I interrupted quickly. 'I think there's something rather moving about him. He has a wonderful faculty of love. One has only to glance at his face when he's looking at you to see how deeply, how devotedly he's attached to you. He loves his children much more than you do.'

'I suppose you're going to say now that I'm not a good mother.'

'On the contrary I think you're an excellent mother. You see that they're well and happy. You watch over their diet and take care that their bowels act regularly. You teach them to behave nicely and you read to them and make them say their prayers. If they were sick you'd send for a doctor at once and nurse them with care. But you're not wrapped up in them as Gray is.'

'It's unnecessary that one should be. I'm a human being and I treat them as human beings. A mother only does her children harm if she makes them the only concern of her life.'

'I think you're quite right.'

'And the fact remains that they worship me.'

'I've noticed that. You're their ideal of all that's graceful and beautiful and wonderful. But they're not cosy and at their ease with you as they are with Gray. They worship you, that's true; but they love him.'

'He's very lovable.'

I liked her for saying that. One of her most amiable traits was that she was never affronted by the naked truth.

'After the crash Gray went all to pieces. For weeks he worked at the office till midnight. I used to sit at home in an agony of fear, I was afraid he'd blow his brains out, he was so ashamed. You see, they'd been so proud of the firm, his father and Gray, they were proud of their integrity and the sureness of their judgment. It wasn't so much that we'd lost all our money, what he couldn't get over was that all those people who'd trusted him had lost theirs. He felt that he ought to have had more foresight. I couldn't get him to see that he wasn't to blame.'

Isabel took a lipstick out of her bag and painted her lips.

'But that's not what I wanted to tell you. The one thing we had left was the plantation and I felt that the only chance for Gray was to get away, so we parked the children with Mamma and went down there. He'd always liked it, but we'd never been there by ourselves; we'd taken a crowd with us and had a grand time. Gray's a good shot, but he hadn't the heart to shoot then. He used to take a boat and go out on the marsh by himself for hours at a time and watch the birds. He'd wander up and down the canals with the pale rushes on each side of him and only the blue sky above. On some days the canals are as blue as the Mediterranean. He used not to say much when he came back. He'd say it was swell. But I could see what he felt. I knew that his heart was moved by the beauty and the vastness and the stillness. There's a moment just before sunset when the light on the marsh is lovely. He used to stand and look at it and it filled him with bliss. He took long rides in those solitary, mysterious woods; they're like the woods in a play of Maeterlinck's, so grey, so silent, it's almost uncanny; and there's a moment in spring–it hardly lasts more than a fortnight–when the dogwood bursts into flower, and the gum trees burst into leaf, and their young fresh green against the grey Spanish moss is like a song of joy; the ground is carpeted with great white lilies and wild azalea. Gray couldn't say what it meant to him, but it meant the world. He was drunk with the loveliness of it. Oh, I know I don't put it well, but I can't tell you how moving it was to see that great hulk of a man uplifted by an emotion so pure and so beautiful that it made me want to cry. If there is a God in heaven Gray was very near Him then.'

Isabel had grown a trifle emotional while she told me this and taking a tiny handkerchief she carefully wiped away a tear that glistened at the corner of each eye.

'Aren't you romanticizing?' I said, smiling. 'I have a notion that you're ascribing to Gray thoughts and emotions that you would have expected him to have.'

'How should I have seen them if they hadn't been there? You know what I am. I'm never really happy unless I feel the cement of a sidewalk under my feet and there are large plate-glass windows all along the street with hats to look at and fur coats and diamond bracelets and gold-mounted dressingcases.'

I laughed and we were silent for a moment. Then she went back to what we had been talking of before.

'I'd never divorce Gray. We've been through too much together. And he's absolutely dependent upon me. It's rather flattering, you know, and it gives you a sense of responsibility. And besides . . .'

'Besides what?'

She gave me a sidelong glance and there was a roguish twinkle in her eyes. I had a notion she didn't quite know how I would take what she had in mind to say.

'He's wonderful in bed. We've been married for ten years and he's as passionate a lover as he was at the beginning. Didn't you say in a play once that no man wants the same woman longer than five years? Well, you didn't know what you were talking about. Gray wants me as much as when we were first married. He's made me very happy in that way. Although you wouldn't think it to look at me, I'm a very sensual woman.'

'You're quite wrong, I would think it.'

'Well, it's not an unattractive trait, is it?'

'On the contrary.' I gave her a searching look. 'Do you regret you didn't marry Larry ten years ago?'

'No. It would have been madness. But of course if I'd known then what I know now I'd have gone away and lived with him for three months, and then I'd have got him out of my system for good and all.'

'I think it's lucky for you you didn't make the experiment; you might have found yourself bound to him by bonds you couldn't break.'

'I don't think so. It was merely a physical attraction. You know, often the best way to overcome desire is to satisfy it.'

'Has it ever struck you that you're a very possessive woman? You've told me that Gray has a deep strain of poetic feeling and you've told me that he's an ardent lover; and I can well believe that both mean a lot to you; but you haven't told me what means much more to you than both of them put together—your feeling that you hold him in the hollow of that beautiful but not so small hand of yours. Larry would always have escaped you. D'you remember that Ode of Keats's? "Bold Lover, never, never canst thou kiss, though winning near the goal."'

'You often think you know a great deal more than you do,' she said, a trifle acidly. 'There's only one way a woman holds a man and you know it. And let me tell you this; it's not the first time she goes to bed with him that counts, it's the second. If she holds him then she holds him for good.'

'You do pick up the most extraordinary bits of information.'

'I get around and I keep my eyes and ears open.'

'May I enquire how you acquired that one?'

She gave me her most teasing smile.

'From a woman I made friends with at a dress show. The *vendeuse* told me she was the smartest kept woman in Paris, so I made up my mind I'd got to know her. Adrienne de Troye. Ever heard of her?'

'Never.'

'How your education has been neglected! She's forty-five and not even pretty, but she looks much more distinguished than any of Uncle Elliott's duchesses. I sat down beside her and put on my impulsive little-American-girl act. I told her I had to speak to her because I'd never seen anyone more ravishing in my life. I told her she had the perfection of a Greek cameo.'

'The nerve you've got.'

'She was rather stiff at first and stand-offish, but I ran on in my simple naïve way and she was thawed. Then we had quite a nice little chat. When the show was over I asked her if she wouldn't come to lunch with me at the Ritz one day. I told her I'd always admired her wonderful chic.'

'Had you ever seen her before?'

'Never. She wouldn't lunch with me, she said they had such malicious tongues in Paris, it would compromise me, but she was pleased that I'd asked her, and when she saw my mouth quiver with disappointment she asked me if I wouldn't come and lunch with her in her house. She patted my hand when she saw I was simply overwhelmed by her affability.'

'And did you go?'

'Of course I went. She has a dear little house off the Avenue Foch and we were waited on by a butler who's the very image of George Washington. I stayed till four o'clock. We took our hair down and our stays off, and had a thorough girls' gossip. I learnt enough that afternoon to write a book.'

'Why don't you? It's just the sort of thing to suit the *Ladies' Home Journal*.'

'You fool,' she laughed.

I was silent for a moment. I pursued my thoughts.

'I wonder if Larry was ever *really* in love with you,' I said presently.

She sat up. Her expression lost its amenity. Her eyes were angry.

'What are you talking about? Of course he was in love with me. D'you think a girl doesn't know when a man's in love with her?'

'Oh, I dare say he was in love with you after a fashion. He didn't know any girl so intimately as he knew you. You'd played around together since you were children. He expected himself to be in love with you. He had the normal sexual instinct. It seemed such a natural thing that you should marry. There wouldn't have been any particular difference in your relations except that you lived under the same roof and went to bed together.'

Isabel, to some extent mollified, waited for me to go on and, knowing that women are always glad to listen when you discourse upon love, I went on.

'Moralists try to persuade us that the sexual instinct hasn't got so very much to do with love. They're apt to speak of it as if it were an epiphenomenon.'

'What in God's name is that?'

'Well, there are psychologists who think that consciousness accompanies brain processes and is determined by them, but doesn't itself exert any influence on them. Something like the reflection of a tree in water; it couldn't exist without the tree, but it doesn't in any way affect the tree. I think it's all stuff and nonsense to say that there can be love without passion; when people say love can endure after passion is dead they're talking of something else, affection, kindliness, community of taste and interest, and habit. Especially habit. Two people can go on having sexual intercourse from habit in just the same way as they grow hungry at the hour they're accustomed to have their meals. Of course there can be desire without love. Desire isn't passion. Desire is the natural consequence of the sexual instinct and it isn't of any more importance than any other function of the human animal. That's why women are foolish to make a song and dance if their husbands have an occasional flutter when the time and the place are propitious.'

'Does that apply only to men?'

I smiled.

'If you insist I'll admit that what is sauce for the gander is sauce for the goose. The only thing to be said against it is that with a man a passing connection of that sort has no emotional significance, while with a woman it has.'

'It depends on the woman.'

I wasn't going to let myself be interrupted.

'Unless love is passion, it's not true, but something else; and passion thrives not on satisfaction, but on impediment. What d'you suppose Keats meant when he told the lover on his Grecian urn not to grieve? "Forever wilt thou love, and she be fair!" Why? Because she was unattainable, and however madly the lover pursued she still eluded him. For they were both imprisoned in the marble of what I suspect was an indifferent work of art. Your love for Larry and his for you were as simple and natural as the love of Paolo and Francesca or Romeo and Juliet. Fortunately for you it didn't come to a bad end. You made a rich marriage and Larry roamed the world to find out what song the Sirens sang. Passion didn't enter into it.'

'How did you know?'

'Passion doesn't count the cost. Pascal said that the heart has its reasons that reason takes no account of. If he meant what I think, he meant that when passion seizes the heart it invents reasons that seem not only plausible but conclusive to prove that the world is well lost for love. It convinces you that honour is well sacrificed and that shame is a cheap price to pay. Passion is destructive. It destroyed Antony and Cleopatra, Tristan and Isolde, Parnell and Kitty O'Shea. And if it doesn't destroy it dies. It may be then that one is faced with the desolation of knowing that one has wasted the years of one's life, that one's brought disgrace upon oneself, endured the frightful pang of jealousy, swallowed every bitter mortification, that one's expended all one's tenderness, poured out all the riches of one's soul on a poor drab, a fool, a peg on which one hung one's dreams, who wasn't worth a stick of chewing gum.'

Before I finished this harangue I knew very well that Isabel wasn't paying any attention to me, but was occupied with her own reflections. But her next remark surprised me.

'Do you think Larry is a virgin?'

'My dear, he's thirty-two.'

'I'm certain he is.'

'How can you be?'

'That's the kind of thing a woman knows instinctively.'

'I knew a young man who had a very prosperous career for some years by convincing one beautiful creature after another that he'd never had a woman. He said it worked like a charm.'

'I don't care what you say. I believe in my intuition.'

It was growing late, Gray and Isabel were dining with friends, and she had to dress. I had nothing to do, so I walked in the pleasant spring evening up the Boulevard Raspail. I have never believed very much in women's intuition; it fits in too neatly with what they want to believe to persuade me that it is trustworthy; and as I thought of the end of my long talk with Isabel I couldn't help but laugh. It put me in mind of Suzanne Rouvier and it occurred to me that I hadn't seen her for several days. I wondered if she was doing anything. If not, she might like to dine with me and go to a movie. I stopped a prowling taxi and gave the address of her apartment.

Seven

I mentioned Suzanne Rouvier at the beginning of this book. I had known her for ten or twelve years and at the date which I have now reached she must have been not far from forty. She was not beautiful; in fact she was rather ugly. She was tall for a Frenchwoman, with a short body, long legs and long arms, and she held herself gawkily as though she didn't know how to cope with the length of her limbs. The colour of her hair changed according to her whim, but most often it was a reddish brown. She had a small square face, with very prominent cheekbones vividly rouged, and a large mouth with heavily-painted lips. None of this sounds attractive, but it was; it is true that she had a good skin, strong white teeth and big, vividly blue eyes. They were her best feature, and she made the most of them by painting her eyelashes and her eyelids. She had a shrewd, roving, friendly look and she combined great good nature with a proper degree of toughness. In the life she had led she needed to be tough. Her mother, the widow of a small official in the government, had on his death returned to her native village in Anjou to live on her pension, and when Suzanne was fifteen she apprenticed her to a dressmaker in the neighbouring town, which was near enough for her to be able to come home on Sundays. It was during her fortnight's holiday, when she had reached the age of seventeen, that she was seduced by an artist who was spending his summer in the village to paint landscape. She already knew very well that without a penny to bless herself with her chance of marriage was remote and when the painter, at the end of the summer, proposed taking her to Paris she consented with alacrity. He took her to live with him in a rabbit-warren of studios in Montmartre, and she spent a very pleasant year in his company.

At the end of this he told her that he had not sold a single canvas and could no longer afford the luxury of a mistress. She had been expecting the news for some time and was not disconcerted by it. He asked her if she wanted to go home and when she said she didn't, told her that another painter in the same block would be glad to have her. The man he named had made a pass at her two or three times and though she had rebuffed him it had been with so much good humour that he was not affronted. She did not dislike him and so accepted the proposition with placidity. It was convenient that she did not have to go to the expense of taking a taxi to transport her trunk. Her second lover, a good deal older than the first, but still presentable, painted her in every conceivable position, clothed and in the nude; and she passed two happy years with him. She was proud to think that with her as a model he had made his first real success and she showed me a reproduction cut out of an illustrated paper of the picture that had brought it about. It had been purchased by an American gallery. It was a nude, lifesize, and she was lying in something of the same position as Manet's Olympe. The artist had been quick to see that there was something modern and amusing in her proportions, and, fining down her thin body to emaciation, he had elongated her long legs and arms, he had emphasized her high cheekbones and made her blue eyes extravagantly large. From the reproduction I naturally could not tell what the colour was like, but I was sensible of the elegance of the design. The picture brought him sufficient notoriety to enable him to marry an admiring widow with money, and Suzanne, well aware that a man had to think of his future, accepted the rupture of their cordial relations without acrimony.

For by now she knew her value. She liked the artistic life, it amused her to pose, and after the day's work was over she found it pleasant to go to the café and sit with painters, their wives and mistresses, while they discussed art, reviled dealers, and told bawdy stories. On this occasion, having seen the break coming, she had made her plans. She picked out a young man who was unattached and who, she thought, had talent. She chose her opportunity when he was alone at the café, explained the circumstances and without further preamble suggested that they should live together.

'I'm twenty and a good housekeeper. I'll save you money there and I'll save you the expense of a model. Look at your shirt, it's a disgrace, and your studio is a mess. You want a woman to look after you.'

He knew she was a good sort. He was amused at her proposal and she saw he was inclined to accept.

'After all, there's no harm in trying,' she said. 'If it doesn't work we shall neither of us be worse off than we are now.'

He was a non-representative artist and he painted portraits of her in squares and oblongs. He painted her with one eye and no mouth. He painted her as a geometrical arrangement in black and brown and grey. He painted her in a criss-cross of lines through which you vaguely saw a human face. She stayed with him for a year and a half and left him of her own accord.

'Why?' I asked her. 'Didn't you like him?'

'Yes, he was a nice boy. I didn't think he was getting any further. He was repeating himself.'

She found no difficulty in discovering a successor. She remained faithful to artists.

'I've always been in painting,' she said. 'I was with a sculptor for six months, but I don't know why, it said nothing to me.'

She was pleased to think that she had never separated from a lover with unpleasantness. She was not only a good model, but a good housewife. She loved working about the studio she happened for a while to be living in and took pride in keeping it in apple-pie order. She was a good cook and could turn out a tasty meal at the smallest possible cost. She mended her lovers' socks and sewed buttons on their shirts.

'I never saw why because a man was an artist he shouldn't be neat and tidy.'

She only had one failure. This was a young Englishman who had more money than anyone she had known before and he had a car.

'But it didn't last long,' she said. 'He used to get drunk and then he was tiresome. I wouldn't have minded that if he'd been a good painter, but, my dear, it was grotesque. I told him I was going to leave him and he began to cry. He said he loved me.

'"My poor friend," I said to him. "Whether you love me or not isn't of the smallest consequence. What is of consequence is that you have no talent. Return to your own country and go into the grocery business. That is all you're fit for."'

'What did he say to that?' I asked.

'He flew into a passion and told me to get out. But it was good advice I gave him, you know. I hope he took it, he wasn't a bad fellow; only a bad artist.'

Common sense and good nature will do a lot to make the pilgrimage of life not too difficult to a light woman, but the profession Suzanne had adopted had its ups and downs like any other. There was the Scandinavian for instance. She was so imprudent as to fall in love with him.

'He was a god, my dear,' she told me. 'He was immensely tall, as tall as the Eiffel Tower, with great broad shoulders and a magnificent chest, a waist that you could almost put your hands round, a belly flat, but flat like the palm of my hand, and muscles like a professional athlete's. He had golden, wavy hair and a skin of honey. And he didn't paint badly. I liked his brush work, it was bold and dashing, and he had a rich vivid palette.'

She had made up her mind to have a child by him. He was against it, but she told him she would take the responsibility.

'He liked it well enough when it was born. Oh, such a lovely baby, rosy, fair-haired and blue-eyed like her papa. It was a girl.'

Suzanne lived with him for three years.

'He was a little stupid and sometimes he bored me, but he was very sweet and so beautiful that I didn't really mind.'

Then he got a telegram from Sweden to say his father was dying and he must come back at once. He promised to return, but she had a premonition that he never would. He left all the money he had. She didn't hear from him for a month and then she got a letter from him saying that his father had died, leaving his affairs in confusion, and that he felt it his duty to remain by his mother and go into the lumber business. He enclosed a draft for ten thousand francs. Suzanne was not the woman to give way to despair. She came to the conclusion very quickly that a child would hamper her activities, so she took the baby girl down to her mother's and left her, along with the ten thousand francs, in her care.

'It was heart-rending, I adored that child, but in life one has to be practical.'

'What happened then?' I asked.

'Oh, I got along. I found a friend.'

But then came her typhoid. She always spoke of it as 'my typhoid' as a millionaire might speak of 'my place at Palm Beach' or 'my grouse moor'. She nearly died of it and was in the hospital for three months. When she left she was nothing but skin and bone, as weak as a rat, and so nervous that she could do nothing but cry. She wasn't much use to anyone then, she wasn't strong enough to pose and she had very little money.

'Oh la, la,' she said, 'I passed through some hard times. Luckily I had good friends. But you know what artists are, it's a struggle for them to make both ends meet, anyway. I was never a pretty woman, I had something of course, but I wasn't twenty any more. Then I ran into the cubist I'd been with; he'd been married and divorced since we lived together, he'd given up cubism and become a surrealist. He thought he could use me and said he was lonely; he said he'd give me board and lodgings and I promise you, I was glad to accept.'

Suzanne stayed with him till she met her manufacturer. The manufacturer was brought to the studio by a friend on the chance that he might buy one of the ex-cubist's pictures, and Suzanne, anxious to effect a sale, set herself out to be as agreeable to him as she knew how. He could not make up his mind to buy on the spur of the moment, but said he would like to come and see the pictures again. He did, a fortnight later, and this time she received the impression that he had come to see her rather than works of art. When he left, still without buying, he pressed her hand with unnecessary warmth. Next day the friend who had brought him waylaid her when she was on her way to market to buy the day's provisions and told her that the manufacturer had taken a fancy to her and wanted to know if she would dine with him next time he came to Paris, because he had a proposition to make to her.

'What does he see in me, d'you suppose?' she asked.

'He's an amateur of modern art. He's seen portraits of you. You intrigue him. He's a provincial and a businessman. You represent Paris to him, art, romance, everything that he misses in Lille.'

'Has he money?' she asked in her sensible way.

'Plenty.'

'Well, I'll dine with him. There's no harm hearing what he's got to say.'

He took her to Maxim's, which impressed her; she had dressed very quietly, and she felt as she looked at the women around her that she could pass very well for a respectable married woman. He ordered a bottle of champagne, and this persuaded her that he was a gentleman. When they came to coffee he put his proposition before her. She thought it very handsome. He told her that he came to Paris regularly once a fortnight to attend a board meeting, and it was tiresome in the evening to dine alone and if he felt the need of feminine society to go to a brothel. Being a married man with two children, he thought that an unsatisfactory arrangement for a man in his position. Their common friend had told him all about her and he knew she was a woman of discretion. He was no longer young and he had no wish to get entangled with a giddy girl. He was something of a collector of the modern school and her connection with it was sympathetic to him. Then he came down to brass tacks. He was prepared to take an apartment for her and furnish and provide her with an income of two thousand francs a month. In return for this he wished to enjoy her company for one night every fourteen days. Suzanne had never had the spending of so much money in her life, and she quickly reckoned that on such a sum she could not only live and dress as such an advancement in the world evidently demanded, but provide for her daughter and put away something for a rainy day. But she hesitated for a moment. She had always been 'in painting', as she put it, and there was no doubt in her mind that it was a come-down to be the mistress of a businessman.

'*Cest à prendre ou à laisser*,' he said. 'You can take it or leave it.'

He was not repulsive to her and the rosette of the Legion of Honour in his buttonhole proved that he was a man of distinction. She smiled.

'*Je prends*,' she replied. 'I'll take it.'

Eight

Though Suzanne had always lived in Montmartre, she decided that it was necessary to break with the past, so she took an apartment in Montparnasse in a house just off the boulevard. It consisted of two rooms, a tiny kitchen and a bathroom; it was on the sixth floor, but there was a lift. To her a bathroom and a lift, even though it only held two persons and moved at a snail's pace and you had to walk downstairs, represented not only luxury but style.

For the first few months of their union Monsieur Achille Gauvain, for such was his name, put up at an hotel on his fortnightly visits to Paris and, after spending such part of the night with Suzanne as his amorous inclination demanded, returned to it to sleep by himself till it was time for him to get up and catch his train to return to his business affairs and the sober pleasures of family life; but then Suzanne pointed out to him that he was throwing away money to no purpose and it would be both more economical and more comfortable if he stayed in the apartment till morning. He could not but see the force of this. He was flattered at Suzanne's thoughtfulness for his comfort—it was true, there was nothing agreeable in going out into the street and finding a taxi on a cold winter night—and he approved of her disinclination to put him to useless expense. It was a good woman who counted not only her own pennies but her lover's.

Monsieur Achille had every reason to feel pleased with himself. In general they went to dine at one of the better restaurants in Montparnasse, but now and then Suzanne prepared dinner for him in the apartment. The tasty food she gave him was very much to his liking. On warm evenings he would dine in his shirt-sleeves and feel deliciously wanton and bohemian. He had always had an inclination for buying pictures, but Suzanne would let him buy nothing that she did not approve of, and he soon found reason to trust her judgment. She would have no truck with dealers, but took him to the studios of the painters and thus enabled him to buy pictures for half the money he would otherwise have to pay. He knew that she was putting something aside, and when she told him that year by year she was buying a bit of land in her native village, he felt a thrill of pride. He knew the desire to own land that is in the heart of every person of French blood, and his esteem for her was increased because she possessed it too.

On her side Suzanne was well satisfied. She was neither faithful to him nor unfaithful; that is to say, she took care not to form any permanent connection with another man, but if she came across one who took her fancy she was not averse from going to bed with him. But it was a point of honour with her not to let him stay the night. She felt she owed that to the man of means and position who had settled her life in such an assured and respectable manner.

I had come to know Suzanne when she was living with a painter who happened to be an acquaintance of mine and had often sat in his studio while she posed; I continued to see her now and then at irregular intervals, but did not enter upon terms of any intimacy with her till she moved to Montparnasse. It appeared that Monsieur Achille, for this was how she always spoke of him and how she addressed him, had read one or two of my books in translation, and one evening he invited me to dine with them at a restaurant. He was a little man, half a head shorter than Suzanne, with iron-grey hair and a neat grey moustache. He was on the plump side, and he had a pot-belly, but only to the extent of giving him an air of substance. He walked with the short fat man's strut and it was plain that he was not displeased with himself. He gave me a fine dinner. He was very polite. He told me he was glad I was a friend of Suzanne's, he could see at a glance that I was *comme il faut* and he would be glad to think that I should see something of her. His affairs, alas! kept him tied to Lille and the poor girl was too often alone; it would be a comfort to him to know that she was in touch with a man of education. He was a businessman, but he had always admired artists.

'*Ah, mon cher monsieur*, art and literature have always been the twin glories of France. Along with her military prowess, of course. And I, a manufacturer of woollen goods, have no hesitation in saying that I put the painter and the writer on a level with the general and the statesman.'

No one could say handsomer than that.

Suzanne would not hear of having a maid to do the house-work, partly for economy's sake and partly because (for reasons best known to herself) she didn't want anyone poking her nose into what was nobody's business but her own. She kept the tiny apartment, furnished in the most modern style of the moment, clean and neat, and she made all her own underclothes. But even then, now that she no longer posed, time hung heavily on her hands, for she was an industrious woman; and presently the idea occurred to her that, after having sat to so many painters, there was no reason why she should not paint too. She bought canvases, brushes and paints and forthwith set to work. Sometimes when I was to take her out to dinner I would go early and find her in a smock busily at work. Just as the embryo in the womb recapitulates in brief the evolution of the species, so did Suzanne recapitulate the styles of all her lovers. She painted landscape like the landscape painter, abstractions like the cubist, and with the help of picture postcards sailing-boats lying at anchor like the Scandinavian. She could not draw, but she had an agreeable sense of colour, and if her pictures were not very good she got a lot of fun out of painting them.

Monsieur Achille encouraged her. It gave him a sense of satisfaction that his mistress should be an artist. It was on his insistence that she sent a canvas to the autumn salon and they were both very proud when it was hung. He gave her one bit of good advice.

'Don't try to paint like a man, my dear,' he said. 'Paint like a woman. Don't aim to be strong; be satisfied to charm. And be honest. In business sharp practice sometimes succeeds, but in art honesty is not only the best but the only policy.'

At the time of which I write the connection had lasted for five years to their mutual content.

'Evidently he doesn't thrill me,' said Suzanne. 'But he's intelligent and in a good position. I've reached an age when it's necessary for me to think of my situation.'

She was sympathetic and understanding and Monsieur Achille conceived a high opinion of her judgment. She lent a willing ear when he discussed with her his business and domestic affairs. She condoled with him when his daughter failed in an examination and rejoiced with him when his son got engaged to a girl with money. He had himself married the only child of a man in his own line of business and the amalgamation of two rival firms had been a source of profit to both parties. It was naturally a satisfaction to him that his son was sensible enough to see that the soundest basis of a happy marriage is community of financial interests. He confided to Suzanne his ambition to marry his daughter into the aristocracy.

'And why not, with her fortune?' said Suzanne.

Monsieur Achille made it possible for Suzanne to send her own daughter to a convent where she would receive a good education, and he promised that at the proper age he would pay to have her suitably trained to earn her living as a typist and stenographer.

'She's going to be a beauty when she grows up,' Suzanne told me, 'but evidently it won't hurt her to have an education and to be able to pound a typewriter. She's so young it's too soon to tell, but it may be that she'll have no temperament.'

Suzanne had delicacy. She left it to my intelligence to infer her meaning. I inferred it all right.

Nine

A week or so after I had so unexpectedly run into Larry, Suzanne and I one night, having dined together and gone to a movie, were sitting in the Sélect on the Boulevard du Montparnasse, having a glass of beer, when he strolled in. She gave a gasp and to my surprise called out to him. He came up to the table, kissed her and shook hands with me. I could see that she could hardly believe her eyes.

'May I sit down?' he said. 'I haven't had any dinner and I'm going to have something to eat.'

'Oh, but it's good to see you, *mon petit*,' she said, her eyes sparkling. 'Where have you sprung from? And why have you given no sign of life all these years? My God, how thin you are! For all I knew you might have been dead.'

'Well, I wasn't,' he answered, his eyes twinkling. 'How is Odette?'

That was the name of Suzanne's daughter.

'Oh, she's growing a big girl. And pretty. She still remembers you.'

'You never told me you knew Larry,' I said to her.

'Why should I? I never knew you knew him. We're old friends.'

Larry ordered himself eggs and bacon. Suzanne told him all about her daughter and then about herself. He listened in his smiling, charming way while she chattered. She told him that she had settled down and was painting. She turned to me.

'I'm improving, don't you think? I don't pretend I'm a genius, but I have as much talent as many of the painters I've known.'

'D'you sell any pictures?' asked Larry.

'I don't have to,' she answered airily. 'I have private means.'

'Lucky girl.'

'No, not lucky: clever. You must come and see my pictures.'

She wrote down her address on a piece of paper and made him promise to go. Suzanne, excited, went on talking nineteen to the dozen. Then Larry asked for his bill.

'You're not going?' she cried.

'I am,' he smiled.

He paid and with a wave of the hand left us. I laughed. He had a way that always amused me of being with you one moment and without explanation gone the next. It was so abrupt; it was almost as if he had faded into the air.

'Why did he want to go away so quickly?' said Suzanne, with vexation.

'Perhaps he's got a girl waiting for him,' I replied mockingly.

'That's an idea like another.' She took her compact out of her bag and powdered her face. 'I pity any woman who falls in love with him. *Oh la, la.*'

'Why do you say that?'

She looked at me for a minute with a seriousness I had not often seen in her.

'I very nearly fell in love with him myself once. You might as well fall in love with a reflection in the water or a ray of sunshine or a cloud in the sky. I had a narrow escape. Even now when I think of it I tremble at the danger I ran.'

Discretion be blowed. It would have been inhuman not to want to know what this was all about. I congratulated myself that Suzanne was a woman who had no notion of reticence.

'How on earth did you ever get to know him?' I asked.

'Oh, it was years ago. Six years, seven years, I forget. Odette was only five. He knew Marcel when I was living with him. He used to come to the studio and sit while I was posing. He'd take us out to dinner sometimes. You never knew when he'd come. Sometimes not for weeks and then two or three days running. Marcel used to like to have him there; he said he painted better when he was there. Then I had my typhoid. I went through a bad time when I came out of the hospital.' She shrugged her shoulders. 'But I've already told you all that. Well, one day I'd been round the studios trying to get work and no one wanted me, and I'd had nothing but a glass of milk and a croissant all day and I didn't know how I was going to pay for my room, and I met him accidentally on the Boulevard Clichy. He stopped and asked me how I was and I told him about my typhoid, and then he said to me: "You look as if you could do with a square meal." And there was something in his voice and in the look of his eyes that broke me; I began to cry.

'We were next door to La Mère Mariette and he took me by the arm and sat me down at a table. I was so hungry I was ready to eat an old boot, but when the omelette came I felt I couldn't eat a thing. He forced me to take a little and he gave me a glass of burgundy. I felt better then and I ate some asparagus. I told him all my troubles. I was too weak to hold a pose. I was just skin and bone and I looked terrible; I couldn't expect to get a man. I asked him if he'd lend me the money to go back to my village. At least I'd have my little girl there. He asked me if I wanted to go, and I said of course not, Mamma didn't want me, she could hardly live on her pension with prices the way they were, and the money I'd sent for Odette had all been spent, but if I appeared at the door she could hardly refuse to take me in, she'd see how ill I looked. He looked at me for a long time, and I thought he was going to say he couldn't lend me anything. Then he said:

'"Would you like me to take you down to a little place I know in the country, you and the kid? I want a bit of a holiday."

'I could hardly believe my ears. I'd known him for ages and he'd never made a pass at me.

'"In the condition I'm in?" I said. I couldn't help laughing. "My poor friend," I said, "I'm no use to any man just now."

'He smiled at me. Have you ever noticed what a wonderful smile he's got? It's as sweet as honey.'

'"Don't be so silly," he said. "I'm not thinking of that."

'I was crying so hard by then, I could hardly speak. He gave me money to fetch the child and we all went to the country together. Oh, it was charming, the place he took us to.'

Suzanne described it to me. It was three miles from a little town the name of which I have forgotten, and they took a car out to the inn. It was a ramshackle building on a river with a lawn that ran down to the water. There were plane trees on the lawn and they had their meals in their shade. In summer artists came there to paint, but it was early for that yet and they had the inn to themselves. The fare was famous, and on Sundays people used to drive from here and there to lunch with abandon, but on weekdays their peace was seldom disturbed. With the rest and the food and wine, Suzanne grew stronger, and she was happy to have her child with her.

'He was sweet with Odette and she adored him. I had to prevent her from making a nuisance of herself, but he never seemed to mind how much she pestered him. It used to make me laugh, they were like two children together.'

'What did you do with yourselves?' I asked.

'Oh, there was always something to do. We used to take a boat and fish and sometimes we'd get the *patron* to lend us his Citroën and we'd go into town. Larry liked it. The old houses and the *place*. It was so quiet that your footsteps on the cobblestones were the only sound you heard. There was a Louis Quatorze *hôtel de ville* and an old church, and at the edge of the town was the château with a garden by Le Nôtre. When you sat at the café on the *place* you had the feeling that you had stepped back three hundred years and the Citroën at the kerb didn't seem to belong to this world at all.'

It was after one of these outings that Larry told her the story of the young airman which I narrated at the beginning of this book.

'I wonder why he told you,' I said.

'I haven't an idea. They'd had a hospital in the town during the war and in the cemetery there were rows and rows of little crosses. We went to see it. We didn't stay long, it gave me the creeps—all those poor boys lying there. Larry was very silent on the way home. He never ate much, but at dinner he hardly touched a thing. I remember so well, it was a beautiful, starry night and we sat on the riverbank, it was pretty with the poplars silhouetted against the darkness, and he smoked his pipe. And suddenly, à *propos de bottes*, he told me about his friend and how he died to save him.' Suzanne took a swig of beer. 'He's a strange creature. I shall never understand him. He used to like to read to me. Sometimes in the daytime, while I sewed things for the little one, and in the evening after I'd put her to bed.'

'What did you read?'

'Oh, all sorts of things. Letters of Madame de Sévigné and bits of Saint-Simon. *Imagine-toi*, I who'd never read anything before but the newspaper and now and then a novel when I heard them talk about it in the studios and didn't want them to think me a fool! I had no idea reading could be so interesting. Those old writers weren't such fatheads as one would think.'

'Who would think?' I chuckled.

'Then he made me read with him. We read Phèdre and Bérénice. He took the men's parts and I took the women's. You can't think how amusing it was,' she added naïvely. 'He used to look at me so strangely when I cried at the pathetic parts. Of course it was only because I hadn't got my strength. And you know, I've still got the books. Even now I can't read some of the letters of Madame de Sévigné that he read to me without hearing his lovely voice and without seeing the river flowing so quietly and the poplars on the opposite bank, and sometimes I can't go on, it gives me such a pain in my heart. I know now that those were the happiest weeks I ever spent in my life. That man, he's an angel of sweetness.'

Suzanne felt she was growing sentimental and feared (wrongly) that I should laugh at her. She shrugged her shoulders and smiled.

'You know, I've always made up my mind that when I've reached the canonical age and no man wants to sleep with me any more I shall make my peace with the Church and repent of my sins. But the sins I committed with Larry nothing in the world will ever induce me to repent of. Never, never, never!'

'But as you've described it I can see nothing you can possibly have to repent of.'

'I haven't told you the half of it yet. You see, I have a naturally good constitution and being out in the air all day eating well, sleeping well, with not a care in the world, in three or four weeks I was as strong as ever I'd been. And I was looking well; I had colour in my cheeks and my hair had recovered its sheen. I felt twenty. Larry swam in the river every morning and I used to watch him. He has a beautiful body, not an athlete's like my Scandinavian, but strong and of an infinite grace.

'He'd been very patient while I was so weak, but now that I was perfectly well I saw no reason to keep him waiting any longer. I gave him a hint or two that I was ready for anything, but he didn't seem to understand. Of course you Anglo-Saxons are peculiar, you're brutal and at the same time you're sentimental; there's no denying it, you're not good lovers. I said to myself, "Perhaps it's his delicacy, he's done so much for me, he's let me have the child here, it may be that he hasn't the heart to ask me for the return that is his right." So one night, as we were going to bed, I said to him, "D'you want me to come to your room tonight?"'

I laughed.

'You put it a bit bluntly, didn't you?'

'Well, I couldn't ask him to come to mine, because Odette was sleeping there,' she answered ingenuously. 'He looked at me with those kind eyes of his for a moment, then he smiled. "D'you want to come," he said.

'"What do you think—with that fine body of yours?"

'"All right, come then."

'I went upstairs and undressed and then I slipped along the passage to his room. He was lying in bed reading and smoking a pipe. He put down his pipe and his book and moved over to make room for me.'

Suzanne was silent for a while and it went against my grain to ask her questions. But after a while she went on.

'He was a strange lover. Very sweet, affectionate and even tender, virile without being passionate, if you understand what I mean, and absolutely without vice. He loved like a hot-blooded schoolboy. It was rather funny and rather touching. When I left him I had the feeling that I should be grateful to him rather than he to me. As I closed the door I saw him take up his book and go on reading from where he had left off.'

I began to laugh.

'I'm glad it amuses you,' she said a trifle grimly. But she was not without a sense of humour. She giggled. 'I soon discovered that if I waited for an invitation I might wait indefinitely, so when I felt like it I just went into his room and got into bed. He was always very nice. He had in short natural human instincts, but he was like a man so preoccupied that he forgets to eat, yet when you put a good dinner before him he eats it with appetite. I know when a man's in love with me, and I should have been a fool if I'd believed that Larry loved me, but I thought he'd get into the habit of me. One has to be practical in life and I said to myself that it would suit me very well if when we went back to Paris he took me to live with him. I knew he'd let me have the child and I should have liked that. My instinct told me I'd be silly to fall in love with him, you know women are very unfortunate, so often when they fall in love they cease to be lovable, and I made up my mind to be on my guard.'

Suzanne inhaled the smoke of her cigarette and blew it out through her nose. It was growing late and many of the tables were now empty, but there was still a group of people hanging around the bar.

'One morning, after breakfast, I was sitting on the riverbank sewing, and Odette was playing with some bricks he'd bought her when Larry came up to me.

'"I've come to say good-bye to you," he said.

'"Are you going somewhere?" I said, surprised.

'"Yes."

'"Not for good?" I said.

'"You're quite well now. Here's enough money to keep you for the rest of the summer and to start you off when you get back to Paris."

'For a moment I was so upset I didn't know what to say. He stood in front of me, smiling in that candid way of his.

'"Have I done something to displease you?" I asked him.

'"Nothing. Don't think that for a moment. I've got work to do. We've had a lovely time down here. Odette, come and say good-bye to your uncle."

'She was too young to understand. He took her up in his arms and kissed her; then he kissed me and walked back into the hotel; in a minute I heard the car drive away. I looked at the banknotes I had in my hand. Twelve thousand francs. It came so quickly I hadn't time to react. "*Zut alors*," I said to myself. I had at least one thing to be thankful for, I hadn't allowed myself to fall in love with him. But I couldn't make head or tail of it.'

I was obliged to laugh.

'You know, at one time I made quite a little reputation for myself as a humorist by the simple process of telling the truth. It came as such a surprise to most people that they thought I was being funny.'

'I don't see the connection.'

'Well, Larry is, I think, the only person I've ever met who's completely disinterested. It makes his actions seem peculiar. We're not used to persons who do things simply for the love of God whom they don't believe in.'

Suzanne stared at me.

'My poor friend, you've had too much to drink.'

Chapter Five

One

I dawdled over my work in Paris. It was very agreeable in the springtime, with the chestnuts in the Champs Elysées in bloom and the light in the streets so gay. There was pleasure in the air, a light transitory pleasure, sensual without grossness, that made your step more springy and your intelligence more alert. I was happy in the various company of my friends and, my heart filled with amiable memories of the past, I regained in spirit at least something of the glow of youth. I thought I should be a fool to allow work to interfere with a delight in the passing moment that I might never enjoy again so fully.

Isabel, Gray, Larry and I went for excursions to places of interest within convenient distance. We went to Chantilly and Versailles, to St Germain and Fontainebleau. Wherever we went, we lunched well and copiously. Gray ate largely to satisfy his enormous frame and was apt to drink a little too much. His health, whether owing to Larry's treatment or merely to the course of time, was certainly improved. He ceased to have racking headaches and his eyes were losing the look of bewilderment that when first I saw him on coming to Paris had been so distressing. He did not talk much except now and then to tell a long-winded story, but laughed with great loud guffaws at the nonsense Isabel and I talked. He enjoyed himself. Though not amusing, he was so good-humoured and so easily pleased that it was impossible not to like him. He was the kind of man with whom one would have hesitated to pass a lonely evening, but with whom one might cheerfully have looked forward to spending six months.

His love for Isabel was a delight to see; he adored her beauty and thought her the most brilliant, fascinating creature in the world; and his devotion, his doglike devotion to Larry was touching. Larry appeared to enjoy himself too; I had a notion that he looked upon this time as a holiday that he was taking from whatever projects he had in mind and was serenely making the most of it. He didn't talk very much either, but it didn't matter, his company was sufficient conversation; he was so easy, so pleasantly cheerful that you didn't ask more of him than what he gave, and I well knew that if the days we spent together were so happy it was due to his being with us. Though he never said a brilliant or a witty thing, we should have been dull without him.

It was on the return from one of these jaunts that I witnessed a scene that somewhat startled me. We had been to Chartres and were on our way back to Paris. Gray was driving and Larry was sitting beside him; Isabel and I were at the back. We were tired after the long day. Larry sat with his arm stretched out along the top of the front seat. His shirt-cuff was pulled back by his position and displayed his slim, strong wrist and the lower part of his brown arm lightly covered with fine hairs. The sun shone goldenly upon them. Something in Isabel's immobility attracted my attention, and I glanced at her. She was so still you might have thought her hypnotized. Her breath was hurried. Her eyes were fixed on the sinewy wrist with its little golden hairs and on that long, delicate, but powerful hand, and I have never seen on a human countenance such a hungry concupiscence as I saw then on hers. It was a mask of lust. I should never have believed that her beautiful features could assume an expression of such unbridled sensuality. It was animal rather than human. The beauty was stripped from her face; the look upon it made her hideous and frightening. It horribly suggested the bitch in heat and I felt rather sick. She was unconscious of my presence; she was conscious of nothing but the hand, lying along the rim so negligently, that filled her with frantic desire. Then as it were a spasm twitched across her face, she gave a shudder and shutting her eyes sank into the corner of the car.

'Give me a cigarette,' she said in a voice I hardly recognized, it was so raucous.

I got one out of my case and lit it for her. She smoked it greedily. For the rest of the drive she looked out of the window and never said a word.

When we arrived at their house, Gray asked Larry to drive me back to the hotel and then take the car to the garage. Larry got into the driver's seat and I sat myself beside him. As they crossed the pavement Isabel took Gray's arm and, snuggling up to him, gave him a look which I could not see, but whose sense I could divine. I guessed that he would have a passionate bedfellow that night, but would never know to what prickings of conscience he owed her ardour.

June was approaching its end and I had to get back to the Riviera. Friends of Elliott's, who were going to America, had lent the Maturins their villa at Dinard and they were going there with the children as soon as their school closed. Larry was staying in Paris to work, but was buying himself a second-hand Citroën and had promised to spend a few days with them in August. On my last night in Paris I asked the three of them to dine with me.

It was on that night that we met Sophie Macdonald.

Two

Isabel had conceived the desire to make a tour of the tough joints, and because I had some acquaintance with them she asked me to be their guide. I did not much like the notion, because in places of that sort in Paris they are apt to make their disapproval of sightseers from another world unpleasantly obvious. But Isabel insisted. I warned her that it would be boring and begged her to dress plainly. We dined late, went to the Folies-Bergère for an hour and then set out. I took them first to a cellar near Nôtre Dame frequented by gangsters and their molls where I knew the proprietor, and he made room for us at a long table at which were sitting some very disreputable people, but I ordered wine for all of them and we drank one another's healths. It was hot, smoky and dirty. Then I took them to the Sphynxs where women, naked under their smart, tawdry evening dresses, their breasts, nipples and all, exposed, sit in a row on two benches opposite one another and when the band strikes up dance together listlessly with their eyes on the lookout for the men who sit round the dance hall at marble-topped tables. We ordered a bottle of warm champagne. Some of the women gave Isabel the eye as they passed us and I wondered if she knew what it meant.

Then we went on to the Rue de Lappe. It is a dingy, narrow street and even as you enter it you get the impression of sordid lust. We went into a café. There was the usual young man, pale and dissipated, playing the piano, while another man, old and tired, scraped away on a fiddle, and a third made discordant noises on a saxophone. The place was packed and it looked as though there wasn't a vacant table, but the *patron*, seeing that we were customers with money to spend, unceremoniously turned a couple out, making them take seats at a table already occupied, and settled us down. The two persons who were hustled away did not take it well, and they made remarks about us that were far from complimentary. A lot of people were dancing, sailors with the red pompon on their hats, men mostly with their caps on and handkerchiefs round their necks, women of mature age and young girls, painted to the eyes, bareheaded, in short skirts and coloured blouses. Men danced with podgy boys with made-up eyes; gaunt, hard-featured women danced with fat women with dyed hair; men danced with women. There was a frowst of smoke and liquor and of sweating bodies. The music went on interminably and that unsavoury mob proceeded round the room, the sweat shining on their faces, with a solemn intensity in which there was something horrible. There were a few big men of brutal aspect, but for the most part they were puny and ill-nourished. I watched the three who were playing. They might have been robots, so mechanical was their performances, and I asked myself if it was possible that at one time, when they were setting out, they had thought they might be musicians whom people would come from far to hear and to applaud. Even to play the violin badly you must take lessons and practise: did that fiddler go to all that trouble just to play fox trots till the small hours of the morning in that stinking squalor? The music stopped and the pianist wiped his face with a dirty handkerchief. The dancers slouched or sidled or squirmed back to their tables. Suddenly we heard an American voice.

'For Christ's sake.'

A woman got up from one of the tables across the room. The man she was with tried to stop her, but she pushed him aside and staggered across the floor. She was very drunk. She came up to our table and stood in front of us, swaying a little and grinning stupidly. She seemed to find the sight of us vastly amusing. I glanced at my companions. Isabel was staring at her blankly, Gray had a sullen frown on his face and Larry gazed as though he couldn't believe his eyes.

'Hello,' she said.

'Sophie,' said Isabel.

'Who the hell did you think it was?' she gurgled. She grabbed the waiter who was passing, 'Vincent, fetch me a chair.'

'Fetch one yourself,' he said, snatching himself away.

'*Salaud*,' she cried, spitting at him.

'*T'en fais pas, Sophie*,' said a big fat fellow with a great head of greasy hair, who was sitting next to us in his shirt-sleeves. 'Here's a chair.'

'Fancy meeting you all like this,' she said, still swaying. 'Hello, Larry. Hello, Gray.' She sank into the chair which the man who had spoken placed behind her. 'Let's all have a drink. *Patron*,' she screamed.

I had noticed that the proprietor had his eye on us and now he came up.
'You know these people, Sophie?' he asked, addressing her in the familiar
second person singular.

'*Ta gueule*,' she laughed drunkenly. 'They're my childhood friends. I'm
buying a bottle of champagne for them. And don't you bring us any *urine de
cheval*. Bring us something one can swallow without vomiting.'

'You're drunk, my poor Sophie,' he said.

'To hell with you.'

He went off, glad enough to sell a bottle of champagne–we for safety's
sake had been drinking brandy and soda–and Sophie stared at me dully for a
moment.

'Who's your friend, Isabel?'

Isabel told her my name.

'Oh? I remember, you came to Chicago once. Bit of a stuffed shirt, aren't
you?'

'Maybe,' I smiled.

I had no recollection of her, but that was not surprising, since I had not
been to Chicago for more than ten years and had met a great many people
then and a great many since.

She was quite tall and, when standing, looked taller still, for she was very
thin. She wore a bright green silk blouse, but it was crumpled and spotted,
and a short black skirt. Her hair, cut short and loosely curled, but tousled,
was brightly hennaed. She was outrageously made up, her cheeks rouged to
the eyes, and her eyelids, upper and lower, heavily blued; her eyebrows and
eyelashes were thick with mascara and her mouth scarlet with lipstick. Her
hands, with their painted nails, were dirty. She looked more of a slut than
any woman there and I had a suspicion that she was not only drunk but
doped. But one couldn't deny that there was a certain vicious attractiveness
about her; she held her head with an arrogant tilt and her make-up
accentuated the startling greenness of her eyes. Sodden with drink as she
was, she had a bold-faced shamelessness that I could well imagine appealed
to all that was base in men. She embraced us in a sardonic smile.

'I can't say you seem so terribly pleased to see me,' she said.

'I heard you were in Paris,' said Isabel lamely, a chilly smile on her face.

'You might have called me. I'm in the phone-book.'

'We haven't been here very long.'

Gray came to the rescue.

'Are you having a good time over here, Sophie?'

'Fine. You went bust, Gray, didn't you?'

His face flushed a deeper red.

'Yes.'

'Tough on you. I guess it's pretty grim in Chicago right now. Lucky for
me I got out when I did. For Christ's sake why doesn't that bastard bring us
something to drink?'

'He's just coming,' I said, seeing the waiter threading his way through the
tables with glasses and wine on a tray.

My remark drew her attention to me.

'My loving in-laws kicked me out of Chicago. Said I was gumming up
their f—— reputations.' She giggled savagely. 'I'm a remittance man.'

The champagne came and was poured out. With a shaking hand she raised
a glass to her lips.

'To hell with stuffed shirts,' she said. She emptied the glass and glanced at

Larry. 'You don't seem to have much to say for yourself, Larry.'

He had been looking at her with an impassive face. He had not taken his eyes off her since she had appeared. He smiled amiably.

'I'm not a very talkative guy.'

The music struck up again and a man came over to us. He was a tallish fellow and well built, with a great hooked nose, a mat of shining black hair and great sensual lips. He looked like an evil Savonarola. Like most of the men there he wore no collar and his tight-fitting coat was closely buttoned to give him a waist.

'Come on, Sophie. We're going to dance.'

'Go away. I'm busy. Can't you see I'm with friends?'

'*J'm en fous de tes amis.* To hell with your friends. You're dancing.'

He took hold of her arm but she snatched it away.

'*Fous-moi la paix, espèce de con,*' she cried, with sudden violence.

'*Merde.*'

'*Mange.*'

Gray did not understand what they were saying, but I saw that Isabel, with that strange knowledge of obscenity that the most virtuous women seem to possess, understood perfectly and her face went hard with a frown of disgust. The man raised his arm with his hand open, the horny hand of a workman, and was about to slap her, when Gray half raised himself from his chair.

'*Allaiz vous ong,*' he shouted, with his execrable accent.

The man stopped and threw Gray a furious glance.

'Take care, Coco,' said Sophie, with a bitter laugh. 'He'll lay you out cold.'

The man took in Gray's great height and weight and strength. He shrugged his shoulders sullenly and, throwing a filthy word at us, slunk off. Sophie giggled drunkenly. The rest of us were silent. I refilled her glass.

'You living in Paris, Larry?' she asked after she had drained it.

'For the present.'

It's always difficult to make conversation with a drunk, and there's no denying it, the sober are at a disadvantage with him. We went on talking for a few minutes in a dreary, embarrassed way. Then Sophie pushed back her chair.

'If I don't go back to my boy friend he'll be mad as hell. He's a sulky brute, but Christ, he's a good screw.' She staggered to her feet. 'So long, folks. Come again. I'm here every night.'

She pushed her way through the dancers and we lost sight of her in the crowd. I almost laughed at the icy scorn on Isabel's classic features. None of us said a word.

'This is a foul place,' said Isabel suddenly. 'Let's go.'

I paid for our drinks and for Sophie's champagne and we trooped out. The crowd was on the dance floor and we got out without remark. It was after two, and to my mind time to go to bed, but Gray said he was hungry, so I suggested that we should go to Graf's in Montmartre and get something to eat. We were silent as we drove up. I sat beside Gray to direct him. We reached the garish restaurant. There were still people sitting on the terrace. We went in and ordered bacon and eggs and beer. Isabel, outwardly at least, had regained her composure. She congratulated me, somewhat ironically perhaps, on my acquaintance with the more disreputable parts of Paris.

'You asked for it,' I said.

'I've thoroughly enjoyed myself. I've had a grand evening.'

'Hell,' said Gray. 'It stank. And Sophie.'

Isabel shrugged an indifferent shoulder.

'D'you remember her at all?' she asked me. 'She sat next to you the first night you came to dinner with us. She hadn't got that awful red hair then. Its natural colour is dingy beige.'

I threw my mind back. I had a recollection of a very young girl with blue eyes that were almost green and an attractive tilt to her head. Not pretty, but fresh and ingenuous, with a mixture of shyness and pertness that I found amusing.

'Of course I remember. I liked her name. I had an aunt called Sophie.'

'She married a boy called Bob Macdonald.'

'Nice fellow,' said Gray.

'He was one of the best-looking boys I ever saw. I never understood what he saw in her. She married just after I did. Her parents were divorced and her mother married a Standard Oil man in China. She lived with her father's people at Marvin and we used to see a lot of her then, but after she married she dropped out of our crowd somehow. Bob Macdonald was a lawyer, but he wasn't making much money, and they had a walk-up apartment on the North Side. But it wasn't that. They didn't want to see anybody. I never saw two people so crazy about one another. Even after they'd been married two or three years and had a baby they'd go to the pictures and he'd sit with his arm round her waist and she with her head on his shoulder just like lovers. They were quite a joke in Chicago.'

Larry listened to what Isabel said, but made no comment. His face was inscrutable.

'What happened then?' I asked.

'One night they were driving back to Chicago in a little open car of theirs, and they had the baby with them. They always had to take the baby along because they hadn't any help, Sophie did everything herself, and, anyway, they worshipped it. And a bunch of drunks in a great sedan driving at eighty miles an hour crashed into them head on. Bob and the baby were killed outright, but Sophie only had concussion and a rib or two broken. They kept it from her as long as they could that Bob and the baby were dead, but at last they had to tell her. They say it was awful. She nearly went crazy. She shrieked the place down. They had to watch her night and day and once she nearly succeeded in jumping out of the window. Of course we did all we could, but she seemed to hate us. After she came out of the hospital they put her in a sanatorium and she was there for months.'

'Poor thing.'

'When they let her go she started to drink, and when she was drunk she'd go to bed with anyone who asked her. It was terrible for her in-laws. They're very nice quiet people and they hated the scandal. At first we all tried to help her, but it was impossible; if you asked her to dine she'd arrive plastered and she was quite likely to pass out before the evening was over. Then she got in with a rotten crowd and we had to drop her. She was arrested once for driving a car when she was drunk. She was with a dago she'd picked up in a speak-easy and it turned out that he was wanted by the cops.'

'There was Bob's insurance; the people who owned the car that smashed into them were insured and she got something from them. But it didn't last long. She spent it like a drunken sailor and in two years she was broke. Her grandmother wouldn't have her back at Marvin. Then her in-laws said they'd make her an allowance if she'd go and live abroad. I suppose that's what she's living on now.'

'The wheel comes full circle,' I remarked. 'There was a time when the black sheep of the family was sent from my country to America; now apparently he's sent from your country to Europe.'

'I can't help feeling sorry for her,' said Gray.

'Can't you?' said Isabel coolly. 'I can. Of course it was a shock and no one could have sympathized with Sophie more than I did. We'd known one another always. But a normal person recovers from a thing like that. If she went to pieces it's because there was a rotten streak in her. She was naturally unbalanced; even her love for Bob was exaggerated. If she'd had character she'd have been able to make something of life.'

'If pots and pans . . . Aren't you very hard, Isabel?' I murmured.

'I don't think so. I have common sense and I see no reason to be sentimental about Sophie. God knows, no one could be more devoted to Gray and the babes than I am, and if they were killed in a motor accident I should go out of my mind, but sooner or later I'd pull myself together. Isn't that what you'd wish me to do, Gray, or would you prefer me to get blind every night and go to bed with every apache in Paris?'

Gray then came as near to making a humorous remark as I ever heard.

'Of course I'd prefer you to hurl yourself on my funeral pyre in a new Molyneux dress, but as that's not done any more, I guess the best thing you could do would be to take bridge. And I'd like you to remember not to go an original no-trump on less than three and half to four quick tricks.'

It was not the occasion for me to point out to Isabel that her love for her husband and her children, thought sincere enough, was scarcely passionate. Perhaps she read the thought that was passing through my mind, for she addressed me somewhat truculently.

'What have you got to say?'

'I'm like Gray, I'm sorry for the girl.'

'She's not a girl, she's thirty.'

'I suppose it was the end of the world for her when her husband and her baby were killed. I suppose she didn't care what became of her and flung herself into the horrible degradation of drink and promiscuous copulation to get even with life that had treated her so cruelly. She'd lived in heaven and when she lost it she couldn't put up with the common earth of common men, but in despair plunged headlong into hell. I can imagine that if she couldn't drink the nectar of the gods any more she thought she might as well drink bathroom gin.'

'That's the sort of thing you say in novels. It's nonsense and you know it's nonsense. Sophie wallows in the gutter because she likes it. Other women have lost their husbands and children. It wasn't that that made her evil. Evil doesn't spring from good. The evil was there always. When that motor accident broke her defences it set her free to be herself. Don't waste your pity on her; she's now what at heart she always was.'

All this time Larry had remained silent. He seemed to be in a brown study and I thought he hardly heard what we were saying. Isabel's words were followed by a brief silence. He began to speak, but in a strange, toneless voice, as though not to us, but to himself; his eyes seemed to look into the dim distance of past time.

'I remember her when she was fourteen with her long hair brushed back off her forehead and a black bow at the back, with her freckled, serious face.

She was a modest, high-minded, idealistic child. She read everything she could get hold of and we used to talk about books.'

'When?' asked Isabel, with a slight frown.

'Oh, when you were out being social with your mother. I used to go up to her grandfather's and we'd sit under a great elm they had there and read to one another. She loved poetry and wrote quite a lot herself.'

'Plenty of girls do that at that age. It's pretty poor stuff.'

'Of course it's a long time ago and I dare say I wasn't a very good judge.'

'You couldn't have been more than sixteen yourself.'

'Of course it was imitative. There was a lot of Robert Frost in it. But I have a notion it was rather remarkable for so young a girl. She had a delicate ear and a sense of rhythm. She had a feeling for the sounds and scents of the country, the first softness of spring in the air and the smell of the parched earth after rain.'

'I never knew she wrote poetry,' said Isabel.

'She kept it a secret, she was afraid you'd all laugh at her. She was very shy.'

'She's not that now.'

'When I came back from the war she was almost grown-up. She'd read a lot about the condition of the working classes and she'd seen something of it for herself in Chicago. She'd got on to Carl Sandburg and was writing savagely in free verse about the misery of the poor and the exploitation of the working classes. I dare say it was rather commonplace, but it was sincere and it had pity in it and aspiration. At that time she wanted to become a social worker. It was moving, her desire for sacrifice. I think she was capable of a great deal. She wasn't silly or mawkish, but she gave one the impression of a lovely purity and a strange loftiness of soul. We saw a lot of one another that year.'

I could see that Isabel listened to him with growing exasperation. Larry had no notion that he was driving a dagger in her heart and with his every detached word twisting it in the wound. But when she spoke it was with a smile on her lips.

'How did she come to choose you for her confidant?'

Larry looked at her with his trustful eyes.

'I don't know. She was a poor girl among all of you who had plenty of dough, and I didn't belong. I was there just because Uncle Bob practised at Marvin. I suppose she felt that gave us something in common.'

Larry had no relations. Most of us have at least cousins whom we may hardly know, but who at least give us a sense that we are part of the human family. Larry's father had been an only son, his mother an only daughter; his grandfather on one side, the Quaker, had been lost at sea when a young man and his grandfather on the other side had neither brother nor sister. No one could be more alone in the world than Larry.

'Did it ever occur to you that Sophie was in love with you?' asked Isabel.

'Never,' he smiled.

'Well, she was.'

'When he came back from the war as a wounded hero half the girls in Chicago had a crush on Larry,' said Gray in his bluff way.

'This was more than a crush. She worshipped you, my poor Larry. D'you mean to say you didn't know it?'

'I certainly didn't and I don't believe it.'

'I suppose you thought she was too high-minded.'

'I can see that skinny little girl with the bow in her hair and her serious face whose voice trembled with tears when she read that ode of Keats's because it was so beautiful. I wonder where she is now.'

Isabel gave a very slight start and threw him a suspicious enquiring glance.

'It's getting frightfully late and I'm so tired I don't know what to do. Let's go.'

Three

On the following evening I took the Blue Train to the Riviera and two or three days later went over to Antibes to see Elliott and give him news of Paris. He looked far from well. The cure at Montecatini had not done him the good he expected, and his subsequent wanderings had exhausted him. He found a baptismal font in Venice and then went on to Florence to buy the triptych he had been negotiating for. Anxious to see these objects duly placed, he went down to the Pontine Marshes and put up at a miserable inn where the heat had been hard to bear. His precious purchases were a long time on the way, but determined not to leave till he had accomplished his purpose, he stayed on. He was delighted with the effect when at last everything was in order, and he showed me with pride the photographs he had taken. The church, though small, had dignity, and the restrained richness of the interior was proof of Elliott's good taste.

'I saw an early Christian sarcophagus in Rome that took my fancy and I deliberated a long time about buying it, but in the end I thought better of it.'

'What on earth did you want with an early Christian sarcophagus, Elliott?'

'To put myself in it, my dear fellow. It was of a very good design and I thought it would balance the font on the other side of the entrance, but those early Christians were stumpy little fellows and I shouldn't have fitted in. I wasn't going to lie there till the Last Trump with my knees doubled up to my chin like a foetus. Most uncomfortable.'

I laughed, but Elliott was serious.

'I had a better idea. I've made all arrangements, with some difficulty, but that was to be expected, to be buried in front of the altar at the foot of the chancel steps, so that when the poor peasants of the Pontine Marshes come up to take the Sacrament they'll clump over my bones with their heavy shoes. Rather chic, don't you think? Just a plain stone slab with my name on it and a couple of dates. *Si monumentum quaeris, circumspice.* If you seek his monument, look around, you know.'

'I do know enough Latin to understand a hackneyed quotation, Elliott,' I said tartly.

'I beg your pardon, my dear fellow. I'm so accustomed to the crass ignorance of the upper classes, I forgot for the moment that I was talking to an author.'

He scored.

'But what I wanted to say to you was this,' he continued. 'I've left proper instructions in my will, but I want you to see they're carried out. I will *not* be buried on the Riviera among a lot of retired colonels and middle-class French people.'

'Of course I'll do what you wish, Elliott, but I don't think we need plan for anything like that for many years to come.'

'I'm getting on, you know, and to tell you the truth I shan't be sorry to go. What are those lines of Landor's? I've warmed both hands . . .'

Though I have a bad verbal memory, the poem is very short and I was able to repeat it.

> *'I strove with none, for none was worth my strife.*
> *Nature I loved, and, next to Nature, Art;*
> *I warmed both hands before the fire of Life;*
> *It sinks, and I am ready to depart.'*

'That's it,' he said.

I could not but reflect that it was only by a violent stretch of the imagination that Elliott could fit the epigram to himself.

'It expresses my sentiments exactly,' he said, however. 'The only thing I could add to it is that I've always moved in the best society in Europe.'

'It would be difficult to squeeze that into a quatrain.'

'Society is dead. At one time I had hopes that America would take the place of Europe and create an aristocracy that the *hoi polloi* would respect, but the depression has destroyed any chance of that. My poor country is becoming hopelessly middle-class. You wouldn't believe it, my dear fellow, but last time I was in America a taxi driver addressed me as brother.'

But though the Riviera, still shaken by the crash of '29, was not what it had been, Elliott continued to give parties and go to parties. He had never frequented Jews, making an exception only for the family of Rothschild, but the grandest parties were being given now by members of the chosen race, and when there was a party Elliott could not bear not to go to it. He wandered through these gatherings, graciously shaking the hand of one or kissing that of another, but with a kind of forlorn detachment like an exiled royalty who felt a trifle embarrassed to find himself in such company. The exiled royalties, however, had the time of their lives and to meet a film star seemed the height of their ambitions. Nor had Elliott ever looked with approval on the modern practice of treating members of the theatrical profession as persons whom you met socially; but a retired actress had built herself a sumptuous residence in his immediate neighbourhood and kept open house. Cabinet ministers, dukes, great ladies stayed with her for weeks on end. Elliott became a constant visitor.

'Of course it's a very mixed crowd,' he told me, 'but one doesn't have to talk to people one doesn't want to. She's a compatriot of mine and I feel I ought to help her out. It must be a relief to her house guests to find someone who can talk their own language.'

Sometimes he was obviously so far from well that I asked him why he didn't take things more easily.

'My dear fellow, at my age one can't afford to fall out. You don't think that I've moved in the highest circles for nearly fifty years without realizing that if you're not seen everywhere you're forgotten.'

I wondered if he realized what a lamentable confession he was then making. I had not the heart to laugh at Elliott any more; he seemed to me a profoundly pathetic object. Society was what he lived for, a party was the breath of his nostrils, not to be asked to one was an affront, to be alone was a mortification; and, an old man now, he was desperately afraid.

So the summer passed. Elliott spent it scurrying from one end of the Riviera to the other, lunching in Cannes, dining in Monte Carlo and exercising all his ingenuity to fit in a tea party here and a cocktail party there; and however tired he felt, taking pains to be affable, chatty and amusing. He was full of gossip and you could trust him to know the details of the latest scandal before anyone but the parties immediately concerned. He would have stared at you with frank amazement had you suggested to him that his existence was futile. He would have thought you distressingly plebian.

Four

The autumn came and Elliott decided to go to Paris for a while, partly to see how Isabel, Gray and the children were getting on, and partly to make what he called *acte de présence* in the capital. Then he meant to go to London to order some new clothes and incidentally to look up some old friends. My own plan was to go straight to London, but he asked me to drive up with him to Paris, and since that is an agreeable thing to do I consented and, having done so, saw no reason why I should not spend at least a few days in Paris myself. We made the journey by easy stages, stopping at places where the food was good; Elliott had something the matter with his kidneys and drank nothing but Vichy, but always insisted on choosing my half-bottle of wine for me and, too good-natured to grudge me a pleasure he could not share, got a genuine satisfaction out of my enjoyment of a fine vintage. He was so generous that I had difficulty in persuading him to let me pay my share of the expenses. Though I grew a little tired of his stories of the great whom he had known in the past I liked the trip. Much of the country we drove through, just touched with the beginning of its autumn beauty, was very lovely. Having lunched at Fontainebleau, we did not arrive in Paris till afternoon. Elliott dropped me at my modest, old-fashioned hotel and went round the corner to the Ritz.

We had warned Isabel of our arriving, so I was not surprised to find a note from her awaiting me, but I was surprised at its contents.

> Come round the moment you get in. Something terrible has happened. Don't bring Uncle Elliott. For God's sake come as soon as you can.

I am not less curious than anyone else, but I had to have a wash and put on a clean shirt; then I took a taxi and went round to the apartment in the Rue St Guillaume. I was shown into the drawing-room. Isabel sprang to her feet.

'Where have you been all this time? I've been waiting for hours.'

It was five o'clock and, before I could answer, the butler brought in the tea things. Isabel, her hands clenched, watched him with impatience. I couldn't imagine what was the matter.

'I've only just arrived. We dawdled over lunch at Fontainebleau.'

'God, how slow he is. Maddening!' said Isabel.

The man placed the salver with the teapot and the sugar basin and the cups on the table and with what really was exasperating deliberation arranged around it plates of bread and butter, cakes and cookies. He went out and closed the door behind him.

'Larry's going to marry Sophie Macdonald.'

'Who's she?'

'Don't be stupid,' cried Isabel, her eyes flashing with anger. 'That drunken slut we met at that filthy café you took us to. God knows why you took us to a place like that. Gray was disgusted.'

'Oh, you mean your Chicago friend?' I said, ignoring her unjust approach.

'How d'you know?'

'How should I know? He came and told me himself yesterday afternoon. I've been frantic ever since.'

'Supposing you sat down, gave me a cup of tea and told me all about it.'

'Help yourself.'

She sat behind the tea-table and watched me irritably while I poured myself out a cup. I made myself comfortable on a small sofa by the fireplace.

'We haven't seen so much of him lately, since we came back from Dinard, I mean; he came up there for a few days, but wouldn't stay with us, he stayed at a hotel. He used to come down to the beach and play with the children. They're crazy about him. We played golf at St Briac. Gray asked him one day if he'd seen Sophie again.

'"Yes, I've seen her several times," he said.

'"Why?" I asked.

'"She's an old friend," he said.

'"If I were you I wouldn't waste my time on her," I said.

'Then he smiled. You know how he smiles, as though he thought what you'd said funny, though it isn't funny at all.

'"But you're not me," he said.

'I shrugged my shoulders and changed the conversation. I never gave the matter another thought. You can imagine my horror when he came here and told me they were going to get married.

'"You can't, Larry," I said. "You can't."

'"I'm going to," he said as calmly as if he said he was going to have a second helping of potatoes. "And I want you to be very nice to her, Isabel."

'"That's asking too much," I said. "You're crazy. She's bad, bad, bad."'

'What makes you think that?' I interrupted.

Isabel looked at me with flashing eyes.

'She's soused from morning till night. She goes to bed with every tough who asks her.'

'That doesn't mean she's bad. Quite a number of highly respected citizens get drunk and have a liking for rough trade. They're bad habits, like biting one's nails, but I don't know that they're worse than that. I call a person bad who lies and cheats and is unkind.'

'If you're going to take her part I'll kill you.'

'How did Larry meet her again?'

'He found her address in the phone-book. He went to see her. She was sick, and no wonder, with the life she leads. He got a doctor and had someone in to look after her. That's how it started. He says she's given up drink; the damned fool thinks she's cured.'

'Have you forgotten what Larry did for Gray? He's cured him, hasn't he?'

'That's different. Gray wanted to be cured. She doesn't.'

'How d'you know?'

'Because I know women. When a woman goes to pieces like that she's done for; she can never get back. If Sophie's what she is, it's because she was like that always. D'you think she'll stick to Larry? Of course not. Sooner or later she'll break out. It's in her blood. It's a brute she wants, that's what excites her, and it's a brute she'll go after. She'll lead Larry a hell of a life.'

'I think that's very probably, but I don't know what you can do about it. He's going into this with his eyes open.'

'*I* can do nothing about it, but you can.'

'I?'

'Larry likes you and he listens to what you say. You're the only person who has any influence over him. You know the world. Go to him and tell him that he can't make such a fool of himself. Tell him that it'll ruin him.'

'He'll only tell me that it's no business of mine and he'll be quite right.'

'But you like him, at least you're interested in him, you can't sit by and let him make a hopeless mess of his life.'

'Gray's his oldest and most intimate friend. I don't think it'll do any good, but I should have thought Gray was the best person to speak to him.'

'Oh, Gray,' she said impatiently.

'You know it may not turn out so badly as you think. I've known two or three fellows, one in Spain and two in the East, who married whores and they made them very good wives. They were grateful to their husbands, for the security they gave them, I mean, and they of course knew what pleases a man.'

'You make me tired. D'you think I sacrificed myself to let Larry fall into the hands of a raging nymphomaniac?'

'How did you sacrifice yourself?'

'I gave Larry up for the one and only reason that I didn't want to stand in his way.'

'Come off it, Isabel. You gave him up for a square-cut diamond and a sable coat.'

The words were hardly out of my mouth when a plate of bread and butter came flying at my head. By sheer luck I caught the plate, but the bread and butter was scattered on the floor. I got up and put the plate back on the table.

'Your uncle Elliott wouldn't have thanked you if you'd broken one of his Crown Derby plates. They were made for the third Duke of Dorset and they're almost priceless.'

'Pick up the bread and butter,' she snapped.

'Pick it up yourself,' I said, seating myself again on the sofa.

She got up and, fuming, picked up the scattered pieces.

'And you call yourself an English gentleman,' she exclaimed savagely.

'No, that's a thing I've never done in all my life.'

'Get the hell out of here. I never want to see you again. I hate the sight of you.'

'I'm sorry for that, because the sight of you always gives me pleasure. Have you ever been told that your nose is exactly like that of the Psyche in the museum of Naples, and that's the loveliest representation of virginal beauty that ever existed. You've got exquisite legs, so long and shapely, and I never cease to be surprised at them, because they were thick and lumpy when you were a girl. I can't imagine how've you managed it.'

'An iron will and the grace of God,' she said angrily.

'But of course your hands are your most fascinating feature. They're so slim and so elegant.'

'I was under the impression you thought them too big.'

'Not for your height and build. I'm always amazed at the infinite grace with which you use them. Whether by nature or by art you never make a gesture without imparting beauty to it. They're like flowers sometimes and sometimes likes birds on the wing. They're more expressive than any words you can say. They're like the hands of El Greco's portraits; in fact, when I look at them I'm inclined to believe Elliott's highly improbable story of your having an ancestor who was a Spanish grandee.'

She looked up crossly.

'What are you talking about? That's the first I've heard of it.'

I told her about the Count de Lauria and Queen Mary's maid of honour from whose issue in the female line Elliott traced his descent. Meanwhile Isabel contemplated her long fingers and her manicured painted nails with complacency.

'One must be descended from someone,' she said. Then with a tiny chuckle, giving me a mischievous look in which no trace of rancour remained, she added: 'You lousy bastard.'

So easy is it to make a woman see reason if you only tell her the truth.

'There are moments when I don't positively dislike you,' said Isabel.

She came and sat on the sofa beside me and, slipping her arm through mine, leant over to kiss me. I withdrew my cheek.

'I will not have my face smeared with lipstick,' I said. 'If you want to kiss me, kiss me on the lips, which is what merciful Providence intended them for.'

She giggled and, her hand turning my head towards her, with her lips pressed a thin layer of paint on mine. The sensation was far from unpleasant.

'Now you've done that, perhaps you'll tell me what it is you want.'

'Advice.'

'I'm quite willing to give you that, but I don't think for a moment you'll take it. There's only one thing you can do and that is to make the best of a bad job.'

Flaring up again, she snatched her arm away and, getting up, flung herself into a chair on the other side of the fireplace.

'I'm not going to sit by and let Larry ruin himself. I'll stick at nothing to prevent him from marrying that slut.'

'You won't succeed. You see, he's enthralled by one of the most powerful emotions that can beset the human breast.'

'You don't mean to say you think he's in love with her?'

'No. That would be trifling in comparison.'

'Well?'

'Have you ever read the New Testament?'

'I suppose so.'

'D'you remember how Jesus was led into the wilderness and fasted forty days? Then, when he was a-hungered, the devil came to him and said: If thou be the son of God, command that these stones be made bread. But Jesus resisted the temptation. Then the devil set him on a pinnacle of the temple and said to him: If thou be the son of God, cast thyself down. For angels had charge of him and would bear him up. But again Jesus resisted. Then the devil took him into a high mountain and showed him the kingdoms of the world and said that he would give them to him if he would fall down and worship him. But Jesus said: Get thee hence, Satan. That's the end of the story according to the good simple Matthew. But it wasn't. The devil was sly and he came to Jesus once more and said: If thou wilt accept shame and disgrace, scourging, a crown of thorns and death on the cross, thou shalt save the human race, for greater love hath no man than this, that a man lay down his life for his friends. Jesus fell. The devil laughed till his sides ached, for he knew the evil men would commit in the name of their redeemer.'

Isabel looked at me indignantly.

'Where on earth did you get that?'

'Nowhere. I've invented it on the spur of the moment.'

'I think it's idiotic and blasphemous.'

'I only wanted to suggest to you that self-confidence is a passion so overwhelming that beside it even lust and hunger are trifling. It whirls its victim to destruction in the highest affirmation of his personality. The object doesn't matter; it may be worth while or it may be worthless. No wine is so intoxicating, no love so shattering, no vice so compelling. When he sacrifices himself man for a moment is greater than God, for how can God, infinite and omnipotent, sacrifice himself? At best he can only sacrifice his only begotten son.'

'Oh, Christ, how you bore me,' said Isabel.

I paid no attention.

'How can you suppose that common sense or prudence will have any effect on Larry when he's in the grip of a passion like that? You don't know what he's been seeking all these years. I don't know either, I only suspect. All these years of labour, all these experiences he garnered weigh nothing in the balance now they're set against his desire—oh, it's more than a desire, his urgent, clamorous need to save the soul of a wanton woman whom he'd known as an innocent child. I think you're right, I think he's undertaking a hopeless job; with his acute sensibility he'll suffer the tortures of the damned; his life's work, whatever it may be, will remain undone. The ignoble Paris killed Achilles by shooting an arrow in his heel. Larry lacks just that touch of ruthlessness that even the saint must have to win his halo.'

'I love him,' said Isabel. 'God knows, I ask nothing of him. I expect nothing. No one could love anyone more unselfishly than I love him. He's going to be so unhappy.'

She began to cry and, thinking it would do her good, I let her be. I diverted myself idly with the idea that had sprung so unexpectedly into my mind. I played with it. I couldn't but surmise that the devil, looking at the cruel wars that Christianity has occasioned, the persecutions, the tortures Christian has inflicted on Christian, the unkindness, the hypocrisy, the intolerance, must consider the balance sheet with complacency. And when he remembers that it has laid upon mankind the bitter burden of the sense of sin that has darkened the beauty of the starry night and cast a baleful shadow on the passing pleasures of a world to be enjoyed, he must chuckle as he murmurs: give the devil his due.

Presently Isabel took a handkerchief from her bag and a mirror and, looking at herself, carefully wiped the corner of her eyes.

'Damned sympathetic, aren't you?' she snapped.

I looked at her pensively, but did not answer. She powdered her face and painted her lips.

'You said just now you suspected what he's been after all these years. What did you mean?'

'I can only guess, you know, and I may be quite wrong. I think he's been seeking for a philosophy, or maybe a religion, and a rule of life that'll satisfy both his head and his heart.'

Isabel considered this for a moment. She sighed.

'Don't you think it's very strange that a country boy from Marvin, Illinois, should have a notion like that?'

'No stranger than that Luther Burbank who was born on a farm in Massachusetts should have produced a seedless orange or that Henry Ford who was born on a farm in Michigan should have invented a Tin Lizzie.'

'But those are practical things. That's in the American tradition.'

I laughed.

'Can anything in the world be more practical than to learn how to live to best advantage?'

Isabel gave a gesture of lassitude.

'You don't want to lose Larry altogether, do you?'

She shook her head.

'You know how loyal he is: if you won't have anything to do with his wife he won't have anything to do with you. If you've got any sense you'll make friends with Sophie. You'll forget the past and be as nice to her as you can be when you like. She's going to be married and I suppose she's buying some clothes. Why don't you offer to go shopping with her? I think she'd jump at it.'

Isabel listened to me with narrowed eyes. She seemed intent upon what I was saying. For a moment she pondered, but I could not guess what was passing through her mind. Then she surprised me.

'Will you ask her to lunch? It would be rather awkward for me after what I said to Larry yesterday.'

'Will you behave if I do?'

'Like an angel of light,' she answered with her most engaging smile.

'I'll fix it up right away.'

There was a phone in the room. I soon found Sophie's number, and after the usual delay which those who use the French telephone learn to put up with patiently, I got her. I mentioned my name.

'I've just arrived in Paris,' I said, 'and heard that you and Larry are going to be married. I want to congratulate you. I hope you'll be very happy.' I smothered a cry as Isabel, who was standing by me, gave the soft of my arm a vicious pinch. 'I'm only here for a very short time and I wonder if you and Larry will come and lunch with me the day after tomorrow at the Ritz. I'm asking Gray and Isabel and Elliott Templeton.'

'I'll ask Larry. He's here now.' There was a pause. 'Yes, we shall be glad to.'

I fixed an hour, made a civil remark, and replaced the receiver on its stand. I caught an expression in Isabel's eyes that caused me some misgiving.

'What are you thinking?' I asked her. 'I don't quite like the look of you.'

'I'm sorry; I thought that was the one thing about me you did like.'

'You haven't got some nefarious scheme that you're hatching, Isabel?'

She opened her eyes very wide.

'I promise you I haven't. As a matter of fact I'm terribly curious to see what Sophie looks like now Larry has reformed her. All I hope is that she won't come to the Ritz with a mask of paint on her face.'

Five

My little party did not go too badly. Gray and Isabel arrived first; Larry and Sophie Macdonald five minutes later. Isabel and Sophie kissed each other warmly and Isabel and Gray congratulated her on her engagement. I caught the appraising sweep of eyes with which Isabel took in Sophie's appearance. I was shocked at it. When I saw her in that dive in the Rue de Lappe, outrageously painted, with hennaed hair, in the bright green coat, though she looked outrageous and was very drunk, there was something provocative and even basely alluring in her; but now she looked drab and, though certainly a year or two younger than Isabel, much older. She still had that gallant tilt of her head, but now, I don't know why, it was pathetic. She was letting her hair go back to its natural colour and it had the slatternly look that hair has when it has been dyed and left to grow. Except for a streak of red on her lips she had no make-up on. Her skin was rough and it had an unhealthy pallor. I remembered how vividly green her eyes had looked, but now they were pale and grey. She wore a red dress, obviously brand-new, with hat, shoes and bag to match; I don't pretend to know anything about women's clothes, but I had a feeling that it was fussy and too elaborate for the occasion. On her breast was a piece of showy artificial jewellery such as you buy in the Rue de Rivoli. Beside Isabel, in black silk, with a string of cultured pearls round her neck and in a very smart hat, she looked cheap and dowdy.

I ordered cocktails, but Larry and Sophie refused them. Then Elliott arrived. His progress through the vast foyer was, however, impeded by the hands he had to shake and the hands he had to kiss as he saw one person after the other whom he knew. He behaved as though the Ritz were his private house and he were assuring his guests of his pleasure that they had been able to accept his invitation. He had been told nothing about Sophie except that she had lost her husband and child in a motor accident and was now going to marry Larry. When at last he reached us he congratulated them both with the elaborate graciousness of which he was a master. We went in to the dining-room and since we were four men and two women I placed Isabel and Sophie opposite one another at the round table, with Sophie between Gray and myself; but the table was small enough for the conversation to be general. I had already ordered the luncheon and the wine waiter came along with the wine card.

'You don't know anything about wine, my dear fellow,' said Elliott. 'Give me the wine card, Albert.' He turned over the pages. 'I drink nothing but Vichy myself, but I can't bear to see people drink wine that isn't perfect.'

He and Albert, the wine waiter, were old friends and after an animated discussion they decided on the wine I should give my guests. Then he turned to Sophie.

'And where are you going for your honeymoon, my dear?'

He glanced at her dress and an almost imperceptible raising of his eyebrows showed me that he had formed an unfavourable opinion of it.

'We're going to Greece.'

'I've been trying to get there for ten years,' said Larry, 'but somehow I've never been able to manage it.'

'It ought to be lovely at this time of the year,' said Isabel, with a show of enthusiasm.

She remembered, as I remembered, that that was where Larry proposed to take her when he wanted her to marry him. It seemed to be an *idée fixe* with Larry to go to Greece on a honeymoon.

The conversation flowed none too easily and I should have found it a difficult row to hoe if it hadn't been for Isabel. She was on her best behaviour. Whenever silence seemed to threaten us and I racked my brain for something fresh to talk about, she broke in with facile chatter. I was grateful to her. Sophie hardly spoke except when she was spoken to and then it seemed an effort to her. The spirit had gone out of her. You would have said that something had died in her and I asked myself if Larry wasn't putting her to a strain greater than she could support. If as I suspected she had doped as well as drunk, the sudden deprivation must have worn her nerves to a frazzle. Sometimes I intercepted a look between them. In his I saw tenderness and encouragement, but in hers an appeal that was pathetic. It may be that Gray with his sweetness of disposition instinctively felt what I thought I saw, for he began to tell her how Larry had cured him of the headaches that had incapacitated him and went on to say how much he had depended on him and how much he owed him.

'Now I'm as fit as a flea,' he continued. 'As soon as ever I can get a job I'm going back to work. I've got several irons in the fire and I'm hoping to land something before long. Gosh, it'll be good to be back home again.'

Gray meant well, but what he had said was perhaps not very tactful if, as I supposed, Larry to cure Sophie of her aggravated alcoholism had used with her the same method of suggestion—for that to my mind was what it was—that had been successful with Gray.

'You never have headaches now, Gray?' asked Elliott.

'I haven't had one for three months and if I think one's coming on I take hold of my charm and I'm all right.' He fished out of his pocket the ancient coin Larry had given him. 'I wouldn't sell it for a million dollars.'

We finished luncheon and coffee was served. The wine waiter came up and asked whether we wanted liqueurs. We all refused except Gray, who said he would have a brandy. When the bottle was brought Elliott insisted on looking at it.

'Yes, I can recommend it. That'll do you no harm.'

'A little glass for Monsieur?' asked the waiter.

'Alas, it's forbidden me.'

Elliott told him at some length that he was having trouble with his kidneys and that his doctor would not allow him to drink alcohol.

'A tear of zubrovka could do Monsieur no harm. It's well known to be very good for the kidneys. We have just received a consignment from Poland.'

'Is that true? It's hard to get nowadays. Let me have a look at the bottle.'

The wine waiter, a portly, dignified creature with a long silver chain round his neck, went away to fetch it, and Elliott explained that it was the Polish form of vodka but in every way superior.

'We used to drink it at the Radziwills when I stayed with them for the shooting. You should have seen those Polish princes putting it away; I'm not exaggerating when I tell you that they'd drink it by the tumbler without turning a hair. Good blood, of course; aristocrats to the tips of their fingers. Sophie, you must try it, and you too, Isabel. It's an experience no one can afford to miss.'

The wine waiter brought the bottle. Larry, Sophie and I refused to be tempted, but Isabel said she would like to try it. I was surprised, for habitually she drank very little and she had had two cocktails and two or three glasses of wine. The waiter poured out of a glass of pale green liquid and Isabel sniffed it.

'Oh, what a lovely smell.'

'Hasn't it?' cried Elliott. 'That's the herbs they put in it; it's they that give it its delicate taste. Just to keep you company I'll have a drop. It can't hurt me for once.'

'It tastes divine,' said Isabel. 'It's like mother's milk. I've never tasted anything so good.'

Elliott raised his glass to his lips.

'Oh, how it brings back the old days! You people who never stayed with the Radziwills don't know what living is. That was the grand style. Feudal, you know. You might have thought yourself back in the Middle Ages. You were met at the station by a carriage with six horses and postilions. And at dinner a footman in livery behind every person.'

He went on to describe the magnificence and luxury of the establishment and the brilliance of the parties; and the suspicion, doubtless unworthy, occurred to me that the whole thing was a put-up job between Elliott and the wine waiter to give Elliott an opportunity to discourse upon the grandeur of this princely family and the host of Polish aristocrats he hobnobbed with in their castle. There was no stopping him.

'Another glass, Isabel?'

'Oh, I daren't. But it is heavenly. I'm so glad to know about it; Gray, we must get some.'

'I'll have some sent round to the apartment.'

'Oh, Uncle Elliott, would you?' cried Isabel enthusiastically. 'You are so kind to us. You must try it, Gray; it smells of freshly mown hay and spring flowers, of thyme and lavender, and it's soft on the palate and so comfortable, it's like listening to music by moonlight.'

It was unlike Isabel to gush inordinately and I wondered if she was a trifle tight. The party broke up. I shook hands with Sophie.

'When are you going to be married?' I asked her.

'The week after next. I hope you'll come to the wedding.'

'I'm afraid I shan't be in Paris. I'm leaving for London tomorrow.'

While I was saying good-bye to the rest of my guests Isabel took Sophie aside and talked to her for a minute, then turned to Gray.

'Oh, Gray, I'm not coming home just yet. There's a dress show at Molyneux's and I'm taking Sophie to it. She ought to see the new models.'

'I'd love to,' said Sophie.

We parted. I took Suzanne Rouvier out to dinner that night and next morning started for England.

Six

Elliott arrived at Claridge's a fortnight later and shortly afterwards I dropped in to see him. He had ordered himself several suits of clothes and at what I thought excessive length told me in detail what he had chosen and why. When at last I could get a word in I asked him how the wedding had gone off.

'It didn't go off,' he answered grimly.

'What *do* you mean?'

'Three days before it was to take place Sophie disappeared. Larry hunted everywhere for her.'

'What an extraordinary thing! Did they have a row?'

'No. Far from it. Everything had been arranged. I was going to give her away. They were taking the Orient Express immediately after the wedding. If you ask me, I think Larry's well out of it.'

I guessed that Isabel had told Elliott everything.

'What exactly happened?' I asked.

'Well, you remember that day we lunched at the Ritz with you. Isabel took her to Molyneux's. D'you remember the dress Sophie wore? Deplorable. Did you notice the shoulders? That's how you tell if a dress is well made, by the way it fits over the shoulders. Of course, poor girl, she couldn't afford Molyneux's prices, and Isabel, you know how generous she is, and after all they've known one another since they were children, Isabel offered to give her a dress so that at least she'd have something decent to be married in. Naturally she jumped at it. Well, to cut a long story short, Isabel asked her to come to the apartment one day at three so that they could go together for the final fitting. Sophie came all right, but unfortunately Isabel had to take one of the children to the dentist's and didn't get in till after four and by that time Sophie had gone. Isabel thought she'd got tired of waiting and had gone on to Molyneux's, so she went there at once, but she hadn't come. At last she gave her up and went home again. They were all going to dine together and Larry came along at dinner-time and the first thing she asked him was where Sophie was.

'He couldn't understand it and he rang up her apartment, but there was no reply, so he said he'd go down there. They held dinner up as long as they could, but neither of them turned up and so they had dinner by themselves. Of course you know what Sophie's life was before you ran into her in the Rue de Lappe; that was a most unfortunate idea of yours to take them down there. Well, Larry spent all night going around her old haunts, but couldn't find her anywhere. He went to the apartment time after time, but the *concierge* said she hadn't been in. He spent three days hunting for her. She'd just vanished. Then on the fourth day he went to the apartment again and the *concierge* told him she'd been in and packed a bag and gone away in a taxi.'

'Was Larry awfully upset?'

'I didn't see him. Isabel tells me he was rather.'

'She didn't write or anything?'

'Nothing.'

I thought it over.

'What do you make of it?' I said.

'My dear fellow, exactly what you make of it. She couldn't stick it out; she went on the booze again.'

That was obvious, but for all that it was strange. I couldn't see why she had chosen just that moment to skip.

'How is Isabel taking it?'

'Of course she's sorry, but she's a sensible girl and she told me she always thought it would be a disaster if Larry married a woman like that.'

'And Larry?'

'Isabel's been very kind to him. She says that what makes it difficult is that he won't discuss it. He'll be all right, you know; Isabel says he was never in love with Sophie. He was only marrying her out of a sort of misguided chivalry.'

I could see Isabel putting a brave face on a turn of events that was certainly causing her a great deal of satisfaction. I well knew that next time I saw her she would not fail to point out to me that she had known all along what would happen.

But it was nearly a year before I saw her again and though by that time I could have told her something about Sophie that would have set her thinking, the circumstances were such that I had no inclination to. I stayed in London till nearly Christmas and then, wanting to get home, went straight down to the Riviera without stopping in Paris. I set to work on a novel and for the next few months lived in retirement. I saw Elliott now and then. It was obvious that his health was failing, and it pained me that he persisted notwithstanding in leading a social life. He was vexed with me because I would not drive thirty miles to go to the constant parties he continued to give. He thought it very conceited of me to prefer to sit at home and work.

'It's an unusually brilliant season, my dear fellow,' he told me. 'It's a crime to shut yourself up in your house and miss everything that's going on. And why you had to choose a part of the Riviera to live in that's completely out of fashion I shan't be able to understand if I live to be a hundred.'

Poor nice silly Elliott; it was clear that he would live to no such age.

By June I had finished the rough draft of my novel and thought I deserved a holiday, so, packing a bag, I got on the cutter from which in summer we used to bathe in the Baie des Fosses and set sail along the coast towards Marseilles. There was only a fitful breeze and for the most part we chugged along with the motor auxiliary. We spent a night at the harbour at Cannes, another at Sainte Maxime, and a third at Sanary. Then we got to Toulon. This is a port I have always had an affection for. The ships of the French fleet give it an air at once romantic and companionable, and I am never tired of wandering about its old streets. I can linger for hours on the quay, watching the sailors on shore leave strolling about in pairs or with their girls, and the civilians who saunter back and forth as though they had nothing in the world to do but enjoy the pleasant sunshine. Because of all these ships and the ferryboats that take the bustling crowd to various points of the vast harbour, Toulon gives you the effect of a terminal to which all the ways of the wide world converge; and as you sit in a café, your eyes a little dazzled by the brightness of sea and sky, your fancy takes golden journeys to the uttermost parts of the earth. You land in a longboat on a coral beach, fringed with coconut palms, in the Pacific; you step off the gangway on to the dock at Rangoon and get into a rickshaw; you watch from the upper deck the noisy, gesticulating crowd of Negroes as your ship is made fast to the pier at Port au Prince.

We got in latish in the morning and towards the middle of the afternoon I landed and walked along the quay, looking at the shops, at the people who passed me and at the people sitting under the awning in the cafés. Suddenly I saw Sophie and at the same moment she saw me. She smiled and said hello. I stopped and shook hands with her. She was by herself at a small table with an empty glass before her.

'Sit down and have a drink,' she said.

'You have one with me,' I replied, taking a chair.

She wore the striped blue-and-white jersey of the French sailor, a pair of bright red slacks and sandals through which protruded the painted nails of her big toes. She wore no hat, and her hair, cut very short and curled, was of so pale a gold that it was almost silver. She was as heavily made up as when we had run across her at the Rue de Lappe. She had had a drink or two as I judged from the saucers on the table, but she was sober. She did not seem displeased to see me.

'How are all the folks in Paris?' she asked.

'I think they're all right. I haven't seen any of them since that day we all lunched together at the Ritz.'

She blew a great cloud of smoke from her nostrils and began to laugh.

'I didn't marry Larry after all.'

'I know. Why not?'

'Darling, when it came to the point I couldn't see myself being Mary Magdalen to his Jesus Christ. No, sir.'

'What made you change your mind at the last moment?'

She looked at me mockingly. With the audacious tilt of the head, with her small breasts and narrow flanks, in that get-up, she looked like a vicious boy; but I must admit that she was much more attractive than in the red dress, with its dismal air of provincial smartness, in which I had last seen her. Face and neck were deeply burnt by the sun, and though the brownness of her skin made the rouge on her cheeks and the black of her eyebrows more aggressive, the effect in its vulgar way was not without lure.

'Would you like me to tell you?'

I nodded. The waiter brought the beer I had ordered for myself and the brandy and seltzer for her. She lit a *caporal* from one she had just finished.

'I hadn't had a drink for three months. I hadn't had a smoke.' She saw my faint look of surprise and laughed. 'I don't mean cigarettes. Opium. I felt awful. You know, sometimes when I was alone I'd shriek the place down; I'd say, "I can't go through with it, I can't go through with it." It wasn't so bad when I was with Larry, but when he wasn't there it was hell.'

I was looking at her and when she mentioned opium I scanned her more sharply; I noticed the pin-point pupils that showed she was smoking it now. Her eyes were startlingly green.

'Isabel was giving me my wedding dress. I wonder what's happened to it now. It was a peach. We'd arranged that I should pick her up and we'd go to Molyneux's together. I will say this for Isabel, what she doesn't know about clothes isn't worth knowing. When I got to the apartment their man said she'd had to take Joan to the dentist's and had left a message that she'd be in directly. I went into the living-room. The coffee things were still on the table and I asked the man if I could have a cup. Coffee was the only thing that kept me going. He said he'd bring me some and took the empty cups and the coffee-pot away. He left a bottle on the tray. I looked at it, and it was that Polish stuff you'd all talked about at the Ritz.'

'Zubrovka. I remember Elliott saying he'd send Isabel some.'

'You'd all raved about how good it smelt and I was curious. I took out the cork and had a sniff. You were quite right; it smelt damned good. I lit a cigarette and in a few minutes the man came in with the coffee. That was good too. They talk a lot about French coffee, they can have it; give me American coffee. That's the only thing I miss here. But Isabel's coffee wasn't bad, I was feeling lousy, and after I'd had a cup I felt better. I looked at that bottle standing there. It was a terrible temptation, but I said, "To hell with it, I won't think of it," and I lit another cigarette. I thought Isabel would be in any minute, but she didn't come; I got frightfully nervous; I hate being kept waiting and there was nothing to read in the room. I started walking about and looking at the pictures, but I kept on seeing that damned bottle. Then I thought I'd just pour out a glass and look at it. It had such a pretty colour.'

'Pale green.'

'That's right. It's funny, its colour is just like its smell. It's like that green you sometimes see in the heart of a white rose. I *had* to see if it tasted like that, I thought just a taste couldn't hurt me; I only meant to take a sip and then I heard a sound, I thought it was Isabel coming in and I swallowed the glassful because I didn't want her to catch me. But it wasn't Isabel after all. Gosh, it made me feel good, I hadn't felt like that since I'd gone on the wagon. I really began to feel alive again. If Isabel had come in then I suppose I'd be married to Larry now. I wonder how it would have turned out.'

'And she didn't come in?'

'No, she didn't. I was furious with her. Who did she think she was, keeping me waiting like that? And then I saw that the liqueur glass was full again; I suppose I must have poured it out without thinking, but, believe it or not, I didn't know I had. It seemed silly to pour it back again, so I drank it. There's no denying it, it was delicious. I felt a different woman; I felt like laughing and I hadn't felt like that for three months. D'you remember that old cissie saying he'd seen fellas in Poland drink it by the tumbler without turning a hair? Well, I thought I could take what any Polish son of a bitch could take and you may as well be hanged for a sheep as a lamb, so I emptied the dregs of my coffee in the fireplace and filled the cup to the brim. Talk of mother's milk—my arse. Then I don't quite know what happened, but I don't believe there was much left in the bottle by the time I was through. Then I thought I'd get out before Isabel came in. She nearly caught me. Just as I got out of the front door I heard Joanie's voice. I ran up the stairs and waited till they were safely in the apartment and then I dashed down and got into a taxi. I told the driver to drive like hell and when he asked where to I burst out laughing in his face. I felt like a million dollars.'

'Did you go back to your apartment?' I asked, though I knew she hadn't.

'What sort of a damn fool d'you take me for? I knew Larry would come and look for me. I didn't dare go to any of the places I used to go to, so I went to Hakim's. I knew Larry'd never find me there. Besides, I wanted a smoke.'

'What's Hakim's?'

'Hakim's. Hakim's an Algerian and he can always get you opium if you've got the dough to pay for it. He was quite a friend of mine. He'll get you anything you want, a boy, a man, a woman or a nigger. He always has half a dozen Algerians on tap. I spent three days there. I don't know how many men I didn't have.' She began to giggle. 'All shapes, sizes and colours. I made up for lost time all right. But you know, I was scared. I didn't feel safe in Paris, I was afraid Larry'd find me, besides I hadn't got any money left, those bastards you have to pay them to go to bed with you, so I got out. I went back to the apartment and gave the *concierge* a hundred francs and told her if anyone came and asked for me to say I'd gone away. I packed my things and that night I took the train to Toulon. I didn't feel really safe till I got here.'

'And have you been here ever since?'

'You betcha, and I'm going to stay here. You can get all the opium you want, the sailors bring it back from the East, and it's good stuff, not that muck they sell you in Paris. I've got a room at the hotel. You know, the Commerce et la Marine. When you go in there at night the corridors just reek of it.' She sniffed voluptuously. 'Sweet and acrid, and you know they're smoking in their rooms, and it gives you a nice homey feeling. And they don't mind who you take in with you. They come and thump at your door at five in the morning to get the sailors up to go back to their ships, so you don't have to worry about that.' And then, without transition: 'I saw a book of yours in the store just along the quay; if I'd known I was going to see you I'd have bought it and got you to sign it.'

When passing the bookshop I had stopped to look in the window and had noticed among other new books the translation of a novel of mine that had recently appeared.

'I don't suppose it would have amused you much,' I said.

'I don't know why it shouldn't. I *can* read, you know.'

'And you can write too, I believe.'

She gave me a rapid glance and began to laugh.

'Yeah, I used to write poetry when I was a kid. I guess it was pretty terrible, but I thought it fine. I suppose Larry told you.' She hesitated for a moment. 'Life's hell anyway, but if there is any fun to be got out of it, you're only a god-damn fool if you don't get it.' She threw back her head defiantly. 'If I buy that book will you write in it?'

'I'm leaving tomorrow. If you really want it, I'll get you a copy and leave it at your hotel.'

'That'd be swell.'

Just then a naval launch came up to the quay and a crowd of sailors tumbled out of it. Sophie embraced them with a glance.

'That'll be my boy friend.' She waved her arm at someone. 'You can stand him a drink and then you better scram. He's a Corsican and as jealous as our old friend Jehovah.'

A young man came up to us, hesitated when he saw me, but on a beckoning gesture came up to our table. He was tall, swarthy, clean-shaven, with splendid dark eyes, an aquiline nose and raven black, wavy hair. He did not look more than twenty. Sophie introduced me as an American friend of her childhood.

'Dumb but beautiful,' she said to me.

'You like 'em tough, don't you?'

'The tougher the better.'

'One of these days you'll get your throat cut.'

'I wouldn't be surprised,' she grinned. 'Good riddance to bad rubbish.'

'One's going to speak French, isn't one?' the sailor said sharply.

Sophie turned upon him a smile in which there was a trace of mockery. She spoke a fluent and slangy French, with a strong American accent, but this gave the vulgar and obscene colloquialisms that she commonly used a comic tang, so that you could not help but laugh.

'I was telling him that you were beautiful, but to spare your modesty I was saying it in English.' She addressed me. 'And he's strong. He has the muscles of a boxer. Feel them.'

The sailor's sullenness was dispelled by the flattery and with a complacent smile he flexed his arm so that the biceps stood out.

'Feel it,' he said. 'Go on, feel it.'

I did so and expressed a proper admiration. We chatted for a few minutes. I paid for the drinks and got up.

'I must be going.'

'It's nice to have seen you. Don't forget the book.'

'I won't.'

I shook hands with them both and strolled off. On my way I stopped at the bookshop, bought the novel and wrote Sophie's name and my own. Then, because it suddenly occurred to me and I could think of nothing else, I wrote the first line of Ronsard's lovely little poem which is in all the anthologies:

Mignonne, allons voir si la rose. . . .

I left it at the hotel. It is on the quay and I have often stayed there because when you are awakened at dawn by the clarion that calls the men on night leave back to duty the sun rising mistily over the smooth water of the harbour invests the wraithlike ships with a shrouded loveliness. Next day we sailed for Cassis, where I wanted to buy some wine, and then to Marseilles to take up a new sail that we had ordered. A week later I got home.

Seven

I found a message from Joseph, Elliott's manservant to tell me that Elliott was ill in bed and would be glad to see me, so next day I drove over to Antibes. Joseph, before taking me up to see his master, told me that Elliott had had an attack of uræmia and that his doctor took a grave view of his condition. He had come through it and was getting better, but his kidneys were diseased and it was impossible that he should ever completely recover. Joseph had been with Elliott for forty years and was devoted to him, but though his manner was regretful it was impossible not to notice the inner satisfaction with which, like so many members of his class, catastrophe in the house filled him.

'*Ce pauvre monsieur*,' he sighed. 'Evidently he had his manias but at bottom he was good. Sooner or later one must die.'

He spoke already as though Elliott were at his last gasp.

'I'm sure he's provided for you, Joseph,' I said grimly.

'One must hope it,' he said mournfully.

I was surprised when he ushered me into the bedroom to find Elliott was very spry. He was pale and looked old, but was in good spirits. He was shaved and his hair was neatly brushed. He wore pale blue silk pyjamas, on the pocket of which were embroided his initials surmounted by his count's crown. These, much larger and again with the crown, were heavily embroidered on the turned-down sheet.

I asked him how he felt.

'Perfectly well,' he said cheerfully. 'It's only a temporary indisposition. I shall be up and about again in a few days. I've got the Grand Duke Dimitri lunching with me on Saturday, and I've told my doctor he must put me to rights by then at all costs.'

I spent half an hour with him, and on my way out asked Joseph to let me know if Elliott had a relapse. I was astonished a week later when I went to lunch with one of my neighbours to find him there. Dressed for a party, he looked like death.

'You oughtn't to be out, Elliott,' I told him.

'Oh, what nonsense, my dear fellow. Frieda is expecting the Princess Mafalda. I've known the Italian royal family for years, ever since poor Luisa was *en poste* at Rome, and I couldn't let poor Frieda down.'

I did not know whether to admire his indomitable spirit or to lament that at his age, stricken with mortal illness, he should still retain his passion for society. You would never have thought he was a sick man. Like a dying actor when he had the grease paint on his face and steps on the stage, who forgets for the time being his aches and pains, Elliott played his part of the polished courtier with his accustomed assurance. He was infinitely amiable, flatteringly attentive to the proper people and amusing with that malicious irony at which he was an adept. I think I had never seen him display his social gift to greater advantage. When the Royal highness had departed (and the grace with which Elliott bowed, managing to combine respect for her exalted rank with an old man's admiration for a comely woman, was a sight to see) I was not surprised to hear our hostess tell him that he had been the life and soul of the party.

A few days later he was in bed again and his doctor forbade him to leave his room. Elliott was exasperated.

'It's too bad this should happen just now. It's a particularly brilliant season.'

He reeled off a long list of persons of importance who were spending the summer on the Riviera.

I went to see him every three or four days. Sometimes he was in bed, but sometimes he lay on a chaise longue in a gorgeous dressing-gown. He seemed to have an inexhaustible supply of them, for I do not remember that I ever saw him in the same one twice. On one of these occasions, it was the beginning of August by now, I found Elliott unusually quiet. Joseph had told me when he let me into the house that he seemed a little better so I was surprised that he was so listless. I tried to amuse him with such gossip of the coast as I had picked up, but he was plainly uninterested. There was a slight frown between his eyes, and a sullenness in his expression that was unusual with him.

'Are you going to Edna Novemali's party?' he asked me suddenly.

'No, of course not.'

'Has she asked you?'

'She's asked everyone on the Riviera.'

The Princess Novemali was an American of immense wealth who had married a Roman prince, but not an ordinary prince such as go for two a penny in Italy, but the head of a great family and the descendant of a *condottiere* who had carved out a principality for himself in the sixteenth century. She was a woman of sixty, a widow, and since the Fascist regime demanded too large a slice of her American income to suit her, she had left Italy and built herself, on a fine estate behind Cannes, a Florentine villa. She had brought marble from Italy with which to line the walls of her great reception rooms and imported painters to paint the ceilings. Her pictures, her bronzes were uncommonly fine and even Elliott, though he didn't like Italian furniture, was obliged to admit that hers was magnificent. The gardens were lovely and the swimming-pool must have cost a small fortune. She entertained largely and you never sat down less than twenty at table. She had arranged to give a fancy-dress party on the night of the August full moon, and although it was still three weeks ahead nothing else was being talked of on the Riviera. There were to be fireworks and she was bringing down a coloured orchestra from Paris. The exiled royalties were telling one another with envious admiration that it would cost her more than they had to live on for a year.

'It's princely,' they said.

'It's crazy,' they said.

'It's in bad taste,' they said.

'What are you going to wear?' Elliott asked me.

'But I told you, Elliott, I'm not going. You don't think I'm going to dress myself up in fancy dress at my time of life.'

'She hasn't asked me,' he said hoarsely.

He looked at me with haggard eyes.

'Oh, she will,' I said coolly. 'I dare say all the invitations haven't gone out yet.'

'She's not going to ask me.' His voice broke. 'It's a deliberate insult.'

'Oh, Elliott, I can't believe that. I'm sure it's an oversight.'

'I'm not a man that people overlook.'

'Anyhow, you wouldn't have been well enough to go.'

'Of course I should. The best party of the season! If I was on my deathbed I'd get up for it. I've got the costume of my ancestor, the Count de Lauria, to wear.'

I did not quite know what to say and so remained silent.

'Paul Barton was in to see me just before you came,' Elliott said suddenly.

I cannot expect the reader to remember who this was, since I had to look back myself to see what name I had given him. Paul Barton was the young American whom Elliott had introduced into London society and who had aroused his hatred by dropping him when he no longer had any use for him. He had been somewhat in the public eye of late, first because he had adopted British nationality and then because he had married the daughter of a newspaper magnate who had been raised to the peerage. With this influence behind him and with his own adroitness it was evident that he would go far. Elliott was very bitter.

'Whenever I wake up in the night and hear a mouse scratching away in the wainscot I say, "That's Paul Barton climbing." Believe me, my dear fellow, he'll end up in the House of Lords. Thank God, I shan't be alive to see it.'

'What did he want?' I asked, for I knew as well as Elliott that this young man did nothing for nothing.

'I'll tell you what he wanted,' said Elliott, snarling. 'He wanted to borrow my Count de Lauria costume.'

'Nerve!'

'Don't you see what it means? I t means he knew Edna hadn't asked me and wasn't going to ask me. She put him up to it. The old bitch. She'd never have got anywhere without me. I gave parties for her. I introduced her to everyone she knows. She sleeps with her chauffeur; you knew that of course. Disgusting! He sat there and told me that she's having the whole garden illuminated and there are going to be fireworks. I love fireworks. And he told me that Edna was being pestered by people who were asking for invitations, but she had turned them all down because she wanted the party to be really brilliant. He spoke as though there were no question of my being invited.'

'And are you lending him the costume?'

'I'd see him dead and in hell first. I'm going to be buried in it.' Elliott, sitting up in bed, rocked to and fro like a woman distraught. 'Oh, it's so unkind,' he said. 'I hate them, I hate them all. They were glad enough to make a fuss of me when I could entertain them, but now I'm old and sick they have no use for me. Not ten people have called to enquire since I've been laid up, and all this week only one miserable bunch of flowers. I've done everything for them. They've eaten my food and drunk my wine. I've run their errands for them. I've made their parties for them. I've turned myself inside out to do them favours. And what have I got out of it? Nothing, nothing, nothing. There's not one of them who cares if I live or die. Oh, it's so cruel.' He began to cry. Great heavy tears trickled down his withered cheeks. 'I wish to God I'd never left America.'

It was lamentable to see that old man, with the grave yawning in front of him, weep like a child because he hadn't been asked to a party: shocking and at the same time almost intolerably pathetic.

'Never mind, Elliott,' I said, 'it may rain on the night of the party. That'll bitch it.'

He caught at my words like the drowning man we've all heard about at a straw. He began to giggle through his tears.

'I've never thought of that. I'll pray to God for rain as I've never prayed before. You're quite right; that'll bitch it.'

I managed to divert his frivolous mind into another channel and left him, if not cheerful, at least composed. But I was not willing to let the matter rest, so on getting home I called up Edna Novemali and, saying I had to come to Cannes next day, asked if I could lunch with her. She sent a message that she'd be pleased but there'd be no party. Nevertheless when I arrived I found ten people there besides herself. She was not a bad sort, generous and hospitable, and her only grave fault was her malicious tongue. She could not help saying beastly things about even her intimate friends, but she did this because she was a stupid woman and knew no other way to make herself interesting. Since her slanders were repeated she was often not on speaking terms with the objects of her venom, but she gave good parties and most of them found it convenient after a while to forgive her. I did not want to expose Elliott to the humiliation of asking her to invite him to her big do, so waited to see how the land lay. She was excited about it and the conversation at luncheon was concerned with nothing else.

'Elliott will be delighted to have an opportunity to wear his Philip the Second costume,' I said as casually as I could.

'I haven't asked him,' she said.

'Why not?' I replied, with an air of surprise.

'Why should I? He doesn't count socially any more. He's a bore and a snob and a scandalmonger.'

Since these accusations could with equal truth be brought against her, I thought this a bit thick. She was a fool.

'Besides,' she added, 'I want Paul to wear Elliott's costume. He'll look simply divine in it.'

I said nothing more, but determined by hook or by crook to get poor Elliott the invitation he hankered after. After luncheon Edna took her friends out into the garden. That gave me the chance I was looking for. On one occasion I had stayed in the house for a few days and knew its arrangement. I guessed that there would still be a number of invitation cards left over and that they would be in the secretary's room. I whipped along there, meaning to slip one in my pocket, write Elliott's name on it and post it. I knew he was much too ill to go, but it would mean a great deal to him to receive it. I was taken aback when I opened the door to find Edna's secretary at her desk. I had expected her to be still at lunch. She was a middle-aged Scotch woman, called Miss Keith, with sandy hair, a freckled face, pince-nez and an air of determined virginity. I collected myself.

'The Princess is taking the crowd around the garden, so I thought I'd come in and smoke a cigarette with you.'

'You're welcome.'

Miss Keith spoke with a Scotch burr and when she indulged in the dry humour which she reserved for her favourites she so broadened it as to make her remarks extremely amusing, but when you were overcome with laughter she looked at you with pained surprise as though she thought you daft to see anything funny in what she said.

'I suppose this party is giving you a hell of a lot of work, Miss Keith,' I said.

'I don't know whether I'm standing on my head or on my heels.'

Knowing I could trust her, I went straight to the point.

'Why hasn't the old girl asked Mr Templeton?'

Miss Keith permitted a smile to cross her grim features.

'You know what she is. She's got a down on him. She crossed his name out on the list herself.'

'He's dying, you know. He'll never leave his bed again. He's awfully hurt at being left out.'

'If he wanted to keep in with the Princess he'd have been wiser not to tell everyone that she goes to bed with her chauffeur. And him with a wife and three children.'

'And does she?'

Miss Keith looked at me over her pince-nez.

'I've been a secretary for twenty-one years, my dear sir, and I've made it a rule to believe all my employers as pure as the driven snow. I'll admit that when one of my ladies found herself three months gone in the family way when his lordship had been shooting lions in Africa for six, my faith was sorely tried, but she took a little trip to Paris, a very expensive little trip it was too, and all was well. Her ladyship and I shared a deep sigh of relief.'

'Miss Keith, I didn't come here to smoke a cigarette with you, I came to snitch an invitation card and send it to Mr Templeton myself.'

'That would have been a very unscrupulous thing to do.'

'Granted. Be a good sport, Miss Keith. Give me a card. He won't come and it'll make the poor old man happy. You've got nothing against him, have you?'

'No, he's always been very civil to me. He's a gentleman, I will say that for him, and that's more than you can say for most of the people who come here and fill their fat bellies at the Princess's expense.'

All important persons have about them someone in a subordinate position who has their ear. These dependants are very susceptible to slights and, when they are not treated as they think they should be, will by well-directed shafts, constantly repeated, poison the minds of their patrons against those who have provoked their animosity. It is well to keep in with them. This Elliott knew better than anybody and he had always a friendly word and a cordial smile for the poor relation, the old maidservant or the trusted secretary. I was sure he had often exchanged pleasant badinage with Miss Keith and at Christmas had not forgotten to send her a box of chocolates, a vanity case or a handbag.

'Come on, Miss Keith, have a heart.'

Miss Keith fixed her pince-nez more firmly on her prominent nose.

'I am sure you wish me to do nothing disloyal to my employer, Mr Maugham, besides which the old cow would fire me if she found out I'd disobeyed her. The cards are on the desk in their envelopes. I am going to look out of the window, partly to stretch my legs which are cramped from sitting too long in one position and also to observe the beauty of the prospect. What happens when my back is turned neither God nor man can hold me responsible for.'

When Miss Keith resumed her seat the invitation was in my pocket.

'It's been nice to see you, Miss Keith,' I said holding out my hand. 'What are you wearing at the fancy-dress party?'

'I am a minister's daughter, my dear sir,' she replied. 'I leave such foolishness to the upper classes. When I have seen that the representatives of the *Herald* and the *Mail* get a good supper and a bottle of our second-best champagne, my duties will be terminated and I shall retire to the privacy of my bed-chamber with a detective story.'

Eight

A couple of days later, when I went to see Elliott, I found him beaming.

'Look,' he said, 'I've had my invitation. It came this morning.'

He took the card out from under his pillow and showed it to me.

'It's what I told you,' I said. 'You see, your name begins with a T. The secretary has evidently only just reached you.'

'I haven't answered yet. I'll do it tomorrow.'

I had a moment's fright at that.

'Would you like me to answer it for you? I could post it when I leave you.'

'No, why should you? I'm quite capable of answering invitations myself.'

Fortunately, I thought, the envelope would be opened by Miss Keith and she would have the sense to suppress it. Elliott rang the bell.

'I want to show you my costume.'

'You're not thinking of going, Elliott?'

'Of course I am. I haven't worn it since the Beaumont's ball.'

Joseph answered the bell and Elliott told him to bring the costume. It was in a large flat box, wrapped in tissue paper. There were long white silk hose, padded trunks of cloth of gold slashed with white satin, a doublet to match, a cloak, a ruff to wear round the neck, a flat velvet cap and a long gold chain from which hung the order of the Golden Fleece. I recognized it as a copy of the gorgeous dress worn by Philip the Second in Titian's portrait at the Prado, and when Elliott told me it was exactly the costume the Count de Lauria had worn at the wedding of the King of Spain with the Queen of England I could not but think that he was giving rein to his imagination.

On the following morning while I was having breakfast I was called on the telephone. It was Joseph to tell me that Elliott had had another attack during the night and the doctor, hurriedly summoned, doubted whether he would last the day. I sent for the car and drove over to Antibes. I found Elliott unconscious. He had resolutely refused to have a nurse, but I found one there, sent for the doctor from the English hospital between Nice and Beaulieu, and was glad to see her. I went out and telegraphed to Isabel. She and Gray were spending the summer with the children at the inexpensive seaside resort of La Baule. It was a long journey and I was afraid they would not get to Antibes in time. Except for her two brothers, whom he had not seen for years, she was Elliott's only living relative.

But the will to live was strong in him, or it may be that the doctor's medicaments were effective, for during the course of the day he rallied. Though shattered, he put on a bold front and amused himself by asking the nurse indecent questions about her sex life. I stayed with him most of the afternoon and next day, on going to see him again, found him, though very weak, sufficiently cheerful. The nurse would only let me stay with him a short time. I was worried at not having received an answer to my telegram. Not knowing Isabel's address at La Baule I had sent it to Paris and feared that the *concierge* had delayed to forward it. It was not till two days later that I got a reply to say that they were starting at once. As ill luck would have it, Gray and Isabel were on a motor trip in Brittany and had only just had my wire. I looked up the trains and saw that they could not arrive for at least thirty-six hours.

Early next morning Joseph called me again to tell me that Elliott had had a very bad night and was asking for me. I hurried over. When I arrived Joseph took me aside.

'Monsieur will excuse me if I speak to him on a delicate subject,' he said to me. 'I am of course a freethinker and believe all religion is nothing but a conspiracy of the priests to gain control over the people, but Monsieur knows what women are. My wife and the chambermaid insist that the poor gentleman should receive the last sacraments and evidently the time is growing short.' He looked at me in rather a shamefaced way. 'And the fact remains, one never knows, perhaps it is better, if one's got to die, to regularize one's situation with the Church.'

I understood him perfectly. However freely they mock, most Frenchmen, when the end comes, prefer to make their peace with the faith that is part of their blood and bones.

'Do you want me to suggest it to him?'

'If Monsieur would have the goodness.'

It was not a job I fancied, but after all Elliott had been for many years a devout Catholic, and it was fitting that he should conform to the obligations of his faith. I went up to his room. He was lying on his back, shrivelled and wan, but perfectly conscious. I asked the nurse to leave us alone.

'I'm afraid you're very ill, Elliott,' I said. I was wondering if you wouldn't like to see a priest?'

He looked at me for a minute without answering.

'D'you mean to say I'm going to die?'

'Oh, I hope not. But it's just as well to be on the safe side.'

'I understand.'

He was silent. It is a terrible moment when you have to tell someone what I had just told Elliott. I could not look at him. I clenched my teeth because I was afraid I was going to cry. I was sitting on the edge of the bed, facing him, with my arm outstretched for support.

He patted my hand.

'Don't be upset, my dear fellow. *Noblesse oblige*, you know.'

I laughed hysterically.

'You ridiculous creature, Elliott.'

'That's better. Now call up the bishop and say that I wish to make my confession and receive Extreme Unction. I would be grateful if he'd send the Abbé Charles. He's a friend of mine.'

The Abbé Charles was the bishop's vicar general whom I have had occasion to mention before. I went downstairs and telephoned. I spoke to the bishop himself.

'Is it urgent?' he asked.

'Very.'

'I will attend to it at once.'

The doctor arrived and I told him what I had done. He went up with the nurse to see Elliott and I waited on the ground floor in the dining-room. It is only twenty minutes' drive from Nice to Antibes and little more than half an hour later a black sedan drew up at the door. Joseph came to me.

'*C'est Monseigneur en personne, Monsieur*,' he said in a flurry. 'It's the bishop himself.'

I went out to receive him. He was not as usual accompanied by his vicar general, but, why I did not know, by a young abbé who bore a casket that contained, I supposed, the utensils needed to administer the sacrament. The chauffeur followed with a shabby black valise. The bishop shook hands with me and presented his companion.

'How is our poor friend?'

'I'm afraid he's very ill, Monseigneur.'

'Will you be so obliging as to show us into a room where we can enrobe.'

'The dining-room is here, Monseigneur, and the drawing-room is on the next floor.'

'The dining-room will do very well.'

I ushered him in. Joseph and I waited in the hall. Presently the door opened and the bishop came out, followed by the abbé holding in both hands the chalice surmounted by a little platter on which lay the consecrated wafer. They were covered by a cambric napkin so fine that it was transparent. I had never seen the bishop but at a dinner or luncheon party, and a very good trencherman he was, who enjoyed his food and a glass of good wine, telling funny and sometimes ribald stories with verve. He had struck me then as a sturdy, thickset man of no more than average height. Now, in surplice and stole, he looked not only tall, but stately. His red face, puckered as a rule with malicious yet kindly laughter, was grave. There was in his appearance nothing left of the cavalry officer he had once been; he looked, what indeed he was, a great dignitary of the Church. I was hardly surprised to see Joseph cross himself. The bishop inclined his head in a slight bow.

'Conduct me to the sick man,' he said.

I made way for him to ascend the stairs before me, but he bade me precede him. We went up in a solemn silence. I entered Elliott's room.

'The bishop has come himself, Elliott.'

Elliott struggled to raise himself to a sitting position.

'Monseigneur, this is an honour I did not venture to expect.'

'Do not move, my friend.' The bishop turned to the nurse and me. 'Leave us.' And then to the abbé: 'I will call you when I am ready.'

The abbé glanced around and I guessed that he was looking for a place to set down the chalice. I pushed aside the tortoise-shell-backed brushes on the dressing-table. The nurse went downstairs and I led the abbé into the adjoining room which Elliott used as a study. The windows were open to the blue sky and he went over and stood by one of them. I sat down. A race of Stars was in progress and their sails gleamed dazzling white against the azure. A big schooner with a black hull, her red sails spread, was beating up against the breeze towards the harbour. I recognized her for a lobster boat, bringing a catch from Sardinia to supply the gala dinners at the casinos with a fish course. Through the closed door I could hear the muffled murmur of voices. Elliott was making his confession. I badly wanted a cigarette, but feared the abbé would be shocked if I lit one. He stood motionless, looking out, a slender young man, and his thick waving black hair, his fine dark eyes, his olive skin revealed his Italian origin. There was the quick fire of the South in his aspect and I asked myself what urgent faith, what burning desire had caused him to abandon the joys of life, the pleasures of his age and the satisfaction of his senses, to devote himself to the service of God.

Suddenly the voices in the next room were still and I looked at the door. It was opened and the bishop appeared.

'*Venez*,' he said to the priest.

I was left alone. I heard the bishop's voice once more and I knew he was saying the prayers that the Church had ordained should be said for the dying. Then there was another silence and I knew that Elliott was partaking of the body and the blood of Christ. From I know not what feeling, inherited, I suppose, from far-away ancestors, though not a Catholic I can never attend Mass without a sense of tremulous awe when the little tinkle of the servitor's bell informs me of the Elevation of the Host; and now, similarly, I shivered as though a cold wind ran through me, I shivered with fear and wonder. The door was opened once more.

'You may come in,' said the bishop.

I entered. The abbé was spreading the cambric napkin over the cup and the little gilt plate on which the consecrated water had lain. Elliott's eyes shone.

'Conduct Monseigneur to his car,' he said.

We descended the stairs. Joseph and the maids were waiting in the hall. The maids were crying. There were three of them and one after the other they came forward and, dropping to their knees, kissed the bishop's ring. He blessed them with two fingers. Joseph's wife nudged him and he advanced, fell to his knees too and kissed the ring. The bishop faintly smiled.

'You are a freethinker, my son?'

I could see Joseph making an effort over himself.

'Yes, Monseigneur.'

'Do not let it trouble you. You have been a good and faithful servant to your master. God will overlook the errors of your understanding.'

I went out into the street with him and opened the door of his car. He gave me a bow and as he stepped in smiled indulgently.

'Our poor friend is very low. His defects were of the surface; he was generous of heart and kindly towards his fellow men.'

Nine

Thinking that Elliott might want to be alone after the ceremony in which he had taken part, I went up to the drawing-room and began to read, but no sooner had I settled myself than the nurse came in to tell me that he wanted to see me. I climbed the flight of stairs to his room. Whether owing to a shot that the doctor had given him to help him to support the ordeal before him or whether from the excitement of it, he was calmly cheerful and his eyes were bright.

'A great honour, my dear fellow,' he said. 'I shall enter the kingdom of heaven with a letter of introduction from a prince of the Church. I fancy that all doors will be open to me.'

'I'm afraid you'll find the company very mixed,' I smiled.

'Don't you believe it, my dear fellow. We know from Holy Writ that there are class distinctions in heaven just as there are on earth. There are seraphim and cherubim, archangels and angels. I have always moved in the best society in Europe and I have no doubt that I shall move in the best society in heaven. Our Lord has said: The House of my Father hath many mansions. It would be highly unsuitable to lodge the *hoi polloi* in a way to which they're entirely unaccustomed.'

I suspected that Elliott saw the celestial habitations in the guise of the châteaux of a Baron de Rothschild with eighteenth-century panelling on the walls, Buhl tables, marquetry cabinets and Louis Quinze suites covered with their original *petit-point*.

'Believe me, my dear fellow,' he went on after a pause, 'there'll be none of this damned equality in heaven.'

He dropped off quite suddenly into a doze. I sat down with a book. He slept off and on. At one o'clock the nurse came in to tell me that Joseph had luncheon ready for me. Joseph was subdued.

'Fancy Monseigneur the Bishop coming himself. It is a great honour he has done our poor gentleman. You saw me kiss his ring?'

'I did.'

'It's not a thing I would have done of myself! I did it to satisfy my poor wife.'

I spent the afternoon in Elliott's room. In the course of it a telegram came from Isabel to say that she and Gray would arrive by the Blue Train next morning. I could hardly hope they would be in time. The doctor came. He shook his head. Towards sunset Elliott awoke and was able to take a little nourishment. It seemed to give him a momentary strength. He beckoned to me and I went up to the bed. His voice was very weak.

'I haven't answered Edna's invitation.'

'Oh, don't bother about that now, Elliott.'

'Why not? I've always been a man of the world; there's no reason why I should forget my manners as I'm leaving it. Where is the card?'

It was on the chimney-piece and I put it in his hand, but I doubt whether he could see it.

'You'll find a pad of writing paper in my study. If you'll get it I'll dictate my answer.'

I went into the next room and came back with writing materials. I sat down by the side of his bed.

'Are you ready?'

'Yes.'

His eyes were closed, but there was a mischievous smile on his lips and I wondered what was coming.

'Mr Elliott Templeton regrets that he cannot accept Princess Novemali's kind invitation owing to a previous engagement with his Blessed Lord.'

He gave a faint, ghostly chuckle. His face was of a strange blue-white, ghastly to behold, and he exhaled the nauseating stench peculiar to his disease. Poor Elliott who had loved to spray himself with the perfumes of Chanel and Molyneux. He was still holding the purloined invitation card and, thinking it incommoded him, I tried to take it out of his hand, but he tightened his grip on it. I was startled to hear him speak quite loudly.

'The old bitch,' he said.

These were the last words he spoke. He sank into a coma. The nurse had been up with him all the previous night and looked very tired, so I sent her to bed, promising to call her if necessary, and said I would sit up. There was indeed nothing to do. I lit a shaded lamp and read till my eyes ached and then, turning it off, I sat in darkness. The night was warm and the windows wide open. At regular intervals the flash of the lighthouse swept the room with a passing glimmer. The moon, which when full would look upon the vacuous, noisy gaiety of Edna Novemali's fancy-dress party, set, and in the sky, a deep, deep blue, the countless stars shone with their terrifying brilliance. I think I may have dropped off into a light sleep, but my senses were still awake, and I was suddenly startled into intense consciousness by a hurried, angry sound, the most awe-inspiring sound that anyone can hear, the death rattle. I went over to the bed and by the gleam of the lighthouse felt Elliott's pulse. He was dead. I lit the lamp by his bedside and looked at him. His jaw had fallen. His eyes were open and before closing them I stared into them for a minute. I was moved and I think a few tears trickled down my cheeks. An old, kind friend. It made me sad to think how silly, useless and trivial his life had been. It mattered very little now that he had gone to so many parties and had hobnobbed with all those princes, dukes and counts. They had forgotten him already.

I saw no reason to wake the exhausted nurse, so I returned to my chair by the window. I was asleep when she came in at seven. I left her to do whatever she thought fit and had breakfast, then I went to the station to meet Gray and Isabel. I told them Elliott was dead and since there was no room for them in his house asked them to stay with me, but they preferred to go to an hotel. I went back to my own house to have a bath, shave and change.

In the course of the morning Gray called me to say that Joseph had given them a letter addressed to me that Elliott had entrusted to him. Since it might contain something for my eyes alone I said I would drive over at once, and so less than an hour later I once more entered the house. The letter, marked on the envelope: *To be delivered immediately after my death*, contained instructions for his obsequies. I knew that he had set his heart on being buried in the church that he had built and I had already told Isabel. He wished to be embalmed and mentioned the name of the firm to which the commission should be given. 'I have made enquiries,' he continued, 'and I am informed that they make a very good job of it. I trust you to see that it is not scamped. I desire to be dressed in the dress of my ancestor the Count de Lauria, with his sword by my side and the order of the Golden Fleece on my breast. I leave the choice of my coffin to you. It should be unpretentious but suitable to my position. In order to give no one unnecessary trouble I desire that Thomas Cook and Son should make all arrangements for the transportation of my remains and that one of their men should accompany the coffin to its final resting-place.'

I remembered that Elliott had said he wanted to be buried in that fancy dress of his, but I had taken it for a passing whim and hadn't thought he meant it seriously. Joseph was insistent that his wishes be carried out and there seemed no reason why they should not be. The body was duly embalmed and then I went with Joseph to dress it in those absurd clothes. It was a gruesome business. We slipped his long legs into the white silk hose and pulled the cloth-of-gold trunks over them. It was a job to get his arms through the sleeves of the doublet. We fixed the great starched ruff and draped the satin cape over his shoulders. Finally we placed the flat velvet cap on his head and the collar of the Golden Fleece round his neck. The embalmer had rouged his cheeks and reddened his lips. Elliott, the costume too large now for his emaciated frame, looked like a chorus man in an early opera of Verdi's. The sad Don Quixote of a worthless purpose. When the undertaker's men had put him in the coffin I laid the property sword down the length of his body, between his legs, with his hands on the pommel as I have seen the sword laid on the sculptured tomb of a Crusader.

Gray and Isabel went to Italy to attend the funeral.

Chapter Six

One

I feel it right to warn the reader that he can very well skip this chapter without losing the thread of the story as I have to tell, since for the most part it is nothing more than the account of a conversation that I had with Larry. I should add, however, that except for this conversation I should perhaps not have thought it worth while to write this book.

Two

That autumn, a couple of months after Elliott's death, I spent a week in Paris on my way to England. Isabel and Gray, after their grim journey to Italy, had returned to Brittany, but were now once more settled in the apartment in the Rue St Guillaume. She told me the details of his will. He left a sum of money for Masses to be said for his soul in the church he had built and a further sum for its upkeep. He had bequeathed a handsome amount to the Bishop of Nice to be spent on charitable purposes. He had left me the equivocal legacy of his eighteenth-century pornographic library and a beautiful drawing by Fragonard of a satyr engaged with a nymph on a performance that is usually conducted in private. It was too indecent to hang on my walls and I am not one to gloat upon obscenity in private. He had provided generously for his servants. His two nephews were to have ten thousand dollars each and the residue of his estate went to Isabel. What this amounted to she did not tell me and I did not enquire; I gathered from her complacency that it was quite a lot of money.

For long, ever since he had regained his health, Gray had been impatient to go back to America and get to work again, and though Isabel was comfortable enough in Paris, his restlessness had affected her too. He had for some time been in communication with his friends, but the best opening that presented itself was contingent on his putting in a considerable amount of capital. That he had not got, but Elliott's death had put Isabel in possession of very much more than was needed; and Gray with her approval was starting negotiations with the view, if everything turned out as well as it was represented, of leaving Paris and going to look into the matter for himself. But before that was possible there was much to attend to. They had to come to a reasonable agreement with the French Treasury over the inheritance tax. They had to get rid of the house at Antibes and the apartment in the Rue St Guillaume. They had to arrange for a sale at the Hôtel Drouot of Elliott's furniture, pictures and drawings. These were valuable and it seemed wise to wait till spring when the great collectors were likely to be in Paris. Isabel was not sorry to spend another winter there; the children by now could chatter French as easily as they could chatter English and she was glad to let them have a few more months at a French school. They had grown in three years and were now long-legged, skinny, vivacious little creatures, with little at present of their mother's beauty, but with nice manners and an insatiable curiosity.

So much for that.

Three

I met Larry by chance. I had asked Isabel about him and she told me that since their return from La Baule they had seen very little of him. She and Gray had by now made a number of friends for themselves, people of their own generation, and they were more often engaged than during the pleasant weeks when the four of us were so much together. One evening I went to the Théâtre Français to see *Bérénice*. I had read it of course, but had never seen it played, and since it is seldom given I was unwilling to miss the opportunity. It is not one of Racine's best plays, for the subject is too tenuous to support five acts, but it is moving and contains passages that are justly famous. The story is founded on a brief passage in Tacitus: Titus, who loved Bérénice, Queen of Palestine, with passion and who had even, as was supposed, promised her marriage, for reasons of state sent away from Rome during the first days of his reign in despite of his desires and in despite of hers. For the Senate and the people of Rome were violently opposed to their Emperor's alliance with a foreign queen. The play is concerned with the struggle in his breast between love and duty, and when he falters, it is Bérénice who in the end, assured that he loves her, confirms his purpose and separates herself from him for ever.

I suppose only a Frenchman can appreciate to the full the grace and grandeur of Racine and the music of his verse, but even a foreigner, once he has accustomed himself to the periwigged formality of the style, can hardly fail to be moved by his passionate tenderness and by the nobility of his sentiment. Racine knew as few have done how much drama is contained in the human voice. To me at all events the roll of those mellifluous Alexandrines is a sufficient substitute for action, and I find the long speeches, worked up with infinite skill to the expected climax, every bit as thrilling as any hair-raising adventure of the movies.

There was an interval after the third act and I went out to smoke a cigarette in the foyer over which presides Houdon's Voltaire with his toothless, sardonic grin. Someone touched me on the shoulder. I turned round, perhaps with a slight movement of annoyance, for I wanted to be left with the exaltation with which those sonorous lines had filled me, and saw Larry. As always, I was glad to see him. It was a year since I had set eyes on him, and I suggested that at the end of the play we should meet and have a glass of beer together. Larry said he was hungry, for he had had no dinner, and proposed that we should go to Montmarte. We found one another in due course and stepped out into the open. The Théâtre Français has a musty fug that is peculiar to it. It is impregnated with the body odour of those unnumbered generations of sour-faced, unwashed women called *ouvreuses* who show you to your seat and domineeringly await their tip. It was a relief to get into the fresh air, and since the night was fine we walked. The arc lamps in the Avenue de l'Opéra glared so defiantly that the stars above, as though too proud to compete, shrouded their brightness in the dark of their infinite distance. As we walked we spoke of the performance we had just seen. Larry was disappointed. He would have liked it to be more natural, the lines spoken as people naturally speak and the gestures less theatrical. I thought his point of view mistaken. It was rhetoric, magnificent rhetoric, and I had a notion that it should be spoken rhetorically. I liked the regular thump of the rhymes; and the stylized gestures, handed down in a long tradition, seemed to me to suit the temper of the formal act. I could not but think that that was how Racine would have wished his play to be played. I had admired the way in which the actors had contrived to be human, passionate and true within the limitations that confined them. Art is triumphant when it can use convention as an instrument of its own purpose.

We reached the Avenue de Clichy and went into the Brasserie Graf. It was not long past midnight and the room was crowded, but we found a table and ordered ourselves eggs and bacon. I told Larry I had seen Isabel.

'Gray will be glad to get back to America,' he said. 'He's a fish out of water here. He won't be happy till he's at work again. I dare say he'll make a lot of money.'

'If he does it'll be due to you. You not only cured him in body, but in spirit as well. You restored his confidence in himself.'

'I did very little. I merely showed him how to cure himself.'

'How did you learn to do that little?'

'By accident. It was when I was in India. I'd been suffering from insomnia and happened to mention it to an old Yogi I knew and he said he'd soon settle that. He did just what you saw me do with Gray and that night I slept as I hadn't slept for months. And then, a year later it must have been, I was in the Himalayas with an Indian friend of mine and he sprained his ankle. It was impossible to get a doctor and he was in great pain. I thought I'd try to do what the old Yogi had done, and it worked. You can believe it or not, he was completely relieved of the pain.' Larry laughed. 'I can assure you, no one was more surprised than I. There's nothing to it really; it only means putting the idea into the sufferer's mind.'

'Easier said than done.'

'Would it surprise you if your arm raised itself from the table without any volition of yours?'

'Very much.'

'It will. My Indian friend told people what I'd done when we got back to civilization and he brought others to see me. I hated doing it, because I couldn't quite understand it, but they insisted. Somehow or other I did them good. I found I was able to relieve people not only of pain but of fear. It's strange how many people suffer from it. I don't mean fear of closed spaces and fear of heights, but fear of death and, what's worse, fear of life. Often they're people who seem in the best of health, prosperous, without any worry, and yet they're tortured by it. I've sometimes thought it was the most besetting humour of men, and I asked myself at one time if it was due to some deep animal instinct that man has inherited from that primeval something that first felt the thrill of life.'

I was listening to Larry with expectation, for it was not often that he spoke at any length, and I had an inkling that for once he felt communicative. Perhaps the play we had just seen had released some inhibition and the rhythm of its sonorous cadences, as music will, had overcome his instinctive reserve. Suddenly I realized that something was happening to my hand. I had not given another thought to Larry's half-laughing question. I was conscious that my hand no longer rested on the table, but was raised an inch above it without my willing it. I was taken aback. I looked at it and saw that it trembled slightly. I felt a queer tingling in the nerves of my arm, a little jerk, and my hand and forearm lifted of themselves, I to the best of my belief neither aiding nor resisting, until they were several inches from the table. Then I felt my whole arm being raised from the shoulder.

'This is very odd,' I said.

Larry laughed. I made the slightest effort of will and my hand fell back on to the table.

'It's nothing,' he said. 'Don't attach any importance to it.'

'Were you taught that by the Yogi you spoke to us about when you first came back from India?'

'Oh no, he had no patience with that kind of thing. I don't know whether he believed that he possessed the powers that some Yogis claim to have, but he would have thought it puerile to exercise them.'

Our eggs and bacon arrived and we ate them with good appetite. We drank our beer. Neither of us spoke. Larry was thinking of I knew not what and I was thinking of him. We finished. I lit a cigarette and he lit a pipe.

'What made you go to India in the first place?' I asked abruptly.

'Chance. At least I thought so at the time. Now I'm inclined to think it was the inevitable outcome of my years in Europe. Almost all the people who've had most effect on me I seem to have met by chance, yet looking back it seems as though I couldn't but have met them. It's as if they were waiting there to be called upon when I needed them. I went to India because I wanted a rest. I'd been working very hard and wished to sort out my thoughts. I got a job as a deck hand on one of those pleasure-cruise ships that go around the world. It was going to the East and through the Panama Canal to New York. I hadn't been to America for five years and I was homesick. I was depressed. You know how ignorant I was when we first met in Chicago all those years ago. I'd read an awful lot in Europe and seen a lot, but I was no nearer than when I started to what I was looking for.'

I wanted to ask him what that was, but had a feeling that he'd just laugh, shrug his shoulders and say it was a matter of no consequence.

'But why did you go as a deck hand?' I asked instead. 'You had money.'

'I wanted the experience. Whenever I've got waterlogged spiritually, whenever I've absorbed all I can for the time, I've found it useful to do something of that sort. That winter, after Isabel and I broke off our engagement, I worked in a coal mine near Lens for six months.'

It was then that he told me of those incidents that I have narrated in a previous chapter.

'Were you sore when Isabel threw you over?'

Before he answered he looked at me for some time with those strangely black eyes of his that seemed then to look inwards rather than out.

'Yes. I was very young. I'd made up my mind that we were going to marry. I'd made plans for the life that we were going to lead together. I expected it to be lovely.' He laughed faintly. 'But it takes two to make a marriage just as it takes two to make a quarrel. It had never occurred to me that the life I offered Isabel was a life that filled her with dismay. If I'd had any sense I'd never have suggested it. She was too young and ardent. I couldn't blame her. I couldn't yield.'

It's just possible that the reader will remember that on his flight from the farm, after that grotesque encounter with the farmer's widowed daughter-in-law, he had gone to Bonn. I was anxious to get him to continue, but knew I must be careful not to ask more direct questions than I could help.

'I've never been to Bonn,' I said. 'When I was a boy I spent some time as a student at Heidelberg. It was, I think, the happiest time of my life.'

'I liked Bonn. I spent a year there. I got a room in the house of the widow of one of the professors at the university who took in a couple of boarders. She and her two daughters, both of them middle-aged, did the cooking and the house-work. I found my fellow boarder was a Frenchman and I was disappointed at first because I wanted to speak nothing but German; but he was an Alsatian and he spoke German, if not more fluently, with a better accent than he spoke French. He was dressed like a German pastor and I was surprised to find out after a few days that he was a Benedictine monk. He'd been granted leave of absence from his monastery to make researches at the university library. He was a very learned man, but he didn't look it any more than he looked like my idea of a monk. He was a tall, stout fellow, with sandy hair, prominent blue eyes and a red, round face. He was shy and reserved and didn't seem to want to have anything much to do with me, but he was very polite in a rather elaborate way and always took a civil part in the conversation at table; I only saw him then; as soon as we had finished dinner he went back to work at the library, and after supper, when I sat in the parlour improving my German with whichever of the two daughters wasn't washing up, he retired to his room.

'I was surprised when one afternoon, after I'd been there at least a month, he asked me if I'd care to take a walk with him. He said he could show me places in the neighbourhood that he didn't think I'd be likely to discover for myself. I'm a pretty good walker, but he could outwalk me any day. We must have covered a good fifteen miles on that first walk. He asked me what I was doing in Bonn, and I said I'd come to learn German and get to know something about German literature. He talked very intelligently. He said he'd be glad to help me in any way he could. After that we went for walks two or three times a week. I discovered that he'd taught philosophy for some years. When I was in Paris I'd read a certain amount, Spinoza and Plato and Descartes, but I hadn't read any of the great German philosophers and I was only too glad to listen while he talked about them. One day, when we'd made an excursion across the Rhine and were sitting in a beer-garden drinking a glass of beer, he asked me if I was a Protestant.

'"I suppose so," I said.

'He gave me a quick look and I thought I saw in his eyes the glimmer of a smile. He began to talk about Aeschylus; I'd been learning Greek, you know, and he knew the great tragedians as I could never hope to know them. It was inspiring to hear him. I wondered why he'd suddenly asked me that question. My guardian, Uncle Bob Nelson, was an agnostic, but he went to church regularly because his patients expected it of him and sent me to Sunday school for the same reason. Martha, our help, was a rigid Baptist and she used to frighten my childhood by telling me of the hell fire to which the sinner would be condemned to all eternity. She took a real delight in picturing to me the agonies that would be endured by the various people in the village whom for some reason or other she had had it in for.

'By winter I'd got to know Father Ensheim very well. I think he was rather a remarkable man. I never saw him vexed. He was good-natured and kindly, far more broad-minded than I would have expected, and wonderfully tolerant. His erudition was prodigious and he must have known how ignorant I was, but he used to talk to me as though I were as learned as he. He was very patient with me. He seemed to want nothing but to be of service to me. One day, I don't know why, I had an attack of lumbago and Frau Grabau, my landlady, insisted on putting me to bed with hot-water bottles. Father Ensheim, hearing I was laid up, came into my room to see me, after supper. Except that I was in a good deal of pain I felt perfectly well. You know what bookish people are, they're inquisitive about books, and as I put down the book I was reading when he came in, he took it up and looked at the title. It was a book about Meister Eckhart that I'd found at a bookseller's in the town. He asked me why I was reading it, so I said that I'd been going through a certain amount of mystical literature and told him about Kosti and how he'd aroused my interest in the subject. He surveyed me with his prominent blue eyes and there was a look in them that I can only describe as amused tenderness. I had the feeling that he found me rather ridiculous, but felt so much loving-kindness towards me that he didn't like me any the less. Anyhow, I've never much minded if people thought me a bit of a fool.

'"What are you looking for in these books?" he asked me.

'"If I knew that," I answered, "I'd at least be on the way to finding it."

'"Do you remember my asking you if you were a Protestant? You said you supposed so. What did you mean by that?"

'"I was brought up as one," I said.

'"Do you believe in God?" he asked.

'I don't like personal questions and my first impulse was to tell him that was no business of his. But there was so much goodness in his aspect that I felt it impossible to affront him. I didn't know what to say; I didn't want to answer yes and I didn't want to answer no. It may have been the pain I was suffering that enabled me to speak or it may have been something in him. Anyhow, I told him about myself.'

Larry hesitated for a moment, and when he went on I knew he wasn't speaking to me but to the Benedictine monk. He had forgotten me. I don't know what there was in the time or the place that enabled him to speak without my prompting, of what his natural reticence had so long concealed.

'Uncle Bob Nelson was very democratic and he sent me to the high school at Marvin. It was only because Louisa Bradley nagged him into it that when I was fourteen he let me go to St Paul's. I wasn't very good at anything, either at work or games, but I fitted in all right. I think I was an entirely normal boy. I was crazy about aviation. Those were the early days of flying and Uncle Bob was as excited about it as I was; he knew some of the airmen, and when I said I wanted to learn to fly he said he'd fix it for me. I was tall for my age and when I was sixteen I could easily pass for eighteen. Uncle Bob made me promise to keep it a secret, because he knew everyone would be down on him like a ton of bricks for letting me go, but as a matter of fact he helped me to get over to Canada and gave me a letter to someone he knew, and the result was that by the time I was seventeen I was flying in France.

'They were terrible gimcrack planes we flew in then, and you practically took your life in your hands each time you went up. The heights we got to were absurd, judged by present standards, but we didn't know any better and thought it wonderful. I loved flying. I couldn't describe the feeling it gave me, I only knew I felt proud and happy. In the air, 'way up, I felt that I was part of something very great and very beautiful. I didn't know what it was all about, I only knew that I wasn't alone any more, by myself as I was, two thousand feet up, but that I belonged. I can't help it if it sounds silly. When I was flying above the clouds and they were like an enormous flock of sheep below me I felt that I was at home with infinitude.'

Larry paused. He gazed at me from the caverns of his impenetrable eyes, but I did not know whether he saw me.

'I'd known that men had been killed by the hundred thousand, but I hadn't seen them killed. It didn't mean very much to me. Then I saw a dead man with my own eyes. The sight filled me with shame.'

'Shame?' I exclaimed involuntarily.

'Shame, because that boy, he was only three or four years older than me, who'd had such energy and daring, who a moment before had had so much vitality, who'd been so good, was now just mangled flesh that looked as if it had never been alive.'

I didn't say anything. I had seen dead men when I was a medical student and I had seen many more during the war. What had dismayed me was how trifling they looked. There was no dignity in them. Marionettes that the showman had thrown into the discard.

'I didn't sleep that night. I cried. I wasn't frightened for myself; I was indignant; it was the wickedness of it that broke me. The war came to an end and I went home. I'd always been keen on mechanics, and if there was nothing doing in aviation, I'd intended to get into an automobile factory. I'd been wounded and had to take it easy for a while. Then they wanted me to go to work. I couldn't do the sort of work they wanted me to do. It seemed futile. I'd had a lot of time to think. I kept on asking myself what life was for. After all it was only by luck that I was alive; I wanted to make something of my life, but I didn't know what. I'd never thought much about God. I began to think about Him now. I couldn't understand why there was evil in the world. I knew I was very ignorant; I didn't know anyone I could turn to and I wanted to learn, so I began to read at haphazard.

'When I told Father Ensheim all this he asked me: "Then you've been reading for four years? Where have you got?"

'"Nowhere," I said.

'He looked at me with an air of such radiant benignity that I was confused. I didn't know what I'd done to arouse so much feeling in him. He softly drummed his fingers on the table as though he were turning a notion over in his mind.

'"Our wise old Church," he said then, "has discovered that if you will act as if you believed belief will be granted to you; if you pray with doubt, but pray with sincerity, your doubt will be dispelled; if you will surrender yourself to the beauty of that liturgy the power of which over the human spirit has been proved by the experience of the ages, peace will descend upon you. I am returning to my monastery in a little while. Why don't you come and spend a few weeks with us? You can work in the fields with our lay brothers; you can read in our library. It will be an experience no less interesting than working in a coal mine or on a German farm."

'"Why do you suggest it?" I asked.

'"I've been observing you for three months," he said. "Perhaps I know you better than you know yourself. The distance that separates you from faith is no greater than the thickness of a cigarette paper."

'I didn't say anything to that. It gave me a funny sort of feeling, as though someone had got hold of my heart-strings and were giving them a tug. At last I said I'd think about it. He dropped the subject. For the rest of Father

Ensheim's stay in Bonn we never spoke of anything connected with religion again, but as he was leaving he gave me the address of his monastery and told me if I made up my mind to come I had only to write him a line and he'd make arrangements. I missed him more than I expected. The year wore on and it was midsummer. I like it well enough in Bonn. I read Goethe and Schiller and Heine. I read Hölderlin and Rilke. Still I wasn't getting anywhere. I thought a lot of what Father Ensheim had said, and at last I decided to accept his offer.

'He met me at the station. The monastery was in Alsace and the country was pretty. Father Ensheim presented me to the abbot and then showed me to the cell that had been assigned to me. It had a narrow iron bed, a crucifix on the wall, and by way of furniture only the barest necessities. The dinner bell rang and I made my way to the refectory. It was a huge vaulted chamber. The abbot stood at the door with two monks, one of whom held a basin and the other a towel, and the abbot sprinkled a few drops of water on the hands of the guests by way of washing them and dried them with the towel one of the two monks handed him. There were three guests besides myself, two priests who were passing that way and had stopped off for dinner and an elderly, grouchy Frenchman who was making a retreat.

'The abbot and the two priors, senior and junior, sat at the head of the room, each at his separate table; the fathers along the two sides of the walls, while the novices, the lay brothers and the guests sat at tables in the middle. Grace was said and we ate. A novice took up his position near the refectory door and in a monotonous voice read from an edifying work. When we had finished grace was said again. The abbot, Father Ensheim, the guests and the monk in charge of them went into a small room where we had coffee and talked of casual things. Then I went back to my cell.

'I stayed there three months. I was very happy. The life exactly suited me. The library was good and I read a great deal. None of the fathers tried in any way to influence me, but they were glad to talk to me. I was deeply impressed by their learning, their piety and their unworldliness. You mustn't think it was an idle life they led. They were constantly occupied. They farmed their own land and worked it themselves and they were glad to have my help. I enjoyed the splendour of the services, but the one I liked best of all was Matins. It was at four in the morning. It was wonderfully moving to sit in the church with the night all around you while the monks, mysterious in their habits, their cowls drawn over their heads, sang with their strong male voices the plain song of the liturgy. There was something reassuring in the regularity of the daily round, and notwithstanding all the energy that was displayed, notwithstanding the activity of thought, you had an abiding sense of repose.'

Larry smiled a trifle ruefully.

'Like Rolla, I've come too late into a world too old. I should have been born in the Middle Ages when faith was a matter of course; then my way would have been clear to me and I'd have sought to enter the order. I couldn't believe. I wanted to believe, but I couldn't believe in a God who wasn't better than the ordinary decent man. The monks told me that God had created the world for his glorification. That didn't seem to me a very worthy object. Did Beethoven create his symphonies for his glorification? I don't believe it. I believe he created them because the music in his soul demanded expression and then all he tried to do was to make them as perfect as he knew how.

'I used to listen to the monks repeating the Lord's Prayer; I wondered how they could continue to pray without misgiving to their heavenly father to give them their daily bread. Do children beseech their earthly father to give them sustenance? They expect him to do it, they neither feel nor need to feel gratitude to him for doing it, and we have only blame for a man who brings children into the world that he can't or won't provide for. It seemed to me that if an omnipotent creator was not prepared to provide his creatures with the necessities of existence, material and spiritual, he'd have done better not to create them.'

'Dear Larry,' I said, 'I think it's just as well you weren't born in the Middle Ages. You'd undoubtedly have perished at the stake.'

He smiled.

'You've had a great deal of success,' he went on. 'Do you want to be praised to your face?'

'It only embarrasses me.'

'That's what I should have thought. I couldn't believe that God wanted it either. We didn't think much in the air corps of a fellow who wangled a cushy job out of his C.O. by buttering him up. It was hard for me to believe that God thought much of a man who tried to wangle salvation by fulsome flattery. I should have thought the worship most pleasing to him was to do your best according to your lights.

'But, that wasn't the chief thing that bothered me: I couldn't reconcile myself with that preoccupation with sin which, so far as I could tell, was never entirely absent from the monks' thoughts. I'd known a lot of fellows in the air corps. Of course they got drunk when they got a chance, and had a girl whenever they could and used foul language; we had one or two bad hats: one fellow was arrested for passing rubber cheques and was sent to prison for six months; it wasn't altogether his fault; he'd never had any money before, and when he got more than he'd ever dreamt of having, it went to his head. I'd known bad men in Paris, and when I got back to Chicago I knew more, but for the most part their badness was due to heredity, which they couldn't help, or to their environment, which they didn't choose: I'm not sure that society wasn't more responsible for their crimes than they were. If I'd been God I couldn't have brought myself to condemn one of them, not even the worst, to eternal damnation. Father Ensheim was broad-minded; he thought that hell was the deprivation of God's presence, but if that is such an intolerable punishment that it can justly be called hell, can one conceive that a good God can inflict it? After all, He created men: if He so created them that it was possible for them to sin, it was because He willed it. If I trained a dog to fly at the throat of any stranger who came into my back yard, it wouldn't be fair to beat him when did so.

'If an all-good and all-powerful God created the world, why did He create evil? The monks said, so that man by conquering the wickedness in him, by resisting temptation, by accepting pain and sorrow and misfortune as the trials sent by God to purify him, might at long last be made worthy to receive His grace. It seemed to me like sending a fellow with a message to some place and just to make it harder for him you constructed a maze that he had to get through, then dug a moat that he had to swim and finally built a wall that he had to scale. I wasn't prepared to believe in an all-wise God who hadn't common sense. I didn't see why you shouldn't believe in a God who hadn't created the world, but had to make the best of the bad job he'd found, a being enormously better, wiser and greater than man, who strove with the evil he hadn't made and who you hoped might in the end overcome it. But on the other hand, I didn't see why you should.

'Those good fathers had no answers that satisfied either my head or my heart to the questions that perplexed me. My place was not with them. When I went to say good-bye to Father Ensheim he didn't ask me whether I had profited by the experience in the way he had been so sure I would. He looked at me with inexpressible kindness.

'"I'm afraid I've been a disappointment to you, Father," I said.

'"No," he answered. "You are a deeply religious man who doesn't believe in God. God will seek you out. You'll come back. Whether here or elsewhere only God can tell."'

Four

'I settled down in Paris for the rest of the winter. I knew nothing of science, and I thought the time had come when I must acquire at least a nodding acquaintance with it. I read a lot. I don't know that I learnt much except that my ignorance was abysmal. But I knew that before. When the spring came I went to the country and stayed at a little inn on a river near one of those beautiful old French towns where life doesn't seem to have moved for two hundred years.'

I guessed that this was the summer Larry had spent with Suzanne Rouvier, but I did not interrupt him.

'After that I went to Spain. I wanted to see Velasquez and El Greco. I wondered if art could point out the way to me that religion hadn't. I wandered about a bit and then came to Seville. I liked it and thought I'd spend the winter there.'

I had myself been to Seville when I was twenty-three and I, too, had liked it. I liked its white, tortuous streets, its cathedral, and the wide-spreading plain of the Guadalquivir; but I liked also those Andalusian girls with their grace and their gaiety, with their dark shining eyes, the carnation in their hair stressing its blackness and by the contrast itself more vivid; I liked the rich colour of their skins and the inviting sensuality of their lips. Then indeed to be young was very heaven. When Larry went there he was only a little older than I had been and I could not but ask myself whether it was possible that he had remained indifferent to the lure of those enchanting creatures. He answered my unspoken question.

'I ran across a French painter I'd known in Paris, a fellow called Auguste Cottet, who'd kept Suzanne Rouvier at one time. He'd come to Seville to paint and was living with a girl he'd picked up there. He asked me to go with them one evening to Eretania to listen to a *flamenco* singer and they brought along with them a friend of hers. She was the prettiest little thing you ever saw. She was only eighteen. She'd got into trouble with a boy and had had to leave her native village because she was going to have a baby. The boy was doing his military service. After she had the baby she put it out to nurse and got a job in the tobacco factory. I took her home with me. She was very gay and very sweet, and after a few days I asked her if she'd like to come and live with me. She said she would, so we took a couple of rooms in a *casa de huéspedes*, a bedroom and a sitting-room. I told her she could leave her job, but she didn't want to, and that suited me because it left me my days to myself. We had the run of the kitchen, so she used to make my breakfast for me before she went to work and then at midday she'd come back and cook the lunch and in the evening we'd dine at a restaurant and go to a movie or to some place to dance. She looked upon me as a lunatic because I had a rubber bath and insisted on having a cold sponge every morning. The baby was farmed out in a village a few miles from Seville and we used to go and see it on Sundays. She made no secret of the fact that she was living with me to make enough money to furnish the lodgings in a tenement they were going to take when her boy friend was through with his military service. She was a dear little thing and I'm sure she's made her Paco a good wife. She was cheerful, good-tempered and affectionate. She looked upon what you delicately call sexual congress as a natural function of the body like any other. She took pleasure in it and she was happy to give pleasure. She was of course a little animal, but a very nice, attractive, domesticated animal.

'Then one evening she told me that she'd had a letter from Paco in Spanish Morocco, where he was doing his service, to say that he was to be released and would arrive in Cadiz in a couple of days. She packed her belongings next morning and slipped her money in her stocking and I took her to the station. She gave me a hearty kiss as I put her into the railway carriage, but she was too excited at the thought of seeing her lover again to have a thought for me and I'm sure that before the train was out of the station she'd forgotten my existence.

'I stayed on in Seville and in the fall I set out on the journey that landed me in India.'

Five

It was getting late. The crowd had thinned out and only a few tables were occupied. The people who had been sitting there because they had nothing else to do had gone home. Those who had been to a play or a picture and had come to have a drink or a bite to eat had left. Now and then latecomers straggled in. I saw a tall man, evidently an Englishman, come in with a young rough. He had the long, washed-out face with thinning wavy hair of the British intellectual and evidently suffered from the delusion common to many that when you are abroad no one you know at home can possibly recognize you. The young rough greedily ate a great plate of sandwiches while his companion watched him with amused benevolence. What an appetite! I saw one man whom I knew by sight because he went to the same barber's at Nice. He was stout, elderly and grey-haired, with a puffy red face and heavy pouches under his eyes. He was a Middle Western banker who had left his native city after the crash rather than face an investigation. I do not know whether he had committed any crime; if he had, he was perhaps too small fry to put the authorities to the trouble of getting him extradited. He had a pompous manner and the false heartiness of a cheap politician, but his eyes were frightened and unhappy. He was never quite drunk and never quite sober. He was always with some harlot who was obviously getting all she could out of him, and he was now with two painted middle-aged women who treated him with a mockery they didn't trouble to conceal while he, only half understanding what they said, giggled fatuously. The gay life! I wondered if he wouldn't have done better to stay at home and take his medicine. One day his women would have squeezed him dry and then there would be nothing left for him but the river or an overdose of veronal.

Between two and three there was a slight increase of custom and I supposed that the night clubs were closing their doors. A bunch of young Americans strolled in, very drunk and noisy, but they didn't stay long. Not far from us two fat, sombre women, tightly fitted into mannish clothes, sat side by side, drinking whiskies and sodas in gloomy silence. A party in evening dress put in an appearance, what they call in French *gens du monde*, who had evidently been doing the rounds and now wanted a spot of supper to finish up with. They came and went. My curiosity had been excited by a little man, quietly dressed, who had been sitting there for an hour or more with a glass of beer in front of him reading the paper. He had a neat black beard and wore pince-nez. At last a woman came in and joined him. He gave a nod devoid of friendliness and conjectured that he was annoyed because she had kept him waiting. She was young, rather shabby, but heavily painted, and looked very tired. Presently I noticed her take something out of her bag and hand it to him. Money. He looked at it and his face darkened. He addressed her in words I could not hear, but from her manner I guessed they were abusive, and she seemed to be making excuses. Suddenly he leant over and gave her a resounding smack on the cheek. She gave a cry and began to sob. The manager, drawn by the disturbance, came up to see what was the matter. It looked as if he were telling them to get out if they couldn't behave. The girl turned on him and shrilly, so that one heard every word, told him in foul language to mind his own business.

'If he slapped my face it's because I deserved it,' she cried.

Women! I had always thought that to live on a woman's immoral earnings you must be a strapping flashy fellow with sex appeal, ready with your knife or your gun; it was astonishing that such a puny creature, who might have been a lawyer's clerk from his appearance, could get a footing in such an overcrowded profession.

Six

The waiter who had served us was going off duty and to get his tip presented the bill. We paid and ordered coffee.

'Well?' I said.

I felt that Larry was in the mood to talk and I knew that I was in the mood to listen.

'Aren't I boring you?'

'No.'

'Well, we got to Bombay. The ship was stopping there for three days to give the tourists a chance to see the sights and make excursions. On the third day I got the afternoon off and went ashore. I walked about for a while, looking at the crowd: what a conglomeration! Chinese, Mohammedans,

Hindus, Tamils as black as your hat; and those great humped bullocks with their long horns that draw the carts! Then I went to Elephanta to see the caves. An Indian had joined us at Alexandria for the passage to Bombay and the tourists were rather sniffy about him. He was a fat little man with a brown round face and he wore a thick tweed suit of black and green check and a clerical collar. I was having a breath of air on deck one night and he came up and spoke to me. I didn't want to talk to anyone just then, I wanted to be alone; he asked me a lot of questions and I'm afraid I was rather short with him. Anyhow I told him I was a student working my passage back to America.

'"You should stop off in India," he said. "The East has more to teach the West than the West conceives."

'"Oh yes?" I said.

'"At any rate," he went on, "be sure you go and see the caves at Elephanta. You'll never regret it."' Larry interrupted himself to ask me a question. 'Have you ever been to India?'

'Never.'

'Well, I was looking at the colossal image with its three heads which is the great sight at Elephanta and wondering what it was all about when I heard someone behind me say: "I see you've taken my advice." I turned round and it took me a minute to realize who it was that had spoken to me. It was the little man in the heavy check suit and the clerical collar, but now he was wearing a long saffron robe, the robe, I knew later, of the Ramakrishna Swamis; and instead of the funny, spluttering little guy he'd been before, he was dignified and rather splendid. We both stared at the colossal bust.

'"Brahma, the Creator," he said. "Vishnu the Preserver and Siva the Destroyer. The three manifestations of the Ultimate Reality."

'"I'm afraid I don't quite understand," I said.

'"I'm not surprised," he answered, with a little smile on his lips and a twinkle in his eyes, as though he were gently mocking me. "A God that can be understood is no God. Who can explain the Infinite in words?"

'He joined the palms of his hands together and with just the indication of a bow strolled on. I stayed looking at those three mysterious heads. Perhaps because I was in a receptive mood, I was strangely stirred. You know how sometimes you try to recall a name; it's on the tip of your tongue, but you can't get it: that was the feeling I had then. When I came out of the caves I sat for a long while on the steps and looked at the sea. All I knew about Brahminism were those verses of Emerson's and I tried to remember them. It exasperated me that I couldn't and when I went back to Bombay I went into a bookshop to see if I could find a volume of poetry that had them in. They're in the Oxford Book of English Verse. D'you remember them?

> 'They reckon ill who leave me out;
> When me they fly, I am the wings;
> I am the doubter and the doubt.
> And I the hymn the Brahmin sings.

'I had supper in a native eating-house and then, as I didn't have to be on board till ten, I went and walked on the Maidan and looked at the sea. I thought I'd never seen so many stars in the sky. The cool was delicious after the heat of the day. I found a public garden and sat on a bench. It was very dark there and silent white figures flitted to and fro. That wonderful day, with the brilliant sunshine, the coloured, noisy crowds, the smell of the East, acrid and aromatic, enchanted me; and like an object, a splash of colour that a painter puts in to pull his composition together, those three enormous heads of Brahma, Vishnu and Siva gave a mysterious significance to it all. My heart began to beat like mad, because I'd suddenly become aware of an intense conviction that India had something to give me that I had to have. It seemed to me that a chance was offered to me and I must take it there and then or it would never be offered me again. I made up my mind quickly. I decided not to go back to the ship. I'd left nothing there but a few things in a grip. I walked slowly back to the native quarter and looked about for an hotel. I found one after a while and took a room. I had the clothes I stood up in, some loose cash, my passport and my letter of credit; I felt so free, I laughed out loud.

'The ship was sailing at eleven and just to be on the safe side I stayed in my room till then. I went down to the quay and watched her pull out. After that I went to the Ramakrishna Mission and routed out the Swami who'd spoken to me at Elephanta. I didn't know his name, but I explained that I wanted to see the Swami who'd just arrived from Alexandria. I told him I'd decided to stay in India and asked him what I ought to see. We had a long talk and at last he said he was going to Benares that night and asked me if I'd like to go with him. I jumped at it. We went third-class. The carriage was full of people eating and drinking and talking and the heat was terrific. I didn't get a wink of sleep and next morning I was pretty tired, but the Swami was as fresh as a daisy. I asked him how come and he said: "By meditation on the formless one; I found rest in the Absolute." I didn't know what to think, but I could see with my own eyes that he was as alert and wide awake as though he'd had a good night's sleep in a comfortable bed.

'When at last we got to Benares a young man of my own age came to meet my companion and the Swami asked him to find me a room. His name was Mahendra and he was a teacher at the university. He was a nice, kindly, intelligent fellow and he seemed to take as great a fancy to me as I took to him. That evening he took me out in a boat on the Ganges; it was a thrill for me, very beautiful with the city crowding down to the water's edge, and awe-inspiring; but next morning he had something better to show me, he fetched me at my hotel before dawn and took me out on the river again. I saw something I could never have believed possible, I saw thousands upon thousands of people come down to take their lustral bath and pray. I saw one tall gaunt fellow, with a mass of tangled hair and a great ragged beard, with nothing but a jock-strap to cover his nakedness, stand with his long arms outstretched, his head up, and in a loud voice pray to the rising sun. I can't tell you what an impression it made on me. I spent six months in Benares and I went over and over again on the Ganges at dawn to see that strange sight. I never got over the wonder of it. Those people believed not halfheartedly, not with reservation or uneasy doubt, but with every fibre of their being.

'Everyone was very kind to me. When they discovered I hadn't come to shoot tigers or to buy or sell anything, but only to learn, they did everything to help me. They were pleased that I should wish to learn Hindustani, and found teachers for me. They lent me books. They were never tired of answering my questions. Do you know anything about Hinduism?'

'Very little,' I answered.

'I should have thought it would interest you. Can there be anything more stupendous than the conception that the universe has no beginning and no end, but passes everlastingly from growth to equilibrium, from equilibrium to decline, from decline to dissolution, from dissolution to growth, and so on to all eternity?'

'And what do the Hindus think is the object of this endless recurrence?'

'I think they'd say that such is the nature of the Absolute. You see, they believe that the purpose of creation is to serve as a stage for the punishment or reward of the deeds of the soul's earlier existences.'

'Which presupposes belief in the transmigration of souls.'

'It's a belief held by two thirds of the human race.'

'The fact that a great many people believe something is no guarantee of its truth.'

'No, but at least it makes it worthy of consideration. Christianity absorbed so much of Neo-Platonism, it might very easily have absorbed that too, and in point of fact there was an early Christian sect that believed in it, but it was declared heretical. Except for that Christians would believe in it as confidently as they believe in the resurrection of Christ.'

'Am I right in thinking that it means that the soul passes from body to body in an endless course of experience occasioned by the merit or demerit of previous works?'

'I think so.'

'But you see, I'm not only my spirit but my body, and who can decide how much I, my individual self, am conditioned by the accident of my body? Would Byron have been Byron but for his club foot, or Dostoevsky Dostoevsky without his epilepsy?'

'The Indians wouldn't speak of an accident. They would answer that it's your actions in previous lives that have determined your soul to inhabit an imperfect body.' Larry drummed idly on the table and, lost in thought, gazed into space. Then, with a faint smile on his lips and a reflective look in his eyes, he went on. 'Has it occurred to you that transmigration is at once an explanation and a justification of the evil of the world? If the evils we suffer are the result of sins committed in our past lives we can bear them with resignation and hope that if in this one we strive towards virtue our future lives will be less afflicted. But it's easy enough to bear our own evils, all we need for that is a little manliness; what's intolerable is the evil, often so unmerited in appearance, that befalls others. If you can persuade yourself that it is the inevitable result of the past you may pity, you may do what you can to alleviate, and you should, but you have no cause to be indignant.'

'But why didn't God create a world free from suffering and misery at the beginning when there was neither merit nor demerit in the individual to determine his actions?'

'The Hindus would say that there was no beginning. The individual soul, co-existent with the universe, has existed from all eternity and owes its nature to some prior existence.'

'And does the belief in the transmigration of souls have a practical effect on the lives of those who believe it? After all, that is the test.'

'I think it has. I can tell you of one man I knew personally on whose life it certainly had a very practical effect. The first two or three years I was in India I lived mostly in native hotels, but now and then someone asked me to stay with him and once or twice I lived in grandeur as the guest of a maharajah. Through one of my friends in Benares I got an invitation to stay in one of the smaller northern states. The capital was lovely; "a rose-bed city half as old as time". I was recommended to the Minister of Finance. He'd had a European education and had been to Oxford. When you talked to him you got the impression of a progressive, intelligent and enlightened man; and he had the reputation of being an extremely efficient minister and a clever, astute politician. He wore European clothes and was very natty in appearance. He was rather a nice-looking fellow, a little on the stout side as Indians tend to become in middle age, with a close-cropped, neat moustache. He often asked me to go to his house. He had a large garden and we'd sit under the shade of great trees and talk. He had a wife and two grown-up children. You'd have taken him for just the ordinary, rather commonplace Anglicized Indian and I was staggered when I found out that in a year, when he reached the age of fifty, he was going to resign his profitable position, dispose of his property to his wife and children and go out into the world as a wandering mendicant. But the most surprising part was that his friends, and the maharajah, accepted it as a settled thing and looked upon it not as an extraordinary proceeding but as a natural one.

'One day I said to him: "You, who are so liberal, who know the world, who've read so much, science, philosophy, literature—do you in your heart of hearts believe in reincarnation?"

'His whole face changed. It became the face of a visionary.

'"My dear friend," he said, "if I didn't believe in it life would have no meaning for me."'

'And do you believe in it, Larry?' I asked.

'That's a very difficult question to answer. I don't think it's possible for us Occidentals to believe in it as implicitly as these Orientals do. It's in their blood and bones. With us it can only be an opinion. I neither believe in it nor disbelieve in it.'

He paused for a moment and with his face resting on his hand looked down at the table. Then he leant back.

'I should like to tell you of a very strange experience I had once. I was practising meditation one night in my little room at the Ashrama as my Indian friends had taught me to do. I had lit a candle and was concentrating my attention on its flame, and after a time, through the flame, but quite clearly, I saw a long line of figures one behind the other. The foremost was an elderly lady in a lace cap with grey ringlets that hung down over her ears. She wore a tight black bodice and a black silk flounced skirt—the sort of clothes, I think, they wore in the seventies, and she was standing full face to me in a gracious, diffident attitude, her arms hanging straight down her sides with the palms towards me. The expression on her lined face was kindly, sweet and mild. Immediately behind her, but sideways so that I saw his profile, with a great hooked nose and thick lips, was a tall gaunt Jew in a yellow gabardine with a yellow skullcap on his thick dark hair. He had the studious look of a scholar and an air of grim and at the same time passionate austerity. Behind him, but facing me and as distinct as though there were no one between us, was a young man with a cheerful ruddy countenance, whom you couldn't have taken for anything but an Englishman of the sixteenth century. He stood firmly on his feet, his legs a little apart, and he had a bold, reckless wanton look. He was dressed all in red, grandly as though it were a court dress, with broad-toed velvet shoes on his feet and a flat velvet cap on his head. Behind those three there was an endless chain of figures, like a queue outside a movie house, but they were dim and I couldn't see what they looked like. I was only aware of their vague shapes and of the movement that passed through them like wheat waving in a summer breeze. In a little while,

I don't know whether it was in a minute, or five, or ten, they faded slowly into the darkness of the night and there was nothing but the steady flame of the candle.'

Larry gave a little smile.

'Of course it may be that I'd fallen into a doze and dreamt. It may be that my concentration on that feeble flame had induced a sort of hypnotic condition in me and that those three figures that I saw as distinctly as I see you were recollections of pictures preserved in my subconscious. But it may be that they were myself in past lives. It may be that I was not so very long ago an old lady in New England and before that a Levantine Jew and somewhere back, soon after Sebastian Cabot had sailed from Bristol, a gallant at the Court of Henry Prince of Wales.'

'What eventually happened to your friend of the rose-red city?'

'Two years later I was down south at a place called Madura. One night in the temple someone touched me on the arm. I looked round and saw a bearded man with long black hair, dressed in nothing but a loincloth, with the staff and the begging-bowl of the holy man. It was not till he spoke that I recognized him. It was my friend. I was so astounded that I didn't know what to say. He asked me what I'd been doing and I told him; he asked me where I was going and I said to Travancore; he told me to go and see Shri Ganesha. "He will give you what you're looking for," he said. I asked him to tell me about him, but he smiled and said I'd find out all that was necessary for me to know when I saw him. I'd got over my surprise by then and asked him what he was doing in Madura. He said he was making a pilgrimage on foot to the holy places of India. I asked him how he ate and how he slept. He told me that when anyone offered him shelter he slept on the veranda, but otherwise under a tree or in the precincts of a temple; and as for food, if people offered him a meal he ate it and if they didn't he went without. I looked at him: "You've lost weight," I said. He laughed and answered that he felt all the better for it. Then he said good-bye to me—it was funny to hear that guy in a loincloth say, "Well, so long, old chap"—and stepped into that part of the temple where I couldn't follow him.

'I stayed in Madura for some time. I think it's the only temple in India in which the white man can walk about freely so long as he doesn't enter the holy of holies. At nightfall it was packed with people. Men, women and children. The men, stripped to the waist, wore dhoties, and their foreheads, and often their chests and arms, were thickly smeared with the white ash of burnt cow dung. You saw them making obeisance at one shrine or another and sometimes lying full length on the ground, face downwards, in the ritual attitude of prostration. They prayed and recited litanies. They called to one another, greeted one another, quarrelled with one another, heatedly argued with one another. There was an ungodly row, and yet in some mysterious way God seemed to be near and living.

'You pass through long halls, the roof supported by sculptured columns, and at the foot of each column a religious mendicant is seated; each has in front of him a bowl for offerings or a small mat on which the faithful now and again throw a copper coin. Some are clad; some are almost naked. Some look at you vacantly as you pass; some are reading, silently or aloud, and appear unconscious of the streaming throng. I looked for my friend among them; I never saw him again. I suppose he proceeded on the journey to his goal.'

'And what was that?'

'Liberation from the bondage of rebirth. According to the Vedanists the self, which they call the atman and we call the soul, is distinct from the body and its senses, distinct from the mind and its intelligence; it is not part of the Absolute, for the Absolute, being infinite, can have no parts, but the Absolute itself. It is uncreated; it has existed from eternity and when at last it has cast off the seven veils of ignorance will return to the infinitude from which it came. It is like a drop of water that has arisen from the sea and in a shower has fallen into a puddle, then drifts into a brook, finds its way into a stream, after that into a river, passing through mountain gorges and wide plains, winding this way and that, obstructed by rocks and fallen trees, till at last it reaches the boundless sea from which it rose.'

'But that poor little drop of water, when it has once more become one with the sea, has surely lost its individuality.'

Larry grinned.

'You want to taste sugar, you don't want to become sugar. What is individuality but the expression of our egoism? Until the soul has shed the last trace of that it cannot become one with the Absolute.'

'You talk very familiarly of the Absolute, Larry, and it's an imposing word. What does it actually signify to you?'

'Reality. You can't say what it is; you can only say what it isn't. It's inexpressible. The Indians call it Brahman. It's nowhere and everywhere. All things imply and depend upon it. It's not a person, it's not a thing, it's not a cause. It has no qualities. It transcends permanence and change; whole and part, finite and infinite. It is eternal because its completeness and perfection are unrelated to time. It is truth and freedom.'

'Golly!' I said to myself, but to Larry: 'But how can a purely intellectual conception be a solace to the suffering human race? Men have always wanted a personal God to whom they can turn in distress for comfort and encouragement.'

'It may be that at some far distant day greater insight will show them that they must look for comfort and encouragement in their own souls. I myself think that the need to worship is no more than the survival of an old remembrance of cruel gods that had to be propitiated. I believe that God is within me or nowhere. If that's so, whom or what am I to worship—myself? Men are on different levels of spiritual development, and so the imagination of India has evolved the manifestations of the Absolute that are known as Brahma, Vishnu, Siva and by a hundred other names. The Absolute is in Isvara, the creator and ruler of the world, and it is in the humble fetish before which the peasant in his sun-baked field places the offering of a flower. The multitudinous gods of India are but expedients to lead to the realization that the self is one with the supreme self.'

I looked at Larry reflectively.

'I wonder just what it was that attracted you to this austere faith,' I said.

'I think I can tell you. I've always felt that there was something pathetic in the founders of religion who made it a condition of salvation that you should believe in them. It's as though they needed your faith to have faith in themselves. They remind you of those old pagan gods who grew wan and faint if they were not sustained by the burnt offerings of the devout. Advaita doesn't ask you to take anything on trust; it asks only that you should have a passionate craving to know Reality; it states that you can experience God as surely as you can experience joy or pain. And there are men in India today—hundreds of them for all I know—who have the certitude that they have done so. I found something wonderfully satisfying in the notion that you can attain Reality by knowledge. In later ages the sages of India in recognition of human infirmity, admitted that salvation may be won by the way of love and the way of works, but they never denied that the noblest way, though the hardest, is the way of knowledge, for its instrument is the most precious faculty of man, his reason.'

Seven

I must interrupt myself to make it plain that I am not attempting here to give anything in the nature of a description of the philosophical system known as Vedanta. I have not the knowledge to do so, but even if I had this would not be the proper place for it. Our conversation was a long one and Larry told me a great deal more than I have felt it possible to set down in what after all purports to be a novel. My concern is with Larry. I should not have touched on such an intricate subject at all except that it seemed to me that without at least some slight account of his speculations and the singular experiences that were perhaps occasioned by them I could not give plausibility to the line of conduct which he was led to adopt and with which I shall presently acquaint the reader. It irks me that I cannot hope with any words of mine to give an idea of the pleasantness of his voice that invested even his most casual utterances with persuasiveness, or of the constant change in his expression, from grave to gently gay, from reflective to playful, that accompanied his thoughts like the ripple of a piano when the violins with a great sweep sing the several themes of a concerto. Although he spoke of serious things he spoke of them quite naturally, in a conversational tone, with a certain diffidence, perhaps, but without any more constraint than if he had been speaking of the weather and the crops. If I have given the impression that there was anything didactic in his manner the fault is mine. His modesty was as evident as his sincerity.

There was no more than a sprinkling of people in the café. The roisterers had long since departed. The sad creatures who make a business of love had gone to their sordid dwellings. Now and then a tired-looking man came in to have a glass of beer and a sandwich, or one, who seemed only half awake, for a cup of coffee. White-collar workers. One had been on a night shift and was going home to bed; the other, roused by the call of an alarm clock, was on his unwilling way to the long day's labour. Larry appeared as unconscious of the time as of the surroundings. I have found myself in the course of my life in many strange situations. More than once I have been within a hair's breadth of death. More than once I have touched hands with romance and known it. I have ridden a pony through Central Asia along the road that Marco Polo took to reach the fabulous lands of Cathay; I have drunk a glass of Russian tea in a prim parlour in Petrograd while a soft-spoken little man in a black coat and striped trousers told me how he had assassinated a grand duke; I have sat in a drawing-room in Westminster and listened to the serene geniality of a piano trio of Haydn's while the bombs were crashing without; but I do not think I have ever found myself in a stranger situation than when

I sat on the red-plush seats of that garish restaurant for hour after hour while Larry talked of God and eternity, of the Absolute and the weary wheel of endless becoming.

Eight

Larry had been silent for a few minutes, and unwilling to hurry him I waited. Presently he gave me a friendly little smile as though he had suddenly once more become aware of me.

'When I got down to Travancore I found I needn't have asked for information about Shri Ganesha. Everyone knew of him. For many years he'd lived in a cave in the hills, but finally he'd been persuaded to move down to the plain where some charitable person had given him a plot of land and had built a little adobe house for him. It was a long way from Trivandrum, the capital, and it took me all day, first by train and then by bullock cart, to get to the Ashrama. I found a young man at the entrance of the compound and asked him if I could see the Yogi. I'd brought with me the basket of fruit which is the customary gift to offer. In a few minutes the young man came back and led me into a long hall with windows all around it. In one corner Shri Ganesha sat in the attitude of meditation on a raised dais covered with a tiger skin. "I've been expecting you," he said. I was surprised, but supposed my friend of Madura had told him something about me. But he shook his head when I mentioned his name. I presented my fruit and he told the young man to take it away. We were left alone and he looked at me without speaking. I don't know how long the silence lasted. It might have been for half an hour. I've told you what he looked like; what I haven't told you is the serenity that he irradiated, the goodness, the peace, the selflessness. I was hot and tired after my journey, but gradually I began to feel wonderfully rested. Before he'd said another word I knew that this was the man I'd been seeking.'

'Did he speak English?' I interrupted.

'No. But you know, I'm pretty quick at languages, I'd picked up enough Tamil to understand and make myself understood in the South. At last he spoke.

'"What have you come here for?" he asked.

'I began to tell him how I'd come to India and how I'd passed my time for three years; how, on report of their wisdom and sanctity, I'd gone to one holy man after another and had found no one to give me what I looked for. He interrupted me.

'"All that I know. There is no need to tell me. What have you come here for?"

'"So that you may be my Guru," I answered.

'"Brahman alone is the Guru," he said.

'He continued to look at me with a strange intensity and then suddenly his body became rigid, his eyes seemed to turn inwards and I saw that he'd fallen into the trance which the Indians call Samadhi and in which they hold the duality of subject and object vanishes and you become Knowledge Absolute. I was sitting cross-legged on the floor, in front of him, and my heart beat violently. After how long a time I don't know he sighed and I realized that he had recovered normal consciousness. He gave me a glance sweet with loving-kindness.

'"Stay," he said. "They will show you where you may sleep."

'I was given as a dwelling-place the shack in which Shri Ganesha had lived when first he came down to the plain. The hall in which he now passed both day and night had been built when disciples gathered around him and more and more people attracted by his fame, came to visit him. So that I mightn't be conspicuous I adopted the comfortable Indian dress and I got so sunburnt that unless your attention was drawn to me you might have taken me for a native. I read a great deal. I meditated. I listened to Shri Ganesha when he chose to talk; he didn't talk very much, but he was always willing to answer questions and it was wonderfully inspiring to listen to him. It was like music in your ears. Though in his youth he had himself practised very severe austerities he did not enjoin them on his disciples. He sought to wean them from the slavery of selfhood, passion and sense, and told them that they could acquire liberation by tranquillity, restraint, renunciation, resignation, by steadfastness of mind and by an ardent desire for freedom. People used to come from the near-by town three or four miles away, where there was a famous temple to which great crowds flocked once a year for a festival; they came from Trivandrum and from far-off places to tell him their troubles, to ask his advice, to listen to his teaching; and all went away strengthened in soul and at peace with themselves. What he taught was very simple. He taught that we are all greater than we know and that wisdom is the means to freedom. He taught that it is not essential to salvation to retire from the world, but only to renounce the self. He taught that work done with no selfish interest purifies the mind and that duties are opportunities afforded to man to sink his separate self and become one with the universal self. But it wasn't his teaching that was so remarkable; it was the man himself, his benignity, his greatness of soul, his saintliness. His presence was a benediction. I was very happy with him. I felt that at last I had found what I wanted. The weeks, the months passed with unimaginable rapidity. I proposed to stay either till he died and he told us that he did not intend very much longer to inhabit his perishable body, or till I received illumination, that state when you have at last burst the bonds of ignorance, and know with a certainty there is no disputing that you and the Absolute are one.'

'And then?'

'Then, if what they say is true, there is nothing more. The soul's course on earth is ended and it will return no more.'

'And is Shri Ganesha dead?' I asked.

'Not so far as I know.'

As he spoke he saw what was implied in my question and gave a light laugh. He went on after a moment's hesitation, but in such a manner as led me at first to suppose that he wished to avoid answering the second question that he well knew was on the tip of my tongue, the question, of course, whether he had received illumination.

'I didn't stay at the Ashrama continuously. I was lucky enough to make the acquaintance of a native forestry officer whose permanent residence was on the outskirts of a village at the foot of the mountains. He was a devotee of Shri Ganesha and when he could get away from his work came and spent two or three days with us. He was a nice fellow and we had long talks. He liked to practise his English on me. After I'd known him for some time, he told me that the forestry service had a bungalow up in the mountains and if ever I wanted to go there to be by myself he would give me the key. I went there now and then. It was a two-day journey; first you had to go by bus to the forestry officer's village, then you had to walk, but when you got there it was magnificent in its grandeur and its solitude. I took what I could in a knapsack on my back and hired a bearer to carry provisions for me, and I stayed till they were exhausted. It was only a log cabin with a cookhouse behind it and for furniture there was nothing but a trestle bed on which to put your sleeping-mat, a table and a couple of chairs. It was cool up there and at times it was pleasant to light a fire at night. It gave me a wonderful thrill to know that there wasn't a living soul within twenty miles of me. At night I used often to hear the roar of a tiger or the racket of elephants as they crashed through the jungle. I used to take long walks in the forest. There was one place where I loved to sit because from it I saw the mountains spread before me and below, a lake to which at dusk the wild animals, deer, pig, bison, elephant, leopard came to drink.

'When I'd been at the Ashrama just two years I went up to my forest retreat for a reason that'll make you smile. I wanted to spend my birthday there. I got there the day before. Next morning I awoke before dawn and I thought I'd go and see the sunrise from the place I've just told you about. I knew the way blindfold. I sat down under a tree and waited. It was night still, but the stars were pale in the sky, and day was at hand. I had a strange feeling of suspense. So gradually that I was hardly aware of it light began to filter through the darkness, slowly, like a mysterious figure slinking between the trees. I felt my heart beating as though at the approach of danger. The sun rose.'

Larry paused and a rueful smile played on his lips.

'I have no descriptive talent, I don't know the words to paint a picture; I can't tell you, so as to make you see it, how grand the sight was that was displayed before me as the day broke in its splendour. Those mountains with their deep jungle, the mist still entangled in the treetops, and the bottomless lake far below me. The sun caught the lake through a cleft in the heights and it shone like burnished steel. I was ravished with the beauty of the world. I'd never known such exaltation and such a transcendent joy. I had a strange sensation, a tingling that arose in my feet and travelled up to my head, and I felt as though I were suddenly released from my body and as pure spirit partook of a loveliness I had never conceived. I had a sense that a knowledge more than human possessed me, so that everything that had been confused was clear and everything that had perplexed me was explained. I was so happy that it was pain and I struggled to release myself from it, for I felt that if it lasted a moment longer I should die; and yet it was such rapture that I was ready to die rather than forgo it. How can I tell you what I felt? No words can tell the ecstasy of my bliss. When I came to myself I was exhausted and trembling. I fell asleep.

'It was high noon when I woke. I walked back to the bungalow, and I was so light at heart that it seemed to me that I hardly touched the ground. I made myself some food, gosh, I was hungry, and I lit my pipe.'

Larry lit his pipe now.

'I dared not think that this was illumination that I, Larry Darrell of Marvin, Illinois, had received when others striving for it for years, with austerity and mortification, still waited.'

'What makes you think that it was anything more than a hypnotic condition induced by your state of mind combined with the solitude, the mystery of the dawn and the burnished steel of your lake?'

'Only my overwhelming sense of its reality. After all it was an experience of the same order as the mystics have had all over the world through all the centuries. Brahmins in India, Sufis in Persia, Catholics in Spain, Protestants in New England; and so far as they've been able to describe what defies description they've described it in similar terms. It's impossible to deny the fact of its occurrence; the only difficulty is to explain it. If I was for a moment one with the Absolute or if it was an inrush from the subconscious of an affinity with the universal spirit which is latent in all of us, I wouldn't know.'

Larry paused for an instant and threw me a quizzical glance.

'By the way, can you touch your little finger with your thumb?' he asked.

'Of course,' I said with a laugh, proving it with the appropriate action.

'Are you aware that that's something that only man and the primates can do? It's because the thumb is opposable to the other digits that the hand is the admirable instrument it is. Isn't it possible that the opposable thumb, doubtless in a rudimentary form, was developed in the remote ancestor of man and the gorilla in certain individuals, and was a characteristic that only became common to all after innumerable generations? Isn't it at least possible that these experiences of oneness with Reality that so many diverse persons have had to point to a development in the human consciousness of a sixth sense which in the far, far future will be common to all men so that they may have as direct a perception of the Absolute as we have now of the objects of sense?'

'And how would you expect that to affect them?' I asked.

'I can as little tell you that as the first creature that found it could touch its little finger with its thumb could have told you what infinite consequences were entailed in that insignificant action. So far as I'm concerned I can only tell you that the intense sense of peace, joy and assurance that possessed me in that moment of rapture abides with me still and that the vision of the world's beauty is as fresh and vivid now as when first my eyes were dazzled by it.'

'But Larry, surely your idea of the Absolute forces you to believe that the world and its beauty are merely an illusion—the fabric of Maya.'

'It's a mistake to think that the Indians look upon the world as an illusion; they don't; all they claim is that it's not real in the same sense as the Absolute. Maya is only a speculation devised by those ardent thinkers to explain how the Infinite could produce the Finite. Samkara, the wisest of them all, decided that it was an insoluble mystery. You see, the difficulty is to explain why Brahman, which is Being, Bliss and Intelligence, which is unalterable, which ever is and forever maintains itself in rest, which lacks nothing and needs nothing and so knows neither charge nor strife, which is perfect, should create the world. Well, if you ask that question the answer you're generally given is that the Absolute created the world in sport without reference to any purpose. But when you think of flood and famine, of earthquake and hurricane and all the ills that flesh is heir to, your moral sense is outraged at the idea that so much that is shocking can have been created in play. Shri Ganesha had too much kindliness of heart to believe that; he looked upon the world as the expression of the Absolute and as the overflow of its perfection. He taught that God cannot help creating and that the world is the manifestation of his nature. When I asked how, if the world was a manifestation of the nature of a perfect being, it should be so hateful that the only reasonable aim man can set before him is to liberate himself from its bondage, Shri Ganesha answered that the satisfactions of the world are transitory and that only the Infinite gives enduring happiness. But endless duration makes good no better, nor white any whiter. If the rose at noon has lost the beauty it had at dawn, the beauty it had then was real. Nothing in the world is permanent, and we're foolish when we ask anything to last, but surely we're still more foolish not to take delight in it while we have it. If change is of the essence of existence one would have thought it only sensible to make it the premise of our philosophy. We can none of us step into the same river twice, but the river flows on and the other river we step into is cool and refreshing too.

'The Aryans when they first came down into India saw that the world we know is but an appearance of the world we know not; but they welcomed it as gracious and beautiful; it was only centuries later, when the exhaustion of conquest, when the debilitating climate had sapped their vitality so that they became a prey to invading hordes, that they saw only evil in life and craved for liberation from its return. But why should we of the West, we Americans especially, be daunted by decay and death, hunger and thirst, sickness, old age, grief and delusion? The spirit of life is strong in us. I felt more alive then, as I sat in my log cabin smoking my pipe, than I had ever felt before. I felt in myself an energy that cried out to be expended. It was not for me to leave the world and retire to a cloister, but to live in the world and love the objects of the world, not indeed for themselves, but for the Infinite that is in them. If in those moments of ecstasy I had indeed been one with the Absolute, then, if what they said was true, nothing could touch me and when I had worked out the karma of my present life I should return no more. The thought filled me with dismay. I wanted to live again and again. I was willing to accept every sort of life, no matter what its pain and sorrow; I felt that only life after life, life after life could satisfy my eagerness, my vigour and my curiosity.

'Next morning I started down the mountain and the day after arrived at the Ashrama. Shri Ganesha was surprised to see me in European clothes. I'd put them on at the forestry officer's bungalow when I started uphill because it was colder there and hadn't thought to change them.

'"I've come to bid you farewell, master," I said. "I am going back to my own people."

'He did not speak. He was sitting, as ever, cross-legged on the tiger skin on the dais. A stick of incense burnt in the brazier before it and scented the air with its faint fragrance. He was alone as he had been on the first day I saw him. He looked at me with an intensity so piercing that I had the impression he saw into the deepest recesses of my being. I know he knew what had happened.

'"It is well," he said. "You have been gone long enough."

'I went down on my knees and he gave me his blessing. When I rose to my feet my eyes were filled with tears. He was a man of noble and saintly character. I shall always look upon it as a privilege to have known him. I said good-bye to the devotees. Some had been there for years; some had come after me. I left my few belongings and my books, thinking they might be useful to someone, and with my knapsack on my back, in the same old slacks and brown coat I had arrived in, a battered topee on my head, I trudged back to the town. A week later I boarded a ship at Bombay and landed at Marseilles.'

Silence fell upon us as we pursued our separate reflections; but, tired though I was, there was one more point which I very much wanted to put to him, and it was I who finally spoke.

'Larry, old boy,' I said, 'this long quest of yours started with the problem of evil. It was the problem of evil that urged you on. You've said nothing all this time to indicate that you've reached even a tentative solution of it.'

'It may be that there is no solution or it may be that I'm not clever enough to find it. Ramakrishna looked upon the world as the sport of God. "It is like a game," he said. "In this game there are joy and sorrow, virtue and vice, knowledge and ignorance, good and evil. The game cannot continue if sin and suffering are altogether eliminated from the creation." I would reject that with all my strength. The best I can suggest is that when the Absolute manifested itself in the world evil was the natural correlation of good. You could never have had the stupendous beauty of the Himalayas without the unimaginable horror of a convulsion of the earth's crust. The Chinese craftsman who makes a vase in what they call eggshell porcelain can give it a lovely shape, ornament it with a beautiful design, stain it a ravishing colour and give it a perfect glaze, but from its very nature he can't make it anything but fragile. If you drop it on the floor it will break into a dozen fragments. Isn't it possible in the same way that the values we cherish in the world can only exist in combination with evil?'

'It's an ingenious notion, Larry. I don't think it's very satisfactory.'

'Neither do I,' he smiled. 'The best to be said for it is that when you've come to the conclusion that something is inevitable all you can do is to make the best of it.'

'What are your plans now?'

'I've got a job of work to finish here and then I shall go back to America.'

'What to do?'

'Live.'

'How?'

He answered very coolly, but with an impish twinkle in his eyes, for he knew very well how little I expected such a reply.

'With calmness, forbearance, compassion, selflessness and continence.'

'A tall order,' I said. 'And why continence? You're a young man; is it wise to attempt to suppress what with hunger is the strongest instinct of the human animal?'

'I am in the fortunate position that sexual indulgence with me has been a pleasure rather than a need. I know by personal experience that in nothing are the wise men of India more dead right than in their contention that chastity intensely enhances the power of the spirit.'

'I should have thought that wisdom consisted in striking a balance between the claims of the body and the claims of the spirit.'

'That is just what the Indians maintain that we in the West haven't done. They think that we with our countless inventions, with our factories and machines and all they produce, have sought happiness in material things, but that happiness rests not in them, but in spiritual things. And they think the way we have chosen leads to destruction.

'And are you under the impression that America is a suitable place to practise the particular virtues you mentioned?'

'I don't see why not. You Europeans know something about America. Because we amass large fortunes you think we care for nothing but money. We care nothing for it; the moment we have it we spend it, sometimes well sometimes ill, but we spend it. Money is nothing to us; it's merely the symbol of success. We are the greatest idealists in the world; I happen to think that we've set our ideal on the wrong objects; I happen to think that the greatest ideal man can set himself is self-perfection.'

'It's a noble one, Larry.'

'Isn't it worth while to try to live up to it?'

'But can you for a moment imagine that you, one man, can have any effect on such a restless, busy, lawless, intensely individualistic people as the people of America? You might as well try to hold back the waters of the Mississippi with your bare hands.'

'I can try. It was one man who invented the wheel. It was one man who discovered the law of gravitation. Nothing that happens is without effect. If you throw a stone in a pond the universe isn't quite the same as it was before. It's a mistake to think that those holy men of India lead useless lives. They are a shining light in the darkness. They represent an ideal that is a refreshment to their fellows; the common run may never attain it, but they respect it and it affects their lives for good. When a man becomes pure and perfect the influence of his character spreads so that they who seek truth are naturally drawn to him. It may be that if I lead the life I've planned for myself it may affect others; the effect may be no greater than the ripple caused by a stone thrown in a pond, but one ripple causes another, and that one a third; it's just possible that a few people will see that my way of life offers happiness and peace, and that they in their turn will teach what they have learnt to others.'

'I wonder if you have any idea what you're up against, Larry. You know, the Philistines have long since discarded the rack and stake as a means of suppressing the opinions they feared: they're discovered a much more deadly weapon of destruction—the wisecrack.'

'I'm a pretty tough guy,' smiled Larry.

'Well, all I can say is that it's damned lucky for you that you have a private income.'

'It's been of great use to me. Except for that I shouldn't have been able to do all I've done. But my apprenticeship is over. From now on it can only be a burden to me. I shall rid myself of it.'

'That would be very unwise. The only thing that may make the kind of life you propose possible is financial independence.'

'On the contrary, financial independence would make the life I propose meaningless.'

I couldn't restrain a gesture of impatience.

'It may be all very well for the wandering mendicant in India; he can sleep under a tree and the pious are willing enough to acquire merit by filling his begging-bowl with food. But the American climate is far from suitable for sleeping out in the open, and though I don't pretend to know much about America, I do know that if there's one thing your countrymen are agreed upon it is that if you want to eat you must work. My poor Larry, you'd be sent to the workhouse as a vagrant before ever you got into your stride.'

He laughed.

'I know. One must adapt oneself to one's environment and of course I'd work. When I get to America I shall try to get a job in a garage. I'm a pretty good mechanic and I don't think it ought to be difficult.'

'Wouldn't you then be wasting energy that might be more usefully employed in other ways?'

'I like manual labour. Whenever I've got waterlogged with study I've taken a spell of it and found it spiritually invigorating. I remember reading a biography of Spinoza and thinking how silly the author was to look upon it as a terrible hardship that in order to earn his scanty living Spinoza had to polish lenses. I'm sure it was a help to his intellectual activity, if only because it diverted his attention for a while from the hard work of speculation. My mind is free when I'm washing a car or tinkering with a carburettor and when the job's done I have the pleasant sensation of having accomplished something. Naturally I wouldn't want to stay in a garage indefinitely. It's many years since I was in America and I must learn it afresh. I shall try to get work as a truck driver. In that way I should be able to travel from end to end of the country.'

'You've forgotten perhaps the most important use of money. It saves time. Life is so short, and there's so much to do, one can't afford to waste a minute; and just think how much you waste, for instance, in walking from place to place instead of going by bus and in going by bus instead of by taxi.'

Larry smiled.

'True enough and I hadn't thought of it, but I could cope with that difficulty by having my own taxi.'

'What d'you mean by that?'

'Eventually I shall settle in New York, among other reasons because of its libraries; I can live on very little, I don't mind where I sleep and I'm quite satisfied with one meal a day; by the time I've seen all I want to of America I should be able to have saved enough to buy a taxi and become a taxi driver.'

'You ought to be shut up, Larry. You're as crazy as a loon.'

'Not at all. I'm very sensible and very practical. As an owner-driver I would need to work only for as many hours as would provide for my board and lodging and for the depreciation on the car. The rest of my time I could devote to other work and if I wanted to go anywhere in a hurry I could always go in my taxi.'

'But, Larry, a taxi is just as much of a possession as a government bond,' I said, to tease him. 'As an owner-driver you'd be a capitalist.

He laughed.

'No. My taxi would be merely the instrument of my labour. It would be an equivalent to the staff and the begging-bowl of the wandering mendicant.'

On this note of banter our conversation ended. I had noticed for some time that people were coming into the café with greater frequency. One man in evening dress sat down not far from us and ordered himself a substantial breakfast. He had the tired but satisfied mien of one who looks back with complacency upon a night of amorous dalliance. A few old gentlemen, early risers, because old age needs little sleep, were drinking their *café au lait* with deliberation while through thick-lensed spectacles they read the morning paper. Younger men, some of them neat and spruce, others in threadbare coats, hurried in to devour a roll and swallow a cup of coffee on their way to a shop or an office. An old crone entered with a pile of newspapers and went round offering them for sale, vainly as far I could see, at the various tables. I looked out of the great plate glass windows and saw that it was broad daylight. A minute or two later the electric light was turned off except at the rear of the huge restaurant. I looked at my watch. It was past seven o'clock.

'What about a spot of breakfast?' I said.

We had croissants, all crisp and hot from the baker's, and *café au lait*. I was tired and listless, and felt certain I looked like the wrath of God, but

Larry seemed as fresh as ever. His eyes were shining, there wasn't a line on his smooth face, and he didn't look a day more than twenty-five. The coffee revived me.

'Will you allow me to give you a piece of advice, Larry? It's not a thing I give often.'

'It's not a thing I often take,' he answered with a grin.

'Will you think very carefully before you dispossess yourself of your very small fortune? When it's gone, it's gone for ever. A time may come when you'll want money very badly, either for yourself or for somebody else, and then you'll bitterly regret that you were such a fool.'

There was a glint of mockery in his eyes as he answered, but it was devoid of malice.

'You attach more importance to money than I do.'

'I can well believe it,' I answered tartly. 'You see, you've always had it and I haven't. It's given me what I value almost more than anything else in life—independence. You can't think what a comfort it's been to me to think that if I wanted to I could tell anyone in the world to go to hell.'

'But I don't want to tell anyone in the world to go to hell, and if I did, the lack of a bank balance wouldn't prevent me. You see, money to you means freedom; to me it means bondage.'

'You're an obstinate brute, Larry.'

'I know. I can't help it. But in any case I have plenty of time to change my mind if I want to. I'm not going back to America till next spring. My friend Auguste Cottet, the painter, has lent me a cottage at Sanary and I'm going to spend the winter there.'

Sanary is an unpretentious seaside resort on the Riviera, between Bandol and Toulon, and it is frequented by artists and writers who do not care for the garish mummery of St Tropez.

'You'll like it if you don't mind its being as dull as ditch-water.'

'I have work to do. I've collected a lot of material and I'm going to write a book.'

'What's it about?'

'You'll see when it comes out,' he smiled.

'If you'd like to send it to me when it's finished I think I can get it published for you.'

'You needn't bother about that. I have some American friends who run a small press in Paris and I've arranged with them to print it for me.'

'But you can't expect a book brought out like that to have any sale and you won't get any reviews.'

'I don't care if it's reviewed and I don't expect it to sell. I'm only printing enough copies to send to my friends in India and the few people I know in France who might be interested in it. It's of no particular importance. I'm only writing it to get all that material out of the way, and I'm publishing it because I think you can only tell what a thing's like when you see it in print.'

'I see the point of both those reasons.'

We had finished our breakfast by now and I called the waiter for the bill. When it came I passed it over to Larry.

'If you're going to chuck your money down the drain you can damn well pay for my breakfast.'

He laughed and paid. I was stiff from sitting for so long and as we walked out of the restaurant my sides ached. It was good to get into the fresh clean air of the autumn morning. The sky was blue, and the Avenue de Clichy, a sordid thoroughfare by night, had a mild jauntiness, like a painted, haggard woman walking with a girl's springy step, that was not displeasing. I signalled a passing taxi.

'Can I give you a lift?' I asked Larry.

'No. I shall walk down to the Seine and have a swim at one of the baths, then I must go to the Bibliothèque, I've got some research to do there.'

We shook hands and I watched him cross the road with his loose, long-legged stride. I, being made of stuff less stern, stepped into the taxi and returned to my hotel. When I got into my sitting-room I noticed that it was after eight.

'This is a nice hour for an elderly gentleman to get home,' I remarked disapprovingly to the nude lady (under a glass case) who had since the year 1813 been lying on top of the clock in what I should have thought was a position of extreme discomfort.

She continued to look at her gilt bronze face in a gilt bronze mirror, and all the clock said was: tick, tick. I turned on a hot bath. When I had lain in it till it was tepid, I dried myself, swallowed a sleeping-tablet, and taking to bed with me Valéry's *Le Cimetière Marin*, which happened to be on the night table, read till I fell asleep.

Chapter Seven

One

One morning, six months later, in April, I was busy writing in my study on the roof of my house at Cap Ferrat when a servant came up to say that the police of St Jean (my neighbouring village) were below and wished to see me. I was vexed at being interrupted and could not imagine what they wanted. My conscience was at ease and I had already given my subscription to the Benevolent Fund. In return I had received a card, which I kept in my car so that if I was stopped for exceeding the speed limit or found parked on the wrong side of a street I could unostentatiously let it be seen while producing my driving licence and so escape with an indulgent caution. I thought it more likely then that one of my servants had been the victim of an anonymous denunciation, that being one of the amenities of French life, because her papers were not in order; but being on good terms with the local cops, whom I never allowed to leave my house without a glass of wine to speed them on their way, I anticipated no great difficulty. But they, for they worked in pairs, had come on a very different errand.

After we had shaken hands and enquired after our respective healths, the senior of the two—he was called a *brigadier* and had one of the most imposing moustaches I ever saw—fished a notebook out of his pocket. He turned over the pages with a dirty thumb.

'Does the name Sophie Macdonald say something to you?' he asked.

'I know a person of that name,' I replied cautiously.

'We have just been in telephonic communication with the police station at Toulon and the chief inspector requests you to betake yourself there [*vous prie de vous y rendre*] without delay.'

'For what reason?' I asked. 'I am only slightly acquainted with Mrs Macdonald.'

I jumped to the conclusion that she had got into trouble, probably connected with opium, but I didn't see why I should be mixed up in it.

'That is not my affair. There is no doubt that you have had dealings with this woman. It appears that she has been missing from her lodgings for five days and a body has been fished out of the harbour which the police have reason to believe is hers. They want you to identify it.'

A cold shiver passed through me. I was not, however, too much surprised. It was likely enough that the life she led would incline her in a moment of depression to put an end to herself.

'But surely she can be identified by her clothes and her papers.'

'She was found stark naked with her throat cut.'

'Good God!' I was horrified. I reflected for an instant. For all I knew the police could force me to go and I thought I had better submit with good grace. 'Very well. I will take the first train I can.'

I looked up a timetable and found that I could catch one that would get me to Toulon between five and six. The *brigadier* said he would phone the chief inspector to that effect and asked me on my arrival to go straight to the police station. I did no more work that morning. I packed a few necessary things in a suitcase and after luncheon drove to the station.

Two

On presenting myself at the headquarters of the Toulon police I was immediately ushered into the room of the chief inspector. He was sitting at a table, a heavy, swarthy man of saturnine appearance whom I took to be a Corsican. He threw me, perhaps from force of habit, a suspicious glance; but noticing the ribbon of the Legion of Honour, which I had taken the precaution to put in my buttonhole, with an unctuous smile asked me to sit down and proceeded to make profuse apologies for having been obliged to incommode a person of my distinction. Adopting a similar tone, I assured him that nothing could make me happier than to be of service to him. Then we got down to brass tacks and he resumed his brusque, rather insolent manner. Looking at some papers before him, he said:

'This is a dirty business. It appears that the woman Macdonald had a very bad reputation. She was a drunkard, a dope fiend and a nymphomaniac. She was in the habit of sleeping not only with sailors off the ships, but with the riffraff of the town. How does it happen that a person of your age and respectability should be acquainted with such a character?'

I was inclined to tell him that it was no business of his, but from a diligent perusal of hundreds of detective stories I have learnt that it is well to be civil with the police.

'I knew her very little. I met her when she was a girl in Chicago, where she afterwards married a man of good position. I met her again in Paris a year or so ago through friends of hers and mine.'

I had been wondering how on earth he had ever connected me with

Sophie, but now he pushed forward a book.

'This volume was found in her room. If you will kindly look at the dedication you will see that it hardly suggests that your acquaintance with her was as slight as you claim.'

It was the translation of that novel of mine that she had seen in the bookshop window and asked me to write in. Under my own name I had written "*Mignonne, allons voir si la rose,*" because it was the first thing that occurred to me. It certainly looked a trifle familiar.

'If you are suggesting that I was her lover, you are mistaken.'

'It would be no affair of mine,' he replied, and then with a gleam in his eye: 'And without wishing to say anything offensive to you I must add that from what I have heard of her proclivities I should not say you were her type. But it is evident that you would not address a perfect stranger as *mignonne.*'

'That line, *monsieur le commissaire,* is the first of a celebrated poem by Ronsard, whose works I am certain are familiar to a man of your education and culture. I wrote it because I felt sure she knew the poem and would recall the following lines, which might suggest to her that the life she was leading was, to say the least of it, indiscreet.'

'Evidently I have read Ronsard at school, but with all the work I have to do I confess that the lines you refer to have escaped my memory.'

I repeated the first stanza and knowing very well he had never heard the poet's name till I mentioned it, had no fear that he would recall the last one which can hardly be taken as an incitement to virtue.

'She was apparently a woman of some education. We found a number of detective stories in her room and two or three volumes of poetry. There was a Baudelaire and a Rimbaud and an English volume by someone called Eliot. Is he known?'

'Widely.'

'I have no time to read poetry. In any case I cannot read English. If he is a good poet it is a pity he doesn't write in French, so that educated people could read him.'

The thought of my chief inspector reading *The Waste Land* filled me with pleasure. Suddenly he pushed a snapshot towards me.

'Have you any idea who that is?'

I immediately recognized Larry. He was in bathing trunks, and the photograph, a recent one, had been taken, I guessed during the summer part of which he had spent with Isabel and Gray at Dinard. My first impulse was to say I did not know, for I wanted nothing less than to get Larry mixed up in this hateful business, but I reflected that if the police discovered his identity my assertion would look as if I thought there was something to hide.

'He's an American citizen called Laurence Darrell.'

'It was the only photograph found among the woman's effects. What was the connection between them?'

'They both came from the same village near Chicago. They were childhood friends.'

'But this photograph was taken not long ago, I suspect at a seaside resort in the North or on the West of France. It would be easy to discover the exact place. What is he, this individual?'

'An author,' I said boldly. The inspector slightly raised his bushy eyebrows and I guessed that he did not attribute high morality to members of my calling. 'Of independent means,' I added to make it sound more respectable.

'Where is he now?'

Again I was tempted to say I didn't know, but again decided it would only make things awkward if I did. The French police may have many faults, but their system enables them to find anyone they want to without delay.

'He's living at Sanary.'

The inspector looked up and it was clear that he was interested.

'Where?'

I had remembered Larry telling me that Auguste Cottet had lent him his cottage and on my return at Christmas I had written to ask him to come and stay with me for a while, but as I fully expected he had refused. I gave the inspector his address.

'I'll telephone to Sanary and have him brought here. It might be worth while to question him.'

I could not but see that the inspector thought that here might be a suspect, but I was only inclined to laugh; I was convinced that Larry could easily prove that he had nothing to do with the affair. I was anxious to hear more about Sophie's lamentable end, but the inspector only told me in somewhat greater detail what I already knew. Two fishermen had brought the body in. It was a romantic exaggeration of my local policeman's that it was stark naked. The murderer had left girdle and brassière. If Sophie had been dressed in the same way as I had seen her he had had to strip her only of her slacks and her jersey. There was nothing to identify her and the police had inserted a description in the local paper. This had brought a woman to the station who kept a small rooming-house in a back street, what the French call a *maison de passe*, to which men could bring women or boys. She was an agent of the police, who liked to know who frequented her house and what for. Sophie had been turned out of the hotel on the quay at which she was living when I ran across her because her conduct was more scandalous than even the tolerant proprietor could put up with. She had offered to engage a room with a tiny sitting-room beside it in the house of the woman I have just mentioned. It was more profitable to let it two or three times a night for short periods, but Sophie offered to pay so handsomely that the woman consented to rent it to her by the month. She came to the police station now to state that her tenant had been absent for several days; she had not bothered, thinking she had gone for a trip to Marseilles or to Villefranche, where ships of the British fleet had lately arrived, an event that always attracted women, young and old, from all along the coast; but she had read the description of the deceased in the paper and thought it might apply to her tenant. She had been taken to see the body and after a trifling hesitation declared it was that of Sophie Macdonald.

'But if the body's been identified, what do you want me for?'

'Madame Bellet is a woman of high honourability and excellent character,' said the inspector, 'but she may have reasons for identifying the dead woman that we do not know; and in any case I think she should be seen by someone who was more closely connected with her so that the fact may be confirmed.'

'Do you think you have any chance of catching the murderer?'

The inspector shrugged his massive shoulders.

'Naturally we are making enquiries. We have questioned a number of persons at the bars she used to go to. She may have been killed out of jealousy by a sailor whose ship has already left the port, or by a gangster for whatever money she had on her. It appears that she always had on her a sum that would seem large to a man of that sort. It may be that some people have a strong suspicion who the culprit is, but in the circles she moved in it is unlikely that anyone will speak unless it is to his advantage. Consorting with the bad characters she did, such an end as she has come to was only too probable.'

I had nothing to say to this. The inspector asked me to come next morning at nine o'clock, by which time he would have seen 'this gentleman of the photograph', after which a policeman would take us to the morgue to see the body.

'And how about burying her?'

'If after identifying the body you claim it as friends of the deceased and are prepared to undertake the expense of the funeral yourselves, you will receive the necessary authorization.'

'I'm sure that Mr Darrell and I would like to have it as soon as possible.'

'I quite understand. It is a sad story and it is better that the poor woman should be laid to rest without delay. And that reminds me that I have here the card of an undertaker who will arrange the matter for you on reasonable terms and with dispatch. I will just write a line on it so that he may give you every attention.'

I was pretty sure he would get a rake-off on the amount paid, but I thanked him warmly, and when he had ushered me out with every expression of esteem I went forthwith to the address on the card. The undertaker was brisk and businesslike. I chose a coffin, neither the cheapest nor the most expensive, accepted his offer to get me two or three wreaths from a florist of his acquaintance – 'to save monsieur a painful duty and out of respect for the dead,' he said – and arranged for the hearse to be at the morgue at two o'clock next day. I could not but admire his efficiency when he told me that I need not trouble to see about a grave, he would do all that was necessary, and 'Madame was a Protestant, I assume,' furthermore he would, if I wished it, have a pastor waiting at the cemetery to read the burial service. But since I was a stranger and a foreigner he was sure that I would not take it amiss if he asked me to be good enough to give him a cheque in advance. He named a larger sum than I had foreseen, evidently expecting me to beat him down, and I discerned a look of surprise, perhaps even of disappointment, on his face when I took out my cheque-book and wrote out a cheque without demur.

I took a room at an hotel and next morning returned to the police station. I was kept waiting for some time and then was bidden to go into the chief inspector's office. I found Larry, looking grave and distressed, sitting in the chair I had sat in the day before. The inspector greeted me with joviality. I might have been a long-lost brother.

'Well, *mon cher monsieur*, your friend has answered all the questions it was my duty to put to him with the utmost frankness. I have no reason to disbelieve his statement that he has not seen this poor woman for eighteen months. He has accounted for his movements during the last week in a perfectly satisfactory manner as well as for the fact that his photograph was found in her room. It was taken at Dinard and he happened to have it in his pocket one day when he was lunching with her. I have had excellent reports of the young man from Sanary and I am besides, I say it without vanity, a good judge of character myself; I am convinced that he is incapable of committing a crime of this nature. I have ventured to offer my sympathy that a friend of his childhood, brought up with all the advantages of a healthy family life, should have turned out so badly. But such is life. And now, my dear gentlemen, one of my men will accompany you to the morgue and when you have identified the body, your time is at your own disposal. Go and have a good lunch. I have a card here of the best restaurant in Toulon and I will just write a word on it which will assure you of the *patron's* best attention. A good bottle of wine will do you both good after this harrowing experience.'

He was by now positively beaming with good will. We walked to the mortuary with a policeman. They were not doing a lively business in that establishment. There was a body on one slab only. We went up to it and the mortuary attendant uncovered the head. It was not a pleasant sight. The sea water had taken the curl out of the dyed silvery hair and it was plastered dankly on the skull. The face was horribly swollen and it was ghastly to look at, but there was no doubt that it was Sophie's. The attendant drew the covering sheet down to show us what we both would rather not have seen, the horrid gash across the throat that stretched from ear to ear.

We went back to the station. The chief inspector was busy, but we said what we had to say to an assistant; he left us and presently returned with the necessary papers. We took them to the undertaker.

'Now let's have a drink,' I said.

Larry hadn't uttered a word since we left the police station to go to the mortuary except on our return there to declare that he identified the body as that of Sophie Macdonald. I led him down to the quay and we sat in the café in which I had sat with her. A strong mistral was blowing and the harbour, usually so smooth, was flecked with white foam. The fishing-boats were gently rocking. The sun shone brightly and, as always happens with a mistral, every object in sight had a peculiar sparkling sharpness as though you looked at it through glasses focused with more than common accuracy. It imparted a nerve-racking, throbbing vitality to everything in sight. I drank a brandy and soda, but Larry never touched the one I had ordered for him. He sat in moody silence and I did not disturb him.

Presently I looked at my watch.

'We'd better go and have something to eat,' I said. 'We've got to be at the mortuary at two.'

'I'm hungry, I didn't have any breakfast.'

Having judged from his appearance that the chief inspector knew where the food was good, I took Larry to the restaurant he had told us of. Knowing that Larry seldom ate meat, I ordered an omelette and a grilled lobster and then, asking for the wine list, chose, again following the policeman's counsel, a vintage wine. When it appeared I poured out a glass for Larry.

'You damn well drink it,' I said. 'It may suggest a topic of conversation to you.'

He obediently did as I bade him.

'Shri Ganesha used to say that silence also is conversation,' he murmured.

'That suggests a jolly social gathering of intellectual dons at the University of Cambridge.'

'I'm afraid you'll have to stand the racket of this funeral by yourself,' he said. 'I haven't any money.'

'I'm quite prepared to do that,' I answered. Then the implication of his remark hit me. 'You haven't been and gone and done it really?'

He did not answer for a moment. I noticed the whimsical, teasing glint in his eyes.

'You haven't got rid of your money?'

'Every cent except what I need to last me till my ship comes in.'

'What ship?'

'The man who has the next cottage to mine at Sanary is the Marseilles agent of a line of freighters that run from the Near East to New York. They've cabled him from Alexandria that they've had to put off a couple of sick men there from a ship that's coming on to Marseilles and asked him to get two more to take their place. He's a buddy of mine and he's promised to get me on. I'm giving him my old Citroën as a parting present. When I step on board I shall have nothing but the clothes I stand up in and a few things in a grip.'

'Well, it's your own money. You're free, white and twenty-one.'

'Free is the right word. I've never been happier or felt more independent in my life. When I get to New York I shall have my wages and they'll carry me on till I can get a job.'

'What about your book?'

'Oh, it's finished and printed. I made a list of people I wanted it sent to—you ought to get a copy in a day or two.'

'Thank you.'

There was not much more to say and we finished our meal in amiable silence. I ordered coffee. Larry lit a pipe and I a cigar. I looked at him thoughtfully. He felt my eyes upon him and threw me a glance; his own were lit with an impish twinkle.

'If you feel like telling me I'm a damned fool, don't hesitate. I wouldn't in the least mind.'

'No, I don't particularly feel like that. I was only wondering if your life wouldn't have fallen into a more perfect pattern if you'd married and had children like everybody else.'

He smiled. I must have remarked twenty times on the beauty of his smile, it was so cosy, trustful and sweet, it reflected the candour, the truthfulness of his charming nature; but I must do so once again, for now, besides all that, there was in it something rueful and tender.

'It's too late for that now. The only woman I've met whom I could have married was poor Sophie.'

I looked at him with amazement.

'Can you say that after all that's happened?'

'She had a lovely soul, fervid, aspiring and generous. Her ideals were greathearted. There was even at the end a tragic nobility in the way she sought destruction.'

I was silent. I did not know what to make of these strange assertions.

'Why didn't you marry her then?' I asked.

'She was a child. To tell you the truth, it never occurred to me when I used to go over to her grandfather's and we read poetry together under the elm tree that there was in that skinny brat the seed of spiritual beauty.'

I could not but think it surprising that at this juncture he made no mention of Isabel. He could not have forgotten that he had been engaged to her and I could only suppose that he regarded the episode as a foolishness without consequence of two young things not old enough to know their own minds. I was ready to believe that the suspicion had never so much as fugitively crossed his mind that ever since she had been eating her heart out for him.

It was time for us to go. We walked to the square where Larry had left his car, very shabby now, and drove to the mortuary. The undertaker was as good as his word. The businesslike efficiency with which everything was accomplished, under the garish sky, with the violent wind bending the cypresses of the cemetery, added a last note of horror to the proceedings. When it was all over the undertaker shook hands with us cordially.

'Well, gentlemen, I hope you are satisfied. It went very well.'

'Very well,' I said.

'Monsieur will not forget that I am always at his disposition if he has need of my services. Distance is no object.'

I thanked him. When we came to the gate of the cemetery Larry asked me if there was anything further I wanted him for.

'Nothing.'

'I'd like to get back to Sanary as soon as possible.'

'Drop me at my hotel, will you?'

We spoke never a word as we drove. When we arrived I got out. We shook hands and he went off. I paid my bill, got my bag and took a taxi to the station. I too wanted to get away.

Three

A few days later I started for England. My intention had been to go straight through, but after what had happened I particularly wanted to see Isabel, so I decided to stop in Paris for twenty-four hours. I wired to her to ask if I could come in late in the afternoon and stay to dinner; when I reached my hotel I found a note from her to say that she and Gray were dining out, but that she would be very glad to see me if I would come not before half past five as she had a fitting.

It was chilly and raining off and on quite heavily, so that I presumed Gray would not have gone to Mortefontaine to play golf. This did not suit me very well, since I wanted to see Isabel alone, but when I arrived at the apartment the first thing she said was that Gray was at the Travellers playing bridge.

'I told him not to be too late if he wanted to see you, but we're not dining till nine, which means we needn't get there before nine-thirty, so we've got plenty of time for a good talk. I've got all sorts of things to tell you.'

They had sublet the apartment and the sale of Elliott's collection was to take place in a fortnight. They wanted to attend it and were moving into the Ritz. Then they were sailing. Isabel was selling everything except the modern pictures that Elliott had had in his house at Antibes. Though she didn't much care for them she thought quite rightly that they would be a prestige item in their future home.

'It's a pity poor Uncle Elliott wasn't more advanced. Picasso, Matisse and Rouault, you know. I suppose his pictures are good in their way, but I'm afraid they'll seem rather old-fashioned.'

'I wouldn't bother about that if I were you. Other painters will come along in a few years and Picasso and Matisse won't seem any more up to date than your Impressionists.'

Gray was in process of concluding his negotiations and with the capital provided by Isabel was to enter a flourishing business as vice-president. It was connected with oil and they were to live at Dallas.

'The first thing we shall have to do is to find a suitable house. I want a nice garden so that Gray can have somewhere to potter about when he comes home from work and I must have a really large living-room so that I can entertain.'

'I wonder you don't take Elliott's furniture over with you.'

'I don't think it would be very suitable. I shall make it all modern, with perhaps just a little touch of Mexican here and there to give it a note. As soon as I get to New York I'll find out who is the decorator everyone's going to now.'

Antoine, the manservant, brought in a tray with an array of bottles and Isabel, always tactful, knowing that nine men out of ten are convinced they can mix a better cocktail than any woman (and they're right), asked me to shake a couple. I poured out the gin and the Noilly-Prat and added the dash of absinthe that transforms a dry Martini from a nondescript drink to one for which the gods of Olympus would undoubtedly have abandoned their home-brewed nectar, a beverage that I had always thought must have been rather like Coca-Cola. I noticed a book on the table as I handed Isabel her glass.

'Hullo!' I said. 'Here's Larry's book.'

'Yes, it came this morning, but I've been so busy, I had a thousand things to do before lunch and I was lunching out and I was at Molyneux's this afternoon. I don't know when I shall have a moment to get down to it.'

I thought with melancholy how an author spends months writing a book, and may be puts his heart's blood into it, and then it lies about unread till the reader has nothing else in the world to do. It was a volume of three hundred pages nicely printed and neatly bound.

'I suppose you know Larry has been in Sanary all the winter. Did you see him by any chance?'

'Yes, we were at Toulon together only the other day.'

'Were you? What were you doing there?'

'Burying Sophie.'

'She's not dead?' cried Isabel.

'If she hadn't been we'd have had no plausible reason to bury her.'

'That's not funny.' She paused for a second. 'I'm not going to pretend I'm sorry. A combination of drink and dope, I suppose.'

'No, she had her throat cut and was thrown into the sea stark naked.'

Like the *brigadier* at St Jean I found myself impelled a trifle to exaggerate her undress.

'How horrible! Poor thing. Of course leading the life she did she was bound to come to a bad end.'

'That's what the *commissaire de police* at Toulon said.'

'Do they know who did it?'

'No, but I do. I think you killed her.'

She gave me a stare of amazement.

'What are you talking about?' Then with the ghost of a chuckle: 'Guess again; I have a cast-iron alibi.'

'I ran across her at Toulon last summer. I had a long talk with her.'

'Was she sober?'

'Sufficiently. She told me how it happened that she'd disappeared so unaccountably just a few days before she was going to be married to Larry.'

I noticed Isabel's face stiffen. I proceeded to tell her exactly what Sophie had told me. She listened warily.

'I've thought of her story a good deal since then and the more I've thought about it the more convinced I am that there's something fishy about it. I've lunched here twenty times and you never have liqueurs for luncheon. You'd been lunching alone. Why should there have been a bottle of zubrovka on the tray with the coffee-cup?'

'Uncle Elliott had just sent it to me. I wanted to see if I liked it as much as when I'd had it at the Ritz.'

'Yes, I remember how you raved about it then. I was surprised, as you never drink liqueurs anyway; you're much too careful of your figure for that. I had at the time an impression that you were trying to tantalize Sophie. I thought it was just malice.'

'Thank you.'

'On the whole you're very good at keeping appointments. Why should you have gone out when you were expecting Sophie for something so important to her and interesting to you as a fitting of her wedding dress?'

'She told you that herself. I wasn't happy about Joan's teeth. Our dentist is very busy and I just had to take the time he could give me.'

'When one goes to a dentist one makes the next appointment before leaving.'

'I know. But he called me up in the morning and said he had to break it, but could give me three o'clock that afternoon instead, so of course I jumped at it.'

'Couldn't the governess have taken Joan?'

'She was scared, poor darling, I felt she'd be happier if I went with her.'

'And when you came back and found the bottle of zubrovka three parts empty and Sophie gone, weren't you rather surprised?'

'I thought she'd got tired of waiting and gone on to Molyneux's by herself. I couldn't make it out when I went there and they told me she hadn't been.'

'And the zubrovka?'

'Well, I did notice that a good deal had been drunk. I thought Antoine had drunk it and I very nearly spoke to him about it, but Uncle Elliott was paying for him and he was a friend of Joseph's, so I thought I'd better ignore it. He's a very good servant and if he takes a little nip now and then who am I to blame him?'

'What a liar you are, Isabel?'

'Don't you believe me?'

'Not for a moment.'

Isabel got up and walked over to the chimney-piece. There was a wood fire and it was pleasant on that dreary day. She stood with one elbow on the mantel-shelf in a graceful attitude which it was one of her most charming gifts to be able to assume without any appearance of intention. Like most French women of distinction she dressed in black in the daytime, which peculiarly suited her rich colouring, and on this occasion she wore a dress the expensive simplicity of which displayed her slender figure to advantage. She puffed at her cigarette for a minute.

'There's no reason why I shouldn't be perfectly frank with you. It was most unfortunate that I had to go out and of course Antoine should never have left the liqueur and the coffee things in the room. They ought to have been taken away when I went out. When I came back and saw the bottle was nearly empty of course I knew what had happened, and when Sophie disappeared I guessed she'd gone off on a bat. I didn't say anything about it because I thought it would only distress Larry, and he was worried enough as it was.'

'Are you sure the bottle wasn't left there on your explicit instructions?'

'Quite.'

'I don't believe you.'

'Don't then.' She flung the cigarette viciously into the fire. Her eyes were dark with anger. 'All right, if you want the truth you can have it and to hell with you. I did it and I'd do it again. I told you I'd stick at nothing to prevent her from marrying Larry. You wouldn't do a thing, either you or Gray. You just shrugged your shoulders and said it was a terrible mistake. You didn't care a damn. I did.'

'If you'd left her alone she'd be alive now.'

'Married to Larry and he'd be utterly miserable. He thought he'd make a new woman of her. What fools men are! I knew that sooner or later she'd break down. It stuck out a mile. You saw yourself when we were all lunching together at the Ritz how jittery she was. I noticed you looking at her when she was drinking her coffee; her hand was shaking so, she was afraid to take the cup with one hand, she had to put both her hands to it to get it up to her mouth. I noticed her watching the wine when the waiter filled our glasses; she followed the bottle with those horrible washed-out eyes of hers like a snake following the fluttering of a new-fledged chick and I knew she'd give her soul for a drink.'

Isabel faced me now, her eyes flashing with passion, and her voice was harsh. She couldn't get the words out quickly enough.

'The idea came to me when Uncle Elliott made all that fuss about the damned Polish liqueur. I thought it beastly, but I pretended it was the most wonderful stuff I'd ever tasted. I was certain that if she got a chance she'd never have the strength to resist. That's why I took her to the dress show. That's why I offered to make her a present of her wedding dress. That day, when she was going to have the last fitting, I told Antoine I'd have the zubrovka after lunch and then I told him I was expecting a lady and to ask her to wait and offer her some cofee and to leave the liqueur in case she fancied a glass. I did take Joan to the dentist's, but of course we hadn't an appointment and he couldn't see us, so I took her to a newsreel. I'd made up my mind that if I found Sophie hadn't touched the stuff I'd make the best of things and try to be friends with her. That's true, I swear it. But when I got home and saw the bottle I knew I'd been right. She'd gone and I'd have bet any money in the world she'd gone for good.'

Isabel was actually panting when she finished.

'That's more or less what I imagined had happened,' I said. 'You see, I was right; you cut her throat as surely as if you'd drawn the knife across it with your own hands.'

'She was bad, bad, bad. I'm glad she's dead.' She threw herself into a chair. 'Give me a cocktail, damn you.'

I went over and mixed another.

'You are a mean devil,' she said as she took it from me. Then she allowed herself to smile. Her smile was like a child's that knows it's been naughty, but thinks it can wheedle you by its ingenuous charm not to be cross. 'You won't tell Larry, will you?'

'I wouldn't dream of it.'

'Cross your heart? Men are so untrustworthy.'

'I promise you I won't. But even if I wanted to, I shouldn't have an opportunity as I don't suppose I shall ever see him again in my life.'

She sat bolt upright.

'What *do* you mean?'

'At this moment, he's on a freighter, either as a deck hand or a stoker, on his way to New York.'

'You don't mean that? What a strange creature he is! He was up here a few weeks ago for something to do with his book that he had to look up at the public library, but he never said a word about going to America. I'm glad; that means we shall see him.'

'I doubt it. His America will be as remote from your America as the Gobi desert.'

Then I told her what he had done and what he intended to do. She listened to me open-mouthed. Consternation was written on her face. She interrupted me now and then with an interjection: 'He's crazy. He's crazy.' When I had finished she hung her head and I saw two tears trickle down her cheeks.

'Now I really have lost him.'

She turned away from me and wept, leaning her face against the back of the chair. Her lovely face was twisted with the grief she did not care to hide. There was nothing I could do. I didn't know what vain, conflicting hopes she had cherished that my tidings had finally shattered. I had a vague notion that to see him occasionally, at least to know that he was part of her world, had been a bond of union, however tenuous, that his action had finally severed so that she knew herself for ever bereft. I wondered what unavailing regret afflicted her. I thought it would do her good to cry. I picked up Larry's book and looked at the table of contents. My copy had not arrived when I left the Riviera and I could not now hope to get it for several days. It was not in the least the sort of thing I expected. It was a collection of essays of about the same length as those in Lytton Strachey's *Eminent Victorians*, upon a number of famous persons. The choice he had made puzzled me. There was one on Sulla, the Roman dictator who, having achieved absolute power, resigned it to return to private life; there was one on Akbar, the Mogul conqueror who won an empire; there was one on Rubens, there was one on Goethe and there was one on the Lord Chesterfield of the Letters. It was obvious that each of the essays had needed a tremendous amount of reading and I was no longer surprised that it had taken Larry so long to produce this book, but I could not see why he had thought it worth while to give it so much time or why he had chosen those particular men to study. Then it occurred to me that every one of them in his own way had made a supreme success of life and I guessed that this was what had interested Larry. He was curious to see what in the end it amounted to.

I skimmed a page to see how he wrote. His style was scholarly, but lucid and easy. There was nothing in it of the pretentiousness or the pedantry that too often characterizes the writing of the amateur. One could tell that he had frequented the best authors as assiduously as Elliott Templeton frequented the nobility and gentry. I was interrupted by a sigh from Isabel. She sat up and finished with a grimace the cocktail which was now lukewarm.

'If I don't stop crying my eyes'll be terrible and we're going out to dinner tonight.' She took a mirror out of her bag and looked at herself anxiously. 'Yes, half an hour with an ice bag over my eyes, that's what I want.' She powdered her face and reddened her lips. Then she looked at me reflectively. 'Do you think any worse of me for what I did?'

'Would you care?'

'Strange as it may seem to you, I would. I want you to think well of me?'

I grinned.

'My dear, I'm a very immoral person,' I answered. 'When I'm really fond of anyone, though I deplore his wrongdoing it doesn't make me less fond of him. You're not a bad woman in your way and you have every grace and every charm. I don't enjoy your beauty any the less because I know how much it owes to the happy combination of perfect taste and ruthless determination. You only lack one thing to make you completely enchanting.'

She smiled and waited.

'Tenderness.'

The smile died on her lips and she gave me a glance that was totally lacking in amenity, but before she could collect herself to reply Gray lumbered into the room. In the three years he had been in Paris Gray had put on a good many pounds, his face had grown redder and his hair was thinning rapidly, but he was in rude health and in high spirits. He was unaffectedly pleased to see me. Gray's conversation was composed of clichés. However shop-worn, he uttered them with an obvious conviction that he was the first person to think of them. He never went to bed, but hit the hay, where he slept the sleep of the just; if it rained, it rained to beat the band and to the very end Paris to him was Gay Paree. But he was so kindly, so unselfish, so upright, so reliable, so unassuming that it was impossible not to like him. I had a real affection for him. He was excited now over their approaching departure.

'Gosh, it'll be great to get into harness again,' he said. 'I'm feeling my oats already.'

'Is it all settled then?'

'I haven't signed on the dotted line yet, but it's on ice. The fella I'm going in with was a roommate of mine at college, and he's a good scout, and I'm dead sure he wouldn't hand me a lemon. But as soon as we get to New York I'll fly down to Texas to give the outfit the once-over, and you bet I'll keep my eyes peeled for a nigger in the woodpile before I cough up any of Isabel's dough.'

'Gray's a very good businessman, you know,' she said.

'I wasn't raised in a barn,' he smiled.

He went on to tell me at somewhat excessive length about the business he was entering, but I understood little of such matters and the only concrete fact I gathered was that he stood a good chance of making a lot of money. He grew so interested in what he was saying that presently he turned to Isabel and said:

'Look here, why shouldn't we cut this lousy party and us three go and have a slap-up dinner at the Tour d'Argent by ourselves?'

'Oh, darling, we can't do that. They're giving the party for us.'

'Anyhow, I couldn't come now,' I interrupted. 'When I heard you were fixed up this evening I called up Suzanne Rouvier and arranged to take her out.'

'Who's Suzanne Rouvier?' asked Isabel.

'Oh, one of Larry's gals,' I said to tease her.

'I always suspected Larry had a little floozie tucked away somewhere,' said Gray, with a fat chuckle.

'Nonsense,' snapped Isabel. 'I know all about Larry's sex life. There isn't any.'

'Well, let's have one more drink before we part,' said Gray.

We had it and then I said good-bye to them. They came into the hall with me and while I was putting on my coat Isabel slipped her arm through Gray's and, nestling up to him, looked into his eyes with an expression that imitated very well the tenderness I had accused her of lacking.

'Tell me, Gray–frankly–do you think I'm hard-boiled?'

'No, darling, far from it. Why, has anybody been saying you were?'

'No.'

She turned her head away so that he shouldn't see, and in a manner that Elliott would certainly have thought very unladylike put out her tongue at me.

'It's not the same thing,' I murmured as I stepped out of the door and closed it behind me.

Four

When I passed through Paris again the Maturins had gone and other people lived in Elliott's apartment. I missed Isabel. She was good to look at and easy to talk to. She was quick on the uptake and bore no malice. I have never seen her since. I am a poor and dilatory correspondent and Isabel was no letter writer. If she could not communicate with you by telephone or telegram she did not communicate with you. I had a Christmas card from her that Christmas with a pretty picture on it of a house with a Colonial portico surrounded by live oaks, which I took to be the house of the plantation that they had been unable to sell when they wanted the money and which now they were probably willing to keep. The post-mark showed that it had been posted at Dallas, so I concluded that the deal had gone through satisfactorily and they were settled there.

I have never been to Dallas, but I suppose that, like other American cities I know, it has a residential district within easy motoring distance of the business section and the country club where the affluent have fine houses in large gardens with a handsome view of hill or dale from the living-room windows. In such a district and in such a house, furnished from cellar to attic in the latest mode by the most fashionable decorator in New York, Isabel certainly dwells. I can only hope that her Renoir, her flower piece by Manet, her landscape by Monet and her Gauguin do not look too dated. The dining-room is doubtless of a convenient size for the women's luncheons which she gives at frequent intervals and at which the wine is good and the food superlative. Isabel learnt a great deal in Paris. She would not have settled on the house unless she had seen at a glance that the living-room would do very well for the sub-deb dances which it would be her pleasant duty to give as her daughters grew older. Joan and Priscilla must be now of a marriageable age. I am sure that they have been admirably brought up; they have been sent to the best schools and Isabel has taken care that they should acquire the accomplishments that must make them desirable in the eyes of eligible young men. Though I suppose Gray by now is still a little redder in the face, more jowly, balder and a good deal heavier, I can't believe that Isabel has changed. She is still more beautiful than her daughters. The Maturins must be a great asset to the community and I have little doubt that they are as popular as they deserve to be. Isabel is entertaining, gracious, complaisant and tactful; Gray, of course, is the quintessence of the Regular Guy.

Five

I continued to see Suzanne Rouvier from time to time until an unexpected change in her condition caused her to leave Paris and she too went out of my life. One afternoon, roughly two years after the events that I have just related, having spent an hour pleasantly browsing over the books in the galleries of the Odéon and with nothing to do for a while, I thought I would call on Suzanne. I had not seen her for six months. She opened the door, a palette on her thumb and a paintbrush between her teeth, clad in a smock covered with paint.

'*Ah, c'est vous, cher ami. Entrez, je vous en prie.*'

I was a little surprised at this formal address, for generally we spoke to one another in the second person singular, but I stepped into the small room that served both as living-room and studio. There was a canvas on the easel.

'I'm so busy, I don't know which way to turn, but sit down and I will go on with my work. I haven't a moment to waste. You wouldn't believe it, but I'm giving a one-man show at Meyerheim's, and I have to get thirty canvases ready.'

'At Meyerheim's? That's wonderful. How on earth have you managed that?'

For Meyerheim is not one of those fly-by-night dealers in the Rue de la Seine who have a small shop that is always on the verge of closing for lack of money to pay the rent. Meyerheim has a fine gallery on the moneyed side of the Seine and he has an international reputation. An artist whom he takes up is well on the way to fortune.

'Monsieur Achille brought him to see my work and he thinks I have a lot of talent.'

'*A d'autres, ma vieille,*' I replied, which I think can best be translated by: 'Tell that to the marines, old girl.'

She threw me a glance and giggled.

'I'm going to be married.'

'To Meyerheim?'

'Don't be an idiot.' She put down her brushes and her palette. 'I've been working all day and I deserve a rest. Let us have a little glass of porto and I'll tell you all about it.'

One of the less agreeable features of French life is that you are apt to be pressed to drink a glass of vinegary port at an unseasonable hour. You must resign yourself to it. Suzanne fetched a bottle and two glasses, filled them and sat down with a sigh of relief.

'I've been standing for hours and my varicose veins are aching. Well, it's like this. Monsieur Achille's wife died at the beginning of this year. She was a good woman and a good Catholic, but he did not marry her from inclination, he married her because it was good business, and though he esteemed and respected her it would be an exaggeration to say that her death left him inconsolable. His son is suitably married and is doing well in the firm and now a marriage has been arranged between his daughter and a count. Belgian it is true, but authentic, with a very pretty château in the neighbourhood of Namur. Monsieur Achille thought his poor wife would not wish the happiness of two young people to be deferred on her account, so the marriage, notwithstanding that they are in mourning, is to take place as soon as the financial arrangements are completed. Evidently Monsieur Achille will be lonely in that large house at Lille, and needs a woman not only to minister to his comfort, but also to run the important establishment necessary to his position. To cut a long story short, he has asked me to take the place of his poor wife, for as he very reasonably said: "I married the first time to eliminate competition between two rival firms, and I do not regret it, but there is no reason why I should not marry the second time to please myself."'

'I congratulate you,' said I.

'Evidently I shall miss my liberty. I have enjoyed it. But one has to think of the future. Between ourselves, I don't mind telling you that I shall never see forty again. Monsieur Achille is at a dangerous age; where should I be if he suddenly took it into his head to run after a girl of twenty? And then there is my daughter to think of. She is now sixteen and promises to be as beautiful as her father. I have given her a good education. But it is no good denying facts that stare you in the face; she has neither the talent to be an actress nor the temperament to be a whore like her poor mother: I ask you then, what has she to look forward to? A secretaryship or a job in the post office. Monsieur Achille has very generously agreed that she should live with us and has promised to give her a handsome *dot* so that she can make a good marriage. Believe me, my dear friend, people can say what they like, but marriage still remains the most satisfactory profession a woman can adopt. Obviously when my daughter's welfare was concerned I could not hesitate to accept a proposition even at the cost of certain satisfactions which in any case, as the years go by, I should find it more difficult to obtain; for I must tell you that when I am married I propose to be of a ferocious virtue [*d'une vertu farouche*], for my long experience has convinced me that the only basis of a happy marriage is complete fidelity on both sides.'

'A highly moral sentiment, my pretty,' I said. 'And will Monsieur Achille continue to make his fortnightly visits to Paris on business?'

'*Oh, la la*, for whom do you take me, my little one? The first thing I said to Monsieur Achille when he asked for my hand was: "Now listen, my dear, when you come to Paris for your board meetings it is understood that I come too. I am not going to trust you here by yourself." "You cannot imagine that I am capable of committing follies at my age," he answered. "Monsieur Achille," I said to him, "you are a man in the prime of life and no one knows better than I that you have a passionate temperament. You have a fine presence and a distinguished air. You have everything to please a woman; in short I think it better that you should not be exposed to temptation." In the end he agreed to give up his place on the board to his son, who will come to Paris instead of his father. Monsieur Achille pretended to think me unreasonable, but he was in point of fact enormously flattered.' Suzanne gave a sigh of satisfaction. 'Life would be even harder for us poor women than it is if it were not for the unbelievable vanity of men.'

'All that is very fine, but what has it got to do with your having a one-man show at Meyerheim's?'

'You are a little stupid today, my poor friend. Have I not told you for years that Monsieur Achille is a highly intelligent man? He has his position to think of and the people of Lille are censorious. Monsieur Achille wishes me to take the place in society which as the wife of a man of his importance it will be my right to occupy. You know what these provincials are, they love to poke their long noses in other people's affairs, and the first thing they will ask is: who is Suzanne Rouvier? Well, they will have their answer. She is the distinguished painter whose recent show at the Meyerheim Gallery had a remarkable and well-deserved success. "Madame Suzanne Rouvier, the widow of an officer in the colonial infantry, has with the courage characteristic of our Frenchwomen for some years supported herself and a charming daughter deprived too soon of a father's care by means of her talent, and we are happy to know that the general public will soon have the opportunity to appreciate the delicacy of her touch and the soundness of her technique at the galleries of the ever perspicacious Monsieur Meyerheim."'

'What gibberish is that?' I said, pricking up my ears.

'That, my dear, is the advance publicity that Monsieur Achille is putting out. It will appear in every paper in France of any consequence. He has been magnificent. Meyerheim's terms were onerous, but Monsieur Achille accepted them as if they were a bagatelle. There will be a *champagne d'honneur* at the private view and the Minister of Fine Arts, who is under an obligation to Monsieur Achille, will open the exhibition with an eloquent speech in which he will dwell upon my virtues as a woman and my talent as a painter and which he will end with the declaration that the state, whose duty and privilege it is to reward merit, has bought one of my pictures for the national collections. All Paris will be there and Meyerheim is looking after the critics himself. He has guaranteed that their notices will be not only favourable but lengthy. Poor devils, they earn so little, it is a charity to give them an opportunity of making something on the side.'

'You've deserved it all, my dear. You've always been a good sort.'

'*Et ta sœur*,' she replied, which is untranslatable. 'But that's not all. Monsieur Achille has bought in my name a villa on the coast at St Rafael, so I shall take my place in Lille society not only as a distinguished artist, but as a woman of property. In two or three years he is going to retire and we shall live on the Riviera like gentlefolks [*comme des gens bien*]. He can paddle in the sea and catch shrimps while I devote myself to my art. Now I will show you my pictures.'

Suzanne had been painting for several years and she had worked through the manner of her various lovers to arrive at a style of her own. She still could not draw, but she had acquired a pretty sense of colour. She showed me landscapes that she had painted while staying with her mother in the province of Anjou, bits of the gardens at Versailles and the forest at Fontainebleau, street scenes that had taken her fancy in the suburbs of Paris. Her painting was vaporous and unsubstantial, but it had a flowerlike grace and even a certain careless elegance. There was one picture that took my fancy and because I thought she would be pleased I offered to buy it. I cannot remember whether it was called A Glade in the Forest or The White Scarf and subsequent examination has left me uncertain to this day. I asked the price, which was reasonable, and said I would take it.

'You're an angel,' she cried. 'My first sale. Of course you can't have it till after the show, but I'll see that it gets into the papers that you've bought it. After all, a little publicity can do you no harm. I'm glad you've chosen that one, I think it's one of my best.' She took a hand mirror and looked at the picture in it. 'It has charm,' she said, screwing up her eyes. No one can deny that. Those greens–how rich they are and yet how delicate! And that white note in the middle, that is a real find; it ties the picture together, it had distinction. There's talent there, there can be no doubt of it, there's real talent.'

I saw that she was already a long way on the road to being a professional painter.

'And now, my little one, we've gossiped long enough, I must get back to work.'

'And I must be going,' I said.

'*A propos*, is that poor Larry still among the Redskins?'

For that was the disrespectful way in which she was accustomed to refer to the inhabitants of God's Own Country.

'So far as I know.'

'It must be hard for someone like him who is so sweet and gentle. If one can believe the movies life is terrible over there with all those gangsters and cowboys and Mexicans. Not that those cowboys haven't physical attraction which says something to you. *Oh, la la!* But it appears that it is *excessively* dangerous to go out into the streets of New York without a revolver in your pocket.'

She came to the door to see me out and kissed me on both cheeks.

'We've had some good times together. Keep a good recollection of me.'

Six

This is the end of my story. I have heard nothing of Larry, nor indeed did I expect to. Since he generally did what he proposed, I think it likely that on his return to America he got a job in a garage and then drove a truck till he had acquired the knowledge he wanted of the country from which he had for so many years absented himself. When he had done that he may very well have carried out his fantastic suggestion of becoming a taxi driver: true, it was only a random idea thrown across a café table in jest, but I shouldn't be altogether surprised if he had put it into effect; and I have never since taken a taxi in New York without glancing at the driver on the chance that I might meet Larry's gravely smiling, deep-set eyes. I never have. War broke out. He would have been too old to fly, but he may be once more driving a truck, at home or abroad; or he may be working in a factory. I should like to think that in his leisure hours he is writing a book in which he is trying to set forth whatever life has taught him and the message he has to deliver to his fellow-men; but if he is, it may be long before it is finished. He has plenty of time, for the years have left no mark on him and to all intents and purposes he is still a young man.

He is without ambition and he has no desire for fame; to become anything of a public figure would be deeply distasteful to him; and so it may be that he is satisfied to lead his chosen life and be no more than just himself. He is too modest to set himself up as an example to others; but it may be he thinks that a few uncertain souls, drawn to him like moths to a candle, will be brought in time to share his own glowing belief that ultimate satisfaction can only be found in the life of the spirit, and that by himself following with selflessness and renunciation the path of perfection he will serve as well as if he wrote books or addressed multitudes.

But this is conjecture. I am of the earth, earthy; I can only admire the radiance of such a rare creature, I cannot step into his shoes and enter into his inmost heart as I sometimes think I can do with persons more nearly allied to the common run of men. Larry has been absorbed, as he wished, into that tumultuous conglomeration of humanity, distracted by so many conflicting interests, so lost in the world's confusion, so wishful of good, so cocksure on the outside, so diffident within, so kind, so hard, so trustful and so cagey, so mean and so generous, which is the people of the United States. That is all I can tell of him: I know it is very unsatisfactory; I can't help it. But as I was finishing this book, uneasily conscious that I must leave my reader in the air and seeing no way to avoid it, I looked back with my mind's eye on my long narrative to see if there was any way in which I could devise a more satisfactory ending; and to my intense surprise it dawned upon me that without in the least intending to I had written nothing more nor less than a success story. For all the persons with whom I have been concerned got what they wanted: Elliott social eminence; Isabel an assured position backed by a substantial fortune in an active and cultured community; Gray a steady and lucrative job, with an office to go to from nine till six every day; Suzanne Rouvier security; Sophie death; and Larry happiness. And however superciliously the highbrows carp, we the public in our heart of hearts all like a success story; so perhaps my ending is not so unsatisfactory after all.

Theatre

W.
Somerset
Maugham

Theatre

The characters in this novel are imaginary. The author
has tried to fit them with names of his own invention;
if he has by chance hit on the name of any living
person he offers his apologies for an accident which,
whatever care is taken, must sometimes occur.

Preface

It is not very difficult to write a preface to a book that you wrote a long time ago, for the hurrying years have made a different man of you and you can look upon it with a stranger's eyes. You see its faults, and for the reader's delectation you can recall, according to your temperament with toleration or with dismay, the defects in your character as it was then which account for the defects of your book; or you can look back, maybe with the pleasure which distance lends the past, upon the conditions under which you wrote; you can draw a pretty picture of your garret or dwell with modest complacency on the stiff upper lip with which you faced neglect. But when, in order to tempt a reader to buy a book that has no longer the merit of novelty, you set about writing a preface to a work of fiction that you composed no more than two or three years back, it is none too easy to find anything that you want to say, for you have said in your book all you had to say upon the theme with which it deals and having done so have never given it another thought. As nothing is more dead than a love that has burnt itself out, so no subject is less interesting to an author than one upon which he has said his say. Of course you can quarrel with your reviewers, but there is little point in that; what such and such a critic thought of a novel that he read the year before last can only matter to an author if his susceptibility is really too tender for the rough and tumble of this queer world; the critic has long forgotten both the book and his criticism, and the generality of readers never trouble their heads with criticism anyhow.

When first I set up as a professional author I used to paste such reviews as I got in great scrap-books, thinking it would amuse me some day to read them again, and I would carefully head each one with the date and the name of the paper in which it had appeared. But in course of time these unwieldy volumes grew very cumbersome, and because for one reason and another I have seldom lived for long in the same house, I found it necessary at last to get the dustman to rid me of them. Since then I have contented myself with reading my notices, as time wore on with sufficient equanimity not to be unduly perturbed by those that were unfavourable nor unduly elated by those that were laudatory, and throwing them into my waste-paper basket. My recollection is that on the whole the criticisms of Theatre were pretty good. Some critics, however, complained that Julia Lambert, my heroine, was not a creature of high moral character, great intelligence and nobility of soul, and concluded from this that she was a mediocre actress. I have been given to understand that a number of leading ladies were of the same opinion. Indeed one old actress, celebrated for her acting when I was a boy, and still remembered by the middle-aged for the amusingly disagreeable things she so often said, chiefly at the expense of her fellow-players, was quite biting in her references to me; but I think her acrimony was due to a misapprehension. I took pains in my novel to make it clear that my heroine, whatever her other faults, was not a snob, and this naturally enough prevented the old person in question from recognizing the fact that my Julia was a fine actress. We are all inclined to think that others can only have our virtues if they also have our vices.

Greatness is rare. During the last fifty years I have seen most of the actresses who have made a name for themselves. I have seen many who had eminent gifts, many who excelled in a domain they had made their own, many who had charm, beauty and knowledge, but I cannot think of more than one to whom I could without hesitation ascribe greatness. This was Eleanora Duse. It may be that Mrs Siddons had it; it may be that Rachel had it; I do not know; I never saw Sarah Bernhardt till she was past her prime; the glory that surrounded her, the extravagance of her legend, made it difficult to judge her coolly; she was often mannered and she could rant at times like any player queen; at her best she may have had greatness, I only saw its appurtenances, the crown, the sceptre and the ermine cloak—the Emperor of China's new clothes, but no Emperor of China. With the one exception I have mentioned I have only seen actresses who could be good, sometimes very good, in certain parts. I have a notion that one's opinion in this matter depends a good deal on how much one is affected by the glamour of the stage. There are many people whom the theatre fills with an excitement which no familiarity can stale. It is to them a world of mystery and delight; it gives them entry into a realm of the imagination which increases their joy in life, and its illusion colours the ordinariness of their daily round with the golden shimmer of romance. When they watch the celebrated actress, her beauty enhanced by make-up, her significance emphasized by spot-lights, uttering her fine phrases as though they came out of her own head, undergoing remarkable experiences and suffering poignant emotions, they feel that they live more fully; and it is natural enough that they should make a somewhat excessive use of hyperbole when they seek to describe the sensations which the skilful interpreter has given them. It is natural also that they should overlook the fact that the performance which has filled them with rapture owes at least something to the costumier, the scene-painter, the electrician and the author.

Even in my early youth I was never stage-struck; but whether because I am by nature of a somewhat sceptical disposition or whether because my mind was filled with private dreams which satisfied my romantic yearnings, I cannot say; and when I began to have plays acted I lost even the few illusions I had. When I discovered how much effort was put to achieving the gesture that had such a spontaneous look, when I realized how often the perfect intonation which moved an audience to tears was due not to the actress's sensibility but to the producer's experience, when in short I learnt from the inside how complicated was the process by which a play is made ready to set before an audience, I found it impossible to regard even the most brilliant members of the profession with the same awed and admiring wonder as the general public. On the other hand I learnt that they had qualities with which the public is little inclined to credit them. I learnt, for example, that with few exceptions they were hard-working, courageous, patient and conscientious. Though dropping with fatigue after a long day's work, I saw them consent with cheerfulness to go through still once more a difficult scene that they had that very day rehearsed half a dozen times already; I saw them, in illness, give a performance when they could hardly stand on their feet rather than let the company down; and I learnt that for all the frills and airs they might put on, when it came down to the business of getting the best out of the play and themselves, they were as reasonable as anyone could desire. Behind their famous 'temperament', which is a combination of selfishness and nerves more or less consciously emphasized under the erroneous impression that it is a proof of artistic sensibility, there is far oftener than the public imagines an abundance of shrewd, practical sense. I have never known a child that didn't like to show off, and in every actor there remains something of the child; it is to this that he owes many of his most charming gifts. He has more than the normal exhibitionism which is common to all but very few of us, and if he hadn't he would not be an actor; it is wiser to regard this particular trait with humour than with disdain. If I had to put in a phrase the impressions I formed of actors during the long time of my connection with the stage, I should say that their virtues are more solid than they pretend and their failings incidental to the hazardous and exacting profession they follow.

Thirty years elapsed between the production of my first play and the production of my last and in that period I was thrown into intimate contact with a great number of distinguished actresses. Julia Lambert is a portrait of none of them. I have taken a trait here and a trait there and sought to create a living person. Because I was not much affected by the glamour of the brilliant creatures I had known in the flesh I drew the creature of my fancy, I daresay, with a certain coolness. It is this, perhaps, which has disconcerted those readers who cannot separate the actress from the limelight that surrounds her and vexed those actresses who have been so dazzled by the limelight that they honestly think there is no more in them than that. They do themselves an injustice. The quality of the artist depends on the quality of the man and no one can excel in the arts who has not, besides his special gifts, moral rectitude; I would not deny, however, that this may exhibit itself in a form that is surprising and fantastic. I think Julia Lambert is true to life. I should like the reader to notice that though her admirers ascribe greatness to her, and though she accepts the flattery greedily, I, speaking in my own person, have not claimed that she was more than highly successful, very talented, serious and industrious. I should add that for my part I feel a great affection for her; I am not shocked by her naughtiness, nor scandalized by her absurdities; I can only consider her, whatever she does, with fond indulgence.

Before I bring this preface to a close I must tell the reader that in the book which I am now inviting him to peruse I have made two errors in fact. The novelist tries to be accurate in every detail, but sometimes he makes a mistake, and there is generally no lack of persons who are prepared to point it out to him. Once I wrote a novel in which I had occasion to mention a beach called Manly, which is a favourite resort during the bathing season of the inhabitants of Sydney, and unfortunately I spelt it Manley. The superfluous 'e' brought me hundreds of angry and derisive letters from New South Wales. You would have thought that the slip, which might after all have been a printer's error, though of course it was due only to my own carelessness, was a deliberate insult that I had offered to the Commonwealth. Indeed one lady told me that it was one more proof of the ignorant superciliousness of the English towards the inhabitants of the English colonies, and that it was people like me who would be responsible if next time Great Britain was embroiled in a Continental war the youth of Australia, instead of flying to her rescue, preferred to stay quietly at home.

She ended her letter on a rhetorical note. What, she asked me, would the English say if an Australian novelist, writing about England, should spell Bournmouth with an 'e'? My first impulse was to answer that to the best of my belief the English wouldn't turn a hair, even if it were incorrect, which in point of fact it wasn't, but I thought it would better become me to suffer the lady's stern rebuke in silence. Now in this book I have made two mistakes; I have made my heroine put down her failure in Beatrice to the fact that she was not at ease with blank verse, and I have made her, when she speaks of Racine's *Phèdre*, complain that the heroine did not appear till the third act. Instead of verifying my facts as I should have done, I trusted my memory, and my memory played me false. Beatrice speaks very little verse; all her important scenes are in prose; and if Julia failed in the part it was not for the reason she gave. Phèdre enters upon the stage in the third scene of the first act. I do not know why only two persons, one apiece, pointed out to me these inexcusable blunders; I like to think that most readers did me the credit of supposing that they were due, not to my ignorance, but to my subtlety, and that in making Julia Lambert speak in this casual and haphazard fashion I was adding a neat touch to my delineation of her character. But I may be unduly flattering myself, and it is just possible that my readers' recollection of the famous plays in which these characters appear was as hazy as my own, and they knew no better.

Chapter One

The door opened and Michael Gosselyn looked up. Julia came in.

'Hulloa! I won't keep you a minute. I was just signing some letters.'

'No hurry. I only came to see what seats had been sent to the Dennorants. What's that young man doing here?'

With the experienced actress's instinct to fit the gesture to the word, by a movement of her neat head she indicated the room through which she had just passed.

'He's the accountant. He comes from Lawrence and Hamphreys. He's been here three days.'

'He looks very young.'

'He's an articled clerk. He seems to know his job. He can't get over the way our accounts are kept. He told me he never expected a theatre to be run on such business-like lines. He says the way some of those firms in the city keep their accounts is enough to turn your hair grey.'

Julia smiled at the complacency on her husband's handsome face.

'He's a young man of tact.'

'He finishes today. I thought we might take him back with us and give him a spot of lunch. He's quite a gentleman.'

'Is that a sufficient reason to ask him to lunch?'

Michael did not notice the faint irony of her tone.

'I won't ask him if you don't want him. I merely thought it would be a treat for him. He admires you tremendously. He's been to see the play three times. He's crazy to be introduced to you.'

Michael touched a button and in a moment his secretary came in.

'Here are the letters, Margery. What appointments have I got for this afternoon?'

Julia with half an ear listened to the list Margery read out and, though she knew the room so well, idly looked about her. It was a very proper room for the manager of a first-class theatre. The walls had been panelled (at cost price) by a good decorator and on them hung engravings of theatrical pictures by Zoffany and de Wilde. The armchairs were large and comfortable. Michael sat in a heavily-carved Chippendale chair, a reproduction but made by a well-known firm, and his Chippendale table, with heavy ball and claw feet, was immensely solid. On it stood in a massive silver frame a photograph of herself and to balance it a photograph of Roger, their son. Between these was a magnificent silver ink-stand that she had herself given him on one of his birthdays and behind it a rack in red morocco, heavily gilt, in which he kept his private paper in case he wanted to write a letter in his own hand. The paper bore the address, Siddons Theatre, and the envelope his crest, a boar's head with the motto underneath: Nemo me impune lacessit. A bunch of yellow tulips in a silver bowl, which he had got through winning the theatrical golf tournament three times running, showed Margery's care. Julia gave her a reflective glance. Notwithstanding her cropped peroxide hair and her heavily-painted lips she had the neutral look that marks the perfect secretary. She had been with Michael for five years. In that time she must have got to know him inside and out. Julia wondered if she could be such a fool as to be in love with him.

But Michael rose from his chair.

'Now, darling, I'm ready for you.'

Margery gave him his black Homburg hat and opened the door for Julia and Michael to go out. As they entered the office the young man Julia had noticed turned round and stood up.

'I should like to introduce you to Miss Lambert,' said Michael. Then with the air of an ambassador presenting an attaché to the sovereign of the court to which he is accredited: 'This is the gentleman who is good enough to put some order into the mess we make of our accounts.'

The young man went scarlet. He smiled stiffly in answer to Julia's warm, ready smile and she felt the palm of his hand wet with sweat when she cordially grasped it. His confusion was touching. That was how people had felt when they were presented to Sarah Siddons. She thought that she had not been very gracious to Michael when he had proposed asking the boy to luncheon. She looked straight into his eyes. Her own were large, of a very dark brown, and starry. It was no effort to her, it was as instinctive as brushing away a fly that was buzzing round her, to suggest now a faintly amused, friendly tenderness.

'I wonder if we could persuade you to come and eat a chop with us. Michael will drive you back after lunch.'

The young man blushed again and his adam's apple moved in his thin neck.

'It's awfully kind of you.' He gave his clothes a troubled look. 'I'm absolutely filthy.'

'You can have a wash and brush up when we get home.'

The car was waiting for them at the stage door, a long car in black and chromium, upholstered in silver leather, and with Michael's crest discreetly emblazoned on the doors. Julia got in.

'Come and sit with me. Michael is going to drive.'

They lived in Stanhope Place, and when they arrived Julia told the butler to show the young man where he could wash his hands. She went up to the drawing-room. She was painting her lips when Michael joined her.

'I've told him to come up as soon as he's ready.'

'By the way, what's his name?'

'I haven't a notion.'

'Darling, we must know. I'll ask him to write in our book.'

'Damn it, he's not important enough for that.' Michael asked only very distinguished people to write in their book. 'We shall never see him again.'

At that moment the young man appeared. In the car Julia had done all she could to put him at his ease, but he was still very shy. The cocktails were waiting and Michael poured them out. Julia took a cigarette and the young man struck a match for her, but his hand was trembling so much that she thought he would never be able to hold the light near enough to her cigarette, so she took his hand and held it.

'Poor lamb,' she thought, 'I suppose this is the most wonderful moment in his whole life. What fun it'll be for him when he tells his people. I expect he'll be a blasted little hero in his office.'

Julia talked very differently to herself and to other people: when she talked to herself her language was racy. She inhaled the first whiff of her cigarette with delight. It was really rather wonderful, when you came to think of it, that just to have lunch with her and talk to her for three-quarters of an hour, perhaps, could make a man quite important in his own scrubby little circle.

The young man forced himself to make a remark.

'What a stunning room this is.'

She gave him the quick, delightful smile, with a slight lift of her fine eyebrows, which he must often have seen her give on the stage.

'I'm so glad you like it.' Her voice was rather low and ever so slightly hoarse. You would have thought his observation had taken a weight off her mind. 'We think in the family that Michael has such perfect taste.'

Michael gave the room a complacent glance.

'I've had a good deal of experience. I always design the sets myself for our plays. Of course, I have a man to do the rough work for me, but the ideas are mine.'

They had moved into that house two years before, and he knew, and Julia knew, that they had put it into the hands of an expensive decorator when they were going on tour, and he had agreed to have it completely ready for them, at cost price in return for the work they promised him in the theatre, by the time they came back. But it was unnecessary to impart such tedious details to a young man whose name even they did not know. The house was furnished in extremely good taste, with a judicious mixture of the antique and the modern, and Michael was right when he said that it was quite obviously a gentleman's house. Julia, however, had insisted that she must have her bedroom as she liked, and having had exactly the bedroom that pleased her in the old house in Regent's Park which they had occupied since the end of the war she brought it over bodily. The bed and the dressing-table were upholstered in pink silk, the chaise-longue and the armchair in Nattier blue; over the bed there were fat little gilt cherubs who dangled a lamp with a pink shade, and fat little gilt cherubs swarmed all round the mirror on the dressing-table. On satinwood tables were signed photographs, richly framed, of actors and actresses and members of the royal family. The decorator had raised his supercilious eyebrows, but it was the only room in the house in which Julia felt completely at home. She wrote her letters at a satinwood desk, seated on a gilt Hamlet stool.

Luncheon was announced and they went downstairs.

'I hope you'll have enough to eat,' said Julia. 'Michael and I have very small appetites.'

In point of fact there was grilled sole, grilled cutlets and spinach, and stewed fruit. It was a meal designed to satisfy legitimate hunger, but not to produce fat. The cook, warned by Margery that there was a guest to luncheon had hurriedly made some fried potatoes. They looked crisp and smelt appetizing. Only the young man took them. Julia gave them a wistful look before she shook her head in refusal. Michael stared at them gravely for a moment as though he could not quite tell what they were, and then with a little start, breaking out of a brown study, said No thank you. They sat at a refectory table, Julia and Michael at either end in very grand Italian chairs and the young man in the middle on a chair that was not at all comfortable, but perfectly in character. Julia noticed that he seemed to be looking at the sideboard and with her engaging smile, leaned forward.

'What is it?'

He blushed scarlet.

'I was wondering if I might have a piece of bread.'

'Of course.'

She gave the butler a significant glance; he was at that moment helping Michael to a glass of dry white wine, and he left the room.

'Michael and I never eat bread. It was stupid of Jevons not to realize that you might want some.'

'Of course bread is only a habit,' said Michael. 'It's wonderful how soon you can break yourself of it if you set your mind to it.'

'The poor lamb's as thin as a rail, Michael.'

'I don't not eat bread because I'm afraid of getting fat. I don't eat it because I see no point in it. After all, with the exercise I take I can eat anything I like.'

He still had at fifty-two a very good figure. As a young man, with a great mass of curling chestnut hair, with a wonderful skin and large deep blue eyes, a straight nose and small ears, he had been the best-looking actor on the English stage. The only thing that slightly spoiled him was the thinness of his mouth. He was just six foot tall and he had a gallant bearing. It was his obvious beauty that had engaged him to go on the stage rather than to become a soldier like his father. Now his chestnut hair was very grey, and he wore it much shorter; his face had broadened and was a good deal lined; his skin no longer had the soft bloom of a peach and his colour was high. But with his splendid eyes and his fine figure he was still a very handsome man. Since his five years at the war he had adopted a military bearing, so that if you had not known who he was (which was scarcely possible, for in one way and another his photograph was always appearing in the illustrated papers) you might have taken him for an officer of high rank. He boasted that his weight had not changed since he was twenty, and for years, wet or fine, he had got up every morning at eight to put on shorts and a sweater and have a run round Regent's Park.

'The secretary told me you were rehearsing this morning, Miss Lambert,' the young man remarked. 'Does that mean you're putting on a new play?'

'Not a bit of it,' answered Michael. 'We're playing to capacity.'

'Michael thought we were getting a bit ragged, so he called a rehearsal.'

'I'm very glad I did. I found little bits of business had crept in that I hadn't given them and a good many liberties were being taken with the text. I'm a great stickler for saying the author's exact words, though, God knows, the words authors write nowadays aren't much.'

'If you'd like to come and see our play,' Julia said graciously, 'I'm sure Michael will be delighted to give you some seats.'

'I'd love to come again,' the young man answered eagerly. 'I've seen it three times already.'

'You haven't?' cried Julia, with surprise, though she remembered perfectly that Michael had already told her so. 'Of course it's not a bad little play, it's served our purpose very well, but I can't imagine anyone wanting to see it three times.'

'It's not so much the play I went to see, it was your performance.'

'I dragged that out of him all right,' thought Julia and then aloud: 'When we read the play Michael was rather doubtful about it. He didn't think my part was very good. You know, it's not really a star part. But I thought I could make something out of it. Of course we had to cut the other woman a lot in rehearsals.'

'I don't say we re-wrote the play,' said Michael, 'but I can tell you it was a very different play we produced from the one the author submitted to us.'

'You're simply wonderful in it,' the young man said.

('He has a certain charm.') 'I'm glad you liked me,' she answered.

'If you're very nice to Julia I daresay she'll give you a photograph of herself when you go.'

'Would you?'

He blushed again and his blue eyes shone ('He's really rather sweet.') He was not particularly good-looking, but he had a frank, open face and his shyness was attractive. He had curly light brown hair, but it was plastered down and Julia thought how much better he would look if, instead of trying to smooth out the wave with brilliantine, he made the most of it. He had a fresh colour, a good skin and small well-shaped teeth. She noticed with approval that his clothes fitted and that he wore them well. He looked nice and clean.

'I suppose you've never had anything to do wtih the theatre from the inside before?' she said.

'Never. That's why I was so crazy to get this job. You can't think how it thrills me.'

Michael and Julia smiled on him kindly. His admiration made them feel a little larger than life-size.

'I never allow outsiders to come to rehearsals, but as you're our accountant you almost belong to the theatre, and I wouldn't mind making an exception in your favour if it would amuse you to come.'

'That would be terribly kind of you. I've never been to a rehearsal in my life. Are you going to act in the next play?'

'Oh, I don't think so. I'm not very keen about acting any more. I find it almost impossible to find a part to suit me. You see, at my time of life I can't very well play young lovers, and authors don't seem to write the parts they used to write when I was a young fellow. What the French call a raisonneur. You know the sort of thing I mean, a duke, or a cabinet minister, or an eminent K.C. who says clever, witty things and turns people round his little finger. I don't know what's happened to authors. They don't seem able to write good lines any more. Bricks without straw; that's what we actors are expected to make nowadays. And are they grateful to us? The authors, I mean. You'd be surprised if I told you the terms some of them have the nerve to ask.'

'The fact remains, we can't do without them,' smiled Julia. 'If the play's wrong no acting in the world will save it.'

'That's because the public isn't really interested in the theatre. In the great days of the English stage people didn't go to see the plays, they went to see the players. It didn't matter what Kemble and Mrs Siddons acted. The public went to see them. And even now, though I don't deny that if the play's wrong you're dished, I do contend that if the play's right, it's the actors the public go to see, not the play.'

'I don't think anyone can deny that,' said Julia.

'All an actress like Julia wants is a vehicle. Give her that and she'll do the rest.'

Julia gave the young man a delightful, but slightly deprecating smile.

'You mustn't take my husband too seriously. I'm afraid we must admit that he's partial where I'm concerned.'

'Unless this young man is a much bigger fool than I think him he must know that there's nothing in the way of acting that you can't do.'

'Oh, that's only an idea that people have got because I take care never to do anything but what I can do.'

Presently Michael looked at his watch.

'I think when you've finished your coffee, young man, we ought to be going.'

The boy gulped down what was left in his cup and Julia rose from the table.

'You won't forget my photograph?'

'I think there are some in Michael's den. Come along and we'll choose one.'

She took him into a fair-sized room behind the dining-room. Though it was supposed to be Michael's private sitting-room—'a fellow wants a room where he can get away by himself and smoke his pipe'—it was chiefly used as a cloak-room when they had guests. There was a noble mahogany desk on which were signed photographs of George V and Queen Mary. Over the chimney-piece was an old copy of Lawrence's portrait of Kemble as Hamlet. On a small table was a pile of typescript plays. The room was surrounded by bookshelves under which were cupboards, and from one of these Julia took a bundle of her latest photographs. She handed one to the young man.

'This one is not so bad.'

'It's lovely.'

'Then it can't be as like me as I thought.'

'But it is. It's exactly like you.'

She gave him another sort of smile, just a trifle roguish; she lowered her eyelids for a second and then raising them gazed at him for a little with that soft expression that people described as her velvet look. She had no object in doing this. She did it, if not mechanically, from an instinctive desire to please. The boy was so young, so shy, he looked as if he had such a nice nature, and she would never see him again, she wanted him to have his money's worth; she wanted him to look back on this as one of the great moments of his life. She glanced at the photograph again. She liked to think she looked like that. The photographer had so posed her, with her help, as to show her at her best. Her nose was slightly thick, but he had managed by his lighting to make it look very delicate, not a wrinkle marred the smoothness of her skin, and there was a melting look in her fine eyes.

'All right. You shall have this one. You know I'm not a beautiful woman, I'm not even a very pretty one; Coquelin always used to say I had the beauté du diable. You understand French, don't you?'

'Enough for that.'

'I'll sign it for you.'

She sat at the desk and with her bold, flowing hand wrote: Yours sincerely, Julia Lambert.

Chapter Two

When the two men had gone she looked through the photographs again before putting them back.

'Not bad for a woman of forty-six,' she smiled. 'They are like me, there's no denying that.' She looked round the room for a mirror, but there wasn't one. 'These damned decorators. Poor Michael, no wonder he never uses this room. Of course I never have photographed well.'

She had an impulse to look at some of her old photographs. Michael was a tidy, business-like man, and her photographs were kept in large cardboard cases, dated and chronologically arranged. His were in other cardboard cases in the same cupboard.

'When someone comes along and wants to write the story of our careers he'll find all the material ready to his hand,' he said.

With the same laudable object he had had all their press cuttings from the very beginning pasted in a series of large books.

There were photographs of Julia when she was a child, and photographs of her as a young girl, photographs of her in her first parts, photographs of her as a young married woman, with Michael, and then with Roger, her son, as a baby. There was one photograph of the three of them, Michael very manly and incredibly handsome, herself all tenderness looking down at Roger with maternal feeling, and Roger a little boy with a curly head, which had been an enormous success. All the illustrated papers had given it a full page and they had used it on the programmes. Reduced to picture-postcard size it had sold in the provinces for years. It was such a bore that Roger when he got to Eton refused to be photographed with her any more. It seemed so funny of him not to want to be in the papers.

'People will think you're deformed or something,' she told him. 'And it's not as if it weren't good form. You should just go to a first night and see the society people how they mob the photographers, cabinet ministers and judges and everyone. They may pretend they don't like it, but just see them posing when they think the camera man's got his eye on them.'

But he was obstinate.

Julia came across a photograph of herself as Beatrice. It was the only Shakespearean part she had ever played. She knew that she didn't look well in costume; she could never understand why, because no one could wear modern clothes as well as she could. She had her clothes made in Paris, both for the stage and for private life, and the dressmakers said that no one brought them more orders. She had a lovely figure, everyone admitted that; she was fairly tall for a woman, and she had long legs. It was a pity she had never had a chance of playing Rosalind, she would have looked all right in boy's clothes, of course it was too late now, but perhaps it was just as well she hadn't risked it. Though you would have thought, with her brilliance, her roguishness, her sense of comedy she would have been perfect. The critics hadn't really liked her Beatrice. It was that damned blank verse. Her voice, her rather low rich voice, with that effective hoarseness, which wrung your heart in an emotional passage or gave so much humour to a comedy line, seemed to sound all wrong when she spoke it. And then her articulation; it was so distinct that, without raising her voice, she could make you hear her every word in the last row of the gallery; they said it made verse sound like prose. The fact was, she supposed, that she was much too modern.

Michael had started with Shakespeare. That was before she knew him. He had played Romeo at Cambridge, and when he came down, after a year at a dramatic school, Benson had engaged him. He toured the country and played a great variety of parts. But he realized that Shakespeare would get him nowhere and that if he wanted to become a leading actor he must gain experience in modern plays. A man called James Langton was running a repertory theatre at Middlepool that was attracting a good deal of attention; and after Michael had been with Benson for three years, when the company was going to Middlepool on its annual visit, he wrote to Langton and asked whether he would see him. Jimmie Langton, a fat, bald-headed, rubicund man of forty-five, who looked like one of Rubens' prosperous burghers, had a passion for the theatre. He was an eccentric, arrogant, exuberant, vain and charming fellow. He loved acting, but his physique prevented him from playing any but a few parts, which was fortunate, for he was a bad actor. He could not subdue his natural flamboyance, and every part he played, though he studied it with care and gave it thought, he turned into a grotesque. He broadened every gesture, he exaggerated every intonation. But it was a very different matter when he rehearsed his cast; then he would suffer nothing artificial. His ear was perfect, and though he could not produce the right intonation himself he would never let a false one pass in anyone else.

'Don't *be* natural,' he told his company. 'The stage isn't the place for that. The stage is make-believe. But *seem* natural.'

He worked his company hard. They rehearsed every morning from ten till two, when he sent them home to learn their parts and rest before the evening's performance. He bullied them, he screamed at them, he mocked them. He underpaid them. But if they played a moving scene well he cried like a child, and when they said an amusing line as he wanted it said he bellowed with laughter. He would skip about the stage on one leg if he was pleased, and if he was angry would throw the script down and stamp on it while tears of rage ran down his cheeks. The company laughed at him and abused him and did everything they could to please him. He aroused a protective instinct in them, so that one and all they felt that they couldn't let him down. Though they said he drove them like slaves, and they never had a moment to themselves, flesh and blood couldn't stand it, it gave them a sort of horrible satisfaction to comply with his outrageous demands. When he wrung an old trooper's hand, who was getting seven pounds a week, and said, by God, laddie, you're stupendous, the old trooper felt like Charles Kean.

It happened that when Michael kept the appointment he had asked for, Jimmie Langton was in need of a leading juvenile. He had guessed why Michael wanted to see him, and had gone the night before to see him play. Michael was playing Mercutio and he had not thought him very good, but when he came into the office he was staggered by his beauty. In a brown coat and grey flannel trousers, even without make-up, he was so handsome it took your breath away. He had an easy manner and he talked like a gentleman. While Michael explained the purpose of his visit Jimmie Langton observed him shrewdly. If he could act at all, with those looks that young man ought to go far.

'I saw your Mercutio last night,' he said. 'What d'you think of it yourself?'

'Rotten.'

'So do I. How old are you?'

'Twenty-five.'

'I suppose you've been told you're good-looking?'

'That's why I went on the stage. Otherwise I'd have gone into the army like my father.'

'By gum, if I had your looks what an actor I'd have been.'

The result of the interview was that Michael got an engagement. He stayed at Middlepool for two years. He soon grew popular with the company. He was good-humoured and kindly; he would take any amount of trouble to do anyone a service. His beauty created a sensation in Middlepool and the girls used to hang about the stage door to see him go out. They wrote him love letters and sent him flowers. He took it as a natural homage, but did not allow it to turn his head. He was eager to get on and seemed determined not to let any entanglement interfere with his career. It was his beauty that saved him, for Jimmie Langton quickly came to the conclusion that, notwithstanding his perseverance and desire to excel, he would never be more than a competent actor. His voice was a trifle thin and in moments of vehemence was apt to go shrill. It gave them more the effect of hysteria than of passion. But his gravest fault as a juvenile lead was that he could not make love. He was easy enough in ordinary dialogue and could say his lines with point, but when it came to making protestations of passion something seemed to hold him back. He felt embarrassed and looked it.

'Damn you, don't hold that girl as if she was a sack of potatoes,' Jimmie Langton shouted at him. 'You kiss her as if you were afraid you were standing in a draught. You're in love with that girl. You must feel that you're in love with her. Feel as if your bones were melting inside you and if an earthquake were going to swallow you up next minute, to hell with the earthquake.'

But it was no good. Notwithstanding his beauty, his grace and his ease of manner, Michael remained a cold lover. This did not prevent Julia from falling madly in love with him. For it was when he joined Langton's repertory company that they met.

Her own career had been singularly lacking in hardship. She was born in Jersey, where her father, a native of that island, practised as a veterinary surgeon. Her mother's sister was married to a Frenchman, a coal merchant, who lived at St Malo, and Julia had been sent to live with her while she attended classes at the local lycée. She learnt to speak French like a Frenchwoman. She was a born actress and it was an understood thing for as long as she could remember that she was to go on the stage. Her aunt, Madame Falloux, was 'en relations' with an old actress who had been a sociétaire of the Comédie Française and who had retired to St Malo to live on the small pension that one of her lovers had settled on her when after many years of faithful concubinage they had parted. When Julia was a child of twelve this actress was a boisterous, fat old woman of more than sixty, but of great vitality, who loved food more than anything else in the world. She had a great, ringing laugh, like a man's, and she talked in a deep, loud voice.

It was she who gave Julia her first lessons. She taught her all the arts that she had herself learnt at the Conservatoire and she talked to her of Reichenberg who had played ingénues till she was seventy, of Sarah Bernhardt and her golden voice, of Mounet-Sully and his majesty, and of Coquelin the greatest actor of them all. She recited to her the great tirades of Corneille and Racine as she had learnt to say them at the Français and taught her to say them in the same way. It was charming to hear Julia in her childish voice recite those languorous, passionate speeches of Phèdre, emphasizing the beat of the Alexandrines and mouthing her words in that manner which is so artificial and yet so wonderfully dramatic. Jane Taitbout must always have been a very stagy actress, but she taught Julia to articulate with extreme distinctness, she taught her how to walk and how to hold herself, she taught her not to be afraid of her own voice, and she made deliberate that wonderful sense of timing which Julia had by instinct and which afterwards was one of her greatest gifts.

'Never pause unless you have a reason for it,' she thundered, banging with her clenched fist on the table at which she sat, 'but when you pause, pause as long as you can.'

When Julia was sixteen and went to the Royal Academy of Dramatic Art in Gower Street she knew already much that they could teach her there. She had to get rid of a certain number of tricks that were out of date and she had to acquire a more conversational style. But she won every prize that was open to her, and when she was finished with the school her good French got her almost immediately a small part in London as a French maid. It looked for a while as though her knowledge of French would specialize her in parts needing a foreign accent, for after this she was engaged to play an Austrian waitress. It was two years later that Jimmie Langton discovered her. She was on tour in a melodrama that had been successful in London; in the part of an Italian adventuress, whose machinations were eventually exposed, she was trying somewhat inadequately to represent a woman of forty. Since the heroine, a blonde person of mature years, was playing a young girl, the performance lacked verisimilitude. Jimmie was taking a short holiday which he spent in going every night to the theatre in one town after another. At the end of the piece he went round to see Julia. He was well enough known in the theatrical world for her to be flattered by the compliments he paid her, and when he asked her to lunch with him next day she accepted.

They had no sooner sat down to table than he went straight to the point.

'I never slept a wink all night for thinking of you,' he said.

'This is very sudden. Is your proposal honourable or dishonourable?'

He took no notice of the flippant rejoinder.

'I've been at this game for twenty-five years. I've been a call-boy, a stage-hand, a stage-manager, an actor, a publicity man, damn it, I've even been a critic. I've lived in the theatre since I was a kid just out of a board school, and what I don't know about acting isn't worth knowing. I think you're a genius.'

'It's sweet of you to say so.'

'Shut up. Leave me to do the talking. You've got everything. You're the right height, you've got a good figure, you've got an indiarubber face.'

'Flattering, aren't you?'

'That's just what I am. That's the face an actress wants. The face that can look anything, even beautiful, the face that can show every thought that passes through the mind. That's the face Duse's got. Last night even though you weren't really thinking about what you were doing every now and then the words you were saying wrote themselves on your face.'

'It's such a rotten part. How could I give it my attention? Did you hear the things I had to say?'

'Actors are rotten, not parts. You've got a wonderful voice, the voice that can wring an audience's heart, I don't know about your comedy, I'm prepared to risk that.'

'What d'you mean by that?'

'Your timing is almost perfect. That couldn't have been taught, you must have that by nature. That's the far, far better way. Now let's come down to brass tacks. I've been making enquiries about you. It appears you speak French like a Frenchwoman and so they give you broken English parts. That's not going to lead you anywhere, you know.'

'That's all I can get.'

'Are you satisfied to go on playing those sort of parts for ever? You'll get stuck in them and the public won't take you in anything else. Seconds, that's all you'll play. Twenty pounds a week at the outside and a great talent wasted.'

'I've always thought that some day or other I should get a chance of a straight part.'

'When? You may have to wait ten years. How old are you now?'

'Twenty.'

'What are you getting?'

'Fifteen pounds a week.'

'That's a lie. You're getting twelve, and it's a damned sight more than you're worth. You've got everything to learn. Your gestures are commonplace. You don't know that every gesture must mean something. You don't know how to get an audience to look at you before you speak. You make up too much. With your sort of face the less make-up the better. Wouldn't you like to be a star?'

'Who wouldn't?'

'Come to me and I'll make you the greatest actress in England. Are you a quick study? You ought to be at your age.'

'I think I can be word-perfect in any part in forty-eight hours.'

'It's experience you want and me to produce you. Come to me and I'll let you play twenty parts a year. Ibsen, Shaw, Barker, Sudermann, Hankin, Galsworthy. You've got magnetism and you don't seem to have an idea how to use it.' He chuckled. 'By God, if you had, that old hag would have had you out of the play you're in now before you could say knife. You've got to take an audience by the throat and say, now, you dogs, you pay attention to me. You've got to dominate them. If you haven't got the gift no one can give it you, but if you have you can be taught how to use it. I tell you, you've got the makings of a great actress. I've never been so sure of anything in my life.'

'I know I want experience. I'd have to think it over of course. I wouldn't mind coming to you for a season.'

'Go to hell. Do you think I can make an actress of you in a season? Do you think I'm going to work my guts out to make you give a few decent performances and then have you go away to play some twopenny-halfpenny part in a commercial play in London? What sort of a bloody fool do you take me for? I'll give you a three years' contract, I'll give you eight pounds a week and you'll have to work like a horse.'

'Eight pounds a week's absurd. I couldn't possibly take that.'

'Oh yes, you could. It's all you're worth and it's all you're going to get.'

Julia had been on the stage for three years and had learnt a good deal. Besides, Jane Taitbout, no strict moralist, had given her a lot of useful information.

'And are you under the impression by any chance, that for that I'm going to let you sleep with me as well?'

'My God, do you think I've got time to go to bed with the members of my company? I've got much more important things to do than that, my girl. And you'll find that after you've rehearsed for four hours and played a part at night to my satisfaction, besides a couple of matinées, you won't have much time or much inclination to make love to anybody. When you go to bed all you'll want to do is to sleep.'

But Jimmie Langton was wrong there.

Chapter Three

Julia, taken by his enthusiasm and his fantastic exuberance, accepted his offer. He started her in modest parts which under his direction she played as she had never played before. He interested the critics in her, he flattered them by letting them think that they had discovered a remarkable actress, and allowed the suggestion to come from them that he should let the public see her as Magda. She was a great hit and then in quick succession he made her play Nora in *The Doll's House*, Ann in *Man and Superman*, and Hedda Gabler. Middlepool was delighted to discover that it had in its midst an actress who it could boast was better than any star in London, and crowded to see her in plays that before it had gone to only from local patriotism. The London paragraphers mentioned her now and then, and a number of enthusiastic patrons of the drama made the journey to Middlepool to see her. They went back full of praise, and two or three London managers sent representatives to report on her. They were doubtful. She was all very well in Shaw and Ibsen, but what would she do in an ordinary play? The managers had had bitter experiences. On the strength of an outstanding performance in one of these queer plays they had engaged an actor, only to discover that in any other sort of play he was no better than anybody else.

When Michael joined the company Julia had been playing in Middlepool for a year. Jimmie started him with Marchbanks in *Candida*. It was the happy choice one would have expected him to make, for in that part his great beauty was an asset and his lack of warmth no disadvantage.

Julia reached over to take out the first of the cardboard cases in which Michael's photographs were kept. She was sitting comfortably on the floor. She turned the early photographs over quickly, looking for that which he had had taken when first he came to Middlepool; but when she came upon it, it gave her a pang. For a moment she felt inclined to cry. It had been just like him then. Candida was being played by an older woman, a sound actress who was cast generally for mothers, maiden aunts or character parts, and Julia with nothing to do but act eight times a week attended the rehearsals. She fell in love with Michael at first sight. She had never seen a more beautiful young man, and she pursued him relentlessly. In due course Jimmie put on *Ghosts*, braving the censure of respectable Middlepool, and Michael played the boy and she played Regina. They heard one another their parts and after rehearsals lunched, very modestly, together so that they might talk of them. Soon they were inseparable. Julia had little reserve; she flattered Michael outrageously. He was not vain of his good looks, he knew he was handsome and accepted compliments, not exactly with indifference, but as he might have accepted a compliment on a fine old house that had been in his family for generations. It was a well-known fact that it was one of the best houses of its period, one was proud of it and took care of it, but it was just there, as natural to possess as the air one breathed. He was shrewd and ambitious. He knew that his beauty was at present his chief asset, but he knew it could not last for ever and was determined to become a good actor so that he should have something besides his looks to depend on. He meant to learn all he could from Jimmie Langton and then go to London.

'If I play my cards well I can get some old woman to back me and go into management. One's got to be one's own master. That's the only way to make a packet.'

Julia soon discovered that he did not much like spending money, and when they ate a meal together, or on a Sunday went for a small excursion, she took care to pay her share of the expenses. She did not mind this. She liked him for counting the pennies, and, inclined to be extravagant herself and always a week or two behind with her rent, she admired him because he hated to be in debt and even with the small salary he was getting managed to save up a little every week. He was anxious to have enough put by so that when he went to London he need not accept the first part that was offered him, but could afford to wait till he got one that gave him a real chance. His father had little more than his pension to live on, and it had been a sacrifice to send him to Cambridge. His father, not liking the idea of his going on the stage, had insisted on this.

'If you want to be an actor I suppose I can't stop you,' he said, 'but damn it all, I insist on your being educated like a gentleman.'

It gave Julia a good deal of satisfaction to discover that Michael's father was a colonel, it impressed her to hear him speak of an ancestor who had gambled away his fortune at White's during the Regency, and she liked the signet ring Michael wore with the boar's head on it and the motto: Nemo me impune lacessit.

'I believe you're prouder of your family than of looking like a Greek god,' she told him fondly.

'Anyone can be good-looking,' he answered, with his sweet smile, 'but not everyone can belong to a decent family. To tell you the truth I'm glad my governor's a gentleman.'

Julia took her courage in both hands.

'My father's a vet.'

For an instant Michael's face stiffened, but he recovered himself immediately and laughed.

'Of course it doesn't really matter what one's father is. I've often heard my father talk of the vet in his regiment. He counted as an officer of course. Dad always said he was one of the best.'

And she was glad he'd been to Cambridge. He had rowed for his College and at one time there was some talk of putting him in the university boat.

'I should have liked to get my blue. It would have been useful to me on the stage. I'd have got a lot of advertisement out of it.'

Julia could not tell if he knew that she was in love with him. He never made love to her. He liked her society and when they found themselves with other people scarcely left her side. Sometimes they were asked to parties on Sunday, dinner at midday or a cold, sumptuous supper, and he seemed to think it natural that they should go together and come away together. He kissed her when he left her at her door, but he kissed her as he might have kissed the middle-aged woman with whom he had played Candida. He was friendly, good-humoured and kind, but it was distressingly clear that she was no more to him than a comrade. Yet she knew that he was not in love with anybody else. The love-letters that women wrote to him he read out to Julia with a chuckle, and when they sent him flowers he immediately gave them to her.

'What blasted fools they are,' he said. 'What the devil do they think they're going to get out of it?'

'I shouldn't have thought it very hard to guess that,' said Julia dryly.

Although she knew he took these attentions so lightly she could not help feeling angry and jealous.

'I should be a damned fool if I got myself mixed up with some woman in Middlepool. After all, they're mostly flappers. Before I knew where I was I'd have some irate father coming along and saying, now you must marry the girl.'

She tried to find out whether he had had any adventures while he was playing with Benson's company. She gathered that one or two of the girls had been rather inclined to make nuisances of themselves, but he thought it was a terrible mistake to get mixed up with any of the actresses a chap was playing with. It was bound to lead to trouble.

'And you know how people gossip in a company. Everyone would know everything in twenty-four hours. And when you start a thing like that you don't know what you're letting yourself in for. I wasn't risking anything.'

When he wanted a bit of fun he waited till they were within a reasonable distance of London and then he would race up to town and pick up a girl at the Globe Restaurant. Of course it was expensive, and when you came to think of it, it wasn't really worth the money; besides, he played a lot of cricket in Benson's company, and golf when he got the chance, and that sort of thing was rotten for the eye.

Julia told a thumping lie.

'Jimmie always says I'd be a much better actress if I had an affair.'

'Don't you believe it. He's just a dirty old man. With him, I suppose. I mean, you might just as well say that I'd give a better performance of Marchbanks if I wrote poetry.'

They talked so much together that it was inevitable for her at last to learn his views on marriage.

'I think an actor's a perfect fool to marry young. There are so many cases in which it absolutely ruins a chap's career. Especially if he marries an actress. He becomes a star and then she's a millstone round his neck. She insists on playing with him, and if he's in management he has to give her leading parts, and if he engages someone else there are most frightful scenes. And of course, for an actress it's insane. There's always the chance of her having a baby and she may have to refuse a damned good part. She's out of the public eye for months, and you know what the public is, unless they see you all the time they forget that you ever existed.'

Marriage? What did she care about marriage? Her heart melted within her when she looked into his deep, friendly eyes, and she shivered with delightful anguish when she considered his shining, russet hair. There was nothing that he could have asked her that she would not gladly have given him. The thought never entered his lovely head.

'Of course he likes me,' she said to herself. 'He likes me better than anyone, he even admires me, but I don't attract him that way.'

She did everything to seduce him except slip into bed with him, and she only did not do that because there was no opportunity. She began to fear that they knew one another too well for it to seem possible that their relations should change, and she reproached herself bitterly because she had not rushed to a climax when first they came in contact with one another. He had too sincere an affection for her now ever to become her lover. She found out when his birthday was and gave him a gold cigarette case which she knew was the thing he wanted more than anything in the world. It cost a good deal more than she could afford and he smilingly reproached her for her extravagance. He never dreamt what ecstatic pleasure it gave her to spend her money on him. When her birthday came along he gave her half a dozen pairs of silk stockings. She noticed at once that they were not of very good quality, poor lamb, he had not been able to bring himself to spring to that, but she was so touched that he should give her anything that she could not help crying.

'What an emotional little thing you are,' he said, but he was pleased and touched to see her tears.

She found his thrift rather an engaging trait. He could not bear to throw his money about. He was not exactly mean, but he was not generous. Once or twice at restaurants she thought he undertipped the waiter, but he paid no attention to her when she ventured to remonstrate. He gave the exact ten per cent, and when he could not make the exact sum to a penny asked the waiter for change.

'Neither a borrower nor a lender be,' he quoted from Polonius.

When some member of the company, momentarily hard up, tried to borrow from him it was in vain. But he refused so frankly, with so much heartiness, that he did not affront.

'My dear old boy, I'd love to lend you a quid, but I'm absolutely stony. I don't know how I'm going to pay my rent at the end of the week.'

For some months Michael was so much occupied with his own parts that he failed to notice how good an actress Julia was. Of course he read the reviews, and their praise of Julia, but he read summarily, without paying much attention till he came to the remarks the critics made about him. He was pleased by their approval, but not cast down by their censure. He was too modest to resent an unfavourable criticism.

'I suppose I was rotten,' he would say ingenuously.

His most engaging trait was his good humour. He bore Jimmie Langton's abuse with equanimity. When tempers grew frayed during a long rehearsal he remained serene. It was impossible to quarrel with him. One day he was sitting in front watching the rehearsal of an act in which he did not appear. It ended with a powerful and moving scene in which Julia had the opportunity to give a fine display of acting. When the stage was being set for the next act Julia came through the pass door and sat down beside Michael. He did not speak to her, but looked sternly in front of him. She threw him a surprised look. It was unlike him not to give her a smile and a friendly word. Then she saw that he was clenching his jaw to prevent its trembling and that his eyes were heavy with tears.

'What's the matter, darling?'

'Don't talk to me. You dirty little bitch, you've made me cry.'

'Angel!'

The tears came to her own eyes and streamed down her face. She was so pleased, so flattered.

'Oh, damn it,' he sobbed. 'I can't help it.'

He took a handkerchief out of his pocket and dried his eyes.

('I love him, I love him, I love him.')

Presently he blew his nose.

'I'm beginning to feel better now. But, my God, you shattered me.'

'It's not a bad scene, is it?'

'The scene be damned, it was you. You just wrung my heart. The critics are right, damn it, you're an actress and no mistake.'

'Have you only just discovered it?'

'I knew you were pretty good, but I never knew you were as good as all that. You make the rest of us look like a piece of cheese. You're going to be a star. Nothing can stop you.'

'Well then, you shall be my leading man.'

'Fat chance I'd have of that with a London manager.'

Julia had an inspiration.

'Then you must go into management yourself and make me your leading lady.'

He paused. He was not a quick thinker and needed a little time to let a notion sink into his mind. He smiled.

'You know that's not half a bad idea.'

They talked it over at luncheon. Julia did most of the talking while he listened to her with absorbed interest.

'Of course the only way to get decent parts consistently is to run one's own theatre,' he said. 'I know that.'

The money was the difficulty. They discussed how much was the least they could start on. Michael thought five thousand pounds was the minimum. But how in heaven's name could they raise a sum like that? Of course some of those Middlepool manufacturers were rolling in money, but you could hardly expect them to fork out five thousand pounds to start a couple of young actors who had only a local reputation. Besides, they were jealous of London.

'You'll have to find your rich old woman,' said Julia gaily.

She only half believed all she had been saying, but it excited her to discuss a plan that would bring her into a close and constant relation with Michael. But he was being very serious.

'I don't believe one could hope to make a success in London unless one were pretty well known already. The thing to do would be to act there in other managements for three or four years first; one's got to know the ropes. And the advantage of that would be that one would have had time to read plays. It would be madness to start in management unless one had at least three plays. One of them out to be a winner.'

'Of course if one did that, one ought to make a point of acting together so that the public got accustomed to seeing the two names on the same bill.'

'I don't know that there's much in that. The great thing is to have good, strong parts. There's no doubt in my mind that it would be much easier to find backers if one had made a bit of a reputation in London.'

Chapter Four

It was getting on for Easter, and Jimmie Langton always closed his theatre for Holy Week. Julia did not quite know what to do with herself; it seemed hardly worth while to go to Jersey. She was surprised to receive a letter one morning from Mrs Gosselyn, Michael's mother, saying that it would give the Colonel and herself so much pleasure if she would come with Michael to spend the week at Cheltenham. When she showed the letter to Michael he beamed.

'I asked her to invite you. I thought it would be more polite than if I just took you along.'

'You are sweet. Of course I shall love to come.'

Her heart beat with delight. The prospect of spending a whole week with Michael was enchanting. It was just like his good nature to come to the rescue when he knew she was at a loose end. But she saw there was something he wanted to say, yet did not quite like to.

'What is it?'

He gave a little laugh of embarrassment.

'Well, dear, you know, my father's rather old-fashioned, and there are some things he can't be expected to understand. Of course I don't want you to tell a lie or anything like that, but I think it would seem rather funny to him if he knew your father was a vet. When I wrote and asked if I could bring you down I said he was a doctor.'

'Oh, that's all right.'

Julia found the Colonel a much less alarming person than she had expected. He was thin and rather small, with a lined face and close-cropped white hair. His features had a worn distinction. He reminded you of a head of an old coin that had been in circulation too long. He was civil, but reserved. He was neither peppery nor tyrannical as Julia, from her knowledge of the stage, expected a colonel to be. She could not imagine him shouting out words of command in that courteous, rather cold voice. He had in point of fact retired with honorary rank after an entirely undistinguished career, and for many years had been content to work in his garden and play bridge at his club. He read *The Times*, went to church on Sunday and accompanied his wife to tea-parties. Mrs Gosselyn was a tall, stoutish, elderly woman, much taller than her husband, who gave you the impression that she was always trying to diminish her height. She had the remains of good looks, so that you said to yourself that when young she must have been beautiful. She wore her hair parted in the middle with a bun on the nape of her neck. Her classic features and her size made her at first meeting somewhat imposing, but Julia quickly discovered that she was very shy. Her movements were stiff and awkward. She was dressed fussily, with a sort of old-fashioned richness which did not suit her. Julia, who was entirely without self-consciousness, found the elder woman's deprecating attitude rather touching. She had never known an actress to speak to and did not quite know how to deal with the predicament in which she now found herself. The house was not at all grand, a small detached stucco house in a garden with a laurel hedge, and since the Gosselyns had been for some years in India there were great trays of brass ware and brass bowls, pieces of Indian embroidery and highly-carved Indian tables. It was cheap bazaar stuff, and you wondered how anyone had thought it worth bringing home.

Julia was quick-witted. It did not take her long to discover that the Colonel, notwithstanding his reserve, and Mrs Gosselyn, notwithstanding her shyness, were taking stock of her. The thought flashed through her mind that Michael had brought her down for his parents to inspect her. Why? There was only one possible reason, and when she thought of it her heart leaped. She saw that he was anxious for her to make a good impression. She felt instinctively that she must conceal the actress, and without effort, without deliberation, merely because she felt it would please, she played the part of the simple, modest, ingenuous girl who had lived a quiet country life. She walked round the garden with the Colonel and listened intelligently while he talked of peas and asparagus; she helped Mrs Gosselyn with the flowers and dusted the ornaments with which the drawing-room was crowded. She talked to her of Michael. She told her how cleverly he acted and how popular he was and she praised his looks. She saw that Mrs Gosselyn was very proud of him, and with a flash of intuition saw that it would please her if she let her see, with the utmost delicacy, as though she would have liked to keep it a secret but betrayed herself unwittingly, that she was head over ears in love with him.

'Of course we hope he'll do well,' said Mrs Gosselyn. 'We didn't much like the idea of his going on the stage; you see, on both sides of the family, we're army, but he was set on it.'

'Yes, of course I see what you mean.'

'I know it doesn't mean so much as when I was a girl, but after all he was born a gentleman.'

'Oh, but some very nice people go on the stage nowadays, you know. It's not like in the old days.'

'No, I suppose not. I'm so glad he brought you down here. I was a little nervous about it. I thought you'd be made-up and . . . perhaps a little loud. No one would dream you were on the stage.'

('I should damn well think not. Haven't I been giving a perfect performance of the village maiden for the last forty-eight hours?')

The Colonel began to make little jokes with her and sometimes he pinched her ear playfully.

'Now you mustn't flirt with me, Colonel,' she cried, giving him a roguish, delicious glance. 'Just because I'm an actress you think you can take liberties with me.'

'George, George,' smiled Mrs Gosselyn. And then to Julia: 'He always was a terrible flirt.'

('Gosh, I'm going down like a barrel of oysters.')

Mrs Gosselyn told her about India, how strange it was to have all those coloured servants, but how nice the society was, only army people and Indian civilians, but still it wasn't like home, and how glad she was to get back to England.

They were to leave on Easter Monday because they were playing that night, and on Sunday evening after supper Colonel Gosselyn said he was going to his study to write letters; a minute or two later Mrs Gosselyn said she must go and see the cook. When they were left alone Michael, standing with his back to the fire, lit a cigarette.

'I'm afraid it's been very quiet down here; I hope you haven't had an awfully dull time.'

'It's been heavenly.'

'You've made a tremendous success with my people. They've taken an enormous fancy to you.'

'God, I've worked for it,' thought Julia, but aloud said: 'How d'you know?'

'Oh, I can see it. Father told me you were very ladylike, and not a bit like an actress, and mother says you're so sensible.'

Julia looked down as though the extravagance of these compliments was almost more than she could bear. Michael came over and stood in front of her. The thought occurred to her that he looked like a handsome young footman applying for a situation. He was strangely nervous. Her heart thumped against her ribs.

'Julia dear, will you marry me?'

For the last week she had asked herself whether or not he was going to propose to her, and now that he had at last done so, she was strangely confused.

'Michael!'

'Not immediately, I don't mean. But when we've got our feet on the ladder. I know that you can act me off the stage, but we get on together like a house on fire, and when we do go into management I think we'd make a pretty good team. And you know I do like you most awfully. I mean, I've never met anyone who's a patch on you.'

('The blasted fool, why does he talk all that rot? Doesn't he know I'm crazy to marry him? Why doesn't he kiss me, kiss me, kiss me? I wonder if I dare tell him I'm absolutely sick with love for him.')

'Michael, you're so handsome. No one could refuse to marry you!'

'Darling!'

('I'd better get up. He wouldn't know how to sit down. God, that scene that Jimmie made him do over and over again!')

She got on her feet and put up her face to his. He took her in his arms and kissed her lips.

'I must tell mother.'

He broke away from her and went to the door.

'Mother, mother!'

In a moment the Colonel and Mrs Gosselyn came in. They bore a look of happy expectancy.

('By God, it was a put-up job.')

'Mother, father, we're engaged.'

Mrs Gosselyn began to cry. With her awkward, lumbering gait she came up to Julia, flung her arms round her, and sobbing, kissed her. The Colonel wrung his son's hand in a manly way and releasing Julia from his wife's embrace kissed her too. He was deeply moved. All this emotion worked on Julia and, though she smiled happily, the tears coursed down her cheeks. Michael watched the affecting scene with sympathy.

'What d'you say to a bottle of pop to celebrate?' he said. 'It looks to me as though mother and Julia were thoroughly upset.'

'The ladies, God bless 'em,' said the Colonel when their glasses were filled.

Chapter Five

Julia now was looking at the photograph of herself in her wedding-dress.

'Christ, what a sight I looked.'

They decided to keep their engagement to themselves, and Julia told no one about it but Jimmie Langton, two or three girls in the company and her dresser. She vowed them to secrecy and could not understand how within forty-eight hours everyone in the theatre seemed to know all about it. Julia was divinely happy. She loved Michael more passionately than ever and would gladly have married him there and then, but his good sense prevailed. They were at present no more than a couple of provincial actors, and to start their conquest of London as a married couple would jeopardize their chances. Julia showed him as clearly as she knew how, and this was very clearly indeed, that she was quite willing to become his mistress, but this he refused. He was too honourable to take advantage of her.

'I could not love thee, dear, so much, loved I not honour more,' he quoted.

He felt sure that when they were married they would bitterly regret it if they had lived together before as man and wife. Julia was proud of his principles. He was a kind and affectionate lover, but in a very short while seemed to take her a trifle for granted; by his manner, friendly but casual, you might have thought they had been married for years. But he showed great good nature in allowing Julia to make love to him. She adored to sit cuddled up to him with his arm round her waist, her face against his, and it was heaven when she could press her eager mouth against his rather thin lips. Though when they sat side by side like that he preferred to talk of the parts they were studying or make plans for the future, he made her very happy. She never tired of praising his beauty. It was heavenly, when she told him how exquisite his nose was and how lovely his russet, curly hair, to feel his hold on her tighten a little and to see the tenderness in his eyes.

'Darling, you'll make me as vain as a peacock.'

'It would be so silly to pretend you weren't divinely handsome.'

Julia thought he was, and she said it because she liked saying it, but she said it also because she knew he liked to hear it. He had affection and admiration for her, he felt at ease with her, and he had confidence in her, but she was well aware that he was not in love with her. She consoled herself by thinking that he loved her as much as he was capable of loving, and she thought that when they were married, when they slept together, her own passion would excite an equal passion in him. Meanwhile she exercised all her tact and all her self-control. She knew she could not afford to bore him. She knew she must never let him feel that she was a burden or a responsibility. He might desert her for a game of golf, or to lunch with a casual acquaintance, she never let him see for a moment that she was hurt. And with an inkling that her success as an actress strengthened his feeling for her she worked like a dog to play well.

When they had been engaged for rather more than a year an American manager, looking for talent and having heard of Jimmie Langton's repertory company, came to Middlepool and was greatly taken by Michael. He sent him round a note asking him to come to his hotel on the following afternoon. Michael, breathless with excitement, showed it to Julia; it could only mean that he was going to offer him a part. Her heart sank, but she pretended that she was as excited as he, and went with him next day to the hotel. She was to wait in the lobby while Michael saw the great man.

'Wish me luck,' he whispered, as he turned from her to enter the lift. 'It's almost too good to be true.'

Julia sat in a great leather armchair willing with all her might the American manager to offer a part that Michael would refuse or a salary that he felt it would be beneath his dignity to accept. Or alternatively that he should get Michael to read the part he had in view and come to the conclusion that he could not touch it. But when she saw Michael coming towards her half an hour later, his eyes bright and his step swinging, she knew he had clicked. For a moment she thought she was going to be sick, and when she forced on her face an eager, happy smile, she felt that her muscles were stiff and hard.

'It's all right. He says it's a damned good part, a boy's part, nineteen. Eight or ten weeks in New York and then on the road. It's a safe forty weeks with John Drew. Two hundred and fifty dollars a week.'

'Oh, darling, how wonderful for you.'

It was quite clear that he had accepted with alacrity. The thought of refusing had never even occurred to him.

'And I—I,' she thought, 'if they'd offered me a thousand dollars a week I wouldn't have gone if it meant being separated from Michael.'

Black despair seized her. She could do nothing. She must pretend to be as delighted as he was. He was too much excited to sit still and took her out into the crowded street to walk.

'It's a wonderful chance. Of course America's expensive, but I ought to be able to live on fifty dollars a week at the outside, they say the Americans are awfully hospitable and I shall get a lot of free meals. I don't see why I shouldn't save eight thousand dollars in the forty weeks and that's sixteen hundred pounds.'

('He doesn't love me. He doesn't care a damn about me. I hate him. I'd like to kill him. Blast that American manager.')

'And if he takes me on for a second year I'm to get three hundred. That means that in two years I'd have the best part of four thousand pounds. Almost enough to start management on.'

'A second year!' For a moment Julia lost control of herself and her voice was heavy with tears. 'D'you mean to say you'll be gone two years?'

'Oh, I should come back next summer of course. They pay my fare back and I'd go and live at home so as not to spend any money.'

'I don't know how I'm going to get on without you.'

She said the words very brightly, so that they sounded polite, but somewhat casual.

'Well, we can have a grand time together in the summer and you know a year, two years at the outside, well, it passes like a flash of lightning.'

Michael had been walking at random, but Julia without his noticing had guided him in the direction she wished, and now they arrived in front of the theatre. She stopped.

'I'll see you later. I've got to pop up and see Jimmie.' His face fell.

'You're not going to leave me now! I must talk to somebody. I thought we might go and have a snack together before the show.'

'I'm terribly sorry. Jimmie's expecting me and you know what he is.' Michael gave her his sweet, good-natured smile.

'Oh, well, go on then. I'm not going to hold it up against you because for once you've let me down.'

He walked on and she went in by the stage door. Jimmie Langton had arranged himself a tiny flat under the roof to which you gained access through the balcony. She rang the bell of his front door and he opened it himself. He was surprised, but pleased, to see her.

'Hulloa, Julia, come in.'

She walked past him without a word, and when they got into his sitting-room, untidy, littered with typescript plays, books and other rubbish, the remains of his frugal luncheon still on a tray by his desk, she turned and faced him. Her jaw was set and her eyes were frowning.

'You devil!'

With a swift gesture she went up to him, seized him by his loose shirt collar with both hands and shook him. He struggled to get free of her, but she was strong and violent.

'Stop it. Stop it.'

'You devil, you swine, you filthy low-down cad.'

He took a swing and with his open hand gave her a great smack on the face. She instinctively loosened her grip on him and put her own hand up to her cheek, for he had hurt her. She burst out crying.

'You brute. You rotten hound to hit a woman.'

'You put that where the monkey put the nuts, dearie. Didn't you know that when a woman hits me I always hit back?'

'I didn't hit you.'

'You damned near throttled me.'

'You deserved it. Oh, my God, I'd like to kill you.'

'Now sit down, duckie, and I'll give you a drop of Scotch to pull you together. And then you can tell me all about it.'

Julia looked round for a big chair into which she could conveniently sink.

'Christ, the place is like a pig-sty. Why the hell don't you get a charwoman in?'

With an angry gesture she swept the books on to the floor from an armchair, threw herself in it, and began to cry in earnest. He poured her out a stiff dose of whisky, added a drop of soda, and made her drink it.

'Now what's all this Tosca stuff about?'

'Michael's going to America.'

'Is he?'

She wrenched herself away from the arm he had round her shoulder.

'How could you? How could you?'

'I had nothing to do with it.'

'That's a lie. I suppose you didn't even know that filthy American manager was in Middlepool. Of course it's your doing. You did it deliberately to separate us.'

'Oh, dearie, you're doing me an injustice. In point of fact I don't mind telling you that I said to him he could have anyone in the company he liked with the one exception of Michael Gosselyn.'

Julia did not see the look in Jimmie's eyes when he told her this, but if she had would have wondered why he was looking as pleased as if he had pulled off a very clever little trick.

'Even me?' she said.

'I knew he didn't want women. They've got plenty of their own. It's men they want who know how to wear their clothes and don't spit in the drawing-room.'

'Oh, Jimmie, don't let Michael go. I can't bear it.'

'How can I prevent it? His contract's up at the end of the season. It's a wonderful chance for him.'

'But I love him. I want him. Supposing he sees someone else in America. Supposing some American heiress falls in love with him.'

'If he doesn't love you any more than that I should have thought you'd be well rid of him.'

The remark revived Julia's fury.

'You rotten old eunuch, what do you know about love?'

'These women,' Jimmie sighed. 'If you try to go to bed with them they say you're a dirty old man, and if you don't they say you're a rotten old eunuch.'

'Oh, you don't understand. He's so frightfully handsome, they'll fall for him like a row of ninepins, and poor lamb, he's so susceptible to flattery. Anything can happen in two years.'

'What's this about two years?'

'If he's a success he's to stay another year.'

'Well, don't worry your head about that. He'll be back at the end of the season and back for good. That manager only saw him in *Candida*. It's the only part he's half-way decent in. Take my word for it, it won't be long before they find out they've been sold a pup. He's going to be a flop.'

'What do you know about acting?'

'Everything.'

'I'd like to scratch your eyes out.'

'I warn you that if you attempt to touch me I shan't give you a little bit of a slap, I shall give you such a biff on the jaw that you won't be able to eat in comfort for a week.'

'By God, I believe you'd do it. Do you call yourself a gentleman?'

'Not even when I'm drunk.'

Julia giggled, and Jimmie felt the worst of the scene was over.

'Now you know just as well as I do that you can act him off his head. I tell you, you're going to be the greatest actress since Mrs Kendal. What do you want to go and hamper yourself with a man who'll always be a millstone round your neck? You want to go into management; he'll want to play opposite you. He'll never be good enough, my dear.'

'He's got looks. I can carry him.'

'You've got a pretty good opinion of yourself, haven't you? But you're wrong. If you want to make a success you can't afford to have a leading man who's not up to the mark.'

'I don't care. I'd rather marry him and be a failure than be a success and married to somebody else.'

'Are you a virgin?'

Julia giggled again.

'I don't know that it's any business of yours, but in point of fact I am.'

'I thought you were. Well, unless it means something to you, why don't you go over to Paris with him for a fortnight when we close? He won't be sailing till August. It might get him out of your system.'

'Oh, he wouldn't. He's not that sort of man. You see, he's by way of being a gentleman.'

'Even the upper classes propagate their species.'

'You don't understand,' said Julia haughtily.

'I bet you don't either.'

Julia did not condescend to reply. She was really very unhappy.

'I can't live without him, I tell you. What am I to do with myself when he's away?'

'Stay on with me. I'll give you a contract for another year. I've got a lot of new parts I want to give you and I've got a juvenile in my eye who's a find. You'll be surprised how much easier you'll find it when you've got a chap opposite you who'll really give you something. You can have twelve pounds a week.'

Julia went up to him and stared into his eyes searchingly.

'Have you done all this to get me to stay on for another year? Have you broken my heart and ruined my whole life just to keep me in your rotten theatre?'

'I swear I haven't. I like you and I admire you. And we've done better business the last two years than we've ever done before. But damn it, I wouldn't play you a dirty trick like that.'

'You liar, you filthy liar.'

'I swear it's the truth.'

'Prove it then,' she said violently.

'How can I prove it? You know I'm decent really.'

'Give me fifteen pounds a week and I'll believe you.'

'Fifteen pounds a week? You know what our takings are. How can I? Oh well, all right. But I shall have to pay three pounds out of my own pocket.'

'A fat lot I care.'

Chapter Six

After a fortnight of rehearsals, Michael was thrown out of the part for which he had been engaged, and for three or four weeks was left to kick his heels about till something else could be found for him. He opened in due course in a play that ran less than a month in New York. It was sent on the road; but languished and was withdrawn. After another wait he was given a part in a costume play where his good looks shone to such advantage that his indifferent acting was little noticed, and in this he finished the season. There was no talk of renewing his contract. Indeed the manager who had engaged him was caustic in his comments.

'Gee, I'd give something to get even with that fellow Langton, the son of a bitch,' he said. 'He knew what he was doing all right when he landed me with that stick.'

Julia wrote to Michael constantly, pages and pages of love and gossip, while he answered once a week, four pages exactly in a neat, precise hand. He always ended up by sending her his best love and signing himself hers very affectionately, but the rest of his letter was more informative than passionate. Yet she awaited its coming in an agony of impatience and read it oer and over again. Though he wrote cheerfully, saying little about the theatre except that the parts they gave him were rotten and the plays in which he was expected to act beneath contempt, news travels in the theatrical world, and Julia knew that he had not made good.

'I suppose it's beastly of me,' she thought, 'but thank God, thank God.'

When he announced the date of his sailing she could not contain her joy. She got Jimmie so to arrange his programme that she might go and meet him at Liverpool.

'If the boat comes in late I shall probably stay the night,' she told Jimmie.

He smiled ironically.

'I suppose you think that in the excitement of home-coming you may work the trick.'

'What a beastly little man you are.'

'Come off it, dear. My advice to you is, get him a bit tight and then lock yourself in a room with him and tell him you won't let him out till he's made a dishonest woman of you.'

But when she was starting he came to the station with her. As she was getting into the carriage he took her hand and patted it.

'Feeling nervous, dear?'

'Oh, Jimmie dear, wild with happiness and sick with anxiety.'

'Well, good luck to you. And don't forget you're much too good for him. You're young and pretty and you're the greatest actress in England.'

When the train steamed out Jimmie went to the station bar and had a whisky and soda, 'Lord, what fools these mortals be,' he sighed. But Julia stood up in the empty carriage and looked at herself in the glass.

'Mouth too large, face too puddingy, nose too fleshy. Thank God, I've got good eyes and good legs. Exquisite legs. I wonder if I've got too much make-up on. He doesn't like make-up off the stage. I look bloody without rouge. My eyelashes are all right. Damn it all, I don't look so bad.'

Uncertain till the last moment whether Jimmie would allow her to go, Julia had not been able to let Michael know that she was meeting him. He was surprised and frankly delighted to see her. His beautiful eyes beamed with pleasure.

'You're more lovely than ever,' she said.

'Oh, don't be so silly,' he laughed, squeezing her arm affectionately. 'You haven't got to go back till after dinner, have you?'

'I haven't got to go back till tomorrow. I've taken a couple of rooms at the Adelphi, so that we can have a real talk.'

'The Adelphi's a bit grand, isn't it?'

'Oh, well, you don't come back from America every day. Damn the expense.'

'Extravagant little thing, aren't you? I didn't know when we'd dock, so I told my people I'd wire when I was getting down to Cheltenham. I'll tell them I'll be coming along tomorrow.'

When they got to the hotel Michael came to Julia's room, at her suggestion, so that they could talk in peace and quiet. She sat on his knees, with her arm round his neck, her cheek against his.

'Oh, it's so good to be home again,' she sighed.

'You don't have to tell me that,' he said, not understanding that she referred to his arms and not to his arrival.

'D'you still like me?'

'Rather.'

She kissed him fondly.

'Oh, you don't know how I've missed you.'

'I was an awful flop in America,' he said. 'I didn't tell you in my letters, because I thought it would only worry you. They thought me rotten.'

'Michael,' she cried, as though she could not believe him.

'The fact is, I suppose, I'm too English. They don't want me another year. I didn't think they did, but just as a matter of form I asked them if they were going to exercise their option and they said no, not at any price.'

Julia was silent. She looked deeply concerned, but her heart was beating with exultation.

'I honestly don't care you know. I didn't like America. It's a smack in the eye of course, it's no good denying that, but the only thing is to grin and bear it. If you only knew the people one has to deal with! Why, compared with some of them, Jimmie Langton's a great gentleman. Even if they had wanted me to stay I should have refused.'

Though he put a brave face on it, Julia felt that he was deeply mortified. He must have had to put up with a good deal of unpleasantness. She hated him to have been made unhappy, but, oh, she was so relieved.

'What are you going to do now?' she asked quietly.

'Well, I shall go home for a bit and think things over. Then I shall go to London and see if I can't get a part.'

She knew that it was no good suggesting that he should come back to Middlepool. Jimmie Langton would not have him.

'You wouldn't like to come with me, I suppose?'

Julia could hardly believe her ears.

'Me? Darling, you know I'd go anywhere in the world with you.'

'Your contract's up at the end of this season, and if you want to get anywhere you've got to make a stab at London soon. I saved every bob I could in America, they all called me a tight-wad but I just let them talk, I've brought back between twelve and fifteen hundred pounds.'

'Michael, how on earth can you have done that?'

'I didn't give much away, you know,' he smiled happily. 'Of course it's not enough to start management on, but it's enough to get married on, I mean we'd have something to fall back on if we didn't get parts right away or happened to be out of a job for a few months.'

It took Julia a second or two to understand what he meant.

'D'you mean to say, get married now?'

'Of course it's a risk, without anything in prospect, but one has to take a risk sometimes.'

Julia took his head in both her hands and pressed his lips with hers. Then she gave a sigh.

'Darling, you're wonderful and you're as beautiful as a Greek god, but you're the biggest damned fool I've ever known in my life.'

They went to a theatre that night and at supper drank champagne to celebrate their reunion and toast their future. When Michael accompanied her to her room she held up her face to his.

'D'you want me to say good night to you in the passage? I'll just come in for a minute.'

'Better not, darling,' she said with quiet dignity.

She felt like a high-born damsel, with all the traditions of a great and ancient family to keep up; her purity was a pearl of great price; she also felt that she was making a wonderfully good impression: of course he was a great gentleman, and 'damn it all' it behoved her to be a great lady. She was so pleased with her performance that when she had got into her room and somewhat noisily locked the door, she paraded up and down bowing right and left graciously to her obsequious retainers. She stretched out her lilly white hand for the trembling old steward to kiss (as a baby he had often dandled her on his knee), and when he pressed it with his pallid lips she felt something fall upon it. A tear.

Chapter Seven

The first year of their marriage would have been stormy except for Michael's placidity. It needed the excitement of getting a part or a first night, the gaiety of a party where he had drunk several glasses of champagne, to turn his practical mind to thoughts of love. No flattery, no allurements, could tempt him when he had an engagement next day for which he had to keep his brain clear or a round of golf for which he needed a steady eye. Julia made him frantic scenes. She was jealous of his friends at the Green Room Club, jealous of the games that took him away from her, and jealous of the men's luncheons he went to under the pretext that he must cultivate people who might be useful to them. It infuriated her that when she worked herself up into a passion of tears he should sit there quite calmly, with his hands crossed and a good-humoured smile on his handsome face, as though she were merely making herself ridiculous.

'You don't think I'm running after any other woman, do you?' he asked.

'How do I know? It's quite obvious that you don't care two straws for me.'

'You know you're the only woman in the world for me.'

'My God!'

'I don't know what you want.'

'I want love. I thought I'd married the handsomest man in England and I've married a tailor's dummy.'

'Don't be so silly. I'm just the ordinary normal Englishman. I'm not an Italian organ-grinder.'

She swept up and down the room. They had a small flat at Buckingham Gate and there was not much space, but she did her best. She threw up her hands to heaven.

'I might be squint-eyed and hump-backed. I might be fifty. Am I so unattractive as all that? It's so humiliating to have to beg for love. Misery, misery.'

'That was a good movement, dear. As if you were throwing a cricket ball. Remember that.'

She gave him a look of scorn.

'That's all you can think of. My heart is breaking, and you can talk of a movement that I made quite accidentally.'

But he saw by the expression of her face that she was registering it in her memory, and he knew that when the occasion arose she would make effective use of it.

'After all love isn't everything. It's all very well at its proper time and in its proper place. We had a lot of fun on our honeymoon, that's what a honeymoon's for, but now we've got to get down to work.'

They had been lucky. They had managed to get fairly good parts together in a play that had proved a success. Julia had one good acting scene in which she had brought down the house, and Michael's astonishing beauty had made a sensation. Michael with his gentlemanly push, with his breezy good-nature, had got them both a lot of publicity and their photographs appeared in the illustrated papers. They were asked to a number of parties and Michael notwithstanding his thriftiness, did not hesitate to spend money on entertaining people who might be of service. Julia was impressed by his lavishness on these occasions. An actor-manager offered Julia the leading part in his next play, and though there was no part for Michael and she was anxious to refuse it, he would not let her. He said they could not afford to let sentiment stand in the way of business. He eventually got a part in a costume play.

They were both acting when war broke out. To Julia's pride and anguish Michael enlisted at once, but with the help of his father, one of whose old brother officers was an important personage at the War Office, he very soon got a commission. When he went out to France Julia bitterly regretted the reproaches she had so often heaped upon him, and made up her mind that if he were killed she would commit suicide. She wanted to become a nurse so that she could go out to France too and at least be on the same soil as he, but he made her understand that patriotism demanded that she should go on acting, and she could not resist what might very well be his dying request. Michael thoroughly enjoyed the war. He was popular in the regimental mess, and the officers of the old army accepted him almost at once, even though he was an actor, as one of themselves. It was as though the family of soldiers from which he was born had set a seal on him so that he fell instinctively into the manner and way of thinking of the professional soldier. He had tact and a pleasant manner, and he knew how to pull strings adroitly; it was inevitable that he should get on the staff of some general. He showed himself possessed of considerable organizing capacity and the last three years of the war he passed at G.H.Q. He ended it as a major, with the Military Cross and the Legion of Honour.

Meanwhile Julia had been playing a succession of important parts and was recognized as the best of the younger actresses. Throughout the war the theatre was very prosperous, and she profited by being seen in plays that had long runs. Salaries went up, and with Michael to advise her she was able to extort eighty pounds a week from reluctant managers. Michael came over to England on his leaves and Julia was divinely happy. Though he was in no more danger than if he had been sheep-farming in New Zealand, she acted as though the brief periods he spent with her were the last days the doomed man would ever enjoy on earth. She treated him as though he had just come from the horror of the trenches and was tender, considerate, and unexacting.

It was just before the end of the war that she fell out of love with him.

She was pregnant at the time. Michael had judged it imprudent to have a baby just then, but she was nearly thirty and thought that if they were going to have one at all they ought to delay no longer; she was so well established on the stage that she could afford not to appear for a few months, and with the possibility that Michael might be killed at any moment—it was true he said he was as safe as a house, he only said that to reassure her, and even generals were killed sometimes—if she was to go on living she must have a child by him. The baby was expected at the end of the year. She looked forward to Michael's next leave as she had never done before. She was feeling very well, but she had a great yearning to feel his arms around her, she felt a little lost, a little helpless, and she wanted his protective strength. He came, looking wonderfully handsome in his well-cut uniform, with the red tabs and the crown on his shoulder-straps. He had filled out a good deal as the result of the hardships of G.H.Q. and his skin was tanned. With his close-cropped hair, breezy manner and military carriage he looked every inch a soldier. He was in great spirits, not only because he was home for a few days, but because the end of the war was in sight. He meant to get out of the army as quickly as possible. What was the good of having a bit of influence if you didn't use it? So many young men had left the stage, either from patriotism or because life was made intolerable for them by the patriotic who stayed at home, and finally owing to conscription, that leading parts had been in the hands either of people who were inapt for military service or those who had been so badly wounded that they had got their discharge. There was a wonderful opening, and Michael saw that if he were available quickly he could get his choice of parts. When he had recalled himself to the recollection of the public they could look about for a theatre, and with the reputation Julia had now acquired it would be safe to start in management.

They talked late into the night and then they went to bed. She cuddled up to him voluptuously and he put his arms round her. After three months of abstinence he was amorous.

'You're the most wonderful little wife,' he whispered.

He pressed his mouth to hers. She was filled on a sudden with a faint disgust. She had to resist an inclination to push him away. Before, to her passionate nostrils his body, his young beautiful body, had seemed to have a perfume of flowers and honey, and this had been one of the things that had most enchained her to him, but now in some strange way it had left him. She realized that he no longer smelt like a youth, he smelt like a man. She felt a little sick. She could not respond to his ardour, she was eager that he should get his desire satisfied quickly, turn over on his side, and go to sleep. For long she lay awake. She was dismayed. Her heart sank because she knew she had lost something that was infinitely precious to her, and pitying herself she was inclined to cry; but at the same time she was filled with a sense of triumph, it seemed a revenge that she enjoyed for the unhappiness he had caused her; she was free of the bondage in which her senses had held her to him and she exulted. Now she could deal with him on equal terms. She stretched her legs out in bed and sighed with relief.

'By God, it's grand to be one's own mistress.'

They had breakfast in their room, Julia in bed and Michael seated at a little table by her side. She looked at him while he read the paper. Was it possible that three months had made so much difference in him, or was it merely that for years she had still seen him with the eyes that had seen him when he came on the stage to rehearse at Middlepool in the glorious beauty of his youth and she had been stricken as with a mortal sickness? He was wonderfully handsome still, after all he was only thirty-six, but he was not a boy any more; with his close-cropped hair and weather-beaten skin, little lines beginning to mark the smoothness of his forehead and to show under his eyes, he was definitely a man. He had lost his coltish grace and his movements were set. Each difference was very small, but taken altogether they amounted, in her shrewd, calculating eyes, to all the difference in the world. He was a middle-aged man.

They still lived in the small flat that they had taken when first they came to London. Though Julia had been for some time earning a good income it had not seemed worth while to move while Michael was on active service, but now that a baby was coming the flat was obviously too small. Julia had found a house in Regent's Park that she liked very much. She wanted to be settled down in good time for her confinement.

The house faced the gardens. Above the drawing-room floor were two bedrooms and above these, two rooms that could be made into a day and a night nursery. Michael was pleased with everything; even the price seemed to him reasonable. Julia had, during the last four years, been earning so much more money than he that she had offered to furnish the house herself. They stood in one of the bedrooms.

'I can make do with a good deal of what we've got for my bedroom,' she said. 'I'll get you a nice suite at Maple's.'

'I wouldn't go to much expense,' he smiled. 'I don't suppose I shall use it much, you know.'

He liked to share a bed with her. Though not passionate he was affectionate, and he had an animal desire to feel her body against his. For long it had been her greatest comfort. The thought now filled her with irritation.

'Oh, I don't think there should be any more nonsense till after the baby's born. Until all that's over and done with I'm going to make you sleep by yourself.'

'I hadn't thought of that. If you think it's better for the kid . . .'

Chapter Eight

Michael got himself demobbed the moment the war was finished and stepped straight into a part. He returned to the stage a much better actor than he left it. The breeziness he had acquired in the army was effective. He was a well set-up, normal, high-spirited fellow, with a ready smile and a hearty laugh. He was well suited to drawing-room comedy. His light voice gave a peculiar effect to a flippant line, and though he never managed to make love convincingly he could carry off a chaffing love scene, making a proposal as if it were rather a joke, or a declaration as though he were laughing at himself, in a manner that the audience found engaging. He never attempted to play anyone but himself. He specialized in men about town, gentlemanly gamblers, guardsmen and young scamps with a good side to them. Managers liked him. He worked hard and was amenable to direction. So long as he could get work he didn't mind much what sort of part it was. He stuck out for the salary he thought he was worth, but if he couldn't get it was prepared to take less rather than be idle.

He was making his plans carefully. During the winter that followed the end of the war there was an epidemic of influenza. His father and mother died. He inherited nearly four thousand pounds, and this with his own savings and Julia's brought up their joint capital to seven thousand. But the rent of theatres had gone up enormously, the salaries of actors and the wages of stage-hands had increased, so that the expense of running a theatre was very much greater than it had been before the war. A sum that would then have been amply sufficient to start management on was now inadequate. The only thing was to find some rich man to go in with them so that a failure or two to begin with would not drive them from the field. It was said that you could always find a mug in the city to write a fat cheque for the production of a play, but when you came down to business you discovered that the main condition was that the leading part should be played by some pretty lady in whom he was interested. Years before, Michael and Julia had often joked about the rich old woman who would fall in love with him and set him up in management. He had long since learnt that no rich old woman was to be found to set up in management a young actor whose wife was an actress to whom he was perfectly faithful. In the end the money was found by a rich woman, and not an old one either, but who was interested not in him but in Julia.

Mrs de Vries was a widow. She was a short stout woman with a fine Jewish nose and fine Jewish eyes, a great deal of energy, a manner at once effusive and timid, and a somewhat virile air. She had a passion for the stage. When Julia and Michael had decided to try their luck in London Jimmie Langton, to whose rescue she had sometimes come when it looked as though he would be forced to close his repertory theatre, had written to her asking her to do what she could for them. She had seen Julia act in Middlepool. She gave parties so that the young actors might get to know managers, and asked them to stay at her grand house near Guildford, where they enjoyed a luxury they had never dreamt of. She did not much like Michael. Julia accepted the flowers with which Dolly de Vries filled her flat and her dressing-room, she was properly delighted with the presents she gave her, bags, vanity cases, strings of beads in semi-precious stones, brooches; but appeared to be unconscious that Dolly's generosity was due to anything but admiration for her talent. When Michael went away to the war Dolly pressed her to come and live in her house in Montagu Square, but Julia, with protestations of extravagant gratitude, refused in such a way that Dolly, with a sigh and a tear, could only admire her the more. When Roger was born Julia asked her to be his godmother.

For some time Michael had been turning over in his mind the possibility that Dolly de Vries might put up the money they needed, but he was shrewd enough to know that while she might do it for Julia she would not do it for him. Julia refused to approach her.

'She's already been so kind to us I really couldn't ask her, and it would be so humiliating if she refused.'

'It's a good gamble, and even if she lost the money she wouldn't feel it. I'm quite sure you could get round her if you tried.'

Julia was pretty sure she could too. Michael was very simple-minded in some ways; she did not feel called upon to point out to him the obvious facts.

But he was not a man who let a thing drop when he had set his mind to it. They were going to Guildford to spend the week-end with Dolly, and were driving down after the Saturday night's performance in the new car that Julia had given Michael for his birthday. It was a warm beautiful night. Michael had bought options, though it wrung his heart to write the cheques, on three plays that they both liked, and he had heard of a theatre that they could get on reasonable terms. Everything was ready for the venture except the capital. He urged Julia to seize the opportunity that the week-end presented.

'Ask her yourself then,' said Julia impatiently. 'I tell you, I'm not going to.'

'She wouldn't do it for me. You can twist her round your little finger.'

'We know a thing or two about financing plays now. People finance plays for two reasons, either because they want notoriety, or because they're in love with someone. A lot of people talk about art, but you don't often find them paying out hard cash unless they're going to get something out of it for themselves.'

'Well, we'll give Dolly all the notoriety she wants.'

'That doesn't happen to be what she's after.'

'What do you mean?'

'Can't you guess?'

Light dawned on him, and he was so surprised that he slowed down. Was it possible that what Julia suspected was true? He had never even thought that Dolly liked him much, and as for supposing she was in love with him—why, the notion had never crossed his mind. Of course Julia had sharp eyes, not much got by her, but she was a jealous little thing, she was always thinking women were making a dead set at him. It was true that Dolly had given him a pair of cuff-links at Christmas, but he thought that was only so that he shouldn't feel left out in the cold because she had given Julia a brooch that must have cost at least two hundred pounds. That might be only her cunning. Well, he could honestly say he'd never done a thing to make her think there was anything doing. Julia giggled.

'No, darling, it's not you she's in love with.'

It was disconcerting the way Julia knew what he was thinking. You couldn't hide a thing from that woman.

'Then why did you put the idea into my head? I wish to goodness you'd express yourself so that a fellow can understand.'

Julia did.

'I never heard such nonsense,' he cried. 'What a filthy mind you've got, Julia!'

'Come off it, dear.'

'I don't believe there's a word of truth in it. After all I've got eyes in my head. Do you mean to say I shouldn't have noticed it?' He was more irritable than she had ever known him. 'And even if it were true I suppose you can take care of yourself. It's a chance in a thousand, and I think it would be madness not to take it.'

'Claudio and Isabella in *Measure for Measure*.'

'That's a rotten thing to say, Julia. God damn it, I am a gentleman.'

'Nemo me impune lacessit.'

They drove the rest of the journey in stormy silence. Mrs de Vries was waiting up for them.

'I didn't want to go to bed till I'd seen you,' she said as she folded Julia in her arms and kissed her on both cheeks. She gave Michael a brisk handshake.

Julia spent a happy morning in bed reading the Sunday papers. She read first the theatrical news, then the gossip columns, after that the woman's pages, and finally cast an eye over the head-lines of the world's news. The book reviews she ignored; she could never understand why so much space was wasted on them. Michael, who had the room next hers, had come in to say good morning, and then gone out into the garden. Presently there was a timid little knock at the door and Dilly came in. Her great black eyes were shining. She sat on the bed and took Julia's hand.

'Darling, I've been talking to Michael. I'm going to put up the money to start you in management.'

Julia's heart gave a sudden beat.

'Oh, you mustn't. Michael shouldn't have asked you. I won't have it. You've been far, far too kind to us already.'

Dolly leant over and kissed Julia on the lips. Her voice was lower than usual and there was a little tremor in it.

'Oh, my love, don't you know there isn't anything in the world I wouldn't do for you? It'll be so wonderful; it'll bring us so close together and I shall be so proud of you.'

They heard Michael come whistling along the passage, and when he came into the room Dolly turned to him with her great eyes misty with tears.

'I've just told her.'

He was brimming over with excitement.

'What a grand woman!' He sat down on the other side of the bed and took Julia's disengaged hand.

'What d'you say, Julia?'

She gave him a little reflective look.

'Vous l'avez voulu, Georges Dandin.'

'What's that?'

'Molière.'

As soon as the deed of partnership had been signed and Michael had got his theatre booked for the autumn he engaged a publicity agent. Paragraphs were sent to the papers announcing the new venture and Michael and the publicity agent prepared interviews for him and Julia to give to the Press. Photographs of them, singly and together, with and without Roger, appeared in the weeklies. The domestic note was worked for all it was worth. They could not quite make up their minds which of the three plays they had it would be best to start with. Then one afternoon when Julia was sitting in her bedroom reading a novel, Michael came in with a manuscript in his hand.

'Look here, I want you to read this play at once. It's just come in from an agent. I think it's a knockout. Only we've got to give an answer right away.'

Julia put down her novel.

'I'll read it now.'

'I shall be downstairs. Let me know when you've finished and I'll come up and talk it over with you. It's got a wonderful part for you.'

Julia read quickly, skimming over the scenes in which she was not concerned, but the principal woman's part, the part of course she would play, with concentration. When she had turned the last page she rang the bell and asked her maid (who was also her dresser) to tell Michael she was ready for him.

'Well, what d'you think?'

'The play's all right. I don't see how it can fail to be a success.'

He caught something doubtful in her tone.

'What's wrong then? The part's wonderful. I mean, it's the sort of thing that you can do better than anyone in the world. There's a lot of comedy and all the emotion you want.'

'It's a wonderful part, I know that; it's the man's part.'

'Well, that's a damned good part too.'

'I know; but he's fifty, and if you make him younger you take all the point out of the play. You don't want to take the part of a middle-aged man.'

'But I wasn't thinking of playing that. There's only one man for that. Monte Vernon. And we can get him. I'll play George.'

'But it's a tiny part. You can't play that.'

'Why not?'

'But I thought the point of going into management was that we should both play leads.'

'Oh, I don't care a hang about that. As long as we can find plays with star parts for you I don't matter. Perhaps in the next play there'll be a good part for me too.'

Julia leant back in her chair, and the ready tears filled her eyes and ran down her cheeks.

'Oh, what a beast I am.'

He smiled, and his smile was as charming as ever. He came over to her and kneeling by her side put his arms round her.

'Lor Lumme, what's the matter with the old lady now?'

When she looked at him now she wondered what there was in him that had ever aroused in her such a frenzy of passion. The thought of having sexual relations with him nauseated her. Fortunately he found himself very comfortable in the bedroom she had furnished for him. He was not a man to whom sex was important, and he was relieved when he discovered that Julia no longer made any demands on him. He thought with satisfaction that the birth of the baby had calmed her down, he was bound to say that he had thought it might, and he was only sorry they had not had one before. When he had two or three times, more out of amiability than out of desire, suggested that they should resume marital relations and she had made excuses, either that she was tired, not very well, or had two performances next day, to say nothing of a fitting in the morning, he accepted the situation with equanimity. Julia was much easier to get on with, she never made scenes any more, and he was happier than he had ever been before. It was a damned satisfactory marriage he had made, and when he looked at other people's marriages he couldn't help seeing he was one of the lucky ones. Julia was a damned good sort and clever, as clever as a bagful of monkeys; you could talk to her about anything in the world. The best companion a chap ever had, my boy. He didn't mind saying this, he'd rather spend a day alone with her than play a round of golf.

Julia was surprised to discover in herself a strange feeling of pity for him because she no longer loved him. She was a kindly woman, and she realized that it would be a bitter blow to his pride if he ever had an inkling how little he meant to her. She continued to flatter him. She noticed that for long now he had come to listen complacently to her praise of his exquisite nose and beautiful eyes. She got a little private amusement by seeing how much he could swallow. She laid it on with a trowel. But now she looked more often at his straight thin-lipped mouth. It grew meaner as he grew older, and by the time he was an old man it would be no more than a cold hard line. His thrift, which in the early days had seemed an amusing, rather touching trait, now revolted her. When people were in trouble, and on the stage they too often are, they got sympathy and kind friendly words from Michael, but very little cash. He looked upon himself as devilish generous when he parted with a guinea, and a five-pound note was to him the extreme of lavishness. He had soon discovered that Julia ran the house extravagantly, and insisting that he wanted to save her trouble took the matter in his own hands. After that nothing was wasted. Every penny was accounted for. Julia wondered why servants stayed with them. They did because Michael was so nice to them. With his hearty, jolly, affable manner he made them anxious to please him, and the cook shared his satisfaction when she had found a butcher from whom they could get meat a penny a pound cheaper than elsewhere. Julia could not but laugh when she thought how strangely his passion for economy contrasted with the devil-may-care, extravagant creatures he portrayed so well on the stage. She had often thought that he was incapable of a generous impulse; and now, as though it were the most natural thing in the world, he was prepared to stand aside so that she might have her chance. She was too deeply moved to speak. She reproached herself bitterly for all the unkind things she had for so long been thinking of him.

Chapter Nine

They put on the play, and it was a success. After that they continued to produce plays year after year. Because Michael ran the theatre with the method and thrift with which he ran his home they lost little over the failures, which of course they sometimes had, and made every possible penny out of their successes. Michael flattered himself that there was not a management in London where less money was spent on the productions. He exercised great ingenuity in disguising old sets so that they looked new, and by ringing the changes on the furniture that he gradually collected in the store-room saved the expense of hiring. They gained the reputation of being an enterprising management because Michael in order not to pay the high royalties of well-known authors was always willing to give an unknown one a trial. He sought out actors who had never been given a chance and whose salaries were small. He thus made some very profitable discoveries.

When they had been in management for three years they were sufficiently well established for Michael to be able to borrow from the bank enough money to buy the lease of a theatre that had just been built. After much discussion they decided to call it the Siddons Theatre. They opened with a failure and this was succeeded by another. Julia was frightened and discouraged. She thought that the theatre was unlucky and that the public were getting sick of her. It was then that Michael showed himself at his best. He was unperturbed.

'In this business you have to take the rough with the smooth. You're the best actress in England. There are only three people who bring money into the theatre regardless of the play, and you're one of them. We've had a couple of duds. The next play's bound to be all right and then we shall get back all we've lost and a packet into the bargain.'

As soon as Michael had felt himself safe he had tried to buy Dolly de Vries out, but she would not listen to his persuasion and was indifferent to his coldness. For once his cunning found its match. Dolly saw no reason to sell out an investment that seemed sound, and her half share in the partnership kept her in close touch with Julia. But now with great courage he made another effort to get rid of her. Dolly indignantly refused to desert them when they were in difficulties, and he gave it up as a bad job. He consoled himself by thinking that Dolly might leave Roger, her godson, a great deal of money. She had no one belonging to her but nephews in South Africa, and you could not look at her without suspecting that she had a high blood pressure. Meanwhile it was convenient to have the house near Guildford to go to whenever they wished. It saved the expense of having a country house of their own. The third play was a winner, and Michael did not hesitate to point out how right he had been. He spoke as though he was directly responsible for its success. Julia could almost have wished that it had failed like the others in order to take him down a peg or two. For his conceit was outrageous. Of course you had to admit that he had a sort of cleverness, shrewdness rather, but he was not nearly so clever as he thought himself. There was nothing in which he did not think that he knew better than anybody else.

As time went on he began to act less frequently. He found himself much more interested in management.

'I want to run my theatre in as business-like a way as a city office,' he said.

And he felt that he could more profitably spend his evenings, when Julia was acting, by going to outlying theatres and trying to find talent. He kept a little book in which he made a note of every actor who seemed to show promise. Then he had taken to directing. It had always grizzled him that directors should ask so much money for rehearsing a play, and of late some of them had even insisted on a percentage on the gross. At last an occasion came when the two directors Julia liked best were engaged and the only other one she trusted was acting and thus could not give them all his time.

'I've got a good mind to have a shot at it myself,' said Michael.

Julia was doubtful. He had no fantasy and his ideas were commonplace. She was not sure that he would have authority over the cast. But the only available director demanded a fee that they both thought exorbitant and there was nothing left but to let Michael try. He made a much better job of it than Julia expected. He was thorough; he worked hard. Julia, strangely enough, felt that he was getting more out of her than any other director had done. He knew what she was capable of, and, familiar with her every inflection, every glance of her wonderful eyes, every graceful movement of her body, he was able to give her suggestions out of which she managed to build up the best performance of her career. With the cast he was at once conciliatory and exacting. When tempers were frayed his good humour, his real kindliness, smoothed things over. After that there was no question but that he should continue to direct their plays. Authors liked him because, being unimaginative, he was forced to let the plays speak for themselves and often not being quite sure what they meant he was obliged to listen to them.

Julia was now a rich woman. She could not but admit that Michael was as careful of her money as of his own. He watched her investments and was as pleased when he could sell stocks at a profit on her account as if he had made the money for himself. He put her down for a very large salary, and was proud to be able to say that she was the most highly-paid actress in London, but when he himself acted he never put himself down for a higher salary than he thought the part was worth. When he directed a play he put down on the expense account the fee that a director of the second rank would have received. They shared the expenses of the house and the cost of Roger's education. Roger had been entered for Eton within a week of his birth. It was impossible to deny that Michael was scrupulously fair and honest. When Julia realized how much richer she was than he she wanted to pay all these expenses herself.

'There's no reason why you should,' said Michael. 'As long as I can pay my whack I'll pay it. You earn more than I do because you're worth more. I put you down for a good salary because you draw it.'

No one could do other than admire the self-abnegation with which he sacrificed himself for her sake. Any ambition he may have had for himself he had abandoned in order to foster her career. Even Dolly, who did not like him, acknowledged his unselfishness. A sort of modesty had always prevented Julia from discussing him with Dolly, but Dolly, with her shrewdness, had long seen how intensely Michael exasperated his wife, and now and then took the trouble to point out how useful he was to her. Everybody praised him. A perfect husband. It seemed to her that none but she knew what it was like to live with a man who was such a monster of vanity. His complacency when he had beaten an opponent at golf or got the better of someone in a business deal was infuriating. He gloried in his artfulness. He was a bore, a crashing bore. He liked to tell Julia everything he did and every scheme that passed through his head; it had been charming when merely to have him with her was a delight, but for years she had found his prosiness intolerable. He could describe nothing without circumstantial detail. Nor was he only vain of his business acumen; with advancing years he had become outrageously vain of his person. As a youth he had taken his beauty for granted: now he began to pay more attention to it and spared no pains to keep what was left of it. It became an obsession. He devoted anxious care to his figure. He never ate a fattening thing and never forgot his exercises. He consulted hair specialists when he thought his hair was thinning, and Julia was convinced that had it been possible to get the operation done secretly he would have had his face lifted. He had got into the way of sitting with his chin slightly thrust out so that the wrinkles in his neck should not show and he held himself with an arched back to keep his belly from sagging. He could not pass a mirror without looking into it. He hankered for compliments and beamed with delight when he had managed to extract one. They were food and drink to him. Julia laughed bitterly when she remembered that it was she who had accustomed him to them. For years she had told him how beautiful he was and now he could not live without flattery. It was the only chink in his armour. An actress out of a job had only to tell him to his face that he was too handsome to be true for him to think that she might do for a part he had in mind. For years, so far as Julia knew, Michael had not bothered with women, but when he reached the middle forties he began to have little flirtations. Julia suspected that nothing much came of them. He was prudent, and all he wanted was admiration. She had heard that when women became pressing he used her as a pretext to get rid of them. Either he couldn't risk doing anything to hurt her, or she was jealous or suspicious and it seemed better that the friendship should cease.

'God knows what they see in him,' Julia exclaimed to the empty room.

She took up half a dozen of his later photographs at random and looked at them carefully one by one. She shrugged her shoulders.

'Well, I suppose I can't blame them, I fell in love with him too. Of course he was better-looking in those days.'

It made Julia a little sad to think how much she had loved him. Because her love had died she felt that life had cheated her. She sighed.

'And my back's aching,' she said.

Chapter Ten

There was a knock at the door.

'Come in,' said Julia.

Evie entered.

'Aren't you going to bed today, Miss Lambert?' She saw Julia sitting on the floor surrounded by masses of photographs. 'Whatever are you doing?'

'Dreaming.' She took up two of the photographs. 'Look here upon this picture, and on this.'

One was of Michael as Mercutio in all the radiant beauty of his youth and the other of Michael in the last part he had played, in a white topper and a morning coat, with a pair of field-glasses slung over his shoulder. He looked unbelievably self-satisfied.

Evie sniffed.

'Oh, well, it's no good crying over spilt milk.'

'I've been thinking of the past and I'm as blue as the devil.'

'I don't wonder. When you start thinking of the past it means you ain't got no future, don't it?'

'You shut your trap, you old cow,' said Julia, who could be very vulgar when she chose.

'Come on now, or you'll be fit for nothing tonight. I'll clear up all this mess.'

Evie was Julia's dresser and maid. She had come to her first at Middlepool and had accompanied her to London. She was a cockney, a thin, raddled, angular woman, with red hair which was always untidy and looked as if it much needed washing; two of her front teeth were missing but, notwithstanding Julia's offer, repeated for years, to provide her with new ones she would not have them replaced.

'For the little I eat I've got all the teeth I want. It'd only fidget me to 'ave a lot of elephant's tusks in me mouth.'

Michael had long wanted Julia at least to get a maid whose appearance was more suitable to their position, and he had tried to persuade Evie that the work was too much for her, but Evie would not hear of it.

'You can say what you like, Mr Gosselyn, but no one's going to maid Miss Lambert as long as I've got me 'ealth and strength.'

'We're all getting on, you know, Evie. We're not so young as we were.'

Evie drew her forefinger across the base of her nostrils and sniffed.

'As long as Miss Lambert's young enough to play women of twenty-five, I'm young enough to dress 'er. And maid 'er.' Evie gave him a sharp look. 'An' what d'you want to pay two lots of wages for, when you can get the work done for one?'

Michael chuckled in his good-humoured way.

'There's something in that, Evie dear.'

She bustled Julia upstairs. When she had no matinée Julia went to bed for a couple of hours in the afternoon and then had a light massage. She undressed now and slipped between the sheets.

'Damn, my hot water bottle's nearly stone cold.'

She looked at the clock on the chimney-piece. It was no wonder. It must have been there an hour. She had no notion that she had stayed so long in Michael's room, looking at those photographs and idly thinking of the past.

'Forty-six. Forty-six. Forty-six. I shall retire when I'm sixty. At fifty-eight South Africa and Australia. Michael says we can clean up there. Twenty thousand pounds. I can play all my old parts. Of course even at sixty I could play women of forty-five. But what about parts? Those bloody dramatists.'

Trying to remember any plays in which there was a first-rate part for a woman of five-and-forty she fell asleep. She slept soundly till Evie came to awake her because the masseuse was there. Evie brought her the evening paper, and Julia, stripped, while the masseuse rubbed her long slim legs and her belly, putting on her spectacles, read the same theatrical intelligence she had read that morning, the gossip column and the woman's page. Presently Michael came in and sat on her bed. He often came at that hour to have a little chat with her.

'Well, what was his name?' asked Julia.

'Whose name?'

'The boy who came to lunch?'

'I haven't a notion. I drove him back to the theatre. I never gave him another thought.'

Miss Phillips, the masseuse, liked Michael. You knew where you were with him. He always said the same things and you knew exactly what to answer. No side to him. And terribly good-looking. My word.

'Well, Miss Phillips, fat coming off nicely?'

'Oh, Mr Gosselyn, there's not an ounce of fat on Miss Lambert. I think it's wonderful the way she keeps her figure.'

'Pity I can't have you to massage me, Miss Phillips. You might be able to do something about mine.'

'How you talk, Mr Gosselyn. Why, you've got the figure of a boy of twenty. I don't know how you do it, upon my word I don't.'

'Plain living and high thinking, Miss Phillips.'

Julia was paying no attention to what they said, but Miss Phillips's reply reached her.

'Of course there's nothing like massage, I always say that, but you've got to be careful of your diet. That there's no doubt about at all.'

'Diet!' she thought. 'When I'm sixty I shall let myself go. I shall eat all the bread and butter I like. I'll have hot rolls for breakfast, I'll have potatoes for lunch and potatoes for dinner. And beer. God, how I like beer. Pea soup and tomato soup; treacle pudding and cherry tart. Cream, cream, cream. And so help me God, I'll never eat spinach again as long as I live.'

When the massage was finished Evie brought her a cup of tea, a slice of ham from which the fat had been cut, and some dry toast. Julia got up, dressed, and went down with Michael to the theatre. She liked to be there an hour before the curtain rang up. Michael went on to dine at his club. Evie had preceded her in a cab and when she got into her dressing-room everything was ready for her. She undressed once more and put on a dressing-gown. As she sat down at her dressing-table to make up she noticed some fresh flowers in a vase.

'Hulloa, who sent them? Mrs de Vries?'

Dolly always sent her a huge basket on her first nights, and on the hundredth night, and the two hundredth if there was one, and in between, whenever she ordered flowers for her own house, had some sent to Julia.

'No, miss.'

'Lord Charles?'

Lord Charles Tamerley was the oldest and most constant of Julia's admirers, and when he passed a florist's he was very apt to drop in and order some roses for her.

'Here's the card,' said Evie.

Julia looked at it. Mr Thomas Fennell. Tavistock Square.

'What a place to live. Who the hell d'you suppose he is, Evie?'

'Some feller knocked all of a heap by your fatal beauty, I expect.'

'They must have cost all of a pound. Tavistock Square doesn't look very prosperous to me. For all you know he may have gone without his dinner for a week to buy them.'

'I don't think.'

Julia plastered her face with grease paint.

'You're so damned unromantic, Evie. Just because I'm not a chorus girl you can't understand why anyone should send me flowers. And God knows, I've got better legs than most of them.'

'You and your legs,' said Evie.

'Well, I don't mind telling you I think it's a bit of all right having an unknown young man sending me flowers at my time of life. I mean it just shows you.'

'If he saw you now 'e wouldn't, not if I know anything about men.'

'Go to hell,' said Julia.

But when she was made up to her satisfaction, and Evie had put on her stockings and her shoes, having a few minutes still to spare she sat down at her desk and in her straggling bold hand wrote to Mr Thomas Fennell a gushing note of thanks for his beautiful flowers. She was naturally polite and it was, besides, a principle with her to answer all fan letters. That was how she kept in touch with her public. Having addressed the envelope she threw the card in the waste-paper basket and was ready to slip into her first act dress. The call-boy came round knocking at the dressing-room doors.

'Beginners, please.'

Those words, though heaven only knew how often she had heard them, still gave her a thrill. They braced her like a tonic. Life acquired significance. She was about to step from the world of make-believe into the world of reality.

Chapter Eleven

Next day Julia had luncheon with Charles Tamerley. His father, the Marquess of Dennorant, had married an heiress and he had inherited a considerable fortune. Julia often went to the luncheon parties he was fond of giving at his house in Hill Street. At the bottom of her heart she had a profound contempt for the great ladies and the noble lords she met there, because she was a working woman and an artist, but she knew the connection was useful. It enabled them to have first nights at the Siddons which the papers described as brilliant, and when she was photographed at week-end parties among a number of aristocratic persons she knew that it was good publicity. There were one or two leading ladies, younger than she, who did not like her any better because she called at least two duchesses by their first names. This caused her no regret. Julia was not a brilliant conversationalist, but her eyes were so bright, her manner so intelligent, that once she had learnt the language of society she passed for a very amusing woman. She had a great gift of mimicry, which ordinarily she kept in check thinking it was bad for her acting, but in these circles she turned it to good account and by means of it acquired the reputation of a wit. She was pleased that they liked her, these smart, idle women, but she laughed at them up her sleeve because they were dazzled by her glamour. She wondered what they would think if they really knew how unromantic the life of a successful actress was, the hard work it entailed, the constant care one had to take of oneself and the regular, monotonous habits which were essential. But she good-naturedly offered them advice on make-up and let them copy her clothes. She was always beautifully dressed. Even Michael, fondly thinking she got her clothes for nothing, did not know how much she really spent on them.

Morally she had the best of both worlds. Everyone knew that her marriage with Michael was exemplary. She was a pattern of conjugal fidelity. At the same time many people in that particular set were convinced that she was Charles Tamerley's mistress. It was an affair that was supposed to have been going on so long that it had acquired respectability, and tolerant hostesses when they were asked to the same house for a week-end gave them adjoining rooms. This belief had been started by Lady Charles, from whom Charles Tamerley had been long separated, and in point of fact there was not a word of truth in it. The only foundation for it was that Charles had been madly in love with her for twenty years, and it was certainly on Julia's account that the Tamerleys, who had never got on very well, agreed to separate. It was indeed Lady Charles who had first brought Julia and Charles together. They happened, all three, to be lunching at Dolly de Vries' when Julia, a young actress, had made her first great success in London. It was a large party and she was being made much of. Lady Charles, a woman of over thirty then, who had the reputation of being a beauty, though except for her eyes she had not a good feature, but by a sort of brazen audacity managed to produce an effective appearance, leant across the table with a gracious smile.

'Oh, Miss Lambert, I think I used to know your father in Jersey. He was a doctor, wasn't he? He used to come to our house quite often.'

Julia felt a slight sickness in the pit of her stomach; she remembered now who Lady Charles was before she married, and she saw the trap that was being set for her. She gave a rippling laugh.

'Not at all,' she answered. 'He was a vet. He used to go to your house to deliver the bitches. The house was full of them.'

Lady Charles for a moment did not quite know what to say.

'My mother was very fond of dogs,' she answered.

Julia was glad that Michael was not there. Poor lamb, he would have been terribly mortified. He always referred to her father as Dr Lambert, pronouncing it as though it were a French name, and when soon after the war he died and her mother went to live with her widowed sister at St Malo he began to speak of her as Madame de Lambert. At the beginning of her career Julia had been somewhat sensitive on the point, but when once she was established as a great actress she changed her mind. She was inclined, especially among the great, to insist on the fact that her father had been a vet. She could not quite have explained why, but she felt that by so doing she put them in their place.

But Charles Tamerley knew that his wife had deliberately tried to humiliate the young woman, and angered, went out of his way to be nice to her. He asked her if he might be allowed to call and brought her some beautiful flowers.

He was then a man of nearly forty, with a small head on an elegant body, not very good-looking but of distinguished appearance. He looked very well-bred, which indeed he was, and he had exquisite manners. He was an amateur of the arts. He bought modern pictures and collected old furniture. He was a lover of music and exceedingly well read. At first it amused him to go to the tiny flat off the Buckingham Palace Road in which these two young actors lived. He saw that they were poor and it excited him to get into touch with what he fondly thought was Bohemia. He came several times and he thought it quite an adventure when they asked him to have a luncheon with them which was cooked and served by a scarecrow of a woman whom they called Evie. This was life. He did not pay much attention to Michael who seemed to him, notwithstanding his too obvious beauty, a somewhat ordinary young man, but he was taken by Julia. She had a warmth, a force of character, and a bubbling vitality which were outside his experience. He went to see her act several times and compared her performance with his recollections of the great foreign actresses. It seemed to him that she had in her something quite individual. Her magnetism was incontestable. It gave him quite a thrill to realize on a sudden that she had genius.

'Another Siddons perhaps. A greater Ellen Terry.'

In those days Julia did not think it necessary to go to bed in the afternoons, she was as strong as a horse and never tired, so he used often to take her for walks in the Park. She felt that he wanted her to be a child of nature. That suited her very well. It was no effort for her to be ingenuous, frank and girlishly delighted with everything. He took her to the National Gallery, and the Tate, and the British Museum, and she really enjoyed it almost as much as she said. He liked to impart information and she was glad to receive it. She had a retentive memory and learnt a great deal from him. If later she was able to talk about Proust and Cézanne with the best of them, so that you were surprised and pleased to find so much culture in an actress, it was to him she owed it. She knew that he had fallen in love with her some time before he knew it himself. She found it rather comic. From her standpoint he was a middle-aged man, and she thought of him as a nice old thing. She was madly in love with Michael. When Charles realized that he loved her his manner changed a little, he seemed struck with shyness and when they were together was often silent.

'Poor lamb,' she said to herself, 'he's such a hell of a gentleman he doesn't know what to do about it.'

But she had already prepared her course of conduct for the declaration which she felt he would sooner or later bring himself to make. One thing she was going to make quite clear to him. She wasn't going to let him think that because he was a lord and she was an actress he had only to beckon and she would hop into bed with him. If he tried that sort of thing she'd play the outraged heroine on him, with the outflung arm and the index extended in the same line, as Jane Taitbout had taught her to make the gesture, pointed at the door. On the other hand if he was shattered and tongue-tied, she'd be all tremulous herself, sobs in the voice and all that, and she'd say it had never dawned on her that he felt like that about her, and no, no, it would break Michael's heart. They'd have a good cry together and then everything would be all right. With his beautiful manners she could count upon him not making a nuisance of himself when she had once got it into his head that there was nothing doing.

But when it happened it did not turn out in the least as she had expected. Charles Tamerley and Julia had been for a walk in St James's Park, they had looked at the pelicans, and the scene suggesting it, they had discussed the possibility of her playing Millamant on a Sunday evening. They went back to Julia's flat to have a cup of tea. They shared a crumpet. Then Charles got up to go. He took a miniature out of his pocket and gave it to her.

'It's a portrait of Clairon. She was an eighteenth-century actress and she had many of your gifts.

Julia looked at the pretty, clever face, with the powdered hair, and wondered whether the stones that framed the little picture were diamonds or only paste.

'Oh, Charles, how can you! You are sweet.'

'I thought you might like it. It's by way of being a parting present.'

'Are you going away?'

She was surprised, for he had said nothing about it. He looked at her with a faint smile.

'No. But I'm not going to see you any more.'

'Why?'

'I think you know just as well as I do.'

Then Julia did a disgraceful thing. She sat down and for a minute looked silently at the miniature. Timing it perfectly, she raised her eyes till they met Charles's. She could cry almost at will, it was one of her most telling accomplishments, and now without a sound, without a sob, the tears poured down her cheeks. With her mouth slightly open, with the look in her eyes of a child that has been deeply hurt and does not know why, the effect was unbearably pathetic. His face was crossed by a twinge of agony. When he spoke his voice was hoarse with emotion.

'You're in love with Michael, aren't you?'

She gave a little nod. She tightened her lips as though she were trying to control herself, but the tears rolled down her cheeks.

'There's no chance for me at all?' He waited for some answer from her, but she gave none, she raised her hand to her mouth and seemed to bite a nail, and still she stared at him with those streaming eyes. 'Don't you know what torture it is to go on seeing you? D'you want me to go on seeing you?'

Again she gave a little nod.

'Clara's making me scenes about you. She's found out I'm in love with you. It's only common sense that we shouldn't see one another any more.'

This time Julia slightly shook her head. She gave a sob. She leant back in the chair and turned her head aside. Her whole body seemed to express the hopelessness of her grief. Flesh and blood couldn't stand it. Charles stepped forward and sinking to his knees took that broken woebegone body in his arms.

'For God's sake don't look so unhappy. I can't bear it. Oh, Julia, Julia, I love you so much, I can't make you so miserable. I'll accept anything. I'll make no demands on you.'

She turned her tear-stained face to him ('God, what a sight I must look now') and gave him her lips. He kissed her tenderly. It was the first time he had ever kissed her.

'I don't want to lose you,' she muttered huskily.

'Darling, darling!'

'It'll be just as it was before?'

'Just.'

She gave a deep sigh of contentment and for a minute or two rested in his arms. When he went away she got up and looked in the glass.

'You rotten bitch,' she said to herself.

But she giggled as though she were not in the least ashamed and then went into the bathroom to wash her face and eyes. She felt wonderfully exhilarated. She heard Michael come in and called out to him.

'Michael, look at that miniature Charles has just given me. It's on the chimney-piece. Are those diamonds or paste?'

Julia was somewhat nervous when Lady Charles left her husband. She threatened to bring proceedings for divorce, and Julia did not at all like the idea of appearing as intervener. For two or three weeks she was very jittery. She decided to say nothing to Michael till it was necessary, and she was glad she had not, for in due course it appeared that the threats had been made only to extract more substantial alimony from the innocent husband. Julia managed Charles with wonderful skill. It was understood between them that her great love for Michael made any close relation between them out of the question, but so far as the rest was concerned he was everything to her, her friend, her adviser, her confidant, the man she could rely on in any emergency or go to for comfort in any disappointment. It was a little more difficult when Charles, with his fine sensitiveness, saw that she was no longer in love with Michael. Then Julia had to exercise a great deal of tact. It was not that she had any scruples about being his mistress; if he had been an actor who loved her so much and had loved her so long she would not have minded popping into bed with him out of sheer good nature; but she just did not fancy him. She was very fond of him, but he was so elegant, so well-bred, so cultured, she could not think of him as a lover. It would be like going to bed with an objet d'art. And his love of art filled her with a faint derision; after all she was a creator, when all was said and done he was only the public. He wished her to elope with him. They would buy a villa at Sorrento on the bay of Naples, with a large garden, and they would have a schooner so that they could spend long days on the beautiful wine-coloured sea. Love and beauty and art; the world well lost.

'The damned fool,' she thought. 'As if I'd give up my career to bury myself in some hole in Italy!'

She persuaded him that she had a duty to Michael, and then there was the baby; she couldn't let him grow up with the burden on his young life that his mother was a bad woman. Orange trees or no orange trees, she would never have a moment's peace in that beautiful Italian villa if she was tortured by the thought of Michael's unhappiness and her baby being looked after by strangers. One couldn't only think of oneself, could one? One had to think of others too. She was very sweet and womanly. She sometimes asked Charles why he did not arrange a divorce with his wife and marry some nice woman. She could not bear the thought of his wasting his life over her. He told her that she was the only woman he had ever loved and that he must go on loving her till the end.

'It seems so sad,' said Julia.

All the same she kept her eyes open, and if she noticed that any woman had predatory intentions on Charles she took care to queer her pitch. She did not hesitate if the danger seemed to warrant it to show herself extremely jealous. It had been long agreed, with all the delicacy that might be expected from his good-breeding and Julia's good heart, in no definite words, but with guarded hints and remote allusiveness, that if anything happened to Michael, Lady Charles should somehow or other be disposed of and they would then marry. But Michael had perfect health.

On this occasion Julia had much enjoyed lunching at Hill Street. The party had been very grand. Julia had never encouraged Charles to entertain any of the actors or authors he sometimes came across, and she was the only person there who had ever had to earn a living. She had sat between an old, fat, bald and loquacious Cabinet Minister who took a great deal of trouble to entertain her, and a young Duke of Westreys who looked like a stable-boy and who flattered himself that he knew French slang better than a Frenchman. When he discovered that Julia spoke French he insisted on conversing with her in that language. After luncheon she was persuaded to recite a tirade from *Phèdre* as it was done at the Comédie Française and the same tirade as an English student at the Royal Academy of Dramatic Art would deliver it. She made the company laugh very much and came away from the party flushed with success. It was a fine bright day and she made up her mind to walk from Hill Street to Stanhope Place. A good many people recognized her as she threaded her way through the crowd in Oxford Street, and though she looked straight ahead of her she was conscious of their glances.

'What a hell of a nuisance it is that one can't go anywhere without people staring at one.'

She slackened her pace a little. It certainly was a beautiful day.

She let herself into her house with a latch-key and as she got in heard the telephone ringing. Without thinking she took up the receiver.

'Yes?'

She generally disguised her voice when she answered, but for once forgot to.

'Miss Lambert?'

'I don't know if Miss Lambert's in. Who is it please?' she asked, assuming quickly a cockney accent.

The monosyllable had betrayed her. A chuckle travelled over the wire.

'I only wanted to thank you for writing to me. You know, you needn't have troubled. It was so nice of you to ask me to lunch, I thought I'd like to send you a few flowers.'

The sound of his voice and the words told her who it was. It was the blushing young man whose name she did not know. Even now, though she had looked at his card, she could not remember it. The only thing that had struck her was that he lived in Tavistock Square.

'It was very sweet of you,' she answered, in her own voice.

'I suppose you wouldn't come to tea with me one day, would you?'

The nerve of it! She wouldn't go to tea with a duchess; he was treating her like a chorus girl. It was rather funny when you came to think of it.

'I don't know why not.'

'Will you really?' his voice sounded eager. He had a pleasant voice. 'When?'

She did not feel at all like going to bed that afternoon.

'Today.'

'O.K. I'll get away from the office. Half-past four? 138, Tavistock Square.'

It was nice of him to have suggested that. He might so easily have mentioned some fashionable place where people would stare at her. It proved that he didn't just want to be seen with her.

She took a taxi to Tavistock Square. She was pleased with herself. She was doing a good action. It would be wonderful for him in after years to be able to tell his wife and children that Julia Lambert had been to tea with him when he was just a little insignificant clerk in an accountant's office. And she had been so simple and so natural. No one to hear her prattling away would have guessed that she was the greatest actress in England. And if they didn't believe him he'd have her photograph to prove it, signed yours sincerely. He'd laugh and say that of course if he hadn't been such a kid he'd never have had the cheek to ask her.

When she arrived at the house and had paid off the taxi she suddenly remembered that she did not know his name and when the maid answered the door would not know whom to ask for. But on looking for the bell she noticed that there were eight of them, four rows of two, and by the side of each was a card or a name written in ink on a piece of paper. It was an old house that had been divided up into flats. She began looking, rather hopelessly, at the names wondering whether one of them would recall something, when the door opened and he stood before her.

'I saw you drive up and I ran down. I'm afraid I'm on the third floor. I hope you don't mind.'

'Of course not.'

She climbed the uncarpeted stairs. She was a trifle out of breath when she came to the third landing. He had skipped up eagerly, like a young goat, she thought, and she had not liked to suggest that she would prefer to go more leisurely. The room into which he led her was fairly large, but dingily furnished. On the table was a plate of cakes and two cups, a sugar basin and a milk-jug. The crockery was of the cheapest sort.

'Take a pew,' he said. 'The water's just on the boil. I'll only be a minute. I've got a gas-ring in the bathroom.'

He left her and she looked about.

'Poor lamb, he must be as poor as a church mouse.'

The room reminded her very much of some of the lodgings she had lived in when she was first on the stage. She noticed the pathetic attempts he had made to conceal the fact that it was a bedroom as well as a sitting-room. The divan against the wall was evidently his bed at night. The years slipped away from her in fancy and she felt strangely young again. What fun they had had in rooms very like that and how they had enjoyed the fantastic meals they had had, things in paper bags and eggs and bacon fried on the gas-ring! He came in with the tea in a brown pot. She ate a square sponge-cake with pink icing on it. That was a thing she had not done for years. The Ceylon tea, very strong, with milk and sugar in it, took her back to days she thought she had forgotten. She saw herself as a young, obscure, struggling actress. It was rather delicious. It needed a gesture, but she could only think of one: she took off her hat and gave her head a shake.

They talked. He seemed shy, much shyer than he had seemed over the telephone; well, that was not to be wondered at, now she was there he must be rather overcome, and she set herself to put him at his ease. He told her that his parents lived at Highgate, his father was a solicitor, and he had lived there too, but he wanted to be his own master and now in the last year of his articles he had broken away and taken his tiny flat. He was working for his final examination. They talked of the theatre. He had seen her in every play she had acted in since he was twelve years old. He told her that once when he was fourteen he had stood outside the stage-door after a matinée and when she came out had asked her to sign her name in his autograph-book. He was sweet with his blue eyes and pale brown hair. It was a pity he plastered it down like that. He had a white skin and rather a high colour; she wondered if he was consumptive. Although his clothes were cheap he wore them well, she liked that, and he looked incredibly clean.

She asked him why he had chosen Tavistock Square. It was central, he explained, and he liked the trees. It was quite nice when you looked out of the window. She got up to look, that would be a good way to make a move, then she would put on her hat and say good-bye to him.

'Yes, it is rather charming, isn't it. It's so London; it gives one a sort of jolly feeling.'

She turned to him, standing by her side, as she said this. He put his arm round her waist and kissed her full on the lips. No woman was ever more surprised in her life. She was so taken aback that she never thought of doing anything. His lips were soft and there was a perfume of youth about him which was really rather delightful. But what he was doing was preposterous. He was forcing her lips apart with the tip of his tongue and now he had both arms round her. She did not feel angry, she did not feel inclined to laugh, she did not know what she felt. And now she had a notion that he was gently drawing her along, his lips still pressing hers, she felt quite distinctly the glow of his body, it was as though there was a furnace inside him, it was really remarkable; and then she found herself laid on the divan and he was beside her, kissing her mouth and her neck and her cheeks and her eyes. Julia felt a strange pang in her heart. She took his head in her hands and kissed his lips.

A few minutes later she was standing at the chimney-piece, in front of the looking-glass, making herself tidy.

'Look at my hair.'

He handed her a comb and she ran it through. Then she put on her hat. He was standing just behind her, and over her shoulder she saw his face with those eager blue eyes and a faint smile in them.

'And I thought you were such a shy young man,' she said to his reflection. He chuckled.

'When am I going to see you again?'

'Do you want to see me again?'

'Rather.'

She thought rapidly. It was too absurd, of course she had no intention of seeing him again, it was stupid of her to have let him behave like that, but it was just as well to temporize. He might be tiresome if she told him that the incident would have no sequel.

'I'll ring up one of these days.'

'Swear.'

'On my honour.'

'Don't be too long.'

He insisted on coming down stairs with her and putting her into a cab. She had wanted to go down alone, so that she could have a look at the cards attached to the bells on the lintel.

'Damn it all, I ought at least to know his name.'

But he gave her no chance. When the taxi drove off she sank into one corner of it and gurgled with laughter.

'Raped, my dear. Practically raped. At my time of life. And without so much as a by your leave. Treated me like a tart. Eighteenth-century comedy, that's what it is. I might have been a waiting-maid. In a hoop, with those funny puffy things—what the devil are they called?—that they wore to emphasize their hips, an apron and a scarf round me neck.' Then with vague memories of Farquhar and Goldsmith she invented the dialogue. 'La, sir, 'tis shame to take advantage of a poor country girl. What would Mrs Abigail, her ladyship's woman, say an she knew her ladyship's brother had ravished me of the most serious treasure a young woman in my station of life can possess, videlicet her innocence. Fie, o fie, sir.'

When Julia got home the masseuse was already waiting for her. Miss Phillips and Evie were having a chat.

'Wherever 'ave you been, Miss Lambert?' said Evie. 'An' what about your rest, I should like to know.'

'Damn my rest.'

Julia tore off her clothes, and flung them with ample gestures all over the room. Then, stark naked, she skipped on to the bed, stood up on it for a moment, like Venus rising from the waves, and then throwing herself down stretched herself out.

'What's the idea?' said Evie.

'I feel good.'

'Well, if I behaved like that people'd say I'd been drinkin'.'

Miss Phillips began to massage her feet. She rubbed gently, to rest and not to tire her.

'When you came in just now, like a whirlwind,' she said, 'I thought you looked twenty years younger. Your eyes were shining something wonderful.'

'Oh, keep that for Mr Gosselyn, Miss Phillips.' And then as an afterthought, 'I feel like a two-year-old.'

And it was the same at the theatre later on. Archie Dexter, who was her leading man, came into her dressing-room to speak about something. She had just finished making-up. He was startled.

'Hulloa, Julia, what's the matter with you tonight? Gosh, you look swell. Why, you don't look a day more than twenty-five.'

'With a son of sixteen it's no good pretending I'm so terribly young any more. I'm forty and I don't care who knows it.'

'What have you done to your eyes? I've never seen them shine like that before.'

She felt in tremendous form. They had been playing the play, it was called *The Powder Puff*, for a good many weeks, but tonight Julia played it as though it were the first time. Her performance was brilliant. She got laughs that she had never got before. She always had magnetism, but on this occasion it seemed to flow over the house in a great radiance. Michael happened to be watching the last two acts from the corner of a box and at the end he came into her dressing-room.

'D'you know the prompter says we played nine minutes longer tonight, they laughed so much.'

'Seven curtain calls. I thought the public were going on all night.'

'Well, you've only got to blame yourself, darling. There's no one in the world who could have given the performance you gave tonight.'

'To tell you the truth I was enjoying myself. Christ, I'm hungry. What have we got for supper?'

'Tripe and onions.'

'Oh, how divine!' She flung her arms round his neck and kissed him. 'I adore tripe and onions. Oh, Michael, Michael, if you love me, if you've got any spark of tenderness in that hard heart of yours, let me have a bottle of beer.'

'Julia.'

'Just this once. It's not often I ask you to do anything for me.'

'Oh well, after the performance you gave tonight I suppose I can't say no, but by God, I'll see that Miss Phillips pitches into you tomorrow.'

Chapter Twelve

When Julia got to bed and slipped her feet down to the comfort of her hot-water bottle, she took a happy look at her room, rose-pink and Nattier-blue, with the gold cherubs of her dressing-table, and sighed with satisfaction. She thought how very Madame de Pompadour it was. She put out the light but she did not feel at all sleepy. She would have liked really to go to Quag's and dance, but not to dance with Michael, to dance with Louis XV or Ludwig of Bavaria or Alfred de Musset. Clairon and the Bal de l'Opéra. She remembered the miniature Charles had once given her. That was how she felt tonight. Such an adventure had not happened to her for ages. The last time was eight years before. That was an episode that she ought to have been thoroughly ashamed of; goodness, how scared she'd been afterwards, but she had in point of fact never been able to think of it since without a chuckle.

That had been an accident too. She had been acting for a long time without a rest and she badly needed one. The play she was in was ceasing to attract and they were about to start rehearsing a new one when Michael got the chance of letting the theatre to a French company for six weeks. It seemed a good opportunity for Julia to get away. Dolly had rented a house at Cannes for the season and Julia could stay with her. It was just before Easter when she started off, and the trains south were so crowded that she had not been able to get a sleeper, but at a travel agency they had said that it would be quite all right and there would be one waiting for her at the station in Paris. To her consternation she found when they got to Paris that nothing seemed to be known about her, and the chef de train told her that every sleeper was engaged. The only chance was that someone should not turn up at the last moment. She did not like the idea of sitting up all night in the corner of a first-class carriage, and went in to dinner with a perturbed mind. She was given a table for two, and soon a man came and sat down opposite her. She paid no attention to him. Presently the chef de train came along and told her that he was very sorry, but he could do nothing for her. She made a useless scene. When the official had gone, the man at her table addressed her. Though he spoke fluent, idioinatic French, she recognized by his accent that he was not a Frenchman. She told him in answer to his polite enquiry the whole story and gave him her opinion of the travel agency, the railway company, and the general inefficiency of the human race. He was very sympathetic. He told her that after dinner he would go along the train and see for himself if something could not be arranged. One never knew what one of the conductors could not manage for a tip.

'I'm simply tired out,' she said. 'I'd willingly give five hundred francs for a sleeper.'

The conversation thus started, he told her that he was an attaché at the Spanish Embassy in Paris and was going down to Cannes for Easter. Though she had been talking to him for a quarter of an hour she had not troubled to notice what he was like. She observed now that he had a beard, a black curly beard and a black curly moustache, but the beard grew rather oddly on his face; there were two bare patches under the corners of his mouth. It gave him a curious look. With his black hair, drooping eyelids and rather long nose, he reminded her of someone she had seen. Suddenly she remembered, and it was such a surprise that she blurted out:

'D'you know, I couldn't think who you reminded me of. You're strangely like Titian's portrait of Francis I in the Louvre.'

'With his little pig's eyes?'

'No, not them, yours are large, I think it's the beard chiefly.'

She glanced at the skin under his eyes; it was faintly violet and unwrinkled. Notwithstanding the ageing beard he was quite a young man; he could not have been more than thirty. She wondered if he was a Spanish Grandee. He was not very well dressed, but then foreigners often weren't, his clothes might have cost a lot even if they were badly cut, and his tie, though rather loud, she recognized as a Charvet. When they came to the coffee he asked her whether he might offer her a liqueur.

'That's very kind of you. Perhaps it'll make me sleep better.'

He offered her a cigarette. His cigarette-case was silver, that put her off a little, but when he closed it she saw that in the corner was a small crown in gold. He must be a count or something. It was rather chic, having a silver cigarette-case with a gold crown on it. Pity he had to wear those modern clothes! If he'd been dressed like Francis I he would really look very distinguished. She set herself to be as gracious as she knew how.

'I think I should tell you,' he said presently, 'that I know who you are. And may I add that I have a great admiration for you?'

She gave him a lingering look of her splendid eyes.

'You've seen me act?'

'Yes, I was in London last month.'

'An interesting little play, wasn't it?'

'Only because you made it so.'

When the man came round to collect the money she had to insist on paying her own bill. The Spaniard accompanied her to the carriage and then said he would go along the train to see if he could find a sleeper for her. He came back in a quarter of an hour with a conductor and told her that he had got her a compartment and if she would give the conductor her things he would take her to it. She was delighted. He threw down his hat on the seat she vacated and she followed him along the corridor. When they reached the compartment he told the conductor to take the portmanteau and the dispatch-case that were in the rack to the carriage madame had just left.

'But it's not your own compartment you're giving up to me?' cried Julia.

'It's the only one on the train.'

'Oh, but I won't hear of it.'

'Allez,' the Spaniard said to the conductor.

'No, no.'

The conductor, on a nod from the stranger, took the luggage away.

'I don't matter. I can sleep anywhere, but I shouldn't sleep a wink if I thought that such a great artist was obliged to spend the night in a stuffy carriage with three other people.'

Julia continued to protest, but not too much. It was terribly sweet of him. She didn't know how to thank him. He would not even let her pay for the sleeper. He begged her, almost with tears in his eyes, to let him have the great privilege of making her that trifling present. She had with her only a dressing-bag, in which were her face creams, her night-dress and her toilet things, and this he put on the table for her. All he asked was that he might be allowed to sit with her and smoke a cigarette or two till she wanted to go to bed. She could hardly refuse him that. The bed was already made up and they sat down on it. In a few minutes the conductor came back with a bottle of champagne and a couple of glasses. It was an odd little adventure and Julia was enjoying it. It was wonderfully polite of him, all that, ah, those foreigners, they knew how to treat a great actress. Of course that was the sort of thing that happened to Bernhardt every day. And Siddons, when she went into a drawing-room everyone stood up as though she were royalty. He complimented her on her beautiful French. Born in Jersey and educated in France? Ah, that explained it. But why hadn't she chosen to act in French rather than in English? She would have as great a reputation as Duse if she had. She reminded him of Duse, the same magnificent eyes and the pale skin, and in her acting the same emotion and the wonderful naturalness.

They half finished the bottle of champagne and Julia realized that it was very late.

'I really think I ought to go to bed now.'

'I'll leave you.'

He got up and kissed her hand. When he was gone Julia bolted the door and undressed. Putting out all the lights except the one just behind her head she began to read. Presently there was a knock at the door.

'Yes?'

'I'm sorry to disturb you. I left my toothbrush in the lavabo. May I get it?'

'I'm in bed.'

'I can't go to sleep unless I brush my teeth.'

'Oh well, he's clean anyway.'

With a little shrug of her shoulders Julia slipped her hand to the door and drew back the bolt. It would be stupid in the circumstances to be prudish. He came in, went into the lavatory and in a moment came out, brandishing a toothbrush. She had noticed it when she brushed her own teeth, but thought it belonged to the person who had the compartment next door. At that period adjoining compartments shared a lavatory. The Spaniard seemed to catch sight of the bottle.

'I'm so thirsty, do you mind if I have a glass of champagne?'

Julia was silent for a fraction of a second. It was his champagne and his compartment. Oh, well, in for a penny, in for a pound.

'Of course not.'

He poured himself out a glass, lit a cigarette and sat down on the edge of her bed. She moved a little to give him more room. He accepted the situation as perfectly natural.

'You couldn't possibly have slept in that carriage,' he said. 'There's a man there who's a heavy breather. I'd almost rather he snored. If he snored one could wake him.'

'I'm so sorry.'

'Oh, it doesn't matter. If the worst comes to the worst I'll curl up in the corridor outside your door.'

'He can hardly expect me to ask him to come and sleep in here,' Julia said to herself. 'I'm beginning to think this was all a put-up job. Nothing doing, my lad.' And then aloud: 'Romantic, of course, but uncomfortable.'

'You're a terribly attractive woman.'

She was just as glad that her night-dress was pretty and that she had put no cream on her face. She had in point of fact not troubled to take off her make-up. Her lips were brightly scarlet, and with the reading light behind her she well knew that she did not look her worst. But she answered ironically.

'If you think that because you've given up your compartment to me I'm going to let you sleep with me, you're mistaken.'

'Just as you say, of course. But why not?'

'I'm not that sort of terribly attractive woman.'

'What sort of woman are you then?'

'A faithful wife and a devoted mother.'

He gave a little sigh.

'Very well. Then I'll say good night to you.'

He crushed the stub of his cigarette on the ashtray and took her hand and kissed it. He slowly ran his lips up her arm. It gave Julia a funny little sensation. The beard slightly tickled her skin. Then he leant over and kissed her lips. His beard had a somewhat musty smell, which she found peculiar; she was not sure if it revolted or thrilled her. It was odd when she came to think of it, she had never been kissed by a man with a beard before. It seemed strangely indecent. He snapped out the light.

He did not leave her till a chink of light through the drawn blind warned them that day had broken. Julia was shattered morally and physically.

'I shall look a perfect wreck when we get to Cannes.'

And what a risk to take! He might have murdered her or stolen her pearl necklace. She went hot and cold all over as she pictured to herself the danger she had incurred. He was going to Cannes too. Supposing he claimed acquaintance with her there, how on earth was she going to explain him to her friends? She felt sure Dolly wouldn't like him. He might try to blackmail her. And what should she do if he wanted to repeat the experience? He was passionate, there was no doubt about that, he had asked her where she was staying, and though she had not told him, he could certainly find out if he tried; in a place like Cannes, it would be almost impossible not to run across him. He might pester her. If he loved her as much as he said it was inconceivable that he should let her alone, and foreigners were so unreliable, he might make frightful scenes. The only comfort was that he was only staying over Easter, she would pretend she was tired and tell Dolly that she preferred to stay quietly at the villa.

'How could I have been such a fool?' she cried angrily.

Dolly would be there to meet her at the station, and if he was tactless enough to come up and say good-bye to her she would tell Dolly that he had given up his compartment to her. There was no harm in that. It was always best to tell as much of the truth as you could. But there was quite a crowd of passengers getting out at Cannes, and Julia got out of the station and into Dolly's car without catching a glimpse of him.

'I've arranged nothing for today,' said Dolly. 'I thought you'd be tired and I wanted to have you all to myself for twenty-four hours.'

Julia gave her arm an affectionate squeeze.

'That'll be too wonderful. We'll just sit about the villa and grease our faces and have a good old gossip.'

But next day Dolly had arranged that they should go out to luncheon, and they were to meet their hosts at one of the bars on the Croisette to have cocktails. It was a beautiful day, clear, warm and sunny. When they got out of the car Dolly stopped to give the chauffeur instructions about fetching them and Julia waited for her. Suddenly her heart gave a great jump, for there was the Spaniard walking towards her, with a woman on one side of him clinging to his arm and on the other a little girl whose hand he held. She had not time to turn away. At that moment Dolly joined her to walk across the pavement. The Spaniard came, gave her a glance in which there was no sign of recognition, he was in animated conversation with the woman on his arm, and walked on. In a flash Julia understood that he was just as little anxious to see her as she was to see him. The woman and the child were obviously his wife and daughter whom he had come down to Cannes to spend Easter with. What a relief! Now she could enjoy herself without fear. But as she accompanied Dolly to the bar, Julia thought how disgusting men were. You simply couldn't trust them for a minute. It was really disgraceful that a man with a charming wife and such a sweet little girl should be willing to pick up a woman in the train. You would think they'd have some sense of decency.

But as time passed Julia's indignation was mitigated, and she had often thought of the adventure since with a good deal of pleasure. After all it had been fun. Sometimes she allowed her reveries to run away with her and she went over in her fancy the incidents of that singular night. He had been a most agreeable lover. It would be something to look back on when she was an old woman. It was the beard that had made such an impression on her, the odd feeling of it on her face and that slightly musty smell which was repulsive and yet strangely exciting. For years she looked out for men with beards, and she had a feeling that if one of them made proposals to her she simply wouldn't be able to resist him. But few men wore beards any more, luckily for her because the sight made her go a little weak at the knees, and none of those that did ever made any advance to her. She would have liked to know who the Spaniard was. She saw him a day or two later playing chemin de fer at the Casino and asked two or three people if they knew him. Nobody did, and he remained in her recollection and in her bones, without a name. It was an odd coincidence that she didn't know the name either of the young man who had that afternoon behaved in so unexpected a manner. It struck her as rather comic.

'If I only knew beforehand that they were going to take liberties with me I'd at least ask for their cards.'

With this thought she fell happily asleep.

Chapter Thirteen

Some days passed, and one morning, while Julia was lying in bed reading a play, they rang through from the basement to ask if she would speak to Mr Fennell. The name meant nothing to her and she was about to refuse when it occurred to her that it might be the young man of her adventure. Her curiosity induced her to tell them to connect him. She recognized his voice.

'You promised to ring me up,' he said. 'I got tired of waiting, so I've rung you up instead.'

'I've been terribly busy the last few days.'

'When am I going to see you?'

'As soon as I have a moment to spare.'

'What about this afternoon?'

'I've got a matinée today.'

'Come to tea after the matinée.'

She smiled. ('No, young feller-me-lad, you don't catch me a second time like that.')

'I can't possibly,' she answered. 'I always stay in my dressing-room and rest till the evening performance.'

'Can't I come and see you while you're resting?'

She hesitated for an instant. Perhaps the best thing would be to let him come; with Evie popping in and out and Miss Phillips due at seven, there would be no chance of any nonsense, and it would be a good opportunity to tell him, amiably, because he was really a sweet little thing, but firmly, that the incident of the other afternoon was to have no sequel. With a few well chosen words she would explain to him that it was quite unreasonable and that he must oblige her by erasing the episode from his memory.

'All right. Come at half-past five and I'll give you a cup of tea.'

There was no part of her busy life that she enjoyed more than those three hours that she spent in her dressing-room between the afternoon and the evening performances. The other members of the cast had gone away; and Evie was there to attend to her wants and the door-keeper to guard her privacy. Her dressing-room was like the cabin of a ship. The world seemed a long way off, and she relished her seclusion. She felt an enchanting freedom. She dozed a little, she read a little, or lying on the comfortable sofa she let her thoughts wander. She reflected on the part she was playing and the favourite parts she had played in the past. She thought of Roger her son. Pleasant reveries sauntered through her mind like lovers wandering in a green wood. She was fond of French poetry and sometimes she repeated to herself verses of Verlaine.

Punctually at half-past five Evie brought her in a card. 'Mr Thomas Fennell,' she read.

'Send him in and bring some tea.'

She had decided how she was going to treat him. She would be amiable, but distant. She would take a friendly interest in his work and ask him about his examination. Then she would talk to him about Roger. Roger was seventeen now and in a year would be going to Cambridge. She would insinuate the fact that she was old enough to be his mother. She would act as if there had never been anything between them and he would go away, never to see her again except across the footlights, half convinced that the whole thing had been a figment of his fancy. But when she saw him, so slight, with his hectic flush and his blue eyes, so charmingly boyish, she felt a sudden pang. Evie closed the door behind him. She was lying on the sofa and she stretched out her arm to give him her hand, the gracious smile of Madame Récamier on her lips, but he flung himself on his knees and passionately kissed her mouth. She could not help herself, she put her arms round his neck, and kissed him as passionately.

('Oh, my good resolutions. My God, I can't have fallen in love with him.')
'For goodness' sake, sit down. Evie's coming in with the tea.'
'Tell her not to disturb us.'
'What do you mean?' But what he meant was obvious. Her heart began to beat quickly. 'It's ridiculous. I can't. Michael might come in.'
'I want you.'
'What d'you suppose Evie would think? It'd be idiotic to take such a risk. No, no, no.'

There was a knock at the door and Evie came in with the tea. Julia gave her instructions to put the table by the side of her sofa and a chair for the young man on the other side of the table. She kept Evie with unnecessary conversation. She felt him looking at her. His eyes moved quickly, following her gestures and the expression of her face; she avoided them, but she felt their anxiety and the eagerness of his desire. She was troubled. It seemed to her that her voice did not sound quite natural.

('What the devil's the matter with me? God, I can hardly breathe.')

When Evie reached the door the boy made a gesture that was so instinctive that her sensitiveness rather than her sight caught it. She could not but look at him. His face had gone quite pale.

'Oh, Evie,' she said. 'This gentleman wants to talk to me about a play. See that no one disturbs me. I'll ring when I want you.'
'Very good, miss.'

Evie went out and closed the door.

('I'm a fool. I'm a bloody fool.')

But he had moved the table, and he was on his knees, and she was in his arms.

She sent him away a little before Miss Phillips was due, and when he was gone rang for Evie.

'Play any good?' asked Evie.
'What play?'
'The play 'e was talkin' to you abaht.'
'He's clever. Of course he's young.'

Evie was looking down at the dressing-table. Julia liked everything always to be in the same place, and if a pot of grease or her eyeblack was not exactly where it should be made a scene.

'Where's your comb?'

He had used it to comb his hair and had carelessly placed it on the tea-table. When Evie caught sight of it she stared at it for a moment reflectively.

'How on earth did it get there?' cried Julia lightly.
'I was just wondering.'

It gave Julia a nasty turn. Of course it was madness to do that sort of thing in the dressing-room. Why, there wasn't even a key in the lock. Evie kept it. All the same the risk had given it a spice. It was fun to think that she could be so crazy. At all events they'd made a date now. Tom, she'd asked him what they called him at home and he said Thomas, she really couldn't call him that, Tom wanted to take her to supper somewhere so that they could dance, and it happened that Michael was going up to Cambridge for a night to rehearse a series of one-act plays written by undergraduates. They would be able to spend hours together.

'You can get back with the milk,' he'd said.
'And what about my performance next day?'
'We can't bother about that.'

She had refused to let him fetch her at the theatre, and when she got to the restaurant they had chosen he was waiting for her in the lobby. His face lit up as he saw her.

'It was getting so late, I was afraid you weren't coming.'

'I'm sorry, some tiresome people came round after the play and I couldn't get rid of them.'

But it wasn't true. She had been as excited all the evening as a girl going to her first ball. She could not help thinking how absurd she was. But when she had taken off her theatrical make-up and made up again for supper she could not satisfy herself. She put blue on her eyelids and took it off again, she rouged her cheeks, rubbed them clean and tried another colour.

'What are you trying to do?' said Evie.

'I'm trying to look twenty, you fool.'

'If you try much longer you'll look your age.'

She had never seen him in evening clothes before. He shone like a new pin. Though he was of no more than average height his slimness made him look tall. She was a trifle touched to see that for all his airs of the man of the world he was shy with the head-waiter when it came to ordering supper. They danced and he did not dance very well, but she found his slight awkwardness rather charming. People recognized her, and she was conscious that he enjoyed the reflected glory of their glances. A pair of young things who had been dancing came up to their table to say how do you do to her. When they had left he asked:

'Wasn't that Lord and Lady Dennorant?'

'Yes. I've known George since he was at Eton.'

He followed them with his eyes.

'She was Lady Cecily Laweston, wasn't she?'

'I've forgotten. Was she?'

It seemed a matter of no interest to her. A few minutes later another couple passed them.

'Look, there's Lady Lepard.'

'Who's she?'

'Don't you remember, they had a big party at their place in Cheshire a few weeks ago and the Prince of Wales was there. It was in the *Bystander*.'

Oh, that was how he got all his information. Poor sweet. He read about grand people in the papers and now and then, at a restaurant or a theatre, saw them in the flesh. Of course it was a thrill for him. Romance. If he only knew how dull they were really. This innocent passion for the persons whose photographs appear in the illustrated papers made him seem incredibly naïve, and she looked at him with tender eyes.

'Have you ever taken an actress out to supper before?'

He blushed scarlet.

'Never.'

She hated to let him pay the bill, she had an inkling that it was costing pretty well his week's salary, but she knew it would hurt his pride if she offered to pay it herself. She asked casually what the time was and instinctively he looked at his wrist.

'I forgot to put on my watch.'

She gave him a searching look.

'Have you pawned it?'

He reddened again.

'No. I dressed in rather a hurry tonight.'

She only had to look at his tie to know that he had done no such thing. He was lying to her. She knew that he had pawned his watch in order to take her out to supper. A lump came into her throat. She could have taken him in her arms then and there and kissed his blue eyes. She adored him.

'Let's go,' she said.

They drove back to his bed-sitting room in Tavistock Square.

Chapter Fourteen

Next day Julia went to Cartier's and bought a watch to send to Tom Fennell instead of the one he had pawned, and two or three weeks later, discovering that it was his birthday, she sent him a gold cigarette-case.

'D'you know, that's the one thing I've wanted all my life.'

She wondered if there were tears in his eyes. He kissed her passionately.

Then, on one excuse and another, she sent him pearl studs and sleeve-links and waistcoat buttons. It thrilled her to make him presents.

'It's so awful that I can't give you anything in return,' he said.

'Give me the watch you pawned to stand me a supper.'

It was a little gold watch that could not have cost more than ten pounds, but it amused her to wear it now and then.

It was not till after that night when they had first supped together that Julia confessed to herself that she had fallen in love with Tom. It came to her as a shock. But she was exhilarated.

'I who thought I could never be in love again. Of course it can't last. But why shouldn't I get what fun out of it I can?'

She decided that he must come again to Stanhope Place. It was not long before an opportunity presented itself.

'You know that young accountant of yours,' she said to Michael. 'Tom Fennell's his name. I met him out at supper the other night and I've asked him to dinner next Sunday. We want an extra man.'

'Oh, d'you think he'll fit in?'

It was rather a grand party. It was on that account she had asked him. She thought it would please him to meet some of the people he had known only from their pictures. She had realized already that he was a bit of a snob. Well, that was all to the good; she could give him all the smart people he wanted. For Julia was shrewd, and she knew very well that Tom was not in love with her. To have an affair with her flattered his vanity. He was a highly-sexed young man and enjoyed sexual exercise. From hints, from stories that she had dragged out of him, she discovered that since he was seventeen he had had a great many women. He loved the act rather than the person. He looked upon it as the greatest lark in the world. And she could understand why he had so much success. There was something appealing in his slightness, his body was just skin and bone, that was why his clothes sat on him well, and something charming in his clean freshness. His shyness and his effrontery combined to make him irresistible. It was strangely flattering for a woman to be treated as a little bit of fluff that you just tumbled on to a bed.

'What he's got, of course, is sex appeal.'

She knew that his good looks were due to his youth. He would grow
wizened as he grew older, dried up and haggard; that charming flush on his
cheeks would turn into a purple glow and his delicate skin would go lined
and sallow; but the feeling that what she loved in him would endure so short
a time increased her tenderness. She felt a strange compassion for him. He
had the high spirits of youth, and she lapped them up as a kitten laps up milk.
But he was not amusing. Though he laughed when Julia said a funny thing
he never said one himself. She did not mind. She found his dullness restful.
She never felt so light-hearted as in his company, and she could be brilliant
enough for two.

People kept on telling Julia that she was looking ten years younger and
that she had never acted better. She knew it was true and she knew the
reason. But it behoved her to walk warily. She must keep her head. Charles
Tamerley always said that what an actress needed was not intelligence, but
sensibility, and he might be right; perhaps she wasn't clever, but her feelings
were alert and she trusted them. They told her now that she must never tell
Tom that she loved him. She was careful to make it plain to him that she laid
no claims on him and that he was free to do whatever he liked. She took up
the attitude that the whole thing was a bit of nonsense to which neither of
them must attach importance. But she left nothing undone to bind him to
her. He liked parties and she took him to parties. She got Dolly and Charles
Tamerley to ask him to luncheon. He was fond of dancing and she got him
cards for balls. For his sake she would go to them herself for an hour, and she
was conscious of the satisfaction he got out of seeing how much fuss people
made of her. She knew that he was dazzled by the great, and she introduced
him to eminent persons. Fortunately Michael took a fancy to him. Michael
liked to talk, and Tom was a good listener. He was clever at his business. One
day Michael said to her:

'Smart fellow, Tom. He knows a lot about income-tax. I believe he's
shown me a way of saving two or three hundred pounds on my next return.'

Michael, looking for new talent, often took him to the play in the evenings,
either in London or the suburbs; they would fetch Julia after the
performance, and the three of them supped together. Now and then Michael
asked Tom to play golf with him on Sundays and then if there was no party
would bring him home to dinner.

'Nice to have a young fellow like that around,' he said. 'It keeps one from
growing rusty.'

Tom was very pleasant about the house. He would play backgammon with
Michael, or patience with Julia, and when they turned on the gramophone
he was always there to change the records.

'He'll be a nice friend for Roger,' said Michael. 'Tom's got his head
screwed on his shoulders the right way, and he's a lot older than Roger. He
ought to have a good influence on him. Why don't you ask him to come and
spend his holiday with us?'

('Lucky I'm a good actress.') But it wanted an effort to keep the joy out of
her voice and to prevent her face from showing the exultation that made her
heart beat so violently. 'That's not a bad idea,' she answered. 'I'll ask him if
you like.'

Their play was running through August, and Michael had taken a house at
Taplow so that they could spend the height of the summer there. Julia was to
come up for her performances and Michael when business needed it, but she
would have the day in the country and Sundays. Tom had a fortnight's

holiday; he accepted the invitation with alacrity.

But one day Julia noticed that he was unusually silent. He looked pale and his buoyant spirits had deserted him. She knew that something was wrong, but he would not tell her what it was; he would only say that he was worried to death. At last she forced him to confess that he had got into debt and was being dunned by tradesmen. The life into which she had led him had made him spend more money than he could afford, and ashamed of his cheap clothes at the grand parties to which she took him, he had gone to an expensive tailor and ordered himself new suits. He had backed a horse hoping to make enough money to get square and the horse was beaten. To Julia it was a very small sum that he owed, a hundred and twenty-five pounds, and she found it absurd that anyone should allow a trifle like that to upset him. She said at once that she would give it to him.

'Oh, I couldn't. I couldn't take money from a woman.'

He went scarlet; the mere thought of it made him ashamed. Julia used all her arts of cajolery. She reasoned, she pretended to be affronted, she even cried a little, and at last as a great favour he consented to borrow the money from her. Next day she sent him a letter in which were bank notes to the value of two hundred pounds. He rang her up and told her that she had sent far more than he wanted.

'Oh, I know people always lie about their debts,' she said with a laugh. 'I'm sure you owe more than you said.'

'I promise you I don't. You're the last person I'd lie to.'

'Then keep the rest for anything that turns up. I hate seeing you pay the bill when we go out to supper. And taxis and all that sort of thing.'

'No, really. It's so humiliating.'

'What nonsense! You know I've got more money than I know what to do with. Can you grudge me the happiness it gives me to get you out of a hole?'

'It's awfully kind of you. You don't know what a relief it is. I don't know how to thank you.'

But his voice was troubled. Poor lamb, he was so conventional. But it was true, it gave her a thrill she had never known before to give him money; it excited in her a surprising passion. And she had another scheme in her head which during the fortnight Tom was to spend at Taplow she thought she could easily work. Tom's bed-sitting room in Tavistock Square had at first seemed to her charming in its sordidness, and the humble furniture had touched her heart. But time had robbed it of these moving characteristics. Once or twice she had met people on the stairs and thought they stared at her strangely. There was a slatternly housekeeper who made Tom's room and cooked his breakfast, and Julia had a feeling that she knew what was going on and was spying on her. Once the locked door had been tried while Julia was in the room, and when she went out the housekeeper was dusting the banisters. She gave Julia a sour look. Julia hated the smell of stale food that hung about the stairs and with her quick eyes she soon discovered that Tom's room was none too clean. The dingy curtains, the worn carpet, the shoddy furniture; it all rather disgusted her. Now it happened that a little while before, Michael, always on the look out for a good investment, had bought a block of garages near Stanhope Place. By letting off those he did not want he found that he could get their own for nothing. There were a number of rooms over. He divided them into two small flats, one for their chauffeur and one which he proposed to let. This was still vacant and Julia suggested to Tom that he should take it. It would be wonderful. She could slip along and see him for an hour when he got back from the office; sometimes she could drop in after the theatre and no one would be any the wiser. They would be free there. She talked to him of the fun they would have furnishing it; she was sure they had lots of things in their house that they did not want, and by storing them he would be doing them a kindness. The rest they would buy together. He was tempted by the idea of having a flat of his own, but it was out of the question; the rent, though small, was beyond his means. Julia knew that. She knew also that if she offered to pay it herself he would indignantly refuse. But she had a notion that during that idle, luxurious fortnight by the river she would be able to overcome his scruples. She saw how much the idea tempted him, and she had little doubt that she could devise some means to persuade him that by falling in with her proposal he was really doing her a service.

'People don't want reasons to do what they'd like to,' she reflected. 'They want excuses.'

Julia looked forward to Tom's visit to Taplow with excitement. It would be lovely to go on the river with him in the morning and in the afternoon sit about the garden with him. With Roger in the house she was determined that there should be no nonsense between her and Tom; decency forbad. But it would be heaven to spend nearly all day with him. When she had matinées he could amuse himself with Roger.

But things did not turn out at all as she expected. It had never occurred to her that Roger and Tom would take a great fancy to one another. There were five years between them and she thought, or would have if she had thought about it at all, that Tom would look upon Roger as a hobbledehoy, quite nice of course, but whom you treated as such, who fetched and carried for you and whom you told to go and play when you did not want to be bothered with him. Roger was seventeen. He was a nice-looking boy, with reddish hair and blue eyes, but that was the best you could say of him. He had neither his mother's vivacity and changing expression nor his father's beauty of feature. Julia was somewhat disappointed in him. As a child when she had been so constantly photographed with him he was lovely. He was rather stolid now and he had a serious look. Really when you came to examine him his only good features were his teeth and his hair. Julia was very fond of him, but she could not but find him a trifle dull. When she was alone with him the time hung somewhat heavily on her hands. She exhibited a lively interest in the things she supposed must interest him, cricket and such like, but he did not seem to have much to say about them. She was afraid he was not very intelligent.

'Of course he's young,' she said hopefully. 'Perhaps he'll improve as he grows older.'

From the time that he first went to his preparatory school she had seen little of him. During the holidays she was always acting at night and he went out with his father or with a boy friend, and on Sundays he and his father played golf together. If she happened to be lunching out it often happened that she did not see him for two or three days together except for a few minutes in the morning when he came to her room. It was a pity he could not always have remained a sweetly pretty little boy who could play in her room without disturbing her and be photographed, smiling into the camera, with his arm round her neck. She went down to see him at Eton occasionally and had tea with him. It flattered her that there were several photographs of her in his room. She was conscious that when she went to Eton it created quite a little excitement, and Mr Brackenbridge, in whose house he was, made a point of being very polite to her. When the half ended Michael and Julia had already moved to Taplow and Roger came straight there. Julia kissed him emotionally. He was not so much excited at getting home as she had expected him to be. He was rather casual. He seemed suddenly to have grown very sophisticated.

He told Julia at once that he desired to leave Eton at Christmas, he thought he had got everything out of it that he could, and he wanted to go to Vienna for a few months and learn German before going up to Cambridge. Michael had wished him to go into the army, but this he had set his face against. He did not yet know what he wanted to be. Both Julia and Michael had from the first been obsessed by the fear that he would go on the stage, but for this apparently he had no inclination.

'Anyhow he wouldn't be any good,' said Julia.

He led his own life. He went out on the river and lay about the garden reading. On his seventeenth birthday Julia had given him a very smart roadster, and in this he careered about the country at breakneck speeds.

'There's one comfort,' said Julia. 'He's no bother. He seems quite capable of amusing himself.'

On Sundays they had a good many people down for the day, actors and actresses, an occasional writer, and a sprinkling of some of their grander friends. Julia found these parties very amusing and she knew that people liked to come to them. On the first Sunday after Roger's arrival there was a great mob. Roger was very polite to the guests. He did his duty as part host like a man of the world. But it seemed to Julia that he held himself in some curious way aloof, as though he were playing a part in which he had not lost himself, and she had an uneasy feeling that he was not accepting all these people, but coolly judging them. She had an impression that he took none of them very seriously.

Tom had arranged to come on the following Saturday and she drove him down after the theatre. It was a moonlit night and at that hour the roads were empty. The drive was enchanting. Julia would have liked it to go on for ever. She nestled against him and every now and then in the darkness he kissed her.

'Are you happy?' she asked.

'Absolutely.'

Michael and Roger had gone to bed, but supper was waiting for them in the dining-room. The silent house gave them the feeling of being there without leave. They might have been a couple of wanderers who had strolled out of the night into a strange house and found a copious repast laid out for them. It was romantic. It had a little the air of a tale in the Arabian Nights. Julia showed him his room, which was next door to Roger's, and then went to bed. She did not wake till late next morning. It was a lovely day. So that she might have Tom all to herself she had not asked anybody down. When she was dressed they would go on the river together. She had her breakfast and her bath. She put on a little white frock that suited the sunny riverside and her, and a large-brimmed red straw hat whose colour threw a warm glow on her face. She was very little made-up. She looked at herself in the glass and smiled with satisfaction.She really looked very pretty and young. She strolled down into the garden. There was a lawn that stretched down to the river, and here she saw Michael surrounded by the Sunday papers. He was alone.

'I thought you'd gone to play golf.'

'No, the boys have gone. I thought they'd have more fun if I let them go alone.' He smiled in his friendly way. 'They're a bit too active for me. They were bathing at eight o'clock this morning, and as soon as they'd swallowed their breakfast they bolted off in Roger's car.'

'I'm glad they've made friends.'

Julia meant it. She was slightly disappointed that she would not be able to go on the river with Tom, but she was anxious that Roger should like him, she had a feeling that Roger did not like people indiscriminately; and after all she had the next fortnight to be with Tom.

'They make me feel damned middle-aged, I don't mind telling you that,' Michael remarked.

'What nonsense. You're much more beautiful than either of them, and well you know it, my pet.'

Michael thrust out his jaw a little and pulled in his belly.

The boys did not come back till luncheon was nearly ready.

'Sorry we're so late,' said Roger. 'There was a filthy crowd and we had to wait on nearly every tee. We halved the match.

They were hungry and thirsty, excited and pleased with themselves.

'It's grand having no one here today,' said Roger. 'I was afraid you'd got a whole gang coming and we'd have to behave liee little gentlemen.'

'I thought a rest would be rather nice,' said Julia.

Roger gave her a glance.

'It'll do you good, mummy. You're looking awfully fagged.'

('Blast his eyes. No, I mustn't show I mind. Thank God, I can act.')

She laughed gaily.

'I had a sleepless night wondering what on earth we were going to do about your spots.'

'I know, aren't they sickening? Tom says he used to have them too.'

Julia looked at Tom. In his tennis shirt open at the neck, with his hair ruffled, his face already caught by the sun, he looked incredibly young. He really looked no older than Roger.

'Anyhow, his nose is going to peel,' Roger went on with a chuckle. 'He'll look a sight then.'

Julia felt slightly uneasy. It seemed to her that Tom had shed the years so that he was become not only in age Roger's contemporary. They talked a great deal of nonsense. They ate enormously and drank tankards of beer. Michael, eating and drinking as sparingly as usual, watched them with amusement. He was enjoying their youth and their high spirits. He reminded Julia of an old dog lying in the sun and gently beating his tail on the ground as he looked at a pair of puppies gambolling about him. They had coffee on the lawn. Julia found it very pleasant to sit there in the shade, looking at the river. Tom was slim and graceful in his long white trousers. She had never seen him smoke a pipe before. She found it strangely touching. But Roger mocked him.

'Do you smoke it because it makes you feel manly or because you like it?'

'Shut up,' said Tom.

'Finished your coffee?'

'Yes.'

'Come on then, let's go on the river.'

Tom gave her a doubtful look. Roger saw it.

'Oh, it's all right, you needn't bother about my respected parents, they've got the Sunday papers. Mummy's just given me a racing punt.'

('I must keep my temper. I must keep my temper. Why was I such a fool as to give him a racing punt?')

'All right,' she said, with an indulgent smile, 'go on the river, but don't fall in.'

'It won't hurt us if we do. We'll be back for tea. Is the court marked out, daddy? We're going to play tennis after tea.'

'I daresay your father can get hold of somebody and you can have a four.'

'Oh, don't bother. Singles are better fun really and one gets more exercise.' Then to Tom. 'I'll race you to the boathouse.'

Tom leapt to his feet and dashed off with Roger in quick pursuit. Michael took up one of the papers and looked for his spectacles.

'They've clicked all right, haven't they?'

'Apparently.'

'I was afraid Roger would be rather bored alone here with us. It'll be fine for him to have someone to play around with.'

'Don't you think Roger's rather inconsiderate?'

'You mean about the tennis? Oh, my dear, I don't really care if I play or not. It's only natural that those two boys should want to play together. From their point of view I'm an old man, and they think I'll spoil their game. After all the great thing is that they should have a good time.'

Julia had a pang of remorse. Michael was prosy, near with his money, self-complacent, but how extraordinarily kind he was and how unselfish! He was devoid of envy. It gave him a real satisfaction, so long as it did not cost money, to make other people happy. She read his mind like an open book. It was true that he never had any but a commonplace thought; on the other hand he never had a shameful one. It was exasperating that with so much to make him worthy of her affection, she should be so excruciatingly bored by him.

'I think you're a much better man than I am a woman, my sweet,' she said.

He gave her his good, friendly smile and slightly shook his head.

'No, dear, I had a wonderful profile, but you've got genius.'

Julia giggled. There was a certain fun to be got out of a man who never knew what you were talking about. But what did they mean when they said an actress had genius? Julia had often asked herself what it was that had placed her at last head and shoulders above her contemporaries. She had had detractors. At one time people had compared her unfavourably with some actress or other who at the moment enjoyed the public favour, but now no one disputed her supremacy. It was true that she had not the world-wide notoriety of the film-stars; she had tried her luck on the pictures, but had achieved no success; her face on the stage so mobile and expressive for some reason lost on the screen, and after one trial she had with Michael's approval refused to accept any of the offers that were from time to time made her. She had got a good deal of useful publicity out of her dignified attitude. But Julia did not envy the film-stars; they came and went; she stayed. When it was possible she went to see the performance of actresses who played leading parts on the London stage. She was generous in her praise of them and her praise was sincere. Sometimes she honestly thought them so very good that she could not understand why people made so much fuss over her. She was much too intelligent not to know in what estimation the public held her, but she was modest about herself. It always surprised her when people raved over something she had done that came to her so naturally that she had never thought it possible to do anything else. The critics admired her variety. They praised especially her capacity for insinuating herself into a part. She was not aware that she deliberately observed people, but when she came to study a new part vague recollections surged up in her from she knew not where, and she found that she knew things about the character she was to represent that she had had no inkling of. It helped her to think of someone she knew or even someone she had seen in the street or at a party; she combined with this recollection her own personality, and thus built up a character founded on fact but enriched with her experience, her knowledge of technique and her amazing magnetism. People thought that she only acted during the two or three hours she was on the stage; they did not know that the character she was playing dwelt in the back of her mind all day long, when she was talking to others with all the appearance of attention, or in whatever business she was engaged. It often seemed to her that she was two persons, the actress, the popular favourite, the best-dressed woman in London, and that was a shadow; and the woman she was playing at night, and that was the substance.

'Damned if I know what genius is,' she said to herself. 'But I know this, I'd give all I have to be eighteen.'

But she knew that wasn't true. If she were given the chance to go back again would she take it? No. Not really. It was not the popularity, the celebrity if you like, that she cared for, nor the hold she had over audiences, the real love they bore her, it was certainly not the money this had brought her; it was the power she felt in herself, her mastery over the medium, that thrilled her. She could step into a part, not a very good one perhaps, with silly words to say, and by her personality, by the dexterity which she had at her fingertips, infuse it with life. There was no one who could do what she could with a part. Sometimes she felt like God.

'And besides,' she chuckled, 'Tom wouldn't be born.'

After all it was very natural that he should like to play about with Roger. They belonged to the same generation. It was the first day of his holiday, she must let him enjoy himself; there was a whole fortnight more. He would soon get sick of being all the time with a boy of seventeen. Roger was sweet, but he was dull; she wasn't going to let maternal affection blind her to that. She must be very careful not to show that she was in the least put out. From the beginning she had made up her mind that she would never make any claim on Tom; it would be fatal if he felt that he owed something to her.

'Michael, why don't you let that flat in the mews to Tom? Now that he's passed his exam and is a chartered accountant he can't go on living in a bed-sitting room.'

'That's not a bad idea. I'll suggest it to him.'

'It would save an agent's fees. We could help him to furnish it. We've got a lot of stuff stored away. We might just as well let him use it as have it moulder away in the attics.'

Tom and Roger came back to eat an enormous tea and then played tennis till the light failed. After dinner they played dominoes. Julia gave a beautiful performance of a still young mother fondly watching her son and his boy friend. She went to bed early. Presently they too went upstairs. Their rooms were just over hers. She heard Roger go into Tom's room. They began talking, her windows and theirs were open, and she heard their voices in animated conversation. She wondered with exasperation what they found to say to one another. She had never found either of them very talkative. After a while Michael's voice interrupted them.

'Now then, you kids, you go to bed. You can go on talking tomorrow.'

She heard them laugh.

'All right, daddy,' cried Roger.

'A pair of damned chatterboxes, that's what you are.'

She heard Roger's voice again.

'Well, good night, old boy.'

And Tom's hearty answer: 'So long, old man.'

'Idiots!' she said to herself crossly.

Next morning while she was having her breakfast Michael came into Julia's room.

'The boys have gone off to play golf at Huntercombe. They want to play a couple of rounds and they asked if they need come back to lunch. I told them that was quite all right.'

'I don't know that I particularly like the idea of Tom treating the house as if it was a hotel.'

'Oh, my dear, they're only a couple of kids. Let them have all the fun they can get, I say.'

She would not see Tom at all that day, for she had to start for London between five and six in order to get to the theatre in good time. It was all very well for Michael to be so damned good-natured about it. She was hurt. She felt a little inclined to cry. He must be entirely indifferent to her, it was Tom she was thinking of now; and she had made up her mind that today was going to be quite different from the day before. She had awakened determined to be tolerant and to take things as they came, but she hadn't been prepared for a smack in the face like this.

'Have the papers come yet?' she asked sulkily.

She drove up to town with rage in her heart.

The following day was not much better. The boys did not go off to play golf, but they played tennis. Their incessant activity profoundly irritated Julia. Tom in shorts, with his bare legs, and a cricket shirt, really did not look more than sixteen. Bathing as they did three or four times a day he could not get his hair to stay down, and the moment it was dry it spread over his head in unruly curls. It made him look younger than ever, but oh, so charming. Julia's heart was wrung. And it seemed to her that his demeanour had strangely changed; in the constant companionship of Roger he had shed the young man about town who was so careful of his dress, so particular about wearing the right thing, and was become again a sloppy little schoolboy. He never gave a hint, no glance even betrayed, that he was her lover; he treated her as if she were no more than Roger's mother. In every remark he made, in his mischievousness, in his polite little ways, he made her feel that she belonged to an older generation. His behaviour had nothing of the chivalrous courtesy a young man might show to a fascinating woman; it was the tolerant kindness he might display to a maiden aunt.

Julia was irritated that Tom should docilely follow the lead of a boy so much younger than himself. It indicated lack of character. But she did not blame him; she blamed Roger. Roger's selfishness revolted her. It was all very well to say he was young. His indifference to anyone's pleasure but his own showed a vile disposition. He was tactless and inconsiderate. He acted as though the house, the servants, his father and mother were there for his particular convenience. She would often have been rather sharp with him, but that she did not dare before Tom assume the rôle of the correcting mother. And when you reproved Roger he had a maddening way of looking deeply hurt, like a stricken hind, which made you feel that you had been unkind and unjust. She could look like that too, it was an expression of the eyes that he had inherited from her; she had used it over and over again on the stage with moving effect, and she knew it need not mean very much, but when she saw it in his it shattered her. The mere thought of it now made her feel tenderly towards him. And that sudden change of feeling showed her the truth; she was jealous of Roger, madly jealous. The realization gave her something of a shock; she did not know whether to laugh or to be ashamed. She reflected a moment.

'Well, I'll cook his goose all right.'

She was not going to let the following Sunday pass like the last. Thank God, Tom was a snob. 'A woman attracts men by her charm and holds them by their vices,' she murmured and wondered whether she had invented the aphorism or remembered it from some play she had once acted in.

She gave instructions for some telephoning to be done. She got the Dennorants to come for the week-end. Charles Tamerley was staying at Henley and accepted an invitation to come over for Sunday and bring his host, Sir Mayhew Bryanston, who was Chancellor of the Exchequer. To amuse him and the Dennorants, because she knew that the upper classes do not want to meet one another in what they think is Bohemia, but artists of one sort or another, she asked Archie Dexter, her leading man, and his pretty wife who acted under her maiden name of Grace Hardwill. She felt pretty sure that with a marquess and marchioness to hover round and a Cabinet Minister to be impressed by, Tom would not go off to play golf with Roger or spend the afternoon in a punt. In such a party Roger would sink into his proper place of a schoolboy that no one took any notice of, and Tom would see how brilliant she could be when she took the trouble. In the anticipation of her triumph she managed to bear the intervening days with fortitude. She saw little of Roger and Tom. On her matinée days she did not see them at all. If they were not playing some game they were careering about the country in Roger's car.

Julia drove the Dennorants down after the play. Roger had gone to bed, but Michael and Tom were waiting up to have supper with them. It was a very good supper. The servants had gone to bed too and they helped themselves. Julia noticed the shy eagerness with which Tom saw that the Dennorants had everything they wanted, and his alacrity to jump up if he could be of service. His civility was somewhat officious. The Dennorants were an unassuming young couple to whom it had never occurred that their rank could impress anyone, and George Dennorant was a little embarrassed when Tom took away his dirty plate and handed him a dish to help himself to the next course.

'No golf for Roger tomorrow, I think,' said Julia to herself.

They stayed up talking and laughing till three in the morning, and when Tom said good night to her his eyes were shining; but whether from love or champagne she did not know. He pressed her hand.

'What a lovely party,' he said.

It was late when Julia, dressed in organdie, looking her best, came down into the garden. She saw Roger in a long chair with a book.

'Reading?' she said, lifting her really beautiful eyebrows. 'Why aren't you playing golf?'

Roger looked a trifle sulky.

'Tom said it was too hot.'

'Oh?' she smiled charmingly. 'I was afraid you thought you ought to stay and entertain my guests. There are going to be so many people, we could easily have managed without you. Where are the others?'

'I don't know. Tom's making chichi with Cecily Dennorant.'

'She's very pretty, you know.'

'It looks to me as though it's going to be a crashing bore today.'

'I hope Tom won't find it so,' she said, as though she were seriously concerned.

Roger remained silent.

The day passed exactly as she had hoped. It was true that she saw little of Tom, but Roger saw less. Tom made a great hit with the Dennorants; he explained to them how they could get out of paying as much income-tax as they did. He listened respectfully to the Chancellor while he discoursed on the stage and to Archie Dexter while he gave his views on the political situation. Julia was at the top of her form. Archie Dexter had a quick wit, a fund of stage stories and a wonderful gift for telling them; between the two of them they kept the table during luncheon laughing uproariously; and after tea, when the tennis players were tired of playing tennis, Julia was persuaded (not much against her will) to do her imitations of Gladys Cooper, Constance Collier and Gertie Lawrence. But Julia did not forget that Charles Tamerley was her devoted, unrewarded lover, and she took care to have a little stroll alone with him in the gloaming. With him she sought to be neither gay nor brilliant, she was tender and wistful. Her heart ached, notwithstanding the scintillating performance she had given during the day; and it was with almost complete sincerity that with sighs, sad looks and broken sentences, she made him understand that her life was hollow and despite the long continued success of her career she could not but feel that she had missed something. Sometimes she thought of the villa at Sorrento on the bay of Naples. A beautiful dream. Happiness might have been hers for the asking, perhaps; she had been a fool; after all what were the triumphs of the stage but illusion? Pagliacci. People never realized how true that was; Vesti la giubba and all that sort of thing. She was desperately lonely. Of course there was no need to tell Charles that her heart ached not for lost opportunities, but because a young man seemed to prefer playing golf with her son to making love to her.

But then Julia and Archie Dexter got together. After dinner when they were all sitting in the drawing-room, without warning, starting with a few words of natural conversation they burst, as though they were lovers, into a jealous quarrel. For a moment the rest did not realize it was a joke till their mutual accusations became so outrageous and indecent that they were consumed with laughter. Then they played an extempore scene of an intoxicated gentleman picking up a French tart in Jermyn Street. After that, with intense seriousness, while their little audience shook with laughter, they did Mrs Alving in *Ghosts* trying to seduce Pastor Manders. They finished with a performance that they had given often enough before at theatrical parties to enable them to do it with effect. This was a Chekov play in English, but in moments of passion breaking into something that sounded exactly like Russian. Julia exercised all her great gift for tragedy, but underlined it with a farcical emphasis, so that the effect was incredibly funny. She put into her performance the real anguish of her heart, and with her lively sense of the ridiculous made a mock of it. The audience rolled about in their chairs; they held their sides; they groaned in an agony of laughter. Perhaps Julia had never acted better. She was acting for Tom and for him alone.

'I've seen Bernhardt and Réjane,' said the Chancellor; 'I've seen Duse and Ellen Terry and Mrs Kendal. Nunc Dimittis.'

Julia, radiant, sank back into a chair and swallowed at a draught a glass of champagne.

'If I haven't cooked Roger's goose I'll eat my hat,' she thought.

But for all that the two lads had gone off to play golf when she came downstairs next morning. Michael had taken the Dennorants up to town. Julia was tired. She found it an effort to be bright and chatty when Tom and Roger came in to lunch. In the afternoon the three of them went on the river, but Julia had the feeling that they took her, not because they much wanted to, but because they could not help it. She stifled a sigh when she reflected how much she had looked forward to Tom's holiday. Now she was counting the days that must pass till it ended. She drew a deep breath of relief when she got into the car to go to London. She was not angry with Tom, but deeply hurt; she was exasperated with herself because she had so lost control over her feelings. But when she got into the theatre she felt that she shook off the obsession of him like a bad dream from which one awoke; there, in her dressing-room, she regained possession of herself and the affairs of the common round of daily life faded to insignificance. Nothing really mattered when she had within her grasp this possibility of freedom.

Thus the week went by. Michael, Roger and Tom enjoyed themselves. They bathed, they played tennis, they played golf, they lounged about on the river. There were only four days more. There were only three days more.

('I can stick it out now. It'll be different when we're back in London again. I mustn't show how miserable I am. I must pretend it's all right.')

'A snip having this spell of fine weather,' said Michael. 'Tom's been a success, hasn't he? Pity he can't stay another week.'

'Yes, a terrible pity.'

'I think he's a nice friend for Roger to have. A thoroughly normal, clean-minded English boy.'

'Oh, thoroughly.' ('Bloody fool, bloody fool.')

'To see the way they eat is a fair treat.'

'Yes, they seem to have enjoyed their food.' ('My God, I wish it could have choked them.')

Tom was to go up to town by an early train on Monday morning. The Dexters, who had a house at Bourne End, had asked them all to lunch on Sunday. They were to go down in the launch. Now that Tom's holiday was nearly over Julia was glad that she had never by so much as a lifted eyebrow betrayed her irritation. She was certain that he had no notion how deeply he had wounded her. After all she must be tolerant, he was only a boy, and if you must cross your t's, she was old enough to be his mother. It was a bore that she had a thing about him, but there it was, she couldn't help it; she had told herself from the beginning that she must never let him feel that she had any claims on him. No one was coming to dinner on Sunday. She would have liked to have Tom to herself on his last evening; that was impossible, but at all events they could go for a stroll by themselves in the garden.

'I wonder if he's noticed that he hasn't kissed me since he came here?'

They might go out in the punt. It would be heavenly to lie in his arms for a few minutes; it would make up for everything.

The Dexters' party was theatrical. Grace Hardwill, Archie's wife, played in musical comedy, and there was a bevy of pretty girls who danced in the piece in which she was then appearing. Julia acted with great naturalness the part of a leading lady who puts on no frills. She was charming to the young ladies, with their waved platinum hair, who earned three pounds a week in the chorus. A good many of the guests had brought kodaks and she submitted with affability to being photographed. She applauded enthusiastically when Grace Hardwill sang her famous song to the accompaniment of the composer. She laughed as heartily as anyone when the comic woman did an imitation of her in one of her best-known parts. It was all very gay, rather rowdy, and agreeably light-hearted. Julia enjoyed herself, but when it was seven o'clock was not sorry to go. She was thanking her hosts effusively for the pleasant party when Roger came up to her.

'I say, mum, there's a whole crowd going on to Maidenhead to dine and dance, and they want Tom and me to go too. You don't mind, do you?'

The blood rushed to her cheeks. She could not help answering rather sharply.

'How are you to get back?'

'Oh, that'll be all right. We'll get someone to drop us.'

She looked at him helplessly. She could not think what to say.

'It's going to be a tremendous lark. Tom's crazy to go.'

Her heart sank. It was with the greatest difficulty that she managed not to make a scene. But she controlled herself.

'All right, darling. But don't be too late. Remember that Tom's got to rise with the lark.'

Tom had come up and heard the last words.

'You're sure you don't mind?' he asked.

'Of course not. I hope you'll have a grand time.'

She smiled brightly at him, but her eyes were steely with hatred.

'I'm just as glad those two kids have gone off,' said Michael when they got into the launch. 'We haven't had an evening to ourselves for ever so long.'

She clenched her hands in order to prevent herself from telling him to hold his silly tongue. She was in a black rage. This was the last straw. Tom had neglected her for a fortnight, he had not even treated her with civility, and she had been angelic. There wasn't a woman in the world who would have shown such patience. Any other woman would have told him that if he couldn't behave with common decency he'd better get out. Selfish, stupid and common, that's what he was. She almost wished he wasn't going tomorrow so that she could have the pleasure of turning him out bag and baggage. And to dare to treat her like that, a twopenny-halfpenny little man in the city; poets, cabinet ministers, peers of the realm would be only too glad to break the most important engagements to have the chance of dining with her, and he threw her over to go and dance with a pack of peroxide blondes who couldn't act for nuts. That showed what a fool he was. You would have thought he'd have some gratitude. Why, the very clothes he had on she'd paid for. That cigarette-case he was so proud of, hadn't she given him that? And the ring he wore. My God, she'd get even with him. Yes, and she knew how she could do it. She knew where he was most sensitive and how she could most cruelly wound him. That would get him on the raw. She felt a faint sensation of relief as she turned the scheme over in her mind. She was impatient to carry out her part of it at once, and they had no sooner got home than she went up to her room. She got four single pounds out of her bag and a ten-shilling note. She wrote a brief letter.

> Dear Tom,
>   I'm enclosing the money for your tips as I shan't see you in the morning. Give three pounds to the butler, a pound to the maid who's been valeting you, and ten shillings to the chauffeur.
> Julia

She sent for Evie and gave instructions that the letter should be given to Tom by the maid who awoke him. When she went down to dinner she felt much better. She carried on an animated conversation with Michael while they dined and afterwards they played six pack bezique. If she had racked her brains for a week she couldn't have thought of anything that would humiliate Tom more bitterly.

But when she went to bed she could not sleep. She was waiting for Roger and Tom to come home. A notion came to her that made her restless. Perhaps Tom would realize that he had behaved rottenly, if he gave it a moment's thought he must see how unhappy he was making her; it might be that he would be sorry and when he came in, after he had said good night to Roger, he would creep down to her room. If he did that she would forgive everything. The letter was probably in the butler's pantry; she could easily slip down and get it back. At last a car drove up. She turned on her light to look at the time. It was three. She heard the two young men go upstairs and to their respective rooms. She waited. She put on the light by her bedside so that when he opened the door he should be able to see. She would pretend she was sleeping and then as he crept forward on tiptoe slowly open her eyes and smile at him. She waited. In the silent night she heard him get into bed and switch off the light. She stared straight in front of her for a minute, then with a shrug of the shoulders opened a drawer by her bedside and from a little bottle took a couple of sleeping-tablets.

'If I don't sleep I shall go mad.'

Chapter Fifteen

Julia did not wake till after eleven. Among her letters was one that had not come by post. She recognized Tom's neat, commercial hand and tore it open. It contained nothing but the four pounds and the ten-shilling note. She felt slightly sick. She did not quite know what she had expected him to reply to her condescending letter and the humiliating present. It had not occurred to her that he would return it. She was troubled, she had wanted to hurt his feelings, but she had a fear now that she had gone too far.

'Anyhow I hope he tipped the servants,' she muttered to reassure herself. She shrugged her shoulders. 'He'll come round. It won't hurt him to discover that I'm not all milk and honey.'

But she remained thoughtful throughout the day. When she got to the theatre a parcel was waiting for her. As soon as she looked at the address she knew what it contained. Evie asked if she should open it.

'No.'

But the moment she was alone she opened it herself. There were the cuff-links and the waistcoat buttons, the pearl studs, the wrist-watch and the cigarette-case of which Tom was so proud. All the presents she had ever given him. But no letter. Not a word of explanation. Her heart sank and she noticed that she was trembling.

'What a damned fool I was! Why didn't I keep my temper?'

Her heart now beat painfully. She couldn't go on the stage with that anguish gnawing at her vitals, she would give a frightful performance; at whatever cost she must speak to him. There was a telephone in his house and an extension to his room. She rang him. Fortunately he was in.

'Tom.'

'Yes?'

He had paused for a moment before answering and his voice was peevish.

'What does this mean? Why have you sent me all those things?'

'Did you get the notes this morning?'

'Yes. I couldn't make head or tail of it. Have I offended you?'

'Oh no,' he answered. 'I like being treated like a kept boy. I like having it thrown in my face that even my tips have to be given me. I thought it rather strange that you didn't send me the money for a third-class ticket back to London.'

Although Julia was in a pitiable state of anxiety, so that she could hardly get the words out of her mouth, she almost smiled at his fatuous irony. He was a silly little thing.

'But you can't imagine that I wanted to hurt your feelings. You surely know me well enough to know that's the last thing I should do.'

'That only makes it worse.' ('Damn and curse,' thought Julia.) 'I ought never to have let you make me those presents. I should never have let you lend me money.'

'I don't know what you mean. It's all some horrible misunderstanding. Come and fetch me after the play and we'll have it out. I know I can explain.'

'I'm going to dinner with my people and I shall sleep at home.'

'Tomorrow then.'

'I'm engaged tomorrow.'

'I must see you, Tom. We've been too much to one another to part like this. You can't condemn me unheard. It's so unjust to punish me for no fault of mine.'

'I think it's much better that we shouldn't meet again.'

Julia was growing desperate.

'But I love you, Tom. I love you. Let me see you once more and then, if you're still angry with me, we'll call it a day.'

There was a long pause before he answered.

'All right. I'll come after the matinée on Wednesday.'

'Don't think unkindly of me, Tom.'

She put down the receiver. At all events he was coming. She wrapped up again the things he had returned to her, and hid them away where she was pretty sure Evie would not see them. She undressed, put on her old pink dressing-gown and began to make-up. She was out of humour: this was the first time she had ever told him that she loved him. It vexed her that she had been forced to humiliate herself by begging him to come and see her. Till then it had always been he who sought her company. She was not pleased to think that the situation between them now was openly reversed.

Julia gave a very poor performance at the matinée on Wednesday. The heat wave had affected business and the house was apathetic. Julia was indifferent. With that sickness of apprehension gnawing at her heart she could not care how the play went. ('What the hell do they want to come to the theatre for on a day like this anyway?') She was glad when it was over.

'I'm expecting Mr Fennell,' she told Evie. 'While he's here I don't want to be disturbed.'

Evie did not answer. Julia gave her a glance and saw that she was looking grim.

('To hell with her. What do I care what she thinks!')

He ought to have been there by now. It was after five. He was bound to come; after all, he'd promised, hadn't he? She put on a dressing-gown, not the one she made up in, but a man's dressing-gown, in plum-coloured silk. Evie took an interminable time to put things straight.

'For God's sake don't fuss, Evie. Leave me alone.'

Evie did not speak. She went on methodically arranging the various objects on the dressing-table exactly as Julia always wanted them.

'Why the devil don't you answer when I speak to you?'

Evie turned round and looked at her. She thoughtfully rubbed her finger along her nostrils.

'Great actress you may be . . .'

'Get the hell out of here.'

After taking off her stage make-up Julia had done nothing to her face except put the very faintest shading of blue under her eyes. She had a smooth, pale skin and without rouge on her cheeks or red on her lips she looked wan. The man's dressing-gown gave an effect at once helpless, fragile and gallant. Her heart was beating painfully and she was very anxious, but looking at herself in the glass she murmured: Mimi in the last act of *Bohème*. Almost without meaning to she coughed once or twice consumptively. She turned off the bright lights on her dressing-table and lay down on the sofa. Presently there was a knock on the door and Evie announced Mr Fennell. Julia held out a white, thin hand.

'I'm lying down. I'm afraid I'm not very well. Find yourself a chair. It's nice of you to come.'

'I'm sorry. What's the matter?'

'Oh, nothing.' She forced a smile to her ashy lips. 'I haven't been sleeping very well the last two or three nights.'

She turned her beautiful eyes on him and for a while gazed at him in silence. His expression was sullen, but she had a notion that he was frightened.

'I'm waiting for you to tell me what you've got against me,' she said at last in a low voice.

It trembled a little, she noticed, but quite naturally. ('Christ, I believe I'm frightened too.')

'There's no object in going back to that. The only thing I wanted to say to you was this: I'm afraid I can't pay you the two hundred pounds I owe you right away, I simply haven't got it, but I'll pay you by degrees. I hate having to ask you to give me time, but I can't help myself.'

She sat up on the sofa and put both her hands to her breaking heart.

'I don't understand. I've lain awake for two whole nights turning it all over in my mind. I thought I should go mad. I've been trying to understand. I can't. I can't.'

('What play did I say that in?')

'Oh yes, you can, you understand perfectly. You were angry with me and you wanted to get back on me. And you did. You got back on me all right. You couldn't have shown your contempt for me more clearly.'

'But why should I want to get back on you? Why should I be angry with you?'

'Because I went to Maidenhead with Roger to that party and you wanted me to come home.'

'But I told you to go. I said I hoped you'd have a good time.'

'I know you did, but your eyes were blazing with passion. I didn't want to go, but Roger was keen on it. I told him I thought we ought to come back and dine with you and Michael, but he said you'd be glad to have us off your hands, and I didn't like to make a song and dance about it. And when I saw you were in a rage it was too late to get out of it.'

'I wasn't in a rage. I can't think how you got such an idea in your head. It was so natural that you should want to go to the party. You can't think I'm such a beast as to grudge you a little fun in your fortnight's holiday. My poor lamb, my only fear was that you would be bored. I so wanted you to have a good time.'

'Then why did you send me that money and write me that letter? It was so insulting.'

Julia's voice faltered. Her jaw began to tremble and the loss of control over her muscles was strangely moving. Tom looked away uneasily.

'I couldn't bear to think of your having to throw away your good money on tips. I know that you're not terribly rich and I knew you'd spent a lot on green fees. I hate women who go about with young men and let them pay for everything. It's so inconsiderate. I treated you just as I'd have treated Roger. I never thought it would hurt your feelings.'

'Will you swear that?'

'Of course I will. My God, is it possible that after all these months you don't know me better than that? If what you think were true, what a mean, cruel, despicable woman I should be, what a cad, what a heartless, vulgar beast! Is that what you think I am?'

A poser.

'Anyhow it doesn't matter. I ought never to have accepted valuable presents from you and allowed you to lend me money. It's put me in a rotten position. Why I thought you despised me is that I can't help feeling that you've got a right to. The fact is I can't afford to run around with people who are so much richer than I am. I was a fool to think I could. It's been fun and I've had a grand time, but now I'm through. I'm not going to see you any more.'

She gave a deep sigh.

'You don't care two hoots for me. That's what that means.'

'That's not fair.'

'You're everything in the world to me. You know that. I'm so lonely and your friendship meant a great deal to me. I'm surrounded by hangers-on and parasites and I knew you were disinterested. I felt I could rely on you. I so loved being with you. You were the only person in the world with whom I could be entirely myself. Don't you know what a pleasure it was to me to help you a little? It wasn't for your sake I made you little presents, it was for my own; it made me so happy to see you using the things I'd given you. If you'd cared for me at all they wouldn't have humiliated you, you'd have been touched to owe me something.'

She turned her eyes on him once more. She could always cry easily, and she was really so miserable now that she did not have to make even a small effort. He had never seen her cry before. She could cry, without sobbing, her wonderful dark eyes wide open, with a face that was almost rigid. Great heavy tears ran down it. And her quietness, the immobility of the tragic body, were terribly moving. She hadn't cried like that since she cried in *The Stricken Heart*. Christ, how that play had shattered her. She was not looking at Tom, she was looking straight in front of her; she was really distracted with grief, but, what was it? another self within her knew what she was doing, a self that shared in her unhappiness and yet watched its expression. She felt him go white. She felt a sudden anguish wring his heartstrings, she felt that his flesh and blood could not support the intolerable pain of hers.

'Julia.'

His voice was broken. She slowly turned her liquid eyes on him. It was not a woman crying that he saw, it was all the woe of human kind, it was the immeasurable, the inconsolable grief that is the lot of man. He threw himself down on his knees and took her in his arms. He was shattered.

'Dearest, dearest.'

For a minute she did not move. It was as if she did not know that he was there. He kissed her streaming eyes and with his mouth sought hers. She gave it to him as though she were powerless, as though, scarcely conscious of what was befalling her, she had no will left. With a scarcely perceptible movement she pressed her body to his and gradually her arms found their way round his neck. She lay in his arms, not exactly inert, but as though all the strength, all the vitality, had gone out of her. In his mouth he tasted the saltness of her tears. At last, exhausted, clinging to him with soft arms she sank back on the sofa. His lips clung to hers.

You would never have thought had you seen her a quarter of an hour later, so quietly gay, flushed a little, that so short a while before she had passed through such a tempest of weeping. They each had a whisky and soda and a cigarette and looked at one another with fond eyes.

'He's a sweet little thing,' she thought.

It occurred to her that she would give him a treat.

'The Duke and Duchess of Rickaby are coming to the play tonight and we're going to have supper at the Savoy. I suppose you wouldn't come, would you? I want a man badly to make a fourth.'

'If you'd like me to, of course I will.'

The heightened colour on his cheeks told her how excited he was to meet such distinguished persons. She did not tell him that the Rickabys would go anywhere for a free meal. Tom took back the presents that he had returned to her rather shyly, but he took them. When he had gone she sat down at the dressing-table and had a good look at herself.

'How lucky I am that I can cry without my eyelids swelling,' she said. She massaged them a little. 'All the same, what mugs men are.'

She was happy. Everything would be all right now. She had got him back. But somewhere, at the back of her mind or in the bottom of her heart, was a feeling of ever so slight contempt for Tom because he was such a simple fool.

Chapter Sixteen

Their quarrel, destroying in some strange way the barrier between them, brought them closer together. Tom offered less resistance than she had expected when she mooted once more the question of the flat. It looked as though, after their reconciliation, having taken back her presents and consented to forget the loan, he had put aside his moral scruples. They had a lot of fun furnishing it. The chauffeur's wife kept it clean for him and cooked his breakfast. Julia had a key and would sometimes let herself in and sit by herself in the little sitting-room till he came back from his office. They supped together two or three times a week and danced, then drove back to the flat in a taxi. Julia enjoyed a happy autumn. The play they put on was a success. She felt alert and young. Roger was coming home at Christmas, but only for a fortnight, and was then going to Vienna. Julia expected him to monopolize Tom and she was determined not to mind. Youth naturally appealed to youth and she told herself that there was no reason for her to feel anxious if for a few days the two of them were so wrapped up in one another that Tom had no thought for her. She held him now. He was proud to be her lover, it gave him confidence in himself, and he was pleased to be on familiar terms with a large number of more or less distinguished persons whom after all he only knew through her. He was anxious now to join a good club and Julia was preparing the ground. Charles had never refused her anything, and with tact she was certain that she could wheedle him into proposing Tom for one of those to which he belonged. It was a new and delicious sensation for Tom to have money to spend; she encouraged him to be extravagant; she had a notion that he would get used to living in a certain way and then would realize that he could not do without her.

'Of course it can't last,' she told herself, 'but when it comes to an end it will have been a wonderful experience for him. It'll really have made a man of him.'

But though she told herself that it could not last she did not see really why it shouldn't. As the years went by and he grew older there wouldn't be any particular difference between them. He would no longer be so very young in ten or fifteen years and she would be just the same age as she was now. They were very comfortable together. Men were creatures of habit; that gave women such a hold on them. She did not feel a day older than he, and she was convinced that the disparity in their ages had never even occurred to him. It was true that on this point she had once had a moment's disquietude. She was lying on his bed. He was standing at the dressing-table, in his shirt sleeves, brushing his hair. She was stark naked and she lay in the position of a Venus by Titian that she remembered to have seen in a country house at which she had stayed. She felt that she made really a lovely picture, and in complete awareness of the charming sight she offered, held the pose. She was happy and satisfied.

'This is romance,' she thought, and a light, quick smile hovered over her lips.

He caught sight of her in the mirror, turned round and without a word, twitched the sheet over her. Though she smiled at him affectionately, it gave her quite a turn. Was he afraid that she would catch cold or was it that his English modesty was shocked at her nakedness? Or could it be that, his boyish lust satisfied, he was a trifle disgusted at the sight of her ageing body? When she got home she again took all her clothes off and examined herself in the looking-glass. She determined not to spare herself. She looked at her neck, there was no sign of age there, especially when she held her chin up; and her breasts were small and firm; they might have been a girl's. Her belly was flat, her hips were small, there was a very small roll of fat there, like a long sausage, but everyone had that, and anyhow Miss Phillips could have a go at it. No one could say that her legs weren't good, they were long and slim and comely; she passed her hands over her body, her skin was as soft as velvet and there wasn't a blemish on it. Of course there were a few wrinkles under her eyes, but you had to peer to see them; they said there was an operation now by which you could get rid of them, it might be worth while to enquire into that; it was lucky that her hair had retained its colour; however well hair was dyed, to dye hardened the face; hers remained a rich, deep brown. Her teeth were all right too.

'Prudishness, that's all it was.'

She had a moment's recollection of the Spaniard with the beard in the wagon-lit and she smiled roguishly at herself in the glass.

'No damned modesty about him.'

But all the same from that day on she took care to act up to Tom's standards of decency.

Julia's reputation was so good that she felt she need not hesitate to show herself with Tom in public places. It was a new experience for her to go to night clubs, she enjoyed it, and though no one could have been better aware than she that she could go nowhere without being stared at, it never entered her head that such a change in her habits must excite comment. With twenty years of fidelity behind her, for of course she did not count the Spaniard, an accident that might happen to any woman, Julia was confident that no one would imagine for a moment that she was having an affair with a boy young enough to be her son. It never occurred to her that perhaps Tom was not always so discreet as he might have been. It never occurred to her that the look in her eyes when they danced together betrayed her. She looked upon her position as so privileged that it never occurred to her that people at last were beginning to gossip.

When this gossip reached the ears of Dolly de Vries she laughed. At Julia's request she had invited Tom to parties and once or twice had him down for a week-end in the country, but she had never paid any attention to him. He seemed a nice little thing, a useful escort for Julia when Michael was busy, but perfectly insignificant. He was one of those persons who everywhere pass unnoticed, and even after you had met him you could not remember what he was like. He was the extra man you invited to dinner to make an odd number even. Julia talked of him gaily as 'me boy friend' or as 'my young man'; she could hardly have been so cool about it, so open, if there were anything in it. Besides, Dolly knew very well that the only two men there had ever been in Julia's life were Michael and Charles Tamerley. But it was funny of Julia, after taking so much care of herself for years, suddenly to start going to night clubs three or four times a week. Dolly had seen little of her of late and indeed had been somewhat piqued by her neglect. She had many friends in theatrical circles and she began to make enquiries. She did not at all like what she heard. She did not know what to think. One thing was evident, Julia couldn't know what was being said about her, and someone must tell her. Not she; she hadn't the courage. Even after all these years she was a little frightened of Julia. Julia was a very good-tempered woman, and though her language was often brusque it was hard to ruffle her; but there was something about her that prevented you from taking liberties with her; you had a feeling that if once you went too far you would regret it. But something must be done. Dolly turned the matter over in her mind for a fortnight, anxiously; she tried to put her own wounded feelings aside and look at it only from the point of view of Julia's career, and at last she came to the conclusion that Michael must speak to her. She had never liked Michael, but after all he was Julia's husband and it was her duty to tell him at least enough to make him put a stop to whatever was going on.

She rang Michael up and made an appointment with him at the theatre. Michael liked Dolly as little as she liked him, though for other reasons, and when he heard that she wanted to see him he swore. He was annoyed that he had never been able to induce her to sell out her shares in the management, and he resented whatever suggestions she made as an unwarrantable interference. But when she was shown into his office he greeted her with cordiality. He kissed her on both cheeks.

'Sit down and make yourself comfy. Come to see that the old firm's still raking in dividends for you?'

Dolly de Vries was now a woman of sixty. She was very fat, and her face, with its large nose and heavy red lips, seemed larger than life. There was a slightly masculine touch in her black satin dress, but she wore a double string of pearls round her neck, a diamond brooch at her waist and another in her hat. Her short hair was dyed a rich copper. Her lips and her finger-nails were bright red. Her voice was loud and deep, but when she got excited the words were apt to tumble over one another and a slight cockney accent revealed itself.

'Michael, I'm upset about Julia.'

Michael, always the perfect gentleman, slightly raised his eyebrows and compressed his thin lips. He was not prepared to discuss his wife even with Dolly.

'I think she's doing a great deal too much. I don't know what's come over her. All these parties she's going to now. These night clubs and things. After all, she's not a young woman any more; she'll just wear herself out.'

'Oh, nonsense. She's as strong as a horse and she's in the best of health. She's looking younger than she has for years. You're not going to grudge her a bit of fun when her day's work is over. The part she's playing just now doesn't take it out of her; I'm very glad that she should want to go out and amuse herself. It only shows how much vitality she has.'

'She never cared for that sort of thing before. It seems so strange that she should suddenly take to dancing till two in the morning in the horrible atmosphere of those places.'

'It's the only exercise she gets. I can't expect her to put on shorts and come for a run with me in the park.'

'I think you ought to know that people are beginning to talk. It's doing her reputation a lot of harm.'

'What the devil d'you mean by that?'

'Well, it's absurd that at her age she should make herself so conspicuous with a young boy.'

He glanced at her for a moment without understanding, and when he caught what she meant he laughed loud.

'Tom? Don't be such a fool, Dolly.'

'I'm not a fool. I know what I'm talking about. When anyone's as well known as Julia and she's always about with the same man naturally people talk.'

'But Tom's just as much my friend as hers. You know very well that I can't take Julia out dancing. I have to get up every morning at eight to get my exercise in before my day's work. Hang it all, I do know something about human nature after thirty years on the stage. Tom's a very good type of clean honest English boy and he's by way of being a gentleman. I daresay he admires Julia, boys of that age often think they're in love with women older than themselves, well, it won't do him any harm, it'll do him good; but to think Julia could possibly give him a thought—my poor Dolly, you make me laugh.'

'He's boring, he's dull, he's common and he's a snob.'

'Well, if you think he's all that doesn't it strike you as rather strange that Julia should be so wrapped up in him as you seem to think?'

'Only a woman knows what a woman can do.'

'That's not a bad line, Dolly. We shall have you writing a play next. Now let's get this straight. Can you look me in the face and tell me that you really think Julia is having an affair with Tom?'

She looked him in the face. Her eyes were anguished. For though at first she had only laughed at what was being said about Julia she had not been able altogether to suppress the doubts that soon assailed her; she remembered a dozen little incidents that at the time had escaped her notice, but when considered in cold blood looked terribly suspicious. She had suffered such torture as she had never thought it possible to endure. Proof? She had no proof; she only had an intuition that she could not mistrust; she wanted to say yes, the impulse to do so was almost uncontrollable; she controlled it. She could not give Julia away. The fool might go and tell her and Julia would never speak to her again. He might have Julia watched and catch her out. No one could tell what might happen if she told the truth.

'No, I don't.'

Her eyes filled with tears and began to roll down her massive cheeks. Michael saw her misery. He thought her ridiculous, but he realized that she was suffering and in the kindness of his heart sought to console her.

'I was sure you didn't really. You know how fond Julia is of you, you mustn't be jealous, you know, if she has other friends.'

'God knows I don't grudge her anything,' she sobbed. 'She's been so different to me lately. She's been so cold. I've been such a loyal friend to her, Michael.'

'Yes, dear, I know you have.'

'Had I but served my God with half the zeal I served my King . . .'

'Oh, come now, it's not so bad as that. You know, I'm not the sort of chap to talk about his wife to other people. I always think that's such frightfully bad form. But you know, honestly you don't know the first thing about Julia. Sex doesn't mean a thing to her. When we were first married it was different, and I don't mind telling you after all these years that she made life a bit difficult for me. I don't say she was a nymphomaniac or anything like that, but she was inclined to be rather tiresome sometimes. Bed's all very well in its way, but there are other things in life. But after Roger was born she changed completely. Having a baby settled her. All those instincts went into her acting. You've read Freud, Dolly; what does he call it when that happens?'

'Oh, Michael, what do I care about Freud?'

'Sublimation. That's it. I often think that's what's made her such a great actress. Acting's a whole time job and if you want to be really good you've got to give your whole self to it. I'm so impatient with the public who think actors and actresses lead a devil of a life. We haven't got the time for that sort of nonsense.'

What Michael was saying made her so angry that she recovered her self-control.

'But Michael, it may be that you and I know that there's nothing wrong in Julia's going about all the time with that miserable little pip-squeak. It's so bad for her reputation. After all, one of your great assets has been your exemplary married life. Everyone has looked up to you. The public has loved to think of you as such a devoted and united couple.'

'And so we are, damn it.'

Dolly was growing impatient.

'But I tell you people are talking. You can't be so stupid as not to see that they're bound to. I mean, if Julia had had one flagrant affair after another, nobody would take any notice, but after the life she's led for so many years suddenly to break out like this—naturally everybody starts chattering. It's so bad for business.'

Michael gave her a swift glance. He smiled a little.

'I see what you mean, Dolly. I daresay there's something in what you say and in the circumstances I feel that you have a perfect right to say it. You were awfully good to us when we started and I should hate to see you let down now. I'll tell you what, I'll buy you out.'

'Buy me out?'

Dolly straightened herself and her face, a moment ago rumpled and discomposed, hardened. She was seized with indignation. He went on suavely.

'I see your point. If Julia's gadding about all night it must tell on her performances. That's obvious. She's got a funny sort of public, a lot of old ladies come to our matinées because they think she's such a sweet good woman. I don't mind admitting that if she gets herself unpleasantly talked about it might have some effect on the takings. I know Julia well enough to know that she wouldn't put up with any interference with her liberty of action. I'm her husband and I've got to put up with it. But you're in a different position altogether. I shouldn't blame you if you wanted to get out while the going was good.'

Dolly was alert now. She was far from a fool and when it came to business was a match for Michael. She was angry, but her anger gave her self-control.

'I should have thought after all these years, Michael, that you knew me better than that. I thought it my duty to warn you, but I'm prepared to take the rough with the smooth, I'm not the woman to desert a sinking ship. I daresay I can afford to lose my money better than you can.'

It gave her a great deal of satisfaction to see the disappointment that was clearly expressed on Michael's face. She knew how much money meant to him and she had a hope that what she had said would rankle. He pulled himself together quickly.

'Well, think it over, Dolly.'

She gathered up her bag and they parted with mutual expressions of affection and good will.

'Silly old bitch,' he said when the door was closed behind her.

'Pompous old ass,' she hissed as she went down in the lift.

But when she got into her magnificent and very expensive car and drove back to Montagu Square she could not hold back the heavy, painful tears that filled her eyes. She felt old, lonely, unhappy, and desperately jealous.

Chapter Seventeen

Michael flattered himself on his sense of humour. On the Sunday evening that followed his conversation with Dolly he strolled into Julia's room while she was dressing. They were going to the pictures after an early dinner.

'Who's coming tonight besides Charles?' he asked her.

'I couldn't find another woman. I've asked Tom.'

'Good! I wanted to see him.'

He chuckled at the thought of the joke he had up his sleeve. Julia was looking forward to the evening. At the cinema she would arrange the seating so that Tom sat next to her and he would hold her hand while she chatted in undertones to Charles on the other side of her. Dear Charles, it was nice of him to have loved her so long and so devotedly; she would go out of her way to be very sweet to him. Charles and Tom arrived together. Tom was wearing his new dinner jacket for the first time and he and Julia exchanged a little private glance, of satisfaction on his part and of compliment on hers.

'Well, young feller,' said Michael heartily, rubbing his hands, 'do you know what I hear about you? I hear that you're compromising my wife.'

Tom gave him a startled look and went scarlet. The habit of flushing mortified him horribly, but he could not break himself of it.

'Oh my dear,' cried Julia gaily, 'how marvellous! I've been trying to get someone to compromise me all my life. Who told you, Michael?'

'A little bird,' he said archly.

'Well, Tom, if Michael divorces me you'll have to marry me, you know.'

Charles smiled with his gentle, rather melancholy eyes.

'What have you been doing, Tom?' he asked.

Charles was gravely, Michael boisterously, diverted by the young man's obvious embarrassment. Julia, though she seemed to share their amusement, was alert and watchful.

'Well, it appears that the young rip has been taking Julia to night clubs when she ought to have been in bed and asleep.'

Julia crowed with delight.

'Shall we deny it, Tom, or shall we brazen it out?'

'Well, I'll tell you what I said to the little bird,' Michael broke in. 'I said to her, as long as Julia doesn't want me to go to night clubs with her . . .'

Julia ceased to listen to what he said. Dolly, she thought, and oddly enough she described her to herself in exactly the words Michael had used a couple of days before. Dinner was announced and their bright talk turned to other things. But though Julia took part in it with gaiety, though she appeared to be giving her guests all her attention and even listened with a show of appreciation to one of Michael's theatrical stories that she had heard twenty times before, she was privately holding an animated conversation with Dolly. Dolly cowered before her while she told her exactly what she thought of her.

'You old cow,' she said to her. 'How dare you interfere with my private concerns? No, don't speak. Don't try to excuse yourself. I know exactly what you said to Michael. It was unpardonable. I thought you were a friend of mine. I thought I could rely on you. Well, that finishes it. I'll never speak to you again. Never. Never. D'you think I'm impressed by your rotten old money? Oh, it's no good saying you didn't mean it. Where would you be except for me, I should like to know. Any distinction you've got, the only importance you have in the world, is that you happen to know me. Who's made your parties go all these years? D'you think that people came to them to see you? They came to see me. Never again. Never.'

It was in point of fact a monologue rather than a conversation.

Later on, at the cinema, she sat next to Tom as she had intended and held his hand, but it seemed to her singularly unresponsive. Like a fish's fin. She suspected that he was thinking uncomfortably of what Michael had said. She wished that she had had an opportunity of a few words with him so that she might have told him not to worry. After all no one could have carried off the incident with more brilliance than she had. Aplomb; that was the word. She wondered what it was exactly that Dolly had told Michael. She had better find out. It would not do to ask Michael, that would look as though she attached importance to it; she must find out from Dolly herself. It would be much wiser not to have a row with her. Julia smiled as she thought of the scene she would have with Dolly. She would be sweetness itself, she would wheedle it all out of her, and never give her an inkling that she was angry. It was curious that it should send a cold shiver down her back to think that people were talking about her. After all if she couldn't do what she liked, who could? Her private life was nobody's business. All the same one couldn't deny that it wouldn't be very nice if people were laughing at her. She wondered what Michael would do if he found out the truth. He couldn't very well divorce her and continue to manage for her. If he had any sense he'd shut his eyes. But Michael was funny in some ways; every now and then he would get up on his hind legs and start doing his colonel stuff. He was quite capable of saying all of a sudden that damn it all, he must behave like a gentleman. Men were such fools; there wasn't one of them who wouldn't cut off his nose to spite his face. Of course it wouldn't really matter very much to her. She could go and act in America for a year till the scandal had died down and then go into management with somebody else. But it would be a bore. And then there was Roger to consider; he'd feel it, poor lamb; he'd be humiliated, naturally; it was no good shutting one's eyes to the fact, at her age she'd look a perfect fool being divorced on account of a boy of three-and-twenty. Of course she wouldn't be such a fool as to marry Tom. Would Charles marry her? She turned and in the half-light looked at his distinguished profile. He had been madly in love with her for years; he was one of those chivalrous idiots that a woman could turn round her little finger; perhaps he wouldn't mind being co-respondent instead of Tom. That might be a very good way out. Lady Charles Tamerley. It sounded all right.

Perhaps she *had* been a little imprudent. She had always been very careful when she went to Tom's flat, but it might be that one of the chauffeurs in the mews had seen her go in or come out and had thought things. That class of people had such filthy minds. As far as the night clubs were concerned, she'd have been only too glad to go with Tom to quiet little places where no one would see them, but he didn't like that. He loved a crowd, he wanted to see smart people, and be seen. He liked to show her off.

'Damn,' she said to herself. 'Damn, damn.'

Julia didn't enjoy her evening at the cinema as much as she had expected.

Chapter Eighteen

Next day Julia got Dolly on her private number.

'Darling, it seems ages since I've seen you. What have you been doing with yourself all this time?'

'Nothing very much.'

Dolly's voice sounded cold.

'Now listen, Roger's coming home tomorrow. You know he's leaving Eton for good. I'm sending the car for him early and I want you to come to lunch. Not a party; only you and me, Michael and Roger.'

'I'm lunching out tomorrow.'

In twenty years Dolly had never been engaged when Julia wanted her to do something with her. The voice at the other end of the telephone was hostile.

'Dolly, how can you be so unkind? Roger'll be terribly disappointed. His first day at home; besides, I want to see you. I haven't seen you for ages and I miss you terribly. Can't you break your engagement, just for this once, darling, and we'll have a good old gossip after lunch, just you and me?'

No one could be more persuasive than Julia when she liked, no one could put more tenderness into her voice, nor a more irresistible appeal. There was a moment's pause and Julia knew that Dolly was struggling with her wounded feelings.

'All right, darling, I'll manage.'

'Darling.' But when she rang off Julia through clenched teeth muttered: 'The old cow.'

Dolly came. Roger listened politely while she told him that he had grown and with his grave smile answered her suitably when she said the sort of things she thought proper to a boy of his age. Julia was puzzled by him. Without talking much he listened, apparently with attention, to what the rest of them were saying, but she had an odd feeling that he was occupied with thoughts of his own. He seemed to observe them with a detached curiosity like that with which he might have observed animals in a zoo. It was faintly disquieting. When the opportunity presented itself she delivered the little bit of dialogue she had prepared for Dolly's benefit.

'Oh, Roger darling, you know your wretched father's busy tonight. I've got a couple of seats for the second house at the Palladium and Tom wants you to dine with him at the Café Royal.'

'Oh!' He paused for a second. 'All right.'

She turned to Dolly.

'It's so nice for Roger to have somebody like Tom to go about with. They're great friends, you know.'

Michael gave Dolly a glance. There was a twinkle in his eyes. He spoke.

'Tom's a very decent sort of boy. He won't let Roger get into any mischief.'

'I should have thought Roger would prefer to go about with his Eton friends,' said Dolly.

'Old cow,' thought Julia. 'Old cow.'

But when luncheon was over she asked her to come up to her room.

'I'll get into bed and you can talk to me while I'm resting. A good old girl's gossip, that's what I want.'

She put her arm affectionately round Dolly's vast waist and led her upstairs. For a while they spoke of indifferent things, clothes and servants, make-up and scandal; then Julia, leaning on her elbow, looked at Dolly with confiding eyes.

'Dolly, there's something I want to talk to you about. I want advice and you're the only person in the world whose advice I would take. I know I can trust you.'

'Of course, darling.'

'It appears that people are saying rather disagreeable things about me. Someone's been to Michael and told him that there's a lot of gossip about me and poor Tom Fennell.'

Though her eyes still wore the charming and appealing look that she knew Dolly found irresistible, she watched her closely for a start or for some change in her expression. She saw nothing.

'Who told Michael?'

'I don't know. He won't say. You know what he is when he starts being a perfect gentleman.'

She wondered if she only imagined that Dolly's features at this slightly relaxed.

'I want the truth, Dolly.'

'I'm so glad you've asked me, darling. You know how I hate to interfere in other people's business and if you hadn't brought the matter up yourself nothing would have induced me to mention it.'

'My dear, if I don't know that you're a loyal friend, who does?'

Dolly slipped off her shoes and settled down massively in her chair. Julia never took her eyes off her.

'You know how malicious people are. You've always led such a quiet, regular life. You've gone out so little, and then only with Michael or Charles Tamerley. He's different; of course everyone knows he's adored you for ages. It seems so funny that all of a sudden you should run around all over the place with a clerk in the firm that does your accounts.'

'He isn't exactly that. His father has bought him a share in the firm and he's a junior partner.'

'Yes, he gets four hundred a year.'

'How d'you know?' asked Julia quickly.

This time she was certain that Dolly was disconcerted.

'You persuaded me to go to his firm about my income-tax. One of the head partners told me. It seems a little strange that on that he should be able to have a flat, dress the way he does and take people to night clubs.'

'For all I know his father may make him an allowance.'

'His father's a solicitor in the North of London. You know very well that if he's bought him a partnership he isn't making him an allowance as well.'

'Surely you don't imagine that I'm keeping him,' said Julia, with a ringing laugh.

'I don't imagine anything, darling. Other people do.'

Julia liked neither the words Dolly spoke nor the way she said them. But she gave no sign of her uneasiness.

'It's too absurd. He's Roger's friend much more than mine. Of course I've been about with him. I felt I was getting too set. I'm tired of just going to the theatre and taking care of myself. It's no life. After all if I don't enjoy myself a little now I never shall. I'm getting on, you know, Dolly, it's no good denying it. You know what Michael is; of course he's sweet, but he is a bore.'

'No more a bore than he's ever been,' said Dolly acidly.

'I should have thought I was the last person anyone would dream would have an affair with a boy twenty years younger than myself.

'Twenty-five,' corrected Dolly. 'I should have thought so too. Unfortunately he's not very discreet.'

'What do you mean by that?'

'Well, he's told Avice Crichton that he'll get her a part in your next play.'

'Who the devil is Avice Crichton?'

'Oh, she's a young actress I know. She's as pretty as a picture.'

'He's only a silly kid. I suppose he thinks he can get round Michael. You know what Michael is with his little bits.'

'He says he can get you to do anything he wants. He says you just eat out of his hand.'

It was lucky for Julia that she was a good actress. For a second her heart stood still. How could he say a thing like that? The fool. The blasted fool. But recovering herself at once she laughed lightly.

'What nonsense! I don't believe a word of it.'

'He's a very commonplace, rather vulgar young man. It's not surprising if all the fuss you've made of him has turned his head.'

Julia, smiling good-naturedly, looked at her with ingenuous eyes.

'But, darling, *you* don't think he's my lover, do you?'

'If I don't, I'm the only person who doesn't.'

'And do you?'

For a minute Dolly did not answer. They looked at one another steadily, their hearts were black with hatred; but Julia still smiled.

'If you give me your solemn word of honour that he isn't, of course I'll believe you.'

Julia dropped her voice to a low, grave note. It had a true ring of sincerity:

'I've never told you a lie yet, Dolly, and I'm too old to begin now. I give you my solemn word of honour that Tom has never been anything more to me than just a friend.'

'You take a great weight off my mind.'

Julia knew that Dolly did not believe her and Dolly was aware that Julia knew it. She went on.

'But in that case, for your own sake, Julia dear, do be sensible. Don't go about with this young man any more. Drop him.'

'Oh, I couldn't do that. That would be an admission that people were right in what they thought. After all, my conscience is clear. I can afford to hold my head high. I should despise myself if I allowed my behaviour to be influenced by malicious gossip.'

Dolly slipped her feet back into her shoes and getting her lipstick out of her bag did her lips.

'Well, dear, you're old enough to know your own mind.'

They parted coldly.

But one or two of Dolly's remarks had been somewhat of a shock to Julia. They rankled. It was disconcerting that gossip had so nearly reached the truth. But did it matter? Plenty of women had lovers and who bothered? And an actress. No one expected an actress to be a pattern of propriety.

'It's my damned virtue. That's at the bottom of the trouble.'

She had acquired the reputation of a perfectly virtuous woman, whom the tongue of scandal could not touch, and now it looked as though her reputation was a prison that she had built round herself. But there was worse. What had Tom meant by saying that she ate out of his hand? That deeply affronted her. Silly little fool. How dare he? She didn't know what to do about it either. She would have liked to tax him with it. What was the good? He would deny it. The only thing was to say nothing; it had all gone too far now, she must accept everything. It was no good not facing the truth, he didn't love her, he was her lover because it gratified his self-esteem, because it brought him various things he cared for and because in his own eyes at least it gave him a sort of position.

'If I had any sense I'd chuck him.' She gave an angry laugh. 'It's easy to say that. I love him.'

The strange thing was that when she looked into her heart it was not Julia Lambert the woman who resented the affront, she didn't care for herself, it was the affront to Julia Lambert the actress that stung her. She had often felt that her talent, genius the critics called it, but that was a very grand word, her gift, if you like, was not really herself, not even part of her, but something outside that used her, Julia Lambert the woman, in order to express itself. It was a strange, immaterial personality that seemed to descend upon her and it did things through her that she did not know she was capable of doing. She was an ordinary, prettyish, ageing woman. Her gift had neither age nor form. It was a spirit that played on her body as the violinist plays on his violin. It was the slight to that that galled her.

She tried to sleep. She was so accustomed to sleeping in the afternoon that she could always drop off the moment she composed herself, but on this occasion she turned restlessly from side to side and sleep would not come. At last she looked at the clock. Tom often got back from his office soon after five. She yearned for him; in his arms was peace, when she was with him nothing else mattered. She dialled his number.

'Hulloa? Yes. Who is it?'

She held the receiver to her ear, panic-stricken. It was Roger's voice. She hung up.

Chapter Nineteen

Nor did Julia sleep well that night. She was awake when she heard Roger come in, and turning on her light she saw that it was four. She frowned. He came clattering down the stone stairs next morning just when she was beginning to think of getting up.

'Can I come in, mummy?'

'Come in.'

He was still in his pyjamas and dressing-gown. She smiled at him because he looked so fresh and young.

'You were very late last night.'

'No, not very. I was in by one.'

'Liar. I looked at my clock. It was four.'

'All right. It was four then,' he agreed cheerfully.

'What on earth were you doing?'

'We went on to some place after the show and had supper. We danced.'

'Who with?'

'A couple of girls we picked up. Tom knew them before.'

'What were their names?'

'One was called Jill and one was called Joan. I don't know what their other names were. Joan's on the stage. She asked me if I couldn't get her an understudy in your next play.'

At all events neither of them was Avice Crichton. That name had been in her thoughts ever since Dolly had mentioned it.

'But those places aren't open till four.'

'No, we went back to Tom's flat. Tom made me promise I wouldn't tell you. He said you'd be furious.'

'Oh, my dear, it takes a great deal more than that to make me furious. I promise you I won't say a word.'

'If anyone's to blame I am. I went to see Tom yesterday afternoon and we arranged it then. All this stuff about love that one hears about in plays and reads in novels. I'm nearly eighteen. I thought I ought to see for myself what it was all about.'

Julia sat up in bed and looked at Roger with wide, enquiring eyes.

'Roger, what *do* you mean?'

He was composed and serious.

'Tom said he knew a couple of girls who were all right. He's had them both himself. They live together and so we phoned and asked them to meet us after the show. He told them I was a virgin and they'd better toss up for me. When we got back to the flat he took Jill into the bedroom and left me the sitting-room and Joan.'

For the moment she did not think of Tom, she was so disturbed at what Roger was saying.

'I don't think it's so much really. I don't see it's anything to make all that fuss about.'

She could not speak. The tears filled her eyes and ran quickly down her face.

'Mummy, what's the matter? Why are you crying?'

'But you're a little boy.'

He came over to her and sitting on the side of her bed took her in his arms.

'Darling, don't cry. I wouldn't have told you if I'd thought it was going to upset you. After all, it had to happen sooner or later.'

'But so soon. So soon. It makes me feel so old.'

'Not you, darling. Age cannot wither her, nor custom stale her infinite variety.'

She giggled through her tears.

'You fool, Roger, d'you think Cleopatra would have liked what that silly old donkey said of her? You might have waited a little longer.'

'It's just as well I didn't. I know all about it now. To tell you the truth I think it's rather disgusting.'

She sighed deeply. It was a comfort to feel him holding her so tenderly. But she felt terribly sorry for herself.

'You're not angry with me, darling?' he asked.

'Angry? No. But if it had to come I wish it hadn't been quite so matter of fact. You talk as though it had just been a rather curious experiment.'

'I suppose it was in a way.'

She gave him a little smile.

'And you really think that was love?'

'Well, it's what most people mean by it, isn't it?'

'No, they don't, they mean pain and anguish, shame, ecstasy, heaven and hell; they mean the sense of living more intensely, and unutterable boredom; they mean freedom and slavery; they mean peace and unrest.'

Something in the stillness with which he listened to her made her give him a glance through her eyelashes. There was a curious expression in his eyes. She did not know what it meant. It was as though he were gravely listening to a sound that came from a long way off.

'It doesn't sound as though it were much fun,' he murmured.

She took his smooth face in her hands and kissed his lips.

'I'm a fool, aren't I? You see, I still see you as a little baby boy that I'm holding in my arms.'

A twinkle shone in his eyes.

'What are you grinning at, you ape?'

'It made a damned good photograph, didn't it?'

She could not but laugh.

'You pig. You filthy pig.'

'I say, about the understudy, is there any chance for Joan?'

'Tell her to come and see me one day.'

But when Roger left her she sighed. She was depressed. She felt very lonely. Her life had always been so full and so exciting that she had never had the time to busy herself much with Roger. She got in a state, of course, when he had whooping-cough or measles, but he was for the most part in robust health, and then he occupied a pleasant place in the background of her consciousness. But she had always felt that he was there to be attended to when she was inclined and she had often thought it would be nice when he was old enough really to share her interests. It came to her as a shock now to realize that, without ever having really possessed him, she had lost him. Her lips tightened when she thought of the girl who had taken him from her.

'An understudy. My foot.'

Her pain absorbed her so that she could not feel the grief she might have felt from her discovery of Tom's perfidy. She had always known in her bones that he was unfaithful to her. At his age, with his wanton temperament, with herself tied down by her performances at the theatre, by all manner of engagements which her position forced upon her, it was plain that he had ample opportunity to gratify his inclinations. She had shut her eyes. All she asked was that she should not know. This was the first time that an actual fact had been thrust upon her notice.

'I must just put up with it,' she sighed. Thoughts wandered through her mind. 'It's like lying and not knowing you're lying, that's what's fatal; I suppose it's better to be a fool and know it than a fool and not know it.'

Chapter Twenty

Tom went to Eastbourne with his family for Christmas. Julia had two performances on Boxing Day, so the Gosselyns stayed in town; they went to a large party at the Savoy that Dolly de Vries gave to see the New Year in; and a few days later Roger set off for Vienna. While he was in London Julia saw little of Tom. She did not ask Roger what they did when they tore about the town together, she did not want to know, she steeled herself not to think and distracted her mind by going to as many parties as she could. And there was always her acting; when once she got into the theatre her anguish, her humiliation, her jealousy were allayed. It gave her a sense of triumphant power to find, as it were in her pot of grease paint, another personality that could be touched by no human griefs. With that refuge always at hand she could support anything.

On the day that Roger left, Tom rang her up from his office.

'Are you doing anything tonight? What about going out on the binge?'

'No, I'm busy.'

It was not true, but the words slipped out of her mouth independent of her will.

'Oh, are you? Well, what about tomorrow?'

If he had expressed disappointment, if he had asked her to cut the date she supposed she had, she might have had strength to break with him then and there. His casualness defeated her.

'Tomorrow's all right.'

'O.K. I'll fetch you at the theatre after the show. Bye-bye.'

Julia was ready and waiting when he was shown into her dressing-room. She was strangely nervous. His face lit up when he saw her, and when Evie went out of the room for a moment he caught her in his arms and warmly kissed her on the lips.

'I feel all the better for that,' he laughed.

You would never have thought to look at him, so young, fresh and ingenuous, in such high spirits, that he was capable of giving her so much pain. You would never have thought that he was so deceitful. It was quite plain that he had not noticed that for more than a fortnight he had hardly seen her.

('Oh, God, if I could only tell him to go to hell.')

But she looked at him with a gay smile in her lovely eyes.

'Where are we going?'

'I've got a table at Quag's. They've got a new turn there, an American conjurer, who's grand.'

She talked with vivacity all through supper. She told him about the various parties she had been to, and the theatrical functions she had not been able to get out of, so that it seemed only on account of her engagements that they had not met. It disconcerted her to perceive that he took it as perfectly natural. He was glad to see her, that was plain, he was interested in what she had been doing and in the people she had seen, but it was plain also that he had not missed her. To see what he would say she told him that she had had an offer to take the play in which she was acting to New York. She told him the terms that had been suggested.

'They're marvellous,' he said, his eyes glittering. 'What a snip! You can't lose and you may make a packet.'

'The only thing is, I don't much care for leaving London.'

'Why on earth not? I should have thought you'd jump at it. The play's had a good long run, for all you know it'll be pretty well through by Easter, and if you want to make a stab at America you couldn't have a better vehicle.'

'I don't see why it shouldn't run through the summer. Besides, I don't like strangers very much. I'm fond of my friends.'

'I think that's silly. Your friends'll get along without you all right. And you'll have a grand time in New York.'

Her gay laugh was very convincing.

'One would think you were terribly anxious to get rid of me.'

'Of course I should miss you like hell. But it would only be for a few months. If I had a chance like that I'd jump at it.'

But when they had finished supper and the commissionaire had called up a taxi for them he gave the address of the flat as if it were an understood thing that they should go back to it. In the taxi he put his arm round her waist and kissed her, and later, when she lay in his arms, in the little single bed, she felt that all the pain she had suffered during that last fortnight was not too great a price to pay for the happy peace that filled her heart.

Julia continued to go to the smart supper places and to night clubs with Tom. If people wanted to think he was her lover, let them; she was past caring. But it happened more than once that he was engaged when she wanted him to go somewhere with her. It had spread around among Julia's grander friends that Tom was very clever at helping one with one's income-tax returns. The Dennorants had asked him down to the country for a week-end, and here he had met a number of persons who were glad to take advantage of his technical knowledge. He began to get invitations from people whom Julia did not know. Acquaintances would mention him to her.

'You know Tom Fennell, don't you? He's very clever, isn't he? I hear he's saved the Gillians hundreds of pounds on their income-tax.'

Julia was none too pleased. It was through her that he had got asked to parties that he wanted to go to. It began to look as if in this respect he could do without her. He was pleasant and unassuming, very well-dressed now, and with a fresh, clean look that was engaging; he was able to save people money; Julia knew the world which he was so anxious to get into well enough to realize that he would soon establish himself in it. She had no very high opinion of the morals of the women he would meet there and she could name more than one person of title who would be glad to snap him up. Julia's comfort was that they were all as mean as cat's meat. Dolly had said he was only earning four hundred a year; he certainly couldn't live in those circles on that.

Julia had with decision turned down the American offer before ever she mentioned it to Tom; their play was playing to very good business. But one of those inexplicable slumps that occasionally affect the theatre now swept over London and the takings suddenly dropped. It looked as though they would not be able to carry on long after Easter. They had a new play on which they set great hopes. It was called *Nowadays*, and the intention had been to produce it early in the autumn. It had a great part for Julia and the advantage of one that well suited Michael. It was the sort of play that might easily run a year. Michael did not much like the idea of producing it in May, with the summer coming on, but there seemed no help for it and he began looking about for a cast.

One afternoon, during the interval at a matinée, Evie brought a note in to Julia. She was surprised to see Roger's handwriting.

> Dear Mother,
>   This is to introduce to you Miss Joan Denver who I talked to you about. She's awfully keen on getting in the Siddons Theatre and would be quite satisfied with an understudy however small.
>   Your affectionate son,
>   Roger

Julia smiled at the formal way in which he wrote; she was tickled because he was so grown up as to try to get jobs for his girl friends. Then she suddenly remembered who Joan Denver was. Joan and Jill. She was the girl who had seduced poor Roger. Her face went grim. But she was curious to see her.

'Is George there?' George was the door-keeper. Evie nodded and opened the door.

'George.'

He came in.

'Is the lady who brought this letter here now?'

'Yes, miss.'

'Tell her I'll see her after the play.'

She wore in the last act an evening dress with a train; it was a very grand dress and showed her beautiful figure to advantage. She wore diamonds in her dark hair and diamond bracelets on her arms. She looked, as indeed the part required, majestic. She received Joan Denver the moment she had taken her last call. Julia could in the twinkling of an eye leap from her part into private life, but now without an effort she continued to play the imperious, aloof, stately and well-bred woman of the play.

'I've kept you waiting so long I thought I wouldn't keep you till I'd got changed.'

Her cordial smile was the smile of a queen; her graciousness kept you at a respectful distance. In a glance she had taken in the young girl who entered her dressing-room. She was young, with a pretty little face and a snub nose, a good deal made-up and not very well made-up.

'Her legs are too short,' thought Julia. 'Very second-rate.'

She had evidently put on her best clothes and the same glance had told Julia all about them.

('Shaftesbury Avenue. Off the nail.')

The poor thing was at the moment frightfully nervous. Julia made her sit down and offered her a cigarette.

'There are matches by your side.'

She saw her hands tremble when she tried to strike one. It broke and she rubbed a second three times against the box before she could get it to light.

('If Roger could only see her now! Cheap rouge, cheap lipstick, and scared out of her wits. Gay little thing, he thought she was.')

'Have you been on the stage long, Miss —— I'm so sorry I've forgotten your name.'

'Joan Denver.' Her throat was dry and she could hardly speak. Her cigarette went out and she held it helplessly. She answered Julia's question. 'Two years.'

'How old are you?'

'Nineteen.'

('That's a lie. You're twenty-two if you're a day.') 'You know my son, don't you?'

'Yes.'

'He's just left Eton. He's gone to Vienna to learn German. Of course he's very young, but his father and I thought it would be good for him to spend a few months abroad before going up to Cambridge. And what parts have you played? Your cigarette's gone out. Won't you have another?'

'Oh, it's all right, thanks. I've been playing on tour. But I'm frightfully anxious to be in town.' Despair gave her courage and she uttered the speech she had evidently prepared. 'I've got the most tremendous admiration for you, Miss Lambert. I always say you're the greatest actress on the stage. I've learnt more from you than I did all the years I was at the R.A.D.A. My greatest ambition is to be in your theatre, Miss Lambert, and if you could see your way to giving me a little something, I know it would be the most wonderful chance a girl could have.'

'Will you take off your hat?'

Joan Denver took the cheap little hat off her head and with a quick gesture shook out her close-cropped curls.

'What pretty hair you have,' said Julia.

Still with that slightly imperious, but infinitely cordial smile, the smile that a queen in royal procession bestows on her subjects, Julia gazed at her. She did not speak. She remembered Jane Taitbout's maxim: Don't pause unless it's necessary, but then pause as long as you can. She could almost hear the girl's heart beating and she felt her shrinking in her ready-made clothes, shrinking in her skin.

'What made you think of asking my son to give you a letter to me?'

Joan grew red under her make-up and she swallowed before she answered.

'I met him at a friend's house and I told him how much I admired you and he said he thought perhaps you'd have something for me in your next play.'

'I'm just turning over the parts in my mind.'

'I wasn't thinking of a part. If I could have an understudy–I mean, that would give me a chance of attending rehearsals and studying your technique. That's an education in itself. Everyone agrees about that.'

('Silly little fool, trying to flatter me. As if I didn't know that. And why the hell should I educate her?') 'It's very sweet of you to put it like that. I'm only a very ordinary person really. The public is so kind, so very kind. You're a pretty little thing. And young. Youth is so beautiful. Our policy has always been to give the younger people a chance. After all we can't go on for ever, and we look upon it as a duty we owe the public to train up actors and actresses to take our place when the time comes.'

Julia said these words so simply, in her beautifully modulated voice, that Joan Denver's heart was warmed. She'd got round the old girl and the understudy was as good as hers. Tom Fennell had said that if she played her cards well with Roger it might easily lead to something.

'Oh, that won't be for a long while yet, Miss Lambert,' she said, her eyes, her pretty dark eyes glowing.

('You're right there, my girl, dead right. I bet I could play you off the stage when I was seventy.')

'I must think it over. I hardly know yet what understudies we shall want in our next play.'

'I hear there's some talk of Avice Crichton for the girl's part. I thought perhaps I could understudy her.'

Avice Crichton. No flicker of the eyes showed that the name meant anything to Julia.

'My husband has mentioned her, but nothing is settled yet. I don't know her at all. Is she clever?'

'I think so. I was at the Academy with her.'

'And pretty as a picture, they tell me.' Rising to her feet to show that the audience was at an end, Julia put off her royalty. She changed her tone and became on a sudden the jolly, good-natured actress who would do a good turn to anyone if she could. 'Well, dear, leave me your name and address and if there's anything doing I'll let you know.'

'You won't forget me, Miss Lambert?'

'No, dear, I promise you I won't. It's been so nice to see you. You have a very sweet personality. You'll find your way out, won't you? Good-bye.'

'A fat chance she's got of ever setting foot in this theatre,' said Julia to herself when she was gone. 'Dirty little bitch to seduce my son. Poor lamb. It's a shame, that's what it is; women like that oughtn't to be allowed.'

She looked at herself in the glass as she slipped out of her beautiful gown. Her eyes were hard and her lips had a sardonic curl. She addressed her reflection.

'And I may tell you this, old girl: there's one person who isn't going to play in *Nowadays* and that's Miss Avice Crichton.''

Chapter Twenty-one

But a week or so later Michael mentioned her.

'I say, have you ever heard of a girl called Avice Crichton?'

'Never.'

'I'm told she's rather good. A lady and all that sort of things. Her father's in the army. I was wondering if she'd do for Honor.'

'How did you hear about her?'

'Through Tom. He knows her, he says she's clever. She's playing in a Sunday night show. Next Sunday, in point of fact. He says he thinks it might be worth while to go and have a look-see.'

'Well, why don't you?'

'I was going down to Sandwich to play golf. Would it bore you awfully to go? I expect the play's rotten, but you'd be able to tell if it was worth while letting her read the part. Tom'll go with you.'

Julia's heart was beating nineteen to the dozen.

'Of course I'll go.'

She phoned to Tom and asked him to come round and have a snack before they went to the theatre. He arrived before she was ready.

'Am I late or were you early?' she said, when she came into the drawing-room.

She saw that he had been waiting impatiently. He was nervous and eager.

'They're going to ring up sharp at eight,' he said. 'I hate getting to a play after it's begun.'

His agitation told her all she wanted to know. She lingered a little over the cocktails.

'What is the name of this actress we're going to see tonight?' she asked.

'Avice Crichton. I'm awfully anxious to know what you think about her. I think she's a find. She knows you're coming tonight. She's frightfully nervous, but I told her she needn't be. You know what these Sunday night plays are; scratch rehearsals and all that; I said you'd quite understand and you'd make allowances.'

All through dinner he kept looking at his watch. Julia acted the woman of the world. She talked of one thing and another and noticed that he listened with distraction. As soon as he could he brought the conversation back to Avice Crichton.

'Of course I haven't said anything to her about it, but I believe she'd be all right for Honor.' He had read *Nowadays*, as he read, before they were produced, all Julia's plays. 'She looks the part all right, I'm sure of that. She's had a struggle and of course it would be a wonderful chance for her. She admires you tremendously and she's terribly anxious to get into a play with you.'

'That's understandable. It means the chance of a year's run and a lot of managers seeing her.'

'She's the right colour, she's very fair; she'd be a good contrast to you.'

'What with platinum and peroxide there's no lack of blondes on the stage.'

'But hers is natural.'

'Is it? I had a long letter from Roger this morning. He seems to be having quite a good time in Vienna.'

Tom's interest subsided. He looked at his watch. When the coffee came Julia said it was undrinkable. She said she must have some more made.

'Oh, Julia, it isn't worth while. We shall be awfully late.'

'I don't suppose it matters if we miss the first few minutes.'

His voice was anguished.

'I promised we wouldn't be late. She's got a very good scene almost at the beginning.'

'I'm sorry, but I can't go without my coffee.'

While they waited for it she maintained a bright flow of conversation. He scarcely answered. He looked anxiously at the door. And when the coffee came she drank it with maddening deliberation. By the time they got in the car he was in a state of cold fury and he stared silently in front of him with a sulky pout on his mouth. Julia was not dissatisfied with herself. They reached the theatre two minutes before the curtain rose and as Julia appeared there was a burst of clapping from the audience. Julia, apologizing to the people she disturbed, threaded her way to her seat in the middle of the stalls. Her faint smile acknowledged the applause that greeted her beautifully-timed entrance, but her downcast eyes modestly disclaimed that it could have any connection with her.

The curtain went up and after a short scene two girls came in, one very pretty and young, the other much older and plain. In a minute Julia turned to Tom and whispered:

'Which is Avice Crichton, the young one or the old one?'

'The young one.'

'Oh, of course, you said she was fair, didn't you?'

She gave his face a glance. He had lost his sulky look; a happy smile played on his lips. Julia turned her attention to the stage. Avice Crichton was very pretty, no one could deny that, with lovely golden hair, fine blue eyes and a little straight nose; but it was a type that Julia did not care for.

'Insipid,' she said to herself. 'Chorus-girly.'

She watched her performance for a few minutes. She watched intently; then she leant back in her stall with a little sigh.

'She can't act for toffee,' she decided.

When the curtain fell Tom turned to her eagerly. He had completely got over his bad temper.

'What do you think of her?'

'She's as pretty as a picture.'

'I know that. But her acting. Don't you think she's good?'

'Yes, clever.'

'I wish you'd come round and tell her that yourself. It would buck her up tremendously.'

'I?'

He did not realize what he was asking her to do. It was unheard-of that she, Julia Lambert, should go behind and congratulate a small-part actress.

'I promised I'd take you round after the second act. Be a sport, Julia. It'll please her so much.'

('The fool. The blasted fool. All right, I'll go through with it.') 'Of course if you think it'll mean anything to her, I'll come with pleasure.'

After the second act they went through the iron door and Tom led her to Avice Crichton's dressing-room. She was sharing it with the plain girl with whom she had made her first entrance. Tom effected the introductions. She held out a limp hand in a slightly affected manner.

'I'm so glad to meet you, Miss Lambert. Excuse this dressing-room, won't you? But it was no good trying to make it look nice just for one night.'

She was not in the least nervous. Indeed, she seemed self,assured.

('Hard as nails. And with an eye to the main chance. Doing the colonel's daughter on me.')

'It's awfully nice of you to come round. I'm afraid it's not much of a play, but when one's starting like I am one has to put up with what one can get. I was rather doubtful about it when they sent it me to read but I took a fancy to the part.'

'You play it charmingly,' said Julia.

'It's awfully nice of you to say so. I wish we could have had a few more rehearsals. I particularly wanted to show *you* what I could do.'

'Well, you know, I've been connected with the profession a good many years. I always think, if one has talent one can't help showing it. Don't you?'

'I know what you mean. Of course I want a lot more experience, I know that, but it's only a chance I want really. I know I can act. If I could only get a part that I could really get my teeth into.'

She waited a little in order to let Julia say that she had in her new play just the part that would suit her, but Julia continued to look at her smilingly. Julia was grimly amused to find herself treated like a curate's wife to whom the squire's lady was being very kind.

'Have you been on the stage long?' she said at last. 'It seems funny I should never have heard of you.'

'Well, I was in revue for a while, but I felt I was just wasting my time. I was out on tour all last season. I don't want to leave London again if I can help it.'

'The theatrical profession's terribly overcrowded,' said Julia.

'Oh, I know. It seems almost hopeless unless you've got influence or something. I hear you're putting a new play on soon.'

'Yes.'

Julia continued to smile with an almost intolerable sweetness.

'If there's a part for me in it, I'd most awfully like to play with you. I'm so sorry Mr Gosselyn couldn't come tonight.'

'I'll tell him about you.'

'D'you really think there's a chance for me?' Through her self-assurance, through the country-house manner she assumed in order to impress Julia, there pierced an anxious eagerness. 'If you'd put in a word for me it would help so much.'

Julia gave her a reflective look.

'I take my husband's advice more often than he takes mine,' she smiled.

When they left the dressing-room so that Avice Crichton might change for the third act, Julia caught the questioning glance she gave Tom as she said good-bye to him. Julia was conscious, though she saw no movement, that he slightly shook his head. Her sensibility at that moment was extraordinarily acute and she translated the mute dialogue into words.

'Coming to supper afterwards?'

'No, damn it, I can't, I've got to see her home.'

Julia listened to the third act grimly. That was in order since the play was serious. When it was over and a pale shattered author had made a halting speech, Tom asked her where she would like to go for supper.

'Let's go home and talk,' she said. 'If you're hungry I'm sure we can find something to eat in the kitchen.'

'D'you mean to Stanhope Place?'

'Yes.'

'All right.'

She felt his relief that she did not want to go back to the flat. He was silent in the car and she knew that it irked him to have to come back with her. She guessed that someone was giving a supper party to which Avice Crichton was going and he wanted to be there. The house was dark and empty when they reached it. The servants were in bed. Julia suggested that they should go down to the basement and forage.

'I don't want anything to eat unless you do.' he said. 'I'll just have a whisky and soda and go to bed. I've got a very heavy day tomorrow at the office.'

'All right. Bring it up to the drawing-room. I'll go and turn on the lights.'

When he came up she was doing her face in front of a mirror and she continued till he had poured out the whisky and sat down. Then she turned round. He looked very young, and incredibly charming, in his beautiful clothes, sitting there in the big armchair, and all the bitterness she had felt that evening, all the devouring jealousy of the last few days, were dissipated on a sudden by the intensity of her passion. She sat down on the arm of his chair and caressingly passed her hand over his hair. He drew back with an angry gesture.

'Don't do that,' he said. 'I do hate having my hair mussed about.'

It was like a knife in her heart. He had never spoken to her in that tone before. But she laughed lightly and getting up took the whisky he had poured out for her and sat down in a chair opposite him. The movement he had made, the words he had spoken, were instinctive and he was a trifle abashed. He avoided her glance and his face once more bore a sulky look. The moment was decisive. For a while they were silent. Julia's heart beat painfully, but at last she forced herself to speak.

'Tell me,' she said, smiling, 'have you been to bed with Avice Crichton?'

'Of course not,' he cried.

'Why not? She's pretty.'

'She's not that sort of girl. I respect her.'

Julia let none of her feelings appear on her face. Her manner was wonderfully casual; she might have been talking of the fall of empires or the death of kings.

'D'you know what I should have said? I should have said you were madly in love with her.' He still avoided her eyes. 'Are you engaged to her by any chance?'

'No.'

He looked at her now, but the eyes that met Julia's were hostile.

'Have you asked her to marry you?'

'How could I? A damned rotter like me.'

He spoke so passionately that Julia was astonished.

'What *are* you talking about?'

'Oh what's the good of beating about the bush? How could I ask a decent girl to marry me? I'm nothing but a kept boy and, God knows, you have a good reason to know it.'

'Don't be so silly. What a fuss to make over a few little presents I've given you.'

'I oughtn't to have taken them. I knew all the time it was wrong. It all came so gradually that I didn't realize what was happening till I was in it up to my neck. I couldn't afford to lead the life you made me lead; I was absolutely up against it. I had to take money from you.'

'Why not? After all, I'm a very rich woman.'

'Damn your money.'

He was holding a glass in his hands and yielding to a sudden impulse, he flung it into the fireplace. It shattered.

'You needn't break up the happy home,' said Julia ironically.

'I'm sorry. I didn't mean to do that.' He sank back into his chair and turned his head away. 'I'm so ashamed of myself. It's not very nice to have lost one's self-respect.'

Julia hesitated. She did not quite know what to say.

'It seemed only natural to help you when you were in a hole. It was a pleasure to me.'

'I know, you were wonderfully tactful about it. You almost persuaded me that I was doing you a service when you paid my debts. You made it easy for me to behave like a cad.'

'I'm sorry you should feel like that about it.'

She spoke rather tartly. She was beginning to feel a trifle irritated.

'There's nothing for you to be sorry about. You wanted me and you bought me. If I was such a skunk as to let myself be bought that was no business of yours.'

'How long have you been feeling like this?'

'From the beginning.'

'That isn't true.'

She knew that what had awakened his conscience was the love that had seized him for a girl who he believed was pure. The poor fool! Didn't he know that Avice Crichton would go to bed with an assistant stage-manager if she thought it would get her a part?

'If you're in love with Avice Crichton why don't you tell me so?' He looked at her miserably, but did not answer. 'Are you afraid it'll crab her chances of getting a part in the new play? You ought to know me well enough by now to know that I would never let sentiment interfere with business.'

He could hardly believe his ears.

'What do you mean by that?'

'I think she's rather a find. I'm going to tell Michael that I think she'll do very well.'

'Oh, Julia, you are a brick. I never knew what a wonderful woman you were.'

'You should have asked me and I'd have told you.'

He gave a sigh of relief.

'My dear, I'm so terribly fond of you.'

'I know, and I'm terribly fond of you. You're great fun to go about with and you're always so well turned out, you're a credit to any woman. I've liked going to bed with you and I've a sort of notion you've liked going to bed with me. But let's face it, I've never been in love with you any more than you've been in love with me. I knew it couldn't last. Sooner or later you were bound to fall in love and that would end it. And you have fallen in love, haven't you?'

'Yes.'

She was determined to make him say it, but when he did the pang it gave her was dreadful. Notwithstanding, she smiled good-humouredly.

'We've had some very jolly times together, but don't you think the moment has come to call it a day?'

She spoke so naturally, almost jestingly, that no one could have guessed that the pain at her heart seemed past bearing. She waited for her answer with sickening dread.

'I'm awfully sorry, Julia; I must regain my self-respect.' He looked at her with troubled eyes. 'You aren't angry with me?'

'Because you've transferred your volatile affections from me to Avice Crichton?' Her eyes danced with mischievous laughter. 'My dear, of course not. After all they stay in the profession.'

'I'm very grateful to you for all you've done for me. I don't want you to think I'm not.'

'Oh, my pet, don't talk such nonsense. I've done nothing for you.' She got up. 'Now you really must go. You've got a heavy day at the office tomorrow and I'm dog-tired.'

It was a load off his mind. But he wasn't quite happy for all that, he was puzzled by her tone, which was so friendly and yet at the same time faintly ironical; he felt a trifle let down. He went up to her to kiss her good night. She hesitated for the fraction of a second, then with a friendly smile gave him first one cheek and then the other.

'You'll find your way out, won't you?' She put her hand to her mouth to hide an elaborate yawn. 'Oh, I'm so sleepy.'

The moment he had gone she turned out the lights and went to the

window. She peered cautiously through the curtains. She heard him slam
the front door and saw him come out. He looked right and left. She guessed
at once that he was looking for a taxi. There was none in sight and he started
to walk in the direction of the Park. She knew that he was going to join Avice
Crichton at the supper party and tell her the glad news. Julia sank into a
chair. She had acted, she had acted marvellously, and now she felt all in.
Tears, tears that nobody could see, rolled down her cheeks. She was
miserably unhappy. There was only one thing that enabled her to bear her
wretchedness, and that was the icy contempt that she could not but feel for
the silly boy who could prefer to her a small-part actress who didn't even
begin to know how to act. It was grotesque. She couldn't use her hands; why,
she didn't even know how to walk across the stage.

'If I had any sense of humour I'd just laugh my head off,' she cried. 'It's
the most priceless joke I've ever heard.'

She wondered what Tom would do now. The rent of the flat would be
falling due on quarter-day. A lot of the things in it belonged to her. He
wouldn't much like going back to his bed-sitting room in Tavistock Square.
She thought of the friends he had made through her. He'd been clever with
them. They found him useful and he'd keep them. But it wouldn't be so easy
for him to take Avice about. She was a hard, mercenary little thing, Julia was
sure of that, she wouldn't be much inclined to bother about him when his
money flowed less freely. The fool to be taken in by her pretence of virtue!
Julia knew the type. It was quite obvious, she was only using Tom to get a
part at the Siddons and the moment she got it she would give him the air.
Julia started when this notion crossed her mind. She had promised Tom that
Avice should have the part in *Nowadays* because it fell into the scene she was
playing, but she had attached no importance to her promise. Michael was
always there to put his foot down.

'By God, she shall have the part,' she said out loud. She chuckled
maliciously. 'Heaven knows, I'm a good-natured woman, but there are
limits to everything.'

It would be a satisfaction to turn the tables on Tom and Avice Crichton.
She sat on, in the darkness, grimly thinking how she would do it. But every
now and then she started to cry again, for from the depths of her
subconscious surged up recollections that were horribly painful.
Recollections of Tom's slim, youthful body against hers, his warm
nakedness and the peculiar feel of his lips, his smile, at once shy and roguish,
and the smell of his curly hair.

'If I hadn't been a fool I'd have said nothing. I ought to know him by now.
It's only an infatuation. He'd have got over it and then he'd have come
hungrily back to me.'

Now she was nearly dead with fatigue. She got up and went to bed. She
took a sleeping-draught.

Chapter Twenty-two

But she woke early next morning, at six, and began to think of Tom. She repeated to herself all she had said to him and all he had said to her. She was harassed and unhappy. Her only consolation was that she had carried the rupture through with so careless a gaiety that he could not guess how miserable she had made him.

She spent a wretched day, unable to think of anything else, and angry with herself because she could not put Tom out of her mind. It would not have been so bad if she could have confided her grief to a friend. She wanted someone to console her, someone to tell her that Tom was not worth troubling about and to assure her that he had treated her shamefully. As a rule she took her troubles to Charles or to Dolly. Of course Charles would give her all the sympathy she needed, but it would be a terrible blow to him, after all he had loved her to distraction for twenty years, and it would be cruel to tell him that she had given to a very ordinary young man what he would gladly have sacrificed ten years of his life for. She was his ideal and it would be heartless on her part to shatter it. It certainly did her good at that moment to be assured that Charles Tamerley, so distinguished, so cultured, so elegant, loved her with an imperishable devotion. Of course Dolly would be delighted if she confided in her. They had not seen much of one another lately, but Julia knew that she had only to call up and Dolly would come running. Even though she more than suspected the truth already she'd be shocked and jealous when Julia made a clean breast of it, but she'd be so thankful that everything was over, she'd forgive. It would be a comfort to both of them to tear Tom limb from limb. Of course it wouldn't be very nice to admit that Tom had chucked her, and Dolly was so shrewd, she would never get away with the lie that she had chucked him. She wanted to have a good cry with somebody, and there didn't seem to be any reason for it if she had made the break herself. It would be a score for Dolly, and however sympathetic she was it was asking too much of human nature to expect that she would be altogether sorry that Julia had been taken down a peg or two. Dolly had always worshipped her. She wasn't going to give her a peep at her feet of clay.

'It almost looks as if the only person I can go to is Michael,' she giggled. 'But I suppose it wouldn't do.'

She knew exactly what he would say.

'My dear girl, I'm really not the sort of feller you ought to come to with a story like that. Damn it all, you put me in a very awkward position. I flatter myself I'm pretty broad-minded, I may be an actor, but when all's said and done I am a gentleman, and well, I mean, I mean it's such damned bad form.'

Michael did not get home till the afternoon, and when he came into her room she was resting. He told her about his week-end and the result of his matches. He had played very well, some of his recoveries had been marvellous, and he described them in detail.

'By the way, what about that girl you saw last night, is she any good?'

'I really think she is, you know. She's very pretty. You're sure to fall for her.'

'Oh, my dear, at my time of life. Can she act?'

'She's inexperienced of course, but I think she's got it in her.'

'Oh well, I'd better have her up and give her the once over. How can I get hold of her?'

'Tom's got her address.'

'I'll phone right away.'

He took off the receiver and dialled Tom's number. Tom was in and Michael wrote down the address on a pad.

The conversation went on.

'Oh, my dear old chap, I'm sorry to hear that. What rotten luck!'

'What's the matter?' asked Julia.

He motioned her to be quiet.

'Oh, well, I don't want to be hard on you. Don't you worry. I'm sure we can come to some arrangement that will be satisfactory to you.' He put his hand over the receiver and turned to Julia. 'Shall I ask him to dinner next Sunday?'

'If you like.'

'Julia says, will you come and dine on Sunday? Oh, I'm sorry. Well, so long, old man.'

He put down the receiver.

'He's got a date. Is the young ruffian having an affair with this girl?'

'He assures me not. He respects her. She's a colonel's daughter.'

'Oh, she's a lady.'

'I don't know that that follows,' said Julia acidly. 'What were you talking to him about?'

'He says they've cut his salary. Bad times. He wants to give up the flat.' Julia's heart gave a sudden sickening beat. 'I've told him not to worry. I'll let him stay there rent free till times improve.'

'I don't know why you should do that. After all, it was a purely business arrangement.'

'It seems rather tough luck on a young chap like that. And you know he's very useful to us; if we want an extra man we can always call upon him, and it's convenient having him round the corner when I want someone to play golf with me. It's only twenty-five pounds a quarter.'

'You're the last person I should expect to see indulge in indiscriminate generosity.'

'Oh, don't you be afraid, if I lose on the swings I'll get back on the roundabouts.'

The masseuse came in and put an end to the conversation. Julia was thankful that it would soon be time to go down to the theatre and so put an end for a while to the misery of that long day; when she got back she would take a sleeping-draught again and so get some hours of forgetfulness. She had a notion that in a few days the worst of her pain would be over; the important thing was to get through them as best she could. She must distract her mind. When she left for the theatre she told the butler to ring up Charles Tamerley and see if she could lunch with him at the Ritz next day.

He was extraordinarily nice at luncheon. His look, his manner bespoke the different world he lived in, and she felt a sudden abhorrence for the circle in which on Tom's account she had moved during the last year. He spoke of politics, of art, of books; and peace entered into her soul. Tom had been an obsession and she saw now that it had been hurtful; but she would escape from it. Her spirits rose. She did not want to be alone, she knew that even though she went home after luncheon she would not sleep, so she asked Charles if he would take her to the National Gallery. She could give him no greater pleasure; he liked to talk about pictures and he talked of them well. It took them back to the old days when she had made her first success in London and they used to spend so many afternoons together, walking in the park or sauntering through museums. The day after that she had matinée and the next a luncheon-party, but when they separated they arranged to lunch again together on the Friday and go to the Tate.

A few days later Michael told her that he had engaged Avice Crichton.

'She has the looks for the part, there's no doubt about that, and she'll be a good contrast to you. I'm taking her acting on the strength of what you said.'

Next morning they rang through from the basement to say that Mr Fennell was on the telephone. It seemed to her that her heart stopped beating.

'Put him through.'

'Julia, I wanted to tell you, Michael has engaged Avice.'

'Yes, I know.'

'He told her he was engaging her on what you'd told him. You are a brick.'

Julia, her heart now beating nineteen to the dozen, made an effort to control her voice.

'Oh, don't talk such nonsense,' she answered gaily. 'I told you it would be all right.'

'I'm awfully glad it's fixed up. She's accepted the part on what I've told her about it. Ordinarily she won't take anything unless she's read the play.'

It was just as well he could not see Julia's face when she heard him say this. She would have liked to answer tartly that it was not their habit when they engaged small-part actresses to let them read the play, but instead she said mildly:

'Well, I think she'll like it, don't you? It's quite a good part.'

'And you know, she'll play it for all it's worth. I believe she'll make a sensation.'

Julia took a long breath.

'It'll be wonderful, won't it? I mean, it may make her.'

'Yes, I've told her that. I say, when am I going to see you again?'

'I'll phone you, shall I? It's such a bore, I'm terribly full of engagements for the next few days.'

'You're not going to drop me just because . . .'

She gave a low, rather hoarse chuckle, that chuckle which so delighted audiences.

'Don't be so silly. Oh lord, there's my bath running. I must go and have it. Good-bye, my sweet.'

She put down the receiver. The sound of his voice! The pain in her heart was unendurable. Sitting up in her bed she rocked to and fro in an agony.

'What shall I do? What shall I do?'

She had thought she was getting over it, and now that brief, silly conversation had shown her that she loved him as much as ever. She wanted him. She missed him every minute of the day. She could not do without him.

'I shall never get over it,' she moaned.

Once again the theatre was her only refuge. By an ironic chance the great scene of the play in which she was then acting, the scene to which the play owed its success, showed the parting of two lovers. It was true that they parted from a sense of duty; and Julia, in the play, sacrificed her love, her hopes of happiness, all that she held dear, to an ideal of uprightness. It was a scene that had appealed to her from the beginning. She was wonderfully moving in it. She put into it now all the agony of her spirit; it was no longer the broken heart of a character that she portrayed but her own. In ordinary life she tried to stifle a passion that she knew very well was ridiculous, a love that was unworthy of the woman she was, and she steeled herself to think as little as possible of the wretched boy who had wrought such havoc with her; but when she came to this scene she let herself go. She gave free rein to her anguish. She was hopeless with her own loss, and the love she poured out on the man who was playing opposite to her was the love she still felt, the passionate, devouring love, for Tom. The prospect of the empty life that confronted the woman of the play was the prospect of her own empty life. There was at least that solace, she felt she had never played so magnificently.

'My God, it's almost worth while to suffer so frightfully to give such a performance.'

She had never put more of herself into a part.

One night a week or two later when she came into her dressing-room at the end of the play, exhausted by all the emotion she had displayed, but triumphant after innumerable curtain calls, she found Michael sitting there.

'Hulloa? You haven't been in front, have you?'

'Yes.'

'But you were in front two or three days ago.'

'Yes, I've sat through the play for the last four nights.'

She started to undress. He got up from his chair and began to walk up and down. She gave him a glance and saw that he was frowning slightly.

'What's the matter?'

'That's what I want to know.'

She gave a start. The thought flashed through her mind that he had once more heard something about Tom.

'Why the devil isn't Evie here?' she asked.

'I told her to get out. I've got something to say to you, Julia. It's no good your flying in a temper. You've just got to listen.'

A cold shiver ran down her spine.

'Well, what is it?'

'I heard something was up and I thought I'd better see for myself. At first I thought it was just an accident. That's why I didn't say anything till I was quite sure. What's wrong with you, Julia?'

'With me?'

'Yes. Why are you giving such a lousy performance?'

'Me?' That was the last thing she expected to hear him say. She faced him with blazing eyes. 'You damned fool, I've never acted better in my life.'

'Nonsense. You're acting like hell.'

Of course it was a relief that he was talking about her acting, but what he was saying was so ridiculous that, angry as she was, she had to laugh.

'You blasted idiot, you don't know what you're talking about. Why, what I don't know about acting isn't worth knowing. Everything you know about it I've taught you. If you're even a tolerable actor it's due to me. After all, the proof of the pudding's in the eating. D'you know how many curtain calls I got tonight? The play's never gone better in all its run.'

'I know all about that. The public are a lot of jackasses. If you yell and scream and throw yourself about you'll always get a lot of damned fools to shout themselves silly. Just barn-storming, that's what you've been doing the last four nights. It was false from beginning to end.'

'False? But I felt every word of it.'

'I don't care what you felt, you weren't acting it. Your performance was a mess. You were exaggerating; you were over-acting; you didn't carry conviction for a moment. It was about as rotten a piece of ham acting as I've ever seen in my life.'

'You bloody swine, how dare you talk to me like that? It's you the ham.'

With her open hand she gave him a great swinging blow on the face. He smiled.

'You can hit me, you can swear at me, you can yell your head off, but the fact remains that your acting's gone all to hell. I'm not going to start rehearsing *Nowadays* with you acting like that.'

'Find someone who can act the part better than I can then.'

'Don't be silly, Julia. I may not be a very good actor myself, I never thought I was, but I know good acting from bad. And what's more there's nothing about *you* I don't know. I'm going to put up the notices on Saturday and then I want you to go abroad. We'll make *Nowadays* our autumn production.'

The quiet, decisive way in which he spoke calmed her. It was true that when it came to acting Michael knew everything there was to know about her.

'Is it true that I'm acting badly?'

'Rottenly.'

She thought it over. She knew exactly what had happened. She had let her emotion run away with her; she had been feeling, not acting. Again a cold shiver ran down her spine. This was serious. It was all very fine to have a broken heart, but if it was going to interfere with her acting . . . no, no, no. That was quite another pair of shoes. Her acting was more important than any love affair in the world.

'I'll try and pull myself together.'

'It's no good trying to force oneself. You're tired out. It's my fault, I ought to have insisted on your taking a holiday long ago. What you want is a good rest.'

'What about the theatre?'

'If I can't let it, I'll revive some play that I can play in. There's *Hearts are Trumps*. You always hated your part in that.'

'Everyone says the season's going to be wonderful. You can't expect much of a revival with me out of the cast; you won't make a penny.'

'I don't care a hang about that. The only thing that matters is your health.'

'Oh, Christ, don't be so magnanimous,' she cried. 'I can't bear it.'

Suddenly she burst into a storm of weeping.

'Darling!'

He took her in his arms and sat her down on the sofa with himself beside her. She clung to him desperately.

'You're so good to me, Michael, and I hate myself. I'm a beast, I'm a slut, I'm just a bloody bitch. I'm rotten through and through.'

'All that may be,' he smiled, 'but the fact remains that you're a very great actress.'

'I don't know how you can have the patience you have with me. I've treated you foully. You've been too wonderful and I've sacrificed you heartlessly.'

'Now, dear, don't say a lot of things that you'll regret later. I shall only bring them up against you another time.'

His tenderness melted her and she reproached herself bitterly because for years she had found him so boring.

'Thank God, I've got you. What should I do without you?'

'You haven't got to do without me.'

He held her close and though she sobbed still she began to feel comforted.

'I'm sorry I was so beastly to you just now.'

'Oh, my dear.'

'Do you really think I'm a ham actress?'

'Darling, Duse couldn't hold a candle to you.'

'Do you honestly think that? Give me your hanky. You never saw Sarah Bernhardt, did you?'

'No, never.'

'She ranted like the devil.'

They sat together for a little while, in silence, and Julia grew calmer in spirit. Her heart was filled with a great love for Michael.

'You're still the best-looking man in England,' she murmured at last. 'No one will ever persuade me to the contrary.'

She felt that he drew in his belly and thrust out his chin, and it seemed to her rather sweet and touching.

'You're quite right. I'm tired out. I feel low and miserable. I feel all empty inside. The only thing is to go away.'

Chapter Twenty-three

After Julia had made up her mind to that she was glad. The prospect of getting away from the misery that tormented her at once made it easier to bear. The notices were put up; Michael collected his cast for the revival and started rehearsals. It amused Julia to sit idly in a stall and watch the actress who had been engaged rehearse the part which she had played herself some years before. She had never lost the thrill it gave her when she first went on the stage to sit in the darkened playhouse, under dust-sheets, and see the characters grow in the actors' hands. Merely to be inside a theatre rested her; nowhere was she so happy. Watching the rehearsals she was able to relax so that when at night she had her own performance to give she felt fresh. She realized that all Michael had said was true. She took hold of herself. Thrusting her private emotion into the background and thus getting the character under control, she managed once more to play with her accustomed virtuosity. Her acting ceased to be a means by which she gave release to her feelings and was again the manifestation of her creative instinct. She got a quiet exhilaration out of thus recovering mastery over her medium. It gave her a sense of power and of liberation.

But the triumphant effort she made took it out of her, and when she was not in the theatre she felt listless and discouraged. She lost her exuberant vitality. A new humility overcame her. She had a feeling that her day was done. She sighed as she told herself that nobody wanted her any more. Michael suggested that she should go to Vienna to be near Roger, and she would have liked that, but she shook her head.

'I should only cramp his style.'

She was afraid he would find her a bore. He was enjoying himself and she would only be in the way. She could not bear the thought that he would find it an irksome duty to take her here and there and occasionally have luncheon or dinner with her. It was only natural that he should have more fun with the friends of his own age that he had made. She decided to go and stay with her mother. Mrs Lambert–Madame de Lambert, as Michael insisted on calling her–had lived for many years now with her sister, Madame Falloux, at St Malo. She spent a few days every year in London with Julia, but this year had not been well enough to come. She was an old lady, well over seventy, and Julia knew that it would be a great joy for her to have her daughter on a long visit. Who cared about an English actress in Vienna? She wouldn't be anyone there. In St Malo she would be something of a figure, and it would be fun for the two old women to be able to show her off to their friends.

'Ma fille, la plus grande actrice d'Angleterre,' and all that sort of thing.

Poor old girls, they couldn't live much longer and they led drab, monotonous lives. Of course it would be fearfully boring for her, but it would be a treat for them. Julia had a feeling that perhaps in the course of her brilliant and triumphant career she had a trifle neglected her mother. She could make up for it now. She would lay herself out to be charming. Her tenderness for Michael and her ever-present sense of having been for years unjust to him filled her with contrition. She felt that she had been selfish and overbearing, and she wanted to atone for all that. She was eager to sacrifice herself, and so wrote to her mother to announce her imminent arrival.

She managed in the most natural way in the world to see nothing of Tom till her last day in London. The play had closed the night before and she was starting for St Malo in the evening. Tom came in about six o'clock to say good-bye to her. Michael was there, Dolly, Charles Tamerley and one or two others, so that there was no chance of their being left even for a moment by themselves. Julia found no difficulty in talking to him naturally. To see him gave her not the anguish she had feared but no more than a dull heartache. They had kept the date and place of her departure secret, that is to say, the Press representative of the theatre had only rung up a very few newspapers, so that when Julia and Michael reached the station there were not more than half a dozen reporters and three camera-men. Julia said a few gracious words to them, and Michael a few more, then the Press representative took the reporters aside and gave them a succinct account of Julia's plans. Meanwhile Julia and Michael posed while the camera-men to the glare of flashes photographed them arm in arm, exchanging a final kiss, and at last Julia, half out of the carriage window, giving her hand to Michael who stood on the platform.

'What a nuisance these people are,' she said. 'One simply cannot escape them.'

'I can't imagine how they knew you were going.'

The little crowd that had assembled when they realized that something was going on stood at a respectful distance. The Press representative came up and told Michael he thought he'd given the reporters enough for a column. The train steamed out.

Julia had refused to take Evie with her. She had a feeling that in order to regain her serenity she must cut herself off completely for a time from her old life. Evie in that French household would be out of place. For Madame Falloux, Julia's Aunt Carrie, married as a girl to a Frenchman, now as an old, old lady spoke French more easily than English. She had been a widow for many years and her only son had been killed in the war. She lived in a tall, narrow stone house on a hill, and when you crossed its threshold from the cobbled street you entered upon the peace of a by-gone age. Nothing had been changed for half a century. The drawing-room was furnished with a Louis XV suite under covers, and the covers were only taken off once a month to give the silk underneath a delicate brushing. The crystal chandelier was shrouded in muslin so that the flies should not spot it. In front of the chimney-piece was a fire-screen of peacocks' feathers artfully arranged and protected by glass. Though the room was never used Aunt Carrie dusted it herself every day. The dining-room was panelled and here too the chairs were under dust-covers. On the sideboard was a silver épergne, a silver coffee-pot, a silver teapot and a silver tray. Aunt Carrie and Julia's mother, Mrs Lambert, lived in the morning-room, a long narrow room, with Empire furniture. On the walls in oval frames were oil portraits of Aunt Carrie and her deceased husband, of his father and mother, and a pastel of the dead son as a child. Here they had their work-boxes, here they read their papers, the *Catholic La Croix*, the *Revue des Deux Mondes* and the local daily, and here they played dominoes in the evening. Except on Thursday evenings when the Abbé and the Commandant La Garde, a retired naval officer, came to dinner, they had their meals there; but when Julia arrived they decided that it would be more convenient to eat in the dining-room.

Aunt Carrie still wore mourning for her husband and her son. It was seldom warm enough for her to leave off the little black tricot that she crocheted herself. Mrs Lambert wore black too, but when Monsieur L'Abbé and the Commandant came to dinner she put over her shoulders a white lace shawl that Julia had given her. After dinner they played plafond for two sous a hundred. Mrs Lambert, because she had lived for so many years in Jersey and still went to London, knew all about the great world, and she said that a game called contract was much played, but the Commandant said it was all very well for Americans, but he was content to stick to plafond, and the Abbé said that for his part he thought it a pity that whist had been abandoned. But there, men were never satisfied with what they had; they wanted change, change, change, all the time.

Every Christmas Julia gave her mother and her aunt expensive presents, but they never used them. They showed them to their friends with pride, these wonderful things that came from London, and then wrapped them up in tissue paper and put them away in cupboards. Julia had offered her mother a car, but she refused it. For the little they went out, they could go on foot; a chauffeur would steal their petrol, if he had his meals out it would be ruinous and if he had them in it would upset Annette. Annette was cook, housekeeper and housemaid. She had been with Aunt Carrie for five-and-thirty years. Her niece was there to do the rough work, but Angèle was young, she wasn't forty yet, and it would hardly do to have a man constantly about the house.

They put Julia in the same room she had had as a girl when she was living with Aunt Carrie for her education. It gave her a peculiar, heart-rending sensation, indeed for a little it made her quite emotional. But she fell into the life very easily. Aunt Carrie had become a Catholic on her marriage and Mrs Lambert, when on losing her husband she settled down in St Malo, having received instructions from the Abbé, in due course took the same step. The two old ladies were very devout. They went to Mass every morning and to High Mass on Sundays. Otherwise they seldom went out. When they did it was to pay a ceremonious call on some old lady who had had a bereavement in the family or one of whose grandchildren was become engaged. They read their papers, and their magazine, did a great deal of sewing for charitable purposes, played dominoes and listened to the radio that Julia had given them. Though the Abbé and the Commandant had dined with them every Thursday for many years they were always in a flutter when Thursday came. The Commandant, with the sailor's downrightness that they expected of him, did not hesitate to say so if something was not cooked to his liking, and even the Abbé, though a saint, had his likes and dislikes. For instance, he was very fond of sole normande, but he insisted on its being cooked with the best butter, and with butter at the price it was since the war that was very expensive. Every Thursday morning Aunt Carrie took the cellar key from the place where she had hidden it and herself fetched a bottle of claret from the cellar. She and her sister finished what was left of it by the end of the week.

They made a great fuss of Julia. They dosed her with tisanes, and were anxious that she should not sit in anything that might be thought a draught. Indeed a great part of their lives was devoted to avoiding draughts. They made her lie on sofas and were solicitous that she should cover her feet. They reasoned with her about the clothes she wore. Those silk stockings that were so thin you could see through them; and what did she wear next to her skin? Aunt Carrie would not have been surprised to learn that she wore nothing but a chemise.

'She doesn't even wear that,' said Mrs Lambert.

'What does she wear then?'

'Panties,' said Julia.

'And a soutien-gorge, I suppose.'

'Certainly not,' cried Julia tartly.

'Then, my niece, under your dress you are naked?'

'Practically.'

'C'est de la folie,' said Aunt Carrie.

'C'est vraiment pas raisonnable, ma fille,' said Mrs Lambert.

'And without being a prude,' added Aunt Carrie, 'I must say that it is hardly decent.'

Julia showed them her clothes, and on the first Thursday after her arrival they discussed what she should wear for dinner. Aunt Carrie and Mrs Lambert grew rather sharp with one another. Mrs Lambert thought that since her daughter had evening dresses with her she ought to wear one, but Aunt Carrie considered it quite unnecessary.

'When I used to come and visit you in Jersey, my dear, and gentlemen were coming to dinner, I remember you would put on a tea-gown.'

'Of course a tea-gown would be very suitable.'

They looked at Julia hopefully. She shook her head.

'I would sooner wear a shroud.'

Aunt Carrie wore a high-necked dress of heavy black silk, with a string of jet, and Mrs Lambert a similar one, but with her lace shawl and a paste necklace. The Commandant, a sturdy little man with a much-wrinkled face, white hair cut en brosse and an imposing moustache dyed a deep black, was very gallant, and though well past seventy pressed Julia's foot under the table during dinner. On the way out he seized the opportunity to pinch her bottom.

'Sex appeal,' Julia murmured to herself as with dignity she followed the two old ladies into the parlour.

They made a fuss of her, not because she was a great actress, but because she was in poor health and needed rest. Julia to her great amazement soon discovered that to them her celebrity was an embarrassment rather than an asset. Far from wanting to show her off, they did not offer to take her with them to pay calls. Aunt Carrie had brought the habit of afternoon tea with her from Jersey, and had never abandoned it. One day, soon after Julia's arrival, when they had invited some ladies to tea, Mrs Lambert at luncheon thus addressed her daughter.

'My dear, we have some very good friends at St Malo, but of course they still look upon us as foreigners, even after all these years, and we don't like to do anything that seems at all eccentric. Naturally we don't want you to tell a lie, but unless you are forced to mention it, your Aunt Carrie thinks it would be better if you did not tell anyone that you are an actress.'

Julia was taken aback, but, her sense of humour prevailing, she felt inclined to laugh.

'If one of the friends we are expecting this afternoon happens to ask you what your husband is, it wouldn't be untrue, would it? to say that he was in business.'

'Not at all,' said Julia, permitting herself to smile.

'Of course, we know that English actresses are not like French ones,' Aunt Carrie added kindly. 'It's almost an understood thing for a French actress to have a lover.'

'Dear, dear,' said Julia.

Her life in London, with its excitements, its triumphs and its pains, began to seem very far away. She found herself able soon to consider Tom and her feeling for him with a tranquil mind. She realized that her vanity had been more wounded than her heart. The days passed monotonously. Soon the only thing that recalled London to her was the arrival on Monday of the Sunday papers. She got a batch of them and spent the whole day reading them. Then she was a trifle restless. She walked on the ramparts and looked at the islands that dotted the bay. The grey sky made her sick for the grey sky of England. But by Tuesday morning she had sunk back once more into the calmness of the provincial life. She read a good deal, novels, English and French, that she bought at the local bookshop, and her favourite Verlaine. There was a tender melancholy in his verses that seemed to fit the grey Breton town, the sad old stone houses and the quietness of those steep and tortuous streets. The peaceful habits of the two old ladies, the routine of their uneventful existence and their quiet gossip, excited her compassion. Nothing had happened to them for years, nothing now would ever happen to them till they died, and then how little would their lives have signified. The strange thing was that they were content. They knew neither malice nor envy. They had achieved the aloofness from the common ties of men that Julia felt in herself when she stood at the footlights bowing to the applause of an enthusiastic audience. Sometimes she had thought that aloofness her most precious possession. In her it was born of pride; in them of humility. In both cases it brought one precious thing, liberty of spirit; but with them it was more secure.

Michael wrote to her once a week, brisk, business-like letters in which he told her what the takings were at the Siddons and the preparations he was making for the next production; but Charles Tamerley wrote to her every day. He told her the gossip of the town, he talked in his charming, cultivated way of the pictures he saw and the books he read. He was tenderly allusive and playfully erudite. He philosophized without pedantry. He told her that he adored her. They were the most beautiful love-letters Julia had ever received, and for the sake of posterity she made up her mind to keep them. One day perhaps someone would publish them and people would go to the National Portrait Gallery and look at her portrait, the one McEvoy had painted, and sigh when they thought of the sad, romantic love-story of which she had been the heroine.

Charles had been wonderful to her during the first two weeks of her bereavement, she did not know what she would have done without him. He had always been at her beck and call. His conversation, by taking her into a different world, had soothed her nerves. Her soul had been muddied, and in his distinction of spirit she had washed herself clean. It had rested her wonderfully to wander about the galleries with him and look at pictures. She had good reason to be grateful to him. She thought of all the years he had loved her. He had waited for her now for more than twenty years. She had not been very kind to him. It would have given him so much happiness to possess her and really it would not have hurt her. She wondered why she had resisted him so long. Perhaps because he was so faithful, because his devotion was so humble, perhaps only because she wanted to preserve in his mind the ideal that he had of her. It was stupid really and she had been selfish. It occurred to her with exultation that she could at last reward him for all his tenderness, his patience and his selflessness. She had not lost the sense of unworthiness which Michael's great kindness had aroused in her, and she was remorseful still because she had been for so long impatient of him. The desire for self-sacrifice with which she left England burnt still in her breast with an eager flame. She felt that Charles was a worthy object for its exercise. She laughed a little, kindly and compassionately, as she thought of his amazement when he understood what she intended; for a moment he would hardly be able to believe it, and then what rapture, then what ecstasy! The love that he had held banked up for so many years would burst its sluices like a great torrent and in a flood o'erwhelm her. Her heart swelled at the thought of his infinite gratitude. But still he could hardly believe in his good fortune; and when it was all over and she lay in his arms she would nestle up to him and whisper tenderly:

'Was it worth waiting for?'

'Like Helen, you make me immortal with a kiss.'

It was wonderful to be able to give so much happiness to a human being.

'I'll write to him just before I leave St Malo,' she decided.

The spring passed into summer, and at the end of July it was time for Julia to go to Paris and see about her clothes. Michael wanted to open with the new play early in September, and rehearsals were to start in August. She had brought the play with her to St Malo, intending to study her part, but the circumstances in which she lived had made it impossible. She had all the leisure she needed, but in that grey, austere and yet snug little town, in the constant company of those two old ladies whose interests were confined to the parish church and their household affairs, though it was a good play, she could take but little interest in it.

'It's high time I was getting back,' she said. 'It would be hell if I really came to the conclusion that the theatre wasn't worth the fuss and bother they make about it.'

She said good-bye to her mother and to Aunt Carrie. They had been very kind to her, but she had an inkling that they would not be sorry when her departure allowed them to return to the life she had interrupted. They were a little relieved besides to know that now there was no more danger of some eccentricity, such as you must always run the risk of with an actress, which might arouse the unfavourable comment of the ladies of St Malo.

She arrived in Paris in the afternoon, and when she was shown into her suite at the Ritz, she gave a sigh of satisfaction. It was a treat to get back to luxury. Three or four people had sent her flowers. She had a bath and changed. Charley Deverill, who always made her clothes for her, an old friend, called to take her to dinner in the Bois.

'I had a wonderful time,' she told him, 'and of course it was a grand treat for those old girls to have me there, but I have a feeling that if I'd stayed a day longer I should have been bored.'

To drive up the Champs Elysées on that lovely evening filled her with exhilaration. It was good to smell once more the smell of petrol. The cars, the taxis, the hooting of horns, the chestnut trees, the street lights, the crowd on the pavement and the crowd sitting outside the cafés; it was an enchantment. And when they got to the Château de Madrid, so gay, so civilized and so expensive, it was grand to see once more well-dresed women, decently made-up, and tanned men in dinner-jackets.

'I feel like a queen returning from exile.'

Julia spent several happy days choosing her clothes and having the first fittings. She enjoyed every moment of them. But she was a woman of character, and when she had come to a decision she adhered to it; before leaving for London she wrote a note to Charles. He had been to Goodwood and Cowes and was spending twenty-four hours in London on his way to Salzburg.

Charles Dear,
    How wonderful that I shall see you so soon. Of course I am free on Wednesday. Shall we dine together and do you love me still?

Your Julia

As she stuck down the envelope she murmured: Bis dat qui cito dat. It was a Latin tag that Michael always quoted when, asked to subscribe to a charity, he sent by return of post exactly half what was expected of him.

Chapter Twenty-four

On Wednesday morning Julia had her face massaged and her hair waved. She could not make up her mind whether to wear for dinner a dress of flowered organdie, very pretty and spring-like with its suggestion of Botticelli's Primavera, or one of white satin beautifully cut to show off her slim young figure, and virginal; but while she was having her bath she decided on the white satin: it indicated rather delicately that the sacrifice she intended was in the nature of an expiation for her long ingratitude to Michael. She wore no jewels but a string of pearls and a diamond bracelet; besides her wedding-ring only one square-cut diamond. She would have liked to put on a slight brown tan, it looked open-air-girl and suited her, but reflecting on what lay before her she refrained. She could not very well, like the actor who painted himself black all over to play Othello, tan her whole body. Always a punctual woman, she came downstairs as the front door was being opened for Charles. She greeted him with a look into which she put tenderness, a roguish charm and intimacy. Charles now wore his thinning grey hair rather long, and with advancing years his intellectual, distinguished features had sagged a little; he was slightly bowed and his clothes looked as though they needed pressing.

'Strange world we live in,' thought Julia. 'Actors do their damnedest to look like gentlemen and gentlemen do all they can to look like actors.'

There was no doubt that she was making a proper effect on him. He gave her the perfect opening.

'Why are you looking so lovely tonight?' he asked.

'Because I'm looking forward to dining with you.'

With her beautiful, expressive eyes she looked deep into his. She parted her lips in the manner that she found so seductive in Romney's portraits of Lady Hamilton.

They dined at the Savoy. The head-waiter gave them a table on the gangway so that they were admirably in view. Though everyone was supposed to be out of town the grill-room was well filled. Julia bowed and smiled to various friends of whom she caught sight. Charles had much to tell her; she listened to him with flattering interest.

'You are the best company in the world, Charles,' she told him.

They had come late, they dined well, and by the time Charles had finished his brandy people were already beginning to come in for supper.

'Good gracious, are the theatres out already?' he said, glancing at his watch. 'How quickly the time flies when I'm with you. D'you imagine they want to get rid of us?'

'I don't feel a bit like going to bed.'

'I suppose Michael will be getting home presently?'

'I suppose so.'

'Why don't you come back to my house and have a talk?'

That was what she called taking a cue.

'I'd love it,' she answered, putting into her tone the slight blush which she felt would have well become her cheek.

They got into his car and drove to Hill Street. He took her into his study. It was on the ground floor and looked on a tiny garden. The french windows were wide open. They sat down on a sofa.

'Put out some of the lights and let the night into the room,' said Julia. She quoted from *The Merchant of Venice*. '"In such a night as this, when the sweet wind did gently kiss the trees . . ."'

Charles switched off everything but one shaded lamp, and when he sat down again she nestled up to him. He put his arm round her waist and she rested her head on his shoulder.

'This is heaven,' she murmured.

'I've missed you terribly all these months.'

'Did you get into mischief?'

'Well, I bought an Ingres drawing and paid a lot of money for it. I must show it you before you go.'

'Don't forget. Where have you put it?'

She had wondered from the moment she got into the house whether the seduction would take place in the study or upstairs.

'In my bedroom,' he answered.

'That's much more comfortable really,' she reflected.

She laughed in her sleeve as she thought of poor old Charles devising a simple little trick like that to get her into his bedroom. What mugs men were! Shy, that was what was the matter with them. A sudden pang shot through her heart as she thought of Tom. Damn Tom. Charles really was very sweet and she was determined to reward him at last for his long devotion.

'You've been a wonderful friend to me, Charles,' she said in her low, rather husky voice. She turned a little so that her face was very near his, her lips, again like Lady Hamilton's, slightly open. 'I'm afraid I haven't always been very kind to you.'

She looked so deliciously yielding, a ripe peach waiting to be picked, that it seemed inevitable that he should kiss her. Then she would twine her soft white arms round his neck. But he only smiled.

'You mustn't say that. You've been always divine.'

('He's afraid, poor lamb.') 'I don't think anyone has ever been so much in love with me as you were.'

He gave her a little squeeze.

'I am still. You know that. There's never been any woman but you in my life.'

Since, however, he did not take the proffered lips she slightly turned. She looked reflectively at the electric fire. Pity it was unlit. The scene wanted a fire.

'How different everything would have been if we'd bolted that time. Heigh-ho.'

She never quite knew what heigh-ho meant, but they used it a lot on the stage, and said with a sigh it always sounded very sad.

'England would have lost its greatest actress. I know now how dreadfully selfish it was of me ever to propose it.'

'Success isn't everything. I sometimes wonder whether to gratify my silly little ambition I didn't miss the greatest thing in the world. After all, love is the only thing that matters.' And now she looked at him again with eyes more beautiful than ever in their melting tenderness. 'D'you know, I think that now, if I had my time over again, I'd say take me.'

She slid her hand down to take his. He gave it a graceful pressure.

'Oh, my dear.'

'I've so often thought of that dream villa of ours. Olive trees and oleanders and the blue sea. Peace. Sometimes I'm appalled by the dullness and vulgarity of my life. What you offered was beauty. It's too late now, I know; I didn't know then how much I cared for you, I never dreamt that as the years went on you would mean more and more to me.'

'It's heavenly to hear you say that, my sweet. It makes up for so much.'

'I'd do anything in the world for you, Charles. I've been selfish. I've ruined your life, I didn't know what I was doing.'

Her voice was low and tremulous and she threw back her head so that her neck was like a white column. Her décolleté showed part of her small firm breasts and with her hands she pressed them forward a little.

'You mustn't say that, you mustn't think that,' he answered gently. 'You've been perfect always. I wouldn't have had you otherwise. Oh, my dear, life is so short and love is so transitory. The tragedy of life is that sometimes we get what we want. Now that I look back on our long past together I know that you were wiser than I. "What leaf-fringed legend haunts about thy shape?" Don't you remember how it goes? "Never, never canst thou kiss, though winning near the goal—yet, do not grieve; she cannot fade, though thou hast not thy bliss. For ever wilt thou love, and she be fair!"'

('Idiotic.') 'Such lovely lines,' she sighed. 'Perhaps you're right. Heigh-ho.'

He went on quoting. That was a trick of his that Julia had always found somewhat tiresome.

> '"Ah, happy, happy boughs! that cannot shed
> Your leaves, nor ever bid the Spring adieu;
> And, happy melodist, unwearied,
> For ever piping songs for ever new! . . ."'

It gave Julia an opportunity to think. She stared in the unlit fire, her gaze intent, as though she were entranced by the exquisite beauty of those words. It was quite obvious that he just hadn't understood. It could hardly be wondered at. She had been deaf to his passionate entreaties for twenty years, and it was very natural if he had given up his quest as hopeless. It was like Mount Everest; if those hardy mountaineers who had tried for so long in vain to reach the summit finally found an easy flight of steps that led to it, they simply would not believe their eyes: they would think there was a catch in it. Julia felt that she must make herself a little plainer; she must, as it were, reach out a helping hand to the weary pilgrim.

'It's getting dreadfully late,' she said softly. 'Show me your new drawing and then I must go home.'

He rose and she gave him both her hands so that he should help her up from the sofa. They went upstairs. His pyjamas and dressing-gown were neatly arranged on a chair.

'How well you single men do yourselves. Such a cosy, friendly bedroom.'

He took the framed drawing off the wall and brought it over for her to look at under the light. It was a portrait in pencil of a stoutish woman in a bonnet and a low-necked dress with puffed sleeves. Julia thought her plain and the dress ridiculous.

'Isn't it ravishing?' she cried.

'I knew you'd like it. A good drawing, isn't it?'

'Amazing.'

He put the little picture back on its nail. When he turned round again she was standing near the bed with her hands behind her back, a little like a Circassian slave introduced by the chief eunuch to the inspection of the Grand Vizier; there was a hint of modest withdrawal in her bearing, a delicious timidity, and at the same time the virgin's anticipation that she was about to enter into her kingdom. Julia gave a sigh that was ever so slightly voluptuous.

'My dear, it's been a wonderful evening. I've never felt so close to you before.'

She slowly raised her hands from behind her back and with the exquisite timing that came so naturally to her moved them forwards, stretching out her arms, and held them palms upwards as though there rested on them, invisibly, a lordly dish, and on the dish lay her proffered heart. Her beautiful eyes were tender and yielding and on her lips played a smile of shy surrender.

She saw Charles's smile freeze on his face. He had understood all right.

('Christ, he doesn't want me. It was all a bluff.') The revelation for a moment staggered her. ('God, how am I going to get out of it? What a bloody fool I must look.')

She very nearly lost her poise. She had to think like lightning. He was standing there, looking at her with an embarrassment that he tried hard to conceal. Julia was panic-stricken. She could not think what to do with those hands that held the lordly dish; God knows, they were small, but at the moment they felt like legs of mutton hanging there. Nor did she know what to say. Every second made her posture and the situation more intolerable.

('The skunk, the dirty skunk. Codding me all these years.')

She did the only thing possible. She continued the gesture. Counting so that she should not go too fast, she drew her hands towards one another, till she could clasp them, and then throwing back her head, raised them, very slowly, to one side of her neck. The attitude she reached was as lovely as the other, and it was the attitude that suggested to her what she had to say. Her deep rich voice trembled a little with emotion.

'I'm so glad when I look back to think that we have nothing to reproach ourselves with. The bitterness of life is not death, the bitterness of life is that love dies. (She'd heard something like that said in a play.) If we'd been lovers you'd have grown tired of me long ago, and what should we have now to look back on but regret for our own weakness? What was that line of Shelley's that you said just now about fading?'

'Keats,' he corrected. 'She cannot fade though thou hast not thy bliss.'

'That's it. Go on.'

She was playing for time.

'For ever wilt thou love, and she be fair.'

She threw her arms wide in a great open gesture and tossed her curly head. She'd got it.

'It's true, isn't it? "For ever wilt thou love and I be fair." What fools we should have been if for a few moments' madness we had thrown away the wonderful happiness our friendship has brought us. We have nothing to be ashamed of. We're clean. We can walk with our heads held high and look the whole world in the face.'

She instinctively felt that this was an exit line, and suiting her movements to the words, with head held high, backed to the door and flung it open. Her power was such that she carried the feeling of the scene all the way down the stairs with her. Then she let it fall and with the utmost simplicity turned to Charles who had followed her.

'My cloak.'

'The car is there,' he said as he wrapped it round her. 'I'll drive you home.'

'No, let me go alone. I want to stamp this hour on my heart. Kiss me before I go.'

She held up her lips to him. He kissed them. But she broke away from him, with a stifled sob, and tearing open the door ran to the waiting car.

When she got home and stood in her own bedroom she gave a great whoof of relief.

'The bloody fool. Fancy me being taken in like that. Thank God, I got out of it all right. He's such an ass, I don't suppose he began to see what I was getting at.' But that frozen smile disconcerted her. 'He may have suspected, he couldn't have been certain, and afterwards he must have been pretty sure he'd made a mistake. My God, the rot I talked. It seemed to do down all right, I must say. Lucky I caught on when I did. In another minute I'd have had me dress off. That wouldn't have been so damned easy to laugh away.'

Julia began to titter. The situation was mortifying of course, he had made a damned fool of her, but if you had any sense of humour you could hardly help seeing that there was a funny side to it. She was sorry that there was nobody to whom she could tell it; even it if was against herself it would make a good story. What she couldn't get over was that she had fallen for the comedy of undying passion that he had played all those years; for of course it was just a pose; he liked to see himself as the constant adorer, and the last thing he wanted, apparently, was to have his constancy rewarded.

'Bluffed me, he did, completely bluffed me.'

But an idea occurred to Julia and she ceased to smile. When a woman's amorous advances are declined by a man she is apt to draw one of two conclusions; one is that he is homosexual and the other is that he is impotent. Julia reflectively lit a cigarette. She asked herself if Charles had used his devotion to her as a cover to distract attention from his real inclinations. But she shook her head. If he had been homosexual she would surely have had some hint of it; after all, in society since the war they talked of practically nothing else. Of course it was quite possible he was impotent. She reckoned out his age. Poor Charles. She smiled again. And if that were the case it was he, not she, who had been placed in an embarrassing and even ridiculous position. He must have been scared stiff, poor lamb. Obviously it wasn't the sort of thing a man liked to tell a woman, especially if he were madly in love with her; the more she thought of it the more probable she considered the explanation. She began to feel very sorry for him, almost maternal in fact.

'I know what I'll do,' she said, as she began to undress, 'I'll send him a huge bunch of white lilies tomorrow.'

Chapter Twenty-five

Julia lay awake next morning for some time before she rang her bell. She thought. When she reflected on her adventure of the previous night she could not but be pleased that she had shown so much presence of mind. It was hardly true to say that she had snatched victory from defeat, but looking upon it as a strategic retreat her conduct had been masterly. She was notwithstanding ill at ease. There might be yet another explanation for Charles's singular behaviour. It was possible that he did not desire her because she was not desirable. The notion had crossed her mind in the night, and though she had at once dismissed it as highly improbable, there was no denying it, at that hour of the morning it had a nasty look. She rang. As a rule, since Michael often came in while Julia had breakfast, Evie when she had drawn the curtains handed her a mirror and a comb, her powder and lipstick. On this occasion, instead of running the comb rapidly through her hair and giving her face a perfunctory dab with the puff, Julia took some trouble. She painted her lips with care and put on some rouge; she arranged her hair.

'Speaking without passion or prejudice,' she said, still looking at herself in the glass, when Evie placed the breakfast tray on her bed, 'would you say I was by way of being a good-looking woman, Evie?'

'I must know what I'm letting myself in for before answering that question.'

'You old bitch,' said Julia.

'You're no beauty you know.'

'No great actress ever has been.'

'When you're all dolled up posh like you was last night, and got the light be'ind you, I've seen worse, you know.'

('Fat lot of good it did me last night.') 'What I want to say is, if I really set my mind on getting off with a man, d'you think I could?'

'Knowing what men are, I wouldn't be surprised. Who d'you want to get off with now?'

'Nobody. I was only talking generally.'

Evie sniffed and drew her forefinger along her nostrils.

'Don't sniff like that. If your nose wants blowing, blow it.'

Julia ate her boiled egg slowly. She was busy with her thoughts. She looked at Evie. Funny-looking old thing of course, but one never knew.

'Tell me, Evie, do men ever try to pick you up in the street?'

'Me? I'd like to see 'em try.'

'So would I, to tell you the truth. Women are always telling me how men follow them in the street and if they stop and look in at a shop window come up and try to catch their eye. Sometimes they have an awful bother getting rid of them.'

'Disgusting, I call it.'

'I don't know about that. It's rather flattering. You know, it's a most extraordinary thing, no one ever follows me in the street. I don't remember a man ever having tried to pick me up.'

'Oh well, you walk along Edgware Road one evening. You'll get picked up all right.'

'I shouldn't know what to do if I was.'

'Call a policeman,' said Evie grimly.

'I know a girl who was looking in a shop window in Bond Street, a hat shop, and a man came up and asked her if she'd like a hat. I'd love one, she said, and they went in and she chose one and gave her name and address, he paid for it on the nail, and then she said, thank you so much, and walked out while he was waiting for the change.'

'That's what she told you.' Evie's sniff was sceptical. She gave Julia a puzzled look. 'What's the idea?'

'Oh, nothing. I was only wondering why in point of fact I never have been accosted by a man. It's not as if I had no sex appeal.'

But had she? She made up her mind to put the matter to the test.

That afternoon, when she had had her sleep, she got up, made up a little more than usual, and without calling Evie put on a dress that was neither plain nor obviously expensive and a red straw hat with a wide brim.

'I don't want to look like a tart,' she said as she looked at herself in the glass. 'On the other hand I don't want to look too respectable.'

She tiptoed down the stairs so that no one should hear her and closed the door softly behind her. She was a trifle nervous, but pleasantly excited; she felt that she was doing something rather shocking. She walked through Connaught Square into the Edgware Road. It was about five o'clock. There was a dense line of buses, taxis and lorries; bicyclists dangerously threaded their way through the traffic. The pavements were thronged. She sauntered slowly north. At first she walked with her eyes straight in front of her, looking neither to the right nor to the left, but soon realized that this was useless. She must look at people if she wanted them to look at her. Two or three times when she saw half a dozen persons gazing at a shop window she paused and gazed too, but none of them took any notice of her. She strolled on. People passed her in one direction and another. They seemed in a hurry. No one paid any attention to her. When she saw a man alone coming towards her she gave him a bold stare, but he passed on with a blank face. It occurred to her that her expression was too severe, and she let a slight smile hover on her lips. Two or three men thought she was smiling at them and quickly averted their gaze. She looked back as one of them passed her and he looked back too, but catching her eye he hurried on. She felt a trifle snubbed and decided not to look round again. She walked on and on. She had always heard that the London crowd was the best behaved in the world, but really its behaviour on this occasion was unconscionable.

'This couldn't happen to one in the streets of Paris, Rome or Berlin,' she reflected.

She decided to go as far as the Marylebone Road, and then turn back. It would be too humiliating to have to go home without being once accosted. She was walking so slowly that passers-by sometimes jostled her. This irritated her.

'I ought to have tried Oxford Street,' she said. 'That fool Evie. The Edgware Road's obviously a wash-out.'

Suddenly her heart gave an exultant leap. She had caught a young man's eye and she was sure that there was gleam in it. He passed, and she had all she could do not to turn round. She started, for a moment he passed her again, he had retraced his steps, and this time he gave her a stare. She shot him a glance and then modestly lowered her eyes. He fell back and she was conscious that he was following her. It was all right. She stopped to look into a shop window and he stopped too. She knew how to behave now. She pretended to be absorbed in the goods that were displayed, but just before she moved on gave him a quick flash of her faintly-smiling eyes. He was rather short, he looked like a clerk or a shop-walker, he wore a grey suit and a brown soft hat. He was not the man she would have chosen to be picked up by, but there it was, he was evidently trying to pick her up. She forgot that she was beginning to feel tired. She did not know what would happen next. Of course she wasn't going to let the thing go too far, but she was curious to see what his next step would be. She wondered what he would say to her. She was excited and pleased; it was a weight off her mind. She walked on slowly and she knew he was close behind her. She stopped at another shop window, and this time when he stopped he was close beside her. Her heart began to beat wildly. It was really beginning to look like an adventure.

'I wonder if he'll ask me to go to a hotel with him. I don't suppose he could afford that. A cinema. That's it. It would be rather fun.'

She looked him full in the face now and very nearly smiled. He took off his hat.

'Miss Lambert, isn't it?'

She almost jumped out of her skin. She was indeed so taken aback that she had not the presence of mind to deny it.

'I thought I recognized you the moment I saw you, that's why I turned back, to make sure, see, and I said to meself, if that's not Julia Lambert I'm Ramsay Macdonald. Then you stopped to look in that shop window and that give me the chance to 'ave a good look at you. What made me 'esitate was seeing you in the Edgware Road. It seems so funny, if you know what I mean.'

It was much funnier than he imagined. Anyhow it didn't matter if he knew who she was. She ought to have guessed that she couldn't go far in London without being recognized. He had a cockney accent and a pasty face, but she gave him a jolly, friendly smile. He mustn't think she was putting on airs.

'Excuse me talking to you, not 'aving been introduced and all that, but I couldn't miss the opportunity. Will you oblige me with your autograph?'

Julia caught her breath. It couldn't be that this was why he had followed her for ten minutes. He must have thought that up as an excuse for speaking to her. Well, she would play up.

'I shall be delighted. But I can't very well give it you in the street. People would stare so.'

'That's right. Look here, I was just going along to 'ave my tea. There's a Lyons at the next corner. Why don't you come in and 'ave a cup too?'

She was getting on. When they'd had tea he'd probably suggest going to the pictures.

'All right,' she said.

They walked along till they came to the shop and took their places at a small table.

'Two teas, please, miss,' he ordered. 'Anything to eat?' And when Julia declined: 'Scone and butter for one, miss.'

Julia was able now to have a good look at him. Though stocky and short he had good features, his black hair was plastered down on his head and he had fine eyes, but his teeth were poor and his pale skin gave him an unhealthy look. There was a sort of impudence in his manner that Julia did not much like, but then, as she sensibly reflected, you could hardly expect the modesty of the violet in a young man who picked you up in the Edgware Road.

'Before we go any further let's 'ave this autograph, eh? Do it now, that's my motto.'

He took a fountain pen from his pocket and from a bulging pocket-book a large card.

'One of our trade cards,' he said. 'That'll do O.K.'

Julia thought it silly to carry the subterfuge to this length, but she good-humouredly signed her name on the back of the card.

'Do you collect autographs?' she asked him with a subtle smile.

'Me? Noa. I think it's a lot of tommy rot. My young lady does. She's got Charlie Chaplin and Douglas Fairbanks and I don't know what all. Show you 'er photo if you like,'

From his pocket-book he extracted a snapshot of a rather pert-looking young woman showing all her teeth in a cinema smile.

'Pretty,' said Julia.

'And how. We're going to the pictures tonight. She will be surprised when I give her your autograph. The first thing I said to meself when I knew it was you was, I'll get Julia Lambert's autograph for Gwen or die in the attempt. We're going to get married in August, when I 'ave my 'oliday, you know; we're going to the Isle of Wight for the 'oneymoon. I shall 'ave a rare lot of fun with 'er over this. She won't believe me when I tell her you 'an me 'ad tea together, she'll think I'm kidding, and then I'll show 'er the autograph, see?'

Julia listened to him politely, but the smile had left her face.

'I'm afraid I shall have to go in a minute,' she said. 'I'm late already.'

'I 'aven't got too much time meself. You see, meeting my young lady, I want to get away from the shop on the tick.'

The check had been put on the table when the girl brought their tea, and when they got up Julia took a shilling out of her bag.

'What are you doing that for? You don't think I'm going to let you pay. I invited you.'

'That's very kind of you.'

'But I'll tell you what you can do, let me bring my young lady to see you in your dressing-room one day. Just shake 'ands with her, see? It would mean a rare lot to her. Why, she'd go on talking about it the rest of her life.'

Julia's manner had been for some minutes growing stiffer and now, though gracious still, it was almost haughty.

'I'm so sorry, but we never allow strangers behind.'

'Oh, sorry. You don't mind my asking though, do you? I mean, it's not as if it was for meself.'

'Not at all. I quite understand.'

She signalled to a cab crawling along the curb and gave her hand to the young man.

'Good-bye, Miss Lambert. So long, good luck and all that sort of thing. And thanks for the autograph.'

Julia sat in the corner of the taxi raging.

'Vulgar little beast. Him and his young lady. The nerve of asking if he could bring her to see ME.'

When she got home she went upstairs to her room. She snatched her hat off her head and flung it angrily on the bed. She strode over to the looking-glass and stared at herself.

'Old, old, old,' she muttered. 'There are no two ways about it; I'm entirely devoid of sex appeal. You wouldn't believe it, would you? You'd say it was preposterous. What other explanation is there? I walk from one end of the Edgware Road to the other and God knows I'd dressed the part perfectly, and not a man pays the smallest attention to me except a bloody little shop-assistant who wants my autograph for his young lady. It's absurd. A lot of sexless bastards. I don't know what's coming to the English. The British Empire!'

The last words she said with a scorn that would have withered a whole front bench of cabinet ministers. She began to gesticulate.

'It's ridiculous to suppose that I could have got to my position if I hadn't got sex appeal. What do people come to see an actress for? Because they want to go to bed with her. Do you mean to tell me that I could fill a theatre for three months with a rotten play if I hadn't got sex appeal? What is sex appeal anyway?'

She paused, looking at herself reflectively.

'Surely I can act sex appeal. I can act anything.'

She began to think of the actresses who notoriously had it, of one especially, Lydia Mayne, whom one always engaged when one wanted a vamp. She was not much of an actress but in certain parts she was wonderfully effective. Julia was a great mimic, and now she began to do an imitation of Lydia Mayne. Her eyelids drooped sensually over her eyes as Lydia's did and her body writhed sinuously in her dress. She got into her eyes the provoking indecency of Lydia's glance and into her serpentine gestures that invitation which was Lydia's speciality. She began to speak in Lydia's voice, with the lazy drawl that made every remark she uttered sound faintly obscene.

'Oh, my dear man, I've heard that sort of thing so often. I don't want to make trouble between you and your wife. Why won't men leave me alone?'

It was a cruel caricature that Julia gave. It was quite ruthless. It amused her so much that she burst out laughing.

'Well, there's one thing, I may not have any sex appeal, but after seeing my imitation there aren't many people who'd think Lydia had either.'

It made her feel much better.

Chapter Twenty-six

Rehearsals began and distracted Julia's troubled mind. The revival that Michael put on when she went abroad had done neither very well nor very badly, but rather than close the theatre he was keeping it in the bill till *Nowadays* was ready. Because he was acting two matinées a week, and the weather was hot, he determined that they should take rehearsals easy. They had a month before them.

Though Julia had been on the stage so long she had never lost the thrill she got out of rehearsing, and the first rehearsal still made her almost sick with excitement. It was the beginning of a new adventure. She did not feel like a leading lady then, she felt as gay and eager as if she were a girl playing her first small part. But at the same time she had a delicious sense of her own powers. Once more she had the chance to exercise them.

At eleven o'clock she stepped on to the stage. The cast stood about idly. She kissed and shook hands with the artists she knew and Michael with urbanity introduced to her those she did not. She greeted Avice Crichton with cordiality. She told her how pretty she was and how much she liked her hat; she told her about the lovely frocks she had chosen for her in Paris.

'Have you seen Tom lately?' she asked.

'No, I haven't. He's away on his holiday.'

'Oh, yes. He's a nice little thing, isn't he?'

'Sweet.'

The two women smiled into one another's eyes. Julia watched her when she read her part and listened to her intonations. She smiled grimly. It was exactly what she had expected. Avice was one of those actresses who were quite sure of themselves from the first rehearsal. She didn't know what was coming to her. Tom meant nothing to Julia any more, but she had a score to settle with Avice and she wasn't going to forget it. The slut!

The play was a modern version of *The Second Mrs Tanqueray*, but with the change of manners of this generation it had been treated from the standpoint of comedy. Some of the old characters were introduced, and Aubrey Tanqueray, now a very old man, appeared in the second act. After Paula's death he had married for the third time. Mrs Cortelyon had undertaken to compensate him for his unfortunate experience with his second wife, and she was now a cantankerous and insolent old lady. Ellean, his daughter, and Hugh Ardale had agreed to let bygones be bygones, for Paula's tragic death had seemed to wipe out the recollection of his lapse into extra-conjugal relations; and they had married. He was now a retired brigadier-general who played golf and deplored the decline of the British Empire—'Gad, sir, I'd stand those damned socialists against a wall and shoot 'em if I had my way'; whereas Ellean, by this time an elderly woman, after a prudish youth had become gay, modern and plain-spoken. The character that Michael played was called Robert Humphreys, and like the Aubrey of Pinero's play he was a widower with an only daughter; he had been a consul in China for many years, and having come into money had retired and was settling on the estate, near where the Tanquerays still lived, which a cousin had left him. His daughter, Honor (this was the part for which Avice Crichton had been engaged), was studying medicine with the intention of practising in India. Alone in London, and friendless after so many years abroad, he had picked up a well-known woman of the town called Mrs Marten. Mrs Marten belonged to the same class as Paula, but she was less exclusive; she 'did' the summer and the winter season at Cannes and in the intervals lived in a flat in Albemarle Street where she entertained the officers of His Majesty's brigade. She played a good game of bridge and an even better game of golf. The part well suited Julia.

The author followed the lines of the old play closely. Honor announced to her father that she was abandoning her medical studies and until her marriage wished to live with him, for she had just become engaged to Ellean's son, a young guardsman. Somewhat disconcerted, Robert Humphreys broke to her his intention of marrying Mrs Marten. Honor took the information with composure.

'Of course you know she's a tart, don't you?' she said coolly.

He, much embarrassed, spoke of the unhappy life she had led and how he wanted to make up to her for all she had suffered.

'Oh, don't talk such rot,' she answered. 'It's grand work if you can get it.'

Ellean's son had been one of Mrs Marten's numerous lovers just as Ellean's husband had been one of Paula Tanqueray's. When Robert Humphreys brought his wife down to his home in the country and this fact was discovered, they decided that Honor must be informed. To their consternation Honor did not turn a hair. She knew already.

'I was as pleased as Punch when I found out,' she told her step-mother. 'You see, darling, you can tell me if he's all right in bed.'

This was Avice Crichton's best scene, it lasted a full ten minutes, and Michael had realized from the beginning that it was effective and important. Avice's cold, matter-of-fact prettiness had been exactly what he had thought would be so telling in the circumstances. But after half a dozen rehearsals he began to think that that was all she had to give. He talked it over with Julia.

'How d'you think Avice is shaping?'

'It's early days to tell yet.'

'I'm not happy about her. You said she could act. I've seen no sign of it yet.'

'It's a cast-iron part. She can't really go wrong in it.'

'You know just as well as I do that there's no such thing as a cast-iron part. However good a part is, it has to be acted for all it's worth. I'm not sure if it wouldn't be better to kick her out and get somebody else.'

'That wouldn't be so easy. I think you ought to give her a chance.'

'She's so awkward, her gestures are so meaningless.'

Julia reflected. She had her reasons for wishing to keep Avice in the cast. She knew her well enough to be sure that if she were dismissed she would tell Tom that it was because Julia was jealous of her. He loved her and would believe anything she said. He might even think that Julia had put this affront on her in revenge for his desertion. No, no, she must stay. She must play the part, and fail; and Tom must see with his own eyes what a bad actress she was. They both of them thought the play would make her. Fools. It would kill her.

'You know how clever you are, Michael, I'm sure you can train her if you're willing to take a little trouble.'

'But that's just it, she doesn't seem able to take direction. I show her exactly how to say a line and then she goes and says it in her own way. You wouldn't believe it, but sometimes I can hardly help thinking she's under the delusion that she knows better than I do.'

'You make her nervous. When you tell her to do something she's in such a dither she doesn't know what she's up to.'

'Good lord, no one could be more easy than I am. I've never even been sharp with her.'

Julia gave him an affectionate smile.

'Are you going to pretend that you really don't know what's the matter with her?'

'No, what?'

He looked at her with a blank face.

'Come off it, darling. Haven't you noticed that she's madly in love with you?'

'With me? But I thought she was practically engaged to Tom. Nonsense. You're always fancying things like that.'

'But it's quite obvious. After all she isn't the first who's fallen for your fatal beauty, and I don't suppose she'll be the last.'

'Heaven knows, I don't want to queer poor Tom's pitch.'

'It's not your fault, is it?'

'What d'you want me to do about it then?'

'Well, I think you ought to be nice to her. She's very young, you know, poor thing. What she wants is a helping hand. If you took her alone a few times and went through the part with her I believe you could do wonders. Why don't you take her out to lunch one day and have a talk to her?'

She saw the gleam in Michael's eyes as he considered the proposition and the shadow of a smile that was outlined on his lips.

'Of course the great thing is to get the play as well acted as we can.'

'I know it'll be a bore for you, but honestly, for the sake of the play I think it'll be worth while.'

'You know that I would never do anything to upset you, Julia. I mean, I'd much sooner fire the girl and get someone else in her place.'

'I think that would be such a mistake. I'm convinced that if you'll only take enough trouble with her she'll give a very good performance.'

He walked up and down the room once or twice. He seemed to be considering the matter from every side.

'Well, I suppose it's my job to get the best performance I can out of every member of my cast. In every case you have to find out which is the best method of approach.'

He threw out his chin and drew in his belly. He straightened his back. Julia knew that Avice Crichton would hold the part, and next day at rehearsal he took her aside and had a long talk with her. She knew by his manner exactly what he was saying and, watching them out of the corner of her eye, presently she saw Avice nod and smile. He had asked her to lunch with him. With a contented mind Julia went on studying her part.'

Chapter Twenty-seven

They had been rehearsing for a fortnight when Roger arrived from Austria. He had been spending a few weeks on a Carinthian lake, and after a day or two in London was to go and stay with friends in Scotland. Since Michael had to dine early to go to the theatre Julia went to meet him by herself. When she was dressing, Evie, sniffing as usual, told her that she was taking as much pains to make herself look nice as if she were going to meet a young man. She wanted Roger to be proud of her, and certainly she looked very young and pretty in her summer frock as she strolled up and down the platform. You would have thought, but wrongly, that she was perfectly unconscious of the attention she attracted. Roger, after a month in the sun, was very brown, but he was still rather spotty and he seemed thinner than when he had left London at the New Year. She hugged him with exuberant affection. He smiled slightly.

They were to dine by themselves. Julia asked him if he would like to go to a play afterwards or to the pictures, but he said he preferred to stay at home.

'That'll be much nicer,' she answered, 'and we'll just talk.'

There was indeed a subject that Michael had invited her to discuss with Roger when the opportunity arose. Now that he was going to Cambridge so soon he ought to make up his mind what he wanted to do. Michael was afraid that he would drift through his time there and then go into a broker's office or even on the stage. Thinking that Julia had more tact than he, and more influence with the boy, he had urged her to put before him the advantages of the Foreign Office and the brilliant possibilities of the Bar. Julia thought it would be strange if in the course of two or three hours' conversation she could not find a way to lead to this important topic. At dinner she tried to get him to talk about Vienna. But he was reticent.

'Oh, I just did the usual things, you know. I saw the sights and worked hard at my German. I knocked about in beer places. I went to the opera a good deal.'

She wondered if he had had any love affairs.

'Anyhow, you haven't come back engaged to a Viennese maiden,' she said, thinking to draw him out.

He gave her a reflective, but faintly amused look. You might almost have thought that he had seen what she was driving at. It was strange; though he was her own son she did not feel quite at home with him.

'No,' he answered, 'I was too busy to bother with that sort of thing.'

'I suppose you went to all the theatres.'

'I went two or three times.'

'Did you see anything that would be any use to me?'

'You know, I never thought about that.'

His answer might have seemed a little ungracious but that it was accompanied by a smile, and his smile was very sweet. Julia wondered again how it was that he had inherited so little of Michael's beauty and of her charm. His red hair was nice, but his pale lashes gave his face a sort of empty look. Heaven only knew where with such a father and such a mother he had got his rather lumpy figure. He was eighteen now; it was time he fined down. He seemed a trifle apathetic; he had none of her sparkling vitality; she could picture the vividness with which she would have narrated her experiences if she had just spent six months in Vienna. Why, already she had made a story about her stay at St Malo with Aunt Carrie and her mother that made people roar with laughter. They all said it was as good as a play, and her own impression was that it was much better than most. She told it to Roger now. He listened with his slow, quiet smile; but she had an uneasy feeling that he did not think it quite so funny as she did. She sighed in her heart. Poor lamb, he could have no sense of humour. Then he made some remark that led her to speak of *Nowadays*. She told him its story, and explained what she was doing with her part; she talked to him of the cast and described the sets. At the end of dinner it suddenly struck her that she had been talking entirely of herself and her own interests. She did not know how she had been led to do this, and the suspicion flashed across her mind that Roger had guided the conversation in that direction so that it should be diverted from him and his affairs. But she put it aside. He really wasn't intelligent enough for that. It was later when they sat in the drawing-room listening to the radio and smoking, that Julia found the chance to slip in, apparently in the most casual fashion, the question she had prepared.

'Have you made up your mind what you're going to be yet?'

'No. Is there any hurry?'

'You know how ignorant I am about everything. Your father says that if you're going to be a barrister you ought to work at law when you go to Cambridge. On the other hand, if you fancy the Foreign Office you should take up modern languages.'

He looked at her for so long, with that queer, reflective air of his, that Julia had some difficulty in holding her light, playful and yet affectionate expression.

'If I believed in God I'd be a priest,' he said at last.

'A priest?'

Julia could hardly believe her ears. She had a feeling of acute discomfort. But his answer sank into her mind and in a flash she saw him as a cardinal, inhabiting a beautiful palazzo in Rome, filled with wonderful pictures, and surrounded by obsequious prelates; and then again as a saint, in a mitre and vestments heavily embroidered with gold, with benevolent gestures distributing bread to the poor. She saw herself in a brocaded dress and a string of pearls. The mother of the Borgias.

'That was all right in the sixteenth century,' she said. 'It's too late in the day for that.'

'Much.'

'I can't think what put such an idea in your head.' He did not answer, so that she had to speak again. 'Aren't you happy?'

'Quite,' he smiled.

'What is it you want?'

Once again he gave her his disconcerting stare. It was hard to know if he was serious, for his eyes faintly shimmered with amusement.

'Reality.'

'What *do* you mean?'

'You see, I've lived all my life in an atmosphere of make-believe. I want to get down to brass tacks. You and father are all right breathing this air, it's the only air you know and you think it's the air of heaven. It stifles me.'

Julia listened to him attentively, trying to understand what he meant.

'We're actors, and successful ones. That's why we've been able to surround you with every luxury since you were born. You could count on the fingers of one hand the actors who've sent their son to Eton.'

'I'm very grateful for all you've done for me.'

'Then what are you reproaching us for?'

'I'm not reproaching you. You've done everything you could for me. Unfortunately for me you've taken away my belief in everything.'

'We've never interfered with your beliefs. I know we're not religious people, we're actors, and after eight performances a week one wants one's Sundays to oneself. I naturally expected they'd see to all that at school.'

He hesitated a little before he spoke again. One might have thought that he had to make a slight effort over himself to continue.

'When I was just a kid, I was fourteen, I was standing one night in the wings watching you act. It must have been a pretty good scene, you said the things you had to say so sincerely, and what you were saying was so moving, I couldn't help crying. I was all worked up. I don't know how to say it quite, I was uplifted; I felt terribly sorry for you, I felt a bloody little hero; I felt I'd never do anything again that was beastly or underhand. And then you had to come to the back of the stage, near where I was standing, the tears were streaming down your face; you stood with your back to the audience and in your ordinary voice you said to the stage-manager: what the bloody hell is that electrician doing with the lights? I told him to leave out the blue. And then in the same breath you turned round and faced the audience with a great cry of anguish and went on with the scene.'

'But, darling, that was acting. If an actress felt the emotions she represented she'd tear herself to pieces. I remember the scene well. It used to bring down the house. I've never heard such applause in my life.'

'I suppose I was a fool to be taken in by it. I believed you meant what you said. When I saw that it was all pretence it smashed something. I've never believed in you since. I'd been made a fool of once; I made up my mind that I wouldn't ever be made a fool of again.'

She gave him her delightful and disarming smile.

'Darling, I think you're talking nonsense.'

'Of course you do. You don't know the difference between truth and make-believe. You never stop acting. It's second nature to you. You act when there's a party here. You act to the servants, you act to father, you act to me. To me you act the part of the fond, indulgent, celebrated mother. You don't exist, you're only the innumerable parts you've played. I've often wondered if there was ever a you or if you were never anything more than a vehicle for all these other people that you've pretended to be. When I've seen you go into an empty room I've sometimes wanted to open the door suddenly, but I've been afraid to in case I found nobody there.'

She looked up at him quickly. She shivered, for what he said gave her an eerie sensation. She listened to him attentively, with a certain anxiety, for he was so serious that she felt he was expressing something that had burdened him for years. She had never in his whole life heard him talk so much.

'D'you think I'm only sham?'

'Not quite. Because sham is all you are. Sham is your truth. Just as margarine is butter to people who don't know what butter is.'

She had a vague feeling of guilt. The Queen in *Hamlet*: 'And let me wring your heart; for so I shall, if it be made of penetrable stuff.' Her thoughts wandered.

('I wonder if I'm too old to play Hamlet. Siddons and Sarah Bernhardt played him. I've got better legs than any of the men I've seen in the part. I'll ask Charles what he thinks. Of course there's that bloody blank verse. Stupid of him not to write it in prose. Of course I might do it in French at the Français. God, what a stunt that would be.')

She saw herself in a black doublet, with long silk hose. 'Alas, poor Yorick.' But she bethought herself.

'You can hardly say that your father doesn't exist. Why, he's been playing himself for the last twenty years.' ('Michael could play the King, not in French, of course, but if we decided to have a shot at it in London.')

'Poor father, I suppose he's good at his job, but he's not very intelligent, is he? He's so busy being the handsomest man in England.'

'I don't think it's very nice of you to speak of your father like that.'

'Have I told you anything you don't know?' he asked coolly.

Julia wanted to smile, but would not allow the look of somewhat pained dignity to leave her face.

'It's our weakness, not our strength, that endears us to those who love us,' she replied.

'In what play did you say that?'

She repressed a gesture of annoyance. The words had come naturally to her lips, but as she said them she remembered that they were out of a play. Little brute! But they came in very appositely.

'You're hard,' she said plaintively. She was beginning to feel more and more like Hamlet's mother. 'Don't you love me?'

'I might if I could find you. But where are you? If one stripped you of your exhibitionism, if one took your technique away from you, if one peeled you as one peels an onion of skin after skin of pretence and insincerity, of tags of old parts and shreds of faked emotions, would one come upon a soul at last?' He looked at her with his grave sad eyes and then he smiled a little. 'I like you all right.'

'Do you believe I love you?'

'In your way.'

Julia's face was suddenly discomposed.

'If you only knew the agony I suffered when you were ill! I don't know what I should have done if you'd died!'

'You would have given a beautiful performance of a bereaved mother at the bier of her only child.'

'Not nearly such a good performance as if I'd had the opportunity of rehearsing it a few times,' Julia answered tartly. 'You see, what you don't understand is that acting isn't nature; it's art, and art is something you create. Real grief is ugly; the business of the actor is to represent it not only with truth but with beauty. If I were really dying as I've died in half a dozen plays, d'you think I'd care whether my gestures were graceful and my faltering words distinct enough to carry to the last row of the gallery? If it's a sham it's no more a sham than a sonata of Beethoven's, and I'm no more of a sham than the pianist who plays it. It's cruel to say that I'm not fond of you. I'm devoted to you. You've been the only thing in my life.'

'No. You were fond of me when I was a kid and you could have me photographed with you. It made a lovely picture and it was fine publicity. But since then you haven't bothered much about me. I've bored you rather than otherwise. You were always glad to see me, but you were thankful that I went my own way and didn't want to take up your time. I don't blame you; you hadn't got time in your life for anyone but yourself.'

Julia was beginning to grow a trifle impatient. He was getting too near the truth for her comfort.

'You forget that young things are rather boring.'

'Crashing, I should think,' he smiled. 'But then why do you pretend that you can't bear to let me out of your sight? That's just acting too.'

'You make me very unhappy. You make me feel as if I hadn't done my duty to you.'

'But you have. You've been a very good mother. You've done something for which I shall always be grateful to you, you've left me alone.'

'I don't understand what you want.'

'I told you. Reality.'

'But where are you going to find it?'

'I don't know. Perhaps it doesn't exist. I'm young still; I'm ignorant. I thought perhaps that at Cambridge, meeting people and reading books, I might discover where to look for it. If they say it only exists in God, I'm done.'

Julia was disturbed. What he said had not really penetrated to her understanding, his words were lines and the important thing was not what they meant, but whether they 'got over', but she was sensitive to the emotion she felt in him. Of course he was only eighteen, and it would be silly to take him too seriously, she couldn't help thinking he'd got all that from somebody else, and that there was a good deal of pose in it. Did anyone have ideas of his own and did anyone not pose just a wee, wee bit? But of course it might be that at the moment he felt everything he said, and it wouldn't be very nice of her to make light of it.

'Of course I see what you mean,' she said. 'My greatest wish in the world is that you should be happy. I'll manage your father, and you can do as you like. You must seek your own salvation, I see that. But I think you ought to make sure that all these ideas of yours aren't just morbid. Perhaps you were too much alone in Vienna and I daresay you read too much. Of course your father and I belong to a different generation and I don't suppose we can help you. Why don't you talk it over with someone more of your own age? Tom, for instance.'

'Tom? A poor little snob. His only ambition in life is to be a gentleman, and he hasn't the sense to see that the more he tries the more hopeless it is.'

'I thought you liked him so much. Why, at Taplow last summer you just lived in his pocket.'

'I didn't dislike him. I made use of him. He could tell me a lot of things that I wanted to know. But I thought him an insignificant, silly little thing.'

Julia remembered how insanely jealous she had been of their friendship. It made her angry to think of all the agony she had wasted.

'You've dropped him, haven't you?' he asked suddenly.

She was startled.

'I suppose I have more or less.'

'I think it's very wise of you. He wasn't up to your mark.'

He looked at her with his calm, reflective eyes, and on a sudden Julia had a sickening fear that he knew that Tom had been her lover. It was impossible, she told herself, it was only her guilty conscience that made her think so; at Taplow there had been nothing; it was incredible that any of the horrid gossip had reached his ears; and yet there was something in his expression that made her certain that he knew. She was ashamed.

'I only asked him to come down to Taplow because I thought it would be nice for you to have a boy of that age to play around with.'

'It was.'

There was in his eyes a faint twinkle of amusement. She felt desperate. She would have liked to ask him what he was grinning at, but dared not; for she knew; he was not angry with her, she could have borne that, he was merely diverted. She was bitterly hurt. She would have cried, but that he would only laugh. And what could she say to him? He believed nothing she said. Acting! For once she was at a loss how to cope with a situation. She was up against something that she did not know, something mysterious and rather frightening. Could that be reality? At that moment they heard a car drive up.

'There's your father,' she exclaimed.

What a relief! The scene was intolerable, and she was thankful that his arrival must end it. In a moment Michael, very hearty, with his chin thrust out and his belly pushed in, looking for all his fifty odd years incredibly handsome, burst into the room and, in his manly way, thrust out his hand to greet, after a six months' absence, his only begotten son.

Chapter Twenty-eight

Three days later Roger went up to Scotland. By the exercise of some ingenuity Julia had managed that they should not again spend any length of time alone together. When they happened to be by themselves for a few minutes they talked of indifferent things. Julia was not really sorry to see him go. She could not dismiss from her mind the curious conversation she had had with him. There was one point in particular that unaccountably worried her; this was his suggestion that if she went into an empty room and someone suddenly opened the door there would be nobody there. It made her feel very uncomfortable.

'I never set out to be a raving beauty, but the one thing no one has ever denied me is personality. It's absurd to pretend that because I can play a hundred different parts in a hundred different ways I haven't got an individuality of my own. I can do that because I'm a bloody good actress.'

She tried to think what happened to her when she went alone into an empty room.

'But I never am alone, even in an empty room. There's always Michael, or Evie, or Charles, or the public; not in the flesh, of course, but in the spirit, as it were. I must speak to Charles about Roger.'

Unfortunately he was away. But he was coming back for the dress-rehearsal and the first night; he had not missed these occasions for twenty years, and they had always had supper together after the dress-rehearsal. Michael would remain in the theatre, busy with the lights and so on, so that they would be alone. They would be able to have a good talk.

She studied her part. Julia did not deliberately create the character she was going to act by observation; she had a knack of getting into the shoes of the woman she had to portray so that she thought with her mind and felt with her senses. Her intuition suggested to her a hundred small touches that afterwards amazed people by their verisimilitude; but when they asked her where she had got them she could not say. Now she wanted to show the courageous yet uneasy breeziness of the Mrs Marten who played golf and could talk to a man like one good chap to another and yet, essentially a respectable, middle-class woman, hankered for the security of the marriage state.

Michael never liked to have a crowd at a dress-rehearsal, and this time, anxious to keep the secret of the play till the first night, he had admitted besides Charles only the people, photographers and dressmakers, whose presence was necessary. Julia spared herself. She had no intention of giving all she had to give till the first night. It was enough if her performance was adequate. Under Michael's business-like direction everything went off without a hitch, and by ten o'clock Julia and Charles were sitting in the Grill Room of the Savoy. The first thing she asked him was what he thought of Avice Crichton.

'Not at all bad and wonderfully pretty. She really looked lovely in that second-class dress.'

'I'm not going to wear the dress I wore in the second act. Charley Deverill has made me another.'

He did not see the slightly humorous glance she gave him, and if he had would not have guessed what it meant. Michael, having taken Julia's advice, had gone to a good deal of trouble with Avice. He had rehearsed her by herself upstairs in his private room and had given her every intonation and every gesture. He had also, Julia had good reason to believe, lunched with her several times and taken her out to supper. The result of all this was that she was playing the part uncommonly well. Michael rubbed his hands.

'I'm very pleased with her. I think she'll make quite a hit. I've half a mind to give her a contract.'

'I wouldn't,' said Julia. 'Not till after the first night. You can never really tell how a performance is going to pan out till you've got an audience.'

'She's a nice girl and a perfect lady.'

'A nice girl, I suppose, because she's madly in love with you, and a perfect lady because she's resisting your advances till she's got a contract.'

'Oh, my dear, don't be so silly. Why, I'm old enough to be her father.'

But he smiled complacently. She knew very well that his love-making went no further than holding hands and a kiss or two in a taxi, but she knew also that it flattered him to imagine that she suspected him capable of infidelity.

But now Julia, having satisfied her appetite with proper regard for her figure, attacked the subject which was on her mind.

'Charles dear, I want to talk to you about Roger.'

'Oh yes, he came back the other day, didn't he? How is he?'

'My dear, a most terrible thing has happened. He's come back a fearful prig and I don't know what to do about it.'

She gave him her version of the conversation. She left out one or two things that it seemed inconvenient to mention, but what she told was on the whole accurate.

'The tragic thing is that he has absolutely no sense of humour,' she finished.

'After all he's only eighteen.'

'You could have knocked me down with a feather when he said all those things to me. I felt just like Balaam when his ass broke into light conversation.'

She gave him a gay look, but he did not even smile. He did not seem to think her remark as funny as she did.

'I can't imagine where he got his ideas. It's absurd to think that he could have thought out all that nonsense for himself.'

'Are you sure that boys of that age don't think more than we older people imagine? It's a sort of puberty of the spirit and its results are often strange.'

'It seems so deceitful of Roger to have harboured thoughts like those all these years and never breathed a word about them. He might have been accusing me.' She gave a chuckle. 'To tell you the truth, when Roger was talking to me I felt just like Hamlet's mother.' Then with hardly a break: 'I wonder if I'm too old to play Hamlet?'

'Gertrude isn't a very good part, is it?'

Julia broke into a laugh of frank amusement.

'Don't be idiotic, Charles. I wouldn't play the Queen. I'd play Hamlet.'

'D'you think it's suited to a woman?'

'Mrs Siddons played it and so did Sarah Bernhardt. It would set a seal on my career, if you know what I mean. Of course there's the difficulty of the blank verse.'

'I have heard actors speak it so that it was indistinguishable from prose,' he answered.

'Yes, but that's not quite the same is it?'

'Were you nice to Roger?'

She was surprised at his going back to that subject so suddenly, but she returned to it with a smile.

'Oh, charming.'

'It's hard not to be impatient with the absurdity of the young; they tell us that two and two make four as though it had never occurred to us, and they're disappointed if we can't share their surprise when they have just discovered that a hen lays an egg. There's a lot of nonsense in their ranting and raving, but it's not all nonsense. One ought to sympathize with them; one ought to do one's best to understand. One has to remember how much has to be forgotten and how much has to be learnt when for the first time one faces life. It's not very easy to give up one's ideals, and the brute facts of everyday are bitter pills to swallow. The spiritual conflicts of adolescence can be very severe and one can do so little to resolve them.'

'But you don't really think there's anything in all this stuff of Roger's? I believe it's all a lot of communist nonsense that he's learnt in Vienna. I wish we'd never sent him there.'

'You may be right. It may be that in a year or two he'll lose sight of the clouds of glory and accept the chain. It may be that he'll find what he's looking for, if not in God, then in art.'

'I should hate him to be an actor if that's what you mean.'

'No, I don't think he'll fancy that.'

'And of course he can't be a playwright, he hasn't a sense of humour.'

'I daresay he'll be quite content to go into the Foreign Office. It would be an asset to him there.'

'What would you advise me to do?'

'Nothing. Let him be. That's probably the greatest kindness you can do him.'

'But I can't help being worried about him.'

'You needn't be. Be hopeful. You thought you'd only given birth to an ugly duckling; perhaps he's going to turn into a white-winged swan.'

Charles was not giving Julia what she wanted. She had expected him to be more sympathetic.

'I suppose he's getting old, poor dear,' she reflected. 'He's losing his grip of things. He must have been impotent for years; I wonder it never struck me before.'

She asked what the time was.

'I think I ought to go. I must get a long night's rest.'

Julia slept well and when she awoke had at once a feeling of exultation. Tonight was the first night. It gave her a little thrill of pleasure to recollect that people had already been assembling at the pit and gallery doors when she left the theatre after the dress-rehearsal, and now at ten in the morning there was probably already a long queue.

'Lucky it's a fine day for them, poor brutes.'

In bygone years she had been intolerably nervous before a first night. She had felt slightly sick all day and as the hours passed got into such a state that she almost thought she would have to leave the stage. But by now, after having passed through the ordeal so many times, she had acquired a certain nonchalance. Throughout the early part of the day she felt only happy and mildly excited; it was not till late in the afternoon that she began to feel ill at ease. She grew silent and wanted to be left alone. She also grew irritable, and Michael, having learnt from experience, took care to keep out of her way. Her hands and feet got cold and by the time she reached the theatre they were like lumps of ice. But still the apprehension that filled her was not unpleasant.

Julia had nothing to do that morning but go down to the Siddons for a word-rehearsal at noon, so she lay in bed till late. Michael did not come back to luncheon, having last things to do to the sets, and she ate alone. Then she went to bed and for an hour slept soundly. Her intention was to rest all the afternoon; Miss Phillips was coming at six to give her a light massage, and by seven she wanted to be at the theatre. But when she awoke she felt so much refreshed that it irked her to stay in bed, so she made up her mind to get up and go for a walk. It was a fine, sunny day. Liking the town better than the country and streets more than trees, she did not go into the Park, but sauntered round the neighbouring squares, deserted at that time of year, idly looking at the houses, and thought how much she preferred her own to any of them. She felt at ease and light-hearted. Then she thought it time to go home. She had just reached the corner of Stanhope Place when she heard her name called in a voice that she could not but recognize.

'Julia.'

She turned round and Tom, his face all smiles, caught her up. She had not seen him since her return from France. He was very smart in a neat grey suit and a brown hat. He was tanned by the sun.

'I thought you were away.'

'I came back on Monday. I didn't ring up because I knew you were busy with the final rehearsals. I'm coming tonight; Michael gave me a stall.'

'Oh, I'm glad.'

It was plain that he was delighted to see her. His face was eager and his eyes shone. She was pleased to discover that the sight of him excited no emotion in her. She wondered as they went on talking what there was in him that had ever so deeply affected her.

'What on earth are you wandering about like this for?'

'I've been for a stroll. I was just going in to tea.'

'Come and have tea with me.'

His flat was just round the corner. Indeed he had caught sight of her just as he was going down the mews to get to it.

'How is it you're back so early?'

'Oh, there's nothing much on at the office just now. You know, one of our partners died a couple of months ago, and I'm getting a bigger share. It means I shall be able to keep on at the flat after all. Michael was jolly decent about it, he said I could stay on rent free till things got better. I hated the idea of turning out. Do come. I'd love to make you a cup of tea.'

He rattled on so vivaciously that Julia was amused. You would never have thought to listen to him that there had ever been anything between them. He seemed perfectly unembarrassed.

'All right. But I can only stay a minute.'

'O.K.'

They turned into the mews and she preceded him up the narrow staircase.

'You toddle along to the sitting-room and I'll put the water on to boil.'

She went in and sat down. She looked round the room that had been the scene of so many emotions for her. Nothing was changed. Her photograph stood in its old place, but on the chimney-piece was a large photograph also of Avice Crichton. On it was written for Tom from Avice. Julia took everything in. The room might have been a set in which she had once acted; it was vaguely familiar, but no longer meant anything to her. The love that had consumed her then, the jealousy she had stifled, the ecstasy of surrender, it had no more reality than one of the innumerable parts she had played in the past. She relished her indifference. Tom came in, with the tea-cloth she had given him, and neatly set out the tea-service which she had also given him. She did not know why the thought of his casually using still all her little presents made her inclined to laugh. Then he came in with the tea and they drank it sitting side by side on the sofa. He told her more about his improved circumstances. In his pleasant, friendly way he acknowledged that it was owing to the work that through her he had been able to bring the firm that he had secured a larger share in the profits. He told her of the holiday from which he had just returned. It was quite clear to Julia that he had no inkling how much he had made her suffer. That too made her now inclined to laugh.

'I hear you're going to have an enormous success tonight.'

'It would be nice, wouldn't it?'

'Avice says that both you and Michael have been awfully good to her. Take care she doesn't romp away with the play.'

He said it chaffingly, but Julia wondered whether Avice had told him that this was what she expected to do.

'Are you engaged to her?'

'No. She wants her freedom. She says an engagement would interfere with her career.'

'With her what?' The words slipped out of Julia's mouth before she could stop them, but she immediately recovered herself. 'Yes, I see what she means of course.'

'Naturally, I don't want to stand in her way. I mean, supposing after tonight she got a big offer for America I can quite see that she ought to be perfectly free to accept.'

Her career! Julia smiled quietly to herself.

'You know, I do think you're a brick, the way you've behaved to her.'

'Why?'

'Oh well, you know what women are!'

As he said this he slipped his arm round her waist and kissed her. She laughed outright.

'What an absurd little thing you are.'

'How about a bit of love?'

'Don't be so silly.'

'What is there silly about it? Don't you think we've been divorced long enough?'

'I'm all for irrevocable divorce. And what about Avice?'

'Oh, she's different. Come on.'

'Has it slipped your memory that I've got a first night tonight?'

'There's plenty of time.'

He put both arms round her and kissed her softly. She looked at him with mocking eyes. Suddenly she made up her mind.

'All right.'

They got up and went into the bedroom. She took off her hat and slipped out of her dress. He held her in his arms as he had held her so often before. He kissed her closed eyes and the little breasts of which she was so proud. She gave him her body to do what he wanted with, but her spirit held aloof. She returned his kisses out of amiability, but she caught herself thinking of the part she was going to play that night. She seemed to be two persons, the mistress in her lover's embrace, and the actress who already saw in her mind's eye the vast vague dark audience and heard the shouts of applause as she stepped on to the stage. When, a little later, they lay side by side, he with his arm round her neck, she forgot about him so completely that she was quite surprised when he broke a long silence.

'Don't you care for me any more?'

She gave him a little hug.

'Of course, darling. I dote on you.'

'You're so strange today.'

She realized that he was disappointed. Poor little thing, she didn't want to hurt his feelings. He was very sweet really.

'With the first night before me I'm not really myself today. You mustn't mind.'

When she came to the conclusion, quite definitely now, that she no longer cared two straws for him she could not help feeling a great pity for him. She stroked his cheek gently.

'Sweetie pie. (I wonder if Michael remembered to have tea sent along to the queues. It doesn't cost much and they do appreciate it so enormously.) You know, I really must get up. Miss Phillips is coming at six. Evie will be in a state, she won't be able to think what's happened to me.'

She chattered brightly while she dressed. She was conscious, although she did not look at him, that Tom was vaguely uneasy. She put her hat on, then she took his face in both her hands and gave him a friendly kiss.

'Good-bye, my lamb. Have a good time tonight.'

'Best of luck.'

He smiled with some awkwardness. She perceived that he did not quite know what to make of her. Julia slipped out of the flat, and if she had not been England's leading actress, and a woman of hard on fifty, she would have hopped on one leg all the way down Stanhope Place till she got to her house. She was as pleased as Punch. She let herself in with her latch-key and closed the front door behind her.

'I daresay there's something in what Roger said. Love isn't worth all the fuss they make about it.'

Chapter Twenty-nine

Four hours later it was all over. The play went well from the beginning; the audience, notwithstanding the season, a fashionable one, were pleased after the holidays to find themselves once more in a playhouse, and were ready to be amused. It was an auspicious beginning for the theatrical season. There had been great applause after each act and at the end a dozen curtain calls; Julia took two by herself, and even she was startled by the warmth of her reception. She had made the little halting speech, prepared beforehand, which the occasion demanded. There had been a final call of the entire company and then the orchestra had struck up the National Anthem. Julia, pleased, excited and happy, went to her dressing-room. She had never felt more sure of herself. She had never acted with greater brilliance, variety and resource. The play ended with a long tirade in which Julia, as the retired harlot, castigated the flippancy, the uselessness, the immorality of the idle set into which her marriage had brought her. It was two pages long, and there was not another actress in England who could have held the attention of the audience while she delivered it. With her exquisite timing, with the modulation of her beautiful voice, with her command of the gamut of emotions, she had succeeded by a miracle of technique in making it a thrilling, almost spectacular climax to the play. A violent action could not have been more exciting, nor an unexpected dénouement more surprising. The whole cast had been excellent with the exception of Avice Crichton. Julia hummed in an undertone as she went into her dressing-room.

Michael followed her in almost at once.

'It looks like a winner all right.' He threw his arms round her and kissed her. 'By God, what a performance you gave.'

'You weren't so bad yourself dear.'

'That's the sort of part I can play on my head,' he answered carelessly, modest as usual about his own acting. 'Did you hear them during your long speech? That ought to knock the critics.'

'Oh, you know what they are. They'll give all their attention to the blasted play and then three lines at the end to me.'

'You're the greatest actress in the world, darling, but by God, you're a bitch.'

Julia opened her eyes very wide in an expression of the most naïve surprise.

'Michael, what do you mean?'

'Don't look so innocent. You know perfectly well. Do you think you can cod an old trooper like me?'

He was looking at her with twinkling eyes, and it was very difficult for her not to burst out laughing.

'I am as innocent as a babe unborn.'

'Come off it. If anyone ever deliberately killed a performance you killed Avice's. I couldn't be angry with you, it was so beautifully done.'

Now Julia simply could not conceal the little smile that curled her lips. Praise is always grateful to the artist. Avice's one big scene was in the second act. It was with Julia, and Michael had rehearsed it so as to give it all to the girl. This was indeed what the play demanded and Julia, as always, had in rehearsals accepted his direction. To bring out the colour of her blue eyes and to emphasize her fair hair they had dressed Avice in pale blue. To contrast with this Julia had chosen a dress of an agreeable yellow. This she had worn at the dress-rehearsal. But she had ordered another dress at the same time, of sparkling silver, and to the surprise of Michael and the consternation of Avice it was in this that she made her entrance in the second act. Its brilliance, the way it took the light, attracted the attention of the audience. Avice's blue looked drab by comparison. When they reached the important scene they were to have together Julia produced, as a conjurer produces a rabbit from his hat, a large handkerchief of scarlet chiffon and with this she played. She waved it, she spread it out as though to look at it, she screwed it up, she wiped her brow with it, she delicately blew her nose. The audience fascinated could not take their eyes away from the red rag. And as she moved up stage so that Avice to speak to her had to turn her back on the audience, and when they were sitting on a sofa together she took her hand, in an impulsive way that seemed to the public exquisitely natural, and sitting well back herself forced Avice to turn her profile to the house. Julia had noticed early in rehearsals that in profile Avice had a sheep-like look. The author had given Avice lines to say that had so much amused the cast at the first rehearsal that they had all burst out laughing. Before the audience had quite realized how funny they were Julia had cut in with her reply, and the audience anxious to hear it suppressed their laughter. The scene which was devised to be extremely amusing took on a sardonic colour, and the character Avice played acquired a certain odiousness. Avice in her inexperience, not getting the laughs she had expected, was rattled; her voice grew hard and her gestures awkward. Julia took the scene away from her and played it with miraculous virtuosity. But her final stroke was accidental. Avice had a long speech to deliver, and Julia nervously screwed her red handkerchief into a ball; the action almost automatically suggested an expression; she looked at Avice with troubled eyes and two heavy tears rolled down her cheeks. You felt the shame with which the girl's flippancy affected her, and you saw her pain because her poor little ideals of uprightness, her hankering for goodness, were so brutally mocked. The episode lasted no more than a minute, but in that minute, by those tears and by the anguish of her look, Julia laid bare the sordid misery of the woman's life. That was the end of Avice.

'And I was such a damned fool, I thought of giving her a contract,' said Michael.

'Why don't you?'

'When you've got your knife into her? Not on your life. You're a naughty little thing to be so jealous. You don't really think she means anything to me, do you? You ought to know by now that you're the only woman in the world for me.'

Michael thought that Julia had played this trick on account of the rather violent flirtation he had been having with Avice, and though, of course, it was hard luck on Avice he could not help being a trifle flattered.

'You old donkey,' smiled Julia, knowing exactly what he was thinking and tickled to death at his mistake. 'After all, you are the handsomest man in London.'

'All that's as it may be. But I don't know what the author'll say. He's a conceited little ape and it's not a bit the scene he wrote.'

'Oh, leave him to me. I'll fix him.'

There was a knock at the door and it was the author himself who came in. With a cry of delight, Julia went up to him, threw her arms round his neck and kissed him on both cheeks.

'Are you pleased?'

'It looks like a success,' he answered, but a trifle coldly.

'My dear, it'll run for a year.' She placed her hands on his shoulders and looked him full in the face. 'But you're a wicked, wicked man.'

'I?'

'You almost ruined my performance. When I came to that bit in the second act and suddenly saw what it meant I nearly broke down. You knew what was in that scene, you're the author; why did you let us rehearse it all the time as if there was no more in it than appeared on the surface? We're only actors, how can you expect us to–to fathom your subtlety? It's the best scene in your play and I almost bungled it. No one in the world could have written it but you. Your play's brilliant, but in that scene there's more than brilliance, there's genius.'

The author flushed. Julia looked at him with veneration. He felt shy and happy and proud.

('In twenty-four hours the mug'll think he really meant the scene to go like that.')

Michael beamed.

'Come along to my dressing-room and have a whisky and soda. I'm sure you need a drink after all that emotion.'

They went out as Tom came in. Tom's face was red with excitement.

'My dear, it was grand. You were simply wonderful. Gosh, what a performance.'

'Did you like it? Avice was good, wasn't she?'

'No, rotten.'

'My dear, what do you mean? I thought she was charming.'

'You simply wiped the floor with her. She didn't even look pretty in the second act.'

Avice's career!

'I say, what are you doing afterwards?'

'Dolly's giving a party for us.'

'Can't you cut it and come along to supper with me? I'm madly in love with you.'

'Oh, what nonsense. How can I let Dolly down?'

'Oh, do.'

His eyes were eager. She could see that he desired her as he had never done before, and she rejoiced in her triumph. But she shook her head firmly. There was a sound in the corridor of a crowd of people talking, and they both knew that a troop of friends were forcing their way down the narrow passage to congratulate her.

'Damn all these people. God, how I want to kiss you. I'll ring you up in the morning.'

The door burst open and Dolly, fat, perspiring and bubbling over with enthusiasm, swept in at the head of a throng that packed the dressing-room to suffocation. Julia submitted to being kissed by all and sundry. Among others were three or four well-known actresses, and they were prodigal of their praise. Julia gave a beautiful performance of unaffected modesty. The corridor was packed now with people who wanted to get at least a glimpse of her. Dolly had to fight her way out.

'Try not to be too late,' she said to Julia. 'It's going to be a heavenly party.'

'I'll come as soon as ever I can.'

At last the crowd was got rid of and Julia, having undressed, began to take off her make-up. Michael came in, wearing a dressing-gown.

'I say, Julia, you'll have to go to Dolly's party by yourself. I've got to see the libraries and I can't manage it. I'm going to sting them.'

'Oh, all right.'

'They're waiting for me now. See you in the morning.'

He went out and she was left alone with Evie. The dress she had arranged to wear for Dolly's party was placed over a chair. Julia smeared her face with cleansing cream.

'Evie, Mr Fennell will be ringing up tomorrow. Will you say I'm out?'

Evie looked in the mirror and caught Julia's eyes.

'And if he rings up again?'

'I don't want to hurt his feelings, poor lamb, but I have a notion I shall be very much engaged for some time now.'

Evie sniffed loudly, and with that rather disgusting habit of hers drew her forefinger across the bottom of her nose.

'I understand,' she said dryly.

'I always said you weren't such a fool as you looked.' Julia went on with her face. 'What's that dress doing on that chair?'

'That? That's the dress you said you'd wear for the party.'

'Put it away. I can't go to the party without Mr Gosselyn.'

'Since when?'

'Shut up, you old hag. Phone through and say that I've got a bad headache and had to go home to bed, but Mr Gosselyn will come if he can.'

'The party's being given special for you. You can't let the poor old gal down like that?'

Julia stamped her feet.

'I don't want to go to a party. I won't go to a party.'

'There's nothing for you to eat at home.'

'I don't want to go home. I'll go and have supper at a restaurant.'

'Who with?'

'By myself.'

Evie gave her a puzzled glance.

'The play's a success, isn't it?'

'Yes. Everything's a success. I feel on the top of the world. I feel like a million dollars. I want to be alone and enjoy myself. Ring up the Berkeley and tell them to keep a table for one in the little room. They'll know what I mean.'

'What's the matter with you?'

'I shall never in all my life have another moment like this. I'm not going to share it with anyone.'

When Julia had got her face clean she left it. She neither painted her lips nor rouged her cheeks. She put on again the brown coat and skirt in which she had come to the theatre and the same hat. It was a felt hat with a brim, and this she pulled down over one eye so that it should hide as much of her face as possible. When she was ready she looked at herself in the glass.

'I look like a working dressmaker whose husband's left her, and who can blame him? I don't believe a soul would recognize me.'

Evie had had the telephoning done from the stage-door, and when she came back Julia asked her if there were many people waiting for her there.

'About three 'undred I should say.'

'Damn.' She had a sudden desire to see nobody and be seen by nobody. She wanted just for one hour to be obscure. 'Tell the fireman to let me out at the front and I'll take a taxi, and then as soon as I've got out let the crowd know there's no use in their waiting.'

'God only knows what I 'ave to put up with,' said Evie darkly.

'You old cow.'

Julia took Evie's face in her hands and kissed her raddled cheeks; then slipped out of her dressing-room, on to the stage and through the iron door into the darkened auditorium.

Julia's simple disguise was evidently adequate, for when she came into the little room at the Berkeley of which she was peculiarly fond, the head-waiter did not immediately know.

'Have you got a corner that you can squeeze me into?' she asked diffidently. Her voice and a second glance told him who she was.

'Your favourite table is waiting for you, Miss Lambert. The message said you would be alone?' Julia nodded and he led her to a table in the corner of the room. 'I hear you've had a big success tonight, Miss Lambert.' How quickly good news travelled. 'What can I order?'

The head-waiter was surprised that Julia should be having supper by herself, but the only emotion that it was his business to show clients was gratification at seeing them.

'I'm very tired, Angelo.'

'A little caviare to begin with, madame, or some oysters?'

'Oysters, Angelo, but fat ones.'

'I will choose them myself, Miss Lambert, and to follow?'

Julia gave a long sigh, for now she could, with a free conscience, order what she had had in mind ever since the end of the second act. She felt she deserved a treat to celebrate her triumph, and for once she meant to throw prudence to the winds.

'Grilled steak and onions, fried potatoes, and a bottle of Bass. Give it me in a silver tankard.'

She probably hadn't eaten fried potatoes for ten years. But what an occasion it was! By happy chance on this day she had confirmed her hold on the public by a performance that she could only describe as scintillating, she had settled an old score, by one ingenious device disposing of Avice and making Tom see what a fool he had been, and best of all had proved to herself beyond all question that she was free from the irksome bonds that had oppressed her. Her thought flickered for an instant round Avice.

'Silly little thing to try to put a spoke in my wheel. I'll let her have her laughs tomorrow.'

The oysters came and she ate them with enjoyment. She ate two pieces of brown bread and butter with the delicious sense of imperilling her immortal soul, and she took a long drink from the silver tankard.

'Beer, glorious beer,' she murmured.

She could see Michael's long face if he knew what she was doing. Poor Michael who imagined she had killed Avice's scene because she thought he was too attentive to that foolish little blonde. Really, it was pitiful how stupid men were. They said women were vain, why they were modest violets in comparison with men. She could not but laugh when she thought of Tom. He had wanted her that afternoon, he had wanted her still more that night. It was wonderful to think that he meant no more to her than a stage-hand. It gave one a grand feeling of confidence to be heart-whole.

The room in which she sat was connected by three archways with the big dining-room where they supped and danced; amid the crowd doubtless were a certain number who had been to the play. How surprised they would be if they knew that the quiet little woman in the corner of the adjoining room, her face half hidden by a felt hat, was Julia Lambert. It gave her a pleasant sense of independence to sit there unknown and unnoticed. They were acting a play for her and she was the audience. She caught brief glimpses of them as they passed the archway, young men and young women, young men and women not so young, men with bald heads and men with fat bellies, old harridans clinging desperately to their painted semblance of youth. Some were in love, and some were jealous, and some were indifferent.

Her steak arrived. It was cooked exactly as she liked it, and the onions were crisp and brown. She ate the fried potatoes delicately, with her fingers, savouring each one as though it were the passing moment that she would bid delay.

'What is love beside steak and onions?' she asked. It was enchanting to be alone and allow her mind to wander. She thought once more of Tom and spiritually shrugged a humorous shoulder. 'It was an amusing experience.'

It would certainly be useful to her one of these days. The sight of the dancers seen through the archway was so much like a scene in a play that she was reminded of a notion that she had first had in St Malo. The agony that she had suffered when Tom deserted her recalled to her memory Racine's *Phèdre* which she had studied as a girl with old Jane Taitbout. She read the play again. The torments that afflicted Theseus' queen were the torments that afflicted her, and she could not but think that there was a striking similarity in their situations. That was a part she could act; she knew what it felt like to be turned down by a young man one had a fancy for. Gosh, what a performance she could give! She knew why in the spring she had acted so badly that Michael had preferred to close down; it was because she was feeling the emotions she portrayed. That was no good. You had to have had the emotions, but you could only play them when you had got over them. She remembered that Charles had once said to her that the origin of poetry was emotion recollected in tranquillity. She didn't know anything about poetry, but it was certainly true about acting.

'Clever of poor old Charles to get hold of an original idea like that. It shows how wrong it is to judge people hastily. One thinks the aristocracy are a bunch of nitwits, and then one of them suddenly comes out with something like that that's so damned good it takes your breath away.'

But Julia had always felt that Racine had made a great mistake in not bringing on his heroine till the third act.

'Of course I wouldn't have any nonsense like that if I played it. Half an act to prepare my entrance if you like, but that's ample.'

There was no reason why she should not get some dramatist to write her a play on the subject, either in prose or in short lines of verse with rhymes at not too frequent intervals. She could manage that, and effectively. It was a good idea, there was no doubt about it, and she knew the clothes she would wear, not those flowing draperies in which Sarah swathed herself, but the short Greek tunic that she had seen on a bas-relief when she went to the British Museum with Charles.

'How funny things are! You go to those museums and galleries and think what a damned bore they are and then, when you least expect it, you find that something you've seen comes in useful. It shows art and all that isn't really waste of time.'

Of course she had the legs for a tunic, but could one be tragic in one? This she thought about seriously for two or three minutes. When she was eating out her heart for the indifferent Hippolytus (and she giggled when she thought of Tom, in his Savile Row clothes, masquerading as a young Greek hunter) could she really get her effects without abundant draperies? The difficulty excited her. But then a thought crossed her mind that for a moment dashed her spirits.

'It's all very well, but where are the dramatists? Sarah had her Sardou, Duse her D'Annunzio. But who have I got? "The Queen of Scots hath a bonnie bairn and I am but a barren stock."'

She did not, however, let this melancholy reflection disturb her serenity for long. Her elation was indeed such that she felt capable of creating dramatists from the vast inane as Deucalion created men from the stones of the field.

'What nonsense that was that Roger talked the other day, and poor Charles, who seemed to take it seriously. He's a silly little prig, that's all.' She indicated a gesture towards the dance room. The lights had been lowered, and from where she sat it looked more than ever like a scene in a play. '"All the world's a stage, and all the men and women merely players." But there's the illusion, through that archway; it's we, the actors, who are reality. That's the answer to Roger. They are our raw material. We are the meaning of their lives. We take their silly little emotions and turn them into art, out of them we create beauty, and their significance is that they form the audience we must have to fulfil ourselves. They are the instruments on which we play, and what is an instrument without somebody to play on it?'

The notion exhilarated her, and for a moment or two she savoured it with satisfaction. Her brain seemed miraculously lucid.

'Roger says we don't exist. Why, it's only we who do exist. They are the shadows and we give them substance. We are the symbols of all this confused, aimless struggling that they call life, and it's only the symbol which is real. They say acting is only make-believe. That make-believe is the only reality.'

Thus Julia out of her own head framed anew the platonic theory of ideas. It filled her with exultation. She felt a sudden wave of friendliness for that immense anonymous public who had being only to give her opportunity to express herself. Aloof on her mountain top she considered the innumerable activities of men. She had a wonderful sense of freedom from all earthly ties, and it was such an ecstasy that nothing in comparison with it had any value. She felt like a spirit in heaven.

The head-waiter came up to her with an ingratiating smile.

'Everything all right, Miss Lambert?'

'Lovely. You know, it's strange how people differ. Mrs Siddons was a rare one for chops; I'm not a bit like her in that; I'm a rare one for steaks.'

The Moon and Sixpence

W. Somerset Maugham

Preface

This novel was suggested by the life of Paul Gauguin. I had been living for some years in London working hard and earning very little money, but enjoying myself. I had written four or five novels, of which two had been not unsuccessful; I was unknown to the general public, but here and there a discerning person was of opinion that I showed promise. I was made much of by elderly women of means who liked to see young men of talent at their tables; old gentlemen were very kind to me and asked me to dine at their clubs. I lunched out a good deal and spent pleasant week-ends in the country. I went to literary tea-parties. I was on the list of various ladies of title who gave balls. I made something of a show on an inadequate income. I had had my first play produced by the Stage Society, and, a great honour, it had been printed in *The Fortnightly Review*. I was just thirty. It seemed to me a solemn moment and I felt called upon to take a decisive step.

I was in a rut. I was exasperated by the quiet and orderly life I had been living. I had had enough of the week-end visits to the houses of the rich and the grand and interminable dinner-parties in Mayfair that I was bidden to. I did not want to go to any more dances. I was growing old (I thought) and the precious years were slipping unprofitably through my fingers. I had a great eagerness for life. I determined to cut myself adrift from the agreeable friends and the monotonous pleasures that were wasting me. I got rid of the little flat near Victoria of which for a moment I had been so proud, sold the furniture and set out for Paris. This, I admit, was far from reckless, but the date was 1904, and Paris then still seemed the home of culture. I had a friend, a painter, who lived there and the life in the Latin Quarter that he described was much to my liking. I looked forward to adventures not only of the spirit. I had known Paris as a boy, for I was born there, and even after my parents' death which sent me to England, I had often, passing through, stayed there for longer or shorter periods; but the Paris I knew was the Paris of the Champs-Elysées and the Boulevards. The Paris of Montparnasse was new to me. I took an apartment of three small rooms near the Lion de Belfort, on the fifth floor, with a spacious view over the cemetery. Montparnasse had at that time very much the air of a provincial town, which even now when you look at it with the eyes of fancy it still charmingly wears. The great handsome streets that have been cut through it did not exist and the Boulevard Raspail was only half built. A horse tram ran down the rue de Rennes. The night life which has made it the haunt of half Paris, foreign and native, was undreamt of. The Dome, the Rotonde, the Closerie des Lilas were there, but their patrons were the inhabitants of the quarter. To go over to the other side of the river, in a bus drawn by three horses, was an excursion. It was rarely made except to go to the Louvre or the Salon and now and then to the theatre. As a rule if one wanted to see a show one went to the Gaîtés Montparnasse. In the rue de Rennes were some good shops, but in the side streets they were the same little smelly grubby shops that had been there for a century. Life on the Montparnasse was intense, for art seemed the most important thing in the world and since everyone was young, love, a light love for the most part, without consequence, added zest to it, but notwithstanding life was quiet, plain and easy. It was also incredibly cheap. However busy one was, there was ample leisure. The air seemed fresher than in the Paris of the Boulevard and the crowd less insistent. When I look back my most vivid recollection is of a feeling of anticipation that danced in one's heart like dust in a sunbeam. It was then that I became aware of Cézanne, van Gogh and Gauguin. Of these I suppose that Cézanne is by far the greater artist, but Gauguin has a singular appeal to the man of letters. Though I do not now so much admire his pictures I still see how much there is in them to excite the literary imagination. I met men who had known him and worked with him in Pont-Aven. I heard much about him. It occurred to me that there was in what I was told the subject of a novel, and I read the only life of him that at that moment existed. I kept the idea in my mind. I kept it for over ten years. When I went to Tahiti, it was with the notion of finding out what I could of Gauguin's life and here again I came across a number of persons who had been more or less connected with him. At last I found myself ready to write the novel I had so long contemplated. It was written during the summer of 1918 while I was recovering on a hill-top in Surrey from the tuberculosis I had contracted earlier in the war.

For the experiences of Charles Strickland in Marseilles I used some passages from an interesting book of travels by Harry Franck, called *A Vagabond Journey round the World*. In a novel it would be absurd to put the source from which you obtain information, it would destroy the illusion you seek to create, but I gave the reader a hint of the truth by suggesting that Captain Nichols, the narrator of the facts in question, had found them in the pages of a magazine. This was apparently not enough, for an angry gentleman wrote a long article condemning my reprehensible behaviour. It left me calm. I gladly acknowledge my debt to Mr Harry Franck. *A Vagabond Journey round the World* is very readable. It contains a dozen incidents that only require imagination, a sense of character, the power to write and the creative impulse to make into stories. The novelist cannot know everything. A great deal of the information necessary to him must be got from other people or from books. It is quite a modern notion that the writer should pretend to invent everything he writes out of his own head. It is an absurd one. The writers of the past took from one another what they wanted. Many went further and without sense of shame copied whole passages. This would be reprehensible now that to write books is a commercial proposition, but to make a fuss because one writer uses an incident that he has found in another's book is nonsense. By turning it to good account he makes it sufficiently his own. Books of facts are a legitimate quarry for the imaginative writer. There is no more reason why he should not make use of them than of the incidents that are told to him in a club smoking-room or at the bar of an hotel. I would go further; I would say that any writer is justified in taking from another whatever can profit him. I have seen scenes on the stage lifted from my own plays and have not turned a hair. It has flattered me that my fellow-dramatists should have studied my work with such care. A little while ago a young man wrote an article called *Down and Out in Marseilles*. It was quite a good article. The publishers of the paper in which it appeared were much concerned when they discovered that it was copied almost word for word from a chapter in *The Moon and Sixpence*. It contained not only the passages I had myself used from Mr Harry Franck's book, but others that I had written from my own observation in the less reputable quarters (now, alas, owing to the economic situation deprived of their garish vivacity) of the ancient city of Marseilles. I calmed the editor's fears (he saw me bringing an action for infringement of copyright) and begged him to congratulate the writer of the article on his ingenuity.

1933   W.M.

Chapter One

I confess that when first I made acquaintance with Charles Strickland I never for a moment discerned that there was in him anything out of the ordinary. Yet now few will be found to deny his greatness. I do not speak of that greatness which is achieved by the fortunate politician or the successful soldier; that is a quality which belongs to the place he occupies rather than to the man; and a change of circumstances reduces it to very discreet proportions. The Prime Minister out of office is seen, too often, to have been but a pompous rhetorician, and the General without an army is but the tame hero of a market town. The greatness of Charles Strickland was authentic. It may be that you do not like his art, but at all events you can hardly refuse it the tribute of your interest. He disturbs and arrests. The time has passed when he was an object of ridicule, and it is no longer a mark of eccentricity to defend or of perversity to extol him. His faults are accepted as the necessary complement to his merits. It is still possible to discuss his place in art, and the adulation of his admirers is perhaps no less capricious than the disparagement of his detractors; but one thing can never be doubtful, and that is that he had genius. To my mind the most interesting thing in art is the personality of the artist; and if that is singular, I am willing to excuse a thousand faults. I suppose Velasquez was a better painter than El Greco, but custom stales one's admiration for him: the Cretan, sensual and tragic, proffers the mystery of his soul like a standing sacrifice. The artist, painter, poet, or musician, by his decoration, sublime or beautiful, satisfies the aesthetic sense; but that is akin to the sexual instinct, and shares its barbarity: he lays before you also the greater gift of himself. To pursue his secret has something of the fascination of a detective story. It is a riddle which shares with the universe the merit of having no answer. The most insignificant of Strickland's works suggests a personality which is strange, tormented, and complex; and it is this surely which prevents even those who do not like his pictures from being indifferent to them; it is this which has excited so curious an interest in his life and character.

It was not till four years after Strickland's death that Maurice Huret wrote that article in the *Mercure de France* which rescued the unknown painter from oblivion and blazed the trail which succeeding writers, with more or less docility, have followed. For a long time no critic has enjoyed in France a more incontestable authority, and it was impossible not to be impressed by the claims he made; they seemed extravagant; but later judgments have confirmed his estimate, and the reputation of Charles Strickland is now firmly established on the lines which he laid down. The rise of this reputation is one of the most romantic incidents in the history of art. But I do not propose to deal with Charles Strickland's work except in so far as it touches upon his character. I cannot agree with the painters who claim superciliously that the layman can understand nothing of painting, and that he can best show his appreciation of their works by silence and a cheque-book. It is a grotesque misapprehension which sees in art no more than a craft comprehensible perfectly only to the craftsman; art is a manifestation of emotion, and emotion speaks a language that all may understand. But I will allow that the critic who has not a practical knowledge of technique is seldom able to say anything on the subject of real value, and my ignorance of painting is extreme. Fortunately, there is no need for me to risk the adventure, since my friend Mr Edward Leggatt, an able writer as well as an admirable painter, has exhaustively discussed Charles Strickland's work in a little book* which is a charming example of a style, for the most part, less happily cultivated in England than in France.

Maurice Huret in his famous article gave an outline of Charles Strickland's life which was well calculated to whet the appetites of the inquiring. With his disinterested passion for art, he had a real desire to call the attention of the wise to a talent which was in the highest degree original; but he was too good a journalist to be unaware that the 'human interest' would enable him more easily to effect his purpose. And when such as had come in contact with Strickland in the past, writers who had known him in London, painters who had met him in the cafés of Montmartre, discovered to their amazement that where they had seen but an unsuccessful artist, like another, authentic genius had rubbed shoulders with them, there began to appear in the magazines of France and America a succession of articles, the reminiscences of one, the appreciation of another, which added to Strickland's notoriety, and fed without satisfying the curiosity of the public. The subject was grateful, and the industrious Weitbrecht-Rotholz in his imposing monograph† has been able to give a remarkable list of authorities.

The faculty for myth is innate in the human race. It seizes with avidity upon any incidents, surprising or mysterious, in the career of those who have at all distinguished themselves from their fellows, and invents a legend to which it then attaches a fanatical belief. It is the protest of romance against the commonplace of life. The incidents of the legend become the hero's surest passport to immortality. The ironic philosopher reflects with a smile that Sir Walter Raleigh is more safely enshrined in the memory of mankind because he set his cloak for the Virgin Queen to walk on than because he carried the English name to undiscovered countries. Charles Strickland lived obscurely. He made enemies rather than friends. It is not strange, then, that those who wrote of him should have eked out their scanty recollections with a lively fancy, and it is evident that there was enough in the little that was known of him to give opportunity to the romantic scribe; there was much in his life which was strange and terrible, in his character something outrageous, and in his fate not a little that was pathetic. In due course a legend arose of such circumstantiality that the wise historian would hesitate to attack it.

But a wise historian is precisely what the Rev. Robert Strickland is not. He wrote his biography‡ avowedly to 'remove certain misconceptions which had gained currency' in regard to the later part of his father's life, and which had 'caused considerable pain to persons still living'. It is obvious that

---

* *A Modern Artist: Notes on the Work of Charles Strickland*, by Edward Leggatt, A.R.H.A. Martin Secker, 1917.

† *Karl Strickland: sein Leben und seine Kunst*, by Hugo Weitbrecht-Rotholz, Ph.D. Schwingel und Hanisch. Leipzig, 1914.

‡ *Strickland: The Man and His Work*, by his son, Robert Strickland. Wm. Heinemann, 1913.

there was much in the commonly received account of Strickland's life to embarrass a respectable family. I have read this work with a good deal of amusement, and upon this I congratulate myself, since it is colourless and dull. Mr Strickland has drawn the portrait of an excellent husband and father, a man of kindly temper, industrious habits, and moral disposition. The modern clergyman has acquired in his study of the science which I believe is called exegesis as astonishing facility for explaining things away, but the subtlety with which the Rev. Robert Strickland has 'interpreted' all the facts in his father's life which a dutiful son might find it inconvenient to remember must surely lead him in the fullness of time to the highest dignities of the Church. I see already his muscular calves encased in the gaiters episcopal. It was a hazardous, though maybe a gallant thing to do, since it is probable that the legend commonly received had had no small share in the growth of Strickland's reputation; for there are many who have been attracted to his art by the detestation in which they held his character or the compassion with which they regarded his death; and the son's well-meaning efforts threw a singular chill upon the father's admirers. It is due to no accident that when one of his most important works, <i>The Woman of Samaria</i>,* was sold at Christie's shortly after the discussion which followed the publication of Mr Strickland's biography, it fetched £235 less than it had done nine months before, when it was bought by the distinguished collector whose sudden death had brought it once more under the hammer. Perhaps Charles Strickland's power and originality would scarcely have sufficed to turn the scale if the remarkable mythopoeic faculty of mankind had not brushed aside with impatience a story which disappointed all its craving for the extraordinary. And presently Dr Weitbrecht-Rotholz produced the work which finally set at rest the misgivings of all lovers of art.

Dr Weitbrecht-Rotholz belongs to that school of historians which believes that human nature is not only about as bad as it can be, but a great deal worse; and certainly the reader is safer of entertainment in their hands than in those of the writers who take a malicious pleasure in representing the great figures of romance as patterns of the domestic virtues. For my part, I should be sorry to think that there was nothing between Antony and Cleopatra but an economic situation; and it will require a great deal more evidence than is ever likely to be available, thank God, to persuade me that Tiberius was as blameless a monarch as King George V. Dr Weitbrecht-Rotholz has dealt in such terms with the Rev. Robert Strickland's innocent biography that it is difficult to avoid feeling a certain sympathy for the unlucky parson. His decent reticence is branded as hypocrisy, his circumlocutions are roundly called lies, and his silence is vilified as treachery. And on the strength of peccadillos, reprehensible in an author but excusable in a son, the Anglo-Saxon race is accused of prudishness, humbug, pretentiousness, deceit, cunning, and bad cooking. Personally I think it was rash of Mr Strickland, in refuting the account which had gained belief of a certain 'unpleasantness' between his father and mother, to state that Charles Strickland in a letter written from Paris had described her as 'an excellent woman', since Dr Weitbrecht-Rotholz was able to print the letter in facsimile, and it appears that the passage referred to ran in fact as follows: <i>God damn my wife. She is an excellent woman. I wish she was in hell.</i> It is not

* This was described in Christie's catalogue as follows: 'A nude woman, a native of the Society Islands, is lying on the ground beside a brook. Behind is a tropical landscape with palm-trees, bananas, etc. 60 in. × 48 in.'

thus that the Church in its great days dealt with evidence that was unwelcome.

Dr Weitbrecht-Rotholz was an enthusiastic admirer of Charles Strickland, and there was no danger that he would whitewash him. He had an unerring eye for the despicable motive in actions that had all the appearance of innocence. He was a psycho-pathologist as well as a student of art, and the subconscious had few secrets from him. No mystic ever saw deeper meaning in common things. The mystic sees the ineffable and the psycho-pathologist the unspeakable. There is a singular fascination in watching the eagerness with which the learned author ferrets out every circumstance which may throw discredit on his hero. His heart warms to him when he can bring forward some example of cruelty or meanness, and he exults like an inquisitor at the *auto-da-fé* of an heretic when with some forgotten story he can confound the filial piety of the Rev. Robert Strickland. His industry has been amazing. Nothing has been too small to escape him, and you may be sure that if Charles Strickland left a laundry bill unpaid it will be given you *in extenso*, and if he forbore to return a borrowed half-crown no detail of the transaction will be omitted.

Chapter Two

When so much has been written about Charles Strickland, it may seem unnecessary that I should write more. A painter's monument is his work. It is true I knew him more intimately than most: I met him first before ever he became a painter, and I saw him not infrequently during the different years he spent in Paris; but I do not suppose I should ever have set down my recollections if the hazards of the war had not taken me to Tahiti. There, as is notorious, he spent the last years of his life; and there I came across persons who were familiar with him. I find myself in a position to throw light on just that part of his tragic career which has remained most obscure. If they who believe in Strickland's greatness are right, the personal narratives of such as knew him in the flesh can hardly be superfluous. What would we not give for the reminiscences of someone who has been as intimately acquainted with El Greco as I was with Strickland?

But I seek refuge in no such excuses. I forget who it was that recommended men for their soul's good to do each day two things they disliked: it was a wise man, and it is a precept that I have followed scrupulously; for every day I have got up and I have gone to bed. But there is in my nature a strain of asceticism, and I have subjected my flesh each week to a more severe mortification. I have never failed to read the Literary Supplement of *The Times*. It is a salutary discipline to consider the vast number of books that are written, the fair hopes with which their authors see them published, and the fate which awaits them. What chance is there that any book will make its way among that multitude? And the successful books are but the successes of a season. Heaven knows what pains the author has been at, what bitter experiences he has endured and what heartache suffered, to give some chance reader a few hours' relaxation or to while away the tedium of a journey. And if I may judge from the reviews, many of these books are well and carefully written; much thought has gone to their composition; to some even has been given the anxious labour of a lifetime. The moral I draw is that the writer should seek his reward in the pleasure of his work and in release from the burden of his thought; and, indifferent to aught else, care nothing for praise or censure, failure or success.

Now the war has come, bringing with it a new attitude. Youth has turned to gods we of an earlier day knew not, and it is possible to see already the direction in which those who come after us will move. The younger generation, conscious of strength and tumultuous, have done with knocking at the door; they have burst in and seated themselves in our seats. The air is noisy with their shouts. Of their elders some, by imitating the antics of youth, strive to persuade themselves that their day is not yet over; they shout with the lustiest, but the war-cry sounds hollow in their mouth; they are like poor wantons attempting with pencil, paint and powder, with shrill gaiety, to recover the illusion of their spring. The wiser go their way with a decent grace. In their chastened smile is an indulgent mockery. They remember that they too trod down a sated generation, with just such clamour and with just such scorn, and they foresee that these brave torch-bearers will presently yield their place also. There is no last word. The new evangel was old when Nineveh reared her greatness to the sky. These gallant words which seemed so novel to those that speak them were said in accents scarcely changed a hundred times before. The pendulum swings backwards and forwards. The circle is ever travelled anew.

Sometimes a man survives a considerable time from an era in which he had his place into one which is strange to him, and then the curious are offered one of the most singular spectacles in the human comedy. Who now, for example, thinks of George Crabbe? He was a famous poet in his day, and the world recognised his genius with a unanimity which the greater complexity of modern life has rendered infrequent. He had learned his craft at the school of Alexander Pope, and he wrote moral stories in rhymed couplets. Then came the French Revolution and the Napoleonic Wars, and the poets sang new songs. Mr Crabbe continued to write moral stories in rhymed couplets. I think he must have read the verse of these young men who were making so great a stir in the world, and I fancy he found it poor stuff. Of course, much of it was. But the odes of Keats and of Wordsworth, a poem or two by Coleridge, a few more by Shelley, discovered vast realms of the spirit that none had explored before. Mr Crabbe was as dead as mutton, but Mr Crabbe continued to write moral stories in rhymed couplets. I have read desultorily the writings of the younger generation. It may be that among them a more fervid Keats, a more ethereal Shelley, has already published numbers the world will willingly remember. I cannot tell. I admire their polish—their youth is already so accomplished that it seems absurd to speak of promise—I marvel at the felicity of their style; but with all their copiousness (their vocabulary suggests that they fingered Roget's *Thesaurus* in their cradles) they say nothing to me; to my mind they know too much and feel too obviously; I cannot stomach the heartiness with which they slap me on the back or the emotion with which they hurl themselves on my bosom; their passion seems to me a little anaemic and their dreams a trifle dull. I do not like them. I am on the shelf. I will continue to write moral stories in rhymed couplets. But I should be thrice a fool if I did it for aught but my own entertainment.

Chapter Three

But all this is by the way.

I was very young when I wrote my first book. By a lucky chance it excited attention, and various persons sought my acquaintance.

It is not without melancholy that I wander among my recollections of the world of letters in London when first, bashful but eager, I was introduced to it. It is long since I frequented it, and if the novels that describe its present singularities are accurate, much in it is now changed. The venue is different. Chelsea and Bloomsbury have taken the place of Hampstead, Notting Hill Gate, and High Street, Kensington. Then it was a distinction to be under forty, but now to be more than twenty-five is absurd. I think in those days we were a littly shy of our emotions, and the fear of ridicule tempered the more obvious forms of pretentiousness. I do not believe that there was in that genteel Bohemia an intensive culture of chastity, but I do not remember so crude a promiscuity as seems to be practised in the present day. We did not think it hypocritical to draw over our vagaries the curtain of a decent silence. The spade was not invariably called a bloody shovel. Woman had not yet altogether come into her own.

I lived near Victoria Station, and I recall long excursions by bus to the hospitable houses of the literary. In my timidity I wandered up and down the street while I screwed up my courage to ring the bell; and then, sick with apprehension, was ushered into an airless room full of people. I was introduced to this celebrated person after that one, and the kind words they said about my book made me excessively uncomfortable. I felt they expected me to say clever things, and I never could think of any till after the party was over. I tried to conceal my embarrassment by handing round cups of tea and rather ill-cut bread-and-butter. I wanted no one to take notice of me, so that I could observe these famous creatures at my ease and listen to the clever things they said.

I have a recollection of large, unbending women with great noses and rapacious eyes, who wore their clothes as though they were armour; and of little, mouse-like spinsters, with soft voices and a shrewd glance. I never ceased to be fascinated by their persistence in eating buttered toast with their gloves on, and I observed with admiration the unconcern with which they wiped their fingers on their chair when they thought no one was looking. It must have been bad for the furniture, but I suppose the hostess took her revenge on the furniture of her friends when, in turn, she visited them. Some of them were dressed fashionably, and they said they couldn't for the life of them see why you should be dowdy just because you had written a novel; if you had a neat figure you might as well make the most of it, and a smart shoe on a small foot had never prevented an editor from taking your 'stuff'. But others thought this frivolous, and they wore 'art fabrics' and barbaric jewellery. The men were seldom eccentric in appearance. They tried to look as little like authors as possible. They wished to be taken for men of the world, and could have passed anywhere for the managing clerks of a city firm. They always seemed a little tired. I had never known writers before, and I found them very strange, but I do not think they ever seemed to me quite real.

I remember that I thought their conversation brilliant, and I used to listen with astonishment to the stinging humour with which they would tear a brother-author to pieces the moment that his back was turned. The artist has this advantage over the rest of the world, that his friends offer not only their appearance and their character to his satire, but also their work. I despaired of ever expressing myself with such aptness or with such fluency. In those days coversation was still cultivated as an art; a neat repartee was more highly valued than the crackling of thorns under a pot; and the epigram, not yet a mechanical appliance by which the dull may achieve a semblance of wit, gave sprightliness to the small talk of the urbane. It is sad that I can remember nothing of all this scintillation. But I think the conversation never settled down so comfortably as when it turned to the details of the trade which was the other side of the art we practised. When we had done discussing the merits of the latest book, it was natural to wonder how many copies had been sold, what advance the author had received, and how much he was likely to make out of it. Then we would speak of this publisher and of that, comparing the generosity of one with the meanness of another; we would argue whether it was better to go to one who gave handsome royalties or to another who 'pushed' a book for all it was worth. Some advertised badly and some well. Some were modern and some were old-fashioned. Then we would talk of agents and the offers they had obtained for us; of editors and the sort of contributions they welcomed, how much they paid a thousand, and whether they paid promptly or otherwise. To me it was all very romantic. It gave me an intimate sense of being a member of some mystic brotherhood.

Chapter Four

No one was kinder to me at that time than Rose Waterford. She combined a masculine intelligence with a feminine perversity, and the novels she wrote were original and disconcerting. It was at her house one day that I met Charles Strickland's wife. Miss Waterford was giving a tea-party, and her small room was more than usually full. Everyone seemed to be talking, and I, sitting in silence, felt awkward; but I was too shy to break into any of the groups that seemed absorbed in their own affairs. Miss Waterford was a good hostess, and seeing my embarrassment came up to me.

'I want you to talk to Mrs Strickland,' she said. 'She's raving about your book.'

'What does she do?' I asked.

I was conscious of my ignorance, and if Mrs Strickland was a well-known writer I thought it as well to ascertain the fact before I spoke to her.

Rose Waterford cast down her eyes demurely to give greater effect to her reply.

'She gives luncheon-parties. You've only got to roar a little, and she'll ask you.'

Rose Waterford was a cynic. She looked upon life as an opportunity for writing novels and the public as her raw material. Now and then she invited members of it to her house if they showed an appreciation of her talent and entertained with proper lavishness. She held their weakness for lions in good-humoured contempt, but played to them her part of the distinguished woman of letters with decorum.

I was led up to Mrs Strickland, and for ten minutes we talked together. I noticed nothing about her except that she had a pleasant voice. She had a flat in Westminster, overlooking the unfinished cathedral, and because we lived in the same neighbourhood we felt friendly disposed to one another. The Army and Navy Stores are a bond of union between all who dwell between the river and St James's Park. Mrs Strickland asked me for my address, and a few days later I received an invitation to luncheon.

My engagements were few, and I was glad to accept. When I arrived, a little late, because in my fear of being too early I had walked three times round the cathedral, I found the party already complete. Miss Waterford was there and Mrs Jay, Richard Twining and George Road. We were all writers. It was a fine day, early in spring, and we were in good humour. We talked about a hundred things. Miss Waterford, torn between the æstheticism of her early youth, when she used to go to parties in sage green, holding a daffodil, and the flippancy of her maturer years, which tended to high heels and Paris frocks, wore a new hat. It put her in high spirits. I had never heard her more malicious about our common friends. Mrs Jay, aware that impropriety is the soul of wit, made observations in tones hardly above a whisper that might well have tinged the snowy tablecloth with a rosy hue. Richard Twining bubbled over with quaint absurdities, and George Road, conscious that he need not exhibit a brilliancy which was almost a byword, opened his mouth only to put food into it. Mrs Strickland did not talk much, but she had a pleasant gift for keeping the conversation general; and when there was a pause she threw in just the right remark to set it going once more. She was a woman of thirty-seven, rather tall, and plump, without being fat; she was not pretty, but her face was pleasing, chiefly, perhaps, on account of her kind brown eyes. Her skin was rather sallow. Her dark hair was elaborately dressed. She was the only woman of the three whose face was free of make-up, and by contrast with the others she seemed simple and unaffected.

The dining-room was in the good taste of the period. It was very severe. There was a high dado of white wood and a green paper on which were etchings by Whistler in neat black frames. The green curtains with their peacock design, hung in straight lines, and the green carpet, in the pattern of which pale rabbits frolicked among leafy trees, suggested the influence of William Morris. There was blue delf on the chimney-piece. At that time there must have been five hundred dining-rooms in London decorated in exactly the same manner. It was chaste, artistic, and dull.

When we left I walked away with Miss Waterford, and the fine day and her new hat persuaded us to saunter through the Park.

'That was a very nice party,' I said.

'Did you think the food was good? I told her that if she wanted writers she must feed them well.'

'Admirable advice,' I answered. 'But why does she want them?'

Miss Waterford shrugged her shoulders.

'She finds them amusing. She wants to be in the movement. I fancy she's rather simple, poor dear, and she thinks we're all wonderful. After all, it pleases her to ask us to luncheon, and it doesn't hurt us. I like her for it.'

Looking back, I think that Mrs Strickland was the most harmless of all the lion-hunters that pursue their quarry from the rarefied heights of Hampstead to the nethermost studies of Cheyne Walk. She had led a very quiet youth in the country, and the books that came down from Mudie's Library brought with them not only their own romance, but the romance of London. She had a real passion for reading (rare in her kind, who for the most part are more interested in the author than in his book, in the painter than in his pictures), and she invented a world of the imagination in which she lived with a freedom she never acquired in the world of every day. When she came to know writers it was like adventuring upon a stage which till then she had only known from the other side of the footlights. She saw them dramatically, and really seemed herself to live a larger life because she entertained them and visited them in their fastnesses. She accepted the rules with which they played the game of life as valid for them, but never for a moment thought of regulating her own conduct in accordance with them. Their moral eccentricities, like their oddities of dress, their wild theories and paradoxes, were an entertainment which amused her, but had not the slightest influence on her convictions.

'Is there a Mr Strickland?' I asked.

'Oh yes; he's something in the city. I believe he's a stockbroker. He's very dull.'

'Are they good friends?'

'They adore one another. You'll meet him if you dine there. But she doesn't often have people to dinner. He's very quiet. He's not in the least interested in literature or the arts.'

'Why do nice women marry dull men?'

'Because intelligent men won't marry nice women.'

I could not think of any retort to this, so I asked if Mrs Strickland had children.

'Yes; she has a boy and a girl. They're both at school.'

The subject was exhausted, and we began to talk of other things.

Chapter Five

During the summer I met Mrs Strickland not infrequently. I went now and then to pleasant little luncheons at her flat, and to rather more formidable tea-parties. We took a fancy to one another. I was very young, and perhaps she liked the idea of guiding my virgin steps on the hard road of letters; while for me it was pleasant to have someone I could go to with my small troubles, certain of an attentive ear and reasonable counsel. Mrs Strickland had the gift of sympathy. It is a charming faculty, but one often abused by those who are conscious of its possession: for there is something ghoulish in the avidity with which they will pounce upon the misfortune of their friends so that they may exercise their dexterity. It gushes forth like an oil-well, and the sympathetic pour out their sympathy with an abandon that is sometimes embarrassing to their victims. There are bosoms on which so many tears have been shed that I cannot bedew them with mine. Mrs Strickland used her advantage with tact. You felt that you obliged her by accepting her sympathy. When, in the enthusiasm of my youth, I remarked on this to Rose Waterford, she said:

'Milk is very nice, especially with a drop of brandy in it, but the domestic cow is only too glad to be rid of it. A swollen udder is very uncomfortable.'

Rose Waterford had a blistering tongue. No one could say such bitter things; on the other hand, no one could do more charming ones.

There was another thing I liked in Mrs Strickland. She managed her surroundings with elegance. Her flat was always neat and cheerful, gay with flowers, and the chintzes in the drawing-room, notwithstanding their severe design, were bright and pretty. The meals in the artistic little dining-room were pleasant; the table looked nice, the two maids were trim and comely, the food was well cooked. It was impossible not to see that Mrs Strickland was an excellent housekeeper. And you felt sure that she was an admirable mother. There were photographs in the drawing-room of her son and daughter. The son—his name was Robert—was a boy of sixteen at Rugby; and you saw him in flannels and a cricket cap, and again in a tail-coat and a stand-up collar. He had his mother's candid brow and fine, reflective eyes. He looked clean, healthy, and normal.

'I don't know that he's very clever,' she said one day, when I was looking at the photograph, 'but I know he's good. He has a charming character.'

The daughter was fourteen. Her hair, thick and dark like her mother's, fell over her shoulders in fine profusion, and she had the same kindly expression and sedate, untroubled eyes.

'They're both of them the image of you,' I said.

'Yes; I think they are more like me than their father.'

'Why have you never let me meet him?' I asked.

'Would you like to?'

She smiled, her smile was really very sweet, and she blushed a little; it was singular that a woman of that age should flush so readily. Perhaps her naïveté was her greatest charm.

'You know, he's not at all literary,' she said. 'He's a perfect philistine.'

She said this not disparagingly, but affectionately rather, as though, by acknowledging the worst about him, she wished to protect him from the aspersions of her friends.

'He's on the Stock Exchange, and he's a typical broker. I think he'd bore you to death.'

'Does he bore you?' I asked.

'You see, I happen to be his wife. I'm very fond of him.'

She smiled to cover her shyness, and I fancied she had a fear that I would make the sort of gibe that such a confession could hardly have failed to elicit from Rose Waterford. She hesitated a little. Her eyes grew tender.

'He doesn't pretend to be a genius. He doesn't even make much money on the Stock Exchange. But he's awfully good and kind.'

'I think I should like him very much.'

'I'll ask you to dine with us quietly some time, but mind, you come at your own risk; don't blame me if you have a very dull evening.'

Chapter Six

But when at last I met Charles Strickland, it was under circumstances which allowed me to do no more than just make his acquaintance. One morning Mrs Strickland sent me round a note to say that she was giving a dinner-party that evening, and one of her guests had failed her. She asked me to stop the gap. She wrote:

> It's only decent to warn you that you will be bored to extinction. It was a thoroughly dull party from the beginning, but if you will come I shall be uncommonly grateful. And you and I can have a little chat by ourselves.

It was only neighbourly to accept.

When Mrs Strickland introduced me to her husband, he gave me a rather indifferent hand to shake. Turning to him gaily, she attempted a small jest.

'I asked him to show him that I really had a husband. I think he was beginning to doubt it.'

Strickland gave the polite little laugh with which people acknowledge a facetiousness in which they see nothing funny, but did not speak. New arrivals claimed my host's attention, and I was left to myself. When at last we were all assembled, waiting for dinner to be announced, I reflected, while I chatted with the woman I had been asked to 'take in', that civilised man practises a strange ingenuity in wasting on tedious exercises the brief span of his life. It was the kind of party which makes you wonder why the hostess has troubled to bid her guests, and why the guests have troubled to come. There were ten people. They met with indifference, and would part with relief. It was, of course, a purely social function. The Stricklands 'owed' dinners to a number of persons, whom they took no interest in, and so had asked them; these persons had accepted. Why? To avoid the tedium of dining *tête-à-tête*, to give their servants a rest, because there was no reason to refuse, because they were 'owed' a dinner.

The dining-room was inconveniently crowded. There was a K.C. and his wife, a Government official and his wife, Mrs Strickland's sister and her husband, Colonel MacAndrew, and the wife of a Member of Parliament. It was because the Member of Parliament found that he could not leave the House that I had been invited. The respectability of the party was portentous. The women were too nice to be well dressed, and too sure of their position to be amusing. The men were solid. There was about all of them an air of well-satisfied prosperity.

Everyone talked a little louder than natural in an instinctive desire to make the party go, and there was a great deal of noise in the room. But there was no general conversation. Each one talked to his neighbour; to his neighbour on the right during the soup, fish and entrée; to his neighbour on the left during the roast, sweet, and savoury. They talked of the political situation and of golf, of their children and the latest play, of the pictures at the Royal

Academy, of the weather and their plans for the holidays. There was never a pause, and the noise grew louder. Mrs Strickland might congratulate herself that her party was a success. Her husband played his part with decorum. Perhaps he did not talk very much, and I fancied there was towards the end a look of fatigue in the faces of the women on either side of him. They were finding him too heavy. Once or twice Mrs Strickland's eyes rested on him somewhat anxiously.

At last she rose and shepherded the ladies out of the room. Strickland shut the door behind her, and, moving to the other end of the table, took his place between the K.C. and the Government official. He passed round the port again and handed us cigars. The K.C. remarked on the excellence of the wine, and Strickland told us where he got it. We began to chat about vintages and tobacco. The K.C. told us of a case he was engaged in, and the Colonel talked about polo. I had nothing to say and so sat silent, trying politely to show interest in the conversation; and because I thought no one was in the least concerned with me, examined Strickland at my ease. He was bigger than I expected: I do not know why I had imagined him slender and of insignificant appearance; in point of fact, he was broad and heavy, with large hands and feet, and he wore his evening clothes clumsily. He gave you somewhat the idea of a coachman dressed up for the occasion. He was a man of forty, not good-looking, and yet not ugly, for his features were rather good; but they were all a little larger than life-size, and the effect was ungainly. He was clean-shaven, and his large face looked uncomfortably naked. His hair was reddish, cut very short, and his eyes were small, blue or grey. He looked commonplace. I no longer wondered that Mrs Strickland felt a certain embarrassment about him; he was scarcely a credit to a woman who wanted to make herself a position in the world of art and letters. It was obvious that he had no social gifts, but these a man can do without; he had no eccentricity even, to take him out of the common run; he was just a good, dull, honest, plain man. One would admire his excellent qualities but avoid his company. He was null. He was probably a worthy member of society, a good husband and father, an honest broker; but there was no reason to waste one's time over him.

Chapter Seven

The season was drawing to its dusty end, and everyone I knew was arranging to go away. Mrs Strickland was taking her family to the coast of Norfolk, so that the children might have the sea and her husband golf. We said good-bye to one another, and arranged to meet in the autumn. But on my last day in town, coming out of the Stores, I met her with her son and daughter; like myself, she had been making her final purchases before leaving London, and we were both hot and tired. I proposed that we should all go and eat ices in the Park.

I think Mrs Strickland was glad to show me her children, and she accepted my invitation with alacrity. They were even more attractive than their photographs had suggested, and she was right to be proud of them. I was young enough for them not to feel shy, and they chattered merrily about one thing and another. They were extraordinarily nice, healthy young children. It was very agreeable under the trees.

When in an hour they crowded into a cab to go home, I strolled idly to my club. I was perhaps a little lonely, and it was with a touch of envy that I thought of the pleasant family life of which I had had a glimpse. They seemed devoted to one another. They had little private jokes of their own which, unintelligible to the outsider, amused them enormously. Perhaps Charles Strickland was dull, judged by a standard that demanded above all things verbal scintillation; but his intelligence was adequate to his surroundings, and that is a passport, not only to reasonable success, but still more to happiness. Mrs Strickland was a charming woman, and she loved him. I pictured their lives, troubled by no untoward adventure, honest, decent, and, by reason of those two upstanding, pleasant children, so obviously destined to carry on the normal traditions of their race and station, not without significance. They would grow old insensibly; they would see their son and daughter come to years of reason, marry in due course–the one a pretty girl, future mother of healthy children; the other a handsome, manly fellow, obviously a soldier; and, at last, prosperous in their dignified retirement, beloved by their descendants, after a happy, not unuseful life, in the fullness of their age they would sink into the grave.

That must be the story of innumerable couples, and the pattern of life it offers has a homely grace. It reminds you of a placid rivulet, meandering smoothly through green pastures and shaded by pleasant trees, till at last it falls into the vasty sea; but the sea is so calm, so silent, so indifferent, that you are troubled suddenly by a vague uneasiness. Perhaps it is only a kink in my nature, strong in me even in those days, that I felt in such an existence, the share of the great majority, something amiss. I recognised its social value, I saw its ordered happiness, but a fever in my blood asked for a wilder course. There seemed to me something alarming in such easy delights. In my heart was a desire to live more dangerously. I was not unprepared for jagged rocks and treacherous shoals if I could only have change–change and the excitement of the unforeseen.

Chapter Eight

On reading over what I have written of the Stricklands, I am conscious that they must seem shadowy. I have been able to invest them with none of those characteristics which make the persons of a book exist with a real life of their own; and, wondering if the fault is mine, I rack my brains to remember idiosyncrasies which might lend them vividness. I feel that by dwelling on some trick of speech or some queer habit I should be able to give them a significance peculiar to themselves. As they stand they are like the figures in an old tapestry; they do not separate themselves from the background, and at a distance seem to lose their pattern, so that you have little but a pleasing piece of colour. My only excuse is that the impression they made on me was no other. There was just that shadowiness about them which you find in people whose lives are part of the social organism, so that they exist in it and by it only. They are like cells in the body, essential, but, so long as they remain healthy, engulfed in the momentous whole. The Stricklands were an average family in the middle class. A pleasant, hospitable woman, with a harmless craze for the small lions of literary society; a rather dull man, doing his duty in that state of life in which a merciful Providence had placed him; two nice-looking, healthy children. Nothing could be more ordinary. I do not know that there was anything about them to excite the attention of the curious.

When I reflect on all that happened later, I ask myself if I was thick-witted not to see that there was in Charles Strickland at least something out of the common. Perhaps. I think I have gathered in the years that intervene between then and now a fair knowledge of mankind, but even if when I first met the Stricklands I had the experience which I have now, I do not believe that I should have judged them differently. But because I have learnt that man is incalculable, I should not at this time of day be so surprised by the news that reached me when in the early autumn I returned to London.

I had not been back twenty-four hours before I ran across Rose Waterford in Jermyn Street.

'You look very gay and sprightly,' I said. 'What's the matter with you?'

She smiled, and her eyes shone with a malice I knew already. It meant that she had heard some scandal about one of her friends, and the instinct of the literary woman was all alert.

'You did meet Charles Strickland, didn't you?'

Not only her face, but her whole body, gave a sense of alacrity. I nodded. I wondered if the poor devil had been hammered on the Stock Exchange or run over by an omnibus.

'Isn't it dreadful? He's run away from his wife.'

Miss Waterford certainly felt that she could not do her subject justice on the kerb of Jermyn Street, and so, like an artist, flung the bare fact at me and declared that she knew no details. I could not do her the injustice of supposing that so trifling a circumstance would have prevented her from giving them, but she was obstinate.

'I tell you I know nothing,' she said, in reply to my agitated questions, and then, with an airy shrug of the shoulders: 'I believe that a young person in a City teashop has left her situation.'

She flashed a smile at me, and, protesting an engagement with her dentist, jauntily walked on. I was more interested than distressed. In those days my experience of life at first hand was small, and it excited me to come upon an incident among people I knew of the same sort as I had read in books. I confess that time has now accustomed me to incidents of this character among my acquaintance. But I was also a little shocked. Strickland was certainly forty, and I thought it disgusting that a man of his age should concern himself with affairs of the heart. With the superciliousness of extreme youth, I put thirty-five as the utmost limit at which a man might fall in love without making a fool of himself. And this news was slightly disconcerting to me personally, because I had written from the country to Mrs Strickland, announcing my return, and had added that unless I heard from her to the contrary, I would come on a certain day to drink a dish of tea with her. This was the very day, and I had received no word from Mrs Strickland. Did she want to see me or did she not? It was likely enough that in the agitation of the moment my note has escaped her memory. Perhaps I should be wiser not to go. On the other hand, she might wish to keep the affair quiet, and it might be highly indiscreet on my part to give any sign that this strange news had reached me. I was torn between the fear of hurting a nice woman's feelings and the fear of being in the way. I felt she must be suffering, and I did not want to see a pain which I could not help; but in my heart was a desire, that I felt a little ashamed of, to see how she was taking it. I did not know what to do.

Finally it occurred to me that I would call as though nothing had happened, and send a message in by the maid asking Mrs Strickland if it was convenient for her to see me. This would give her the opportunity to send me away. But I was overwhelmed with embarrassment when I said to the maid the phrase I had prepared, and while I waited for the answer in a dark passage I had to call up all my strength of mind not to bolt. The maid came back. Her manner suggested to my excited fancy a complete knowledge of the domestic calamity.

'Will you come this way, sir?' she said.

I followed her into the drawing-room. The blinds were partly drawn to darken the room, and Mrs Strickland was sitting with her back to the light. Her brother-in-law, Colonel MacAndrew, stood in front of the fireplace, warming his back at an unlit fire. To myself my entrance seemed excessively awkward. I imagined that my arrival had taken them by surprise, and Mrs Strickland had let me come in only because she had forgotten to put me off. I fancied that the Colonel resented the interruption.

'I wasn't quite sure if you expected me,' I said, trying to seem unconcerned.

'Of course I did. Anne will bring the tea in a minute.'

Even in the darkened room, I could not help seeing that Mrs Strickland's face was all swollen with tears. Her skin, never very good, was earthy.

'You remember my brother-in-law, don't you? You met at dinner here, just before the holidays.'

We shook hands. I felt so shy that I could think of nothing to say, but Mrs Strickland came to my rescue. She asked me what I had been doing with myself during the summer, and with this help I managed to make some conversation till tea was brought in. The Colonel asked for a whisky-and-soda.

'You'd better have one too, Amy,' he said.

'No; I prefer tea.'

This was the first suggestion that anything untoward had happened. I took no notice, and did my best to engage Mrs Strickland in talk. The Colonel, still standing in front of the fireplace, uttered no word. I wondered how soon I could decently take my leave, and I asked myself why on earth Mrs Strickland had allowed me to come. There were no flowers, and various knick-knacks, put away during the summer, had not been replaced; there was something cheerless and stiff about the room which had always seemed so friendly; it gave you an odd feeling, as though someone were lying dead on the other side of the wall. I finished tea.

'Will you have a cigarette?' asked Mrs Strickland.

She looked about for the box, but it was not to be seen.

'I'm afraid there are none.'

Suddenly she burst into tears, and hurried from the room.

I was startled. I suppose now that the lack of cigarettes, brought as a rule by her husband, forced him back upon her recollection, and the new feeling that the small comforts she was used to were missing gave her a sudden pang. She realised that the old life was gone and done with. It was impossible to keep up our social pretences any longer.

'I dare say you'd like me to go,' I said to the Colonel, getting up.

'I suppose you've heard that blackguard has deserted her,' he cried explosively.

I hesitated.

'You know how people gossip,' I answered. 'I was vaguely told that something was wrong.'

'He's bolted. He's gone off to Paris with a woman. He's left Amy without a penny.'

'I'm awfully sorry,' I said, not knowing what else to say.

The Colonel gulped down his whisky. He was a tall, lean man of fifty, with a drooping moustache and grey hair. He had pale blue eyes and a weak mouth. I remembered from my previous meeting with him that he had a foolish face, and was proud of the fact that for ten years before he left the army he had played polo three days a week.

'I don't suppose Mrs Strickland wants to be bothered with me just now,' I said. 'Will you tell her how sorry I am? If there's anything I can do, I shall be delighted to do it.'

He took no notice of me.

'I don't know what's to become of her. And then there are the children. Are they going to live on air? Seventeen years.'

'What about seventeen years?'

'They've been married,' he snapped. 'I never liked him. Of course he was my brother-in-law, and I made the best of it. Did you think him a gentleman? She ought never to have married him.'

'Is it absolutely final?'

'There's only one thing for her to do, and that's to divorce him. That's what I was telling her when you came in. "Fire in with your petition, my dear Amy," I said. "You owe it to yourself and you owe it to the children." He'd better not let me catch sight of him. I'd thrash him within an inch of his life.'

I could not help thinking that Colonel MacAndrew might have some difficulty in doing this, since Strickland had struck me as a hefty fellow, but I did not say anything. It is always distressing when outraged morality does not possess the strength of arm to administer direct chastisement on the sinner. I was making up my mind to another attempt at going when Mrs Strickland came back. She had dried her eyes and powdered her nose.

'I'm sorry I broke down,' she said. 'I'm glad you didn't go away.'

She sat down. I did not at all know what to say. I felt a certain shyness at referring to matters which were no concern of mine. I did not then know the besetting sin of woman, the passion to discuss her private affairs with anyone who is willing to listen. Mrs Strickland seemed to make an effort over herself.

'Are people talking about it?' she asked.

I was taken aback by her assumption that I knew all about her domestic misfortune.

'I've only just come back. The only person I've seen is Rose Waterford.'

Mrs Strickland clasped her hands.

'Tell me exactly what she said.' And when I hesitated, she insisted. 'I particularly want to know.'

'You know the way people talk. She's not very reliable, is she? She said your husband had left you.'

'Is that all?'

I did not choose to repeat Rose Waterford's parting reference to a girl from a tea-shop. I lied.

'She didn't say anything about his going with anyone?'

'No.'

'That's all I wanted to know.'

I was a little puzzled, but at all events I understood that I might now take my leave. When I shook hands with Mrs Strickland I told her that if I could be of any use to her I should be very glad. She smiled wanly.

'Thank you so much. I don't know that anybody can do anything for me.'

Too shy to express my sympathy, I turned to say goodbye to the colonel. He did not take my hand.

'I'm just coming. If you're walking up Victoria Street, I'll come along with you.'

'All right,' I said. 'Come on.'

Chapter Nine

'This is a terrible thing,' he said, the moment we got out into the street.

I realised that he had come away with me in order to discuss once more what he had been already discussing for hours with his sister-in-law.

'We don't know who the woman is, you know,' he said. 'All we know is that the blackguard's gone to Paris.'

'I thought they got on so well.'

'So they did. Why, just before you came in Amy said they'd never had a quarrel in the whole of their married life. You know Amy. There never was a better woman in the world.'

Since these confidences were thrust on me, I saw no harm in asking a few questions.

'But do you mean to say she suspected nothing?'

'Nothing. He spent August with her and the children in Norfolk. He was just the same as he'd always been. We went down for two or three days, my wife and I, and I played golf with them. He came back to town in September to let his partner go away, and Amy stayed on in the country. They'd taken a house for six weeks, and at the end of her tenancy she wrote to tell him on which day she was arriving in London. He answered from Paris. He said he'd made up his mind not to live with her any more.'

'What explanation did he give?'

'My dear fellow, he gave no explanation. I've seen the letter. It wasn't more than ten lines.'

'But that's extraordinary.'

We happened then to cross the street, and the traffic prevented us from speaking. What Colonel MacAndrew had told me seemed very improbable, and I suspected that Mrs Strickland, for reasons of her own, had concealed from him some part of the facts. It was clear that a man after seventeen years of wedlock did not leave his wife without certain occurrences which must have led her to suspect that all was not well with their married life. The Colonel caught me up.

'Of course, there was no explanation he could give except that he'd gone off with a woman. I suppose he thought she could find that out for herself. That's the sort of chap he was.'

'What is Mrs Strickland going to do?'

'Well, the first thing is to get our proofs. I'm going over to Paris myself.'

'And what about his business?'

'That's where he's been so artful. He's been drawing in his horns for the last year.'

'Did he tell his partner he was leaving?'

'Not a word.'

Colonel MacAndrew had a very sketchy knowledge of business matters, and I had none at all, so I did not quite understand under what conditions Strickland had left his affairs. I gathered that the deserted partner was very angry and threatened proceedings. It appeared that when everything was settled he would be four or five hundred pounds out of pocket.

'It's lucky the furniture in the flat is in Amy's name. She'll have that at all events.'

'Did you mean it when you said she wouldn't have a bob?'

'Of course I did. She's got two or three hundred pounds and the furniture.'

'But how is she going to live?'

'God knows.'

The affair seemed to grow more complicated, and the Colonel, with his expletives and his indignation, confused rather than informed me. I was glad that, catching sight of the clock at the Army and Navy Stores, he remembered an engagement to play cards at his club, and so left me to cut across St James's Park.

Chapter Ten

A day or two later Mrs Strickland sent me round a note asking if I could go and see her that evening after dinner. I found her alone. Her black dress, simple to austerity, suggested her bereaved condition, and I was innocently astonished that notwithstanding a real emotion she was able to dress the part she had to play according to her notions of seemliness.

'You said that if I wanted you to do anything you wouldn't mind doing it,' she remarked.

'It was quite true.'

'Will you go over to Paris and see Charlie?'

'I?'

I was taken aback. I reflected that I had only seen him once. I did not know what she wanted me to do.

'Fred is set on going.' Fred was Colonel MacAndrew. 'But I'm sure he's not the man to go. He'll only make things worse. I don't know who else to ask.'

Her voice trembled a little, and I felt a brute even to hesitate.

'But I've not spoken ten words to your husband. He doesn't know me. He'll probably just tell me to go to the devil.'

'That wouldn't hurt you,' said Mrs Strickland, smiling.

'What is it exactly you want me to do?'

She did not answer directly.

'I think it's rather an advantage that he doesn't know you. You see, he never really liked Fred; he thought him a fool; he didn't understand soldiers. Fred would fly into a passion, and there'd be a quarrel, and things would be worse instead of better. If you said you came on my behalf, he couldn't refuse to listen to you.'

'I haven't known you very long,' I answered. 'I don't see how anyone can be expected to tackle a case like this unless he knows all the details. I don't want to pry into what doesn't concern me. Why don't you go and see him yourself?'

'You forget he isn't alone.'

I held my tongue. I saw myself calling on Charles Strickland and sending in my card; I saw him come into the room, holding it between finger and thumb:

'To what do I owe this honour?'

'I've come to see you about your wife.'

'Really. When you are a little older you will doubtless learn the advantage of minding your own business. If you will be so good as to turn your head slightly to the left, you will see the door. I wish you good afternoon.'

I foresaw that it would be difficult to make my exit with dignity and I wished to goodness that I had not returned to London till Mrs Strickland had composed her difficulties. I stole a glance at her. She was immersed in thought. Presently she looked up at me, sighed deeply, and smiled.

'It was all so unexpected,' she said. 'We'd been married seventeen years. I never dreamed that Charlie was the sort of man to get infatuated with anyone. We always got on well together. Of course, I had a great many interests that he didn't share.'

'Have you found out who'—I did not quite know how to express myself—'who the person, who it is he's gone away with?'

'No. No one seems to have an idea. It's so strange. Generally when a man falls in love with someone people see them about together, lunching or something, and her friends always come and tell the wife. I had no warning—nothing. His letter came like a thunderbolt. I thought he was perfectly happy.'

She began to cry, poor thing, and I felt very sorry for her. But in a little while she grew calmer.

'It's no good making a fool of myself,' she said, drying her eyes. 'The only thing is to decide what is the best thing to do.'

She went on, talking somewhat at random, now of the recent past, then of their first meeting and their marriage; but presently I began to form a fairly coherent picture of their lives; and it seemed to me that my surmises had not been incorrect. Mrs Strickland was the daughter of an Indian civilian, who on his retirement had settled in the depths of the country, but it was his habit every August to take his family to Eastbourne for change of air; and it was here, when she was twenty, that she met Charles Strickland. He was twenty-three. They played tennis together, walked on the front together, listened together to the nigger minstrels; and she had made up her mind to accept him a week before he proposed to her. They lived in London, first in Hampstead, and then, as he grew more prosperous, in town. Two children were born to them.

'He always seemed very fond of them. Even if he was tired of me, I wonder that he had the heart to leave them. It's all so incredible. Even now I can hardly believe it's true.'

At last she showed me the letter he had written. I was curious to see it, but had not ventured to ask for it.

> My dear Amy,
>   I think you will find everything all right in the flat. I have given Anne your instructions, and dinner will be ready for you and the children when you come. I shall not be there to meet you. I have made up my mind to live apart from you, and I am going to Paris in the morning. I shall post this letter on my arrival. I shall not come back. My decision is irrevocable.
>   Yours always,
>   Charles Strickland

'Not a word of explanation or regret. Don't you think it's inhuman?'

'It's a very strange letter under the circumstances,' I replied.

'There's only one explanation, and that is that he's not himself. I don't know who this woman is who's got hold of him, but she's made him into another man. It's evidently been going on a long time.'

'What makes you think that?'

'Fred found that out. My husband said he went to the club three or four nights a week to play bridge. Fred knows one of the members, and said something about Charles being a great bridge-player. The man was surprised. He said he'd never even seen Charles in the card-room. It's quite clear now that when I thought Charles was at his club he was with her.'

I was silent for a moment. Then I thought of the children.

'It must have been very difficult to explain to Robert,' I said.

'Oh, I never said a word to either of them. You see, we only came up to town the day before they had to go back to school. I had the presence of mind to say that their father had been called away on business.'

It could not have been very easy to be bright and careless with that sudden secret in her heart, nor to give her attention to all the things that needed doing to get her children comfortably packed off. Mrs Strickland's voice broke again.

'And what is to happen to them, poor darlings? How are we going to live?'

She struggled for self-control, and I saw her hands clench and unclench spasmodically. It was dreadfully painful.

'Of course I'll go over to Paris if you think I can do any good, but you must tell me exactly what you want me to do.'

'I want him to come back.'

'I understand from Colonel MacAndrew that you'd made up your mind to divorce him.'

'I'll never divorce him,' she answered with a sudden violence. 'Tell him that from me. He'll never be able to marry that woman. I'm as obstinate as he is, and I'll never divorce him. I have to think of my children.'

I think she added this to explain her attitude to me, but I thought it was due to a very natural jealousy rather than to maternal solicitude.

'Are you in love with him still?'

'I don't know. I want him to come back. If he'll do that we'll let bygones be bygones. After all, we've been married for seventeen years. I'm a broad-minded woman. I wouldn't have minded what he did as long as I knew nothing about it. He must know that his infatuation won't last. If he'll come back now everything can be smoothed over, and no one will know anything about it.'

It chilled me a little that Mrs Strickland should be concerned with gossip, for I did not know then how great a part is played in women's life by the opinion of others. It throws a shadow of insincerity over their most deeply felt emotions.

It was known where Strickland was staying. His partner, in a violent letter, sent to his bank, had taunted him with hiding his whereabouts; and Strickland, in a cynical and humorous reply, had told his partner exactly where to find him. He was apparently living in an hotel.

'I've never heard of it,' said Mrs Strickland. 'But Fred knows it well. He says it's very expensive.'

She flushed darkly. I imagined that she saw her husband installed in a luxurious suite of rooms, dining at one smart restaurant after another, and she pictured his days spent at race-meetings, and his evenings at the play.

'It can't go on at his age,' she said. 'After all, he's forty. I could understand it in a young man, but I think it's horrible in a man of his years, with children who are nearly grown up. His health will never stand it.'

Anger struggled in her breast with misery.

'Tell him our home cries out for him. Everything is just the same, and yet everything is different. I can't live without him. I'd sooner kill myself. Talk to him about the past, and all we've gone through together. What am I to say to the children when they ask for him? His room is exactly as it was when he left it. It's waiting for him. We're all waiting for him.'

Now she told me exactly what I should say. She gave me elaborate answers to every possible observation of his.

'You will do everything you can for me?' she said pitifully. 'Tell him what a state I'm in.'

I saw that she wished me to appeal to his sympathies by every means in my power. She was weeping freely. I was extraordinarily touched. I felt indignant at Strickland's cold cruelty, and I promised to do all I could to bring him back. I agreed to go over on the next day but one, and to stay in Paris till I had achieved something. Then, as it was growing late and we were both exhausted by so much emotion, I left her.

Chapter Eleven

During the journey I thought over my errand with misgiving. Now that I was free from the spectacle of Mrs Strickland's distress I could consider the matter more calmly. I was puzzled by the contradictions that I saw in her behaviour. She was very unhappy, but to excite my sympathy she was able to make a show of her unhappiness. It was evident that she had been prepared to weep, for she had provided herself with a sufficiency of handkerchiefs; I admired her forethought, but in retrospect it made her tears perhaps less moving. I could not decide whether she desired the return of her husband because she loved him, or because she dreaded the tongue of scandal; and I was perturbed by the suspicion that the anguish of love contemned was alloyed in her broken heart with the pangs, sordid to my young mind, of wounded vanity. I had not yet learnt how contradictory is human nature; I did not know how much pose there is in the sincere, how much baseness in the noble, nor how much goodness in the reprobate.

But there was something of an adventure in my trip, and my spirits rose as I approached Paris. I saw myself, too, from the dramatic standpoint, and I was pleased with the rôle of the trusted friend bringing back the errant husband to his forgiving wife. I made up my mind to see Strickland the following evening, for I felt instinctively that the hour must be chosen with delicacy. An appeal to the emotions is little likely to be effectual before luncheon. My own thoughts were then constantly occupied with love, but I never could imagine connubial bliss till after tea.

I enquired at my hotel for that in which Charles Strickland was living. It was called the Hôtel des Belges. But the concierge, somewhat to my surprise, had never heard of it. I had understood Mrs Strickland that it was a large and sumptuous place at the back of the Rue de Rivoli. We looked it out in the directory. The only hotel of that name was in the Rue des Moines. The quarter was not fashionable; it was not even respectable. I shook my head.

'I'm sure that's not it,' I said.

The concierge shrugged his shoulders. There was no other hotel of that name in Paris. It occurred to me that Strickland had concealed his address, after all. In giving his partner the one I knew he was perhaps playing a trick on him. I do not know why I had an inkling that it would appeal to Strickland's sense of humour to bring a furious stockbroker over to Paris on a fool's errand to an ill-famed house in a mean street. Still, I thought I had better go and see. Next day about six o'clock I took a cab to the Rue des Moines, but dismissed it at the corner, since I preferred to walk to the hotel and look at it before I went in. It was a street of small shops subservient to the needs of poor people, and about the middle of it, on the left as I walked down, was the Hôtel des Belges. My own hotel was modest enough, but it was magnificent in comparison with this. It was a tall, shabby building, that cannot have been painted for years, and it had so bedraggled an air that the houses on each side of it looked neat and clean. The dirty windows were all shut. It was not here that Charles Strickland lived in guilty splendour with the unknown charmer for whose sake he had abandoned honour and duty. I was vexed, for I felt that I had been made a fool of, and I nearly turned away without making an enquiry. I went in only to be able to tell Mrs Strickland that I had done my best.

The door was at the side of a shop. It stood open, and just within was a sign: *Bureau au premier.* I walked up narrow stairs, and on the landing found a sort of box, glassed in, within which were a desk and a couple of chairs. There was a bench outside, on which it might be presumed the night porter passed uneasy nights. There was no one about, but under an electric bell was written *Garçon.* I rang, and presently a waiter appeared. He was a young man with furtive eyes and a sullen look. He was in shirt-sleeves and carpet slippers.

I do not know why I made my enquiry as casual as possible.

'Does Mr Strickland live here by any chance?' I asked.

'Number thirty-two. On the sixth floor.'

I was so surprised that for a moment I did not answer.

'Is he in?'

The waiter looked at a board in the *bureau.*

'He hasn't left his key. Go up and you'll see.'

I thought it as well to put one more question.

'*Madame est là!*'

'*Monsieur est seul.*'

The waiter looked at me suspiciously as I made my way upstairs. They were dark and airless. There was a foul and musty smell. Three flights up a woman in a dressing-gown, with touzled hair, opened a door and looked at me silently as I passed. At length I reached the sixth floor, and knocked at the door numbered thirty-two. There was a sound within, and the door was partly opened. Charles Strickland stood before me. He uttered not a word. He evidently did not know me.

I told him my name. I tried my best to assume an airy manner.

'You don't remember me. I had the pleasure of dining with you last July.'

'Come in,' he said cheerily. 'I'm delighted to see you. Take a pew.'

I entered. It was a very small room, overcrowded with furniture of the style which the French know as Louis Philippe. There was a large wooden bedstead on which was a billowing red eiderdown, and there was a large wardrobe, a round table, a very small washstand, and two stuffed chairs covered with red rep. Everything was dirty and shabby. There was no sign of the abandoned luxury that Colonel MacAndrew had so confidently described. Strickland threw on the floor the clothes that burdened one of the chairs, and I sat down on it.

'What can I do for you?' he asked.

In that small room he seemed even bigger than I remembered him. He wore an old Norfolk jacket, and he had not shaved for several days. When last I saw him he was spruce enough, but he looked ill at ease: now, untidy and ill-kempt, he looked perfectly at home. I did not know how he would take the remark I had prepared.

'I've come to see you on behalf of your wife.'

'I was just going out to have a drink before dinner. You'd better come too. Do you like absinthe?'

'I can drink it.'

'Come on, then.'

He put on a bowler hat much in need of brushing.

'We might dine together. You owe me a dinner, you know.'

'Certainly. Are you alone?'

I flattered myself that I had got in that important question very naturally.

'Oh yes. In point of fact I've not spoken to a soul for three days. My French isn't exactly brilliant.'

I wondered as I preceded him downstairs what had happened to the little lady in the tea-shop. Had they quarrelled already, or was his infatuation passed? It seemed hardly likely if, as appeared, he had been taking steps for a year to make his desperate plunge. We walked to the Avenue de Clichy, and sat down at one of the tables on the pavement of a large café.

Chapter Twelve

The Avenue de Clichy, was crowded at that hour, and a lively fancy might see in the passers-by the personages of many a sordid romance. There were clerks and shop-girls; old fellows who might have stepped out of the pages of Honoré de Balzac; members, male and female, of the professions which make their profit of the frailties of mankind. There is in the streets of the poorer quarters of Paris a thronging vitality which excites the blood and prepares the soul for the unexpected.

'Do you know Paris well?' I asked.

'No. We came on our honeymoon. I haven't been since.'

'How on earth did you find out your hotel?'

'It was recommended to me. I wanted something cheap.'

The absinthe came, and with due solemnity we dropped water over the melting sugar.

'I thought I'd better tell you at once why I had come to see you,' I said, not without embarrassment.

His eyes twinkled.

'I thought somebody would come along sooner or later. I've had a lot of letters from Amy.'

'Then you know pretty well what I've got to say.'

'I've not read them.'

I lit a cigarette to give myself a moment's time. I did not quite know how to set about my mission. The eloquent phrases I had arranged, pathetic or indignant, seemed out of place on the Avenue de Clichy. Suddenly he gave a chuckle.

'Beastly job for you this, isn't it?'

'Oh, I don't know,' I answered.

'Well, look here, you get it over, and then we'll have a jolly evening.'

I hesitated.

'Has it occurred to you that your wife is frightfully unhappy?'

'She'll get over it.'

I cannot describe the extraordinary callousness with which he made this reply. It disconcerted me, but I did my best not to show it. I adopted the tone used by my Uncle Henry, a clergyman, when he was asking one of his relatives for a subscription to the Additional Curates Society.

'You don't mind my talking to you frankly?'

He shook his head, smiling.

'Has she deserved that you should treat her like this?'

'No.'

'Have you any complaint to make against her?'

'None.'

'Then, isn't it monstrous to leave her in this fashion, after seventeen years of married life, without a fault to find with her?'

'Monstrous.'

I glanced at him with surprise. His cordial agreement with all I said cut the ground from under my feet. It made my position complicated, not to say ludicrous. I was prepared to be persuasive, touching, and hortatory, admonitory and expostulating, if need be vituperative even, indignant and sarcastic; but what the devil does a mentor do when the sinner makes no bones about confessing his sin? I had no experience, since my own practice has always been to deny everything.

'What, then?' asked Strickland.

I tried to curl my lip.

'Well, if you acknowledge that, there doesn't seem much more to be said.'

'I don't think there is.'

I felt I was not carrying out my embassy with any great skill. I was distinctly nettled.

'Hang it all, one can't leave a woman without a bob.'

'Why not?'

'How is she going to live?'

'I've supported her for seventeen years. Why shouldn't she support herself for a change?'

'She can't.'

'Let her try.'

Of course there were many things I might have answered to this. I might have spoken of the economic position of woman, of the contract, tacit and overt, which a man accepts by his marriage, and of much else; but I felt that there was only one point which really signified.

'Don't you care for her any more?'

'Not a bit,' he replied.

The matter was immensely serious for all the parties concerned, but there was in the manner of his answers such a cheerful effrontery that I had to bite my lips in order not to laugh. I reminded myself that his behaviour was abominable. I worked myself up into a state of moral indignation.

'Damn it all, there are your children to think of. They've never done you any harm. They didn't ask to be brought into the world. If you chuck everything like this, they'll be thrown on the streets.'

'They've had a good many years of comfort. It's much more than the majority of children have. Besides, somebody will look after them. When it comes to the point, the MacAndrews will pay for their schooling.'

'But aren't you fond of them? They're such awfully nice kids. Do you mean to say you don't want to have anything more to do with them?'

'I liked them all right when they were kids, but now they're growing up I haven't got any particular feeling for them.'

'It's just inhuman.'

'I dare say.'

'You don't seem in the least ashamed.'

'I'm not.'

I tried another tack.

'Everyone will think you a perfect swine.'

'Let them.'

'Won't it mean anything to you to know that people loathe and despise you?'

'No.'

His brief answer was so scornful that it made my question, natural though it was, seem absurd. I reflected for a minute or two.

'I wonder if one can live quite comfortably when one's conscious of the disapproval of one's fellows? Are you sure it won't begin to worry you? Everyone has some sort of conscience, and sooner or later it will find you out. Supposing your wife died, wouldn't you be tortured by remorse?'

He did not answer, and I waited for some time for him to speak. At last I had to break the silence myself.

'What have you to say to that?'

'Only that you're a damned fool.'

'At all events, you can be forced to support your wife and children,' I retorted, somewhat piqued. 'I suppose the law has some protection to offer them.'

'Can the law get blood out of a stone? I haven't any money. I've got about a hundred pounds.'

I began to be more puzzled than before. It was true that his hotel pointed to the most straitened circumstances.

'What are you going to do when you've spent that?'

'Earn some.'

He was perfectly cool, and his eyes kept that mocking smile which made all I said seem rather foolish. I paused for a little while to consider what I had better say next. But it was he who spoke first.

'Why doesn't Amy marry again? She's comparatively young, and she's not unattractive. I can recommend her as an excellent wife. If she wants to divorce me I don't mind giving her the necessary grounds.'

Now it was my turn to smile. He was very cunning, but it was evidently this that he was aiming at. He had some reason to conceal the fact that he had run away with a woman, and he was using every precaution to hide her whereabouts. I answered with decision.

'Your wife says that nothing you can do will ever induce her to divorce you. She's quite made up her mind. You can put any possibility of that definitely out of your head.'

He looked at me with an astonishment that was certainly not feigned. The smile abandoned his lips, and he spoke quite seriously.

'But, my dear fellow, I don't care. It doesn't matter a twopenny damn to me one way or the other.'

I laughed.

'Oh, come now; you mustn't think us such fools as all that. We happen to know that you came away with a woman.'

He gave a little start, and then suddenly burst into a shout of laughter. He laughed so uproariously that the people sitting near us looked round, and some of them began to laugh too.

'I don't see anything very amusing in that.'

'Poor Amy,' he grinned.

Then his face grew bitterly scornful.

'What poor minds women have got! Love. It's always love. They think a man leaves them only because he wants others. Do you think I should be such a fool as to do what I've done for a woman?'

'Do you mean to say you didn't leave your wife for another woman?'

'Of course not.'

'On your word of honour?'

I don't know why I asked for that. It was very ingenuous of me.

'On my word of honour.'

'Then, what in God's name have you left her for?'

'I want to paint.'

I looked at him for quite a long time. I did not understand. I thought he was mad. It must be remembered that I was very young, and I looked upon him as a middle-aged man. I forgot everything but my own amazement.

'But you're forty.'

'That's what made me think it was high time to begin.'

'Have you ever painted?'

'I rather wanted to be a painter when I was a boy, but my father made me go into business because he said there was no money in art. I began to paint a bit a year ago. For the last year I've been going to some classes at night.'

'Was that where you went when Mrs Strickland thought you were playing bridge at your club?'

'That's it.'

'Why didn't you tell her?'

'I preferred to keep it to myself.'

'Can you paint?'

'Not yet. But I shall. That's why I've come over here. I couldn't get what I wanted in London. Perhaps I can here.'

'Do you think it's likely that a man will do any good when he starts at your age? Most men begin painting at eighteen.'

'I can learn quicker than I could when I was eighteen.'

'What makes you think you have any talent?'

He did not answer for a minute. His gaze rested on the passing throng, but I do not think he saw it. His answer was no answer.

'I've got to paint.'

'Aren't you taking an awful chance?'

He looked at me then. His eyes had something strange in them, so that I felt rather uncomfortable.

'How old are you? Twenty-three?'

It seemed to me that the question was beside the point. It was natural that I should take chances; but he was a man whose youth was past, a stockbroker with a position of respectability, a wife and two children. A course that would have been natural for me was absurd for him. I wished to be quite fair.

'Of course a miracle may happen, and you may be a great painter, but you must confess the chances are a million to one against it. It'll be an awful sell if at the end you have to acknowledge you've made a hash of it.'

'I've got to paint,' he repeated.

'Supposing you're never anything more than third-rate, do you think it will have been worth while to give up everything? After all, in any other walk of life it doesn't matter if you're not very good: you can get along quite comfortably if you're just adequate; but it's different with an artist.'

'You blasted fool,' he said.

'I don't see why, unless it's folly to say the obvious.'

'I tell you I've got to paint. I can't help myself. When a man falls into the water it doesn't matter how he swims, well or badly: he's got to get out or else he'll drown.'

There was real passion in his voice, and in spite of myself I was impressed. I seemed to feel in him some vehement power that was struggling within him; it gave me the sensation of something very strong, overmastering, that held him, as it were, against his will. I could not understand. He seemed really to be possessed of a devil, and I felt that it might suddenly turn and rend him. Yet he looked ordinary enough. My eyes, resting on him curiously, caused him no embarrassment. I wondered what a stranger would have taken him to be, sitting there in his old Norfolk jacket and his unbrushed bowler; his trousers were baggy, his hands were not clean; and his face, with the red stubble of the unshaved chin, the little eyes, and the large, aggressive nose, was uncouth and coarse. His mouth was large, his lips were heavy and sensual. No; I could not have placed him.

'You won't go back to your wife?' I said at last.

'Never.'

'She's willing to forget everything that's happened and start afresh. She'll never make you a single reproach.'

'She can go to hell.'

'You don't care if people think you an utter blackguard? You don't care if she and your children have to beg their bread?'

'Not a damn.'

I was silent for a moment in order to give greater force to my next remark. I spoke as deliberately as I could.

'You are a most unmitigated cad.'

'Now that you've got that off your chest, let's go and have dinner.'

Chapter Thirteen

I dare say it would have been more seemly to decline this proposal. I think perhaps I should have made a show of the indignation I really felt, and I am sure that Colonel MacAndrew at least would have thought well of me if I had been able to report my stout refusal to sit at the same table with a man of such character. But the fear of not being able to carry it through effectively has always made me shy of assuming the moral attitude; and in this case the certainty that my sentiments would be lost on Strickland made it peculiarly embarrassing to utter them. Only the poet or the saint can water an asphalt pavement in the confident anticipation that lilies will reward his labour.

I paid for what we had drunk, and we made our way to a cheap restaurant, crowded and gay, where we dined with pleasure. I had the appetite of youth and he of a hardened conscience. Then we went to a tavern to have coffee and liqueurs.

I had said all I had to say on the subject that had brought me to Paris, and though I felt it in a manner treacherous to Mrs Strickland not to pursue it, I could not struggle against his indifference. It requires the feminine temperament to repeat the same thing three times with unabated zest. I solace myself by thinking that it would be useful for me to find out what I could about Strickland's state of mind. It also interested me much more. But this was not an easy thing to do, for Strickland was not a fluent talker. He seemed to express himself with difficulty, as though words were not the medium with which his mind worked; and you had to guess the intentions of his soul by hackneyed phrases, slang, and vague, unfinished gestures. But though he said nothing of any consequence, there was something in his personality which prevented him from being dull. Perhaps it was sincerity. He did not seem to care much about the Paris he was now seeing for the first time (I did not count the visit with his wife), and he accepted sights which must have been strange to him without any sense of astonishment. I have been to Paris a hundred times, and it never fails to give me a thrill of excitement; I can never walk its streets without feeling myself on the verge of adventure. Strickland remained placid. Looking back, I think now that he was blind to everything but to some disturbing vision in his soul.

One rather absurd incident took place. There were a number of harlots in the tavern: some were sitting with men, others by themselves; and presently I noticed that one of these was looking at us. When she caught Strickland's eye she smiled. I do not think he saw her. In a little while she went out, but in a minute returned and, passing our table, very politely asked us to buy her something to drink. She sat down and I began to chat with her; but it was plain that her interest was in Strickland. I explained that he knew no more than two words of French. She tried to talk to him, partly by signs, partly in pidgin French, which, for some reason, she thought would be more comprehensible to him, and she had half a dozen phrases of English. She made me translate what she could only express in her own tongue, and eagerly asked for the meaning of his replies. He was quite good-tempered, a little amused, but his indifference was obvious.

'I think you've made a conquest,' I laughed.

'I'm not flattered.'

In his place I should have been more embarrassed and less calm. She had laughing eyes and a most charming mouth. She was young. I wondered what she found so attractive in Strickland. She made no secret of her desires, and I was bidden to translate.

'She wants you to go home with her.'

'I'm not taking any,' he replied.

I put his answer as pleasantly as I could. It seemed to me a little ungracious to decline an invitation of that sort, and I ascribed his refusal to lack of money.

'But I like him,' she said. 'Tell him it's for love.'

When I translated this, Strickland shrugged his shoulders impatiently.

'Tell her to go to hell,' he said.

His manner made his answer quite plain, and the girl threw back her head with a sudden gesture. Perhaps she reddened under her paint. She rose to her feet.

'*Monsieur n'est pas poli,*' she said.

She walked out of the inn. I was slightly vexed.

'There wasn't any need to insult her that I can see,' I said. 'After all, it was rather a compliment she was paying you.'

'That sort of thing makes me sick,' he said roughly.

I looked at him curiously. There was real distaste in his face, and yet it was the face of a coarse and sensual man. I suppose the girl had been attracted by a certain brutality in it.

'I could have got all the women I wanted in London. I didn't come here for that.'

Chapter Fourteen

During the journey back to England I thought much of Strickland. I tried to set in order what I had to tell his wife. It was unsatisfactory, and I could not imagine that she would be content with me; I was not content with myself. Strickland perplexed me. I could not understand his motives. When I had asked him what first gave him the idea of being a painter, he was unable or unwilling to tell me. I could make nothing of it. I tried to persuade myself that an obscure feeling of revolt had been gradually coming to a head in his slow mind, but to challenge this was the undoubted fact that he had never shown any impatience with the monotony of his life. If, seized by an intolerable boredom, he had determined to be a painter merely to break with irksome ties, it would have been comprehensible, and commonplace; but commonplace is precisely what I felt he was not. At last, because I was romantic, I devised an explanation which I acknowledged to be far-fetched, but which was the only one that in any way satisfied me. It was this: I asked myself whether there was not in his soul some deep-rooted instinct of creation, which the circumstances of his life had obscured, but which grew relentlessly, as a cancer may grow in the living tissues, till at last it took possession of his whole being and forced him irresistibly to action. The cuckoo lays its egg in the strange bird's nest, and when the young one is hatched it shoulders its foster-brothers out and breaks at last the nest that has sheltered it.

But how strange it was that the creative instinct should seize upon this dull stockbroker, to his own ruin, perhaps; and to the misfortune of such as were dependent on him, and yet no stranger than the way in which the spirit of God has seized men, powerful and rich, pursuing them with stubborn vigilance till at last, conquered, they have abandoned the joy of the world and the love of women for the painful austerities of the cloister. Conversion may come under many shapes, and it may be brought about in many ways. With some men it needs a cataclysm, as a stone may be broken to fragments by the fury of a torrent; but with some it comes gradually, as a stone may be worn away by the ceaseless fall of a drop of water. Strickland had the directness of the fanatic and the ferocity of the apostle.

But to my practical mind it remained to be seen whether the passion which obsessed him would be justified of its works. When I asked him what his brother-students at the night classes he had attended in London thought of his painting, he answered with a grin:

'They thought it a joke.'

'Have you begun to go to a studio here?'

'Yes. The blighter came round this morning–the master, you know; when he saw my drawing he just raised his eyebrows and walked on.'

Strickland chuckled. He did not seem discouraged. He was independent of the opinion of his fellows.

And it was just that which had most disconcerted me in my dealings with him. When people say they do not care what others think of them, for the most part they deceive themselves. Generally they mean only that they will do as they choose, in the confidence that no one will know their vagaries; and at the utmost only that they are willing to act contrary to the opinion of the majority because they are supported by the approval of their neighbours. It is not difficult to be unconventional in the eyes of the world when your unconventionality is but the convention of your set. It affords you then an inordinate amount of self-esteem. You have the self-satisfaction of courage without the inconvenience of danger. But the desire for approbation is perhaps the most deeply seated instinct of civilised man. No one runs so hurriedly to the cover of respectabilty as the unconventional woman who has exposed herself to the slings and arrows of outraged propriety. I do not believe the people who tell me they do not care a row of pins for the opinion of their fellows. It is the bravado of ignorance. They mean only that they do not fear reproaches for peccadillos which they are convinced none will discover.

But here was a man who sincerely did not mind what people thought of him, and so convention had no hold on him; he was like a wrestler whose body is oiled; you could not get a grip on him; it gave him a freedom which was an outrage. I remember saying to him:

'Look here, if everyone acted like you, the world couldn't go on.'

'That's a damned silly thing to say. Everyone doesn't want to act like me. The great majority are perfectly content to do the ordinary thing.'

And once I sought to be satirical.

'You evidently don't believe in the maxim: Act so that every one of your actions is capable of being made into a universal rule.'

'I never heard it before, but it's rotten nonsense.'

'Well, it was Kant who said it.'

'I don't care; it's rotten nonsense.'

Nor with such a man could you expect the appeal to conscience to be effective. You might as well ask for a reflection without a mirror. I take it that conscience is the guardian in the individual of the rules which the community has evolved for its own preservation. It is the policeman in all our hearts, set there to watch that we do not break its laws. It is the spy seated in the central stronghold of the ego. Man's desire for the approval of his fellows is so strong, his dread of their censure so violent, that himself has brought his enemy within his gates; and it keeps watch over him, vigilant always in the interests of its master to crush any half-formed desire to break away from the herd. It will force him to place the good of society before his own. It is the very strong link that attaches the individual to the whole. And man, subservient to interests he has persuaded himself are greater than his own, makes himself a slave to his taskmaster. He sits him in a seat of honour. At last, like a courtier fawning on the royal stick that is laid about his shoulders, he prides himself on the sensitiveness of his conscience. Then he has no words hard enough for the man who does not recognise its sway; for, a member of society now, he realises accurately enough that against him he is powerless. When I saw that Strickland was really indifferent to the blame his conduct must excite, I could only draw back in horror as from a monster of hardly human shape.

The last words he said to me when I bade him good night were:

'Tell Amy it's no good coming after me. Anyhow, I shall change my hotel, so she wouldn't be able to find me.'

'My own impression is that she's well rid of you,' I said.

'My dear fellow, I only hope you'll be able to make her see it. But women are very unintelligent.'

Chapter Fifteen

When I reached London I found waiting for me an urgent request that I should go to Mrs Strickland's as soon after dinner as I could. I found her with Colonel MacAndrew and his wife. Mrs Strickland's sister was older than she, not unlike her, but more faded; and she had the efficient air, as though she carried the British Empire in her pocket, which the wives of senior officers acquire from the consciousness of belonging to a superior caste. Her manner was brisk, and her good breeding scarcely concealed her conviction that if you were not a soldier you might as well be a counter-jumper. She hated the Guards, whom she thought conceited and she could not trust herself to speak of their ladies, who were so remiss in calling. Her gown was dowdy and expensive.

Mrs Strickland was plainly nervous.

'Well, tell us your news,' she said.

'I saw your husband. I'm afraid he's quite made up his mind not to return.' I paused a little. 'He wants to paint.'

'What do you mean?' cried Mrs Strickland, with the utmost astonishment.

'Did you never know that he was keen on that sort of thing?'

'He must be as mad as a hatter,' exclaimed the Colonel.

Mrs Strickland frowned a little. She was searching among her recollections.

'I remember before we were married he used to potter about with a paint-box. But you never saw such daubs. We used to chaff him. He had absolutely no gift for anything like that.'

'Of course it's only an excuse,' said Mrs MacAndrew.

Mrs Strickland pondered deeply for some time. It was quite clear that she could not make head or tail of my announcement. She had put some order into the drawing-room by now, her housewifely instincts having got the better of her dismay; and it no longer bore that deserted look, like a furnished house long to let, which I had noticed on my first visit after the catastrophe. But now that I had seen Strickland in Paris it was difficult to imagine him in those surroundings. I thought it could hardly have failed to strike them that there was something incongruous in him.

'But if he wanted to be an artist, why didn't he say so?' asked Mrs Strickland at last. 'I should have thought I was the last person to be unsympathetic to—to aspirations of that kind.'

Mrs MacAndrew tightened her lips. I imagine that she had never looked with approval on her sister's leaning towards persons who cultivated the arts. She spoke of 'culchaw' derisively.

Mrs Strickland continued:

'After all, if he had any talent I should be the first to encourage it. I wouldn't have minded sacrifices. I'd much rather be married to a painter than to a stockbroker. If it weren't for the children, I wouldn't mind anything. I could be just as happy in a shabby studio in Chelsea as in this flat.'

'My dear, I have no patience with you,' cried Mrs MacAndrew. 'You don't mean to say you believe a word of this nonsense?'

'But I think it's true,' I put it mildly.

She looked at me with good-humoured contempt.

'A man doesn't throw up his business and leave his wife and children at the age of forty to become a painter unless there's a woman in it. I suppose he met one of your—artistic friends, and she's turned his head.'

A spot of colour rose suddenly to Mrs Strickland's pale cheeks.

'What is she like?'

I hesitated a little. I knew that I had a bombshell.

'There isn't a woman.'

Colonel MacAndrew and his wife uttered expressions of incredulity, and Mrs Strickland sprang to her feet.

'Do you mean to say you never saw her?'

'There's no one to see. He's quite alone.'

'That's preposterous,' cried Mrs MacAndrew.

'I knew I ought to have gone over myself,' said the Colonel. 'You can bet your boots I'd have routed her out fast enough.'

'I wish you had gone over,' I replied, somewhat tartly. 'You'd have seen that every one of your suppositions was wrong. He's not at a smart hotel. He's living in one tiny room in the most squalid way. If he's left his home, it's not to live a gay life. He's got hardly any money.'

'Do you think he's done something that we don't know about, and is lying doggo on account of the police?'

The suggestion sent a ray of hope in all their breasts, but I would have nothing to do with it.

'If that were so, he would hardly have been such a fool as to give his partner his address,' I retorted acidly. 'Anyhow, there's one thing I'm positive of, he didn't go away with anyone. He's not in love. Nothing is farther from his thoughts.'

There was a pause while they reflected over my words.

'Well, if what you say is true,' said Mrs MacAndrew at last, 'things aren't so bad as I thought.'

Mrs Strickland glanced at her, but said nothing. She was very pale now, and her fine brow was dark and lowering. I could not understand the expression of her face. Mrs MacAndrew continued:

'If it's just a whim, he'll get over it.'

'Why don't you go over to him, Amy?' hazarded the Colonel. 'There's no reason why you shouldn't live with him in Paris for a year. We'll look after the children. I dare say he'd got stale. Sooner or later he'll be quite ready to come back to London, and no great harm will have been done.'

'I wouldn't do that,' said Mrs MacAndrew. 'I'd give him all the rope he wants. He'll come back with his tail between his legs and settle down again quite comfortably.' Mrs MacAndrew looked at her sister coolly. 'Perhaps you weren't very wise with him sometimes. Men are queer creatures, and one has to know how to manage them.'

Mrs MacAndrew shared the common opinion of her sex that a man is always a brute to leave a woman who is attached to him, but that a woman is much to blame if he does. *Le cœur a ses raisons que le raison ne connaît pas.*

Mrs Strickland looked slowly from one to another of us.

'He'll never come back,' she said.

'Oh, my dear, remember what we've just heard. He's been used to comfort and to having someone to look after him. How long do you think it'll be before he gets tired of a scrubby room in a scrubby hotel? Besides, he hasn't any money. He must come back.'

'As long as I thought he'd run away with some woman I thought there was a chance. I don't believe that sort of thing ever answers. He'd have got sick to death of her in three months. But if he hasn't gone because he's in love, then it's finished.'

'Oh, I think that's awfully subtle,' said the Colonel, putting into the word all the contempt he felt for a quality so alien to the traditions of his calling. 'Don't you believe it. He'll come back, and, as Dorothy says, I dare say he'll be none the worse for having had a bit of a fling.'

'But I don't want him back,' she said.

'Amy!'

It was anger that had seized Mrs Strickland, and her pallor was the pallor of a cold and sudden rage. She spoke quickly now, with little gasps.

'I could have forgiven it if he'd fallen desperately in love with someone and gone off with her. I should have thought that natural. I shouldn't really have blamed him. I should have thought he was led away. Men are so weak, and women are so unscrupulous. But this is different. I hate him. I'll never forgive him now.'

Colonel MacAndrew and his wife began to talk to her together. They were astonished. They told her she was mad. They could not understand. Mrs Strickland turned desperately to me.

'Don't *you* see?' she cried.

'I'm not sure. Do you mean that you could have forgiven him if he'd left you for a woman, but not if he's left you for an idea? You think you're a match for the one, but against the other you're helpless?'

Mrs Strickland gave me a look in which I read no great friendliness, but did not answer. Perhaps I had struck home. She went on in a low and trembling voice:

'I never knew it was possible to hate anyone as much as I hate him. Do you know, I've been comforting myself by thinking that however long it lasted he'd want me at the end? I knew when he was dying he'd send for me, and I was ready to go; I'd have nursed him like a mother, and at the last I'd have told him that it didn't matter, I'd loved him always, and I forgave him everything.'

I have always been a little disconcerted by the passion women have for behaving beautifully at the death-bed of those they love. Sometimes it seems as if they grudge the longevity which postpones their chance of an effective scene.

'But now—now it's finished. I'm as indifferent to him as if he were a stranger. I should like him to die miserable, poor, and starving, without a friend. I hope he'll rot with some loathsome disease. I've done with him.'

I thought it as well then to say what Strickland had suggested.

'If you want to divorce him, he's quite willing to do whatever is necessary to make it possible.'

'Why should I give him his freedom?'

'I don't think he wants it. He merely thought it might be more convenient to you.'

Mrs Strickland shrugged her shoulders impatiently. I think I was a little disappointed in her. I expected then people to be more of a piece than I do now, and I was distressed to find so much vindictiveness in so charming a creature. I did not realise how motley are the qualities that go to make up a human being. Now I am well aware that pettiness and grandeur, malice and charity, hatred and love, can find place side by side in the same human heart.

I wondered if there was anything I could say that would ease the sense of bitter humiliation which at present tormented Mrs Strickland. I thought I would try.

'You know, I'm not sure that your husband is quite responsible for his actions. I do not think he is himself. He seems to me to be possessed by some power which is using him for its own ends, and in whose hold he is helpless as a fly in a spider's web. It's as though someone had cast a spell over him. I'm reminded of those strange stories one sometimes hears of another personality entering into a man and driving out the old one. The soul lives unstably in the body, and is capable of mysterious transformations. In the old days they would say Charles Strickland had a devil.'

Mrs MacAndrew smoothed down the lap of her gown, and gold bangles fell over her wrists.

'All that seems to me very far-fetched,' she said acidly. 'I don't deny that perhaps Amy took her husband a little too much for granted. If she hadn't been so busy with her own affairs, I can't believe that she wouldn't have suspected something was the matter. I don't think that Alec could have something on his mind for a year or more without my having a pretty shrewd idea of it.'

The Colonel stared into vacancy, and I wondered whether anyone could be quite so innocent of guile as he looked.

'But that doesn't prevent the fact that Charles Strickland is a heartless beast.' She looked at me severely. 'I can tell you why he left his wife–from pure selfishness and nothing else whatever.'

'That is certainly the simplest explanation,' I said. But I thought it explained nothing. When, saying I was tired, I rose to go, Mrs Strickland made no attempt to detain me.

Chapter Sixteen

What followed showed that Mrs Strickland was a woman of character. Whatever anguish she suffered she concealed. She saw shrewdly that the world is quickly bored by the recital of misfortune, and willingly avoids the sight of distress. Whenever she went out–and compassion for her misadventure made her friends eager to entertain her–she bore a demeanour that was perfect. She was brave, but not too obviously; cheerful, but not brazenly; and she seemed more anxious to listen to the troubles of others than to discuss her own. Whenever she spoke of her husband it was with pity. Her attitude towards him at first perplexed me. One day she said to me:

'You know, I'm convinced you were mistaken about Charles being alone. From what I've been able to gather from certain sources that I can't tell you, I know that he didn't leave England by himself.'

'In that case he has a positive genius for covering up his tracks.'

She looked away and slightly coloured.

'What I mean is, if anyone talks to you about it, please don't contradict it if they say he eloped with somebody.'

'Of course not.'

She changed the conversation as though it were a matter to which she attached no importance. I discovered presently that a peculiar story was circulating among her friends. They said that Charles Strickland had become infatuated with a French dancer, whom he had first seen in the ballet at the Empire, and had accompanied her to Paris. I could not find out how this had arisen, but, singularly enough, it created much sympathy for Mrs Strickland, and at the same time gave her not a little prestige. This was not without its use in the calling which she had decided to follow. Colonel MacAndrew had not exaggerated when he said she would be penniless, and it was necessary for her to earn her living as quickly as she could. She made up her mind to profit by her acquaintance with so many writers and without loss of time began to learn shorthand and typewriting. Her education made it likely that she would be a typist more efficient than the average, and her story made her claims appealing. Her friends promised to send her work, and took care to recommend her to all theirs.

The MacAndrews, who were childless and in easy circumstances, arranged to undertake the care of the children, and Mrs Strickland had only herself to provide for. She let her flat and sold her furniture. She settled in two tiny rooms in Westminster, and faced the world anew. She was so efficient that it was certain she would make a success of the adventure.

Chapter Seventeen

It was about five years after this that I decided to live in Paris for a while. I was growing stale in London. I was tired of doing much the same thing every day. My friends pursued their course with uneventfulness; they had no longer any surprises for me, and when I met them I knew pretty well what they would say; even their love-affairs had a tedious banality. We were like tram-cars running on their lines from terminus to terminus, and it was possible to calculate within small limits the number of passengers they would carry. Life was ordered too pleasantly. I was seized with panic. I gave up my small apartment, sold my few belongings, and resolved to start afresh.

I called on Mrs Strickland before I left. I had not seen her for some time, and I noticed changes in her; it was not only that she was older, thinner, and more lined; I think her character had altered. She had made a success of her business, and now had an office in Chancery Lane, she did little typing herself, but spent her time correcting the work of the four girls she employed. She had had the idea of giving it a certain daintiness, and she made much use of blue and red inks; she bound the copy in coarse paper, that looked vaguely like watered silk, in various pale colours; and she had acquired a reputation for neatness and accuracy. She was making money. But she could not get over the idea that to earn her living was somewhat undignified, and she was inclined to remind you that she was a lady by birth.

She could not help bringing into her conversation the names of people she knew which would satisfy you that she had not sunk in the social scale. She was a little ashamed of her courage and business capacity, but delighted that she was going to dine the next night with a K.C. who lived in South Kensington. She was pleased to be able to tell you that her son was at Cambridge, and it was with a little laugh that she spoke of the rush of dances to which her daughter, just out, was invited. I suppose I said a very stupid thing.

'Is she going into your business?' I asked.

'Oh no; I wouldn't let her do that,' Mrs Strickland answered. 'She's so pretty. I'm sure she'll marry well.'

'I should have thought it would be a help to you.'

'Several people have suggested that she should go on the stage, but of course I couldn't consent to that. I know all the chief dramatists, and I could get her a part tomorrow, but I shouldn't like her to mix with all sorts of people.'

I was a little chilled by Mrs Strickland's exclusiveness.

'Do you ever hear of your husband?'

'No; I haven't heard a word. He may be dead for all I know.'

'I may run across him in Paris. Would you like me to let you know about him?'

She hesitated a minute.

'If he's in any real want I'm prepared to help him a little. I'd send you a certain sum of money, and you could give it him gradually, as he needed it.'

'That's very good of you,' I said.

But I knew it was not kindness that prompted the offer. It is not true that suffering ennobles the character; happiness does that sometimes, but suffering, for the most part, makes men petty and vindictive.

Chapter Eighteen

In point of fact, I met Strickland before I had been a fortnight in Paris.

I quickly found myself a tiny apartment on the fifth floor of a house in the Rue des Dames, and for a couple of hundred francs bought at a second-hand dealer's enough furniture to make it habitable. I arranged with the concierge to make my coffee in the morning and to keep the place clean. Then I went to see my friend Dirk Stroeve.

Dirk Stroeve was one of those persons whom, according to your character, you cannot think of without derisive laughter or an embarrassed shrug of the shoulders. Nature had made him a buffoon. He was a painter, but a very bad one, whom I had met in Rome, and I still remembered his pictures. He had a genuine enthusiasm for the commonplace. His soul palpitating with love of art, he painted the models who hung about the stairway of Bernini in the Piazzi di Spagna, undaunted by their obvious picturesqueness; and his studio was full of canvases on which were portrayed moustachioed, large-eyed peasants in peaked hats, urchins in becoming rags, and women in bright petticoats. Sometimes they lounged at the steps of a church, and sometimes dallied among cypresses against a cloudless sky; sometimes they made love by a Renaissance well-head, and sometimes they wandered through the Campagna by the side of an ox-waggon. They were carefully drawn and carefully painted. A photograph could not have been more exact. One of the painters at the Villa Medici had called him *Le Maître de la Boîte à Chocolats*. To look at his pictures you would have thought that Monet, Manet, and the rest of the Impressionists had never been.

'I don't pretend to be a great painter,' he said. 'I'm not a Michael Angelo, no, but I have something. I sell. I bring romance into the homes of all sorts of people. Do you know, they buy my pictures not only in Holland, but in Norway and Sweden and Denmark? It's mostly merchants who buy them, and rich tradesmen. You can't imagine what the winters are like in those countries, so long and dark and cold. They like to think that Italy is like my pictures. That's what they expect. That's what I expected Italy to be before I came here.'

And I think that was the vision that had remained with him always, dazzling his eyes so that he could not see the truth; and notwithstanding the brutality of fact, he continued to see with the eyes of the spirit an Italy of romantic brigands and picturesque ruins. It was an ideal that he painted–a poor one, common, and shop-soiled, but still it was an ideal; and it gave his character a definite charm. ,

It was because I felt this that Dirk Stroeve was not to me, as to others, merely an object of ridicule. His fellow-painters made no secret of their contempt for his work, but he earned a fair amount of money, and they did not hesitate to make free use of his purse. He was generous, and the needy, laughing at him because he believed so naïvely their stories of distress, borrowed from him with effrontery. He was very emotional, yet his feeling, so easily aroused, had in it something absurd, so that you accepted his kindness, but felt no gratitude. To take money from him was like robbing a child, and you despised him because he was so foolish. I imagine that a pickpocket, proud of his light fingers, must feel a sort of indignation with the careless woman who leaves in a cab a vanity-bag with all her jewels in it. Nature had made him a butt, but had denied him insensibility. He writhed under the jokes, practical and otherwise, which were perpetually made at his expense, and yet never ceased, it seemed wilfully, to expose himself to them. He was constantly wounded, and yet his good-nature was such that he could not bear malice: the viper might sting him, but he never learned by experience, and had no sooner recovered from his pain than he tenderly placed it once more in his bosom. His life was a tragedy written in the terms of knock-about farce. Because I did not laugh at him he was grateful to me, and he used to pour into my sympathetic ear the long list of his troubles. The saddest thing about them was they they were grotesque, and the more pathetic they were, the more you wanted to laugh.

But though so bad a painter, he had a very delicate feeling for art, and to go with him to picture-galleries was a rare treat. His enthusiasm was sincere and his criticism acute. He was catholic. He had not only a true appreciation of the old masters, but sympathy with the moderns. He was quick to discover talent, and his praise was generous. I think I have never known a man whose judgment was surer. And he was better educated than most painters. He was not, like most of them, ignorant of kindred arts, and his taste for music and literature gave depth and variety to his comprehension of painting. To a young man like myself his advice and guidance were of incomparable value.

When I left Rome I corresponded with him, and about once in two months received from him long letters in queer English, which brought before me vividly his spluttering, enthusiastic, gesticulating conversation. Some time before I went to Paris he had married an Englishwoman, and was now settled in a studio in Montmartre. I had not seen him for four years, and had never met his wife.

Chapter Nineteen

I had not announced my arrival to Stroeve, and when I rang the bell of his studio, on opening the door himself, for a moment he did not know me. Then he gave a cry of delighted surprise and drew me in. It was charming to be welcomed with so much eagerness. His wife was seated near the stove at her sewing, and she rose as I came in. He introduced me.

'Don't you remember?' he said to her. 'I've talked to you about him often.' And then to me: 'But why didn't you let me know you were coming? How long have you been here? How long are you going to stay? Why didn't you come here an hour earlier, and we would have dined together?'

He bombarded me with questions. He sat me down in a chair, patting me as though I were a cushion, pressed cigars upon me, cakes, wine. He could not leave me alone. He was heart-broken because he had no whisky, wanted to make coffee for me, racked his brain for something he could possibly do for me, and beamed and laughed, and in the exuberance of his delight sweated at every pore.

'You haven't changed,' I said, smiling, as I looked at him.

He had the same absurd appearance that I remembered. He was a fat little man, with short legs, young still–he could not have been more than thirty–but prematurely bald. His face was perfectly round, and he had a very high colour, a white skin, red cheeks, and red lips. His eyes were blue and round, too, he wore large gold-rimmed spectacles, and his eyebrows were so fair you could not see them. He reminded you of those jolly fat merchants that Rubens painted.

When I told him that I meant to live in Paris for a while, and had taken an apartment, he reproached me bitterly for not having let him know. He would have found me an apartment himself, and lent me furniture–did I really mean that I had gone to the expense of buying it?–and he would have helped me to move in. He really looked upon it as unfriendly that I had not given him the opportunity of making himself useful to me. Meanwhile, Mrs Stroeve sat quietly mending her stockings, without talking, and she listened to all he said with a quiet smile on her lips.

'So, you see, I'm married,' he said suddenly; 'what do you think of my wife?'

He beamed at her, and settled his spectacles on the bridge of his nose. The sweat made them constantly slip down.

'What on earth do you expect me to say to that?' I laughed.

'Really, Dirk,' put in Mrs Stroeve, smiling.

'But isn't she wonderful? I tell you, my boy, lose no time; get married as soon as ever you can. I'm the happiest man alive. Look at her sitting there.

Doesn't she make a picture? Chardin, eh? I've seen all the most beautiful women in the world; I've never seen anyone more beautiful than Madame Dirk Stroeve.'

'If you don't be quiet, Dirk, I shall go away.'

'*Mon petit choux*,' he said.

She flushed a little, embarrassed by the passion of his tone. His letters had told me that he was very much in love with his wife, and I saw that he could hardly take his eyes off her. I could not tell if she loved him. Poor pantaloon, he was not an object to excite love, but the smile in her eyes was affectionate, and it was possible that her reserve concealed a very deep feeling. She was not the ravishing creature that his love-sick fancy saw, but she had a grave comeliness. She was rather tall, and her grey dress, simple and well-cut, did not hide the fact that her figure was beautiful. It was a figure that might have appealed more to the sculptor than to the costumier. Her hair, brown and abundant, was plainly done, her face was very pale, and her features were good without being distinguished. She had quiet grey eyes. She just missed being beautiful, and in missing it was not even pretty. But when Stroeve spoke of Chardin it was not without reason, and she reminded me curiously of that pleasant housewife in her mob-cap and apron whom the great painter has immortalised. I could imagine her sedately busy among her pots and pans, making a ritual of her household duties, so that they acquired a moral significance; I did not suppose that she was clever or could ever be amusing, but there was something in her grave intentness which excited my interest. Her reserve was not without mystery. I wondered why she had married Dirk Stroeve. Though she was English, I could not exactly place her, and it was not obvious from what rank in society she sprang, what had been her upbringing, or how she had lived before her marriage. She was very silent, but when she spoke it was with a pleasant voice, and her manners were natural.

I asked Stroeve if he was working.

'Working? I'm painting better than I've ever painted before.'

We sat in the studio, and he waved his hand to an unfinished picture on an easel. I gave a little start. He was painting a group of Italian peasants, in the costume of the Campagna, lounging on the steps of a Roman church.

'Is that what you're doing now?' I asked.

'Yes. I can get my models here just as well as in Rome.'

'Don't you think it's very beautiful?' said Mrs Stroeve.

'This foolish wife of mine thinks I'm a great artist,' said he.

His apologetic laugh did not disguise the pleasure that he felt. His eyes lingered on the picture. It was strange that his critical sense, so accurate and unconventional when he dealt with the work of others, should be satisfied in himself with what was hackneyed and vulgar beyond belief.

'Show him some more of your pictures,' she said.

'Shall I?'

Though he had suffered so much from the ridicule of his friends, Dirk Stroeve, eager for praise and naïvely self-satisfied, could never resist displaying his work. He brought out a picture of two curly-headed Italian urchins playing marbles.

'Aren't they sweet?' said Mrs Stroeve.

And then he showed me more. I discovered that in Paris he had been painting the same stale, obviously picturesque things that he had painted for years in Rome. It was all false, insincere, shoddy; and yet no one was more honest, sincere, and frank than Dirk Stroeve. Who could resolve the contradiction?

I do not know what put it into my head to ask:

'I say, have you by any chance run across a painter called Charles Strickland?'

'You don't mean to say you know him?' cried Stroeve.

'Beast,' said his wife.

Stroeve laughed.

'*Ma pauvre chérie.*' He went over to her and kissed both her hands. 'She doesn't like him. How strange that you should know Strickland!'

'I don't like bad manners,' said Mrs Stroeve.

Dirk, laughing still, turned to me to explain.

'You see, I asked him to come here one day and look at my pictures. Well, he came, and I showed him everything I had.' Stroeve hesitated a moment with embarrassment. I do not know why he had begun a story against himself; he felt an awkwardness at finishing it. 'He looked at–at my pictures, and he didn't say anything. I thought he was reserving his judgment till the end. And at last I said: "There, that's the lot!" He said: "I came to ask you to lend me twenty francs."'

'And Dirk actually gave it him,' said his wife indignantly.

'I was so taken aback. I didn't like to refuse. He put the money in his pocket, just nodded, said "Thanks", and walked out.'

Dirk Stroeve, telling the story, had such a look of blank astonishment on his round, foolish face that it was almost impossible not to laugh.

'I shouldn't have minded if he'd said my pictures were bad, but he said nothing–nothing.'

'And you *will* tell the story, Dirk,' said his wife.

It was lamentable that one was more amused by the ridiculous figure cut by the Dutchman than outraged by Strickland's brutal treatment of him.

'I hope I shall never see him again,' said Mrs Stroeve.

Stroeve smiled and shrugged his shoulders. He had already recovered his good-humour.

'The fact remains that he's a great artist, a very great artist.'

'Strickland?' I exclaimed. 'It can't be the same man.'

'A big fellow with a red beard. Charles Strickland. An Englishman.'

'He had no beard when I knew him, but if he has grown one it might well be red. The man I'm thinking of only began painting five years ago.'

'That's it. He's a great artist.'

'Impossible.'

'Have I ever been mistaken?' Dirk asked me. 'I tell you he has genius. I'm convinced of it. In a hundred years if you and I are remembered at all, it will be because we knew Charles Strickland.'

I was astonished, and at the same time I was very much excited. I remembered suddenly my last talk with him.

'Where can one see his work?' I asked. 'Is he having any success? Where is he living?'

'No; he has no success. I don't think he's ever sold a picture. When you speak to men about him they only laugh. But I *know* he's a great artist. After all, they laughed at Manet. Corot never sold a picture. I don't know where he lives, but I can take you to see him. He goes to a café in the Avenue de Clichy at seven o'clock every evening. If you like we'll go there to-morrow.'

'I'm not sure if he'll wish to see me. I think I may remind him of a time he prefers to forget. But I'll come all the same. Is there any chance of seeing any of his pictures?'

'Not from him. He won't show you a thing. There's a little dealer I know who has two or three. But you mustn't go without me, you wouldn't understand. I must show them to you myself.'

'Dirk, you make me impatient,' said Mrs Stroeve. 'How can you talk like that about his pictures when he treated you as he did?' She turned to me. 'Do you know, when some Dutch people came here to buy Dirk's pictures he tried to persuade them to buy Strickland's? He insisted on bringing them here to show.'

'What did *you* think of them?' I asked her, smiling.

'They were awful.'

'Ah, sweetheart, you don't understand.'

'Well, your Dutch people were furious with you. They thought you were having a joke with them.'

Dirk Stroeve took off his spectacles and wiped them. His flushed face was shining with excitement.

'Why should you think that beauty, which is the most precious thing in the world, lies like a stone on the beach for the careless passer-by to pick up idly? Beauty is something wonderful and strange that the artist fashions out of the chaos of the world in the torment of his soul. And when he has made it, it is not given to all to know it. To recognise it you must repeat the adventure of the artist. It is a melody that he sings to you, and to hear it again in your own heart you want knowledge and sensitiveness and imagination.'

'Why did I always think your pictures beautiful, Dirk? I admired them the very first time I saw them.'

Stroeve's lips trembled a little.

'Go to bed, my precious. I will walk a few steps with our friend, and then I will come back.'

Chapter Twenty

Dirk Stroeve agreed to fetch me on the following evening and take me to the café at which Strickland was most likely to be found. I was interested to learn that it was the same as that at which Strickland and I had drunk absinthe when I had gone over to Paris to see him. The fact that he had never changed suggested a sluggishness of habit which seemed to me characteristic.

'There he is,' said Stroeve, as we reached the café.

Though it was October, the evening was warm, and the tables on the pavement were crowded. I ran my eyes over them, but did not see Strickland.

'Look. Over there, in the corner. He's playing chess.'

I noticed a man bending over a chess-board, but could see only a large felt hat and a red beard. We threaded our way among the tables till we came to him.

'Strickland.'

He looked up.

'Hulloa, fatty. What do you want?'

'I've brought an old friend to see you.'

Strickland gave me a glance, and evidently did not recognise me. He resumed his scrutiny of the chess-board.

'Sit down, and don't make a noise,' he said.

He moved a piece and straightway became absorbed in the game. Poor Stroeve gave me a troubled look, but I was not disconcerted by so little. I ordered something to drink, and waited quietly till Strickland had finished. I welcomed the opportunity to examine him at my ease. I certainly should never have known him. In the first place his red beard, ragged and untrimmed, hid much of his face, and his hair was long; but the most surprising change in him was his extreme thinness. It made his great nose protrude more arrogantly; it emphasised his cheek-bones; it made his eyes seem larger. There were deep hollows at his temples. His body was cadaverous. He wore the same suit that I had seen him in five years before; it was torn and stained, threadbare, and it hung upon him loosely, as though it had been made for someone else. I noticed his hands, dirty, with long nails; they were merely bone and sinew, large and strong; but I had forgotten that they were so shapely. He gave me an extraordinary impression as he sat there, his attention riveted on his game—an impression of great strength; and I could not understand why it was that his emaciation somehow made it more striking.

Presently, after moving, he leaned back and gazed with a curious abstraction at his antagonist. This was a fat, bearded Frenchman. The Frenchman considered the position, then broke suddenly into jovial expletives, and with an impatient gesture, gathering up the pieces, flung them into their box. He cursed Strickland freely, then, calling for the waiter, paid for the drinks, and left. Stroeve drew his chair closer to the table.

'Now I suppose we can talk,' he said.

Strickland's eyes rested on him, and there was in them a malicious expression. I felt sure he was seeking for some gibe, could think of none, and so was forced to silence.

'I've brought an old friend to see you,' repeated Stroeve, beaming cheerfully.

Strickland looked at me thoughtfully for nearly a minute. I did not speak.

'I've never seen him in my life,' he said.

I do not know why he said this, for I felt certain I had caught a gleam of recognition in his eyes. I was not so easily abashed as I had been some years earlier.

'I saw you wife the other day,' I said. 'I felt sure you'd like to have the latest news of her.'

He gave a short laugh. His eyes twinkled.

'We had a jolly evening together,' he said. 'How long ago is it?'

'Five years.'

He called for another absinthe. Stroeve, with voluble tongue, explained how he and I had met, and by what an accident we discovered that we both knew Strickland. I do not know if Strickland listened. He glanced at me once or twice reflectively, but for the most part seemed occupied with his own thoughts; and certainly without Stroeve's babble the conversation would have been difficult. In half an hour the Dutchman, looking at his watch, announced that he must go. He asked whether I would come too. I thought, alone, I might get something out of Strickland, and so answered that I would stay.

When the fat man had left I said:

'Dirk Stroeve thinks you're a great artist.'

'What the hell do you suppose I care?'

'Will you let me see your pictures?'

'Why should I?'

'I might feel inclined to buy one.'

'I might not feel inclined to sell one.'

'Are you making a good living?' I asked, smiling. He chuckled.

'Do I look it?'

'You look half starved.'

'I am half starved.'

'Then come and let's have a bit of dinner.'

'Why do you ask me?'

'Not out of charity,' I answered coolly. 'I don't really care a twopenny damn if you starve or not.'

His eyes lit up again.

'Come on, then,' he said, getting up. 'I'd like a decent meal.'

Chapter Twenty-one

I let him take me to a restaurant of his choice, but on the way I bought a paper. When we had ordered our dinner, I propped it against a bottle of St Galmier and began to read. We ate in silence. I felt him looking at me now and again, but I took no notice. I meant to force him to conversation.

'Is there anything in the paper?' he said, as we approached the end of our silent meal.

I fancied there was in his tone a slight note of exasperation.

'I always like to read the *feuilleton* on the drama,' I said.

I folded the paper and put it down beside me.

'I've enjoyed my dinner,' he remarked.

'I think we might have our coffee here, don't you?'

'Yes.'

We lit our cigars. I smoked in silence. I noticed that now and then his eyes rested on me with a faint smile of amusement. I waited patiently.

'What have you been up to since I saw you last?' he asked at length.

I had not very much to say. It was a record of hard work and of little adventure; of experiments in this direction and in that; of the gradual acquisition of the knowledge of books and of men. I took care to ask Strickland nothing about his own doings. I showed not the least interest in him, and at last I was rewarded. He began to talk of himself. But with his poor gift of expression he gave but indications of what he had gone through, and I had to fill up the gaps with my own imagination. It was tantalising to get no more than hints into a character that interested me so much. It was like making one's way through a mutilated manuscript. I received the impression of a life which was a bitter struggle against every sort of difficulty; but I realised that much which would have seemed horrible to most people did not in the least affect him. Strickland was distinguished from most Englishmen by his perfect indifference to comfort; it did not irk him to live always in one shabby room; he had no need to be surrounded by beautiful things. I do not suppose he had ever noticed how dingy was the paper on the wall of the room in which on my first visit I found him. He did not want arm-chairs to sit in; he really felt more at his ease on a kitchen chair. He ate with appetite, but was indifferent to what he ate; to him it was only food that he devoured to still the pangs of hunger; and when no food was to be had he seemed capable of doing without it. I learned that for six months he had lived on a loaf of bread and a bottle of milk a day. He was a sensual man, and yet was indifferent to sensual things. He looked upon privation as no hardship. There was something impressive in the manner in which he lived a life wholly of the spirit.

When the small sum of money which he brought with him from London came to an end he suffered from no dismay. He sold no pictures; I think he made little attempt to sell any; he set about finding some way to make a bit of money. He told me with grim humour of the time he had spent acting as guide to Cockneys who wanted to see the night side of life in Paris; it was an occupation that appealed to his sardonic temper; and somehow or other he had acquired a wide acquaintance with the more disreputable quarters of the city. He told me of the long hours he spent walking about the Boulevard de la Madeleine on the look-out for Englishmen, preferably the worse for liquor, who desired to see things which the law forbade. When in luck he was able to make a tidy sum; but the shabbiness of his clothes at last frightened the sightseers, and he could not find people adventurous enough to trust themselves to him. Then he happened on a job to translate the advertisements of patent medicines which were sent broadcast to the medical profession in England. During a strike he had been employed as a house-painter.

Meanwhile he had never ceased to work at his art; but soon tiring of the studios, entirely by himself. He had never been so poor that he could not buy canvas and paint, and really he needed nothing else. So far as I could make out, he painted with great difficulty, and in his unwillingness to accept help from anyone lost much time in finding out for himself the solution of technical problems which preceding generations had already worked out one by one. He was aiming at something, I knew not what, and perhaps he hardly knew himself; and I got again more strongly the impression of a man possessed. He did not seem quite sane. It seemed to me that he would not show his pictures because he was really not interested in them. He lived in a dream, and the reality meant nothing to him. I had the feeling that he worked on a canvas with all the force of his violent personality, oblivious of everything in his effort to get what he saw with the mind's eye; and then, having finished, not the picture perhaps, for I had an idea that he seldom brought anything to completion, but the passion that fired him, he lost all care for it. He was never satisfied with what he had done; it seemed to him of no consequence compared with the vision that obsessed his mind.

'Why don't you ever send your work to exhibitions?' I asked. 'I should have thought you'd like to know what people thought about it.'

'Would you?'

I cannot describe the unmeasurable contempt he put into the two words.

'Don't you want fame? It's something that most artists haven't been indifferent to.'

'Children. How can you care for the opinion of the crowd, when you don't care twopence for the opinion of the individual?'

'We're not all reasonable beings,' I laughed.

'Who makes fame? Critics, writers, stockbrokers, women.'

'Wouldn't it give you a rather pleasant sensation to think of people you didn't know and had never seen receiving emotions, subtle and passionate, from the work of your hands? Everyone likes power. I can't imagine a more wonderful exercise of it than to move the souls of men to pity or terror.'

'Melodrama.'

'Why do you mind if you paint well or badly?'

'I don't. I only want to paint what I see.'

'I wonder if I could write on a desert island, with the certainty that no eyes but mine would ever see what I had written.'

Strickland did not speak for a long time, but his eyes shone strangely, as though he saw something that kindled his soul to ecstasy.

'Sometimes I've thought of an island lost in a boundless sea, where I could live in some hidden valley, among strange trees, in silence. There I think I could find what I want.'

He did not express himself quite like this. He used gestures instead of adjectives, and he halted. I have put into my own words what I think he wanted to say.

'Looking back on the last five years, do you think it was worth it?' I asked.

He looked at me, and I saw that he did not know what I meant. I explained.

'You gave up a comfortable home and a life as happy as the average. You were fairly prosperous. You seem to have had a rotten time in Paris. If you had your time over again would you do what you did?'

'Rather.'

'Do you know that you haven't asked anything about your wife and children? Do you ever think of them?'

'No.'

'I wish you weren't so damned monosyllabic. Have you never had a moment's regret for all the unhappiness you caused them?'

His lips broke into a smile, and he shook his head.

'I should have thought sometimes you couldn't help thinking of the past. I don't mean the past of seven or eight years ago, but further back still, when you first met your wife, and loved her, and married her. Don't you remember the joy with which you first took her in your arms?'

'I don't think of the past. The only thing that matters is the everlasting present.'

I thought for a moment over this reply. It was obscure, perhaps, but I thought that I saw dimly his meaning.

'Are you happy?' I asked.

'Yes.'

I was silent. I looked at him reflectively. He held my stare, and presently a sardonic twinkle lit up his eyes.

'I'm afraid you disapprove me?'

'Nonsense,' I answered promptly; 'I don't disapprove of the boa-constrictor; on the contrary, I'm interested in his mental processes.'

'It's a purely professional interest you take in me?'

'Purely.'

'It's only right that you shouldn't disapprove of me. You have a despicable character.'

'Perhaps that's why you feel at home with me,' I retorted.

He smiled dryly, but said nothing. I wish I knew how to describe his smile. I do not know that it was attractive, but it lit up his face, changing the expression, which was generally sombre, and gave it a look of not ill-natured malice. It was a slow smile, starting and sometimes ending in the eyes; it was very sensual, neither cruel nor kindly, but suggested rather the inhuman glee of the satyr. It was his smile that made me ask him:

'Haven't you been in love since you came to Paris?'

'I haven't got time for that sort of nonsense. Life isn't long enough for love and art.'

'Your appearance doesn't suggest the anchorite.'

'All that business fills me with disgust.'

'Human nature is a nuisance, isn't it?' I said.

'Why are you sniggering at me?'

'Because I don't believe you.'

'Then you're a damned fool.'

I paused, and I looked at him searchingly.

'What's the good of trying to humbug me?' I said.

'I don't know what you mean.'

I smiled.

'Let me tell you. I imagine that for months the matter never comes into your head, and you're able to persuade yourself that you've finished with it for good and all. You rejoice in your freedom, and you feel that at last you can call your soul your own. You seem to walk with your head among the stars. And then, all of a sudden you can't stand it any more, and you notice that all the time your feet have been walking in the mud. And you want to roll yourself in it. And you find some woman, coarse and low and vulgar, some beastly creature in whom all the horror of sex is blatant, and you fall upon her like a wild animal. You drink till you're blind with rage.'

He stared at me without the slightest movement. I held his eyes with mine. I spoke very slowly.

'I'll tell you what must seem strange, that when it's over you feel so extraordinarily pure. You feel like a disembodied spirit, immaterial; and you seem to be able to touch beauty as though it were a palpable thing; and you feel an intimate communion with the breeze, and with the trees breaking into leaf, and with the iridescence of the river. You feel like God. Can you explain that to me?'

He kept his eyes fixed on mine till I had finished, and then he turned away. There was on his face a strange look, and I thought that so might a man look when he had died under the torture. He was silent. I knew that our conversation was ended.

Chapter Twenty-two

I settled down in Paris and began to write a play. I led a very regular life, working in the morning, and in the afternoon lounging about the gardens of the Luxembourg or sauntering through the streets. I spent long hours in the Louvre, the most friendly of all galleries and the most convenient for meditation; or idled on the quays, fingering second-hand books that I never meant to buy. I read a page here and there, and made acquaintance with a great many authors whom I was content to know desultorily. In the evenings I went to see my friends. I looked in often on the Stroeves, and sometimes shared their modest fare. Dirk Stroeve flattered himself on his skill in cooking Italian dishes, and I confess that his *spaghetti* were very much better than his pictures. It was a dinner for a King when he brought in a huge dish of it, succulent with tomatoes, and we ate it together with the good household bread and a bottle of red wine. I grew more intimate with Blanche Stroeve, and I think, because I was English and she knew few English people, she was glad to see me. She was pleasant and simple, but she remained always rather silent, and, I knew not why, gave me the impression that she was concealing something. But I thought that was perhaps no more than a natural reserve accentuated by the verbose frankness of her husband. Dirk never concealed anything. He discussed the most intimate matters with a complete lack of self-consciousness. Sometimes he embarrassed his wife, and the only time I saw her put out of countenance was when he insisted on telling me that he had taken a purge, and went into somewhat realistic details on the subject. The perfect seriousness with which he narrated his misfortunes convulsed me with laughter, and this added to Mrs Stroeve's irritation.

'You seem to like making a fool of yourself,' she said.

His round eyes grew rounder still, and his brow puckered in dismay as he saw that she was angry.

'Sweetheart, have I vexed you? I'll never take another. It was only because I was bilious. I lead a sedentary life. I don't take enough exercise. For three days I hadn't . . .'

'For goodness' sake, hold your tongue,' she interrupted, tears of annoyance in her eyes.

His face fell, and he pouted his lips like a scolded child. He gave me a look of appeal, so that I might put things right, but, unable to control myself, I shook with helpless laughter.

We went one day to the picture-dealer in whose shop Stroeve thought he could show me at least two or three of Strickland's pictures, but when we arrived were told that Strickland himself had taken them away. The dealer did not know why.

'But don't imagine to yourself that I make myself bad blood on that account. I took them to oblige Monsieur Stroeve, and I said I would sell them if I could. But really—' He shrugged his shoulders. 'I'm interested in the young men, but *voyons*, you yourself, Monsieur Stroeve, you don't think there's any talent there.'

'I give you my word of honour, there's no one painting today in whose talent I am more convinced. Take my word for it, you are missing a good affair. Some day those pictures will be worth more than all you have in your shop. Remember Monet, who could not get anyone to buy his pictures for a hundred francs. What are they worth now?'

'True. But there were a hundred as good painters as Monet who couldn't sell their pictures at that time, and their pictures are worth nothing still. How can one tell? Is merit enough to bring success? Don't believe it. *Du reste*, it has still to be proved that this friend of yours has merit. No one claims it for him but Monsieur Stroeve.'

'And how, then, will you recognise merit?' asked Dirk, red in the face with anger.

'There is only one way—by success.'

'Philistine,' cried Dirk.

'But think of the great artists of the past—Raphael, Michael Angelo, Ingres, Delacroix—they were all successful.'

'Let us go,' said Stroeve to me, 'or I shall kill this man.'

Chapter Twenty-three

I saw Strickland not infrequently, and now and then played chess with him. He was of uncertain temper. Sometimes he would sit silent and abstracted, taking no notice of anyone; and at others, when he was in a good humour, he would talk in his own halting way. He never said a clever thing, but he had a vein of brutal sarcasm which was not ineffective, and he always said exactly what he thought. He was indifferent to the susceptibilities of others, and when he wounded them was amused. He was constantly offending Dirk Stroeve so bitterly that he flung away, vowing he would never speak to him again; but there was a solid force in Strickland that attracted the fat Dutchman against his will, so that he came back, fawning like a clumsy dog, though he knew that his only greeting would be the blow he dreaded.

I do not know why Strickland put up with me. Our relations were peculiar. One day he asked me to lend him fifty francs.

'I wouldn't dream of it,' I replied.

'Why not?'

'It wouldn't amuse me.'

'I'm frightfully hard up, you know.'

'I don't care.'

'You don't care if I starve?'

'Why on earth should I?' I asked in my turn.

He looked at me for a minute or two, pulling his untidy beard. I smiled at him.

'What are you amused at?' he said, with a gleam of anger in his eyes.

'You're so simple. You recognise no obligations. No one is under any obligation to you.'

'Wouldn't it make you uncomfortable if I went and hanged myself because I'd been turned out of my room as I couldn't pay the rent?'

'Not a bit.'

He chuckled.

'You're bragging. If I really did you'd be overwhelmed with remorse.'

'Try it, and we'll see,' I retorted.

A smile flickered in his eyes, and he stirred his absinthe in silence.

'Would you like to play chess?' I asked.

'I don't mind.'

We set up the pieces, and when the board was ready he considered it with a comfortable eye. There is a sense of satisfaction in looking at your men all ready for the fray.

'Did you really think I'd lend you money?' I asked.

'I didn't see why you shouldn't.'

'You surprise me.'

'Why?'

'It's disappointing to find that at heart you are sentimental. I should have liked you better if you hadn't made that ingenuous appeal to my sympathies.'

'I should have despised you if you'd been moved by it,' he answered.

'That's better,' I laughed.

We began to play. We were both absorbed in the game. When it was finished I said to him:

'Look here, if you're hard up, let me see your pictures. If there's anything I like I'll buy it.'

'Go to hell,' he answered.

He got up and was about to go away. I stopped him.

'You haven't paid for your absinthe,' I said, smiling.

He cursed me, flung down the money, and left.

I did not see him for several days after that, but one evening, when I was sitting in the café, reading a paper, he came up and sat beside me.

'You haven't hanged yourself after all,' I remarked.

'No. I've got a commission. I'm painting the portrait of a retired plumber for two hundred francs.'*

'How did you manage that?'

'The woman where I get my bread recommended me. He'd told her he was looking out for someone to paint him. I've got to give her twenty francs.'

'What's he like?'

'Splendid. He's got a great red face like a leg of mutton, and on his right cheek there's an enormous mole with long hairs growing out of it.'

Strickland was in a good humour, and when Dirk Stroeve came up and sat down with us he attacked him with ferocious banter. He showed a skill I should never have credited him with in finding the places where the unhappy Dutchman was most sensitive. Strickland employed not the rapier of sarcasm but the bludgeon of invective. The attack was so unprovoked that Stroeve, taken unawares, was defenceless. He reminded you of a frightened sheep running aimlessly hither and thither. He was startled and amazed. At last the tears ran from his eyes. And the worst of it was that, though you hated Strickland, and the exhibition was horrible, it was impossible not to laugh. Dirk Stroeve was one of those unlucky persons whose most sincere emotions are ridiculous.

But after all when I look back upon that winter in Paris, my pleasantest recollection is of Dirk Stroeve. There was something very charming in his little household. He and his wife made a picture which the imagination gratefully dwelt upon, and the simplicity of his love for her had a deliberate grace. He remained absurd, but the sincerity of his passion excited one's sympathy. I could understand how his wife must feel for him, and I was glad that her affection was so tender. If she had any sense of humour, it must amuse her that he should place her on a pedestal and worship her with such an honest idolatry, but even while she laughed she must have been pleased and touched. He was the constant lover, and though she grew old, losing her rounded lines and her fair comeliness, to him she would certainly never alter. To him she would always be the loveliest woman in the world. There was a pleasing grace in the orderliness of their lives. They had but the studio,

---

* This picture, formerly in the possession of a wealthy manufacturer at Lille, who fled from that city on the approach of the Germans, is now in the National Gallery at Stockholm. The Swede is adept at the gentle pastime of fishing in troubled waters.

a bedroom, and a tiny kitchen. Mrs Stroeve did all the housework herself; and while Dirk painted bad pictures, she went marketing, cooked the luncheon, sewed, occupied herself like a busy ant all the day; and in the evening sat in the studio, sewing again, while Dirk played music which I am sure was far beyond her comprehension. He played with taste, but with more feeling than was always justified, and into his music poured all his honest, sentimental, exuberant soul.

Their life in its own way was an idyll, and it managed to achieve a singular beauty. The absurdity that clung to everything connected with Dirk Stroeve gave it a curious note, like an unresolved discord, but made it somehow more modern, more human; like a rough joke thrown into a serious scene, it heightened the poignancy which all beauty has.

Chapter Twenty-four

Shortly before Christmas Dirk Stroeve came to ask me to spend the holiday with him. He had a characteristic sentimentality about the day and wanted to pass it among his friends with suitable ceremonies. Neither of us had seen Strickland for two or three weeks—I because I had been busy with friends who were spending a little while in Paris, and Stroeve because, having quarrelled with him more violently than usual, he had made up his mind to have nothing more to do with him. Strickland was impossible, and he swore never to speak to him again. But the season touched him with gentle feeling, and he hated the thought of Strickland spending Christmas Day by himself; he ascribed his own emotions to him, and could not bear that on an occasion given up to good-fellowship the lonely painter should be abandoned to his own melancholy. Stroeve had set up a Christmas tree in his studio, and I suspected that we should both find absurd little presents hanging on its festive branches; but he was shy about seeing Strickland again; it was a little humiliating to forgive so easily insults so outrageous, and he wished me to be present at the reconciliation on which he was determined.

We walked together down the Avenue de Clichy, but Strickland was not in the café. It was too cold to sit outside, and we took our places on leather benches within. It was hot and stuffy, and the air was grey with smoke. Strickland did not come, but presently we saw the French painter who occasionally played chess with him. I had formed a casual acquaintance with him, and he sat down at our table. Stroeve asked him if he had seen Strickland.

'He's ill,' he said. 'Didn't you know?'

'Seriously?'

'Very, I understand.'

Stroeve's face grew white.

'Why didn't he write and tell me? How stupid of me to quarrel with him! We must go to him at once. He can have no one to look after him. Where does he live?'

'I have no idea,' said the Frenchman.

We discovered that none of us knew how to find him. Stroeve grew more and more distressed.

'He might die, and not a soul would know anything about it. It's dreadful. I can't bear the thought. We must find him at once.'

I tried to make Stroeve understand that it was absurd to hunt vaguely about Paris. We must first think of some plan.

'Yes; but all this time he may be dying, and when we get there it may be too late to do anything.'

'Sit still and let us think,' I said impatiently.

The only address I knew was the Hôtel des Belges, but Strickland had long left that, and they would have no recollection of him. With that queer idea of his to keep his whereabouts secret, it was unlikely that, on leaving, he had said where he was going. Besides, it was more than five years ago. I felt pretty sure that he had not moved far. If he continued to frequent the same café as when he had stayed at the hotel, it was probably because it was the most convenient. Suddenly I remembered that he had got his commission to paint a portrait through the baker from whom he bought his bread, and it struck me that there one might find his address. I called for a directory and looked out the bakers. There were five in the immediate neighbourhood, and the only thing was to go to all of them. Stroeve accompanied me unwillingly. His own plan was to run up and down the streets that led out of the Avenue de Clichy and ask at every house if Strickland lived there. My commonplace scheme was, after all, effective, for in the second shop we asked at the woman behind the counter acknowledged that she knew him. She was not certain where he lived, but it was in one of the three houses opposite. Luck favoured us, and in the first we tried the concierge told us that we should find him on the top floor.

'It appears that he's ill,' said Stroeve.

'It may be,' answered the concierge indifferently. '*En effet*, I have not seen him for several days.'

Stroeve ran up the stairs ahead of me, and when I reached the top floor I found him talking to a workman in his shirtsleeves who had opened a door at which Stroeve had knocked. He pointed to another door. He believed that the person who lived there was a painter. He had not seen him for a week. Stroeve made as though he were about to knock, and then turned to me with a gesture of helplessness. I saw that he was panic-stricken.

'Supposing he's dead?'

'Not he,' I said.

I knocked. There was no answer. I tried the handle, and found the door unlocked. I walked in, and Stroeve followed me. The room was in darkness. I could only see that it was an attic, with a sloping roof; and a faint glimmer, no more than a less profound obscurity, came from a skylight.

'Strickland,' I called.

There was no answer. It was really rather mysterious, and it seemed to me that Stroeve, standing just behind, was trembling in his shoes. For a moment I hesitated to strike a light. I dimly perceived a bed in the corner, and I wondered whether the light would disclose lying on it a dead body.

'Haven't you got a match, you fool?'

Strickland's voice, coming out of the darkness, harshly, made me start. Stroeve cried out:

'Oh, my God, I thought you were dead.'

I struck a match, and looked about for a candle. I had a rapid glimpse of a tiny apartment, half room, half studio, in which was nothing but a bed, canvases with their faces to the wall, an easel, a table, and a chair. There was no carpet on the floor. There was no fireplace. On the table, crowded with paints, palette-knives, and litter of all kinds, was the end of a candle. I lit it. Strickland was lying in the bed, uncomfortably because it was too small for him, and he had put all his clothes over him for warmth. It was obvious at a glance that he was in a high fever. Stroeve, his voice cracking with emotion, went up to him.

'Oh, my poor friend, what is the matter with you? I had no idea you were ill. Why didn't you let me know? You must know I'd have done anything in the world for you. Were you thinking of what I said? I didn't mean it. I was wrong. It was stupid of me to take offence.'

'Go to hell,' said Strickland.

'Now, be reasonable. Let me make you comfortable. Haven't you anyone to look after you?'

He looked round the squalid attic in dismay. He tried to arrange the bed-clothes. Strickland, breathing laboriously, kept an angry silence. He gave me a resentful glance. I stood quite quietly, looking at him.

'If you want to do something for me, you can get me some milk,' he said at last. 'I haven't been able to get out for two days.'

There was an empty bottle by the side of the bed, which had contained milk, and in a piece of newspaper a few crumbs.

'What have you been having?' I asked.

'Nothing.'

'For how long?' cried Stroeve. 'Do you mean to say you've had nothing to eat or drink for two days? It's horrible.'

'I've had water.'

His eyes dwelt for a moment on a large can within reach of an outstretched arm.

'I'll go immediately,' said Stroeve. 'Is there anything you fancy?'

I suggested that he should get a thermometer, and a few grapes, and some bread. Stroeve, glad to make himself useful, clattered down the stairs.

'Damned fool,' muttered Strickland.

I felt his pulse. It was beating quickly and feebly. I asked him one or two questions, but he would not answer, and when I pressed him he turned his face irritably to the wall. The only thing was to wait in silence. In ten minutes Stroeve, panting, came back. Besides what I had suggested, he brought candles, and meat-juice, and a spirit-lamp. He was a practical little fellow, and without delay set about making bread-and-milk. I took Strickland's temperature. It was a hundred and four. He was obviously very ill.

Chapter Twenty-five

Presently we left him. Dirk was going home to dinner, and I proposed to find a doctor and bring him to see Strickland; but when we got down into the street, fresh after the stuffy attic, the Dutchman begged me to go immediately to his studio. He had something in mind which he would not tell me, but he insisted that it was very necessary for me to accompany him. Since I did not think a doctor could at the moment do any more than we had done, I consented. We found Blanche Stroeve laying the table for dinner. Dirk went up to her, and took both her hands.

'Dear one, I want you to do something for me,' he said.

She looked at him with the grave cheerfulness which was one of her charms. His red face was shining with sweat, and he had a look of comic agitation, but there was in his round, surprised eyes an eager light.

'Strickland is very ill. He may be dying. He is alone in a filthy attic, and there is not a soul to look after him. I want you to let me bring him here.'

She withdrew her hands quickly, I had never seen her make so rapid a movement, and her cheeks flushed.

'Oh no.'

'Oh, my dear one, don't refuse. I couldn't bear to leave him where he is. I shouldn't sleep a wink for thinking of him.'

'I have no objection to your nursing him.'

Her voice was cold and distant.

'But he'll die.'

'Let him.'

Stroeve gave a little gasp. He wiped his face. He turned to me for support, but I did not know what to say.

'He's a great artist.'

'What do I care? I hate him.'

'Oh, my love, my precious, you don't mean that. I beseech you to let me bring him here. We can make him comfortable. Perhaps we can save him. He shall be no trouble to you. I will do everything. We'll make him up a bed in the studio. We can't let him die like a dog. It would be inhuman.'

'Why can't he go to a hospital?'

'A hospital! He needs the care of loving hands. He must be treated with infinite tact.'

I was surprised to see how moved she was. She went on laying the table, but her hands trembled.

'I have no patience with you. Do you think if you were ill he would stir a finger to help you?'

'But what does that matter? I should have you to nurse me. It wouldn't be necessary. And besides, I'm different; I'm not of any importance.'

'You have no more spirit than a mongrel cur. You lie down on the ground and ask people to trample on you.'

Stroeve gave a little laugh. He thought he understood the reason for his wife's attitude.

'Oh, my poor dear, you're thinking of that day he came here to look at my pictures. What does it matter if he didn't think them any good? It was stupid of me to show them to him. I dare say they're not very good.'

He looked round the studio ruefully. On the easel was a half-finished picture of a smiling Italian peasant, holding a bunch of grapes over the head of a dark-eyed girl.

'Even if he didn't like them he should have been civil. He needn't have insulted you. He showed that he despised you, and you lick his hand. Oh, I hate him.'

'Dear child, he has genius. You don't think I believe that I have it. I wish I had; but I know it when I see it, and I honour it with all my heart. It's the most wonderful thing in the world. It's a great burden to its possessors. We should be very tolerant with them, and very patient.'

I stood apart, somewhat embarrassed by the domestic scene, and wondered why Stroeve had insisted on my coming with him. I saw that his wife was on the verge of tears.

'But it's not only because he's a genius that I ask you to let me bring him here; it's because he's a human being, and he is ill and poor.'

'I will never have him in my house—never.'

Stroeve turned to me.

'Tell her that it's a matter of life and death. It's impossible to leave him in that wretched hole.'

'It's quite obvious that it would be much easier to nurse him here,' I said, 'but of course it would be very inconvenient. I have an idea that someone will have to be with him day and night.'

'My love, it's not you who would shirk a little trouble.'

'If he comes here, I shall go,' said Mrs Stroeve violently.

'I don't recognise you. You're so good and kind.'

'Oh, for goodness' sake, let me be. You drive me to distraction.'

Then at last the tears came. She sank into a chair, and buried her face in her hands. Her shoulders shook convulsively. In a moment Dirk was on his knees beside her, with his arms round her, kissing her, calling her all sorts of pet names, and the facile tears ran down his own cheeks. Presently she released herself and dried her tears.

'Leave me alone,' she said, not unkindly; and then to me, trying to smile: 'What must you think of me?'

Stroeve, looking at her with perplexity, hesitated. His forehead was all puckered, and his red mouth set in a pout. He reminded me oddly of an agitated guinea-pig.

'Then it's No, darling?' he said at last.

She gave a gesture of lassitude. She was exhausted.

'The studio is yours. Everything belongs to you. If you want to bring him here, how can I prevent you?'

A sudden smile flashed across his round face.

'Then you consent? I knew you would. Oh, my precious.'

Suddenly she pulled herself together. She looked at him with haggard eyes. She clasped her hands over her heart as though its beating were intolerable.

'Oh, Dirk, I've never since we met asked you to do anything for me.'

'You know there's nothing in the world that I wouldn't do for you.'

'I beg you not to let Strickland come here. Anyone else you like. Bring a thief, a drunkard, any outcast off the streets, and I promise you I'll do everything I can for them gladly. But I beseech you not to bring Strickland here.'

'But why?'

'I'm frightened of him. I don't know why, but there's something in him that terrifies me. He'll do us some great harm. I know it. I feel it. If you bring him here it can only end badly.'

'But how unreasonable!'

'No, no. I know I'm right. Something terrible will happen to us.'

'Because we do a good action?'

She was panting now, and in her face was a terror which was inexplicable. I do not know what she thought. I felt that she was possessed by some shapeless dread which robbed her of all self-control. As a rule she was so calm; her agitation now was amazing. Stroeve looked at her for a while with puzzled consternation.

'You are my wife; you are dearer to me than anyone in the world. No one shall come here without your entire consent.'

She closed her eyes for a moment, and I thought she was going to faint. I was a little impatient with her; I had not suspected that she was so neurotic a woman. Then I heard Stroeve's voice again. It seemed to break oddly on the silence.

'Haven't you been in bitter distress once when a helping hand was held out to you? You know how much it means. Wouldn't you like to do someone a good turn when you have the chance?'

The words were ordinary enough, and to my mind there was in them something so hortatory that I almost smiled. I was astonished at the effect they had on Blanche Stroeve. She started a little, and gave her husband a long look. His eyes were fixed on the ground. I did not know why he seemed embarrassed. A faint colour came into her cheeks, and then her face became white—more than white, ghastly; you felt that the blood had shrunk away from the whole surface of her body; and even her hands were pale. A shiver passed through her. The silence of the studio seemed to gather body, so that it became an almost palpable presence. I was bewildered.

'Bring Strickland here, Dirk. I'll do my best for him.'

'My precious,' he smiled.

He wanted to take her in his arms, but she avoided him.

'Don't be affectionate before strangers, Dirk,' she said. 'It makes me feel such a fool.'

Her manner was quite normal again, and no one could have told that so shortly before she had been shaken by such a great emotion.

Chapter Twenty-six

Next day we moved Strickland. It needed a good deal of firmness and still more patience to induce him to come, but he was really too ill to offer any effective resistance to Stroeve's entreaties and to my determination. We dressed him, while he feebly cursed us, got him downstairs, into a cab, and eventually to Stroeve's studio. He was so exhausted by the time we arrived that he allowed us to put him to bed without a word. He was ill for six weeks. At one time it looked as though he could not live more than a few hours, and I am convinced that it was only through the Dutchman's doggedness that he pulled through. I have never known a more difficult patient. It was not that he was exacting and querulous; on the contrary, he never complained, he asked for nothing, he was perfectly silent; but he seemed to resent the care that was taken of him; he received all enquiries about his feelings or his needs with a jibe, a sneer, or an oath. I found him detestable, and as soon as he was out of danger I had no hesitation in telling him so.

'Go to hell,' he answered briefly.

Dirk Stroeve, giving up his work entirely, nursed Strickland with tenderness and sympathy. He was dexterous to make him comfortable, and he exercised a cunning of which I should never have thought him capable to induce him to take the medicines prescribed by the doctor. Nothing was too much trouble for him. Though his means were adequate to the needs of himself and his wife, he certainly had no money to waste; but now he was wantonly extravagant in the purchase of delicacies, out of season and dear, which might tempt Strickland's capricious appetite. I shall never forget the tactful patience with which he persuaded him to take nourishment. He was never put out by Strickland's rudeness; if it was merely sullen, he appeared not to notice it; if it was aggressive, he only chuckled. When Strickland, recovering somewhat, was in a good humour and amused himself by laughing at him, he deliberately did absurd things to excite his ridicule. Then he would give me little happy glances, so that I might notice in how much better form the patient was. Stroeve was sublime.

But it was Blanche who most surprised me. She proved herself not only a capable, but a devoted nurse. There was nothing in her to remind you that she had so vehemently struggled against her husband's wish to bring Strickland to the studio. She insisted on doing her share of the offices needful to the sick. She arranged his bed so that it was possible to change the sheet without disturbing him. She washed him. When I remarked on her competence, she told me with that pleasant little smile of hers that for a while she had worked in a hospital. She gave no sign that she hated Strickland so desperately. She did not speak to him much, but she was quick to forestall his wants. For a fortnight it was necessary that someone should stay with him all night, and she took turns watching with her husband. I wondered what she thought during the long darkness as she sat by the bedside. Strickland was a weird figure as he lay there, thinner than ever, with his ragged red beard and his eyes staring feverishly into vacancy; his illness seemed to have made them larger, and they had an unnatural brightness.

'Does he ever talk to you in the night?' I asked her once.

'Never.'

'Do you dislike him as much as you did?'

'More, if anything.'

She looked at me with her calm grey eyes. Her expression was so placid, it was hard to believe that she was capable of the violent emotion I had witnessed.

'Has he ever thanked you for what you do for him?'

'No,' she smiled.

'He's inhuman.'

'He's abominable.'

Stroeve was, of course, delighted with her. He could not do enough to show his gratitude for the whole-hearted devotion with which she had accepted the burden he laid on her. But he was a little puzzled by the behaviour of Blanche and Strickland towards one another.

'Do you know, I've seen them sit there for hours together without saying a word?'

On one occasion, when Strickland was so much better that in a day or two he was to get up, I sat with them in the studio. Dirk and I were talking. Mrs Stroeve sewed, and I thought I recognised the shirt she was mending as Strickland's. He lay on his back; he did not speak. Once I saw that his eyes were fixed on Blanche Stroeve, and there was in them a curious irony. Feeling their gaze, she raised her own, and for a moment they stared at one another. I could not quite understand her expression. Her eyes had in them a strange perplexity, and perhaps—but why?—alarm. In a moment Strickland looked away and idly surveyed the ceiling, but she continued to stare at him, and now her look was quite inexplicable.

In a few days Strickland began to get up. He was nothing but skin and bone. His clothes hung upon him like rags on a scarecrow. With his untidy beard and long hair, his features, always a little larger than life, now emphasised by illness, he had an extraordinary aspect; but it was so odd that it was not quite ugly. There was something monumental in his ugliness. I do not know how to express precisely the impression he made upon me. It was not exactly spirituality that was obvious, though the screen of the flesh seemed almost transparent, because there was in his face an outrageous sensuality; but, though it sounds nonsense, it seemed as though his sensuality were curiously spiritual. There was in him something primitive. He seemed to partake of those obscure forces of nature which the Greeks personified in shapes part human and part beast, the satyr and the faun. I thought of Marsyas, whom the god flayed because he had dared to rival him in song. Strickland seemed to bear in his heart strange harmonies and unadventured patterns, and I foresaw for him an end of torture and despair. I had again the feeling that he was possessed of a devil; but you could not say that it was a devil of evil, for it was a primitive force that existed before good and ill.

He was still too weak to paint, and he sat in the studio, silent, occupied with God knows what dreams, or reading. The books he liked were queer; sometimes I would find him poring over the poems of Mallarmé, and he read them as a child reads, forming the words with his lips, and I wondered what strange emotion he got from those subtle cadences and obscure phrases; and again I found him absorbed in the detective novels of Gaboriau. I amused myself by thinking that in his choice of books he showed pleasantly the irreconcilable sides of his fantastic nature. It was singular to notice that even in the weak state of his body he had no thought for its comfort. Stroeve liked his ease, and in his studio were a couple of heavily upholstered arm-chairs and a large divan. Strickland would not go near them, not from any affectation of stoicism, for I found him seated on a three-legged stool when I went into the studio one day and he was alone, but because he did not like them. For choice he sat on a kitchen chair without arms. It often exasperated me to see him. I never knew a man so entirely indifferent to his surroundings.

Chapter Twenty-seven

Two or three weeks passed. One morning, having come to a pause in my work, I thought I would give myself a holiday, and I went to the Louvre. I wandered about looking at the pictures I knew so well, and let my fancy play idly with the emotions they suggested. I sauntered into the long gallery, and there suddenly saw Stroeve. I smiled, for his appearance, so rotund and yet so startled, could never fail to excite a smile, and then as I came nearer I noticed that he seemed singularly disconsolate. He looked woebegone and yet ridiculous, like a man who has fallen into the water with all his clothes on, and, being rescued from death, frightened still, feels that he only looks a fool. Turning round, he stared at me, but I perceived that he did not see me. His round blue eyes looked harassed behind his glasses.

'Stroeve,' I said.

He gave a little start, and then smiled, but his smile was rueful.

'Why are you idling in this disgraceful fashion?' I asked gaily.

'It's a long time since I was at the Louvre. I thought I'd come and see if they had anything new.'

'But you told me you had to get a picture finished this week.'

'Strickland's painting in my studio.'

'Well?'

'I suggested it myself. He's not strong enough to go back to his own place yet. I thought we could both paint there. Lots of fellows in the Quarter share a studio. I thought it would be fun. I've always thought it would be jolly to have someone to talk to when one was tired of work.'

He said all this slowly, detaching statement from statement with a little awkward silence, and he kept his kind, foolish eyes fixed on mine. They were full of tears.

'I don't think I understand,' I said.

'Strickland can't work with anyone else in the studio.'

'Damn it all, it's your studio. That's his look-out.'

He looked at me pitifully. His lips were trembling.

'What happened?' I asked, rather sharply.

He hesitated and flushed. He glanced unhappily at one of the pictures on the wall.

'He wouldn't let me go on painting. He told me to get out.'

'But why didn't you tell him to go to hell?'

'He turned me out. I couldn't very well struggle with him. He threw my hat after after me, and locked the door.'

I was furious with Strickland, and was indignant with myself, because Dirk Stroeve cut such an absurd figure that I felt inclined to laugh.

'But what did your wife say?'

'She'd gone out to do the marketing.'

'Is he going to let her in?'

'I don't know.'

I gazed at Stroeve with perplexity. He stood like a schoolboy with whom a master is finding fault.

'Shall I get rid of Strickland for you?' I asked.

He gave a little start, and his shining face grew very red.

'No. You'd better not do anything.'

He nodded to me and walked away. It was clear that for some reason he did not want to discuss the matter. I did not understand.

Chapter Twenty-eight

The explanation came a week later. It was about ten o'clock at night; I had been dining by myself at a restaurant, and having returned to my small apartment, was sitting in my parlour, reading. I heard heard the cracked tinkling of the bell, and, going into the corridor, opened the door. Stroeve stood before me.

'Can I come in?' he asked.

In the dimness of the landing I could not see him very well, but there was something in his voice that surprised me. I knew he was of abstemious habit or I should have thought he had been drinking. I led the way into my sitting-room and asked him to sit down.

'Thank God I've found you,' he said.

'What's the matter?' I asked in astonishment at his vehemence.

I was able now to see him well. As a rule he was neat in his person, but now his clothes were in disorder. He looked suddenly bedraggled. I was convinced he had been drinking, and I smiled. I was on the point of chaffing him on his state.

'I didn't know where to go,' he burst out. 'I came here earlier, but you weren't in.'

'I dined late,' I said.

I changed my mind: it was not liquor that had driven him to this obvious desperation. His face, usually so rosy, was now strangely mottled. His hands trembled.

'Has anything happened?' I asked.

'My wife has left me.'

He could hardly get the words out. He gave a little gasp, and the tears began to trickle down his round cheeks. I did not know what to say. My first thought was that she had come to the end of her forbearance with his infatuation for Strickland, and, goaded by the latter's cynical behaviour, had insisted that he should be turned out. I knew her capable of temper, for all the calmness of her manner; and if Stroeve still refused, she might easily have flung out of the studio with vows never to return. But the little man was so distressed that I could not smile.

'My dear fellow, don't be unhappy. She'll come back. You mustn't take very seriously what women say when they're in a passion.'

'You don't understand. She's in love with Strickland.'

'What!' I was startled at this, but the idea had no sooner taken possession of me than I saw it was absurd.

'How can you be so silly? You don't mean to say you're jealous of Strickland?' I almost laughed. 'You know very well that she can't bear the sight of him.'

'You don't understand,' he moaned.

'You're an hysterical ass,' I said a little impatiently. 'Let me give you a whisky-and-soda, and you'll feel better.'

I supposed that for some reason or other—and Heaven knows what ingenuity men exercise to torment themselves—Dirk had got it into his head that his wife cared for Strickland, and with his genius for blundering he might quite well have offended her so that, to anger him, perhaps, she had taken pains to foster his suspicion.

'Look here,' I said, 'let's go back to your studio. If you've made a fool of yourself you must eat humble pie. Your wife doesn't strike me as the sort of woman to bear malice.'

'How can I go back to the studio?' he said wearily. 'They're there. I've left it to them.'

'Then it's not your wife who's left you; it's you who've left your wife.'

'For God's sake don't talk to me like that.'

Still I could not take him seriously. I did not for a moment believe what he had told me. But he was in very real distress.

'Well, you've come here to talk to me about it. You'd better tell me the whole story.'

'This afternoon I couldn't stand it any more. I went to Strickland and told him I thought he was quite well enough to go back to his own place. I wanted the studio myself.'

'No one but Strickland would have needed telling,' I said. 'What did he say?'

'He laughed a little; you know how he laughs, not as though he were amused, but as though you were a damned fool, and said he'd go at once. He began to put his things together. You remember I fetched from his room what I thought he needed, and he asked Blanche for a piece of paper and some string to make a parcel.'

Stroeve stopped, gasping, and I thought he was going to faint. This was not at all the story I had expected him to tell me.

'She was very pale, but she brought the paper and the string. He didn't say anything. He made the parcel and he whistled a tune. He took no notice of either of us. His eyes had an ironic smile in them. My heart was like lead. I was afraid something was going to happen, and I wished I hadn't spoken. He looked round for his hat. Then she spoke:

'"I'm going with Strickland, Dirk," she said. "I can't live with you any more."'

'I tried to speak, but the words wouldn't come. Strickland didn't say anything. He went on whistling as though it had nothing to do with him.'

Stroeve stopped again and mopped his face. I kept quite still. I believed him now, and I was astounded. But all the same I could not understand.

Then he told me, in a trembling voice, with the tears pouring down his cheeks, how he had gone up to her, trying to take her in his arms, but she had drawn away and begged him not to touch her. He implored her not to leave him. He told her how passionately he loved her, and reminded her of all the devotion he had lavished upon her. He spoke to her of the happiness of their life. He was not angry with her. He did not reproach her.

'Please let me go quietly, Dirk,' she said at last. 'Don't you understand that I love Strickland? Where he goes I shall go.'

'But you must know that he'll never make you happy. For your own sake don't go. You don't know what you've got to look forward to.'

'It's your fault. You insisted on his coming here.'

He turned to Strickland.

'Have mercy on her,' he implored him. 'You can't let her do anything so mad.'

'She can do as she chooses,' said Strickland. 'She's not forced to come.'

'My choice is made,' she said, in a dull voice.

Strickland's injurious calm robbed Stroeve of the rest of his self-control. Blind rage seized him, and without knowing what he was doing he flung himself on Strickland. Strickland was taken by surprise and he staggered, but he was very strong, even after his illness, and in a moment, he did not exactly know how, Stroeve found himself on the floor.

'You funny little man,' said Strickland.

Stroeve picked himself up. He noticed that his wife had remained perfectly still, and to be made ridiculous before her increased his humiliation. His spectacles had tumbled off in the struggle, and he could not immediately see them. She picked them up and silently handed them to him. He seemed suddenly to realise his unhappiness, and though he knew he was making himself still more absurd, he began to cry. He hid his face in his hands. The others watched him without a word. They did not move from where they stood.

'Oh, my dear,' he groaned at last, 'how can you be so cruel?'

'I can't help myself, Dirk,' she answered.

'I've worshipped you as no woman was ever worshipped before. If in anything I did I displeased you, why didn't you tell me, and I'd have changed. I've done everything I could for you.'

She did not answer. Her face was set, and he saw that he was only boring her. She put on a coat and her hat. She moved towards the door, and he saw that in a moment she would be gone. He went up to her quickly and fell on his knees before her, seizing her hands: he abandoned all self-respect.

'Oh, don't go, my darling. I can't live without you; I shall kill myself. If I've done anything to offend you I beg you to forgive me. Give me another chance. I'll try harder still to make you happy.'

'Get up, Dirk. You're making yourself a perfect fool.'

He staggered to his feet, but still he would not let her go.

'Where are you going?' he said hastily. 'You don't know what Strickland's place is like. You can't live there. It would be awful.'

'If I don't care, I don't see why you should.'

'Stay a minute longer. I must speak. After all, you can't grudge me that.'

'What is the good? I've made up my mind. Nothing that you can say will make me alter it.'

He gulped, and put his hand to his heart to ease its painful beating.

'I'm not going to ask you to change your mind, but I want you to listen to me for a minute. It's the last thing I shall ever ask you. Don't refuse me that.'

She paused, looking at him with those reflective eyes of hers, which now were so indifferent to him. She came back into the studio and leaned against the table.

'Well?'

Stroeve made a great effort to collect himself.

'You must be a little reasonable. You can't live on air, you know. Strickland hasn't got a penny.'

'I know.'

'You'll suffer the most awful privations. You know why he took so long to get well. He was half starved.'

'I can earn money for him.'

'How?'

'I don't know. I shall find a way.'

A horrible thought passed through the Dutchman's mind, and he shuddered.

'I think you must be mad. I don't know what has come over you.'

She shrugged her shoulders.

'Now may I go?'

'Wait one second longer.'

He looked round his studio wearily; he had loved it because her presence had made it gay and home-like; he shut his eyes for an instant; then he gave her a long look as though to impress on his mind the picture of her. He got up and took his hat.

'No; I'll go.'

'You?'

She was startled. She did not know what he meant.

'I can't bear to think of you living in that horrible, filthy attic. After all, this is your home just as much as mine. You'll be comfortable here. You'll be spared at least the worst privations.'

He went to the drawer in which he kept his money and took out several bank-notes.

'I would like to give you half what I've got here.'

He put them on the table. Neither Strickland nor his wife spoke.

Then he recollected something else.

'Will you pack up my clothes and leave them with the concierge? I'll come and fetch them tomorrow.' He tried to smile. 'Good-bye, my dear. I'm grateful for all the happiness you gave me in the past.'

He walked out and closed the door behind him. With my mind's eye I saw Strickland throw his hat on a table, and, sitting down, begin to smoke a cigarette.

Chapter Twenty-nine

I kept silence for a little while, thinking of what Stroeve had told me. I could not stomach his weakness, and he saw my disapproval.

'You know as well as I do how Strickland lived,' he said tremulously. 'I couldn't let her live in those circumstances—I simply couldn't.'

'That's your business,' I answered.

'What would *you* have done?' he asked.

'She went with her eyes open. If she had to put up with certain inconveniences it was her own look-out.'

'Yes; but, you see, you don't love her.'

'Do you love her still?'

'Oh, more than ever. Strickland isn't the man to make a woman happy. It can't last. I want her to know that I shall never fail her.'

'Does that mean that you're prepared to take her back?'

'I shouldn't hesitate. Why, she'll want me more than ever then. When she's alone and humiliated and broken it would be dreadful if she had nowhere to go.'

He seemed to bear no resentment. I suppose it was commonplace in me that I felt slightly outraged at his lack of spirit. Perhaps he guessed what was in my mind, for he said:

'I couldn't expect her to love me as I loved her. I'm a buffoon. I'm not the sort of man that women love. I've always known that. I can't blame her if she's fallen in love with Strickland.'

'You certainly have less vanity than any man I've ever known,' I said.

'I love her so much better than myself. It seems to me that when vanity comes into love it can only be because really you love yourself best. After all, it constantly happens that a man when he's married falls in love with somebody else; when he gets over it he returns to his wife, and she takes him back, and everyone thinks it very natural. Why should it be different with women?'

'I dare say that's logical,' I smiled, 'but most men are made differently, and they can't.'

But while I talked to Stroeve I was puzzling over the suddenness of the whole affair. I could not imagine that he had had no warning. I remembered the curious look I had seen in Blanche Stroeve's eyes; perhaps its explanation was that she was growing dimly conscious of a feeling in her heart that surprised and alarmed her.

'Did you have no suspicion before today that there was anything between them?' I asked.

He did not answer for a while. There was a pencil on the table, and unconsciously he drew a head on the blotting-paper.

'Please say so, if you hate my asking you questions,' I said.

'It eases me to talk. Oh, if you knew the frightful anguish in my heart.' He threw the pencil down. 'Yes, I've known it for a fortnight. I knew it before she did.'

'Why on earth didn't you send Strickland packing?'

'I couldn't believe it. It seemed so improbable. She couldn't bear the sight of him. It was more than improbable; it was incredible. I thought it was merely jealousy. You see, I've always been jealous, but I trained myself never to show it; I was jealous of every man she knew; I was jealous of you. I knew she didn't love me as I loved her. That was only natural, wasn't it? But she allowed me to love her, and that was enough to make me happy. I forced myself to go out for hours together in order to leave them by themselves; I wanted to punish myself for suspicions which were unworthy of me; and when I came back I found they didn't want me–not Strickland, he didn't care if I was there or not, but Blanche. She shuddered when I went to kiss her. When at last I was certain, I didn't know what to do; I knew they'd only laugh at me if I made a scene. I thought if I held my tongue and pretended not to see, everything would come right. I made up my mind to get him away quietly, without quarrelling. Oh, if you only knew what I've suffered!'

Then he told me again of his asking Strickland to go. He chose his moment carefully, and tried to make his request sound casual; but he could not master the trembling of his voice, and he felt himself that into words that he wished to seem jovial and friendly there crept the bitterness of his jealousy. He had not expected Strickland to take him up on the spot and make his preparations to go there and then; above all, he had not expected his wife's decision to go with him. I saw that now he wished with all his heart that he had held his tongue. He preferred the anguish of jealousy to the anguish of separation.

'I wanted to kill him, and I only made a fool of myself.'

He was silent for a long time, and then he said what I knew was in his mind.

'If I'd only waited, perhaps it would have gone all right. I shouldn't have been so impatient. Oh, poor child, what have I driven her to?'

I shrugged my shoulders, but did not speak. I had no sympathy for Blanche Stroeve, but knew that it would only pain poor Dirk if I told him exactly what I thought of her.

He had reached the stage of exhaustion when he could not stop talking. He went over again every word of the scene. Now something occurred to him that he had not told me before; now he discussed what he ought to have said instead of what he did say; then he lamented his blindness. He regretted that he had done this, and blamed himself that he had omitted the other. It grew later and later, and at last I was as tired as he.

'What are you going to do now?' I said finally.

'What can I do? I shall wait till she sends for me.'

'Why don't you go away for a bit?'

'No, no; I must be at hand when she wants me.'

For the present he seemed quite lost. He had made no plans. When I suggested that he should go to bed he said he could not sleep; he wanted to go out and walk the streets till day. He was evidently in no state to be left alone. I persuaded him to stay the night with me, and I put him into my own bed. I had a divan in my sitting-room, and could very well sleep on that. He was by now so worn out that he could not resist my firmness. I gave him a sufficient dose of veronal to insure his unconsciousness for several hours. I thought that was the best service I could render him.

Chapter Thirty

But the bed I made up for myself was sufficiently uncomfortable to give me a wakeful night, and I thought a good deal of what the unlucky Dutchman had told me. I was not so much puzzled by Blanche Stroeve's action, for I saw in that merely the result of a physical appeal. I do not suppose she had ever really cared for her husband, and what I had taken for love was no more than the feminine response to caresses and comfort which in the minds of most women passes for it. It is a passive feeling capable of being roused for any object, as the vine can grow on any tree; and the wisdom of the world recognises its strength when it urges a girl to marry the man who wants her with the assurance that love will follow. It is an emotion made up of the satisfaction in security, pride of property, the pleasure of being desired, the gratification of a household, and it is only by an amiable vanity that women ascribe to it spiritual value. It is an emotion which is defenceless against passion. I suspected that Blanche Stroeve's violent dislike of Strickland had in it from the beginning a vague element of sexual attraction. Who am I that I should seek to unravel the mysterious intricacies of sex? Perhaps Stroeve's passion excited without satisfying that part of her nature, and she hated Strickland because she felt in him the power to give her what she needed. I think she was quite sincere when she struggled against her husband's desire to bring him into the studio; I think she was frightened of him, though she knew not why; and I remembered how she had foreseen disaster. I think in some curious way the horror which she felt for him was a transference of the horror which she felt for herself because he so strangely troubled her. His appearance was wild and uncouth; there was aloofness in his eyes and sensuality in his mouth; he was big and strong; he gave the impression of untamed passion; and perhaps she felt in him, too, that sinister element which had made me think of those wild beings of the world's early history when matter, retaining its early connection with the earth, seemed to possess yet a spirit of its own. If he affected her at all, it was inevitable that she should love or hate him. She hated him.

And then I fancy that the daily intimacy with the sick man moved her strangely. She raised his head to give him food, and it was heavy against her hand; when she had fed him she wiped his sensual mouth and his red beard. She washed his limbs; they were covered with thick hair; and when she dried his hands, even in his weakness they were strong and sinewy. His fingers were long; they were the capable, fashioning fingers of the artist; and I know not what troubling thoughts they excited in her. He slept very quietly, without a movement, so that he might have been dead, and he was like some wild creature of the woods, resting after a long chase; and she wondered what fancies passed through his dreams. Did he dream of the nymph flying through the woods of Greece with the satyr in hot pursuit? She fled, swift of foot and desperate, but he gained on her step by step, till she felt his hot breath on her cheek; and still she fled silently, and silently he pursued, and when at last he seized her was it terror that thrilled her heart or was it ecstasy?

Blanche Stroeve was in the cruel grip of appetite. Perhaps she hated Strickland still, but she hungered for him, and everything that had made up her life till then became of no account. She ceased to be a woman, complex, kind and petulant, considerate and thoughtless; she was a Mænad. She was desire.

But perhaps this is very fanciful; and it may be that she was merely bored with her husband and went to Strickland out of a callous curiosity. She may have had no particular feeling for him, but succumbed to his wish from propinquity or idleness, to find then that she was powerless in a snare of her own contriving. How did I know what were the thoughts and emotions behind that placid brow and those cool grey eyes?

But if one could be certain of nothing in dealing with creatures so incalculable as human beings, there were explanations of Blanche Stroeve's behaviour which were at all events plausible. On the other hand, I did not understand Strickland at all. I racked my brain, but could in no way account for an action so contrary to my conception of him. It was not strange that he should so heartlessly have betrayed his friend's confidence, nor that he hesitated not at all to gratify a whim at the cost of another's misery. That was in his character. He was a man without any conception of gratitude. He had no compassion. The emotions common to most of us simply did not exist in him, and it was as absurd to blame him for not feeling them as for blaming the tiger because he is fierce and cruel. But it was the whim I could not understand.

I could not believe that Strickland had fallen in love with Blanche Stroeve. I did not believe him capable of love. That is an emotion in which tenderness is an essential part, but Strickland had no tenderness either for himself or for others; there is in love a sense of weakness, a desire to protect, an eagerness to do good and to give pleasure—if not unselfishness, at all events a selfishness which marvellously conceals itself; it has in it a certain diffidence. These were not traits which I could imagine in Strickland. Love is absorbing; it takes the lover out of himself; the most clear-sighted, though he may know, cannot realise that his love will cease; it gives body to what he knows is illusion, and, knowing it is nothing else, he loves it better than reality. It makes a man a little more than himself, and at the same time a little less. He ceases to be himself. He is no longer an individual, but a thing, an instrument to some purpose foreign to his ego. Love is never quite devoid of sentimentality, and Strickland was the least inclined to that infirmity of any man I have known. I could not believe that he would ever suffer that possession of himself which love is; he could never endure a foreign yoke. I believed him capable of uprooting from his heart, though it might be with agony, so that he was left battered and ensanguined, anything that came between himself and that uncomprehended craving that urged him constantly to he knew not what. If I have succeeded at all in giving the complicated impression that Strickland made on me, it will not seem outrageous to say that I felt he was at once too great and too small for love.

But I suppose that everyone's conception of the passion is formed on his own idiosyncrasies, and it is different with every different person. A man like Strickland would love in a manner peculiar to himself. It was vain to seek the analysis of his emotion.

Chapter Thirty-one

Next day, though I pressed him to remain, Stroeve left me. I offered to fetch his things from the studio, but he insisted on going himself; I think he hoped they had not thought of getting them together, so that he would have an opportunity of seeing his wife again and perhaps inducing her to come back to him. But he found his traps awaiting for him in the porter's lodge, and the concierge told him that Blanche had gone out. I do not think he resisted the temptation of giving her an account of his troubles. I found that he was telling them to everyone he knew; he expected sympathy, but only excited ridicule.

He bore himself most unbecomingly. Knowing at what time his wife did her shopping, one day, unable any longer to bear not seeing her, he waylaid her in the street. She would not speak to him, but he insisted on speaking to her. He spluttered out words of apology for any wrong he had committed towards her; he told her he loved her devotedly and begged her to return to him. She would not answer; she walked hurriedly, with averted face. I imagined him with his fat little legs trying to keep up with her. Panting a little in his haste, he told her how miserable he was; he besought her to have mercy on him; he promised, if she would forgive him, to do everything she wanted. He offered to take her for a journey. He told her that Strickland would soon tire of her. When he repeated to me the whole sordid little scene I was outraged. He had shown neither sense nor dignity. He had omitted nothing that could make his wife despise him. There is no cruelty greater than a woman's to a man who loves her and whom she does not love; she has no kindness then, no tolerance even, she has only an insane irritation. Blanche Stroeve stopped suddenly, and as hard as she could slapped her husband's face. She took advantage of his confusion to escape, and ran up the stairs to the studio. No word had passed her lips.

When he told me this he put his hand to his cheek as though he still felt the smart of the blow, and in his eyes was a pain that was heartrending and an amazement that was ludicrous. He looked like an overblown schoolboy, and though I felt so sorry for him, I could hardly help laughing.

Then he took to walking along the street which she must pass through to get to the shops, and he would stand at the corner, on the other side, as she went along. He dared not speak to her again, but sought to put into his round eyes the appeal that was in his heart. I suppose he had some idea that the sight of his misery would touch her. She never made the smallest sign that she saw him. She never even changed the hour of her errands or sought an alternative route. I have an idea that there was some cruelty in her indifference. Perhaps she got enjoyment out of the torture she inflicted. I wondered why she hated him so much.

I begged Stroeve to behave more wisely. His want of spirit was exasperating.

'You're doing no good at all by going on like this,' I said. 'I think you'd have been wiser if you'd hit her over the head with a stick. She wouldn't have despised you as she does now.'

I suggested that he should go home for a while. He had often spoken to me of the silent town, somewhere up in the north of Holland, where his parents still lived. They were poor people. His father was a carpenter, and they dwelt in a little old red-brick house, neat and clean, by the side of a sluggish canal. The streets were wide and empty; for two hundred years the place had been dying, but the houses had the homely stateliness of their time. Rich merchants, sending their wares to the distant Indies, had lived in them calm and prosperous lives, and in their decent decay they kept still an aroma of their splendid past. You could wander along the canal till you came to broad green fields, with windmills here and there, in which cattle, black and white, grazed lazily. I thought that among those surroundings, with their recollections of his boyhood, Dirk Stroeve would forget his unhappiness. But he would not go.

'I must be here when she needs me,' he repeated. 'It would be dreadful if something terrible happened and I were not at hand.'

'What do you think is going to happen?' I asked.

'I don't know. But I'm afraid.'

I shrugged my shoulders.

For all his pain, Dirk Stroeve remained a ridiculous object. He might have excited sympathy if he had grown worn and thin. He did nothing of the kind. He remained fat, and his round, red cheeks shone like ripe apples. He had great neatness of person, and he continued to wear his spruce black coat and his bowler hat, always a little too small for him, in a dapper, jaunty manner. He was getting something of a paunch, and sorrow had no effect on it. He looked more than ever like a prosperous bagman. It is hard that a man's exterior should tally so little sometimes with his soul. Dirk Stroeve had the passion of Romeo in the body of Sir Toby Belch. He had a sweet and generous nature, and yet was always blundering; a real feeling for what was beautiful and the capacity to create only what was commonplace; a peculiar delicacy of sentiment and gross manners. He could exercise tact when dealing with the affairs of others, but none when dealing with his own. What a cruel practical joke old Nature played when she flung so many contradictory elements together, and left the man face to face with the perplexing callousness of the universe.

Chapter Thirty-two

I did not see Strickland for several weeks. I was disgusted with him, and if I had had an opportunity should have been glad to tell him so, but I saw no object in seeking him out for the purpose. I am a little shy of any assumption of moral indignation; there is always in it an element of self-satisfaction which makes it awkward to anyone who has a sense of humour. It requires a very lively passion to steel me to my own ridicule. There was a sardonic sincerity in Strickland which made me sensitive to anything that might suggest a pose.

But one evening when I was passing along the Avenue de Clichy in front of the café which Strickland frequented and which I now avoided, I ran straight into him. He was accompanied by Blanche Stroeve, and they were just going to Strickland's favourite corner.

'Where the devil have you been all this time?' said he. 'I thought you must be away.'

His cordiality was proof that he knew I had no wish to speak to him. He was not a man with whom it was worth while wasting politeness.

'No,' I said; 'I haven't been away.'

'Why haven't you been here?'

'There are more cafés in Paris than one, at which to trifle away an idle hour.'

Blanche then held out her hand and bade me good evening. I do not know why I had expected her to be somehow changed; she wore the same grey dress that she wore so often, neat and becoming, and her brow was as candid, her eyes as untroubled, as when I had been used to see her occupied with her household duties in the studio.

'Come and have a game of chess,' said Strickland.

I do not know why at the moment I could think of no excuse. I followed them rather sulkily to the table at which Strickland always sat, and he called for the board and the chessmen. They both took the situation so much as a matter of course that I felt it absurd to do otherwise. Mrs Stroeve watched the game with inscrutable face. She was silent, but she had always been silent. I looked at her mouth for an expression that could give me a clue to what she felt; I watched her eyes for some tell-tale flash, some hint of dismay or bitterness; I scanned her brow for any passing line that might indicate a settling emotion. Her face was a mask that told nothing. Her hands lay on her lap motionless, one in the other loosely clasped. I knew from what I had heard that she was woman of violent passions; and that injurious blow that she had given Dirk, the man who had loved her so devotedly, betrayed a sudden temper and a horrid cruelty. She had abandoned the safe shelter of her husband's protection and the comfortable ease of a well-provided estab-lishment for what she could not but see was an extreme hazard. It showed an eagerness for adventure, a readiness for the hand-to-mouth, which the care she took of her home and her love of good housewifery made not a little remarkable. She must be a woman of complicated character, and there was something dramatic in the contrast of that with her demure appearance.

I was excited by the encounter, and my fancy worked busily while I sought to concentrate myself on the game I was playing. I always tried my best to beat Strickland, because he was a player who despised the opponent he vanquished; his exultation in victory made defeat more difficult to bear. On the other hand, if he was beaten he took it with complete good-humour. He was a bad winner and a good loser. Those who think that man betrays his character nowhere more clearly than when he is playing a game might on this draw subtle inferences.

When he had finished I called the waiter to pay for the drinks, and left them. The meeting had been devoid of incident. No word had been said to give me anything to think about and any surmises I might make were unwarranted. I was intrigued. I could not tell how they were getting on. I would have given much to be a disembodied spirit so that I could see them in the privacy of the studio and hear what they talked about. I had not the smallest indication on which to let my imagination work.

Chapter Thirty-three

Two or three days later Dirk Stroeve called on me.

'I hear you've seen Blanche,' he said.

'How on earth did you find out?'

'I was told by someone who saw you sitting with them. Why didn't you tell me?'

'I thought it would only pain you.'

'What do I care if it does? You must know that I want to hear the smallest thing about her.'

I waited for him to ask me questions.

'What does she look like?' he said.

'Absolutely unchanged.'

'Does she seem happy?'

I shrugged my shoulders.

'How can I tell? We were in a café; we were playing chess; I had no opportunity to speak to her.'

'Oh, but couldn't you tell by her face?'

I shook my head. I could only repeat that by no word, by no hinted gesture, had she given an indication of her feelings. He must know better than I how great were her powers of self-control. He clasped his hands emotionally.

'Oh, I'm so frightened. I know something is going to happen, something terrible, and I can do nothing to stop it.'

'What sort of thing?' I asked.

'Oh, I don't know,' he moaned, seizing his head with his hands. 'I foresee some terrible catastrophe.'

Stroeve had always been excitable, but now he was beside himself; there was no reasoning with him. I thought it probable enough that Blanche Stroeve would not continue to find life with Strickland tolerable, but one of the falsest of proverbs is that you must lie on the bed that you have made. The experience of life shows that people are constantly doing things which must lead to disaster, and yet by some chance manage to evade the result of their folly. When Blanche quarrelled with Strickland she had only to leave him, and her husband was waiting humbly to forgive and forget. I was not prepared to feel any great sympathy for her.

'You see, you don't love her,' said Stroeve.

'After all, there's nothing to prove that she is unhappy. For all we know they may have settled down into a most domestic couple.'

Stroeve gave me a look with his woeful eyes.

'Of course it doesn't much matter to you, but to me it's so serious, so intensely serious.'

I was sorry if I had seemed impatient or flippant.

'Will you do something for me?' asked Stroeve.

'Willingly.'

'Will you write to Blanche for me?'

'Why can't you write yourself?'

'I've written over and over again. I didn't expect her to answer. I don't think she reads the letters.'

'You make no account of feminine curiosity. Do you think she could resist?'

'She could—mine.'

I looked at him quickly. He lowered his eyes. That answer of his seemed to me strangely humiliating. He was conscious that she regarded him with an indifference so profound that the sight of his handwriting would have not the slightest effect on her.

'Do you really believe that she'll ever come back to you?' I asked.

'I want her to know that if the worst comes to the worst she can count on me. That's what I want you to tell her.'

I took a sheet of paper.

'What is it exactly you wish me to say?'

This is what I wrote:

> Dear Mrs Stroeve,
>   Dirk wishes me to tell you that if at any time you want him he will be grateful for the opportunity of being of service to you. He has no ill-feeling towards you on account of anything that has happened. His love for you is unaltered. You will always find him at the following address.

Chapter Thirty-four

But though I was no less convinced than Stroeve that the connection between Strickland and Blanche would end disastrously, I did not expect the issue to take the tragic form it did. The summer came, breathless and sultry, and even at night there was no coolness to rest one's jaded nerves. The sun-baked streets seemed to give back the heat that had beat down on them during the day, and the passers-by dragged their feet along them wearily. I had not seen Strickland for weeks. Occupied with other things, I had ceased to think of him and his affairs. Dirk, with his vain lamentations, had begun to bore me, and I avoided his society. It was a sordid business, and I was not inclined to trouble myself with it further.

One morning I was working. I sat in my pyjamas. My thoughts wandered, and I thought of the sunny beaches of Brittany and the freshness of the sea. By my side was the empty bowl in which the concierge had brought me my *café au lait* and the fragment of *croissant* which I had not had appetite enough to eat. I heard the concierge in the next room emptying my bath. There was a tinkle at my bell, and I left her to open the door. In a moment I heard Stroeve's voice asking if I was in. Without moving, I shouted to him to come in. He entered the room quickly, and came up to the table at which I sat.

'She's killed herself,' he said hoarsely.

'What do you mean?' I cried, startled.

He made movements with his lips as though he were speaking, but no sound issued from them. He gibbered like an idiot. My heart thumped against my ribs, and, I do not know why, I flew into a temper.

'For God's sake, collect yourself, man,' I said. 'What on earth are you talking about?'

He made despairing gestures with his hands, but still no words came from his mouth. He might have been struck dumb. I do not know what came over me; I took him by the shoulders and shook him. Looking back, I am vexed that I made such a fool of myself; I suppose the last restless nights had shaken my nerves more than I knew.

'Let me sit down,' he gasped at length.

I filled a glass with St Galmier, and gave it to him to drink. I held it to his mouth as though he were a child. He gulped down a mouthful, and some of it was spilt on his shirt-front.

'Who's killed herself?'

I do not know why I asked, for I knew whom he meant. He made an effort to collect himself.

'They had a row last night. He went away.'

'Is she dead?'

'No; they've taken her to the hospital.'

'Then what are you talking about?' I cried impatiently. 'Why did you say she'd killed herself?'

'Don't be cross with me. I can't tell you anything if you talk to me like that.'

I clenched my hands, seeking to control my irritation. I attempted a smile.

'I'm sorry. Take your time. Don't hurry, there's a good fellow.'

His round blue eyes behind the spectacles were ghastly with terror. The magnifying-glasses he wore distorted them.

'When the concierge went up this morning to take a letter she could get no answer to her ring. She heard someone groaning. The door wasn't locked, and she went in. Blanche was lying on the bed. She'd been frightfully sick. There was a bottle of oxalic acid on the table.'

Stroeve hid his face in his hands and swayed backwards and forwards, groaning.

'Was she conscious?'

'Yes. Oh, if you knew how she's suffering! I can't bear it. I can't bear it.' His voice rose to a shriek.

'Damn it all, you haven't got to bear it,' I cried impatiently. 'She's got to bear it.'

'How can you be so cruel?'

'What have you done?'

'They sent for a doctor and for me, and they told the police. I'd given the concierge twenty francs, and told her to send for me if anything happened.'

He paused a minute, and I saw that what he had to tell me was very hard to say.

'When I went she wouldn't speak to me. She told them to send me away. I swore that I forgave her everything, but she wouldn't listen. She tried to beat her head against the wall. The doctor told me that I mustn't remain with her. She kept on saying, "Send him away!" I went, and waited in the studio. And when the ambulance came and they put her on a stretcher, they made me go in the kitchen so that she shouldn't know I was there.'

While I dressed–for Stroeve wished me to go at once with him to the hospital–he told me that he had arranged for his wife to have a private room, so that she might at least be spared the sordid promiscuity of a ward. On our way he explained to me why he desired my presence; if she still refused to see him, perhaps she would see me. He begged me to repeat to her that he loved her still; he would reproach her for nothing, but desired only to help her; he made no claim on her, and on her recovery would not seek to induce her to return to him; she would be perfectly free.

But when we arrived at the hospital, a gaunt, cheerless building, the mere sight of which was enough to make one's heart sick, and after being directed from this official to that, up endless stairs and through long, bare corridors, found the doctor in charge of the case, we were told that the patient was too ill to see anyone that day. The doctor was a little bearded man in white, with an off-hand manner. He evidently looked upon a case as a case, and anxious relatives as a nuisance which must be treated with firmness. Moreover, to him the affair was commonplace; it was just an hysterical woman who had quarrelled with her lover and taken poison; it was constantly happening. At first he thought that Dirk was the cause of the disaster, and he was needlessly brusque with him. When I explained that he was the husband, anxious to forgive, the doctor looked at him suddenly, with curious, searching eyes. I seemed to see in them a hint of mockery; it was true that Stroeve had the head of the husband who is deceived. The doctor faintly shrugged his shoulders.

'There is no immediate danger,' he said, in answer to our questioning. 'One doesn't know how much she took. It may be that she will get off with a fright. Women are constantly trying to commit suicide for love, but generally they take care not to succeed. It's generally a gesture to arouse pity or terror in their lover.'

There was in his tone a frigid contempt. It was obvious that to him Blanche Stroeve was only a unit to be added to the statistical list of attempted suicides in the city of Paris during the current year. He was busy, and could waste no more time on us. He told us that if we came at a certain hour next day, should Blanche be better, it might be possible for her husband to see her.

Chapter Thirty-five

I scarcely know how we got through that day. Stroeve could not bear to be alone, and I exhausted myself in efforts to distract him. I took him to the Louvre, and he pretended to look at pictures, but I saw that his thoughts were constantly with his wife. I forced him to eat, and after luncheon I induced him to lie down, but he could not sleep. He accepted willingly my invitation to remain for a few days in my apartment. I gave him books to read, but after a page or two he would put the book down and stare miserably into space. During the evening we played innumerable games of piquet, and bravely, not to disappoint my efforts, he tried to appear interested. Finally I gave him a draught, and he sank into uneasy slumber.

When we went again to the hospital we saw a nursing sister. She told us that Blanche seemed a little better, and she went in to ask if she would see her husband. We heard voices in the room in which she lay, and presently the nurse returned to say that the patient refused to see anyone. We told her that if she refused to see Dirk the nurse was to ask if she would see me, but this she refused also. Dirk's lips trembled.

'I dare not insist,' said the nurse. 'She is too ill. Perhaps in a day or two she may change her mind.'

'Is there anyone else she wants to see?' asked Dirk, in a voice so low it was almost a whisper.

'She says she only wants to be left in peace.'

Dirk's hands moved strangely, as though they had nothing to do with his body, with a movement of their own.

'Will you tell her that if there is anyone else she wishes to see I will bring him? I only want her to be happy.'

The nurse looked at him with her calm, kind eyes, which had seen all the horror and pain of the world, and yet, filled with the vision of a world without sin, remained serene.

'I will tell her when she is a little calmer.'

Dirk, filled with compassion, begged her to take the message at once.

'It may cure her. I beseech you to ask her now.'

With a faint smile of pity, the nurse went back into the room. We heard her low voice, and then, in a voice I did not recognise, the answer:

'No. No. No.'

The nurse came out again and shook her head.

'Was that she who spoke then?' I asked. 'Her voice sounded so strange.'

'It appears that her vocal cords have been burnt by the acid.'

Dirk gave a low cry of distress. I asked him to go on and wait for me at the entrance, for I wanted to say something to the nurse. He did not ask what it was, but went silently. He seemed to have lost all power of will; he was like an obedient child.

'Has she told you why she did it?' I asked.

'No. She won't speak. She lies on her back quite quietly. She doesn't move for hours at a time. But she cries always. Her pillow is all wet. She's too weak to use a handkerchief, and the tears just run down her face.'

It gave me a sudden wrench of the heart-strings. I could have killed Strickland then, and I knew that my voice was trembling, when I bade the nurse good-bye.

I found Dirk waiting for me on the steps. He seemed to see nothing, and did not notice that I had joined him till I touched him on the arm. We walked along in silence, I tried to imagine what had happened to drive the poor creature to that dreadful step. I presumed that Strickland knew what had happened, for someone must have been to see him from the police, and he must have made his statement. I did not know where he was. I supposed he had gone back to the shabby attic which served him as a studio. It was curious that she should not wish to see him. Perhaps she refused to have him sent for because she knew he would refuse to come. I wondered what an abyss of cruelty she must have looked into that in horror she refused to live.

Chapter Thirty-six

The next week was dreadful. Stroeve went twice a day to the hospital to enquire after his wife, who still declined to see him; and came away at first relieved and hopeful because he was told that she seemed to be growing better, and then in despair because, the complication which the doctor had feared having ensued, recovery was impossible. The nurse was pitiful to his distress, but she had little to say that could console him. The poor woman lay quite still, refusing to speak, with her eyes intent, as though she watched for the coming of death. It could now be only a question of a day or two; and when, late one evening Stroeve came to see me I knew it was to tell me that she was dead. He was absolutely exhausted. His volubility had left him at last, and he sank down wearily on my sofa. I felt that no words of condolence availed, and I let him lie there quietly. I feared he would think it heartless if I read, so I sat by the window, smoking a pipe, till he felt inclined to speak.

'You've been very kind to me,' he said at last. 'Everyone's been very kind.'

'Nonsense,' I said, a little embarrassed.

'At the hospital they told me I might wait. They gave me a chair, and I sat outside the door. When she became unconscious they said I might go in. Her mouth and chin were all burnt by the acid. It was awful to see her lovely skin all wounded. She died very peacefully, so that I didn't know she was dead till the sister told me.'

He was too tired to weep. He lay on his back limply, as though all the strength had gone out of his limbs, and presently I saw that he had fallen asleep. It was the first natural sleep he had had for a week. Nature, sometimes so cruel is sometimes merciful. I covered him and turned down the light. In the morning when I awoke he was still asleep. He had not moved. His gold-rimmed spectacles were still on his nose.

Chapter Thirty-seven

The circumstances of Blanche Stroeve's death necessitated all manner of dreadful formalities, but at last we were allowed to bury her. Dirk and I alone followed the hearse to the cemetery. We went at a foot-pace, but on the way back we trotted, and there was something to my mind singularly horrible in the way the driver of the hearse whipped up his horses. It seemed to dismiss the dead with a shrug of the shoulders. Now and then I caught sight of the swaying hearse in front of us, and our own driver urged his pair so that we might not remain behind. I felt in myself, too, the desire to get the whole thing out of my mind. I was beginning to be bored with a tragedy that did not really concern me, and pretending to myself that I spoke in order to distract Stroeve, I turned with relief to other subjects.

'Don't you think you'd better go away for a bit?' I said. 'There can be no object in your staying in Paris now.' He did not answer, but I went on ruthlessly:

'Have you made any plans for the immediate future?'

'No.'

'You must try and gather together the threads again. Why don't you go down to Italy and start working?'

Again he made no reply, but the driver of our carriage came to my rescue. Slackening his pace for a moment, he leaned over and spoke. I could not hear what he said, so I put my head out of the window; he wanted to know where we wished to be set down. I told him to wait a minute.

'You'd better come and have lunch with me,' I said to Dirk. 'I'll tell him to drop us in the Place Pigalle.'

'I'd rather not. I want to go to the studio.'

I hesitated a moment.

'Would you like me to come with you?' I asked then.

'No; I should prefer to be alone.'

'All right.'

I gave the driver the necessary direction, and in renewed silence we drove on. Dirk had not been to the studio since the wretched morning on which they had taken Blanche to the hospital. I was glad he did not want me to accompany him, and when I left him at the door I walked away with relief. I took a new pleasure in the streets of Paris, and I looked with smiling eyes at the people who hurried to and fro. The day was fine and sunny, and I felt in myself a more acute delight in life. I could not help it; I put Stroeve and his sorrows out of my mind. I wanted to enjoy.

Chapter Thirty-eight

I did not see him again for nearly a week. Then he fetched me soon after seven one evening and took me out to dinner. He was dressed in the deepest mourning, and on his bowler was a broad black band. He had even a black border to his handkerchief. His garb of woe suggested that he had lost in one catastrophe every relation he had in the world, even to cousins by marriage twice removed. His plumpness and his red, fat cheeks made his mourning not a little incongruous. It was cruel that his extreme unhappiness should have in it something of buffoonery.

He told me he had made up his mind to go away, though not to Italy, as I had suggested, but to Holland.

'I'm starting to-morrow. This is perhaps the last time we shall ever meet.'

I made an appropriate rejoinder, and he smiled wanly.

'I haven't been home for five years. I think I'd forgotten it all; I seemed to have come so far away from my father's house that I was shy at the idea of revisiting it; but now I feel it's my only refuge.'

He was sore and bruised, and his thoughts went back to the tenderness of his mother's love. The ridicule he had endured for years seemed now to weigh him down, and the final blow of Blanche's treachery had robbed him of the resiliency which had made him take it so gaily. He could no longer laugh with those who laughed at him. He was an outcast. He told me of his childhood in the tidy brick house, and of his mother's passionate orderliness. Her kitchen was a miracle of clean brightness. Everything was always in its place, and nowhere could you see a speck of dust. Cleanliness, indeed, was a mania with her. I saw a neat little old woman, with cheeks like apples, toiling away from morning to night, through the long years, to keep her house trim and spruce. His father was a spare old man, his hands gnarled after the work of a lifetime, silent and upright; in the evening he read the paper aloud, while his wife and daughter (now married to the captain of a fishing smack), unwilling to lose a moment, bent over their sewing. Nothing ever happened in that little town, left behind by the advance of civilisation, and one year followed the next till death came, like a friend, to give rest to those who had laboured so diligently.

'My father wished me to become a carpenter like himself. For five generations we've carried on the same trade, from father to son. Perhaps that is the wisdom of life, to tread in your father's steps, and look neither to the right nor to the left. When I was a little boy I said I would marry the daughter of the harness-maker who lived next door. She was a little girl with blue eyes and a flaxen pigtail. She would have kept my house like a new pin, and I should have had a son to carry on the business after me.'

Stroeve sighed a little and was silent. His thoughts dwelt among pictures of what might have been, and the safety of the life he had refused filled him with longing.

'The world is hard and cruel. We are here none knows why, and we go none knows whither. We must be very humble. We must see the beauty of quietness. We must go through life so inconspicuously that Fate does not notice us. And let us seek the love of simple, ignorant people. Their ignorance is better than all our knowledge. Let us be silent, content in our little corner, meek and gentle like them. That is the wisdom of life.'

To me it was his broken spirit that expressed itself, and I rebelled against his renunciation. But I kept my own counsel.

'What made you think of being a painter?' I asked.

He shrugged his shoulders.

'It happened that I had a knack for drawing. I got prizes for it at school. My poor mother was very proud of my gift, and she gave me a box of water-colours as a present. She showed my sketches to the pastor and the doctor and the judge. And they sent me to Amsterdam to try for a scholarship, and I won it. Poor soul, she was so proud; and though it nearly broke her heart to part from me, she smiled, and would not show me her grief. She was pleased that her son should be an artist. They pinched and saved so that I should have enough to live on, and when my first picture was exhibited they came to Amsterdam to see it, my father and mother and my sister, and my mother cried when she looked at it.' His kind eyes glistened. 'And now on every wall of the old house there is one of my pictures in a beautiful gold frame.'

He glowed with happy pride. I thought of those cold scenes of his, with their picturesque peasants and cypresses and olive-trees. They must look queer in their garish frames on the walls of the peasant house.

'The dear soul thought she was doing a wonderful thing for me when she made me an artist, but perhaps, after all, it would have been better for me if my father's will had prevailed and I were now but an honest carpenter.'

'Now that you know what art can offer, would you change your life? Would you have missed all the delight it has given you?'

'Art is the greatest thing in the world,' he answered, after a pause.

He looked at me for a minute reflectively; he seemed to hesitate; then he said:

'Did you know that I had been to see Strickland?'

'You?'

I was astonished. I should have thought he could not bear to set eyes on him. Stroeve smiled faintly.

'You know already that I have no proper pride.'

'What do you mean by that?'

He told me a singular story.

Chapter Thirty-nine

When I left him, after we had buried poor Blanche, Stroeve walked into the house with a heavy heart. Something impelled him to go to the studio, some obscure desire for self-torture, and yet he dreaded the anguish that he foresaw. He dragged himself up the stairs; his feet seemed unwilling to carry him; and outside the door he lingered for a long time, trying to summon up courage to go in. He felt horribly sick. He had an impulse to run down the stairs after me and beg me to go in with him; he had a feeling that there was somebody in the studio. He remembered how often he had waited for a minute or two on the landing to get his breath after the ascent, and how absurdly his impatience to see Blanche had taken it away again. To see her was a delight that never staled, and even though he had not been out an hour he was as excited at the prospect as if they had been parted for a month. Suddenly he could not believe that she was dead. What had happened could only be a dream, a frightful dream; and when he turned the key and opened the door, he would see her bending slightly over the table in the gracious attitude of the woman in Chardin's *Bénédicité*, which always seemed to him so exquisite. Hurriedly he took the key out of his pocket, opened, and walked in.

The apartment had no look of desertion. His wife's tidiness was one of the traits which had so much pleased him; his own upbringing had given him a tender sympathy for the delight in orderliness; and when he had seen her instinctive desire to put each thing in its appointed place it had given him a little warm feeling in his heart. The bedroom looked as though she had just left it: the brushes were neatly placed on the toilet-table, one on each side of the comb; someone had smoothed down the bed on which she had spent her last night in the studio: and her nightdress in a little case lay on the pillow. It was impossible to believe that she would never come into that room again.

But he felt thirsty, and went into the kitchen to get himself some water. Here, too, was order. On a rack were the plates that she had used for dinner on the night of her quarrel with Strickland, and they had been carefully washed. The knives and forks were put away in a drawer. Under a cover were the remains of a piece of cheese, and in a tin box was a crust of bread. She had done her marketing from day to day, buying only what was strictly needful, so that nothing was left over from one day to the next. Stroeve knew from the enquiries made by the police that Strickland had walked out of the house immediately after dinner, and the fact that Blanche had washed up the things as usual gave him a little thrill of horror. Her methodicalness made her suicide more deliberate. Her self-possession was frightening. A sudden pang seized him, and his knees felt so weak that he almost fell. He went back into the bedroom and threw himself on the bed. He cried out her name:

'Blanche. Blanche.'

The thought of her suffering was intolerable. He had a sudden vision of her standing in the kitchen—it was hardly larger than a cupboard—washing the plates and glasses, the forks and spoons, giving the knives a rapid polish on the knife-board; and then putting everything away, giving the sink a scrub, and hanging the dish-cloth up to dry—it was there still, a grey, torn rag; then looking round to see that everything was clean and nice. He saw her roll down her sleeves and remove her apron—the apron hung on a peg behind the door—and take the bottle of oxalic acid and go with it into the bedroom.

The agony of it drove him up from the bed and out of the room. He went into the studio. It was dark, for the curtains had been drawn over the great window, and he pulled them quickly back; but a sob broke from him as with a rapid glance he took in the place where he had been so happy. Nothing was changed here, either. Strickland was indifferent to his surroundings, and he had lived in the other's studio without thinking of altering a thing. It was deliberately artistic. It represented Stroeve's idea of the proper environment for an artist. There were bits of old brocade on the walls, and the piano was covered with a piece of silk, beautiful and tarnished; in one corner was a copy of the *Venus of Milo*, and in another of the *Venus of the Medici*. Here and there was an Italian cabinet surmounted with delf, and here and there a bas-relief. In a handsome gold frame was a copy of Velasquez' *Innocent X*, that Stroeve had made in Rome, and placed so as to make the most of their decorative effect were a number of Stroeve's pictures, all in splendid frames. Stroeve had always been very proud of his taste. He had never lost his appreciation for the romantic atmosphere of a studio, and though now the sight of it was like a stab in his heart, without thinking what he was at, he changed slightly the position of a Louis XV table which was one of his treasures. Suddenly he caught sight of a canvas with its face to the wall. It was a much larger one than he himself was in the habit of using, and he wondered what it did there. He went over to it and leaned it towards him so that he could see the painting. It was a nude. His heart began to beat quickly, for he guessed at once that it was one of Strickland's pictures. He flung it back against the wall angrily—what did he mean by leaving it there?—but his movement caused it to fall, face downwards, on the ground. No matter whose the picture, he could not leave it there in the dust, and he raised it; but then curiosity got the better of him. He thought he would like to have a proper look at it, so he brought it along and set it on the easel. Then he stood back in order to see it at his ease.

He gave a gasp. It was the picture of a woman lying on a sofa, with one arm beneath her head and the other along her body; one knee was raised, and the other leg was stretched out. The pose was classic. Stroeve's head swam. It was Blanche. Grief and jealousy and rage seized him, and he cried out hoarsely; he was inarticulate; he clenched his fists and raised them threateningly at an invisible enemy. He screamed at the top of his voice. He was beside himself. He could not bear it. That was too much. He looked round wildly for some instrument; he wanted to hack the picture to pieces; it should not exist another minute. He could see nothing that would serve his purpose; he rummaged about his painting things; somehow he could not find a thing; he was frantic. At last he came upon what he sought, a large scraper, and he pounced on it with a cry of triumph. He seized it as though it were a dagger, and ran to the picture.

As Stroeve told me this he became as excited as when the incident occurred, and he took hold of a dinner-knife on the table between us, and brandished it. He lifted his arm as though to strike, and then, opening his hand, let it fall with a clatter to the ground. He looked at me with a tremulous smile. He did not speak.

'Fire away,' I said.

'I don't know what happened to me. I was just going to make a great hole in the picture, I had my arm all ready for the blow, when suddenly I seemed to see it.'

'See what?'

'The picture. It was a work of art. I couldn't touch it. I was afraid.'

Stroeve was silent again, and he stared at me with his mouth open and his round blue eyes starting out of his head.

'It was a great, a wonderful picture. I was seized with awe. I had nearly committed a dreadful crime. I moved a little to see it better, and my foot knocked against the scraper. I shuddered.'

I really felt something of the emotion that had caught him. I was strangely impressed. It was as though I were suddenly transported into a world in which the values were changed. I stood by, at a loss, like a stranger in a land where the reactions of man to familiar things are all different from those he has known. Stroeve tried to talk to me about the picture, but he was incoherent, and I had to guess at what he meant. Strickland had burst the bonds that hitherto had held him. He had found, not himself, as the phrase goes, but a new soul with unsuspected powers. It was not only the bold simplification of the drawing which showed so rich and so singular a personality; it was not only the painting, though the flesh was painted with a passionate sensuality which had in it something miraculous; it was not only the solidity, so that you felt extraordinarily the weight of the body; there was also a spirituality, troubling and new, which led the imagination along unsuspected ways, and suggested dim empty spaces, lit only by the eternal stars, where the soul, all naked, adventured fearful to the discovery of new mysteries.

If I am rhetorical it is because Stroeve was rhetorical. (Do we not know that man in moments of emotion expresses himself naturally in the terms of a novelette?) Stroeve was trying to express a feeling which he had never known before, and he did not know how to put it into common terms. He was like the mystic seeking to describe the ineffable. But one fact he made clear to me: people talk of beauty lightly, and having no feeling for words, they use that one carelessly, so that it loses its force; and the thing it stands for, sharing its name with a hundred trivial objects, is deprived of dignity. They call beautiful a dress, a dog, a sermon; and when they are face to face with Beauty cannot recognise it. The false emphasis with which they try to deck their worthless thoughts blunts their susceptibilities. Like the charlatan who counterfeits a spiritual force he has some times felt, they lose the power they have abused. But Stroeve, the unconquerable buffoon, had a love and an understanding of beauty which were as honest and sincere as was his own sincere and honest soul. It meant to him what God means to the believer, and when he saw it he was afraid.

'What did you say to Strickland when you saw him?'

'I asked him to come with me to Holland.'

I was dumbfounded. I could only look at Stroeve in stupid amazement.

'We both loved Blanche. There would have been room for him in my mother's house. I think the company of poor, simple people would have done his soul a great good. I think he might have learnt from them something that would be very useful to him.'

'What did he say?'

'He smiled a little. I suppose he thought me very silly. He said he had other fish to fry.'

I could have wished that Strickland had used some other phrase to indicate his refusal.

'He gave me the picture of Blanche.'

I wondered why Strickland had done that. But I made no remark, and for some time we kept silence.

'What have you done with all your things?' I said at last.

'I got a Jew in, and he gave me a round sum for the lot. I'm taking my pictures home with me. Beside them I own nothing in the world now but a box of clothes and a few books.'

'I'm glad you're going home,' I said.

I felt that his chance was to put all the past behind him. I hoped that the grief which now seemed intolerable would be softened by the lapse of time, and a merciful forgetfulness would help him to take up once more the burden of life. He was young still, and in a few years he would look back on all his misery with a sadness in which there would be something not unpleasurable. Sooner or later he would marry some honest soul in Holland, and I felt sure he would be happy. I smiled at the thought of the vast number of bad pictures he would paint before he died.

Next day I saw him off for Amsterdam.

Chapter Forty

For the next month, occupied with my own affairs, I saw no one connected with this lamentable business, and my mind ceased to be occupied with it. But one day, when I was walking along, bent on some errand, I passed Charles Strickland. The sight of him brought back to me all the horror which I was not unwilling to forget, and I felt in me a sudden repulsion for the cause of it. Nodding, for it would have been childish to cut him, I walked on quickly; but in a minute I felt a hand on my shoulder.

'You're in a great hurry,' he said cordially.

It was characteristic of him to display geniality with anyone who showed a disinclination to meet him, and the coolness of my greeting can have left him in little doubt of that.

'I am,' I answered briefly.

'I'll walk along with you,' he said.

'Why?' I asked.

'For the pleasure of your society.'

I did not answer, and he walked by my side silently. We continued thus for perhaps a quarter of a mile. I began to feel a little ridiculous. At last we passed a stationer's, and it occurred to me that I might as well buy some paper. It would be an excuse to be rid of him.

'I'm going in here,' I said. 'Good-bye.'

'I'll wait for you.'

I shrugged my shoulders, and went into the shop. I reflected that French paper was bad, and that, foiled of my purpose, I need not burden myself with a purchase that I did not need. I asked for something I knew could not be provided, and in a minute came out into the street.

'Did you get what you wanted?' he asked.

'No.'

We walked on in silence, and then came to a place where several streets met. I stopped at the kerb.

'Which way do you go?' I enquired.

'Your way,' he smiled.

'I'm going home.'

'I'll come along with you and smoke a pipe.'

'You might wait for an invitation,' I retorted frigidly.

'I would if I thought there was any chance of getting one.'

'Do you see that wall in front of you?' I said, pointing.

'Yes.'

'In that case I should have thought you could see also that I don't want your company.'

'I vaguely suspected it, I confess.'

I could not help a chuckle. It is one of the defects of my character that I cannot altogether dislike anyone who makes me laugh. But I pulled myself together.

'I think you're detestable. You're the most loathsome beast that it's ever been my misfortune to meet. Why do you seek the society of someone who hates and despises you?'

'My dear fellow, what the hell do you suppose I care what you think of me?'

'Damn it all,' I said, more violently because I had an inkling my motive was none too creditable, 'I don't want to know you.'

'Are you afraid I shall corrupt you?'

His tone made me feel not a little ridiculous. I knew that he was looking at me sideways, with a sardonic smile.

'I suppose you are hard up,' I remarked insolently.

'I should be a damned fool if I thought I had any chance of borrowing money from you.'

'You've come down in the world if you can bring yourself to flatter.'

He grinned.

'You'll never really dislike me so long as I give you the opportunity to get off a good thing now and then.'

I had to bite my lip to prevent myself from laughing. What he said had a hateful truth in it, and another defect of my character is that I enjoy the company of those, however depraved, who can give me a Roland for my Oliver. I began to feel that my abhorrence for Strickland could only be sustained by an effort on my part. I recognised my moral weakness, but saw that my disapprobation had in it already something of a pose; and I knew that if I felt it, his own keen instinct had discovered it too. He was certainly laughing at me up his sleeve. I left him the last word, and sought refuge in a shrug of the shoulders and taciturnity.

Chapter Forty-one

We arrived at the house in which I lived. I would not ask him to come in with me, but walked up the stairs without a word. He followed me, and entered the apartment on my heels. He had not been in it before, but he never gave a glance at the room I had been at pains to make pleasing to the eye. There was a tin of tobacco on the table, and, taking out his pipe, he filled it. He sat down on the only chair that had no arms and tilted himself on the back legs.

'If you're going to make yourself at home, why don't you sit in an arm-chair?' I asked irritably.

'Why are you concerned about my comfort?'

'I'm not,' I retorted, 'but only about my own. It makes me uncomfortable to see someone sit on an uncomfortable chair.'

He chuckled, but did not move. He smoked on in silence, taking no further notice of me, and apparently was absorbed in thought. I wondered why he had come.

Until long habit has blunted the sensibility, there is something disconcerting to the writer in the instinct which causes him to take an interest in the singularities of human nature so absorbing that his moral sense is powerless against it. He recognises in himself an artistic satisfaction in the contemplation of evil which a little startles him; but sincerity forces him to confess that the disapproval he feels for certain actions is not nearly so strong as his curiosity in their reasons. The character of a scoundrel, logical and complete, has a fascination for his creator which is an outrage to law and order. I expect that Shakespeare devised Iago with a gusto which he never knew when, weaving moonbeams with his fancy, he imagined Desdemona. It may be that in his rogues the writer gratifies instincts deep-rooted in him, which the manners and customs of a civilised world have forced back to the mysterious recesses of the subconscious. In giving to the character of his invention flesh and bones he is giving life to that part of himself which finds no other means of expression. His satisfaction is a sense of liberation.

The writer is more concerned to know than to judge.

There was in my soul a perfectly genuine horror of Strickland, and side by side with it a cold curiosity to discover his motives. I was puzzled by him, and I was eager to see how he regarded the tragedy he had caused in the lives of people who had used him with so much kindness. I applied the scalpel boldly.

'Stroeve told me that picture you painted of his wife was the best thing you've ever done.'

Strickland took his pipe out of his mouth, and a smile lit up his eyes.

'It was great fun to do.'

'Why did you give it him?'

'I'd finished it. It wasn't any good to me.'

'Do you know that Stroeve nearly destroyed it?'

'It wasn't altogether satisfactory.'

He was quiet for a moment or two, then he took his pipe out of his mouth again, and chuckled.

'Do you know that the little man came to see me?'

'Weren't you rather touched by what he had to say?'

'No; I thought it damned silly and sentimental.'

'I suppose it escaped your memory that you'd ruined his life?' I remarked.

He rubbed his bearded chin reflectively.

'He's a very bad painter.'

'But a very good man.'

'And an excellent cook,' Strickland added derisively.

His callousness was inhuman, and in my indignation I was not inclined to mince my words.

'As a mere matter of curiosity I wish you'd tell me, have you felt the smallest twinge of remorse for Blanche Stroeve's death?'

I watched his face for some change of expression, but it remained impassive.

'Why should I?' he asked.

'Let me put the facts before you. You were dying, and Dirk Stroeve took you into his own house. He nursed you like a mother. He sacrificed his time and his comfort and his money for you. He snatched you from the jaws of death.'

Strickland shrugged his shoulders.

'The absurd little man enjoys doing things for other people. That's his life.'

'Granting that you owed him no gratitude, were you obliged to go out of your way to take his wife from him? Until you came on the scene they were happy. Why couldn't you leave them alone?'

'What makes you think they were happy?'

'It was evident.'

'You are a discerning fellow. Do you think she could ever have forgiven him for what he did for her?'

'What do you mean by that?'

'Don't you know why he married her?'

I shook my head.

'She was a governess in the family of some Roman prince, and the son of the house seduced her. She thought he was going to marry her. They turned her out into the street neck and crop. She was going to have a baby, and she tried to commit suicide. Stroeve found her and married her.'

'It was just like him. I never knew anyone with so compassionate a heart.'

I had often wondered why that ill-assorted pair had married, but just that explanation had never occurred to me. That was perhaps the cause of the peculiar quality of Dirk's love for his wife. I had noticed in it something more than passion. I remembered also how I had always fancied that her reserve concealed I knew not what; but now I saw in it more than the desire to hide a shameful secret. Her tranquillity was like the sullen calm that broods over an island which has been swept by a hurricane. Her cheerfulness was the cheerfulness of despair. Strickland interrupted my reflections with an observation the profound cynicism of which startled me.

'A woman can forgive a man for the harm he does her,' he said, 'but she can never forgive him for the sacrifice he makes on her account.'

'It must be reassuring to you to know that you certainly run no risk of incurring the resentment of the women you come in contact with,' I retorted.

A slight smile broke on his lips.

'You are always prepared to sacrifice your principles for a repartee,' he answered.

'What happened to the child?'

'Oh, it was still-born, three or four months after they were married.'

Then I came to the question which had seemed to me most puzzling.

'Will you tell me why you bothered about Blanche Stroeve at all?'

He did not answer for so long that I nearly repeated it.

'How do I know?' he said at last. 'She couldn't bear the sight of me. It amused me.'

'I see.'

He gave a sudden flash of anger.

'Damn it all, I wanted her.'

But he recovered his temper immediately, and looked at me with a smile.

'At first she was horrified.'

'Did you tell her?'

'There wasn't any need. She knew. I never said a word. She was frightened. At last I took her.'

I do not know what there was in the way he told me this that extraordinarily suggested the violence of his desire. It was disconcerting and rather horrible. His life was strangely divorced from material things, and it was as though his body at times wreaked a fearful revenge on his spirit. The satyr in him suddenly took possession, and he was powerless in the grip of an instinct which had all the strength of the primitive forces of nature. It was an obsession to complete that there was no room in his soul for prudence or gratitude.

'But why did you want to take her away with you?' I asked.

'I didn't,' he answered, frowning. 'When she said she was coming I was nearly as surprised as Stroeve. I told her that when I'd had enough of her she'd have to go, and she said she'd risk that.' He paused a little. 'She had a wonderful body, and I wanted to paint a nude. When I'd finished my picture I took no more interest in her.'

'And she loved you with all her heart.'

He sprang to his feet and walked up and down the small room.

'I don't want love. I haven't time for it. It's weakness. I am a man, and sometimes I want a woman. When I've satisfied my passion I'm ready for other things. I can't overcome my desire, but I hate it; it imprisons my spirit; I look forward to the time when I shall be free from all desire and can give myself without hindrance to my work. Because women can do nothing except love, they've given it a ridiculous importance. They want to persuade us that it's the whole of life. It's an insignificant part. I know lust. That's normal and healthy. Love is a disease. Women are the instruments of my pleasure; I have no patience with their claim to be helpmates, partners, companions.'

I had never heard Strickland speak so much at one time. He spoke with a passion of indignation. But neither here nor elsewhere do I pretend to give his exact words; his vocabulary was small, and he had no gift for framing sentences, so that one had to piece his meaning together out of interjections, the expression of his face, gestures and hackneyed phrases.

'You should have lived at a time when women were chattels and men the masters of slaves,' I said.

'It just happens that I am a completely normal man.'

I could not help laughing at this remark, made in all seriousness; but he went on, walking up and down the room like a caged beast, intent on expressing what he felt, but found such difficulty in putting coherently.

'When a woman loves you she's not satisfied until she possesses your soul. Because she's weak she has a rage for domination, and nothing less will satisfy her. She has a small mind, and she resents the abstract which she is unable to grasp. She is occupied with material things, and she is jealous of the ideal. The soul of man wanders through the uttermost regions of the universe, and she seeks to imprison it in the circle of her account-book. Do you remember my wife? I saw Blanche little by little trying all her tricks. With infinite patience she prepared to snare me and bind me. She wanted to bring me down to her level; she cared nothing for me, she only wanted me to be hers. She was willing to do everything in the world for me except the one thing I wanted: to leave me alone.'

I was silent for a while.

'What did you expect her to do when you left her?'

'She could have gone back to Stroeve,' he said irritably. 'He was ready to take her.'

'You're inhuman,' I answered. 'It's as useless to talk to you about these things as to describe colours to a man who was born blind.'

He stopped in front of my chair, and stood looking down at me with an expression in which I read a contemptuous amazement.

'Do you really care a twopenny damn if Blanche Stroeve is alive or dead?'

I thought over his question, for I wanted to answer it truthfully, at all events to my soul.

'It may be a lack of sympathy in myself if it does not make any great difference to me that she is dead. Life had a great deal to offer her. I think it's terrible that she should have been deprived of it in that cruel way, and I am ashamed because I do not really care.'

'You have not the courage of your convictions. Life has no value. Blanche Stroeve didn't commit suicide because I left her, but because she was a foolish and unbalanced woman. But we've talked about her quite enough; she was an entirely unimportant person. Come, and I'll show you my pictures.'

He spoke as though I were a child that needed to be distracted. I was sore, but not with him so much as with myself. I thought of the happy life that pair had led in the cosy studio in Montmartre, Stroeve and his wife, their simplicity, kindness, and hospitality; it seemed to me cruel that it should have been broken to pieces by a ruthless chance; but the cruellest thing of all was that in fact it made no great difference. The world went on, and no one was a penny the worse for all that wretchedness. I had an idea that Dirk, a man of greater emotional reactions than depth of feeling, would soon forget; and Blanche's life, begun with who knows what bright hopes and what dreams, might just as well have never been lived. It all seemed useless and inane.

Strickland had found his hat, and stood looking at me.

'Are you coming?'

'Why do you seek my acquaintance?' I asked him. 'You know that I hate and despise you.'

He chuckled good-humouredly.

'Your only quarrel with me really is that I don't care a twopenny damn what you think about me.'

I felt my cheeks grow red with sudden anger. It was impossible to make him understand that one might be outraged by his callous selfishness. I longed to pierce his armour of complete indifference. I knew also that in the end there was truth in what he said. Unconsciously, perhaps, we treasure the power we have over people by their regard for our opinion of them, and we hate those upon whom we have no such influence. I suppose it is the bitterest wound to human pride. But I would not let him see that I was put out.

'Is it possible for any man to disregard others entirely?' I said, though more to myself than to him. 'You're dependent on others for everything in existence. It's a preposterous attempt to try to live only for yourself and by yourself. Sooner or later you'll be ill and tired and old, and then you'll crawl back into the herd. Won't you be ashamed when you feel in your heart the desire for comfort and sympathy? You're trying an impossible thing. Sooner or later the human being in you will yearn for the common bonds of humanity.'

'Come and look at my pictures.'

'Have you ever thought of death?'

'Why should I? It doesn't matter.'

I stared at him. He stood before me, motionless, with a mocking smile in his eyes; but for all that, for a moment I had an inkling of a fiery, tortured spirit, aiming at something greater than could be conceived by anything that was bound up with the flesh. I had a fleeting glimpse of a pursuit of the ineffable. I looked at the man before me in his shabby clothes, with his great nose and shining eyes, his red beard and untidy hair; and I had a strange sensation that it was only an envelope, and I was in the presence of a disembodied spirit.

'Let us go and look at your pictures,' I said.

Chapter Forty-two

I did not know why Strickland had suddenly offered to show them to me. I welcomed the opportunity. A man's work reveals him. In social intercourse he gives you the surface that he wishes the world to accept, and you can only gain a true knowledge of him by inferences from little actions, of which he is unconscious, and from fleeting expressions, which cross his face unknown to him. Sometimes people carry to such perfection the mask they have assumed that in due course they actually become the person they seem. But in his book or his picture the real man delivers himself defenceless. His pretentiousness will only expose his vacuity. The lath painted to look like iron is seen to be but a lath. No affectation of peculiarity can conceal a commonplace mind. To the acute observer no one can produce the most casual work without disclosing the innermost secrets of his soul.

As I walked up the endless stairs of the house in which Strickland lived, I confess that I was a little excited. It seemed to me that I was on the threshold of a surprising adventure. I looked about the room with curiosity. It was even smaller and more bare than I remembered it. I wondered what those friends of mine would say who demanded vast studios, and vowed they could not work unless all the conditions were to their liking.

'You'd better stand there,' he said, pointing to a spot from which, presumably, he fancied I could see to best advantage what he had to show me.

'You don't want me to talk, I suppose,' I said.

'No, blast you; I want you to hold your tongue.'

He placed a picture on the easel, and let me look at it for a minute or two; then took it down and put another in its place. I think he showed me about thirty canvases. It was the result of the six years during which he had been painting. He had never sold a picture. The canvases were of different sizes. The smaller were pictures of still-life and the largest were landscapes. There were about half a dozen portraits.

'That is the lot,' he said at last.

I wish I could say that I recognised at once their beauty and their great originality. Now that I have seen many of them again and the rest are familiar to me in reproductions, I am astonished that at first sight I was bitterly disappointed. I felt nothing of the peculiar thrill which it is the property of art to give. The impression that Strickland's pictures gave me was disconcerting; and the fact remains, always to reproach me, that I never even thought of buying any. I missed a wonderful chance. Most of them have found their way into museums, and the rest are the treasured possessions of wealthy amateurs. I try to find excuses for myself. I think that my taste is good, but I am conscious that it has no originality. I know very little about painting, and I wander along trails that others have blazed for me. At that time I had the greatest admiration for the Impressionists. I longed to possess a Sisley and a Degas, and I worshipped Manet. His *Olympia* seemed to me the greatest picture of modern times, and *Le Déjeuner sur l'Herbe* moved me profoundly. These works seemed to me the last word in painting.

I will not describe the pictures that Strickland showed me. Descriptions of pictures are always dull, and, these, besides, are familiar to all who take an interest in such things. Now that his influence has so enormously affected modern painting, now that others have charted the country which he was among the first to explore, Strickland's pictures, seen for the first time, would find the mind more prepared for them; but it must be remembered that I had never seen anything of the sort. First of all I was taken aback by what seemed to me the clumsiness of his technique. Accustomed to the drawing of the old masters, and convinced that Ingres was the greatest draughtsman of recent times, I thought that Strickland drew very badly. I knew nothing of the simplification at which he aimed. I remember a still-life of oranges on a plate, and I was bothered because the plate was not round and the oranges were lop-sided. The portraits were a little larger than life-size, and this gave them an ungainly look. To my eyes the faces looked like caricatures. They were painted in a way that was entirely new to me. The landscapes puzzled me even more. There were two or three pictures of the forest of Fontainebleau and several of streets in Paris: my first feeling was that they might have been painted by a drunken cab-driver. I was perfectly bewildered. The colour seemed to me extraordinarily crude. It passed through my mind that the whole thing was a stupendous, incomprehensible farce. Now that I look back I am more than ever impressed by Stroeve's acuteness. He saw from the first that here was a revolution in art, and he recognised in its beginnings the genius which now all the world allows.

But if I was puzzled and disconcerted, I was not unimpressed. Even I, in my colossal ignorance, could not but feel that here, trying to express itself, was real power. I was excited and interested. I felt that these pictures had something to say to me that was very important for me to know, but I could not tell what it was. They seemed to me ugly, but they suggested without disclosing a secret of momentous significance. They were strangely tantalising. They gave me an emotion that I could not analyse. They said something that words were powerless to utter. I fancy that Strickland saw vaguely some spiritual meaning in material things that was so strange that he could only suggest it with halting symbols. It was as though he found in the chaos of the universe a new pattern, and were attempting clumsily, with anguish of soul, to set it down. I saw a tormented spirit striving for the release of expression.

I turned to him.

'I wonder if you haven't mistaken your medium,' I said.

'What the hell do you mean?'

'I think you're trying to say something, I don't quite know what it is, but I'm not sure that the best way of saying it is by means of painting.'

When I imagined that on seeing his pictures I should get a clue to the understanding of his strange character I was mistaken. They merely increased the astonishment with which he filled me. I was more at sea than ever. The only thing that seemed clear to me—and perhaps even this was fanciful—was that he was passionately striving for liberation from some power that held him. But what the power was and what line the liberation would take remained obscure. Each one of us is alone in the world. He is shut in a tower of brass, and can communicate with his fellows only by signs, and the signs have no common value, so that their sense is vague and uncertain. We seek pitifully to convey to others the treasures of our heart, but they have not the power to accept them and so we go, lonely, side by side but not together, unable to know our fellows and unknown by them. We are like people living in a country whose language they know so little that, with all manner of beautiful and profound things to say, they are condemned to the banalities of the conversation manual. Their brain is seething with ideas, and they can only tell you that the umbrella of the gardener's aunt is in the house.

The final impression I received was of a prodigious effort to express some state of the soul, and in this effort, I fancied, must be sought the explanation of what so utterly perplexed me. It was evident that colours and forms had a significance for Strickland that was peculiar to himself. He was under an intolerable necessity to convey something that he felt, and he created them with that intention alone. He did not hesitate to simplify or to distort if he could get nearer to that unknown thing he sought. Facts were nothing to him, for beneath the mass of irrelevant incidents he looked for something significant to himself. It was as though he had become aware of the soul of the universe and were compelled to express it. Though these pictures confused and puzzled me, I could not be unmoved by the emotion that was patent in them; and, I knew not why, I felt in myself a feeling that with regard to Strickland was the last I had ever expected to experience. I felt an overwhelming compassion.

'I think I know now why you surrendered to your feeling for Blanche Stroeve,' I said to him.

'Why?'

'I think your courage failed. The weakness of your body communicated itself to your soul. I do not know what infinite yearning possesses you, so that you are driven to a perilous, lonely search for some goal where you expect to find a final release from the spirit that torments you. I see you as the eternal pilgrim to some shrine that perhaps does not exist. I do not know to what inscrutable Nirvana you aim. Do you know yourself? Perhaps it is Truth and Freedom that you seek, and for a moment you thought that you might find release in Love. I think your tired soul sought rest in a woman's arms, and when you found no rest there you hated her. You had no pity for her, because you have no pity for yourself. And you killed her out of fear, because you trembled still at the danger you had barely escaped.'

He smiled dryly and pulled his beard.

'You are a dreadful sentimentalist, my poor friend.'

A week later I heard by chance that Strickland had gone to Marseilles. I never saw him again.

Chapter Forty-three

Looking back, I realise that what I have written about Charles Strickland must seem very unsatisfactory. I have given incidents that came to my knowledge, but they remain obscure because I do not know the reasons that led to them. The strangest, Strickland's determination to become a painter, seems to be arbitrary; and though it must have had causes in the circumstances of his life, I am ignorant of them. From his own conversation I was able to glean nothing. If I were writing a novel, rather than narrating such facts as I know of a curious personality, I should have invented much to account for this change of heart. I think I should have shown a strong vocation in boyhood, crushed by the will of his father or sacrificed to the necessity of earning a living, I should have pictured him impatient of the restraints of life; and in the struggle between his passion for art and the duties of his station I could have aroused sympathy for him. I should so have made him a more imposing figure. Perhaps it would have been possible to see in him a new Prometheus. There was here, maybe, the opportunity for a modern version of the hero who for the good of mankind exposes himself to the agonies of the damned. It is always a moving subject.

On the other hand, I might have found his motives in the influence of the married relation. There are a dozen ways in which this might be managed. A latent gift might reveal itself on acquaintance with the painters and writers whose society his wife sought; or domestic incompatibility might turn him upon himself; a love affair might fan into bright flame a fire which I could have shown smouldering dimly in his heart. I think then I should have drawn Mrs Strickland quite differently. I should have abandoned the facts and made her a nagging, tiresome woman, or else a bigoted one with no sympathy for the claims of the spirit. I should have made Strickland's marriage a long torment from which escape was the only possible issue. I think I should have emphasised his patience with the unsuitable mate, and the compassion which made him unwilling to throw off the yoke that oppressed him. I should certainly have eliminated the children.

An effective story might also have been made by bringing him into contact with some old painter whom the pressure of want or the desire for commercial success had made false to the genius of his youth, and who, seeing in Strickland the possibilities which himself had wasted, influenced him to forsake all and follow the divine tyranny of art. I think there would have been something ironic in the picture of the successful old man, rich and honoured, living in another the life which he, though knowing it was the better part, had not had the strength to pursue.

The facts are much duller. Strickland, a boy fresh from school, went into a broker's office without any feeling of distaste. Until he married he led the ordinary life of his fellows, gambling mildly on the Exchange, interested to the extent of a sovereign or two on the result of the Derby or the Oxford and Cambridge Race. I think he boxed a little in his spare time. On his chinmney-piece he had photographs of Mrs Langtry and Mary Anderson. He read *Punch* and the *Sporting Times*. He went to dances in Hampstead.

It matters less that for so long I should have lost sight of him. The years during which he was struggling to acquire proficiency in a difficult art were monotonous, and I do not know that there was anything significant in the shifts to which he was put to earn enough money to keep him. An account of them would be an account of the things he had seen happen to other people. I do not think they had any effect on his own character. He must have acquired experiences which would form abundant material for a picaresque novel of modern Paris, but he remained aloof, and judging from his conversation there was nothing in those years that had made a particular impression on him. Perhaps when he went to Paris he was too old to fall a victim to the glamour of his environment. Strange as it may seem, he always appeared to me not only practical, but immensely matter of fact. I suppose his life during this period was romantic, but he certainly saw no romance in it. It may be that in order to realise the romance of life you must have something of the actor in you; and, capable of standing outside yourself, you must be able to watch your actions with an interest at once detached and absorbed. But no one was more single-minded than Strickland. I never knew anyone who was less self-conscious. But it is unfortunate that I can give no description of the arduous steps by which he reached such mastery over his art as he ever acquired; for if I could show him undaunted by failure, by an unceasing effort of courage holding despair at bay, doggedly persistent in the face of self-doubt, which is the artist's bitterest enemy, I might excite some sympathy for a personality which, I am all too conscious, must appear singularly devoid of charm. But I have nothing to go on. I never once saw Strickland at work, nor do I know that anyone else did. He kept the secret of his struggles to himself. If in the loneliness of his studio he wrestled desperately with the Angel of the Lord he never allowed a soul to divine his anguish.

When I come to his connection with Blanche Stroeve I am exasperated by the fragmentariness of the facts at my disposal. To give my story coherence I should describe the progress of their tragic union, but I know nothing of the three months during which they lived together. I do not know how they got on or what they talked about. After all, there are twenty-four hours in the day, and the summits of emotion can only be reached at rare intervals. I can only imagine how they passed the rest of the time. While the light lasted and so long as Blanche's strength endured I suppose that Strickland painted, and it must have irritated her when she saw him absorbed in his work. As a mistress she did not then exist for him, but only as a model; and then there were long hours in which they lived side by side in silence. It must have frightened her. When Strickland suggested that in her surrender to him there was a sense of triumph over Dirk Stroeve, because he had come to her help in her extremity, he opened the door to many a dark conjecture. I hope it was not true. It seems to me rather horrible. But who can fathom the subtleties of the human heart? Certainly not those who expect from it only decorous sentiments and normal emotions. When Blanche saw that, notwithstanding his moments of passion, Strickland remained aloof, she must have been filled with dismay, and even in those moments I surmise that she realised that to him she was not an individual, but an instrument of pleasure; he was a stranger still, and she tried to bind him to herself with pathetic arts. She strove to ensnare him with comfort and would not see that comfort meant nothing to him. She was at pains to get him the things to eat that he liked, and would not see that he was indifferent to food. She was afraid to leave him alone. She pursued him with attentions, and when his passion was dormant sought to excite it, for then at least she had the illusion of holding him. Perhaps she knew with her intelligence that the claims she forged only aroused his instinct of destruction, as the plate-glass window makes your fingers itch for half a brick; but her heart, incapable of reason, made her continue on a course she knew was fatal. She must have been very unhappy. But the blindness of love led her to believe what she wanted to be true, and her love was so great that it seemed impossible to her that it should not in return awake an equal love.

But my study of Strickland's character suffers from a graver defect than my ignorance of many facts. Because they were obvious and striking, I have written of his relations to women; and yet they were but an insignificant part of his life. It is an irony that they should so tragically have affected others. His real life consisted of dreams and of tremendously hard work.

Here lies the unreality of fiction. For in men, as a rule, love is but an episode which takes its place among the other affairs of the day, and the emphasis laid on it in novels gives it an importance which is untrue to life. There are few men to whom it is the most important thing in the world, and they are not very interesting ones; even women, with whom the subject is of paramount interest, have a contempt for them. They are flattered and excited by them, but have an uneasy feeling that they are poor creatures. But even during the brief intervals in which they are in love, men do other things which distract their mind; the trades by which they earn their living engage their attention; they are absorbed in sport; they can interest themselves in art. For the most part, they keep their various activities in various compartments, and they can pursue one to the temporary exclusion of the other. They have a faculty of concentration on that which occupies them at the moment, and it irks them if one encroaches on the other. As lovers, the difference between men and women is that women can love all day long, but men only at times.

With Strickland the sexual appetite took a very small place. It was unimportant. It was irksome. His soul aimed elsewhither. He had violent passions, and on occasion desire seized his body so that he was driven to an orgy of lust, but he hated the instincts that robbed him of his self-possession. I think, even, he hated the inevitable partner in his debauchery. When he had regained command over himself, he shuddered at the sight of the woman he had enjoyed. His thoughts floated then serenely in the empyrean, and he felt towards her the horror that perhaps the painted butterfly, hovering about the flowers, feels to the filthy chrysalis from which it has triumphantly emerged. I suppose that art is a manifestation of the sexual instinct. It is the same emotion which is excited in the human heart by the sight of a lovely woman, the Bay of Naples under the yellow moon, and the *Entombment* of Titian. It is possible that Strickland hated the normal release of sex because it seemed to him brutal by comparison with the satisfaction of artistic creation. It seems strange even to myself, when I have described a man who was cruel, selfish, brutal and sensual, to say that he was a great idealist. The fact remains.

He lived more poorly than an artisan. He worked harder. He cared nothing for those things which with most people make life gracious and beautiful. He was indifferent to money. He cared nothing about fame. You cannot praise him because he resisted the temptation to make any of those compromises with the world which most of us yield to. He had no such temptation. It never entered his head that compromise was possible. He lived in Paris more lonely than an anchorite in the deserts of Thebes. He asked nothing from his fellows except that they should leave him alone. He was single-hearted in his aim, and to pursue it he was willing to sacrifice not only himself—many can do that—but others. He had a vision.

Strickland was an odious man, but I still think he was a great one.

Chapter Forty-four

A certain importance attaches to the views on art of painters, and this is the natural place for me to set down what I know of Strickland's opinions of the great artists of the past. I am afraid I have very little worth noting. Strickland was not a conversationalist, and he had no gift for putting what he had to say in the striking phrase that the listener remembers. He had no wit. His humour, as will be seen if I have in any way succeeded in reproducing the manner of his conversation, was sardonic. His repartee was rude. He made one laugh sometimes by speaking the truth, but this is a form of humour which gains its force only by its unusualness; it would cease to amuse if it were commonly practised.

Strickland was not, I should say, a man of great intelligence, and his views on painting were by no means out of the ordinary. I never heard him speak of those whose work had a certain analogy with his own—of Cézanne, for instance, or of Van Gogh; and I doubt very much if he had ever seen their pictures. He was not greatly interested in the Impressionists. Their technique impressed him, but I fancy that he thought their attitude commonplace. When Stroeve was holding forth at length on the excellence of Monet, he said: 'I prefer Winterhalter.' But I dare say he said it to annoy, and if he did he certainly succeeded.

I am disappointed that I cannot report any extravagances in his opinions on the old masters. There is so much in his character which is strange that I feel it would complete the picture if his views were outrageous. I feel the need to ascribe to him fantastic theories about his predecessors, and it is with a certain sense of disillusion that I confess he thought about them pretty much as does everybody else. I do not believe he knew El Greco. He had a great but somewhat impatient admiration for Velasquez. Chardin delighted him, and Rembrandt moved him to ecstasy. He described the impression that Rembrandt made on him with a coarseness I cannot repeat. The only painter that interested him who was at all unexpected was Brueghel the Elder. I knew very little about him at that time, and Strickland had no power to explain himself. I remember what he said about him because it was so unsatisfactory.

'He's all right,' said Strickland. 'I bet he found it hell to paint.'

When later, in Vienna, I saw several of Peter Brueghel's pictures, I thought I understood why he had attracted Strickland's attention. Here, too, was a man with a vision of the world peculiar to himself. I made somewhat copious notes at the time, intending to write something about him, but I have lost them, and have now only the recollection of an emotion. He seemed to see his fellow-creatures grotesquely, and he was angry with them because they were grotesque; life was a confusion of ridiculous, sordid happenings, a fit subject for laughter, and yet it made him sorrowful to laugh. Brueghel gave me the impression of a man striving to express in one medium feelings more appropriate to expression in another, and it may be that it was the obscure consciousness of this that excited Strickland's sympathy. Perhaps both were trying to put down in paint ideas which were more suitable to literature.

Strickland at this time must have been nearly forty-seven.

Chapter Forty-five

I have said already that but for the hazard of a journey to Tahiti I should doubtless never have written this book. It is thither that after many wanderings Charles Strickland came, and it is there that he painted the pictures on which his fame most securely rests. I suppose no artist achieves completely the realisation of the dream that obsesses him, and Strickland, harassed incessantly by his struggle with technique, managed, perhaps, less than others to express the vision that he saw with his mind's eye; but in Tahiti the circumstances were favourable to him; he found in his surroundings the accidents necessary for his inspiration to become effective, and his later pictures give at least a suggestion of what he sought. They offer the imagination something new and strange. It is as though in this far country his spirit, that had wandered disembodied, seeking a tenement, at last was able to clothe itself in flesh. To use the hackneyed phrase, here he found himself.

It would seem natural that my visit to this remote island should immediately revive my interest in Strickland, but the work I was engaged in occupied my attention to the exclusion of whatever was irrelevant, and it was not till I had been there some days that I even remembered his connection with it. After all, I had not seen him for fifteen years, and it was nine since he died. But I think my arrival at Tahiti would have driven out of my head matters of much more immediate importance to me, and even after a week I found it not easy to order myself soberly. I remember that on my first morning I awoke early, and when I came on to the terrace of the hotel no one was stirring. I wandered round to the kitchen, but it was locked, and on a bench outside it a native boy was sleeping. There seemed no chance of breakfast for some time, so I sauntered down to the water-front. The Chinamen were already busy in their shops. The sky had still the pallor of dawn, and there was a ghostly silence on the lagoon. Ten miles away the island of Murea, like some high fastness of the Holy Grail, guarded its mystery.

I did not altogether believe my eyes. The days that had passed since I left Wellington seemed extraordinary and unusual. Wellington is trim and neat and English; it reminds you of a seaport town on the South Coast. And for three days afterwards the sea was stormy. Grey clouds chased one another across the sky. Then the wind dropped, and the sea was calm and blue. The Pacific is more desolate than other seas; its spaces seem more vast, and the most ordinary journey upon it has somehow the feeling of an adventure. The air you breathe is an elixir which prepares you for the unexpected. Nor is it vouchsafed to man in the flesh to know aught that more nearly suggests the approach to the golden realms of fancy than the approach to Tahiti. Murea, the sister isle, comes into view in rocky splendour, rising from the desert sea mysteriously, like the unsubstantial fabric of a magic wand. With its jagged outline it is like a Montserrat of the Pacific, and you may imagine that there Polynesian knights guard with strange rites mysteries unholy for men to know. The beauty of the island is unveiled as diminishing distance shows you in distincter shape its lovely peaks, but it keeps its secret as you sail by, and, darkly inviolable, seems to fold itself together in a stony, inaccessible grimness. It would not surprise you if, as you came near seeking for an opening in the reef, it vanished suddenly from your view, and nothing met your gaze but the blue loneliness of the Pacific.

Tahiti is a lofty green island, with deep folds of a darker green, in which you divine silent valleys; there is mystery in their sombre depths, down which murmur and plash cool streams, and you feel that in those umbrageous places life from immemorial times has been led according to immemorial ways. Even here is something sad and terrible. But the impression is fleeting, and serves only to give a greater acuteness to the enjoyment of the moment. It is like the sadness which you may see in the jester's eyes when a merry company is laughing at his sallies; his lips smile and his jokes are gayer because in the communion of laughter he finds himself more intolerably alone. For Tahiti is smiling and friendly; it is like a lovely woman graciously prodigal of her charm and beauty; and nothing can be more conciliatory than the entrance into the harbour at Papeete. The schooners moored to the quay are trim and neat, the little town along the bay is white and urbane, and the flamboyants, scarlet against the blue sky, flaunt their colour like a cry of passion. They are sensual with an unashamed violence that leaves you breathless. And the crowd that throngs the wharf as the steamer draws alongside is gay and debonair; it is a noisy, cheerful, gesticulating crowd. It is a sea of brown faces. You have an impression of coloured movement against the flaming blue of the sky. Everything is done with a great deal of bustle, the unloading of the baggage, the examination of the customs; and everyone seems to smile at you. It is very hot. The colour dazzles you.

Chapter Forty-six

I had not been in Tahiti long before I met Captain Nichols. He came in one morning when I was having breakfast on the terrace of the hotel and introduced himself. He had heard that I was interested in Charles Strickland, and announced that he was come to have a talk about him. They are as fond of gossip in Tahiti as in an English village, and one or two enquiries I had made for pictures by Strickland had been quickly spread. I asked the stranger if he had breakfasted.

'Yes; I have my coffee early,' he answered, 'but I don't mind having a drop of whisky.'

I called the Chinese boy.

'You don't think it's too early?' said the Captain.

'You and your liver must decide that between you,' I replied.

'I'm practically a teetotaller,' he said, as he poured himself out a good half-tumbler of 'Canadian Club'.

When he smiled he showed broken and discoloured teeth. He was a very lean man, of no more than average height, with grey hair cut short and a stubby grey moustache. He had not shaved for a couple of days. His face was deeply lined, burned brown by long exposure to the sun, and he had a pair of small blue eyes which were astonishingly shifty. They moved quickly, following my smallest gesture, and they gave him the look of a very thorough rogue. But at the moment he was all heartiness and good-fellowship. He was dressed in a bedraggled suit of khaki, and his hands would have been all the better for a wash.

'I knew Strickland well,' he said, as he leaned back in his chair and lit the cigar I had offered him. 'It's through me he came out to the islands.'

'Where did you meet him?' I asked.

'In Marseilles.'

'What were you doing there?'

He gave me an ingratiating smile.

'Well, I guess I was on the beach.'

My friend's appearance suggested that he was now in the same predicament, and I prepared myself to cultivate an agreeable acquaintance. The society of beach-combers always repays the small pains you need be at to enjoy it. They are easy of approach and affable in conversation. They seldom put on airs, and the offer of a drink is a sure way to their hearts. You need no laborious steps to enter upon familiarity with them, and you can earn not only their confidence, but their gratitude, by turning an attentive ear to their discourse. They look upon conversation as the great pleasure of life, thereby proving the excellence of their civilisation, and for the most part they are entertaining talkers. The extent of their experience is pleasantly balanced by the fertility of their imagination. It cannot be said that they are without guile, but they have a tolerant respect for the law, when the law is supported by strength. It is hazardous to play with them, but their ingenuity adds a peculiar excitement to the best game in the world. I came to know Captain Nichols very well before I left Tahiti, and I am the richer for his acquaintance. I do not consider that the cigars and whisky he consumed at my expense (he always refused cocktails, since he was practically a teetotaller), and the few dollars, borrowed with a civil air of conferring a favour upon me, that passed from my pocket to his, were in any way equivalent to the entertainment he afforded me. I remained his debtor. I should be sorry if my conscience, insisting on a rigid attention to the matter in hand, forced me to dismiss him in a couple of lines.

I do not know why Captain Nichols first left England. It was a matter upon which he was reticent, and with persons of his kidney a direct question is never very discreet. He hinted at undeserved misfortune, and there is no doubt that he looked upon himself as the victim of injustice. My fancy played with the various forms of fraud and violence, and I agreed with him sympathetically when he remarked that the authorities in the old country were so damned technical. But it was nice to see that any unpleasantness he had endured in his native land had not impaired his ardent patriotism. He frequently declared that England was the finest country in the world, sir, and he felt a lively superiority over Americans, Colonials, Dagos, Dutchmen, and Kanakas.

But I do not think he was a happy man. He suffered from dyspepsia, and he might often be seen sucking a tablet of pepsin; in the morning his appetite was poor; but this affliction alone would hardly have impaired his spirits. He had a greater cause of discontent with life than this. Eight years before he had rashly married a wife. There are men whom a merciful Providence has undoubtedly ordained to a single life, but who from wilfulness or through circumstances they could not cope with have flown in the face of its decrees. There is no object more deserving of pity than the married bachelor. Of such was Captain Nichols. I met his wife. She was a woman of twenty-eight, I should think, though of a type whose age is always doubtful; for she cannot have looked different when she was twenty, and at forty would look no older. She gave me an impression of extraordinary tightness. Her plain face with its narrow lips was tight, her skin was stretched tightly over her bones, her smile was tight, her hair was tight, her clothes were tight, and the white drill she wore had all the effect of black bombazine. I could not imagine why Captain Nichols had married her, and having married her why he had not deserted her. Perhaps he had, often, and his melancholy arose from the fact that he could never succeed. However far he went and in howsoever secret a place he hid himself, I felt sure that Mrs Nichols, inexorable as fate and remorseless as conscience, would presently rejoin him. He could as little escape her as the cause can escape the effect.

The rogue, like the artist and perhaps the gentleman, belongs to no class. He is not embarrassed by the *sans gêne* of the hobo, nor put out of countenance by the etiquette of the prince. But Mrs Nichols belonged to the well-defined class, of late become vocal, which is known as the lower-middle. Her father, in fact, was a policeman. I am certain that he was an efficient one. I do not know what her hold was on the Captain, but I do not think it was love. I never heard her speak, but it may be that in private she had a copious conversation. At any rate, Captain Nichols was frightened to death of her. Sometimes, sitting with me on the terrace of the hotel, he would become conscious that she was walking in the road outside. She did

not call him; she gave no sign that she was aware of his existence; she merely
walked up and down composedly. Then a strange uneasiness would seize the
Captain; he would look at his watch and sigh.

'Well, I must be off,' he said.

Neither wit nor whisky could detain him then. Yet he was a man who had
faced undaunted hurricane and typhoon, and would not have hesitated to
fight a dozen unarmed niggers with nothing but a revolver to help him.
Sometimes, Mrs Nichols would send her daughter, a pale-faced, sullen child
of seven, to the hotel.

'Mother wants you,' she said, in a whining tone.

'Very well, my dear,' said Captain Nichols.

He rose to his feet at once, and accompanied his daughter along the road. I
suppose it was a very pretty example of the triumph of spirit over matter,
and so my digression has at least the advantage of a moral.

Chapter Forty-seven

I have tried to put some connection into the various things Captain Nichols
told me about Strickland, and I here set them down in the best order I can.
They made one another's acquaintance during the latter part of the winter
following my last meeting with Strickland in Paris. How he had passed the
intervening months I do not know, but life must have been very hard, for
Captain Nichols saw him first in the Asile de Nuit. There was a strike at
Marseilles at the time, and Strickland, having come to the end of his
resources, had apparently found it impossible to earn the small sum he
needed to keep body and soul together.

The Asile de Nuit is a large stone building where pauper and vagabond
may get a bed for a week, provided their papers are in order and they can
persuade the friars in charge that they are working-men. Captain Nichols
noticed Strickland for his size and his singular appearance among the crowd
that waited for the doors to open; they waited listlessly, some walking to and
fro, some leaning against the wall, and others seated on the kerb with their
feet in the gutter; and when they filed into the office he heard the monk who
read his papers address him in English. But he did not have a chance to speak
to him, since, as he entered the common-room, a monk came in with a huge
Bible in his arms, mounted a pulpit which was at the end of the room, and
began the service which the wretched outcasts had to endure as the price of
their lodging. He and Strickland were assigned to different rooms and when,
thrown out of bed at five in the morning by a stalwart monk, he had made his
bed and washed his face, Strickland had already disappeared. Captain
Nichols wandered about the streets for an hour of bitter cold, and then made
his way to the Place Victor Gélu, where the sailor-men are wont to
congregate. Dozing against the pedestal of a statue, he saw Strickland again.
He gave him a kick to awaken him.

'Come and have breakfast, mate,' he said.

'Go to hell,' answered Strickland.

I recognised my friend's limited vocabulary, and I prepared to regard
Captain Nichols as a trustworthy witness.

'Busted?' asked the Captain.

'Blast you,' answered Strickland.

'Come along with me. I'll get you some breakfast.'

After a moment's hesitation, Strickland scrambled to his feet, and together they went to the Bouchée de Pain, where the hungry are given a wedge of bread, which they must eat there and then, for it is forbidden to take it away; and then to the Cuillère de Soupe, where for a week, at eleven and four, you may get a bowl of thin, salt soup. The two buildings are placed far apart, so that only the starving should be tempted to make use of them. So they had breakfast, and so began the queer companionship of Charles Strickland and Captain Nichols.

They must have spent something like four months at Marseilles in one another's society. Their career was devoid of adventure, if by adventure you mean unexpected or thrilling incident, for their days were occupied in the pursuit of enough money to get a night's lodging and such food as would stay the pangs of hunger. But I wish I could give here the pictures, coloured and racy, which Captain Nichols' vivid narrative offered to the imagination. His account of their discoveries in the low life of a seaport town would have made a charming book, and in the various characters that came their way the student might easily have found matter for a very complete dictionary of rogues. But I must content myself with a few paragraphs. I received the impression of a life intense and brutal, savage, multi-coloured, and vivacious. It made the Marseilles that I knew, gesticulating and sunny, with its comfortable hotels and its restaurants crowded with the well-to-do, tame and commonplace. I envied men who had seen with their own eyes the sights that Captain Nichols described.

When the doors of the Asile de Nuit were closed to them, Strickland and Captain Nichols sought the hospitality of Tough Bill. This was the master of a sailors' boarding-house, a huge mulatto with a heavy fist, who gave the stranded mariner food and shelter till he found him a berth. They lived with him a month, sleeping with a dozen others, Swedes, negroes, Brazilians, on the floor of the two bare rooms in his house which he assigned to his charges; and every day they went with him to the Place Victor Gélu, whither came ships' captains in search of a man. He was married to an American woman, obese and slatternly, fallen to this pass by Heaven knows what process of degradation, and every day the boarders took it in turns to help her with the housework. Captain Nichols looked upon it as a smart piece of work on Strickland's part that he had got out of this by painting a portrait of Tough Bill. Tough Bill not only paid for the canvas, colours, and brushes, but gave Strickland a pound of smuggled tobacco into the bargain. For all I know, this picture may still adorn the parlour of the tumble-down little house somewhere near the Quai de la Joliette, and I suppose it could now be sold for fifteen hundred pounds. Strickland's idea was to ship on some vessel bound for Australia or New Zealand, and from there make his way to Samoa or Tahiti. I do not know how he had come upon the notion of going to the South Seas, though I remember that his imagination had long been haunted by an island, all green and sunny, encircled by a sea more blue than is found in Northern latitudes. I suppose that he clung to Captain Nichols because he was acquainted with those parts, and it was Captain Nichols who persuaded him that he would be more comfortable in Tahiti.

'You see, Tahiti's French,' he explained to me. 'And the French aren't so damned technical.'

I thought I saw his point.

Strickland had no papers, but that was not a matter to disconcert Tough Bill when he saw a profit (he took the first month's wages of the sailor for whom he found a berth), and he provided Strickland with those of an English stoker who had providentially died on his hands. But both Captain Nichols and Strickland were bound East, and it chanced that the only opportunities for signing on were with ships sailing West. Twice Strickland refused a berth on tramps sailing for the United States, and once on a collier going to Newcastle. Tough Bill had no patience with an obstinacy which could only result in loss to himself, and on the last occasion he flung both Strickland and Captain Nichols out of his house without more ado. They found themselves once more adrift.

Tough Bill's fare was seldom extravagant, and you rose from his table almost as hungry as you sat down, but for some days they had good reason to regret it. They learned what hunger was. The Cuillère de Soupe and the Asile de Nuit were both closed to them, and their only sustenance was the wedge of bread which the Bouchée de Pain provided. They slept where they could, sometimes in an empty truck on a siding near the station, sometimes in a cart behind a warehouse; but it was bitterly cold, and after an hour or two of uneasy dozing they would tramp the streets again. What they felt the lack of most bitterly was tobacco, and Captain Nichols, for his part, could not do without it; he took to hunting the 'Can o' Beer', for cigarette-ends and the butt-ends of cigars which the promenaders of the night before had thrown away.

'I've tasted worse smoking mixture in a pipe,' he added, with a philosophic shrug of his shoulders, as he took a couple of cigars from the case I offered him, putting one in his mouth and the other in his pocket.

Now and then they made a bit of money. Sometimes a mail steamer would come in, and Captain Nichols, having scraped acquaintance with the time-keeper, would succeed in getting the pair of them a job as stevedores. When it was an English boat, they would dodge into the forecastle and get a hearty breakfast from the crew. They took the risk of running against one of the ship's officers and being hustled down the gangway with the toe of a boot to speed their going.

'There's no harm in a kick in the hindquarters when your belly's full,' said Captain Nichols, 'and personally I never take it in bad part. An officer's got to think about discipline.'

I had a lively picture of Captain Nichols flying headlong down a narrow gangway before the uplifted foot of an angry mate, and, like a true Englishman, rejoicing in the spirit of the Mercantile Marine.

There were often odd jobs to be got about the fish-market. Once they each earned a franc by loading trucks with innumerable boxes of oranges that had been dumped down on the quay. One day they had a stroke of luck: one of the boarding-masters got a contract to paint a tramp that had come in from Madagascar round the Cape of Good Hope, and they spent several days on a plank hanging over the side, covering the rusty hull with paint. It was a situation that must have appealed to Strickland's sardonic humour. I asked Captain Nichols how he bore himself during these hardships.

'Never knew him say a cross word,' answered the Captain. 'He'd be a bit surly sometimes, but when we hadn't had a bite since morning, and we hadn't even got the price of a lie-down at the Chink's, he'd be as lively as a cricket.'

I was not surprised at this. Strickland was just the man to rise superior to circumstances, when they were such as to occasion despondency in most; but whether this was due to equanimity of soul or to contradictoriness it would be difficult to say.

The Chink's Head was a name the beach-combers gave to a wretched inn off the Rue Bouterie, kept by a one-eyed Chinaman, where for six sous you could sleep in a cot and for three on the floor. Here they made friends with others in as desperate condition as themselves, and when they were penniless and the night was bitter cold, they were glad to borrow from anyone who had earned a stray franc during the day the price of a roof over their heads. They were not niggardly, these tramps, and he who had money did not hesitate to share it among the rest. They belonged to all the countries in the world, but this was no bar to good-fellowship; for they felt themselves freemen of a country whose frontiers include them all, the great country of Cockaigne.

'But I guess Strickland was an ugly customer when he was roused,' said Captain Nichols, reflectively. 'One day we ran into Tough Bill in the Place, and he asked Charlie for the paper's he'd given him.

'"You'd better come and take them if you want them,' says Charlie.

'He was a powerful fellow, Tough Bill, but he didn't quite like the look of Charlie, so he began cursing him. He called him pretty near every name he could lay hands on, and when Tough Bill began cursing it was worth listening to him. Well, Charlie stuck it for a bit, then he stepped forward and he just said: "Get out, you bloody swine." It wasn't so much what he said, but the way he said it. Tough Bill never spoke another word; you could see him go yellow, and he walked away as if he'd remembered he had a date.'

Strickland, according to Captain Nichols, did not use exactly the words I have given, but since this book is meant for family reading I have thought it better, at the expense of truth, to put into his mouth expressions familiar to the domestic circle.

Now, Tough Bill was not the man to put up with humiliation at the hands of a common sailor. His power depended on his prestige, and first one, then another, of the sailors who lived in his house told them he had sworn to do Strickland in.

One night Captain Nichols and Strickland were sitting in one of the bars of the Rue Bouterie. The Rue Bouterie is a narrow street of one-storeyed houses, each house consisting of but one room: they are like the booths in a crowded fair or the cages of animals in a circus. At every door you see a woman. Some lean lazily against the side-posts, humming to themselves or calling to the passer-by in a raucous voice, and some listlessly read. They are French, Italian, Spanish, Japanese, coloured; some are fat and some are thin; and under the thick paint on their faces, the heavy smears on their eyebrows, and the scarlet of their lips, you see the lines of age and the scars of dissipation. Some wear black shifts and flesh-coloured stockings; some with curly hair, dyed yellow, are dressed like little girls in short muslin frocks. Through the open door you see a red-tiled floor, a large wooden bed, and on a deal table a ewer and a basin. A motley crowd saunters along the street—Lascars off a P. & O., blond Northmen from a Swedish barque, Japanese from a man-of-war, English sailors, Spaniards, pleasant-looking fellows from a French cruiser, negroes off an American tramp. By day it is merely sordid, but at night, lit only by the lamps in the little huts, the street has a sinister beauty. The hideous lust that pervades the air is oppressive and horrible, and yet there is something mysterious in the sight which haunts and troubles you. You feel I know not what primitive force which repels and yet fascinates you. Here all the decencies of civilisation are swept away, and you feel that men are face to face with a sombre reality. There is an atmosphere that is at once intense and tragic.

In the bar in which Strickland and Nichols sat a mechanical piano was loudly grinding out dance music. Round the room people were sitting at tables, here half a dozen sailors uproariously drunk, there a group of soldiers; and in the middle, crowded together, couples were dancing. Bearded sailors with brown faces and large horny hands clasped their partners in a tight embrace. The women wore nothing but a shift. Now and then two sailors would get up and dance together. The noise was deafening. People were singing, shouting laughing, and when a man gave a long kiss to the girl sitting on his knees, cat-calls from the English sailors increased the din. The air was heavy with the dust beaten up by the heavy boots of the men, and grey with smoke. It was very hot. Behind the bar was seated a woman nursing her baby. The waiter, an undersized youth with a flat, spotty face, hurried to and fro carrying a tray laden with glasses of beer.

In a little while Tough Bill, accompanied by two huge negroes, came in, and it was easy to see that he was already three parts drunk. He was looking for trouble. He lurched against a table at which three soldiers were sitting and knocked over a glass of beer. There was an angry altercation, and the owner of the bar stepped forward and ordered Tough Bill to go. He was a hefty fellow, in the habit of standing no nonsense from his customers, and Tough Bill hesitated. The landlord was not a man he cared to tackle, for the police were on his side, and with an oath he turned on his heel. Suddenly he caught sight of Strickland. He rolled up to him. He did not speak. He gathered the spittle in his mouth and spat full in Strickland's face. Strickland seized his glass and flung it at him. The dancers stopped suddenly still. There was an instant of complete silence, but when Tough Bill threw himself on Strickland the lust of battle seized them all, and in a moment there was a confused scrummage. Tables were overturned, glasses crashed to the ground. There was a hellish row. The women scattered to the door and behind the bar. Passers-by surged in from the street. You heard curses in every tongue, the sound of blows, cries; and in the middle of the room a dozen men were fighting with all their might. On a sudden the police rushed in, and everyone who could made for the door. When the bar was more or less cleared, Tough Bill was lying insensible on the floor with a great gash in his head. Captain Nichols dragged Strickland, bleeding from a wound in his arm, his clothes in rags, into the street. His own face was covered with blood from a blow on the nose.

'I guess you'd better get out of Marseilles before Tough Bill comes out of hospital,' he said to Strickland, when they had got back to the Chink's Head and were cleaning themselves.

'This beats cock-fighting,' said Strickland.

I could see his sardonic smile.

Captain Nichols was anxious. He knew Tough Bill's vindictiveness. Strickland had downed the mulatto twice, and the mulatto, sober, was a man to be reckoned with. He would bide his time stealthily. He would be in no hurry, but one night Strickland would get a knife-thrust in his back, and in a day or two the corpse of a nameless beach-comber would be fished out of the dirty water of the harbour. Nichols went next evening to Tough Bill's house and made enquiries. He was in hospital still, but his wife, who had been to see him, said he was swearing hard to kill Strickland when they let him out.

A week passed.

'That's what I always say,' reflected Captain Nichols, 'when you hurt a man, hurt him bad. It gives you a bit of time to look about and think what you'll do next.'

Then Strickland had a bit of luck. A ship bound for Australia had sent to the Sailors' Home for a stoker in place of one who had thrown himself overboard off Gibraltar in an attack of delirium tremens.

'You double down to the harbour, my lad,' said the Captain to Strickland, 'and sign on. You've got your papers.'

Strickland set off at once, and that was the last Captain Nichols saw of him. The ship was only in port for six hours, and in the evening Captain Nichols watched the vanishing smoke from her funnels as she ploughed East through the wintry sea.

I have narrated all this as best I could, because I like the contrast of these episodes with the life that I had seen Strickland live in Ashley Gardens when he was occupied with stocks and shares; but I am aware that Captain Nichols was an outrageous liar, and I dare say there is not a word of truth in anything he told me. I should not be surprised to learn that he had never seen Strickland in his life, and owed his knowledge of Marseilles to the pages of a magazine.

Chapter Forty-eight

It is here that I purposed to end my book. My first idea was to begin it with the account of Strickland's last years in Tahiti and with his horrible death, and then to go back and relate what I knew of his beginnings. This I meant to do, not from wilfulness, but because I wished to leave Strickland setting out with I know not what fancies in his lonely soul for the unknown islands which fired his imagination. I liked the picture of him, starting at the age of forty-seven, when most men have already settled comfortably in a groove, for a new world. I saw him, the sea grey under the mistral and foam-flecked, watching the vanishing coast of France, which he was destined never to see again; and I thought there was something gallant in his bearing and dauntless in his soul. I wished so to end on a note of hope. It seemed to emphasise the unconquerable spirit of man. But I could not manage it. Somehow I could not get into my story, and after trying once or twice I had to give it up; I started from the beginning in the usual way, and made up my mind I could only tell what I knew of Strickland's life in the order in which I learnt the facts.

Those that I have now are fragmentary. I am in the position of a biologist who from a single bone must reconstruct not only the appearance of an extinct animal, but its habits. Strickland made no particular impression on the people who came in contact with him in Tahiti. To them he was no more than a beach-comber in constant need of money, remarkable only for the peculiarity that he painted pictures which seemed to them absurd; and it was not till he had been dead for some years and agents came from the dealers in

Paris and Berlin to look for any pictures which might still remain on the island, that they had any idea that among them had dwelt a man of consequence. They remembered then that they could have bought for a song canvases which now were worth large sums, and they could not forgive themselves for the opportunity which had escaped them. There was a Jewish trader called Cohen, who had come by one of Strickland's pictures in a singular way. He was a little old Frenchman, with soft kind eyes and a pleasant smile, half trader and half seaman, who owned a cutter in which he wandered boldly among the Paumotus and the Marquesas, taking out trade goods and bringing back copra, shell, and pearls. I went to see him because I was told he had a large black pearl which he was willing to sell cheaply, and when I discovered that it was beyond my means I began to talk to him about Strickland. He had known him well.

'You see, I was interested in him because he was a painter,' he told me. 'We don't get many painters in the islands, and I was sorry for him because he was such a bad one. I gave him his first job. I had a plantation on the peninsula, and I wanted a white overseer. You never get any work out of the natives unless you have a white man over them. I said to him: "You'll have plenty of time for painting, and you can earn a bit of money." I knew he was starving, but I offered him good wages.'

'I can't imagine that he was a very satisfactory overseer,' I said, smiling.

'I made allowances. I have always had a sympathy for artists. It is in our blood, you know. But he only remained a few months. When he had enough money to buy paints and canvases he left me. The place had got hold of him by then, and he wanted to get away to into the bush. But I continued to see him now and then. He would turn up in Papeete every few months and stay a little while; he'd get money out of someone or other and then disappear again. It was on one of these visits that he came to me and asked for the loan of two hundred francs. He looked as if he hadn't had a meal for a week, and I hadn't the heart to refuse him. Of course, I never expected to see my money again. Well, a year later he came to see me once more, and he brought a picture with him. He did not mention the money he owed me, but he said: "Here is a picture of your plantation that I've painted for you." I looked at it. I did not know what to say, but of course I thanked him, and when he had gone away I showed it to my wife.'

'What was it like?' I asked.

'Do not ask me. I could not make head or tail of it. I never saw such a thing in my life. "What shall we do with it?" I said to my wife. "We can never hang it up," she said. "People would laugh at us." So she took it into an attic and put it away with all sorts of rubbish, for my wife can never throw anything away. It is her mania. Then, imagine to yourself, just before the war my brother wrote to me from Paris, and said: "Do you know anything about an English painter who lived in Tahiti? It appears that he was a genius, and his pictures fetch large prices. See if you can lay your hands on anything and send it to me. There's money to be made." So I said to my wife: "What about that picture that Strickland gave me? Is it possible that it is still in the attic?" "Without doubt," she answered, "for you know that I never throw anything away. It is my mania." We went up to the attic, and there, among I know not what rubbish that had been gathered during the thirty years we have inhabited that house, was the picture. I looked at it again, and I said: "Who would have thought that the overseer of my plantation on the peninsula, to whom I lent two hundred francs, had genius? Do you see anything in the picture?" "No," she said, "it does not resemble the plantation and I have never seen coconuts with blue leaves; but they are mad in Paris, and it may be that your brother will be able to sell it for the two hundred francs you lent Strickland." Well, we packed it up and we sent it to my brother. And at last I received a letter from him. What do you think he said? "I received your picture," he said, "and I confess I thought it was a joke that you had played on me. I would not have given the cost of postage for the picture. I was half afraid to show it to the gentleman who had spoken to me about it. Imagine my surprise when he said it was a masterpiece, and offered me thirty thousand francs. I dare say he would have paid more, but frankly I was so taken aback that I lost my head; I accepted the offer before I was able to collect myself.""

Then Monsieur Cohen said an admirable thing.

'I wish that poor Strickland had been still alive. I wonder what he would have said when I gave him twenty-nine thousand eight hundred francs for his picture.'

Chapter Forty-nine

I lived at the Hôtel de la Fleur, and Mrs Johnson, the proprietress, had a sad story to tell of lost opportunity. After Strickland's death certain of his effects were sold by auction in the market-place at Papeete, and she went to it herself because there was among the truck an American stove she wanted. She paid twenty-seven francs for it.

'There were a dozen pictures,' she told me, 'but they were unframed, and nobody wanted them. Some of them sold for as much as ten francs, but mostly they went for five or six. Just think, if I had bought them I should be a rich woman now.'

But Tiaré Johnson would never under any circumstances have been rich. She could not keep money. The daughter of a native and an English sea-captain settled in Tahiti, when I knew her she was a woman of fifty, who looked older, and of enormous proportions. Tall and extremely stout, she would have been of imposing presence if the great good-nature of her face had not made it impossible for her to express anything but kindliness. Her arms were like legs of mutton, her breasts like giant cabbages; her face, broad and fleshy, gave you an impression of almost indecent nakedness, and vast chin succeeded to vast chin. I do not know how many of them there were. They fell away voluminously into the capaciousness of her bosom. She was dressed usually in a pink Mother Hubbard, and she wore all day long a large straw hat. But when she let down her hair, which she did now and then, for she was vain of it, you saw that it was long and dark and curly; and her eyes had remained young and vivacious. Her laughter was the most catching I ever heard; it would begin, a low peal in her throat, and would grow louder and louder till her whole vast body shook. She loved three things—a joke, a glass of wine, and a handsome man. To have known her is a privilege.

She was the best cook on the island, and she adored good food. From morning till night you saw her sitting on a low chair in the kitchen, surrounded by a Chinese cook and two or three native girls, giving her orders, chatting sociably with all and sundry, and tasting the savoury messes she devised. When she wished to do honour to a friend she cooked the dinner with her own hands. Hospitality was a passion with her, and there was no one on the island who need go without a dinner when there was anything to eat at the Hôtel de la Fleur. She never turned her customers out of her house because they did not pay their bills. She always hoped they would pay when they could. There was one man there who had fallen on adversity, and to him she had given board and lodging for several months. When the Chinese laundryman refused to wash for him without payment she had sent his things to be washed with hers. She could not allow the poor fellow to go about in a dirty shirt, she said, and since he was a man, and men must smoke, she gave him a franc a day for cigarettes. She used him with the same affability as those of her clients who paid their bills once a week.

Age and obesity had made her inapt for love, but she took a keen interest in the amatory affairs of the young. She looked upon venery as the natural occupation for men and women, and was ever ready with precept and example from her own wide experience.

'I was not fifteen when my father found that I had a lover,' she said. 'He was third mate on the *Tropic Bird*. A good-looking boy.'

She sighed a little. They say a woman always remembers her first lover with affection; but perhaps she does not always remember him.

'My father was a sensible man.'

'What did he do?' I asked.

'He thrashed me within an inch of my life, and then he made me marry Captain Johnson. I did not mind. He was older, of course, but he was good-looking too.'

Tiaré—her father had called her by the name of the white, scented flower which, they tell you, if you have once smelt, will always draw you back to Tahiti in the end, however far you may have roamed—Tiaré remembered Strickland very well.

'He used to come here sometimes, and I used to see him walking about Papeete. I was sorry for him, he was so thin, and he never had any money. When I heard he was in town, I used to send a boy to find him and make him come to dinner with me. I got him a job once or twice, but he couldn't stick to anything. After a little while he wanted to get back to the bush, and one morning he would be gone.'

Strickland reached Tahiti about six months after he left Marseilles. He worked his passage on a sailing vessel that was making the trip from Auckland to San Francisco, and he arrived with a box of paints, an easel, and a dozen canvases. He had a few pounds in his pocket, for he had found work in Sydney, and he took a small room in a native house outside the town. I think the moment he reached Tahiti he felt himself at home. Tiaré told me that he said to her once:

'I'd been scrubbing the deck, and all at once a chap said to me: "Why, there it is." And I looked up and I saw the outline of the island. I knew right away that there was the place I'd been looking for all my life. Then we came near, and I seemed to recognise it. Sometimes when I walk about it all seems familiar. I could swear I've lived here before.'

'Sometimes it takes them like that,' said Tiaré. 'I've known men come on shore for a few hours while their ship was taking in cargo, and never go back. And I've known men who came here to be in an office for a year, and they cursed the place, and when they went away they took their dying oath they'd hang themselves before they came back again, and in six months you'd see them land once more, and they'd tell you they couldn't live anywhere else.'

Chapter Fifty

I have an idea that some men are born out of their due place. Accident has cast them amid certain surroundings, but they have always a nostalgia for a home they know not. They are strangers in their birthplace, and the leafy lanes they have known from childhood or the populous streets in which they have played, remain but a place of passage. They may spend their whole lives aliens among their kindred and remain aloof among the only scenes they have ever known. Perhaps it is this sense of strangeness that sends men far and wide in the search for something permanent, to which they may attach themselves. Perhaps some deep-rooted atavism urges the wanderer back to lands which his ancestors left in the dim beginnings of history. Sometimes a man hits upon a place to which he mysteriously feels that he belongs. Here is the home he sought, and he will settle amid scenes that he has never seen before, among men he has never known, as though they were familiar to him from his birth. Here at last he finds rest.

I told Tiaré the story of a man I had known at St Thomas's Hospital. He was a Jew named Abraham, a blond, rather stout young man, shy and very unassuming; but he had remarkable gifts. He entered the hospital with a scholarship and during the five years of the curriculum gained every prize that was open to him. He was made house-physician and house-surgeon. His brilliance was allowed by all. Finally he was elected to a position on the staff, and his career was assured. So far as human things can be predicted, it was certain that he would rise to the greatest heights in his profession. Honours and wealth awaited him. Before he entered upon his new duties he wished to take a holiday, and, having no private means, he went as surgeon on a tramp steamer to the Levant. It did not generally carry a doctor, but one of the senior surgeons at the hospital knew a director of the line, and Abraham was taken as a favour.

In a few weeks the authorities received his resignation of the coveted position on the staff. It created profound astonishment, and wild rumours were current. Whenever a man does anything unexpected, his fellows ascribe it to the most discreditable motives. But there was a man ready to step into Abraham's shoes, and Abraham was forgotten. Nothing more was heard of him. He vanished.

It was perhaps ten years later that one morning on board ship, about to land at Alexandria, I was bidden to line up with the other passengers for the doctor's examination. The doctor was a stout man in shabby clothes, and when he took off his hat I noticed that he was very bald. I had an idea that I had seen him before. Suddenly I remembered.

'Abraham,' I said.

He turned to me with a puzzled look, and then, recognising me, seized my hand. After expressions of surprise on either side, hearing that I meant to spend the night in Alexandria, he asked me to dine with him at the English

Club. When we met again I declared my astonishment at finding him there. It was a very modest position that he occupied, and there was about him an air of straitened circumstance. Then he told me his story. When he set out on his holiday in the Mediterranean he had every intention of returning to London and his appointment at St Thomas's. One morning the tramp docked at Alexandria, and from the deck he looked at the city, white in the sunlight, and the crowd on the wharf; he saw the natives in their shabby gabardines, the blacks from the Soudan, the noisy throng of Greeks and Italians, the grave Turks in tarbooshes, the sunshine and the blue sky; and something happened to him. He could not describe it. It was like a thunder-clap, he said, and then, dissatisfied with this, he said it was like a revelation. Something seemed to twist his heart, and suddenly he felt an exultation, a sense of wonderful freedom. He felt himself at home, and he made up his mind there and then, in a minute, that he would live the rest of his life in Alexandria. He had no great difficulty in leaving the ship, and in twenty-four hours, with all his belongings, he was on shore.

'The Captain must have thought you as mad as a hatter,' I smiled.

'I didn't care what anybody thought. It wasn't I that acted, but something stronger within me. I thought I would go to a little Greek hotel, while I looked about, and I felt I knew where to find one. And do you know, I walked straight there, and when I saw it I recognised it at once.'

'Had you been to Alexandria before?'

'No; I'd never been out of England in my life.'

Presently he entered the Government service, and there he had been ever since.

'Have you never regretted it?'

'Never, not for a minute. I earn just enough to live upon, and I'm satisfied. I ask nothing more than to remain as I am till I die. I've had a wonderful life.'

I left Alexandria next day, and I forgot about Abraham till a little while ago, when I was dining with another old friend in the profession, Alec Carmichael, who was in England on short leave. I ran across him in the street and congratulated him on the knighthood with which his eminent services during the war had been rewarded. We arranged to spend an evening together for old time's sake, and when I agreed to dine with him, he proposed that he should ask nobody else, so that we could chat without interruption. He had a beautiful old house in Queen Anne Street, and being a man of taste he had furnished it admirably. On the walls of the dining-room I saw a charming Bellotto, and there was a pair of Zoffanys that I envied. When his wife, a tall, lovely creature in cloth of gold, had left us, I remarked laughingly on the change in his present circumstances from those when we had both been medical students. We had looked upon it then as an extravagance to dine in a shabby Italian restaurant in the Westminster Bridge Road. Now Alec Carmichael was on the staff of half a dozen hospitals. I should think he earned ten thousand a year, and his knighthood was but the first of the honours which must inevitably fall to his lot.

'I've done pretty well,' he said, 'but the strange thing is that I owe it all to one piece of luck.'

'What do you mean by that?'

'Well, do you remember Abraham? He was the man who had the future. When we were students he beat me all along the line. He got the prizes and the scholarships that I went in for. I always played second fiddle to him. If he'd kept on he'd be in the position I'm in now. That man had a genius for surgery. No one had a look in with him. When he was appointed Registrar at Thomas's I hadn't a chance of getting on the staff. I should have had to become a G.P., and you know what likelihood there is for a G.P. ever to get out of the common rut. But Abraham fell out, and I got the job. That gave me my opportunity.'

'I dare say that's true.'

'It was just luck. I suppose there was some kink in Abraham. Poor devil, he's gone to the dogs altogether. He's got some twopenny-halfpenny job in the medical at Alexandria—sanitary officer or something like that. I'm told he lives with an ugly old Greek woman and has half a dozen scrofulous kids. The fact is, I suppose, that it's not enough to have brains. The thing that counts is character. Abraham hadn't got character.'

Character? I should have thought it needed a good deal of character to throw up a career after half an hour's meditation, because you saw in another way of living a more intense significance. And it required still more character never to regret the sudden step. But I said nothing, and Alec Carmichael proceeded reflectively:

'Of course it would be hypocritical for me to pretend that I regret what Abraham did. After all, I've scored by it.' He puffed luxuriously at the long Corona he was smoking. 'But if I weren't personally concerned I should be sorry at the waste. It seems a rotten thing that a man should make such a hash of life.'

I wondered if Abraham really had made a hash of life. Is to do what you most want, to live under the conditions that please you, in peace with yourself, to make a hash of life; and is it success to be an eminent surgeon with ten thousand a year and a beautiful wife? I suppose it depends on what meaning you attach to life, the claim which you acknowledge to society, and the claim of the individual. But again I held my tongue, for who am I to argue with a knight?

Chapter Fifty-one

Tiaré, when I told her this story, praised my prudence, and for a few minutes we worked in silence, for we were shelling peas. Then her eyes, always alert for the affairs of her kitchen, fell on some action of the Chinese cook which aroused her violent disapproval. She turned on him with a torrent of abuse. The Chink was not backward to defend himself, and a very lively quarrel ensued. They spoke in the native language, of which I had learnt but half a dozen words, and it sounded as though the world would shortly come to an end; but presently peace was restored and Tiaré gave the cook a cigarette. They both smoked comfortably.

'Do you know, it was I who found him his wife?' said Tiaré suddenly, with a smile that spread all over her immense face.

'The cook?'

'No, Strickland.'

'But he had one already.'

'That is what he said, but I told him she was in England, and England is at the other end of the world.'

'True,' I replied.

'He would come to Papeete every two or three months, when he wanted paints or tobacco or money, and then he would wander about like a lost dog. I was sorry for him. I had a girl here then called Ata to do the rooms; she was some sort of a relation of mine, and her father and mother were dead, so I had her to live with me. Strickland used to come here now and then to have a square meal or to play chess with one of the boys. I noticed that she looked at him when he came, and I asked her if she liked him. She said she liked him well enough. You know what these girls are; they're always pleased to go with a white man.'

'Was she a native?' I asked.

'Yes; she hadn't a drop of white blood in her. Well, after I'd talked to her I sent for Strickland, and I said to him: Strickland, it's time for you to settle down. A man of your age shouldn't go playing with the girls down at the front. They're bad lots, and you'll come to no good with them. You've got no money, and you can never keep a job for more than a month or two. No one will employ you now. You say you can always live in the bush with one or other of the natives, and they're glad to have you because you're a white man, but it's not decent for a white man. Now, listen to me, Strickland."'

Tiaré mingled French with English in her conversation, for she used both languages with equal facility. She spoke them with a singing accent which was not unpleasing. You felt that a bird would speak in these tones if it could speak English.

'"Now, what do you say to marrying Ata? She's a good girl and she's only seventeen. She's never been promiscuous like some of these girls—a captain or a first mate, yes, but she's never been touched by a native. *Elle se respecte, vois-tu?* The purser of the *Oahu* told me last journey that he hadn't met a nicer girl in the islands. It's time she settled down too, and besides, the captains and the first mates like a change now and then. I don't keep my girls too long. She has a bit of property down by Taravao, just before you come to the peninsula, and with copra at the price it is now you could live quite comfortably. There's a house, and you'd have all the time you wanted for your painting. What do you say to that?"'

Tiaré paused to take breath.

'It was then he told me of his wife in England. "My poor Strickland," I said to him, "they've all got a wife somewhere; that is generally why they come to the islands. Ata is a sensible girl, and she doesn't expect any ceremony before the Mayor. She's a Protestant, and you know they don't look upon these things like the Catholics."

'Then he said: "But what does Ata say to it?" "It appears that she has a *béguin* for you," I said. "She's willing if you are. Shall I call her?" He chuckled in a funny, dry way he had, and I called her. She knew what I was talking about, the hussy, and I saw her out of the corner of my eyes listening with all her ears, while she pretended to iron a blouse that she had been washing for me. She came. She was laughing, but I could see that she was a little shy, and Strickland looked at her without speaking.'

'Was she pretty?' I asked.

'Not bad. But you must have seen pictures of her. He painted her over and over again, sometimes with a *pareo* on and sometimes with nothing at all. Yes, she was pretty enough. And she knew how to cook. I taught her myself. I saw Strickland was thinking of it, so I said to him: "I've given her good wages and she's saved them, and the captains and the first mates she's known have given her a little something now and then. She's saved several hundred francs.'

'He pulled his great red beard and smiled.

'"Well, Ata," he said. "do you fancy me for a husband?"

'She did not say anything, but just giggled.

'"But I tell you, my poor Strickland, the girl has a *béguin* for you," I said.

'"I shall beat you," he said, looking at her.

'"How else should I know you loved me?" she answered.'

Tiaré broke off her narrative and addressed herself to me reflectively.

'My first husband, Captain Johnson, used to thrash me regularly. He was a man. He was handome, six foot three, and when he was drunk there was no holding him. I would be black and blue all over for days at a time. Oh, I cried when he died. I thought I should never get over it. But it wasn't till I married George Rainey that I knew what I'd lost. You can never tell what a man is like till you live with him. I've never been so deceived in a man as I was in George Rainey. He was a fine, upstanding fellow too. He was nearly as tall as Captain Johnson, and he looked strong enough. But it was all on the surface. He never drank. He never raised his hand to me. He might have been a missionary. I made love with the officers of every ship that touched at the island, and George Rainey never saw anything. At last I was disgusted with him, and I got a divorce. What was the good of a husband like that? It's a terrible thing the way some men treat women.'

I condoled with Tiaré, and remarked feelingly that men were deceivers ever, then asked her to go on with her story of Strickland.

'"Well," I said to him, "there's no hurry about it. Take your time and think it over. Ata has a very nice room in the annexe. Live with her for a month, and see how you like her. You can have your meals here. And at the end of a month, if you decide you want to marry her, you can just go and settle down on her property.'

'Well, he agreed to that. Ata continued to do the housework, and I gave him his meals as I said I would. I taught Ata how to make one or two dishes I knew he was fond of. He did not paint much. He wandered about the hills and bathed in the stream. And he sat about the front looking at the lagoon, and at sunset he would go down and look at Murea. He used to go fishing on the reef. He loved to moon about the harbour talking to the natives. He was a nice quiet fellow. And every evening after dinner he would go down to the annexe with Ata. I saw he was longing to get away to the bush, and at the end of the month I asked him what he intended to do. He said if Ata was willing to go, he was willing to go with her. So I gave them a wedding dinner. I cooked it with my own hands. I gave them a pea soup and lobster *à la portugaise*, and a curry, and a coconut salad—you've never had one of my coconut salads, have you? I must make you one before you go—and then I made them an ice. We had all the champagne we could drink and liqueurs to follow. Oh, I'd made up my mind to do things well. And afterwards we danced in the drawing-room. I was not so fat then, and I always loved dancing.'

The drawing-room at the Hôtel de la Fleur was a small room, with a cottage piano, and a suite of mahogany furniture, covered in stamped velvet, neatly arranged round the walls. On round tables were photograph albums, and on the walls enlarged photographs of Tiaré and her first husband, Captain Johnson. Still, though Tiaré was old and fat, on occasion we rolled back the Brussels carpet, brought in the maids and one or two friends of

Tiaré's, and danced, though now to the wheezy music of a gramophone. On the verandah the air was cented with the heavy perfume of the tiaré, and over-head the Southern Cross shone in a cloudless sky.

Tiaré smiled indulgently as she remembered the gaiety of a time long passed.

'We kept it up till three, and when we went to bed I don't think anyone was very sober. I had told them they could have my trap to take them as far as the road went, because after that they had a long walk. Ata's property was right away in a fold of the mountain. They started at dawn, and the boy I sent with them didn't come back till next day.

'Yes, that's how Strickland was married.'

Chapter Fifty-two

I supposed the next three years were the happiest of Strickland's life. Ata's house stood about eight kilometres from the road that runs round the island, and you went to it along a winding pathway shaded by the luxuriant trees of the tropics. It was a bungalow of unpainted wood, consisting of two small rooms, and outside was a small shed that served as a kitchen. There was no furniture except the mats they used as beds and a rocking-chair, which stood on the verandah. Bananas with their great ragged leaves, like the tattered habiliments of an empress in adversity, grew close up to the house. There was a tree just behind which bore alligator pears, and all about were the coconuts which gave the land its revenue. Ata's father had planted crotons round his property, and they grew in coloured profusion, gay and brilliant; they fenced the land with flame. A mango grew in front of the house, and at the edge of the clearing were two flamboyants, twin trees, that challenged the gold of the coconuts with their scarlet flowers.

Here Strickland lived, coming seldom to Papeete, on the produce of the land. There was a little stream that ran not far away, in which he bathed, and down this on occasion would come a shoal of fish. Then the natives would assemble with spears, and with much shouting would transfix the great startled things as they hurried down to the sea. Sometimes Strickland would go down to the reef, and come back with a basket of small, coloured fish that Ata would fry in coconut oil, or with a lobster; and sometimes she would make a savoury dish of the great land-crabs that scuttled away under your feet. Up the mountain were wild-orange trees, and now and then Ata would go with two or three women from the village and return laden with the green, sweet, luscious fruit. Then the coconuts would be ripe for picking, and her cousins (like all the natives, Ata had a host of relatives) would swarm up the trees and throw down the big ripe nuts. They split them open and put them in the sun to dry. Then they cut out the copra and put it into sacks, and the women would carry it down to the trader at the village by the lagoon, and he would give in exchange for it rice and soap and tinned meat and a little money. Sometimes there would be a feast in the neighbourhood, and a pig would be killed. Then they would go and eat themselves sick, and dance, and sing hymns.

But the house was a long way from the village, and the Tahitians are lazy. They love to travel and they love to gossip, but they do not care to walk, and for weeks at a time Strickland and Ata lived alone. He painted and he read, and in the evening, when it was dark, they sat together on the verandah, smoking and looking at the night. Then Ata had a baby, and the old woman who came up to help her through her trouble stayed on. Presently the grand-daughter of the old woman came to stay with her, and then a youth appeared—none quite knew wherefrom or to whom be belonged—but he settled down with them in a happy-go-lucky way, and they all lived together.

Chapter Fifty-three

'*Tenez, voilà le capitaine Brunot*,' said Tiaré, one day when I was fitting together what she could tell me of Strickland. 'He knew Strickland well; he visited him at his house.'

I saw a middle-aged Frenchman with a big black beard, streaked with grey, a sunburned face, and large, shining eyes. He was dressed in a neat suit of ducks. I had noticed him at luncheon, and Ah Lin, the Chinese boy, told me he had come from the Paumotus on the boat that had that day arrived. Tiaré introduced me to him, and he handed me his card, a large card on which was printed *René Brunot*, and underneath, *Capitaine au Long Cours*. We were sitting on a little verandah outside the kitchen, and Tiaré was cutting out a dress that she was making for one of the girls about the house. He sat down with us.

'Yes; I knew Strickland well,' he said. 'I am very fond of chess, and he was always glad of a game. I come to Tahiti three or four times a year for my business, and when he was at Papeete he would come here and we would play. When he married'—Captain Brunot smiled and shrugged his shoulders—'*enfin*, when he went to live with the girl that Tiaré gave him, he asked me to go and see him. I was one of the guests at the wedding feast.' He looked at Tiaré, and they both laughed. 'He did not come much to Papeete after that, and about a year later it chanced that I had to go to that part of the island for I forget what business, and when I had finished it I said to myself: "*Voyons*, why should I not go and see that poor Strickland?" I asked one or two natives if they knew anything about him, and I discovered that he lived not more than five kilometres from where I was. So I went. I shall never forget the impression my visit made on me. I live on an atoll, a low island, it is a strip of land surrounding a lagoon, and its beauty is the beauty of the sea and sky, and the varied colour of the lagoon, and the grace of the coconut trees; but the place where Strickland lived had the beauty of the Garden of Eden. Ah, I wish I could make you see the enchantment of that spot, a corner hidden away from all the world, with the blue sky overhead and the rich, luxuriant trees. It was a feast of colour. And it was fragrant and cool. Words cannot describe that paradise. And here he lived, unmindful of the world and by the world forgotten. I suppose to European eyes it would have seemed astonishingly sordid. The house was dilapidated and none too clean. When I approached I saw three or four natives lying on the verandah. You know how natives love to herd together. There was a young man lying full length, smoking a cigarette, and he wore nothing but a *pareo*.'

The *pareo* is a long strip of trade cotton, red or blue, stamped with a white pattern. It is worn round the waist and hangs to the knees.

'A girl of fifteen, perhaps, was plaiting pandanus-leaf to make a hat, and an old woman was sitting on her haunches smoking a pipe. Then I saw Ata. She was suckling a newborn child, and another child, stark naked, was playing at her feet. When she saw me she called out to Strickland, and he came to the door. He, too, wore nothing but a *pareo*. He was an extraordinary figure, with his red beard and matted hair, and his great hairy chest. His feet were horny and scarred, so that I knew he went always bare-foot. He had gone native with a vengeance. He seemed pleased to see me, and told Ata to kill a chicken for our dinner. He took me into the house to show me the picture he was at work on when I came in. In one corner of the room was the bed, and in the middle was an easel with the canvas upon it. Because I was sorry for him, I had bought a couple of his pictures for small sums, and I had sent others to friends f mine in France. And though I had bought them out of compassion, after living with them I began to like them. Indeed, I found a strange beauty in them. Everyone thought I was mad, but it turns out that I was right. I was his first admirer in the islands.'

He smiled maliciously at Tiaré, and with lamentations she told us again the story of how at the sale of Strickland's effects she had neglected the pictures, but bought an American stove for twenty-seven francs.

'Have you the pictures still?' I asked.

'Yes; I am keeping them till my daughter is of marriageable age, and then I shall sell them. They will be her *dot*.'

Then he went on with the account of his visit to Strickland.

'I shall never forget the evening I spent with him. I had not intended to stay more than an hour, but he insisted that I should spend the night. I hesitated, for I confess I did not much like the look of the mats on which he proposed that I should sleep; but I shrugged my shoulders. When I was building my house in the Paumotus I had slept out for weeks on a harder bed than that, with nothing to shelter me but wild shrubs; and as for vermin, my tough skin should be proof against their malice.

'We went down to the stream to bathe while Ata was preparing the dinner, and after we had eaten it we sat on the verandah. We smoked and chatted. The young man had a concertina, and he played the tunes popular on the music-halls a dozen years before. They sounded strangely in the tropical night thousands of miles from civilisation. I asked Strickland if it did not irk him to live in that promiscuity. No, he said; he liked to have his models under his hand. Presently, after loud yawning, the natives went away to sleep, and Strickland and I were left alone. I cannot describe to you the intense silence of the night. On my island in the Paumotus there is never at night the complete stillness that there was here. There is the rustle of the myriad animals on the beach, all the little shelled things that crawl about ceaselessly, and there is the noisy scurrying of the land-crabs. Now and then in the lagoon you hear the leaping of a fish, and sometimes a hurried noisy splashing as a brown shark sends all the other fish scampering for their lives. And above all, ceaseless like time, is the dull roar of the breakers on the reef. But here there was not a sound, and the air was scented with the white flowers of the night. It was a night so beautiful that your soul seemed hardly able to bear the prison of the body. You felt that it was ready to be wafted away on the immaterial air, and death bore all the aspect of a beloved friend.'

Tiaré sighed.

'Ah, I wish I were fifteen again.'

Then she caught sight of a cat trying to get at a dish of prawns on the kitchen table, and with a dexterous gesture and a lively volley of abuse flung a book at its scampering tail.

'I asked him if he was happy with Ata.

'"She leaves me alone," he said. "She cooks my food and looks after her babies. She does what I tell her. She gives me what I want from a woman."

'"And do you never regret Europe? Do you not yearn sometimes for the light of the streets in Paris or London, the companionship of your friends and equals, *que sais-je?* for theatres and newspapers, and the rumble of omnibuses on the cobbled pavements?"

'For a long time he was silent. Then he said:

'"I shall stay here till I die."

'"But are you never bored or lonely?" I asked.

'He chuckled.

'"*Mon pauvre ami*," he said. 'It is evident that you do not know what it is to be an artist."'

Capitaine Brunot turned to me with a gentle smile, and there was a wonderful look in his dark, kind eyes.

'He did me an injustice, for I too know what it is to have dreams. I have my visions too. In my way I also am an artist.'

We were all silent for a while, and Tiaré fished out of her capacious pocket a handful of cigarettes. She handed one to each of us, and we all three smoked. At last she said:

'Since *ce monsieur* is interested in Strickland, why do you not take him to see Dr Coutras? He can tell him something about his illness and death.'

'*Volontiers*,' said the Captain, looking at me.

I thanked him, and he looked at his watch.

'It is past six o'clock. We should find him at home if you care to come now.'

I got up without further ado, and we walked along the road that led to the doctor's house. He lived out of the town, but the Hôtel de la Fleur was on the edge of it, and we were quickly in the country. The broad road was shaded by pepper-trees, and on each side were the plantations, coconut and vanilla. The pirate birds were screeching among the leaves of the palms. We came to a stone bridge over a shallow river, and we stopped for a few minutes to see the native boys bathing. They chased one another with shrill cries and laughter, and their bodies, brown and wet, gleamed in the sunlight.

Chapter Fifty-four

As we walked along I reflected on a circumstance which all that I had lately heard about Strickland forced on my attention. Here, on this remote island, he seemed to have aroused none of the detestation with which he was regarded at home, but compassion rather; and his vagaries were accepted with tolerance. To these people, native and European, he was a queer fish, and they took him for granted; the world was full of odd persons, who did odd things; and perhaps they knew that a man is not what he wants to be, but what he must be. In England and France he was the square peg in the round hole, but here the holes were any sort of shape, and no sort of peg was quite amiss. I do not think he was any gentler here, less selfish or less brutal, but the circumstances were more favourable. If he had spent his life amid these surroundings he might have passed for no worse a man than another. He received here what he neither expected nor wanted among his own people—sympathy.

I tried to tell Captain Brunot something of the astonishment with which this filled me, and for a little while he did not answer.

'It is not strange that I, at all events, should have had sympathy for him,' he said at last, 'for, though perhaps neither of us knew it, we were both aiming at the same thing.'

'What on earth can it be that two people so dissimilar as you and Strickland could aim at?' I asked, smiling.

'Beauty.'

'A large order,' I murmured.

'Do you know how men can be so obsessed by love that they are deaf and blind to everything else in the world? They are as little their own masters as the slaves chained to the benches of a galley. The passion that held Strickland in bondage was no less tyrannical than love.'

'How strange that you should say that!' I answered. 'For long ago I had the idea that he was possessed of a devil.'

'And the passion that held Strickland was a passion to create beauty. It gave him no peace. It urged him hither and thither. He was eternally a pilgrim, haunted by a divine nostalgia, and the demon within him was ruthless. There are men whose desire for truth is so great that to attain it they will shatter the very foundation of their world. Of such was Strickland, only beauty with him took the place of truth. I could only feel for him profound compassion.'

'That is strange also. A man whom he had deeply wronged told me that he felt a great pity for him.' I was silent for a moment. 'I wonder if there you have found the explanation of a character which has always seemed to me inexplicable. How did you hit on it?'

He turned to me with a smile.

'Did I not tell you that I, too, in my way was an artist? I realised in myself the same desire as animated him. But whereas his medium was paint, mine has been life.'

Then Captain Brunot told me a story which I must repeat, since, if only by way of contrast, it adds something to my impression of Strickland. It has also to my mind a beauty of its own.

Captain Brunot was a Breton, and had been in the French Navy. He left it on his marriage, and settled down on a small property he had near Quimper to live for the rest of his days in peace; but the failure of an attorney left him suddenly penniless, and neither he nor his wife was willing to live in penury where they had enjoyed consideration. During his seafaring days he had cruised the South Seas, and he determined now to seek his fortune there. He spent some months in Papeete to make his plans and gain experience; then, on money borrowed from a friend in France, he bought an island in the Paumotus. It was a ring of land round a deep lagoon, uninhabited, and covered only with scrub and wild guava. With the intrepid woman who was his wife, and a few natives, he landed there, and set about building a house, and clearing the scrub so that he could plant coconuts. That was twenty years before, and now what had been a barren island was a garden.

'It was hard and anxious work at first, and we worked strenuously, both of us. Every day I was up at dawn, clearing, planting, working on my house, and at night when I threw myself on my bed it was to sleep like a log till morning. My wife worked as hard as I did. Then children were born to us, first a son and then a daughter. My wife and I have taught them all they know. We had a piano sent out from France, and she has taught them to play and to speak English, and I have taught them Latin and mathematics, and we read history together. They can sail a boat. They can swim as well as the natives. There is nothing about the land of which they are ignorant. Our trees have prospered, and there is shell on my reef. I have come to Tahiti now to buy a schooner. I can get enough shell to make it worth while to fish for it, and, who knows? I may find pearls. I have made something where there was nothing. I too have made beauty. Ah, you do not know what it is to look at those tall, healthy trees and think that every one I planted myself.'

'Let me ask you the question that you asked Strickland. Do you never regret France and your old home in Brittany?'

'Some day, when my daughter is married and my son has a wife and is able to take my place on the island, we shall go back and finish our days in the old house in which I was born.'

'You will look back on a happy life,' I said.

'*Évidemment*, it is not exciting on my island, and we are very far from the world—imagine, it takes me four days to come to Tahiti—but we are happy there. It is given to few men to attempt a work and to achieve it. Our life is simple and innocent. We are untouched by ambition, and what pride we have is due only to our contemplation of the work of our hands. Malice cannot touch us, nor envy attack. Ah, *mon cher monsieur*, they talk of the blessedness of labour, and it is a meaningless phrase, but to me it has the most intense significance. I am a happy man.'

'I am sure you deserve to be,' I smiled.

'I wish I could think so. I do not know how I have deserved to have a wife who was the perfect friend and helpmate, the perfect mistress and the perfect mother.'

I reflected for a while on the life that the Captain suggested to my imagination.

'It is obvious that to lead such an existence and make so great a success of it, you must both have needed a strong will and a determined character.'

'Perhaps; but without one other factor we could have achieved nothing.'

'And what was that?'

He stopped, somewhat dramatically, and stretched out his arm.

'Belief in God. Without that we should have been lost.'

Then we arrived at the house of Dr Coutras.

Chapter Fifty-five

Dr Coutras was an old Frenchman of great stature and exceeding bulk. His body was shaped like a huge duck's egg; and his eyes, sharp, blue, and good-natured, rested now and then with self-satisfaction on his enormous paunch. His complexion was florid and his hair white. He was a man to attract

immediate sympathy. He received us in a room that might have been in a
house in a provincial town in France, and the one or two Polynesian curios
had an odd look. He took my hand in both of his–they were huge–and gave
me a hearty look, in which, however, was great shrewdness. When he shook
hands with Capitaine Brunot he enquired politely after *Madame et les
enfants*. For some minutes there was an exchange of courtesies and some
local gossip about the island, the prospects of the copra and the vanilla crop;
then we came to the object of my visit.

I shall not tell what Dr Coutras related to me in his words, but in my own,
for I cannot hope to give at second hand any impression of his vivacious
delivery. He had a deep, resonant voice, fitted to his massive frame, and a
keen sense of the dramatic. To listen to him was, as the phrase goes, as good
as a play; and much better than most.

It appears that Dr Coutras had gone one day to Taravao in order to see an
old chiefess who was ill, and he gave a vivid picture of the obese old lady,
lying in a huge bed, smoking cigarettes, and surrounded by a crowd of dark-
skinned retainers. When he had seen her he was taken into another room and
given dinner–raw fish, fried bananas, and chicken–*que sais-je*? the typical
dinner of the *indigène*–and while he was eating it he saw a young girl being
driven away from the door in tears. He thought nothing of it, but when he
went out to get into his trap and drive home, he saw her again, standing a
little way off; she looked at him with a woebegone air, and tears streamed
down her cheeks. He asked someone what was wrong with her, and was told
that she had come down from the hills to ask him to visit a white man who
was sick. They had told her that the doctor could not be disturbed. He called
her, and himself asked what she wanted. She told him that Ata had sent her,
she who used to be at the Hôtel de la Fleur, and that the Red One was ill. She
thrust into his hand a crumpled piece of newspaper, and when he opened it
he found in it a hundred-franc note.

'Who is the Red One?' he asked of one of the bystanders.

He was told that that was what they called the Englishman, a painter, who
lived with Ata up in the valley seven kilometres from where they were. He
recognised Strickland by the description. But it was necessary to walk. It
was impossible for him to go; that was why they had sent the girl away.

'I confess,' said the doctor, turning to me, 'that I hesitated. I did not relish
fourteen kilometres over a bad pathway, and there was no chance that I
could get back to Papeete that night. Besides, Strickland was not
sympathetic to me. He was an idle, useless scoundrel, who preferred to live
with a native woman rather than work for his living like the rest of us. *Mon
Dieu*, how was I to know that one day the world would come to the
conclusion that he had genius? I asked the girl if he was not well enough to
have come down to see me. I asked her what she thought was the matter with
him. She would not answer. I pressed her, angrily perhaps, but she looked
down on the ground and began to cry. Then I shrugged my shoulders; after
all, perhaps it was my duty to go, and in a very bad temper I bade her lead the
way.'

His temper was certainly no better when he arrived, perspiring freely and
thirsty. Ata was on the look-out for him, and came a little way along the path
to meet him.

'Before I see anyone give me something to drink or I shall die of thirst,' he
cried out. '*Pour l'amour de Dieu*, get me a coconut.'

She called out, and a boy came running along. He swarmed up a tree, and presently threw down a ripe nut. Ata pierced a hole in it, and the doctor took a long, refreshing draught. Then he rolled himself a cigarette and felt in a better humour.

'Now, where is the Red One?' he asked.

'He is in the house, painting. I have not told him you were coming. Go in and see him.'

'But what does he complain of? If he is well enough to paint, he is well enough to have come down to Taravao and save me this confounded walk. I presume my time is no less valuable than his.'

Ata did not speak, but with the boy followed him to the house. The girl who had brought him was by this time sitting on the verandah, and here was lying an old woman, with her back to the wall, making native cigarettes. Ata pointed to the door. The doctor, wondering irritably why they behaved so strangely, entered, and there found Strickland cleaning his palette. There was a picture on the easel. Strickland, clad only in a *pareo*, was standing with his back to the door, but he turned round when he heard the sound of boots. He gave the doctor a look of vexation. He was surprised to see him, and resented the intrusion. But the doctor gave a gasp, he was rooted to the floor, and he stared with all his eyes. This was not what he expected. He was seized with horror.

'You enter without ceremony,' said Strickland. 'What can I do for you.'

The doctor recovered himself, but it required quite an effort for him to find his voice. All his irritation was gone, and he felt—*eh bien, oui, je ne le nie pas*—he felt an overwhelming pity.

'I am Dr Coutras. I was down at Taravao to see the chiefess, and Ata sent for me to see you.'

'She's a damned fool. I have had a few aches and pains lately and a little fever, but that's nothing; it will pass off. Next time anyone went to Papeete I was going to send for some quinine.'

'Look at yourself in the glass.'

Strickland gave him a glance, smiled, and went over to a cheap mirror in a little wooden frame, that hung in the wall.

'Well?'

'Do you not see a strange change in your face? Do you not see the thickening of your features and a look—how shall I describe it?—the books call it lion-faced. *Mon pauvre ami*, must I tell you that you have a terrible disease?'

'I?'

'When you look at yourself in the glass you see the typical appearance of the leper.'

'You are jesting,' said Strickland.

'I wish to God I were.'

'Do you intend to tell me that I have leprosy?'

'Unfortunately, there can be no doubt about it.'

Dr Coutras had delivered sentence of death on many men, and he could never overcome the horror with which it filled him. He felt always the furious hatred that must seize a man condemned when he compared himself with the doctor, sane and healthy, who had the inestimable privilege of life. Strickland looked at him in silence. Nothing of emotion could be seen on his face, disfigured already by the loathsome disease.

'Do they know?' he asked at last, pointing to the persons on the verandah, now sitting in unusual, unaccountable silence.

'These natives know the signs so well,' said the doctor. 'They were afraid to tell you.'

Strickland stepped to the door and looked out. There must have been something terrible in his face, for suddenly they all burst out into loud cries and lamentation. They lifted up their voices and they wept. Strickland did not speak. After looking at them for a moment, he came back into the room.

'How long do you think I can last?'

'Who knows? Sometimes the disease continues for twenty years. It is a mercy when it runs its course quickly.'

Strickland went to his easel and looked reflectively at the picture that stood on it.

'You have had a long journey. It is fitting that the bearer of important tidings should be rewarded. Take this picture. It means nothing to you now, but it may be that one day you will be glad to have it.'

Dr Coutras protested that he needed no payment for his journey; he had already given back to Ata the hundred-franc note, but Strickland insisted that he should take the picture. Then together they went out on the verandah. The natives were sobbing violently.

'Be quiet, woman. Dry thy tears,' said Strickland, addressing Ata. 'There is no great harm. I shall leave thee very soon.'

'They are not going to take thee away?' she cried.

At that time there was no rigid sequestration on the islands, and lepers, if they chose, were allowed to go free.

'I shall go up into the mountain,' said Strickland.

Then Ata stood up and faced him.

'Let the others go if they choose, but I will not leave thee. Thou art my man and I am thy woman. If thou leavest me I shall hang myself on the tree that is behind the house. I swear it by God.'

There was something immensely forcible in the way she spoke. She was no longer the meek, soft native girl, but a determined woman. She was extraordinarily transformed.

'Why shouldst thou stay with me? Thou canst go back to Papeete, and thou wilt soon find another white man. The old woman can take care of thy children, and Tiaré will be glad to have thee back.'

'Thou art my man and I am thy woman. Whither thou goest I will go too.'

For a moment Strickland's fortitude was shaken, and a tear filled each of his eyes and trickled slowly down his cheeks. Then he gave the sardonic smile which was usual with him.

'Women are strange little beasts,' he said to Dr Coutras. 'You can treat them like dogs, you can beat them till your arm aches, and still they love you.' He shrugged his shoulders. 'Of course, it is one of the most absurd illusions of Christianity that they have souls.'

'What is it that thou art saying to the doctor?' asked Ata suspiciously. 'Thou wilt not go?'

'If it please thee I will stay, poor child.'

Ata flung herself on her knees before him, and clasped his legs with her arms and kissed them. Strickland looked at Dr Coutras with a faint smile.

'In the end they get you, and you are helpless in their hands. White or brown, they are all the same.'

Dr Coutras felt that it was absurd to offer expressions of regret in so terrible a disaster, and he took his leave. Strickland told Tané, the boy, to lead him to the village. Dr Coutras paused for a moment, and then he addressed himself to me.

'I did not like him, I have told you he was not sympathetic to me, but as I walked slowly down to Taravao I could not prevent an unwilling admiration for the stoical courage which enabled him to bear perhaps the most dreadful of human afflictions. When Tané left me I told him I would send some medicine that might be of service; but my hope was small that Strickland would consent to take it, and even smaller that, if he did, it would do him good. I gave the boy a message for Ata that I would come whenever she sent for me. Life is hard, and Nature takes sometimes a terrible delight in torturing her children. It was with a heavy heart that I drove back to my comfortable home in Papeete.'

For a long time none of us spoke.

'But Ata did not send for me,' the doctor went on, at last, 'and it chanced that I did not go to that part of the island for a long time. I had no news of Strickland. Once or twice I heard that Ata had been to Papeete to buy painting materials, but I did not happen to see her. More than two years passed before I went to Taravao again, and then it was once more to see the old chiefess. I asked them whether they had heard anything of Strickland. By now it was known everywhere that he had leprosy. First Tané, the boy, had left the house, and then, a little time afterwards, the old woman and her grandchild. Strickland and Ata were left alone with their babies. No one went near the plantation, for, as you know, the natives have a very lively horror of the disease, and in the old days when it was discovered the sufferer was killed; but sometimes when the village boys were scrambling about the hills, they would catch sight of the white man, with his great red beard, wandering about. They fled in terror. Sometimes Ata would come down to the village at night and arouse the trader, so that he might sell her various things of which she stood in need. She knew that the natives looked upon her with the same horrified aversion as they looked upon Strickland, and she kept out of their way. Once some women, venturing nearer than usual to the plantation, saw her washing clothes in the brook, and they threw stones at her. After that the trader was told to give her the message that if she used the brook again men would come and burn down her house.'

'Brutes,' I said.

'*Mais non, mon cher monsieur*, men are always the same. Fear makes them cruel. . . . I decided to see Strickland, and when I had finished with the chiefess asked for a boy to show me the way. But none would accompany me, and I was forced to find it alone.'

When Dr Coutras arrived at the plantation he was seized with a feeling of uneasiness. Though he was hot from walking, he shivered. There was something hostile in the air which made him hesitate, and he felt that invisible forces barred his way. Unseen hands seemed to draw him back. No one would go near now to gather the coconuts, and they lay rotting on the ground. Everywhere was desolation. The bush was encroaching, and it looked as though very soon the primeval forest would regain possession of that strip of land which had been snatched from it at the cost of so much labour. He had the sensation that here was the abode of pain. As he approached the house he was struck by the unearthly silence, and at first he thought it was deserted. Then he saw Ata. She was sitting on her haunches in the lean-to that served her as kitchen, watching some mess cooking in a pot. Near her a small boy was playing silently in the dirt. She did not smile when she saw him.

'I have come to see Strickland,' he said.

'I will go and tell him.'

She went to the house, ascended the few steps that led to the verandah, and entered. Dr Coutras followed her, but waited outside in obedience to her gesture. As she opened the door he smelt the sickly sweet which makes the neighbourhood of the leper nauseous. He heard her speak, and then he heard Strickland's answer, but he did not recognise the voice. It had become hoarse and indistinct. Dr Coutras raised his eyebrows. He judged that the disease had already attacked the vocal cords. Then Ata came out again.

'He will not see you. You must go away.'

Dr Coutras insisted, but she would not let him pass. Dr Coutras shrugged his shoulders, and after a moment's reflection turned away. She walked with him. He felt that she too wanted to be rid of him.

'Is there nothing I can do at all?' he asked.

'You can send him some paints,' she said. 'There is nothing else he wants.'

'Can he paint still?'

'He is painting the walls of the house.'

'This is a terrible life for you, my poor child.'

Then at last she smiled, and there was in her eyes a look of superhuman love. Dr Coutras was startled by it, and amazed. And he was awed. He found nothing to say.

'He is my man,' she said.

'Where is your other child?' he asked. 'When I was here last you had two.'

'Yes; it died. We buried it under the mango.'

When Ata had gone with him a little way she said she must turn back. Dr Coutras surmised she was afraid to go farther in case she met any of the people from the village. He told her again that if she wanted him she had only to send and he would come at once.

Chapter Fifty-six

Then two years more went by, or perhaps three, for time passes imperceptibly in Tahiti, and it is hard to keep count of it; but at last a message was brought to Dr Coutras that Strickland was dying. Ata had waylaid the cart that took the mail into Papeete, and besought the man who drove it to go at once to the doctor. But the doctor was out when the summons came, and it was evening when he received it. It was impossible to start at so late an hour, and so it was not till next day soon after dawn that he set out. He arrived at Taravao, and for the last time tramped the seven kilometres that led to Ata's house. The path was overgrown, and it was clear that for years now it had remained all but untrodden. It was not easy to find the way. Sometimes he had to stumble along the bed of the stream, and sometimes he had to push through shrubs, dense and thorny; often he was obliged to climb over rocks in order to avoid the hornet-nests that hung on the trees over his head. The silence was intense.

It was with a sigh of relief that at last he came upon the little unpainted house, extraordinarily bedraggled now, and unkempt; but here too was the same intolerable silence. He walked up, and a little boy, playing unconcernedly in the sunshine, started at his approach and fled quickly away: to him the stranger was the enemy. Dr Coutras had a sense that the child was stealthily watching him from behind a tree. The door was wide open. He called out, but no one answered. He stepped in. He knocked at a door, but again there was no answer. He turned the handle and entered. The stench that assailed him turned him horribly sick. He put his handkerchief to his nose and forced himself to go in. The light was dim, and after the brilliant sunshine for a while he could see nothing. Then he gave a start. He could not make out where he was. He seemed on a sudden to have entered a magic world. He had a vague impression of a great primeval forest and of naked people walking beneath the trees. Then he saw that there were paintings on the walls.

'*Mon Dieu*, I hope the sun hasn't affected me,' he muttered.

A slight movement attracted his attention, and he saw that Ata was lying on the floor, sobbing quietly.

'Ata,' he called. 'Ata.'

She took no notice. Again the beastly stench almost made him faint, and he lit a cheroot. His eyes grew accustomed to the darkness, and now he was seized by an overwhelming sensation as he stared at the painted walls. He knew nothing of pictures, but there was something about these that extraordinarily affected him. From floor to ceiling the walls were covered with a strange and elaborate composition. It was indescribably wonderful and mysterious. It took his breath away. It filled him with an emotion which he could not understand nor analyse. He felt the awe and the delight which a man might feel who watched the beginning of a world. It was tremendous, sensual, passionate; and yet there was something horrible there too, something which made him afraid. It was the work of a man who had delved into the hidden depths of nature and had discovered secrets which were beautiful and fearful too. It was the work of a man who knew things which it is unholy for men to know. There was something primeval there and terrible. It was not human. It brought to his mind vague recollections of black magic. It was beautiful and obscene.

'*Mon Dieu*, this is genius.'

The words were wrung from him, and he did not know he had spoken.

Then his eyes fell on the bed of mats in the corner, and he went up, and he saw the dreadful, mutilated, ghastly object which had been Strickland. He was dead. Dr Coutras made an effort of will and bent over that battered horror. Then he started violently, and terror blazed in his heart, for he felt that someone was behind him. It was Ata. He had not heard her get up. She was standing at his elbow, looking at what he looked at.

'Good Heavens, my nerves are all distraught,' he said. 'You nearly frightened me out of my wits.'

He looked again at the poor dead thing that had been man, and then he started back in dismay.

'But he was blind.'

'Yes; he has been blind for nearly a year.'

Chapter Fifty-seven

At that moment we were interrupted by the appearance of Madame Coutras, who had been paying visits. She came in, like a ship in full sail, an imposing creature, tall and stout, with an ample bust and an obesity girthed in alarmingly by straight-fronted corsets. She had a bold hooked nose and three chins. She held herself upright. She had not yielded for an instant to the enervating charm of the tropics, but contrariwise was more active, more worldly, more decided that anyone in a temperate clime would have thought it possible to be. She was evidently a copious talker, and now poured forth a breathless stream of anecdote and comment. She made the conversation we had just had seem far away and unreal.

Presently Dr Coutras turned to me.

'I still have in my *bureau* the picture that Strickland gave me,' he said. 'Would you like to see it?'

'Willingly.'

We got up, and he led me on to the verandah which surrounded his house. We paused to look at the gay flowers that rioted in his garden.

'For a long time I could not get out of my head the recollection of the extraordinary decoration with which Strickland had covered the walls of his house,' he said reflectively.

I had been thinking of it too. It seemed to me that here Strickland had finally put the whole expression of himself. Working silently, knowing that it was his last chance, I fancied that here he must have said all that he knew of life and all that he divined. And I fancied that perhaps here he had at last found peace. The demon which possessed him was exorcised at last, and with the completion of the work, for which all his life had been a painful preparation, rest descended on his remote and tortured soul. He was willing to die, for he had fulfilled his purpose.

'What was the subject?' I asked.

'I scarcely know. It was strange and fantastic. It was a vision of the beginnings of the world, the Garden of Eden, with Adam and Eve—*que sais-je?*—it was a hymn to the beauty of the human form, male and female, and the praise of Nature, sublime, indifferent, lovely, and cruel. It gave you an awful sense of the infinity of space and of the endlessness of time. Because he painted the trees I see about me every day, the coconuts, the banyans, the flamboyants, the alligator-pears, I have seen them ever since differently, as though there were in them a spirit and a mystery which I am ever on the point of seizing and which for ever escapes me. The colours were the colours familiar to me, and yet they were different. They had a significance which was all their own. And those nude men and women. They were on the earth, and yet apart from it. They seemed to possess something of the clay of which they were created, and at the same time something divine. You saw man in the nakedness of his primeval instincts, and you were afraid, for you saw yourself.'

Dr Coutras shrugged his shoulders and smiled.

'You will laugh at me. I am a materialist, and I am a gross, fat man—Falstaff, eh?—the lyrical mode does not become me. I make myself ridiculous. But I have never seen painting which made so deep an impression upon me. *Tenez*, I had just the same feeling as when I went to the Sistine Chapel in Rome. There too I was awed by the greatness of the man who had painted that ceiling. It was genius, and it was stupendous and overwhelming. I felt small and insignificant. But you are prepared for the greatness of Michael Angelo. Nothing had prepared me for the immense surprise of these pictures in a native hut, far away from civilisation, in a fold of the mountain above Taravao. And Michael Angelo is sane and healthy. Those great works of his have the calm of the sublime; but here, notwithstanding beauty, was something troubling. I do not know what it was. It made me uneasy. It gave me the impression you get when you are sitting next door to a room that you know is empty, but in which, you know not why, you have a dreadful consciousness that notwithstanding there is someone. You scold yourself; you know it is only your nerves—and yet, and yet ... In a little while it is impossible to resist the terror that seizes you, and you are helpless in the clutch of an unseen horror. Yes; I confess I was not altogether sorry when I heard that those strange masterpieces had been destroyed.'

'Destroyed?' I cried.

'*Mais oui*; did you not know?'

'How should I know? It is true I had never heard of this work; but I thought perhaps it had fallen into the hands of a private owner. Even now there is no certain list of Strickland's paintings.'

'When he grew blind he would sit hour after hour in those two rooms that he had painted, looking at his works with sightless eyes, and seeing, perhaps, more than he had ever seen in his life before. Ata told me that he never complained of his fate, he never lost courage. To the end his mind remained serene and undisturbed. But he made her promise that when she had buried him—did I tell you that I dug his grave with my own hands, for none of the natives would approach the infected house, and we buried him, she and I, sewn up in three *pareos* joined together, under the mango-tree—he made her promise that she would set fire to the house and not leave it till it was burned to the ground and not a stick remained.'

I did not speak for a while, for I was thinking. Then I said:

'He remained the same to the end, then.'

'Do you understand? I must tell you that I thought it my duty to dissuade her.'

'Even after what you have just said?'

'Yes; for I knew that here was a work of genius, and I did not think we had the right to deprive the world of it. But Ata would not listen to me. She had promised. I would not stay to witness the barbarous deed, and it was only afterwards that I heard what she had done. She poured paraffin on the dry floors and on the pandanus-mats, and then she set fire. In a little while nothing remained but smouldering embers, and a great masterpiece existed no longer.

'I think Strickland knew it was a masterpiece. He had achieved what he wanted. His life was complete. He had made a world and saw that it was good. Then, in pride and contempt, he destroyed it.'

'But I must show you my picture,' said Dr Coutras, moving on.

'What happened to Ata and the child?'

'They went to the Marquesas. She had relations there. I have heard that the boy works on one of Cameron's schooners. They say he is very like his father in appearance.'

At the door that led from the verandah to the doctor's consulting-room, he paused and smiled.

'It is a fruit-piece. You would think it not a very suitable picture for a doctor's consulting-room, but my wife will not have it in the drawing-room. She says it is frankly obscene.'

'A fruit-piece!' I exclaimed in surprise.

We entered the room, and my eyes fell at once on the picture. I looked at it for a long time.

It was a pile of mangoes, bananas, oranges, and I know not what; and at first sight it was an innocent picture enough. It would have been passed in an exhibition of the Post-Impressionists by a careless person as an excellent but not very remarkable example of the school; but perhaps afterwards it would come back to his recollection, and he would wonder why. I do not think then he could ever entirely forget it.

The colours were so strange that words can hardly tell what a troubling emotion they gave. There were sombre blues, opaque like a delicately carved bowl in lapis lazuli, and yet with a quivering lustre that suggested the palpitation of mysterious life; there were purples, horrible like raw and putrid flesh, and yet with a glowing, sensual passion that called up vague memories of the Roman Empire of Heliogabalus; there were reds, shrill like the berries of holly—one thought of Christmas in England, and the snow, the good cheer, and the pleasure of children—and yet by some magic softened till they had the swooning tenderness of a dove's breast; there were deep yellows that died with an unnatural passion into a green as fragrant as the spring and as pure as the sparkling water of a mountain brook. Who can tell what anguished fancy made these fruits? They belonged to a Polynesian garden of the Hesperides. There was something strangely alive in them, as though they were created in a stage of the earth's dark history when things were not irrevocably fixed to their forms. They were extravagantly luxurious. They were heavy with tropical odours. They seemed to possess a sombre passion of their own. It was enchanted fruit, to taste which might open the gateway to God knows what secrets of the soul and to mysterious palaces of the imagination. They were sullen with unawaited dangers, and to eat them might turn a man to beast or god. All that was healthy and natural, all that clung to happy relationships and the simple joys of simple men, shrunk from them in dismay; and yet a fearful attraction was in them, and, like the fruit on the Tree of the Knowledge of Good and Evil they were terrible with the possibilities of the Unknown.

At last I turned away. I felt that Strickland had kept his secret to the grave.

'*Voyons, René, mon ami*,' came the loud, cheerful voice of Madame Coutras, 'what are you doing all this time? Here are the *apéritifs*. Ask *Monsieur* if he will not drink a little glass of Quinquina Dubonnet.'

'*Volontiers, Madame*,' I said, going out on to the verandah.

The spell was broken.

Chapter Fifty-eight

The time came for my departure from Tahiti. According to the gracious custom of the island, presents were given me by the persons with whom I had been thrown in contact—baskets made of the leaves of the coconut tree, mats of pandanus, fans; and Tiaré gave me three little pearls and three jars of guava-jelly made with her own plump hands. When the mail-boat, stopping for twenty-four hours on its way from Wellington to San Francisco, blew the whistle that warned the passengers to get on board, Tiaré clasped me to her vast bosom, so that I seemed to sink into a billowy sea, and pressed her red lips to mine. Tears glistened in her eyes. And when we steamed slowly out of the lagoon, making our way gingerly through the opening in the reef, and then steered for the open sea, a certain melancholy fell upon me. The breeze was laden still with the pleasant odours of the land. Tahiti is very far away, and I knew that I should never see it again. A chapter of my life was closed, and I felt a little nearer to inevitable death.

Not much more than a month later I was in London; and after I had arranged certain matters which claimed my immediate attention, thinking Mrs Strickland might like to hear what I knew of her husband's last years, I wrote to her. I had not seen her since long before the war, and I had to look out her address in the telephone-book. She made an appointment, and I went to the trim little house on Campden Hill which she now inhabited. She was by this time a woman of hard on sixty, but she bore her years well, and no one would have taken her for more than fifty. Her face, thin and not much lined, was of the sort that ages gracefully, so that you thought in youth she must have been a much handsomer woman than in fact she was. Her hair, not yet very grey, was becomingly arranged, and her black gown was modish. I remembered having heard that her sister, Mrs MacAndrew, outliving her husband but a couple of years, had left money to Mrs Strickland; and by the look of the house and the trim maid who opened the door I judged that it was a sum adequate to keep the widow in modest comfort.

When I was ushered into the drawing-room I found that Mrs Strickland had a visitor, and when I discovered who he was, I guessed that I had been asked to come at just that time not without intention. The caller was Mr Van Busche Taylor, an American, and Mrs Strickland gave me particulars with a charming smile of apology to him.

'You know, we English are so dreadfully ignorant. You must forgive me if it's necessary to explain.' Then she turned to me. 'Mr Van Busche Taylor is the distinguished American critic. If you haven't read his book your education has been shamefully neglected, and you must repair the omission at once. He's writing something about dear Charlie, and he's come to ask me if I can help him.'

Mr Van Busche Taylor was a very thin man with a large, bald head, bony and shining; and under the great dome of his skull his face, yellow, with deep lines in it, looked very small. He was quiet and exceedingly polite. He spoke with the accent of New England, and there was about his demeanour a bloodless frigidity which made me ask myself why on earth he was busying himself with Charles Strickland. I had been slightly tickled at the gentleness which Mrs Strickland put into her mention of her husband's name, and while the pair conversed I took stock of the room in which we sat. Mrs Strickland had moved with the times. Gone were the Morris papers and gone the severe cretonnes, gone were the Arundel prints that had adorned the walls of her drawing-room in Ashley Gardens; the room blazed with fantastic colour, and I wondered if she knew that those varied hues, which fashion had imposed upon her, were due to the dreams of a poor painter in a South Sea island. She gave me the answer herself.

'What wonderful cushions you have,' said Mr Van Busche Taylor.

'Do you like them?' she said, smiling. 'Bakst, you know.'

And yet on the walls were coloured reproductions of several of Strickland's best pictures, due to the enterprise of a publisher in Berlin.

'You're looking at my pictures,' she said, following my eyes. 'Of course, the originals are out of my reach, but it's a comfort to have these. The publisher sent them to me himself. They're a great consolation to me.'

'They must be very pleasant to live with,' said Mr Van Busche Taylor.

'Yes; they're so essentially decorative.'

'That is one of my profoundest convictions,' said Mr Van Busche Taylor. 'Great art is always decorative.'

Their eyes rested on a nude woman suckling a baby, while a girl was kneeling by their side holding out a flower to the indifferent child. Looking over them was a wrinkled, scraggy hag. It was Strickland's version of the Holy Family. I suspected that for the figures had sat his household above Taravao, and the woman and the baby were Ata and his first son. I asked myself if Mrs Strickland had any inkling of the facts.

The conversation proceeded, and I marvelled at the tact with which Mr Van Busche Taylor avoided all subjects that might have been in the least embarrassing, and at the ingenuity with which Mrs Strickland, without saying a word that was untrue, insinuated that her relations with her husband had always been perfect. At last Mr Van Busche Taylor rose to go. Holding his hostess's hand, he made her a graceful, though perhaps too elaborate, speech of thanks, and left us.

'I hope he didn't bore you,' she said, when the door closed behind him. 'Of course it's a nuisance sometimes, but I feel it's only right to give people any information I can about Charlie. There's a certain responsibility about having been the wife of a genius.'

She looked at me with those pleasant eyes of hers, which had remained as candid and as sympathetic as they had been more than twenty years before. I wondered if she was making a fool of me.

'Of course you've given up your business?' I said.

'Oh yes,' she answered airily. 'I ran it more by way of a hobby than for any other reason, and my children persuaded me to sell it. They thought I was overtaxing my strength.'

I saw that Mrs Strickland had forgotten that she had ever done anything so disgraceful as to work for her living. She had the true instinct of the nice woman that it is only really decent for her to live on other people's money.

'They're here now,' she said. 'I thought they'd like to hear what you had to say about their father. You remember Robert, don't you? I'm glad to say he's been recommended for the Military Cross.'

She went to the door and called them. There entered a tall man in khaki, with the parson's collar, handsome in a somewhat heavy fashion, but with the frank eyes that I remembered in him as a boy. He was followed by his sister. She must have been the same age as was her mother when first I knew her, and she was very like her. She too gave one the impression that as a girl she must have been prettier than indeed she was.

'I suppose you don't remember them in the least,' said Mrs Strickland, proud and smiling. 'My daughter is now Mrs Ronaldson. Her husband's a Major in the Gunners.'

'He's by way of being a pukka soldier, you know,' said Mrs Ronaldson gaily. 'That's why he's only a Major.'

I remembered my anticipation long ago that she would marry a soldier. It was inevitable. She had all the graces of the soldier's wife. She was civil and affable, but she could hardly conceal her intimate conviction that she was not quite as others were. Robert was breezy.

'It's a bit of luck that I should be in London when you turned up,' he said. 'I've only got three days' leave.'

'He's dying to get back,' said his mother.

'Well, I don't mind confessing it, I have a rattling good time at the front. I've made a lot of good pals. It's a first-rate life. Of course war's terrible, and all that sort of thing; but it does bring out the best qualities in a man, there's no denying that.'

Then I told them what I had learnt about Charles Strickland in Tahiti. I thought it unnecessary to say anything of Ata and her boy, but for the rest I was as accurate as I could be. When I had narrated his lamentable death I ceased. For a minute or two we were all silent. Then Robert Strickland struck a match and lit a cigarette.

'The mills of God grind slowly, but they grind exceeding small,' he said, somewhat impressively.

Mrs Strickland and Mrs Ronaldson looked down with a slightly pious expression which indicated, I felt sure, that they thought the quotation was from Holy Writ. Indeed, I was unconvinced that Robert Strickland did not share their illusion. I do not know why I suddenly thought of Strickland's son by Ata. They had told me he was a merry, light-hearted youth. I saw him, with my mind's eye, on the schooner on which he worked, wearing nothing but a pair of dungarees; and at night, when the boat sailed along easily before a light breeze, and the sailors were gathered on the upper deck, while the captain and the supercargo lolled in deck-chairs, smoking their pipes, I saw him dance with another lad, dance wildly, to the wheezy music of the concertina. Above was the blue sky, and the stars, and all about the desert of the Pacific Ocean.

A quotation from the Bible came to my lips, but I held my tongue, for I know that clergymen think it a little blasphemous when the laity poach upon their preserves. My Uncle Harry, for twenty-seven years Vicar of Whitstable, was on these occasions in the habit of saying that the devil could always quote scripture to his purpose. He remembered the days when you could get thirteen Royal Natives for a shilling.